ED
McBAIN

ED McBAIN

Heinemann/Octopus

Cop Hater first published in Great Britain in 1966
by Hamish Hamilton Ltd
Give the Boys a Great Big Hand first published in Great Britain in 1960
by Hamish Hamilton Ltd
Doll first published in Great Britain in 1966
by Hamish Hamilton Ltd
Eighty Million Eyes first published in Great Britain in 1966
by Hamish Hamilton Ltd
Hail, Hail, the Gang's all Here! first published in Great Britain in 1971
by Hamish Hamilton Ltd
Sadie When She Died first published in Great Britain in 1972
by Hamish Hamilton Ltd
Let's Hear It for the Deaf Man first published in Great Britain in 1973
by Hamish Hamilton Ltd

This edition first published jointly in
Great Britain by

William Heinemann Limited   Secker & Warburg Limited
15/16 Queen Street   54 Poland Street
London W1   London W1

and

Octopus Books Limited
59 Grosvenor Street
London W1

ISBN 0 905712 36 6

Printed in the United States

CONTENTS

COP HATER

"The alarm
sounded at
eleven p.m.
He reached
out for it,
groping in
the dark-
ness, find-
ing the
lever and
pressing it
against the
back of the
clock...."

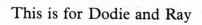

This is for Dodie and Ray

Chapter One

The alarm sounded at eleven p.m.

He reached out for it, groping in the darkness, finding the lever and pressing it against the back of the clock. The buzzing stopped. The room was very silent. Beside him, he could hear May's even breathing. The windows were wide open, but the room was hot and damp, and he thought again about the air conditioning unit he'd wanted to buy since the summer before. Reluctantly, he sat up and rubbed hamlike fists into his eyes.

He was a big man, his head topped with straight blond hair that was unruly now. His eyes were normally grey, but they were virtually colourless in the darkness of the room, puffed with sleep. He stood up and stretched. He slept only in pyjama pants, and when he raised his arms over his head, the pants slipped down over the flatness of his hard belly. He let out a grunt, pulled up the pants, and then glanced at May again.

The sheet was wadded at the foot of the bed, a soggy lifeless mass. May lay curled into a sprawling C, her gown twisted up over her thigh. He went to the bed and put his hand on her thigh for an instant. She murmured and rolled over. He grinned in the darkness and then went into the bathroom to shave.

He had timed every step of the operation, and so he knew just how long it took to shave, just how long it took to dress, just how long it took to gulp a quick cup of coffee. He took off his wrist watch before he began shaving, leaving it on the wash-basin where he could glance at it occasionally. At eleven-ten, he began dressing. He put on an Aloha shirt his brother had sent him from Hawaii. He put on a pair of tan gabardine slacks, and a light poplin windbreaker. He put a handkerchief in his left hip pocket, and then scooped his wallet and change off the dresser.

He opened the top drawer of the dresser and took the .38 from where it lay next to May's jewellery box. His thumb passed over the hard leather of the holster, and then he shoved the holster and gun into his right hip pocket, beneath the poplin jacket. He lighted a cigarette, went into the kitchen to put up the coffee water, and then went to check on the kids.

Mickey was asleep, his thumb in his mouth as usual. He passed his hand over the boy's head. He was sweating like a pig. He'd have to talk to May about the air conditioning again. It wasn't fair to the kids, cooped up like this in a sweat box. He walked to Cathy's bed and went through the same ritual. She wasn't as perspired as her brother. Well, she was a girl, girls didn't sweat as much. He heard the kettle in the kitchen whistling loudly. He glanced at his watch, and then grinned.

He went into the kitchen, spooned two teaspoonfuls of instant coffee into a large cup, and then poured the boiling water over the powder. He drank the coffee black, without sugar. He felt himself coming awake at last, and he vowed for the hundredth time that he wouldn't try to catch any sleep before this tour, it was plain stupid. He should sleep when he got home, hell, what did he average this way? A couple of hours? And then it was time to go in. No, it was foolish. He'd have to talk to May about it. He gulped the coffee down, and then went into his bedroom again.

He liked to look at her asleep. He always felt a little sneaky when he took advantage of her that way. Sleep was a kind of private thing, and it wasn't right to pry when somebody was completely unaware. But, God, she was beautiful when she was asleep, so what the hell, it wasn't fair. He watched her for several moments, the dark hair spread out over the pillow, the rich sweep of her hip and thigh, the femaleness of the raised gown and the exposed white flesh. He went to the side of the bed, and brushed the hair back from her temple. He kissed her very gently, but she stirred and said, 'Mike?'

'Go back to sleep, honey.'

'Are you leaving?' she murmured hoarsely.

'Yes.'

'Be careful, Mike.'

'I will.' He grinned. 'And you be good.'

'Uhm,' she said, and then she rolled over into the pillow. He sneaked a last look at her from the doorway, and then went through the living room and out of the house. He glanced at his watch. It was eleven-thirty. Right on schedule, and damn if it wasn't a lot cooler in the street.

At eleven forty-one, when Mike Reardon was three blocks away from his place of business, two bullets entered the back of his skull and ripped away half his face when they left his body. He felt only impact and sudden unbearable pain, and then vaguely heard the shots, and then everything inside him went dark, and he crumpled to the sidewalk.

He was dead before he struck the ground.

He had been a citizen of the city, and now his blood poured from his broken face and spread around him in a sticky red smear.

Another citizen found him at eleven fifty-six, and went to call the police. There was very little difference between the citizen who rushed down the street to a phone booth, and the citizen named Mike Reardon who lay crumpled and lifeless against the concrete.

Except one.

Mike Reardon was a cop.

Chapter Two

The two Homicide cops looked down at the body on the sidewalk. It was a hot night, and the flies swarmed around the sticky blood on the sidewalk. The Assistant Medical Examiner was kneeling alongside the body, gravely studying it. A photographer from the Bureau of Identification was busily popping flash bulbs. Cars 23 and 24 were parked across the street, and the patrolmen from those cars were unhappily engaged in keeping back spectators.

The call had gone to one of the two switchboards at Headquarters where a sleepy patrolman had listlessly taken down the information and then shot it via pneumatic tube to the radio room. The dispatcher in the radio room, after consulting the huge precinct map on the wall behind him, had sent Car 23 to investigate and report on the allegedly bleeding man in the street. When Car 23 had reported back with a homicide, the dispatcher had contacted Car 24 and sent it to the scene. At the same time, the patrolman on the switchboard had called Homicide North and also the 87th Precinct, in which territory the body had been found.

The body lay outside an abandoned, boarded-up theatre. The theatre had started as a first-run movie house, many years back when the neighbourhood had still been fashionable. As the neigbourhood began rotting, the theatre began showing second-run films, and then old movies, and finally foreign language films. There was a door to the left of the movie house, and the door had once been boarded, too, but the planks had been ripped loose and the staircase inside was littered with cigarette butts, empty pint whisky bottles, and contraceptives. The marquee above the theatre stretched to the sidewalk, punched with jagged holes, the victim of thrown rocks, tin cans, hunks of pipe, and general debris.

Across the street from the theatre was an empty lot. The lot had once owned an apartment house, and the house had been a good one with high rents. It had not been unusual, in the old days, to see an occasional mink coat drifting from the marbled doorway of that apartment house. But the crawling tendrils of the slum had reached out for the brick, clutching it with tenacious fingers, pulling it into the ever-widening circle it called its own. The old building had succumbed, becoming a part of the slum, so that people rarely remembered it had once been a proud and elegant dwelling. And then it had been condemned, and the building had been razed to the ground, and now the lot was clear and open, except for the scattered brick rubble that still clung to the ground in some places. A City housing project, it was rumoured, was going up in the lot. In the meantime, the kids used the lot for various purposes. Most of the purposes were concerned with bodily functions, and so a stench hung on the air over the lot, and the stench was particularly strong on a hot summer night, and it drifted towards the theatre, captured beneath the canopy of the overhanging marquee, smothering the sidewalk with its smell of life, mingling with the smell of death on the sidewalk.

One of the Homicide cops moved away from the body and began scouring the sidewalk. The second cop stood with his hands in his back pockets. The Assistant M.E. went through the ritual of ascertaining the death of a man who was certainly dead. The first cop came back.

'You see these?' he asked.

'What've you got?'

'Couple of ejected cartridge cases.'

'Mm?'

'Remington slugs. .45 calibre.'

'Put 'em in an envelope and tag 'em. You about finished, Doc?'

'In a minute.'

The flash bulbs kept popping. The photographer worked like the press agent for a hit musical. He circled the star of the show, and he snapped his pictures from different angles, and all the while his face showed no expression, and the sweat streamed down his back, sticking his shirt to his flesh. The Assistant M.E. ran his hand across his forehead.

'What the hell's keeping the boys from the 87th?' the first cop asked.

'Big poker game going probably. We're better off without them.' He turned to the Assistant M.E. 'What do you say, Doc?'

'I'm through.' He rose wearily.

'What've you got?'

'Just what it looks like. He was shot twice in the back of the head. Death was probably instantaneous.'

'Want to give us a time?'

'On a gunshot wound? Don't kid me.'

'I thought you guys worked miracles.'

'We do. But not during the summer.'

'Can't you even guess?'

'Sure, guessing's free. No rigor mortis yet, so I'd say he was killed maybe a half-hour ago. With this heat, though ... hell, he might maintain normal body warmth for hours. You won't get us to go out on a limb with this one. Not even after the autopsy is ...'

'All right, all right. Mind if we find out who he is?'

'Just don't mess it up for the Lab boys. I'm taking off.' The Assistant M.E. glanced at his watch. 'For the benefit of the timekeeper, it's 12:19.'

'Short day today,' the first Homicide cop said. He jotted the time down on the time table he'd kept since his arrival at the scene.

The second cop was kneeling near the body. He looked up suddenly. 'He's heeled,' he said.

'Yeah?'

The Assistant M.E. walked away, mopping his brow.

'Looks like a .38,' the second cop said. He examined the holstered gun more closely. 'Yeah. Detective's Special. Want to tag this?'

'Sure.' The first cop heard a car brake to a stop across the street. The front doors opened, and two men stepped out and headed for the knot around the body. 'Here's the 87th now.'

'Just in time for tea,' the second cop said drily. 'Who'd they send?'

'Looks like Carella and Bush.' The first cop took a packet of rubber-banded tags from his right hand jacket pocket. He slipped one of the tags free from the rubber band, and then returned the rest to his pocket. The tag was a three-by-five rectangle of an oatmeal colour. A hole was punched in one end of the tag, and a thin wire was threaded through the hole and twisted to form two loose ends. The tag read POLICE DEPARTMENT, and beneath that in bolder type: EVIDENCE.

Carella and Bush, from the 87th Precinct, walked over leisurely. The Homicide cop glanced at them cursorily, turned to the *Where found* space on the tag, and began filling it out. Carella wore a blue suit, his grey tie neatly clasped to his white shirt. Bush was wearing an orange sports shirt and khaki trousers.

'If it ain't Speedy Gonzales and Whirlaway,' the second Homicide cop said. 'You guys certainly move fast, all right. What do you do on a bomb scare?'

'We leave it to the Bomb Squad,' Carella said drily. 'What do you do?'

'You're very comical,' the Homicide cop said.

'We got hung up.'

'I can see that.'

'I was catching alone when the squeal came in,' Carella said. 'Bush was out with Foster on a bar knifing. Reardon didn't show.' Carella paused. 'Ain't that right, Bush?' Bush nodded.

'If you're catching, what the hell are you doing here?' the first Homicide cop said.

Carella grinned. He was a big man, but not a heavy one. He gave an impression of great power, but the power was not a meaty one. It was, instead, a fine-honed muscular power. He wore his brown hair short. His eyes were brown, with a peculiar downward slant that gave him a clean-shaven Oriental appearance. He had wide shoulders and narrow hips, and he managed to look well-dressed and elegant even when he was dressed in a leather jacket for a waterfront plant. He had thick wrists and big hands, and he spread the hands wide now and said, 'Me answer the phone when there's a homicide in progress?' His grin widened. 'I left Foster to catch. Hell, he's practically a rookie.'

'How's the graft these days?' the second Homicide cop asked.

'Up yours,' Carella answered drily.

'Some guys get all the luck. You sure as hell don't get anything from a stiff.'

'Except *tsores*,' the first cop said.

'Talk English,' Bush said genially. He was a soft-spoken man, and his quiet voice came as a surprise because he was all of six feet four inches and weighed at least two-twenty, bone dry. His hair was wild and unkempt, as if a wise Providence had fashioned his unruly thatch after his surname. His hair was also red, and it clashed violently against the orange sports shirt he wore. His arms hung from the sleeves of the shirt, muscular and thick. A jagged knife scar ran the length of his right arm.

The photographer walked over to where the detectives were chatting.

'What the hell are you doing?' he asked angrily.

'We're trying to find out who he is,' the second cop said. 'Why? What's the matter?'

'I didn't say I was finished with him yet.'

'Well, ain't you?'

'Yeah, but you should've asked.'

'For Pete's sake, who are you working for? Conover?'

'You Homicide dicks give me a pain in the ...'

'Go home and emulsify some negatives or something, will you?'

The photographer glanced at his watch. He grunted and withheld the time purposely, so that the first cop had to glance at his own watch before jotting down the time on his time table. He subtracted a few minutes, and indicated a t.o.a. for Carella and Bush, too.

Carella looked down at the back of the dead man's head. His face remained expressionless, except for a faint, passing film of pain which covered his eyes for a moment, and then darted away as fleetingly as a jack-rabbit.

'What'd they use?' he asked. 'A cannon?'

'A .45,' the first cop said. 'We've got the cartridge cases.'

'How many?'

'Two.'

'Figures,' Carella said. 'Why don't we flip him over?'

'Ambulance coming?' Bush asked quietly.

'Yeah,' the first cop said. 'Everybody's late tonight.'

'Everybody's drowning in sweat tonight,' Bush said. 'I can use a beer.'

'Come on,' Carella said, 'give me a hand here.'

The second cop bent down to help Carella. Together they rolled the body over. The flies swarmed up angrily, and then descended to the sidewalk again, and to the bloody broken flesh that had once been a face. In the darkness, Carella saw a gaping hole where the left eye should have been. There was another hole beneath the right eye, and the cheek bone was splintered outward, the jagged shards piercing the skin.

'Poor bastard,' Carella said. He would never get used to staring death in the face. He had been a cop for twelve years now, and he had learned to stomach the sheer, overwhelming, physical impact of death – but he would never get used to the other thing about death, the invasion of privacy that came with death, the reduction of pulsating life to a pile of bloody, fleshy rubbish.

'Anybody got a flash?' Bush asked.

The first cop reached into his left hip pocket. He thumbed a button, and a circle of light splashed onto the sidewalk.

'On his face,' Bush said.

The light swung up onto the dead man's face.

Bush swallowed. 'That's Reardon,' he said, his voice very quiet. And then, almost in a whisper, 'My God, that's Mike Reardon.'

Chapter Three

There were sixteen detectives assigned to the 87th Precinct, and David Foster was one of them. The precinct, in all truth, could have used a hundred and sixteen detectives and even then been understaffed. The precinct area spread South from the River Highway and the tall buildings which still boasted doormen and elevator operators to the Stem with its delicatessens and movie houses, on South to Culver Avenue and the Irish section, still South to the Puerto Rican section and then into Grover's Park, where muggers and rapists ran rife. Running East and West, the precinct covered a long total of some thirty-five streets. And packed into this rectangle – North and South from the river to the park, East and West for thirty-five blocks – was a population of 90,000 people.

David Foster was one of those people.

David Foster was a Negro.

He had been born in the precinct territory, and he had grown up there, and when he'd turned 21, being of sound mind and body, being four inches over the minimum requirement of five feet eight inches, having 20/20 vision without glasses, and not having any criminal record, he had taken the competitive Civil Service examination and had been appointed a patrolman.

The starting salary at the time had been $3,725 per annum, and Foster had earned his salary well. He had earned it so well that in the space of five years he had been appointed to the Detective Division. He was now a 3rd Grade Detective, and his salary was now $5,230 per annum, and he still earned it.

At one a.m., on the morning of July 24th, while a colleague named Mike Reardon lay spilling his blood into the gutter, David Foster was earning his salary by interrogating the man he and Bush had picked up in the bar knifing.

The interrogation was being conducted on the second floor of the precinct house. To the right of the desk on the first floor, there was an inconspicuous and dirty white sign with black letters which announced DETECTIVE DIVISION, and a pointing hand advised any visitor that the bulls hung out upstairs.

The stairs were metal, and narrow, but scrupulously clean. They went up for a total of sixteen risers, then turned back on themselves and continued on up for another sixteen risers, and there you were.

Where you were was a narrow, dimly-lighted corridor. There were two doors on the right of the open stairway, and a sign labelled them LOCKERS. If you turned left and walked down the corridor, you passed a wooden slatted bench on your left, a bench without a back on your right (set into a narrow alcove before the sealed doors of what had once been an elevator shaft), a door on your right marked MEN'S LAVATORY, and a door on your left over which a small sign hung, and the sign simply read CLERICAL.

At the end of the corridor was the detective squadroom.

You saw first a slatted rail divider. Beyond that, you saw desks and telephones, and a bulletin board with various photographs and notices on it, and a hanging light globe and beyond that more desks and the grilled windows that opened on the front of the building. You couldn't see very much that went on beyond the railing on your right because two huge metal filing cabinets blocked the desks on that side of the room. It was on that side of the room that Foster was interrogating the man he'd picked up in the bar earlier that night.

'What's your name?' he asked the man.

'*No hablo inglés,*' the man said.

'Oh, hell,' Foster said. He was a burly man with a deep chocolate colouring and warm brown eyes. He wore a white dress shirt, open at the throat. His sleeves were rolled up over muscular forearms.

'*Cuál es su nombre?*' he asked in hesitant Spanish.

'Thomas Perillo.'

'Your address?' He paused, thinking. '*Dirección?*'

'*Tres-tres-cuatro Mei-son.*'

'Age? *Edad?*'

Perillo shrugged.

'All right,' Foster said, 'where's the knife? Oh, God, we'll never get anywhere tonight. Look, *dónde está el cuchillo? Puede usted decirme?*'

'*Creo que no.*'

'Why not? For God's sake, you had a knife, didn't you?'

'*No sé.*'

'Look, you son of a bitch, you know damn well you had a knife. A dozen people saw you with it. Now how about it?'

Perillo was silent.

'*Tiene usted un cuchillo?*' Foster asked.

'*No.*'

'You're a liar!' Foster said. 'You *do* have a knife. What'd you do with it after you slashed that guy in the bar?'

'*Dónde está el servicio?*' Perillo asked.

'Never mind where the hell the men's room is,' Foster snapped. 'Stand up straight. What the hell do you think this is, the pool room? Take your hands out of your pockets.'

Perillo took his hands from his pockets.

'Now where's the knife?'

'*No sé.*'

'You don't know, you don't know,' Foster mimicked. 'All right, get the hell out of here. Sit down on the bench outside. I'm gonna get a cop in here who really speaks your language, pal. Now go sit down. Go ahead.'

'*Bien,*' Perillo said. '*Dónde está el servicio?*'

'Down the hall on your left. And don't take all night in there.'

Perillo went out. Foster grimaced. The man he'd cut hadn't been cut bad at all. If they knocked themselves out over every goddamn knifing they got, they'd be busy running down nothing but knifings. He wondered what it would be like to be stationed in a precinct where carving was something you did to a turkey. He grinned at his own humour, wheeled a typewriter over, and began typing up a report on the burglary they'd had several days back.

When Carella and Bush came in, they seemed in a big hurry. Carella walked directly to the phone, consulted a list of phone numbers beside it, and began dialling.

'What's up?' Foster said.

'That homicide,' Carella answered.

'Yeah?'

'It was Mike.'

'What do you mean? Huh?'

'Mike Reardon.'

'What?' Foster said. 'What?'

'Two slugs at the back of his head. I'm calling the Lieutenant. He's gonna want to move fast on this one.'

'Hey, is he kidding?' Foster said to Bush, and then he saw the look on Bush's face, and he knew this was not a joke.

Lieutenant Byrnes was the man in charge of the 87th Detective Squad. He had a small, compact body and a head like a rivet. His eyes were blue and tiny, but those eyes had seen a hell of a lot, and they didn't miss very much that went on around the lieutenant. The lieutenant knew his precinct was a trouble spot, and that was the way he liked it. It was the bad neighbourhoods that needed policemen, he was fond of saying, and he was proud to be a part of a squad that really earned its keep. There had once been sixteen men in his squad now there were fifteen.

Ten of those fifteen were gathered around him in the squadroom, the remaining five being out on plants from which they could not be yanked. The men sat in their chairs, or on the edges of desks, or they stood near the grilled windows, or they leaned against filing cabinets. The squadroom looked the way it might look at any of the times when the new shift was coming in to relieve the old one, except that there were no dirty jokes now. The men all knew that Mike Reardon was dead.

Acting Lieutenant Lynch stood alongside Byrnes while Byrnes filled his pipe. Byrnes had thick capable fingers, and he wadded the tobacco with his thumb, not looking up at the men.

Carella watched him. Carella admired and respected the lieutenant, even though many of the other men called him 'an old turd'. Carella knew cops who worked in precincts where the old man wielded a whip instead of a cerebellum. It wasn't good to work for a tyrant. Byrnes was all right, and Byrnes was also a good cop and a smart cop, and so Carella gave him his undivided attention, even though the lieutenant had not yet begun speaking.

Byrnes struck a wooden match and lighted his pipe. He gave the appearance of an unhurried man about to take his port after a heavy meal, but the wheels were grinding furiously inside his compact skull, and every fibre in his body was outraged at the death of one of his best men.

'No pep talk,' he said suddenly. 'Just go out and find the bastard.' He blew out a cloud of smoke and then waved it away with one of his short, wide hands. 'If you read the newspapers, and if you start believing them, you'll know that cops hate cop killers. That's the law of the jungle. That's the law of survival. The newspapers are wrong if they think any revenge motive is attached. We can't let a cop be killed because a cop is a symbol of law and order. If you take away the symbol, you get animals in the streets. We've got enough animals in the streets now.

'So I want you to find Reardon's killer, but not because Reardon was a cop assigned to this precinct, and not even because Reardon was a good cop. I want you to find that bastard because Reardon was a *man* – and a damned fine man.

'Handle it however you want to, you know your jobs. Give me progress reports on whatever you get from the files, and whatever you get in the streets. But find him. That's all.'

The lieutenant went back into his office with Lynch, and some of the cops went to the *modus operandi* file and began digging for information on thugs who used .45's. Some of the cops went to the Lousy File, the file of known criminals in the precinct, and they began searching for any cheap thieves who may have crossed Mike Reardon's path at one time or another. Some of the cops went to the Convictions File and began a methodical search of cards listing every conviction for which the precinct had been responsible, with a special eye out for cases on which Mike Reardon had worked. Foster went out into the corridor and told the suspect he'd questioned to get the hell home and to keep his nose clean. The rest of the cops took to the streets, and Carella and Bush were among them.

'He gripes me,' Bush said. 'He thinks he's Napoleon.'

'He's a good man,' Carella said.

'Well, *he* seems to think so, anyway.'

'Everything gripes you,' Carella said. 'You're maladjusted.'

'I'll tell you one thing,' Bush said. 'I'm getting an ulcer in this goddamn precinct. I never had trouble before, but since I got assigned to this precinct, I'm getting an ulcer. Now how do you account for that?'

There were a good many possible ways to account for Bush's ulcer and none of them had anything whatever to do with the precinct. But Carella didn't feel like arguing at the moment, and so he kept his peace. Bush simply nodded sourly.

'I want to call my wife,' he said.

'At two in the morning?' Carella asked incredulously.

'What's the matter with that?' Bush wanted to know. He was suddenly antagonistic.

'Nothing. Go ahead, call her.'

'I just want to check,' Bush said, and then he said, 'Check in.'

'Sure.'

'Hell, we may be going for days on this one.'

'Sure.'

'Anything wrong with calling her to let her know what's up?'

'Listen, are you looking for an argument,' Carella asked, smiling.

'No.'

'Then go call your wife, and get the hell off my back.'

Bush nodded emphatically. They stopped ouside an open candy store on Culver, and Bush went in to make his call. Carella stood outside, his back to the open counter at the store's front.

The city was very quiet. The tenements stretched grimy fingers towards the soft muzzle of the sky. Occasionally, a bathroom light winked like an opening eye in an otherwise blinded face. Two young Irish girls walked past the candy store, their high heels clattering on the pavement. He glanced momentarily at their legs and the thin summer frocks they wore. One of the girls winked unashamedly at him, and then both girls began giggling, and for no good reason he remembered something about lifting the skirts of an Irish lass, and the thought came to him full-blown so that he knew it was stored somewhere in his memory, and it seemed to him he had read it. Irish lasses, *Ulysses*? That had been one hell of a book to get through, pretty little lasses and all. I wonder what Bush reads? Bush is too busy to read. Bush is too busy worrying about his wife. God, does that man worry.

He glanced over his shoulder. Bush was still in the booth, talking rapidly. The man behind the counter leaned over a racing form, a toothpick angling up out of his mouth. A young kid sat at the end of the counter drinking an egg cream. Carella sucked in a breath of fetid air. The door to the phone booth opened, and Bush stepped out, mopping his brow. He nodded at the counterman, and then went out to join Carella.

'Hot as hell in that booth,' he said.

'Everything okay?' Carella asked.

'Sure,' Bush said. He looked at Carella suspiciously. 'Why shouldn't it be?'

'No reason. Any ideas where we should start?'

'This isn't going to be such a cinch,' Bush said. 'Any stupid son of a bitch with a grudge could've done it.'

'Or anybody in the middle of committing a crime.'

'We ought to leave it to Homicide. We're in over our heads.'

'We haven't even started yet, and you say we're in over our heads. What the hell's wrong with you, Hank?'

'Nothing,' Bush said, 'only I don't happen to think of cops as masterminds, that's all.'

'That's a nice thing for a cop to say.'

'It's the truth. Look, this detective tag is a laugh, and you know it as well as I do. All you need to be a detective is a strong pair of legs, and a stubborn streak. The legs take you around to all the various dumps you have to go to, and the stubborn streak keeps you from quitting. You follow each separate trail mechanically, and if you're lucky, one of the trails pays off. If you're not lucky, it doesn't. Period.'

'And brains don't enter into it at all, huh?'

'Only a little. It doesn't take much brains to be a cop.'

'Okay.'

'Okay what?'

'Okay, I don't want to argue. If Reardon got it trying to stop somebody in the commission of a crime ...'

'That's another thing that burns me up about cops,' Bush said.

'You're a regular cop hater, aren't you?' Carella asked.

'This whole goddamn city is full of cop haters. You think anybody respects a cop? Symbol of law and order! The old man ought to get out there and face life. Anybody who ever got a parking tag is automatically a cop hater. That's the way it is.'

'Well, it sure as hell shouldn't be that way,' Carella said, somewhat angrily.

Bush shrugged. 'What burns me up about cops is they don't speak English.'

'What?'

'In the commission of a crime!' Bush mocked. 'Cop talk. Did you ever hear a cop say "We caught him"? No. He says, "We apprehended him".'

'I never heard a cop say "We apprehended him",' Carella said.

'I'm talking about for official publication,' Bush said.

'Well, that's different. Everybody talks fancy when it's for official publication.'

'Cops especially.'

'Why don't you turn in your shield? Become a hackie or something?'

'I'm toying with the idea.' Bush smiled suddenly. His entire tirade had been delivered in his normally hushed voice, and now that he was smiling, it was difficult to remember that he'd been angry at all.

'Anyway, I thought the bars,' Carella said. 'I mean, if this *is* a grudge kind of thing, it might've been somebody from the neighbourhood. And we may be able to pick up something in the bars. Who the hell knows?'

'I can use a beer, anyway,' Bush said. 'I've been wanting a beer ever since I come on tonight.'

The Shamrock was one of a million bars all over the world with the same name. It squatted on Culver Avenue between a pawn shop and a Chinese laundry. It was an all-night joint, and it catered to the Irish clientele that lined Culver. Occasionally, a Puerto Rican wandered into *The Shamrock*, but such offtrail excursions were discouraged by those among *The Shamrock*'s customers who owned quick tempers and powerful fists. The cops stopped at the bar often, not to wet their whistles – because drinking on duty was strictly forbidden by the rules and regulations – but to make sure that too many quick tempers did not mix with too much whisky or too many fists. The flareups within the gaily decorated walls of the bar were now few and far between, or – to be poetic – less frequent than they had been in the good old days when the neighbourhood had first succumbed to the Puerto Rican assault wave. In those days, not speaking English too well, not reading signs too well, the Puerto Ricans stumbled into *The Shamrock* with remarkably ignorant rapidity. The staunch defenders of America for the Americans, casually ignoring the fact that Puerto Ricans were and are Americans, spent many a pugilistic evening proving their point. The bar was often brilliantly decorated with spilled blood. But that was in the good old days. In the bad new days, you could go into *The Shamrock* for a week running, and not see more than one or two broken heads.

There was a Ladies Invited sign in the window of the bar, but not many ladies accepted the invitation. The drinkers were, instead, neighbourhood men who tired of the four walls of their dreary tenement flats, who sought the carefree camaraderie of other men who had similarly grown weary of their own homes. Their wives were out playing Bingo on Tuesdays, or at the movies collecting a piece of china on Wednesdays, or across the street with the Sewing Club ('We so and so and so and so') on Thursdays, and so it went. So what was wrong with a friendly brew in a neighbourhood tavern? Nothing.

Except when the cops showed.

Now there was something very disgusting about policemen in general, and bulls in particular. Sure, you could go through the motions of saying, 'How are yuh, this evenin', Officer Dugan?' and all that sort of rot, and you could really and truly maybe hold a fond spot in the old ticker for the new rookie, but you still couldn't deny that a cop sitting next to you when you were half-way towards getting a snootful was a somewhat disconcerting thing and would likely bring on the goblins in the morning. Not that anyone had anything against cops. It was just that cops should not loiter around bars and spoil a man's earnest drinking. Nor should cops hang around book joints and spoil a man's earnest gambling. Nor should they hang around brothels and spoil a man's earnest endeavours too, cops simply shouldn't hang around, that was all.

And bulls, bulls were cops in disguise, only worse.

So what did those two big jerks at the end of the bar want?

'A beer, Harry,' Bush said.

'Comin' up,' Harry the bartender answered. He drew the beer and brought it over to where Bush and Carella were seated. 'Good night for a beer, ain't it?' Harry said.

'I never knew a bartender who didn't give you a commercial when you ordered a beer on a hot night,' Bush said quietly.

Harry laughed, but only because his customer was a cop. Two men at the shuffleboard table were arguing about an Irish free state. The late movie on television was about a Russian empress.

'You fellows here on business?' Harry asked.

'Why?' Bush said. 'You got any for us?'

'No, I was just wonderin'. I mean, it ain't often we get the bu ... it ain't often a detective drops by,' Harry said.

'That's because you run such a clean establishment,' Bush said.

'Ain't none cleaner on Culver.'

'Not since they ripped your phone booth out,' Bush said.

'Yeah, well, we were gettin' too many phone calls.'

'You were taking too many bets,' Bush said, his voice even. He picked up the glass of beer, dipped his upper lip into the foam, and then downed it.

'No, no kiddin',' Harry said. He did not like to think of the close call he'd had with that damn phone booth and the State Attorney's Commission. 'You fellows lookin' for somebody?'

'Kind of quiet tonight,' Carella said.

Harry smiled, and a gold tooth flashed at the front of his mouth. 'Oh, always quiet in here, fellows, you know that.'

'Sure,' Carella said, nodding. 'Danny Gimp drop in?'

'No, haven't seen him tonight. Why? What's up?'

'That's good beer,' Bush said.

'Like another?'

'No, thanks.'

'Say, are you sure nothing's wrong?' Harry asked.

'What's with you, Harry? Somebody do something wrong here?' Carella asked.

'What? No, hey, no I hope I didn't give you that impression. It's just kind of strange, you fellows dropping in. I mean, we haven't had any trouble here or anything.'

'Well, that's good,' Carella said. 'See anybody with a gun lately.'

'A gun?'

'Yeah.'

'What kind of gun?'

'What kind did you see?'

'I didn't see any kind.' Harry was sweating. He drew a beer for himself and drank it hastily.

'None of the young punks in with zip guns or anything?' Bush asked quietly.

'Oh, well zip guns,' Harry said, wiping the foam from his lip, 'I mean, you see them all the time.'

'And nothing bigger?'

'Bigger like what? Like you mean a .32 or a .38?'

'Like we mean a .45,' Carella said.

'The last .45 I seen in here,' Harry said, thinking, 'was away back in . . .' He shook his head. 'No, that wouldn't help you. What happened? Somebody get shot?'

'Away back *when*?' Bush asked.

'Fifty, fifty-one, it must've been. Kid discharged from the Army. Come in here wavin' a .45 around. He was lookin' for trouble all right, that kid. Dooley busted it up. You remember Dooley? He used to have this beat before he got transferred out to another precinct. Nice kid. Always used to stop by and . . .'

'He still live in the neighbourhood?' Bush asked.

'Huh? Who?'

'The guy who was in here waving the .45 around.'

'Oh, him.' Harry's brows swooped down over his eyes. 'Why?'

'I'm asking you,' Bush said. 'Does he or doesn't he?'

'Yeah. I guess. Why?'

'Where?'

'Listen,' Harry said, 'I don't want to get nobody in trouble.'

'You're not getting anybody in trouble,' Bush said. 'Does this guy still own the .45?'

'I don't know.'

'What happened that night? When Dooley busted it up.'

'Nothing. The kid had a load on. You know, just out of the Army, like that.'

'Like what?'

'Like he was wavin' the gun around. I don't even think it was loaded. I think the barrel was leaded.'

'Are you sure it was?'

'Well, no.'

'Did Dooley take the gun away from him?'

'Well . . .' Harry paused and mopped his brow. 'Well, I don't think Dooley even saw the gun.'

'If he busted it up . . .'

'Well,' Harry said, 'one of the fellows saw Dooley comin' down the street, and they kind of calmed the kid down and got him out of here.'

'*Before* Dooley came in?'

'Well, yeah. Yeah.'

'And the kid took the gun with him when he left?'

'Yeah,' Harry said. 'Look, I don't want no trouble in my place, you follow?'

'I follow,' Bush said. 'Where does he live?'

Harry blinked his eyes. He looked down at the bar top.

'Where?' Bush repeated.

'On Culver.'

'Where on Culver?'

'The house on the corner of Culver and Mason. Look, fellows ...'

'This guy mention anything about not liking cops?' Carella asked.

'No, no,' Harry said. 'He's a fine boy. He just had a couple of sheets to the wind that night, that's all.'

'You know Mike Reardon?'

'Oh, sure,' Harry said.

'This kid know Mike?'

'Well, I can't say as I know. Look, the kid was just squiffed that night, that's all.'

'What's his name?'

'Look, he was only tanked up, that's all. Hell, it was away back in 1950.'

'What's his name?'

'Frank. Frank Clarke. With an "e".'

'What do you think Steve?' Bush asked Carella.

Carella shrugged. 'It came too easy. It's never good when it comes that easy.'

'Let's check it, anyway,' Bush said.

Chapter Four

There are smells inside a tenement, and they are not only the smell of cabbage. The smell of cabbage, to many, is and always will be a good wholesome smell and there are many who resent the steady propaganda which links cabbage with poverty.

The smell inside a tenement is the smell of life.

It is the smell of every function of life, the sweating, the cooking, the elimination, the breeding. It is all these smells, and they are wedded into one gigantic smell which hits the nostrils the moment you enter the downstairs doorway. For the smell has been inside the building for decades. It has seeped through the floorboards and permeated the walls. It clings to the banister and the linoleum-covered steps. It crouches in corners and it hovers about the naked light bulbs on each landing. The smell is always there, day and night. It is the stench of living, and it never sees the light of day, and it never sees the crisp brittleness of starlight.

It was there on the morning of July 24 at 3:00 a.m. It was there in full force because the heat of the day had baked it into the walls. It hit Carella as he and

Bush entered the building. He snorted through his nostrils and then struck a match and held it to the mailboxes.

'There it is,' Bush said. 'Clarke. 3B.'

Carella shook out the match and they walked towards the steps. The garbage cans were in for the night, stacked on the ground floor landing behind the steps. Their aroma joined the other smells to clash in a medley of putridity. The building slept, but the smells were awake. On the second floor, a man – or a woman – snored loudly. On each door, close to the floor, the circular trap for a milk bottle lock hung despondently, awaiting the milkman's arrival. On one of the doors hung a plaque, and the plaque read IN GOD WE TRUST. And behind that door, there was undoubtedly the unbending steel bar of a police lock, embedded in the floor and tilted to lean against the door.

Carella and Bush laboured up to the third floor. The light bulb on the third floor landing was out. Bush struck a match.

'Down the hall there.'

'You want to do this up big?' Carella asked.

'He's got a .45 in there, hasn't he?'

'Still.'

'What the hell, my wife doesn't need my insurance money,' Bush said.

They walked to the door and flanked it. They drew their service revolvers with nonchalance. Carella didn't for a moment believe he'd need his gun, but caution never hurt. He drew back his left hand and knocked on the door.

'Probably asleep,' Bush said.

'Betokens a clear conscience,' Carella answered. He knocked again.

'Who is it?' a voice answered.

'Police. Want to open up?'

'Oh, for God's sake,' the voice mumbled. 'Just a minute.'

'We won't need these,' Bush said. He holstered his gun, and Carella followed suit. From within the apartment, they could hear bed springs creaking, and then a woman's voice asking 'What is it?' They heard footsteps approaching the door, and then someone fumbled with the police lock on the inside, and the heavy steel bar clattered when it was dropped to the floor. The door opened a crack.

'What do you want?' the voice said.

'Police. We'd like to ask you a few questions.'

'At this time of the morning? Can't it wait?'

'Afraid it can't.'

'Well, what's the matter? There a burglar in the building?'

'No. We'd just like to ask you some questions. You're Frank Clarke, aren't you?'

'Yeah.' Clarke paused. 'Let me see your badge.'

Carella reached into his pocket for the leather case to which his shield was pinned. He held it up to the crack in the door.

'I can't see nothing,' Clarke said. 'Just a minute.'

'Who is it?' the woman asked.

'The cops,' Clarke mumbled. He stepped away from the door, and then a light flashed inside the apartment. He came back to the door. Carella held up the badge again.

'Yeah, okay,' Clarke said. 'What do you want?'

'You own a .45, Clarke?'

'What?'

'A .45. Do you own one?'

'My God, is that what you want to know? Is that what you come banging on the door for in the middle of the night? Ain't you guys got any sense at all? I got to go to work in the morning.'

'Do you have a .45, or don't you?'

'Who said I had one?'

'Never mind who. How about it?'

'Why do you want to know? I been here all night.'

'Anybody to swear for that?'

Clarke's voice lowered. 'Hey, look, fellows, I got somebody with me, you know what I mean? Look, give me a break, will you?'

'What about the gun?'

'Yeah. I got one.'

'A .45?'

'Yeah. Yeah, it's a .45.'

'Mind if we take a look at it?'

'What for? I've got a permit for it.'

'We'd like to look at it anyway.'

'Hey, look, what the hell kind of a routine is this, anyway? I told you I got a permit for the gun. What did I do wrong? Whattya want from me, anyway?'

'We want to see the .45,' Bush said. 'Get it.'

'You got a search warrant?' Clarke asked.

'Never mind that,' Bush said. 'Get the gun.'

'You can't come in here without a search warrant. And you can't bulldoze me into gettin' the gun, either. I don't want to get that gun, then you can whistle.'

'How old's the girl in there?' Bush asked.

'What?'

'You heard me. Wake up, Clarke!'

'She's 21, and you're barkin' up the wrong tree,' Clarke said. 'We're engaged.'

From down the hall, someone shouted, 'Hey, shut up, willya? For Christ's sake! Go down to the poolroom, you want to talk!'

'How about letting us in, Clarke?' Carella asked gently. 'We're waking your neighbours.'

'I don't have to let you in noplace. Go get a search warrant.'

'I know you don't, Clarke. But a cop's been killed, and he was killed with a .45, and if I were you I wouldn't play this so goddamn cosy. Now how about opening that door and showing us you're clean? How about it, Clarke?'

'A cop? You say, a cop! Why didn't you say so? Just a ... just a minute, willya? Just a minute.' He moved away from the door. Carella could hear him talking to the woman, and he could hear the woman's whispered answer. Clarke came back to the door and took off the night chain. 'Come on in,' he said.

There were dishes stacked in the kitchen sink. The kitchen was a six-by-eight rectangle, and adjoining that was the bedroom. The girl stood in the bedroom doorway. She was a short blonde, somewhat dumpy. She wore a man's bathrobe. Her eyes were puffed with sleep, and she wore no makeup.

She blinked her eyes and stared at Carella and Bush as they moved into the kitchen.

Clarke was a short man with bushy black brows and brown eyes. His nose was long, broken sharply in the middle. His lips were thick, and he needed a shave badly. He was wearing pyjama pants and nothing else. He stood bare-chested and bare-footed in the glare of the kitchen light. The water tap dripped its tattoo on the dirty dishes in the sink.

'Let's see the gun,' Bush said.

'I got a permit for it,' Clarke answered. 'Okay if I smoke?'

'It's your apartment.'

'Gladys,' Clarke said, 'there's a pack on the dresser. Bring some matches, too, willya?' The girl moved into the darkness of the bedroom, and Clarke whispered, 'You guys sure picked a hell of a time to come calling, all right.' He tried a smile, but neither Carella or Bush seemed amused, and so he dropped it instantly. The girl came back with the package of cigarettes. She hung one on her lip, and then handed the pack to Clarke. He lighted his own cigarette and then handed the matches to the blonde.

'What kind of a permit?' Carella asked. 'Carry or premises?'

'Carry,' Clarke said.

'How come?'

'Well, it used to be premises. I registered the gun when I got out of the Army. It was a gift,' he said quickly. 'From my captain.'

'Go ahead.'

'So I got a premises permit when I was discharged. That's the law, ain't it?'

'You're telling the story,' Bush said.

'Well, that's the way I understood it. Either that, or I had to get the barrel leaded up. I don't remember. Anyway, I got the permit.'

'*Is* the barrel leaded?'

'Hell, no. What do I need a permit for a dead gun for? I had this premises permit, and then I got a job with a jeweller, you know? Like I had to make a lot of valuable deliveries, things like that. So I had it changed to a carry permit.'

'When was this?'

'Couple of months back.'

'Which jeweller do you work for?'

'I quit that job,' Clarke said.

'All right, get the gun. And get the permit, too, while you're at it.'

'Sure,' Clarke said. He went to the sink, held his cigarette under the dripping tap, and then dropped the soggy butt in with the dishes. He walked past the girl and into the bedroom.

'This is some time of night to be asking questions,' the girl said angrily.

'We're sorry, Miss,' Carella said.

'Yeah, I'll bet you are.'

'We didn't mean to disturb your beauty sleep,' Bush said nastily.

The girl raised one eyebrow. 'Then why did you?' She blew out a cloud of smoke, the way she had seen movie sirens do. Clarke came back into the room holding the .45. Bush's hand moved imperceptibly towards his right hip and the holster there.

'Put it on the table,' Carella said.

Clarke put the gun on the table.

'Is it loaded?'- Carella asked.

'I think so.'

'Don't you know?'

'I ain't even looked at the thing since I quit that job.'

Carella draped a handkerchief over his spread fingers and picked up the gun. He slid the magazine out. 'It's loaded, all right,' he said. Quickly, he sniffed the barrel.

'You don't have to smell,' Clarke said. 'It ain't been fired since I got out of the Army.'

'It came close once, though, didn't it?'

'Huh?'

'That night in *The Shamrock*.'

'Oh, that,' Clarke said. 'Is that why you're here? Hell, I was looped that night. I didn't mean no harm.'

Carella slammed the magazine back into place. 'Where's the permit, Clarke?'

'Oh, yeah. I looked around in there. I couldn't find it.'

'You're sure you've got one?'

'Yeah, I'm sure. I just can't find it.'

'You'd better take another look. A good one, this time.'

'I did take a good look. I can't find it. Look, I got a permit. You can check on it. I wouldn't kid you. Who was the cop got killed?'

'Want to take another look for the permit?'

'I already told you, I can't find it. Look, I got one.'

'You *had* one, pal,' Carella said. 'You just lost it.'

'Huh? What? What'd you say?'

'When a cop asks you for your permit, you produce it or you lose it.'

'Well, hell, I just misplaced it temporarily. Look, you can check all this. I mean . . . look, what's the matter with you guys, anyway? I didn't do nothing. I been here all night. You can ask Gladys. Ain't that right, Gladys?'

'He's been here all night,' Gladys said.

'We're taking the gun,' Carella said. 'Give him a receipt for it, Hank.'

'That ain't been fired in years,' Clarke said. 'You'll see. And you check on that permit. I got one. You check on it.'

'We'll let you know,' Carella said. 'You weren't planning on leaving the city were you?'

'Hell, no. Where would I go?'

'Back to sleep is as good a place as any,' the blonde said.

Chapter Five

The pistol permit was on Steve Carella's desk when he reported for work at 4:00 p.m. on the afternoon of July 24. He had worked until eight in the morning, gone home for six hours' sleep, and was back at his desk now, looking a little bleary-eyed but otherwise none the worse for wear.

The heat had persisted all day long, a heavy yellow blanket that smothered the city in its woolly grip. Carella did not like the heat. He had never liked summer, even as a kid, and now that he was an adult and a cop, the only memorable characteristic summer seemed to have was that it made dead bodies decompose more quickly.

He loosened his collar the instant he entered the squadroom, and when he got to his desk, he rolled up his sleeves, and then picked up the pistol permit.

Quickly, he scanned the printed form.

License No.	Date	Police Department	Year	

PISTOL LICENSE APPLICATION

(APPLICATION MUST BE MADE IN DUPLICATE)

I Hereby Apply for License to Carry a Revolver or Pistol upon my person or Possession on premises

37-12 Culver Avenue

For the following reasons: Make deliveries for jewelry firm.

Clarke	Francis D.		37 -12 Culver Ave.
(PRINT) Surname	**Given Name**	**Initials**	**Number** **Street**

There was more, a lot more, but it didn't interest Carella. Clarke had indeed owned a pistol permit – but that didn't mean he hadn't used the pistol on a cop named Mike Reardon.

Carella shoved the permit to one side of his desk, glanced at his watch, and then reached for the phone automatically. Quickly, he dialled Bush's home number and then waited, his hand sweating on the receiver. The phone rang six times, and then a woman's voice said, 'Hello?'

'Alice?'

'Who's this?'

'Steve Carella.'

'Oh. Hello, Steve.'

'Did I wake you?'

'Yes.'

'Hank's not here yet. He's all right, isn't he?'

'He left a little while ago,' Alice said. The sleep was beginning to leave her voice already. Alice Bush was a cop's wife who generally slept when her husband did, adjusting her schedule to fit his. Carella had spoken to her on a good many mornings and afternoons, and he always marvelled at the way she could come almost instantly awake within the space of three or four sentences. Her voice invariably sounded like the first faint rattle of impending death when she picked up the receiver. As the conversation progressed, it modulated into the dulcet whine of a middle-aged Airedale, and then into the disconcertingly sexy voice which was the normal speaking voice of Hank's wife. Carella had met her on one occasion, when he and Hank had shared a late snack with her, and he knew that she was a dynamic blonde with a magnificent figure and the brownest eyes he'd ever seen. From what Bush had expansively delivered about personal aspects of his home life, Carella knew that Alice slept in clinging black, sheer nightgowns. The knowledge was unnerving, for whenever Carella roused her out of bed, he automatically formed a mental picture of the well-rounded blonde he'd met, and the picture was always dressed as Hank had described it.

He generally, therefore, cut his conversations with Alice short, feeling somewhat guilty about the artistic inclinations of his mind. This morning, though, Alice seemed to be in a talkative mood.

'I understand one of your colleagues got knocked off,' she said.

Carella smiled, in spite of the topic's grimness. Alice sometimes had a peculiar way of mixing the King's English with choice bits of underworld and police vernacular.

'Yes,' he said.

'I'm awfully sorry,' she answered, her voice changing. 'Please be careful, you and Hank. If a cheap hood is shooting up the streets . . .'

'We'll be careful,' he said. 'I've got to go now, Alice.'

'I leave Hank in capable hands,' Alice said, and she hung up without saying goodbye.

Carella grinned and shrugged, and then put the receiver back into the cradle. David Foster, his brown face looking scrubbed and shining, ambled over to the desk. 'Afternoon Steve,' he said.

'Hi, Dave. What've you got?'

'Ballistics report on that .45 you brought in last night.'

'Any luck?'

'Hasn't been fired since Old King Cole ordered the bowl.'

'Well, that narrows it down,' Carella said. 'Now we've only got the nine million, nine hundred ninety-nine thousand other people in this fair city to contend with.'

'I don't like it when cops get killed,' Foster said. His brow lowered menacingly, giving him the appearance of a bull ducking his head to charge at the *muleta*. 'Mike was my partner. He was a good guy.'

'I know.'

'I been trying to think who,' Foster said. 'I got my personal I.B. right up here, and I been leafing through them mug shots one by one.' He tapped his temple. 'I been turning them over and studying them, and so far I haven't got anything, but give me time. Somebody musta had it in for Mike, and when that face falls into place, that guy's gonna wish he was in Alaska.'

'Tell you the truth,' Carella said, 'I wish I was there right now.'

'Hot, ain't it?' Foster said, classically understating the temperature and humidity.

'Yeah.' From the corner of his eye, Carella saw Bush walk down the corridor, push through the railing, and sign in. He walked to Carella's desk, pulled over a swivel chair and plopped into it disconsolately.

'Rough night?' Foster asked, grinning.

'The roughest,' Bush said in his quiet voice.

'Clarke was a blank,' Carella told him.

'I figured as much. Where do we go from here?'

'That's a good question.'

'Coroner's report in yet?'

'No.'

'The boys picked up some hoods for questioning,' Foster said. 'We might give them the once over.'

'Where are they? Downstairs?' Carella asked.

'In the Waldorf Suite,' Foster said, referring to the detention cells on the first floor of the building.

'Why don't you call down for them?'

'Sure,' Foster said.

'Where's the Skipper?'

'He's over at Homicide North. He's trying to goose them into some real action on this one.'

'You see the paper this morning?' Bush asked.

'No,' Carella said.

'Mike made the front page. Have a look.' He put the paper on Carella's desk. Carella held it up so that Foster could see it while he spoke on the phone.

'Shot him in the back,' Foster mumbled. 'That lousy bastard.' He spoke into the phone and then hung up. The men lighted cigarettes, and Bush phoned out for coffee, and then they sat around gassing. The prisoners arrived before the coffee did.

There were two men, both unshaven, both tall, both wearing short-sleeved sports shirts. The physical resemblance ended there. One of the men owned a handsome face, with regular features and white, even teeth. The other man looked as if his face had challenged a concrete mixer and lost. Carella recognized both of them at once. Mentally, he flipped over their cards in the Lousy File.

'Were they picked up together?' he asked the uniformed cop who brought them into the squadroom.

'Yeah,' the cop said.

'Where?'

'13th and Shippe. They were sitting in a parked car.'

'Any law against that?' the handsome one asked.

'At three in the morning,' the uniformed cop added.

'Okay,' Carella said. 'Thanks.'

'What's your name?' Bush asked the handsome one.

'You know my name, cop.'

'Say it again. I like the sound.'

'I'm tired.'

'You're gonna be a lot more tired before this is finished. Now cut the comedy, and answer the questions. Your name?'

'Terry.'

'Terry what?'

'Terry McCarthy. What the hell is this, a joke? You know my name.'

'How about your buddy?'

'You know him, too. He's Clarence Kelly.'

'What were you doing in that car?' Carella asked.

'Looking at dirty pictures,' McCarthy said.

'Possession of pornography,' Carella said dully. 'Take that down, Hank.'

'Hey, wait a minute,' McCarthy said. 'I was only wisecrackin'.'

'DON'T WISECRACK ON MY TIME!!' Carella shouted.

'Okay, okay, don't get sore.'

'What were you doing in that car?'

'Sitting.'

'You always sit in parked cars at three in the a.m.?' Foster asked.

'Sometimes,' McCarthy said.

'What else were you doing?'

'Talking.'

'What about?'

'Everything.'

'Philosophy?' Bush asked.

'Yeah,' McCarthy said.

'What'd you decide?'

'We decided it ain't wise to sit in parked cars at three in the morning. There's always some cop who's got to fill his pinch book.'

Carella tapped a pencil on the desk. 'Don't get me mad, McCarthy,' he said. 'I just come from six hours' sleep, and I don't feel like listening to a vaudeville routine. Did you know Mike Reardon?'

'Who?'

'Mike Reardon. A detective attached to this precinct.'

McCarthy shrugged. He turned to Kelly. 'We know him, Clarence?'

'Yeah,' Clarence said. 'Reardon. That rings a bell.'

'How big a bell?' Foster asked.

'Just a tiny tinkle so far,' Kelly said, and he began laughing. The laugh died when he saw the bulls weren't quite appreciating his humour.

'Did you see him last night?'

'No.'

'How do you know?'

'We didn't run across any bulls last night,' Kelly said.

'Do you usually?'

'Well, sometimes.'

'Were you heeled when they pulled you in?'

'What?'

'Come on,' Foster said.

'No.'

'We'll check that.'

'Yeah, go ahead,' McCarthy said. 'We didn't even have a water pistol between us.'

'What were you doing in the car?'

'I just told you,' McCarthy said.

'The story stinks. Try again,' Carella answered.

Kelly sighed. McCarthy looked at him.

'Well?' Carella said.

'I was checkin' up on my dame,' Kelly said.

'Yeah?' Bush said.

'Truth,' Kelly said. 'So help me God, may I be struck dead right this goddamn minute.'

'What's there to check up on?' Bush asked.

'Well, you know.'

'No, I don't know. Tell me.'

'I figured she was maybe slippin' around.'

'Slipping around with who?' Bush asked.

'Well, that's what I wanted to find out.'

'And what were you doing with him, McCarthy?'

'I was helping him check,' McCarthy said, smiling.

'Was she?' Bush asked, a bored expression on his face.

'No, I don't think so,' Kelly said.

'Don't check again,' Bush said. 'Next time we're liable to find you with the burglar's tools.'

'Burglar's tools!' McCarthy said, shocked.

'Gee, Detective Bush,' Kelly said, 'you know us better than that.'

'Get the hell out of here,' Bush said.

'We can go home?'

'You can go to hell, for my part,' Bush informed them.

'Here's the coffee,' Foster said.

The released prisoners sauntered out of the squadroom. The three detectives paid the delivery boy for the coffee and then pulled chairs up to one of the desks.

'I heard a good one last night,' Foster said.

'Let's hear it,' Carella prompted.

'This guy is a construction worker, you see?'

'Yeah.'

'Working up on a girder about sixty floors above the street.'

'Yeah?'

'The lunch whistle blows. He knocks off, goes to the end of the girder, sits down, and puts his lunch box on his lap. He opens the box, takes out a sandwich and very carefully unwraps the waxed paper. Then he bites into it. "Goddamn!" he says, "peanut butter!" and he throws the sandwich down the sixty floors to the street.'

'I don't get it,' Bush said, sipping his coffee.

'I'm not finished yet,' Foster said, grinning, hardly able to contain his glee.

'Go ahead,' Carella said.

'He reaches into the box,' Foster said, 'for the next sandwich. He very carefully unwraps the waxed paper. He bites into the sandwich. "Goddamn!" he says again, "peanut butter!" and he flings that second sandwich down the sixty floors to the street.'

'Yeah,' Carella said.

'He opens the third sandwich,' Foster said. 'This time it's ham. This time he likes it. He eats the sandwich all up.'

'This is gonna go on all night,' Bush said. 'You shoulda stood in bed, Dave.'

'No wait a minute, wait a minute,' Foster said. 'He opens the fourth sandwich. He bites into it. "Goddamn!" he says again, "peanut butter!" and he flings that sandwich too down the sixty floors to the street. Well, there's another construction worker sitting on a girder just a little bit above this fellow. He looks down and says, "Say, fellow, I've been watching you with them sandwiches."'

'"So what?" the first guy says.

'"You married?" the second guy asks.

'"Yes, I'm married."

'The second guy shakes his head, "How long you been married?"

'"Ten years," the first guy says.

'"And your wife still doesn't know what kind of sandwiches you like?"

'The first guy points his finger up at the guy above him and yells, "You leave my wife out of this. I made those goddamn sandwiches myself!"'

Carella burst out laughing, almost choking on his coffee. Bush stared at Foster dead-panned.

'I still don't get it,' Bush said. 'What's so funny about a guy married ten years whose wife doesn't know what kind of sandwiches he likes? That's not funny. That's a tragedy.'

'He made the sandwiches *himself*,' Foster said.

'So then it's a psycho joke. Psycho jokes don't appeal to me. You got to be nuts to appreciate a psycho joke.'

'I appreciate it,' Carella said.

'So? That proves my point,' Bush answered.

'Hank didn't get enough sleep,' Carella said to Foster. Foster winked.

'I got plenty of sleep,' Bush said.

'Ah-ha,' Carella said. 'Then that explains it.'

'What the hell do you mean by that?' Bush said, annoyed.

'Oh, forget it. Drink your coffee.'

'A man doesn't get a joke, right away his sex life gets dragged in. Do I ask you how much sleep you get or don't get?'

'No,' Carella said.

'Okay. Okay.'

One of the patrolmen walked into the squadroom. 'Desk sergeant asked me to give you this,' he said. 'Just came up from Downtown.'

'Probably that Coroner's report,' Carella said, taking the manila envelope. 'Thanks.'

The patrolman nodded and went out. Carella opened the envelope.

'Is it?' Foster asked.

BULLET

Calibre	Weight	Twist	No. of Grooves
.45	230grms.	16L	6

Width of land marks		Width of groove marks	
	.071		.158

Metal Case		Half Metal		Soft Point	
	Brass				No

Deceased	Michael Reardon		Date	July 24th

Remarks: Remington bullet taken from wooden booth

behind body of Michael Reardon

'Yeah. Something else, too.' He pulled a card from the envelope. 'Oh, report on the slugs they dug out of the theatre booth.'

'Let's see it,' Hank said.

Carella handed him the card.

'Argh, so what does it tell us?' Bush said, still smarting from the earlier badinage.

'Nothing,' Carella answered, 'until we get the gun that fired it.'

'What about the Coroner's report?' Foster asked.

Carella slipped it out of the envelope.

CORONER'S PRELIMINARY
AUTOPSY REPORT

MICHAEL REARDON

Male, apparent age 42; chronological age 38. Approximate weight 210 pounds; height 289 cm.

GROSS INSPECTION

HEAD: 1.0 × 1.25 cm circular perforation visible 3.1 centimetres laterally to the left of external occipital protuberance (inion). Wound edges slightly inverted. Flame zone and second zone reveal heavy embedding of powder grains. A number 22 catheter inserted through the wound in the occipital region of the skull transverses ventrally and emerges through the right orbit. Point of emergence has left a gaping rough-edged wound measuring 3.7 centimetres in diameter.

There is a second perforation located 6.2 centimetres laterally to the left of the tip of the right mastoid process of the temporal bone, measuring 1.0 × 1.33 centimetres. A number 22 catheter inserted through this second wound passes anteriorly and ventrally and emerges through a perforation measuring approximately 3.5 centimetres in diameter through the right maxilla. The edges of the remaining portion of the right maxilla are splintered.

BODY: Gross inspection of remaining portion of body is negative for demonstrable pathology.

REMARKS: On craniotomy with brain examination, there is evidence of petechiae along course of projectile; splinters of cranial bone are embedded within the brain substance.

MICROSCOPIC: Examination of brain reveals minute petechiae as well as bone substance within brain matter. Microscopic examination of brain tissue is essentially negative for pathology.

'He did a good job,' Foster said.

'Yeah,' Bush answered.

Carella sighed and looked at his watch. 'It's going to be a long night, fellers,' he said.

Chapter Six

He had not seen Teddy Franklin since Mike took the slugs.

Generally, in the course of running down something, he would drop in to see her spending a few minutes with her before rushing off again. And, of course, he spent all his free time with her because he was in love with the girl.

He had met her less than six months ago, when she'd been working addressing envelopes for a small firm on the fringe of the precinct territory. The firm reported a burglary, and Carella had been assigned to it. He had been taken instantly with her buoyant beauty, asked her out, and that had been the beginning. He had also, in the course of investigation, cracked the burglary – but that didn't seem important now. The important thing now was Teddy. Even the firm had gone the way of most small firms, fading into the abyss of a corporate dissolution, leaving her without a job but with enough saved money to maintain herself for a while. He honestly hoped it would only be for a while, a short while at that. This was the girl he wanted to marry. This was the girl he wanted for his own.

Thinking of her, thinking of the progression of slow traffic lights which kept him from racing to her side, he cursed Ballistics Reports and Coroner's Reports, and people who shot cops in the back of the head, and he cursed the devilish instrument known as the telephone and the fact that the instrument was worthless with a girl like Teddy. He glanced at his watch. It was close to midnight, and she didn't know he was coming, but he'd take the chance, anyway. He wanted to see her.

When he reached her apartment building in Riverhead, he parked the car and locked it. The street was very quiet. The building was old and sedate, covered with lush ivy. A few windows blinked wide-eyed at the stifling heat of the night, but most of the tenants were asleep or trying to sleep. He glanced up at her window, pleased when he saw the light was still burning. Quickly, he mounted the steps, stopping outside her door.

He did not knock.

Knocking was no good with Teddy.

He took the knob in his hand and twisted it back and forth, back and forth. In a few moments, he heard her footsteps, and then the door opened a crack, and then the door opened wide.

She was wearing prisoner pyjamas, white-and-black striped cotton top and pants she'd picked up as a gag. Her hair was raven black, and the light in the foyer put a high sheen onto it. He closed the door behind him, and she went instantly into his arms, and then she moved back from him, and he marvelled at the expressiveness of her eyes and her mouth. There was joy in her eyes, pure soaring joy. Her lips parted, edging back over small white teeth, and then she lifted her face to his, and he took her kiss, and he felt the warmth of her body beneath the cotton pyjamas.

'Hello,' he said, and she kissed the words on his mouth and then broke away, holding only his hand, pulling him into the warmly-lighted living room.

She held her right index finger alongside her face, calling for his attention.

'Yes?' he said, and then she shook her head, changing her mind, wanting him to sit first. She fluffed a pillow for him, and he sat in the easy chair, and she perched herself on the arm of the chair and cocked her head to one side, repeating the extended index finger gesture.

'Go ahead,' he said, 'I'm listening.'

She watched his lips carefully, and then she smiled. Her index finger dropped. There was a white tag sewed onto the prisoner pyjama top close to the mound of her left breast. She ran the extended finger across the tag. He looked at it closely.

'I'm not examining your feminine attributes,' he said, smiling, and she shook her head, understanding. She had inked numbers onto the tag, carrying out the prison garb motif. He studied the numbers closely.

'My shield numbers,' he said, and the smile flowered on her mouth. 'You deserve a kiss for that,' he told her.

She shook her head.

'No kiss?'

She shook her head again.

'Why not?'

She opened and closed the fingers on her right hand.

'You want to talk?' he asked.

She nodded.

'What about?'

She left the arm of the chair suddenly. She went to an end-table and picked up a newspaper. She carried it back to him and then pointed to the picture of Mike Reardon on page one, his brains spilling out onto the sidewalk.

'Yeah,' he said dully.

There was sadness on her face now, an exaggerated sadness because Teddy could not give tongue to words, Teddy could neither hear words, and so her face was her speaking tool, and she spoke in exaggerated syllables, even to Carella, who understood the slightest nuance of expression in her eyes or on her mouth. But the exaggeration did not lie, for there was genuineness to the grief she felt. She had never met Mike Reardon, but Carella had talked of him often, and she felt that she knew him well.

She raised her eyebrows and spread her hands simultaneously, asking Carella 'Who?' and Carella, understanding instantly, said, 'We don't know yet. That's why I haven't been around. We've been working on it.' He saw puzzlement in her eyes. 'Am I going too fast for you?' he asked.

She shook her head.

'What then? What's the matter?'

She threw herself into his arms and she was weeping suddenly and fiercely, and he said, 'Hey, hey, come on, now,' and then realized she could not read his lips because her head was buried in his shoulder. He lifted her chin.

'You're getting my shirt wet,' he said.

She nodded, trying to hold back the tears.

'What's the matter?'

She lifted her hand slowly, and she touched his cheek gently, so gently that it felt like the passing of a mild breeze, and then her fingers touched his lips and lingered there, caressing them.

'You're worried about me?'

She nodded.

'There's nothing to worry about.'

She tossed her hair at the first page of the newspaper again.

'That was probably some crackpot,' Carella said.

She lifted her face, and her eyes met his fully, wide and brown, still moist from the tears.

'I'll be careful,' he said. 'Do you love me?'

She nodded, and then ducked her head.

'What's the matter?'

She shrugged and smiled, an embarrassed, shy smile.

'You missed me?'

She nodded again.

'I missed you, too.'

She lifted her head again, and there was something else in her eyes this time, a challenge to him to read her eyes correctly this time, because she had truly missed him but he had not uncovered the subtlety of her meaning as yet. He studied her eyes, and then he knew what she was saying, and he said only, 'Oh.'

She knew that he knew then, and she cocked one eyebrow saucily and slowly gave one exaggerated nod of her head, repeating his 'oh,' soundlessly rounding her lips.

'You're just a fleshpot,' he said jokingly.

She nodded.

'You only love me because I have a clean, strong, young body.'

She nodded.

'Will you marry me?'

She nodded.

'I've only asked you about a dozen times so far.'

She shrugged and nodded, enjoying herself immensely.

'When?'

She pointed at him.

'All right, I'll set the date. I'm getting my vacation in August. I'll marry you then, okay?'

She sat perfectly still, staring at him.

'I mean it.'

She seemed ready to cry again. He took her in his arms and said, 'I mean it, Teddy. Teddy, darling, I mean it. Don't be silly about this, Teddy, because I honestly, truly mean it. I love you, and I want to marry you, and I've wanted to marry you for a long, long time now, and if I have to keep asking you, I'll go nuts. I love you just the way you are, I wouldn't change any of you, darling, so don't get silly, please don't get silly again. It ... it doesn't matter to me, Teddy. Little Teddy, little Theodora, it doesn't matter to me, can you understand that? You're *more* than any other woman, so much more, so please marry me.'

She looked up at him, wishing she could speak because she could not trust her eyes now, wondering why someone as beautiful as Steve Carella, as wonderful as Steve Carella, as brave and as strong and as marvellous as Steve Carella would want to marry a girl like her, a girl who could never say, 'I love you, darling, I adore you.' But he has asked her again, and now, close in the circle of his arms, now she could believe that it didn't really matter to him, that to him she was as whole as any woman, 'more than any other woman,' he had said.

'Okay?' he asked. 'Will you let me make you honest?'

She nodded. The nod was a very small one.

'You mean it this time?'

She did not nod again. She lifted her mouth, and she put her answer into her lips, and his arms tightened around her, and she knew that he understood her. She broke away from him, and he said, 'Hey!' but she trotted away from his reach and went to the kitchen.

When she brought back the champagne, he said, 'I'll be damned!'

She sighed, agreeing that he undoubtedly would be damned, and he slapped her playfully on the fanny.

She handed him the bottle, did a deep curtsy which was ludicrous in the prisoner pyjamas and then sat on the floor cross-legged while he struggled with the cork.

The champagne exploded with an enormous pop, and though she did not hear the sound, she saw the cork leave the neck of the bottle and ricochet off the ceiling, and she saw the bubbly white fluid overspilling the lip and running over his hands.

She began to clap, and then she got to her feet and went for glasses, and he poured first a little of the wine into his saying, 'That's the way it's done, you know. It's supposed to take off the skim and the bugs and everything,' and then filling her glass, and then going back to pour his to the brim.

'To us,' he toasted.

She opened her arms slowly, wider and wider and wider.

'A long, long, happy love,' he supplied.

She nodded happily.

'And our marriage in August.' They clinked glasses, and then sipped at the wine, and she opened her eyes wide in pleasure and cocked her head appreciatively.

'Are you happy?' he asked.

Yes, her eyes said, yes, yes.

'Did you mean what you said before?'

She raised one brow inquisitively.

'About ... missing me?'

Yes, yes, yes, yes, her eyes said.

'You're beautiful.'

She curtsied again.

'Everything about you. I love you, Teddy. God, how I love you.'

She put down the wine glass and then took his hand. She kissed the palm of his hand, and the back, and then she led him into the bedroom, and she unbuttoned his shirt and pulled it out of his trousers, her hands moving gently. He lay down on the bed, and she turned off the light and then, unselfconsciously, unembarrassedly, she took off the pyjamas and went to him.

And while they made gentle love in a small room in a big apartment house, a man named David Foster walked towards his own apartment, an apartment he shared with his mother.

And while their love grew fierce and then gentle again, a man named David Foster thought about his partner Mike Reardon, and so immersed in his thoughts was he that he did not hear the footsteps behind him, and when he finally did hear them, it was too late.

He started to turn, but a .45 automatic spat orange flame into the night, once, twice, again, again, and David Foster clutched at his chest, and the red blood burst through his brown fingers, and then he hit the concrete – dead.

Chapter Seven

There is not much you can say to a man's mother when the man is dead. There is not much you can say at all.

Carella sat in the doilied easy chair and looked across at Mrs Foster. The early afternoon sunlight seeped through the drawn blinds in the small, neat living room, narrow razor-edge bands of brilliance against the cool dimness. The heat in the streets was still insufferable, and he was thankful for the cool living room, but his topic was death, and he would have preferred the heat.

Mrs Foster was a small, dried-up woman. Her face was wrinkled and seamed, as brown as David's had been. She sat hunched in the chair, a small withered woman with a withered face and withered hands, and he thought *A strong wind would blow her away, poor woman*, and he watched the grief that lay quietly contained behind the expressionless withered face.

'David was a good boy,' she said. Her voice was hollow, a narrow sepulchral voice. He had come to talk of death, and now he could smell death on this woman, could hear death in the creak of her voice, and he thought it strange that David Foster, her son, who was alive and strong and young several hours ago was now dead – and his mother, who had probably longed for the peaceful sleep of death many a time, was alive and talking to Carella.

'Always a good boy. You raise 'em in a neighbourhood like this one,' Mrs Foster said, 'and you fear for how they'll turn out. My husband was a good worker, but he died young, and it wasn't always easy to see that David wasn't needing. But he was a good boy, always. He would come home and tell me what the other boys were doing, the stealing and all the things they were doing, and I knew he was all right.'

'Yes, Mrs Foster,' Carella said.

'And they all liked him around here, too,' Mrs Foster went on, shaking her head. 'All the boys he grew up with, and all the old folks, too. The people around here, Mr Carella, they don't take much to cops. But they liked my David because he grew up among them, and he was a part of them, and I guess they were sort of proud of him, the way I was proud.'

'We were all proud of him, Mrs Foster,' Carella said.

'He was a good cop, wasn't he?'

'Yes, he was fine cop.'

'Then why should anyone want to kill him?' Mrs Foster asked. 'Oh, I know his job was a dangerous one, yes, but this is different, this is senseless. He wasn't even on duty. He was coming home. Who would want to shoot my boy, Mr Carella? Who would want to shoot my boy?'

'That's what I wanted to talk to you about, Mrs Foster. I hope you don't mind if I ask a few questions.'

'If it'll help you find the man who killed David, I'll answer questions all day for you.'

'Did he ever talk about his work?'

'Yes, he did. He always told me what happened around the precinct, what you were working on. He told me about his partner being killed, and he told me he was leafing through pictures in his mind, just waiting until he hit the right one.'

'Did he say anything else about the pictures? Did he say he suspected anyone?'

'No.'

'Mrs Foster, what about his friends?'

'Everyone was his friend.'

'Did he have an address book or anything in which their names might be listed?'

'I don't think he had an address book, but there's a pad near the telephone he always used.'

'May I have that before I leave?'

'Certainly.'

'Did he have a sweetheart?'

'No, not anyone steady. He went out with a lot of different girls.'

'Did he keep a diary?'

'No.'

'Does he have a photograph collection?'

'Yes, he liked music a lot. He was always playing his records whenever he ...'

'No, not phonograph. Photograph.'

'Oh. No. He carried a few pictures in his wallet, but that's all.'

'Did he ever tell you where he went on his free time?'

'Oh, lots of different places. He like the theatre a lot. The stage, I mean. He went often.'

'These boyhood friends of his. Did he pal around with them much?'

'No, I don't think so.'

'Did he drink?'

'Not heavily.'

'I mean, would you know whether or not he frequented any of the bars in the neighbourhood? Social drinking, of course.'

'I don't know.'

'Had he received any threatening letters or notes that you know of?'

'He never mentioned any.'

'Ever behave peculiarly on the telephone?'

'Peculiarly? What do you mean?'

'Well, as if he were trying to hide something from you. Or as if he were worried ... anything like that. I'm thinking of threatening calls, Mrs Foster.'

'No, I don't ever remember him acting strange on the phone.'

'I see. Well ...' Carella consulted his notes. 'I guess that's about it. I want to get going, Mrs Foster, because there's a lot of work to do. If you could get me that telephone pad ...'

'Yes, of course.' She rose, and he watched her slight body as she moved out of the cool living room into one of the bedrooms. When she returned, she handed him the pad and said, 'Keep it as long as you like.'

'Thank you. Mrs Foster, please know that we all share your sorrow,' he said lamely.

'Find my boy's killer,' Mrs Foster said. She extended one of her withered hands and took his hand in a strong, firm grip, and he marvelled at the strength of the grip, and at the strength in her eyes and on her face. Only when he was in the hallway, with the door locked behind him, did he hear the gentle sobs that came from within the apartment.

He went downstairs and out to the car. When he reached the car, he took off his jacket, wiped his face, and then sat behind the wheel to study his worksheet:

STATEMENT OF EYEWITNESSES: None.

MOTIVE: Revenge? Con? Nut? Tie-in with Mike? Check Ballistics report.

NUMBER OF MURDERERS: Two? One Mike, one David. Or tie-in? B.R. again.

WEAPONS: .45 automatic.

ROUTE OF MURDERER: ?

DIARIES, JOURNALS, LETTERS, ADDRESSES, TELEPHONE NUMBERS, PHOTO-GRAPHS: Check with David's mthr.

ASSOCIATES, RELATIVES, SWEETHEARTS, ENEMIES, ETC: Ditto.

PLACES FREQUENTED, HANG-OUTS: Ditto.

HABITS: Ditto.

TRACES AND CLUES FOUND ON THE SCENE: Heelprint in dog faeces. At lab now. Four shells. Two bullets. Ditto.

FINGERPRINTS FOUND: None.

Carella scratched his head, sighed against the heat, and then headed back for the precinct house to see if the new Ballistics report had come in yet.

The widow of Michael Reardon was a full-breasted woman in her late thirties. She had dark hair and green eyes, and an Irish nose spattered with a clichéful of freckles. She had a face for merry-go-rounds and roller-coaster rides, a face that could split in girlish glee when water was splashed on her at the seashore. She was a girl who could get drunk sniffing the vermouth cork before it was passed over a martini. She was a girl who went to church on Sundays, a girl who'd belonged to the Newman Club when she was younger. She had good legs, very white, and a good body, and her name was May.

She was dressed in black on the hot afternoon of July 25, and her feet were planted firmly on the floor before her, and her hands were folded in her lap, and there was no laughter on the face made for roller-coaster rides.

'I haven't told the children yet,' she said to Bush. 'The children don't know. How can I tell them? What can I say?'

'It's a rough thing,' Bush said in his quiet voice. His scalp felt sticky and moist. He needed a haircut, and his wild red hair was shrieking against the heat.

'Yes,' May said. 'Can I get you a beer or something? It's very hot. Mike used to take a beer when he got home. No matter what time it was, he always took a beer. He was a very well-ordered person. I mean, he did things carefully and on schedule. I think he wouldn't have been able to sleep if he didn't have that glass of beer when he got home.'

'Did he ever stop in the neighbourhood bars?'

'No. He always drank here, in the house. And never whisky. Only one or two glasses of beer.'

Mike Reardon, Bush thought. *He used to be a cop and a friend. Now he's a victim and a corpse, and I ask questions about him.*

'We were supposed to get an air-conditioning unit,' May said. 'At least, we talked about it. This apartment gets awfully hot. That's because we're so close to the building next door.'

'Yes,' Bush said. 'Mrs Reardon, did Mike have any enemies that you know of? I mean, people he knew outside his line of duty?'

'No, I don't think so. Mike was a very easy-going sort. Well, you worked with him. You know.'

'Can you tell me what happened the night he was killed? Before he left the house?'

'I was sleeping when he left. Whenever he had the twelve-to-eight tour, we argued about whether we should try to get any sleep before he went in.'

'Argued?'

'Well, you know, we discussed it. Mike preferred staying up, but I have two children, and I'm beat when it hits ten o'clock. So he usually compromised on those nights, and we both got to bed early – at about nine, I suppose.'

'Were you asleep when he left?'

'Yes. But I woke up just before he went out.'

'Did he say anything to you? Anything that might indicate he was worried about an ambush? Had he received a threat or anything?'

'No.' May Reardon glanced at her watch. 'I have to be leaving soon, Detective Bush. I have an appointment at the funeral parlour. I wanted to ask you about that. I know you're doing tests on ... on the body and all ... but the family ... Well, the family is kind of old-fashioned and we want to ... we want to make arrangements. Do you have any idea when ... when you'll be finished with him?'

'Soon, Mrs Reardon. We don't want to miss any bets. A careful autopsy may put us closer to finding his killer.'

'Yes, I know. I didn't want you to think ... it's just the family. They ask questions. They don't understand. They don't know what it means to have him gone, to wake up in the morning and not ... not have him here.' She bit her lip and turned her face from Bush. 'Forgive me. Mike wouldn't ...

wouldn't like this. Mike wouldn't want me to ...' She shook her head and swallowed heavily. Bush watched her, feeling sudden empathy for this woman who was Wife, feeling sudden compassion for all women everywhere who had ever had their men torn from them by violence. His thoughts wandered to Alice, and he wondered idly how she would feel if he stopped a bullet, and then he put the thought out of his mind. It wasn't good to think like that. Not these days. Not after two in a row. Was it possible there was a nut loose? Somebody who'd marked the whole goddamn precinct as his special target?

Yes, it was possible.

It was very damn possible, and so it wasn't good to think about things like Alice's reaction to his own death. You thought about things like that, and they consumed your mind, and then when you needed a clear mind which could react quickly to possible danger, you didn't have it. And that's when you were up the creek without a paddle.

What had Mike Reardon been thinking of when he'd been gunned down?

What had been in the mind of David Foster when the four slugs ripped into his body?

Of course, it was possible the two deaths were unrelated. Possible, but not very probable. The m.o. was remarkably similar, and once the Ballistics report came through they'd know for sure whether they were dealing with one man or two.

Bush's money was on the one-man possibility.

'If there's anything else you want to ask me,' May said. She had pulled herself together now, and she faced him squarely, her face white, her eyes large.

'If you'll just collect any address books, photographs, telephone numbers, newspaper clippings he may have saved, anything that may give us a lead onto his friends or even his relatives, I'd be much obliged.'

'Yes, I can do that,' May said.

'And you can't remember anything unusual that may have some bearing on this, is that right?'

'No, I can't. Detective Bush, what am I going to tell the kids? I sent them off to a movie. I told them their daddy was out on a plant. But how long can I keep it from them? How do you tell a pair of kids that their father is dead? Oh God, what am I going to do?'

Bush remained silent. In a little while, May Reardon went for the stuff he wanted.

At 3:42 p.m. on July 25, the Ballistics report reached Carella's desk. The shells and bullets found at the scene of Mike Reardon's death had been put beneath the comparison microscope together with the shells and bullets used in the killing of David Foster.

The Ballistics report stated that the same weapon had been used in both murders.

Chapter Eight

On the night that David Foster was killed, a careless mongrel searching for food in garbage cans, had paused long enough to sully the sidewalk of the city. The dog had been careless, to be sure, and a human being had been just as careless, and there was a portion of a heelprint for the Lab boys to work over, solely because of this combined record of carelessness. The Lab boys turned to with something akin to distaste.

The heelprint was instantly photographed, not because the boys liked to play with cameras, but simply because they knew accidents frequently occurred in the making of a cast. The heelprint was placed on a black-stained cardboard scale, marked off in inches. The camera, supported above the print by a reversible tripod, the lens parallel to the print to avoid any false perspectives, clicked merrily away. Satisfied that the heelprint was now prescrved for posterity – photographically, at least – the Lab boys turned to the less antiseptic task of making the cast.

One of the boys filled a rubber cup with half a pint of water. Then he spread plaster of Paris over the water, taking care not to stir it, allowing it to sink to the bottom of its own volition. He kept adding plaster of Paris until the water couldn't absorb any more of it, until he'd dumped about ten ounces of it into the cup. Then he brought the cup to one of the other boys who was preparing the print to take the mixture.

Because the print was in a soft material, it was sprayed first with shellac and then with a thin coat of oil. The plaster of Paris mixture was stirred and then carefully applied to the prepared print. It was applied with a spoon in small portions. When the print was covered to a thickness of about one-third of an inch, the boys spread pieces of twine and sticks onto the plaster to reinforce it, taking care that the debris did not touch the bottom of the print and destroy its details. They then applied another coat of plaster to the print, and allowed the cast to harden. From time to time, they touched the plaster, feeling for warmth, knowing that warmth meant the cast was hardening.

Since there was only one print, and since it was not even a full print, and since it was impossible to get a Walking Picture from this single print, and since the formula $H\frac{r}{l}BS\frac{ra\ rv\ raa\ ll\ lb}{la\ lv\ laa\ rl\ rb}X$, a formula designed to give the complete picture of a man's walk in terms of step length, breadth of step length of left foot, right foot, greatest width of left foot, right foot, wear on heel and sole – since the formula could not be applied to a single print, the Lab boys did all they could with what they had.

And they decided, after careful study, that the heel was badly worn on the outside edge, a peculiarity which told them the man belonging to that heel undoubtedly walked with a somewhat duck-like waddle. They also decided that the heel was not the original heel of the shoe, that it was a rubber heel which had been put on during a repair job, and that the third nail from the shank side of the heel, on the left, had been bent when applying the new heel.

And – quite coincidentally *if* the heelprint happened to have been left by the murderer – the heel bore the clearly stamped trade name 'O'Sullivan', and everyone knows that O'Sullivan is America's Number One Heel.

The joke was an old one. The Lab boys hardly laughed at all.

The newspapers were not laughing very much, either.

The newspapers were taking this business of cop-killing quite seriously. Two morning tabloids, showing remarkable versatility in headlining the same incident, respectively reported the death of David Foster with the words SECOND COP SLAIN and KILLER SLAYS 2ND COP.

The afternoon tabloid, a newspaper hard-pressed to keep up with the circulation of the morning sheets, boldly announced KILLER ROAMS STREETS. And then, because this particular newspaper was vying for circulation, and because this particular newspaper made it a point to 'expose' anything which happened to be in the public's eye at the moment – anything from Daniel Boone to long winter underwear, anything which gave them a free circulation ride on the then-popular bandwagon – their front page carried a red banner that day, and the red banner shouted 'The Police Jungle – What Goes On In Our Precincts' and then in smaller white type against the red, 'See Murray Schneider, p. 4.'

And anyone who had the guts to wade through the first three pages of cheesecake and chest-thumping liberalism, discovered on page four that Murray Schneider blamed the deaths of Mike Reardon and David Foster upon 'the graft-loaded corruptness of our filth-ridden Gestapo.'

In the graft-loaded squadroom of the corrupt 87th Precinct, two detectives named Steve Carella and Hank Bush stood behind a filth-ridden desk and pored over several cards their equally corrupt fellow-officers had dug from the Convictions File.

'Try this for size,' Bush said.

'I'm listening,' Carella said.

'Some punk gets pinched by Mike and Dave, right?'

'Right.'

'The judge throws the book at him, and he gets room and board from the State for the next five or ten years. Okay?'

'Okay.'

'Then he gets out. He's had a lot of time to mull this over, a lot of time to build up his original peeve into a big hate. The one thing in his mind is to get Mike and Dave. So he goes out for them. He gets Mike first and then he tries to get Dave quick, before this hate of his cools down. Wham, he gets Dave, too.'

'It reads good,' Carella said.

'That's why I don't buy this Flannagan punk.'

'Why not?'

'Take a look at the card. Burglary, possession of burglary tools, a rape

Cop Hater

NAME OF PRISONER

Precinct	(Surname)	(First Name and Init.)
87th	ORDIZ	LUIS "DIZZY"

Date & Time of Arrest
May 2, 1952 7.00PM

Address of Prisoner
635 6th St. South

Sex	Colour	Date of Birth Mo. Day Year	Place of Birth	Alien ~~Citizen~~
M	White	8 12 1912	San Juan Puerto Rico	

Social Condition Married (Single)	Read and Write Yes (No)	Occupation Dishwasher	Employed Yes (No)

Charge	Specific Offense	Date-Time Occurrence
Violation PL 1751 Subdiv. 1	Poss. of nar- cotics with intent to sell.	5/2/52 7:00 PM

Pct. Complaint No.
33A-411

D.B. Complaint No.
DD179-52

Place of Occurrence
635 6th St. South

Precinct
87th

Name of Complainant

Address of Complainant

Arresting Officer(s) (Name-s) Michael Reardon & David Foster

(Rank) Det. 3rd & Det. 2nd Gr.

(Command) Det. Bureau

Authority

(Pickup)   Complaint   Warrant   F.O.A.

Action of Court

Sentenced for four years at state penitentiary, Ossining, New York

Date	Judge	Court
7/6/52	Fields	

away back in '47. Mike and Dave got him on the last burglary pinch. This was the first time he got convicted, and he drew ten, just got out last month on parole after doing five years.'

'So.'

'So I don't figure a guy with a big hate is going to be good enough to cut ten years to five. Besides, Flannagan never carried a gun all the while he was working. He was a gent.'

'Guns are easy to come by.'

'Sure. But I don't figure him for our man.'

'I'd like to check him out, anyway,' Carella said.

'Okay, but I want to check this other guy out first. Ordiz. Luis "Dizzy" Ordiz. Take a look at the card.'

Carella pulled the conviction card closer. The card was a 4 × 6 white rectangle, divided into printed rectangles of various sizes and shapes.

'A hophead,' Carella said.

'Yeah. Figure the hate a hophead can build in four years' time.'

'He went the distance?'

'Got out the beginning of the month,' Bush said. 'Cold turkey all that time. This don't build brotherly love for the cops who made the nab.'

'No, it doesn't.'

'Figure this, too. Take a look at his record. He was picked up in '51 on a dis cond charge. This was before he got on the junk, allegedly. But he was carrying a .45. The gun had a busted hammer, but it was still a .45. Go back to '49. Again, dis cond, fighting in a bar. Had a .45 on him, no busted hammer this time. He got off lucky that time. Suspended sentence.'

'Seems to favour .45's.'

'Like the guy who killed Mike and Dave. What do you say?'

'I say we take a look. Where is he?'

Bush shrugged. 'Your guess is as good as mine.'

Danny Gimp was a man who'd had polio when he was a child. He was lucky in that it had not truly crippled him. He had come out of the disease with only a slight limp, and a nickname which would last him the rest of his life. His real surname was Nelson, but very few people knew that, and he was referred to in the neighbourhood as Danny Gimp. Even his letters came addressed that way.

Danny was fifty-four years old, but it was impossible to judge his age from his face or his body. He was very small, small all over, his bones, his features, his eyes, his stature. He moved with the loose-hipped walk of an adolescent, and his voice was high and reedy, and his face bore hardly any wrinkles or other telltale signs of age.

Danny Gimp was a stool pigeon.

He was a very valuable man, and the men of the 87th Precinct called him in regularly, and Danny was always ready to comply – whenever he could. It was a rare occasion when Danny could not supply the piece of information the bulls were looking for. On these occasions, there were other stoolies to talk to. Somewhere somebody had the goods. It was simply a question of finding the right man at the right time.

Danny could usually be found in the third booth on the right hand side of a bar name *Andy's Pub*. He was not an alcoholic, nor did he even drink to excess. He simply used the bar as a sort of office. It was cheaper than paying rent someplace downtown, and it had the added attraction of a phone booth which he used regularly. The bar, too, was a good place to listen – and listening was one-half of Danny's business. The other half was talking.

He sat opposite Carella and Bush, and first he listened.

Then he talked.

'Dizzy Ordiz,' he said. 'Yeah, yeah.'

'You know where he is?'

'What's he do?'

'We don't know.'

'Last I heard, he was on the state.'

'He got out at the beginning of the month.'

'Parole?'

'No.'

'Ordiz, Ordiz. Oh, yeah. He's a junkie.'

'That's right.'

'Should be easy to locate. What'd he do?'

'Maybe nothing,' Bush said. 'Maybe a hell of a lot.'

'Oh, you thinking of these cop kills?' Danny asked.

Bush shrugged.

'Not Ordiz. You're barkin' up the wrong tree.'

'What makes you say so?'

Danny sipped at his beer, and then glanced up at the rotating fan. 'You'd never know there was a fan going in this dump, would you? If this heat don't break soon. I'm headin' for Canada. I got a friend up there. Quebec. You ever been to Quebec?'

'No,' Bush said.

'Nice there. Cool.'

'What about Ordiz?'

'Take him with me, he wants to come,' Danny said, and then he began laughing at his own joke.

'He's cute today,' Carella said.

'I'm cute all the time,' Danny said.

'How much love you got for Ordiz?'

'Don't know him from a hole in the wall. Don't care to, either. Hopheads make me want to vomit.'

'Okay, then where is he?'

'I don't know yet. Give me some time.'

'How much time?'

'Hour, two hours. Junkies are easy to trace. Talk to a few pushers, zing, you're in. He got out the beginning of the month, huh? That means he's back on it strong by now. This should be a cinch.'

'He may have kicked it,' Carella said. 'It may not be such a cinch.'

'They never kick it,' Danny said. 'Don't pay attention to fairy tales. He was probably gettin' the stuff sneaked in even up the river. I'll find him. But if you think he knocked off your buddies, you're wrong.'

'Why?'

'I seen this jerk around. He's a nowhere. A real *trombenik*, if you dig foreign. He don't know enough to come in out of an atom bomb attack. He got one big thing in his life. Horse. That's Ordiz. He lives for the White God. Only thing on his mind.'

'Reardon and Foster sent him away,' Carella said.

'So what? You think a junkie bears a grudge? All part of the game. He ain't got time for grudges. He only got time for meetin' his pusher and makin' the buy. This guy Ordiz, he was always half-blind on the stuff. He couldn't see straight enough to shoot off his own big toe. So he's gonna cool two cops? Don't be ridic.'

'We'd like to see him, anyway,' Bush said.

'Sure. Do I tell you how to run headquarters? Am I the commissioner? But this guy is from Squaresville, fellas, I'm telling you. He wouldn't know a .45 from a cement mixer.'

'He's owned a few in his life,' Carella said.

'Playing with them, playing with them. If one of them things ever went off within a hundred yards of him, he'd be scared for a week. Take it from me, he don't care about nothin' but heroin. Listen, they don't call him Dizzy for nothin'. He's dizzy. He's got butterflies up here. He chases them away with H.'

'I don't trust junkies,' Bush said.

'Neither do I,' Danny answered. 'But this guy ain't a killer, take it from me. He don't even know how to kill time.'

'Do us a favour,' Carella said.

'Sure.'

'Find him for us. You know our number.'

'Sure. I'll buzz you in an hour or so. This is gonna be a cinch. Hopheads are a cinch.'

Chapter Nine

The heat on that July 26 reached a high of 95.6 at twelve noon. At the precinct house, two fans circulated the soggy air that crawled past the open windows and the grilles behind them. Everything in the Detective squadroom seemed to wilt under the steady, malignant pressure of the heat. Only the file cabinets and the desks stood at strict attention. Reports, file cards, carbon paper, envelopes, memos, all of these were damp and sticky to the touch, clinging to wherever they were dropped, clinging with a moist limpidity.

The men in the squadroom worked in their shirt sleeves. Their shirts were stained with perspiration, large dark amoeba blots which nibbled at the cloth, spreading from beneath the armpits, spreading from the hollow of the spinal column. The fans did not help the heat at all. The fans circulated the suffocating breath of the city, and the men sucked in the breath and typed up their reports in triplicate, and checked their worksheets, and dreamt of summers in the White Mountains or summers in Atlantic City with the ocean slapping their faces. They called complainants, and they called suspects, and their hands sweated on the black plastic of the phone, and they feel Heat like a living thing which invaded their bodies and seared them with a million white-hot daggers.

Lieutenant Byrnes was as hot as any man in the squadroom. His office was just to the left of the slatted dividing railing, and it had a large corner window, but the window was wide open and not a breath of a breeze came through it. The reporter sitting opposite him looked cool. The reporter's name was Savage, and the reporter was wearing a blue seersucker suit and a dark blue Panama, and the reporter was smoking a cigarette and casually puffing the smoke up at the ceiling where the heat held it in a solid blue-grey mass.

'There's nothing more I can tell you,' Byrnes said. The reporter annoyed him immensely. He did not for a moment believe that any man on this earth had been born with a name like 'Savage'. He further did not believe that any man on this earth, on this day, could actually be as cool as Savage pretended he was.

'Nothing more, Lieutenant?' Savage asked, his voice very soft. He was a handsome man with close-cropped blond hair and a straight, almost-feminine nose. His eyes were grey, cool. Cool.

'Nothing,' the Lieutenant said. 'What the hell did you expect? If we knew who did it, we'd have him in here, don't you think?'

'I should imagine so,' Savage said. 'Suspects?'

'We're working on it.'

'Suspects?' Savage repeated.

'A few. The suspects are our business. You splash them on your front page, and they'll head for Europe.'

'Think a kid did it?'

'What do you mean, a kid?'

'A teen-ager.'

'Anybody could've done it,' Brynes said. 'For all I know *you* did it.'

Savage smiled, exposing bright white teeth. 'Lots of teen-age gangs in this precinct, aren't there?'

'We've got the gangs under control. This precinct isn't the garden spot of the city, Savage, but we like to feel we're doing the best job possible here. Now I realize your newspaper may take offence at that, but we really try, Savage, we honestly try to do our little jobs.'

'Do I detect sarcasm in you voice, Lieutenant?' Savage asked.

'Sarcasm is a weapon of the intellectual, Savage. Everybody, especially your newspaper, knows that cops are just stupid, plodding beasts of burden.'

'My paper never said that, Lieutenant.'

'No?' Byrnes shrugged. 'Well, you can use it in tomorrow's edition.'

'We're trying to help,' Savage said. 'We don't like cops getting killed any more than you do.' Savage paused. 'What about the teen-age gang idea?'

'We haven't even considered it. This isn't the way those gangs operate. Why the hell do you guys try to pin everything that happens in this city on the teen-agers? My son is a teen-ager, and he doesn't go around killing cops.'

'That's encouraging,' Savage said.

'The gang phenomenon is a peculiar one to understand,' Byrnes said. 'I'm not saying we've got it licked, but we do have it under control. If we've stopped the street rumbles, and the knifings and shootings, then the gangs have become nothing more than social clubs. As long as they stay that way, I'm happy.'

'Your outlook is a strangely optimistic one,' Savage said coolly. 'My newspaper doesn't happen to believe the street rumbles have stopped. My newspaper is of the opinion that the death of those two cops may be traced directly to these "social clubs".'

'Yeah?'

'Yeah.'

'So what the hell do you want me to do about it? Round up every kid in the city and shake him down? So your goddamn newspaper can sell another million copies?'

'No. But we're going ahead with our own investigation. And if we crack this, it won't make the 87th Precinct look too good.'

'It won't make Homicide North look too good, either. And it won't make the Police Commissioner look good. It'll make everybody in the department look like amateurs as contrasted with the super-sleuths of your newspaper.'

'Yes, it might,' Savage agreed.

'I have a few words of advice for you, Savage.'

'Yes?'

'The kids around here don't like questions asked. You're not dealing with Snob Hill teen-agers who tie on a doozy by drinking a few cans of beer. You're dealing with kids whose code is entirely different from yours or mine. Don't get yourself killed.'

'I won't,' Savage said, smiling resplendently.

'And one other thing.'

'Yes?'

'Don't foul up my precinct. I got enough headaches without you and your half-witted reporters stirring up more trouble.'

'What's more important to you, Lieutenant?' Savage asked. 'My not fouling up your precinct – or my not getting killed?'

Byrnes smiled and then began filling his pipe. 'They both amount to about the same thing,' he said.

The call from Danny Gimp came in fifty minutes. The desk Sergeant took the call, and then plugged it in to Carella's line.

'87th Detective Squad,' he said. 'Carella here.'

'Danny Gimp.'

'Hello, Danny, what've you got?'

'I found Ordiz.'

'Where?'

'This a favour, or business?' Danny asked.

'Business,' Carella said tersely. 'Where do I meet you?'

'You know *Jenny's*?'

'You kidding?'

'I'm serious.'

'If Ordiz is a junkie, what's he doing on Whore Street?'

'He's blind in some broad's pad. You're lucky you get a few mumbles out of him.'

'Whose pad?'

'That's what we meet for, Steve. No?'

'Call me "Steve" face-to-face, and you'll lose some teeth, pal,' Carella said.

'Okay, *Detective* Carella. You want this dope, I'll be in Jenny's in five minutes. Bring some loot.'

'Is Ordiz heeled?'

'He may be.'

'I'll see you,' Carella said.

La Vi de Putas was a street which ran North and South for a total of three blocks. The Indians probably had their name for it, and the teepees that lined the path in those rich days of beaver pelts and painted beads most likely did a thriving business even then. As the Indians retreated to their happy hunting grounds and the well-worn paths turned to paved roads, the teepees gave way to apartment buildings, and the practitioners of the world's oldest profession claimed the plush-lined cubby holes as their own. There was a time when the street was called *Piazza Putana* by the Italian immigrants, and *The Hussy Hole* by the Irish immigrants. With the Puerto Rican influx, the street had changed its language – but not its sole source of income. The Puerto Ricans referred to it as *La Via de Putas*. The Cops called it 'Whore Street.' In any language, you paid your money, and you took your choice.

The gals who ran the sex emporiums called themselves Mama-this or Mama-that. Mama Theresa's was the best-known joint on the Street. Mama Carmen's was the filthiest. Mama Luz's had been raided by the cops sixteen times because of some of the things that went on behind its crumbling brick façade. The cops were not above visiting any of the various Mamas on social calls, too. The business calls included occasional raids and occasional rake-offs. The raids were interesting sometimes, but they were usually conducted by members of the Vice Squad who were unfamiliar with the working arrangements some of the 87th Precinct cops had going with the madams. Nothing can mess up a good deal like an ignorant cop.

Carella, perhaps, was an ignorant cop. Or an honest one, depending how you looked at it. He met Danny Gimp at Jenny's, which was a small cafe on the corner of Whore Street, a cafe which allegedly served old world absinthe, complete with wormwood and water to mix the stuff in. No old-world absinthe drinker had ever been fooled by Jenny's stuff, but the cafe still served as a sort of no-man's land between the respectable workaday world of the proletariat, and the sinful shaded halls of the brothels. A man could hang his hat in Jenny's, and a man could have a drink there, and a man could pretend he was on a fraternity outing there, and with the third drink, he was ready to rationalize what he was about to do. Jenny's was something necessary to the operation of the Street. Jenny's, to stretch a point, served the same purpose as the shower stall does in a honeymoon suite.

On July 26, with the heat baking the black paint that covered the lower half of Jenny's front window – a window which had been smashed in some dozen times since the establishment was founded – Carella and Danny were not interested in the Crossing-the-Social-Barrier aspect of Jenny's bistro. They were interested in a man named Luis 'Dizzy' Ordiz, who may or may not have pumped a total of six bullets into a total of two cops. Bush was out checking on the burglar named Flannagan. Carella had come down in a squad car driven by a young rookie named Kling. The squad car was parked outside now, with Kling leaning against the fender, his head erect, sweltering even in his Summer blues. Tufts of blond hair stuck out of his lightweight hat. He was hot. He was hot as hell.

Inside, Carella was hot, too. 'Where is he?' he asked Danny.

Danny rolled the ball of his thumb against the ball of his forefinger. 'I haven't had a square meal in days,' he said.

Carella took a ten spot from his wallet and fed it to Danny.

'He's at Mama Luz's,' Danny said. 'He's with a broad they call La Flamenca. She ain't so hot.'

'What's he doing there?'

'He copped from a pusher a couple of hours back. Three decks of H. He stumbled over to Mama Luz with amorous intentions, but the H won the battle. Mama Luz tells me he's been dozing for the past sixty.'

'And La Flamenca?'

'She's with him, probably cleaned out his wallet by this time. She's a big red-headed job with two gold teeth in the front of her mouth, damn near blind you with them teeth of hers. She's got mean hips, a big job, real big. Don't get rough with her, less she swallow you up in one gobble.'

'Is he heeled?' Carella asked.

'Mama Luz don't know. She don't think so.'

'Doesn't the red-head know?'

'I didn't ask the red-head,' Danny said. 'I don't deal with the hired help.'

'Then how come you know about her hips?' Carella asked.

'Your ten spot don't buy my sex life,' Danny said, smiling.

'Okay,' Carella said, 'thanks.'

He left Danny at the table and went over to where Kling was leaning on the fender.

'Hot,' Kling said.

'You want a beer, go ahead,' Carella told him.

'No, I just want to go home.'

'Everybody wants to go home,' Carella said. 'Home is where you pack your rod.'

'I never understand detectives,' Kling said.

'Come on, we have a visit to make,' Carella said.

'Where?'

'Up the street, Mama Luz. Just point the car; it knows the way.'

Kling took off his hat and ran one hand through his blond hair. 'Phew,' he said, and then he put on his hat and climbed in behind the wheel. 'Who are we looking for?'

'Man named Dizzy Ordiz.'

'Never heard of him.'

'He never heard of you either,' Carella said.

'Yeah,' Kling said drily, 'well, I'd appreciate it if you introduced us.'

'I will,' Carella said, and he smiled as Kling set the car in motion.

Mama Luz was standing in the doorway when they pulled up. The kids on the sidewalk wore big grins, expecting a raid. Mama Luz smiled and said, 'Hello, Detective Carella. Hot, no?'

'Hot,' Carella agreed, wondering why in hell everybody and his brother commented about the weather. It was certainly obvious to anyone but a half-wit that this was a very hot day, that this was a suffocatingly hot day, that this was probably hotter than a day in Manilla, or even if you thought Calcutta hotter, this was still a lotta hotter heat than that.

Mama Luz was wearing a silk kimono. Mama Luz was a big fat woman with a mass of black hair pulled into a bun at the back of her head. Mama Luz used to be a well-known prostitute, allegedly one of the best in the city, but now she was a madam. She was scrupulously clean, and always smelled of lilacs. Her complexion was as white as any complexion can be, more white because it rarely saw the sun. Her features were patrician, her smile was angelic. If you didn't know she ran one of the wildest brothels on the Street, you might have thought she was somebody's mother.

She wasn't.

'You come on a social call?' she asked Carella, winking.

'If I can't have you, Mama Luz,' Carella said, 'I don't want anybody.'

Kling blinked, and then wiped the sweatband of his hat.

'For you, *toro*,' Mama Luz said, winking again, 'Mama Luz does anything. For you, Mama Luz is a young girl again.'

'You've always been a young girl,' Carella said, and he slapped her on the backside, and then said, 'Where's Ordiz?'

'With *la roja*,' Mama Luz said. 'She has picked his eyes out by now.' She shrugged. 'These new girls, all they are interested in is money. In the old days ...' Mama Luz cocked her head wistfully. 'In the old days, *toro*, there was sometimes love, do you know? What has happened to love nowadays, eh?'

'It's all locked up in that fat heart of yours,' Carella said. 'Does Ordiz have a gun?'

'Do I shake down my guests?' Mama Luz said. 'I don't think he has a gun, Stevie. You will not shoot up the works, will you? This has been a quiet day.'

'No, I will not shoot up the works,' Carella said. 'Show me where he is.'

'This way. Upstairs.'

The stairs shook beneath her. She turned her head over her shoulder, winked at Carella, and said, 'I trust you behind me, Stevie.'

'*Gracias*,' Carella said.

'Don't look up my dress.'

'It's a temptation, I'll admit,' Carella said, and behind him he heard Kling choke back a cross between a sob and a gasp.

Mama Luz stopped on the first landing. 'The door at the end of the hall. No blood, Stevie, please. With this one, you do not need blood. He is half-dead already.'

'Okay,' Carella said. 'Get downstairs, Mama Luz.'

'And later, when the work is done,' Mama Luz said suggestively, and she bumped one fleshy hip against Carella, almost knocking him off his feet. She went past Kling, laughing, her laughter trailing up the stairwell.

Carella sighed and looked at Kling. 'What're you gonna do, kid,' he said, 'I'm in love.'

'I never understand detectives,' Kling said.

They went down the hallway. Kling drew his service revolver when he saw Carella's was already in his hand.

'She said no shooting,' he reminded Carella.

'So far, she only runs a whore house,' Carella said. 'Not the Police Department.'

'Sure,' Kling said.

Carella rapped on the door with the butt of his .38.

'*Quién es?*' a girl's voice asked.

'Police,' Carella said. 'Open up.'

'*Momento,*' the voice said.

'She's getting dressed,' Kling advised Carella.

In a few moments, the door opened. The girl standing there was a big redhead. She was not smiling, so Carella did not have the opportunity to examine the gold teeth in the front of her mouth.

'What you want?' she asked.

'Clear out,' Carella said. 'We want to talk to the man in there.'

'Sure,' she said. She threw Carella a look intended to convey an attitude of virginity offended, and then she swivelled past him and slithered down the hallway. Kling watched her. When he turned back to the door, Carella was already in the room.

There was a bed in the room, and a night table, and a metal washbasin. The shade was drawn. The room smelled badly. A man lay in the bed in his trousers. His shoes and socks were off. His chest was bare. His eyes were closed, and his mouth was open. A fly buzzed around his nose.

'Open the window,' Carella said to Kling. 'This place stinks.'

The man on the bed stirred. He lifted his head and looked at Carella.

'Who are you?' he said.

'Your name Ordiz?' Carella asked.

'Yeah. You a cop?'

'Yes.'

'What did I do wrong now?'

Kling opened the window. From the streets below came the sound of children's voices.

'Where were you Sunday night?'

'What time?'

'Close to midnight.'

'I don't remember.'

'You better, Ordiz. You better start remembering damn fast. You shoot up just now?'

'I don't know what you mean.'

'You're an H-man, Ordiz, and we know it, and we know you copped three decks a little while back. Are you stoned now, or can you read me?'

'I hear you,' Ordiz said.

He passed a hand over his eyes. He owned a thin face with a hatchet nose and thick, rubbery lips. He needed a shave badly.

'Okay, talk.'

'Friday night, you said?'

'I said Sunday.'

'Sunday. Oh yeah. I was at a poker game.'

'Where?'

'South 4th. What's the matter, you don't believe me?'

'You got witnesses?'

'Five guys in the game. You can check with any one of them.'

'Give me their names.'

'Sure. Louie DeScala, and his brother, John. Kid named Pete Diaz. Another kid they call Pepe. I don't know his last name.'

'That's four,' Carella said.

'I was the fifth.'

'Where do these guys live?'

Ordiz reeled off a string of addresses.

'Okay, what about Monday night?'

'I was home.'

'Anybody with you?'

'My landlady.'

'What?'

'My landlady was with me. What's the matter, don't you hear good?'

'Shut up, Dizzy. What's her name?'

'Olga Pazio.'

'Address?'

Ordiz gave it to him. 'What am I supposed to done?' he asked.

'Nothing. You got a gun?'

'No. Listen, I been clean since I got out.'

'What about those three decks?'

'I don't know where you got that garbage. Somebody's fooling you, cop.'

'Sure. Get dressed, Dizzy.'

'What for? I paid for the use of this pad.'

'Okay, you used it already. Get dressed.'

'Hey, listen, what for? I tell you I've been clean since I got out. What the hell, cop?'

'I want you at the precinct while I check these names. You mind?'

'They'll tell you I was with them, don't worry. And that junk about the three decks, I don't know where you got that from. Hell, I ain't been near the stuff for years now.'

'That's plain to see,' Carella said. 'Those scabs on you arm are from beri-beri or something, I guess.'

'Huh?' Ordiz asked.

'Get dressed.'

Carella checked with the men Ordiz had named. Each of them was willing to swear that he'd been at the poker game from ten-thirty on the night of July 23, to four a.m. on the morning of July 24. Ordiz' landlady reluctantly admitted she had spent the night of the 24th and the morning of the 25th in Ordiz' room. Ordiz had solid alibis for the times someone had spent killing Reardon and Foster.

When Bush came back with his report on Flannagan, the boys were right back where they'd started.

'He's got an alibi as long as the Texas panhandle,' Bush said.

Carella sighed, and then took Kling down for a beer before heading over to see Teddy.

Bush cursed the heat, and then went home to his wife.

Chapter Ten

From where Savage sat at the end of the bar, he could plainly see the scripted lettering on the back of the boy's brightly coloured jacket. The boy had caught his eye the moment Savage entered the bar. He'd been sitting in a booth with a dark-haired girl, and they'd both been drinking beer. Savage had seen the purple and gold jacket and then sat at the bar and ordered a gin and tonic. From time to time, he'd glanced over at the couple. The boy was thin and pale, a shock of black hair crowning his head. The collar of the jacket was turned up, and Savage could not see the lettering across the back at first because the boy sat with his back tight against the padded cushioning of the booth.

The girl finished her beer and left, but the boy did not vacate the booth. He turned slightly, and that was when Savage saw the lettering, and that was when the insistent idea at the back of his mind began to take full shape and form.

The lettering on the jacket read: The Grovers.

The name had undoubtedly been taken from the name of the park that hemmed in the 87th Precinct, but it was a name that rang a bell in Savage's head, and it didn't take long for that bell to begin echoing and re-echoing. The Grovers had been responsible for a good many of the street rumbles in the area, including an almost titanic struggle on one section of the park, a struggle featuring knives, broken bottles, guns, and sawed-off stickball bats. The Grovers had made their peace with the cops, or so the story went, but the persistent idea that one of the gangs was responsible for the deaths of Reardon and Foster would not leave Savage's mind.

And here was a Grover.

Here was a boy to talk to.

Savage finished his gin and tonic, left his stool, and walked over to where the boy was sitting alone in the booth.

'Hi,' he said.

The boy did not move his head. He raised only his eyes. He said nothing.

'Mind if I sit down?' Savage asked.

'Beat it, mister,' the boy said.

Savage reached into his jacket pocket. The boy watched him silently. He took out a package of cigarettes, offered one to the boy and, facing the silent refusal, hung one on his own lip.

'My name's Savage,' he said.

'Who cares?' the boy answered.

'I'd like to talk to you.'

'Yeah? What about?'

'The Grovers.'

'Mister, you don't live around here, do you?'

'No.'

'Then, Dad, go home.'

'I told you. I want to talk.'

'I don't. I'm waitin' for a deb. Take off while you still got legs.'

'I'm not scared of you, kid, so knock off the rough talk.'

The boy appraised Savage coolly.

'What's your name?' Savage asked.

'Guess, Blondie.'

'You want a beer?'

'You buying?'

'Sure,' Savage said.

'Then make it a rum-coke.'

Savage turned towards the bar. 'Rum-coke,' he called, 'and another gin and tonic.'

'You drink gin, huh?' the boy said.

'Yes. What's your name, son?'

'Rafael,' the boy said, still studying Savage closely. 'The guys call me Rip.'

'Rip. That's a good name.'

'Good as any. What's the matter, you don't like it?'

'I like it,' Savage said.

'You a nab?'

'A what?'

'A cop.'

'No.'

'What then?'

'I'm a reporter.'

'Yeah?'

'Yes.'

'So whatya want from me?'

'I only want to talk.'

'What about?'

'Your gang.'

'What gang?' Rip said. 'I don't belong to no gang.'

The waiter brought the drinks. Rip tasted his and said, 'That bartender's a crook. He cuts the juice here. This tastes like cream soda.'

'Here's luck,' Savage said.

'You're gonna need it,' Rip replied.

'About the Grovers ...'

'The Grovers are a club.'

'Not a gang?'

'Whatta we need a gang for? We're a club, that's all.'

'Who's president?' Savage asked.

'That's for me to know and you to find out,' Rip answered.

'What's the matter? You ashamed of the club?'

'Hell, no.'

'Don't you want to see it publicized in a newspaper? There isn't another club in the neighbourhood that ever got a newspaper's full treatment.'

'We don't need no treatment. We got a big rep as it is. Ain't nobody in this city who ain't heard of The Grovers. Who you tryin' to snow, mister?'

'Nobody. I just thought you'd like some public relations work.'

'What the hell's that?'

'A favourable press.'

'You mean . . .' Rip furrowed his brow. 'What do you mean?'

'An article telling about your club.'

'We don't need no articles. You better cut out, Dad.'

'Rip. I'm trying to be your friend.'

'I got plenty of friends in The Grovers.'

'How many?'

'There must be at least . . .' Rip stopped short. 'You're a wise bastard, ain't you?'

'You don't have to tell me anything you don't want to, Rip. Why do the boys call you "Rip"?'

'We all got nicknames. That's mine.'

'But why?'

'Because I can handle a blade good.'

'Did you ever have to?'

'Handle one? You're kidding? In this neighbourhood, you don't carry a knife or a piece, you're dead. Dead, man.'

'What's a piece, Rip?'

'A gun.' Rip opened his eyes wide. 'You don't know what a piece is? Man, you ain't been.'

'Do The Grovers have many pieces?'

'Enough.'

'What kind?'

'All kinds. What do you want? We got it.'

'.45's?'

'Why do you ask?'

'Nice gun, a .45.'

'Yeah, it's big,' Rip said.

'Do you ever use these pieces?'

'You got to use them. Man, you think these diddlebops are for fun? You got to use whatever you can get you hands on. Otherwise, you wind up with a tag on your toe.' Rip drank a little more of the rum. 'This neighbourhood ain't a cream puff, Dad. You got to watch yourself all the time. That's why it helps to belong to The Grovers. They see this jacket comin' down the street, they got respect. They know if they mess with me, they got *all* The Grovers to mess with.'

'The police, you mean?'

'Naw, who wants Law trouble? We steer away from them. Unless they bother us.'

'Any cops bother you lately?'

'We got a thing on with the cops. They don't bother us, we don't bother them. Man, there ain't been a rumble in months. Things are very quiet.'

'You like it that way?'

'Sure, why not? Who wants his skull busted? The Grovers want peace. We never punk out, but we never go lookin' for trouble, either. Only time we get involved is when we're challenged, or when a stud from another club tries to make it with one of our debs. We don't go for that.'

'So you've had no trouble with the police lately?'

'Few little skirmishes. Nothing to speak of.'

'What kind of skirmishes?'

'Agh, one of the guys was on mootah. So he got a little high, you know. So he busted a store window, for kicks, you know? So one of the cops put the arm on him. He got a suspended sentence.'

'*Who* put the arm on him?'

'Why you want to know?'

'I'm just curious.'

'One of the bulls, I don't remember who.'

'A detective?'

'I said a bull, didn't I?'

'How'd the rest of The Grovers feel about this?'

'How do you mean?'

'About this detective pulling in one your boys?'

'Agh, the kid was a Junior, didn't know his ass from his elbow. Nobody shoulda given him a reefer to begin with. You don't handle a reefer right . . . well, you know, the guy was just a kid.'

'And you felt no resentment for the cop who'd pulled him in?'

'Huh?'

'You had nothing against the cop who pulled him in?'

Rip's eyes grew suddenly wary. 'What're you drivin' at, mister?'

'Nothing, really.'

'What'd you say your name was?'

'Savage.'

'Why you askin' about how we feel about cops?'

'No reason.'

'Then why you askin'?'

'I was just curious.'

'Yeah,' Rip said flatly. 'Well, I got to go now, I guess that deb ain't comin' back.'

'Listen, stick around a while,' Savage said. 'I'd like to talk some more.'

'Yeah?'

'Yes, I would.'

'That's tough pal,' Rip said. 'I wouldn't.' He got out of the booth. 'Thanks for the drink. I see you around.'

'Sure,' Savage said.

He watched the boy's shuffling walk as he moved out of the bar. The door closed behind him, and he was gone.

Savage studied his drink. There *had* been trouble between The Grovers and a cop – a detective, in fact. So his theory was not quite as far-fetched as the good lieutenant tried to make it.

He sipped at his drink, thinking, and when he'd finished it, he ordered another. He walked out of the bar about ten minutes later, passing two neatly dressed men on his way out.

The two men were Steve Carella and a patrolman in street clothes – a patrolman named Bert Kling.

Chapter Eleven

Bush was limp when he reached the apartment.

He hated difficult cases, but only because he felt curiously inadequate to cope with them. He had not been joking when he told Carella he felt detectives weren't particularly brilliant men. He thoroughly believed this, and whenever a difficult case popped up, his faith in his own theory was reaffirmed.

Legwork and stubbornness, that was all it amounted to.

So far, the legwork they'd done had brought them no closer to the killer than they originally were. The stubbornness? Well, that was another thing again. They would keep at it of course. Until the break came. When would the break come? Today? Tomorrow? Never?

The hell with the case, he thought. I'm home. A man is entitled to the luxury of leaving his goddamn job at the office. A man is entitled to a few peaceful hours with his wife.

He pushed his key into the lock, twisted it, and then threw the door open.

'Hank?' Alice called.

'Yes.' Her voice sounded cool. Alice always sounded cool. Alice was a remarkable woman.

'Do you want a drink?'

'Yes. Where are you?'

'In the bedroom. Come on in, there's a nice breeze here.'

'A breeze? You're kidding.'

'No, seriously.'

He took off his jacket and threw it over the back of a chair He was pulling off his shirt as he went into the bedroom. Bush never wore undershirts. He did not believe in the theory of sweat absorption. An undershirt, he held, was simply an additional piece of wearing apparel, and in this weather the idea was to get as close to the nude as possible. He ripped off his shirt with almost savage intensity. He had a broad chest matted with curling red hair that matched the thatch on his head. The knife scar ran its crooked path down his right arm.

Alice lay in chaise near the open window. She wore a white blouse and a straight black skirt. She was barefoot, and her legs were propped up on the window sill, and the black skirt rustled mildly with the faint breeze that came through the window, She had drawn her blonde hair back into a pony tail. He went to her, and she lifted her face for his kiss, and he noticed the thin film of perspiration on her upper lip.

'Where's that drink?' he asked.

'I'll mix it,' she said. She swung her feet off the window sill, and the skirt pulled back for an instant, her thigh winking at him. He watched her silently, wondering what it was about this woman that was so exciting, wondering if all married men felt this way about their wives even after ten years of marriage.

'Get that gleam out of your eyes,' she said, reading his face.

'Why?'

'It's too damn hot.'

'I know a fellow who claims the best way ...'

'I know about that fellow.'

'Is in a locked room on the hottest day of the year with the windows closed under four blankets.'

'Gin and tonic?'

'Good.'

'I heard that vodka and tonic is better.'

'We'll have to get some.'

'Busy day at the mine?'

'Yes. You?'

'Sat around and worried about you,' Alice said.

'I see all those grey hairs sprouting.'

'He belittles my concern,' Alice said to the air. 'Did you find that killer yet?'

'No.'

'Do you want a lime in this?'

'If you like.'

'Means going into the kitchen. Be a doll and drink it this way.'

'I'm a doll,' Bush said.

She handed him the drink. Bush sat on the edge of the bed. He sipped at the drink, and then leaned forward, the glass dangling at the ends of his muscular long arms.

'Tired?'

'Pooped.'

'You don't look very tired.'

'I'm so pooped, I'm peeped.'

'You always say that,' Alice said. 'I wish you wouldn't always say that. There are things you always say.'

'Like what?'

'Well, like that, for one.'

'Name another.'

'When we're driving in the car and there are fixed traffic signals. Whenever you begin hitting the lights right, you say "We're in with the boys".'

'So what's wrong with that?'

'Nothing, the first hundred times.'

'Oh, hell.'

'Well, it's true.'

'All right, all right. I'm not peeped. I'm not even pooped.'

'I'm hot,' Alice said.

'So am I.'

She began unbuttoning her blouse, and even before he looked up, she said, 'Don't get ideas.'

She took off the blouse and draped it over the back of the chaise.

'What'd you do all day?' he asked.

'Nothing much.'

'Were you in?'

'Most of the time.'

'So what'd you do?'

'Sat around, mostly.'

'Mmmm.' He could not take his eyes from her brassiere. 'Did you miss me?'

'I always miss you,' she said flatly.

'I missed you.'

'Drink your drink.'

'No, really.'

'Well, good,' she said, and she smiled fleetingly. He studied the smile. It was gone almost instantly, and he had the peculiar feeling that it had been nothing more than a duty smile.

'Why don't you get some sleep?' she asked.

'Not yet,' he said, watching her.

'Hank, if you think . . .'

'What?'

'Nothing.'

'I've got to go in again later,' he said.

'They're really pushing on this one, aren't they?'

'Lots of pressure,' he said. 'I think the Old Man is scared he's next.'

'I'll bet it's all over,' Alice said. 'I don't think there'll be another killing.'

'You can never tell,' Bush said.

'Do you want something to eat before you turn in?' she asked.

'I'm not turning in yet.'

Alice sighed. 'You can't escape this damn heat,' she said. 'No matter what you do, it's always with you.' Her hand went to the button at the side of her skirt. She undid it, and then pulled down the zipper. The skirt slid to her feet, and she stepped out of it. She walked to the window, and he watched her. Her legs were long and clean.

'Come here,' he said.

'No. I don't want to, Hank.'

'All right,' he said.

'Do you think it'll cool off tonight?'

'I doubt it.' He watched her closely. He had the distinct impression that she was undressing for him, and yet she'd said . . . He tweaked his nose, puzzled.

She turned from the window. 'You need a haircut,' she said.

'I'll try to get one tomorrow. We haven't had a minute.'

'Oh, goddamn this heat, anyway.' She walked to mix herself another drink, and he could not take his eyes from her. *What's she trying to do?* he wondered. *What the hell is she trying to do to me?*

He rose swiftly, walking to where she stood. He put his arms around her.

'Don't,' she said.

'Baby . . .'

'Don't.' Her voice was firm, a cold edge to it.

'Why not?'

'Because I say so.'

'Well, then why the hell are you parading around like ...'

'Take you hands off me, Hank. Let me go.'

'Aw, baby ...'

She broke away from him. 'Get some sleep,' she said. 'You're tired.' There was something strange in her eyes, an almost malicious gleam.

'Can't ...'

'No.'

'For God's sake. Alice ...'

'No!'

'All right.'

She smiled quickly. 'All right,' she repeated.

'Well ...' Bush paused. 'I'd ... I'd better get to bed.'

'Yes. You'd better.'

'What I can't understand is why ...'

'You won't even need a sheet in this weather,' Alice interrupted.

'No, I guess not.'

He went to the bed and took off his shoes and socks. He didn't want to undress because he didn't want to give her the satisfaction, now that he'd been denied, of knowing how she'd affected him. He took off his trousers and quickly got into the bed, pulling the sheet to his throat.

Alice watched him, smiling. 'I'm reading *Anapurna*,' she said.

'So?'

'I just happened to think of it.'

Bush rolled over onto his side.

'I'm still hot,' Alice said. 'I think I'll take a shower. And then maybe I'll catch an air-conditioned movie. You don't mind, do you?'

'No,' Bush mumbled.

She walked to the side of the bed and stood there for a moment, looking down at him. 'Yes, I think I'll take a shower.'

He did not move. He kept his eyes on the floor, but he could see her feet and her legs, but he did not move.

'Sleep tight, darling,' she whispered, and then she went into the bathroom.

He heard the shower when it began running. He lay on the soggy sheet and listened to the steady machine-gunning of the water. Then, over the sound of the shower, came the sound of the telephone, splitting the silence of the room.

He sat up and reached for the instrument.

'Hello?'

'Bush?'

'Yes?'

'This is Havilland. You better get down here right away.'

'What's the matter?' Bush asked.

'You know that young rookie Kling?'

'Yeah?'

'He was just shot in a bar on Culver.'

Chapter Twelve

The squadroom of the 87th resembled nothing so much as the locker room of the Boys' Club when Bush arrived. There must have been at least two dozen teen-agers crammed in behind the dividing rail and the desks beyond it. Add to this a dozen or so detectives who were firing questions, the answers to which were coming in two languages, and the bedlam was equivalent to the hush of a hydrogen bomb explosion.

The boys were all wearing brilliantly contrasting purple and gold jackets, and the words 'The Grovers' decorated the back of each jacket. Bush looked for Carella in the crowded room, spotted him, and walked over towards him quickly. Havilland, a tough cop with a cherubic face, shouted at one of the boys, 'Don't give me any guff, you little punk, or I'll break your goddamn arm.'

'You try it, dick,' the kid answered, and Havilland cuffed him across the mouth. The boy staggered back, slamming into Bush as he went by. Bush shrugged his shoulders, and the boy flew back into Havilland's arms, as if he'd been brushed aside by a rhinoceros.

Carella was talking to two boys when Bush approached him.

'Who fired the gun?' he asked.

The boys shrugged.

'We'll throw you all in jail as accessories,' Carella promised.

'What the hell happened?' Bush wanted to know.

'I was having a beer with Kling. Nice and peaceful off-duty beer. I left him there, and ten minutes later, when he's leaving the joint, he gets jumped by these punks. One of them put a slug in him.'

'How is he?'

'He's at the hospital. The slug was a .22, went through his right shoulder. We figure a zip gun.'

'You think this ties with the other kills?'

'I doubt it. The m.o.'s 'way off.'

'Then why?'

'How the hell do I know? Looks like the whole city figures it's open season on cops.' Carella turned back to the boys. 'Were you with the gang when the cop was jumped?'

The boys would not answer.

'Okay, fellas,' Carella said, 'play it smart. See what that gets you. See how long The Grovers are gonna last under a rap like this one.

'We din' shoot no cop,' one of the boys said.

'No? What happened, he shoot himself?'

'You ting we crazy?' the other boy said. 'Shoot a bull?'

'This was a patrolman,' Carella said, 'not a detective.'

'He wass wear a suit,' the first boy said.

'Cops wear suits off-duty,' Bush said. 'Now how about it?'

'Nobody shoot a cop,' the first boy said.

'No, except somebody did.'

Lieutenant Byrnes came out of his office and shouted, 'All right, knock it off! KNOCK IT OFF!'

The room fell immediately silent.

'Who's your talk man?' Byrnes asked.

'I am,' a tall boy answered.

'What's your name?'

'Do-Do.'

'What's your full name?'

'Salvador Jesus Santez.'

'All right, come here, Salvador.'

'The guys call me Do-Do.'

'Okay, come here.'

Santez walked over to where Byrnes was standing. He walked with a shuffle which was considered both hip and cool. The boys in the room visibly relaxed. This was their talk man, and Do-Do was a real gone stud. Do-Do would know how to handle this jive.

'What happened?' Byrnes asked.

'Little skirmish, that's all,' Santez said.

'Why?'

'Jus' like that. We got the word passed down, so we joined the fray.'

'What word?'

'You know, like a scout was out.'

'No, I don't know. What the hell are you talking about?'

'Look, Dad ...' Santez started.

'You call me "Dad" again,' Byrnes warned, 'and I'll beat you black and blue.'

'Well, gee, Da ...' Santez stopped dead. 'What you want to know?'

'I want to know why you jumped a cop.'

'What cop? What're you talkin' about?'

'Look, Santez, don't play this too goddamn cute. You jumped one of our patrolmen as he came out of a bar. You beat him up, and one of your boys put a bullet in his shoulder. Now what the hell's the story?'

Santez considered Byrnes' question gravely.

'Well?'

'He's a cop?'

'What the hell did you think he was?'

'He was wearing a light blue summer suit!' Santez said, his eyes opening wide.

'What the hell's that got to do with it? Why'd you jump him? Why'd you shoot him?'

A mumbling was starting behind Santez. Byrnes heard the mumble and shouted. 'Shut up! You've got your talk man, let *him* talk!'

Santez was still silent.

'What about it, Santez?'

'A mistake,' Santez said.

'That's for damn sure.'

'I mean, we didn't know he was a cop.'

'Why'd you jump him?'

'A mistake, I tell you.'

'Start from the beginning.'

'Okay,' Santez said. 'We been giving you trouble lately?'

'No.'

'Okay. We been minding our own business, right? You never hear from The Grovers, except when we protectin' our own, right? The last rumble you get is over there in The Silver Culvers' territory when they pick on one of our Juniors. Am I right?'

'Go ahead, Santez.'

'Okay. Early today, there's a guy snooping around. He grabs one of our Seniors in a bar, and starts pumpin' him.'

'Which Senior?'

'I forget,' Santez said.

'Who was the guy?'

'Said he was from a newspaper.'

'What?'

'Yeah. Said his name was Savage, you know him?'

'I know him,' Byrnes said tightly.

'Okay, so he starts askin' like how many pieces we got, and whether we got .45's and whether we don't like the Law, things like that. This Senior, he's real hip. He tips right off this guy is trying to mix in The Grovers with the two bulls got knocked off around here. So he's on a newspaper, and we got a rep to protect. We don't want Law trouble. If this jerk goes back to his paper and starts printing lies about how we're mixed in, that ain't good for our rep.'

'So what'd you do, Santez?' Byrnes asked wearily, thinking of Savage, and thinking of how he'd like to wring the reporter's neck.

'So this Senior comes back, and we planned to scare off the reporter before he goes printing any story. We went back to the bar and waited for him. When he come out, we jumped him. Only he pulled a gun, so one of the boys plugged him in self defence.'

'Who?'

'Who knows?' Santez said. 'One of the boys burned him.'

'Thinking he was Savage.'

'Sure. How the hell we supposed to know he's a cop instead? He had on a light blue suit, and he had blond hair, like this reporter creep. So we burned him. It was a mistake.'

'You keep saying that, Santez, but I don't think you know just how big a mistake it was. Who fired that shot?'

Santez shrugged.

'Who was the Senior Savage talked to?'

Santez shrugged.

'Is he here?'

Santez had stopped talking, it seemed.

'You know we've got a list of every damn member in your gang, don't you, Santez?'

'Sure.'

'Okay. Havilland, get the list. I want a roll call. Whoever's not here, pick him up.'

'Hey, wait a minute,' Santez said. 'I told you it was all a mistake. You going to get somebody in trouble just 'cause we mistake a cop?'

'Listen to me, Santez, and listen hard. Your gang hasn't been in any trouble recently, and that's fine with us. Call it a truce, call it whatever you want to. But don't ever think and mean *ever*, Santez, that you or your boys can shoot anybody in this goddamn precinct and get away with it. You're a bunch of hoods as far as I'm concerned, Santez. You're a bunch of hoods with fancy jackets, and a seventeen-year-old hood is no less dangerous than a fifty-year-old hood. The only reason we haven't been bearing down on you is because you've been behaving yourself. All right, today you stopped behaving yourself. You shot a man in my precinct territory – and that means you're in trouble. That means you're in big trouble.'

Santez blinked.

'Put them all downstairs and call the roll there,' Byrnes said. 'Then get whoever we missed.'

'All right, let's go,' Havilland said. He began herding the boys out of the room.

Miscolo, one of the patrolmen from Clerical, pushed his way through the crowd and walked over to the Lieutenant.

'Lieutenant, fella outside wants to see you,' he said.

'Who?'

'Guy named Savage. Claims he's a reporter. Wants to know what the rumble was about this aft ...'

'Kick him down the steps,' Byrnes said, and he went back into his office.

Chapter Thirteen

Homicide, if it doesn't happen too close to home, is a fairly interesting thing.

You can really get involved in the investigation of a homicide case because it is the rare occurrence in the everyday life of a precinct. It is the most exotic crime because it deals with the theft of something universal – a man's life.

Unfortunately, there are other less interesting and more mundane matters to deal with in a precinct, too. And in a precinct like the 87th, these mundane matters can consume a lot of time. There are the rapes, and the muggings, and the rollings, and the knifings, and the various types of disorderly conducts, and the breakings and entries, and the burglaries, and the car thefts, and the street rumbles, and the cats caught in sewers, and oh, like that. Many of these choice items of crime are promptly turned over to special squads within the department, but the initial squeal nonetheless goes to the precinct in which the crime is being committed, and these squeals can keep a man hopping.

It's not so easy to hop when the temperature is high.

For cops, shocking as the notion may sound at first, are human beings. They sweat like you and me, and they don't like to work when it's hot. Some of them don't like to work even when it's cool. None of them like to draw Lineup, especially when it's hot.

Steve Carella and Hank Bush drew Lineup on Thursday, July 27.

They were especially displeased about it because Lineup is held only from Mondays to Thursdays, and if they had missed it this Thursday, chances were they would not pull the duty until the following week and perhaps – just perhaps the heat would have broken by then.

The morning started the way most mornings were starting that week. There was a deceptive coolness at first, a coolness which – despite the prognostications of television's various weather men and weather women – seemed to promise a delightful day ahead. The delusions and flights of fancy fled almost instantly. It was apparent within a half-hour of being awake that this was going to be another scorcher, that you would meet people who asked, 'Hot enough for you?' or who blandly and informatively remarked, 'It's not the heat; it's the humidity.'

Whatever it was, it was hot.

It was hot where Carella lived in the suburb of Riverhead, and it was hot in the heart of the city – on High Street, where Headquarters and the line-up awaited.

Since Bush lived in another suburb – Calm's Point, west a little south of Riverhead – they chose to meet at Headquarters at 8:45, fifteen minutes before the linup began. Carella was there on the dot.

At 8:50, Bush strolled up. That is to say, he more or less crawled onto the pavement and slouched over to where Carella was standing and puffing on a cigarette.

'Now I know what Hell is like,' he said.

'Wait until the sun really starts shining,' Carella said.

'You cheerful guys are always good for an early-morning laugh,' Bush answered. 'Let me have a cigarette, will you?'

Carella glanced at his watch. 'Time we were up there.'

'Let it wait. We've got a few minutes yet.' He took the cigarette Carella offered, lighted it, and blew out a stream of smoke. 'Any new corpses today?'

'None yet.'

'Pity. I'm getting so I miss my morning coffee and corpse.'

'The city,' Carella said.

'What?'

'Look at it. What a goddamn monster.'

'A hairy bastard,' Bush agreed.

'But I love her.'

'Yeah,' Bush said noncommittally.

'It's too hot to work today. This is a day for the beach.'

'The beaches'll be jammed. You're lucky you've got a nice lineup to attend.'

'Sure, I know. Who wants a cool, sandy beach with the breakers rolling in and . . .'

'You Chinese?'

'Huh?'

'You know your torture pretty good.'

'Let's go upstairs.'

They flipped their cigarettes away and entered the Headquarters building. The building had once boasted clean red brick and architecture which was modern. The brick was now covered with the soot of five decades, and the architecture was as modern as a suit of armour.

They walked into the first-floor marbled entryway, past the dick squadroom, past the lab, past the various records rooms. Down a shaded hallway, a frosted glass door announced 'Commissioner of Police.'

'I'll bet *he's* at the beach,' Carella said.

'He's in there hiding behind his desk,' Bush said. 'He's afraid the 87th's maniac is going to get him next.'

'Maybe he's not at the beach,' Carella amended. 'I understand this building has a swimming pool in the basement.'

'Two of them,' Bush said. He rang for the elevator. They waited in hot, suffering silence for several moments. The elevator doors slid open. The patrolman inside was sweating.

'Step into the iron coffin,' he said.

Carella grinned. Bush winced. Together they got into the car.

'Lineup?' the patrolman asked.

'No, the swimming pool,' Bush cracked.

'Jokes I can't take in this heat,' the patrolman said.

'Then don't supply straight lines,' Bush said.

'Abbott and Costello I've got with me,' the patrolman said, and he lapsed into silence. The elevator crawled up the intestinal tract of the building. It creaked. It whined. Its walls were moist with the beaded exhalations of its occupants.

'Nine,' the patrolman said.

The doors slid open. Carella and Bush stepped into a sunlit corridor. Simultaneously, they reached for the leather cases to which their shields were pinned. Again simultaneously, they pinned the tin to their collars and then walked towards the desk behind which another patrolman was seated.

The patrolman eyed the tin, nodded, and they passed the desk and walked into a large room which served many purposes at Headquarters. The room was built with the physical proportions of a gymnasium, and did indeed have two basketball hoops, one at each end of the room. The windows were wide and tall, covered with steel mesh. The room was used for indoor sport, lectures, swearing in of rookies, occasional meetings of the Police Benevolent Association or the Police Honor Legion and, of course, the lineups.

For the purpose of these Monday-to-Thursday parades of felony offenders, a permanent stage had been set up at the far end of the room, beneath the balcony there, and beyond the basketball hoop. The stage was brilliantly lighted. Behind the stage was a white wall, and upon the wall in black numerals was the graduated height scale against which the prisoners stood.

In front of the stage, and stretching back towards the entrance doorways for about ten rows, was an array of folding chairs, most of which were occupied by detectives from all over the city when Bush and Carella entered. The blinds at the windows had already been drawn, and a look at the raised dais and speaking stand behind the chairs showed that the Chief of Detectives was already in position and the strawberry festival would start in a few moments. To the left of the stage, the felony offenders huddled in a group, lightly guarded by several patrolmen and several detectives, the men who had made the arrests. Every felony offender who'd been picked up in the city the day before would be paraded across the stage this morning.

The purpose of the lineup, you see – despite popular misconception about the identification of suspects by victims, a practice which was more helpful in theory than in actual usage – was simply to acquaint as many detectives as possible with the men who were doing evil in their city. The ideal set-up would have been to have each detective in each precinct at each scheduled lineup, but other pressing matters made this impossible. So two men were chosen each day from each precinct, on the theory that if you can't acquaint all of the people all of the time, you can at least acquaint some of them some of the time.

'All right,' the Chief of Detectives said into his microphone, 'let's start.'

Carella and Bush took seats in the fifth row as the first two offenders walked onto the stage. It was the practice to show the offenders as they'd been picked up, in pairs, in a trio, a quartet, whatever. This simply for the purpose of establishing an m.o. If a crook works in a pair once, he will generally work in a pair again.

The police stenographer poised his pen above his pad. The Chief of Detectives intoned, 'Diamondback, One,' calling off the area of the city in which the arrest had been made, and the number of the case from that area that day. 'Diamondback, One. Anselmo, Joseph, 17 and Di Palermo, Frederick, 16. Forced the door of an apartment on Cambridge and Gribble. Occupant screamed for help, bringing patrolman to scene. No statement. How about it, Joe?'

Joseph Anselmo was a tall, thin boy with dark black hair and dark brown eyes. The eyes seemed darker than they were because they were set against a pale, white face. The whiteness was attributable to one emotion, and one emotion alone. Joseph Anselmo was scared.

'How about it, Joe?' the Chief of Detectives asked again.

'What do you want to know?' Anselmo said.

'Did you force the door to that apartment?'

'Yes.'

'Why?'

'I don't know.'

'Well, you forced a door, you must have had a reason for doing it. Did you know somebody was in the apartment?'

'No.'

'Did you force it alone.'

Anselmo did not answer.

'How about it, Freddie? Were you with Joe when you broke that lock?'

Frederick Di Palermo was blond and blue-eyed. He was shorter than Anselmo, and he looked cleaner. He shared two things in common with his friend. First, he had been picked up on a felony offence. Second, he was scared.

'I was with him,' Di Palermo said.

'How'd you force the door?'

'We hit the lock.'

'What with.'

'A hammer.'

'Weren't you afraid it would make a noise?'

'We only give it a quick rap,' Di Palermo said. 'We didn't know somebody was home.'

'What'd you expect to get in that apartment?' the Chief of Detectives asked.

'I don't know,' Di Palermo said.

'Now, look,' the Chief of Detectives said patiently, 'you both broke into an apartment. Now we know that, and you just admitted it, so you must have had a reason for going in there. What do you say?'

'The girls told us,' Anselmo said.

'What girls?'

'Oh, some chicks,' Di Palermo answered.

'What'd they tell you?'

'To bust the door.'

'Why?'

'Like that,' Anselmo said.

'Like what?'

'Like for kicks.'

'Only for kicks?'

'I don't know why we busted the door,' Anselmo said, and he glanced quickly at Di Palermo.

'To take something out of the apartment?' the Chief asked.

'Maybe a . . .' Di Palermo shrugged.

'Maybe what?'

'A couple of bucks. You know, like that.'

'You were planning a burglary then, is that right?'

'Yeah, I guess.'

'What'd you do when you discovered the apartment was occupied?'

'The lady screamed,' Anselmo said.

'So we run,' Di Palermo said.

'Next case,' the Chief of Detectives said.

The boys shuffled off the stage to where their arresting officer was waiting for them. Actually, they had said a hell of a lot more than they should have. They'd have been within their rights if they'd insisted on not saying a word at the lineup. Not knowing this, not even knowing that their position was fortified because they'd made no statement when they'd been collared, they had answered the Chief of Detectives with remarkable naïveté. A good lawyer, with a simple charge of unlawfully entering under circumstances or in a manner not amounting to a burglary, would have had his clients plead guilty to a misdemeanor. The Chief of Detectives, however, had asked the boys if they were planning to commit a burglary, and the boys had answered in the affirmative. And the Penal Law, Section 402, defines Burglary in first degree thusly:

A person, who, with intent to commit some crime therein, breaks and enters, in the night time, the dwelling-house of another, in which there is at the time a human being:

1. Being armed with a dangerous weapon; or

2. Arming himself therein with such a weapon: or

3. Being assisted by a confederate actually present; or ...

Well, no matter. The boys had very carelessly tied the knot of a felony about their youthful necks, perhaps not realizing that burglary in the first degree is punishable by imprisonment in a state prison for an indeterminate term the minimum of which shall not be less than ten years and the maximum of which shall not be more than thirty years.

Apparently, 'the girls' had told them wrong.

'Diamondback, Two,' the Chief of Detectives said. 'Pritchett, Virginia, 34. Struck her quote husband unquote about the neck and head with a hatchet at three a.m. in the morning. No statement.'

Virginia Pritchett had walked onto the stage while the Chief of Detectives was talking. She was a small woman, barely clearing the five-foot-one-inch marker. She was thin, narrow-boned, with red hair of the fine, spider-webby type She wore no lipstick. She wore no smile. Her eyes were dead.

'Virginia?' the Chief of Detectives said.

She raised her head. She kept her hands close to her waist, one fist folded over the other. Her eyes did not come to life. They were grey, and she stared into the glaring lights unblinkingly.

'Virginia?'

'Yes, sir?' Her voice was very soft, barely audible. Carella leaned forward to catch what she was saying.

'Have you ever been in trouble before, Virginia?' the Chief of Detectives asked.

'No, sir.'

'What happened, Virginia?'

The girl shrugged, as if she too could not comprehend what had happened. The shrug was a small one, a gesture that would have been similar to passing a hand over the eyes.

'What happened, Virginia?'

The girl raised herself up to her full height, partly to speak into the permanently fixed microphone which dangled several inches before her face on a solid steel pipe, partly because there were eyes on her and because she apparently realized her shoulders were slumped. The room was deathly still. There was not a breeze in the city. Beyond the glaring lights, the detectives sat.

'We argued,' she said sighing.

'Do you want to tell us about it?'

'We argued from the morning, from when we first got up. The heat. It's ... it was very hot in the apartment. Right from the morning. You ... you lose your temper quickly in the heat.'

'Go on.'

'He started with the orange juice. He said the orange juice wasn't cold enough. I told him I'd had it in the ice box all night, it wasn't my fault it wasn't cold. Diamondback isn't ritzy, sir. We don't have refrigerators in Diamondback, and with this heat, the ice melts very fast. Well, he started complaining about the orange juice.'

'Were you married to this man?'

'No, sir.'

'How long have you been living together?'

'Seven years, sir.'

'Go on.'

'He said he was going down for breakfast, and I said he shouldn't go down because it was silly to spend money when you didn't have to. He stayed, but he complained about the orange juice all the while he ate. It went on like that all day.'

'About the orange juice, you mean?'

'No, other things. I don't remember what. He was watching the ball game on TV, and drinking beer, and he'd pick on little things all day long. He was sitting in his undershorts because of the heat. I had hardly anything on myself.'

'Go on.'

'We had supper late, just cold cuts. He was picking on me all that time. He didn't want to sleep in the bedroom that night, he wanted to sleep on the kitchen floor. I told him it was silly, even though the bedroom is very hot. He hit me.'

'What do you mean, he hit you?'

'He hit me about the face. He closed one eye for me. I told him not to touch me again, or I would push him out the window. He laughed. He put a blanket on the kitchen floor, near the window, and he turned on the radio, and I went into the bedroom to sleep.'

'Yes, go ahead, Virginia.'

'I couldn't sleep because it was so hot. And he had the radio up loud. I went into the kitchen to tell him to please put the radio a little lower, and he said to go back to bed. I went into the bathroom, and I washed my face, and that was when I spied the hatchet.'

'Where was the hatchet?'

'He keeps tools on a shelf in the bathroom, wrenches and a hammer, and the hatchet was with them. I thought I would go out and tell him to put the radio lower again, because it was very hot and the radio was very loud, and I wanted to try to get some sleep. But I didn't want him to hit me again, so I took the hatchet, to protect myself with, in case he tried to get rough again.'

'Then what did you do?'

'I went out into the kitchen with the hatchet in my hands. He had got up off the floor and was sitting in a chair near the window, listening to the radio. His back was to me.'

'Yes.'

'I walked over to him, and he didn't turn around, and I didn't say anything to him.'

'What did you do?'

'I struck him with the hatchet.'

'Where?'

'On his head and on his neck.'

'How many times?'

'I don't remember exactly. I just kept hitting him.'

'Then what?'

'He fell off the chair, and I dropped the hatchet, and I went next door to Mr Alanos, he's our neighbour, and I told him I had hit my husband with a hatchet, and he didn't believe me. He came into the apartment, and then he called the police, and an officer came.'

'Your husband was taken to the hospital, did you know that?'

'Yes.'

'Do you know the disposition of his case?'

Her voice was very low. 'I heard he died,' she said. She lowered her head and did not look out past the lights again. Her fists were still folded at her waist. Her eyes were still dead.

'Next case,' the Chief of Detectives said.

'She *murdered* him,' Bush whispered, his voice curiously loaded with awe. Carella nodded.

'Majesta, One,' the Chief of Detectives said. 'Bronckin, David, 27. Had a lamp outage report at 10:24 p.m. last night, corner of Weaver and 69th North. Electric company notified at once, and then another lamp outage two blocks south reported, and then gunfire reported. Patrolman picked up Bronckin on Dicsen and 69th North. Bronckin was intoxicated, was going down the street shooting out lamp-post fixtures. What about it, Dave?'

'I'm only Dave to my friends,' Bronckin said.

'What about it?'

'What do you want from me? I got high, I shot out a few lights. I'll pay for the goddamn lights.'

'What were you doing with the gun?'

'You *know* what I was doing. I was shooting at lamp-posts.'

'Did you start out with that idea? Shooting at the lamp-posts?'

'Yeah. Listen, I don't have to say anything to you. I want a lawyer.'

'You'll have plenty opportunity for a lawyer.'

'Well, I ain't answering any questions until I get one.'

'Who's asking questions? We're trying to find out what possessed you to do a damn fool thing like shooting at light fixtures.'

'I was high. What the hell, you never been high?'

'I don't go shooting at lamp-posts when I'm high,' the Chief said.

'Well, I do. That's what makes horse races.'

'About the gun.'

'Yeah, I knew we'd get down to the gun sooner or later.'

'Is it yours?'

'Sure, it's mine.'

'Where'd you get it?'

'My brother sent it home to me.'

'Where's your brother?'

'In Korea.'

'Have you got a permit for the gun?'

'It was a gift.'

'I don't give a damn if you *made* it! Have you got a permit?'

'No.'

'Then what gave you the idea you could go around carrying it?'

'I just got the idea. Lots of people carry guns. What the hell are you picking on me for? All I shot was a few lights. Why don't you go after the bastards who are shooting people?'

'How do we know you're not one of them, Bronckin?'

'Maybe I am. Maybe I'm Jack the Ripper.'

'Maybe not. But maybe you were carrying that .45 and planning a little worse mischief that shooting out a few lights.'

'Sure. I was gonna shoot the Mayor.'

'A .45,' Carella whispered to Bush.

'Yeah,' Bush said. He was already out of his chair and walking back to the Chief of Detectives.

'All right, smart guy,' the Chief of Detectives said. 'You violated the Sullivan Law, do you know what that means?'

'No, what does it mean, smart guy?'

'You'll find out,' the Chief said. 'Next case.'

At his elbow, Bush said, 'Chief, we'd like to question that man further.

'Go ahead,' the Chief said. 'Hillside, One. Matheson, Peter, 45 ...'

Chapter Fourteen

David Bronckin did not apreciate the idea of being detained from his visit to the Criminal Courts Building, whereto he was being led for arraignment when Carella and Bush intercepted him.

He was a tall man, at least six-three, and he had a very loud voice and a very pugnacious attitude, and he didn't like Carella's first request at all.

'Lift your foot,' Carella said.

'What?'

The men were seated in the Detective squadroom at Headquarters, a room quite similar to the room of the same name back at the 87th. A small fan atop one of the filing cabinets did its best to whip up the air, but the room valiantly upheld its attitude of sleazy limpidity.

'Lift your foot,' Carella repeated.

'What for?'

'Because I say so,' Carella answered tightly.

Bronckin looked at him for a moment and then said, 'You take off that badge and I'll ...'

'I'm not taking it off,' Carella said. 'Lift your foot.'

Bronkin mumbled something and then raised his right foot; Carella held his ankle and Bush looked at the heel.

'Cat's Paw,' Bush said.

'You got any other shoes?' Carella asked.

'Sure, I got other shoes.'

'Home?'

'Yeah. What's up?'

'How long have you owned that .45?'

'Couple of months now.'

'Where were you Sunday night?'

'Listen, I want a lawyer.'

'Never mind the lawyer,' Bush said. 'Answer the question.'

'What was the question?'

'Where were you Sunday night?'
'What time Sunday night?'
'About 11:40 or so.'
'I think I was at a movie.'
'Which movie?'
'The Strand. Yeah. I was at a movie.'
'Did you have the .45 with you?'
'I don't remember.'
'Yes or no.'
'I don't remember. If you want a yes or no, it'll have to be no. I'm no dope.'
'What picture did you see?'
'An old one.'
'Name it.'
'The Creature from the Black Lagoon.'
'What was it about?'
'A monster that comes up from the water.'
'What was the co-feature?'
'I don't remember.'
'Think.'
'Something with John Garfield.'
'What?'
'A prize-fight picture.'
'What was the title?'
'I don't remember. He's a bum, and then he gets to be champ, and then he takes a dive.'
'Body and Soul?'
'Yeah, that was it.'
'Call The Strand, Hank,' Carella said.
'Hey, what're you gonna do that for?' Bronckin asked.
'To check and see if those movies were playing Sunday night.'
'They were playing, all right.'
'We're also going to check that .45 with Ballistics, Bronckin.'
'What for?'
'To see how it matches up against some slugs we've got. You can save us a lot of time.'
'How?'
'What were you doing Monday night?'
'Monday, Monday? Who remembers?'
Bush had located the number in the directory, and was dialling.
'Listen,' Bronckin said, 'you don't have to call them. Those were the pictures, all right.'
'What were you doing Monday night?'
'I ... I went to a movie.'
'Another movie? Two nights in a row?'
'Yeah. The movies are air-conditioned. It's better than hanging around and suffocating, ain't it?'
'What'd you see?'
'Some more old ones.'
'You like old movies, don't you?'

'I don't care about the picture. I was only tryin' to beat the heat. The places showing old movies are cheaper.'

'What were the pictures?'

'Seven Brides for Seven Brothers and Violent Saturday.'

'You remember those all right, do you?'

'Sure, it was more recent.'

'Why'd you say you couldn't remember what you did Monday night?'

'I said that?'

'Yes.'

'Well, I had to think.'

'What movie house was this?'

'On Monday night, you mean?'

'Yeah.'

'One of the RKO's. The one on North 80th.'

Bush put the receiver back into its cradle. 'Checks out, Steve,' he said. 'Creature from the Black Lagoon, and Body and Soul. Like he said.' Bush didn't mention that he'd also taken down a timetable for the theatre, or that he knew exactly what times each picture started and ended. He nodded briefly at Carella, passing on the information.

'What time did you go in?'

'Sunday or Monday?

'Sunday.'

'About 8:30.'

'Exactly 8:30?'

'Who remembers exactly? It was getting hot, so I went into The Strand.'

'What makes you think it was 8:30?'

'I don't know. It was about that time.'

'What time did you leave?'

'About – musta been about a quarter to twelve.'

'Where'd you go then?'

'For some coffee and ...'

'Where?'

'The White Tower.'

'How long did you stay?'

'Half-hour, I guess.'

'What'd you eat?'

'I told you. Coffee and ...'

'Coffee and *what*?'

'My God, a jelly doughnut,' Bronckin said.

'This took you a half-hour?'

'I had a cigarette while I was there.'

'Meet anybody you know there?'

'No.'

'At the movie?'

'No.'

'And you didn't have the gun with you, that right?'

'I don't think I did.'

'Do you usually carry it around?'

'Sometimes.'

'You ever been in trouble with the Law?'

'Yeah.'
'Spell it.'
'I served two at Sing Sing.'
'What for?'
'Assault with a deadly weapon.'
'What was the weapon?'
Bronckin hesitated.
'I'm listening,' Carella said.
'A .45.'
'This one?'
'No.'
'Which?'
'Another one I had.'
'Have you still got it?'
Again, Bronckin hesitated.
'Have you still got it?' Carella repeated.
'Yes.'
'How come? Didn't the police ...'
'I ditched the gun. They never found it. A friend of mine picked it up for me.'
'Did you use the business end?'
'No. The butt.'
'On who?'
'What difference does it make?'
'I want to know. Who?'
'A ... a lady.'
'A woman?'
'Yes.'
'How old?'
'Forty. Fifty.'
'Which?'
'Fifty.'
'You're a nice guy.'
'Yeah,' Bronckin said.
'Who collared you? Which precinct?'
'Ninety-second, I think.'
'Was it?'
'Yes.'
'Who were the cops?'
'I don't know.'
'The ones who made the arrest, I mean.'
'There was only one.'
'A dick?'
'No.'
'When was this?' Bush asked.
'Fifty-two.'
'Where's that other .45?'
'Back at my room.'
'Where?'
'831 Haven.'

Carella jotted down the address.

'What else have you got there?'

'You guys going to help me?'

'What help do you need?'

'Well, I keep a few guns.'

'How many?'

'Six,' Bronckin said.

'What?'

'Yeah.'

'Name them.'

'The two .45's. Then there's a Luger, and a Mauser, and I even got a Tokarev.'

'What else?'

'Oh, just a .22.'

'All in your room?'

'Yeah, it's quite a collection.'

'Your shoes there, too?'

'Yeah. What's with my shoes?'

'No permits for any of these guns, huh?'

'No. Slipped my mind.'

'I'll bet. Hank, call the Ninety-second. Find out who collared Bronckin in '52. I think Foster started at our house, but Reardon may have been a transfer.'

'Oh,' Bronckin said suddenly.

'What?'

'That's what this is all about, huh? Those two cops.'

'Yes.'

'You're way off,' Bronckin said.

'Maybe. What time'd you get out of that RKO?'

'About the same. Eleven-thirty, twelve.'

'The other one check, Hank?'

'Yep.'

'Better call the RKO on North 8oth and check this one, too. You can go now, Bronckin. Your escort's in the hall.'

'Hey,' Bronckin said, 'how about a break? I helped you, didn't I? How about a break?'

Carella blew his nose.

None of the shoes in Bronckin's apartment owned heels even faintly resembling the heel-print cast the Lab boys had.

Ballistics reported that neither of the .45's in Bronckin's possession could have fired any of the fatal bullets.

The 92nd Precinct reported that neither Michael Reardon or David Foster had ever worked there.

There was only one thing the investigators could bank on.

The heat.

Chapter Fifteen

At seven twenty-six that Thursday night, the city looked skyward.

The city had heard a sound, and it paused to identify the sound. The sound was the roll of distant thunder.

And it seemed, simultaneously, as if a sudden breeze sprang up from the North and washed the blistering face of the city. The ominous rolling in the sky grew closer, and now there were lightning flashes, erratic, jagged streaks that knifed the sky.

The people of the city turned their faces upward and waited.

It seemed the rain would never come. The lightning was wild in its fury, lashing the tall buildings, arcing over the horizon. The thunder answered the spitting anger of the lightning, booming its own furious epithets.

And then, suddenly, the sky split open and the rain poured down. Huge drops, and they pelted the sidewalks and the gutters and the streets; and the asphalt and concrete sizzled when the first drops fell; and the citizens of the city smiled and watched the rain, watched the huge drops – God, how big the drops were! – splattering against the ground. And the smiles broadened, and the people slapped each other on the back, and it looked as if everything was going to be all right again.

Until the rain stopped.

It stopped as suddenly as it had begun. It had burst from the sky like water that had broken through a dam. It rained for four minutes and thirty-six seconds. And then, as though someone had suddenly plugged the broken wall of the dam, it stopped.

The lightning still flashed across the sky, and the thunder still growled in response, but there was no rain.

The cool relief the rain had brought lasted no more than ten minutes. At the end of that time, the streets were baking again, and the citizens were swearing and mumbling and sweating.

Nobody likes practical jokes.

Even when God is playing them.

She stood by the window when the rain stopped.

She swore mentally, and she reminded herself that she would have to teach Steve sign language, so that he'd know when she was swearing. He had promised to come tonight, and the promise filled her now, and she wondered what she should wear for him.

'Nothing' was probably the best answer. She was pleased with her joke. She must remember it. To tell him when he came.

The street was suddenly very sad. The rain had brought gaiety, but now
the rain was gone, and there was only the solemn grey of the street, as solemn
as death.

Death.

Two dead, two men he worked with and knew well, why couldn't he have
been a streetcleaner or a flagpole sitter or something, why a policeman, why a
cop?

She turned to look at the clock wondering what time it was, wondering
how long it would be before he came, how long it would be before she
spotted the slow, back-and-forth twisting of the knob, before she rushed to
the door to open it for him. The clock was no comfort. It would be hours yet.
If he came, of course. If nothing else happened, something to keep him at the
station house, another killing, another . . .

No, I mustn't think of that.

It's not fair to Steve to think that.

If I think of harm coming to him . . .

Nothing will happen to him . . . no. Steve is strong, Steve is a good cop,
Steve can take care of himself. But Reardon was a good cop, and Foster, and
they're dead now, how good can a cop be when he's shot in the back with a
.45? How good is any cop against a killer in ambush?

No, don't think these things.

The murders are over now. There will be no more. Foster was the end. It's
done. Done.

Steve, hurry.

She sat facing the door, knowing it would be hours yet, but waiting for the
knob to turn, waiting for the knob to tell her he was there.

The man rose.

He was in his undershorts. They were gaily patterned, and they fitted him
snugly, and he walked from the bed to the dresser with a curiously ducklike
motion. He was a tall man, excellently built. He examined his profile in the
mirror over the dresser, looked at the clock, sighed heavily, and then went
back to bed.

There was time yet.

He lay and looked at the ceiling, and then he suddenly desired a cigarette.
He rose and walked to the dresser again, walking with the strange ducklike
waddle which was uncomplimentary to a man of his physique. He lighted
the cigarette and then went back to bed, where he lay puffing and thinking.

He was thinking about the cop he would kill later that night.

Lieutenant Byrnes stopped in to chat with Captain Frick, commanding
officer of the precinct, before he checked out that night.

'How's it going?' Frick asked.

Byrnes shrugged. 'Looks like we've got the only cool thing in this city.'

'Huh?'

'This case.'

'Oh. Yeah,' Frick said. Frick was tired. He wasn't as young as he used to
be, and all this hullaballoo made him tired. If cops got knocked off, those
were the breaks. Here today, gone tomorrow. You can't live forever, and you
can't take it with you. Find the perpetrator, sure, but don't push a man too

hard. You can't push a man too hard in this heat, especially when he's not as young as he used to be, and tired.

To tell the truth, Frick was a tired man even when he was twenty, and Byrnes knew it. He didn't particularly care for the captain, but he was a conscientious cop, and a conscientious cop checked with the precinct commander every now and then, even if he felt the commander was an egghead.

'You're really working the boys, aren't you?' Frick asked.

'Yes,' Byrnes said, thinking that should have been obvious even to an egghead.

'I figure this for some screwball,' Frick said. 'Got himself a peeve, figured he'd go out and shoot somebody.'

'Why cops?' Byrnes asked.

'Why not? How can you figure what a screwball will do? Probably knocked off Reardon by accident, not even knowing he was a cop. Then saw all the publicity the thing got in the papers, figured it was a good idea, and purposely gunned for another cop.'

'How'd he know Foster was a cop? Foster was in street clothes, same as Reardon.'

'Maybe he's a screwball who's had run-ins with the law before, how do I know? One thing's for sure, though. He's a screwball.'

'Or a mighty shrewd guy,' Byrnes said.

'How do you figure that? What brains does it take to pull a trigger?'

'It doesn't take any brains,' Byrnes said. 'Unless you get away with it.'

'He won't,' Frick answered. He sighed expansively. He was tired. He was getting old. Even his hair was white. Old men shouldn't have to solve mysteries in hot weather.

'Hot, ain't it?' Frick said.

'Yes indeed,' Byrnes replied.

'You heading for home now?'

'Yes.'

'Good for you. I'll be taking off in a little while, too. Some of the boys are out on an attempted suicide, though. Want to find out how it turns out. Some dame on the roof, supposed to be ready to jump.' Frick shook his head. 'Screwballs, huh?'

'Yeah,' Byrnes said.

'Sent my wife and kids away to the mountains,' Frick said. 'Damn glad I did. This heat ain't fit for man nor beast.'

'No, it's not,' Byrnes agreed.

The phone on Frick's desk rang. Frick picked it up.

'Captain Frick,' he said. 'What? Oh. Okay, fine. Right.' He replaced the receiver. 'Not a suicide at all,' he said to Byrnes. 'The dame was just drying her hair, had it sort of hanging over the edge of the roof. Screwball, huh?'

'Yes. Well, I'm taking off.'

'Better keep your gun handy. Might get you next.'

'Who?' Byrnes asked, heading for the door.

'Him.'

'Huh?'

'The screwball.'

Roger Havilland was a bull.

Even the other bulls called him a bull. A real bull. He was a 'bull' as differentiated from a 'bull' which was a detective. Havilland was built like a bull, and he ate like a bull, and he even snorted like a bull. There were no two ways about it. He was a real bull.

He was also not a very nice guy.

There was a time when Havilland was a nice guy, but everyone had forgotten that time, including Havilland. There was a time when Havilland could talk to a prisoner for hours on end without once having to use his hands. There was a time when Havilland did not bellow every other syllable to leave his mouth. Havilland had once been a gentle cop.

But Havilland had once had a most unfortunate thing happen to him. Havilland had tried to break up a street fight one night, being on his way home at the time and being, at the time, that sort of conscientious cop who recognized his duty twenty-four hours a day. The street fight had not been a very big one, as street fights go. As a matter of fact, it was a friendly sort of argument, more or less, with hardly a zip gun in sight.

Havilland stepped in and very politely attempted to bust it up. He drew his revolver and fired a few shots over the heads of the brawlers and somehow or other one of the brawlers hit Havilland on the right wrist with a piece of lead pipe. The gun left Havilland's hand, and then the unfortunate thing happened.

The brawlers, content until then to be bashing in their own heads, suddenly decided a cop's head would be more fun to play upon. They turned on the disarmed Havilland, dragged him into an alley, and went to work on him with remarkable dispatch.

The boy with the lead pipe broke Havilland's arm in four places.

The compound fracture was a very painful thing to bear, more painful in that the damned thing would not set properly and the doctors were forced to rebreak the bones and set them all over again.

For a while there, Havilland doubted if he'd be able to keep his job on the force. Since he'd only recently made Detective 3rd Grade, the prospect was not a particularly pleasant one to him. But the arm healed, as arms will, and he came out of it just about as whole as he went into it – except that his mental attitude had changed somewhat.

There is an old adage which goes something like this: 'One guy can screw it up for the whole company.'

Well, the fellow with the lead pipe certainly screwed it up for the whole company, if not the whole city. Havilland became a bull, a real bull. He had learned his lesson. He would never be cornholed again.

In Havilland's book, there was only one way to beat down a prisoner's resistance. You forgot the word 'down', and you concentrated on beating in the opposite direction: 'up'.

Not many prisoners liked Havilland.

Not many *cops* liked him either.

It is even doubtful whether or not Havilland liked himself.

'Heat,' he said to Carella, 'is all in the mind.'

'My mind is sweating the same as the rest of me,' Carella said.

'If I told you right this minute that you were sitting on a cake of ice in the middle of the Arctic Ocean, you'd begin to feel cool.'

'I don't feel any cooler,' Carella said.

'That's because you're a jackass,' Havilland said, shouting. Havilland always shouted. When Havilland whispered, he shouted. 'You don't want to feel cool. You want to feel hot. It makes you think you're working.'

'I am working.'

'I'm going home,' Havilland shouted abruptly.

Carella glanced at his watch. It was 10:17.

'What's the matter?' Havilland shouted.

'Nothing.'

'It's a quarter after ten, that's what you're looking sour about?' Havilland bellowed.

'I'm not looking sour.'

'Well, I don't care how you look,' Havilland roared. 'I'm going home.'

'So go home. I'm waiting for my relief.'

'I don't like the way you said that,' Havilland answered.

'Why not?'

'It implied that *I* am *not* waiting for my relief.'

Carella shrugged and blithely said, 'Let your conscience be your guide, brother.'

'Do you know how many hours I've been on this job?'

'How many?'

'Thirty-six,' Havilland said. 'I'm so sleepy I could crawl into a sewer and not wake up until Christmastime.'

'You'll pollute our water supply,' Carella said.

'Up yours!' Havilland shouted. He signed out and was leaving when Carella said, 'Hey!'

'What?'

'Don't get killed out there.'

'Up yours,' Havilland said again, and then he left.

The man dressed quietly and rapidly. He put on black trousers and a clean white shirt, and a gold-and-black striped tie. He put on dark blue socks, and then he reached for his shoes. His shoes carried O'Sullivan heels.

He put on the black jacket to his suit, and then he went to the dresser and opened the top drawer. The .45 lay on his handkerchiefs, lethal and blue-black. He pushed a fresh clip into the gun, and then put the gun into his jacket pocket.

He walked to the door in a ducklike waddle, opened it, took a last look around the apartment, flicked out the lights, and went into the night.

Steve Carella was relieved at 11:33 by a detective named Hal Willis. He filled Willis in on anything that was urgent, left him to catch and then walked downstairs.

'Going to see the girlfriend, Steve?' the desk sergeant asked.

'Yep,' Carella answered.

'Wish I was as young as you,' the sergeant said.

'Ah, come on,' Carella replied. 'You can't be more than seventy.'

The sergeant chuckled. 'Not a day over,' he answered.

'Good night,' Carella said.

'Night.'

Carella walked out of the building and headed for his car, which was parked two blocks away in a 'No Parking' zone.

Hank Bush left the precinct at 11:52 when his relief showed up.
'I thought you'd never get here,' he said.
'I thought so, too.'
'What happened?'
'It's too hot to run.'
Bush grimaced, went to the phone, and dialled his home number. He waited several moments. The phone kept ringing on the other end.
'Hello?'
'Alice?'
'Yes.' She paused. 'Hank?'
'I'm on my way,. honey. Why don't you make some iced coffee?'
'All right, I will.'
'Is it very hot there?'
'Yes. Maybe you should pick up some ice cream.'
'All right.'
'No, never mind. No. Just come home. The iced coffee will do.'
'Okay. I'll see you later.'
'Yes, darling.'
Bush hung up. He turned to his relief. 'I hope you don't get relieved 'til nine,' he said.
'The heat's gone to his head,' the detective said to the air.
Bush snorted, signed out, and left the building.

The man with the .45 waited in the shadows.
His hand sweated on the walnut stock of the .45 in his jacket pocket. Wearing black, he knew he blended with the void of the alley mouth, but he was nonetheless nervous and a little frightened. Still, this had to be done.
He heard footsteps approaching. Long firm strides. A man in a hurry. He stared up the street. Yes.
Yes, this was his man.
His hand tightened on the .45.
The cop was closer now. The man in black stepped out of the alleyway abruptly. The cop stopped in his tracks. They were almost of the same height. A street lamp on the corner cast their shadows onto the pavement.
'Have you got a light, Mac?'
The cop was staring at the man in black. Then, suddenly, the cop was reaching for his back pocket. The man in black saw what was happening, and he brought up the .45 quickly, wrenching it free from his pocket. Both men fired simultaneously.
He felt the cop's bullet rip into his shoulder, but the .45 was bucking now, again and again, and he saw the cop clutch at his chest and fall for the pavement. The Detective's Special lay several feet from the cop's body now.
He backed away from the cop, ready to run.
'You son of a bitch,' the cop said.
He whirled. The cop was on his feet, rushing for him. He brought up the .45 again, but he was too late. The cop had him, his thick arms churning. He fought, pulling free, and the cop clutched at his head, and he felt hair wrench

loose, and then the cop's fingers clawed at his face, ripping, gouging.

He fired again. The cop doubled over and then fell to the pavement, his face colliding with the harsh concrete.

His shoulder was bleeding badly. He cursed the cop, and he stood over him, and his blood dripped onto the lifeless shoulders, and he held the .45 out at arm's length and squeezed the trigger again. The cop's head gave a sideways lurch and then was still.

The man in black ran off down the street.

The cop on the sidewalk was Hank Bush.

Chapter Sixteen

Sam Grossman was a police lieutenant. He was also a lab technician. He was tall and angular, a man who'd have looked more at home on a craggy New England farm than in the sterile orderliness of the Police Laboratory which stretched almost half the length of the first floor at Headquarters.

Grossman wore glasses, and his eyes were a guileless blue behind them. There was a gentility to his manner, a quiet warmth reminiscent of a long-lost era, even though his speech bore the clipped stamp of a man who is used to dealing with cold scientific fact.

'Hank was a smart cop,' he said to Carella.

Carella nodded. It was Hank who'd said that it didn't take much brain power to be a detective.

'The way I figure it,' Grossman went on, 'Hank thought he was a goner. The autopsy disclosed four wounds altogether, three in the chest, one at the back of the head. We can safely assume, I think, that the head shot was the last one fired, a *coup de grâce*.'

'Go ahead,' Carella said.

'Figure he'd been shot two or three times already, and possibly knew he'd be a dead pigeon before this was over. Whatever the case, he knew we could use more information on the bastard doing the shooting.'

'The hair, you mean?' Carella asked.

'Yes. We found clumps of hair on the sidewalk. All the hairs had living roots, so we'd have known they were pulled away by force even if we hadn't found some in the palms and fingers of Hank's hands. But he was thinking overtime. He also tore a goodly chunk of meat from the ambusher's face. That told us a few things, too.'

'And what else?'

'Blood. Hank shot this guy, Steve. Well, undoubtedly you know that already.'

'Yes. What does it all add up to?'

'A lot,' Grossman said. He picked up a report from his desk, 'This is what we know for sure, from what we were able to piece together, from what Hank gave us.'

Grossman cleared his throat and began reading.

'The killer is a male, white, adult, not over say fifty years of age. He is a mechanic, possibly highly skilled and highly paid. He is dark complexioned, his skin is oily, he has a heavy beard which he tries to disguise with talc. His hair is dark brown, and he is approximately six feet tall. Within the past two days, he took a haircut and a singe. He is fast, possibly indicating a man who is not overweight. Judging from the hair, he should weigh about 180. He is wounded, most likely above the waist, and not superficially.'

'Break it down for me,' Carella said, somewhat amazed – as he always was – by what the Lab. boys could do with a rag, a bone, and a hank of hair.

'Okay,' Grossman said. 'Male. In this day and age, this sometimes poses a problem, especially if we've got only hair from the head. Luckily, Hank solved that one for us. The *head* hairs of either a male or a female will have an average diameter of less than 0.08 mm. Okay, having only a batch of head hairs to go on, we've got to resort to other measurements to determine whether or not the hair came from a male or a female. Length of the hair used to be a good gauge. If the length was more than 8 cm., we could assume the hair came from a woman. But the goddamn women nowadays are wearing their hair as short as, if not shorter than, the men. So we could have been fooled on this one, if Hank hadn't scratched this guy's face.'

'What's the scratch have to do with it?'

'It gave us a skin sample, to begin with. That's how we knew the man was white, dark complexioned, and oily. But it also gave us a beard hair.'

'How do you know it was a beard hair?'

'Simple,' Grossman said. 'Under the microscope, it showed up in cross-section as being triangular, with concave sides. Only beard hairs are shaped that way. The diameter, too, was greater than 0.1 mm. Simple. A beard hair. Had to be a man.'

'How do you know he was a mechanic?'

'The head hairs were covered with metal dust.'

'You said possibly a highly skilled and highly paid one. Why?'

'The head hairs were saturated with a hair preparation. We broke it down and checked it against our sample sheets. It's very expensive stuff. Five bucks the bottle when sold singly. Ten bucks when sold in a set with the after-shave talc. This customer was wearing both the hair gook *and* the talc. What mechanic can afford ten bucks for such luxuries – unless he's highly paid? If he's highly paid, chances are he's highly skilled.'

'How do you know he's not over fifty?' Carella asked.

'Again, by the diameter of the hair and also the pigmentation. Here, take a look at this chart.' He extended a sheet to Carella.

Age	Diameter
12 days	0.024 mm.
6 months	0.037 mm.
18 months	0.038 mm.
15 years	0.053 mm.
Adults	0.07 mm.

'Fellow's head hair had a diameter of 0.071,' Grossman said.

'That only shows he's an adult.'

'Sure. But if we get a hair with a living root, and there are hardly any pigment grains in the cortex, we can be pretty sure the hair comes from an old person. This guy had plenty of pigment grains. Also, even though we rarely make any age guesses on such single evidence, an older person's hair has a tendency to become finer. This guy's hair is coarse and thick.'

Carella sighed.

'Am I going too fast for you?'

'No,' Carella said. 'How about the singe and the haircut?'

'The singe was simple. The hairs were curled, slightly swelled, and greyish in colour. Not naturally grey, you understand.'

'The haircut?'

'If the guy had had a haircut just before he did the shooting, the head hairs would have shown clean-cut edges. After forty-eight hours, the cut begins to grow round. We can pretty well determine just when a guy's had his last haircut.'

'You said he was six feet tall.'

'Well, Ballistics helped us on that one.'

'Spell it,' Carella said.

'We had the blood to work with. Did I mention the guy has type O blood?'

'You guys ...' Carella started.

'Aw come on, Steve, that was simple.'

'Yeah.'

'Yeah,' Grossman said. 'Look, Steve, the blood serum of one person has the ability to agglutinate ...' He paused. 'That means clump, or bring together the red blood cells of certain other people. There are four blood groups: Group O, Group A, Group B, Group AB. Okay?'

'Okay,' Carella said.

'We take the sample of blood, and we mix a little of it with samples from the four groups. Oh, hell, here's another chart for you to look at.' He handed it to Carella.

1. Group O – no agglutination in either serum.
2. Group A – agglutination in serum B only.
3. Group B – agglutination in serum A only.
4. Group AB – agglutination in both serums.

'This guy's blood – and he left a nice trail of it when he was running away, in addition to several spots on the back of Hank's shirt – would not agglutinate, or clump, in any of the samples. Hence, type O. Another indication that he's white incidentally. A and O are most common in white people. 45% of all white people are in the O group.'

'How do figure he's six feet tall? You still haven't told me.'

'Well, as I said, this is where Ballistics came in. In addition to what we had, of course. The blood spots on Hank's shirt weren't of much value in determining from what height they had fallen since the cotton absorbed them when they hit. But the blood stains on the pavement told us several things.'

'What'd they tell you?'

'First that he was going pretty fast. You see, the faster a man is walking, the narrower and longer will be the blood drops and the teeth on those drops. They look something like a small gear, if you can picture that, Steve.'

'I can.'

'Okay. These were narrow and also sprinkled in many small drops, which told us that he was moving fast and also that the drops were falling from a height of somewhere around two yards or so.'

'So?'

'So, if he was moving fast, he wasn't hit in the legs or the stomach. A man doesn't move very fast under those conditions. If the drops came from a height of approximately two yards, chances are the man was hit high above the waist. Ballistics pried Hank's slug out of the brick wall of the building, and from the angle – assuming Hank only had time to shoot from a draw – they figured the man was struck somewhere around the shoulder. This indicates a tall man, I mean when you put the blood drops and the slug together.'

'How do you know he wasn't wounded superficially?'

'All the blood, man. He left a long trail.'

'You said he weighs about 180. How ...'

'The hair was healthy hair. The guy was going fast. The speed tells us he wasn't overweight. A healthy man of six feet should weigh about 180, no?'

'You've given me a lot, Sam,' Carella said. 'Thanks.'

'Don't mention it. I'm glad I'm not the guy who has to check on doctors' gunshot wound reports, or absentee mechanics. Not to mention this hair lotion and talc. It's called "Skylark", by the way.'

'Well, thanks, anyway.'

'Don't thank me,' Grossman said.

'Huh?'

'Thank Hank.'

Chapter Seventeen

The teletype alarm went out to fourteen states.

It read:

XXXXX APPREHEND SUSPICION OF MURDER XXX UNIDENTIFIED MALE WHITE CAUCASIAN ADULT BELOW FIFTY XXXXX POSSIBLE HEIGHT SIX FEET OR OVER XXX POSSIBLE WEIGHT ONE HUNDRED EIGHTY XXX DARK HAIR SWARTHY COMPLEXION HEAVY BEARD XXXX USES HAIR PREPARATION AND TALC TRADENAME 'SKYLARK' XXXX SHOES MAY POSSIBLY CARRY HEELS WITH 'O'SULLIVAN' TRADENAME XXXX MAN ASSUMED TO BE SKILLED MECHANIC MAY POSSIBLY SEEK SUCH WORK XXXXX GUNWOUND ABOVE WAIST POSSIBLE SHOULDER HIGH MAN MAY SEEK DOCTOR XXXX THIS MAN IS DANGEROUS AND ARMED WITH COLT .45 AUTOMATIC XX

'Those are a lot of "possiblys",' Havilland said.

'Too damn many,' Carella agreed. 'But at least it's a place to start.'

It was not so easy to start.

They could, of course, have started by calling all the doctors in the city, on the assumption that one or more of them had failed to report a gunshot wound, as specified by law. However, there were quite a few doctors in the city. To be exact, there were:

4,283 doctors in Calm's Point
1,975 doctors in Riverhead
8,728 doctors in Isola (including the Diamondback and Hillside sectors)
2,614 doctors in Majesta
and 264 doctors in Bethtown
for a grand total of

COUNT 'EM!

17,864 DOCTORS 17,864

Those are a lot of medical men. Assuming each call would take approximately five minutes, a little multiplication told the cops it would take them approximately 89,320 minutes to call each doctor in the classified directory. Of course, there were 22,000 policemen on the force. If each cop took on the job of calling four doctors, every call could have been made before twenty minutes had expired. Unfortunately, many of the other cops had other tidbits of crime to occupy themselves with. So, faced with the overwhelming number of healers, the detectives decided to wait – instead – for one of them to call with a gunshot wound report. Since the bullet had exited the killer's body, the wound was in all likelihood a clean one, anyway, and perhaps the killer would *never* seek the aid of a doctor. In which case the waiting would all be in vain.

If there were 17,864 doctors in the city, it was virtually impossible to tally the number of mechanics plying their trade there. So this line of approach was also abandoned.

There remained the hair lotion and talc with the innocent-sounding name 'Skylark'.

A quick check showed that both masculine beauty aids were sold over the counter of almost every drug store in the city. They were as common as – if higher-priced than – aspirin tablets.

Good for a cold.

If you don't like them . . .

The police turned, instead, to their own files in the Bureau of Identification, and to the voluminous files in the Federal Bureau of Investigation.

And the search was for a male, white Caucasian, under fifty years in age, dark-haired, dark-complexioned, six feet tall, weighing one-hundred-eighty pounds, addicted to the use of a Colt .45 automatic.

The needle may have been in the city.

But the entire United States was the haystack.

'Lady to see you, Steve,' Miscolo said.

'What about?'

'Said she wanted to talk to the people investigating the cop killer.' Miscolo wiped his brow. There was a big fan in the Clerical Office, and he hated leaving it. Not that he didn't enjoy talking to the DD men. It was simply that Miscolo was a heavy sweater, and he didn't like the armpits of his uniform shirts ruined by unnecessary talk.

'Okay, send her in,' Carella said.

Miscolo vanished, and then reappeared with a small bird-like woman whose head jerked in short arcs as she surveyed first the dividing railing and then the file cabinets and then the desks and the grilled windows and then the detectives on phones everywhere in the squadroom, most of them in various stages of sartorial inelegance.

'This is Detective Carella,' Miscolo said. 'He's one of the detectives on the investigation.' Miscolo sighed heavily and then fled back to the big fan in the small Clerical office.

'Won't you come in, ma'am?' Carella said.

'*Miss*,' the woman corrected. Carella was in his shirt sleeves, and she noticed this with obvious distaste, and then glanced sharply around the room again and said, 'Don't you have a private office?'

'I'm afraid not,' Carella said.

'I don't want them to hear me.'

'Who?' Carella asked.

'Them,' she said. 'Could we go to a desk somewhere in the corner?'

'Certainly,' Carella said. 'What did you say your name was, Miss?'

'Oreatha Bailey,' the woman said. She was at least fifty-five or so, Carella surmised, with the sharp-featured face of a sterotyped witch. He led her through the gate in the railing and to an unoccupied desk in the far right corner of the room, a corner which – unfortunately – did not receive any ventilation from the windows.

When they were seated, Carella asked, 'What can I do for you, Miss Bailey?'

'You don't have a bug in this corner, do you?'

'A ... bug?'

'One of them dictaphone things.'

'No.'

'What did you say your name was?'

'Detective Carella.'

'And you speak English?'

Carella suppressed a smile. 'Yes, I ... I picked up the language from the natives.'

'I'd have preferred an American policeman,' Miss Bailey said in all seriousness.

'Well, I sometimes pass for one,' Carella answered, amused.

'Very well.'

There was a long pause. Carella waited.

Miss Bailey showed no signs of continuing the conversation

'Miss ... ?'

'Shh!' she said sharply.

Carella waited.

After several moments, the woman said. 'I know who killed those policemen.'

Carella leaned forward, interested. The best leads sometimes came from the most unexpected sources. 'Who?' he asked.

'Never you mind,' she answered.

Carella waited.

'They are going to kill a lot more policemen,' Miss Bailey said. 'That's their plan.'

'Whose plan?'

'If they can do away with law enforcement, the rest will be easy,' Miss Bailey said. 'That's their plan. First the police, then the National Guard, and then the regular Army.'

Carella looked at Miss Bailey suspiciously.

'They've been sending messages to me,' Miss Bailey said. 'They think I'm one of them, I don't know why. They come out of the walls and give me messages.'

'Who comes out of the walls?' Carella asked.

'The cockroach-men. That's why I asked if there was a bug in this corner.'

'Oh, the ... the cockroach-men.'

'Yes.'

'I see.'

'Do I look like a cockroach?' she asked.

'No,' Carella said. 'Not particularly.'

'Then why have they mistaken me for one of them? They look like cockroaches, you know.'

'Yes, I know.'

'They talk by radio-nuclear thermics. I think they must be from another planet, don't you?'

'Possibly,' Carella said.

'It's remarkable that I can understand them. Perhaps they've overcome my mind, do you think that's possible?'

'Anything's possible,' Carella agreed.

'They told me about Reardon the night before they killed him. They said they would start with him because he was the Commissar of Sector Three. They used a thermo-disintegrator on him, you know that, don't you?' Miss Bailey paused, and then nodded. '.45 calibre.'

'Yes,' Carella said.

'Foster was the Black Prince of Argaddon. They had to get him. That's what they told me. The signals they put out are remarkably clear, considering the fact that they're in an alien tongue. I do wish you were an American, Mr Carella. There are so many aliens around these days that one hardly knows who to trust.'

'Yes,' Carella said. He could feel the sweat blotting the back of his shirt. 'Yes.'

'They killed Bush because he wasn't a bush, he was a tree in disguise. They hate all plant life.'

'I see.'

'Especially trees. They need the carbon dioxide, you see, and plants consume it. Especially trees. Trees consume a great deal of carbon dioxide.'

'Certainly.'

'Will you stop them, now that you know?' Miss Bailey asked.

'We'll do everything in our power,' Carella said.

'The best way to stop them . . .' Miss Bailey paused and rose, clutching her purse to her narrow bosom. 'Well, I don't want to tell you how to run your business.'

'We appreciate your help,' Carella said. He began walking her to the railing. Miss Bailey stopped.

'Would you like to know the best way to stop these cockroach-men? Guns are no good against them, you know. Because of the thermal heat.'

'I didn't know that,' Carella said. They were standing just inside the railing. He opened the gate for her, and she stepped through.

'There's only one way to stop them,' she said.

'What's that?' Carella asked.

Miss Bailey pursed her mouth. 'Step on them!' she said, and she turned on her heel and walked past Clerical, and then down the steps to the first floor.

Bert Kling seemed to be in high spirits that night.

When Carella and Havilland came into the hospital room, he was sitting up in bed, and aside from the bulky bandage over his right shoulder, you'd never know anything was wrong with him. He beamed a broad smile, and then sat up to talk to the two visiting detectives.

He chewed on the candy they'd brought him, and he said this hospital duty was real jazzy, and that they should get a look at some of the nurses in their tight white uniforms.

He seemed to bear no grudge whatever against the boy who'd shot him. Those breaks were all part of the game, he supposed. He kept chewing candy, and joking, and talking until it was almost time for the cops to leave.

Bert Kling seemed to be in high spirits that night.

Chapter Eighteen

The three funerals followed upon each other's heels with remarkable rapidity. The heat did not help the classical ceremonies of death. The mourners followed the caskets and sweated. An evil, leering sun grinned its blistering grin, and freshly turned soil – which should have been cool and moist – accepted the caskets with dry, dusty indifference.

The beaches that week were jammed to capacity. In Calm's Point at Mott's Island, the scorekeeper recorded a record-breaking crowd of two million four hundred and seventy thousand surf seekers. The police had problems. The police had traffic problems because everyone who owned any sort of a jalopy had put it on the road. The police had fire-hydrant problems, because kids all over the city were turning on the johnny pumps, covering the spout with a flattened coffee can, and romping beneath the improvised shower. The police had burglary problems, because people were sleeping with their windows open; people were leaving parked cars unlocked, windows wide; shopkeepers were stepping across the street for a moment to catch a quick Pepsi Cola. The police had 'floater' problems, because the scorched and heat-weary citizens sometimes sought relief in the polluted currents of the rivers that bound Isola – and some of them drowned, and some of them turned up with bloated bodies and bulging eyes.

On Walker Island, in the River Dix, the police had prisoner problems because the cons there decided the heat was too much for them to bear, and they banged their tin cups on the sweating bars of their hot cells, and the cops listened to the clamour and rushed for riot guns.

The police had all sorts of problems.

Carella wished she were not wearing black.

He knew this was absurd. When a woman's husband is dead, the woman wears black.

But Hank and he had talked a lot in the quiet hours of the midnight tour, and Hank had many times described Alice in the black nightgowns she wore to bed. And try as he might, Carella could not disassociate the separate concepts of black: black as sheer and frothy raiment of seduction; black as the ashy garment of mourning.

Alice Bush sat across from him in the living room of the Calm's Point apartment. The windows were wide open, and he could see the tall Gothic structures of the Calm's Point College campus etched against the merciless, glaring blue of the sky. He had worked with Bush for many years, but this was the first time he'd been inside his apartment, and the association of Alice Bush in black cast a feeling of guilt over his memories of Hank.

The apartment was not at all what he would have expected for a man like Hank. Hank was big, rough-hewn. The apartment was somehow frilly, a woman's apartment. He could not believe that Hank had been comfortable in these rooms. His eyes had scanned the furniture, small-scaled stuff, stuff in which Hank could never have spread his legs. The curtains at the windows were ruffled chintz. The walls of the living room were a sickeningly pale lemon shade. The end tables were heavy with curlicues and inlaid patterns. The corners of the room contained knick-knack shelves, and the shelves were loaded with fragile glass figurines of dogs and cats and gnomes and one of Little Bo Peep holding a delicately blown, slender glass shepherd's crook.

The room, the apartment, seemed to Carella to be the intricately cluttered design for a comedy of manners. Hank must have been as out of place here as a plumber at a literary tea.

Not so Mrs Bush.

Mrs Bush lounged on a heavily padded chartreuse love-seat, her long legs tucked under her, her feet bare. Mrs Bush belonged in this room. This room had been designed for Mrs Bush, designed for femininity, and the Male Animal be damned.

She wore black silk. She was uncommonly big-busted, incredibly narrow-waisted. Her hip bones were wide, flesh-padded, a woman whose body had been designed for the bearing of children – but somehow she didn't seem the type. He could not visualize her squeezing life from her loins. He could only visualize her as Hank had described her – in the role of a seductress. The black silk dress strengthened the concept. The frou-frou room left no doubt. This was a stage set for Alice Bush.

The dress was not low-cut. It didn't have to be.

Nor was it particularly tight, and it didn't have to be that, either.

It was not expensive, but it fitted her figure well. He had no doubt that anything she wore would fit her figure well. He had no doubt that even a potato sack would look remarkably interesting on the woman who had been Hank's wife.

'What do I do now?' Alice asked. 'Make up beds at the precinct? That's the usual routine for a cop's widow, isn't it?'

'Did Hank leave any insurance?' Carella asked.

'Nothing to speak of. Insurance doesn't come easily to cops, does it? Besides . . . Steve, he was a young man. Who thinks of things like this? Who thinks these things are going to happen?' She looked at him wide-eyed. Her eyes were very brown, her hair was very blonde, her complexion was fair and unmarred. She was a beautiful woman, and he did not like considering her such. He wanted her to be dowdy and forlorn. He did not want her looking fresh and lovely. Goddamnit, what was there about this room that suffocated a man? He felt like the last male alive, surrounded by bare-breasted beauties on a tropical island surrounded by man-eating sharks. There was no place to run to. The island was called Amazonia or something, and the island was female to the core, and he was the last man alive.

The room and Alice Bush.

The femaleness reached out to envelop him in a cloying clinging embrace.

'Change your mind, Steve,' Alice said. 'Have a drink.'

'All right, I will,' he answered.

She rose, displaying a long white segment of thigh as she got to her feet, displaying an almost indecent oblivion to the way she handled her body. She had lived with it for a long time, he supposed. She no longer marvelled at its allure. She accepted it, and lived with it, and others could marvel. A thigh was a thigh, what the hell! What was so special about the thigh of Alice Bush?

'Scotch?'

'All right.'

'How does it feel, something like this?' she asked. She was standing at the bar across from him. She stood with the loose-hipped stance of a fashion model, incongruous because he always pictured fashion models as willowy and thin and flat-chested. Alice Bush was none of these.

'Something like what?'

'Investigating the death of a colleague and friend.'

'Weird,' Carella said.

'I'll bet.'

'You're taking it very well,' Carella said.

'I have to,' Alice answered briefly.

'Why?'

'Because I'll fall all to pieces if I don't. He's in the ground, Steve. It's not going to help for me to wail and moan all over the place.'

'I suppose not.'

'We've got to go on living, haven't we? We can't simply give up because someone we love is gone, can we?'

'No,' Carella agreed.

She walked to him and handed him the drink. Their fingers touched for an instant. He looked up at her. Her face was completely guileless. The contact, he was sure, had been accidental.

She walked to the window and looked out towards the college. 'It's lonely here without him,' she said.

'It's lonely at the house without him, too,' Carella said, surprised. He had not realized, before this, how really attached he had become to Hank.

'I was thinking of taking a trip,' Alice said, 'getting away from things that remind me of him.'

'Things like what?' Carella asked.

'Oh, I don't know,' Alice said. 'Like ... last night I saw his hair brush on the dresser, and there was some of the wild red hair of his caught in the bristles, and all at once it reminded me of him, of the wildness of him. He was a wild person, Steve.' She paused. 'Wild.'

The word was female somehow. He was reminded again of the word portrait Hank had drawn, of the real portrait before him, standing by the window, of the femaleness everywhere around him on this island. He could not blame her, he knew that. She was only being herself, being Alice Bush, being Woman. She was only a pawn of fate, a girl who automatically embodied womanhood, a girl who ... hell!

'How far have you come along on it?' she asked. She whirled from the window, went back to the love seat and collapsed into it. The movement was not a gracious one. It was feline, however. She sprawled in the love seat like a big jungle cat, and then she tucked her legs under her again, and he would not have been surprised if she'd begun purring in that moment.

He told her what they thought they knew about the suspected killer. Alice nodded.

'Quite a bit to go on,' she said.

'Not really.'

'I mean, if he should seek a doctor's aid.'

'He hasn't yet. Chances are he won't. He probably dressed the wound himself.'

'Badly shot?'

'Apparently. But clean.'

'Hank should have killed him,' she said. Surprisingly, there was no viciousness attached to the words. The words themselves bore all the lethal potential of a coiled rattler, but the delivery made them harmless.

'Yes,' Carella agreed. 'He should have.'

'But he didn't.'

'No.'

'What's your next step?' she asked.

'Oh, I don't know. Homicide North is up a tree on these killings, and I guess we are, too. I've got a few ideas kicking around, though.'

'A lead?' she asked.

'No. Just ideas.'

'What kind of ideas?'

'They'd bore you.'

'My husband's been killed,' Alice said coldly. 'I assure you I will not be bored by anything that may lead to finding his killer.'

'Well, I'd prefer not to air any ideas until I know what I'm talking about.'

Alice smiled. 'That's different. You haven't touched your drink.'

He raised the glass to his lips. The drink was very strong.

'Wow!' he said. 'You don't spare the alcohol, do you?'

'Hank liked his strong,' she said. 'He liked everything strong.'

And again, like an interwoven thread of personality, a personality dictated by the demands of a body that could look nothing but blatantly inviting, Alice Bush had inadvertently lighted another fuse. He had the feeling that she would suddenly explode into a thousand flying fragments of breast and hip and thigh, splashing over the landscape like a Dali painting.

'I'd better be getting along,' he said. 'The City doesn't pay me for sipping drinks all morning.'

'Stay a while,' she said. 'I have a few ideas myself.'

He glanced up quickly, almost suspecting an edge of *double entendre* in her voice. He was mistaken. She had turned away from him and was looking out the window again, her face in profile, her body in profile.

'Let me hear them,' he said.

'A cop hater,' she replied.

'Maybe.'

'It has to be. Who else would senselessly take three lives? It has to be a cop hater, Steve. Doesn't Homicide North think so?'

'I haven't talked to them in the past few days. That's what they thought in the beginning, I know.'

'What do they think now?'

'That's hard to say.'

'What do *you* think now?'

'Maybe a cop hater. Reardon and Foster, yes, a cop hater. But Hank ... I don't know.'

'I'm not sure I follow you.'

'Well, Reardon and Foster were partners, so we could assume that possibly some jerk was carrying a grudge against them. They worked together ... maybe they rubbed some idiot the wrong way.'

'Yes?'

'But Hank *never* worked with them. Oh, well maybe not never. Maybe once or twice on a plant or something. He never made an important arrest with either of them along, though. Our records show that.'

'Who says it has to be someone with a personal grudge, Steve? This may simply be some goddamned lunatic.' She seemed to be getting angry. He didn't know why she was getting angry because she'd certainly been calm enough up to this point. But her breath was coming heavier now, and her breasts heaved disconcertingly. 'Just some crazy, rotten, twisted fool who's taken it into his mind to knock off every cop in the 87th Precinct. Does that sound so far-fetched?'

'No, not at all. As a matter of fact, we've checked all the mental institutions in the area for people who were recently released who might possibly have had a history of ...' He shook his head. 'You know, we figured perhaps a paranoiac, somebody who'd go berserk at the sight of a uniform. Except these men weren't in uniform.'

'No, they weren't. What'd you get?'

'We thought we had one lead. Not anyone with a history of dislike for policemen, but a young man who had a lot of officer trouble in the Army. He was recently released from Bramlook as cured, but that doesn't mean a goddamned thing. We checked with the psychiatrists there, and they felt his illness would never break out in an act of violence, no less a prolonged rampage of violence.'

'And you let it drop?'

'No, we looked the kid up. Harmless. Alibis a mile long.'

'Who else have you checked?'

'We've got feelers out to all our underworld contacts. We thought this might be a gang thing, where some hood has an alleged grievance against something we've done to hamper him, and so he's trying to show us we're not so high and mighty. He hires a torpedo and begins methodically putting us in our places. But there's been no rumble so far, and underworld revenge is not something you can keep very quiet.'

'What else?'

'I've been wading through FBI photos all morning. You'd never realize how many men there are who fit the possible description we have.' He sipped at the scotch. He was beginning to feel a little more comfortable with Alice. Maybe she wasn't so female, after all. Or maybe her femaleness simply enveloped you after a while, causing you to lose all perspective. Whatever it was, the room wasn't as oppressive now.

'Turn up anything? From the photos?'

'Not yet. Half of them are in jail, and the rest are scattered all over the country. You see, the hell of this thing is ... well ...'

'What?'

'How'd the killer know that these men were cops? They were all in plainclothes. Unless he'd had contact with them before, how could he know?'

'Yes, I see what you mean.'

'Maybe he sat in a parked car across from the house and watched everyone who went in and out. If he did that for a while, he'd get to know who worked there and who didn't.'

'He could have done that,' Alice said thoughtfully. 'Yes he could have.' She crossed her legs unconsciously. Carella looked away.

'Several things against that theory, though,' Carella said. 'That's what makes this case such a bitch.' The word had sneaked out, and he glanced up apprehensively. Alice Bush seemed not to mind the profanity. She had probably heard enough of it from Hank. Her legs were still crossed. They were very good legs. Her skirt had fallen into a funny position. He looked away again.

'You see, if somebody had been watching the house, we'd have noticed him. That is, if he'd been watching it long enough to know who worked there and who was visiting ... that would take time. We'd surely have spotted him.'

'Not if he were hidden.'

'There are no buildings opposite the house. Only the park.'

'He could have been somewhere in the park ... with binoculars, maybe.'

'Sure. But how could he tell the detectives from the patrolmen, then?'

'What?'

'He killed three detectives. Maybe it was chance. I don't think so. All right, how the hell could he tell the patrolmen from the detectives?'

'Very simply,' Alice said. 'Assuming he was watching, he'd see the men when they arrived, and he'd see them after muster when they went out to their beats. They'd be in uniform then. I'm talking about the patrolmen.'

'Yes, I suppose.' He took a deep swallow of the drink. Alice moved on the love seat.

'I'm hot,' she said.

He did not look at her. He knew that his eyes would have been drawn downward if he did, and he did not want to see what Alice was unconsciously, obliviously showing.

'I don't suppose this heat has helped the investigation any,' she said.

'This heat hasn't helped *anything* any.'

'I'm changing to shorts and a halter as soon as you get out of here.'

'There's a hint if ever I heard one,' Carella said.

'No, I didn't mean ... oh hell, Steve, I'd change to them now if I thought you were going to stay longer. I just thought you were leaving soon. I mean ...' She made a vague motion with one hand. 'Oh, nuts.'

'I am leaving, Alice. Lots of photos to look through back there.' He rose. 'Thanks for the drink.' He started for the door, not looking back when she got up, not wanting to look at her legs again.

She took his hand at the door. Her grip was firm and warm. Her hand was fleshy. She squeezed his hand.

'Good luck, Steve. If there's anything I can do to help ...'

'We'll let you know. Thanks again.'

He left the apartment and walked down to the street. It was very hot in the street.

Chapter Nineteen

'Now here's what I call a real handsome one,' Hal Willis said. Hal Willis was the only really small detective Carella had ever known. He passed the minimum height requirement of five eight, of course, but just barely. And contrasted against the imposing bulk of the other bulls in the division, he looked more like a soft shoe dancer than a tough cop. That he was a tough cop, there was no doubt. His bones were slight, and his face was thin, and he looked as if he would have trouble swatting a fly, but anyone who'd ever tangled with Hal Willis did not want the dubious pleasure again. Hal Willis was a Judo expert.

Hal Willis could shake your hand and break your backbone in one and the same motion. Were you not careful with Hal Willis, you might find yourself enwrapped in the excruciating pain of a Thumb Grip. Were you even less careful, you might discover yourself hurtling through space in the fury of either a Rugby or a Far-Eastern Capsize. Ankle Throws, Flying Mares, Back Wheels, all were as much a part of Hal Willis's personality as the sparkling brown eyes in his face.

Those eyes were amusedly turned now towards the FBI photo which he shoved across the desk towards Carella.

The photo was of a man who was indeed a 'real handsome one.' His nose had been fractured in at least four places. A scar ran the length of his left cheek. Scar tissue hooded his eyes. He owned cauliflower ears and hardly any teeth. His name, of course, was 'Pretty-Boy Krajak'.

'A doll,' Carella said. 'Why'd they send him to us?'

'Dark hair, six feet two, weight one-eighty-five. How'd you like to run across him some dark and lonely night?'

'I wouldn't. Is he in the city?'

'He's in L.A.,' Willis said.

'Then we'll leave him to Joe Friday,' Carella cracked.

'Have another Chesterfield,' Willis countered. 'The only living cigarette with 60,000 filter dragnets.'

Carella laughed. The phone rang. Willis picked it up.

'87th Squad,' he said. 'Detective Willis.'

Carella looked up.

'What?' Willis said. 'Give me the address.' He scribbled something hastily on his pad. 'Hold him there, we'll be right over.' He hung up, opened the desk drawer and removed his holster and service revolver.

'What is it?' Carella asked.

'Doctor on 35th North. Has a man in his office with a bullet wound in his left shoulder.'

A squad car was parked in front of the brownstone on 35th North when Carella and Willis arrived.

'The rookies beat us here,' Willis said.

'So long as they've got him,' Carella answered, and he made it sound like a prayer. A sign on the door read, 'DOCTOR IS IN. RING BELL AND PLEASE BE SEATED.'

'Where?' Willis asked. 'On the doorstep?'

They rang the bell, opened the door, and entered the office. The office was situated off the small courtyard on the street level of the brownstone. A patrolman was seated on the long leather couch, reading a copy of *Esquire*. He closed the magazine when the detective entered and said, 'Patrolman Curtis, sir.'

'Where's the doctor?' Carella asked.

'Inside, sir. Country is asking him some questions.'

'Who's Country?'

'My partner, sir.'

'Come on,' Willis said. He and Carella went into the doctor's office. Country, a tall gangling boy with a shock of black hair, snapped to attention when they entered.

'Goodbye, Country,' Willis said drily. The patrolman eased himself towards the door and left the office.

'Dr Russell?' Willis asked.

'Yes,' Dr Russell replied. He was a man of about fifty, with a head of hair that was silver white, giving the lie to his age. He stood as straight as a telephone pole, broad-shouldered, immaculate in his white office tunic. He was a handsome man, and he gave an impression of great competence. For all Carella knew, he may have been a butcher, but he'd have trusted this man to cut out his heart.

'Where is he?'

'Gone,' Dr Russell said.

'How ...'

'I called as soon as I saw the wound. I excused myself, went out to my private office and placed the call. When I came back, he was gone.'

'Nuts,' Willis said. 'Want to tell us from the beginning, doctor?'

'Certainly. He came in ... oh, not more than twenty minutes ago. The office was empty, unusual for this time of day, but I rather imagine people with minor ailments are curing them at the seashore.' He smiled briefly. 'He said he'd shot himself while cleaning his hunting rifle. I took him into the Examination Room – that's *this* room, gentlemen – and asked him to take off his shirt. He did.'

'What happened then?'

'I examined the wound. I asked him when he had had the accident. He said it had occurred only this morning. I knew instantly that he was lying. The wound I was examining was not a fresh one. It was already highly infected. That was when I remembered the newspaper stories.'

'About the cop killer?'

'Yes. I recalled having read something about the man having a pistol wound above the waist. That was when I excused myself to call you.'

'Was this definitely a gunshot wound?'

'Without a doubt. It had been dressed, but very badly. I didn't examine it very closely, you understand, because I rushed off to make the call. But it seemed to me that iodine had been used as a disinfectant.'

'Iodine?'

'Yes.'

'But it was infected nonetheless?'

'Oh, definitely. That man is going to have to find another doctor, sooner or later.'

'What did he look like?'

'Well, where should I begin?'

'How old?'

'Thirty-five or thereabouts.'

'Height?'

'A little over six feet, I should say.'

'Weight?'

'About one-ninety.'

'Black hair?' Willis asked.

'Yes.'

'Colour of eyes?'

'Brown.'

'Any scars, birthmarks, other identifying characteristics?'

'His face was very badly scratched.'

'Did he touch anything in the office?'

'No. Wait, yes.'

'What?'

'I had him sit on the table here. When I began probing the wound, he winced and gripped the stirrups here at the foot of the table.'

'This may be a break, Hal,' Carella said.

'It sounds like one. What was he wearing, Dr Russell?'

'Black.'

'Black suit?'

'Yes.'

'What colour shirt?'

'White. It was stained over the wound.'

'Tie.'

'A striped tie. Gold and black.'

'Tie clasp?'

'Yes. Some sort of design on it.'

'What kind?'

'A bugle? Something like that.'

'Trumpet, hunting horn, horn of plenty?'

'I don't know. I couldn't identify it. It only stuck in my mind because it was an unusual clasp. I noticed it when he was undressing.'

'What colour shoes?'

'Black.'

'Clean-shaven?'

'Yes. That is, you meant was he wearing a beard?'

'Yes.'

'Well then, yes, he was clean-shaven. But he needed a shave.'

'Uh-huh. Wearing any rings?'

'None that I noticed.'

'Undershirt?'

'No undershirt.'

'Can't say I blame him in this heat. Mind if I make a call, Doc?'

'Please help yourself. Do you think he's the man?'

'I hope so,' Willis said. 'God, I hope so.'

When a man is nervous, he perspires – even if the temperature is not hovering somewhere in the nineties.

There are sweat pores on the fingertips, and the stuff they secrete contains 98.5 per cent water and 0.5 to 1.5 per cent solid material. This solid material breaks down to about one-third of inorganic matter – mainly salt – and two-thirds of organic substances like urea, albumin and formic, butyric and acetic acids. Dust, dirt, grease cling to the secretion from a man's fingertips.

The perspiration, mixed with whatever happens to be clinging to it at the moment, leaves a filmy impression on whatever the man happens to touch.

The suspected killer happened to touch the smooth chromium surfaces of the stirrups in Dr Russell's office.

The tech crew dusted the latent fingerprints with one of the commercial black powders. The excess powder was allowed to fall on a sheet of paper. The prints were lightly brushed with an ostrich feather. They were then photographed.

There were two good thumbprints, one for each hand where the suspect had pressed down on the top surfaces of the stirrups. There were good second-joint prints for each hand where the suspect had gripped the undersides of the stirrups.

The prints were sent to the Bureau of Identification. A thorough search was made of the files. The search proved fruitless, and the prints were sent to the Federal Bureau of Investigation while the detectives sat back to wait.

In the meantime, a police artist went to see Dr Russell. Listening to Dr Russell's description, he began drawing a picture of the suspect. He made changes as Dr Russell suggested them – 'No, the nose is a little too long; yes, that's better. Try to give a little curl to his lip there, yes, yes, that's it' – and he finally came up with a drawing which tallied with Dr Russell's recollection of the man he had examined. The picture was sent to each metropolitan daily and to each television station in the area, together with a verbal description of the wanted man.

All this while, the detectives waited for the FBI report. They were still waiting the next day.

Willis looked at the drawing on the first page of one of the morning tabloids.

The headline screamed: HAVE YOU SEEN THIS MAN?

'He's not bad-looking,' Willis said.

'Pretty-Boy Krajak,' Carella said.

'No, I'm serious.'

'He may be handsome, but he's a killer,' Carella said. 'I hope his arm falls off.'

'It very well might,' Willis said drily.

'Where the hell's that FBI report?' Carella asked edgily. He had been answering calls all morning, calls from citizens who reported having seen the killer. Each call had to be checked out, of course, but thus far the man had been seen all over the city at simultaneous times. 'I thought those G-men were supposed to be fast.'

'They are,' Willis said.

'I'm going to check with the Lieutenant.'

'Go ahead,' Willis said.

Carella went to the Lieutenant's door. He knocked and Byrnes called, 'Come.' Carella went into the office. Byrnes was on the phone. He signalled for Carella to stand by. He nodded then and said, 'But, Harriet, I can't see anything wrong with that.'

He listened patiently.

'Yes, but ...'

Carella walked to the window and stared out at the park.

'No, I can't see any reason for ...'

Marriage, Carella thought. And then he thought of Teddy. *It'll be different with us.*

'Harriet, let him go,' Byrnes said. 'He's a good boy, and he won't get into any trouble. Look, take my word for it. For God's sake, it's only an amusement park.'

Byrnes sighed patiently.

'All right, then.' He listened. 'I'm not sure yet, honey. We're waiting for an FBI report. If I'll be home, I'll call you. No, nothing special. It's too damn hot to eat, anyway. Yes, dear, 'bye.'

He hung up. Carella came from the window.

'Women,' Byrnes said, not disagreeably. 'My son wants to go out to Jollyland tonight with some of the boys. She doesn't think he should. Can't see why he wants to go there in the middle of the week. She says she's read newspaper stories about boys getting into fights with other boys at these places. For Pete's sake, it's just an amusement park. The kid is seventeen.'

Carella nodded.

'If you're going to watch them every minute, they'll feel like prisoners. Okay, what are the odds on a fight starting at a place like that? Larry knows enough to avoid trouble. He's a good kid. You met him, didn't you, Steve?'

'Yes,' Carella said. 'He seemed very level-headed.'

'Sure, that's what I told Harriet. Ah, what the hell! These women never cut the apron strings. We get raised by one woman, and then when we're ripe, we get turned over to another woman.'

Carella smiled. 'It's a conspiracy,' he said.

'Sometimes I think so,' Byrnes said. 'But what would we do without them, huh?' He shook his head sadly, a man trapped in the labial folds of a society structure.

'Anything from the Feds yet?' Carella asked.

'No, not yet. I'm praying for a break.'

'Mmmm.'

'We deserve a break, don't we?' Byrnes asked. 'We've worked this one right into the ground. We deserve a break.'

There was a knock on the door.

'Come,' Byrnes said.

Willis entered the room with an envelope. 'This just arrived, sir,' he said.

'FBI?'

'Yes.'

Byrnes took the envelope. Hastily, he tore open the flap and pulled out the folded letter.

'Hell!' he erupted. 'Hell and damnation!'

'Bad?'

'They've got nothing on him!' Byrnes shouted. 'Goddamnit! Goddamnit to hell!'

'Not even Service prints?'

'Nothing. He was probably 4-F!'

'We know *everything* about this guy,' Willis said vehemently, beginning to pace the office. 'We know what he looks like, we know his height, his weight, his blood type, when he got his last haircut.' He slammed his fist into the opposite hand. 'The only thing we don't know is who the hell he is! Who is he, damnit, who is he?'

Neither Carella or Byrnes answered.

That night, a boy named Miguel Aretta was taken to Juvenile House. The police had picked him up as one of the boys who'd been missing from the roundup of The Grovers. It did not take the police long to discover that Miguel was the boy who'd zip-gunned Bert Kling.

Miguel had been carrying a zip-gun on the night that Kling got it. When a Senior Grover named Rafael 'Rip' Desanga had reported to the boys that a smart guy had been around asking questions, Miguel went with them to teach the smart guy a lesson.

As it turned out, the smart guy – or the person they assumed to be the smart guy – had pulled a gun outside the bar. Miguel had taken his own piece from his pocket and burned him.

Bert Kling, of course, had not been that smart guy. He turned out to be, of all things, a cop. So Miguel Aretta was now in Juvenile House, and the people there were trying to understand what made him tick so that they could present his case fairly when it came up in Children's Court.

Miguel Aretta was fifteen years old. It could be assumed that he just didn't know any better.

The real smart guy – a reporter named Cliff Savage – was thirty-seven
years old, and he should have know better.

He didn't.

Chapter Twenty

Savage was waiting for Carella when he left the precinct at 4:00 p.m. the next
day.

He was wearing a brown Dupioni silk suit, a gold tie, and a brown straw
with a pale yellow band. 'Hello,' he said, shoving himself off the side of the
building.

'What can I do for you?' Carella asked.

'You're a detective, aren't you?'

'If you've got a complaint,' Carella said, 'take it to the desk sergeant. I'm
on my way home.'

'My name's Savage.'

'Oh,' Carella said. He regarded the reporter sourly.

'You in the fraternity, too?' Savage asked.

'Which one?'

'The Fraternity against Savage. Eeta Piecea Cliff.'

'I'm Phi Beta Kappa myself,' Carella said.

'Really?'

'No.' He began walking towards his car. Savage fell in step with him.

'Are you sore at me, too, is what I meant,' Savage said.

'You stuck your nose in the wrong place,' Carella answered. 'Because you
did, a cop is in the hospital and a kid is in Juvenile House, awaiting trial.
What do you want me to do, give you a medal?'

'If a kid shoots somebody, he deserves whatever he gets.'

'Maybe he wouldn't've shot anybody if you'd kept you nose out of it.'

'I'm a reporter. My job is getting facts.'

'The lieutenant told me he'd already discussed the possibility of teen-
agers being responsible for the deaths. He said he told you he considered the
possibility extremely remote. But you went ahead and put your fat thumb in
the pie, anyway. You realize Kling could have been killed?'

'He wasn't. Do you realize *I* could have been killed?' Savage said.

Carella made no comment.

'If you people cooperated more with the press ...'

Carella stopped walking. 'Listen,' he said, 'what are you doing in this
neighbourhood? Looking for more trouble? If any of The Grovers recognize
you, we're going to have another rhubarb. Why don't you go back to your
newspaper office and write a column on garbage collection?'

'Your humour doesn't ...'

'I'm not trying to be funny,' Carella said, 'nor do I particularly feel like
discussing anything with you. I just came off duty. I'm going home to
shower and then I have a date with my fiancée. I'm theoretically on duty
twenty-four hours a day, every day of the week, but fortunately that duty

does not include extending courtesy to every stray cub reporter in town.'

'Cub?' Savage was truly offended. 'Now, listen ...'

'What the hell do you want from me?' Carella asked.

'I want to discuss the killings.'

'I don't.'

'Why not?'

'You're a real leech, aren't you?'

'I'm a reporter, and a damned good one. Why don't you want to talk about the killings?'

'I'm perfectly willing to discuss them with anyone who knows what I'm talking about.'

'I'm a good listener,' Savage said.

'Sure. You turned a fine ear towards Rip Desanga.'

'Okay, I made a mistake, I'm willing to admit that. I thought it was the kids, and it wasn't. We know now it was an adult. What else do we know about him? Do we know why he did it?'

'Are you going to follow me all the way home?'

'I'd prefer buying you a drink,' Savage said. He looked at Carella expectantly. Carella weighed the offer.

'All right,' he said.

Savage extended his hand. 'My friends call me Cliff. I didn't get your name.'

'Steve Carella.'

They shook. 'Pleased to know you. Let's get that drink.'

The bar was air-conditioned, a welcome sanctuary from the stifling heat outdoors. They ordered their drinks and then sat opposite each other at the booth alongside the left-hand wall.

'All I want to know,' Savage said, 'is what you think.'

'Do you mean me personally, or the department?'

'You, or course. I can't expect you to speak for the department.'

'Is this for publication?' Carella asked.

'Hell, no. I'm just trying to jell my own ideas on it. Once this thing is broken, there'll be a lot of feature coverage. To do a good job, I want to be acquainted with every facet of the investigation.'

'It'd be a little difficult for a layman to understand every facet of police investigation,' Carella said.

'Of course, of course. But you can at least tell me what you think.'

'Sure. Provided it's not for publication.'

'Scout's honour,' Savage said.

'The department doesn't like individual cops trying to glorify ...'

'Not a word of this will get into print,' Savage said. 'Believe me.'

'What do you want to know?'

'We've got the means, we've got the opportunity,' Savage said. 'What's the motive?'

'Every cop in the city would like the answer to that one,' Carella said.

'A nut maybe.'

'Maybe.'

'You don't think so?'

'No. Some of us do. I don't.'

'Why not?'

'Just like that.'

'Do you have a reason?'

'No, just a feeling. When you've been working on a case for any length of time, you begin to get feelings about it. I just don't happen to believe a maniac's involved here.'

'What *do* you believe?'

'Well, I have a few ideas.'

'Like what?'

'I'd rather not say right now.'

'Oh, come on, Steve.'

'Look, police work is like any other kind of work – except we happen to deal with crime. If you run an import-export business, you play certain hunches and others you don't. It's the same with us. If you have a hunch, you don't go around making a million dollar deal on it until you've checked it.'

'Then you do have a hunch you want to check?'

'Not even a hunch, really. Just an idea.'

'What kind of an idea?'

'About motive.'

'What about motive?'

Carella smiled. 'You're a pretty tenacious guy, aren't you?'

'I'm a good reporter. I already told you that.'

'All right, look at it this way. These men were cops. Three of them were killed in a row. What's the automatic conclusion?'

'Somebody doesn't like cops.'

'Right. A cop hater.'

'So?'

'Take off their uniforms. What have you got then?'

'They weren't wearing uniforms. None of them were uniform cops.'

'I know. I was speaking figuratively. I meant, make them ordinary citizens. Not cops. What do you have then? Certainly not a cop hater.'

'But they *were* cops.'

'They were men first. Cops only coincidentally and secondarily.'

'You feel, then, that the fact that they were cops had nothing to do with the reason they were killed.'

'Maybe. That's what I want to dig into a little deeper.'

'I'm not sure I understand you.'

'It's this,' Carella said. 'We knew these men well, we worked with them every day. Cops. We knew them as cops. We didn't know them as *men*. They may have been killed because they were men, and not because they were cops.'

'Interesting,' Savage said.

'It means digging into their lives on a more personal level. It won't be fun because murder has a strange way of dragging skeletons out of the neatest closets.'

'You mean, for example ...' Savage paused. 'Well, let's say Reardon was playing around with another dame, or Foster was a horse player, or Bush was taking money from a racketeer, something like that.'

'To stretch the point, yes.'

'And somehow, their separate activities were perhaps tied together to one person who wanted them all dead for various reasons. Is that what you're saying?'

'That's a little complicated,' Carella said. 'I'm not sure the deaths are connected in such a complicated way.'

'But we do know the same person killed all three cops.'

'Yes, we're fairly certain of that.'

'Then the deaths are connected.'

'Yes, of course. But perhaps . . .' Carella shrugged. 'It's difficult to discuss this with you because I'm not sure I know what I'm talking about. I only have this idea, that's all. This idea that motive may go deeper than the shield these men wore.'

'I see.' Savage sighed. 'Well, you can console yourself with the knowledge that every cop in the city probably has his own ideas on how to solve this one.'

Carella nodded, not exactly understanding Savage, but not willing to get into a lengthier discussion. He glanced at his watch.

'I've got to go soon,' he said. 'I've got a date.'

'Your girlfriend?'

'Yes.'

'What's her name?'

'Teddy. Well, Theodora really.'

'Theodora what?'

'Franklin.'

'Nice,' Savage said. 'Is this a serious thing?'

'As serious as they come.'

'These ideas of yours,' Savage said. 'About motive. Have you discussed them with your superiors?'

'Hell, no. You don't discuss every little pang of inspiration you get. You look into it, and then if you turn up anything that looks remotely promising, well, then you air the idea.'

'I see. Have you discussed it with Teddy?'

'Teddy? Why, no not yet.'

'Think she'll go for it?'

Carella smiled uneasily. 'She thinks I can do no wrong.'

'Sounds like a wonderful girl.'

'The best. And I'd better get to her before I lose her.'

'Certainly,' Savage said understandingly. Carella glanced at his watch again. 'Where does she live?'

'Riverhead,' Carella said.

'Theodora Franklin of Riverhead,' Savage said.

'Yes.'

'Well, I've appreciated listening to your ideas.'

Carella rose. 'None of that was for print, remember,' he said.

'Of course not,' Savage assured him.

'Thanks for the drink,' Carella said.

They shook hands. Savage stayed in the booth and ordered another Tom Collins. Carella went home to shower and shave for his date with Teddy.

She was dressed resplendently when she opened the door. She stood back, waiting for him to survey her splendour. She was wearing a white linen suit, white straw pumps, a red-stoned pin on the collar of the suit, bright scarlet oval ear-rings picking up the scream of the pin.

'Shucks,' he said, 'I was hoping I'd catch you in your slip.'

She made a motion to unbutton her jacket, smiling.

'We have reservations,' he said.

Where? her face asked.

'Ah Lum Fong,' he replied.

She nodded exuberantly.

'Where's your lipstick?' he asked.

She grinned and went to him, and he took her in his arms and kissed her, and then she clung to him as if he were leaving for Siberia in the next ten minutes.

'Come on,' he said, 'put on your face.'

She went into the other room, applied her lipstick and emerged carrying a small red purse.

'They carry those on the Street,' he said. 'It's a badge of the profession,' and she slapped him on the fanny as they left the apartment.

The Chinese restaurant boasted excellent food and an exotic decor. To Carella, the food alone would not have been enough. When he ate in a Chinese restaurant, he wanted it to look and feel Chinese. He did not appreciate an expanded, upholstered version of a Culver Avenue diner.

They ordered fried wonton soup, and lobster rolls, and barbecued spare ribs and Hon Shu Gai and Steak Kew and sweet and pungent pork. The wonton soup was crisp with Chinese vegetables; luscious snow peas, and water chestnuts, and mushrooms, and roots he could not have named if he'd tried. The wontons were brown and crisp, the soup itself had a rich tangy taste. They talked very little while they ate. They dug into the lobster rolls, and then they attacked the spare ribs, succulently brown.

'Do you know that Lamb thing?' he asked 'A Dissertation on . . .'

She nodded, and then went back to the spare ribs.

The chicken in the Hon Shu Gai was snappingly crisp. They polished off the dish. They barely had room for the Steak Kew, but they did their best with it, and when Charlie – their waiter – came to collect their dishes, he looked at them reproachfully because they had left over some of the delicious cubes of beef.

He cut a king pineapple for them in the kitchen, cut it so that the outside shell could be lifted off in one piece, exposing the ripe yellow meat beneath the prickly exterior, the fruit sliced and ready to be lifted off in long slender pieces. They drank their tea, savouring the aroma and the warmth, their stomachs full, their minds and their bodies relaxed.

'How's August nineteenth sound to you?'

Teddy shrugged.

'It's a Saturday. Would you like to get married on a Saturday?'

Yes, her eyes said.

Charlie brought them their fortune cookies and replenished the teapot.

Carella broke open his cookie. Then, before he read the message on the narrow slip of paper, he said, 'Do you know the one about the man who opened one of these in a Chinese restaurant?'

Teddy shook her head.

'It said, "Don't eat the soup. Signed, a friend."'

Teddy laughed and then gestured to his fortune slip. Carella read it aloud to her:

'You are the luckiest man alive. You are about to marry Theodora Franklin.'

She said 'Oh!' in soundless exasperation, and then took the slip from him. The slender script read: 'You are good with figures.'

'Your figure,' he said.

Teddy smiled and broke open her cookie. Her face clouded momentarily.

'What is it?' he asked.

She shook her head.

'Let me see it.'

She tried to keep the fortune slip from him, but he got it out of her hand and read it.

'Leo will roar – sleep no more.'

Carella stared at the printed slip. 'That's a hell of a thing to put in a cookie,' he said. 'What does it mean?' He thought for a moment. 'Oh, Leo. Leo the Lion. July 22 to August something, isn't it?'

Teddy nodded.

'Well, the meaning here is perfectly clear then. Once we're married, you're going to have a hell of a time sleeping.'

He grinned, and the worry left her eyes. She smiled, nodded, and then reached across the table for his hand.

The broken cookie rested alongside their hands, and beside that the curled fortune slip.

Leo will roar – sleep no more.

Chapter Twenty-One

The man's name was not Leo.

The man's name was Peter.

His last name was Byrnes.

He was roaring.

'What the hell kind of a story is this, Carella?'

'What?'

'Today's issue of this ... this goddamn rag!' he shouted, pointing to the afternoon tabloid on his desk. 'August 4th!'

Leo, Carella thought. 'What ... what do you mean, Lieutenant?'

'What do I mean?' Byrnes shouted. 'WHAT DO I MEAN? Who the hell gave you the authority to reel off this nonsense to that idiot Savage?'

'What?'

'There are cops walking beats in Bethtown because they spouted off nonsense like ...'

'Savage? Let me see that ...' Carella started.

Byrnes flipped open the newspaper angrily. 'Cop Defies Department!' he shouted. 'That's the headline. COP DEFIES DEPARTMENT! What's the matter, Carella, aren't you happy here?'

'Let me see ...'

'And under that "MAY KNOW MURDERER," DETECTIVE SAYS.'

'May know ...'

'Did you tell this to Savage?'

'That I may know who the murderer is? Of course not. Honest, Pete ...'

'Don't call me Pete! Here, read the goddamn story.'

Carella took the newspaper. For some strange reason, his hands were trembling.

Sure enough, the story was on page four, and it was headlined:

COP DEFIES DEPARTMENT
'MAY KNOW MURDERER,'
DETECTIVE SAYS

'But this is ...'

'Read it,' Byrnes said.

Carella read it.

The bar was cool and dim.

We sat opposite each other, Detective Stephen Carella and I. He toyed with his drink, and we talked of many things, but mostly we talked of murder.

'I've got an idea I know who killed those three cops,' Carella said. 'It's not the kind of idea you can take to your superiors, though. They wouldn't understand.'

And so came the first ray of hope in the mystery which has baffled the masterminds of Homicide North and tied the hands of stubborn, opinionated Detective-Lieutenant Peter Byrnes of the 87th Precinct.

'I can't tell you very much more about it right now,' Carella said, 'because I'm still digging. But this cop-hater theory is all wrong. It's something in the personal lives of these three men, of that I'm sure. It needs work, but we'll crack it.'

So spoke Detective Carella yesterday afternoon in a bar in the heart of the Murder Belt. He is a shy, withdrawn man, a man who – in his own words – is 'not seeking glory.'

'Police work is like any other kind of work,' he told me, 'except that we deal in crime. When you've got a hunch, you dig into it. If it pans out, then you bring it to your superiors, and maybe they'll listen, and maybe they won't.'

Thus far, he had confided his 'hunch' only to his fiancée, a lovely young lady named Theodora Franklin, a girl from Riverhead. Miss Franklin feels that Carella can 'do no wrong,' and is certain he will crack the case despite the inadequate fumblings of the department to date.

'There are skeletons in the closets,' Carella said. 'And those skeletons point to our man. We've got to dig deeper. It's just a matter of time now.'

We sat in the cool dimness of the bar, and I felt the quiet strength emanating from this man who has the courage to go ahead with his investigation in spite of the Cop-Hater Theory which pervades the dusty minds of the men working around him.

This man will find the murderer, I thought.

This man will relieve the city of its constant fear, its dread of an unknown killer roaming the streets with a wanton .45 automatic in his blood-stained fist. This man ...

'Good God!' Carella said.

'Yeah,' Byrnes answered. 'Now what about it?'

'I never said these things. I mean, not this way. And he said it wasn't for print!' Carella suddenly exploded. 'Where's the phone? I'm going to sue this son of a bitch for libel! He can't get away with ...'

'Calm down,' Byrnes said.

'Why'd he drag Teddy into this? Does he want to make her a sitting duck for that stupid bastard with the .45? Is he out of his mind?'

'Calm down,' Byrnes repeated.

'Calm down? I never said I knew who the murderer was! I never ...'

'What did you say?'

'I only said I had an idea that I wanted to work on.'

'And what's the idea?'

'That maybe this guy wasn't after cops at all. Maybe he was just after men. And maybe not even that. Maybe he was just after *one* man.'

'Which one?'

'How the hell do I know? Why'd he mention Teddy? What's the matter with this guy?'

'Nothing that a head doctor couldn't cure,' Byrnes said.

'Listen, I want to go up and see Teddy. God knows ...'

'What time is it?' Byrnes asked.

Carella looked at the wall clock. 'Six-fifteen.'

'Wait until six-thirty. Havilland will be back from supper by then.'

'If I ever meet this guy Savage again,' Carella promised, 'I'm going to rip him in half.'

'Or at least give him a speeding ticket,' Byrnes commented.

The man in the black suit stood outside the apartment door, listening. A copy of the afternoon newspaper stuck up from the right-hand pocket of his jacket. His left shoulder throbbed with pain, and the weight of the .45 automatic tugged at the other pocket of his jacket, so that – favouring the wound, bearing the weight of the gun – he leaned slightly to his left while he listened.

There was no sound from within the apartment.

He had read the name very carefully in the newspaper, Theodora Franklin, and then he had checked the Riverhead directory and come up with the address. He wanted to talk to this girl. He wanted to find out how much Carella knew. He had to find out.

She's very quiet in there, he thought. *What's she doing?*

Cautiously, he tried the door knob. He wiggled it slowly from side to side. The door was locked.

He heard footsteps. He tried to back away from the door too late. He reached for the gun in his pocket. The door was opening, wide, wider.

The girl stood there, surprised. She was a pretty girl, small, dark-haired, wide brown eyes. She wore a white chenille robe. The robe was damp in spots. He assumed she had just come from the shower. Her eyes went to his face, and then to the gun in his hand. Her mouth opened, but no sound came from it. She tried to slam to door, but he rammed his foot into the wedge and then shoved it back.

She moved away from him, deeper into the room. He closed the door and locked it.

'Miss Franklin?' he asked.

She nodded, terrified. She had seen the drawing on the front pages of all the newspapers, had seen it broadcast on all the television programmes. There was no mistake, this was the man Steve was looking for.

'Let's have a little talk, shall we?' he asked.

His voice was a nice voice, smooth, almost suave. He was a good-looking man, why had he killed those cops? Why would a man like this ...?

'Did you hear me?' he asked.

She nodded. She could read his lips, could understand everything he said, but ...

'What does your boyfriend know?' he asked.

He held the .45 loosely, as if he were accustomed to its lethal power now, as if he considered it a toy more than a dangerous weapon.

'What's the matter, you scared?'

She touched her hands to her lips, pulled them away in a gesture of futility.

'What?'

She repeated the gesture.

'Come on,' he said, 'talk, for God's sake! You're not that scared!'

Again, she repeated the gesture, shook her head this time. He watched her curiously.

'I'll be damned,' he said at last. 'A dummy!' He began laughing. The laugh filled the apartment, reverberating from the walls. 'A dummy! If that don't take the cake! A dummy!' His laughter died. He studied her carefully. 'You're not trying to pull something, are you?'

She shook her head vigorously. Hands went to the opening of her robe, clutching the chenille to her more tightly.

'Now this has definite advantages, doesn't it?' he said, grinning. 'You can't scream, you can't use the phone, you can't do a damned thing, can you?'

Teddy swallowed, watching him.

'What does Carella know?' he asked.

She shook her head.

'The paper said he's got a lead. Does he know about me? Does he have any idea who I am?'

Again she shook her head.

'I don't believe you.'

She nodded, trying to convince him that Steve knew nothing. What paper was he referring to? What did he mean? She spread her hands wide, indicating innocence, hoping he would understand.

He reached into his jacket pocket and tossed the newspaper to her.

'Page four,' he said. 'Read it. I've got to sit down. This goddamn shoulder ...'

He sat, the gun levelled at her. She opened the paper and read the story, shaking her head as she read.

'Well?' he asked.

She kept shaking her head. No, *this is not true. No. Steve would never say things like these. Steve would . . .*

'What'd he tell you?' the man asked.

Her eyes opened wide with pleading. *Nothing, he told me nothing.*

'The newspaper says . . .'

She hurled the paper to the floor.

'Lies, huh?'

Yes, she nodded.

His eyes narrowed. 'Newspapers don't lie,' he said.

They do, they do!

'When's he coming here?'

She stood motionless, controlling her face, not wanting her face to betray anything to the man with the gun.

'Is he coming?'

She shook her head.

'You're lying. It's all over your face. He's coming here, isn't he?'

She bolted for the door. He caught her arm and flung her back across the room. The robe pulled back over her legs when she fell to the floor. She pulled it together quickly and stared up at him.

'Don't try that again,' he said.

Her breath came heavily now. She sensed a coiled spring within this man, a spring which would unleash itself at the door the moment Steve opened it. But he'd said he would not be there until midnight. He had told her that, and there were a lot of hours between now and midnight. In that time . . .

'You just get out of the shower?' he asked.

She nodded.

'Those are good legs,' he said, and she felt his eyes on her. 'Dames,' he said philosophically. 'What've you got on under that robe?'

Her eyes widened.

He began laughing. 'Just what I thought. Smart. Good way to beat the heat. When's Carella coming?'

She did not answer.

'Steve, eight, nine? Is he on duty today?' He watched her. 'Nothing from you, huh? What's he got, the four to midnight? Sure, otherwise he'd probably be with you right this minute. Well, we might as well make ourselves comfortable, we got a long wait. Anything to drink in this place?'

Teddy nodded.

'What've you got? Gin? Rye? Bourbon?' He watched her. 'Gin? You got tonic? No, huh? Club soda? Okay, mix me a Collins. Hey, where you going?'

Teddy gestured to the kitchen.

'I'll come with you,' he said. He followed her into the kitchen. She opened the refrigerator and took out an opened bottle of club soda.

'Haven't you got a fresh one?' he asked. Her back was to him, and so she could not read his lips. He seized her shoulder and swung her around. His hand did not leave her shoulder.

'I asked you if you had a fresh bottle,' he said.

She nodded and bent, taking an unopened bottle from the lowest shelf of the refrigerator. She took lemons from the fruit drawer, and then went to the cupboard for the bottle of gin.

'Dames,' he said again.

She poured a double shot of gin into a tall glass. She spooned sugar into the glass, and then she went to one of the drawers.

'Hey!'

He saw the knife in her hand.

'Don't get ideas with that. Just slice the lemon.'

She sliced the lemon and squeezed both halves into the glass. She poured club soda until the glass was three-quarters full, and then she went back to the refrigerator for the ice cubes. When the drink was finished, she handed it to him.

'Make one for yourself,' he said.

She shook her head.

'I said make one for yourself! I don't like to drink alone.'

Patiently, wearily, she made herself a drink.

'Come on. Back in the living room.'

They went into the living room, and he sat in an easy chair, wincing as he adjusted himself so that his shoulder was comfortable.

'When the knock comes on that door,' he said, 'you just sit tight, understand? Go unlock it now.'

She went to the door and unlocked it. And now, knowing that the door was open, knowing that Steve would enter and be faced with a blazing .45, she felt fear crawl into her head like a nest of spiders.

'What are you thinking?' he asked.

She shrugged. She walked back into the room and sat opposite him, facing the door.

'This is a good drink,' he said. 'Come on, drink.'

She sipped at the Collins, her mind working ahead to the moment of Steve's arrival.

'I'm going to kill him, you know,' he said.

She watched him, her eyes wide.

'Won't make any difference now, anyway, will it? One cop more or less. Make it look a little better, don't you think?'

She was puzzled, and the puzzlement showed on her face.

'It's the best way,' he explained. 'If he knows something, well, it won't do to have him around. And if he doesn't know anything, it'll round out the picture.' He struggled in the chair. 'I've got to get this shoulder fixed. How'd you like that lousy doctor? That was something, wasn't it? I thought they were supposed to be healers.'

He talks the way anyone does, she thought. *Except that he talks so casually of death. He is going to kill Steve.*

'We were figuring on Mexico, anyway. Going to leave this afternoon, until your boyfriend came up with his bright idea. We'll take off in the morning, though. Soon as I take care of this.' He paused. 'Do you suppose I can get a good doctor in Mexico? The things a guy will do, huh?' He watched her face carefully. 'You ever been in love?'

She studied him, puzzled, confused. He did not seem like a killer. She nodded.

'Who with? This cop?'

She nodded again.

'Well, that's a shame.' He seemed sincerely sorry. 'It's a damn shame, honey, but what hasta be hasta be. There's no other way, you can see that, can't you? I mean, there was no other way right from the start, from the minute I started this thing. And when you start something, you've got to see it through right to the finish. It's a matter of survival now, you realize that? The things a guy will do. Well, you know.' He paused. 'You'd kill for him, wouldn't you?'

She hesitated.

'To keep him, you'd kill for him, wouldn't you?' he repeated.

She nodded.

'So? So there.' He smiled. 'I'm not a professional, you know. I'm a mechanic. That's my line. I'm a damn good mechanic, too. Think I'll be able to get work in Mexico?'

Teddy shrugged.

'Sure, they must have cars down there. They've got cars everywhere. Then, later, when things have cooled down, we'll come back to the States. Hell, things should cool down sooner or later. But what I'm trying to tell you, I'm not a professional killer, so don't get that idea. I'm just a regular guy.'

Her eyes did not believe him.

'No, huh? Well, I'm telling you. Sometimes, there's no other way out. If you see something's hopeless, and somebody explains to you where there's some hope, okay, you take it. I never harmed nobody until I killed those cops. You think I wanted to kill them? Survival, that's all. Some things, you've got to do. Agh, what the hell do you understand? You're just a dummy.'

She sat silent, watching him.

'A woman gets under your skin. Some women are like that. Listen, I've been around. I've been around plenty. I had me more dames than you could count. But this one – different. Different right from the beginning. She just got under my skin. Right under it. When it gets you like that, you can't eat, you can't sleep, nothing. You just think about her all day long. And what can you do when you realize you can't really have her ... well ... unless you ... hell, didn't she ask him for a divorce? Is it my fault he was stubborn? Well, he's still stubborn – only now he's dead.'

Teddy's eyes moved from his face. They covered the door behind him, and then dropped to the doorknob.

'And he took two of his pals with him.' He stared into his glass. 'Those are the breaks. He should've listened to reason. A woman like her ... You'd do anything for a woman like her. Anything! Just being in the same room with her, you want to ...'

Teddy watched the knob with fascination. She rose suddenly. She brought back her glass and then threw it at him. It grazed his forehead, the liquid splashing out of the glass and cascading over his shoulder. He leaped to his feet, his face twisted in fury, the .45 pointed at her.

'You stupid bitch!' he bellowed. 'Why the hell did you do that?'

Chapter Twenty-Two

Carella left the precinct at 6:30 on the button. Havilland had not yet come back from supper, but he could wait no longer. He did not want to leave Teddy alone in that apartment, not after the fool stunt Savage had pulled.

He drove to Riverhead quickly. He ignored traffic lights and full stop signs. He ignored everything. There was an all-consuming thought in his mind, and that thought included a man with a .45 and a girl with no tongue.

When he reached her apartment building, he glanced up at the window. The shades were not drawn. The apartment looked very quiet. He breathed a little more easily, and then entered the building. He climbed the steps, his heart pounding. He knew he shouldn't be alarmed but he could not shake the persistent feeling that Savage's column had invited danger for Teddy.

He stopped outside her door. He could hear the persistent drone of what sounded like the radio going inside. He reached for the knob. In his usual manner, he twisted it slowly from side to side, waiting for her footsteps, knowing she would come to the door the moment she saw his signal. He heard the sound of a chair scraping back and then someone shouted, 'You stupid bitch! Why the hell did you do that?'

His brain came alive. He reached for his .38 and snapped the door open with his other hand.

The man turned.

'You ...!' he shouted, and the .45 bucked in his hand.

Carella fired low, dropping to the floor the instant he entered the room. His first two shots took the man in the thigh. The man fell face forward, the .45 pitching out of his fist. Carella kicked back the hammer on the .38, waiting.

'You bastard,' the man on the floor said. 'You bastard.'

Carella got to his feet. He picked up the .45 and stuck it into his back pocket.

'Get up,' he said. 'You all right, Teddy?'

Teddy nodded. She was breathing heavily, watching the man on the floor.

'Thanks for the warning,' Carella said. He turned to the man again. 'Get up!'

'I can't, you bastard. Why'd you shoot me? For God's sake, why'd you shoot me?'

'Why'd you shoot three cops?'

The man went silent.

'What's your name?' Carella asked.

'Mercer. Paul Mercer.'

'Don't you like cops?'

'I love them.'

'What's the story then?'

'I suppose you're going to check my gun with what you've already got.'

'Damn right,' Carella said. 'You haven't got a chance, Mercer.'

'She put me up to it,' Mercer said, a scowl on his dark face. 'She's the real murderer. All I done was pull the trigger. She said we had to kill him, said it was the only way. We threw the others in just to make it look good, just to make it look as if a cop hater was loose. But it was her idea. Why should I take the rap alone?'

'Whose idea?' Carella asked.

'Alice's,' Mercer said. 'You see ... we wanted to make it look like a cop hater. We wanted ...'

'It was,' Carella said.

When they brought Alice Bush in, she was dressed in grey, a quiet grey. She sat in the squadroom, crossing her legs.

'Do you have a cigarette, Steve?' she asked.

Carella gave her one. He did not light it for her. She sat with the cigarette dangling from her lips until it was apparent she would have to light it herself. Unruffled, she struck a match.

'What about it?' Carella asked.

'What about it?' she repeated, shrugging. 'It's all over, isn't it?'

'You must have really hated him. You must have hated him like poison.'

'You're directing,' Alice said. 'I'm only the star.'

'Don't get glib, Alice!' Carella said angrily. 'I've never hit a woman in my life, but I swear to God ...'

'Relax,' she told him. 'It's all over. You'll get your gold star, and then you'll ...'

'Alice ...'

'What the hell do you want me to do? Break down and cry? I hated him, all right? I hated his big, pawing hands and I hated his stupid red hair, and I hated everything about him, all right?'

'Mercer said you'd asked for a divorce. Is that true?'

'No, I didn't ask for a divorce. Hank would've never agreed to one.'

'Why didn't you give him a chance?'

'What for? Did he ever give me a chance? Cooped up in that goddamned apartment, waiting for him to come off some burglary or some knifing or some mugging? What kind of life is that for a woman?'

'You knew he was a cop when you married him.'

Alice didn't answer.

'You could've asked for a divorce, Alice. You could've tried.'

'I didn't want to, damnit. *I wanted him dead.*'

'Well, you've got him dead. Him and two others. You must be tickled now.'

Alice smiled suddenly. 'I'm not too worried, Steve.'

'No?'

'There have to be *some* men on the jury.' She paused. 'Men like me.'

There were, in fact, eight men on the jury.

The jury brought in a verdict in six minutes flat.

Mercer was sobbing as the jury foreman read off the verdict and the judge gave sentence. Alice listened to the judge with calm indifference, her shoulders thrown back, her head erect.

The jury had found them both guilty of murder in the first degree, and the judge sentenced them to death in the electric chair.

On August nineteenth, Stephen Carella and Theodora Franklin listened to their own sentence.

'Do either of you know of any reason why you both should not be legally joined in marriage, or if there be any present who can show any just cause why these parties should not be legally joined together, let him now speak or hereafter hold his peace.'

Lieutenant Byrnes held his peace. Detective Hal Willis said nothing. The small gathering of friends and relatives watched, dewy-eyed.

The city clerk turned to Carella.

'Do you, Stephen Louis Carella, take this woman as your lawfully wedded wife to live together in the state of matrimony? Will you love, honour and keep her as a faithful man is bound to do, in health, sickness, prosperity and adversity, and forsaking all others keep you alone unto her as long as you both shall live?'

'Yes,' Carella said. 'Yes, I will. I do. Yes.'

'Do you, Theodora Franklin, take this man as your lawfully wedded husband to live together in the state of matrimony? Will you love, honour, and cherish him as a faithful woman is bound to do, in health, sickness, prosperity and adversity, and forsaking all others keep you alone unto him as long as you both shall live?'

Teddy nodded. There were tears in her eyes, but she could not keep the ecstatic smile off her face.

'For as you both have consented in wedlock and have acknowledged it before this company, I do by virtue of the authority vested in me by the laws of this state now pronounce you husband and wife. And may God bless your union.'

Carella took her in his arms and kissed her. The clerk smiled. Lieutenant Byrnes cleared his throat. Willis looked up at the ceiling. The clerk kissed Teddy when Carella released her. Byrnes kissed her. Willis kissed her. All the male relatives and friends came up to kiss her.

Carella smiled idiotically.

'You hurry back,' Byrnes said to him.

'Hurry back? I'm going on my honeymoon, Pete!'

'Well, hurry anyway. How are we going to run that precinct without you? You're the only cop in the city who has the courage to buck the decisions of stubborn, opinionated Detective-Lieutenant Byrnes of the ...'

'Oh, go to hell,' Carella said, smiling.

Willis shook his hand. 'Good luck, Steve. She's a wonderful gal.'

'Thank you, Hal.'

Teddy came to him. He put his arm around her.

'Well,' he said, 'let's go.'

They went out of the room together.

Byrnes stared after them wistfully.

'He's a good cop,' he said.

'Yeah,' Willis answered.

'Come on,' Byrnes said, 'let's go see what's brewing back at the house.'
They went down into the street together.

'Want to get a paper,' Byrnes said. He stopped at a news-stand and picked
up a copy of Savage's tabloid. The trial news had been crowded right off the
front pages. There was more important news.

The headlines simply read:

HEAT WAVE BREAKS!
HAPPY DAY!

GIVE THE BOYS A GREAT BIG HAND

"It was raining. It had been raining for three days now, an ugly March rain that washed the brilliance of near-spring with a monochromatic, unrelenting grey...."

This is for Phyllis and Rick

Chapter One

It was raining.

It had been raining for three days now, an ugly March rain that washed the brilliance of near-spring with a monochromatic, unrelenting grey. The television forecasters had correctly predicted rain for today and estimated that it would rain tomorrow also. Beyond that, they would not venture an opinion.

But it seemed to Patrolman Richard Genero that it had been raining forever, and that it would continue to rain forever, and that eventually he would be washed away into the gutters and then carried into the sewers of Isola and dumped unceremoniously with the other garbage into either the River Harb or the River Dix. North or south, it didn't make a damn bit of difference: both rivers were polluted; both stank of human waste.

Like a man up to his ankles in water in a rapidly sinking rowboat, Genero stood on the corner and surveyed the near-empty streets. His rubber rain cape was as black and as shining as the asphalt that stretched before him. It was still early afternoon, but there was hardly a soul in sight, and Genero felt lonely and deserted. He felt, too, as if he were the only human being in the entire city who didn't know enough to come in out of the rain. I'm going to drown here in the goddamn streets, he thought, and he belched sourly, consoling himself with the fact that he would be relieved on post at 3:45. It would take him about five minutes to get back to the station house and no more than ten minutes to change into his street clothes. Figure a half hour on the subway to Riverhead, and he would be home at 4:30. He wouldn't have to pick up Gilda until 7:30, so that gave him time for a little nap before dinner. Thinking of the nap, Genero yawned, tilting his head.

A drop of cold water ran down his neck, and he said, 'Oh hell!' out loud, and then hurriedly glanced around him to make sure he hadn't been overheard by any conscientious citizen of the city. Satisfied that the image of the pure American law-enforcer had not been destroyed, Genero began walking up the street, his rubber-encased shoes sloshing water every inch of the way.

Rain, rain, go away, he thought.

Oddly, the rain persisted.

Well, rain isn't so bad, he thought. It's better than snow, anyway. The thought made him shudder a little, partially because the very thought of snow was a chilling one, and partially because he could never think of snow or winter without forming an immediate association with the boy he had found in the basement so long ago.

Now cut that out, he thought. It's bad enough it's raining. We don't have to start thinking of creepy cadavers.

The boy's face had been blue, really blue, and he'd been leaning forward on the cot, and it had taken Genero several moments to realize that a rope was around the boy's neck and that the boy was dead.

Listen, let's not even think about it. It makes me itchy.

Well, listen, you're a cop, he reminded himself. What do you think cops do? Turn off fire hydrants all the time? Break up stickball games? I mean, now let's face it, every now and then a cop has got to find a stiff.

Listen, this makes me itchy.

I mean, that's what you get paid for, man. I mean, let's face it. A cop has every now and then got to come up against a little violence. And besides, that kid was a long time ago, all water under the . . .

Water. Jesus, ain't it never going to stop raining?

I'm getting out of this rain, he thought. I'm going over to Max's tailor shop and maybe I can get him to take out some of that sweet Passover wine, and we'll drink a toast to Bermuda. Man, I wish I was in Bermuda. He walked down the street and opened the door to the tailor shop. A bell tinkled. The shop smelled of steam and clean garments. Genero felt better the moment he stepped inside.

'Hello, Max,' he said.

Max was a round-faced man with a fringe of white hair that clung to his balding pate like a halo. He looked up from his sewing machine and said, 'I ain't got no wine.'

'Who wants wine?' Genero answered, grinning a bit sheepishly. 'Would you kick me out of your shop on a miserable day like this?'

'On any day, miserable or otherwise, I wouldn't kick you out mine shop,' Max said, 'so don't make wisecracks. But I warn you, already, even before you begin, I ain't got no wine.'

'So who wants wine?' Genero said. He moved closer to the radiator and pulled off his gloves. 'What are you doing, Max?'

'What does it look like I'm doing? I'm making a plan for the White House. I'm going to blow it up. What else would I be doing on a sewing machine?'

'I mean, what's that thing your working on?'

'It's a Salvation Army uniform,' Max said.

'Yeah? How about that?'

'There's still a few *tailors* left in this city, you know,' Max said. 'It ain't by all of us a matter of cleaning and pressing. Cleaning and pressing is for machines. Tailoring is for men. Max Mandel is a tailor, not a pressing machine.'

'And a damn good tailor,' Genero said, and he watched for Max's reaction.

'I still ain't got no wine,' Max said. 'Why ain't you in the street stopping crime already?'

'On a day like this, nobody's interested in crime,' Genero said. 'The only crime going on today is prostitution.'

Genero watched Max's face, saw the quick gleam of appreciation in the old man's eyes and grinned. He was getting closer to that wine all the time. Max was beginning to enjoy his jokes, and that was a good sign. Now all he had to do was work up a little sympathy.

'A rain like today's,' Genero said, 'it seeps right into a man's bones. Right into his bones.'

'So?'

'So nothing. I'm just saying. Right to the marrow. And the worst part is, a man can't even stop off in a bar or something to get a shot. To warm him up, I mean. It ain't allowed, you know.'

'So?'

'So nothing. I'm just saying.' Genero paused. 'You're sure doing a fine job with that uniform, Max.'

'Thanks.'

The shop went silent. Outside, the rain spattered against the sidewalk in continuous drumming monotony.

'Right to the marrow,' Genero said.

'All right already. Right to the marrow.'

'Chills a man.'

'All right, it chills a man.'

'Yes, sir,' Genero said, shaking his head.

'The wine is in the back near the pressing machine,' Max said without looking up. 'Don't drink too much, you'll get drunk already and I'll be arrested for corrupting an officer.'

'You mean you have wine, Max?' Genero asked innocently.

'Listen to Mr Baby-Blue Eyes, he's asking if I got wine. Go, go in the back. Drink, choke, but leave some in the bottle.'

'That's awfully nice of you, Max,' Genero said, beaming. 'I had no idea you –'

'Go, go before I change my mind.'

Genero went into the back room and found the bottle of wine on the table near the pressing machine. He uncapped it, rinsed a glass at the sink near the small grime-smeared window and poured it full to the brim. He tilted the glass to his mouth, drank until it was empty, and then licked his lips.

'You want some of this, Max?' he called.

'The Salvation Army doesn't like I should drink when I'm sewing their uniforms.'

'It's very good, Max,' Genero said teasingly.

'So have another glass and stop bothering me. You're making my stitches go all *fermisht*.'

Genero drank another glassful, recapped the bottle, and came out into the shop again, rubbing his hands briskly.

'Now I'm ready for anything,' he said, grinning.

'What is there to be ready for? On a day like this, you already said there's nothing but prostitution.'

'I'm ready for that, too,' Genero answered. 'Come on, Max. Close up the shop, and we'll go find two delicious broads. What do you say?'

'Stop giving an old man ideas. My wife should only find me with a delicious broad. A knife she'll stick in my back. Get out, get out, go walk your beat. Go arrest the other drunkards and vagrants. Leave me in peace. I'm running here a bar and grill instead of a tailor shop. Every drunkard cop on the beat, he stops in for wine. The government should allow me to deduct the wine as part of my overhead. One day, in the wine bottle, I'm going to

put poison instead of wine. Then maybe the *fercockteh* cops of the 87th will
leave me alone, already. Go. Get lost. Go.'

'Ahhh, you know you love us, Max.'

'I love you like cockroaches.'

'Better than cockroaches.'

'That's right. I love you like water rats.'

Genero pulled on his gloves. 'Well, back to the bridge,' he said.

'What bridge?'

'The bridge of the ship. That's a joke, Max. The rain, get it? Water. A
ship. Get it?'

'Already the television world lost a great comic when you decided to be a
cop,' Max said, shaking his head. 'Back to the bridge.' He shook his head
again. 'Do me a favour, will you?'

'What's that?' Genero asked, opening the door.

'From the bridge of this ship ...'

'Yeah?'

'Jump!'

Genero grinned and closed the door behind him. It was still pouring
outside, but he felt a lot better now. The sweet wine fumed in his stomach,
and he could feel a warm lassitude seeping through his limbs. He sloshed
through the puddles in an almost carefree manner, squinting through the
driving rain, whistling tunelessly.

The man – or perhaps the tall woman, it was difficult to tell – was standing
at the bus stop. The tall woman – or perhaps the man, it was impossible to
see clearly in the rain – was dressed entirely in black. Black raincoat, black
slacks, black shoes, black umbrella which effectively hid the head and hair.
The bus pulled to the kerb, spreading a huge canopy of water. The doors
snapped open. The person – man or woman – boarded the bus and the rain-
streaked doors closed again, hiding the black-shrouded figure from view.
The bus pulled away from the kerb, spreading another canopy of water
which soaked Genero's trouser legs.

'You stupid ...' he shouted, and he began brushing water from his
trousers, and that was when he saw the bag resting on the sidewalk alongside
the bus stop sign.

'Hey! Hey!' he yelled after the bus. 'You forgot your bag!'

His words were drowned in the gunning roar of the bus's engine and the
steady drumming of the rain.

'Damnit,' he muttered, and he walked to the sign and picked up the bag. It
was a small, blue overnight bag, obviously issued by an airline. In a white
circle on the side of the bag, stencilled there in red letters, were the words:
CIRCLE AIRLINES.

Beneath that, in white script lettering, was the slogan: *We circle the globe.*

Genero studied the bag. It was not very heavy. A small leather fob was
attached to the carrying straps, and an identification tag showed behind a
celluloid panel. But whoever owned the bag had neglected to fill in the NAME
and ADDRESS spaces. The identification tag was blank.

Sourly, Genero unzipped the bag and reached into it.

He drew back his hand in terror and revulsion. An instant thought rushed
across his mind – God, not again – and then he gripped the bus stop sign for
support because he was suddenly dizzy.

Chapter Two

In the detective squadroom of the 87th Precinct, the boys were swapping reminiscences about their patrolman days.

Now you may quarrel with the use of the word 'boys' to describe a group of men who ranged in age from twenty-eight to forty-two, who shaved daily, who went to bed with various and assorted mature and immature women, who swore like pirates, and who dealt with some of the dirtiest humans since Neanderthal. The word 'boys', perhaps, connotes a simplicity, an innocence which would not be entirely accurate.

There was, however, a spirit of boyish innocence in the squadroom on that dreary, rainy March day. It was difficult to believe that these men who stood in a fraternal knot around Andy Parker's desk, grinning, listening in attentiveness, were men who dealt daily with crime and criminals. The squadroom, in effect, could have been a high-school locker room. The chatter could have been that of a high-school football team on the day of the season's last game. The men stood drinking coffee from cardboard containers, completely at ease in the grubby shopworn comfort of the squadroom. Andy Parker, like a belligerent fullback remembering a difficult time in the game against Central High, kept his team huddled about him, leaned back in his swivel chair, and shook his head dolefully.

'I had a pipperoo one time, believe me,' he said. 'I stopped her coming off the River Highway. Right near Pier 17, do you know the spot?'

The boys nodded.

'Well, she crashed the light at the bottom of the ramp, and then made a U-turn under the highway. I blew the whistle, and she jammed on the brakes, and I strolled over to the car and said, "Lady, you must be the Mayor's daughter to be driving like that."'

'Was she?' Steve Carella asked. Sitting on the edge of the desk, a lean muscular man with eyes that slanted peculiarly downward to present an Oriental appearance, he held his coffee container in big hands and studied Parker intently. He did not particularly care for the man or his methods of police investigation, but he had to admit he told a story with gusto.

'No, no. Mayor's daughter, my eye. What she was – well, let me tell the story, will you?'

Parker scratched his heavy beard. He had shaved that morning, but five o'clock shadow came at an earlier hour for him, so that he always looked somewhat unkempt, a big shaggy man with dark hair, dark eyes, dark beard. In fact, were it not for the shield Parker carried pinned to his wallet, he could easily have passed for many of the thieves who found their way into the 87th. He was so much the Hollywood stereotype of the gangster that he'd often been stopped by over-zealous patrolmen seeking suspicious characters. On those occasions, he immediately identified himself as a detective and then proceeded to bawl out the ambitious rookie, which pastime – though he never admitted it to himself – gave him a great deal of pleasure. In truth, it was possible that Andy Parker purposely roamed around in other precincts hoping to be stopped by an unsuspecting patrolman upon whom he could then pull his rank.

'She was sitting in the front seat with a two-piece costume on,' Parker said, 'a two-piece costume and these long black net stockings. What the costume was, it was these little black panties covered with sequins, and this tiny little bra that tried to cover the biggest set of bubs I ever seen on any woman in my entire life I swear to God. I did a double take, and I leaned into the car and said, "You just passed a stop light, lady, and you made a U-turn over a double white line. And for all I know, we got a good case against you for indecent exposure. Now how about that?"'

'What did she say?' Cotton Hawes asked. He alone of the detectives surrounding Parker's desk was not drinking coffee. Hawes was a tea drinker, a habit he'd picked up as a growing boy. His father had been a Protestant minister, and having members of the congregation in for tea had been a daily routine. The boy Hawes, for reasons best known to his father, had been included in the daily congregational tea-drinking visits. The tea, hefty, hot and hearty, had not stunted his growth at all. The man Hawes stood six feet two inches in his stocking feet, a red-headed giant who weighed in at a hundred and ninety pounds.

'She looked at me with these big blue eyes set in a face made for a doll,' Parker said, 'and she batted her eyelashes at me and said, "I'm in a hurry. If you're going to give me the goddamn ticket, give it to me!"'

'Wow!' Hawes said.

'So I asked her what the hurry was, and she said she had to be on stage in five minutes flat.'

'What kind of stage? One of the burly houses?'

'No, no, she was a dancer in a musical comedy. A big hit, too. And it was just about eight-thirty, and she was breaking her neck to catch the curtain. So I pulled out my fountain pen and my pad, and she said, "Or would you prefer two tickets to the biggest hit in town?" and she started digging into her purse, those bubs about to spill out of that tiny little bra and stop traffic away the hell up to the Aquarium.'

'So how was the show?' Carella asked.

'I didn't take the tickets.'

'Why not?'

'Because this way I had a private show of my own. It took me twenty minutes to write that ticket, and all that time she was squirming and wiggling on the front seat with those gorgeous pineapples ready to pop. Man, what an experience!'

'You're not only mean,' Carella said, 'you're also horny.'

'That I am,' Parker admitted proudly.

'I caught a guy once on Freeman Lewis Boulevard,' Carella said. 'He was doing eighty miles an hour. I had to put on the siren before he'd stop. I got out of the squad car and was walking over to his car when the door popped open, and he leaped out and started running towards me.'

'A hood?' Hawes asked.

'No, but that's just what I thought. I figured I'd stumbled on a guy who was running from the law. I expected him to pull a gun any minute.'

'What *did* he do?'

'He came up to me hopping up and down, first one leg, then the other. He said he knew he was speeding, but he'd just had an acute attack of diarrhoea, and he had to find a gas station with a men's room in a hurry.'

Parker burst out laughing. 'Oh, brother, that takes it,' he said.

'Did you let him go?' Hawes asked.

'Hell, no. I just wrote the ticket in a hurry, that's all.'

'I'll tell you one I let go,' Hawes said. 'This was when I was a patrolman with the 30th. The guy was clipping along like a madman, and when I stopped him he just looked at me and said, "You going to give me a ticket?" So I looked right back at him and said, "Damn right, I'm going to give you a ticket." He stared at me for a long time, just nodding his head. Then he said, "That's it, then. You give me a ticket, and I'll kill myself."'

'What the hell did he mean?'

'That's just what I said. I said, "What do you mean, mister?" But he just kept staring at me, and he didn't say another word, just kept staring and nodding his head, over and over again, as if this ticket was the last straw, do you know what I mean? I had the feeling that this had just been one of those days where everything in the world had gone wrong for him, and I knew – I just knew as sure as I was standing there – that if I slapped a summons on him, he would actually go home and turn on the gas or jump out the window or slit his throat. I just knew it. I could just sense it about the guy.'

'So you let him go. The Good Samaritan.'

'Yeah, yeah, Samaritan,' Hawes said. 'You should have seen that guy's eyes. You'd have known he wasn't kidding.'

'I had a woman once,' Kling, the youngest of the detectives started, and Patrolman Dick Genero burst into the squadroom carrying the small, blue overnight bag. One look at his eyes, and anyone would have known he wasn't kidding. He carried the bag in his right hand, far away from his body, as if afraid to be contaminated by it. He pushed his way through the gate in the slatted railing which separated the squadroom from the corridor outside, went directly to Parker's desk, and plunked the bag down in the middle of it with a finality that indicated he had done his duty and was now glad to be rid of it.

'What have you got, Dick?' Hawes asked.

Genero could not speak. His face was white, his eyes were wide. He swallowed several times, but no words came from his mouth. He kept shaking his head and pointing at the bag. Hawes stared at the bag in puzzlement, and then began to unzip it. Genero turned away. He seemed ready to vomit momentarily.

Hawes looked into the bag and said, 'Oh Jesus, where'd you get this?'

'What is it?' Kling asked.

'Oh, Jesus,' Hawes said. 'What a goddamn thing. Get it out of here. Jesus, get it out of the squadroom. I'll call the morgue.' The rugged planes of his face were twisted in pain. He could not look into the bag again. 'I'll call the morgue,' he said again. 'Jesus, get it out of here. Take it downstairs. Get it out of here.'

Carella picked up the bag and started out of the room.

He did not look into it. He did not have to.

He had been a cop for a long time now, and he knew instantly from the expression on Hawes's face that the bag must contain a segment of a human body.

Chapter Three

Now that's pretty damn disgusting.

But let's get something straight. Death *is* pretty damn disgusting, and there are no two ways about it. If you are one of those people who like motion pictures where a man fires a gun and a small spurt of dust explodes on the victim's chest — just a small spurt of dust, no blood – then police work is not the line for you. Similarly, if you are one of those people who believe that corpses look 'just like they're sleeping', it is fortunate you are not a cop. If you are a cop, you know that death is seldom pretty, that it is in fact the ugliest and most frightening event that can overtake a human being.

If you are a cop, you have seen death at its ugliest because you have seen it as the result of violent upheaval. You have, more than likely, puked more than once at the things you have seen. You have, more than likely, trembled with fear, because death has a terrifying way of reminding the strongest human that his flesh can bleed and his bones can break. If you are a cop, you will never get used to the sight of a corpse or a part of a corpse – no matter how long you deal with them, no matter how strong you are, no matter how tough you become.

There is nothing reassuring about the sight of a man who has been worked over with a hatchet. The skull, a formidable piece of bone, assuming the characteristics of a melon, the parallel wounds, the criss-crossing wounds, the bleeding ugly wounds covering the head and the face and the neck, the windpipe exposed and raw, throbbing with colour so bright, but throbbing only with colour because life is gone, life has fled beneath the battering rigidity of an impersonal hatchet blade; there is nothing reassuring.

There is nothing beautiful about the post-mortem decomposition of a body, man or woman, child or adult, the gas formation, the discoloration of head and trunk tissues, the separation of epidermis, the staining of veins, the protrusion of tongue, decomposed liquefied fat soaking through the skin resulting in large yellow-stained areas; there is nothing beautiful.

There is nothing tender about bullet wounds, the smeared and lacerated flesh of contact wounds, the subcutaneous explosion of gases, the tissues seared and blackened by flame and smoke, the embedded powder grains, the gaping holes in the flesh; there is nothing tender.

If you are a cop, you learn that death is ugly, and frightening, and disgusting. If you are a cop, you learn to deal with what is ugly, frightening and disgusting or you quit the force.

The object in the overnight bag was a human hand, ugly, frightening and disgusting.

The man who received it at the morgue was an assistant medical examiner named Paul Blaney, a short man with a scraggly black moustache and violet eyes. Blaney didn't particularly enjoy handling the remains of dead people, and he often wondered why he – the junior member on the medical examiner's staff – was invariably given the most particularly obnoxious stiffs to examine, those who had been in automobile accidents, or fires, or whose remains had been chewed to ribbons by marauding rats. But he knew that he had a job to do. And that job was – given a human hand which has been severed at the wrist from the remainder of the body, how can I determine the race, sex, age, probable height and probable weight of the person to whom it belonged?

That was the job.

With a maximum of dispatch, and a minimum of emotional involvement, Blaney set to work.

Fortunately, the hand was still covered with skin. A lot of bodies he received simply weren't. And so it was quite simple to determine the race of the person to whom the hand had belonged. Blaney determined that race rather quickly, and then jotted the information on a slip of paper.

RACE: White.

Sex was another thing again. It was simple to identify the sex of an individual if the examiner was presented with remains of the breasts or sexual organs, but all Blaney had was a hand. Period. Just a hand. In general, Blaney knew, the female of the species usually had less body hair than the male, more delicate extremities, more subcutaneous fat and less muscula-ture. Her bones, too, were smaller and lighter, with thinner shafts and wider medullary spaces.

The hand on the autopsy table was a huge one. It measured twenty-five centimetres from the tip of the middle finger to the base of the severed wrist, and that came to something more than nine and a half inches when translated into laymen's English. Blaney could not conceive of such a hand having belonged to a woman, unless she were a masseuse or a female wrestler. And even granting such exotic occupations, the likelihood was remote. He had, nonetheless, made errors in determining the sex of a victim from sex-unrelated parts in the past, and he did not wish to make such an error now.

The hand was covered with thick, black, curling hair, another fact which seemed to point towards a male identification; but Blaney carried the ex-amination to its conclusion, measuring the bone shafts, studying the medul-lary spaces, and jotting down his estimate at last.

SEX: Male.

Well, we're getting someplace, he thought. We now know that this gruesome and severed member of a human body once belonged to a white male. Wiping his forehead with a towel, he got back to work again.

A microscopic examination of the hand's skin told Blaney that there had been no loss of elasticity due to the decrease of elastic fibres in the dermis. Since he was making his microscopic examination in an effort to determine the victim's age, he automatically chalked off the possibility of the man's having been a very old one. He knew, further, that he was not likely to get anything more from a closer examination of the skin. The changes in skin throughout the growth and decline of a human being very seldom provide accurate criteria of age. And so he turned to the bones.

The hand had been severed slightly above the wrist so that portions of the radius and ulna, the twin bones which run from the wrist to the elbow, were still attached to the hand. Moreover, Blaney had all the various bones of the hand itself to examine: the carpus, the metacarpal, the phalanx.

He mused, as he worked, that the average layman would – just about now – begin to consider all of his devious machinations as scientific mumbo jumbo, the aimless meanderings of a pseudo-wizard. Well, he thought, the hell with the average layman. I know damn well that the ossification centres of bones go through a sequence of growth and fusion, and that this growth and fusion takes place at certain age levels. I know further that by studying these bones, I can come pretty close to estimating the age of this dead white male, and that is just what I am going to do, average layman be damned.

The entire examination which Blaney conducted on the bones took close to three hours. His notes included such esoteric terms as 'proximal epiphysial muscle' and 'os magnum' and 'multangulum majus' and the like. His final note simply read:

AGE: 18–24.

When it came to the probable height and weight of the victim, Blaney threw up his hands in despair. If he had been presented with a femur, a humerus, or a radius in its entirety, he would have measured any one of them in centimetres from joint surface to joint surface with the cartilage in place, and then made an attempt at calculating the height using Pearson's formula. For the radius, if he'd had a whole one and not just a portion of one, the table would have read like this:

MALE	FEMALE
86.465 plus 3.271 times length of radius.	82.189 plus 3.343 times length of radius.

Then, to arrive at an estimate of the height of the *living* body, he'd have subtracted 1.5 centimetres from the final result for a male, and 2 centimetres for a female.

Unfortunately, he didn't have a whole radius, so he didn't even make an attempt. And although the hand gave him a good knowledge of the size of the victim's bones, he could not make a guess at the weight of the victim without a knowledge of the muscular development and the adipose tissue, so he quit. He wrapped the hand and tagged it for delivery to Lieutenant Samuel G. Grossman at the Police Laboratory. Grossman, he knew, would perform an iso-reaction test on a blood specimen in order to determine the blood group. And Grossman would undoubtedly try to get fingerprint impressions from the severed hand. In this respect, Blaney was positively certain that Grossman would fail. Each finger tip had been nearly sliced away from the rest of the hand by the unknown assailant. A magician couldn't have got a set of prints from that hand, and Grossman was no magician.

So Blaney shipped off the hand, and he concluded his notes; and what he finally transmitted to the bulls of the 87th was this:

RACE: White.

SEX: Male.

AGE: 18–24.

The boys had to take it from there.

Chapter Four

Detective Steve Carella was the first of the boys to take it from there.

He took it early the next morning. Sitting at his desk near the grilled squadroom windows, watching the rain ooze along the glass panes, he dialled Blaney's office and waited.

'Dr Blaney,' a voice on the other end of the wire said.

'Blaney, this is Carella up at the 87th.'

'Hello,' Blaney said.

'I've got your report on that hand, Blaney.'

'Yeah? What's wrong with it?' Blaney asked, immediately on the defensive.

'Nothing at all,' Carella said. 'In fact, it's very helpful.'

'Well, I'm glad to hear that,' Blaney said. 'It's very rare that anyone in the goddamn department admits a medical examination was helpful.'

'We feel differently here at the 87th,' Carella said smoothly. 'We've always relied very heavily upon information provided by the medical examiner's office.'

'Well, I'm certainly glad to hear that,' Blaney said. 'A man works here with stiffs all day long, he begins to have his doubts. It's no fun cutting up dead bodies, you know.'

'You fellows do a wonderful job,' Carella said.

'Well, thank you.'

'I mean it,' Carella said fervently. 'There isn't much glory in what you fellows do, but you can bet your life it's appreciated.'

'Well, thank you. Thank you.'

'I wish I had a nickel for every case you fellows made easier for us to crack,' Carella said, more fervently this time, almost carried away by himself.

'Well, gosh, thanks. What can I do for you, Carella?'

'Your report was an excellent one,' Carella said, 'and very helpful, too. But there was just one thing.'

'Yes?'

'I wonder if you can tell me anything about the person who did the job.'

'Did the job?'

'Yes. Your report told us a lot about the victim, and that's excellent ...'

'Yes?'

'Yes, and very helpful. But what about the perpetrator?'

'The perpetrator?'

'Yes, the man or woman who did the surgery.'

'Oh. Oh, yes, of course,' Blaney said. 'You know, after you've been examining corpses for a while, you forget that someone was responsible for the corpse, do you know what I mean? It becomes ... well, sort of a mathematical problem.'

'I can understand that,' Carella said. 'But about the person responsible for this particular corpse, could you tell anything from the surgery?'

'Well, the hand was severed slightly above the wrist.'

'Could you tell what kind of a tool was used?'

'Either a meat cleaver or a hatchet, I would say. Or something similar.'

'Was it a clean job?'

'Fairly. Whoever did it had to hack through those bones. But there were no hesitation cuts anywhere on the hand, so the person who severed it from the body was probably determined and sure.'

'Skilful?'

'How do you mean?'

'Well, would you say the person had any knowledge of anatomy?'

'I wouldn't think so,' Blaney answered. 'The logical place for the cut would have been at the wrist itself, where the radius and ulna terminate. That certainly would have been easier than hacking through those bones. No, I would discount anyone with a real knowledge of anatomy. In fact, I can't understand why the hand was dismembered, can you?'

'I don't think I follow you, Blaney?'

'You've seen dismemberment cases before, Carella. We usually find the head, and then the trunk, and then the four extremities. But if a person is going to cut off an arm, why then cut off the hand? Do you know what I mean? It's an added piece of work that doesn't accomplish very much.'

'Yeah, I see,' Carella said.

'Most bodies are dismembered or mutilated because the criminal is attempting to avoid identification of the body. That's why the fingertips of that hand were mutilated.'

'Of course.'

'And sometimes your killer will cut up the body to make disposal easier. But cutting off a hand at the wrist? How would that serve either purpose?'

'I don't know,' Carella said. 'In any case, we're not dealing with a surgeon or a doctor here, is that right?'

'I would say not.'

'How about a butcher?'

'Maybe. The bones were severed with considerable force. That might imply a man familiar with his tools. The fingertips were neatly sliced.'

'Okay, Blaney, thanks a lot.'

'Any time,' Blaney said happily, and hung up.

Carella thought for a moment about dismembered bodies. There was suddenly a very sour taste in his mouth. He went into the Clerical Office and asked Miscolo to make a pot of coffee.

In Captain Frick's office downstairs a patrolman named Richard Genero was on the carpet. Frick, who was technically in command of the entire precinct – his command, actually, very rarely intruded upon the activities of the detective squad – was not a very imaginative man, nor in truth a very intelligent one. He liked being a policeman, he supposed, but he would rather have been a movie star. Movie stars got to meet glamorous women. Police captains only got to bawl out patrolmen.

'Am I to understand, Genero,' he said, 'that you don't know whether the person who left this bag on the sidewalk was a man or a woman, is that what I am made to understand, Genero?'

'Yes, sir,' Genero said.

'You can't tell a man from a woman, Genero?'

'No, sir. I mean, yes, sir, I can sir, but it was raining.'

'So?'

'And this person's face was covered. By an umbrella, sir.'

'Was this person wearing a dress?'

'No, sir.'

'A skirt?'

'No, sir.'

'Pants?'

'Do you mean trousers, sir?'

'Yes, of course I mean trousers!' Frick shouted.

'Well, sir, yes, sir. That is, they could have been slacks. Like women wear, sir. Or they could have been trousers. Like men wear, sir.'

'And what did you do when you saw the bag on the sidewalk?'

'I yelled after the bus, sir.'

'And then what?'

'Then I opened the bag.'

'And when you saw what was inside it?'

'I . . . I guess I got a little confused, sir.'

'Did you go after the bus?'

'N . . . n . . . no, sir.'

'Are you aware that there was another bus stop three blocks away?'

'No, sir.'

'There was, Genero. Are you aware that you could have hailed a passing car, and caught that bus, and boarded it, and arrested the person who left this bag on the sidewalk? Are you aware of that, Genero?'

'Yes, sir. I mean, I wasn't aware of it at the time, sir. I am now, sir.'

'And saved us the trouble of sending this bag to the laboratory, or of having the detective division trot all the way out to International Airport?'

'Yes, sir.'

'Or of trying to find the other pieces of that body, of hoping we can identify the body *after* we have all the pieces, are you aware of all this, Genero?'

'Yes, sir.'

'Then how can you be so goddamn stupid, Genero?'

'I don't know, sir.'

'We contacted the bus company,' Frick said. 'The bus that passed that corner at two-thirty – was that the time, Genero?'

'Yes, sir.'

'– at two-thirty was bus number 8112. We talked to the driver. He doesn't remember anyone in black boarding the bus at that corner, man or woman.'

'There was a person, sir. I saw him. Or her, sir.'

'No one's doubting your word, Genero. A bus driver can't be expected to remember everyone who gets on and off his goddamn bus. In any case,

Genero, we're right back where we started. And all because you didn't think. Why didn't you think, Genero?'

'I don't know, sir. I was too shocked, I guess.'

'Boy, there are times I wish I was a movie star or something,' Frick said. 'All right, get out. Look alive, Genero. Keep on your goddamn toes.'

'Yes, sir.'

'Go on, get out.'

'Yes, sir.' Genero saluted and left the captain's office hurriedly, thanking his lucky stars that no one had discovered he'd had two glasses of wine in Max Mandel's shop just before finding the bag. Frick sat at his desk and sighed heavily. Then he buzzed Lieutenant Byrnes upstairs and told him he could deliver the bag to the lab whenever he wanted to. Byrnes said he would send a man down for it at once.

The photograph of the bag lay on Nelson Piat's desk.

'Yes, that's one of our bags, all right,' he said. 'Nice photograph, too. Did you take the photograph?'

'Me, personally, do you mean?' Detective Meyer Meyer asked.

'Yes.'

'No. A police photographer took it.'

'Well, it's our bag, all right,' Piat said. He leaned back in his leather covered swivel chair, dangerously close to the huge sheet of glass that formed one wall of his office. The office was on the fourth floor of the Administration Building at International Airport, overlooking the runway. The runway now was drenched with lashing curtains of rain that swept its slick surface. 'Damn rain,' Piat said. 'Bad for our operation.'

'Can't you fly when it rains?' Meyer asked.

'Oh, *we* can fly all right. *We* can fly in almost everything. But will the *people* fly, that's the question. The minute it begins raining, we get more damn cancellations than you can shake a stick at. Afraid. They're all afraid.' Piat shook his head and studied the photo of the bag again. It was an $8\frac{1}{2} \times 11$ glossy print. The bag had been photographed against a white backdrop. It was an excellent picture, the company's name and slogan leaping out of the print as if they were moulded in neon. 'Well, what about this bag, gentlemen?' Piat said. 'Did some burglar use it for his tools or something?' He chuckled at his own little joke and looked first to Kling and then to Meyer.

Kling answered for both of them. 'Well, not exactly, sir,' he said. 'Some murderer used it for part of a corpse.'

'Part of a . . . ?' Oh. I see. Well, that's not too good. Bad for our operation.' He paused. 'Or is it?' He paused again, calculating. 'Will this case be getting into the newspapers?'

'I doubt it,' Meyer said. 'It's a little too gory for the public, and so far it doesn't contain either a rape or a pretty girl in bloomers. It would make dull copy.'

'I was thinking . . . you know . . . a photo of the bag on the front pages of a mass circulation newspaper, that might not be bad for our operation. Hell, you can't buy that kind of advertising space, now can you? It might be very good for our operation, who knows?'

'Yes, sir,' Meyer said patiently.

If there was one virtue Meyer Meyer possessed, that virtue was patience. And it was, in a sense, a virtue he was born with or, at the very least, a virtue he was named with. Meyer's father, you see, was something of a practical joker, the kind of man who delighted in telling kosher dinner guests during the middle of a meat meal that they were eating off the dairy dishes. Oh, yes, he was a gasser, all right. Well, when this gasser was well past the age when changing diapers or wiping runny noses was a possibility, when his wife had in fact experienced that remarkable female phenomenon euphemistically known as change of life, they were both somewhat taken aback to learn that she was pregnant.

This was a surprising turn of events indeed, the practical joke supreme upon the king of the jesters. Meyer's father fretted, pouted and sulked about it. His jokes suffered while he planned his revenge against the vagaries of nature and birth control. The baby was born, a bouncing, blue-eyed boy delivered by a midwife and weighing in at seven pounds six ounces. And then Meyer's pop delivered the final hilarious thrust. The baby's first name would be Meyer, he decreed, and this handle when coupled with the family name would give the boy a title like a ditto mark: Meyer Meyer.

Well, that's pretty funny. Meyer's old man didn't stop laughing for a week after the briss. Meyer, on the other hand, found it difficult to laugh through bleeding lips. The family was, you understand, practising Orthodox Judaism and they lived in a neighbourhood which housed a large Gentile population, and if the kids in the neighbourhood needed another reason besides Meyer's Jewishness for beating him up every day of the week, his name provided that reason. 'Meyer Meyer, Jew on fire!' the kids would chant, and POW! Meyer got it in the kisser.

Over the years, he learned that it was impossible to fight twelve guys at once, but that it was sometimes possible to talk this even dozen out of administering a beating. Patiently, he talked. Sometimes it worked. Sometimes it didn't. But patience became a way of life. And patience is a virtue, we will all admit. But if Meyer Meyer had not been forced to sublimate, if he had for example just once, just once when he was a growing boy been called Charlie or Frank or Sam and been allowed to stand up against one other kid, not a dozen or more, and bash that kid squarely on the nose, well perhaps, just perhaps, Meyer Meyer would not have been completely bald at the tender age of thirty-seven.

On the other hand, who would have been so cruel as to deprive an ageing comedian of a small practical joke?

Patiently, Meyer Meyer said, 'How are these bags distributed, Mr Piat?'

'Distributed? Well, they're not exactly distributed. That is to say, they are given to people who fly with our airline. It's good for the operation.'

'These bags are given to every one of your passengers, is that correct?'

'No, not exactly. We have several types of flights, you see.'

'Yes?'

'Yes. We have our Luxury flight which gives more space between the seats, a big big twenty inches to stretch those legs in, and drinks en route, and a choice of several dinners, and special baggage accommodations – in short, the finest service our operation can offer.'

'Yes.'

'Yes. And then we have our First-Class flight which offers the same accommodations and the same seating arrangement except that drinks are not provided – you can buy them, of course, if you desire – and there is only one item on the dinner menu, usually roast beef, or ham, or something of the sort.'

'I see.'

'And then we have our Tourist flight.'

'Tourist flight, yes,' Meyer said.

'Our Tourist flight which gives only sixteen inches of leg room, but the same accommodations otherwise, including the same dinner as on the First-Class flight.'

'I see. And this bag ...'

'And then there is our Economy flight, same amount of leg room, but there are three seats on one side of the aisle, instead of two, and the dinner is not a hot meal, just sandwiches and, of course, no drinks.'

'And of all these flights, which ...'

'Then there's our Thrift flight which is not too comfortable, I'm afraid, that is to say not as comfortable as the other flights, but certainly comfortable enough, with only twelve inches of leg room, and ...'

'Is that the last flight?' Meyer asked patiently.

'We're now working on one called the Piggy Bank flight, which will be even less expensive. What we're trying to do, you see, we're trying to put our operation within reach of people who wouldn't ordinarily consider flying, who would take the old-fashioned means of conveyance, like trains, or cars, or boats. Our operation ...'

'Who gets the bags?' Kling asked impatiently.

'What? Oh, yes, the bags. We give them to all passengers on the Luxury or First-Class flights.'

'*All* passengers?'

'All.'

'And when did you start doing this?'

'At least six years ago,' Piat said.

'Then anyone who rode either Luxury or First-Class in the past six years could conceivably have one of these bags, is that right?' Meyer asked.

'That is correct.'

'And how many people would you say ...'

'Oh, thousands and thousands and thousands,' Piat said. 'You must remember, Detective Meyer ...'

'Yes?'

'We circle the globe.'

'Yes,' Meyer said. 'Forgive me. With all those flights zooming around, I guess I lost sight of the destinations.'

'Is there any possibility this might get into the newspapers?'

'There's always a possibility,' Meyer said, rising.

'If it does, would you contact me? I mean, if you know about it beforehand. I'd like to get our promotion department to work.'

'Sure thing,' Meyer said. 'Thank you for your time, Mr Piat.'

'Not at all,' Piat said, shaking hands with Meyer and Kling. 'Not at all.' As they walked across the room to the door, he turned to the huge window and looked out over the rain-soaked runway. 'Damn rain,' he said.

Chapter Five

Friday morning.

Rain.

When he was a kid, he used to walk six blocks to the library in the rain, wearing a mackinaw with the collar turned up, and feeling very much like Abraham Lincoln. Once there, he would sit in the warmth of the wood-panelled reading room, feeling strangely and richly rewarded while he read and the rain whispered against the streets outside.

And sometimes, at the beach, it would begin raining suddenly, the clouds sweeping in over the ocean like black horsemen in a clanging cavalry charge, the lightning scraping the sky like angry scimitar slashes. The girls would grab for sweaters and beach bags, and someone would reach for the portable record player and the stack of 45-rpms, and the boys would hold the blanket overhead like a canopy while they all ran to the safety of the boardwalk restaurant. They would stand there and look out at the rain-swept beach, the twisted, lipsticked straws in deserted Coca Cola bottles, and there was comfort to the gloom somehow.

In Korea, Bert Kling learned about a different kind of rain. He learned about a rain that was cruel and driving and bitter, a rain that turned the earth to a sticky clinging mud that halted machines and men. He learned what it was to be constantly wet and cold. And ever since Korea, he had not liked the rain.

He did not like it on that late Friday morning, either.

He had started the day by paying a visit to the Missing Persons Bureau and renewing his acquaintance there with Detectives Ambrose and Bartholdi.

'Well, well, look who is here,' Bartholdi had said.

'The Sun God of the 87th,' Ambrose added.

'The Blond Wonder himself.'

'In person,' Kling said drily.

'What can we do for you today, Detective Kling?'

'Who did you lose this week, Detective Kling?'

'We're looking for a white male between the ages of eighteen and twenty-four,' Kling said.

'Did you hear that, Romeo?' Ambrose said to Bartholdi.

'I heard it, Mike,' Bartholdi answered.

'That is an awful lot to go on. Now how many white males between the ages of eighteen and twenty-four do you suppose we have records on?'

'At a conservative estimate,' Bartholdi answered, 'I would say approximately six thousand seven hundred and twenty-three.'

'Not counting the ones we ain't had time to file yet.'

'With bulls from all over the city popping in here at every hour of the day, we don't get much time to do filing, Detective Kling.'

'That's a shame,' Kling said drily. He wished he could shake the feeling he constantly experienced in the presence of older cops who'd been on the force longer than he. He knew he was a young detective and a new detective, but he resented the automatic assumption that because of his age and inexperience he must, ipso facto, be an inept detective. He did not consider himself inept. In fact, he thought of himself as being a pretty good cop, Romeo and Mike be damned.

'Can I look through the files?' he asked.

'But of course!' Bartholdi said enthusiastically. 'That's why they're here! So that every dirty-fingered cop in the city can pore over them. Ain't that right, Mike?'

'Why, certainly. How else would we keep busy? If we didn't have dog-eared record cards to retype, we might have to go outside on a lousy day like this. We might have to actually use a gun now and then.'

'We prefer leaving the gunplay to you younger, more agile fellows, Kling.'

'To the heroes,' Ambrose said.

'Yeah,' Kling answered, and he searched for a more devastating reply, but none came to mind.

'Be careful with our cards,' Bartholdi cautioned. 'Did you wash your hands this morning?'

'I washed them,' Kling said.

'Good. Obey the sign.' He pointed to the large placard resting atop the green filing cabinets.

SHUFFLE THEM, JUGGLE THEM, MAUL THEM, CARESS THEM – BUT LEAVE THEM THE WAY YOU FOUND THEM!

'Got it?' Ambrose asked.

'I've been here before,' Kling said. 'You ought to change your sign. It gets kind of dull the hundredth time around.'

'It ain't there for entertainment,' Bartholdi said. 'It's there for information.'

'Take care of the cards,' Ambrose said. 'If you get bored, look up a dame named Barbara Cesare, also known as Bubbles Caesar. She was reported missing in February. That's over there near the window. She was a stripper in Kansas City, and she came here to work some of our own clubs. There are some very fine art photos in her folder.'

'He is just a boy, Mike,' Bartholdi said. 'You shouldn't call his attention to matters like that.'

'Forgive me, Romeo,' Ambrose said. 'You're right. Forget I mentioned Bubbles Caesar, Kling. Forget all about them lovely pictures in the February file over there near the window. You hear?'

'I'll forget all about her,' Kling said.

'We got typing to do,' Bartholdi said, opening the door. 'Have fun.'

'That's Caesar,' Ambrose said as he went out. 'C-A-E-S-A-R.'

'Bubbles,' Bartholdi said, and he closed the door behind him.

Kling, of course, did not have to look through 6,723 missing persons cards. If anything, the haphazard estimate given by Bartholdi was somewhat exaggerated. Actually, some 2,500 persons were reported missing annually in the city for which Kling worked. If this was broken down on a monthly basis, perhaps a little more than 200 people per month found their way into the files of the Missing Persons Bureau. The peak months for disappearances are May and September, but Kling, fortunately, was not particularly concerned with those months. He restricted himself to scouring the files covering January, February, and the early part of March, and so he didn't have very many folders to wade through.

The job, nonetheless, did get somewhat boring, and he did – since he was studying the February file, anyway – take a peek into the folder of the missing exotic dancer, Bubbles Caesar. He had to admit, after studying the several photos of her in the folder, that whoever had named this performer had a decided knack for the *mot juste*. Looking at the pictures of the stripper made him think of Claire Townsend, and thinking of Claire made him wish it was tonight instead of this morning.

He lighted another cigarette, ruefully put away Miss Caesar's folder, and got back to work again.

By eleven o'clock that morning, he had turned up only two possible nominations for the Missing Persons Award. He went down the hall and had both sheets photostated. Bartholdi, who did the job for him, seemed to be in a more serious frame of mind now.

'These what you were looking for, kid?' he asked.

'Well, they're only possibilities. We'll see how they turn out.'

'What's the case, anyway?' Bartholdi asked.

'One of our patrolmen found a severed hand in a bag.'

'Psssssss,' Bartholdi said and he pulled a face.

'Yeah. Right in the street. Near a bus stop.'

'Psssssss,' Bartholdi said again.

'Yeah.'

'A man or a woman? The hand, I mean.'

'A man,' Kling said.

'What kind of a bag? A shopping bag?'

'No, no,' Kling said. 'An airlines bag. You know these bags they give out? These little blue ones? This one came from an outfit called Circle Airlines.'

'A high-flying killer, huh?' Bartholdi said. 'Well, here are the stats, kid. Good luck with them.'

'Thanks,' Kling said. He took the proffered manila envelope and went down the corridor to a phone booth. He dialled Frederick 7–8024 and asked to talk to Steve Carella.

'Some weather, huh?' Carella said.

'The end,' Kling answered. 'Listen, I dug up two possibles from the files here. Thought I'd hit the first before lunch. You want to come with me?'

'Sure,' Carella said. 'Where shall I meet you?'

'Well, the first guy is a merchant seaman, vanished on February 14, Valentine's Day. His wife reported him missing. She lives on Detavoner, near South Eleventh.'

'Meet you on the corner there?'

'Fine,' Kling said. 'Were there any calls for me?'

'Claire called.'

'Yeah?'

'Said you should call her back as soon as you got a chance.'

'Oh? Okay, thanks,' Kling said. 'I'll see you in about a half-hour, okay?'

'Right. Stay out of the rain.' And he hung up.

Now, standing in the rain on what was probably the most exposed corner in the entire city, Kling tried to crawl deep into his trench coat, tried to form an airtight, watertight seal where his hands were thrust deep into his coat pockets, tried to pull in his neck like a turtle, but nothing worked against the goddamn rain, everything was wet and cold and clammy, and where the hell was Carella?

I wish I wore a hat, he thought. I wish I were that kind of American advertising executive who could feel comfortable in a hat.

Hatless, his blond hair soaked and plastered to his skull, Kling stood on the street corner observing:

a) the open parking lot on one corner.

b) the skyscraper under construction on the opposite corner.

c) the fenced-in park on the third corner.

d) the blank wall of a warehouse on the fourth corner.

No canopies under which to stand. No doorways into which a man could duck. Nothing but the wide open spaces of Isola and the rain driving across those spaces like a Cossack charge in an Italian-made spectacle. Damn you, Carella, where are you?

Aw, come on, Steve, he thought. Have a heart.

The unmarked police sedan pulled to the kerb. A sign on the lamp-post read NO PARKING OR STANDING 8:00 A.M. TO 6:00 P.M. Carella parked the car and got out.

'Hi,' he said. 'Been waiting long?'

'What the hell kept you?' Kling wanted to know.

'Grossman called from the lab just as I was leaving.'

'Yeah? So what ...?'

'He's working on both the hand and the bag now, says he'll have a report for us sometime tomorrow.'

'Will he get any prints from the hand?'

'He doubts it. The finger tips are cut to ribbons. Listen, can't we discuss this over a cup of coffee? Must we stand here in the rain? And I'd also like to take a look at that Missing Person sheet before we see this woman.'

'I can use a cup of coffee,' Kling said.

'Does she know we're coming? The guy's wife?'

'No. You think I should have called?'

'No, better this way. Maybe we'll find her with a body in a trunk and a meat cleaver in her dainty fist.'

'Sure. There's a diner in the middle of the block. Let's get the coffee there. You can look over the sheet while I buzz Claire.'

'Good,' Carella said.

They walked to the diner, sat in one of the booths, and ordered two cups of coffee. While Kling went to call his fiancée, Carella sipped at his coffee and studied the report. He read it through once, and then he read it through a second time. This is what it said:

POLICE DEPARTMENT
REPORT OF MISSING PERSON

DET. DISTRICT ____2nd____ SQD. __26th__

CASE NO. _____DD25-1143_____

BUS. NO. _____34A-1762_____

DATE OF THIS REPORT ____2/16____

SURNAME ANDROVICH	FIRST NAME, INITIALS KARL F.		NATIVITY U.S.A.	SEX M	AGE 22	COLOR White
ADDRESS 537 Detavoner Avenue		LAST SEEN AT Home address		DATE AND TIME SEEN 2/14		6:30 A.M. P.M.
PROBABLE DESTINATION S.S. Farren, Pier 6		CAUSE OF ABSENCE ?		DATE AND TIME REPORTED 2/15		9:00 A.M. P.M.

PHYSICAL NOTE PECULIARITIES	CLOTHING—GIVE COLOR, FABRIC, STYLE, LABEL, WHERE POSSIBLE	STRIKE OUT IRRELEVANT WORDS	MISCELLANEOUS INFORMATION
HEIGHT FT. 6 IN. 4½	HEADGEAR Watchcap, blue wool		OCCUPATION OR SCHOOL Wiper, S.S. Farren
WEIGHT 210	OVER OR TOP COAT None		EVER FINGERPRINTED? WHERE AND WHEN? Yes. Morch-Mar. 2/4/58
BUILD Husky	SUIT OR DRESS		DRY CLEANER MARKS In jacket. Detavoner Cleaners. 001 Detavoner Avenue
COMPLEXION Sallow	JACKET Peajacket, Blue		LAUNDRY MARKS
HAIR Brown	TROUSERS Dungarees, blue, faded		PHOTO RECEIVED Yes / PREVIOUSLY MISSING? No
EYES Brown	SHIRT white, cotton, long-sleeved, Manhatten label		PUBLICITY DESIRED? Yes / SOCIAL SECURITY NO. 119-16-4683
GLASSES, TYPE	TIE OR FUR PIECE SCARF		PRELIMINARY INVESTIGATION Ptlm Ralph Cinnetar
MUSTACHE Brown, close trimmed	HOSE GLOVES Black socks, cotton dacron, Esquire		DESK OFFICER Lt. E. Neal
TEETH No dental chart	SHOES Black, untrimmed		TELEGRAPH BUSINESS Sgt. N. Abronoff
	HANDBAG		BUREAU OF INFORMATION Det. 1st/Or D. Nicholson
SCARS	LUGGAGE Duffel bag, canvas, white, stenciled "K. F. ANDROVICH"		OTHERS
	JEWELRY WORN		
DEFORMITIES			
	MONEY CARRIED $30		NOTIFICATION TO MISSING PERSONS BUR. BY Det./Lt.Franklin Canavan, 26DetSq
TATTOO MARKS "MEG" in heart on left biceps	CHARACTERISTICS, HABITS, MANNERISMS Slight tic left eye. Stammers when excited. Very hot-tempered.		RECEIVED AT MISSING PERSONS BUREAU BY Sgt.Sean O'Rourke
			ASSIGNED SQUAD
CONDITION PHYSICAL Good / MENTAL Good			ASSIGNED Det.2/Or Jonah Fredericks
REPORTED BY Margaret Androvich	ADDRESS 537 Detavoner Avenue	TELEPHONE NO. IS 4-7361	RELATIONSHIP Wife

Androvich left his apartment at 537 Detavoner Avenue at 6:30 A.M. on February 14 apparently to board his ship, the SS Farren, wher it was docked at Pier 6. He was scheduled to sail for South America at 8:00 A.M. that morning, and gave every indication of wanting to catch the ship. His wife noticed nothing strange about his behavior at breakfast, which they ate together in the apartment. At 7:45 A.M., the chief officer of the Farren called to inquire of Androvich's whereabouts. His wife told the officer that Androvich had left the apartment at 6:30. She did not report his absence to the police during the remainder of that day, because she was hopeful he would return by morning. This was the first time, except when on cruises, that he had been gone for any prolonged period of time.

Det. Jonah Fredericks
Signature of Assigned Detective

Lt. Samuel Barker.
Commanding Officer

When Kling came back to the table, there was a smile on his face.

'What's up?' Carella asked.

'Oh, nothing much. Claire's father left for New Jersey this morning, that's all. Won't be back until Monday.'

'Which gives you an empty apartment for the weekend, huh?' Carella said.

'Well, I wasn't thinking anything like that,' Kling said.

'No, of course not.'

'But it might be nice,' Kling admitted.

'When are you going to marry that girl?'

'She wants to get her master's degree before we get married.'

'Why?'

'How do I know? She's insecure.' Kling shrugged. 'She's psychotic. How do I know?'

'What does she want after the master's? A doctorate?'

'Maybe.' Kling shrugged. 'Listen, I ask her to marry me every time I see her. She wants the master's. So what can I do? I'm in love with her. Can I tell her to go to hell?'

'I suppose not.'

'Well, I can't.' Kling paused. 'I mean, what the hell, Steve, if a girl wants an education, it's not my right to say no, is it?'

'I guess not.'

'Well, would you have said no to Teddy?'

'I don't think so.'

'Well, there you are.'

'Sure.'

'I mean, what the hell else can I do, Steve? I either wait for her, or I decide not to marry her, right?'

'Right,' Carella said.

'And since I want to marry her, I have no choice. I wait.' He paused thoughtfully. 'Jesus, I hope she isn't one of those perennial schoolgirl types.' He paused again. 'Well, there's nothing I can do about it. I'll just have to wait, that's all.'

'That sounds like sound deduction.'

'Sure. The only thing is . . . well, to be absolutely truthful with you, Steve, I'm afraid she'll get pregnant or something, and then we'll *have* to get married, do you know what I mean? And that'll be different than if we just got married because we felt like it. I mean, even though we love each other and all, it'd be different. Oh, Jesus, I don't know what to do.'

'Just be careful, that's all,' Carella said.

'Oh, I am. I mean, we are, we are. You want to know something Steve?'

'What?'

'I wish I could keep my hands off her. You know, I wish we didn't have to . . . well, you know, my landlady looks at me cockeyed every time I bring Claire upstairs. And then I have to rush her home because her father is the strictest guy who ever walked the earth. I'm surprised he's leaving her alone this weekend. But what I mean is . . . well, damnit, what the hell does she need that master's for, Steve? I mean, I wish I could leave her alone until we were married, but I just can't. I mean, all I have to do is be with her, and my mouth goes dry. Is it that way with . . . well, never mind, I didn't mean to get personal.'

'It's that way,' Carella said.

'Yeah,' Kling said, and he nodded. He seemed lost in thought for a moment. Then he said, 'I've got tomorrow off, but not Sunday. Do you think somebody would want to switch with me? Like for a Tuesday or something? I hate to break up the weekend.'

'Where'd you plan to spend the weekend?' Carella asked.

'Well, you know ...'

'*All* weekend?' Carella said, surprised.

'Well, you know ...'

'Starting *tonight*?' he asked, astonished.

'Well, you know ...'

'I'd give you my Sunday, but I'm afraid ...'

'Will you?' Kling said, leaning forward.

'... you'll be a wreck on Monday morning.' Carella paused. '*All* weekend?' he asked again.

'Well, it isn't often the old man goes away. You know.'

'Flaming Youth, where have you gone?' Carella said, shaking his head. 'Sure, you can have my Sunday if the Skipper says okay.'

'Thanks, Steve.'

'Or did Teddy have something planned?' Carella asked himself.

'Now don't change your mind,' Kling said anxiously.

'Okay, okay.' He tapped the Missing Persons report with his forefinger. 'What do you think?'

'He looks good, I would say. He's big enough, anyway. Six-four and weighs two-ten. That's no midget, Steve.'

'And that hand belonged to a big man.' Carella finished his coffee and said, 'Come on, Lover Man, let's go see Mrs Androvich.'

As they rose, Kling said, 'It's not that I'm a great lover or anything, Steve. It's just ... well ...'

'What?'

Kling grinned. 'I *like* it,' he said.

Chapter Six

Margaret Androvich was a nineteen-year-old blonde who, in the hands of our more skilful novelists, would have been described as willowy. That is to say, she was skinny. The diminutive 'Meg' did not exactly apply to her because she was five feet seven and a half inches tall with all the cuddly softness of a steel cable. In the current fashion of naming particularly svelte women with particularly ugly names, 'Maggie' would have been more appropriate than the 'Meg' which Karl Androvich wore tattooed in a heart on his left arm. But Meg she was, all five feet seven and a half inches of her, and she greeted the detectives at the door with calm and assurance, ushered them into her living room, and asked them to sit.

They sat.

She was indeed skinny with that angular sort of femininity which is usually attributed to fashion models. She was not, at the moment, attired for the pages of *Vogue* Magazine. She was wearing a faded pink quilted robe and furry pink slippers which somehow seemed out of place on a girl so tall. Her face was as angular as her body, with high cheekbones and a mouth which looked pouting even without the benefit of lipstick. Her eyes were blue and large, dominating the narrow face. She spoke with a mild, barely discernible Southern accent. She carried about her the air of a person who knows she is about to be struck in the face with a closed fist but who bears the eventuality with calm expectation.

'Is this about Karl?' she asked gently.

'Yes, Mrs Androvich,' Carella answered.

'Have you heard anything? Is he all right?'

'No, nothing definite,' Carella said.

'But something?'

'No, no. We just wanted to find out a little more about him, that's all.'

'I see.' She nodded vaguely. 'Then you haven't heard anything about him.'

'No, not really.'

'I see.' Again she nodded.

'Can you tell us what happened on the morning he left here?'

'Yes,' she said. 'He just left, that was all. There was nothing different between this time and all the other times he left to catch his ship. It was just the same. Only this time he didn't catch the ship.' She shrugged. 'And I haven't heard from him since.' She shrugged again. 'It's been almost a month now.'

'How long have you been married, Mrs Androvich?'

'To Karl? Six months.'

'Had you been married before? I mean, is Karl your second husband?'

'No. He's my first husband. Only husband I ever had.'

'Where did you meet him, Mrs Androvich?'

'Atlanta.'

'Six months ago?'

'Seven months ago, really.'

'And you got married?'

'Yes.'

'And you came to this city?'

'Yes.'

'Where is your husband from originally?'

'Here. This city.' She paused. 'Do you like it here?'

'The city, do you mean?'

'Yes. Do you like it?'

'Well, I was born and raised here,' Carella said. 'Yes, I guess I like it.'

'I don't,' Meg said flatly.

'Well, that's what makes horse races, Mrs Androvich,' Carella said, and he tried a smile and then pulled it back quickly when he saw her face.

'Yes, that's what makes horse races, all right,' she said. 'I tried to tell Karl that I didn't like it here, that I wanted to go back to Atlanta. But he was born and raised here, too.' She shrugged. 'I guess it's different if you know the place. And with him gone so often, I'm alone a lot, and the streets confuse me. I mean, Atlanta isn't exactly a one-horse town, but it's small compared to here. I can never figure out how to *get* any place here. I'm always getting lost. I wander three blocks from the apartment, and I get lost. Would you like some coffee?'

'Well ...'

'Have some coffee,' Meg said. 'You're not going to rush right off, are you? You all are the first two people I've had here in a long time.'

'I think we can stay for some coffee,' Carella said.

'It won't take but a minute. Would you excuse me, please?'

She went into the kitchen. Kling rose from where he was sitting and walked to the television set. A framed photograph of a man rested atop the receiver. He was studying the photo when Meg came back into the room.

'That's Karl,' she said. 'That's a nice picture. That's the one I sent to the Missing Persons Bureau.' She paused. 'They asked me for a picture, you know.' She paused again. 'Coffee won't take a but a minute. I'm warming some rolls, too. You men must he half-froze, wandering about in that cold rain.'

'That's very nice of you, Mrs Androvich.'

She smiled fleetingly. 'Working man needs sustenance,' she said, and the smile vanished.

'Mrs Androvich, about that morning he left ...'

'Yes. It was Valentine's Day.' She paused. 'There was a big box of candy on the kitchen table when I woke up. And flowers came later. While we were having breakfast.'

'From Karl?'

'Yes. Yes, from Karl.'

'While you were having breakfast?'

'Yes.'

'But ... didn't he leave the house at 6:30?'

'Yes.'

'And flowers arrived before he left?'

'Yes.'

'That's pretty early, isn't it?'

'I guess he made some sort of arrangement with the florist,' Meg said. 'To have them delivered so early.' She paused. 'They were roses. Two dozen red roses.'

'I see,' Carella said.

'Anything out of the ordinary happen during breakfast?' Kling asked.

'No. No, he was in a very cheerful frame of mind.'

'But he wasn't always in a cheerful frame of mind, is that also right? You told someone earlier that he was very hot-tempered.'

'Yes. I told that to Detective Fredericks. At the Missing Persons Bureau. Do you know him?'

'No, not personally.'

'He's a very nice man.'

'And you told Detective Fredericks that your husband stammers, is that right? And he has a slight tic in the right eye, is that correct?'

'The left eye.'

'Yes, the left eye.'

'That's correct.'

'Is he a nervous person, would you say?'

'He's pretty tense, yes.'

'Was he tense on that morning?'

'The morning he left, do you mean?'

'Yes. Was he tense or nervous then?'

'No. He was very calm.'

'I see. And what did you do with the flowers when they arrived?'

'The flowers? I put them in a vase.'

'On the table?'

'Yes.'

'The breakfast table?'

'Yes.'

'They were there while you ate breakfast?'

'Yes.'

'Did he eat a good meal?'

'Yes.'

'His appetite was all right?'

'It was fine. He was very hungry.'

'And nothing seemed unusual or strange?'

'No.' She turned her head towards the kitchen. 'I think the coffee's perking,' she said. 'Will you excuse me, please?'

She went out of the room. Kling and Carella sat staring at each other. Outside, the rain slithered down the windowpane.

She came back into the living room carrying a tray with a coffeepot, three cups and saucers, and a dish of hot rolls. She put these down, studied the tray, and then said, 'Butter. I forgot butter.' In the doorway to the kitchen, she paused and said, 'Would you all like some jam or something?'

'No, this is fine, thanks,' Carella said.

'Would you pour?' she said, and she went out for the butter. From the kitchen, she called, 'Did I bring out the cream?'

'No,' Carella said.

'Or the sugar?'

'No.'

They heard her rummaging in the kitchen. Carella poured coffee into the three cups. She came into the room again and put down the butter, the cream and the sugar.

'There,' she said. 'Do you take anything in yours, Detective – Carella, was it?'

'Yes, Carella. No thank you, I'll have it black.'

'Detective Kling?'

'A little cream and one sugar, thank you.'

'Help yourself to the rolls before they get cold,' she said.

The detectives helped themselves. She sat opposite them, watching.

'Take your coffee, Mrs Androvich,' Carella said.

'Oh, yes. Thank you.' She picked up her cup, put three spoonfuls of sugar into it, and sat stirring it idly.

'Do you think you'll find him?' she asked.

'We hope so.'

'Do you think anything's happened to him?'

'That's hard to say, Mrs Androvich.'

'He was such a big man.' She shrugged.

'*Was*, Mrs Androvich?'

'Did I say "was"? I guess I did. I guess I think of him as gone for good.'

'Why should you think that?'

'I don't know.'

'It sounds as if he was very much in love with you.'

'Oh, yes. Yes, he was.' She paused. 'Are the rolls all right?'

'Delicious,' Carella said.

'Fine,' Kling added.

'I get them delivered. I don't go out much. I'm here most of the time. Right here in this apartment.'

'Why do you think your husband went off like that, Mrs Androvich?'

'I don't know.'

'You didn't quarrel or anything that morning, did you?'

'No. No, we didn't quarrel.'

'I don't mean a real fight or anything,' Carella said. 'Just a quarrel, you know. Anyone who's married has a quarrel every now and then.'

'Are you married, Detective Carella?'

'Yes, I am.'

'Do you quarrel sometimes?'

'Yes.'

'Karl and I didn't quarrel that morning,' she said flatly.

'But you did quarrel sometimes?'

'Yes. About going back to Atlanta mostly. That was all. Just about going back to Atlanta. Because I don't like this city, you see.'

'That's understandable,' Carella said. 'Not being familiar with it, and all. Have you ever been uptown?'

'Uptown where?'

'Culver Avenue? Hall Avenue?'

'Where the big department stores are?'

'No, I was thinking of a little further uptown. Near Grover Park.'

'No. I don't know where Grover Park is.'

'You've never been uptown?'

'Not that far uptown.'

'Do you have a raincoat, Mrs Androvich?'

'A what?'

'A raincoat.'

'Yes, I do. Why?'

'What colour is it, Mrs Androvich?'

'My *raincoat*?'

'Yes.'

'It's blue.' She paused. 'Why?'

'Do you have a black one?'

'No. Why?'

'Do you ever wear slacks?'

'Hardly ever.'

'But sometimes you do wear slacks?'

'Only in the house sometimes. When I'm cleaning. I never wear them in the street. Where I was raised, in Atlanta, a girl wore dresses and skirts and pretty things.'

'Do you have an umbrella, Mrs Androvich?'

'Yes, I do.'

'What colour is it?'

'Red. I don't think I understand all this, Detective Carella.'

'Mrs Androvich, I wonder if we could see the raincoat and the umbrella.'

'What for?'

'Well, we'd like to.'

She stared at Carella and then turned her puzzled gaze on Kling. 'All right,' she said at last. 'Would you come into the bedroom, please?' They followed her into the other room. 'I haven't made the bed yet, you'll have to forgive the appearance of the house.' She pulled the blanket up over the rumpled sheets as she passed the bed on the way to the closet. She threw open the closet door and said, 'There's the raincoat. And there's the umbrella.'

The raincoat was blue. The umbrella was red.

'Thank you,' Carella said. 'Do you have your meat delivered, too, Mrs Androvich?'

'My what?'

'Meat. From the butcher.'

'Yes, I do. Detective Carella, would you mind please telling me what this is all about? All these questions, you make it sound as if ...'

'Well, it's just routine, Mrs Androvich, that's all. Just trying to learn a little about your husband's habits, that's all.'

'What's my raincoat and my umbrella got to do with Karl's habits?'

'Well, you know.'

'No, I don't know.'

'Do you own a meat cleaver, Mrs Androvich?'

She stared at Carella a long time before answering. Then she said, 'What's that got to do with Karl?'

Carella did not answer.

'Is Karl dead?' she said. 'Is that it?'

He did not answer.

'Did someone use a meat cleaver on him? Is that it? Is that it?'

'We don't know, Mrs Androvich.'

'Do you think I did it? Is that what you're saying?'

'We have no knowledge whatever about your husband's whereabouts, Mrs Androvich. Dead or alive. This is all routine.'

'Routine, huh? What happened? Did someone wearing a raincoat and carrying an umbrella hit my husband with a cleaver? Is that what happened?'

'No, Mrs Androvich. *Do* you own a meat cleaver?'

'Yes, I do,' she said. 'It's in the kitchen. Would you like to see it? Maybe you can find some of Karl's skull on it. Isn't that what you'd like to find?'

'This is just a routine investigation, Mrs Androvich.'

'Are all detectives as subtle as you?' she wanted to know.

'I'm sorry if I've upset you, Mrs Androvich. May I see that cleaver? If it's not too much trouble.'

'This way,' she said coldly, and she led them out of the bedroom, through the living room, and into the kitchen. The cleaver was a small one, its cutting edge dull and nicked. 'That's it,' she said.

'I'd like to take this with me, if you don't mind,' Carella said.
'Why?'
'What kind of candy did your husband bring you on Valentine's Day, Mrs Androvich?'
'Nuts. Fruits. A mixed assortment.'
'From where? Who made the candy?'
'I don't remember.'
'Was it a large box?'
'A pound.'
'But you called it a big box of candy when you first spoke of it. You said there was a big box of candy on the kitchen table when you woke up. Isn't that what you said?'
'Yes. It was in the shape of a heart. It looked big to me.'
'But it was only a pound box of candy, is that right?'
'Yes.'
'And the dozen red roses? When did they arrive?'
'At about six A.M.'
'And you put them in a vase?'
'Yes.'
'Do you have a vase big enough to hold a dozen roses?'
'Yes, of course I do. Karl was always bringing me flowers. So I bought a vase one day.'
'Big enough to hold a dozen red roses, right?'
'Yes.'
'They *were* red roses, a dozen of them?'
'Yes.'
'No *white* ones? Just a dozen red roses?'
'Yes, yes, a dozen red roses. All red. And I put them in a vase.'
'You said two dozen, Mrs Androvich. When you first mentioned them, you said there were two dozen.'
'What?'
'Two dozen.'
'I ...'
'Were there any flowers at all, Mrs Androvich?'
'Yes, yes. Yes, there were flowers. I must have made a mistake. It was only a dozen. Not two dozen. I must have been thinking of something else.'
'Was there candy, Mrs Androvich?'
'Yes, of course there was candy.'
'Yes, and you didn't quarrel at the breakfast table. Why didn't you report his absence until the next day?'
'Because I thought ...'
'Had he ever wandered off before?'
'No, he ...'
'Then this was rather unusual for him, wasn't it?'
'Yes, but ...'
'Then why didn't you report it immediately?'
'I thought he'd come back.'
'Or did you think he had reason for staying away?'
'What reason?'
'You tell me, Mrs Androvich.'

The room went silent.

'There was no reason,' she said at last. 'My husband loved me. There was a box of candy on the table in the morning. A heart. The florist delivered a dozen red roses at six o'clock. Karl kissed me goodbye and left. And I haven't seen him since.'

'Give Mrs Androvich a receipt for this meat cleaver, Bert,' Carella said. 'Thank you very much for the coffee and rolls. And for your time. You were very kind.'

As they went out, she said, 'He *is* dead, isn't he?'

Claire Townsend was easily as tall as Meg Androvich, but the similarity between the two girls ended there. Meg was skinny – or, if you prefer, willowy; Claire was richly endowed with flesh that padded the big bones of her body. Meg, in the fashion-model tradition, was flat-chested. Claire was not one of those over-extended cowlike creatures, but she was rightfully proud of a bosom capable of filling a man's hand. Meg was a blue-eyed blonde. Claire's eyes were brown and her hair was as black as sin. Meg, in short, gave the impression of someone living in the pallor of a hospital sickroom; Claire looked like a girl who would be at home on a sunwashed haystack.

There was one other difference.

Bert Kling was madly in love with Claire.

She kissed him the moment he entered the apartment. She was wearing black slacks and a wide, white, smocklike blouse which ended just below her waist.

'What kept you?' she said.

'Florists,' he answered.

'You bought me flowers?'

'No. A lady we talked to said her husband bought her a dozen red roses. We checked about ten florists in the immediate and surrounding neighbourhoods. Result? No red roses on Valentine's Day. Not to Mrs Karl Androvich, anyway.'

'So?'

'So Steve Carella is uncanny. Can I take off my shoes?'

'Go ahead. I bought two steaks. Do you feel like steaks?'

'Later.'

'How is Carella uncanny?'

'Well, he lit into this skinny, pathetic dame as if he were going to rip all the flesh from her bones. When we got outside, I told him I thought he was a little rough with her. I mean, I've seen him operate before, and he usually wears kid gloves with the ladies. So with this one, he used a sledge hammer, and I wondered why. And told him I disapproved.'

'So what did he say?'

'He said he knew she was lying from the minute she opened her mouth, and he began wondering why?'

'How did he know?'

'He just knew. That's what was so uncanny about it. We checked all those damn florists, and nobody made a delivery at six in the morning, and none of them were even *open* before nine.'

'The husband could have ordered the flowers anywhere in the city, Bert.'

'Sure, but that's pretty unlikely, isn't it? He's not a guy who works in an office some place. He's a seaman, and when he's not at sea, he's home. So the logical place to order flowers would be a neighbourhood florist.'

'So?'

'So nothing. I'm tired. Steve sent a meat cleaver to the lab.' He paused. 'She didn't look like the kind of a dame who'd use a meat cleaver on a man. Come here.'

She went to him, climbing into his lap. He kissed her and said, 'I've got the whole weekend. Steve's giving me his Sunday.'

'Oh? Yes?'

'You feel funny,' he said.

'Funny? How?'

'I don't know. Softer.'

'I'm not wearing a bra.'

'How come?'

'I wanted to feel free. Keep your hands off me!' she said suddenly, and she leaped out of his lap.

'Now you are the kind of a dame who would use a meat cleaver on a man,' Kling said, appraising her from the chair in which he sat.

'Am I?' she answered coolly. 'When do you want to eat?'

'Later.'

'Where are we going tonight?' Claire asked.

'No place.'

'Oh?'

'I don't have to be back at the squad until Monday morning,' Kling said.

'Oh, is that right?'

'Yes, and what I planned was ...'

'Yes?'

'I thought we could get into bed right now and stay in bed all weekend. Until Monday morning. How does that sound to you?'

'It sounds pretty strenuous.'

'Yes, it does. But I vote for it.'

'I'll have to think about it. I had my heart set on a movie.'

'We can always see a movie,' Kling said.

'Anyway, I'm hungry right now,' Claire said, studying him narrowly. 'I'm going to make the steaks.'

'I'd rather go to bed.'

'Bert,' she said, 'man does not live by bed alone.'

Kling rose suddenly. They stood at opposite ends of the room, studying each other. 'What did *you* plan on doing tonight?' he asked.

'Eating steaks,' she said.

'And what else?'

'A movie.'

'And tomorrow?'

Claire shrugged.

'Come here,' he said.

'Come get me,' she answered.

He went across the room to her. She tilted her head to his and then crossed her arms tightly over her breasts.

'All weekend,' he said.

'You're a braggart,' she whispered.

'You're a doll.'

'Am I?'

'You're a lovely doll.'

'You going to kiss me?'

'Maybe.'

They stood not two inches from each other, not touching, staring at each other, savouring this moment, allowing desire to leap between them in a mounting wave.

He put his hands on her waist, but he did not kiss her.

Slowly, she uncrossed her arms.

'You really have no bra on?' he asked.

'Big weekend lover,' she murmured. 'Can't even find out for himself whether or not I have a ...'

His hands slid under the smock and he pulled Claire to him.

The next time anyone saw Bert Kling would be on Monday morning.

It would still be raining.

Sam Grossman studied the airlines bag for a long time, and then took off his eyeglasses. Grossman was a police lieutenant, a laboratory technician, and the man in charge of the police lab downtown on High Street. In his years of service with the lab, he had seen bodies or portions of bodies in trunks, valises, duffel bags, shopping bags, boxes, and even wrapped in old newspapers. He had never come across one in an airline's overnight bag, but he experienced no sensation of surprise or shock. The inside of the bag was covered with dried blood, but he did not reel back at the sight of it. He knew there was work to be done, and he set about doing it. He was somewhat like a New England farmer discovering that one of his fields would make an excellent pasture if only it were cleared of rocks and stumps. The only way to clear the field was to clear it.

He had already examined the severed hand, and reached the conclusion that it was impossible to get any fingerprint impressions from the badly mutilated fingertips. He had then taken a sampling of blood from the hand for an isoreaction test, and concluded that the blood was in the 'O' group.

Now he examined the bag for latent fingerprints, and found none. He had not, in all truth, expected to find any. The person who'd mutilated that hand was a person who was very conscious of fingerprints, a person who would have shown the same caution in handling the bag.

He checked the bag next for microscopic traces of hair or fibres or dust which might give some clue to either the killer's or the victim's identity, occupation, or hobby. He found nothing of value on the outside surface of the bag.

He slit the bag open with a scalpel and studied its inner surface and bottom with a magnifying glass. In one corner of the bag he found what appeared to be remnants of orange chalk dust. He collected several grains for a specimen, put them aside, and then studied the bloodstains on the bottom of the bag.

The average layman might have considered Grossman's examination absurd. He was, after all, examining a stain which had obviously been left in the bag by the severed hand. What in the hell was he trying to ascertain? That the hand had been in the bag? Everyone knew that already.

But Grossman was simply trying to determine whether or not the stain on the bottom of the bag was actually human blood; and if not blood, then what? There was the possibility, too, that an apparent bloodstain could have mingled with, or covered, another stain on the bag. And so Grossman really wasn't wasting his time. He was simply doing a thorough job.

The stain was a dark reddish brown in colour and, because of the nonabsorbent surface of the bag's bottom, it was somewhat cracked and chipped, resembling a dried mud flat. Grossman gingerly cut out a portion of the stain, and cut this into two smaller portions which he labelled Stain One and Stain Two, for want of a more imaginative nomenclature. He dropped his two specimens into an 0.9 per cent solution of physiologic salt, and then placed them on separate slides. The slides had to stand in a covered dish for several hours, so he left them and began performing his microscopic and spectroscopic tests on the orange chalk he had found in a corner of the bag. When he returned to the slides later that day, he covered one of them with a coverslip and studied it under a high-power microscope. What he saw was a number of non-nucleated discs, and he knew instantly that the suspect blood was mammalian in origin.

He then took the second slide and poured Wright's Stain onto the un-fixed smear, letting it stand for one minute while he timed the operation. Drop by drop, he added distilled water to the slide, waiting for a metallic scum to form on its surface. When the scum had formed, he again consulted his watch, waiting three minutes before he washed and dried the slide.

Using a micrometer eyepiece, he then measured the various cells on the slide. The human red blood corpuscle is about 1/3200 of an inch in diameter. The cell diameter will vary in other animals of the mammalian group, the erythrocyte of the dog – at 1/3500 of an inch – being closest to the human's.

The specimen Grossman examined under his microscope measured 1/3200 of an inch in diameter.

But where measurement dealt with error in thousandths of an inch, Grossman did not want to take any chances. And so he followed the usual laboratory procedure of using a precipitin reaction after either a chemical, microscopic, or spectroscopic test. The precipitin reaction would determine with certainty whether or not the stain was indeed human blood.

The precipitin reaction is a simple one. If you take a rabbit, and if you inject into this rabbit's blood a specimen of whole human blood or human blood serum, something is going to happen. The something that will happen is this: an antibody called a 'precipitin' will develop in the rabbit's own serum. This will then react with the proteins of the injected serum. If the reaction is a positive one, the proteins can then be identified as having come from a human being.

The specific reaction to Grossman's stain was positive.

The blood was human.

When he performed his isoreaction test, he learned that it was in the 'O' blood group, and he therefore made the logical assumption that the stain on the bottom of the bag had been left by blood dripping from the severed hand and by nothing else.

As for the bits of orange chalk dust, they turned out to be something quite other than chalk. The particles were identified as a woman's cosmetic, further identified through a chemical breakdown and a comparison with the cards in the files as a preparation called Skinglow.

Skinglow was a liquid powder base designed to retain face powder in a clinging veil, further designed to add a slight pink glow to very fair skin under makeup.

It was hardly likely that a man would have used it.

And yet the hand in the bag had definitely belonged to a man.

Grossman sighed and passed the information on to the boys of the 87th.

Chapter Seven

Saturday.

Rain.

Once, when he was a boy, he and some friends had crawled under the iceman's cart on Colby Avenue. It had been pouring bullets, and the three of them sat under the wooden cart and watched the spikes of rain pounding the cobblestones, feeling secure and impervious. Steve Carella caught pneumonia, and shortly afterwards the family moved from Isola to Riverhead. He'd always felt the move had been prompted by the fact that he'd caught pneumonia under the iceman's cart on Colby Avenue.

It rained in Riverhead, too. Once he necked with a girl named Grace McCarthy in the basement of her house while the record player oozed 'Perfidia' and 'Santa Fe Trail', and 'Green Eyes', and the rain stained the small crescent-shaped basement window. They were both fifteen, and they had started by dancing, and he had kissed her suddenly and recklessly in the middle of a dip, and then they had curled up on the sofa and listened to Glenn Miller and necked like crazy fools, expecting Grace's mother to come down to the basement at any moment.

Rain wasn't so bad, he supposed.

Sloshing through the puddles with Meyer Meyer on the way to question the second possibility Kling had pulled from the M.P.B. files, Carella cupped his hand around a match, lighted a cigarette, and flipped the match into the water streaming alongside the kerb.

'You know that cigarette commercial?' Meyer asked.

'Which one?'

'Where the guy is a Thinking Man. You know, a nuclear physicist really, but when we first see him he's developing snap-shots in a darkroom? You know the one?'

'Yeah, what about it?'

'I got a good one for their series.'

'Yeah, let's hear it,' Carella said.

'We see this guy working on a safe, you know? He's drilling a hole in the face of the safe, and he's got his safe-cracking tools on the floor, and a couple of sticks of dynamite, like that.'

'Yeah, go ahead.'

'And the announcer's voice comes in and says, "Hello there, sir." The guy looks up from his work and lights a cigarette. The announcer says, "It must take years of training to become an expert safe-cracker." The guy smiles politely. "Oh, I'm not a safe-cracker," he says. "Safe-cracking is just a hobby with me. I feel a man should have diversified interests." The announcer is very surprised. "Not a safe-cracker?" he asks. "Just a hobby? May I ask then, sir, what you actually do for a living?"'

'And what does the man at the safe answer?' Carella said.

'The man at the safe blows out a stream of smoke,' Meyer said, 'and again he smiles politely. "Certainly, you may ask," he says. "I'm a pimp."' Meyer grinned broadly. 'You like it, Steve?'

'Very good. Here's the address. Don't tell jokes to this lady or she may not let us in.'

'Who's telling jokes? I may quit this lousy job one day and get a job with an advertising agency.'

'Don't do it, Meyer. We couldn't get along without you.'

Together, they entered the tenement. The woman they were looking for was named Martha Livingston, and she had reported the absence of her son, Richard, only a week ago. The boy was nineteen years old, six feet two inches tall, and weighed a hundred and ninety-four pounds. These facts, and these alone, qualified him as a candidate for the person who had once owned the severed hand.

'Which apartment is it?' Meyer asked.

'Twenty-four. Second floor front.'

They climbed to the second floor. A cat in the hallway mewed and then eyed them suspiciously.

'She smells the law on us,' Meyer said. 'She thinks we're from the A.S.P.C.A.'

'She doesn't know we're really street cleaners,' Carella said.

Meyer stooped down to pet the cat as Carella knocked on the door. 'Come on, kitty,' he said. 'Come on, little kitty.'

'Who is it?' a woman's voice shouted. The voice sounded startled.

'Mrs Livingston?' Carella said to the door.

'Yes? Who is it?'

'Police,' Carella said. 'Would you open the door, please?'

'Po –'

And then there was silence.

The silence was a familiar one. It was the silence of sudden discovery and hurried pantomime. Whatever was going on behind that tenement door, Mrs Livingston was not in the apartment alone. The silence persisted. Meyer's hand left the cat's head and went up to the holster clipped to the right side of his belt. He looked at Carella curiously. Carella's .38 was already in his hand.

'Mrs Livingston?' Carella called.

There was no answer from within the apartment.

'Mrs Livingston?' he called again, and Meyer braced himself against the opposite wall, waiting. 'Okay, kick it in,' Carella said.

Meyer brought back his right leg, shoved himself off the wall with his left shoulder, and smashed his foot against the lock in a flat-footed kick that sent the door splintering inward. He rushed into the room behind the opening door, gun in hand.

'Hold it!' he yelled, and a thin man in the process of stepping out onto the fire escape, one leg over the sill, the other still in the room, hesitated for a moment, undecided.

'You'll get wet out there, mister,' Meyer said.

The man hesitated a moment longer, and then came back into the room. Meyer glanced at his feet. He was wearing no socks. He glanced sheepishly at the woman who stood opposite him near the bed. The woman was wearing a slip. There was nothing under it. She was a big blowsy dame of about forty-five with hennaed hair and a drunkard's faded eyes.

'Mrs Livingston?' Carella asked.

'Yeah,' she said. 'What the hell do you mean busting in here?'

'What was your friend's hurry?' Carella asked.

'I'm in no hurry,' the thin man answered.

'No? You always leave a room by the window?'

'I wanted to see if it was still raining.'

'It's still raining. Get over here.'

'What did I do?' the man asked, but he moved quickly to where the two detectives were standing. Methodically, Meyer frisked him, his hands pausing when he reached the man's belt. He pulled a revolver from the man's waist and handed it to Carella.

'You got a permit for this?' Carella asked.

'Yeah,' the man said.

'You'd better have. What's your name, mister?'

'Cronin,' he said. 'Leonard Cronin.'

'Why were you in such a hurry to get out of here, Mr Cronin?'

'You don't have to answer nothing, Lennie,' Mrs Livingston said.

'You a lawyer, Mrs Livingston?' Meyer said.

'No, but . . .'

'Then stop giving advice. We asked you a question, Mr Cronin.'

'Don't tell him nothing, Lennie.'

'Look, Lennie,' Meyer said patiently, 'we got all the time in the world, either here or up at the squad, so you just decide what you're going to say, and then say it. In the meantime, go put on your socks, and you better put on a robe or something, Mrs Livingston, before we get the idea a little hanky-panky was going on in this room. Okay?'

'I don't need no robe,' Mrs Livingston said. 'What I got, you seen before.'

'Yeah, but put on the robe anyway. We wouldn't want you to catch cold.'

'Don't worry about me catching cold, you son-of-a-bitch,' Mrs Livingston said.

'Nice talk,' Meyer answered, shaking his head. Cronin, sitting on the edge of the bed, was pulling on his socks. He was wearing black trousers. A black raincoat was draped over a wooden chair in the corner of the room. A black umbrella dripped water onto the floor near the night-table.

'You were forgetting your raincoat and umbrella, weren't you, Lennie?' Carella said.

Cronin looked up from lacing his shoes. 'I guess so.'

'You'd both better come along with us,' Carella said. 'Put on some clothes, Mrs Livingston.'

◦ Mrs Livingston seized her left breast with her left hand. She aimed it like a pistol at Carella, squeezed it briefly and angrily, and shouted, 'In your eye, cop!'

'Okay, then, come along the way you are. We can add indecent exposure to the prostitution charge the minute we hit the street.'

'Prosti – ! What the hell are you talking about? Boy, you got a nerve!'

'Yeah, I know,' Carella said. 'Let's go, let's go.'

'Why'd you have to bust in here anyway?' Mrs Livingston said. 'What do you want?'

'We come to ask you some questions about your missing son, that's all,' Carella said.

'My son? Is that what this is all about? I hope the bastard is dead. Is that why you broke down the door, for Christ's sake?'

'If you hope he's dead, why'd you bother to report him missing?'

'So I could get relief checks. He was my sole means of support. The minute he took off, I applied for relief. And I had to report him missing to make it legit. That's why. You think I care whether he's dead or alive? Some chance!'

'You're a nice lady, Mrs Livingston,' Meyer said.

'I am a nice lady,' she answered. 'Is there something wrong about a matinee with the man you love?'

'Not if your husband doesn't disapprove.'

'My husband is dead,' she said. 'And in hell.'

'You both behave as if there was a little more than that going on, Mrs Livingston,' Carella said. 'Get dressed. Meyer, take a look through the apartment.'

'You got a search warrant?' the little man asked. 'You got no right to go through this place without a warrant.'

'You're absolutely right, Lennie,' Carella said. 'We'll come back with one.'

'I know my rights,' Cronin said.

'Sure.'

'I know my rights.'

'How about it, lady? Dressed or naked, you're coming over to the station house. Now which will it be?'

'In your eye!' Lady Livingston said.

The patrolmen downstairs all managed to drop up to the Interrogation Room on one pretence or another to take a look at the fat red-headed slob who sat answering questions in her slip. Andy Parker said to Miscolo in the Clerical Office, 'We take a mug shot of her like that, and we'll be able to peddle the photos for five bucks apiece.'

'This precinct got glamour, that's what it's got,' Miscolo answered, and he went back to his typing.

Parker and Hawes went downtown for the search warrant. Upstairs, Meyer and Carella and Lieutenant Byrnes interrogated the two suspects. Byrnes, because he was an older man and presumably less susceptible to the mammalian display, interrogated Martha Livingston in the Interrogation Room off the corridor. Meyer and Carella talked to Leonard Cronin in a corner of the squadroom, far from Lennie's over-exposed paramour.

'Now, how about it, Lennie?' Meyer said. 'You really got a permit for this rod, or are you just snowing us? Come on, you can talk to us.'

'Yeah, I got a permit,' Cronin said. 'Would I kid you guys?'

'I don't think you'd try to kid us, Lennie,' Meyer said gently, 'and we won't try to kid you, either. I can't tell you very much about this, but it can be very serious, take my word for it.'

'How do you mean serious?'

'Well, let's say there could be a lot more involved here than just a Sullivan Act violation. Let's put it that way.'

'You mean because I was banging Martha when you come in? Is that what you mean?'

'No, not that, either. Let's say there is a very big juicy crime involved here maybe. And let's say you could find yourself right in the middle of it. Okay? So level with us from the start, and things may go easier for you.'

'I don't know what big juicy crime you're talking about,' Cronin said.

'Well, you think about it a little,' Carella said.

'You mean the gat? Okay, I ain't got a permit. Is that what you mean?'

'Well, that's not too serious, Lennie,' Meyer said. 'No, we're not thinking about the pistol.'

'Then what? You mean like because Martha's husband ain't really croaked? You mean like because you got us on adultery?'

'Well, even that isn't too serious, Lennie,' Carella said. '*That* we can talk about.'

'Then what? The junk?'

'The *junk*, Lennie?'

'Yeah, in the room.'

'Heroin, Lennie?'

'No, no, hey, no, nothing big like that. The mootah. Just a few sticks, though. Just for kicks. That ain't so serious, now is it?'

'No, that could be very minor, Lennie. Depending on how much marijuana you had there in the room.'

'Oh, just a few sticks.'

'Well then, you've only got a possession rap to worry about. You weren't planning on selling any of that stuff, were you, Lennie?'

'No, no, hey, no, it was just for kicks, just for me and Martha, like you know for kicks. We lit a few sticks before we hopped between the sheets.'

'Then that's not too serious, Lennie.'

'So what's so serious?'

'The boy.'

'What boy?'

'Martha's son. Richard, that's his name, isn't it?'

'How do I know? I never even met the kid.'

'You never met him? How long have you known Martha?'

'I met her last night. In a bar. A joint called The Short-Snorter, you know it? It's run by these two guys, they used to be in the China-Burma-India ...'

'You only met her last night?'

'Sure.'

'She said you were the man she loved,' Carella said.

'Yeah, it was love at first sight.'

'And you never met her son?'

'Never.'

'You ever fly, Lennie?'

'Fly? How do you mean fly? You talking about the marijuana again?'

'No, fly. In an airplane.'

'Never. Just catch me dead in one of them things!'

'How long have you gone for black, Lennie?'

'Black? How do you mean black?'

'Your clothes. Your pants, your tie, your raincoat, your umbrella. Black.'

'I bought them for a funeral,' Cronin said.

'Whose funeral?'

'A buddy of mine. We used to run a crap game together.'

'You ran a crap game, too, Lennie? You've been a busy little man, haven't you?'

'Oh, this wasn't nothing illegal. We never played for money.'

'And your friend died recently, is that right?'

'Yeah. The other day. So I bought the black clothes. Out of respect. You can check. I can tell you the place where I bought them.'

'We'd appreciate that, Lennie. But you didn't own these clothes on Wednesday, did you?'

'Wednesday. Now let me think a minute. What's today?'

'Today is Saturday.'

'Yeah, that's right, Saturday. No. I bought the clothes Thursday. You can check it. They probably got a record.'

'How about you, Lennie?'

'How about me? How so you mean how about me?'

'Have *you* got a record?'

'Well, a little one.'

'How little?'

'I done a little time once. A stickup. Nothing serious.'

'You may do a little more,' Carella said. 'But nothing serious.'

In the Interrogation Room, Lieutenant Byrnes said, 'You're a pretty forthright woman, Mrs Livingston, aren't you?'

'I don't like being dragged out of my house in the middle of the morning,' Martha said.

'Weren't you embarrassed about going downstairs in your slip?'

'No. I keep my body good. I got a good body.'

'What were you and Mr Cronin trying to hide, Mrs Livingston?'

'Nothing. We're in love. I'll shout it from the rooftops.'

'Why did he try to get out of that room?'

'He wasn't trying to get out. He told them what he was trying to do. He wanted to see if it was still raining.'

'So he was climbing out on the fire escape to do that, right?'

'Yeah.'

'Are you aware that your son Richard could be dead at this moment, Mrs Livingston?'

'Who cares? Good riddance to bad rubbish. The people he was hanging around with, he's better off dead. I raised a bum instead of a son.'

'What kind of people was he hanging around with?'

'A gang, a street gang, it's the same story every place in this lousy city. You try to raise a kid right, and what happens? Please, don't get me started.'

'Did your son tell you he was leaving home?'

'No. I already gave all this to another detective when I reported him missing. I don't know where he is, and I don't give a damn, as long as I get my relief cheques. Now that's that.'

'You told the arresting officers your husband was dead. Is that true?'

'He's dead.'

'When did he die?'

'Three years ago.'

'Did he die, or did he leave?'

'It's the same thing, isn't it?'

'Not exactly.'

'He left.'

The room was suddenly very silent.

'Three years ago?'

'Three years ago. When Dickie was just sixteen. He packed up and left. It ain't so easy to raise a boy alone. It ain't so easy. And now he's gone, too. Men stink. They all stink. They all want one thing. Okay, I'll give it to them. But not here.' She tapped her chest. 'Not here inside, where it counts. They all stink. Every single one of them.'

'Do you think your son might have run off with some of his friends?'

'I don't know what he done, the little bastard, and I don't care. Gratitude. I raised him alone after his father left. And this is what I get. He runs out on me. Quits his job and runs out. He's just like all the rest of them, they all stink. You can't trust any man alive. I hope he drops dead, wherever he is. I hope the little bastard drops ...'

And suddenly she was weeping.

She sat quite still in the chair, a woman of forty-five with ridiculously flaming red hair, a big-breasted woman who sat attired only in a silk slip, a fat woman with the faded eyes of a drunkard, and her shoulders did not move, and her face did not move, and her hands did not move, she sat quite still in the hard-backed wooden chair while the tears ran down her face and her nose got red and her teeth clamped into her lips.

'Running out on me,' she said, and then she didn't say anything else. She sat stiffly in the chair, fighting the tears that coursed down her cheeks and her neck and stained the front of her slip.

'I'll get you a coat or something, Mrs Livingston,' Byrnes said.

'I don't need a coat. I don't care who sees me. I don't care. Everybody can see what I am. One look, and everybody can see what I am. I don't need a coat. A coat ain't going to hide nothing.'

Byrnes left her alone in the room, weeping stiffly in the hard-backed chair.

They found exactly thirty-four ounces of marijuana in Martha Livingston's apartment. Apparently, Leonard Cronin was not a very good mathematician. Apparently, too, he was in slightly more serious trouble than he had originally presumed. If, as he'd stated, there had only been a stick or two of marijuana in the room – enough to have made at least two ounces of the stuff – he'd have been charged with possession, which particular crime was punishable by imprisonment of from two to ten years. Now *thirty-four* ounces ain't *two* ounces. And possession of sixteen ounces or more of narcotics other than heroin, morphine, or cocaine created a *rebuttable* presumption of intent to sell, the 'rebuttable' meaning that Cronin could claim he hadn't intended selling it at all, at all. And the maximum term of imprisonment for possession with intent to sell was ten years, the difference between the two charges being that a simple possession rap would usually draw a lesser prison term whereas an intent to sell rap usually drew the limit.

But Cronin had a few other things to worry about. By his own admission, he and Martha Livingston had lit a few sticks before hopping into bed together and Section 2010 of the Penal Law quite bluntly stated: 'Perpetration of an act of intercourse with a female not one's wife who is under the influence of narcotics is punishable by an indeterminate sentence of one day to life or a maximum of twenty years.'

When the gun charge was added to this, and the running of an illegal crap game considered, even if one wished to forget the simple charge of simple adultery – a misdemeanour punishable by imprisonment in a penitentiary or county jail for not more than six months, or by a fine of not more than two hundred and fifty bucks, or by both – even if one wished to forget this minor infraction, Leonard Cronin was going to be a busier little man than he had ever been.

As for Martha Livingston, she'd have been better off exploring Africa. Even allowing for her own conviction that all men stank, she had certainly chosen a prize this time. The narcotics, whomever they belonged to, had been found in her pad. The lady who'd fallen in love at first sight was going to have a hell of a tough row to hoe.

But whatever else lay ahead for the hapless lovers, homicide and butchery would not be included in the charges against them. A check with the clothing store Leonard Cronin named proved that he had indeed purchased his funeral outfit on Thursday. A further check of his rooming-house closet showed that he owned no other black garments. And neither did Mrs Livingston.

There must be a God, after all.

Chapter Eight

On Sunday morning, Cotton Hawes went to church in the rain before reporting to work.

When he came out, it was still raining and he felt much the same as he'd felt before the services. He didn't know why he expected to feel any different; he'd certainly never been washed by any of the great religious fervour which had possessed his minister father. But every Sunday, rain or shine, Cotton Hawes went to church. And every Sunday he sat and listened to the sermon, and he recited the psalms, and he waited. He didn't know exactly what he was waiting for. He suspected he was waiting for a bolt of lightning and an earsplitting crash of thunder which would suddenly reveal the face of God. He supposed that all he really wanted to see was a glimpse of something which was not quite so *real* as the things that surrounded him every day of the week.

For whatever else could be said about police work – and there were countless things to be said, and countless things being said – no one could deny that it presented its practitioners with a view of life which was as real as bread crumbs. Police work dealt with essentials, raw instincts and basic motives, stripped of all the hoop-dee-dah of the sterilized, compressed-in-a-vacuum civilization of the twentieth century. As he walked through the rain, Hawes thought it odd that most of the time consumed by people was spent in sharing the fantasies of another. A thousand escape hatches from reality were available to every manjack in the world – books, the motion pictures, television, magazines, plays, concerts, ballets, anything or everything designed to substitute a pretence of reality, a semblance of real life, a fantasy world for a flesh-and-blood one.

Now perhaps it was wrong for a cop to be thinking this way, Hawes realized, because a cop was one of the fantasy figures in one of the world's escapes: the mystery novel. The trouble was, he thought, that only the fantasy cop was the hero while the *real* cop was just a person. It seemed somehow stupid to him that the most honoured people in the world were those who presented the fantasies, the actors, the directors, the writers, all the various performers whose sole reason for being was to entertain. It was as if a very small portion of the world was actually alive, and these people were alive only in so far as they performed in created fantasies. The rest of the people were observing; the rest of the people were spectators. It would not have been half so sad if these people were viewing the spectacle of real life. Instead, they were observing only a representation of life, so that they became twice-removed from life itself.

Even conversation seemed to concern itself primarily with the fantasy world, and not the real. Did you see Jack Paar last night? Have you read *Doctor Zhivago*? Wasn't *Dragnet* exciting? Did you see the review of *Sweet Bird of Youth*? Talk, talk, talk, but all of the talk had as its nucleus the world of make-believe. And now the television programmes had carried this a step further. More and more channels were featuring people who simply talked about things, so that even the burden of talking about the make-believe world had been removed from the observer's shoulders – there were now other people who would talk it over *for* him. Life became thrice-removed.

And in the midst of this thrice-removed existence, there was reality, and reality for a cop was a hand severed at the wrist.

Now what the hell would they do with that hand on *Naked City*?

He didn't know. He only knew that every Sunday he went to church and looked for something.

On this Sunday, he came out feeling the same as when he'd gone in, and he walked along the shining wet sidewalk bordering the park, heading for the station house. The green globes had been turned on in defence against the rain, the numerals '87' glowing feebly against the slanting grey. He looked up at the dripping stone façade, climbed the low flat steps and entered the muster room. Dave Murchison was sitting behind the desk, reading a movie magazine. The cover showed a picture of Debbie Reynolds, and the headline asked the provocative question *What Will Debbie Do Now?*

He followed the pointing arrow of the DETECTIVE DIVISION sign, climbed the metal steps to the second story, and walked down the long, dim corridor. He shoved through the gate in the slatted railing, tossed his hat at the rack in the corner, and went to his desk. The squadroom was oddly silent. He felt almost as if he were in church again. Frankie Hernandez, a Puerto Rican cop who'd been born and raised in the precinct neighbourhood, looked up and said, 'Hi, Cotton.'

'Hello, Frankie,' he said. 'Steve come in yet?'

'He called in about ten minutes ago,' Hernandez answered. 'Said to tell you he was going straight to the docks to talk to the captain of the *Farren*.'

'Okay,' Hawes said. 'Anything else?'

'Got a report from Grossman on the meat cleaver.'

'What mea – oh yeah, yeah, the Androvich woman.' He paused. 'Any luck?'

'Negative. Not a thing on it but yesterday's roast.'

'Where is everybody, anyway?' Hawes asked. 'It's so quiet around here.'

'There was a burglary last night, grocery store on Culver. Andy and Meyer are out on it. The loot called in to say he'd be late. Wife's got a fever, and he's waiting for the doctor.'

'Isn't Kling supposed to be in today?'

Hernandez shook his head. 'Swapped with Carella.'

'Who's catching, anyway?' Hawes said. 'You got a copy of the duty sheet around?'

'I'm catching,' Hernandez said.

'Boy, it sure is quiet around here,' Hawes said. 'Is Miscolo around? I'd like some tea.'

'He was here a little while ago. I think he went down to talk to the Captain.'

'Days like this . . .' Hawes started, and then let the sentence trail. After a while, he said, 'Frankie, you ever get the feeling that life just isn't real?'

Perhaps he'd asked the wrong person. Life, to Frankie Hernandez, was very real indeed. Hernandez, you see, had taken upon himself the almost impossible task of proving to the world at large that Puerto Ricans could be the *good* guys in life's little drama. He did not know who'd been handling his people's press relations before he happened upon the scene, but he did know that someone was handling it all wrong. He had never had the urge to mug anyone, or knife anyone, or even to have a single puff of a marijuana cigarette. He had grown up in the territory of the 87th Precinct, in one of the worst slums in the world, and he had never so much as stolen a postage stamp, or even a sidelong glance at the whores who paraded *La Via de Putas*. He was a devout Catholic whose father worked hard for a living, and whose mother was concerned solely with the proper upbringing of the four children she had brought into the world. When Hernandez decided to become a cop, his mother and father approved heartily. He became a rookie when he was twenty-two years old, after having served a four-year hitch in the Marines and distinguishing himself in combat during the hell that was Iwo Jima. In his father's candy store, a picture of Frankie Hernandez in full battle dress was pasted to the mirror behind the counter, alongside the Coca Cola sign. Frankie's father never failed to tell any stranger in the store that the picture was of his son Frankie who was now 'a detective in the city's police.'

It hadn't been easy for Hernandez to become a detective in the city's police. To begin with, he'd found a certain amount of prejudice within the department itself, brotherhood edicts notwithstanding. And, coupled with this was a rather peculiar attitude on the part of some of the citizens of the precinct. They felt, he soon discovered, that since he was 'one of them' he was expected to look the other way whenever they became involved in police trouble. Well, unfortunately, Frankie Hernandez was incapable of looking the other way. He had sworn the oath, and he was now wearing the uniform, and he had a job to perform.

And besides, there was The Cause.

Frankie Hernandez had to prove to the neighbourhood, the people of the neighbourhood, the police department, the city, and maybe even the world that Puerto Ricans were people. Colleagues the likes of Andy Parker sometimes made The Cause difficult. Before Andy Parker, there had been patrolmen colleagues who'd made The Cause just as difficult. Hernandez imagined that if he ever became Chief of Detectives or even Police Commissioner, there would be Andy Parker surrounding those high offices, too, ever ready to remind him that The Cause was something to be fought constantly, day and night.

So for Frankie Hernandez, life was always real. Sometimes, in fact, it got too goddamn real.

'No, I never got that feeling, Cotton,' he said.

'I guess it's the rain,' Hawes answered, and he yawned.

The *S.S. Farren* had been named after a famous and honourable White Plains gentleman called Jack Farren. But whereas the flesh-and-blood Farren was a kind, amiable, sympathetic, lovable coot who always carried a clean handkerchief, the namesake looked like a ship which was mean, rotten, rusty, dirty and snot-nosed.

The captain of the ship looked the same way.

He was a hulk of a man with a three-days' beard stubble on his chin. He picked his teeth with a matchbook cover all the while Carella talked to him, sucking air interminably in an attempt to loosen breakfast from his molars. They sat in the captain's cabin, a coffin of a compartment, the bulkheads of which dripped sweat and rust. The captain sucked at his teeth and prodded with his soggy matchbook cover. The rain slanted outside the single porthole. The compartment stank of living, of food, of human waste.

'What can you tell me about Karl Androvich?' Carella asked.

'What do you want to know?' the captain said. His name was Kissovsky. He sounded like a bear. He moved with all the subtle grace of a Panzer division.

'Has he been sailing with you long?'

Kissovsky shrugged. 'Two, three years. He in trouble? What did he get himself into since he jumped ship?'

'Nothing that we know of. Is he a good sailor?'

'Good as most. Sailors ain't worth a damn today. When I was a young man, sailors was sailors.' He sucked air between his teeth.

'Ships were made of wood,' Carella said, 'and men were made of iron.'

'What? Oh, yeah.' Kissovsky tried a smile which somehow formed as a leer. 'I ain't that old, buddy,' he said. 'But we had sailors when I was a kid, not beatniks looking for banana boats so they can practise that ... what do you call it ... Zen? And then come back to write about it. We had men! Men!'

'Then Androvich wasn't a good sailor?'

'Good as most until he jumped ship,' Kissovsky said. 'The minute he jumped ship, he became a bad sailor. I had to make the run down with a man short in the crew. I had the crew stretched tight as it was. One man short didn't help the situation any, I can tell you. A ship is like a little city, buddy. There's guys that sweep the streets, and guys that run the trains, and guys that turn on the lights at night, and guys that run the restaurants, and that's what makes the city go, you see. Okay. You lose the guy who turns on the lights, so nobody can see. You lose the guy who runs the restaurant, so nobody eats. Either that, or you got to find somebody else to do the job, and that means taking him away from another job, so no matter how you slice it, it screws up the china closet. Androvich screwed up the china closet real fine. Besides, he was a lousy sailor, anyway.'

'How so?'

'Out for kicks,' Kissovsky said, tossing one hand upward in a salute to God. 'Live, live, burn, burn, bright like a Roman candle, bullshit! Every port we hit, Androvich went ashore and come back drunk as a fish. And dames? All over the lot! It's a wonder this guy didn't come down with the Oriental Crud or something, the way he was knocking around. Kicks! That's all he was looking for. Kicks!'

'A girl in every port, huh?' Carella said.

'Sure, and drunk as a pig. I used to tell him you got a sweet little wife waiting for you home, you want to bring her back a present from one of these exotic tomatoes, is that what you want to do? He used to laugh at me. Ha, ha, ha. Big joke. Life was a big joke. So he jumps ship, and he screws up the chocolate pudding. That's a sailor, huh?'

'Did he have a girl in this city, too, Captain Kissovsky?'

'Lay off the captain crap, huh?' Kissovsky said. 'Call me Artie, okay, and I'll call you George or whatever the hell your name is, and that way we cut through the fog, okay?'

'It's Steve.'

'Okay. Steve. That's a good name. I got a brother named Steve. He's strong as an ox. He can lift a Mack truck with his bare hands, that kid.'

'Artie, did Androvich have a girl in this city?'

Kissovsky sucked air through his teeth, manoeuvred the matchbook folder around the back of his mouth, and thought. He spit a sliver of food onto the deck, shrugged, and said, 'I don't know.'

'Who *would* know?'

'Maybe the other guys in the crew, but I doubt it. Anything happens on this tub, I know about it. I can tell you one thing. He didn't spend his nights sitting around holding hands with little Lulu Belle or whatever the hell her name is.'

'Meg? His wife?'

'Yeah, Meg. The one he's got tattooed on his arm there. The one he picked up in Atlanta. Beats me how she ever got him to come up with a ring.' Kissovsky shrugged. 'Anyway, she did get him to marry her, but that don't

mean she also got him to sit home tatting doilies. No, sir. This kid was out to
live! No doilies for him. Doilies are for the Sands Spit commuters, not for
the Karl Androviches. You know what he'd do?'

'What?' Carella asked.

'We'd pull into port, you know. I mean here, this city. So he'd wait like
two weeks, living it up all over town, shooting his roll, before he'd call home
to say we were in. And maybe this was like about two days before we were
going to pull out again. Buddy, this kid was giving that girl the business in
both ears. She seems like a nice kid, too. I feel a little sorry for her.' He
shrugged and spit onto the deck again.

'Where'd he go?' Carella asked. 'When he wasn't home? Where'd he hang
out?'

'Wherever there are dames,' Kissovsky said.

'There are dames all over the city.'

'Then that's where he hung out. All over the city. I'll bet you a five-dollar
bill he's with some dame right now. He'll drop in on little Scarlett O'Hara or
whatever the hell her name is, the minute he runs out of money.'

'He only had thirty dollars with him when he vanished,' Carella said.

'Thirty dollars, my eye! Who told you that? There was a big crap game on
the way up from Pensacola. Androvich was one of the winners. Took away
something like seven hundred bucks. That ain't hay, Steve-oh. Add to that
all of January's pay, you know we were holding it until we hit port, and that
adds up to quite a little bundle. And we were only in port here two days. We
docked on the twelfth, and we were shoving off on the fourteenth,
Valentine's Day. So a guy can't spend more than a grand in two days, can
he?' Kissovsky paused thoughtfully. 'The way I figure it, he started back for
the ship, picked up some floozie, and has been living it high on the hog with
her for the past month or so. When the loot runs out, Androvich'll be home.'

'You think he's just having himself a fling, is that it?'

'Just running true to form, that's all. In Nagasaki, when we was there, this
guy . . . well, that's another story.' He paused. 'You ain't worried about him,
are you?'

'Well . . .'

'Don't be. Check the whore houses, and the strip joints, and the bars, anu
Skid Row. You'll find him, all right. Only thing is, I don't think he *wants* to
be found. So what're you gonna do when you latch onto him? *Force* him to go
back to Melissa Lee, or whatever the hell her name is?'

'No, we couldn't do that,' Carella said.

'So what the hell are you bothering for?' Kissovsky sucked air through his
teeth and then spat on the deck. 'Stop worrying,' he said. 'He'll turn up.'

The garbage cans were stacked in the areaway between the two tenements,
and the rain had formed small pools of water on the lid of each can. The old
woman was wearing house slippers, and so she stepped gingerly into the
areaway and tried to avoid the water underfoot, walking carefully to the
closest garbage can, carrying her bag of garbage clutched to her breast like a
sucking infant.

She lifted the lid of the can and shook the water free and was about to drop
her bag into the can when she saw that it was filled. The old lady was Irish,
and she unleashed a torrent of swear words which would have turned a

leprechaun blue, replaced the lid and went to the second garbage can. She was thoroughly drenched now, and she cursed the fact that she hadn't thought to bring an umbrella down with her, cursed the lid of the second garbage can because it seemed to be stuck, finally wrenched it free, soaking herself anew with the water that had been resting on it, and prepared to toss her bag into it and run like hell for the building.

Then she saw the newspaper.

She hesitated for a moment.

The newspaper had been wrapped around something, but the wrapping had come loose. Curiously, the old lady bent closer to the garbage can.

And then she let out a shriek.

Chapter Nine

Everything happened on Monday.

To begin with, Blaney – the Assistant Medical Examiner – officially studied the delightful little package which the patrolman had dug out of the garbage can after a frantic call from the old lady.

The bloody newspaper contained a human hand.

And after duly examining this hand, Blaney phoned the 87th to say that it had belonged to a white male between the ages of 18 and 24, and that unless he was greatly mistaken, it was the mate to the hand he had examined the week before.

Bert Kling took the telephoned message. He barely had strength enough to hold the pencil in his hand as he wrote down the information.

That was the first thing that happened on Monday, and it happened at 9:30 in the morning.

The second thing happened at 11:30 a.m. and it seemed as if the second occurrence would solve once and for all the problem of identification. The second occurrence involved a body which had been washed ashore on the banks of the River Harb. The body had no arms and no head. It was promptly shipped off to the morgue where several things were learned about it.

To begin with, the body was clothed and a wallet in the right hip pocket of the trousers carried a sopping-wet identification card and a driver's licence. The man in the water was known as George Rice. A call to the number listed on the identification card confirmed Blaney's estimate that the body had been in the river for close to two weeks. Apparently, Mr Rice had failed to come home from work one night two weeks ago. His wife had reported him missing, and a sheet on him was allegedly in the files of the M.P.B. Mrs Rice was asked to come down to identify the remains as soon as she was able to. In the meantime, Blaney continued his examination.

And he decided, even though Mr Rice had been only twenty-six years old, and even though Mr Rice was lacking arms and a head, and even though Mr Rice was a good possibility for the person who had owned the two hands that had turned up – he decided after a thorough examination that the body had apparently lost its head and arms through contact with the propeller blades of either a ship or a large boat. And whereas the bloodstain on the bottom of the airline bag had belonged to the 'O' group, the blood of Mr Rice checked out as belonging to the 'AB' group. And whereas the hugeness of the two hands indicated a big fellow, Mr Rice, allowing for his missing head, added up to five feet eight and a half inches, and that is not big.

When Mrs Rice identified the remains through her husband's clothing and a scar on his abdomen – the clothing was not in such excellent shape after having been put through the rigorous test of contact with a boat's propeller and submersion for two weeks, but the scar was still intact – when she made the identification, she also stated that Mr Rice worked in the next state and that he took a ferry to work each morning and returned by ferry each evening, and it therefore seemed more than likely that Mr Rice had either jumped, been pushed, or had fallen from the stern of the ferry and thereby been mutilated by the boat's propellers. A thorough search of the Rice apartment that same day uncovered a suicide note.

And so it was Blaney's unfortunate duty to call the 87th once more and report to Kling, the weary weekend horseman, that the hands he'd been examining over the past few days did *not* belong to the body which had been washed ashore that morning.

So that was that, and the problem of identification still remained to be solved, with the young son of Martha Livingston and the young sailor Karl Androvich still shaping up as pretty good possibilities.

But it was still Monday, a very blue Monday at that because it was raining, and everything was going to happen on Monday.

At 2:00 p.m. the third thing happened.

Two hoodlums were picked up in the next state, and both gave the police an address in Isola. A teletype to City headquarters requesting information netted a B-sheet for one of them, but no record for the other. The boys, it seemed, had held up a Shell station and then tried a hasty escape in a beat-up automobile. So hasty was their departure that they neglected to notice a police car which was cruising along the highway, with the result that they smacked right into the front right fender of the approaching black-and-white sedan, and that was the end of *that* little caper. The boy carrying the gun, the one with the record, was named Robert Germaine.

The other boy, the sloppy driver who'd slammed into the motor patrol car, was named Richard Livingston.

No matter how sloppily you drive a car, it takes two hands – and Richard Livingston was in possession of both of his.

Kling got the information at 3:00 p.m. With weary, shaking fingers, he wrote it down and reminded himself to tell Carella to chalk off a possible victim.

At 4:10 p.m. the telephone rang again.

'Hello,' Kling said.

'Who's this?' a woman's voice asked.

'This is Detective Kling, 87th Squad. Who's this?'

'Mrs Androvich,' the voice said. 'Mrs Karl Androvich.'

'Oh. Hello, Mrs Androvich. What's wrong?'

'Nothing's wrong,' she said.

'I mean, what ...'

'My husband's back,' Meg Androvich said.

'Karl?'

'Yes.'

'He's back?'

'Yes.'

'When did he return?'

'Just a few minutes ago,' she said. She paused for a long time. Then she said, 'He brought me flowers.'

'I'm glad he's back,' Kling said. 'I'll notify the Missing Persons Bureau. Thank you for calling.'

'Not at all,' Meg said. 'Would you do me a favour, please?'

'What's that, Mrs Androvich?'

'Would you please tell that other detective? Carella? Was that his name?'

'Yes ma'am.'

'Would you please tell him?'

'That your husband's back? Yes, ma'am, I'll tell him.'

'No, not that. That's not what I want you to tell him.'

'What *do* you want me to tell him, Mrs Androvich?'

'That Karl brought me flowers. Tell him that, would you? That Karl brought me flowers.' And she hung up.

So that was what happened on Monday.

And that was everything.

The boys still had a pair of hands to work with, and nobody seemed to belong to those hands.

On Tuesday, there was a street rumble, and a fire in the neighbourhood, and a woman who clobbered her husband with a frying pan, and so everybody was pretty busy.

On Wednesday, Steve Carella came back to work. It was still raining. It seemed as if it would never stop raining. A week had gone by since Patrolman Genero had found the first hand.

A whole week had gone by, and the boys were right back where they'd started.

Chapter Ten

The old woman who'd discovered the second hand in the garbage can was named Colleen Brady. She was sixty-four years old, but there was about her a youthfulness which complied faithfully to her given name, so that indeed she seemed to be a colleen.

There is an image that comes instantly to mind whenever an Irish girl is mentioned, an image compounded of one part Saint Patrick's Day to three parts John Huston's *The Quiet One*. The girl has red hair and green eyes, and she runs through the heather beneath a sky of shrieking blue billowing with clouds of pure white, and there is a wild smile on her mouth and you know she will slap you silly if you try to touch her. She is Irish and wild and savage and pure and young, forever young, forever youthful.

And so was Colleen Brady.

She entertained Carella and Hawes as if they were beaux come to call on her with sprigs of hollyhock. She served them tea, and she told them jokes in a brogue as thick as good Irish coffee. Her eyes were green and bright and her skin was as smooth and as fair as a seventeen-year-old's. Her hair was white, but you knew with certainty that it had once been red, and her narrow waist could still be spanned by a man with big hands.

'I saw no one,' she told the detectives. 'Nary a soul. It was a day to keep indoors, it was. I saw no one in the hallway, and no one on the stairs, and no one in the courtyard. It was a right bitter day, and I should have carried down me umbrella, but I didn't. I like to have died from faint when I saw what was in that garbage can. Will y'have more tea?'

'No, thank you, Mrs Brady. You saw no one?'

'No one, aye. And I'm sorry I can't be of more help, for 'tis a gruesome thing to cut a man apart, a gruesome thing. 'Tis a thing for barbarians.' She paused, sipping at her tea, her green eyes alert in her narrow face. 'Have you tried the neighbours? Have you asked them? Perhaps they saw.'

'We wanted to talk to you first, Mrs Brady,' Hawes said.

She nodded. 'Are you Irish, young man?' she asked.

'Part.'

Her green eyes glowed. She nodded secretly and said nothing more, but she studied Hawes with the practised eye of a young girl who'd been chased around the village green more than once.

'Well, we'll be going now, Mrs Brady,' Carella said. 'Thank you very much.'

'Try the neighbours,' she told them. 'Maybe they saw. Maybe one of them saw.'

None of them had seen.

They tried every apartment in Mrs Brady's building and the building adjoining it. Then, wearily, they trudged back to the squadroom in the rain. Hernandez had a message for Carella the moment he walked in.

'Steve, got a call about a half-hour ago from a guy at the M.P.B. He asked for Kling, but I told him he was out, and he wanted to know who else was on the case of the hand in the airline bag, so I told him you were. He said either you or Kling should call him the minute either of you got in.'

'What's his name?'

'It's on the pad there. Bartholomew or something.'

Carella sat at his desk and pulled the pad over. 'Romeo Bartholdi,' he said aloud, and he dialled the Missing Persons Bureau.

'Hello,' he said, 'this is Carella at the 87th Precinct. We got a call here a little while ago from some guy named Bartholdi, said he ...'

'This is Bartholdi.'

'Hi. What's up?'

'What'd you say your name was?'

'Carella.'

'Hello, *paisan*.'

'Hello,' Carella said, smiling. 'What's this all about?'

'Look, I know this is none of my business. But something occurred to me.'

'What is it?'

'A guy named Kling was in last week some time looking through the files. I got to talking to him later, and he told me how you guys found a hand in an airline overnight bag. A guy's hand.'

'Yeah, that's right,' Carella said. 'What about it?'

'Well, *paisan*, this is none of my business. Only he was looking for a possible connection with a disappearance, and he was working through the February stuff, you know.'

'Yeah?'

'He said the bag belonged to an outfit called Circle Airlines, am I right?'

'That's right,' Carella said.

'Okay. This may be reaching, but here it is anyway, for whatever it's worth. My partner and I have been trying to track down a dame who vanished about three weeks ago. She's a stripper, came here from Kansas City in January. Name's Bubbles Caesar. That's not the straight handle, Carella. She was born Barbara Cesare, the Bubbles is for the stage. She's *got* them, too, believe me.'

'Well, what about her?' Carella asked.

'She was reported missing by her agent, a guy named Charles Tudor, on February thirteenth, day before Valentine's Day. What's today's date, anyway?'

'The eleventh,' Carella said.

'Yeah, that's right. Well, that makes it longer than three weeks. Anyway, we've been looking for her all this time, and checking up on her past history, all that. What we found out is this. She flew here from K.C.'

'She did?'

'Yeah, and you can guess the rest. She flew with this Circle Airlines. Now this can be sheer coincidence, or it can amount to something, I don't know. But I thought I'd pass it on.'

'Yeah,' Carella said.

'It's a long shot, I'll admit it. Only there may be a tie-in.'

'How'd she fly?' Carella asked. 'Luxury, Tourist?'

'First Class,' Bartholdi said. 'That's another thing. They give them little bags to First Class passengers, don't they?'

'Yeah,' Carella said.

'Yeah. You know, this may be really far out, but suppose this dame vanished because she done some guy in? I mean, the hand *was* in a Circle Airlines ...' Bartholdi let the sentence trail. 'Well, I admit it's a long shot.'

'We've run out of the other kind,' Carella said. 'What's Tudor's address.'

The Creo Building was situated in midtown Isola, smack on The Stem, and served as an unofficial meeting place for every musician and performer in town. The building was flanked by an all-night cafeteria and a movie house, and its wide entrance doors opened on a marble lobby which would not have seemed out of place in St Peter's. Beyond the lobby, the upper storeys of the building deteriorated into the lesser splendour of unfurnished rehearsal halls and the cubbyhole offices of music publishers, composers, agents, and an occasional ambulance chaser renting telephone and desk space. The men and women who congregated before the entrance doors and in the lobby were a mixed lot.

Here could be seen the hip musicians with the dizzy kicks and the tenor sax cases and the trombone cases discussing openings on various bands, some of them passing around sticks of marijuana, others lost in the religion that was music and needing no outside stimulation. Here, too, were the long-haired classicists carrying oboe cases, wearing soft felt hats, discussing the season in Boston or Dallas, and wondering whether Bernstein would make it at the Philharmonic. Here were the women singers, the canaries, the thrushes whose grins were as trained as their voices, who – no matter how minuscule the band they sang with – entered the arcade like Hollywood movie queens.

Here were the ballet dancers and the modern dancers, wearing short black skirts which permitted freer movement, their high heels clicking on the marble floor, walking with that peculiar duck waddle which seems to be the stamp of all professional dancers. Here were the strippers, the big pale women untouched by the sun, wearing dark glasses and lipstick slashes. Here were the publishers, puffing on cigars and looking like the Russian concept of the American capitalist. And here were the unsuccessful composers, needing haircuts, and here were the slightly successful composers carrying demo records, and here were the really successful composers who sang badly and who played piano more badly but who walked with the cool assurance of jukebox loot spilling out of their ears.

Upstairs, everybody was rehearsing, rehearsing with small combos and big bands, rehearsing with pianos, rehearsing with drums, rehearsing dances and symphonies and improvised jam sessions. The only thing that wasn't rehearsed in the Creo Building was the dialogue going on in the lobby and before the entrance doors.

The dialogue of Charles Tudor may or may not have been rehearsed, it was difficult to tell. His small office was on the eighteenth floor of the building. Two tall, pale, buxom girls carrying hatboxes were sitting on a wooden bench in the waiting room. A short, rosy-cheeked, flat-chested girl was sitting behind a desk at the far end of the room. Carella went to her, flashed the tin, and said, 'We're from the police. We'd like to talk to Mr Tudor, please.'

The receptionist studied first Hawes, then Carella. The two pale strippers on the bench turned a few shades paler. The taller of the two rose abruptly, picked up her hatbox, and hastily departed. The second busied herself with a copy of *Variety*.

'What's this in reference to?' the receptionist asked.

'We'll discuss that with Mr Tudor,' Carella said. 'Would you mind telling him we're here?'

The girl pulled a face and pressed a stud in the phone on her desk. 'Mr Tudor,' she said into the mouthpiece, 'there are a couple of gentlemen here who *claim* to be detectives. Well, they said they'd discuss that with you, Mr Tudor. I couldn't say, I've never met a detective before. Yes, he showed me a badge. Yes, sir.' She hung up.

'You'll have to wait a minute. He's got somebody with him.'

'Thank you,' Carella said.

They stood near the desk and looked around the small waiting room. The second stripper sat motionless behind her *Variety*, not even daring to turn the page. The walls of the room were covered with black-and-white photos of strippers in various provocative poses. Each of the photographs was signed. Most of them started with the words 'To Charlie, who...' and ended with exotic names like Flame or Torch or Maja or Exota or Bali. Hawes walked around the room looking at the photos. The girl behind the copy of *Variety* followed him with her eyes.

Finally, in a very tiny voice which seemed even smaller issuing from such a big woman, she said, 'That's me.'

Hawes turned. 'Huh?' he asked.

'With the furs. The picture you were looking at. It's me.'

'Oh. Oh,' Hawes said. He turned to look at the picture again. Turning back to the girl, he said, 'I didn't recognize you with your ...' and then stopped and grinned.

The girl shrugged.

'Marla? Is that your name? The handwriting isn't too clear.'

'Marla, that's it,' she said. 'It's really Mary Lou, but my first agent changed it to Marla. That sounds exotic, don't you think?'

'Yes, yes, very,' Hawes agreed.

'What's your name?'

'Hawes.'

'That's all?'

'Well, no. Cotton is my first name. Cotton Hawes.'

The girl stared at him for a moment. Then she asked, 'Are *you* a stripper, too?' and burst out laughing. 'Excuse me,' she said, 'but you have to admit that's a pretty exotic name.'

'I guess so,' Hawes said, grinning.

'Is Mr Tudor in some trouble?' Marla asked.

'No.' Hawes shook his head. 'No trouble.'

'Then why do you want to see him?'

'Why do *you* want to see him?' Hawes asked.

'To get a booking.'

'Good luck,' Hawes said.

'Thank you. He's a good agent. He handles a lot of exotic dancers. I'm sure he'll get me something.'

'Good,' Hawes said. 'I hope so.'

The girl nodded and was silent for a while. She picked up the copy of *Variety*, thumbed through it, and then put it down again. 'You still haven't told me why you want to see Mr Tudor,' she said, and at that moment the door to the inner office opened and a statuesque brunette wearing heels which made her four inches taller stepped into the waiting room, bust first.

'Thanks a lot, Charlie,' she yelled, almost colliding with Carella to whom she hastily said, 'Oh, pardon me, dearie,' and then clattered out of the room.

The phone on the receptionist's desk buzzed. She lifted the receiver. 'Yes, Mr Tudor,' she said, and then hung up. 'Mr Tudor will see you now,' she said to Carella.

'Good luck,' Marla said to Hawes as he moved past the bench.

'Thank you,' Hawes said. 'The same to you.'

'If I ever need a cop or something,' she called after him, 'I'll give you a ring.'

'Do that,' Hawes said, and he followed Carella into Tudor's office. The office was decorated with more photographs of exotic dancers, so many photographs that both Tudor and his desk were almost lost in the display. Tudor was a huge man in his late forties wearing a dark-brown suit and a pale-gold tie. He possessed a headful of short black hair which was turning white at the temples, and a black Ernie Kovacs moustache. He was smoking a cigarette in a gold-and-black cigarette holder. He gestured the detectives to chairs, and a diamond pinky ring glistened on his right hand.

'I understand you're policemen,' he said. 'Does this have anything to do with Barbara?'

'Yes, sir,' Carella said. 'We understand that you were the gentleman who reported Miss Caesar missing.'

'Yes,' Tudor said. 'You must forgive my rudeness when my receptionist announced you. I sometimes get calls from policemen which have nothing whatever to do with ... well, something as serious as Barbara.'

'What kind of calls, Mr Tudor?' Hawes asked.

'Oh, you know. A show is closed down someplace, and some of my girls are in it, and immediately the police make an association. I only find employment for these girls. I don't tell them how to observe the rules of propriety.' Tudor shrugged. His speech was curious in that it was absolutely phony. He spoke with the clipped precision of an Englishman, and one received the impression that he chose his words carefully before allowing them to leave his mouth. But the elegant tones and rounded vowels were delivered in the harshest, most blatant city accent Carella had ever heard. And the odd part was that Tudor didn't seem at all aware of the accent that stamped him as a native of either Isola or Calm's Point. Blithely, he clipped his words immaculately and seemed under the impression that he was a member of the House of Lords delivering a speech to his fellow peers.

'I really am not responsible for whatever acts my clients wish to concoct,' Tudor said. 'I wish the police would realize that. I am a booking agent, not a choreographer.' He smiled briefly. 'About Barbara,' he said. 'What have you heard?'

'Nothing at all, Mr Tudor. We were hoping you could tell us a little more about her.'

'Oh.'

Tudor uttered only that single word, but disappointment was evident in it, and disappointment showed immediately afterward on his face.

'I'm sorry if we raised your hopes, Mr Tudor,' Carella said.

'That's all right,' Tudor said. 'It's just ...'

'She meant a lot to you, this girl?'

'Yes,' Tudor answered. He nodded his head. 'Yes.'

'In a business way?' Hawes asked.

'Business?' Tudor shook his head again. 'No, not business. I've handled better strippers. *Am* handling better ones now. That little girl who just left my office. Her name is Pavan, got here from Frisco last July and has just about set this metropolis on fire. Excellent. Absolutely excellent, and she's only twenty years old, would you believe it? She has a long future ahead of her, that girl. Barbara was no child, you know.'

'How old is she?'

'Thirty-four. Of course, there are strippers who keep performing until they're well into their fifties. I don't know of any performers, or of any *women* for that matter, who take as much pride in their bodies as exotic dancers do. I suppose there's an element of narcissism involved. Or perhaps we're looking too deep. They know their bodies are their fortunes. And so they take care of themselves. Barbara, though she was thirty-four, possessed ...' Tudor stopped short. 'Forgive me. I must get out of the habit of using the past tense in speaking about her. It's simply that, when a person leaves, disappears, that person is thought of as being *gone*, and the tongue plays its trick. Forgive me.'

'Are we to understand, Mr Tudor, that there was something more than a strict business relationship between you and Miss Caesar?'

'More?' Tudor said.

'Yes, was there ...'

'I love her,' Tudor said flatly.

The room was silent.

'I see,' Carella said.

'Yes,' Tudor paused for a long time. 'I love her. I still love her. I must keep remembering that. I must keep remembering that I still love her, and that she is still here.'

'Here?'

'Yes. Here. Somewhere. In this city. She is still here.' Tudor nodded. 'Nothing has happened to her. She is the same Barbara, laughing, lovely ...' He stopped himself. 'Have you seen her picture, gentlemen?'

'No,' Carella said.

'I have some, I believe. Would they help you?'

'Yes, they would.'

'I have already given some to the Missing Persons Bureau. Are you from the Missing Persons Bureau?'

'No.'

'No, I didn't think you were. Then what is your interest in Barbara?'

'We're acting in an advisory capacity,' Carella lied.

'I see,' Tudor stood up. He seemed taller on his feet, a man bigger than six feet who walked with economy and grace to the filing cabinet in one corner of the room. 'I think there are some in here,' he said. 'I usually have pictures taken as soon as I put a girl under contract. I had quite a few taken of Barbara when she first came to me.'

'When was this, Mr Tudor?'

Tudor did not look up from the files. His hands worked busily as he spoke. 'January. She came here from Kansas City. A friend of hers in a show there recommended me to her. I was the first person she met in this city.'

'She came to you first, is that correct, Mr Tudor?'

'Straight from the airport. I helped her get settled. I fell in love with her the moment I saw her.'

'Straight from the airport?' Carella asked.

'What? Yes. Ah, here are the pictures.' He turned from the files and carried several glossy prints to his desk. 'This is Barbara, gentlemen. Bubbles Caesar. Beautiful, isn't she?'

Carella did not look at the pictures. 'She came straight from the airport, you say?'

'Yes. Most of these pictures ...'

'Was she carrying any luggage?'

'Luggage? Yes, I believe so. Why?'

'What kind of luggage?'

'A suitcase, I believe. A large one.'

'Anything else?'

'I don't remember.'

'Was she carrying a small, blue overnight bag?' Hawes asked.

Tudor thought for a moment. 'Yes, I think she was. One of those small bags the airlines give you. Yes, she was.'

'Circle Airlines, Mr Tudor?'

'I don't remember. I have the impression it was Pan American.'

Carella nodded and picked up the photographs. The girl Barbara 'Bubbles' Caesar did not seem to be thirty-four years old, not from the photographs, at any rate. The pictures showed a clear-eyed, smiling brunette loosely draped in what seemed to be a fisherman's net. The net did very little to hide the girl's assets. The girl had assets in abundance. And coupled with these was the provocative look that all strippers wore after they'd ceased to wear anything else. Bubbles Caesar looked out of the photographs with an expression that clearly invited trouble. Studying the photos, Carella was absolutely certain that this was the identical look which Eve had flashed at Adam after taking her midday fruit. The look spelled one thing and one thing alone and, even realizing that the look was an acquired one, a trick of the girl's trade, Carella studied the photos and found that his palms were getting wet.

'She's pretty,' he said inadequately.

'The pictures don't do her justice,' Tudor said. 'She has a complexion like a peach and . . . and a vibration that can only be sensed through knowing her. There are people who vibrate, gentlemen. Barbara is one of them.'

'You said you helped her get settled, Mr Tudor. What, exactly, did you do?'

'I got a hotel for her, to begin with. Until she found a place of her own. I advanced her some money. I began seeing her regularly. And, of course, I got a job for her.'

'Where?'

'The King and Queen. It's an excellent club.'

'Where's that, Mr Tudor?'

'Downtown, in The Quarter. I've placed some very good girls there. Pavan started there when she came here from Frisco. But, of course, Pavan had big-time quality, and I moved her out very fast. She's working on The Street now. A place called The String of Pearls. Do you know it?'

'It sounds familiar,' Carella said. 'Miss Caesar was not bigtime in your opinion, is that right?'

'No. Not bad. But not Big-time.'

'Despite those . . . vibrations.'

'The vibrations were a part of her personality. Sometimes they come over on the stage, sometimes they don't. Believe me, if Barbara could have incorporated this . . . this inner glow into her act, she'd have been the biggest ever, the biggest. Bar none. Gypsy Rose Lee, Margie Hart, Zorita, Lili St Cyr, I tell you Barbara would have outshone them all. But no.' He shook his head. 'She was a second-rate stripper. Nothing came across the footlights but that magnificent body and, of course, the look that all strippers wear. But not the glow, not the vibrations, not the . . . the life force, call it what you will.

These only came from knowing her. There is a difference, you understand.'

'Was she working at The King and Queen when she disappeared?'

'Yes. She didn't show up for the show on February twelfth. The owner of the club reported this to me as her agent, and I called her apartment. She was living at the time with two other girls. The one who answered the phone told me that she hadn't seen her since early that morning. I got alarmed, and I went out to look for her. This is a big city, gentlemen.'

'Yes.'

'The next morning, the thirteenth, I called the police.' Tudor paused. He looked past the detectives and through the window where the rain dripped steadily against the red brick of the Creo Building. 'I had bought her a necklace for Valentine's Day. I was going to give it to her on Valentine's Day.' He shook his head. 'And now she's gone.'

'What kind of a necklace, Mr Tudor?'

'A ruby necklace. She has black hair, you know, very black, and deep brown eyes. I thought rubies, I thought the fire of rubies ...' He paused again. 'But she's gone, isn't she?'

'Who owns The King and Queen, Mr Tudor?'

'A man named Randy Simms. Randolph is his full name, I believe, but everyone calls him Randy. He runs a very clean establishment. Do you plan to call on him?'

'Yes. Maybe he can give us some help.'

'Find her, would you?' Tudor said. 'Oh, God, please find her.'

Chapter Eleven

The King and Queen was actually on the outermost fringe of The Quarter, really closer to the brownstone houses which huddled in the side streets off Hall Avenue than to the restaurants, coffee houses, small theatres and art shops which were near Canopy Avenue.

The place was a step-down club, its entrance being one step down from the pavement. To the right of the entrance doorway was a window which had been constructed of pieces of coloured glass in an attempt to simulate a stained-glass window. The coloured panes showed a playing-card portrait of a king on the left, and a playing-card portrait of a queen on the right. The effect was startling, lighted from within so that it seemed as if strong sunlight were playing in the glass. The effect, too, was dignified and surprising. Surprising because one expected something more blatant of a strip joint, the life-sized placards out front featuring an Amazonian doll in the middle of a bump or a grind. There were no placards outside this club. Nor was there a bold display of typography announcing the name of the place. A small, round, gold escutcheon was set off centre in the entrance door, and this was the only indication of the club's name. The address – '12N.' – was engraved onto another round gold plaque set in the lower half of the door.

Hawes and Carella opened the door and walked in.

The club had that same slightly tired, unused look that most night clubs had during the daytime. The look was always startling to Carella. It was as if one suddenly came across a middle-aged woman dressed in black satin and wearing diamonds at ten o'clock in the morning in Schrafft's. The King and Queen looked similarly overdressed and weary during the daylight hours, and perhaps more lonely. There wasn't a sign of life in the place.

'Hello!' Carella called. 'Anybody home?'

His voice echoed into the long room. A window at the far end admitted a single grey shaft of rain-dimmed light. Dust motes slid down the shaft of light, settled silently on the bottoms of deserted chairs stacked on round tables.

'Hello?' he called again.

'Empty,' Hawes said.

'Looks that way. Anybody here?' Carella yelled again.

'Who is it?' a voice answered. 'We don't open until SIX p.m.'

'Where are you?' Carella shouted to the voice.

'In the kitchen. We're closed.'

'Come on out here a minute, will you?'

A man appeared suddenly in the gloom, wiping his hands on a dish towel. He stepped briefly into the narrow shaft of light and then walked to where the two detectives were standing.

'We're closed,' he said.

'We're cops,' Carella answered.

'We're still closed. Especially to cops. If I served you, I'd get my liquor licence yanked.'

'You Randy Simms?' Hawes asked.

'That's me,' Simms said. 'Why? What'd I do?'

'Nothing. Can we sit down and talk someplace?'

'Anyplace,' Simms said. 'Choose your table.'

They pulled chairs off one of the tables and sat. Simms was a sandy-haired man in his late forties, wearing a white dress shirt open at the throat, the sleeves rolled up. There was a faintly bored expression on his handsome face. He looked like a man who spent his summers at St Tropez at home among the girls in the bikinis, his winters at St Moritz skiing without safety bindings. Carella was willing to bet he owned a Mercedes-Benz and a collection of Oriental jade.

'What's this about?' Simms asked. 'Some violation? I had the other doors put in, and I put up the occupancy signs. So what is it this time?'

'We're not firemen,' Carella said. 'We're cops.'

'What difference does it make? Cops or firemen, whenever either of them come around, it costs me money. What is it?'

'You know a girl named Bubbles Caesar?'

'I do,' Simms said.

'She work for you?'

'She used to work for me, yes.'

'Any idea where she is?'

'Not the vaguest. Why? Did she do something?'

'She seems to have disappeared.'

'Is that a crime?'

'Not necessarily.'

'Then why do you want her?'

'We want to talk to her.'

'You're not alone,' Simms said.

'What do you mean?'

'Only that everybody who ever walked into this joint wanted to talk to Barbara, that's all. She's a very attractive girl. A pain in the ass, but very attractive.'

'She gave you trouble?'

'Yes, but not in a professional sense. She always arrived on time, and she did her act when she was supposed to, and she was friendly with the customers, so there was no trouble that way.'

'Then what way *was* there trouble?'

'Well, there were a couple of fights in here.'

'Over Barbara?'

'Yes.'

'Who?'

'What do you mean, who?'

'Who did the fighting?'

'Oh, I don't remember,' Simms said. 'Customers. It's a funny thing with strippers. A man watches a woman take off her clothes, and he forgets he's in a public place and that the girl is a performer. He enters a fantasy in which he is alone with this girl, and she's taking off her clothes only for *him*. Well, sometimes the fantasy persists after the lights go up. And when two guys share the same fantasy, there can be trouble. A man who thinks the girl belongs to *him*, is undressing for *him*, doesn't like the idea of another guy sharing the same impression. Bang, the fists explode. So we heave them out on the sidewalk. Or at least we did. No more now.'

'Now you let them fight?' Hawes asked.

'No. Now we don't give them a chance to fantasize.'

'How do you prevent that?'

'Simple. No strippers.'

'Oh? Have you changed the club's policy?'

'Yep. No strippers, no band, no dancing. Just a high-class jazz pianist, period. Drinks, dim lights, and cool music. You bring your own broad, and you hold hands with *her*, not with some dame wiggling on the stage. We haven't had a fight in the past two weeks.'

'What made you decide on this new policy, Mr Simms?'

'Actually, Barbara had a lot to do with it. She provoked a lot of the fights. I think she did it purposely. She'd pick out two of the biggest guys in the audience, and split her act between them. First one guy, then the other. Afterwards, when she came out front, she'd play up to both of them, and bang, came the fists. Then she didn't show up for work one night, so I was left with a string of second-run strippers and no headliner. It looked like amateur night at The King and Queen. And the trouble with the band, believe me, it wasn't worth it.'

'What kind of trouble with the band?'

'Oh, all kinds. One of the guys on the band was a hophead, the trombone player. So I never knew whether he was going to show up for work or be found puking in some gutter. And then the drummer took off without a word, just didn't show up one night. The drummer is a very important man in a band that accompanies strippers. So I was stuck without a headliner and without a drummer. So you can imagine what kind of a show I had that night.'

'Let me get this straight,' Carella said. 'Are you saying that Barbara and this drummer both disappeared at the same time?'

'The same night, yes.'

'This was when?'

'I don't remember when exactly. A few days before Valentine's Day, I think.'

'What was this drummer's name?'

'Mike something. An Italian name. A real tongue twister. I can't remember it. It started with a C.'

'Were Barbara and Mike very friendly?'

'They didn't seem to be, no. At least, I never noticed anything going on between them. Except the usual patter that goes on between the girls in the show and the band. But nothing special. Oh, I see,' Simms said. 'You think they took off together, is that it?'

'I don't know,' Carella said. 'It's a possibility.'

'Anything's possible with strippers and musicians,' Simms agreed. 'I'm better off without them, believe me. This piano player I've got now, he plays very cool music, and everybody sits and listens in the dark, and it's great. Quiet. I don't need fist fights and intrigue.'

'You can't remember this drummer's last name.'

'No.'

'Try.'

'It began with a C, that's all I can tell you. Italian names throw me.'

'What was the name of the band?' Carella said.

'I don't think it had a name. It was a pickup band.'

'It had a leader, didn't it?'

'Well, he wasn't exactly a leader. Not the type anybody would want to be taken to, if you follow me. He was just the guy who rounded up a bunch of musicians for the job.'

'And what was his name?'

'Elliot. Elliot Chambers.'

'One other thing, Mr Simms,' Carella said. 'Barbara's agent told us she was living with two other girls when she disappeared. Would you know who those girls were?'

'I know one of them,' Simms said without hesitation. 'Marla Phillips. She used to be in the show, too.'

'Would you know where she lives?'

'She's in the book,' Simms said. He paused and looked at the detectives. 'Is that it?'

'That's it,' Carella said.

Outside, Hawes said, 'What do you make of it?'

Carella shrugged. 'I'm going to check with the musician's local, see if I can't get a last name for this Mike the drummer.'

'Do drummers have big hands?'

'Search me. But it looks like more than coincidence, doesn't it? Both of them taking a powder on the same night?'

'Yeah, it does,' Hawes said. 'What about Marla Phillips?'

'Why don't you drop in and pay a visit?'

'All right,' Hawes said.

'See what a nice guy I am? I tackle the musicians' union, and I leave the stripper to you.'

'You're a married man,' Hawes said.

'And a father,' Carella added.

'*And* a father, that's right.'

'If you need any help, I'll be back at the squad.'

'What help could I possibly need?' Hawes asked.

Marla Phillips lived on the ground floor of a brownstone four blocks from The King and Queen. The name plate on the mailboxes listed a hyphenated combination of three names: Phillips-Caesar-Smith. Hawes rang the bell, waited for the responding buzz that opened the inner door, and then stepped into the hallway. The apartment was at the end of the hall. He walked to it, rang the bell set in the door jamb, and waited. The door opened almost instantly.

Marla Phillips looked at him and said, 'Hey!'

He recognized her instantly, of course, and then wondered where his mind was today. He had made no connection with the name when Simms had first mentioned it.

'Aren't you the cop who was in Mr Tudor's office?' Marla asked.

'That's me,' he said.

'Sure. Cotton something. Well, come on in, Cotton. Boy, this is a surprise. I just got home a minute ago. You're lucky you caught me. I have to leave in about ten minutes. Come in, come in. You'll catch cold standing in the hallway.'

Hawes went into the apartment. Standing next to Marla, he realized how tall she truly was. He tried to visualize her on a runway, but the thought was staggering. He followed her into the apartment instead.

'Don't mind the underwear all over the place,' Marla said. 'I live with another girl. Taffy Smith. She's an actress. Legit. Would you like a drink?'

'No, thank you,' Hawes said.

'Too early, huh? Look, will you do me a favour?'

'Sure,' Hawes said.

'I have to call my service to see if there was anything for me while I was out. Would you feed the cat, please? The poor thing must be starved half to death.'

'The cat?'

'Yeah, he's a Siamese, he's wandering around here somewhere. He'll come running into the kitchen the minute he hears you banging around out there. The cat food is under the sink. Just open up a can and put some in his bowl. And would you heat some milk for him? He can't stand cold milk.'

'Sure,' Hawes said.

'You're a honey,' she told him. 'Go ahead now, feed him. I'll be with you in a minute.'

She went to the telephone and Hawes went into the kitchen. As he opened the can of cat food under the watchful eyes of the Siamese who had materialized instantly, he listened to Marla in the other room.

'A Mr Who?' she asked the telephone. 'Well, I don't know anybody by that name, but I'll give him a ring later in the afternoon. Anyone else? Okay, thank you.'

She hung up and walked into the kitchen.

'Are you still warming the milk?' she asked. 'It'll be too hot. You'd better take it off now.' Hawes took off the saucepan and poured the milk into the bowl on the floor.

'Okay, now come with me,' Marla said. 'I have to change, do you mind? I've got a sitting in about five minutes. I do modelling on the side. Cheesecake, you know. For the men's magazines. I've got to put on some fancy lingerie. Come on, come on, please hurry. This way.'

He followed her into a bedroom that held two twin beds, a huge dresser, several chairs, and an assortment of soiled cardboard coffee containers, wooden spoons, and clothing piled haphazardly on the floor and on the top of every available surface.

'Forgive the mess,' Marla said. 'My roommate is a slob.' She took off her suit jacket and threw it on the floor, slipping out of her pumps at the same time. She began pulling her blouse out of her skirt and then said, 'Would you mind turning your back? I hate to be a prude, but I am.'

Hawes turned his back, wondering why Marla Phillips thought it perfectly all right to take off her clothes in a night club before the eyes of a hundred men, but considered it indecent to perform the same act in a bedroom before the eyes of a single man. *Women*, he thought, and he shrugged mentally. Behind him, he could hear the frantic swishing of cotton and silk.

'I hate garter belts,' she said. 'I'm a big girl. I need something to hold me in. What's supposed to be so damn sexy about a garter belt, anyway, would you mind telling me? What was it you wanted, Cotton?'

'Somebody told us you used to room with Bubbles Caesar. Is that right?'

'Yes, that's right. Oh, goddamnit, I've got a run.' She pushed past him half-naked, bent over to pull a pair of stockings from the bottom drawer of the dresser, and then vanished behind his back again. 'Excuse me,' she said. 'What about Barbara?'

'Did she live with you?'

'Yes. Her name is still in the mailbox. There, that's better. Whenever I'm in a hurry, I tear stockings. I don't know what they make them out of these days. Tissue paper, I think. I'll have to take her name out, I suppose. When I get the time. Boy, if I only had time to do all the things I want to do. What about Barbara?'

'When did she move out?'

'Oh, you know. When there was that big fuss. When Mr Tudor reported her missing and all.'

'Around St Valentine's Day.'

'Yes, around that time.'

'Did she tell you she was going?'

'No.'

'Did she take her clothes with her?'

'No.'

'Her clothes are still here?'

'Yes.'

'Then she didn't really *move* out, she just never showed up again.'

'Yes, but she'll probably be back. Okay, you can turn now.'

Hawes turned. Marla was wearing a simple black dress, an offshade of black nylon stockings, and high-heeled black pumps. 'Are my seams straight?' she asked.

'Yes, they seem perfectly straight.'

'Do you like my legs? Actually, my legs are too skinny for the rest of me.'

'They seem okay to me,' Hawes said. 'What makes you think Barbara will be back?'

'I have the feeling she's shacking up with somebody. She likes men, Barbara does. She'll be back. I guess that's why I really haven't taken her name out of the mailbox.'

'These men she likes,' Hawes said. 'Was Mike the drummer one of them?'

'Not that I know of. At least, she never talked about him or anything. And he never called here. Excuse me, I have to put on a new face.'

She shoved Hawes aside and sat at the counter top before the large mirror. The counter was covered with cosmetics. Among the other jars and bottles, Hawes noticed a small jar labelled Skinglow. He picked it up and turned it over in his hands.

'This yours?' he asked.

'What?' Marla turned, lipstick brush in one hand. 'Oh. Yes. Mine, *and* Taffy's, *and* Barbara's. We all use it. It's very good stuff. It doesn't fade out under the lights. Sometimes, under the lights, your body looks *too* white, do you know? It's all right to look white, but not ghostly. So we use the Skinglow, and it takes off the pallor. A lot of strippers and actresses use it.'

'Do you know Mike's last name?'

'Sure. Chirapadano. It's a beaut, isn't it?'

'Does he have big hands?'

'All men have big hands,' Marla said.

'I mean, did you notice that his hands were unusually large?'

'I never noticed. The only thing I noticed about that band was that they all had six hands.'

'Mike included?'

'Mike included.' She turned to him. 'How do I look? What time is it?'

'You look fine. It's –' he glanced at his watch – 'twelve-fifteen.'

'I'm late,' she said flatly. 'Do I look sexy?'

'Yes.'

'Well, okay then.'

'Do you know any of the men Barbara saw?' Hawes asked. 'Any she might run away with?'

'Well, there was one guy who called her an awful lot. Listen, I'm sorry I'm giving you this bum's rush act, but I really have to get out of here. Why don't you call me sometime? You're awfully cute. Or if you're in the neighbourhood some night, drop in. She's always serving coffee, that goddamn screwy roommate of mine.'

'I might do that,' Hawes said. 'Who was this person who called Barbara a lot?'

'Oh, what was his name? He sounded like a Russian or something. Just a minute,' she said, 'I'll think of it.' She opened a drawer, took a black purse from it, and hastily filled it with lipstick, mascara, change, and a small woman's wallet. 'There, that's that,' she said. 'Do I have the address? Yes.'

She paused. 'Androvich, that was the name. Karl Androvich. A sailor or something. Look, Cotton, will you call me sometime? You're not married or anything, are you?'

'No. Did you say Androvich?'

'Yes. Karl Androvich. Will you call me? I think it might be fun. I'm not always in such a crazy rush.'

'Well, sure, but ...'

'Come on, I've got to go. You can stay if you want to, just slam the door on the way out, it locks itself.'

'No, I'll come with you.'

'Are you going uptown?'

'Yes.'

'Good, we can share a cab. Come on, hurry. Would you like to come to the sitting? No, don't, I'll get self-conscious. Come on, come on. Slam the door! Slam the door, Cotton!'

He slammed the door.

'I'm wearing this black stuff that's supposed to be imported from France. The bra is practically nonexistent. These pictures ought to ...'

'When did Androvich last call her?' Hawes asked.

'A few days before she took off,' Marla said. 'There's a cab. Can you whistle?'

'Yes, sure, but ...'

'Whistle!'

Hawes whistled. They got into the cab together.

'Oh, where the hell did I put that address?' Marla said. 'Just a minute,' she told the cabbie. 'Start driving uptown on Hall, I'll have the address for you in a minute. Do you think she ran off with Androvich? Is that possible, Cotton?'

'I doubt it. Androvich is home. Unless ...'

'Unless what?'

'I don't know. I guess we'll have to talk to Androvich.'

'Here's the address,' Marla said to the cabbie, '695 Hall Avenue. Would you hurry, please? I'm terribly late.'

'Lady,' the cabbie answered. 'I have never carried a passenger in this vehicle who *wasn't* terribly late.'

Chapter Twelve

At the squadroom, Hawes told Carella, 'I found out the drummer's name.'

'So did I. I got Chambers' number from the union, and I called him. Drummer's name is Mike Chirapadano. I called the union back and got an address and telephone number for him, too.'

'Call him yet?' Hawes asked.

'Yes. No answer. I'd like to stop by there later this afternoon. Have you had lunch yet?'

'No.'

'Let's.'

'Okay. We've got another stop to make, too.'

'Where?'

'Androvich.'

'What for? Lover Boy is back, isn't he?'

'Sure. But Bubbles' roommate told me Androvich was in the habit of calling her.'

'The roommate?'

'No. Bubbles.'

'Androvich? Androvich was calling Bubbles Caesar?'

'Uh-huh.'

'So *he's* back in it again, huh?'

'It looks that way. He called her a few days before she vanished, Steve.'

'Mmm. So what does that mean?'

'He's the only guy who would know, it seems to me.'

'Yeah. Okay. Lunch first, then Chirapadano – Jesus, that *is* a tongue twister – and then our amorous sailor friend. Cotton, there are times when I get very very weary.'

'Have you ever tried running a footrace with a stripper?' Hawes asked.

Mike Chirapadano lived in a furnished room on North Sixth. He was not in when the detectives dropped by, and his landlady told them he had not been around for the past month.

The landlady was a thin bird of a woman in a flowered housedress. She kept dusting the hallway while they spoke to her.

'He owes me almost two months' rent,' she said. 'Is he in some trouble?'

'When did you last see him, Mrs Marsten?' Hawes asked.

'In Feb-uary,' she answered. 'He owes me for Feb-uary, and he also owes me for March, if he's still living here. The way it looks to me, he ain't living here no more. Don't it look that way to you?'

'Well, I don't know. I wonder if we could take a look at his room.'

'Sure. Don't make no nevermind to me. What's he done? He a dope fiend? All these musicians are dope fiends, you know.'

'Is that right?' Carella asked as they walked upstairs.

'Sure. Main-liners. That means they shoot it right into their veins.'

'Is that right?'

'Sure. It's poison you know. That hero-in they shoot into their veins. That stuff. It's poison. His room is on the third floor. I was up there cleaning only yesterday.'

'Is his stuff still up there?'

'Yep, his clothes and his drums, too. Now why would a man take off like that and leave his belongs behind? He must be a dope fiend is the only way I can figure it. Here, it's down the end of the hall. What did you say he done?'

'Would you know exactly when in February he left, Mrs Marsten?'

'I would know exactly to the day,' the landlady said, but she did not offer the information.

'Well when?' Hawes asked.

'Feb-uary twelfth. It was the day before Friday the thirteenth, and that's how I remember. Friday the thirteenth, that's a hoodoo day if ever there was one. Here's his room. Just a second now, while I unlock the door.'

She took a key from the pocket of her dress and fitted it into the keyhole. 'There's something wrong with this lock; I have to get it fixed. There, that does it.' She threw open the door. 'Spic and span; I just cleaned it yesterday. Even picked up his socks and underwear from all over the floor. One thing I can't stand it's a sloppy-looking room.'

They went into the room together.

'There's his drums over there by the window. The big one is the bass drum, and that round black case is what they call the snare. The other thing there is the high hat. All his clothes is still in the closet and his shaving stuff is in the bathroom, just the way he left them. I can't figure it, can you? What'd you say it was that he done?'

'Did you see him when he left, Mrs Marsten?'

'No.'

'How old a man is he?'

'He's just a young fellow, it's a shame the way these young fellows get to be main-liners and dope fiends, shooting all that there hero-in poison into their systems.'

'How young, Mrs Marten?'

'Twenty-four, twenty-five, no older than that.'

'A big man?'

'More than six feet, I guess.'

'Big hands?'

'What?'

'His hands. Were they big, did you notice?'

'I never noticed. Who looks at a man's hands?'

'Well, some women do,' Carella said.

'All I know is he owes me almost two months' rent,' Mrs Marsten said, shrugging.

'Would you know whether or not he had a lot of girl friends, Mrs Marsten? Did he ever bring a girl here?'

'Not to my house,' the landlady said. 'Not to my house, mister! I don't allow any of that kind of stuff here. No, sir. If he had girl friends, he wasn't fooling around with them under my roof. I keep a clean house. Both the rooms *and* the roomers.'

'I see,' Carella said. 'You mind if we look around a little?'

'Go right ahead. Call me when you're done, and I'll lock the room. Don't make a mess. I just cleaned it yesterday.'

She went out. Carella and Hawes stared at each other.

'Do you suppose they went to Kansas City, maybe?' Hawes asked.

'I don't know. I'm beginning to wish both of them went to hell. Let's shake down the room. Maybe he left a clue.'

He hadn't.

Karl Androvich was a moustached giant who could have been a breathing endorsement for Marlboro cigarettes. He sat in a T-shirt at the kitchen table, his muscles bulging bronze against the clean white, the tattoo showing on his left biceps, 'Meg' in a heart. His hair was a reddish brown, and his moustache was a curious mixture of red, brown and blond hairs, a carefully trimmed, very elegant moustache which – reflecting its owner's pride – was constantly touched by Androvich during the course of the conversation. His hands were immense. Every time they moved up to stroke the moustache, Carella flinched as if he were about to be hit. Meg Androvich hovered about the kitchen, preparing dinner, her ears glued to the conversation.

'There are a few things we'd like to know, Mr Androvich,' Carella said.

'Yeah, what's that?'

'To begin with, where were you between February fourteenth and Monday when you came back to this house?'

'That's my business,' Androvich said. 'Next question.'

Carella was silent for a moment.

'Are you going to answer our questions here, Mr Androvich, or shall we go up to the squadroom where you might become a little more talkative?'

'You going to use a rubber hose on me? Man, I've been worked over with a hose before. You don't scare me.'

'You going to tell us where you were?'

'I told you that's my business.'

'Okay, get dressed.'

'What the hell for? You can't arrest me without a charge.'

'I've got a whole bagful of charges. You're withholding information from the police. You're an accessory before a murder. You're ...'

'A what? A murder? Are you out of your bloody mind?'

'Get dressed Androvich. I don't want to play around.'

'Okay,' Androvich said angrily. 'I was on the town.'

'On the town where?'

'Everywhere. Bars. I was drinking.'

'Why?'

'I felt like it.'

'Did you know your wife had reported you missing?'

'No. How the hell was I supposed to have known that?'

'Why didn't you call her?'

'What are you, a marriage counsellor? I didn't feel like calling her, okay?'

'He didn't have to call me if he didn't feel like it,' Meg said from the stove. 'He's home now. Why don't you all leave him alone?'

'Keep out of this, Meg,' Androvich warned.

'Which bars did you go to?' Hawes asked.

'I went all over the city. I don't remember the names of the bars.'

'Did you go to a place called The King and Queen?'

'No.'

'I thought you didn't remember the names.'

'I don't.'

'Then how do you know you *didn't* go to The King and Queen?'

'It doesn't sound familiar.' A slight tic had begun in Androvich's left eye.

'Does the name Bubbles Caesar sound familiar?'

'No.'

'Or Barbara Cesare?'

'No,' Androvich answered, the muscle of his eye jerking.

'How about Marla Phillips?'

'Never heard of her.'

'How about this phone number, Androvich? Sperling 7–0200. Mean anything to you?'

'No.' The muscle was twitching wildly now.

'Mrs Androvich,' Carella said, 'I think you'd better leave the room.'

'Why?'

'We're about to pull out a few skeletons. Go on in the other room.'

'My wife can hear anything you've got to say,' Androvich said.

'Okay. Sperling 7–0200 is the telephone number of three girls who share an apartment. One of them is named ...'

'Go on in the other room, M-M-Meg,' Androvich said.

'I want to stay here.'

'Do what I t-t-tell you to do.'

'Why is he asking you about that phone number? What have you got to do with those three ...?'

'G-G-Get the hell in the other room, Meg, before I slap you silly. Now do what I say!'

Meg Androvich stared at her husband sullenly, and then went out of the kitchen.

'Damn S-S-Southern t-t-trash,' Androvich muttered under his breath, the stammering more marked now, the tic beating at the corner of his eye.

'You ready to tell us a few things, Androvich?'

'Okay. I knew her.'

'Bubbles?'

'Bubbles.'

'How well did you know her?'

'Very well.'

'How well is that, Androvich?'

'You want a d-d-diagram?'

'If you've got one.'

'We were making it together. Okay?'

'Okay. When did you last see her?'

'February twelfth.'

'You remember the date pretty easily.'

'I ought to.'

'What does that mean?'

'I ... look, what the hell d-d-difference does all this make? The last time I saw her was on the t-t-twelfth. Last month. I haven't seen her since.'

'You sure about that?'

'I'm positive.'

'You sure you haven't been with her all this time?'

'I'm sure. Man, I wish I had been with her. I was *supposed* ...' Androvich cut himself off.

'Supposed to do what?' Hawes asked.

'N-N-Nothing.'

'You called her on the twelfth after your ship docked, is that right?'

'Yes.'

'And you saw her afterwards?'

'Yes, but only for about a half-hour or so.'

'That morning?'

'No. It was in the afternoon.'

'Where'd you see her?'

'At her p-p-p-place.'

'Was anybody else there? Either of her roommates?'

'No. I never met her roommates.'

'But you spoke to them on the telephone?'

'Yeah. I spoke to one of them.'

'Marla Phillips?'

'I d-d-don't know which one it was.'

'Did you speak to the roommate on the morning of the twelfth?'

'Yeah. I spoke to her, and then she called B-B-Bubbles to the phone.'

'And then you went to the apartment that afternoon, right?'

'Right. For a half-hour.'

'And then what?'

'Then I left. One of the r-r-r-roommates was supposed to be coming back. That d-d-damn place is like the middle of Main Street.'

'And you haven't seen her since that afternoon?'

'That's right.'

'Have you tried to contact her?'

Androvich hesitated. Then he said, 'No.'

'How come?'

'I just haven't. I figure she must have gone back to Kansas City.'

'What makes you figure that?'

'I just figure. She isn't around, is she?'

'How do you know?'

'Huh?'

'If you haven't tried contacting her, how do you know she isn't around?'

'Well, m-m-maybe I did try to reach her once or twice.'

'When?'

'I don't remember. During the past few weeks.'

'And you couldn't reach her?'

'No.'

'Who did you reach?'

'The g-g-goddamn answering service.'

'Now, let's go back a little, Androvich. You said you visited Miss Caesar in her apartment on the afternoon of the twelfth. All right, why?'

'I wanted to talk to her.'

'What about?'

'Various things.'

'Like what? Come on, Androvich, let's stop the teethpulling!'

'What d-d-difference does it make to you guys?'

'It may make a lot of difference. Miss Caesar has disappeared. We're trying to find her.'

'You're telling me she's disappeared! Boy, has she disappeared! Well, I d-d-don't know where she is. If I did know ...' Again, he cut himself off.

'If you did know, then what?'

'Nothing.'

'What did you talk about that afternoon?'

'Nothing.'

'You spent a half-hour talking about nothing, is that right?'

'That's right.'

'Did you go to bed with her that afternoon?'

'No. I told you her r-r-roommate was expected back.'

'So you just sat and looked at each other, right?'

'More or less.'

'Get dressed, Androvich. We're going to have to take a little ride.'

'Ride, my ass! I don't know anything about where she is, dammit! If I knew, do you think I'd ...'

'What? Finish it, Androvich! Say what you've got to say!'

'Do you think I'd be here? Do you think I'd be playing hubby and wifey with that mealy-mouthed hunk of Southern garbage? Do you think I'd be listening to this molasses dribble day in and day out? Kahl, honeh, cain't we-all go back t'Atlanta, honeh? Cain't we, Kahl? Do you think I'd be here listening to that crap if I knew where Bubbles was?'

'What would you be doing, Androvich?'

'I'd be with her, goddamnit! Where do you think I spent the last month?'

'Where?'

'Looking for her. Searching this city, every c-c-corner of it. Do you know how big this city is?'

'We've got some idea.'

'Okay, I p-p-picked through it like somebody looking through a scalp for lice. And I didn't find her. And if I couldn't find her, she isn't here, believe me, because I covered every place, *every* place. I went to places you guys have never even heard of, l-l-looking for that broad. She's gone.'

'She was that important to you, huh?'

'Yeah, she was that important to me.'

Androvich fell silent. Carella stared at him.

'What did you talk about that afternoon, Karl?' he asked gently.

'We made plans,' Androvich said. His voice was curiously low now. The tic had stopped suddenly. The stammer had vanished. He did not look up at the detectives. He fastened his eyes on his big hands, and he twisted those hands in his lap, and he did not look up.

'What kind of plans?'

'We were going to run away together.'

'Where?'

'Miami.'

'Why there?'

'She knew of a job she could get down there. In one of the clubs. And Miami's a big port. Not as big as this city, but big enough. I could always get work out of Miami. Or maybe I could get a job on one of the yachts. Anyway, we figured Miami was a good place for us.'

'When were you supposed to leave?'

'Valentine's Day.'

'Why then?'

'Well, my ship was pulling out on the fourteenth, so we figured that would give us a head start. We figured Meg would think I was in South America, and then by the time she realized I wasn't, she wouldn't know where the hell I was. That was the way we figured it.'

'But instead, the chief officer called here to find out where you were.'

'Yeah, and Meg reported me missing.'

'Why *aren't* you in Miami, Karl? What happened?'

'She didn't show.'

'Bubbles?'

'Yeah. I waited at the train station all morning. Then I called her apartment, and all I got was the goddamn answering service. I called all that day, and all that day I got that answering service. I went down to The King and Queen, and the bartender there told me she hadn't showed up for work the past two nights. That was when I began looking for her.'

'Did you plan to marry this girl, Karl?'

'Marry her? How could I do that? I'm already married. Bigamy is against the law.'

'Then what did you plan to do?'

'Just have fun, that's all. I'm a young guy. I deserve a little fun, don't I? Miami is a good town for fun.'

'Do you think she could have gone to Miami without you?'

'I don't think so. I wired the club she mentioned, and they said she hadn't showed up. Besides, why would she do that?'

'Women do funny things.'

'Not Bubbles.'

'We'd better check with the Miami cops, Steve,' Hawes said. 'And maybe a teletype to Kansas City, huh?'

'Yeah.' He paused and looked at Androvich. 'You think she isn't here any more, huh? You think she's left the city?'

'That's the way I figure it. I looked everywhere. She couldn't be here. It'd be impossible.'

'Maybe she's hiding,' Carella said. 'Maybe she did something and doesn't want to be found.'

'Bubbles? No, not Bubbles.'

'Ever hear of a man called Mike Chirapadano?'

'No, Who's he?'

'A drummer.'

'I never heard of him.'

'Bubbles ever mention him?'

'No. Listen, she ain't in this city, that much I can tell you. She just ain't here. Nobody can hide that good.'

'Maybe not,' Carella said. 'But maybe she's here, anyway.'

'What sense does that make? If she ain't out in the open, and she ain't hiding, what does that leave?'

'The river,' Carella said.

Chapter Thirteen

It stopped raining that Thursday.

Nobody seemed to notice the difference.

It was strange. For the past nine days, it had rained steadily and everyone in the city talked about the rain. There were jokes about building arks and jokes about the rain hurting the rhubarb, and it was impossible to go anywhere or do anything without someone mentioning the rain.

On Thursday morning, the sun came out. There was no fanfare of trumpets heralding the sun's appearance, and none of the metropolitan dailies shrieked about it in four-point headlines. The rain just went, and the sun just came, and everyone in the city trotted about his business as if nothing had happened. The rain had been with them too long. It had become almost a visiting relative whose departure is always promised but never really expected. At last, the relative had left and – as with most promised things in life – there was no soaring joy accompanying the event. If anything, there was almost a sense of loss.

Even the bulls of the 87th who quite naturally detested legwork in the rain did not greet the sun with any noticeable amount of enthusiasm.

They had got their teletypes out to Miami and Kansas City, and they had received their answering teletypes, and the answering teletypes told them that Barbara 'Bubbles' Caesar was not at the moment gainfully employed in any of the various clubs in either of the cities. This did not mean that she wasn't living in either of the cities. It simply meant she wasn't working.

It was impossible to check bus or train transportation, but a call to every airline servicing both of the cities revealed that neither Bubbles Caesar nor a Mike Chirapadano had reserved passage out of Isola during the past month.

On Thursday afternoon, the Federal Bureau of Investigation delivered a photostatic copy of Mike Chirapadano's service record.

He had been born in Riverhead twenty-three years ago. He was white, and he was obviously male. Height, six feet three inches. Weight, 185. Eyes, blue. Hair, brown. When the Korean War broke out, he was only thirteen years old. When it ended, he was sixteen, and so he had been spared the Oriental bout. He had joined the Navy for a two-year hitch in July of 1956, had spent all of his service career – except for his boot training at the Great Lakes Naval Station – playing with the ComSerDiv band in Miami. When he got out of the navy in 1958, he came back to Isola. His record listed an honourable discharge in Miami, the Navy providing his transportation back to his home city. A copy of his fingerprint record was included in the data from the FBI but the prints were worthless for comparison purposes since the fingertips on both discovered hands had been mutilated. The Navy listed his blood as belonging to the 'O' group.

Carella studied the information and went home to his wife.

Teddy Carella was a deaf mute.

She was not a tall woman but she somehow managed to give the impression of height – a woman with black hair and brown eyes and a figure which, even after the bearing of twin children, managed to evoke street-corner whistles that – unfortunately – Teddy could not hear.

The twins, Mark and April, had been born on a Sunday in June. June 22, to be exact. Carella would never forget the date because, aside from it being the day on which he'd been presented with two lovely children, it had also been the day of his sister Angela's wedding, and there had been quite a bit of excitement on that day, what with a sniper trying to pick off the groom and all. Happily, the groom had survived. He had survived very well. Angela, less than a year after her marriage, was already pregnant.

Now the problems of the care and feeding of twins are manifold even for a mother who possesses the powers of speech and hearing. The feeding problem is perhaps the least difficult because the eventuality of twins was

undoubtedly considered in the design of the female apparatus and allow-
ances made therefore. For which, thank God. But any mother who has tried
to cope with the infantile madness of even one child must surely recognize
that the schizophrenic rantings of twins present a situation exactly doubled in
potential frenzy.

When Steve Carella discovered that his wife was pregnant, he was not
exactly the happiest man in the world. His wife was a deaf mute. Would the
children be similarly afflicted? He was assured that his wife's handicap was
not an inherited trait, and that in all probability a woman as healthy in all
other respects as Teddy would deliver an equally healthy baby. He had felt
somewhat ashamed of his doubts later. In all truth, he never really
considered Teddy either 'handicapped' or 'afflicted'. She was, to him, the
most beautiful and desirable woman on the face of the earth. Her eyes, her
face, spoke more words to him than could be found in the languages of a
hundred different nations. And when he spoke, she heard him, she heard
him with more than ears, she heard him with her entire being. And so he'd
felt some guilt at his earlier unhappiness, a guilt which slowly dissipated as
the time of the birth drew near.

But he was not expecting twins, and when he was informed that he was
now the father of a boy and a girl, the boy weighing in at six pounds four
ounces, the girl being two ounces lighter than her brother, all of his old fears
and anxieties returned. The fears became magnified when he visited the
hospital the next morning and was told by the obstetrician that the firstborn,
Mark, had broken his collarbone during delivery and that the doctor was
placing him in an incubator until the collarbone healed. Apparently, the
birth had been a difficult one and Mark had gallantly served as a trailblazer
for his wombmate, suffering the fractured clavicle in his progress towards
daylight. As it turned out, the fracture was simply a chipped bone, and it
healed very rapidly, and the babies Carella and Teddy carried home from
the hospital ten days later were remarkably healthy; but Carella was still
frightened.

How will we manage? he wondered. How will Teddy manage to feed them
and take care of them? How will they learn to speak? Wasn't speech a process
of imitation? Oh, God, what will we do?

The first thing they had to do, they discovered, was to move. The
Riverhead apartment on Dartmouth Road seemed to shrink the moment the
babies and their nurse were put into the place. The nurse had been a gift
from Teddy's father, a month's respite from the task of getting a household
functioning again. The nurse was a marvellous woman in her fifties named
Fanny. She had blue hair and she wore pincenez and she weighed a hundred
and fifty pounds and she ran that house like an Army sergeant. She took an
instant liking to Carella and his wife, and her fondness for the twins included
such displays of affection as the embroidering of two pillow slips with their
names, action clearly above and beyond the call of duty.

Whenever Carella had a day off, he and Teddy went looking for a house.
Carella was a Detective 2nd/Grade and his salary – before the various
deductions which decimated it – was exactly $5,555 a year. That is not a lot
of loot. They had managed to save over the past years the grand total of two
thousand bucks, and they were rapidly discovering that this paltry sum
could barely cover the down payment on a lawn mower, much less a full-

fledged house. For the first time in his life, Carella felt completely inadequate. He had brought two children into the world, and now he was faced with the possibility of being unable to house them properly, to give them the things they needed. And suddenly the Carellas discovered that their luck, by George, she was running good!

They found a house that could be had simply by paying the back taxes on it, which taxes amounted to ten thousand dollars. The house was a huge rambling monster in Riverhead, close to Donnegan's Bluff, a house which had undoubtedly held a large family and an army of servants in the good old days. These were the bad new days, however, and with servants and fuel costs being what they were, no one was very anxious to take over a white elephant like this one. Except the Carellas.

They arranged a loan through the local bank (a civil service employee is considered a good risk) and less than a month after the twins were born, they found themselves living in a house of which Charles Adams would have been ecstatically proud. Along about this time, their second stroke of good luck presented itself. Fanny, who had helped them move and helped them get settled, was due to terminate her month's employment when she offered the Carellas a proposition. She had, she told them, been making a study of the situation in the Carella household, and she could not visualize poor little Theodora (these were Fanny's words) raising those two infants alone, nor did she understand how the children were to learn to talk if they could not intimate their mother, and how was Theodora to hear either of the infants yelling, suppose one of them got stuck with a safety pin or something, my God?

Now she understood that a detective's salary was somewhere around five thousand a year – 'You *are* a 2nd/grade detective, aren't you, Steve?' – and that such a salary did not warrant a full-time nurse and governess. But at the same time, she had the utmost faith that Carella would eventually make 1st/grade – 'That *does* pay six thousand a year, doesn't it, Steve? – and until the time when the Carellas could afford to pay her a decent wage, she would be willing to work for room and board, supplementing this with whatever she could earn making night calls and the like.

The Carellas would not hear of it.

She was, they insisted, a trained nurse, and she would be wasting her time by working for the Carellas at what amounted to no salary at all when she could be out earning a damned good living. And besides, she was not a truck horse, how could she possibly work all day long with the children and then hope to take on odd jobs at night? No, they would not hear of it.

But neither would Fanny hear of their not hearing of it.

'I am a very strong woman,' she said, 'and all I'll be doing all day long is taking care of the children under the supervision of Theodora who is their mother. I speak English very well, and the children could do worse for someone to imitate. And besides, I'm fifty-three years old, and I've never had a family of my own, and I rather like this family and so I think I'll stay. And it'll take a bigger man than you, Steve Carella, to throw me into the street. So that settles that.'

And, that indeed, did settle that.

Fanny had stayed. The Carellas had sectioned off one corner of the house and disconnected the heating to it so that their fuel bills were not exorbitant.

Slowly but surely, the bank loan was being paid off. The children were almost a year old and showed every sign of being willing to imitate the sometimes colourful speech of their nurse. Fanny's room was on the second floor of the house, near the children's room, and the Carellas slept downstairs in a bedroom off the living room so that even their sex life went uninterrupted after that grisly six-weeks' postnatal wait. Everything was rosy.

But sometimes a man came home looking for an argument, and you can't very well argue with a woman who cannot speak. There are some men who might agree that such a state of matrimony is surely a state approaching paradise, but on that Thursday night, with the sky peppered with stars, with a springlike breeze in the air, Carella walked up the path to the old house bristling for a fight.

Teddy greeted him at the doorway. He kissed her briefly and stamped into the house, and she stared after him in puzzlement and then followed him.

'Where's Fanny?' he asked.

He watched Teddy's fingers as they rapidly told him, in sign language, that Fanny had left early for a nursing job.

'And the children?' he asked.

She read his lips, and then signalled that the children were already in bed, asleep.

'I'm hungry,' he said. 'Can we eat, please?'

They went into the kitchen, and Teddy served the meal – pork chops, his favourite. He picked sullenly at his food, and after dinner he went into the living room, turned on the television set, watched a show featuring a private eye who was buddy-buddy with a police lieutenant and who was also buddy-buddy with at least eighteen different women of assorted provocative shapes, and then snapped off the show and turned to Teddy and shouted, 'If any police lieutenant in the country ran his squad the way that jerk does, the thieves would overrun the streets! No wonder he needs a private eye to tell him what to do!'

Teddy stared at her husband and said nothing.

'I'd like to see what the pair of them would do with a real case. I'd like to see how they'd manage without a dozen clues staring them in the face.'

Teddy rose and went to her husband, sitting on the arm of his chair.

'I'd like to see what they'd do with a pair of goddamn severed hands. They'd probably both faint dead away,' Carella said.

Teddy stroked his hair.

'We're back to Androvich again,' he shouted. It occurred to him that it didn't matter whether or not he shouted because Teddy was only reading his lips and the decibels didn't matter one little damn. But he shouted nonetheless. 'We're right back to Androvich, and where does that leave us? You want to know where that leaves us?'

Teddy nodded.

'Okay. We've got a pair of hands belonging to a white male who is somewhere between the ages of eighteen and twenty-four. We've got a bum of a sailor who flops down with any girl he meets, bong, bong, there goes Karl Androvich, who allegedly made a date to run off with a stripper named Bubbles Caesar. You listening?'

Yes Teddy nodded.

'So they set the date for Valentine's Day, which is very romantic. All the tramps of the world are always very romantic. Only this particular tramp didn't show up. She left our sailor friend Androvich waiting in the lurch.' He saw the frown on Teddy's face. 'What's the matter? You don't like my calling Bubbles a tramp? She reads that way to me. She's provoked fights in the joint where she stripped by leading on two men simultaneously. She had this deal going with Androvich, and she also probably had something going with a drummer named Mike Chirapadano. At any rate, she and Chirapadano vanished on exactly the same day, so that stinks of conspiracy. And she's also got her agent, a guy named Charlie Tudor, all butterflies in the stomach over her. So it seems to me she was playing the field in six positions. And if that doesn't spell tramp, it comes pretty close.'

He watched his wife's fingers as she answered him.

He interrupted, shouting, 'What do you mean, maybe she's just a friendly girl? We know she was shacking up with the sailor, and probably with the drummer, and probably with the agent as well. All big men, too. She goes for them big. A tramp with ...'

The drummer and the agent are only supposition, Teddy spelled with her hands. *The only one you have any sure knowledge of is the sailor.*

'I don't need any sure knowledge. I can read Bubbles Caesar from clear across the bay on a foggy day.'

I thought sure knowledge was the only thing a detective used.

'You're thinking of a lawyer who never asks a question unless he's sure of what the answer will be. I'm not a lawyer, I'm a cop. I have to ask the questions.'

Then ask them, and stop assuming that all strippers are ...

Carella interrupted her with a roar that almost woke the children. 'Assuming! Who's assuming?' he bellowed, finally involved in the argument he'd been seeking ever since he came home, a curious sort of argument in that Teddy's hands moved unemotionally, filled with words, while he yelled and ranted to her silent fingers. 'What does a girl have to do before I figure her for rotten? For all I know, she knocked off this guy Chirapadano and won't be happy until she's dropped his hands and his legs and his heart and his liver into the little paper sacks all over town! I won't be surprised if she cuts off his ...'

Don't be disgusting, Steve, Teddy cautioned with her hands.

'Where the hell is she? That's what I'd like to know,' Carella said. 'And where's Chirapadano? And whose damn hands are those? And where's the rest of the body? And what's the motive in this thing? There has to be a motive, doesn't there? People just don't go around killing other people, do they?'

You're the detective. You tell me.

'There's always a motive,' Carella said, 'that's for sure. Always. Dammit, if we only *knew* more. Did Bubbles and the drummer go off together? Did she dump the sailor because she wanted the drummer? And if so, did she get tired of him and knock him off? Then why cut off his hands, and where's the rest of the body? And if they aren't his hands, then whose are they? Or are Bubbles and the drummer even connected with the hands? Maybe we're off on a wild goose chase altogether. Boy, I wish I was a shoemaker.'

You do not wish you were a shoemaker, Teddy told him.

'Don't tell me what I wish,' Carella said. 'Boy, you're the most argumentative female I've ever met in my life. Come here and kiss me before we start a real fight. You've been looking for one ever since I got home.'

And Teddy, smiling, went into his arms.

Chapter Fourteen

The very next day, Carella got the fight he was spoiling for.

Oddly, the fight was with another cop.

This was rather strange because Carella was a fairly sensible man who realized how much his colleague could contribute to his job. He had certainly avoided any trouble on the squad prior to this, so it could only be assumed that the Hands Case – as the men had come to call it – was really getting him down.

The fight started very early in the morning, and it was one of those fights which seem to come about full-blown, with nothing leading up to them, like a summer storm which suddenly blackens the streets with rain. Carella was putting a call in to Taffy Smith, the other girl who'd shared the apartment with Bubbles Caesar. He mused that this damned case was beginning to resemble the cases of television's foremost private eye, with voluptuous cuties popping out of the woodwork wherever a man turned. He could not say he objected to the female pulchritude. It was certainly a lot more pleasant than investigating a case at an old ladies' home. At the same time, all these broads seemed to be leading nowhere, and it was this knowledge which rankled in him, and which probably led to the fight.

Hernandez was sitting at the desk alongside Carella's, typing a report. Sunshine sifted through the grilled windows and threw a shadowed lacework on the squadroom floor. The door to Lieutenant Byrnes' office was open. Someone had turned on the standing electric fan, not because it was really hot but only because the sunshine – after so much rain – created an illusion of heat.

'Miss Smith?' Carella said into the phone.

'Yes. Who's this, please?'

'Detective Carella of the 87th Detective Squad.'

'Oh, my goodness,' Taffy Smith said.

'Miss Smith, we'd like to talk to you about your missing roommate, Bubbles Caesar. Do you suppose we could stop by sometime today?'

'Oh. Well, gee, I don't know. I'm supposed to go to rehearsal.'

'What time is your rehearsal, Miss Smith?'

'Eleven o'clock.'

'And when will you be through?'

'Gee, that's awfully hard to say. Sometimes they last all day long. Although maybe this'll be a short one. We got an awful lot done yesterday.'

'Can you give me an approximate time?'

'I'd say about three o'clock. But I can't be sure. Look, let's say three, and you can call here before you leave your office, okay? Then if I'm delayed or anything, my service can give you the message. Okay? Would that be okay?'

'That'd be fine.'

'Unless you want me to leave the key. Then you could go in and make yourself a cup of coffee. Would you rather do that?'

'No, that's all right.'

'Okay, then, I'll see you at three, okay?'

'Fine,' Carella said.

'But be sure to call first, okay? And if I can't make it, I'll leave a message. Okay?'

'Thank you, Miss Smith,' Carella said, and he hung up.

Andy Parker came through the slatted rail divider and threw his hat at his desk. 'Man, what a day,' he said. 'Supposed to hit seventy today. Can you imagine that? In March? I guess all that rain drove winter clear out of the city.'

'I guess so,' Carella said. He listed the appointment with Taffy on his pad and made a note to call her at 2:30 before leaving the squadroom.

'This is the kind of weather you got back home, hey, Chico?' Parker said to Hernandez.

Frankie Hernandez, who'd been typing, did not hear Parker. He stopped the machine, looked up, and said, 'Huh? You talking to me, Andy?'

'Yeah. I said this is the kind of weather you got back home, ain't it?'

'Back home?' Hernandez said. 'You mean Puerto Rico?'

'Sure.'

'I was born here,' Hernandez said.

'Sure, I know,' Parker said. 'Every Puerto Rican you meet in the streets, he was born here. To hear them tell it, none of them ever came from the island. You'd never know there was a place called Puerto Rico, to hear them tell it.'

'That's not true, Andy,' Hernandez said gently. 'Most Puerto Ricans are very proud to have come from the island.'

'But not you, huh? You deny it.'

'I don't come from the island,' Hernandez said.

'No, that's right. You were born here, right?'

'That's right,' Hernandez said, and he began typing again.

Hernandez was not angry, and Parker didn't seem to be angry, and Carella hadn't even been paying any attention to the conversation. He was making out a tentative schedule of outside calls which he hoped he and Hawes could get to that day. He didn't even look up when Parker began speaking again.

'So that makes you an American, right, Chico?' Parker said.

This time, Hernandez heard him over the noise of the typewriter. This time, he looked up quickly and said, 'You talking to me?' But whereas the words were exactly the words he'd used the first time Parker had spoken, Hernandez delivered them differently this time, delivered them with a tightness, an intonation of unmistakable annoyance. His heart had begun to pound furiously. He knew that Parker was calling upon him to defend The Cause once more, and he did not particularly feel like defending anything on a beautiful morning like this one, but the gauntlet had been dropped, and there it lay, and so Hernandez hurled back his words.

'You talking to me?'

'Yes, I am talking to you, Chico,' Parker said. 'It's amazing how you damn people never hear anything when you don't want to hear ...'

'Knock it off, Andy,' Carella said suddenly.

Parker turned towards Carella's desk. 'What the hell's the matter with you?' he said.

'Knock it off, that's all. You're disturbing my squadroom.'

'When the hell did this become *your* squadroom?'

'I'm catching today, and it looks like your name isn't even listed on the duty chart. So why don't you go outside and find some trouble in the streets, if trouble is what you want?'

'When did you become the champion of the people?'

'Right this minute,' Carella said, and he shoved back his chair and stood up to face Parker.

'Yeah?' Parker said.

'Yeah,' Carella answered.

'Well, you can just blow it out your ...'

And Carella hit him.

He did not know he was going to throw the punch until after he had thrown it, until after it had collided with Parker's jaw and sent him staggering backwards against the railing. He knew then that he shouldn't have hit Parker, but at the same time he told himself he didn't feel like sitting around listening to Hernandez take a lot of garbage on a morning like this, and yet he knew he shouldn't have thrown the punch.

Parker didn't say a word. He shoved himself off the railing and lunged at Carella who chopped a short right to Parker's gut, doubling him over. Parker grabbed for his midsection and Carella delivered a rabbit punch to the back of Parker's neck, sending him sprawling over the desk.

Parker got up and faced Carella with new respect and with renewed malice. It was as if he'd forgotten for a moment that his opponent was as trained and as skilled as he himself was, forgotten that Carella could fight as clean or as dirty as the situation warranted, and that the situation generally warranted the dirtiest sort of fighting, and that this sort of fighting had become second nature.

'I'm gonna break you in half, Steve,' Parker said, and there was almost a chiding tone in his voice, the tone of warning a father uses to a child who is acting up.

He feinted with his left and as Carella moved to dodge the blow, he slammed a roundhouse right into his nose, bringing blood to it instantly. Carella touched his nose quickly, saw the blood, and then brought up his guard.

'Cut it out, you crazy bastards,' Hernandez said, stepping between them. 'The skipper's door is open. You want him to come out here?'

'Sure. Steve-oh doesn't care, do you, Steve? You and the skipper are real buddies, aren't you?'

Carella dropped his fists. Angrily, he said, 'We'll finish this another time, Andy.'

'You're damn right we will,' Parker said, and he stormed out of the squadroom.

Carella took a handkerchief from his back pocket and began dabbing at his nose. Hernandez put a cold key at the back of his neck.

'Thanks, Steve,' he said.

'Don't mention it,' Carella answered.

'You shouldn't have bothered. I'm used to Andy.'

'Yeah, but I guess I'm not.'

'Anyway, thanks.'

Hawes walked into the squadroom, saw Carella's bloody handkerchief, glanced hastily at the lieutenant's door, and then whispered, 'What happened?'

'I saw red,' Carella said.

Hawes glanced at the handkerchief again. 'You're *still* seeing red,' he said.

Taffy Smith was neither voluptuous, overblown, *zoftik*, nor even pretty. She was a tiny little girl with ash blonde hair trimmed very close to her head. She had the narrow bones of a sparrow, and a nose covered with freckles, and she wore harlequin glasses which shielded the brightest blue eyes Carella or Hawes had ever seen.

There was, apparently, great Freudian meaning to this girl's penchant for making coffee for strangers. Undoubtedly, as a child, she had witnessed her mother clobbering her father with a coffeepot. Or perhaps a pot of coffee had overturned, scalding her, and she now approached it as a threat to be conquered. Or perhaps she had been raised by a tyrannical aunt in Brazil where, so the song says, coffee beans grow by the millions. Whatever the case, she trotted into the kitchen and promptly got a pot going while the detectives sat down in the living room. The Siamese cat, remembering Hawes, sidled over to him and purred idiotically against his leg.

'Friend of yours?' Carella asked.

'I fed him once,' Hawes answered.

Taffy Smith came back into the living room. 'Gee, I'm bushed,' she said. 'We've been rehearsing all day long. We're doing *Detective Story* at the Y. I'm playing the shoplifter. It's an exhausting role, believe me.' She paused. 'We're all Equity players, you understand. This is just between jobs.'

'I understand,' Carella said.

'How do you like living with a pair of strippers?' Hawes asked.

'Fine,' Taffy said. 'Gee, what's wrong with strippers? They're swell girls.' She paused. 'I've been out of work for a long time now. Somebody's got to keep up the rent. They've been swell about it.'

'They?' Carella said.

'Barbara and Marla. Of course, Barbara's gone now. You know that. Listen, what does a B-sheet look like?'

'Huh?' Carella said.

'A B-sheet. It's mentioned in the play, it takes place in a detective squadroom, you know.'

'Yes, I know.'

'Sure, and a B-sheet is mentioned, and our prop man is going nuts trying to figure out what it looks like. Could you send me one?'

'Well, we're not supposed to give out official documents,' Hawes said.

'Gee, I didn't know that.' She paused. 'But we got a real pair of handcuffs. *They're* official, aren't they?'

'Yes. Where'd you get them?'

'Some fellow who used to be a cop. He's got connections.' She winked.

'Well, maybe we can send you a B-sheet,' Carella said. 'If you don't tell anyone where you got it.'

'Gee, that would be swell,' Taffy answered.

'About your roommate. Barbara. You said she was nice to live with. Didn't she seem a little wild at times?'

'Wild?'

'Yes.'

'You mean, did she break dishes? Something like that?'

'No. I mean men.'

'Barbara? Wild?'

'Yes. Didn't she entertain a lot of men here?'

'Barbara?' Taffy grinned infectiously. 'She never had a man in this apartment all the while I've been living here.'

'But she received telephone calls from men, didn't she?'

'Oh, sure.'

'And none of these men ever came here?'

'I never saw any. Oh, excuse me. That's the coffee.'

She went into the kitchen and returned instantly with the coffeepot and three cardboard containers.

'You'll have to excuse the paper cups,' she said, 'but we try to keep from washing too many dishes around here. We usually get a mob in every night for coffee, kids from all over who feel like talking or who just feel like sitting on a comfortable chair. We've got a nice place, don't you think?'

'Yes,' Carella said.

'I love to make coffee,' Taffy said. 'I guess I got in the habit when I was first married. I used to think that was the dream of marriage, do you know? I had the idea that marriage meant you could make a cup of coffee in your own house whenever you wanted to.' She grinned again. 'I guess that's why I'm divorced right now. Marriage is a lot more than making coffee, I suppose. Still I like to make coffee.'

She poured, went back to the kitchen with the pot, and then returned with cream, sugar, and wooden spoons.

'At these midnight get-togethers,' Carella said, 'where you make coffee – did Barbara hang around?'

'Oh, sure.'

'And she was friendly?'

'Oh, sure.'

'But she never brought any men here?'

'Never.'

'Never entertained any men here?'

'Never. You see, we only have the three rooms. The kitchen, the living room, and the bedroom. The bedroom has two beds, and this sofa opens into a bed, so that makes three beds. So we had to figure out a sort of a schedule. If one of the girls had a date and she thought she might be asking him in for a drink later, we had to keep the living room free. This really wasn't such a problem because Barbara never brought anyone home. So only Marla and I had to worry about it.'

'But Barbara *did* date men?'

'Oh, sure. Lots of them.'

'And if she felt like asking someone in for a drink, she didn't ask them in here, is that right?'

'That's right. Some more coffee?'

'No, thank you,' Hawes said. He had only taken a sip of the first cup.

'Then where did she take them?' Carella asked.

'I beg your pardon?'

'Her boy friends. Where did she go with them?'

'Oh, all over. Clubs, theatres, wherever they wanted to take her.'

'I meant, for that nightcap.'

'Maybe she went to their apartments.'

'She couldn't have gone to Androvich's apartment,' Carella said out loud.

'What was that?'

'There are hotels all over the city, Steve,' Hawes said.

'Yeah,' Carella said. 'Miss Smith, did Barbara ever say anything which would lead you to believe she had *another* apartment?'

'Another one? Why would she need another one? Do you know how much apartments cost in this city?'

'Yes, I do. But did she ever mention anything like that?'

'Not to me, she didn't. Why would she need another apartment?'

'Apparently, Miss Smith, Barbara was seeing a few men and was on ... rather friendly terms with them. An apartment shared with two other girls might have ... well, limited her activities somewhat.'

'Oh, I see what you mean,' Taffy said. She thought about this for a moment. Then she said, 'You're talking about Barbara? Bubbles?'

'Yes.'

Taffy shrugged. 'I never got the idea she was man-crazy. She didn't seem that interested in men.'

'She was ready to run off with one when she disappeared,' Carella said. 'And it's possible she disappeared with a second one.'

'Barbara?' Taffy said. 'Bubbles?'

'Barbara, yes. Bubbles.' Carella paused for a moment. 'I wonder if I could use your phone, Miss Smith?'

'Go right ahead. You can use this one, or the extension in the bedroom. Forgive the mess in there. My roommate is a slob.'

Carella went into the bedroom.

'Marla told me all about you,' Taffy said to Hawes in a whisper.

'She did?'

'Yes. Are you going to call her?'

'Well, I don't know. We've got to wrap up this case first.'

'Oh, sure,' Taffy agreed. 'She's a nice girl. Very sweet.'

'Yes, she seemed nice,' Hawes said. He felt very uncomfortable all at once.

'Do you work nights?' Taffy asked,

'Sometimes, yes.'

'Well, when you're off, why don't you stop by for a cup of coffee?'

'All right, maybe I will.'

'Good,' Taffy said, and she grinned.

Carella came back into the room. 'I just called Androvich's apartment,' he said. 'Thought he might be able to tell us whether or not Barbara was keeping another place.'

'Any luck?'

'He shipped out this morning,' Carella said. 'For Japan.'

Chapter Fifteen

There is a certain look that all big cities take on as five o'clock claims the day. It is a look reserved exclusively for big cities. If you were raised in a small town or a hamlet, you have never seen the look. If you were raised in one of those places that pretend to be huge metropolitan centres but which are in reality only overgrown small towns, you have only seen an imitation of the five o'clock big city look.

The city is a woman, you understand. It could be nothing but a woman. A small town can be the girl next door or an old man creaking in a rocker or a gangly teenager growing out of his dungarees, but the city could be none of these things, the city *is* and can only be a woman. And, like a woman, the city generates love and hate, respect and disesteem, passion and indifference. She is always the same city, always the same woman, but oh the faces she wears, oh the magic guile of this strutting bitch. And if you were born in one of her buildings, and if you know her streets and know her moods, then you love her. Your loving her is not a thing you can control. She has been with you from the start, from the first breath of air you sucked into your lungs, the air mixing cherry blossoms with carbon monoxide, the air of cheap perfume and fresh spring rain, the something in the city air that comes from nothing you can visualize or imagine, the *feel* of city air, the feel of life which you take into your lungs and into your body, this is the city.

And the city is a maze of sidewalks upon which you learned to walk, cracked concrete and sticky asphalt and cobblestones, a hundred thousand corners to turn, a hundred million surprises around each and every one of those corners. This is the city, she grins, she beckons, she cries, her streets are clean sometimes, and sometimes they rustle with fleeing newspapers that rush along the kerbstones in time to the beat of her heart. You look at her, and there are so many things to see, so many things to take into your mind and store there, so many things to remember, a myriad things to pile into a memory treasure chest, and you are in love with everything you see, the city can do no wrong, she is your lady love, and she is yours. You remember every subtle mood that crosses her face, you memorize her eyes, now startled, now tender, now weeping; you memorize her mouth in laughter, her windblown hair, the pulse in her throat. This is no casual love affair. She is as much a part of you as your fingerprints.

You are hooked.

You are hooked because she can change her face, this woman, and change her body, and all that was warm and tender can suddenly become cold and heartless – and still you are in love. You will be in love with her forever, no matter how she dresses, no matter how they change her, no matter who claims her, she is the same city you saw with the innocent eyes of youth, and she is yours.

And at five o'clock, she puts on a different look and you love this look, too; you love everything about her, her rages, her sultry petulance, everything; this is total love that seeks no excuses and no reasons. At five o'clock, her empty streets are suddenly alive with life. She has been puttering in a dusty drawing room all day long, this woman, this city, and now it is five o'clock and suddenly she emerges and you are waiting for her, waiting to clutch her in your arms. There is a jauntiness in her step, and yet it veils a weariness, and together they combine to form an image of past and present merged with a future promise. Dusk sits on the skyline, gently touching the sabre-edged buildings. Starlight is waiting to bathe her streets in silver. The lights of the city, incandescent and fluorescent and neon, are waiting to bracelet her arms and necklace her throat, to hang her with a million gaudy trappings which she does not need. You listen to the hurried purposeful click of her high-heeled pumps and somewhere in the distance there is the growl of a tenor saxophone, far in the distance because this is still five o'clock and the music will not really begin until later, the growl is still deep in the throat. For now, for the moment, there are the cocktail glasses and the muted hum of conversation, the chatter, the light laughter that floats on the air like the sound of shattering glass. And you sit with her, and you watch her eyes, meaningful and deep, and you question her every word, you want to know who she is and what she is, but you will never know. You will love this woman until the day you die, and you will never know her, never come even close to knowing her. Your love is a rare thing bordering on patriotic fervour. For in this city, in this woman, in this big brawling wonderful glittering tender heartless gentle cruel dame of a lady, there is the roar of a nation. If you were born and raised in the city, you cannot think of your country as anything but a giant metropolis. There are no small towns in your nation, there are no waving fields of grain, no mountains, no lakes, no seashores. For you, there is only the city, and she is yours, and love is blind.

Two men in love with the city, Detective Carella and Detective Hawes, joined the throng that rushed along her pavements at five o'clock that afternoon. They did not speak to each other for they were rivals for the same hand, and honourable men do not discuss the woman they both love. They walked into the lobby of the Creo Building and they took the elevator up to the eighteenth floor, and they walked down the deserted corridor to the end of the hall, and then they entered the office of Charles Tudor.

There was no one in the waiting room.

Tudor was locking the door to his inner office as they came in. He turned, still stooping over, the key in the keyhole. He nodded in recognition, finished locking the door, put the keys into his pocket, walked to them with an extended hand and said, 'Gentlemen. Any news?'

Carella took the proffered hand. 'Afraid not, Mr Tudor,' he answered. 'But we'd like to ask you a few more questions.'

'Certainly,' Tudor said. 'You don't mind if we sit here in the waiting room, do you? I've already locked up my private office.'

'This'll be fine,' Carella said.

They sat on the long couch against the wall covered with strippers.

'You said you were in love with Bubbles Caesar, Mr Tudor,' Carella said. 'Did you know that she was seeing at least one other man for certain, and possibly two other men?'

'Barbara?' Tudor asked.

'Yes. Did you know that?'

'No. I didn't.'

'Did you see her very often, Mr Tudor? We're not referring to your business relationship right now.'

'Yes. I saw her quite often.'

'How often?'

'Well, as often as I could.'

'Once a week? Twice a week? More than that? How often, Mr Tudor?'

'I suppose, on the average, I saw her three or four times a week.'

'And what did you do when you saw her, Mr Tudor?'

'Oh, various things.' Tudor gave a small shrug of puzzlement. 'What do people do when they go out? Dinner, dancing, the theatre, a motion picture, a drive in the country. All those things. Whatever we felt like doing.'

'Did you go to bed with her, Mr Tudor?'

'That is my business,' Tudor said flatly. '*And* Barbara's.'

'It might be ours, too, Mr Tudor. Oh, I know, it's a hell of a thing to ask, very personal. We don't like to ask, Mr Tudor. There are a lot of things we don't like to ask, but unfortunately we have to ask those things, whether we like to or not. I'm sure you can understand.'

'No, I'm afraid I cannot,' Tudor said with finality.

'Very well, we'll assume you were intimate with her.'

'You may assume whatever you wish,' Tudor said.

'Where do you live, Mr Tudor?'

'On Blakely Street.'

'Downtown? In The Quarter?'

'Yes.'

'Near Barbara's apartment?'

'Fairly close to it, yes.'

'Did you ever go to Barbara's apartment?'

'No.'

'You never picked her up there?'

'No.'

'But you were seeing her?'

'Yes, of course I was seeing her.'

'And yet you never went to her apartment. Isn't that a little odd?'

'Is it? I despise the housing facilities of most working girls, Detective Carella. When I call on a young lady, I find the curiosity of her roommates unbearable. And so, whenever a young lady shares an apartment with someone else, I prefer to meet her away from the apartment. That is the arrangement I had with Barbara.'

'And apparently an arrangement she preferred. The girls she lived with tell us no man ever came to that apartment to pick her up or take her home. What do you think of that, Mr Tudor?'

Tudor shrugged. 'I am certainly not responsible for Barbara's idiosyncrasies.'

'Certainly not. Did Barbara ever come to your apartment?'

'No.'

'Why not?'

'I live with my father,' Tudor said. 'He's a very old man. Practically ... well, he's very sick. I'm not sure he would have understood Barbara. Or approved of her. And so he never met her.'

'You kept her away from your apartment. Is that right?'

'That is correct.'

'I see.' Carella thought for a moment. He looked at Hawes.

'Where'd you neck, Mr Tudor?' Hawes asked. 'In the back seat of an automobile?'

'That is none of your business,' Tudor said.

'Would you know whether or not Barbara had another apartment?' Hawes asked. 'Besides the one she shared with the two girls?'

'If she had one, I never saw it,' Tudor said.

'You're not married, of course,' Carella said.

'No, I'm not married.'

'Ever married, Mr Tudor?'

'Yes.'

'What's the status now? Separated? Divorced?'

'Divorced. For a long time now, Detective Carella. At least fifteen years.'

'What's your ex-wife's name?'

'Toni Traver. She's an actress. Rather a good one, too.'

'She in this city?'

'I'm sure I don't know. I was divorced from her fifteen years ago. I ran into her in Philadelphia once about eight years ago. I haven't seen her since. Nor do I care to.'

'You paying her alimony, Mr Tudor?'

'She didn't want any. She has money of her own.'

'Does she know about you and Barbara?'

'I don't know. She couldn't care less, believe me.'

'Mmmm,' Carella said. 'And you didn't know about these two other guys Barbara was seeing, right?'

'Right.'

'But surely, if she was seeing them, and if you called for a date or something, she must have said she was busy on that night, no? Didn't you ever ask how come? Didn't you want to know *why* she was busy?'

'I am not a possessive man,' Tudor said.

'But you loved her.'

'Yes. I loved her, and I still love her.'

'Well, how do you feel about it now? Now that you know she was dating two other men, maybe sleeping with both of them, how do you feel about it?'

'I ... naturally, I'm not pleased.'

'No, I didn't think you would be. Did you ever meet a man named Karl Androvich, Mr Tudor?'

'No.'

'How about a man named Mike Chirapadano?'

'No.'

'Ever go to The King and Queen?'

'Yes, of course. I sometimes picked Barbara up at the club.'

'Mike was a drummer in the band there.'

'Really?'

'Yes.' Carella paused. 'He seems to have vanished, Mr Tudor.'

'Really?'

'Yes. At the same time that Barbara did. What do you think of that?'

'I don't know what to think.'

'Think they ran off together?'

'I'm sure I don't know.'

'Do you have a black raincoat and umbrella, Mr Tudor?'

'No, I don't. A what? A black raincoat, did you say?'

'Yes, that's what I said.'

'No, I don't have one.'

'But you do have a raincoat?'

'Yes. A trench coat. It's grey. Or beige. You know, a neutral sort of ...'

'And the umbrella? Is it a man's umbrella?'

'I don't have an umbrella. I detest umbrellas.'

'Never carry one, right?'

'Never.'

'And you don't know of any other apartment Barbara might have kept, right?'

'I don't know of any, no.'

'Well, thank you very much, Mr Tudor,' Carella said. 'You've been most helpful.'

'Not at all,' Tudor answered.

Outside in the hallway, Carella said, 'He smells, Cotton. Wait for him downstairs and tail him, will you? I'll be back at the squadroom. I want to check on his ex-wife, see if I can get a line on her.'

'What are you thinking of? Jealousy?'

'Who knows? But some torches have been known to burn for more than fifteen years. Why not hers?'

'The way he put it ...'

'Sure, but every word he spoke could have been a lie.'

'True.'

'Trail him. Get back to me. I'll be waiting for your call.'

'Where do you expect him to lead me?'

'I don't know, Cotton.'

Carella went back to the squadroom. He learned that Toni Traver was a fairly good character actress and that she was at the moment working in a stock playhouse in Sarasota, Florida. Carella talked to her agent who told him that Miss Traver was not accepting alimony from her ex-husband. In fact, the agent said, he and Miss Traver had wedding plans of their own. Carella thanked him and hung up.

At eight p.m. that night, Cotton Hawes called in to report that Tudor had shaken the tail at seven-thirty.

'I'm sorry as hell,' he said.

'Yeah,' Carella answered.

Chapter Sixteen

The clothes turned up the next morning.

They were wrapped in a copy of the *New York Times*. A patrolman in Calm's Point found them in a trash basket. His local precinct called Headquarters because there was a bloodstain on the black raincoat, and Headquarters promptly called the 87th. The clothes were sent to the lab where Grossman inspected them thoroughly.

Besides the raincoat, there was a black flannel suit, a pair of black lisle socks, and a black umbrella.

An examination of the clothing turned up some rather contradictory facts, and all of these were passed on to Carella who studied them and then scratched his head in puzzlement.

To begin with, the bloodstain on the raincoat belonged to the 'O' group, which seemed to tie it in with the hands, and to further tie in with Mike Chirapadano whose service record had listed him as belonging to that blood group. But a careful examination of the black suit had turned up a subsequent small bloodstain on the sleeve. And this bloodstain belonged to the 'B' group. That was the first contradiction.

The second contradiction seemed puzzling all over again. It had to do with three other stains which were found on the black suit. The first of these was of a hair preparation, found on the inside of the collar where the collar apparently brushed against the nape of the neck. The stain was identified as coming from a tonic called Strike. It was allegedly designed for men who had oily scalps and who did not wish to compound the affliction by using an oily hair tonic.

But side by side with this stain was the second stain, and it had been caused by a preparation known as Dram, which was a hair tonic designed to fight dandruff and dry, flaky scalps. It seemed odd that these two scalp conditions could exist in one and the same man. It seemed contradictory that a person with a dry, flaky scalp would also be a person with an oily scalp. Somehow, the two hair preparations did not seem very compatible.

The third stain on the suit jacket was identified as coming from the selfsame Skinglow cosmetic which had been found in the corner of the airline bag, and this led to some confusion as to whether a man or a woman had worn the damn suit. Carella concluded that a man had worn it, but that he had embraced a woman wearing Skinglow. This accounted for that stain, but not for the hair tonic stains which were still puzzling and contradictory.

But there were more contradictions. The human hairs that clung to the fibre of the suit, for example. Some were brown and thin. Others were black and thick and short. And still others were black and thin and very long. The very long black ones presumably were left on the suit by the dame who'd worn the Skinglow. That embrace was shaping up as a very passionate one. But the thin brown hairs? And the thick black short ones? Puzzlement upon puzzlement.

About one thing, there was no confusion. There was a label inside the jacket, and the label clearly read: *Urban-Suburban Clothes*.

Carella looked up the name in the telephone directory, came up with a winner, clipped on his holster, and left the squadroom.

Cotton Hawes was somewhere in the city glued to Charles Tudor, whose trail he had picked up again early in the morning.

Urban-Suburban Clothes was one of those tiny shops which are sandwiched in between two larger shops and which would be missed entirely were it not for the colourful array of offbeat clothes in the narrow window. Carella opened the door and found himself in a long narrow cubicle which had been designed as a coffin for one man and which now held twelve men, all of whom were pawing through ties and feeling the material of sports coats and holding Italian sports shirts up against their chests. He felt an immediate attack of claustrophobia, which he controlled, and then he began trying to determine which of the twelve men in the shop was the owner. It occurred to him that thirteen was an unlucky number, and he debated leaving. He was carrying the bundle of clothes wrapped in brown paper and the bundle was rather bulky and this did not ease the crowded atmosphere of the shop at all. He squeezed past two men who were passing out cold over the off-orange tint of a sports shirt which had no buttons.

'Excuse me,' he said, 'excuse me.' And he executed an off-tackle run around a group of men who were huddled at the tie rack. The ties apparently were made of Indian madras in colours the men were declaring to be simultaneously 'cool', 'wild', and 'crazy'. Carella felt hot, tamed, and very sane.

He kept looking for the owner of the shop, and finally a voice came at his elbow. 'May I help you, sir?' And a body materialized alongside the voice. Carella whirled to face a thin man with a Fu Manchu beard, wearing a tight brown suit over a yellow weskit, and leering like a sex maniac in a nudist camp.

'Yes, yes, you can,' Carella said. 'Are you the owner of this shop?'

'Jerome Jerralds,' the young man said, and he grinned.

'How do you do, Mr Jerralds?' Carella said. 'I'm ...'

'Trouble?' Jerralds said, eyeing the bundle of wrapped clothes. 'One of our garments didn't fit you properly?'

'No, it's ...'

'Did you make the purchase yourself, or was it a gift?'

'No, this ...'

'You didn't buy the garment yourself?'

'No,' Carella said. 'I'm a ...'

'Then it was a gift?'

'No, I'm ...'

'Then how did you get it, sir?'

'The police lab sent the clothes over,' Carella answered.

'The poli –?' Jerralds started, and his hand went up to stroke the Chinese beard, a cat's-eye ring gleaming on his pinky.

'I'm a cop,' Carella explained.

'Oh?'

'Yeah. I've got a pile of clothes here. I wonder if you can tell me anything about them.'

'Well, I ...'

'I know you're busy, and I won't take much of your time.'

'Well, I ...'

Carella had already unwrapped the package. 'There's a label in the suit,' he said. '*Urban-Suburban Clothes*. This your suit?'

Jerralds studied it. 'Yes, that is our suit.'

'How about the raincoat? It looks like the kind of thing you might sell, but the label's been torn out. Is it your coat?'

'What do you mean, it looks like the kind of thing we might sell?'

'Stylish,' Carella said.

'Oh, I see.'

'With a flair,' Carella said.

'Yes, I see.'

'Important-looking,' Carella said.

'Yes, yes.'

'Cool,' Carella said. 'Wild. Crazy.'

'That's our raincoat, all right,' Jerralds said.

'How about this umbrella?'

'May I see it, please?'

Carella handed him the tagged umbrella.

'No, that's not ours,' Jerralds said. 'We try to offer something different in men's umbrellas. For example, we have one with a handle made from a ram's horn, and another fashioned from a Tibetan candlestick which ...'

'But this one is yours, right?'

'No. Were you interested in ...'

'No, I don't need an umbrella,' Carella said. 'It's stopped raining, you know.'

'Oh, has it?'

'Several days ago.'

'Oh. It gets so crowded in here sometimes ...'

'Yes I can understand. About this suit and this raincoat, can you tell me who bought them?'

'Well, that would be difficult to ...' Jerralds stopped. His hand fluttered to the jacket of the suit, landed on the sleeve, scraped at the stain there. 'Seem to have got something on the sleeve,' he said.

'Blood,' Carella answered.

'Wh –?'

'Blood. That's a bloodstain. You sell many of these suits, Mr Jerralds?'

'Blood, well it's a popular ... blood? Blood?' He stared at Carella.

'It's a popular number?' Carella said.

'Yes.'

'In this size?'

'What size is it?'

'A forty-two.'

'That's a big size.'

'Yes. The suit was worn by a big man. The raincoat's big, too. Can you remember selling both these items to anyone? There's also a pair of black socks here someplace. Just a second.' He dug up the socks. 'These look familiar?'

'Those are our socks, yes. Imported from Italy. They have no seam, you see, manufactured all in one ...'

'Then the suit, the raincoat and the socks are yours. So the guy is either a steady customer, or else someone who stopped in and made all the purchases at one time. Can you think of anyone? Big guy, size forty-two suit?'

'May I see the suit again, please?'

Carella handed him the jacket.

'This is a very popular number,' Jerralds said, turning the jacket over in his hands. 'I really couldn't estimate how many of them we sell each week. I don't see how I could possibly identify the person who bought it.'

'There wouldn't be any serial numbers on it anywhere?' Carella asked. 'On the label maybe? Or sewn into the suit someplace?'

'No, nothing like that,' Jerralds said. He flipped the suit over and studied both shoulders. 'There's a high padding on this right shoulder,' he said almost to himself. To Carella, he said, 'That's odd because the shoulders are supposed to be unpadded, you see. That's the look we try to achieve. A natural, flowing ...'

'So what does the padding on that right shoulder mean?'

'I don't know, unless ... Oh, wait a minute, wait a minute. Yes, yes, I'll bet this is the suit.'

'Go ahead,' Carella said.

'This gentlemen came in, oh, it must have been shortly after Christmas. A very tall man, very well built. A very handsome man.'

'Yes?'

'He ... well, one leg was slightly shorter than the other. A half-inch, a quarter-inch, something like that. Not serious enough to produce a limp, you understand, but just enough to throw the line of his body slightly out of kilter. I understand there are a great number of men whose ...'

'Yes, but what about this particular man?'

'Nothing special. Except that we had to build up the right shoulder of the jacket, pad it, you know. To compensate for that shorter leg.'

'And this is that jacket?'

'I would think so, yes.'

'Who bought it?'

'I don't know.'

'He wasn't a regular customer of yours?'

'No. He came in off the street. Yes, I remember now. He bought the suit, and the raincoat, and several pairs of socks, and black knit tie. I remember now.'

'But you don't remember his name?'

'No, I'm sorry.'

'Do you keep sales slips?'

'Yes, but ...'

'Do you list a customer's name on the slip?'

'Yes, but ...'

'But what?'

'This was shortly after Christmas. January. The beginning of January.'

'So?'

'Well, I'd have to go through a pile of records to get to ...'

'I know,' Carella said.

'We're very busy now,' Jerralds said. 'As you can see ...'

'Yes, I can see.'

'This is Saturday, one of our busiest days. I'm afraid I couldn't take the time to ...'

'Mr Jerralds, we're investigating a murder,' Carella said.

'Oh.'

'Do you think you can take the time?'

'Well ...' Jerralds hesitated. 'Very well, would you come into the back of the store, please?'

He pushed aside a curtain. The back of the store was a small cubbyhole piled high with goods in huge cardboard boxes. A man in jockey shorts was pulling on a pair of pants in front of a full length mirror.

'This doubles as a dressing room,' Jerralds explained. 'Those trousers are just for you, sir,' he said to the half-clad man. 'This way; my desk is over here.'

He led Carella to a small desk set before a dirty, barred window.

'January, January,' he said, 'now where would the January stuff be?'

'Is this supposed to be so tight?' the man in trousers said.

'Tight?' Jerralds asked. 'It doesn't look at all tight, sir.'

'It feels tight to me,' the man said. 'Maybe I'm not used to these pants without pleats. What do you think?' he asked Carella.

'Look okay to me,' Carella said.

'Maybe I'm just not used to it,' the man answered.

'Maybe so.'

'They look wonderful,' Jerralds said. 'That colour is a new one. It's sort of off-green. Green and black, a mixture.'

'I thought it was grey,' the man said, studying the trousers more carefully.

'Well, it looks like grey, and it looks like green, and it also looks like black. That's the beauty of it,' Jerralds said.

'Yeah?' The man looked at the trousers again. 'It's a nice colour,' he said dubiously. He thought for a moment, seeking an escape. 'But they're too tight,' and he began pulling off the trousers. 'Excuse me,' he said, hopping on one leg and crashing into Carella. 'It's a little crowded back here.'

'The January file should be ...' Jerralds touched one temple with his forefinger and knotted his brow. The finger came down like the finger of doom circling in the air and then dived, tapping a carton which rested several feet from the desk. Jerralds opened the carton and began rummaging among the sales slips.

The man threw the trousers onto the desk and said, 'I like the colour, but they're too tight.' He walked to the carton over which he had draped his own trousers and began pulling them on. 'I can't stand tight pants, can you?' he asked Carella.

'No,' Carella answered.

'I like a lot of room,' the man said.

'No, this is February,' Jerralds said. 'Now where the devil did I put the January slips? Let me think,' and again the finger touched his temple, hesitated there until the light of inspiration crossed his bearded face, and then zoomed like a Stuka to a new target. He opened the second carton and pulled out a sheaf of sales slips.

'Here we are,' he said. 'January. Oh, God, this is going to be awful. We had a clearance sale in January. After Christmas, you know. There are *thousands* of slips here.'

'Well, thanks a lot,' the man said, secure in his own loose trousers now. 'I like a lot of room, you understand.'

'I understand,' Jerralds said as he leafed through the sales slips.

'I'll drop in again sometime. I'm a cab driver, you see. I need a lot of room. After all, I sit on my ass all day long.'

'I understand,' Jerralds said. 'I think it was the second week in January. After the sale. Let me try those first.'

'Well, so long,' the cab driver said. 'Nice meeting you.'

'Take it easy,' Carella answered, and the cabbie pushed through the hanging curtains and into the front of the shop.

'Three shirts at four-fifty per ... no, that's not it. This *is* a job, you know. If you weren't such a nice person, I doubt if I'd ... one pair of swim trunks at ... no ... ties, no ... one raincoat black one suit charcoal, three pair lisle ... here it is, here it is,' Jerralds said. 'I thought so. January tenth. Yes, it was a cash sale.'

'And the man's name?'

'It should be on the top of the slip here. It's a little difficult to read. The carbon isn't too clear.'

'Can you make it out?' Carella asked.

'I'm not sure. Chirapadano, does that sound like a name? Michael Chirapadano?'

Chapter Seventeen

The landlady said, 'Are you here again? Where's your redheaded friend?'

'Working on something,' Carella said. 'I'd like to go through Chirapadano's room again. That okay with you?'

'Why? You got a clue?'

'Maybe.'

'He owes me two months' rent,' the landlady said. 'Come on, I'll take you up.'

They walked upstairs. She cleaned the banister with an oily cloth as they went up. She led Carella to the apartment and was taking out the key when she stopped. Carella had heard the sound, too. His gun was already in his hand. He moved the landlady to one side and was backing off against the opposite wall when she whispered, 'For God's sake, don't break it in. Use my key, for God's sake.'

He took the key from her, inserted it into the lock, and twisted it as quietly as he could. He turned the knob then and shoved against the door. The door would not budge. He heard a frantic scurrying inside the apartment, and he shouted, 'Goddamnit!' and hurled his shoulder against the door, snapping it inward.

A tall man stood in the centre of the room, a bass drum in his hand.

'Hold it, Mike!' Carella shouted, and the man threw the bass drum at him, catching him full in the chest, knocking him backwards and against the landlady who kept shouting, 'I told you not to break it in! Why didn't you use the key!'

The man was on Carella now. He did not say a word. There was a wild gleam in his eyes as he rushed Carella, disregarding the gun in Carella's fist as the landlady screamed her admonitions. He threw a left that caught Carella on the cheek and was drawing back his right when Carella swung the .38 in a side-swiping swing that opened the man's cheek. The man staggered backwards, struggling for balance, tripping over the rim of the bass drum and crashing through the skin. He began crying suddenly, a pitiful series of sobs that erupted from his mouth.

'Now you broke it,' he said. 'Now you went and broke it.'

'Are you Mike Chirapadano?' Carella asked.

'That ain't him,' the landlady said. 'Why'd you break the door in? You cops are all alike! Why didn't you use the key like I told you?'

'I *did* use the damn key,' Carella said angrily. 'All it did was lock the door. The door was already open. You sure this isn't Chirapadano?'

'Of course I'm sure. How could the door have been open? I locked it myself.'

'Our friend here probably used a skeleton key on it. How about that, Mac?' Carella asked.

'Now you broke it,' the man said. 'Now you went and broke it.'

'Broke what?'

'The drum. You broke the damn drum.'

'You're the one who broke it,' Carella said.

'You hit me,' the man said. 'I wouldn't have tripped if you hadn't hit me.'

'Who are you? What's your name? How'd you get in here?'

'You figure it out, big man.'

'Why'd you leave the door unlocked?'

'Who expected anyone to come up here?'

'What do you want here anyway? Who are you?'

'I wanted the drums.'

'Why?'

'To hock them.'

'Mike's drums?'

'Yes.'

'All right, now who are you?'

'What do you care? You broke the bass drum. Now I can't hock it.'

'Did Mike ask you to hock his drums?'

'No.'

'You were stealing them?'

'I was borrowing them.'

'Sure. What's your name?'

'Big man. Has a gun, so he thinks he's a big man.' He touched his bleeding face. 'You cut my cheek.'

'That's right,' Carella said. 'What's your name?'

'Larry Daniels.'

'How do you know Chirapadano?'

'We played in the same band.'

'Where?'

'The King and Queen.'

'You a good friend of his?'

Daniels shrugged.

'What instrument do you play?'

'Trombone.'

'Do you know where Mike is?'

'No.'

'But you knew he wasn't here, didn't you? Otherwise you wouldn't have sneaked up here with your skeleton key and tried to steal his drums. Isn't that right?'

'I wasn't stealing them. I was borrowing them. I was going to give him the pawn ticket when I saw him.'

'Why'd you want to hock the drums?'

'I need some loot.'

'Why don't you hock your trombone?'

'I already hocked the horn.'

'You the junkie Randy Simms was talking about?'

'Who?'

'Simms. Randy Simms. The guy who owns The King and Queen. He said the trombone player on the band was a junkie. That you, Daniels?'

'Okay, that's me. It ain't no crime to be an addict. Check the law. It ain't no crime. And I got no stuff on me, so put that in your pipe and smoke it. You ain't got me on a goddamn thing.'

'Except attempted burglary,' Carella said.

'Burglary, my ass. I was borrowing the drums.'

'How'd you know Mike wouldn't be here?'

'I knew, that's all.'

'Sure. But how? Do you know where he is right this minute?'

'No, I don't know.'

'But you knew he wasn't here.'

'I don't know nothing.'

'A dope fiend,' the landlady said. 'I knew it.'

'Where is he, Daniels?'

'Why do you want him?'

'We want him.'

'Why?'

'Because he owns a suit of clothes that may be connected with a murder. And if you withhold information from us, you can be brought in as an accessory after the fact. Now how about that, Daniels? Where is he?'

'I don't know. That's the truth.'

'When did you see him last?'

'Just before he made it with the dame.'

'What dame?'

'The stripper.'

'Bubbles Caesar?'

'That's her name.'

'When was this, Daniels?'

'I don't remember the date exactly. It was around Valentine's Day. A few days before.'

'The twelfth?'

'I don't remember.'

'Mike didn't show up for work on the night of the twelfth. Was that the day you saw him?'

'Yeah. That's right.'

'When did you see him?'

'In the afternoon sometime.'

'And what did he want?'

'He told me he wouldn't be on the gig that night, and he gave me the key to his pad.'

'Why'd he do that?'

'He said he wanted me to take his drums home for him. So when we quit playing that night, that's what I done. I packed up his drums and took them here.'

'So that's how you got in today. You still have Mike's key.'

'Yeah.'

'And that's how you knew he wouldn't be here. He never did get that key back from you, did he?'

'Yeah, that's right.' Daniels paused. 'I was supposed to call him the next day and we was supposed to meet so I could give him the key. Only I called, and there was no answer. I called all that day, but nobody answered the phone.'

'This was the thirteenth of February?'

'Yeah, the next day.'

'And he had told you he would be with Bubbles Caesar?'

'Well, not directly. But when he give me the key and the telephone number, he made a little joke, you know? He said, "Larry, don't be calling me in the middle of the night because Bubbles and me, we are very deep sleepers." Like that. So I figured he would be making it with Bubbles that night. Listen, I'm beginning to get itchy. I got to get out of here.'

'Relax, Daniels. What was the phone number Mike gave you?'

'I don't remember. Listen, I got to get a shot. I mean, now listen, I ain't kidding around here.'

'What was the number?'

'For Christ's sake, who remembers? This was last month, for Christ's sake. Look, now look, I ain't kidding here. I mean, I got to get out of here. I know the signs, and this is gonna be bad unless I get ...'

'Did you write the number down?'

'What?'

'The number. Did you write it down?'

'I don't know, I don't know,' Daniels said, but he pulled out his wallet and began going through it, muttering all the while, 'I have to get a shot, I have to get fixed, I have to get out of here,' his hands trembling as he riffled through the wallet's compartments. 'Here,' he said at last, 'here it is, here's the number. Let me out of here before I puke.'

Carella took the card.

'You can puke at the station house,' he said.

The telephone number was Economy 8–3165.

At the squadroom, Carella called the telephone company and got an operator who promptly told him she had no record of any such number.

'It may be an unlisted number,' Carella said. 'Would you please check it?'

'If it's an unlisted number, sir, I would have no record of it.'

'Look, this is the police department,' Carella said. 'I know you're not supposed to divulge ...'

'It is not a matter of not divulging the number, sir. It is simply that I would have no record of it. What I'm trying to tell you, sir, is that we do *not* have a list labelled "Unlisted Numbers". Do you understand me, sir?'

'Yes, I understand you,' Carella said. 'But the telephone company has a record of it someplace, doesn't it? Somebody pays the damn bill. Somebody *gets* the bill each month. All I want to know is who gets it?'

'I'm sorry, sir, but I wouldn't know who ...'

'Let me talk to your supervisor,' Carella said.

Charles Tudor had begun walking from his home in The Quarter, and Cotton Hawes walked directly behind him. At a respectable distance, to be sure. It was a wonderful day for walking, a day that whetted the appetite for spring. It was a day for idling along and stopping at each and every store window, a day for admiring the young ladies who had taken off their coats and blossomed earlier than the flowers.

Tudor did not idle, and Tudor did not admire. Tudor walked at a rapid clip, his head ducked, his hands thrust into the pockets of his topcoat, a big man who shouldered aside any passerby who got in his way. Hawes, an equally big man, had a tough time keeping up with him. The sidewalks of The Quarter on that lovely Saturday were cluttered with women pushing baby carriages, young girls strutting with high-tilted breasts, young men wearing faded tight jeans and walking with the lope of male dancers, young men sporting beards and paint-smeared sweat shirts, girls wearing leotards over which were Bermuda shorts, old men carrying canvases decorated with pictures of the ocean, Italian housewives from the neighbourhood carrying shopping bags bulging with long breads, young actresses wearing make-up to rehearsals in the many little theatres that dotted the side streets, kids playing Johnny-on-the-Pony.

Hawes could have done without the display of humanity. If he were to keep up with Tudor, he'd have to ...

He stopped suddenly.

Tudor had gone into a candy store on the corner. Hawes quickened his pace. He didn't know whether or not there was a back entrance to the store, but he had lost Tudor the night before, and he didn't want to lose him again. He walked past the candy store and around the corner. There was only one entrance, and he could see Tudor inside making a purchase. He crossed the street quickly, took up a post in the doorway of a tenement, and waited for Tudor to emerge. When Tudor came out, he was tearing the cellophane top from a package of cigarettes. He did not stop to light the cigarette. He lighted it as he walked along, three matches blowing out before he finally got a stream of smoke.

Doggedly, Hawes plodded along behind him.

'Good afternoon, sir, this is your supervisor; may I help you, sir?'

'Yes,' Carella said. 'This is Detective Carella of the 87th Squad up here in Isola,' he said, pulling his rank. 'We have a telephone number we're trying to trace, and it seems . . .'

'Did the call originate from a dial telephone, sir?'

'What call?'

'Because if it did, sir, it would be next to impossible to trace it. A dial telephone utilizes automatic equipment and . . .'

'Yes I know that. We're not trying to trace a call, operator, we're trying to . . .'

'I'm the supervisor, sir.'

'Yes, I know. We're . . .'

'On the other hand, if the call was made from a manual instrument, the possibilities of tracing it would be a little better. Unless it got routed eventually through automatic . . .'

'Lady, I'm a cop, and I know about tracing telephone calls, and all I want you to do is look up a number and tell me the party's name and address. That's all I want you to do.'

'I see.'

'Good. The number is Economy 8–3165. Now would you please look that up and give me the information I want?'

'Just one moment, sir.'

Her voice left the line. Carella drummed impatiently on the desk top. Bert Kling, fully recovered, furiously typed up a D.D. report at the adjoining desk.

Tudor was making another stop. Hawes cased the shop from his distant vantage point. It was set between two other shops in a row of tenements, and so the possibility of another entrance was unlikely. If there *was* another entrance, it would not be one accessible to customers of the shop.

Hawes lighted a cigarette and waited for Tudor to make his purchase and come into the street again.

He was in the shop for close to fifteen minutes.

When he came out, he was carrying some white gardenias.

Oh great, Hawes thought, *he's going to see a dame.*

And then he wondered if the dame could be Bubbles Caesar.

'Sir, this is your supervisor.'

'Yes?' Carella said. 'Have you got . . . ?'

'You understand, sir, that when a person requests an unlisted or un-published telephone number, we . . .'

'I'm not a person,' Carella said, 'I'm a cop.' He wrinkled his brow and thought that one over for a second.

'Yes, sir, but I'm referring to the person whose telephone number this is. When that person requests an unpublished number, we make certain that he understands what this means. It means that there will be no record of the listing available, and that no one will be able to get the number from anyone in the telephone company, even upon protest of an emergency condition existing. You understand that, sir?'

'Yes, I do. Lady, I'm a cop investigating a murder. Now will you please ...'

'Oh, I'll give you the information you requested. I certainly will.'

'Then what ...?'

'But I want you to know that an ordinary citizen could not under any circumstances get the same information. I simply wanted to make the telephone company's policy clear.'

'Oh, it's perfectly clear, operator.'

'Supervisor,' she corrected.

'Yes, sure. Now who's that number listed for, and what's the address?'

'The phone is in a building on Canopy Street. The address is 1611.'

'Thank you. And the owner of the phone?'

'No one *owns* our telephones, sir. You realize that our instruments are provided on a rental basis, and that ...'

'Whose name is that phone listed under, oper – supervisor? Would you please ...'

'The listing is for a man named Charles Tudor,' the supervisor said.

'Charles Tudor?' Carella said. 'Now what the hell ...?'

'Sir?' the supervisor asked.

'Thank you,' Carella said, and he hung up. He turned to Kling. 'Bert,' he said, 'get your hat.'

'I don't wear any,' Kling said, so he clipped on his holster instead.

Charles Tudor had gone into 1611 Canopy Street, unlocked the inner vestibule door, and vanished from sight.

Hawes stood in the hallway now and studied the mailboxes. None of them carried a nameplate for Bubbles Caesar or Charles Tudor or Mike Chirapadano or anyone at all with whom Hawes was familiar. Hawes examined the mailboxes again, relying upon one of the most elementary pieces of police knowledge in his second study of the nameplates. For reasons known only to God and psychiatrists, when a person assumes a fictitious name, the assumed name will generally have the same initials as the person's real name. Actually, this isn't a mystery worthy of supernatural or psychiatric secrecy. The simple fact is that a great many people own monogrammed handkerchiefs, or shirts, or suitcases, or dispatch cases, or whatever. And if a man named Benjamin Franklin who has the initials B. F. on his bags and his shirts and his underwear and maybe tattooed on his forehead should suddenly register in a hotel as George Washington, a curious clerk might wonder whether or not Benjy came by his luggage in an illegal manner. Since a man using an assumed name is a man who is not anxious to attract attention, he will do everything possible to make things easier for himself. And so he will use the initials of his real name in choosing an alias.

One of the mailboxes carried a nameplate for a person called Christopher Talley.

It sounded phoney, and it utilized the C. T. initials, and so Hawes made a mental note of the apartment number: 6B.

Then he pressed the bell for apartment 2A, waited for the answering buzz that released the inner door lock, and rapidly climbed the steps to the sixth floor. Outside apartment 6B, he put his ear to the door and listened. Inside the apartment, a man was talking.

'Barbara,' the man said, 'I brought you some more flowers.'

In the police sedan, Carella said, 'I don't get it, Bert. I just don't get it.'

'What's the trouble?' Kling asked.

'No trouble. Only confusion. We find a pair of hands, and the blood group is identified as "O", right?'

'Right.'

'Okay. Mike Chirapadano is in that blood group. He's also a big guy, and he vanished last month, and so that would make him a good prospect for the *victim*, am I right?'

'Right,' Kling said.

'Okay. But when we find the clothes the murderer was wearing, it turns out they belonged to Mike Chirapadano. So it turns out that he's a good prospect for the *murderer*, too.'

'Yeah?' Kling said.

'Yeah. Then we get a line on Bubbles Caesar's hideout, the place she and Chirapadano used, the place we're going to right now ...'

'Yeah?'

'Yeah; and it turns out the phone is listed for Charles Tudor, Bubbles' agent. Now how does that figure?'

'There's 1611 up ahead,' Kling said.

Standing in the hallway, Hawes could hear only the man's voice, and the voice definitely belonged to Charles Tudor. He wondered whether or not he should crash the apartment. Scarcely daring to breathe, trying desperately to hear the girl's replies, he kept his ear glued to the wood of the door, listening.

'Do you like the flowers, Barbara?' Tudor said.

There was a pause. Hawes listened, but could hear no reply.

'I didn't know whether or not you liked gardenias, but we have so many of the others in here. Well, a beautiful woman should have lots of flowers.'

Another pause.

'You *do* like gardenias?' Tudor said. 'Good. You look beautiful today, Barbara. Beautiful. I don't think I've ever seen you looking so beautiful. Did I tell you about the police?'

Hawes listened for the reply. He thought instantly of Marla Phillips' tiny voice, and he wondered if all big girls were naturally endowed with the same voices. He could not hear a word.

'You don't want to hear about the police?' Tudor said. 'Well, they came to see me again yesterday. Asking about you and me. And Mike. And asking whether or not I owned a black raincoat and umbrella. I told them I didn't. That's the truth, Barbara. I really don't own a black raincoat, and I've never liked umbrellas. You didn't know that, did you? Well, there are a lot of things you don't know about me. I'm a very complex person. But we have lots of time. You can learn all about me. You look so lovely. Do you mind my telling you how beautiful you look?'

This time, Hawes heard something.

But the sound had come from behind him, in the hallway.

He whirled, drawing his .38 instantly.

'Put up the gun, Cotton,' Carella whispered.

'Man, you scared the hell out of me!' Hawes whispered back. He peered past Carella, saw Kling standing there behind him.

'Tudor in there?' Carella asked.

'Yeah. He's with the girl.'

'Bubbles?'

'That's right.'

'Okay, let's break it open,' Carella said.

Kling took up a position to the right of the door, Hawes to the left. Carella braced himself and kicked in the lock. The door swung open. They burst into the room with their guns in their hands, and they saw Charles Tudor on his knees at one end of the room. And then they saw what was behind Tudor, and each of the men separately felt identical waves of shock and terror and pity, and Carella knew at once that they would not need their guns.

Chapter Eighteen

The room was filled with flowers. Bouquets of red roses and white roses and yellow roses, smaller bouquets of violets, long-stemmed gladioli, carnations, gardenias, rhododendron leaves in water-filled vases. The room was filled with the aroma of flowers – fresh flowers and dying flowers, flowers that were new, and flowers that had lost their bloom. The room was filled with the overwhelming scent of flowers and the overwhelming stench of something else.

The girl, Bubbles Caesar, lay quite still on the table around which the flowers were massed. Her black hair trailed behind her head, her long body was clad only in a nightgown, her slender hands were crossed over her bosom. A ruby necklace circled her throat. She lay on the table and stared at the ceiling, and she saw nothing, because she was stone cold dead and she'd been that way for a month and her decomposing body stank to high heaven.

Tudor, on his knees, turned to look at the detectives.

'So you found us,' he said quietly.

'Get up, Tudor.'

'You found us,' he repeated. He looked at the dead girl again. 'She's beautiful, isn't she?' he asked of no one. 'I've never known anyone as beautiful as she.'

In the closet, they found the body of a man. He was wearing only his underpants. Both of his hands had been amputated.

The man was Mike Chirapadano.

Oh, he knew that she was dead; he knew that he had killed them both. They stood around him in the squadroom, and they asked their questions in hushed voices because it was all over now and, killer or not, Charles Tudor was a human being, a man who had loved. Not a cheap thief, and not a punk, only a murderer who had loved. But yes, he knew she was dead. Yes, he knew that. Yes, he knew he had killed her, killed them both. He knew.

And yet, as he talked, as he answered the almost whispered questions of the detectives, it seemed he did not know, it seemed he wandered from the cruel reality of murder to another world, a world where Barbara Caesar was still alive and laughing. He crossed the boundary line into this other world with facility, and then recrossed it to reality, and then lost it again until there were no boundaries any more, there was only a man wandering between two alien lands, a native of neither, a stranger to both.

'When they called me from the club,' he said, 'when Randy Simms called me from the club, I didn't know what to think. Barbara was usually very reliable. So I called her apartment, the one she shared with the other girls, and I spoke to one of her roommates, and the roommate told me she hadn't seen her since early that morning. This was the twelfth, February twelfth; I'll remember that day as long as I live, it was the day I killed Barbara.'

'What did you do after you spoke to the roommate, Mr Tudor?'

'I figured perhaps she'd gone to the other apartment, the one on Canopy Street.'

'Were you paying for that apartment, Mr Tudor?'

'Yes. Yes, I was. Yes. But it was *our* apartment, you know. We shared it. We share a lot of things, Barbara and I. We like to do a lot of things together. I have tickets for a show next week. A musical. She likes music. We'll see that together. We do a lot of things together.'

The detectives stood in a silent knot around him. Carella cleared his throat.

'Did you go to the apartment, Mr Tudor? The one on Canopy Street?'

'Yes, I did. I got there sometime around ten o'clock. In the night. It was night-time. And I went right upstairs, and I used my key, and I ... well, she was there. With this man. This man was touching her. In our apartment. Barbara was in *our* apartment with another man.' Tudor shook his head. 'She shouldn't do things like that. She knows I love her. I bought her a ruby necklace for Valentine's Day. Did you see the necklace? It's quite beautiful. She wears it very well.'

'What did you do when you found them, Mr Tudor?'

'I ... I was shocked. I ... I ... I wanted to know. She ... she told me I didn't own her. She told me she was free, she said nobody owned her, not me, not ... not the man she was with and ... and ... and not Karl either, she said, not Karl, I didn't even know who Karl was. She ...

she said she had promised this Karl she'd go away with him, but he didn't own her either, nobody owned her, she said, and ... and ...'

'Yes, Mr Tudor?'

'I couldn't believe it because ... well, I love her. You know that. And she was saying these terrible things, and this man, this Mike, stood there grinning. In his underwear, he was in his underwear, and she had on a nightgown I'd given her, the one *I'd* given her. I ... I ... I hit him. I kept hitting him, and Barbara laughed, she laughed all the while I was hitting him. I'm a very strong man, I hit him and I kept banging his head against the floor and then Barbara stopped laughing and she said, "You've killed him." I ... I ...'

'Yes?'

'I took her in my arms, and I kissed her and ... and ... I ... my hands ... her throat ... she didn't scream ... nothing ... I simply squeezed and ... and she ... she ... she went limp in my arms. It was his fault I thought, his fault, touching her, he shouldn't have touched her, he had no right to touch the woman I loved and so I ... I went into the kitchen looking for a ... a knife or something. I found a meat cleaver in one of the drawers and I ... I went into the other room and cut off both his hands.' Tudor paused. 'For touching her. I cut off his hands so that he would never touch her again.' His brow wrinkled with the memory. 'There ... there was a lot of blood. I ... picked up the hands and put them in ... in Barbara's overnight bag. Then I dragged his body into the closet and tried to clean up a little. There ... there was a lot of blood all over.'

They got the rest of the story from him in bits and pieces. And the story threaded the boundary line, wove between reality and fantasy. And the men in the squadroom listened in something close to embarrassment, and some of them found other things to do, downstairs, away from the big man who sat in the hard-backed chair and told them of the woman he'd loved, the woman he still loved.

He told them he had begun disposing of Chirapadano's body last week. He had started with the hands, and he decided it was best to dispose of them separately. The overnight bag would be safe, he'd thought, because so many people owned similar bags. He had decided to use that for the first hand. But it occurred to him that identification of the body could be made through the finger tips, and so he had sliced those away with a kitchen knife.

'I cut myself,' he said. 'When I was working on the fingertips. Just a small cut, but it bled a lot. My finger.'

'What type blood do you have, Mr Tudor?' Carella asked.

'What? B, I think. Yes, B. Why?'

'That might explain the contradictory stain on the suit, Steve,' Kling said.

'What?' Tudor said. 'The suit? Oh, yes. I don't know why I did that, really. I don't know why. It was just something I had to do, something I ... I just *had* to do.'

'What was it you had to do, Mr Tudor?'

'Put on his clothes,' Tudor said. 'The dead man's. I ... I put on his suit, and his socks, and I wore his raincoat, and I carried his umbrella. When I went out to ... to get rid of the hands.' He shrugged. 'I don't know why. Really, I don't know why.' He paused. 'I threw the clothes away as soon as I realized you knew about them. I went all the way out to Calm's Point, and I threw them in a trash basket.' Tudor looked at the circle of faces around him. 'Will you be keeping me much longer?' he asked suddenly.

'Why, Mr Tudor?'

'Because I want to get back to Barbara,' he told the cops.

They took him downstairs to the detention cells, and then they sat in the curiously silent squadroom.

'There's the answer to the conflicting stuff we found on the suit,' Kling said.

'Yeah.'

'They both wore it. The killer *and* the victim.'

'Yeah.'

'Why do you suppose he put on the dead man's clothes?' Kling shuddered. 'Jesus, this whole damn case ...'

'Maybe he knew,' Carella said.

'Knew what?'

'That he was a victim, too.'

Miscolo came in from the Clerical Office. The men in the squadroom were silent.

'Anybody want some coffee?' he asked.

Nobody wanted any coffee.

"The child Anna
sat on the floor
close to the
wall and played
with her

DOLL

talking to it,
listening...."

This, too is for Dodie and Ray Crane

Chapter One

The child Anna sat on the floor close to the wall and played with her doll, talking to it, listening. She could hear the voices raised in anger coming from her mother's bedroom through the thin separating wall, but she busied herself with the doll and tried not to be frightened. The man in her mother's bedroom was shouting now. She tried not to hear what he was saying. She brought the doll close to her face and kissed its plastic cheek, and then talked to it again, and listened.

In the bedroom next door, her mother was being murdered.

Her mother was called Tinka, a chic and lacquered label concocted by blending her given name, Tina, with her middle name, Karin. Tinka was normally a beautiful woman, no question about it. She'd have been a beautiful woman even if her name were Beulah. Or Bertha. Or perhaps even Brunhilde. The Tinka tag only enhanced her natural good looks, adding an essential gloss, a necessary polish, an air of mystery and adventure.

Tinka Sachs was a fashion model.

She was, no question about it, a very beautiful woman. She possessed a finely sculptured face that was perfectly suited to the demands of her profession, a wide forehead, high pronounced cheekbones, a generous mouth, a patrician nose, slanted green eyes flecked with chips of amber; oh, she was normally a beauty, no question about it. Her body was a model's body, lithe and loose and gently angled, with long slender legs, narrow hips, and a tiny bosom. She walked with a model's insinuating glide, pelvis tilted, crotch cleaving the air, head erect. She laughed with a model's merry shower of musical syllables, painted lips drawing back over capped teeth, amber eyes glowing. She sat with a model's carelessly draped ease, posing even in her own living room, invariably choosing the wall or sofa that best offset her clothes, or her long blonde hair, or her mysterious green eyes flecked with chips of amber; oh, she was normally a beauty.

She was not so beautiful at the moment.

She was not so beautiful because the man who followed her around the room shouting obscenities at her, the man who stalked her from wall to wall and boxed her into the narrow passage circumscribed by the king-sized bed and the marble-topped dresser opposite, the man who closed in on her oblivious to her murmuring, her pleading, her sobbing, the man was grasping a kitchen knife with which he had been slashing her repeatedly for the past three minutes.

The obscenities spilled from the man's mouth in a steady unbroken torrent, the anger having reached a pitch that was unvaried now, neither rising nor falling in volume or intensity. The knife blade swung in a short, tight arc, back and forth, its rhythm as unvaried as that of the words that poured from the man's mouth. Obscenities and blade, like partners in an evil copulation, moved together in perfect rhythm and pitch, enveloping Tinka in alternating splashes of blood and spittle. She kept murmuring the man's name pleadingly, again and again, as the blade ripped into her flesh. But the glittering arc was relentless. The razor-sharp blade, the monotonous flow of obscenities, inexorably forced her bleeding and torn into the far corner of the room, where the back of her head collided with an original Chagall, tilting it slightly askew, the knife moving in again in its brief terrifying arc, the blade slicing parallel bleeding ditches across her small breasts and moving lower across the flat abdomen, her peignoir tearing again with a clinging silky blood-sotted sound as the knife blade plunged deeper with each step closer he took. She said his name once more, she shouted his name, and then she murmured the word 'Please,' and then she fell back against the wall again, knocking the Chagall from its hook so that a riot of framed colour dropped heavily over her shoulder, falling in a lopsided angle past the long blonde hair, and the open red gashes across her throat and naked chest, the tattered blue peignoir, the natural brown of her exposed pubic hair, the blue satin slippers. She fell gasping for breath, spitting blood, headlong over the painting, her forehead colliding with the wide oaken frame, her blonde hair covering the Chagall reds and yellows and violets with a fine misty golden haze, the knife slash across her throat pouring blood onto the canvas, setting her hair afloat in a pool of red that finally overspilled the oaken frame and ran onto the carpet.

Next door, the child Anna clung fiercely to her doll.

She said a reassuring word to it, and then listened in terror as she heard footfalls in the hall outside her closed bedroom door. She kept listening breathlessly until she heard the front door to the apartment open and then close again.

She was still sitting in the bedroom, clutching her doll, when the superintendent came up the next morning to change a faucet washer Mrs Sachs had complained about the day before.

April is the fourth month of the year.

It is important to know that – if you are a cop, you can sometimes get a little confused.

More often than not, your confusion will be compounded of one part exhaustion, one part tedium, and one part disgust. The exhaustion is an ever present condition and one to which you have become slowly accustomed over the years. You know that the department does not recognize Saturdays, Sundays or legal holidays, and so you are even prepared to work on Christmas morning if you have to, especially if someone intent on committing mischief is inconsiderate enough to plan it for that day – witness General George Washington and the unsuspecting Hessians, those drunks. You know that a detective's work schedule does not revolve around a fixed day, and so you have learned to adjust to your odd waking hours and your shorter sleeping time, but you have never been able to adjust to the nagging feeling of exhaustion that is the result of too much crime and too few hours, too few men to pit against it. You are sometimes a drag at home with your wife and children, but that is only because you are tired, boy what a life, all work and no play, wow.

The tedium is another thing again, but it also helps to generate confusion. Crime is the most exciting sport in the world, right? Sure, ask anybody. Then how come it can be so boring when you're a working cop who is typing reports in triplicate and legging it all over the city talking to old ladies in flowered house dresses in apartments smelling of death? How can the routine of detection become something as proscribed as the ritual of a bullfight, never changing, so that even a gun duel in a night-time alley can assume familiar dimensions and be regarded with the same feeling of ennui that accompanies a routine request to the B.C.I.? The boredom is confusing as hell. It clasps hands with the exhaustion and makes you wonder whether this is January or Friday.

The disgust comes into it only if you are a human being. Some cops aren't. But if you are a human being, you are sometimes appalled by what your fellow human beings are capable of doing. You can understand lying because you practise it in a watered-down form as a daily method of smoothing the way, helping the machinery of mankind to function more easily without getting fouled by too much truth-stuff. You can understand stealing because when you were a kid you sometimes swiped pencils from the public school supply closet, and once a toy aeroplane from the five and ten. You can even understand murder because there is a dark and secret place in your own heart where you have hated deeply enough to kill. You can understand all these things, but you are nonetheless disgusted when they are piled upon you in profusion, when you are constantly confronted with liars, thieves and slaughterers, when all human decency seems in a state of suspension for the eight or twelve or thirty-six hours you are in the squadroom or out answering a squeal. Perhaps you could accept an occasional corpse – death is only a part of life, isn't it? It is corpse heaped upon corpse that leads to disgust and further leads to confusion. If you can no longer tell one corpse from another, if you can no longer distinguish one open bleeding head from the next, then how is April any different from October?

It was April.

The torn and lovely woman lay in profile across the bloody face of the Chagall painting. The lab technicians were dusting for latent prints, vacuuming for hairs and traces of fibre, carefully wrapping for transportation the knife found in the corridor just outside the bedroom door, and the dead girl's pocketbook, which seemed to contain everything but money.

Detective Steve Carella made his notes and then walked out of the room and down the hall to where the little girl sat in a very big chair, her feet not touching the floor, her doll sleeping across her lap. The little girl's name was Anna Sachs – one of the patrolmen had told him that the moment Carella arrived. The doll seemed almost as big as she did.

'Hello,' he said to her, and felt the old confusion once again, the exhaustion because he had not been home since Thursday morning, the tedium because he was embarking on another round of routine questioning, and the disgust because the person he was about to question was only a little girl and her mother was dead and mutilated in the room next door. He tried to smile. He was not very good at it. The little girl said nothing. She looked up at him out of very big eyes. Her lashes were long and brown, her mouth drawn in stoic silence beneath a nose she had inherited from her mother. Unblinkingly, she watched him. Unblinkingly, she said nothing.

'Your name is Anna, isn't it?' Carella said.

The child nodded.

'Do you know what my name is?'

'No.'

'Steve.'

The girl nodded again.

'I have a little girl about your age,' Carella said. 'She's a twin. How old *are* you, Anna?'

'Five.'

'That's just how old my daughter is.'

'Mmm,' Anna said. She paused a moment, and then asked, 'Is Mommy killed?'

'Yes,' Carella said. 'Yes, honey, she is.'

'I was afraid to go in and look.'

'It's better you didn't.'

'She got killed last night, didn't she?' Anna asked.

'Yes.'

There was a silence in the room. Outside, Carella could hear the muted sounds of a conversation between the police photographer and the M.E. An April fly buzzed against the bedroom window. He looked into the child's upturned face.

'Were you here last night?' he asked.

'Um-huh.'

'Where?'

'Here. Right here in my room.' She stroked the doll's cheek, and then looked up at Carella and asked, 'What's a twin?'

'When two babies are born at the same time.'

'Oh.'

She continued looking up at him, her eyes tearless, wide, and certain in the small white face. At last she said, 'The man did it.'

'What man?' Carella asked.

'The one who was with her.'

'Who?'

'Mummy. The man who was with her in her room.'

'Who was the man?'

'I don't know.'

'Did you see him?'

'No. I was here playing with Chatterbox when he came in.'

'Is Chatterbox a friend of yours?'

'Chatterbox is my *dolly*,' the child said, and she held up the doll and giggled, and Carella wanted to scoop her into his arms, hold her close, tell her there was no such thing as sharpened steel and sudden death.

'When was this, honey?' he asked. 'Do you know what time it was?'

'I don't know,' she said, and shrugged. 'I only know how to tell twelve o'clock and seven o'clock, that's all.'

'Well ... was it dark?'

'Yes, it was after supper.'

'This man came in after supper, is that right?'

'Yes.'

'Did your mother know this man?'

'Oh, yes,' Anna said. 'She was laughing and everything when he first came in.'

'Then what happened?'

'I don't know.' Anna shrugged again. 'I was here playing.'

There was another silence.

The first tears welled into her eyes suddenly, leaving the rest of the face untouched; there was no trembling of lip, no crumbling of features, the tears simply overspilled her eyes and ran down her cheeks. She sat as still as a stone, crying soundlessly while Carella stood before her helplessly, a hulking man who suddenly felt weak and ineffective before this silent torrent of grief.

He gave her his handkerchief.

She took it wordlessly and blew her nose, but she did not dry her eyes. Then she handed it back to him and said, 'Thank you,' with the tears still running down her face endlessly, sitting stunned with her small hands folded over the doll's chest.

'He was hitting her,' she said. 'I could hear her crying, but I was afraid to go in. So I . . . I made believe I didn't hear. And then . . . then I *really* didn't hear. I just kept talking with Chatterbox, that was all. That way I couldn't hear what he was doing to her in the other room.'

'All right, honey,' Carella said. He motioned to the patrolman standing in the doorway. When the patrolman joined him, he whispered, 'Is her father around? Has he been notified?'

'Gee, I don't know,' the patrolman said. He turned and shouted, 'Anybody know if the husband's been contacted?'

A Homicide cop standing with one of the lab technicians looked up from his notebook and said, 'He's in Arizona. They been divorced for three years now.'

Lieutenant Peter Byrnes was normally a patient and understanding man, but there were times lately when Bert Kling gave him a severe pain in the ass. And whereas Byrnes, being patient and understanding, could appreciate the reasons for Kling's behaviour, this in no way made Kling any nicer to have around the office. The way Byrnes figured it, psychology was certainly an important factor in police work because it helped you to recognize that there were no longer any villains in the world, there were only disturbed people. Psychology substituted understanding for condemnation. It was a very nice tool to possess, psychology was, until a cheap thief kicked you in the groin one night. It then became somewhat difficult to imagine the thief as a put-upon soul who'd had a shabby childhood. In much the same way, though Byrnes completely understood the trauma that was responsible for Kling's current behaviour, he was finding it more and more difficult to accept Kling as anything but a cop who was going to hell with himself.

'I want to transfer him out,' he told Carella that morning.

'Why?'

'Because he's disrupting the whole damn squadroom, that's why,' Byrnes said. He did not enjoy discussing this, nor would he normally have asked for consultation on any firm decision he had made. His decision, however, was anything but final, that was the damn thing about it. He liked Kling, and yet he no longer liked him. He thought he could be a good cop, but was turning into a bad one. 'I've got enough bad cops around here,' he said aloud.

'Bert isn't a bad cop,' Carella said. He stood before Byrnes's cluttered desk in the corner office and listened to the sounds of early spring on the street outside the building, and he thought of the five-year-old girl named Anna Sachs who had taken his handkerchief while the tears streamed down her face.

'He's a surly shit,' Byrnes said. 'Okay, I know what happened to him, but people have died before, Steve, people have been killed before. And if you're a man you grow up to it, you don't act as if everybody's responsible for it. We didn't have anything to do with his girl friend's death, that's the plain and simple truth, and I personally am sick and tired of being blamed for it.'

'He's not blaming you for it, Peter. He's not blaming any of us.'

'He's blaming the *world*, and that's worse. This morning, he had a big argument with Meyer just because Meyer picked up the phone on his desk. I mean, the goddamn phone was ringing, so instead of crossing the room to his own desk, Meyer picked up the closest phone, which was on Kling's desk, so Kling starts a row. Now you can't have that kind of attitude in a squadroom where men are working together, you can't have it, Steve. I'm going to ask for his transfer.'

'That'd be the worst thing that could happen to him.'

'It'd be the best thing for the squad.'

'I don't think so.'

'Nobody's asking your advice,' Byrnes said flatly.

'Then why the hell did you call me in here?'

'You see what I mean?' Byrnes said. He rose from his desk abruptly and began pacing the floor near the meshed-grill windows. He was a compact man and he moved with an economy that belied the enormous energy in his powerful body. Short for a detective, muscular, with a bullet-shaped head and small blue eyes set in a face seamed with wrinkles, he paced briskly behind his desk and shouted. 'You see the trouble he's causing? Even you and I can't sit down and have a sensible discussion about him without starting to yell. That's *just* what I mean, that's *just* why I want him out of here.'

'You don't throw away a good watch because it's running a little slow,' Carella said.

'Don't give me any goddamn similes,' Byrnes said. 'I'm running a squadroom here, not a clock shop.'

'Metaphors,' Carella corrected.

'What*ever*,' Byrnes said. 'I'm going to call the Chief tomorrow and ask him to transfer Kling out. That's it.'

'Where?'

'What do you mean *where*? What do I care where? Out of here, that's all.'

'But *where*? To another squadroom with a bunch of strange guys, so he can get on *their* nerves even more than he does ours? So he can –'

'Oh, so you admit it.'

'That Bert gets on my nerves? Sure, he does.'

'And the situation isn't improving, Steve, you know that too. It gets worse every day. Look, what the hell am I wasting my breath for? He goes, and that's it.' Byrnes gave a brief emphatic nod, and then sat heavily in his chair again, glaring up at Carella with an almost childish challenge on his face.

Carella sighed. He had been on duty for close to fifty hours now, and he was tired. He had checked in at eight-forty-five Thursday morning, and been out all that day gathering information for the backlog of cases that had been piling up all through the month of March. He had caught six hours' sleep on a cot in the locker room that night, and then been called out at seven on Friday morning by the fire department, who suspected arson in a three-alarm blaze they'd answered on the South Side. He had come back to the squadroom at noon to find four telephone messages on his desk. By the time he had returned all the calls – one was from an assistant M.E. who took a full hour to explain the toxicological analysis of a poison they had found in the stomach contents of a beagle, the seventh such dog similarly poisoned in the past week – the clock on the wall read one-thirty. Carella sent down for a pastrami on rye, a container of milk, and a side of French fries. Before the order arrived, he had to leave the squadroom to answer a burglary squeal on North Eleventh. He did not come back until five-thirty, at which time he turned the phone over to a complaining Kling and went down to the locker room to try to sleep again. At eleven o'clock Friday night, the entire squad, working in flying wedges of three detectives to a team, culminated a two-month period of surveillance by raiding twenty-six known numbers banks in the area, a sanitation project that was not finished until five on Saturday morning. At eight-thirty a.m., Carella answered the Sachs squeal and questioned a crying little girl. It was now ten-thirty a.m., and he was tired, and he wanted to go home, and he didn't want to argue in favour of a man who had become everything the lieutenant said he was, he was just too damn weary. But earlier this morning he had looked down at the body of a woman he had not known at all, had seen her ripped and lacerated flesh, and felt a pain bordering on nausea. Now – weary, bedraggled, unwilling to argue – he could remember the mutilated beauty of Tinka Sachs, and he felt something of what Bert Kling must have known in the Culver Avenue bookshop not four years ago when he'd held the bullet-torn body of Claire Townsend in his arms.

'Let him work with me,' he said.

'What do you mean?'

'On the Sachs case. I've been teaming with Meyer lately. Give me Bert instead.'

'What's the matter, don't you like Meyer?'

'I *love* Meyer, I'm tired, I want to go home to bed, will you please let me have Bert on this case?'

'What'll that accomplish?'

'I don't know.'

'I don't approve of shock therapy,' Byrnes said. 'This Sachs woman was brutally murdered. All you'll do is remind Bert –'

'Therapy, my ass,' Carella said. 'I want to be with him, I want to talk to him, I want to let him know he's still got some people on this goddamn squad who think he's a decent human being worth saving. Now, Pete, I *really* am very very tired and I don't want to argue this any further, I mean it. If you want to send Bert to another squad, that's your business, you're the boss here,

I'm not going to argue with you, that's all. I mean it. Now just make up your mind, okay?'

'Take him,' Byrnes said.

'Thank you,' Carella answered. He went to the door. 'Good night', he said, and walked out.

Chapter Two

Sometimes a case starts like sevens coming out.

The Sachs case started just that way on Monday morning when Steve Carella and Bert Kling arrived at the apartment building on Stafford Place to question the elevator operator.

The elevator operator was close to seventy years old, but he was still in remarkable good health, standing straight and tall, almost as tall as Carella and of the same general build. He had only one eye, however – he was called Cyclops by the superintendent of the building and by just about everyone else he knew – and it was this single fact that seemed to make him a somewhat less than reliable witness. He had lost his eye, he explained, in World War I. It had been bayoneted out of his head by an advancing German in the Ardennes Forest. Cyclops – who up to that time had been called Ernest – had backed away from the blade before it had a chance to pass completely through his eye and into his brain, and then had carefully and passionlessly shot the German three times in the chest, killing him. He did not realize his eye was gone until he got back to the aid station. Until then, he thought the bayonet had only gashed his brow and caused a flow of blood that made it difficult to see. He was proud of his missing eye, and proud of the nickname Cyclops. Cyclops had been a giant, and although Ernest Messner was only six feet tall, he had lost his eye for democracy, which is as good a cause as any for which to lose an eye. He was also very proud of his remaining eye, which he claimed was capable of twenty/twenty vision. His remaining eye was a clear penetrating blue, as sharp as the mind lurking somewhere behind it. He listened intelligently to everything the two detectives asked him, and then he said, 'Sure, I took him up myself.'

'You took a man up to Mrs Sachs's apartment Friday night?' Carella asked.

'That's right.'

'What time was this?'

Cyclops thought for a moment. He wore a black patch over his empty socket, and he might have looked a little like an ageing Hathaway Shirt man in an elevator uniform, except that he was bald. 'Must have been nine or nine-thirty, around then.'

'Did you take the man *down*, too?'

'Nope.'

'What time did you go off?'

'I didn't leave the building until eight o'clock in the morning.'

'You work from when to when, Mr Messner?'

'We've got three shifts in the building,' Cyclops explained. 'The morning shift is eight a.m. to four p.m. The afternoon shift is four p.m. to midnight. And the graveyard shift is midnight to eight a.m.'

'Which shift is yours?' Kling asked.

'The graveyard shift. You just caught me, in fact. I'll be relieved here in ten minutes.'

'If you start work at midnight, what were you doing here at nine p.m. Monday?'

'Fellow who has the shift before mine went home sick. The super called me about eight o'clock, asked if I could come in early. I did him the favour. That was a long night, believe me.'

'It was an even longer night for Tinka Sachs,' Kling said.

'Yeah. Well anyway, I took that fellow up at nine, nine-thirty, and he still hadn't come down by the time I was relieved.'

'At eight in the morning,' Carella said.

'That's right.'

'Is that usual?' Kling asked.

'What do you mean?'

'Did Tinka Sachs usually have men coming here who went up to her apartment at nine, nine-thirty and weren't down by eight the next morning?'

Cyclops blinked with his single eye. 'I don't like to talk about the dead,' he said.

'We're here precisely so you *can* talk about the dead,' Kling answered. 'And about the living who visited the dead. I asked a simple question, and I'd appreciate a simple answer. Was Tinka Sachs in the habit of entertaining men all night long?'

Cyclops blinked again. 'Take it easy, young fellow,' he said. 'You'll scare me right back into my elevator.'

Carella chose to laugh at this point, breaking the tension. Cyclops smiled in appreciation.

'You understand, don't you?' he said to Carella. 'What Mrs Sachs did up there in her apartment was *her* business, not anyone else's.'

'Of course,' Carella said. 'I guess my partner was just wondering why you weren't suspicious. About taking a man up who didn't come down again. That's all.'

'Oh.' Cyclops thought for a moment. Then he said, 'Well, I didn't give it a second thought.'

'Then it *was* usual, is that right?' Kling asked.

'I'm not saying it was usual, and I'm not saying it wasn't. I'm saying if a woman over twenty-one wants to have a man in her apartment, it's not for me to say how long he should stay, all day or all night, it doesn't matter to me, sonny. You got that?'

'I've got it,' Kling said flatly.

'And I don't give a damn what they do up there, either, all day or all night, that's their business if they're old enough to vote. You got that, too?'

'I've got it,' Kling said.

'Fine,' Cyclops answered, and he nodded.

'Actually,' Carella said, 'the man didn't *have* to take the elevator down, did he? He could have gone up to the roof, and crossed over to the next building.'

'Sure,' Cyclops said. 'I'm only saying that neither me nor anybody else working in this building has the right to wonder about what anybody's doing up there or how long they're taking to do it, or whether they choose to leave the building by the front door or the roof or the steps leading to the basement or even by jumping out of the window, it's none of our business. You close that door, you're private. That's my notion.'

'That's a good notion,' Carella said.

'Thank you.'

'You're welcome.'

'What'd the man look like?' Kling asked. 'Do you remember?'

'Yes, I remember,' Cyclops said. He glanced at Kling coldly, and then turned to Carella. 'Have you got a pencil and some paper?'

'Yes,' Carella said. He took a notebook and a slender gold pen from his inside jacket pocket. 'Go ahead.'

'He was a tall man, maybe six-two or six-three. He was blond. His hair was very straight, the kind of hair Sonny Tufts has, do you know him?'

'Sonny *Tufts*?' Carella said.

'That's right, the movie star, him. This fellow didn't look at all like him, but his hair was the same sort of straight blond hair.'

'What colour were his eyes?' Kling asked.

'Didn't see them. He was wearing sunglasses.'

'At night?'

'Lots of people wear sunglasses at night nowadays,' Cyclops said.

'That's true,' Carella said.

'Like masks,' Cyclops added.

'Yes.'

'He was wearing sunglasses, and also he had a very deep tan, as if he's just come back from down south someplace. He had on a light grey raincoat; it was drizzling a little Friday night, do you recall?'

'Yes, that's right,' Carella said. 'Was he carrying an umbrella?'

'No umbrella.'

'Did you notice any of his clothing under the raincoat?'

'His suit was a dark grey, charcoal grey, I could tell that by his trousers. He was wearing a white shirt – it showed up here, in the opening of the coat – and a black tie.'

'What colour were his shoes?'

'Black.'

'Did you notice any scars or other marks on his face or hands?'

'No.'

'Was he wearing any rings?'

'A gold ring with a green stone on the pinky of his right hand – no, wait a minute, it was his left hand.'

'Any other jewellery you might have noticed? Cuff links, tie clasp?'

'No, I didn't see any.'

'Was he wearing a hat?'

'No hat.'

'Was he clean-shaven?'

'What do you mean?'

'Did he have a beard or a moustache?' Kling said.

'No. He was clean-shaven.'

'How old would you say he was?'

'Late thirties, early forties.'

'What about his build? Heavy, medium, or slight?'

'He was a big man. He wasn't fat, but he was a big man, muscular. I guess I'd have to say he was heavy. He had very big hands. I noted the ring on his pinky looked very small for his hand. He was heavy, I'd say, yes, very definitely.'

'Was he carrying anything? Briefcase, suitcase, attaché –'

'Nothing.'

'Did he speak to you?'

'He just gave me the floor number, that's all. Nine, he said. That was all.'

'What sort of voice did he have? Deep, medium, high?'

'Deep.'

'Did you notice any accent or regional dialect?'

'He only said one word. He sounded like anybody else in the city.'

'I'm going to say that word several ways,' Carella said. 'Would you tell me which way sounded most like him?'

'Sure, go ahead.'

'Ny-un,' Carella said.

'Nope.'

'Noin.'

'Nope.'

'Nahn.'

'Nope.'

'Nan.'

'Nope.'

'Nine.'

'That's it. Straight out. No decorations.'

'Okay, good,' Carella said. 'You got anything else, Bert?'

'Nothing else,' Kling said.

'You're a very observant man,' Carella said to Cyclops.

'All I do every day is look at the people I take up and down,' Cyclops answered. He shrugged. 'It makes the job a little more interesting.'

'We appreciate everything you've told us,' Carella said. 'Thank you.'

'Don't mention it.'

Outside the building, Kling said, 'The snotty old bastard.'

'He gave us a lot,' Carella said mildly.

'Yeah.'

'We've really got a good description now.'

'*Too* good, if you ask me.'

'What do you mean?'

'The guy has one eye in his head, and one foot in the grave. So he reels off details even a trained observer would have missed. He might have been making up the whole thing, just to prove he's not a worthless old man.'

'Nobody's worthless,' Carella said mildly. 'Old or otherwise.'

'The humanitarian school of criminal detection,' Kling said.

'What's wrong with humanity?'

'Nothing. It was a human being who slashed Tinka Sachs to ribbons, wasn't it?' Kling asked.

And to this, Carella had no answer.

        ★   ★   ★

A good modelling agency serves as a great deal more than a booking office for the girls it represents. It provides an answering service for the busy young girl about town, a baby-sitting service for the working mother, a guidance-and-counselling service for the man-beleaguered model, a *pied-à-terre* for the harried and hurried between-sittings beauty.

Art and Leslie Cutler ran a good modelling agency. They ran it with the precision of a computer and the understanding of an analyst. Their offices were smart and walnut-panelled, a suite of three rooms on Carrington Avenue, near the bridge leading to Calm's Point. The address of the agency was announced over a doorway leading to a flight of carpeted steps. The address plate resembled a Parisian street sign, white enamelled on a blue field, 21 Carrington, with the blue-carpeted steps beyond leading to the second story of the building. At the top of the stairs there was a second blue-and-white enamelled sign, Paris again, except that this one was lettered in lowercase and it read: the cutlers.

Carella and Kling climbed the steps to the second floor, observed the chic nameplate without any noticeable show of appreciation, and walked into a small carpeted entrance foyer in which stood a white desk starkly fashionable against the walnut walls, nothing else. A girl sat behind the desk. She was astonishingly beautiful, exactly the sort of receptionist one would expect in a modelling agency; if she was only the receptionist, my God, what did the *models* look like?

'Yes, gentlemen, may I help you?' she asked. Her voice was Vassar out of finishing school out of country day. She wore eyeglasses with exaggerated black frames that did nothing whatever to hide the dazzling brilliance of her big blue eyes. He makeup was subdued and wickedly innocent, a touch of pale pink on her lips, a blush of rose at her cheeks, the frames of her spectacles serving as liner for her eyes. Her hair was black and her smile was sunshine. Carella answered with a sunshine smile of his own, the one he usually reserved for movie queens he met at the governor's mansion.

'We're from the police,' he said. 'I'm Detective Carella; this is my partner, Detective Kling.'

'Yes?' the girl said. She seemed completely surprised to have policemen in her reception room.

'We'd like to talk to either Mr or Mrs Cutler,' Kling said. 'Are they in?'

'Yes, but what is this in reference to?' the girl asked.

'It's in reference to the murder of Tinka Sachs,' Kling said.

'Oh,' the girl said. 'Oh, yes.' She reached for a button on the executive phone panel, hesitated, shrugged, looked up at them with radiant blue-eyed innocence, and said, 'I suppose you have identification and all that.'

Carella showed her his shield. The girl looked expectantly at Kling. Kling sighed, reached into his pocket, and opened his wallet to where his shield was pinned to the leather.

'We never get detectives up here,' the girl said in explanation, and pressed the button on the panel.

'Yes?' a voice said.

'Mr Cutler, there are two detectives to see you, a Mr King and a Mr Coppola.'

'Kling and Carella,' Carella corrected.

'Kling and Capella,' the girl said.

Carella let it go.

'Ask them to come right in,' Cutler said.

'Yes, sir.' The girl clicked off and looked up at the detectives. 'Won't you go in, please? Through the bull pen and straight back.'

'Through the what?'

'The bull pen. Oh, that's the main office, you'll see it. It's right inside the door there.' The telephone rang. The girl gestured vaguely towards what looked like a solid walnut wall, and then picked up the receiver. 'The Cutlers,' she said. 'One moment, please.' She pressed a button and then said, 'Mrs Cutler, it's Alex Jamison on five-seven, do you want to take it?' She nodded, listened for a moment, and then replaced the receiver. Carella and Kling had just located the walnut knob on the walnut door hidden in the walnut wall. Carella smiled sheepishly at the girl (blue eyes blinked back radiantly) and opened the door.

The bull pen, as the girl had promised, was just behind the reception room. It was a large open area with the same basic walnut-and-white decor, broken by the colour of the drapes and the upholstery fabric on two huge couches against the left-hand window wall. The windows were draped in diaphanous saffron nylon, and the couches were done in a complementary brown, the fabric nubby and coarse in contrast to the nylon. Three girls sat on the couches, their long legs crossed. All of them were reading *Vogue*. One of them had her head inside a portable hair dryer. None of them looked up as the men came into the room. On the right-hand side of the room, a fourth woman sat behind a long white Formica counter, a phone to her ear, busily scribbling on a pad as she listened. The woman was in her early forties, with the unmistakable bones of an ex-model. She glanced up briefly as Carella and Kling hesitated inside the doorway, and then went back to her jottings, ignoring them.

There were three huge charts affixed to the wall behind her. Each chart was divided into two-by-two-inch squares, somewhat like a colourless checkerboard. Running down the extreme left-hand side of each chart was a column of small photographs. Running across the top of each chart was a listing for every working hour of the day. The charts were covered with plexiglass panels, and a black crayon pencil hung on a cord to the right of each one. Alongside the photographs, crayoned onto the charts in the appropriate time slots, was a record and a reminder of any model's sittings for the week, readable at a glance. To the right of the charts, and accessible through an opening in the counter, there was a cubbyhole arrangement of mailboxes, each separate slot marked with similar small photographs.

The wall bearing the door through which Carella and Kling had entered was covered with eight-by-ten black-and-white photos of every model the agency represented, some seventy-five in all. The photos bore no identifying names. A waist-high runner carried black crayon pencils spaced at intervals along the length of the wall. A wide white band under each photograph, plexiglass-covered, served as the writing area for telephone messages. A model entering the room could, in turn, check her eight-by-ten photo for any calls, her photo-marked mailbox for any letters, and her photo-marked slot on one of the three charts for her next assignment. Looking into the room, you somehow got the vague impression that photography played a major part in the business of this agency. You also had the disquieting feeling that you had seen all of these faces a hundred times before, staring down at you from billboards and up at you from magazine covers. Putting an identifying name under any single one of them would have been akin to labelling the Taj Mahal or the Empire State Building. The only naked wall was the one facing them as they entered, and it – like the reception-room wall – seemed to be made of solid walnut, with nary a door in sight.

'I think I see a knob,' Carella whispered, and they stared across the room towards the far wall. The woman behind the counter glanced up as they passed, and then pulled the phone abruptly from her ear with a 'Just a second, Alex,' and said to the two detectives, 'Yes, may I help you?'

'We're looking for Mr Cutler's office,' Carella said.

'Yes?' she said.

'Yes, we're detectives. We're investigating the murder of Tinka Sachs.'

'Oh. Straight ahead,' the woman said. 'I'm Leslie Cutler. I'll join you as soon as I'm off the phone.'

'Thank you,' Carella said. He walked to the walnut wall, Kling following close behind him, and knocked on what he supposed was the door.

'Come in,' a man's voice said.

Art Cutler was a man in his forties with straight blond hair like Sonny Tufts, and with at least six feet four inches of muscle and bone that stood revealed in a dark blue suit as he rose behind his desk, smiling, and extended his hand.

'Come in, gentlemen,' he said. His voice was deep. He kept his hand extended while Carella and Kling crossed to the desk, and then he shook hands with each in turn, his grip firm and strong. 'Sit down, won't you?' he said, and indicated a pair of Saarinen chairs, one at each corner of his desk. 'You're here about Tinka,' he said dolefully.

'Yes,' Carella said.

'Terrible thing. A maniac must have done it, don't you think?'

'I don't know,' Carella said.

'Well, it *must* have been, don't you think?' he said to Kling.

'I don't know,' Kling said.

'That's why we're here, Mr Cutler,' Carella explained. 'To find out what we can about the girl. We're assuming that an agent would know a great deal about the people he repre –'

'Yes, that's true,' Cutler interrupted, 'and especially in Tinka's case.'

'Why especially in her case?'

'Well, we'd handled her career almost from the very beginning.'

'How long would that be, Mr Cutler?'

'Oh, at least ten years. She was only nineteen when we took her on, and she was . . . well, let me see, she was thirty in February, no, it'd be almost *eleven* years, that's right.'

'February what?' Kling asked.

'February third,' Cutler replied. 'She'd done a little modelling on the coast before she signed with us, but nothing very impressive. We got her into all the important magazines, *Vogue*, *Harper's*, *Mademoiselle*, well, you name them. Do you know what Tinka Sachs was earning?'

'No, what?' Kling said.

'Sixty dollars an hour. Multiply that by an eight- or ten-hour day, an average of six days a week, and you've got somewhere in the vicinity

of a hundred and fifty thousand dollars a year.' Cutler paused. 'That's
a lot of money. That's more than the president of the United States
earns.'

'With none of the headaches,' Kling said.

'Mr Cutler,' Carella said, 'when did you last see Tinka Sachs alive?'

'Late Friday afternoon,' Cutler said.

'Can you give us the circumstances?'

'Well, she had a sitting at five, and she stopped in around seven to pick up
her mail and to see if there had been any calls. That's all.'

'Had there?' Kling asked.

'Had there what?'

'Been any calls?'

'I'm sure I don't remember. The receptionist usually posts all calls
shortly after they're received. You may have seen our photo wall –'

'Yes,' Kling said.

'Well, our receptionist takes care of that. If you want me to check with her,
she may have a record, though I doubt it. Once a call is crayoned onto the
wall –'

'What about mail?'

'I don't know if she had any or ... wait a minute, yes, I think she did pick
some up. I remember she was leafing through some envelopes when I came
out of my office to chat with her.'

'What time did she leave here?' Carella asked.

'About seven-fifteen.'

'For another sitting?'

'No, she was heading home. She has a daughter, you know. A five-year-
old.'

'Yes, I know,' Carella said.

'Well, she was going home,' Cutler said.

'Do you know where she lives?' Kling asked.

'Yes.'

'Where?'

'Stafford Place.'

'Have you ever been there?'

'Yes, of course.'

'How long do you suppose it would take to get from this office to her
apartment?'

'No more than fifteen minutes.'

'Then Tinka would have been home by seven-thirty ... *if* she went
directly home.'

'Yes, I suppose so.'

'Did she say she was going directly home?'

'Yes. No, she said she wanted to pick up some cake, and *then* she was going
home.'

'Cake?'

'Yes. There's a shop up the street that's exceptionally good. Many of our
mannequins buy cakes and pastry there.'

'Did she say she was expecting someone later on in the evening?' Kling
asked.

'No, she didn't say what her plans were.'

'Would your receptionist know if any of those telephone messages related to her plans for the evening?'

'I don't know, we can ask her.'

'Yes, we'd like to,' Carella said.

'What were *your* plans for last Friday night, Mr Cutler?' Kling asked.

'*My* plans?'

'Yes.'

'What do you mean?'

'What time did *you* leave the office?'

'Why would you possibly want to know *that*?' Cutler asked.

'You were the last person to see her alive,' Kling said.

'No, her *murderer* was the last person to see her alive,' Cutler corrected. 'And if I can believe what I read in the newspapers, her *daughter* was the *next*-to-last person to see her alive. So I really can't understand how Tinka's visit to the agency or *my* plans for the evening are in any way germane, or even related, to her death.'

'Perhaps they're not, Mr Cutler,' Carella said, 'but I'm sure you realize we're obliged to investigate every possibility.'

Cutler frowned, including Carella in whatever hostility he had originally reserved for Kling. He hesitated a moment and then grudgingly said, 'My wife and I joined some friends for dinner at *Les Trois Chats*.' He paused and added caustically, 'That's a French restaurant.'

'What time was that?' Kling asked.

'Eight o'clock.'

'Where were you at nine?'

'Still having dinner.'

'And at nine-thirty?'

Cutler sighed and said, 'We didn't leave the restaurant until a little after ten.'

'And then what did you do?'

'Really, is this necessary?' Cutler said, and scowled at the detectives. Neither of them answered. He sighed again and said, 'We walked along Hall Avenue for a while, and then my wife and I left our friends and took a cab home.'

The door opened.

Leslie Cutler breezed into the office, saw the expression on her husband's face, weighed the silence that greeted her entrance, and immediately said, 'What is it?'

'Tell them where we went when we left here Friday night,' Cutler said. 'The gentlemen are intent on playing cops and robbers.'

'You're joking,' Leslie said, and realized at once that they were not. 'We went to dinner with some friends,' she said quickly. 'Marge and Daniel Ronet – she's one of our mannequins. Why?'

'What time did you leave the restaurant, Mrs Cutler?'

'At ten.'

'Was your husband with you all that time?'

'Yes, of course he was.' She turned to Cutler and said, 'Are they allowed to do this? Shouldn't we call Eddie?'

'Who's Eddie?' Kling said.

'Our lawyer.'

'You won't need a lawyer.'

'Are you a new detective?' Cutler asked Kling suddenly.

'What's that supposed to mean?'

'It's supposed to mean your interviewing technique leaves something to be desired.'

'Oh? In what respect? What do you find lacking in my approach, Mr Cutler?'

'Subtlety, to coin a word.'

'That's very funny,' Kling said.

'I'm glad it amuses you.'

'Would it amuse you to know that the elevator operator at 791 Stafford Place gave us an excellent description of the man he took up to Tinka's apartment on the night she was killed? And would it amuse you further to know that the description fits you to a tee? How does *that* hit your funny bone, Mr Cutler?'

'I was nowhere near Tinka's apartment last Friday night.'

'Apparently not. I know you won't mind our contacting the friends you had dinner with, though – just to check.'

'The receptionist will give you their number,' Cutler said coldly.

'Thank you.'

Cutler looked at his watch. 'I have a lunch date,' he said. 'If you gentlemen are finished with your –'

'I wanted to ask your receptionist about those telephone messages,' Carella said. 'And I'd also appreciate any information you can give me about Tinka's friends and acquaintances.'

'My wife will have to help you with that.' Cutler glanced sourly at Kling and said, 'I'm not planning to leave town. Isn't that what you always warn a suspect not to do?'

'Yes, don't leave town,' Kling said.

'Bert,' Carella said casually, 'I think you'd better get back to the squad. Grossman promised to call with a lab report sometime this afternoon. One of us ought to be there to take it.'

'Sure,' Kling said. He went to the door and opened it. 'My partner's a little more subtle than I am,' he said, and left.

Carella, with his work cut out for him, gave a brief sigh, and said, 'Could we talk to your receptionist now, Mrs Cutler?'

Chapter Three

When Carella left the agency at two o'clock that Monday afternoon, he was in possession of little more than he'd had when he first climbed those blue-carpeted steps. The receptionist, radiating wide-eyed helpfulness, could not remember any of the phone messages that had been left for Tinka Sachs on the day of her death. She knew they were all personal calls, and she remembered that some of them were from men, but she could not recall any of the men's names. Neither could she remember the names of the women callers – yes, some of them were women, she said, but she didn't know exactly how many – nor could she remember why *any* of the callers were trying to contact Tinka.

Carella thanked her for her help, and then sat down with Leslie Cutler – who was still fuming over Kling's treatment of her husband – and tried to compile a list of men Tinka knew. He drew another blank here because Leslie informed him at once that Tinka, unlike most of the agency's mannequins (the word 'mannequin' was beginning to rankle a little) kept her private affairs to herself, never allowing a date to pick her up at the agency, and never discussing the men in her life, not even with any of the other mannequins (in fact, the word was beginning to rankle a lot). Carella thought at first that Leslie was suppressing information because of the jackass manner in which Kling had conducted the earlier interview. But as he questioned her more completely, he came to believe that she really knew nothing at all about Tinka's personal matters. Even on the few occasions when she and her husband had been invited to Tinka's home, it had been for a simple dinner for three, with no one else in attendance, and with the child Anna asleep in her own room. Comparatively charmed to pieces by Carella's patience after Kling's earlier display, Leslie offered him the agency flyer on Tinka, the composite that went to all photographers, advertising agency art directors, and prospective clients. He took it, thanked her, and left.

Sitting over a cup of coffee and a hamburger now, in a luncheonette two blocks from the squadroom, Carella took the composite out of its manila envelope and remembered again the way Tinka Sachs had looked the last time he'd seen her. The composite was an eight-by-ten black-and-white presentation consisting of a larger sheet folded in half to form two pages, each printed front and back with photographs of Tinka in various poses.

Carella studied the composite from first page to last:

TINKA
SACHS

SIZE 10-12
HEIGHT (S/F) 5'8"
BUST 34
WAIST 23
HIPS 34
HAIR BLONDE
EYES GREEN
SHOE 7-½ AA
GLOVE 7
HAT 22

The Cutlers
21 CARRINGTON ST.

The only thing the composite told him was that Tinka posed fully clothed, modelling neither lingerie nor swimwear, a fact he considered interesting, but hardly pertinent. He put the composite into the manila envelope, finished his coffee, and went back to the squadroom.

Kling was waiting and angry.

'What was the idea, Steve?' he asked immediately.

'Here's a composite on Tinka Sachs,' Carella said. 'We might as well add it to our file.'

'Never mind the composite. How about answering my question?'

'I'd rather not. Did Grossman call?'

'Yes. The only prints they've found in the room so far are the dead girl's. They haven't yet examined the knife, or her pocketbook. Don't try to get me off this, Steve. I'm goddamn good and sore.'

'Bert, I don't want to get into an argument with you. Let's drop it, okay?'

'No.'

'We're going to be working on this case together for what may turn out to be a long time. I don't want to start by –'

'Yes, that's right, and I don't like being ordered back to the squadroom just because someone doesn't like my line of questioning.'

'Nobody ordered you back to the squadroom.'

'Steve, you outrank me, and you told me to come back, and that was *ordering* me back. I want to know why.'

'Because you were behaving like a jerk, okay?'

'I don't think so.'

'Then maybe you ought to step back and take an objective look at yourself.'

'Dammit, it was *you* who said the old man's identification seemed reliable! Okay, so we walk into the office and we're face to face with the man who'd just been *described* to us! What'd you expect me to do? Serve him a cup of tea?'

'No, I expected you to accuse him –'

'Nobody accused him of anything!'

'– of murder and take him right up here to book him,' Carella said sarcastically. '*That's* what I expected.'

'I asked perfectly reasonable questions!'

'You asked questions that were snotty and surly and hostile and amateurish. You treated him like a criminal from go, when you had no reason to. You immediately put him on the defensive instead of disarming him. If I were in his place, I'd have lied to you just out of spite. You made an enemy instead of a friend out of someone who might have been able to help us. That means if I need any further information about Tinka's professional life, I'll have to beg it from a man who now has good reason to hate the police.'

'He fit our description! Anyone would have asked –'

'Why the hell couldn't you ask in a civil manner? And *then* check on those friends he said he was with, and *then* get tough if you had something to work with? What did you accomplish your way? Not a goddamn thing. Okay, you asked me, so I'm telling you. I had work to do up there, and I couldn't afford to waste more time while you threw mud at the walls. *That's* why I sent you back here. Okay? Good. Did you check Cutler's alibi?'

'Yes.'

'*Was* he with those people?'

'Yes.'

'And *did* they leave the restaurant at ten and walk around for a while?'

'Yes.'

'Then Cutler couldn't have been the man Cyclops took up in his elevator.'

'Unless Cyclops got the time wrong.'

'That's a possibility, and I suggest we check it. But the checking should have been done *before* you started hurling accusations around.'

'I didn't accuse anybody of anything!'

'Your entire approach did! Who the hell do you think you are, a Gestapo agent? You can't go marching into a man's office with nothing but an idea and start –'

'I was doing my best!' Kling said. 'If that's not good enough, you can go to hell.'

'It's not good enough,' Carella said, 'and I don't plan to go to hell, either.'

'I'm asking Pete to take me off this,' Kling said.

'He won't.'

'Why not?'

'Because I outrank you, like you said, and *I* want you on it.'

'Then don't ever try that again, I'm warning you. You embarrass me in front of a civilian again and –'

'If you had any sense, you'd have been embarrassed long before I asked you to go.'

'Listen, Carella –'

'Oh, it's *Carella* now, huh?'

'I don't have to take any crap from you, just remember that. I don't care what your badge says. Just remember I don't have to take any crap from you.'

'Or from anybody.'

'Or from anybody, right.'

'I'll remember.'

'See that you do,' Kling said, and he walked through the gate in the slatted railing and out of the squadroom.

Carella clenched his fists, unclenched them again, and then slapped one open hand against the top of his desk.

Detective Meyer Meyer came out of the men's room in the corridor, zipping up his fly. He glanced to his left towards the iron-runged steps and cocked his head, listening to the angry clatter of Kling's descending footfalls. When he came into the squadroom, Carella was leaning over, straightarmed, on his desk. A dead, cold expression was on his face.

'What was all the noise about?' Meyer asked.

'Nothing,' Carella said. He was seething with anger, and the word came out as thin as a razor blade.

'Kling again?' Meyer asked.

'Kling again.'

'Boy,' Meyer said, and shook his head, and said nothing more.

On his way home late that afternoon, Carella stopped at the Sachs apartment, showed his shield to the patrolman still stationed outside her door, and then went into the apartment to search for anything that might give him a line on the men Tinka Sachs had known – correspondence, a memo pad, an address book, anything. The apartment was empty and still. The child Anna Sachs had been taken to the Children's Shelter on Saturday and then released into the custody of Harvey Sadler – who was Tinka's lawyer – to await the arrival of the little girl's father from Arizona. Carella walked through the corridor past Anna's room, the same route the murderer must have taken, glanced in through the open door at the rows of dolls lined up in the bookcase, and then went past the room and into Tinka's spacious bedroom. The bed had been stripped, the blood-stained sheets and blanket sent to the police laboratory. There had been blood stains on the drapes as well, and these too had been taken down and shipped off to Grossman. The windows were bare now, overlooking the rooftops below, the boats moving slowly on the River Dix. Dusk was coming fast, a reminder that it was still only April. Carella flicked on the lights and walked around the chalked outline of Tinka's body on the thick green carpet, the blood soaked into it and dried to an ugly brown. He went to an oval table serving as a desk on the wall opposite the bed, sat in the pedestal chair before it, and began rummaging through the papers scattered over its top. The disorder told him that detectives from Homicide had already been through all this and found nothing they felt worthy of calling to his attention. He sighed and picked up an envelope with an airmal border, turned it over to look at the flap, and saw that it had come from Dennis Sachs – Tinka's ex-husband – in Rainfield, Arizona. Carella took the letter from the envelope, unfolded it, and began reading:

Tuesday, April 6

My darling Tinka —

Here I am in the middle of the desert, writing by the light of a flickering kerosene lamp, and listening to the howl of the wind outside my tent. The others are all asleep already. I have never felt farther away from the city — or from you.

I become more impatient with Oliver's project every day of the week, but perhaps that's because I know what you are trying to do, and everything seems insignificant beside your monumental struggle. Who cares whether or not the Hohokam traversed this desert on their way from Old Mexico? Who cares whether we uncover any of their lodges here? All I know is that I miss you enormously, and respect you,

and pray for you. My only hope is that your ordeal
will soon be ended, and we can go back to the way
it was in the beginning; before the nightmare began,
before our love was shattered.
   I will call East again on Saturday. All my
love to Anna...

                              ... and to you.

                                 Dennis

Carella refolded the letter and put it back into the envelope. He had just learned that Dennis Sachs was out in the desert on some sort of project involving the Hohokam, whoever the hell they were, and that apparently he was still carrying the torch for his ex-wife. But beyond that, Carella also learned that Tinka had been going through what Dennis called a 'monumental struggle' and 'ordeal'. What ordeal? Carella wondered. What struggle? And what exactly was the 'nightmare' Dennis mentioned later in his letter? Or was the nightmare the struggle itself, the ordeal, and not something that predated it? Dennis Sachs had been phoned in Arizona this morning by the authorities at the Children's Shelter, and was presumably already on his way East. Whether he yet realized it or not, he would have a great many questions to answer when he arrived.

Carella put the letter in his jacket pocket and began leafing through the other correspondence on the desk. There were bills from the electric company, the telephone company, most of the city's department stores, the Diner's Club, and many of the local merchants. There was a letter from a woman who had done house cleaning for Tinka and was writing to say she could no longer work for her because she and her family were moving back to Jamaica, B.W.I. There was a letter from the editor of one of the fashion magazines, outlining her plans for shooting the new Paris line with Tinka and several other mannequins that summer, and asking whether she would be available or not. Carella read these cursorily, putting them into a small neat pile at one edge of the oval table, and then found Tinka's address book.

There were a great many names, addresses, and telephone numbers in the small red leather book. Some of the people listed were men. Carella studied each name carefully, going through the book several times. Most of the names were run-of-the-mill Georges and Franks and Charlies, while others were a bit more rare like Clyde and Adrian, and still others were pretty exotic like Rion and Dink and Fritz. None of them rang a bell. Carella closed the book, put it into his jacket pocket and then went through the remainder of the papers on the desk. The only other item of interest was a partially completed poem in Tinka's handwriting:

When I think of what I am
And of what I might have been,
I tremble.
I fear the night.
Throughout the day,
I push from dragons confused in the dark
Why will they not

He folded the poem carefully and put it into his jacket pocket together with the address book. Then he rose, walked to the door, took a last look into the room, and snapped out the light. He went down the corridor towards the front door. The last pale light of day glanced through Anna's windows into her room, glowing feebly on the faces of her dolls lined up in rows on the bookcase shelves. He went into the room and gently lifted one of the dolls from the top shelf, replaced it, and then recognized another doll as the one Anna had been holding in her lap on Saturday when he'd talked to her. He lifted the doll from the shelf.

The patrolman outside the apartment was startled to see a grown detective rushing by him with a doll under his arm. Carella got into the elevator, hurriedly found what he wanted in Tinka's address book, and debated whether he should call the squad to tell them where he was headed, possibly get Kling to assist him with the arrest. He suddenly remembered that Kling had left the squadroom early. His anger boiled to the surface again. The *hell* with him, he thought, and came out into the street at a trot, running for his car. His thoughts came in a disorderly jumble, one following the next, the brutality of it, the goddamn stalking animal brutality of it, should I try making the collar alone, God that poor kid listening to her mother's murder, maybe I ought to go back to the office first, get Meyer to assist, but suppose my man is getting ready to cut out, why doesn't Kling shape up, oh God, slashed again and again. He started the car. The child's doll was on the seat beside him. He looked again at the name and address in Tinka's book. Well? he thought. Which? Get help or go it alone?

He stepped on the accelerator.

There was an excitement pounding inside him now, coupled with the anger, a high anticipatory clamour that drowned out whatever note of caution whispered automatically in his mind. It did not usually happen this way, there were usually weeks or months of drudgery. The surprise of his windfall, the idea of a sudden culmination to a chase barely begun, unleashed a wild energy inside him, forced his foot onto the gas pedal more firmly. His hands were tight on the wheel. He drove with a recklessness that would have brought a summons to a civilian, weaving in and out of traffic, hitting the horn and the brake, his hands and his feet a part of the machine that hurtled steadily downtown towards the address listed in Tinka's book.

He parked the car, and came out onto the sidewalk, leaving the doll on the front seat. He studied the name plates in the entrance hallway – yes, this was it. He pushed a bell button at random, turned the knob on the locked inside door when the answering buzz sounded. Swiftly he began climbing the steps to the third floor. On the second-floor landing, he drew his service revolver, a .38 Smith & Wesson Police Model 10. The gun had a two-inch barrel that made it virtually impossible to snag on clothing when drawn. It weighed only two ounces and was six and seven-eighths of an inch long, with a blue finish and a checked walnut Magna stock with the familiar S&W monogram. It was capable of firing six shots without reloading.

He reached the third floor and started down the hallway. The mailbox had told him the apartment number was 34. He found it at the end of the hall, and put his ear to the door, listening. He could hear the muted voices of a man and a woman inside the apartment. Kick it in, he thought. You've got enough for an arrest. Kick in the door, and go in shooting if necessary – he's your man. He backed away from the door. He braced himself against the corridor wall opposite the door, lifted his right leg high, pulling back the knee, and then stepped forward and simultaneously unleashed a piston kick, aiming for the lock high on the door.

The wood splintered, the lock ripped from the jamb, the door shot inwards. He followed the opening door into the room, the gun levelled in his right hand. He saw only a big beautiful dark-haired woman sitting on a couch facing the door, her legs crossed, a look of startled surprise on her face. But he had heard a man from outside. Where –?

He turned suddenly. He had abruptly realized that the apartment fanned out on both sides of the entrance door, and that the man could easily be to his right or his left, beyond his field of vision. He turned naturally to the right because he was right-handed, because the gun was in his right hand, and made the mistake that could have cost him his life.

The man was on his left.

Carella heard the sound of his approach too late, reversed his direction, caught a single glimpse of straight blond hair like Sonny Tufts, and then felt something hard and heavy smashing into his face.

Chapter Four

There was no furniture in the small room, save for a wooden chair to the right of the door. There were two windows on the wall facing the door, and these were covered with drawn green shades. The room was perhaps twelve feet wide by fifteen long, with a radiator in the centre of one of the fifteen-foot walls.

Carella blinked his eyes and stared into the semi-darkness.

There were night-time noises outside the windows, and he could see the intermittent flash of neon around the edges of the drawn shades. He wondered what time it was. He started to raise his left hand for a look at his watch, and discovered that it was handcuffed to the radiator. The handcuffs were his own. Whoever had closed the cuff onto his wrist had done so quickly and viciously; the metal was biting sharply into his flesh. The other cuff was clasped shut around the radiator leg. His watch was gone, and he seemed to have been stipped as well of his service revolver, his billet, his cartridges, his wallet and loose change, and even his shoes and socks. The side of his face hurt like hell. He lifted his right hand in exploration and found that his cheek and temple were crusted with dried blood. He looked down again at the radiator leg around which the second cuff was looped. Then he moved to the right of the radiator and looked behind it to see how it was fastened to the wall. If the fittings were loose –

He heard a key being inserted into the door lock. It suddenly occurred to him that he was still alive, and the knowledge filled him with a sense of impending dread rather than elation. *Why* was he still alive? And was someone opening the door right this minute in order to remedy that oversight?

The key turned.

The overhead light snapped on.

A big brunette girl came into the room. She was the same girl who had been sitting on the couch when he'd bravely kicked in the front door. She was carrying a tray in her hands, and he caught the aroma of coffee the moment she entered the room, that and the overriding scent of the heavy perfume the girl was wearing.

'Hello,' she said.

'Hello,' he answered.

'Have a nice sleep?'

'Lovely.'

She was very big, much bigger than she had seemed seated on the couch. She had the bones and body of a showgirl, five feet eight or nine inches tall, with firm full breasts threatening a low-cut peasant blouse, solid thighs sheathed in a tight black skirt that ended just above her knees. Her legs were long and very white, shaped like a dancer's with full calves and slender ankles. She was wearing black slippers, and she closed the door behind her and came into the room silently, the slippers whispering across the floor.

She moved slowly, almost as though she were sleepwalking. There was a current of sensuality about her, emphasized by her dreamlike motion. She seemed to possess an acute awareness of her lush body, and this in turn seemed coupled with the knowledge that whatever she might be – housewife or whore, slattern or saint – men would try to do things to that body, and succeed, repeatedly and without mercy. She was a victim, and she moved with the cautious tread of someone who had been beaten before and now expects attack from any quarter. Her caution, her awareness, the ripeness of

her body, the certain knowledge that it was available, the curious look of
inevitability the girl wore, all invited further abuses, encouraged fantasies,
drew dark imaginings from hidden corners of the mind. Rinsed raven-black
hair framed the girl's white face. It was a face hard with knowledge. Smoky
Cleopatra makeup shaded her eyes and lashes, hiding the deeper-toned flesh
there. Her nose had been fixed once, a long time ago, but it was beginning to
fall out of shape so that it looked now as if someone had broken it, and this
too added to the victim's look she wore. Her mouth was brightly painted, a
whore's mouth, a doll's mouth. It had said every word ever invented. It had
done everything a mouth was ever forced to do.

'I brought you some coffee,' she said.

Her voice was almost a whisper. He watched her as she came closer. He
had the feeling that she could kill a man as readily as kiss him, and he
wondered again why he was still alive.

He noticed for the first time that there was a gun on the tray, alongside the
coffee pot. The girl lifted the gun now, and pointed it at his belly, still
holding the tray with one hand. 'Back,' she said.

'Why?'

'Don't fuck around with me,' she said. 'Do what I tell you to do when I tell
you to do it.'

Carella moved back as far as his cuffed wrist would allow him. The girl
crouched, the tight skirt riding up over her thighs, and pushed the tray
towards the radiator. Her face was dead serious. The gun was a super .38-
calibre Llama automatic. The girl held it steady in her right hand. The
thumb safety on the left side of the gun had been thrown. The automatic was
ready for firing.

The girl rose and backed away towards the chair near the entrance door,
the gun still trained on him. She sat, lowered the gun, and said, 'Go ahead.'

Carella poured coffee from the pot into the single mug on the tray. He took
a swallow. The coffee was hot and strong.

'How is it?' the girl asked.

'Fine.'

'I made it myself.'

'Thank you.'

'I'll bring you a wet towel later,' she said. 'So you can wipe off that blood.
It looks terrible.'

'It doesn't feel so hot, either,' Carella said.

'Well, who invited you?' the girl asked. She seemed about to smile, and
then changed her mind.

'No one, that's true.' He took another sip of coffee. The girl watched him
steadily.

'Steve Carella,' she said. 'Is that it?'

'That's right. What's *your* name?'

He asked the question quickly and naturally, but the girl did not step into
the trap.

'Detective second/grade,' she said. '87th Squad.' She paused. 'Where's
that?'

'Across from the park.'

'What park?'

'Grover Park.'

'Oh, yeah,' she said. 'That's a nice park. That's the nicest park in this whole damn city.'

'Yes,' Carella said.

'I saved your life, you know,' the girl said conversationally.

'Did you?'

'Yeah. *He* wanted to kill you.'

'I'm surprised he didn't.'

'Cheer up, maybe he will.'

'When?'

'You in a hurry?'

'Not particularly.'

The room went silent. Carella took another swallow of coffee. The girl kept staring at him. Outside, he could hear the sounds of traffic.

'What time is it?' he asked.

'About nine. Why? You got a date?'

'I'm wondering how long it'll be before I'm missed, that's all,' Carella said, and watched the girl.

'Don't try to scare me,' she said. 'Nothing scares me.'

'I wasn't trying to scare you.'

The girl scratched her leg idly, and then said, 'There're some questions I have to ask you.'

'I'm not sure I'll answer them.'

'You will,' she said. There was something cold and deadly in her voice. 'I can guarantee that. Sooner or later, you will.'

'Then it'll have to be later.'

'You're not being smart, mister.'

'I'm being very smart.'

'How?'

'I figure I'm alive only because you don't know the answers.'

'Maybe you're alive because I *want* you to be alive,' the girl said.

'Why?'

'I've never had anything like you before,' she said, and for the first time since she'd come into the room, she smiled. The smile was frightening. He could feel the flesh at the back of his neck beginning to crawl. He wet his lips and looked at her, and she returned his gaze steadily, the tiny evil smile lingering on her lips. 'I'm life or death to you,' she said. 'If I tell him to kill you, he will.'

'Not until you know all the answers,' Carella said.

'Oh, we'll get the answers. We'll have plenty of time to get the answers.' The smile dropped from her face. She put one hand inside her blouse and idly scratched her breast, and then looked at him again, and said, 'How'd you get here?'

'I took the subway.'

'That's a lie,' the girl said. There was no rancour in her voice. She accused him matter-of-factly, and then said, 'Your car was downstairs. The registration was in the glove compartment. There was also a sign on the sun visor, something about a law officer on a duty call.'

'All right, I drove here,' Carella said.

'Are you married?'

'Yes.'

'Do you have any children?'

'Two.'

'Girls?'

'A girl and a boy.'

'Then that's who the doll is for,' the girl said.

'What doll?'

'The one that was in the car. On the front seat of the car.'

'Yes,' Carella lied. 'It's for my daughter. Tomorrow's her birthday.'

'He brought it upstairs. It's outside in the living room.' The girl paused. 'Would you like to give your daughter that doll?'

'Yes.'

'Would you like to see her ever again?'

'Yes.'

'Then answer whatever I ask you, without any more lies about the subway or anything.'

'What's my guarantee?'

'Of what?'

'That I'll stay alive.'

'*I'm* your guarantee.'

'Why should I trust you?'

'You have to trust me,' the girl said. 'You're mine.' And again she smiled, and again he could feel the hairs stiffening at the back of his neck.

She got out of the chair. She scratched her belly, and then moved towards him, that same slow and cautious movement, as though she expected someone to strike her and was bracing herself for the blow.

'I haven't got much time,' she said. 'He'll be back soon.'

'Then what?'

The girl shrugged. 'Who knows you're here?' she asked suddenly.

Carella did not answer.

'How'd you get to us?'

Again, he did not answer.

'Did somebody see him leaving Tinka's apartment?'

Carella did not answer.

'How did you know where to come?'

Carella shook his head.

'Did someone identify him? How did you trace him?'

Carella kept watching her. She was standing three feet away from him now, too far to reach, the Llama dangling loosely in her right hand. She raised the gun.

'Do you want me to shoot you?' she asked conversationally.

'No.'

'I'll aim for your balls, would you like that?'

'No.'

'Then answer my questions.'

'You're not going to kill me,' Carella said. He did not take his eyes from the girl's face. The gun was pointed at his groin now, but he did not look at her finger curled inside the trigger guard.

The girl took a step closer. Carella crouched near the radiator, unable to get to his feet, his left hand manacled close to the floor. 'I'll enjoy this,' the girl promised, and struck him suddenly with the butt of the heavy gun, turning the butt up swiftly as her hand lashed out. He felt the numbing shock of metal against bone as the automatic caught him on the jaw and his head jerked back.

'You like?' the girl asked.

He said nothing.

'You *no* like, huh, baby?' She paused. 'How'd you find us?'

Again, he did not answer. She moved past him swiftly, so that he could not turn in time to stop the blow that came from behind him, could not kick out at her as he had planned to do the next time she approached. The butt caught him on the ear, and he felt the cartilage tearing as the metal rasped downwards. He whirled towards her angrily, grasping at her with his right arm as he turned, but she danced out of his reach and around to the front of him again, and again hit him with the automatic, cutting him over the left eye this time. He felt the blood start down his face from the open gash.

'What do you say?' she asked.

'I say go to hell,' Carella said, and the girl swung the gun again. He thought he was ready for her this time. But she was only feinting, and he grabbed out at empty air as she moved swiftly to his right and out of reach. The manacled hand threw him off balance. He fell forward, reaching for support with his free hand, the handcuff biting sharply into his other wrist. The gun butt caught him again just as his hand touched the floor. He felt it colliding with the base of his skull, a two-pound-six-and-a-half-ounce weapon swung with all the force of the girl's substantial body behind it. The pain shot clear to the top of his head. He blinked his eyes against the sudden dizziness. Hold on, he told himself, hold on, and was suddenly nauseous. The vomit came up into his throat, and he brought his right hand to his mouth just as the girl hit him again. He fell back dizzily against the radiator. He blinked up at the girl. Her lips were pulled back taut over her teeth, she was breathing harshly, the gun hand went back again, he was too weak to turn his head aside. The tried to raise his right arm, but it fell limply into his lap.

'Who saw him?' the girl asked.

'No,' he mumbled.

'I'm going to break your nose,' she said. Her voice sounded very far away. He tried to hold the floor for support, but he wasn't sure where the floor was any more. The room was spinning. He looked up at the girl and saw her spinning face and breasts, smelled the heavy cloying perfume and saw the gun in her hand. 'I'm going to break your nose, mister.'

'No.'

'Yes,' she said.

'No.'

He did not see the gun this time. He felt only the excruciating pain of bones splintering. His head rocked back with the blow, colliding with the cast-iron ribs of the radiator. The pain brought him back to raging consciousness. He lifted his right hand to his nose, and the girl hit him again, at the base of the skull again, and again he felt sensibility slipping away from him. He smiled stupidly. She would not let him die, and she would not let him live. She would not allow him to become unconscious, and she would not allow him to regain enough strength to defend himself.

'I'm going to knock out all of your teeth,' the girl said.

He shook his head.

'Who told you where to find us? Was it the elevator operator? Was it that one-eyed bastard?'

He did not answer.

'Do you want to lose all your teeth?'

'No.'

'Then tell me.'

'No.'

'You have to tell me,' she said. 'You *belong* to me.'

'No,' he said.

There was a silence. He knew the gun was coming again. He tried to raise his hand to his mouth, to protect his teeth, but there was no strength in his arm. He sat with his left wrist caught in the fierce biting grip of the handcuff, swollen, throbbing, with blood pouring down his face and from his nose, his nose a throbbing mass of splintered bone, and waited for the girl to knock out his teeth as she had promised, helpless to stop her.

He felt her lips upon him.

She kissed him fiercely and with her mouth open, her tongue searching his lips and his teeth. Then she pulled away from him, and he heard her whisper, 'In the morning, they'll find you dead.'

He lost consciousness again.

On Tuesday morning, they found the automobile at the bottom of a steep cliff some fifty miles across the River Harb, in a sparsely populated area of the adjoining state. Most of the paint had been burned away by what must have been an intensely hot fire, but it was still possible to tell that the car was a green 1961 Pontiac sedan bearing the licence plate RI 7-3461.

The body on the front seat of the car had been incinerated. They knew by what remained of the lower portions that the body had once been a man, but the face and torso had been cooked beyond recognition, the hair and clothing gone, the skin black and charred, the arms drawn up into the typical pugilistic attitude caused by post-mortem contracture of burned muscles, the fingers hooked like claws. A gold wedding band was on the third finger of the skeletal left hand. The fire had eaten away the skin and charred the remaining bones and turned the gold of the ring to a dull black. A .38 Smith & Wesson was caught in the exposed springs of the front seat, together with the metal parts that remained of what had once been a holster.

All of the man's teeth were missing from his mouth.

In the cinders of what they supposed had been his wallet, they found a detective's shield with the identifying number 714-5632.

A call to headquarters across the river informed the investigating police that the shield belonged to a detective second/grade named Stephen Louis Carella.

Chapter Five

Teddy Carella sat in the silence of her living room and watched the lips of Detective Lieutenant Peter Byrnes as he told her that her husband was dead. The scream welled up into her throat, she could feel the muscles there contracting until she thought she would strangle. She brought her hand to her mouth, her eyes closed tight so that she would no longer have to watch the words that formed on the lieutenant's lips, no longer have to see the words that confirmed what she had known was true since the night before when her husband had failed to come home for dinner.

She would not scream, but a thousand screams echoed inside her head. She felt faint. She almost swayed out of the chair, and then she looked up into the lieutenant's face as she felt his supporting arm around her shoulders. She nodded. She tried to smile up at him sympathetically, tried to let him know she realized this was an unpleasant task for him. But the tears were streaming down her face and she wished only that her husband were there to comfort her, and then abruptly she realized that her husband would never be there to comfort her again, the realization circling back upon itself, the silent screams ricochetting inside her.

The lieutenant was talking again.

She watched his lips. She sat stiff and silent in the chair, her hands clasped tightly in her lap, and wondered where the children were, how would she tell the children, and saw the lieutenant's lips as he said his men would do everything possible to uncover the facts of her husband's death. In the meantime, Teddy, if there's anything I can do, anything I can do personally I mean, I think you know how much Steve meant to me, to all of us, if there's anything Harriet or I can do to help in any way, Teddy, I don't have to tell you we'll do anything we can, anything.

She nodded.

There's a possibility this was just an accident, Teddy, though we doubt it, we think he was, we don't think it was an accident, why would he be across the river in the next state, fifty miles from here?

She nodded again. Her vision was blurred by the tears. She could barely see his lips as he spoke.

Teddy, I loved that boy. I would rather have a bullet in my heart than be here in this room today with this, with this information. I'm sorry. Teddy I am sorry.

She sat in the chair as still as a stone.

Detective Meyer Meyer left the squadroom at two p.m. and walked across the street and past the stone wall leading into the park. It was a fine April day, the sky a clear blue, the sun shining overhead, the birds chirping in the newly leaved trees.

He walked deep into the park, and he found an empty bench and sat upon it, crossing his legs, one arm stretched out across the top of the bench, the other hanging loose in his lap. There were young boys and girls holding hands and whispering nonsense, there were children chasing each other and laughing, there were nannies wheeling baby carriages, there were old men reading books as they walked, there was the sound of a city hovering on the air.

There was life.

Meyer Meyer sat on the bench and quietly wept for his friend.

Detective Cotton Hawes went to a movie.

The movie was a western. There was a cattle drive in it, thousands of animals thundering across the screen, men sweating and shouting, horses rearing, bullwhips cracking. There was also an attack on a wagon train, Indians circling, arrows and spears whistling through the air, guns answering, men screaming. There was a fight in a saloon, too, chairs and bottles flying, tables collapsing, women running for cover with their skirts pulled high, fists connecting. Altogether, there was noise and colour and loud music and plenty of action.

When the end titles flashed onto the screen, Hawes rose and walked up the aisle and out into the street.

Dusk was coming.

The city was hushed.

He had not been able to forget that Steve Carella was dead.

Andy Parker, who had hated Steve Carella's guts when he was alive, went to bed with a girl that night. The girl was a prostitute, and he got into her bed and her body by threatening to arrest her if she didn't come across. The girl had been hooking in the neighbourhood for little more than a week. The other working hustlers had taken her aside and pointed out all the Vice Squad bulls and also all the local plainclothes fuzz so that she wouldn't make the mistake of propositioning one of them. But Parker had been on sick leave for two weeks with pharyngitis and had not been included in the girl's original briefing by her colleagues. She had approached what looked like a sloppy drunk in a bar on Ainsley, and before the bartender could catch her eye to warn her, she had given him the familiar 'Wanna have some fun, baby?' line and then had compounded the error by telling Parker it would cost him a fin for a single roll in the hay or twenty-five bucks for all night. Parker had accepted the girl's proposition, and had left the bar with her while the owner of the place frantically signalled his warning. The girl didn't know why the hell he was waving his arms at her. She knew only that she had a John who said he wanted to spend the night with her. She didn't know the John's last name was Law.

She took Parker to a rented room on Culver. Parker was very drunk – he had begun drinking at twelve noon when word of Carella's death reached the squadroom – but he was not drunk enough to forget that he could not arrest this girl until she exposed her 'privates'. He waited until she took off her clothes, and then he showed her his shield and said she could take her choice, a possible three years in the jug, or a pleasant hour or two with a very nice fellow. The girl, who had met very nice fellows like Parker before, all of whom had been Vice Squad cops looking for fleshy handouts, figured this was only a part of her normal overhead, nodded briefly, and spread out on the bed for him.

Parker was very very drunk.

To the girl's great surprise, he seemed more interested in talking than in making love, as the euphemism goes.

'What's the sense of it all, would you tell me?' he said, but did not wait for an answer. 'Son of a bitch like Carella gets cooked in a car by some son of a bitch, what's the sense of it? You know what I see every day of the week, you know what we *all* of us see every day of the week, how do you expect us to stay human, would you tell me? Son of a bitch gets cooked like that, doing his job is all, how do you expect us to stay human? What am I doing here with you, a two-bit whore, is that something for me to be doing? I'm a nice fellow. Don't you know I'm a nice fellow?'

'Sure, you're a nice fellow,' the girl said, bored.

'Garbage every day,' Parker said. 'Filth and garbage, I have the stink in my nose when I go home at night. You know where I live? I live in a garden apartment in Majesta. I've got three and a half rooms, a nice little kitchen, you know, a nice apartment. I've got a hi-fi set and also I belong to the Classics Club, I've got all those books by the big writers, the important writers. I haven't got much time to read them, but I got them all there on a shelf, you should see the books I've got. There are nice people living in that apartment building, not like here, not like what you find in this crumby precinct, how old are you anyway, what are you nineteen, twenty?'

'I'm twenty-one,' the girl said.

'Sure, look at you, the shit of the city.'

'Listen, mister –'

'Shut up, shut up, who the hell's asking you? I'm *paid* to deal with it, all the shit that gets washed into the sewers, that's my job. My neighbours in the building know I'm a detective, they respect me, they look up to me. They don't know that all I do is handle shit all day long until I can't stand the stink of it any more. The kids riding their bikes in the courtyard, they all say, "Good morning, Detective Parker." That's me, a detective. They watch television, you see. I'm one of the good guys. I carry a gun. I'm brave. So look what happens to that son of a bitch Carella. What's the sense?'

'I don't know what you're talking about,' the girl said.

'What's the sense, what's the sense?' Parker said. 'People, boy, I could tell you about people. You wouldn't believe what I could tell you about people.'

'I've been around a little myself,' the girl said drily.

'You can't blame me,' he said suddenly.

'What?'

'You can't blame me. It's not my fault.'

'Sure. Look, mister, I'm a working girl. You want some of this, or not? Because if you –'

'Shut up, you goddamn whore, don't tell me what to do.'

'Nobody's –'

'I can pull you in and make your life miserable, you little slut. I've got the power of life and death over you, don't forget it.'

'Not quite,' the girl said with dignity.

'Not quite, not quite, don't give me any of that crap.'

'You're drunk,' the girl said. 'I don't even think you can –'

'Never mind what I am, I'm not drunk.' He shook his head. 'All right, I'm drunk, what the hell do you care what I am? You think I care what *you* are? You're *nothing* to me, you're *less* than nothing to me.'

'Then what are you doing here?'

'Shut up,' he said. He paused. 'The kids all yell good morning at me,' he said.

He was silent for a long time. His eyes were closed. The girl thought he had fallen asleep. She started to get off the bed, and he caught her arm and pulled her down roughly beside him.

'Stay where you are.'

'Okay,' she said. 'But look, you think we could get this over with? I mean it, mister, I've got a long night ahead of me. I got expenses to meet.'

'Filth,' Parker said. 'Filth and garbage.'

'Okay, already, filth and garbage, do you want it or not?'

'He was a good cop,' Parker said suddenly.

'What?'

'He was a good cop,' he said again, and rolled over quickly and put his head into the pillow.

Chapter Six

At seven-thirty Wednesday morning, the day after the burned wreckage was found in the adjoining state, Bert Kling went back to the apartment building on Stafford Place, hoping to talk again to Ernest Cyclops Messner. The lobby was deserted when he entered the building.

If he had felt alone the day that Claire Townsend was murdered, if he had felt alone the day he held her in his arms in a bookshop demolished by gunfire, suddenly bereft in a world gone cold and senselessly cruel, he now felt something curiously similar and yet enormously different.

Steve Carella was dead.

The last words he had said to the man who had been his friend were angry words. He could not take them back now, he could not call upon a dead man, he could not offer apologies to a corpse. On Monday, he had left the squadroom earlier than he should have, in anger, and sometime that night Carella had met his death. And now there was a new grief within him, a new feeling of helplessness, but it was coupled with an overriding desire to set things right again – for Carella, for Claire, he did not really know. He knew he could not reasonably blame himself for what had happened, but neither could he stop blaming himself. He had to talk to Cyclops again. Perhaps there was something further the man could tell him. Perhaps Carella had contacted him again that Monday night, and uncovered new information that had sent him rushing out to investigate alone.

The elevator doors opened. The operator was not Cyclops.

'I'm looking for Mr Messner,' Kling told the man. 'I'm from the police.'

'He's not here,' the man said.

'He told us he has the graveyard shift.'

'Yeah, well, he's not here.'

'It's only seven-thirty,' Kling said.

'I know what time it is.'

'Well, where is he, can you tell me that?'

'He lives some place here in the city,' the man said, 'but I don't know where.'

'Thank you,' Kling said, and left the building.

It was still too early in the morning for the rush of white-collar workers to subways and buses. The only people in the streets were factory workers hurrying to punch an eight-a.m. timeclock; the only vehicles were delivery trucks and an occasional passenger car. Kling walked swiftly, looking for a telephone booth. It was going to be another beautiful day; the city had been blessed with lovely weather for the past week now. He saw an open drugstore on the next corner, a telephone plaque fastened to the brick wall outside. He went into the store and headed for the directories at the rear.

Ernest Cyclops Messner lived 1117 Gainesborough Avenue in Riverhead, not far from the County Court Building. The shadow of the elevated-train structure fell over the building, and the frequent rumble of trains pulling in and out of the station shattered the silence of the street. But it was a good low-to-middle-income residential area, and Messner's building was the newest on the block. Kling climbed the low flat entrance steps, went into the lobby, and found a listing for E. Messner. He rang the bell under the mailbox, but there was no answering buzz. He tried another bell. A buzz sounded, releasing the lock mechanism on the inner lobby door. He pushed open the door, and began climbing to the seventh floor. It was a little after eight a.m., and the building still seemed asleep.

He was somewhat winded by the time he reached the seventh floor. He paused on the landing for a moment, and then walked into the corridor, looking for apartment 7A. He found it just off the stairwell, and rang the bell.

There was no answer.

He rang the bell again.

He was about to ring it a third time when the door to the apartment alongside opened and a young girl rushed out, looking at her wrist watch and almost colliding with Kling.

'Oh, hi,' she said, surprised. 'Excuse me.'

'That's all right.' He reached for the bell again. The girl had gone past him and was starting down the steps. She turned suddenly.

'Are you looking for Mr Messner?' she asked.

'Yes, I am.'

'He isn't home.'

'How do you know?'

'Well, he doesn't get home until about nine,' she said. 'He works nights, you know.'

'Does he live here alone?'

'Yes, he does. His wife died a few years back. He's lived here a long time, I know him from when I was a little girl.' She looked at her watch again. 'Listen, I'm going to be late. Who *are* you, anyway?'

'I'm from the police,' Kling said.

'Oh, hi.' The girl smiled. 'I'm Marjorie Gorman.'

'Would you know where I can reach him, Marjorie?'

'Did you try his building? He works in a fancy apartment house on –'

'Yes, I just came from there.'

'Wasn't he there?'

'No.'

'That's funny,' Marjorie said. 'Although, come to think of it, we didn't hear him last night, either.'

'What do you mean?'

'The television. The walls are very thin, you know. When he's home, we can hear the television going.'

'Yes, but he works nights.'

'I mean before he leaves. He doesn't go to work until eleven o'clock. He starts at midnight, you know.'

'Yes, I know.'

'Well, that's what I meant. Listen, I really do have to hurry. If you want to talk, you'll have to walk me to the station.'

'Okay,' Kling said, and they started down the steps. 'Are you sure you didn't hear the television going last night?'

'I'm positive.'

'Does he usually have it on?'

'Oh, *con*stantly,' Marjorie said. 'He lives alone, you know, the poor old man. He's got to do *some*thing with his time.'

'Yes, I suppose so.'

'Why did you want to see him?'

She spoke with a pronounced Riverhead accent that somehow marred her clean good looks. She was a tall girl, perhaps nineteen years old, wearing a dark-grey suit and a white blouse, her auburn hair brushed back behind her ears, the lobes decorated with tiny pearl earrings.

'There are some things I want to ask him,' Kling said.

'About the Tinka Sachs murder?'

'Yes.'

'He was telling me about that just recently.'

'When was that?'

'Oh, I don't know. Let me think.' They walked out of the lobby and into the street. Marjorie had long legs, and she walked very swiftly. Kling, in fact, was having trouble keeping up with her. 'What's today, anyway?'

'Wednesday,' Kling said.

'Wednesday, mmm, boy where does the week go? It must have been Monday. That's right. When I got home from the movies Monday night, he was downstairs putting out his garbage. So we talked awhile. He said he was expecting a detective.'

'A detective? Who?'

'What do you mean?'

'Did he say *which* detective he was expecting? Did he mention a name?'

'No, I don't think so. He said he'd talked to some detectives just that morning – that was Monday, right? – and that he'd got a call a few minutes ago saying another detective was coming up to see him.'

'Did he say that exactly? That *another* detective was coming up to see him? A *different* detective?'

'Oh. I don't know if he said just that. I mean, it could have been one of the detectives he'd talked to that morning. I really don't know for sure.'

'Does the name Carella mean anything to you?'

'No.' Marjorie paused. 'Should it?'

'Did Mr Messner use that name when he was talking about the detective who was coming to see him?'

'No, I don't think so. He only said he'd had a call from a detective, that was all. He seemed very proud. He told me they probably wanted him to describe the man again, the one he saw going up to her apartment. The dead girl's. Brrrr, it gives you the creeps, doesn't it?'

'Yes,' Kling said. 'It does.'

They were approaching the elevated station now. They paused at the bottom of the steps.

'This was Monday afternoon, you say?'

'No. Monday night. Monday *night*, I said.'

'What time Monday night?'

'About ten-thirty, I guess. I told you, I was coming home from the movies.'

'Let me get this straight,' Kling said. 'At ten-thirty Monday night, Mr Messner was putting out his garbage, and he told you he had just received a call from a detective who was on his way over? Is that it?'

'That's it.' Marjorie frowned. 'It *was* kind of late, wasn't it? I mean, to be making a business visit. Or do you people work that late?'

'Well, yes, but . . .' Kling shook his head.

'Listen, I really have to go,' Marjorie said. 'I'd like to talk to you, but –'

'I'd appreciate a few more minutes of your time, if you can –'

'Yes, but my boss –'

'I'll call him later and explain.'

'Yeah, you don't *know* him,' Marjorie said, and rolled her eyes.

'Can you just tell me whether Mr Messner mentioned anything about this detective the next time you saw him. I mean, *after* the detective was there.'

'Well, I haven't seen him since Monday night.'

'You didn't see him at *all* yesterday?'

'Nope. Well, I usually miss him in the morning, you know, because I'm gone before he gets home. But sometimes I drop in at night, just to say hello, or he'll come in for something, you know, like that. And I told you about the television. We just didn't hear it. My mother commented about it, as a matter of fact. She said Cyclops was probably – that's what we call him, Cyclops, everybody does, he doesn't mind – she said Cyclops was probably out on the town.'

'Does he often go out on the town?'

'Well, I don't think so – but who knows? Maybe he felt like having himself a good time, you know? Listen, I really have to –'

'All right, I won't keep you. Thank you very much, Marjorie. If you'll tell me where you work, I'll be happy to –'

'Oh, the hell with him. I'll tell him what happened, and he can take it or leave it. I'm thinking of quitting, anyway.'

'Well, thank you again.'

'Don't mention it,' Marjorie said, and went up the steps to the platform.

Kling thought for a moment, and then searched in his pocket for a dime. He went into the cafeteria on the corner, found a phone booth, and identified himself to the operator, telling her he wanted the listing for the lobby phone in Tinka's building on Stafford Place. She gave him the number, and he dialled it. A man answered the phone. Kling said, 'I'd like to talk to the superintendent, please.'

'This is the super.'

'This is Detective Kling of the 87th Squad,' Kling said. 'I'm investigating –'

'Who?' the superintendent said.

'Detective Kling. Who's this I'm speaking to?'

'I'm the super of the building. Emmanuel Farber. Manny. Did you say this was a detective?'

'That's right.'

'Boy, when are you guys going to give us some rest here?'

'What do you mean?'

'Don't you have nothing to do but call up here?'

'I haven't called you before, Mr Farber.'

'No, not you, never mind. This phone's being going like sixty.'

'Who called you?'

'Detectives, never mind.'

'Who? Which detectives?'

'The other night.'

'When?'

'Monday. Monday night.'

'A detective called you Monday night?'

'Yeah, wanted to know where he could reach Cyclops. That's one of our elevator operators.'

'Did you tell him?'

'Sure, I did.'

'Who was he? Did he give you his name?'

'Yeah, some Italian fellow.'

Kling was silent for a moment.

'Would the name have been Carella?' he asked.

'That's right.'

'Carella?'

'Yep, that's the one.'

'What time did he call?'

'Oh, I don't know. Sometime in the evening.'

'And he said his name was Carella?'

'That's right, Detective Carella, that's what he said. Why? You know him?'

'Yes,' Kling said. 'I know him.'

'Well, you ask him. He'll tell you.'

'What time in the evening did he call? Was it early or late?'
'What do you mean by early or late?' Farber asked.
'Was it before dinner?'
'No. Oh no, it was after dinner. About ten o'clock, I suppose. Maybe a little later.'
'And what did he say to you?'
'He wanted Cyclops' address, said he had some questions to ask him.'
'About what?'
'About the murder.'
'He said that specifically? He said, "I have some questions to ask Cyclops about the murder?"'
'About the Tinka Sachs murder, is what he actually said.'
'He said, "This is Detective Carella, I want to know –"'
'That's right, this is Detective Carella –'
'"– I want to know Cyclops Messner's address because I have some questions to ask him about the Tinka Sachs murder."'
'No, that's not it exactly.'
'What's wrong with it?' Kling asked.
'He didn't say the name.'
'You just said he *did* say the name. The Tinka Sachs murder. You said –'
'Yes, that's right. That's not what I mean.'
'Look, what –?'
'He didn't say Cyclops' name.'
'I don't understand you.'
'All he said was he wanted the address of the one-eyed elevator operator because he had some questions to ask him about the Tinka Sachs murder. That's what he said.'
'He referred to him as the one-eyed elevator operator?'
'That's right.'
'You mean he didn't know the name?'
'Well, I don't know about that. He didn't know how to *spell* it, though, that's for sure.'
'Excuse me,' the telephone operator said. 'Five cents for the next five minutes, please.'
'Hold on,' Kling said. He reached into his pocket, and found only two quarters. He put one into the coin slot.
'Was that twenty-five cents you deposited, sir?' the operator asked.
'That's right.'
'If you'll let me have your name and address, sir, we'll –'
'No, forget it.'
'– send you a refund in stamps.'
'No, that's all right, operator, thank you. Just give me as much time as the quarter'll buy, okay?'
'Very well, sir.'
'Hello?' Kling said. 'Mr Farber?'
'I'm still here,' Farber said.
'What makes you think this detective couldn't spell Cyclops' name?'
'Well, I gave him the address, you see, and I was about to hang up when he asked me about the spelling. He wanted to know the correct spelling of the name.'

'And what did you say?'

'I said it was Messner, M-E-S-S-N-E-R, Ernest Messner, and I repeated the address for him again, 1117 Gainesborough Avenue in Riverhead.'

'And then what?'

'He said thank you very much and hung up.'

'Sir, was it your impression that he did not know Cyclops' name until you gave it to him?'

'Well, I couldn't say that for sure. All he wanted was the correct spelling.'

'Yes, but he asked for the address of the one-eyed elevator operator, isn't that what you said?'

'That's right.'

'If he knew the name, why didn't he use it?'

'You got me. What's *your* name?' the superintendent asked.

'Kling. Detective Bert Kling.'

'Mine's Farber, Emmanuel Farber, Manny.'

'Yes, I know. You told me.'

'Oh. Okay.'

There was a long silence on the line.

'Was that all, Detective Kling?' Farber said at last. 'I've got to get these lobby floors waxed and I'm –'

'Just a few more questions,' Kling said.

'Well, okay, but could we –?'

'Cyclops had his usual midnight-to-eight-a.m. shift Monday night, is that right?'

'That's right, but –'

'When he came to work, did he mention anything about having seen a detective?'

'He *didn't*,' Farber said.

'He didn't mention a detective at all? He didn't say –'

'No, he didn't come to work.'

'What?'

'He didn't come to work Monday nor yesterday, either,' Farber said. 'I had to get another man to take his place.'

'Did you try to reach him?'

'I waited until twelve-thirty, with the man he was supposed to relieve taking a fit, and finally I called his apartment, three times in fact, and there was no answer. So I phoned one of the other men. Had to run the elevator myself until the man got here. That must've been about two in the morning.'

'Did Cyclops contact you at all any time yesterday?'

'Nope. You think he'd call, wouldn't you?'

'Did he contact you today?'

'Nope.'

'But you're expecting him to report to work tonight, aren't you?'

'Well, he's due at midnight, but I don't know. I hope he shows up.'

'Yes, I hope so, too,' Kling said. 'Thank you very much, Mr Farber. You've been very helpful.'

'Sure thing,' Farber said, and hung up.

Kling sat in the phone booth for several moments, trying to piece together what he had just learned. Someone had called Farber on Monday night at about ten, identifying himself as Detective Carella, and asking for the address of the one-eyed elevator operator. Carella knew the man was named Ernest Messner and nicknamed Cyclops. He would not have referred to him as the one-eyed elevator operator. But more important than that, he would never have called the superintendent at all. Knowing the man's name, allegedly desiring his address, he would have done exactly what Kling had done this morning. He would have consulted the telephone directories and found a listing for Ernest Messner in the Riverhead book, as simple as that, as routine as that. No, the man who had called Farber was not Carella. But he had known Carella's name, and had made good use of it.

At ten-thirty Monday night, Marjorie Gorman had met Cyclops in front of the building and he had told her he was expecting a visit from a detective. That could only mean that 'Detective Carella' had already called Cyclops and told him he would stop by. And now, Cyclops was missing, had indeed been missing since Monday night.

Kling came out of the phone booth, and began walking back towards the building on Gainesborough Avenue.

The landlady of the building did not have a key to Mr Messner's apartment. Mr Messner has his own lock on the door, she said, the same as any of the other tenants in the building, and she certainly did not have a key to Mr Messner's lock, nor to the locks of any of the other tenants. Moreover, she would *not* grant permission to try his skeleton key on the door, and she warned him that if he forced entry into Mr Messner's apartment, she would sue the city. Kling informed her that if she cooperated, she would save him the trouble of going all the way downtown for a search warrant, and she said she didn't *care* about his going all the way downtown, suppose Mr Messner came back and learned she had let the police in there while he was away, *who'd* get the lawsuit then, would he mind telling her?

Kling said he would go downtown for the warrant.

Go ahead then, the landlady told him.

It took an hour to get downtown, twenty minutes to obtain the warrant, and another hour to get back to Riverhead again. His skeleton key would not open Cyclops' door, so he kicked it in.

The apartment was empty.

Chapter Seven

Dennis Sachs seemed to be about forty years old. He was tall and deeply tanned, with massive shoulders and an athlete's easy stance. He opened the door of his room at the Hotel Capistan, and said, 'Detective Kling? Come in, won't you?'

'Thank you,' Kling said. He studied Sachs's face. The eyes were blue, with deep ridges radiating from the edges, starkly white against the bronzed skin. He had a large nose, an almost feminine mouth, a cleft chin. He needed a shave. His hair was brown.

The little girl, Anna, was sitting on a couch at the far end of the large living room. She had a doll across her lap, and she was watching television when Kling came in. She glanced up at him briefly, and then turned her attention back to the screen. A give-away programme was in progress, the M.C. unveiling a huge motor launch to the delighted shrieks of the studio audience. The couch was upholstered in a lush green fabric against which the child's blonde hair shone lustrously. The place was oppressively over-furnished, undoubtedly part of a suite, with two doors leading from the living room to the adjoining bedrooms. A small cooking alcove was tucked discreetly into a corner near the entrance door, a screen drawn across it. The dominant colours of the suite were pale yellows and deep greens, the rugs were thick, the furniture was exquisitely carved. Kling suddenly wondered how much all this was costing Sachs per day, and then tried to remember where he'd picked up the notion that archaeologists were poverty-stricken.

'Sit down,' Sachs said. 'Can I get you a drink?'

'I'm on duty,' Kling said.

'Oh, sorry. Something soft then? A Coke? Seven-Up? I think we've got some in the refrigerator.'

'Thank you, no,' Kling said.

The men sat. From his wing chair, Kling could see through the large windows and out over the park to where the skyscrapers lined the city. The sky behind the buildings was a vibrant blue. Sachs sat facing him, limned with the light flowing through the windows.

'The people at the Children's Shelter told me you got to the city late Monday, Mr Sachs. May I ask where in Arizona you were?'

'Well, part of the time I was in the desert, and the rest of the time I was staying in a little town called Rainfield, have you ever heard of it?'

'No.'

'Yes. Well, I'm not surprised,' Sachs said. 'It's on the edge of the desert. Just a single hotel, a depot, a general store, and that's it.'

'What were you doing in the desert?'

'We're on a dig, I thought you knew that. I'm part of an archaeological team headed by Dr Oliver Tarsmith. We're trying to trace the route of the Hohokam in Arizona.'

'The Hohokam?'

'Yes, That's a Pima Indian word meaning "those who have vanished". The Hohokam were a tribe once living in Arizona, haven't you ever heard of them?'

'No, I'm afraid I haven't.'

'Yes, well. In any case, they seem to have had their origins in Old Mexico. In fact, archaeologists like myself have found copper bells and other objects that definitely link the Hohokam to the Old Mexican civilization. And, of course, we've excavated ball courts – an especially large one at Snaketown – that are definitely Mexican or Mayan in origin. At one site, we found a rubber ball buried in a jar, and it's our belief that it must have been traded through tribes all the way from southern Mexico. That's where the wild rubber grows, you know.'

'No, I didn't know that.'

'Yes, well. The point is that we archaeologists don't know what route the Hohokam travelled from Mexico to Arizona and then to Snaketown. Dr Tarsmith's theory is that their point of entry was the desert just outside Rainfield. We are now excavating for archaeological evidence to support this theory.'

'I see. That sounds like interesting work.'

Sachs shrugged.

'Isn't it?'

'I suppose so.'

'You don't sound very enthusiastic.'

'Well, we haven't had too much luck so far. We've been out there for close to a year, and we've uncovered only the flimsiest sort of evidence, and ... well, frankly, it's getting a bit tedious. We spend four days a week out on the desert, you see, and then come back into Rainfield late Thursday night. There's nothing much in Rainfield, and the nearest big town is a hundred miles from there. It can get pretty monotonous.'

'Why only *four* days in the desert?'

'Instead of five, do you mean? We usually spend Fridays making out our reports. There's a lot of paperwork involved, and it's easier to do at the hotel.'

'When did you learn of your wife's death, Mr Sachs?'

'Monday morning.'

'You had not been informed up to that time?'

'Well, as it turned out, a telegram was waiting for me in Rainfield. I guess it was delivered to the hotel on Saturday, but I wasn't there to take it.'

'Where were you?'

'In Phoenix.'

'What were you doing there?'

'Drinking, seeing some shows. You can get very sick of Rainfield, you know.'

'Did anyone go with you?'

'No.'

'How did you get to Phoenix?'

'By train.'

'Where did you stay in Phoenix?'

'At the Royal Sands.'

'From when to when?'

'Well, I left Rainfield late Thursday night. I asked Oliver – Dr Tarsmith – if he thought he'd need me on Friday, and he said he wouldn't. I guess he realized I was stretched a little thin. He's a very perceptive man that way.'

'I see. In effect, then, he gave you Friday off.'

'That's right.'

'No reports to write?'

'I took those with me to Phoenix. It's only a matter of organizing one's notes, typing them up, and so on.'

'Did you manage to get them done in Phoenix?'

'Yes, I did.'

'Now, let me understand this, Mr Sachs ...'

'Yes?'

'You left Rainfield sometime late Thursday night ...'

'Yes, I caught the last train out.'

'What time did you arrive in Phoenix?'

'Sometime after midnight. I had called ahead to the Sands for a reservation.'

'I see. When did you leave Phoenix?'

'Mr Kling,' Sachs said suddenly, 'are you just making small talk, or is there some reason for your wanting to know all this?'

'I was simply curious, Mr Sachs. I knew Homicide had sent a wire off to you, and I was wondering why you didn't receive it until Monday morning.'

'Oh. Well, I just explained that. I didn't get back to Rainfield until then.'

'You left Phoenix Monday morning?'

'Yes. I caught a train at about six a.m. I didn't want to miss the jeep.' Sachs paused. 'The expedition's jeep. We usually head out to the desert pretty early, to get some heavy work in before the sun gets too hot.'

'I see. But when you got back to the hotel, you found the telegram.'

'That's right.'

'What did you do then?'

'I immediately called the airport in Phoenix to find out what flights I could get back here.'

'And what did they tell you?'

'There was a TWA flight leaving at eight in the morning, which would get here at four-twenty in the afternoon – there's a two-hour time difference, you know.'

'Yes, I know that. Is that the flight you took?'

'No, I didn't. It was close to six-thirty when I called the airport. I might have been able to make it to Phoenix in time, but it would have been a very tight squeeze, and I'd have had to borrow a car. The trains out of Rainfield aren't that frequent, you see.'

'So what *did* you do?'

'Well, I caught American's eight-thirty flight, instead. Not a through flight; we made a stop at Chicago. I didn't get here until almost five o'clock that night.'

'That was Monday night?'

'Yes, that's right.'

'When did you pick up your daughter?'

'Yesterday morning. Today is Wednesday, isn't it?'

'Yes.'

'You lose track of time when you fly cross-country,' Sachs said.

'I suppose you do.'

The television M.C. was giving away a fourteen-cubic-foot refrigerator with a big, big one-hundred-and-sixty-pound freezer. The studio audience was applauding. Anna sat with her eyes fastened to the screen.

'Mr Sachs, I wonder if we could talk about your wife.'

'Yes, please.'

'The child ...'

'I think she's absorbed in the programme.' He glanced at her, and then said, 'Would you prefer we discussed it in one of the other rooms?'

'I thought that might be better, yes,' Kling said.

'Yes, you're right. Of course,' Sachs said. He rose and led Kling towards the larger bedroom. His valise, partially unpacked, was open on the stand alongside the bed. 'I'm afraid everything's a mess,' he said. 'It's been hurry up, hurry up from the moment I arrived.'

'I can imagine,' Kling said. He sat in an easy chair near the bed. Sachs sat on the edge of the bed and leaned over intently, waiting for him to begin. 'Mr Sachs, how long had you and your wife been divorced?'

'Three years. And we separated a year before that.'

'The child is how old?'

'Anna? She's five.'

'Is there another child?'

'No.'

'The way you said "Anna," I thought –'

'No, there's only the one child. Anna. That's all.'

'As I understand it, then, you and your wife separated the year after she was born.'

'That's right, yes. Actually, it was fourteen months. She was fourteen months old when we separated.'

'Why was that, Mr Sachs?'

'Why was what?'

'Why did you separate?'

'Well, you know.' Sachs shrugged.

'No, I don't.'

'Well, that's personal. I'm afraid.'

The room was very silent. Kling could hear the M.C. in the living room leading the audience in a round of applause for one of the contestants.

'I can understand that divorce is a personal matter, Mr Sachs, but –'

'Yes, it is.'

'Yes, I understand that.'

'I'd rather not discuss it, Mr Kling. Really, I'd rather not. I don't see how it would help you in solving ... in solving my wife's murder. Really.'

'I'm afraid *I'll* have to decide what would help us, Mr Sachs.'

'We had a personal problem, let's leave it at that.'

'What sort of a personal problem?'

'I'd rather not say. We simply couldn't live together any longer, that's all.'

'Was there another man involved?'

'Certainly not!'

'Forgive me, but I think you can see how another man might be important in a murder case.'

'I'm sorry. Yes. Of course. Yes, it would be important. But it wasn't anything like that. There was no one else involved. There was simply a . . . a personal problem between the two of us and we . . . we couldn't find a way to resolve it, so . . . so we thought it best to split up. That's all there was to it.'

'What was the personal problem?'

'Nothing that would interest you.'

'Try me.'

'My wife is dead,' Sachs said.

'I know that.'

'Any problem she might have had is certainly –'

'Oh, it was *her* problem then, is that right? Not yours?'

'It was *our* problem,' Sachs said. 'Mr Kling, I'm not going to answer any other questions along these lines. If you insist that I do, you'll have to arrest me, and I'll get a lawyer, and we'll see about it. In the meantime, I'll just have to refuse to cooperate if that's the tack you're going to follow. I'm sorry.'

'All right, Mr Sachs, perhaps you can tell me whether or not you mutually agreed to the divorce.'

'Yes, we did.'

'Whose idea was it? Yours or hers?'

'Mine.'

'Why?'

'I can't answer that.'

'You know, of course, that adultery is the only grounds for divorce in this state.'

'Yes, I know that. There was no adultery involved. Tinka went to Nevada for the divorce.'

'Did you go with her?'

'No. She knew people in Nevada. She's from the West Coast originally. She was born in Los Angeles.'

'Did she take the child with her?'

'No. Anna stayed here with me while she was gone.'

'Have you kept in touch since the divorce, Mr Sachs?'

'Yes.'

'How?'

'Well, I see Anna, you know. We share the child. We agreed to that before the divorce. Stuck out in Arizona there, I didn't have much chance to see her this past year. But usually, I see quite a bit of her. And I talk to Tinka on the phone, I *used* to talk to her on the phone, and I also wrote to her. We kept in touch, yes.'

'Would you have described your relationship as a friendly one?'

'I loved her,' Sachs said flatly.

'I see.'

Again, the room was silent. Sachs turned his head away.

'Do you have any idea who might have killed her?' Kling asked.

'No.'

'None whatever?'

'None whatever.'

'When did you communicate with her last?'

'We wrote to each other almost every week.'

'Did she mention anything that was troubling her?'

'No.'

'Did she mention any of her friends who might have had reason to ...?'

'No.'

'When did you write to her last?'

'Last week sometime.'

'Would you remember exactly when?'

'I think it was ... the fifth or the sixth, I'm not sure.'

'Did you send the letter by air?'

'Yes.'

'Then it should have arrived here before her death.'

'Yes, I imagine it would have.'

'Did she usually save your letters?'

'I don't know. Why?'

'We couldn't find any of them in the apartment.'

'Then I guess she didn't save them.'

'Did *you* save *her* letters?'

'Yes.'

'Mr Sachs, would you know one of your wife's friends who answers this description: Six feet two or three inches tall, heavily built, in his late thirties or early forties, with straight blond hair and –'

'I don't know who Tinka saw after we were divorced. We led separate lives.'

'But you still loved her.'

'Yes.'

'Then why did you divorce her?' Kling asked again, and Sachs did not answer. 'Mr Sachs, this may be very important to us ...'

'It isn't.'

'Was your wife a dyke?'

'No.'

'Are you a homosexual?'

'No.'

'Mr Sachs, *whatever* it was, believe me, it won't be something new to us. Believe me, Mr Sachs, and please trust me.'

'I'm sorry. It's none of your business. It has nothing to do with anything but Tinka and me.'

'Okay,' Kling said.

'I'm sorry.'

'Think about it. I know you're upset at the moment, but –'

'There's nothing to think about. There are some things I will never discuss with anyone, Mr Kling. I'm sorry, but I owe at least that much to Tinka's memory.'

'I understand,' Kling said, and rose. 'Thank you for your time. I'll leave my card, in case you remember anything that might be helpful to us.'

'All right,' Sachs said.

'When will you be going back to Arizona?'

'I'm not sure. There's so much to be arranged. Tinka's lawyer advised me to stay for a while, at least to the end of the month, until the estate can be settled, and plans made for Anna ... there's so much to do.'

'*Is* there an estate?' Kling asked.

'Yes.'

'A sizeable one?'

'I wouldn't imagine so.'

'I see.' Kling paused, seemed about to say something, and then abruptly extended his hand. 'Thank you again, Mr Sachs,' he said. 'I'll be in touch with you.'

Sachs saw him to the door. Anna, her doll in her lap, was still watching television when he went out.

At the squadroom, Kling sat down with a pencil and pad, and then made a call to the airport, requesting a list of all scheduled flights to and from Phoenix, Arizona. It took him twenty minutes to get all the information, and another ten minutes to type it up in chronological order. He pulled the single sheet from his machine and studied it:

AIRLINE SCHEDULES FROM PHOENIX AND RETURN

EASTBOUND:

Frequency	Airline & Flt.	Departing Phoenix	Arriving Here	Stops		
Exc. Sat.	American #946	12:25 AM	10:45 AM	(Tucson	12:57 AM-	1:35 AM
				(Chicago	6:35 AM-	8:00 AM
Daily	American # 98	7:25 AM	5:28 PM	(Tucson	7:57 AM-	8:25 AM
				(El Paso	9:10 AM-	9:40 AM
				(Dallas	12:00 PM-	12:30 PM
Daily	TWA #146	8:00 AM	4:20 PM	Chicago	12:58 PM-	1:30 PM
Daily	American # 68	8:30 AM	4:53 PM	Chicago	1:27 PM-	2:00 PM
Daily	American # 66	2:00 PM	10:23 PM	Chicago	6:57 PM-	7:30 PM

WESTBOUND:

Frequency	Airline & Flt.	Departing Here	Arriving Phoenix	Stops		
Exc. Sun.	American #965	8:00 AM	11:05 AM	Chicago	9:12 AM-	9:55 AM
Daily	TWA #147	8:30 AM	11:25 AM	Chicago	9:31 AM-	10:15 AM
Daily	American #981	4:00 PM	6:55 PM	Chicago	5:12 PM-	5:45 PM
Daily	TWA #143	4:30 PM	7:40 PM	Chicago	5:41 PM-	6:30 PM
Daily	American # 67	6:00 PM	10:10 PM	(Chicago	7:12 PM-	7:45 PM
				(Tucson	9:08 PM-	9:40 PM

It seemed entirely possible to him that Dennis Sachs could have taken either the twelve-twenty-five flight from Phoenix late Thursday night, or any one of three flights early Friday morning, and still have been here in the city in time to arrive at Tinka's apartment by nine or nine-thirty p.m. He could certainly have killed his wife and caught an early flight back the next

morning. Or any one of four flights on Sunday, all of which – because of the
time difference – would have put him back in Phoenix that same night and in
Rainfield by Monday to pick up the telegram waiting there for him. It was a
possibility – remote, but a possibility nonetheless. The brown hair, of course,
was a problem. Cyclops had said the man's hair was blond. But a commercial
dye or bleach –

One thing at a time, Kling thought. Wearily, he pulled the telephone
directory to him and began a methodical check of the two airlines flying to
Phoenix. He told them he wanted to know if a man named Dennis Sachs, or
any man with the initials D.S., had flown here from Phoenix last Thursday
night or Friday morning, and whether or not he had made the return flight
any time during the weekend. The airlines were helpful and patient. They
checked their flight lists, Something we don't ordinarily do, sir, is this a case
involving a missing person? No, Kling said, this is a case involving a murder.
Oh, well in that case, sir, but we don't ordinarily do this, sir, even for the
police, our flight lists, you see ... Yes, well I appreciate your help, Kling
said.

Neither of the airlines had any record of either a Dennis Sachs, or a D.S.
taking a trip from or to Phoenix at any time before Monday, April 12th.
American Airlines had him listed as a passenger on Flight 68, which had left
Phoenix at eight-thirty a.m. Monday morning, and had arrived here at four-
fifty-three p.m. that afternoon. American reported that Mr Sachs had not as
yet booked return passage.

Kling thanked American and hung up. There was still the possibility that
Sachs had flown here and back before Monday, using an assumed name. But
there was no way of checking that – and the only man who could make any
sort of a positive identification had been missing since Monday night.

The meeting took place in Lieutenant Byrnes's office at five o'clock that
afternoon. There were five detectives present in addition to Byrnes himself.
Miscolo had brought in coffee for most of the men, but they sipped at it only
distractedly, listening intently to Byrnes as he conducted the most un-
orthodox interrogation any of them had ever attended.

'We're here to talk about Monday afternoon,' Byrnes said. His tone was
matter-of-fact, his face expressed no emotion. 'I have the duty chart for
Monday, April twelfth, and it shows Kling, Meyer and Carella on from eight
to four, with Meyer catching. Is that the way it was?'

The men nodded.

'What time did you get here, Cotton?'

Hawes, leaning against the lieutenant's filing cabinet, the only one of the
detectives drinking tea, looked up and said, 'It must've been about five.'

'Was Steve still here?'

'No.'

'What about you, Hal?'

'I got here a little early, Pete,' Willis said. 'I had some calls to make.'

'What time?'

'Four-thirty.'

'Was Steve still here?'

'Yes.'

'Did you talk to him?'

'Yes.'

'What about?'

'He said he was going to a movie with Teddy that night.'

'Anything else?'

'That was about it.'

'I talked to him, too, Pete,' Brown said. He was the only Negro cop in the room. He was sitting in the wooden chair to the right of Byrnes's desk, a coffee container clasped in his huge hands.

'What'd he say to you, Art?'

'He told me he had to make a stop on the way home.'

'Did he say where?'

'No.'

'All right, now let's get this straight. Of the relieving team, only two of you saw him, and he said nothing about where he might have been headed. Is that right?'

'That's right,' Willis said.

'Were you in the office when he left, Meyer?'

'Yes. I was making out a report.'

'Did he say anything to you?'

'He said good night, and he made some joke about bucking for a promotion, you know, because I was hanging around after I'd been relieved.'

'What else?'

'Nothing.'

'Did he say anything to you at any time during the afternoon? About where he might be going later on?'

'Nothing.'

'How about you, Kling?'

'No, he didn't say anything to me, either.'

'Were you here when he left?'

'No.'

'Where were you?'

'I was on my way home.'

'What time did you leave?'

'About three o'clock.'

'Why so early?'

There was a silence in the room.

'Why so early?' Byrnes said again.

'We had a fight.'

'What about?'

'A personal matter.'

'The man is dead,' Byrnes said flatly. 'There are no personal matters any more.'

'He sent me back to the office because he didn't like the way I was behaving during an interview. I got sore.' Kling paused. 'That's what we argued about.'

'So you left here at three o'clock?'

'Yes.'

'Even though you were supposed to be working with Carella on the Tinka Sachs case, is that right?'

'Yes.'

'Did you know where he was going when he left here?'

'No, sir.'

'Did he mention anything about wanting to question anyone, or about wanting to see anyone again?'

'Only the elevator operator. He thought it would be a good idea to check him again.'

'What for?'

'To verify a time he'd given us.'

'Do you think that's where he went?'

'I don't know, sir.'

'Have you talked to this elevator operator?'

'No, sir, I can't locate him.'

'He's been missing since Monday night,' Meyer said. 'According to Bert's report, he was expecting a visit from a man who said he was Carella.'

'Is that right?' Byrnes asked.

'Yes,' Kling said. 'But I don't think it *was* Carella.'

'Why not?'

'It's all in my report, sir.'

'You've read this, Meyer?'

'Yes.'

'What's your impression?'

'I agree with Bert.'

Byrnes moved away from his desk. He walked to the window and stood with his hands clasped behind his back, looking at the street below. 'He found something, that's for sure,' he said, almost to himself. 'He found *something* or *somebody*, and he was killed for it.' He turned abruptly. 'And not a single goddamn one of you knows where he was going. Not even the man who was allegedly working this case with him.' He walked back to his desk. 'Kling, you stay. The rest of you can leave.'

The men shuffled out of the room. Kling stood uncomfortably before the lieutenant's desk. The lieutenant sat in his swivel chair, and turned it so that he was no looking directly at Kling. Kling did not know where he was looking. He eyes seemed unfocused.

'I guess you know that Steve Carella was a good friend of mine,' Byrnes said.

'Yes, sir.'

'A good friend,' Byrnes repeated. He paused for a moment, still looking off somewhere past Kling, his eyes unfocused, and then said, 'Why'd you let him go out alone, Kling?'

'I told you, sir. We had an argument.'

'So you left here at three o'clock, when you knew goddamn well you weren't going to be relieved until four-forty-five. Now what the hell do you call that, Kling?'

Kling did not answer.

'I'm kicking you off this goddamn squad,' Byrnes said. 'I should have done it long ago. I'm asking for your transfer, now get the hell out of here.'

Kling turned and started for the door.

'No, wait a minute,' Byrnes said. He turned directly to Kling now, and there was a terrible look on his face, as though he wanted to cry, but the tears were being checked by intense anger.

'I guess you know, Kling, that I don't have the power to suspend you, I guess you know that. The power rests with the commissioner and his deputies, and they're civilians. But a man can be suspended if he's violated the rules and regulations or if he's committed a crime. The way I look at it, Kling, you've done *both* those things. You violated the rules and regulations by leaving this squadroom and heading home when you were supposed to be on duty, and you committed a crime by allowing Carella to go out there alone and get killed.'

'Lieutenant, I –'

'If I could personally take away your gun and your shield, I'd do it, Kling, believe me. Unfortunately, I can't. But I'm going to call the Chief of Detectives the minute you leave this office. I'm going to tell him I'd like you suspended pending a complete investigation, and I'm going to ask that he recommend that to the commissioner. I'm going to *get* that suspension, Kling, if I have to go to the mayor for it. I'll get departmental charges filed, and a departmental trial, and I'll get you dismissed from the force. I'm *promising* you. Now get the hell out of my sight.'

Kling walked to the door silently, opened it, and stepped into the squadroom. He sat at his desk silently for several moments, staring into space. He heard the buzzer sound on Meyer's phone, heard Meyer lifting the instrument to his ear. 'Yeah?' Meyer said. 'Yeah, Pete. Right. Right. Okay, I'll tell him.' He heard Meyer putting the phone back onto its cradle. Meyer rose and came to his desk. 'That was the lieutenant,' he said. 'He wants me to take over the Tinka Sachs case.'

Chapter Eight

The message went out on the teletype at a little before ten Thursday morning:

MISSING PERSON WANTED FOR QUESTIONING CONNECTION HOMICIDE XXX ERNEST MESSNER ALIAS CYCLOPS MESSNER XXX WHITE MALE AGE 68 XXX HEIGHT 6 FEET XXX WEIGHT 170 LBS XXX COMPLETELY BALD XXX EYES BLUE LEFT EYE MISSING AND COVERED BY PATCH XXX LAST SEEN VICINITY 1117 GAINESBOROUGH AVENUE RIVERHEAD MONDAY APRIL 12 TEN THIRTY PM EST XXX CONTACT MISPERBUR OR DET/2G MEYER MEYER EIGHT SEVEN SQUAD XXXXXXXXX

A copy of the teletype was pulled off the squadroom machine by Detective Meyer Meyer who wondered why it had been necessary for the detective at the Missing Persons Bureau to insert the word 'completely' before the word 'bald'. Meyer, who was bald himself, suspected that the description was redundant, over-emphatic, and undoubtedly derogatory. It was his understanding that a bald person had no hair. None. Count them. None. Why, then, had the composer of this bulletin (Meyer visualized him as a bushy-headed man with thick black eyebrows, a black moustache and a full beard) insisted on inserting the word 'completely', if not to point a deriding finger at all hairless men everywhere? Indignantly, Meyer went to the squadroom dictionary, searched through balas, balata, Balaton, Balboa, balbriggan, and came to:

> **bald** (bôld) adj. **1.** lacking hair on some part of the scalp: *a bald head or person.* **2.** destitute of some natural growth or covering: *a bald mountain.* **3.** bare; plain; unadorned: *a bald prose style.* **4.** open; undisguised: *a bald lie.* **5.** *Zool.* having white on the head: *bald eagle.*

Meyer closed the book, reluctantly admitting that whereas it was impossible to be a little pregnant, it was not equally impossible to be a little bald. The composer of the bulletin, bushy-haired bastard that he was, had been right in describing Cyclops as 'completely bald'. If ever Meyer turned up missing one day, they would describe him in exactly the same way. In the meantime, his trip to the dictionary had not been a total loss. He would hereafter look upon himself as a person who lacked hair on his scalp, a person destitute of some natural growth, bare, plain and unadorned, open and undisguised, having white on the head. Hereafter, he would be known zoologically as The Bald Eagle – Nemesis of All Evil, Protector of the Innocent, Scourge of the Underworld!

'Beware The Bald Eagle!' he said aloud, and Arthur Brown looked up from his desk in puzzlement. Happily, the telephone rang at that moment. Meyer picked it up and said, '87th Squad.'

'This is Sam Grossman at the lab. Who'm I talking to?'

'You're talking to The Bald Eagle,' Meyer said.

'Yeah?'

'Yeah.'

'Well, this is The Hairy Ape,' Grossman said. 'What's with you? Spring fever?'

'Sure, it's such a beautiful day out,' Meyer said, looking through the window at the rain.

'Is Kling there? I've got something for him on this Tinka Sachs case.'

'I'm handling that one now,' Meyer said.

'Oh? Okay. You feel like doing a little work, or were you planning to fly up to your aerie?'

'Up *your* aerie, Mac,' Meyer said, and burst out laughing.

'Oh boy, I see I picked the wrong time to call,' Grossman said. 'Okay, Okay. When you've got a minute later, give me a ring, okay? I'll –'

'The Bald Eagle *never* has a minute later,' Meyer said. 'What've you got for me?'

'This kitchen knife. The murder weapon. According to the tag, it was found just outside her bedroom door, guy probably dropped it on his way out.'

'Okay, what about it?'

'Not much. Only it matches a few other knives in the girl's kitchen, so it's reasonable to assume it belonged to her. What I'm saying is the killer didn't go up there with his own knife, if that's of any use to you.'

'He took the knife from a bunch of other knives in the kitchen, is that it?

'No, I don't think so. I think the knife was in the bedroom.'

'What would a knife be doing in the bedroom?'

'I think the girl used it to slice some lemons.'

'Yeah?'

'Yeah. There was a pitcher of tea on the dresser. Two lemons, sliced in half, were floating in it. We found lemon-juice stains on the tray, as well as faint scratches left by the knife. We figure she carried the tea, the lemons, and the knife into the bedroom on that tray. Then she sliced the lemons and squeezed them into the tea.'

'Well, that seems like guesswork to me,' Meyer said.

'Not at all. Paul Blaney is doing the medical examination. He says he's found citric-acid stains on the girl's left hand, the hand she'd have held the lemons with while slicing with the right. We've checked, Meyer. She was right-handed.'

'Okay, so she was drinking tea before she got killed,' Meyer said.

'That's right. The glass was on the night table near her bed, covered with her prints.'

'Whose prints were covering the knife?'

'Nobody's,' Grossman said. 'Or I should say *everybody's*. A whole mess of them, all smeared.'

'What about her pocketbook? Kling's report said –'

'Same thing, not a good print on it anywhere. There was no money in it, you know. My guess is that the person who killed her also robbed her.'

'Mmm, yeah,' Meyer said. 'Is that all?'

'That's all. Disappointing, huh?'

'I hoped you might come up with something more.'

'I'm sorry.'

'Sure.'

Grossman was silent for a moment. Then he said, 'Meyer?'

'Yeah?'

'You think Carella's death is linked to this one?'

'I don't know,' Meyer said.

'I liked that fellow,' Grossman said, and hung up.

Harvey Sadler was Tinka Sachs's lawyer and the senior partner in the firm of Sadler, McIntyre and Brooks, with offices uptown on Fisher Street. Meyer arrived there at ten minutes to noon, and discovered that Sadler was just about to leave for the YMCA. Meyer told him he was there to find out whether or not Tinka Sachs had left a will, and Sadler said she had indeed. In fact, they could talk about it on the way to the Y, if Meyer wanted to join him. Meyer said he wanted to, and the two men went downstairs to catch a cab.

Sadler was forty-five years old, with a powerful build and craggy features. He told Meyer he had played offensive back for Dartmouth in 1940, just before he was drafted into the army. He kept in shape nowadays, he said, by playing handball at the Y two afternoons a week, Mondays and Thursdays. At least, he *tried* to keep in shape. Even handball twice a week could not completely compensate for the fact that he sat behind a desk eight hours a day.

Meyer immediately suspected a deliberate barb. He had become over-sensitive about his weight several weeks back when he discovered what his fourteen-year-old son Alan meant by the nickname 'Old Crisco'. A bit of off-duty detective work uncovered the information that 'Old Crisco' was merely high school jargon for 'Old Fat-in-the-Can', a disrespectful term of affection if ever he'd heard one. He would have clobbered the boy, naturally, just to show who was boss, had not his wife Sarah agreed with the little vontz. You *are* getting fat, she told Meyer; you should begin exercising at the police gym. Meyer, whose boyhood had consisted of a series of taunts and jibes from Gentiles in his neighbourhood, never expected to be put down by vipers in his own bosom. He looked narrowly at Sadler now, a soldier in the enemy camp, and suddenly wondered if he was becoming a paranoid Jew. Worse yet, an *obese* paranoid Jew.

His reservations about Sadler and also about himself vanished the moment they entered the locker room of the YMCA, which smelled exactly like the locker room of the YMCA. Convinced that nothing in the world could eliminate suspicion and prejudice as effectively as the aroma of a men's locker room, swept by a joyous wave of camaraderie, Meyer leaned against the lockers while Sadler changed into his handball shorts, and listened to the details of Tinka's will.

'She leaves everything to her ex-husband,' Sadler said. 'That's the way she wanted it.'

'Nothing to her daughter?'

'Only if Dennis predeceased Tinka. In that case, a trust was set up for the child.'

'Did Dennis know this?' Meyer asked.

'I have no idea.'

'Was a copy of the will sent to him?'

'Not by me.'

'How many copies did you send to Tinka?'

'Two. The original was kept in our office safe.'

'Did she *request* two copies?'

'No. But it's our general policy to send two copies of any will to the testator. Most people like to keep one at home for easy reference, and the other in a safe deposit box. At least, that's been our experience.'

'We went over Tinka's apartment pretty thoroughly, Mr Sadler. We didn't find a copy of any will.'

'Then perhaps she *did* send one to her ex-husband. That wouldn't have been at all unusual.'

'Why not?'

'Well, they're on very good terms, you know. And, after all, he *is* the only real beneficiary. I imagine Tinka would have wanted him to know.'

'Mmm,' Meyer said. 'How large an estate is it?'

'Well, there's the painting.'

'What do you mean?'

'The Chagall.'

'I still don't understand.'

'The Chagall painting. Tinka bought it many years ago, when she first

Doll

began earning top money as a model. I suppose it's worth somewhere around fifty thousand dollars today.'

'That's a sizeable amount.'

'Yes,' Sadler said. He was in his shorts now, and he was putting on his black gloves and exhibiting signs of wanting to get out on the court. Meyer ignored the signs.

'What about the rest of the estate?' he asked.

'That's it,' Sadler said.

'That's what?'

'The Chagall painting *is* the estate, or at least the substance of it. The rest consists of household furnishings, some pieces of jewellery, clothing, personal effects – none of them worth very much.'

'Let me get this straight, Mr Sadler. It's my understanding that Tinka Sachs was earning somewhere in the vicinity of a hundred and fifty thousand dollars a year. Are you telling me that all she owned of value at her death was a Chagall painting valued at fifty thousand dollars?'

'That's right.'

'How do you explain that?'

'I don't know. I wasn't Tinka's financial adviser. I was only her lawyer.'

'As her lawyer, did you ask her to define her estate when she asked you to draw this will?'

'I did.'

'How did she define it?'

'Essentially as I did a moment ago.'

'When was this, Mr Sadler?'

'The will is dated March twenty-fourth.'

'March twenty-fourth? You mean just last month?'

'That's right.'

'Was there any specific reason for her wanting a will drawn at that time?'

'I have no idea.'

'I mean, was she worried about her health or anything?'

'She seemed in good health.'

'Did she seem frightened about anything? Did she seem to possess a foreknowledge of what was going to happen?'

'No, she did not. She seemed very tense, but not frightened.'

'Why was she tense?'

'I don't know.'

'Did you ask her about it?'

'No, I did not. She came to me to have a will drawn. I drew it.'

'Had you ever done any legal work for her prior to the will?'

'Yes. Tinka once owned a house in Mavis County. I handled the papers when she sold it.'

'When was that?'

'Last October.'

'How much did she get for the sale of the house?'

'Forty-two thousand, five hundred dollars.'

'Was there an existing mortgage?'

'Yes. Fifteen thousand dollars went to pay it off. The remainder went to Tinka.'

'Twenty . . .' Meyer hesitated, calculating. 'Twenty-seven thousand, five hundred dollars went to Tinka, is that right?'

'Yes.'

'In cash?'

'Yes.'

'Where is it, Mr Sadler?'

'I asked her that when we were preparing the will. I was concerned about estate taxes, and about who would inherit the money she had realized on the sale of the house. But she told me she had used it for personal needs.'

'She had spent it?'

'Yes.' Sadler paused. 'Mr Meyer, I only play here two afternoons a week, and I'm very jealous of my time. I was hoping . . .'

'I won't be much longer, please bear with me. I'm only trying to find out what Tinka did with all this money that came her way. According to you, she didn't have a penny of it when she died.'

'I'm only reporting what she told me. I listed her assets as she defined them for me.'

'Could I see a copy of the will, Mr Sadler?'

'Certainly. But it's in my safe at the office, and I won't be going back there today. If you'd like to come by in the morning . . .'

'I'd hoped to get a look at it before –'

'I assure you that I've faithfully reported everything in the will. As I told you, I was only her lawyer, not her financial adviser.'

'Did she *have* a financial adviser?'

'I don't know.'

'Mr Sadler, did you handle Tinka's divorce for her?'

'No. I began representing her only last year, when she sold the house. I didn't know her before then, and I don't know who handled the divorce.'

'One last question,' Meyer said. 'Is anyone else mentioned as a beneficiary in Tinka's will, other than Dennis or Anna Sachs?'

'They are the only beneficiaries,' Sadler said. 'And Anna only if her father predeceased Tinka.'

'Thank you,' Meyer said.

Back at the squadroom, Meyer checked over the typewritten list of all the personal belongings found in Tinka's apartment. There was no listing for either a will or a bankbook, but someone from Homicide had noted that a key to a safety deposit box had been found among the items on Tinka's workdesk. Meyer called Homicide to ask about the key, and they told him it had been turned over to the Office of the Clerk, and he could pick it up there if he was interested and if he was willing to sign a receipt for it. Meyer was indeed interested, so he went all the way downtown to the Office of the Clerk, where he searched through Tinka's effects, finding a tiny red snap-envelope with the safety deposit box key in it. The name of the bank was printed on the face of the miniature envelope. Meyer signed out the key and then – since he was in the vicinity of the various court buildings, anyway – obtained a court order authorizing him to open the safety deposit box. In the company of a court official, he went uptown again by subway and then ran through a pouring rain, courtesy of the vernal equinox, to the First Northern

National Bank on the corner of Phillips and Third, a few blocks from where
Tinka had lived.

A bank clerk removed the metal box from a tier of similar boxes, asked
Meyer if he wished to examine the contents in private, and then led him and
the court official to a small room containing a desk, a chair, and a chained
ballpoint pen. Meyer opened the box.

There were two documents in the box. The first was a letter from an art
dealer, giving an appraisal of the Chagall painting. The letter stated simply
that the painting had been examined, that it was undoubtedly a genuine
Chagall, and that it could be sold at current market prices for anywhere
between forty-five and fifty thousand dollars.

The second document was Tinka's will. It was stapled inside a lawyer's
blueback, the firm name Sadler, McIntyre and Brooks printed on the
bottom of the binder, together with the address, 80 Fisher Street.
Typewritten and centred on the page was the legend LAST WILL AND
TESTAMENT OF TINKA SACHS. Meyer opened the will and began reading:

LAST WILL AND TESTAMENT
of
TINKA SACHS

   I, Tinka Sachs, a resident of this city,
county, and state, hereby revoke all wills and
codicils by me at any time heretofore made and
do hereby make, publish and declare this as and
for my Last Will and Testament.

   FIRST: I give, devise and bequeath to my
former husband, DENNIS R. SACHS, if he shall
survive me, and, if he shall not survive me, to
my trustee, hereinafter named, all of my
property and all of my household and personal
effects including without limitation, clothing,
furniture and furnishings, books, jewelry, art
objects, and paintings.

   SECOND: If my former husband Dennis shall
not survive me, I give, devise and bequeath my
said estate to my Trustee hereinafter named, IN
TRUST NEVERTHELESS, for the following uses and
purposes:
   (1) My Trustee shall hold, invest and
re-invest the principal of said trust and shall
collect the income therefrom until my daughter,
ANNA SACHS, shall attain the age of twenty-one
(21) years, or sooner die.

(2) My Trustee shall, from time to time;
distribute to my daughter ANNA before she has
attained the age of twenty-one (21) so much of
the net income (and the net income of any year
not so distributed shall be accumulated and
shall, after the end of such year, be deemed
principal for purposes of this trust) and so
much of the principal of this trust as my Trustee
may in his sole and unreviewable discretion
determine for any purposes deemed advisable or
convenient by said Trustee, provided, however,
that no principal or income in excess of an
aggregate amount of Five Thousand Dollars
($5,000) in any one year shall be used for the
support of the child unless the death of the
child's father, DENNIS R. SACHS, shall have left
her financially unable to support herself. The
decision of my Trustee with respect to the dates
of distribution and the sums to be distributed
shall be final.

(3) If my daughter, ANNA, shall die before
attaining the age of twenty-one (21) years, my
Trustee shall pay over the then principal of the
trust fund and any accumulated income to the
issue of my daughter, ANNA, then living, in equal
shares, and if there be no such issue then to
those persons who would inherit from me had I
died intestate immediately after the death of
ANNA.

THIRD: I nominate, constitute and appoint
my former husband, DENNIS R. SACHS, Executor of
this my Last Will and Testament. If my said
former husband shall predecease me or shall fail
to qualify or cease to act as Executor, then I
appoint my agent and friend, ARTHUR G. CUTLER,
in his place as successor or substitute executor
and, if my former husband shall predecease me,
as TRUSTEE of the trust created hereby. If my
said friend and agent shall fail to qualify or
cease to act as Executor or Trustee, then I
appoint his wife, LESLIE CUTLER, in his place
as successor or substitute executor and/or

```
trustee, as the case may be.  Unless otherwise
provided by law, no bond or other security shall
be required to permit any Executor or Trustee to
qualify or act in any jurisdiction.
```

The rest of the will was boilerplate. Meyer scanned it quickly, and then turned to the last page where Tinka had signed her name below the words 'IN WITNESS WHEREOF, I sign, seal, publish and declare this as my Last Will and Testament' and where, below that, Harvey Sadler, William McIntyre and Nelson Brooks had signed as attesting witnesses. The will was dated March twenty-fourth.

The only thing Sadler had forgotten to mention – or perhaps Meyer hadn't asked him about it – was that Art Cutler had been named trustee in the event of Dennis Sachs's death.

Meyer wondered if it meant anything.

And then he calculated how much money Tinka had earned in eleven years at a hundred and fifty thousand dollars a year, and wondered again why her only possession of any real value was the Chagall painting she had drenched with blood on the night of her death.

Something stank.

Chapter Nine

He had checked and rechecked his own findings against the laboratory's reports on the burned wreckage, and at first only one thing seemed clear to Paul Blaney. Wherever Steve Carella had been burned to death, it had not been inside that automobile. The condition of the corpse was unspeakably horrible; it made Blaney queasy just to look at it. In his years as medical examiner, Blaney had worked on cases of thaermic trauma ranging from the simplest burns to cases of serious and fatal exposure to flame, light, and electric energy – but these were the worst fourth-degree burns he had ever seen. The body had undoubtedly been cooked for hours: The face was unrecognizable, all of the features gone, the skin black and tight, the single remaining cornea opaque, the teeth undoubtedly loosened and then lost in the fire; the skin on the torso was brittle and split; the hair had been burned away, the flesh completely gone in many places, showing dark red-brown skeletal muscles and charred brittle bones. Blaney's internal examination revealed pale, cooked involuntary muscles, dull and shrunken viscera. Had the body been reduced to its present condition inside that car, the fire would have had to rage for hours. The lab's report indicated that the automobile, ignited by an explosion of gasoline, had burned with extreme intensity, but only briefly. It was Blaney's contention that the body had been burned elsewhere, and then put into the automobile to simulate death there by explosion and subsequent fire.

Blaney was not paid to speculate on criminal motivation, but he wondered now why someone had gone to all this trouble, especially when the car fire would undoubtedly have been hot enough to eliminate adequately and for ever any intended victim. Being a methodical man, he continued to probe. His careful and prolonged investigation had nothing to do with the fact that the body belonged to a policeman, or even to a policeman he had known. The corpse on the table was not to him a person called Steve Carella; it was instead a pathological puzzle.

He did not solve that puzzle until late Friday afternoon.

Bert Kling was alone in the squadroom when the telephone rang. He lifted the receiver.

'Detective Kling, 87th Squad,' he said.

'Bert, this is Paul Blaney.'

'Hello, Paul, how are you?'

'Fine, thanks. Who's handling the Carella case?'

'Meyer's in charge. Why?'

'Can I talk to him?'

'Not here right now.'

'I think this is important,' Blaney said. 'Do you know where I can reach him?'

'I'm sorry, I don't know where he is.'

'If I give it to you, will you make sure he gets it sometime tonight?'

'Sure,' Kling said.

'I've been doing the autopsy,' Blaney said. 'I'm sorry I couldn't get back to you people sooner, but a lot of things were bothering me about this, and I wanted to be careful. I didn't want to make any statements that might put you on the wrong track, do you follow?'

'Yes, sure,' Kling said.

'Well, if you're ready, I'd like to trace this for you step by step. And I'd like to say at the onset that I'm absolutely convinced of what I'm about to say. I mean, I know how important this is, and I wouldn't dare commit myself on guesswork alone – not in a case of this nature.'

'I've got a pencil,' Kling said. 'Go ahead.'

'To begin with, the comparative conditions of vehicle and cadaver indicated to me that the body had been incinerated elsewhere for a prolonged period of time, and only later removed to the automobile where it was found. I now have further evidence from the lab to support this theory. I sent them some recovered fragments of foreign materials that were embedded in the burned flesh. The fragments proved to be tiny pieces of wood charcoal. It seems certain now that the body was consumed in a *wood* fire, and not a gasoline fire such as would have occurred in the automobile. It's my opinion that the victim was thrust headfirst into a fireplace.'

'What makes you think so?'

'The upper half of the body was severely burned, whereas most of the pelvic region and all of the lower extremities are virtually untouched. I think the upper half of the body was pushed into the fireplace and kept there for many hours, possibly throughout the night. Moreover, I think the man was murdered *before* he was thrown into the fire.'

'Before?'

'Yes, I examined the air passages for possible inhaled soot, and the blood for carboxyhaemoglobin. The presence of either would have indicated that the victim was alive during the fire. I found neither.'

'Then how *was* he killed?' Kling asked.

'That would involve guesswork,' Blaney said. 'There's evidence of extradural haemorrhage, and there are also several fractures of the skull vault. But these may only be post-mortem fractures resulting from charring, and I wouldn't feel safe in saying the victim was murdered by a blow to the head. Let's simply say he was dead before he was incinerated, and leave it at that.'

'Then why was he thrown into the fire?' Kling asked.

'To obliterate the body beyond recognition.'

'Go on.'

'The teeth, as you know, were missing from the head, making dental identification impossible. At first I thought the fire had loosened them, but upon further examination, I found bone fragments in the upper gum. I now firmly believe that the teeth were knocked out of the mouth before the body was incinerated, and I believe this was done to further prevent identification.'

'What are you saying, Blaney?'

'May I go on? I don't want any confusion about this later.'

'Please,' Kling said.

'There was no hair on the burned torso. Chest hair, underarm hair, and even the upper region of pubic hair had been singed away by the fire. Neither was there any hair on the scalp, which would have been both reasonable and obvious had the body been thrust into a fireplace head first, as I surmise it was. But upon examination, I was able to find surviving hair roots in the subcutaneous fat below the dermis on the torso and arms, even though the shaft and epithelial sheath had been destroyed. In other words, though the fire had consumed whatever hair had once existed on the torso and arms, there was nonetheless evidence that hair *had been growing* there. I could find no such evidence on the victim's scalp.'

'What do you mean?'

'I mean that the man who was found in that automobile was bald to begin with.'

'What?'

'Yes, nor was this particularly surprising. The atrophied internal viscera, the distended aorta of the heart, the abundant fatty marrow, large medullary cavities, and dense compact osseous tissue all indicated a person well on in years. Moreover, it was my initial belief that only one eye had survived the extreme heat – the right eye – and that it had been rendered opaque whereas the left eye had been entirely consumed by the flames. I have now carefully examined that left socket and it is my conclusion that there had not been an eye in it for many many years. The optic nerve and tract simply do not exist, and there is scar tissue present which indicates removal of the eye long before –'

'Cyclops!' Kling said. 'Oh my God, it's Cyclops!'

'Whoever it is,' Blaney said, 'it is *not* Steve Carella.'

He lay naked on the floor near the radiator.

He could hear rain lashing against the window panes, but the room was warm and he felt no discomfort. Yesterday, the girl had loosened the handcuff a bit, so that it no longer was clamped so tightly on his wrist. His nose was still swollen, but the throbbing pain was gone now, and the girl had washed his cuts and promised to shave him as soon as they were healed.

He was hungry.

He knew that the girl would come with food the moment it grew dark; she always did. There was one meal a day, always at dusk, and the girl brought it to him on a tray and then watched him while he ate, talking to him. Two days ago, she had showed him the newspapers, and he had read them with a peculiar feeling of unreality. The picture in the newspapers had been taken when he was still a patrolman. He looked very young and very innocent. The headline said he was dead.

He listened for the sound of her heels now. He could hear nothing in the other room; the apartment was silent. He wondered if she had gone, and felt a momentary pang. He glanced again at the waning light around the edges of the window shades. The rain drummed steadily against the glass. There was the sound of traffic below, tyres hushed on rainswept streets. In the room, the gloom of dusk spread into the corners. Neon suddenly blinked against the drawn shades. He waited, listening, but there was no sound.

He must have dozed again. He was awakened by the sound of the key being inserted in the door lock. He sat upright, his left hand extended behind him and manacled to the radiator, and watched as the girl came into the room. She was wearing a short silk dressing gown belted tightly at the waist. The gown was a bright red, and she wore black high-heeled pumps that added several inches to her height. She closed the door behind her, and put the tray down just inside the door.

'Hello, doll,' she whispered.

She did not turn on the overhead light. She went to one of the windows instead and raised the shade. Green neon rainsnakes slithered along the glass pane. The floor was washed with melting green, and then the neon blinked out and the room was dark again. He could hear the girl's breathing. The sign outside flashed again. The girl stood near the window in the red gown, the green neon behind her limning her long legs. The sign went out.

'Are you hungry, doll?' she whispered, and walked to him swiftly and kissed him on the cheek. She laughed deep in her throat, then moved away from him and went to the door. The Llama rested on the tray alongside the coffeepot. A sandwich was on a paper plate to the right of the gun.

'Do I still need this?' she asked, hefting the gun and pointing it at him.

Carella did not answer.

'I guess not,' the girl said, and laughed again, that same low throaty laugh that was somehow not at all mirthful.

'Why am I alive?' he said. He was very hungry, and he could smell the coffee deep and strong in his nostrils, but he had learned not to ask for his food. He had asked for it last night, and the girl had deliberately postponed feeding him talking to him for more than an hour before she reluctantly brought the tray to him.

'You're not alive,' the girl said. 'You're dead. I showed you the papers, didn't I? You're dead.'

'Why didn't you really kill me?'

'You're too valuable.'

'How do you figure that?'

'You know who killed Tinka.'

'Then you're better off with me dead.'

'No.' The girl shook her head. 'No, doll. We want to know how you found out.'

'What difference does it make?'

'Oh, a lot of difference,' the girl said. 'He's very concerned about it, really he is. He's getting very impatient. He figures he made a mistake some place, you see, and he wants to know what it was. Because if *you* found out, chances are somebody else will sooner or later. Unless you tell us what it was, you see. Then we can make sure nobody else finds out. Ever.'

'There's nothing to tell you.'

'There's plenty to tell,' the girl said. She smiled. 'You'll tell us. Are you hungry?'

'Yes.'

'Tch,' the girl said.

'Who was that in the burned car?'

'The elevator operator. Messner.' The girl smiled again. 'It was my idea. Two birds with one stone.'

'What do you mean?'

'Well, I thought it would be a good idea to get rid of Messner just in case he was the one who led you to us. Insurance. And I also figured that if everybody thought you were dead, that'd give us more time to work on you.'

'If Messner was my source, why do you have to work on me?'

'Well, there are a lot of unanswered questions,' the girl said. 'Gee, that coffee smells good, doesn't it?'

'Yes,' Carella said.

'Are you cold?'

'No.'

'I can get you a blanket if you're cold.'

'I'm fine, thanks.'

'I thought, with the rain, you might be a little chilly.'

'No.'

'You look good naked,' the girl said.

'Thank you.'

'I'll feed you, don't worry,' she said.

'I know you will.'

'But about those questions, they're really bothering him, you know. He's liable to get bugged completely and just decide the hell with the whole thing. I mean, I like having you and all, but I don't know if I'll be able to control him much longer. If you don't cooperate, I mean.'

'Messner was my source,' Carella said. 'He gave me the description.'

'Then it's a good thing we killed him, isn't it?'

'I suppose so.'

'Of course, that still doesn't answer those questions I was talking about.'

'What questions?'

'For example, how did you get the name? Messner may have given you a description, but where did you get the name? Or the address, for that matter?'

'They were in Tinka's address book. Both the name *and* the address.'

'Was the description there, too?'

'I don't know what you mean.'

'You know what I mean, doll. Unless Tinka had a *description* in that book of hers, how could you match a name to what Messner had told you?' Carella was silent. The girl smiled again. 'I'm *sure* she didn't have descriptions of people in her address book, did she?'

'No.'

'Good, I'm glad you're telling the truth. Because we found the address book in your pocket the night you came busting in here, and we know damn well there're no descriptions of people in it. You hungry?'

'Yes, I'm very hungry,' Carella said.

'I'll feed you, don't worry,' she said again. She paused. 'How'd you know the name and address?'

'Just luck. I was checking each and every name in the book. A process of elimination, that's all.'

'That's another lie,' the girl said. 'I wish you wouldn't lie to me.' She lifted the gun from the tray. She held the gun loosely in one hand, picked up the tray with the other, and then said, 'Back off.'

Carella moved as far back as the handcuff would allow. The girl walked to him, crouched, and put the tray on the floor.

'I'm not wearing anything under this robe,' she said.

'I can see that.'

'I thought you could,' the girl said, grinning, and then rose swiftly and backed towards the door. She sat in the chair and crossed her legs, the short robe riding up on her thighs. 'Go ahead,' she said, and indicated the tray with a wave of the gun.

Carella poured himself a cup of coffee. He took a quick swallow, and then picked up the sandwich and bit into it.

'Good?' the girl asked, watching.

'Yes.'

'I made it myself. You have to admit I take good care of you.'

'Sure,' Carella said.

'I'm going to take even better care of you,' she said. 'Why'd you lie to me? Do you think it's nice to lie to me?'

'I didn't lie.'

'You said you reached us by luck, a process of elimination. That means you didn't know who or what to expect when you got here, right? You were just looking for someone in Tinka's book who would fit Messner's description.'

'That's right.'

'Then why'd you kick the door in? Why'd you have a gun in your hand? See what I mean? You knew who he was *before* you got here. You knew he was the one. How?'

'I told you. It was just luck.'

'Ahh, gee, I wish you wouldn't lie. Are you finished there?'

'Not yet.'

'Let me know when.'

'All right.'

'I have things to do.'

'All right.'

'To *you*,' the girl said.

Carella chewed on the sandwich. He washed it down with a gulp of coffee. He did not look at the girl. She was jiggling her foot now, the gun hand resting in her lap.

'Are you afraid?' she asked.

'Of what?'

'Of what I might do to you.'

'No. Should I be?'

'I might break your nose all over again, who knows?'

'That's true, you might.'

'Or I might even keep my promise to knock out all your teeth.' The girl smiled. '*That* was my idea, too, you know, knocking out Messner's teeth. You people can make identifications from dental charts, can't you?'

'Yes.'

'That's what I thought. That's what I told him. *He* thought it was a good idea, too.'

'You're just *full* of good ideas.'

'Yeah, I have a lot of good ideas,' the girl said. 'You're not scared, huh?'

'No.'

'I would be, if I were you. Really, I would be.'

'The worst you can do is kill me,' Carella said. 'And since I'm already dead, what difference will it make?'

'I like a man with a sense of humour,' the girl said, but she did not smile. 'I can do worse than kill you.'

'What can you do?'

'I can corrupt you.'

'I'm incorruptible,' Carella said, and smiled.

'Nobody's incorruptible,' she said. 'I'm going to make you *beg* to tell us what you know. Really. I'm warning you.'

'I've told you everything I know.'

'Uh-uh,' the girl said, shaking her head. 'Are you finished there?'

'Yes.'

'Shove the tray away from you.'

Carella slid the tray across the floor. The girl went to it, stooped again, and picked it up. She walked back to the chair and sat. She crossed her legs. She began jiggling her foot.

'What's your wife's name?' she asked.

'Teddy.'

'That's a nice name. But you'll forget it soon enough.'

'I don't think so,' Carella said evenly.

'You'll forget her name, and you'll forget her, too.'

He shook his head.

'I promise,' the girl said. 'In a week's time, you won't even remember your *own* name.'

The room was silent. The girl sat quite still except for the jiggling of her foot. The green neon splashed the floor, and then blinked out. There were seconds of darkness, and then the light came on again. She was standing now. She had left the gun on the seat of the chair and moved to the centre of the room. The neon went out. When it flashed on again, she had moved closer to where he was manacled to the radiator.

'What would you like me to do to you?' she asked.

'Nothing.'

'What would you like to do to me?'

'Nothing,' he said.

'No?' she smiled. 'Look, doll.'

She loosened the sash at her waist. The robe parted over her breasts and naked belly. Neon washed the length of her body with green, and then blinked off. In the intermittent flashes, he saw the girl moving – as though in a silent movie – towards the light switch near the door, the open robe flapping loose around her. She snapped on the overhead light, and then walked slowly back to the centre of the room and stood under the bulb. She held the front of the robe open, the long pale white sheath of her body exposed, the red silk covering her back and her arms, her fingernails tipped with red as glowing as the silk.

'What do you think?' she asked. Carella did not answer. 'You want some of it?'

'No,' he said.

'You're lying.'

'I'm telling you the absolute truth,' he said.

'I could make you forget her in a minute,' the girl said. 'I know things you never dreamed of. You want it?'

'No.'

'Just try and get it,' she said, and closed the robe and tightened the sash around her waist. 'I don't like it when you lie to me.'

'I'm not lying.'

'You're naked, mister, don't tell *me* you're not lying.' She burst out laughing and walked to the door, opening it, and then turned to face him again. Her voice was very low, her face serious. 'Listen to me, doll,' she said. 'You are *mine*, do you understand that? I can do whatever I want with you, don't you forget it. I'm promising you right here and now that in a week's time you'll be crawling on your hands and knees to me, you'll be licking my feet, you'll be *begging* for the opportunity to tell me what you know. And once you tell me, I'm going to throw you away, doll, I'm going to throw you broken and cracked in the gutter, doll, and you're going to wish, believe me, you are just going to *wish* it was you they found dead in that car, believe me.' She paused. 'Think about it,' she said, and turned out the light and went out of the room.

He heard the key turning in the lock.

He was suddenly very frightened.

Chapter Ten

The car had been found at the bottom of a steep embankment off Route 407. The road was winding and narrow, a rarely used branch connecting the towns of Middlebarth and York, both of which were serviced by wider, straighter highways. 407 was an oiled road, potholed and frost-heaved, used almost entirely by teenagers searching for a night-time necking spot. The shoulders were muddy and soft, except for one place where the road widened and ran into the approach to what had once been a gravel pit. It was at the bottom of this pit that the burned vehicle and its more seriously burned passenger had been discovered.

There was only one house on Route 407, five and half miles from the gravel pit. The house was built of native stone and timber, a rustic affair with a screened back porch overlooking a lake reportedly containing bass. The house was surrounded by white birch and flowering forsythia. Two dogwoods flanked the entrance driveway, their buds ready to burst. The rain had stopped but a fine mist hung over the lake, visible from the turn in the driveway. A huge oak dripped clinging raindrops onto the ground. The countryside was still. The falling drops clattered noisily.

Detectives Hal Willis and Arthur Brown parked the car at the top of the driveway, and walked past the dripping oak to the front door of the house. The door was painted green with a huge brass doorknob centred in its lower panel and a brass knocker centred in the top panel. A locked padlock still hung in a hinge hasp and staple fastened to the door. But the hasp staple had been pried loose of the jamb, and there were deep gouges in the wood where a heavy tool had been used for the job. Willis opened the door, and they went into the house.

There was the smell of contained woodsmoke, and the stench of something else. Brown's face contorted. Gagging, he pulled a handkerchief from his back pocket and covered his nose and mouth. Willis had backed away towards the door again, turning his face to the outside air. Brown took a quick look at the large stone fireplace at the far end of the room, and then caught Willis by the elbow and led him outside.

'Any question in your mind?' Willis asked.

'None,' Brown said. 'That's the smell of burned flesh.'

'We got any masks in the car?'

'I don't know. Let's check the trunk.'

They walked back to the car. Willis took the keys from the ignition and leisurely unlocked the trunk. Brown began searching.

'Everything in here but the kitchen sink,' he said. 'What the hell's this thing?'

'That's mine,' Willis said.

'Well, what is it?'

'It's a hat, what do you think it is?'

'It doesn't look like any hat I've ever seen,' Brown said.

'I wore it on a plant couple of weeks ago.'

'What were you supposed to be?'

'A foreman.'

'Of what?'

'A chicken market.'

'That's *some* hat, man,' Brown said, and chuckled.

'That's a good hat,' Willis said. 'Don't make fun of my hat. All the ladies who came in to buy chickens said it was a darling hat.'

'Oh, no question,' Brown said. 'It's a cunning hat.'

'Any masks in there?'

'Here's *one*. That's all I see.'

'The canister with it?'

'Yeah, it's all here.'

'Who's going in?' Willis said.

'I'll take it,' Brown said.

'Sure, and then I'll have the NAACP down on my head.'

'We'll just have to chance that,' Brown said, returning Willis' smile. 'We'll just have to chance it, Hal.' He pulled the mask out of its carrier, found the small tin of antidim compound, scooped some onto the provided cloth, and wiped it onto the eyepieces. He seated the facepiece on his chin, moved the canister and head harness into place with an upward, backward sweep of his hands, and then smoothed the edges of the mask around his face.

'Is it fogging?' Willis said.

'No, it's okay.'

Brown closed the outlet valve with two fingers and exhaled, clearing the mask. 'Okay,' he said, and began walking towards the house. He was a huge man, six feet four inches tall and weighing two hundred and twenty pounds, with enormous shoulders and chest, long arms, big hands. His skin was very dark, almost black, his hair was kinky and cut close to his scalp, his nostrils were large, his lips were thick. He looked like a Negro, which is what he was, take him or leave him. He did not at all resemble the white man's pretty concept of what a Negro *should* look like, the image touted in a new wave of magazine and television ads. He looked like himself. His wife Caroline liked the way he looked, and his daughter Connie liked the way he looked, and – more important – *he* liked the way he looked, although he didn't look so great at the moment with a mask covering his face and hoses running to the canister resting at the back of his neck. He walked into the house and paused just inside the door. There were parallel marks on the floor beginning at the jamb and running vertically across the room. He stooped to look at the marks more closely. They were black and evenly spaced, and he recognized them immediately as scuff marks. He rose and followed the marks to the fireplace, where they ended. He did not touch anything in or near the open mouth of the hearth; he would leave that for the lab boys. But he was convinced now that a man wearing shoes, if nothing else, had been dragged across the room from the door to the fireplace. According to what they'd learned yesterday,

Ernest Messner had been incinerated in a wood-burning fire. Well, there had certainly been a wood-burning fire in this room, and the stink he and Willis had encountered when entering was sure as hell the stink of burned human flesh. And now there were heel marks leading from the door to the fireplace. Circumstantially, Brown needed nothing more.

The only question was whether the person cooked in this particular fireplace was Ernest Messner or somebody else.

He couldn't answer that one, and anyway his eyepieces were beginning to fog. He went outside, took off the mask, and suggested to Willis that they drive into either Middlebarth or York to talk to some real estate agents about who owned the house with the smelly fireplace.

Elaine Hinds was a small, compact redhead with blue eyes and long fingernails. Her preference ran to small men, and she was charmed to distraction by Hal Willis, who was the shortest detective on the squad. She sat in a swivel chair behind her desk in the office of Hinds Real Estate in Middlebarth, and crossed her legs, and smiled, and accepted Willis's match to her cigarette, and graciously murmured, 'Thank you,' and then tried to remember what question he had just asked her. She uncrossed her legs, crossed them again, and then said, 'Yes, the house on 407.'

'Yes, do you know who owns it?' Willis asked. He was not unaware of the effect he seemed to be having on Miss Elaine Hinds, and he suspected he would never hear the end of it from Brown. But he was also a little puzzled. He had for many years been the victim of what he called the Mutt and Jeff phenomenon, a curious psychological and physiological reversal that made him irresistibly attractive to very big girls. He had never dated a girl who was shorter than five-nine in heels. One of his girl friends was five-eleven in her stockinged feet, and she was hopelessly in love with him. So he could not now understand why tiny little Elaine Hinds seemed so interested in a man who was only five feet eight inches tall, with the slight build of a dancer and the hands of a Black Jack dealer. He had, of course, served with the Marines and was an expert at judo, but Miss Hinds had no way of knowing that he was a giant among men, capable of breaking a man's back by the mere flick of an eyeball – well, almost. What then had caused her immediate attraction? Being a conscientious cop, he sincerely hoped it would not impede the progress of the investigation. In the meantime, he couldn't help noticing that she had very good legs and she kept crossing and uncrossing them like an undecided virgin.

'The people who own that house,' she said, uncrossing her legs, 'are Mr and Mrs Jerome Brandt, would you like some coffee or something? I have some going in the other room.'

'No, thank you,' Willis said. 'How long have –'

'Mr Brown?'

'No, thank you.'

'How long have the Brandts been living there?'

'Well, they haven't. Not really.'

'I don't think I understand,' Willis said.

Elaine Hinds crossed her legs, and leaned close to Willis, as though about to reveal something terribly intimate. 'They bought it to use as a summer place,' she said. 'Mavis County is a marvellous resort area, you know, with many many lakes and streams and with the ocean not too far from any point in the county. We're supposed to have less rainfall per annum than –'

'When did they buy it, Miss Hinds?'

'Last year. I expect they'll open the house after Memorial Day, but it's been closed all winter.'

'Which explains the broken hasp on the front door,' Brown said.

'Has it been broken?' Elaine said. 'Oh, dear,' and she uncrossed her legs.

'Miss Hinds, would you say that many people in the area knew the house was empty?'

'Yes, I'd say it was common knowledge, do you enjoy police work?'

'Yes, I do,' Willis said.

'It must be terribly exciting.'

'Sometimes the suspense is unbearable,' Brown said.

'I'll just *bet* it is,' Elaine said.

'It's my understanding,' Willis said, glancing sharply at Brown, 'that 407 is a pretty isolated road, and hardly ever used. Is that correct?'

'Oh, yes,' Elaine said. 'Route 126 is a much better connection between Middlebarth and York, and of course the new highway runs past both towns. As a matter of fact, most people in the area *avoid* 407. It's not a very good road, have you been on it?'

'Yes. Then, actually anyone living around here would have known the house was empty, and would also have known the road going by it wasn't travelled too often. Would you say that?'

'Oh, yes, Mr Willis, I definitely *would* say that,' Elaine said.

Willis looked a little startled. He glanced at Brown, and then cleared his throat. 'Miss Hinds, what sort of people are the Brandts? Do you know them?'

'Yes, I sold the house to them. Jerry's an executive at IBM.'

'And his wife?'

'Maxine's a woman of about fifty, three or four years younger than Jerry. A lovely person.'

'Respectable people, would you say?'

'Oh, yes, *entirely* respectable,' Elaine said. 'My goodness, of *course* they are.'

'Would you know if either of them were up here Monday night?'

'I don't know. I imagine they would have called if they were coming. I keep the keys to the house here in the office, you see. I have to arrange for maintenance, and it's necessary –'

'But they didn't call to say they were coming up?'

'No, they didn't.' Elaine paused. 'Does this have anything to do with the auto wreck on 407?'

'Yes, Miss Hinds, it does.'

'Well, how could Jerry or Maxine be even *remotely* connected with that?'

'You don't think they could?'

'Of course not. I haven't seen them for quite some time now, but we did work closely together when I was handling the deal for them last October. Believe me, you couldn't find a sweeter couple. That's unusual, especially with people who have their kind of money.'

'Are they wealthy, would you say?'

Doll

'The house cost forty-two thousand five hundred dollars. They paid for it in cash.'

'Who'd they buy it from?' Willis asked.

'Well, you probably wouldn't know her, but I'll bet your wife would.'

'I'm not married,' Willis said.

'Oh? *Aren't* you?'

'Who'd they buy it from?' Brown asked.

'A fashion model named Tinka Sachs. Do you know her?'

If they had lacked, before this, proof positive that the man in the wrecked automobile was really Ernest Messner, they now possessed the single piece of information that tied together the series of happenings and eliminated the possibility of reasonable chance or coincidence:

1. Tinka Sachs had been murdered in an apartment on Stafford Place on Friday, April ninth.
2. Ernest Messner was the elevator operator on duty there the night of her murder.
3. Ernest Messner had taken a man up to her apartment and had later given a good description of him.
4. Ernest Messner had vanished on Monday night, April twelfth.
5. An incinerated body was found the next day in a wrecked auto on Route 407, the connecting road between Middlebarth and York, in Mavis County.
6. The medical examiner had stated his belief that the body in the automobile had been incinerated in a wood fire elsewhere and only later placed in the automobile.
7. There was only one house on Route 407, five and a half miles from where the wrecked auto was found in the gravel pit.
8. There had been a recent wood fire in the fireplace of that house, and the premises smelled of burned flesh. There were also heel marks on the floor, indicating that someone had been dragged to the fireplace.
9. The house had once been owned by Tinka Sachs, and was sold only last October to its new owners.

It was now reasonable to assume that Tinka's murderer knew he had been identified, and had moved with frightening dispatch to remove the man who'd seen him. It was also reasonable to assume that Tinka's murderer knew of the empty house in Mavis County and had transported Messner's body there for the sole purpose of incinerating it beyond recognition, the further implication being that the murderer had known Tinka at least as far back as last October when she'd still owned the house. There were still a few unanswered questions, of course, but they were small things and nothing that would trouble any hard-working police force anywhere. The cops of the 87th wondered, for example, who had killed Tinka Sachs, and who had killed Ernest Messner, and who had taken Carella's shield and gun from him and wrecked his auto, and whether Carella was still alive, and where?

It's the small things in life that can get you down.

Those airline schedules kept bothering Kling.

He knew he had been taken off the case, but he could not stop thinking about those airline schedules, or the possibility that Dennis Sachs had flown from Phoenix and back sometime between Thursday night and Monday morning. From his apartment that night, he called Information and asked for the name and number of the hotel in Rainfield, Arizona. The local operator connected him with Phoenix Information, who said the only hotel listing they had in Rainfield was for the Major Powell on Main Street, was this the hotel Kling wanted? Kling said it was, and they asked if they should place the call. He knew that if he was eventually suspended, he would lose his gun, his shield and his salary until the case was decided, so he asked the operator how much the call would cost, and she said it would cost two dollars and ten cents for the first three minutes, and sixty-five cents for each additional minute. Kling told her to go ahead and place the call, station to station.

The man who answered the phone identified himself as Walter Blount, manager of the hotel.

'This is Detective Bert Kling,' Kling said. 'We've had a murder here, and I'd like to ask you some questions, if I may. I'm calling long distance.'

'Go right ahead, Mr Kling,' Blount said.

'To begin with, do you know Dennis Sachs?'

'Yes, I do. He's a guest here, part of Dr Tarsmith's expedition.'

'Were you on duty a week ago last Thursday night, April eighth?'

'I'm on duty *all* the time,' Blount said.

'Do you know what time Mr Sachs came in from the desert?'

'Well, I couldn't rightly say. They usually come in at about seven, eight o'clock, something like that.'

'Would you say they came in at about that time on April eighth?'

'I would say so, yes.'

'Did you see Mr Sachs leaving the hotel at any time that night?'

'Yes, he left, oh, ten-thirty or so, walked over to the railroad station.'

'Was he carrying a suitcase?'

'He was.'

'Did he mention where he was going?'

'The Royal Sands in Phoenix, I'd reckon. He asked us to make a reservation for him there, so I guess that's where he was going, don't you think?'

'Did you make the reservation for him personally, Mr Blount?'

'Yes, sir, I did. Single with a bath, Thursday night to Sunday morning. The rates —'

'What time did Mr Sachs return on Monday morning?'

'About six a.m. Had a telegram waiting for him here, his wife got killed. Well, I guess you know that, I guess that's what this is all about. He called the airport right away, and then got back on the train for Phoenix, hardly unpacked at all.'

'Mr Blount, Dennis Sachs told me that he spoke to his ex-wife on the telephone at least once a week. Would you know if that was true?'

'Oh, sure, he was always calling back east.'

'How often, would you say?'

'At least once a week, that's right. Even more than that, I'd say.'

'How much more?'

'Well ... in the past two months or so, he'd call her three, maybe four times a week, something like that. He spent a hell of a lot of time making calls back east, ran up a pretty big phone bill here.'

'Calling his wife, you mean.'

'Well, not only her.'

'Who else?'

'I don't know who the other party was.'

'But he *did* make calls to other numbers here in the city?'

'Well, *one* other number.'

'Would you happen to know that number off-hand, Mr Blount?'

'No, but I've got a record of it on our bills. It's not his wife's number because I've got that one memorized by heart, he's called it regular ever since he first came here a year ago. This other one is new to me.'

'When did he start calling it?'

'Back in February, I reckon.'

'How often?'

'Once a week, usually.'

'May I have the number please?'

'Sure, just let me look it up for you.'

Kling waited. The line crackled. His hand on the receiver was sweating.

'Hello?' Blount said.

'Hello?'

'The number is SE – I think that stands for Sequoia – SE 3-1402.'

'Thank you,' Kling said.

'Not at all,' Blount answered.

Kling hung up, waited patiently for a moment with his hand on the receiver, lifted it again, heard the dial tone, and instantly dialled SE 3-1402. The phone rang insistently. He counted each separate ring, four, five, six, and suddenly there was an answering voice.

'Dr Levi's wire,' the woman said.

'This is Detective Kling of the 87th Squad here in the city,' Kling said. 'Is this an answering service?'

'Yes, sir, it is.'

'Whose phone did you say this was?'

'Dr Levi's.'

'And the first name?'

'Jason.'

'Do you know where I can reach him?'

'I'm sorry, sir, he's away for the weekend. He won't be back until Monday morning.' The woman paused. 'Is this in respect to a police matter, or are you calling for a medical appointment?'

'A police matter,' Kling said.

'Well, the doctor's office hours begin at ten Monday morning. If you'd care to call him then, I'm sure –'

'What's his home number?' Kling asked.

'Calling him there won't help you. He really is away for the weekend.'

'Do you know where?'

'No, I'm sorry.'

'Well, let me have his number, anyway,' Kling said.

'I'm not supposed to give out the doctor's home number. I'll try it for you, if you like. If the doctor's there – which I know he isn't – I'll ask him to call you back. May I have your number, please?'

'Yes, it's Roxbury 2, that's RO 2, 7641.'

'Thank you.'

'Will you please call me in any event, to let me know if you reached him or not?'

'Yes, sir, I will.'

'Thank you.'

'What did you say your name was?'

'Kling, Detective Bert Kling.'

'Yes, sir, thank you,' she said, and hung up.

Kling waited by the phone.

In five minutes' time, the woman called back. She said she had tried the doctor's home number and – as she'd known would be the case all along – there was no answer. She gave him the doctor's office schedule and told him he could try again on Monday, and then she hung up.

It was going to be a long weekend.

Teddy Carella sat in the living room alone for a long while after Lieutenant Byrnes left, her hands folded in her lap, staring into the shadows of the room and hearing nothing but the murmur of her own thoughts.

We now know, the lieutenant had said, that the man we found in the automobile definitely wasn't Steve. He's a man named Ernest Messner, and there is no question about it, Teddy, so I want you to know that. But I also want you to know this doesn't mean Steve is still alive. We just don't know anything about that yet, although we're working on it. The only thing it *does* indicate is that at least he's not for certain dead.

The lieutenant paused. She watched his face. He looked back at her curiously, wanting to be sure she understood everything he had told her. She nodded.

I knew this yesterday, the lieutenant said, but I wasn't sure, and I didn't want to raise your hopes until I had checked it out thoroughly. The medical examiner's office gave this top priority, Teddy. They still haven't finished the autopsy on the Sachs case because, well, you know, when we thought this was Steve, well, we put a lot of pressure on them. Anyway, it isn't. It isn't Steve, I mean. We've got Paul Blaney's word for that, and he's an excellent man, and we've also got the corroboration – what? Corroboration, did you get it? the corroboration of the chief medical examiner as well. So now I'm sure, so I'm telling you. And about the other, we're working on it, as you know, and as soon as we've got anything, I'll tell you that, too. So that's about all, Teddy. We're doing our best.

She had thanked him and offered him coffee, which he refused politely, he was expected home, he had to run, he hoped she would forgive him. She had shown him to the door, and then walked past the playroom, where Fanny was watching television, and then past the room where the twins were sound asleep and then into the living room. She turned out the lights and went to sit near the old piano Carella had bought in a secondhand store downtown, paying sixteen dollars for it and arranging to have it delivered by a furniture man in the precinct. He had always wanted to play the piano, he told her, and was going to start lessons – you're never too old to learn, right, sweetheart?

The lieutenant's news soared within her, but she was fearful of it, suspicious: Was it only a temporary gift that would be taken back? Should she tell the children, and then risk another reversal and a second revelation that their father was dead? 'What does that mean?' April had asked. 'Does dead mean he's never coming back?' And Mark had turned to his sister and angrily shouted, 'Shut up, you stupid dope!' and had run to his room where his mother could not see his tears.

They deserved hope.

They had the right to know there was hope.

She rose and went into the kitchen and scribbled a note on the telephone pad, and then tore off the sheet of paper and carried it out to Fanny. Fanny looked up when she approached, expecting more bad news, the lieutenant brought nothing but bad news nowadays. Teddy handed her the sheet of paper, and Fanny looked at it:

> *Wake the children.*
> *Tell them their father*
> *may still be alive.*

Fanny looked up quickly.

'Thank God,' she whispered, and rushed out of the room.

Chapter Eleven

The patrolman came up to the squadroom on Monday morning, and waited outside the slatted rail divider until Meyer signalled him in. Then he opened the gate and walked over to Meyer's desk.

'I don't think you know me,' he said. 'I'm Patrolman Angieri.'

'I think I've seen you around,' Meyer said.

'I feel funny bringing this up because maybe you already know it. My wife said I should tell you, anyway.'

'What is it?'

'I only been here at this precinct for six months, this is my first precinct, I'm a new cop.'

'Um-huh,' Meyer said.

'If you already know this, just skip it, okay? My wife says maybe you don't know it, and maybe it's important.'

'Well, what is it?' Meyer asked patiently.

'Carella.'

'What about Carella?'

'Like I told you, I'm new in the precinct, and I don't know all the detectives by name, but I recognized him later from his picture in the paper, though it was a picture from when he was a patrolman. Anyway, it was him.'

'What do you mean? I don't think I'm with you, Angieri.'

'Carrying the doll,' Angieri said.

'I still don't get you.'

'I was on duty in the hall, you know? Outside the apartment. I'm talking about the Tinka Sachs murder.'

Meyer leaned forward suddenly. 'Yeah, go ahead,' he said.

'Well, he come up there last Monday night, it must've been five-thirty, six o'clock, and he flashed the tin, and went inside the apartment. When he come out, he was in a hell of a hurry, and he was carrying a doll.'

'Are you telling me Carella was at the Sachs apartment last Monday night?'

'That's right.'

'Are you sure?'

'Positive.' Angieri paused. 'You *didn't* know this, huh? My wife was right.' He paused again. 'She's *always* right.'

'What did you say about a doll?'

'A doll, you know? Like kids play with? Girls? A big doll. With blonde hair, you know? A *doll*.'

'Carella came out of the apartment carrying a child's doll?'

'That's right.'

'Last Monday night?'

'That's right.'

'Did he say anything to you?'

'Nothing.'

'A doll,' Meyer said, puzzled.

It was nine a.m. when Meyer arrived at the Sachs apartment on Stafford Place. He spoke briefly to the superintendent of the building, a man named Manny Farber, and then took the elevator up to the fourth floor. There was no longer a patrolman on duty in the hallway. He went down the corridor and let himself into the apartment, using Tinka's own key, which had been lent to the investigating precinct by the Office of the Clerk.

The apartment was still.

He could tell at once that death had been here. There are different silences in an empty apartment, and if you are a working policeman, you do not scoff at poetic fallacy. An apartment vacated for the summer has a silence unlike one that is empty only for the day, with its occupants expected back that night. And an apartment that has known the touch of death possesses a silence unique and readily identifiable to anyone who has ever stared down at a corpse. Meyer knew the silence of death, and understood it, though he could not have told you what accounted for it. The disconnected humless electrical appliances; the unused, undripping water taps; the unringing telephone; the stopped unticking clocks; the sealed windows shutting out all street noises; these were all a part of it, but they only contributed to the whole and were not its sum and substance. The real silence was something only felt, and had nothing to do with the absence of sound. It touched something deep within him the moment he stepped through the door. It seemed to be carried on the air itself, a shuddering reminder that death had passed this way, and that some of its frightening grandeur was still locked inside these rooms. He paused with his hand on the doorknob, and then sighed and closed the door behind him and went into the apartment.

Sunlight glanced through closed windows, dust beams silently hovered on the unmoving air. He walked softly, as though reluctant to stir whatever ghostly remnants still were here. When he passed the child's room he looked through the open door and saw the dolls lined up in the bookcase beneath the windows, row upon row of dolls, each dressed differently, each staring back at him with unblinking glass eyes, pink cheeks glowing, mute red mouths frozen on the edge of articulation, painted lips parted over even plastic teeth, nylon hair in black, and red, and blonde, and the palest silver.

He was starting into the room when he heard a key turning in the front door.

The sound startled him. It cracked into the silent apartment like a crash of thunder. He heard the tumblers falling, the sudden click of the knob being turned. He moved into the child's room just as the front door opened. His eyes swept the room – bookcases, bed, closet, toy chest. He could hear heavy footsteps in the corridor, approaching the room. He threw open the closet door, drew his gun. The footsteps were closer. He eased the door towards him, leaving it open just a crack. Holding his breath, he waited in the darkness.

The man who came into the room was perhaps six feet two inches tall, with massive shoulders and a narrow waist. He paused just inside the doorway, as though sensing the presence of another person, seemed almost to be sniffing the air for a telltale scent. Then, visibly shrugging away his own correct intuition, he dismissed the idea and went quickly to the bookcases. He stopped in front of them and began lifting dolls from the shelves, seemingly at random, bundling them into his arms. He gathered up seven or eight of them, rose, turned towards the door, and was on his way out when Meyer kicked open the closet door.

The man turned, startled, his eyes opening wide. Foolishly, he clung to the dolls in his arms, first looking at Meyer's face, and then at the Colt .38 in Meyer's hand, and then up at Meyer's face again.

'Who are you?' he asked.

'Good question,' Meyer said. 'Put those dolls down, hurry up, on the bed there.'

'What . . . ?'

'Do as I say, mister!'

The man walked to the bed. He wet his lips, looked at Meyer, frowned, and then dropped the dolls.

'Get over against the wall,' Meyer said.

'Listen, what the hell . . . ?'

'Spread your legs, bend over, lean against the wall with your palms flat. Hurry up!'

'All right, take it easy.' The man leaned against the wall. Meyer quickly and carefully frisked him – chest, pockets, waist, the insides of his legs. Then he backed away from the man and said, 'Turn around, keep your hands up.'

The man turned, his hands high. He wet his lips again, and again looked at the gun in Meyer's hand.

'What are you doing here?' Meyer asked.

'What are *you* doing here?'

'I'm a police officer. Answer my –'

'Oh. Oh, okay,' the man said.

'What's okay about it?'

'I'm Dennis Sachs.'

'Who?'

'Dennis –'

'Tinka's husband?'

'Well, her ex-husband.'

'Where's your wallet?'

'Right here in my –'

'Don't reach for it! Bend over against the wall again, go ahead.'

The man did as Meyer ordered. Meyer felt for the wallet and found it in his right hip pocket. He opened it to the driver's licence. The name on the licence was Dennis Robert Sachs. Meyer handed it back to him.

'All right, put your hands down. What are you doing here?'

'My daughter wanted some of her dolls,' Sachs said. 'I came back to get them.'

'How'd you get in?'

'I have a key. I used to live here, you know.'

'It was my understanding you and your wife were divorced.'

'That's right.'

'And you still have a key?'

'Yes.'

'Did she know this?'

'Yes, of course.'

'And that's all you wanted here, huh? Just the dolls.'

'Yes.'

'Any doll in particular?'

'No.'

'Your daughter didn't specify any particular doll?'

'No, she simply said she'd like some of her dolls, and she asked if I'd come get them for her.'

'How about *your* preference?'

'*My* preference?'

'Yes. Did *you* have any particular doll in mind?'

'Me?'

'That's right, Mr Sachs. You.'

'No. What do you mean? Are you talking about *dolls*?'

'That's right, that's what I'm talking about.'

'Well, what would I want with any *specific* doll?'

'That's what *I'd* like to know.'

'I don't think I understand you.'

'Then forget it.'

Sachs frowned and glanced at the dolls on the bed. He hesitated, then shrugged and said, 'Well, is it all right to take them?'

'I'm afraid not.'

'Why not? They belong to my daughter.'

'We want to look them over, Mr Sachs.'

'For what?'

'I don't know for what. For *anything*.'

Sachs looked at the dolls again, and then he turned to Meyer and stared at him silently. 'I guess you know this has been a pretty bewildering conversation,' he said at last.

'Yeah, well, that's the way mysteries are,' Meyer answered. 'I've got work to do, Mr Sachs. If you have no further business here, I'd appreciate it if you left.'

Sachs nodded and said nothing. He looked at the dolls once again, and then walked out of the room, and down the corridor, and out of the apartment. Meyer waited, listening. The moment he heard the door close behind Sachs, he sprinted down the corridor, stopped just inside the door, counted swiftly to ten, and eased the door open no more than an inch. Peering out into the hallway, he could see Sachs waiting for the elevator. He looked angry as hell. When the elevator did not arrive, he pushed at the button repeatedly and then began pacing. He glanced once at Tinka's supposedly closed door, and then turned back to the elevator again. When it finally arrived, he said to the operator, 'What took you so long?' and stepped into the car.

Meyer came out of the apartment immediately, closed the door behind him, and ran for the service steps. He took the steps down at a gallop, pausing only for an instant at the fire door leading to the lobby, and then opening the door a crack. He could see the elevator operator standing near the building's entrance, his arms folded across his chest. Meyer came out into the lobby quickly, glanced back once at the open elevator doors, and then ran past the elevator and into the street. He spotted Sachs turning the corner up the block, and broke into a run after him. He paused again before turning the corner. When he sidled around it, he saw Sachs getting into a taxi. There was no time for Meyer to go to his own parked car. He hailed another cab and said to the driver, just like a cop, 'Follow that taxi,' sourly reminding himself that he would have to turn in a chit for the fare, even though he knew Petty Cash would probably never reimburse him. The taxi driver turned for a quick look at Meyer, just to see who was pulling all this cloak and dagger nonsense, and then silently began following Sachs's cab.

'You a cop?' he asked at last.

'Yeah,' Meyer said.

'Who's that up ahead?'

'The Boston Strangler,' Meyer said.

'Yeah?'

'Would I kid you?'

'You going to pay for this ride, or is it like taking apples from a pushcart?'

'I'm going to pay for it,' Meyer said. 'Just don't lose him, okay?'

It was almost ten o'clock, and the streets were thronged with traffic. The lead taxi moved steadily uptown and then crosstown, with Meyer's driver skilfully following. The city was a bedlam of noise – honking horns, grinding gears, squealing tyres, shouting drivers and pedestrians. Meyer leaned forward and kept his eye on the taxi ahead, oblivious to the sounds around him.

'He's pulling up, I think,' the driver said.

'Good. Stop about six car lengths behind him.' The taxi meter read eighty-five cents. Meyer took a dollar bill from his wallet, and handed it to the driver the moment he pulled over the kerb. Sachs had already gotten out of his cab and was walking into an apartment building in the middle of the block.

'Is this all the city tips?' the driver asked. 'Fifteen cents on an eighty-five-cent ride?'

'The city, my ass,' Meyer said, and leaped out of the cab. He ran up the street, and came into the building's entrance alcove just as the inner glass door closed behind Sachs. Meyer swung back his left arm and swiftly ran his hand over every bell in the row on the wall. Then, while waiting for an answering buzz, he put his face close to the glass door, shaded his eyes against the reflective glare, and peered inside. Sachs was nowhere in sight; the elevators were apparently around a corner of the lobby. A half-dozen answering buzzes sounded at once, releasing the lock mechanism on the door. Meyer pushed it open, and ran into the lobby. The floor indicator over the single elevator was moving, three, four, five – and stopped. Meyer nodded and walked out to the entrance alcove again, bending to look at the bells there. There were six apartments on the fifth floor. He was studying the names under the bells when a voice behind him said, 'I think you're looking for Dr Jason Levi.'

Meyer looked up, startled.

The man standing behind him was Bert Kling.

Dr Jason Levi's private office was painted an antiseptic white, and the only decoration on its wall was a large, easily readable calendar. His desk was functional and unadorned, made of grey steel, its top cluttered with medical journals and books, X-ray photographs, pharmaceutical samples, tongue depressors, prescription pads. There was a no-nonsense look about the doctor as well, the plain face topped with leonine white hair, the thick-lensed spectacles, the large cleaving nose, the thin-lipped mouth. He sat behind his desk and looked first at the detectives and then at Dennis Sachs, and waited for someone to speak.

'We want to know what you're doing here, Mr Sachs,' Meyer said.

'I'm a patient,' Sachs said.

'Is that true, Dr Levi?'

Levi hesitated. Then he shook his massive head. 'No,' he said. 'That is not true.'

'Shall we start again?' Meyer asked.

'I have nothing to say,' Sachs answered.

'Why'd you find it necessary to call Dr Levi from Arizona once a week?' Kling asked.

'Who said I did?'

'Mr Walter Blount, manager of the Major Powell Hotel in Rainfield.'

'He was lying.'

'Why would he lie?'

'I don't *know* why,' Sachs said. 'Go ask *him*.'

'No, we'll do it the easy way,' Kling said. 'Dr Levi, *did* Mr Sachs call you from Arizona once a week?'

'Yes,' Levi said.

'We seem to have a slight difference of opinion here,' Meyer said.

'Why'd he call you?' Kling asked.

'Don't answer that, Doctor!'

'Dennis, what are we trying to hide? She's dead.'

'You're a doctor, you don't have to tell them anything. You're like a priest. They can't force you to –'

'Dennis, she is dead.'

'Did your calls have something to do with your wife?' Kling asked.

'No,' Sachs said.

'Yes,' Levi said.

'Was *Tinka* your patient, Doctor, is that it?'

'Yes.'

'Dr Levi, I *forbid* you to tell these men anything more about –'

'She was my patient,' Levi said. 'I began treating her at the beginning of the year.'

'In January?'

'Yes. January fifth. More than three months ago.'

'Doctor, I swear on my dead wife that if you go ahead with this, I'm going to ask the AMA to –'

'Nonsense!' Levi said fiercely. 'Your wife is dead! If we can help them find her killer –'

'You're not helping them with anything! All you're doing is dragging her memory through the muck of a criminal investigation.'

'Mr Sachs,' Meyer said, 'whether you know it or not, her memory is already in the muck of a criminal investigation.'

'Why did she come to you, Doctor?' Kling asked. 'What was wrong with her?'

'She said she had made a New Year's resolution, said she had decided once and for all to seek medical assistance. It was quite pathetic, really. She was so helpless, and so beautiful, and so alone.'

'I *couldn't* stay with her any longer!' Sachs said. 'I'm not made of iron! I couldn't handle it. That's why we got the divorce. It wasn't my fault, what happened to her.'

'No one is blaming you for anything,' Levi said. 'Her illness went back a long time, long before she met you.'

'What was this illness, Doctor?' Meyer asked.

'Don't tell them!'

'Dennis, I *have* to –'

'You *don't* have to! Leave it the way it is. Let her live in everyone's memory as a beautiful exciting woman instead of –'

Dennis cut himself off.

'Instead of what?' Meyer asked.

The room went silent.

'Instead of what?' he said again.

Levi sighed and shook his head.

'Instead of a drug addict.'

Chapter Twelve

In the silence of the squadroom later that day, they read Dr Jason Levi's casebook:

January 5

The patient's name is Tina Karin Sachs. She is divorced, has a daughter aged five. She lives in the city and leads an active professional life, which is one of the reasons she was reluctant to seek assistance before now. She stated, however, that she had made a New Year's resolution, and that she is determined to break the habit. She has been a narcotics user since the time she was seventeen, and is now addicted to heroin.

I explained to her that the methods of withdrawal which I had thus far found most satisfactory were those employing either morphine or methadone, both of which had proved to be adequate substitutes for whatever drugs or combinations of drugs my patients had previously been using. I told her, too, that I personally preferred the morphine method.

She asked if there would be much pain involved. Apparently she had once tried cold-turkey withdrawal and had found the attempt too painful to bear. I told her that she would experience withdrawal symptoms – nausea, vomiting, diarrhoea, lacrimation, dilation of pupils, rhinorrhoea, yawning, gooseflesh, sneezing, sweating – with either method. With morphine, the withdrawal would be more severe, but she could expect relative comfort after a week or so. With methadone, the withdrawal would be easier, but she might still feel somewhat tremulous for as long as a month afterwards.

She said she wanted to think it over, and would call me when she had decided.

January 12

I had not expected to see or hear from Tinka Sachs again, but she arrived here today and asked my receptionist if I could spare ten minutes. I said I could, and she was shown into my private office, where we talked for more than forty-five minutes.

She said she had not yet decided what she should do, and wanted to discuss it further with me. She is, as she had previously explained, a fashion model. She receives top fees for her modelling and was now afraid that treatment might entail either pain or sickness which would cause her to lose employment, thereby endangering her career. I told her that her addiction to heroin had made her virtually careerless anyway, since she was spending much of her income on the purchase of drugs. She did not particularly enjoy this observation, and quickly rejoindered that she thoroughly relished all the fringe benefits of modelling – the fame, the recognition, and so on. I asked her if she really enjoyed anything but heroin, or really thought of anything but heroin, and she became greatly agitated and seemed about to leave the office.

Instead, she told me that I didn't know what it was like, and she hoped I understood she had been using narcotics since she was seventeen, when she'd first tried marijuana at a beach party in Malibu. She had continued smoking marijuana for almost a year, never tempted to try any of 'the real shit' until a photographer offered her a sniff of heroin shortly after she'd begun modelling. He also tried to rape her afterwards, a side effect that nearly caused her to abandon her beginning career as a model. Her near-rape, however, did not dissuade her from using marijuana or from sniffing heroin every now and then, until someone warned her that inhaling the drug could damage her nose. Since her nose was part of her face, and her face was part of what she hoped would become her fortune, she promptly stopped the sniffing process.

The first time she tried injecting the drug was with a confirmed addict, male, in a North Hollywood apartment. Unfortunately, the police broke in on them, and they were both arrested. She was nineteen years old at the time, and was luckily released with a suspended sentence. She came to this city the following month, determined never to fool with drugs again, hoping to put three thousand miles between herself and her former acquaintances. But she discovered, almost immediately upon arrival, that the drug was as readily obtainable here as it was in Los Angeles. Moreover, she began her association with the Cutler Agency several weeks after she got here, and found herself in possession of more money than she would ever need to support both herself *and* a narcotics habit. She began injecting the drug under her skin, into the soft tissue of her body. Shortly afterwards, she abandoned the subcutaneous route and began shooting heroin directly into her veins. She has been using it intravenously ever since, has for all intents and purposes been hopelessly hooked since she first began skin-popping. How, then, could I expect to cure her? How could she wake up each morning without knowing that a supply of narcotics was available, in fact accessible? I explained that hers was the common fear of all addicts about to undergo treatment, a reassurance she accepted without noticeable enthusiasm.

I'll think about it, she said again, and again left. I frankly do not believe she will ever return again.

January 20

Tinka Sachs began treatment today.

She has chosen the morphine method (even though she understands the symptoms will be more severe) because she does not want to endanger her career by a prolonged withdrawal, a curious concern for someone who has been endangering her career ever since it started. I had previously explained that I wanted to hospitalize her for several months, but she flatly refused hospitalization of any kind, and stated that the deal was off if that was part of the treatment. I told her that I could not guarantee lasting results unless she allowed me to hospitalize her, but she said we would have to hope for the best because she wasn't going to admit herself to any damn hospital. I finally extracted from her an agreement to stay at home under a nurse's care at least during the first several days of withdrawal, when the symptoms would be most severe. I warned her against making any illegal purchases and against associating with any know addicts or pushers. Our schedule is a rigid one. To start, she will receive $\frac{1}{4}$ grain of morphine four times daily – twenty minutes before each meal. The doses will be administered hypodermically, and the morphine will be dissolved in thiamine hydrochloride.

It is my hope that withdrawal will be complete within two weeks.

January 21

I have prescribed Thorazine for Tinka's nausea, and belladonna and pectin for her diarrhoea. The symptoms are severe. She could not sleep at all last night. I have instructed the nurse staying at her apartment to administer three grains of Nembutal tonight before Tinka retires, with further instructions to repeat $1\frac{1}{2}$ grains if she does not sleep through the night.

Tinka has taken excellent care of her body, a factor on our side. She is quite beautiful and I have no doubt she is a superior model, though I am at a loss to explain how photographers can have missed her obvious addiction. How did she keep from 'nodding' before the cameras? She has scrupulously avoided marking either her lower legs or her arms, but the insides of her thighs (she told me she does not model either lingerie or bathing suits) are covered with hit marks.

Morphine continues at $\frac{1}{4}$ grain four times daily.

January 22

I have reduced the morphine injections to $\frac{1}{4}$ grain twice daily, alternating with $\frac{1}{8}$ grain twice daily. Symptoms are still severe. She has cancelled all of her sittings, telling the agency she is menstruating and suffering cramps, a complaint they have apparently heard from their models before. She shows no desire to eat. I have begun prescribing vitamins.

January 23

The symptoms are abating. We are now administering $\frac{1}{8}$ grain four times daily.

January 24

Treatment continuing with $\frac{1}{8}$ grain four times daily. The nurse will be discharged tomorrow, and Tinka will begin coming to my office for her injections, a procedure I am heartily against. But it is either that or losing her entirely, and I must go along.

January 25

Started one grain codeine twice daily, alternating with $\frac{1}{8}$ grain morphine twice daily. Tinka came to my office at eight-thirty, before breakfast, for her first injection. She came again at twelve-thirty, and at six-thirty. I administered the last injection at her home at eleven-thirty. She seems exceptionally restless, and I have prescribed $\frac{1}{2}$ grain of phenobarbital daily to combat this.

January 26

Tinka Sachs did not come to the office today. I called her apartment several times, but no one answered the telephone. I did not dare call the modelling agency lest they suspect she is undergoing treatment. At three o'clock, I spoke to her daughter's governess. She had just picked the child up at the playschool she attends. She said she did not know where Mrs Sachs was, and suggested that I try the agency. I called again at midnight. Tinka was still not home. The governess said I had awakened her. Apparently, she saw nothing unusual about her employer's absence. The working arrangement calls for her to meet the child after school and to spend as much time with her as is necessary. She said that Mrs Sachs is often gone the entire night, in which case she is supposed to take the child to school in the morning, and then call for her again at two-thirty. Mrs Sachs was once gone for three days, she said.

I am worried.

February 4

Tinka returned to the office again today, apologizing profusely, and explaining that she had been called out of town on an assignment; they were shooting some new tweed fashions and wanted a woodland background. I accused her of lying, and she finally admitted that she had not been out of town at all, but had instead spent the past week in the apartment of a friend from California. After further questioning, she conceded that her California friend is a drug addict, is in fact the man with whom she was arrested when she was nineteen years old. He arrived in the city last September, with very little money, and no place to live. She staked him for a while, and allowed him to live in her Mavis County house until she sold it in October. She then helped him to find an apartment on South Fourth, and she still sees him occasionally.

It was obvious that she had begun taking heroin again.

She expressed remorse, and said that she is more than ever determined to break the habit. When I asked if her friend expects to remain in the city, she said that he does, but that he has a companion with him, and no longer needs any old acquaintance to help him pursue his course of addiction.

I extracted a promise from Tinka that she would never see this man again, nor try to contact him.

We begin treatment again tomorrow morning. This time I insisted that a nurse remain with her for at least two weeks.

We will be starting from scratch.

February 9

We have made excellent progress in the past five days. The morphine injections have been reduced to $\frac{1}{8}$ grain four times daily, and tomorrow we begin alternating with codeine.

Tinka talked about her relationship with her husband for the first time today, in connection with her resolve to break the habit. He is, apparently, an archaeologist working with an expedition somewhere in Arizona. She is in frequent touch with him, and in fact called him yesterday to say she had begun treatment and was hopeful of a cure. It is her desire, she said, to begin a new life with him once the withdrawal is complete. She knows he still loves her, knows that had it not been for her habit they would never have parted.

She said he did not learn of her addiction until almost a year after the child was born. This was all the more remarkable since the baby – fed during pregnancy by the bloodstream of her mother, metabolically dependent on heroin – was quite naturally an addict herself from the moment she was born. Dennis, and the family pediatrician as well, assumed she was a colicky baby, crying half the night through, vomiting, constantly fretting. Only Tinka knew that the infant was experiencing all the symptoms of cold-turkey withdrawal. She was tempted more than once to give the child a secret fix, but she restrained from doing so, and the baby survived the torment of force withdrawal only to face the subsequent storm of separation and divorce.

Tinka was able to explain the hypodermic needle Dennis found a month later by saying she was allergic to certain dyes in the nylon dresses she was modelling and that her doctor had prescribed an antihistamine in an attempt to reduce the allergic reaction. But she could not explain the large sums of money that seemed to be vanishing from their joint bank account, nor could she explain his ultimate discovery of three glassine bags of a white powder secreted at the back of her dresser drawer. She finally confessed that she was a drug addict, that she had been a drug addict for close to seven years and saw nothing wrong with it so long as she was capable of supporting the habit. He goddamn well knew she was earning most of the money in his household, anyway, so what the fuck did he want from her?

He cracked her across the face and told her they would go to see a doctor in the morning.

In the morning, Tinka was gone.

She did not return to the apartment until three weeks later, dishevelled and bedraggled, at which time she told Dennis she had been on a party with three coloured musicians from a club downtown, all of them addicts. She could not remember what they had done together. Dennis had meanwhile consulted a doctor, and he told Tinka that drug addiction was by no means incurable, that there were ways of treating it, that success was almost certain if the patient – Don't make me laugh, Tinka said. I'm hooked through the bag and back, and what's more I like it, now what the hell do you think about that? Get off my back, you're worse than the monkey!

He asked for the divorce six months later.

During that time, he tried desperately to reach this person he had taken for a wife, this stranger who was nonetheless the mother of his child, this driven animal whose entire life seemed bounded by the need for heroin. Their expenses were overwhelming. She could not let her career vanish because without her career she could hardly afford the enormous amounts of heroin she required. So she dressed the part of the famous model, and lived in a lavishly appointed apartment, and rode around town in hired limousines, and ate at the best restaurants, and was seen at all the important functions – while within her the clamour for heroin raged unabated. She worked slavishly, part of her income going towards maintaining the legend that was a necessary adjunct of her profession, the remainder going towards the purchase of drugs for herself and her friends.

There were always friends.

She would vanish for weeks at a time, lured by a keening song she alone heard, compelled to seek other addicts, craving the approval of people like herself, the comradeship of the dream society, the anonymity of the shooting gallery where scars were not stigmata and addiction was not a curse.

He would have left her sooner but the child presented a serious problem. He knew he could not trust Anna alone with her mother, but how could he take her with him on archaeological expeditions around the world? He realized that if Tinka's addiction were allowed to enter the divorce proceedings, he would be granted immediate custody of the child. But Tinka's career would automatically be ruined, and who knew what later untold hurt the attendant publicity could bring to Anna? He promised Tinka that he would not introduce the matter of her addiction if she would allow him to hire a responsible governess for the child. Tinka readily agreed. Except for her occasional binges, she considered herself to be a devoted and exemplary mother. If a governess would make Dennis happy and keep this sordid matter of addiction out of the proceedings, she was more than willing to go along with the idea. The arrangements were made.

Dennis, presumably in love with his wife, presumably concerned about his daughter's welfare, was nonetheless content to abandon one to eternal drug addiction, and the other to the vagaries and unpredictabilities of living with a confirmed junkie. Tinka, for her part, was glad to see him leave. He had become a puritanical goad, and she wondered why she'd ever married him in the first place. She supposed it had had something to do with the romantic notion of one day kicking the habit and starting a new life.

Which is what you're doing now, I told her.

Yes, she said, and her eyes were shining.

February 12

Tinka is no longer dependent on morphine, and we have reduced the codeine intake to one grain twice daily, alternating with $\frac{1}{2}$ grain twice daily.

February 13

I received a long-distance call from Dennis Sachs today. He simply wanted to know how his wife was coming along and said that if I didn't mind he would call once a week – it would have to be either Friday or Saturday since he'd be in the desert the rest of the time – to check on her progress. I told him that the prognosis was excellent, and I expressed the hope that withdrawal would be complete by the twentieth of the month.

February 14

Have reduced the codeine to $\frac{1}{2}$ grain twice daily, and have introduced thiamine twice daily.

February 15

Last night, Tinka slipped out of the apartment while her nurse was dozing. She has not returned, and I do not know where she is.

February 20

Have been unable to locate Tinka.

March 1

Have called the apartment repeatedly. The governess continues to care for Anna – but there has been no word from Tinka.

March 8

In desperation, I called the Cutler Agency today to ask if they have any knowledge of Tinka's whereabouts. They asked me to identify myself, and I said I was a doctor treating her for a skin allergy (Tinka's own lie!) They said she had gone to the Virgin Islands on a modelling assignment and would not be back until the twentieth of March. I thanked them and hung up.

March 22

Tinka came back to my office today.

The assignment had come up suddenly, she said, and she had taken it, forgetting to tell me about it.

I told her I thought she was lying.

All right, she said. She had seized upon the opportunity as a way to get away from me and the treatment. She did not know why, but she had suddenly been filled with panic. She knew that in several days, a week at most, she would be off even the thiamine – and then what would there be? How could she possibly get through a day without a shot of *something*?

Art Cutler had called and proposed the St Thomas assignment, and the idea of sun and sand had appealed to her immensely. By coincidence, her friend from California called that same night, and when she told him where she was going he said that he'd pack a bag and meet her down there.

I asked her exactly what her connection is with this 'friend from California', who now seems responsible for two lapses in her treatment. What lapse? she asked, and then swore she had not touched anything while she was away. This friend was simply *that*, a good friend.

But you told me he is an addict, I said.

Yes, he's an addict, she answered. But he didn't even *suggest* drugs while we were away. As a matter of fact, I think I've kicked it completely. That's really the only reason I came here, to tell you that it's not necessary to continue treatment any longer. I haven't had anything, heroin or morphine or *anything*, all the while I was away. I'm cured.

You're lying, I said.

All right, she said. If I wanted the truth, it was her California friend who'd kept her out of prison those many years ago. He had told the arresting officers that he was a pusher, a noble and dangerous admission to make, and that he had forced a shot on Tinka. She had got off with the suspended sentence while he'd gone to prison; so naturally she was indebted to him. Besides, she saw no reason why she shouldn't spend some time with him on a modelling assignment, instead of running around with a lot of faggot designers and photographers, not to mention the Lesbian editor of the magazine. Who the hell did I think I was, her keeper?

I asked if this 'friend from California' had suddenly struck it rich.

What do you mean? she said.

Well, isn't it true that he was in need of money and a place to stay when he first came to the city?

Yes, that's true.

Then how can he afford to support a drug habit and also manage to take a vacation in the Virgin Islands? I asked.

She admitted that she paid for the trip. If the man had saved her from a prison sentence, what was so wrong about paying his fare and his hotel bill?

I would not let it go.

Finally, she told me the complete story. She had been sending him money over the years, not because he asked her for it, but simply because she felt she owed something to him. His lie had enabled her to come here and start a new life. The least she could do was send him a little money every now and then. Yes, she had been supporting him ever since he arrived here. Yes, yes, it was she who'd invited him along on the trip; there had been no coincidental phone call from him that night. Moreover, she had not only paid for *his* plane fare and hotel bill, but also for that of his companion, whom she described as 'an extremely lovely young woman.'

And no heroin all that while, right?

Tears, anger, defence.

Yes, there had been heroin! There had been enough heroin to sink the island, and she had paid for every drop of it. There had been heroin morning, noon, and night. It was amazing that she had been able to face the cameras at all, she had blamed her drowsiness on the sun. That needle had been stuck in her thigh constantly, like a glittering glass cock! Yes, there had been heroin, and she had loved every minute of it! What the hell did I want from her?

I want to cure you, I said.

March 23

She accused me today of trying to kill her. She said that I have been trying to kill her since the first day we met, that I know she is not strong enough to withstand the pains of withdrawal, and that the treatment will eventually result in her death.

Her lawyer has been preparing a will, she said, and she would sign it tomorrow. She would begin treatment after that, but she knew it would lead to her ultimate death.

March 24

Tinka signed her will today.

She brought me a fragment of a poem she wrote last night:

> *When I think of what I am*
> *And of what I might have been,*
> *I tremble.*
> *I fear the night.*
> *Throughout the day,*
> *I rush from dragons conjured in the dark.*
> *Why will they not*

I asked her why she hadn't finished the poem. She said she couldn't finish it until she knew the outcome herself. What outcome do you want? I asked her.

I want to be cured, she said.

You *will* be cured, I told her.

We began treatment once more.

Dennis Sachs called from Arizona again to enquire about his wife. I told him she had suffered a relapse but that she had begun treatment anew, and that we were hoping for complete withdrawal by April 15th at the very latest. He asked if there was anything he could do for Tinka. I told him that the only person who could do anything for Tinka was Tinka.

Treatment continues.
$\frac{1}{4}$ grain morphine twice daily.
$\frac{1}{8}$ grain morphine twice daily.

$\frac{1}{8}$ grain morphine four times daily.
Prognosis good.

$\frac{1}{8}$ grain morphine twice daily.
One grain codeine twice daily.

Tinka confessed today that she has begun buying heroin on the sly, smuggling it in, and has been taking it whenever the nurse isn't watching. I flew into a rage. She shouted 'April Fool!' and began laughing.
I think there is a chance this time.

One grain codeine four times daily.

One grain codeine twice daily.
$\frac{1}{2}$ grain codeine twice daily.

$\frac{1}{2}$ grain codeine four times daily.

$\frac{1}{2}$ grain codeine twice daily, thiamine twice daily.

Thiamine four times daily. Nurse was discharged today.

Thiamine three times daily.
We are going to make it!

April 8
Thiamine twice daily.

April 9
She told me today that she is certain the habit is almost kicked. This is my feeling as well. The weaning from hypodermics is virtually complete. There is only the promise of a new and rewarding life ahead.

That was where the doctor's casebook ended because that was when Tinka Sachs was murdered.

Meyer glanced up to see if Kling had finished the page. Kling nodded, and Meyer closed the book.

'He took two lives from her,' Meyer said. 'The one she was ending, and the one she was beginning.'

That afternoon Paul Blaney earned his salary for the second time in four days. He called to say he had completed the post-mortem examination of Tinka Sachs and had discovered a multitude of scars on both upper front thighs. It seemed positive that the scars had been caused by repeated intravenous injections, and it was Blaney's opinion that the dead girl had been a drug addict.

Chapter Thirteen

She had handcuffed both hands behind his back during one of his periods of unconsciousness, and then had used a leather belt to lash his feet together. He lay naked on the floor now and waited for her arrival, trying to tell himself he did not need her, and knowing that he needed her desperately.

It was very warm in the room, but he was shivering. His skin was beginning to itch but he could not scratch himself because his hands were manacled behind his back. He could smell his own body odours – he had not been bathed or shaved in three days – but he did not care about his smell or his beard, he only cared that she was not here yet, what was keeping her?

He lay in the darkness and tried not to count the minutes.

The girl was naked when she came into the room. She did not put on the light. There was the familiar tray in her hands, but it did not carry food any more. The Llama was on the left-hand side of the tray. Alongside the gun were a small cardboard box, a book of matches, a spoon with its handle bent back towards the bowl, and a glassine envelope.

'Hello, doll,' she said. 'Did you miss me?'

Carella did not answer.

'Have you been waiting for me?' the girl asked. 'What's the matter, don't you feel like talking?' She laughed her mirthless laugh. 'Don't worry, baby,' she said. 'I'm going to fix you.'

She put the tray down on the chair near the door, and then walked to him.

'I think I'll play with you awhile,' she said. 'Would you like me to play with you?'

Carella did not answer.

'Well, if you're not even going to talk to me, I guess I'll just have to leave. After all, I know when I'm not –'

'No, don't go,' Carella said.

'Do you want me to stay?'

'Yes.'

'Say it.'

'I want you to stay.'

'That's better. What would you like, baby? Would you like me to play with you a little?'

'No.'

'Don't you like being played with?'

'No.'

'What do you like, baby?'

He did not answer.

'Well, you have to tell me,' she said, 'or I just won't give it to you.'

'I don't know,' he said.

'You don't know what you like?'

'Yes.'

'Do you like the way I look without any clothes on?'

'Yes, you look all right.'

'But that doesn't interest you, does it?'

'No.'

'What *does* interest you?'

Again, he did not answer.

'Well, you *must* know what interests you. Don't you know?'

'No, I don't know.'

'Tch,' the girl said, and rose and began walking towards the door.

'Where are you going?' he asked quickly.

'Just to put some water in the spoon, doll,' she said soothingly. 'Don't worry. I'll be back.'

She took the spoon from the tray and walked out of the room, leaving the door open. He could hear the water tap running in the kitchen. Hurry up, he thought, and then thought, No, I don't need you, leave me alone, goddamn you, leave me alone!

'Here I am,' she said. She took the tray off the seat of the chair and then sat and picked up the glassine envelope. She emptied its contents into the spoon, and then struck a match and held it under the blackened bowl. 'Got to cook it up,' she said. 'Got to cook it up for my baby. You getting itchy for it, baby? Don't worry, I'll take care of you. What's your wife's name?'

'Teddy,' he said.

'Oh my,' she said, 'you still remember. That's a shame.' She blew out the match. She opened the small box on the tray, and removed the hypodermic syringe and needle from it. She affixed the needle to the syringe, and depressed the plunger to squeeze any air out of the cylindrical glass tube. From the same cardboard box, which was the original container in which the syringe had been marketed, she took a piece of absorbent cotton, which she placed over the milky white liquid in the bowl of the spoon. Using the cotton as a filter, knowing that even the tiniest piece of solid matter would clog the tiny opening in the hypodermic needle, she drew the liquid up into the syringe, and then smiled and said. 'There we are, all ready for my doll.'

'I don't want it,' Carella said suddenly.

'Oh, honey, please don't lie to me,' she said calmly. 'I *know* you want it, what's your wife's name?'

'Teddy.'

'Teddy, tch, tch, well, well,' she said. From the cardboard box, she took a loop of string, and then walked to Carella and put the syringe on the floor beside him. She looped the piece of string around his arm, just above the elbow joint.

'What's your wife's name?' she asked.

'Teddy.'

'You want this, doll?'

'No.'

'Oooh, it's very good,' she said. 'We had some this afternoon, it was very good stuff. Aren't you just aching all over for it, what's your wife's name?'

'Teddy.'

'Has she got tits like mine?'

Carella did not answer.

'Oh, but that doesn't interest you, does it? All that interests you is what's right here in this syringe, isn't that right?'

'No.'

'This is a very high-class shooting gallery, baby. No eyedroppers here, oh no. Everything veddy veddy high-tone. Though I don't know how we're going to keep ourselves in junk now that little Sweetass is gone. He shouldn't have killed her, he really shouldn't have.'

'Then why did he?'

'I'll ask the questions, doll. Do you remember your wife's name?'

'Yes.'

'What is it?'

'Teddy.'

'Then I guess I'll go. I can make good use of this myself.' She picked up the syringe. 'Shall I go?'

'Do what you want to do.'

'If I leave this room,' the girl said, 'I won't come back until tomorrow morning. That'll be a long long night, baby. You think you can last the night without a fix?' She paused. 'Do you want this or not?'

'Leave me alone,' he said.

'No. No, no, we can't leave you alone. In a little while, baby, you are going to tell us everything you know, you are going to tell us exactly how you found us, you are going to tell us because if you don't we'll leave you here to drown in your own vomit. Now what's you wife's name?'

'Teddy.'

'No.'

'Yes. Her name is Teddy.'

'How can I give you this if your memory's so good?'

'Then don't give it to me.'

'Okay,' the girl said, and walked towards the door. 'Goodnight, doll. I'll see you in the morning.'

'Wait.'

'Yes?' The girl turned. There was no expression on her face.

'You forgot your tourniquet,' Carella said.

'So I did,' the girl answered. She walked back to him and removed the string from his arm. 'Play it cool,' she said. 'Go ahead. See how far you get by playing it cool. Tomorrow morning you'll be rolling all over the floor when I come in.' She kissed him swiftly on the mouth. She sighed deeply. 'Ahh,' she said, 'why do you force me to be mean to you?'

She went back to the door and busied herself with putting the string and cotton back into the box, straightening the book of matches and the spoon, aligning the syringe with the other items.

'Well, goodnight,' she said, and walked out of the room, locking the door behind her.

Detective Sergeant Tony Kreisler of the Los Angeles Police Department did not return Meyer's call until nine o'clock that Monday night, which meant it was six o'clock on the Coast.

'You've had me busy all day long,' Kreisler said. 'It's tough to dig in the files for these ancient ones.'

'Did you come up with anything?' Meyer asked.

'I'll tell you the truth, if this hadn't been a homicide you're working on, I'd have given up long ago, said the hell with it.'

'What've you got for me?' Meyer asked patiently.

'This goes back twelve, thirteen years. You really think there's a connection?'

'It's all we've got to go on,' Meyer said. 'We figured it was worth a chance.'

'Besides, the city paid for the long-distance call, right?' Kreisler said, and began laughing.

'That's right,' Meyer said, and bided his time, and hoped that *Kreisler's* city was paying for *his* call, too.

'Well, anyway,' Kreisler said, when his laughter had subsided, 'you were right about that arrest. We picked them up on a violation of Section 11500 of the Health and Safety Code. The girl's name wasn't Sachs then, we've got her listed as Tina Karin Grady, you suppose that's the same party?'

'Probably her maiden name,' Meyer said.

'That's what I figure. They were holed up in an apartment in North Hollywood with more than twenty-five caps of H, something better than an eighth of an ounce, not that it makes any difference out here. Out here, there's no minimum quantity constituting a violation. Any amount that can be analysed as a narcotic is admissible in court. It's different with you guys, I know that.'

'That's right,' Meyer said.

'Anyway, the guy was a mainliner, hit marks all over his arms. The Grady girl looked like sweet young meat, it was tough to figure what she was doing with a creep like him. She claimed she didn't know he was an addict, claimed he'd invited her up to the apartment, got her drunk, and then forced a shot on her. There were no previous marks on her body, just that one hit mark in the crook of her el —'

'What a minute,' Meyer said.

'Yeah, what's the matter?'

'The *girl* claimed he'd forced the shot on her?'

'That's right. Said he got her drunk.'

'It wasn't the *man* who alibied her?'

'What do you mean?'

'Did the man claim he was a pusher and that he'd forced a fix on the girl?'

Kreisler began laughing again. 'Just catch a junkie who's willing to take a fall as a pusher. Are you kidding?'

'The girl told her doctor that the man alibied her.'

'Absolute lie,' Kreisler said. '*She* was the one who did all the talking, convinced the judge she was innocent, got off with a suspended sentence.'

'And the man?'

'Convicted, served his time at Soledad, minimum of two, maximum of ten.'

'Then *that's* why she kept sending him money. Not because she was indebted to him, but only because she felt guilty as hell.'

'She deserved a break,' Kreisler said. 'What the hell, she was a nineteen-year-old kid. How do you know? Maybe he *did* force a blast on her.'

'I doubt it. She'd been sniffing the stuff regularly and using pot since she was seventeen.'

'Yeah, well, we didn't know that.'

'What was the man's name?' Meyer asked.

'Fritz Schmidt.'

'Fritz? Is that a nickname?'

'No, that's his square handle. Fritz Schmidt.'

'What's the last you've got on him?'

'He was paroled in four. Parole Office gave him a clean bill of health, haven't had any trouble from him since.'

'Do you know if he's still in California?'

'Couldn't tell you.'

'Okay, thanks a lot,' Meyer said.

'Don't mention it,' Kreisler said, and hung up.

There were no listings for Fritz Schmidt in any of the city's telephone directories. But according to Dr Levi's casebook, Tinka's 'friend from California' had only arrived here in September. Hardly expecting any positive results, Meyer dialled the Information operator, identified himself as a working detective, and aksed if she had anything for a Mr Fritz Schmidt in her new listings.

Two minutes later, Meyer and Kling clipped on their holsters and left the squadroom.

The girl came back into the room at nine-twenty-five. She was fully clothed. The Llama was in her right hand. She closed the door gently behind her, but did not bother to switch on the overhead light. She watched Carella silently for several moments, the neon blinking around the edges of the drawn shade across the room. Then she said, 'You're shivering, baby.'

Carella did not answer.

'How tall are you?' she asked.

'Six-two.'

'We'll get some clothes to fit you.'

'Why the sudden concern?' Carella asked. He was sweating profusely, and shivering at the same time, wanting to tear his hands free of the cuffs, wanting to kick out with his lashed feet, helpless to do either, feeling desperately ill and knowing the only thing that would cure him.

'No concern at all, baby,' she said. 'We're dressing you because we've got to take you away from here.'

'Where are you taking me?'

'Away.'

'Where?'

'Don't worry,' she said. 'We'll give you a nice big fix first.'

He felt suddenly exhilarated. He tried to keep the joy from showing on his face, tried not to smile, hoping against hope that she wasn't just teasing him again. He lay shivering on the floor, and the girl laughed and said, 'My, it's rough when a little jolt is overdue, isn't it?'

Carella said nothing.

'Do you know what an overdose of heroin is?' she asked suddenly.

The shivering stopped for just a moment, and then began again more violently. Her words seemed to echo in the room, do you know what an overdose of heroin is, overdose, heroin, do you, do you?

'Do you?' the girl persisted.

'Yes.'

'It won't hurt you,' she said. 'It'll *kill* you, but it won't hurt you.' She laughed again. 'Think of it, baby. How many addicts would you say there are in this city? Twenty thousand, twenty-one thousand, what's your guess?'

'I don't know,' Carella said.

'Let's make it twenty thousand, okay? I like round numbers. Twenty thousand junkies out there, all hustling around and wondering where their next shot is coming from, and here we are about to give you a fix that'd take care of seven or eight of them for a week. How about that? That's real generosity, baby.'

'Thanks,' Carella said. 'What do you think,' he started, and stopped because his teeth were chattering. He waited. He took a deep breath and tried again. 'What do you think you'll . . . you'll accomplish by killing me?'

'Silence,' the girl said.

'How?'

'You're the only one in the world who knows who we are or where we are. Once you're dead, silence.'

'No.'

'Ah, *yes*, baby.'

'I'm telling you no. They'll find you.'

'Uh-uh.'

'Yes.'

'How?'

'The same way I did.'

'Uh-uh. Impossible.'

'If *I* uncovered your mistake –'

'There *was* no mistake, baby.' The girl paused. 'There was only a little girl playing with her doll.'

The room was silent.

'We've got the doll, honey. We found it in your car, remember? It's a very nice doll. Very expensive, I'll bet.'

'It's a present for my daughter,' Carella said. 'I told you –'

'You weren't going to give your daughter a *used* doll for a present, were you? No, honey.' The girl smiled. 'I happened to look under the doll's dress a few minutes ago. Baby, it's all over for you, believe me.' She turned and opened the door. 'Fritz,' she yelled to the other room, 'come in here and give me a hand.'

The mailbox downstairs told them Fritz Schmidt was in apartment 34. They took the steps up two at a time, drawing their revolvers when they were on the third floor, and then scanning the numerals on each door as they moved down the corridor. Meyer put his ear to the door at the end of the hall. He could hear nothing. He moved away from the door, and then nodded to Kling. Kling stepped back several feet, bracing himself, his legs widespread. There was no wall opposite the end door, nothing to use as a launching support for a flat-footed kick at the latch. Meyer used Kling's body as the support he needed, raising his knee high as Kling shoved him out and forwards. Meyer's foot connected. The lock sprang and the door swung wide. He followed it into the apartment, gun in hand, Kling not three feet behind him. They fanned out the moment they were inside the room, Kling to the right, Meyer to the left.

A man came running out of the room to the right of the large living room. He was a tall man with straight blond hair and huge shoulders. He looked at the detectives and then thrust one hand inside his jacket and down towards his belt. Neither Meyer nor Kling waited to find out what he was reaching for. They opened fire simultaneously. The bullets caught the man in his enormous chest and flung him back against the wall, which he clung to for just a moment before falling headlong to the floor. A second person appeared in the doorway. The second person was a girl, and she was very big, and she held a pistol in her right hand. A look of panic was riding her face, but it was curiously coupled with a fixed smile, as though she'd been expecting them all along and was ready for them, was in fact welcoming their arrival.

'Watch it, she's loaded!' Meyer yelled, but the girl swung around swiftly, pointing the gun into the other room instead, aiming it at the floor. In the split second it took her to turn and extend her arm, Kling saw the man lying trussed near the radiator. The man was turned away from the door, but Kling knew instinctively it was Carella.

He fired automatically and without hesitation, the first time he had ever shot a human being in the back, placing the shot high between the girl's shoulders. The Llama in her hand went off at almost the same instant, but the impact of Kling's slug sent her falling halfway across the room, her own bullet going wild. She struggled to rise as Kling ran into the room. She turned the gun on Carella again, but Kling's foot struck her extended hand, kicking the gun up as the second shot exploded. The girl would not let go. Her fingers were still tight around the stock of the gun. She swung it back a third time and shouted, 'Let me *kill* him, you bastard!' and tightened her finger on the trigger.

Kling fired again.

His bullet entered her forehead just above the right eye. The Llama went off as she fell backwards, the bullet spanging against the metal of the radiator and then ricocheting across the room and tearing through the drawn window shade and shattering the glass behind it.

Meyer was at his side.

'Easy,' he said.

Kling had not cried since that time almost four years ago when Claire was killed, but he stood in the centre of the neon-washed room now with the dead and bleeding girl against the wall and Carella naked and shivering near the radiator, and he allowed the hand holding the pistol to drop limply to his side, and then he began sobbing, deep bitter sobs that racked his body.

Meyer put his arm around Kling's shoulders.

'Easy,' he said again. 'It's all over.'

'The doll,' Carella whispered. 'Get the doll.'

Chapter Fourteen

The doll measured thirty inches from the top of her blonde head to the bottoms of her black patent-leather shoes. She wore white bobby socks, a ruffled white voile dress with a white underslip, a black velveteen bodice, and a ruffled lace bib and collar. What appeared at first to be a simulated gold brooch was centred just below the collar.

The doll's trade name was Chatterbox.

There were two D-size flashlight batteries and one 9-volt transistor battery in a recess in the doll's plastic belly. The recess was covered with a flesh-coloured plastic top that was kept in place by a simple plastic twist-lock. Immediately above the battery box, there was a flesh-coloured, open plastic grid that concealed the miniature electronic device in the doll's chest. It was this device after which the doll had been named by its creators. The device was a tiny recorder.

The brooch below the doll's collar was a knob that activated the recording mechanism. To record, a child simply turned the decorative knob counter-clockwise, waited for a single beep signal, and began talking until the beep sounded again, at which time the knob had to be turned once more to its centre position. In order to play back what had just been recorded, the child had only to turn the knob clockwise. The recorded message would continue to play back over and over again until the knob was once more returned to the centre position.

When the detectives turned the brooch-knob clockwise, they heard three recorded voices. One of them belonged to Anna Sachs. It was clear and distinct because the doll had been in Anna's lap when she'd recorded her message on the night of her mother's murder. The message was one of reassurance. She kept saying over and over again to the doll lying across her lap, 'Don't be frightened, Chatterbox, please don't be frightened. It's nothing, Chatterbox, don't be frightened,' over and over again.

The second voice was less distinct because it had been recorded through the thin wall separating the child's bedroom from her mother's. Subsequent tests by the police laboratory showed the recording mechanism to be extremely sensitive for a device of its size, capable of picking up shouted words at a distance of twenty-five feet. Even so, the second voice would not have been picked up at all had Anna not been sitting very close to the thin dividing wall. And, of course, especially towards the end, the words next door had been screamed.

From beep to beep, the recording lasted only a minute and a half. Throughout the length of the recording, Anna talked reassuringly to her doll. 'Don't be frightened, Chatterbox, please don't be frightened. It's nothing, Chatterbox, don't be frightened.' Behind the child's voice, a running counterpoint of horror, was the voice of Tinka Sachs, her mother. Her words were almost inaudible at first. The presented only a vague murmur of faraway terror, the sound of someone repeatedly moaning, the pitiable rise and fall of a voice imploring – but all without words because the sound had been muffled by the wall between the rooms. And then, as Tinka became more and more desperate, as her killer followed her unmercifully around the room with a knife blade, her voice became louder, the words became more distinct. 'Don't! Please don't!' always behind the child's soothing voice in the foreground, 'Don't be frightened, Chatterbox, please don't be frightened,' and her mother shrieking, 'Don't! Please don't! Please,' the voices intermingling, 'I'm bleeding, please, it's nothing, Chatterbox, don't be frightened, Fritz, stop, please, Fritz, stop, stop, oh please, it's nothing, Chatterbox, don't be frightened.'

The third voice sounded like a man's. It was nothing more than a rumble on the recording. Only once did a word come through clearly, and that was the word 'Slut!' interspersed between the child's reassurances to her doll, and Tinka's weakening cries for mercy.

In the end, Tinka shouted the man's name once again, 'Fritz!' and then her voice seemed to fade. The next word she uttered could have been a muted 'please,' but it was indistinct and drowned out by Anna's 'Don't cry, Chatterbox, try not to cry.'

The detectives listened to the doll in silence, and then watched while the ambulance attendants carried Carella out on one stretcher and the still-breathing Schmidt out on another.

'The girl's dead,' the medical examiner said.

'I know,' Meyer answered.

'Who shot her?' one of the Homicide cops asked.

'I did,' Kling answered.

'I'll need the circumstances.'

'Stay with him,' Meyer said to Kling. 'I'll get to the hospital. Maybe that son of a bitch wants to make a statement before he dies.'

```
     I didn't intend to kill her.
     She was happy as hell when I came in,
laughing and joking because she thought she was
off the junk at last.
     I told her she was crazy, she would never
kick it.
     I had not had a shot since three o'clock
that afternoon, I was going out of my head.  I
told her I wanted money for a fix, and she said
```

she couldn't give me money any more, she said she
wanted nothing more to do with me or Pat, that's
the name of the girl I'm living with. She had no
right to hold out on me like that, not when I was
so sick. She could see I was ready to climb the
walls, so she sat there sipping her goddamn iced
tea, and telling me she was not going to keep me
supplied any more, she was not going to spend
half her income keeping me in shit. I told her
she owed it to me. I spent four years in Soledad
because of her, the little bitch, she owed it to
me! She told me to leave her alone. She told
me to get out and leave her alone. She said she
was finished with me and my kind. She said she
had kicked it, did I understand, she had kicked
it!

Am I going to die?

I

I picked

I picked the knife up from the tray.

I didn't intend to kill her, it was just I
needed a fix, couldn't she see that? For
Christ's sake, the times we used to have
together. I stabbed her, I don't know how many
times.

Am I going to die?

The painting fell off the wall, I remember
that.

I took all the bills out of her pocketbook
on the dresser, there was forty dollars in tens.
I ran out of the bedroom and dropped the knife
someplace in the hall, I guess, I don't even
remember. I realized I couldn't take the
elevator down, that much I knew, so I went up to
the roof and crossed over to the next building
and got down to the street that way. I bought
twenty caps with the forty dollars. Pat and me
got very high afterwards, very high.

I didn't know Tina's kid was in the
apartment until tonight, when Pat accidentally
tipped to that goddamn talking doll.

If I'd known she was there, I might have
killed her, too. I don't know.

Fritz Schmidt never got to sign his dictated confession because he died seven minutes after the police stenographer began typing it.

The lieutenant stood by while the two Homicide cops questioned Kling. They had advised him not to make a statement before Byrnes arrived, and now that he was here they went about their routine task with despatch. Kling could not seem to stop crying. The two Homicide cops were plainly embarrassed as they questioned him, a grown man, a cop no less, crying that way. Byrnes watched Kling's face, and said nothing.

The two Homicide cops were called Carpenter and Calhoun. They looked very much alike. Byrnes had never met any Homicide cops who did not look exactly alike. He supposed it was a trademark of their unique speciality. Watching them, he found it difficult to remember who was Carpenter and who was Calhoun. Even their voices sounded alike.

'Let's start with your name, rank, and shield number,' Carpenter said.

'Bertram Kling, detective/third, 74-579.'

'Squad?' Calhoun said.

'The Eight-Seven.' He was still sobbing. The tears rolled down his face endlessly.

'Technically, you just committed a homicide, Kling.'

'It's excusable homicide,' Calhoun said.

'Justifiable,' Carpenter corrected.

'Excusable,' Calhoun repeated. 'Penal Law 1054.'

'Wrong,' Carpenter said. 'Justifiable, P.L. 1055. "Homicide is justifiable when committed by a public officer in arresting a person who has committed a felony and is fleeing from justice." *Justi*fiable.'

'Was the broad committing a felony?' Calhoun asked.

'Yes,' Kling said. He nodded. He tried to wipe the tears from his eyes. 'Yes. Yes, she was.' The tears would not stop.

'Explain it.'

'She was ... she was ready to shoot Carella. She was trying to kill him.'

'Did you fire a warning shot?'

'No. Her back was turned to me and she was ... she was levelling the gun at Carella, so I fired the minute I came into the room. I caught her between the shoulders, I think. With my first shot.'

'Then what?'

Kling wiped the back of his hand across his eyes. 'Then she ... she started to fire again, and I kicked out at her hand, and the slug went wild. When she ... when she got ready to fire the third time, I ... I ...'

'You killed her,' Carpenter said flatly.

'Justifiable,' Calhoun said.

'Absolutely,' Carpenter agreed.

'I said so all along,' Calhoun said.

'She'd already committed a felony by abducting a police officer, what the hell. And then she fired two shots at him. If that ain't a felony, I'll eat all the law books in this crumby state.'

'You got nothing to worry about.'

'Except the Grand Jury. This has to go to the Grand Jury, Kling, same as if you were an ordinary citizen.'

'You still got nothing to worry about,' Calhoun said.

'She was going to kill him,' Kling said blankly. His tears suddenly stopped. He stared at the two Homicide cops as though seeing them for the first time. 'Not again,' he said. 'I couldn't let it happen again.'

Neither Carpenter nor Calhoun knew what the hell Kling was talking about. Byrnes knew, but he didn't particularly feel like explaining. He simply went to Kling and said, 'Forget those departmental charges I mentioned. Go home and get some rest.'

The two Homicide cops didn't know what the hell *Byrnes* was talking about, either. They looked at each other, shrugged, and chalked it all up to the eccentricities of the 87th.

'Well,' Carpenter said. 'I guess that's that.'

'I guess that's that,' Calhoun said. Then, because Kling seemed to have finally gotten control of himself, he ventured a small joke. 'Stay out of jail, huh?' he said.

Neither Byrnes nor Kling even smiled.

Calhoun and Carpenter cleared their throats and walked out without saying good-night.

She sat in the darkness of the hospital room and watched her sedated husband, waiting for him to open his eyes, barely able to believe that he was alive, praying now that he would be well again soon.

The doctors had promised to begin treatment at once. They had explained to her that it was difficult to fix the length of time necessary for anyone to become an addict, primarily because heroin procured illegally varied in its degree of adulteration. But Carella had told them he'd received his first injection sometime late Friday night, which meant he had been on the drug for slightly more than three days. In their opinion, a person psychologically prepared for addiction could undoubtedly become a habitual user in that short a time, if he was using pure heroin of normal strength. But they were working on the assumption that Carella had never used drugs before and had been injected only with narcotics acquired illegally and therefore greatly adulterated. If this was the case, anywhere between two and three weeks would have been necessary to transform him into a confirmed addict. At any rate, they would begin withdrawal (if so strong a word was applicable at all) immediately, and they had no doubt that the cure (and again they apologized for using so strong a word) would be permanent. They had explained that there was none of the addict's usual psychological dependence evident in Carella's case, and then had gone on at great length about personality disturbances, and tolerance levels, and physical dependence – and then one of the doctors suddenly and quietly asked whether or not Carella had ever expressed a prior interest in experimenting with drugs.

Teddy had emphatically shaken her head.

Well, fine then, they said. We're sure everything will work out fine. We're confident of that, Mrs Carella, as for his nose, we'll have to make a more thorough examination in the morning. We don't know when he sustained the injury, you see, or whether or not the broken bones have already knitted. In any case, we should be able to reset it, though it may involve an operation. Please be assured we'll do everything in our power. Would you like to see him now?

She sat in the darkness.

When at last he opened his eyes, he seemed surprised to see her. He smiled and then said, 'Teddy.'

She returned the smile. She touched his face tentatively.

'Teddy,' he said again, and then – because the room was dark and because she could not see his mouth too clearly – he said something which she was sure she misunderstood.

'That's your name,' he said. 'I didn't forget.'

EIGHTY MILLION EYES

"The man was sitting on a bench in the reception room when Miles Vollner came back from lunch that Wednesday afternoon...."

This is for Judy and Fred Underhill

Chapter One

The man was sitting on a bench in the reception room when Miles Vollner came back from lunch that Wednesday afternoon. Vollner glanced at him, and then looked quizzically at his receptionist. The girl shrugged slightly and went back to her typing. The moment Vollner was inside his private office, he buzzed her.

'Who's that waiting outside?' he asked.

'I don't know, sir,' the receptionist said.

'What do you mean, you don't know?'

'He wouldn't give me his name, sir.'

'Did you ask him?'

'Yes, I did.'

'What did he say?'

'Sir, he's sitting right here,' the receptionist said, her voice lowering to a whisper. 'I'd rather not –'

'What's the matter with you?' Vollner said. 'This is *my* office, not *his*. What did he say when you asked him his name?'

'He – he told me to go to hell, sir.'

'What?'

'Yes, sir.'

'I'll be right out,' Vollner said.

He did not go right out because his attention was caught by a letter on his desk, the afternoon mail having been placed there some five minutes ago by his secretary. He opened the letter, read it quickly, and then smiled because it was a large order from a retailer in the Midwest, a firm Vollner had been trying to get as a customer for the past six months. The company Vollner headed was small but growing. It specialized in audio-visual components, with its factory across the River Harb in the next state, and its business and administrative office here on Shepherd Street in the city. Fourteen people worked in the business office – ten men and four women. Two hundred and six people worked in the plant. It was Vollner's hope and expectation that both office and factory staffs would have to be doubled within the next year, and perhaps trebled the year after that. The large order from the Midwest retailer confirmed his beliefs, and pleased him enormously. But then he remembered the man sitting outside, and the smile dropped from his face. Sighing, he went to the door, opened it, and walked down the corridor to the reception room.

The man was still sitting there.

He could not have been older than twenty-three or twenty-four, a sinewy man with a pale narrow face and hooded brown eyes. He was clean-shaven and well dressed, wearing a grey topcoat open over a darker grey suit. A pearl-grey fedora was on top of his head. He sat on the bench with his arms folded across his chest, his legs outstretched, seemingly quite at ease. Vollner went to the bench and stood in front of him.

'Can I help you?' he said.

'Nope.'

'What do you want here?'

'That's none of your business,' the man said.

'I'm sorry,' Vollner answered, 'but it is my business. I happen to own this company.'

'Yeah?' He looked around the reception room, and smiled. 'Nice place you've got.'

The receptionist, behind her desk, had stopped typing and was watching the byplay. Vollner could feel her presence behind him.

'Unless you can tell me what you want here,' he said, 'I'm afraid I'll have to ask you to leave.'

The man was still smiling. 'Well,' he said, 'I'm not about to tell you what I want here, and I'm not about to leave, either.'

For a moment, Vollner was speechless. He glance at the receptionist, and then turned back to the man. 'In that case,' he said, 'I'll have to call the police.'

'You call the police, and you'll be very sorry.'

'We'll see about that,' Vollner said. He walked to the receptionist's desk and said, 'Miss Di Santo, will you get me the police, please?'

The man rose from the bench. He was taller than he had seemed while sitting, perhaps six feet two or three inches, with wide shoulders and enormous hands. He moved towards the desk and, still smiling, said, 'Miss Di Santo, I wouldn't pick up that phone if I was you.'

Miss Di Santo wet her lips and looked at Vollner.

'Call the police,' Vollner said.

'Miss Di Santo, if you so much as put your hand on that telephone, I'll break your arm. I promise that.'

Miss Di Santo hesitated. She looked again to Vollner, who frowned and then said, 'Never mind, Miss Di Santo,' and without saying another word, walked to the entrance door and out into the corridor and towards the elevator. His anger kept building inside him all the way down to the lobby floor. He debated calling the police from a pay phone, and then decided he would do better to find a patrolman on the beat and bring him back upstairs personally. It was two o'clock, and the city streets were thronged with afternoon shoppers. He found a patrolman on the corner of Shepherd and Seventh, directing traffic. Vollner stepped out into the middle of the intersection and said, 'Officer, I'd –'

'Hold it a minute, mister,' the patrolman said. He blew his whistle and waved at the oncoming automobiles. Then he turned back to Vollner and said, 'Now, what is it?'

'There's a man up in my office, won't tell us what his business is.'

'Yeah?' the patrolman said.

'Yes. He threatened me and my receptionist, and he won't leave.'

'Yeah?' The patrolman kept looking at Vollner curiously, as though only half-believing him.

'Yes. I'd like you to come up and help me get him out of there.'
'You would, huh?'
'Yes.'
'And who's gonna handle the traffic on this corner?' the patrolman said.
'This man is threatening us,' Vollner said. 'Surely that's more important than –'
'This is one of the biggest intersections in the city right here, and you want me to leave it.'
'Aren't you supposed to –'
'Mister, don't bug me, huh?' the patrolman said, and blew his whistle, and raised his hand, and then turned and signalled to the cars on his right.
'What's your shield number?' Vollner said.
'Don't bother reporting me,' the patrolman answered. 'This is my post, and I'm not supposed to leave it. You want a cop, go use the telephone.'
'Thanks,' Vollner said tightly. 'Thanks a lot.'
'Don't mention it,' the patrolman said breezily, and looked up at the traffic light, and then blew his whistle again. Vollner walked back to the kerb and was about to enter the cigar store on the corner, when he spotted a second policeman. Still fuming, he walked to him rapidly and said, 'There's a man up in my office who refuses to leave and who is threatening my staff. Now just what the hell do you propose to do about it?'
The patrolman was startled by Vollner's outburst. He was a new cop and a young cop, and he blinked his eyes and then immediately said, 'Where's your office, sir? I'll go back there with you.'
'This way,' Vollner said, and they began walking towards the building. The patrolman introduced himself as Ronnie Fairchild. He seemed brisk and efficient until they entered the lobby, where he began to have his first qualms.
'Is the man armed?' he asked.
'I don't think so,' Vollner said.
'Because if he is, maybe I ought to get some help.'
'I think you can handle it,' Vollner said
'You think so?' Fairchild said dubiously, but Vollner had already led him into the elevator. They got out of the car on the tenth floor, and again Fairchild hesitated. 'Maybe I ought to call this in,' he said. 'After all ...'
'By the time you call it in, the man may *kill* someone,' Vollner suggested.
'Yeah, I suppose so,' Fairchild said hesitantly, thinking that if he *didn't* call this in and ask for help, the person who got killed might very well be himself. He paused outside the door to Vollner's office. 'In there, huh?' he said.
'That's right.'
'Well, okay, let's go.'
They entered the office. Vollner walked directly to the man, who had taken his seat on the bench again, and said, 'Here he is, officer.'
Fairchild pulled back his shoulders. He walked to the bench. 'All right, what's the trouble here?' he asked.
'No trouble, officer.'
'This man tells me you won't leave his office.'
'That's right. I came here to see a girl.'

'Oh,' Fairchild said, ready to leave at once now that he knew this was only a case of romance. 'If that's all . . .'

'What girl?' Vollner said.

'Cindy.'

'Get Cindy out here,' Vollner said to his receptionist, and she rose immediately and hurried down the corridor. 'Why didn't you tell me you were a friend of Cindy's?'

'You didn't ask me,' the man said.

'Listen, if this is just a private matter –'

'No, wait a minute,' Vollner said, putting his hand on Fairchild's arm. 'Cindy'll be out here in a minute.'

'That's good,' the man said. 'Cindy's the one I want to see.'

'Who are you?' Vollner asked.

'Well, who are *you*?'

'I'm Miles Vollner. Look, young man –'

'Nice meeting you, Mr Vollner,' the man said, and smiled again.

'What's your name?'

'I don't think I'd like to tell you that.'

'Officer, ask him what his name is.'

'What's your name, mister?' Fairchild said, and at that moment the receptionist came back, followed by a tall blonde girl wearing a blue dress and high-heeled pumps. She stopped just alongside the receptionist's desk and said, 'Did you want me, Mr Vollner?'

'Yes, Cindy. There's a friend of yours here to see you.'

Cindy looked around the reception room. She was a strikingly pretty girl of twenty-two, full-breasted and wide-hipped, her blonde hair cut casually close to her head, her eyes a cornflower blue that echoed the colour of her dress. She studied Fairchild and then the man in grey. Puzzled, she turned again to Vollner.

'A friend of *mine*?' she asked.

'This man says he came here to see you.'

'Me?'

'He says he's a friend of yours.'

Cindy looked at the man once more, and then shrugged. 'I don't know you,' she said.

'No, huh?'

'No.'

'That's too bad.'

'Listen, what is this?' Fairchild said.

'You're *going* to know me, baby,' the man said.

Cindy looked at him coldly, and said, 'I doubt that very much,' and turned and started to walk away. The man came off the bench immediately, catching her by the arm.

'Just a second,' he said.

'Let go of me.'

'Honey, I'm *never* gonna let go of you.'

'Leave that girl alone,' Fairchild said.

'We don't need fuzz around here,' the man answered. 'Get lost.'

Fairchild took a step towards him, raising his club. The man whirled suddenly, planting his left fist in Fairchild's stomach. As Fairchild doubled over, the man unleashed a vicious uppercut that caught him on the point of his jaw and sent him staggering back towards the wall. Groggily, Fairchild reached for his gun. The man kicked him in the groin, and he fell to the floor groaning. The man kicked him again, twice in the head, and then repeatedly in the chest. The receptionist was screaming now. Cindy was running down the corridor, shouting for help. Vollner stood with his fists clenched, waiting for the man to turn and attack him next.

Instead, the man only smiled and said, 'Tell Cindy I'll be seeing her,' and walked out of the office.

Vollner immediately went to the phone. Men and women were coming out of their private offices all up and down the corridor now. The receptionist was still screaming. Quickly, Vollner dialled the police and was connected with the 87th Precinct.

Sergeant Murchison took the call and advised Vollner that he'd send a patrolman there immediately and that a detective would stop by either later that day or early tomorrow morning.

Vollner thanked him and hung up. His hand was trembling, and his receptionist was still screaming.

In another part of the 87th Precinct, on a side street off Culver Avenue, in the midst of a slum as rank as a cesspool, there stood an innocuous-looking brick building that had once served as a furniture loft. It was now magnanimously called a television studio. The Stan Gifford Show originated from this building each and every Wednesday night of the year, except during the summer hiatus.

It was a little incongruous to see dozens of ivy-league, narrow-tied advertising and television men trotting through a slum almost every day of the week in an attempt to put together Gifford's weekly comedy hour. The neighbourhood citizens watched the procession of creators with a jaundiced eye; the show had been on the air for three solid years, and they had grown used to seeing these aliens in their midst. There had never been any trouble between the midtown masterminds and the uptown residents, and there probably never would be – a slum has enough troubles without picking on a network. Besides, most of the people in the neighbourhood liked the Stan Gifford Show, and would rush indoors the moment it took to the air. If all these nuts were required to put together the show every week, who were they to complain? It was a good show, and it was free.

The good show, and the free one, had been rehearsing since the previous Friday in the loft of North Eleventh, and it was now 3:45 p.m. on Wednesday afternoon, which meant that in exactly four hours and fifteen minutes, a telop would flash in homes across the continent announcing the Stan Gifford Show to follow, and then there would be a station break with commercial, and then the introductory theme music, and then organized bedlam would once again burst forth from approximately twenty million television sets. The network, gratuitously giving itself the edge in selling prime time to potential sponsors, estimated that in each viewing home there were at least two people, which meant that every Wednesday night at 8:00 p.m., eighty million eyes would draw a bead on the smiling coutenance of Stan Gifford as he waved from the screen and said, 'Back for more, huh?' In the hands of a lesser personality, this opening remark – even when delivered with a smile – might have caused many viewers to switch to another channel or even turn off the set completely. But Stan Gifford was charming, intelligent, and born with an intuitive sense of comedy. He knew what was funny and what was not, and he could even turn a bad joke into a good one simply by acknowledging its failure with a deadpan nod and slightly contrite look at his adoring fans. He exuded an ease that seemed totally unrehearsed, a calm that could only be natural.

'Where the hell is Art Wetherley?' he shouted frantically at his assistant director.

'Here just a minute ago, Mr Gifford,' the A.D. shouted back, and then instantly yelled for quiet on the set. The moment quiet was achieved, he broke the silence by shouting, 'Art Wetherley! Front and centre, on the double!'

Wetherley, a diminutive gag writer who had been taking a smoke on one of the fire escapes, came into the studio, walked over to Gifford and said, 'What's up, Stan?'

Gifford was a tall man, with a pronounced widow's peak – he was actually beginning to bald, but he preferred to think of his receding hairline as a pronounced widow's peak – penetrating brown eyes, and a generous mouth. When he smiled, his eyes crinkled up from coast to coast, and he looked like a youthful, beardless Santa Claus about to deliver a bundle of goodies to needy waifs. He was not smiling now, and Wetherley had seen the unsmiling Gifford often enough to know that his solemn countenance meant trouble.

'Is this supposed to be a joke?' Gifford asked. He asked the question politely and quietly, but there was enough menace in his voice to blow up the entire city.

Wetherley, who could be as polite as anyone in television when he wanted to, quietly said, 'Which one is that, Stan?'

'This mother-in-law line,' Gifford said. 'I thought mother-in-law jokes went out with nuclear fission.'

'I wish *my* mother-in-law had gone out with nuclear fission,' Wetherley said, and then instantly realized this was not a time for adding one bad joke to another. 'We can cut the line,' he said quickly.

'I don't want it cut. I want a substitute for it.'

'That's what I meant.'

'Then why didn't you say what you meant?' Gifford looked across the studio at the wall clock, which was busily ticking off minutes to air time. 'You'd better hurry,' he said. 'Stay away from mother-in-law, and stay away from Liz Taylor, and stay away from the astronauts.'

'Gee,' Wetherley said, deadpan, 'what does that leave?'

'Some people actually think you're funny, you know that?' Gifford said, and he turned his broad back on Wetherley and walked away.

The assistant director, who had been standing near one of the booms throughout the entire conversation, sighed heavily and said, 'Boy, I hope he calms down.'

'*I* hope he drops dead,' Wetherley answered.

Steve Carella watched as his wife poured coffee into his cup. 'You're beautiful,' he said, but her head was bent over the coffeepot, and she could not see his lips. He reached out suddenly and cupped her chin with his hand,

and she lifted her head curiously, a faint half smile on her mouth. He said again, 'Teddy, you're beautiful,' and this time she watched his lips, and this time she saw the words on his mouth, and understood them and nodded in acknowledgment. And then, as if his voice had thundered into her silent world, as if she had been waiting patiently all day long to unleash a torrent of words, she began moving her fingers rapidly in the deaf-mute alphabet.

He watched her hands as they told him of the day's events. Behind the hands, her face formed a backdrop, the intense brown eyes adding meaning to each silent word she delivered, the head of black hair cocking suddenly to one side to emphasize a point, the mouth sometimes moving into a pout, or a grimace, or a sudden radiant smile. He watched her hands and her face, interpolating a word or a grunt every now and then, sometimes stopping her when she formed a sentence too quickly, and marvelling all the while at the intense concentration in her eyes, the wonderful animation she brought to the telling of the simplest story. When in turn she listened, her eyes watched intently, as if afraid of missing a syllable, her face mirroring whatever was being said. Because she never heard the intonations or subtleties of any voice, her imagination supplied emotional content that sometimes was not there at all. She could be moved to tears or laughter by a single innocuous sentence; she was like a child listening to a fairy tale, her mind supplying every fantastic unspoken detail. As they did the dishes together, their conversation was a curious blend of household plans and petty larceny, problems with the butcher and the lineup, a dress marked down to twelve ninety-five and a suspect's .38-calibre pistol. Carella kept his voice very low. Volume meant nothing to Teddy, and he knew the twins were asleep in the other room. There was a hushed warmth to that kitchen, as if it gently echoed a city that was curling up for the night.

In ten minutes' time, in twenty million homes, forty million people would turn eighty million eyes on a smiling Stan Gifford who would look out at the world and say, 'Back for more, huh?'

Carella, who did not ordinarily enjoy watching television, had to admit that he was one of those forty million hopeless unwashed addicts who turned to Gifford's channel every Wednesday night. Unconsciously, he kept one eye on the clock as he dried the dishes. For whatever perverse reasons, he derived great pleasure from Gifford's taunting opening statement, and he would have felt cheated if he had tuned in too late to hear it. His reaction to Gifford surprised even himself. He found most television a bore, an attitude undoubtedly contracted from Teddy, who derived little if any pleasure from watching the home screen. She was perfectly capable of reading the lips of a performer when the director chose to show him in a close shot. But whenever an actor turned his back or moved into a long shot, she lost the thread of the story and began asking Carella questions. Trying to watch her moving hands and the screen at the same time was an impossible task. Her frustration led to his entanglement which in turn led to further frustration, so he decided the hell with it.

Except for Stan Gifford.

At three minutes to eight that Wednesday night, Carella turned on the television set, and then made himself comfortable in an easy chair. Teddy opened a book and began reading. He watched the final moments of the show immediately preceding Gifford's (a fat lady won a refrigerator) and then read the telop stating STAN GIFFORD IS NEXT, and then watched the station break and commercial (a very handsome, dark-haired man was making love to a cigarette with each ecstatic puff he took), and then there was a slight electronic pause, and Gifford's theme music started.

'Okay if I turn this light a little lower?' Carella asked. Teddy, her nose buried in her book, did not see him speak. He touched her hand gently, and she looked up. 'Okay to dim this light?' he asked again, and she nodded just as Gifford's face filled the screen.

The smile broke like thunder over Mandalay.

'Back for more, huh?' Gifford said, and Carella burst out laughing and then turned down the lights. The single lamp behind Teddy's chair cast a warm glow over the room. Directly opposite it the colder light of the electronic tube threw a bluish rectangle on the floor directly beneath it. Gifford walked to a table, sat, and immediately went into a monologue, his customary manner of opening the show.

'I was talking to Julius the other day,' he said immediately, and the line, for some curious reason, brought a laugh from the studio audience as well as from Carella. 'He's got a persecution complex, I'll swear to it. An absolute paranoiac.' Another laugh. 'I said to him, "Look, Julie –" I call him Julie because, after all, we've known each other for a long time, some people say I'm almost like a son to him. "Look, Julie," I said to him, "what are you getting all upset about? So a lousy soothsayer stops you on the way to the forum and gives you a lot of baloney about the ides of March, why do you let this upset you, huh? Julie baby, the people *love* you." Well, he turned to me and said, "Brutus, I know you think I'm being foolish, but ...'

And that's the way it went. For ten solid minutes, Gifford held the stage alone, pausing only to garner his laughs, or to deliver his contrite look when a joke fell flat. At the end of the ten minutes he introduced his dance ensemble, who held the stage for another five minutes. He then paraded his first guest, a buxom Hollywood blonde who sang a torch song and did a skit with him, and before anyone at home realized it, the first half of the show was over. Station break, commercial. Carella got a bottle of beer from the refrigerator, and settled down to enjoy the remaining half hour.

Gifford came on to introduce a group of folk singers who sang *Greensleeves* and *Scarlet Ribbons,* a most colourful combination. He walked onto the stage again as soon as they were finished, and then went to work in earnest. His next guest was a male Hollywood personality. The male Hollywood personality seemed to be somewhat at a loss because he could neither sing nor dance nor, according to some critics, even act. But Gifford engaged him in some very high-priced banter for a few minutes, and then personally began a commercial about triple-roasted coffee while the Hollywood visitor went off to change his costume for a promised skit. Gifford finished the commercial and then motioned to someone standing just off camera. A stagehand carried a chair into viewing range. Gifford thanked him with a small bow, and then placed the chair in the centre of the enormous, empty stage.

He had been on camera for perhaps five minutes now, a relatively short time, and when he sat in the chair and heaved a weary sigh, everyone was a little surprised. He kept sitting in the chair, saying nothing, doing nothing.

There was no music behind him. He was simply a man sitting in a chair in the middle of an empty stage, but Carella felt himself beginning to smile because he knew Gifford was about to do one of his pantomimes. He touched Teddy's arm, and she looked up from her book. 'The pantomime,' he said, and she nodded, put down her book, and turned her eyes towards the screen.

Gifford continued doing nothing. He simply sat there and looked out at the audience. But he seemed to be watching something in the very far distance. The stage was silent as Gifford kept watching this something in the distance, a something that seemed to be getting closer and closer. Then, suddenly, Gifford got out of the chair, pulled it aside, and watched the something as it roared past him. He wiped his brow, faced his chair in another direction, and sat again. Now he leaned forward. It was coming from the other direction. Closer it came, closer, and again Gifford got up, pulled his chair aside at the last possible moment, and watched the imaginary thing speed past him. He sat again, facing another direction.

Carella burst into laughter as Gifford spotted it coming at him once more. This time, he got out of the chair with a determined and fierce look on his face. He held the chair in front of him like a lion tamer, defying the something to attack. But again at the last moment he pulled out of the way to let the something roar past. It was now on his left. He turned, whipping the chair around. The camera came in for a tight shot of his perplexed and completely helpless face.

Another look crossed that face.

The camera eye was in tight for the closeup, and it caught the sudden faintness that flashed across the puzzled features. Gifford seemed to sway for an instant, and then he put one hand to his eyes, as if he weren't seeing too clearly, as if the something rushing from the left had taken on real dimensions all at once. He squeezed his eyes shut tightly, and then shook his head, and then staggered back several paces and dropped the chair, just as the something streaked by him.

It was all part of the act, of course. Everyone knew that. But somehow, Gifford's pantomime had taken on a reality that transcended humour. Somehow, there was real confusion in his eyes as he watched the nameless something begin another charge. The camera stayed on him in a tight closeup. Gifford looked directly into the camera, and there was a pathetically pleading look on his face, and suddenly contact was made again, suddenly the audience began laughing. This was the same sweet and gentle man being pursued by a persistent nemesis. This was comedy again.

Carella did not laugh.

Gifford reached down for the chair. The close shot on one camera yielded to a long shot on another camera. His fingers closed around the chair. He righted it, and then sat in it weakly, his head drooping, and again the audience howled, but Carella was leaning forward now, watching Gifford with a deadly cold impersonal fixed stare.

Gifford clutched his abdomen, as if struck there by the invisible juggernaut. He seemed suddenly dizzy, and his face went pale, and he seemed in danger of falling out of the chair. And then, all at once, for eighty million eyes to see, he became violently ill. The camera was caught unaware for a moment. It lingered on his helpless sickness an instant longer, and then suddenly cut away.

Carella stared at the screen numbly as the orchestra struck up a sprightly tune.

Chapter Two

There were two squad cars and an ambulance parked in the middle of the street when Detective Meyer pulled up in front of the loft. Five patrolmen were standing before the single entrance to the building, trying valiantly to keep back the crowd of reporters, photographers, and just plain sightseers who thronged the sidewalk. The newspapermen were making most of the noise, shouting some choice Anglo-Saxon phrases at the policemen who had heard it all already and who refused to budge an inch. Meyer got out of the car and looked for Patrolman Genero, who had called the squadroom not five minutes before. He spotted him almost at once, and then elbowed his way through the crowd, squeezing past an old lady who had thrown a bathrobe over her nightgown, 'I beg your pardon, ma'am,' and then shoving aside a fat man smoking a cigar, 'Would you mind getting the hell out of my way?' and finally reaching Genero, who looked pale and tired as he stood guarding the entrance doorway.

'Boy, am I glad to see you!' Genero said.

'I'm glad to see you, too,' Meyer answered. 'Did you let anyone get by?'

'Only Gifford's doctor and the people from the hospital.'

'Who do I talk to in there?'

'The producer of the show. His name's David Krantz. Meyer, it's bedlam in there. You'd think God dropped dead.'

'Maybe he did,' Meyer said patiently, and he entered the building.

The promised bedlam started almost at once. There were people on the iron-runged stairways, and people in the corridor, and they all seemed to be talking at once, and they all seemed to be saying exactly the same thing. Meyer cornered a bright-eyed young man wearing thick-lensed spectacles and said, 'Where do I find David Krantz?'

'Who wants to know?' the young man answered.

'Police,' Meyer said wearily.

'Oh. Oh! He's upstairs. Third floor.'

'Thanks,' Meyer said. He began climbing the steps. On the third floor, he stopped a girl in a black leotard and said, 'I'm looking for David Krantz.'

'Straight ahead,' the girl answered. 'The man with the moustache.'

The man with the moustache was in the centre of a circle of people standing under a bank of hanging lights. At least five other girls in black leotards, a dozen or so more in red spangled dresses, and a variety of men in suits, sweaters, and work clothes were standing in small clusters around the wide expanse of the studio floor. The floor itself was covered with the debris of television production: cables, cameras, hanging mikes, booms, dollies, cue cards, crawls, props and painted scenery. Beyond the girls, and beyond the knot of men surrounding the man with the moustache, Meyer could see a hospital intern in white talking to a tall man in a business suit. He debated looking at the body first, decided it would be best to talk to the head man, and broke into the circle.

'Mr Krantz?'

Krantz turned with an economy and swiftness of movement that was a little startling. 'Yes, what is it?' he said, snapping the words like a whip. He was dressed smartly, quietly, neatly. His moustache was narrow and thin. He gave an immediate impression of wastelessness in a vast wasteland.

Meyer, who was pretty quick on the draw himself, immediately flipped open his wallet to his shield. 'Detective Meyer, 87th Squad,' he said. 'I understand you're the producer.'

'That's right,' Krantz answered. 'What now?'

'What do you mean what now, Mr Krantz?'

'I mean what are the police doing here?'

'Just a routine check,' Meyer said.

'For a man who died of an obvious heart attack?'

'Well, I didn't know you were a doctor, Mr Krantz.'

'I'm not. But any fool –'

'Mr Krantz, it's very hot in here, and I've been working all day, and I'm tired, you know? Don't start bugging me right off the bat. From what I understand –'

'Here we go,' Krantz said to the circle of people around him.

'Here we go *where*?' Meyer said.

'If a maiden lady dies of old age in her own bed, every cop in the city is convinced it's homicide.'

'Oh? Who told you that, Mr Krantz?'

'I used to produce a half-hour mystery show. I'm familiar with the routine.'

'And what's the routine?'

'Look, Detective Meyer, what do you want from me?'

'I want you to cut it out, first of all. I'm trying to ask some pretty simple questions about what seems to be an accidental –'

'*Seems*? See what I mean?' he said to the crowd.

'Yeah, *seems*, Mr Krantz. And you're making it pretty difficult. Now if you'd like me to get a subpoena for your arrest, we can talk it over at the station house. It's up to you.'

'Now you're kidding, Detective Meyer. You've got no grounds for arresting me.'

'Try Section 1851 of the Penal Law,' Meyer said flatly. '"*Resisting public officer in the discharge of his duty*: A person who, in any case or under any circumstances not otherwise specially provided for, wilfully resists, delays, or obstructs a public officer in dis –"'

'All right, all right,' Krantz said. 'You've made your point.'

'Then get rid of your yes-men, and let's talk.'

The crowd disappeared without a word. In the distance, Meyer could see the tall man arguing violently with the intern in white. He turned his full attention to Krantz and said, 'I thought the show had a studio audience.'

'It does.'

'Well, where are they?'

'We put them all upstairs. Your patrolman said to hold them.'

'I want one of your people to take all their names and tell them to go home.'

'Can't the police take –'

'I've got a mad house in the street outside, and only five men to take care of it. Would you mind helping me, Mr Krantz? I didn't want him dead any more than you did.'

'All right, I'll take care of it.'

'Thanks. Now, what happened?'

'He died of a heart attack.'

'How do you know? Had he ever had one before this?'

'Not that I know of, but –'

'Then let's leave that open for the time being, okay? What time was it when he collapsed?'

'I can get that for you. Somebody was probably keeping a timetable. Hold it a second. George! Hey, George!'

A man wearing a cardigan sweater and talking to one of the dancers turned abruptly at the sound of his name. He peered around owlishly for a moment, obviously annoyed, trying to locate the person who'd called him. Krantz raised his hand in signal, and the man picked up a battery-powered megaphone from the seat of the chair beside him and, still annoyed, walked towards the two men.

'This is George Cooper, our assistant director,' Krantz said. 'Detective Meyer.'

Cooper extended his hand cautiously. Meyer realized at once that the scowl on Cooper's face was a perpetual one, a mixed look of terrible inconvenience and unspeakable injury, as if he were a man trying to think in the midst of a revolution.

'How do you do?' he said.

'Mr Meyer wants to know what time Stan collapsed.'

'What do you mean?' Cooper said, making the sentence sound like a challenge to a duel. 'It was after the folk singers went off.'

'Yes, but what time? Did anybody keep a record?'

'I can run the tape,' Cooper said grudgingly. 'Do you want me to do that?'

'Please,' Meyer said.

'What happened?' Cooper asked. 'Is it a heart attack?'

'We don't –'

'What else could it be?' Krantz interrupted.

'Well, I'll run the tape,' Cooper said. 'You going to be around?'

'I'll be here,' Meyer assured him.

Cooper nodded once, briefly, and walked away scowling.

'Who's that arguing with the intern over there?' Meyer asked.

'Carl Nelson,' Krantz replied. 'Stan's doctor.'

'Was he here all night?'

'No. I reached him at home and told him to come over here in a hurry. That was after I'd called the ambulance.'

'Get him over here, will you?'

'Sure,' Krantz said. He raised his arm and shouted, 'Carl? Have you got a minute?'

Nelson broke away from the intern, turned back to hurl a last word at him, and then walked briskly to where Meyer and Krantz were waiting. He was broad as well as tall, with thick black hair greying at the temples. There was a serious expression on his face as he approached, and a high colour in his cheeks. His lips were pressed firmly together, as if he had made a secret decision and was now ready to defend it against all comers.

'That idiot wants to move the body,' he said immediately. 'I told him I'd report him to the AMA if he did. What do you want, Dave?'

'This is Detective Meyer. Dr Nelson.'

Nelson shook hands briefly and firmly. 'Are you getting the medical examiner to perform an autopsy?' he asked.

'Do you think I should, Dr Nelson?'

'Didn't you see the way Stan died?'

'No. How did he die?'

'It was a heart attack, wasn't it?' Krantz said.

'Don't be ridiculous. Stan's heart was in excellent condition. When I arrived here at about nine o'clock, he was experiencing a wide range of symptoms. Laboured respiration, rapid pulse, nausea, vomiting. We tried a stomach pump, but that didn't help at all. He went into convulsion at about nine-fifteen. The third convulsion killed him at nine-thirty.'

'What are you suggesting, Dr Nelson?'

'I'm suggesting he was poisoned,' Nelson said flatly.

In the phone booth on the third-floor landing, Meyer deposited his dime and then dialled the home number of Lieutenant Peter Byrnes. The booth was hot and smelly. He waited while the phone rang on the other end. Byrnes himself answered, his voice sounding fuzzy with sleep.

'Pete, this is Meyer.'

'What time is it?' Byrnes asked.

'I don't know. Ten-thirty, eleven o'clock.'

'I must have dozed off. Harriet went to a movie. What's the matter?'

'Pete, I'm investigating this Stan Gifford thing, and I thought I ought to –'

'What Stan Gifford thing?'

'The television guy. He dropped dead tonight, and –'

'What television guy?'

'He's a big comic.'

'Yeah?'

'Yeah. Anyway, his doctor thinks we ought to have an autopsy done right away. Because he had a convulsion, and –'

'Strychnine?' Byrnes asked immediately.

'I doubt it. He was vomiting before he went into convulsion.'

'Arsenic?'

'Could be. Anyway, I think the autopsy's a good idea.'

'Go ahead, ask the M.E. to do it.'

'Also, I'm going to need some help on this. I've got some more questions to ask here, and I thought we might get somebody over to the hospital right away. To be there when the body arrives, you see? Get a little action from them.'

'That's a good idea.'

'Yeah, well, Cotton's out on a plant, and Bert was just answering a squeal when I left the office. Could you call Steve for me?'

'Sure.'

'Okay, that's all. I'll ring you later if it's not too late.'

'What time did you say it was?'

Meyer looked at his watch. 'Ten-forty-five.'

'I must have dozed off,' Byrnes said wonderingly, and then hung up.

George Cooper was waiting for Meyer when he came out of the booth. The same look was on his face, as if he had swallowed something thoroughly distasteful and was allowing his anger to feed his nausea.

'I ran that tape,' he said.

'Okay.'

'I timed the second half with a stop watch. What do you want to know?'

'When he collapsed.'

Cooper looked sourly at the pad in his hand and said, 'The folk singers went off at eight-thirty-seven. Stan came on immediately afterwards. He was on camera with that Hollywood ham for two minutes and twelve seconds. When the guest went off to change, Stan did the coffee commercial. He ran a little over the paid-for minute, actually a minute and forty seconds. He started his pantomime at eight-forty-one prime fifty-two. He was two minutes and fifty-five seconds into it when he collapsed. That means he was on camera for a total time of seven minutes and seventeen seconds. He collapsed at eight-forty-four prime seventeen.'

'Thanks,' Meyer said. 'I appreciate your help.' He started walking towards the door leading to the studio floor. Cooper stepped into his path. His eyes met Meyer's, and he stared into them searchingly.

'Somebody poisoned him, huh?' he said.

'What makes you think that, Mr Cooper?'

'They're all talking about it out there.'

'That doesn't necessarily make it true, does it?'

'Dr Nelson says you'll be asking for an autopsy.'

'That's right.'

'Then you *do* think he was poisoned.'

Meyer shrugged. 'I don't think anything yet, Mr Cooper.'

'Listen,' Cooper said, and his voice dropped to a whisper. 'Listen, I . . . I don't want to get anybody in trouble but . . . before the show tonight, when we were rehearsing –' He stopped abruptly. He glanced into the studio. A man in a sports jacket was approaching the hallway, reaching for the package of cigarettes in his pocket.

'Go ahead, Mr Cooper,' Meyer said.

'Skip it,' Cooper answered and walked away quickly. The man in the sports jacket came into the hallway. He nodded briefly to Meyer, put the cigarette into his mouth, leaned against a wall, and struck a match. Meyer took out a cigarette of his own, and then said, 'Excuse me. Do you have a light?'

'Sure,' the man said. He was a small man, with piercing blue eyes and crew-cut hair that gave his face a sharp triangular shape. He struck a match for Meyer, shook it out, and then leaned back against the wall again.

'Thanks,' Meyer said.

'Don't mention it.'

Meyer walked to where Krantz was standing with Nelson and the hospital intern. The intern was plainly confused. He had answered an emergency call, and now no one seemed to know what they wanted him to do with the body. He turned to Meyer pleadingly, hoping for someone who would forcefully take command of the situation.

'You can move the body,' Meyer said. 'Take it to the morgue for autopsy. Tell your man one of our detectives'll be down there soon. Carella's his name.'

The intern left quickly, before anybody could change his mind. Meyer glanced casually towards the corridor, where the man in the sports jacket was still leaning against the wall, smoking.

'Who's that in the hallway?' he asked.

'Art Wetherley,' Krantz answered. 'One of our writers.'

'Was he here tonight?'

'Sure,' Krantz said.

'All right, who else is connected with the show?'

'Where do you want me to start?'

'I want to know who was here tonight, that's all.'

'Why?'

'Oh, Mr Krantz, *please*. Gifford could have died from the noise alone in this place, but there's a possibility he was poisoned. Now who was here tonight?'

'All right, *I* was here. And my secretary. And my associate producer and his secretary. And the unit manager and his secretary. And the –'

'Does everybody have a secretary?'

'Not everybody.'

'Let me hear the rest.'

Krantz folded his arms, and then began reciting by rote. 'The director, and the assistant director. The two Hollywood stars, and the folk singers. Two scenic designers, a costume designer, the booking agent, the choral director, the chorus – seventeen people in it – the orchestra conductor, two arrangers, thirty-three musicians, five writers, four librarians and copyists, the music contractor, the dance accompanist, the choreographer, six dancers, the rehearsal pianist, the lighting director, the audio man, two stage managers, twenty-nine engineers, twenty-seven electricians and stage-hands, three network policemen, thirty-five pages, three makeup men, a hair stylist, nine wardrobe people, four sponsors' men, and six guests.' Krantz nodded in quiet triumph. 'That's who was here tonight.'

'What were you trying to do?' Meyer asked. 'Start World War III?'

Paul Blaney, the assistant medical examiner, had never performed an autopsy on a celebrity before. The tag on the corpse's wrist told him, as if he had not already been told by Carella and Meyer, who were waiting outside in the corridor, that the man lying on the stainless-steel table was Stan Gifford, the television comedian. Blaney shrugged. A corpse was a corpse, and he was only thankful that this one hadn't been mangled in an automobile accident. He never watched television, anyway. Violence upset him.

He picked up his scalpel.

He didn't like the idea of two detectives waiting outside while he worked. The next thing he knew, they'd be coming into the autopsy room with him and giving their opinions on the proper way to hold a forceps. Besides, he rather resented the notion that a corpse, simply because it was a celebrity corpse, was entitled to preferential treatment – like calling a man in the middle of the goddamn night to make an examination. Oh, sure, Meyer had patiently explained that this was an unusual case and likely to attract a great deal of publicity. And yes, the symptoms certainly seemed to indicate poisoning of some sort, but still Blaney didn't like it.

It smacked of pressure. A man should be allowed to remove a liver or a set of kidneys in a calm, unhurried way. Not with anxious policemen breathing down his neck. The usual routine was to perform the autopsy, prepare the report, and then send it on to the investigating team of detectives. If a homicide was indicated, it was sometimes necessary to prepare additional reports, which Blaney did whenever he felt like it, more often not. These were sent to Homicide North or South, the chief of police, the commander of the detective division, the district commander, and the technical police laboratory. Sometimes, and only when Blaney was feeling in a particularly generous mood, he would call the investigating precinct detective and give him a verbal necropsy report over the phone. But he had never had cops waiting in the corridor before. He didn't like the idea. He didn't like it at all.

Viciously, he made his incision.

In the corridor outside, Meyer sat on a bench alongside one green-tinted wall and watched Carella, who paced back and forth before him like an expectant father. Patiently, Meyer turned his head in a slow cycle, following Carella's movement to the end of the short corridor and back again. He was almost as tall as Carella, but more heavily built, so that he seemed squat and burly, especially when he was sitting.

'How'd Mrs Gifford take it?' Carella asked.

'Nobody likes the idea of an autopsy,' Meyer said. 'But I drove out to her house, and told her why we were going ahead, and she agreed it seemed necessary.'

'What kind of a woman?'

'Why?'

'If someone poisoned him ...'

'She's about thirty-eight or thirty-nine, tall, attractive, I guess. It was a little hard to tell. Her mascara was running all over her face.' Meyer paused. 'Besides, she wasn't at the studio, if that means anything.'

'Who *was* at the studio?' Carella asked.

'I had Genero take down all their names before they were released.' Meyer paused. 'I'll tell you the truth, Steve, I hope this autopsy comes up with a natural cause of death.'

'How many people were in the studio?' Carella said.

'Well, I think we can safely discount the studio audience, don't you?'

'I guess so. How many were in the studio audience?'

'Five hundred and sixty.'

'All right, let's safely discount them.'

'So that leaves everyone who was connected with the show, and present tonight.'

'And how many is that?' Carella asked. 'A couple of dozen?'

'Two hundred and twelve people,' Meyer said.

The door to the autopsy room opened, and Paul Blaney stepped into the corridor, pulling off a rubber glove the way he had seen doctors do in the movies. He looked at Meyer and Carella sourly, greatly resenting their presence, and then said, 'Well, what is it you'd like to know?'

'Cause of death,' Meyer said.

'Acute poisoning,' Blaney answered flatly.

'Which poison?'

'Did the man have a history of cardiac ailments?'

'Not according to his doctor.'

'Mmmmm,' Blaney said.

'Well?' Carella said.

'That's very funny because ... well, the poison was strophanthin. I recovered it in the small intestine, and I automatically assumed –'

'What's strophanthin?'

'It's a drug similar to digitalis, but more powerful.'

'Why'd you ask about a possible cardiac ailment?'

'Well, both drugs are used therapeutically in the treatment of cardiac cases. Digitalis by infusion, usually, and strophanthin intravenously or intramuscularly. The normal dose is very small.'

'Of strophanthin, do you mean?'

'Yes.'

'Is it ever given by pill or capsule?'

'I doubt it. It may have been produced as a pill years ago, but it's been replaced by other drugs today. As a matter of fact, I don't know any doctors who'd normally prescribe it.'

'What do you mean?'

'Well, whenever there's a rhythmical disturbance or a structural lesion, digitalis is the more commonly prescribed stimulant. But strophanthin ...' Blaney shook his head.

'Why not strophanthin?'

'I'm not saying it's *never* used, don't misunderstand me. I'm saying it's *rarely* used. A hospital pharmacy may get a call for it once in five years. A doctor would prescribe it only if he wanted immediate results. It acts much faster than digitalis.' Blaney paused. 'Are you sure this man didn't have a cardiac history?'

'Positive.' Carella hesitated a moment and then said, 'Well, what form *does* it come in today?'

'An ampule, usually.'

'Liquid?'

'Yes, ready for injection. You've seen ampules of penicillin, haven't you? Similar to that.'

'Does it come in powder form?'

'It could, yes.'

'What kind of powder?'

'A white crystalline. But I doubt if any pharmacy, even a hospital pharmacy, would stock the powder. Oh, you might find one or two, but it's very rare.'

'What's the lethal dose?' Carella asked.

'Anything over a milligram is considered dangerous. That's one one-thousand of a gram. Compare that to the fatal dose of digitalis, which is about two and a half grams, and you'll understand what I mean about power.'

'How large a dose did Gifford have?'

'I couldn't say exactly. Most of it, of course, had already been absorbed, or he wouldn't have died. It's not easy to recover strophanthin from the organs, you know. It's very rapidly absorbed, and very easily destroyed. Do you want me to guess?'

'Please,' Meyer said.

'Judging from the results of my quantitative analysis, I'd say he ingested at least two full grains.'

'Is that a lot?' Meyer asked.

'It's about a hundred and thirty times the lethal dose.'

'What!'

'Symptoms would have been immediate,' Blaney said. 'Nausea, vomiting, eventual convulsion.'

The corridor was silent for several moments. Then Carella said, 'What do you mean by immediate?'

Blaney looked surprised. 'Immediate,' he answered. 'What else does immediate mean but immediate? Assuming the poison was injected –'

'He was out there for maybe ten minutes,' Carella said, 'with the camera on him every second. He certainly didn't –'

'It was exactly seven minutes and seventeen seconds,' Meyer corrected.

'Whatever it was, he didn't take an injection of strophanthin.'

Blaney shrugged. 'Then maybe the poison was administered orally.'

'How?'

'Well . . .' Blaney hesitated. 'I suppose he could have broken open one of the ampules and swallowed the contents.'

'He didn't. He was on camera. You said the dose was enough to bring on immediate symptoms.'

'Perhaps not so immediate if the drug was taken orally. We really don't know very much about the oral dose. In tests with rabbits, *forty* times the normal intramuscular dose and *eighty* times the normal intravenous dose proved fatal when taken by mouth. Rabbits aren't humans.'

'But you said Gifford probably had *a hundred and thirty* times the normal dose.'

'That's my estimate.'

'How long would that have taken to bring on symptoms?'

'Minutes.'

'How many minutes?'

'Five minutes perhaps, I couldn't say exactly.'

'And he was on camera for more than seven minutes. So the poison must have got into him just before he came on.'

'I would say so, yes.'

'What about this ampule?' Meyer said. 'Could it have been dumped into something he drank?'

'Yes, it could have.'

'Any other way he could have taken the drug?'

'Well,' Blaney said, 'if he'd got hold of the drug in powder form somehow, I suppose two grains could have been placed in a gelatin capsule.'

'What's a gelatin capsule?' Meyer asked.

'You've seen them,' Blaney said. 'Vitamins, tranquillizers, stimulants . . . many pharmaceuticals are packed in gelatin capsules.'

'Let's get back to "immediate" again,' Carella said.

'Are we still –'

'How long does it take for a gelatin capsule to dissolve in the body?'

'I have no idea. Several minutes, I would imagine. Why?'

'Well, the capsule would have had to dissolve before any poison could be released, isn't that right?'

'Yes, of course.'

'So immediate doesn't always mean immediate, does it? In this case, immediately means after the capsule dissolves.'

'I just told you it would have dissolved within minutes.'

'How *many* minutes?' Carella asked.

'I don't know. You'll have to check that with the lab.'

'We will,' Carella said.

Chapter Three

The man assigned to investigate the somewhat odd incident in Miles Vollner's office was Detective Bert Kling. Early Thursday morning, while Carella and Meyer were still asleep, Kling took the subway down to the precinct, stopped at the squadroom to see if there were any messages for him on the bulletin board, and then bused over to Shepherd Street. Vollner's office was on the tenth floor. The lettering on the frosted-glass door disclosed that the name of the firm was VOLLNER AUDIO-VISUAL COMPONENTS, unimaginative but certainly explicit. Kling opened the door and stepped into the reception room. The girl behind the reception desk was a small brunette, her hair cut in bangs across her forehead. She looked up as Kling walked in, smiled, and said, 'Yes, sir, may I help you?'

'I'm from the police,' Kling said. 'I understand there was some trouble here yesterday.'

'Oh, *yes*,' the girl said, 'there *certainly was!*'

'Is Mr Vollner in yet?'

'No, he isn't,' the girl said. 'Was he expecting you?'

'Well, not exactly. The desk sergeant –'

'Oh, he doesn't usually come in until about ten o'clock,' the girl said. 'It's not even nine-thirty yet.'

'I see,' Kling said. 'Well, I have some other stops to make, so maybe I can catch him later on in the –'

'Cindy's here, though,' the girl said.

'Cindy?'

'Yes. She's the one he came to see.'

'What do you mean?'

'The one he *said* he came to see, anyway.'

'The assailant, do you mean?'

'Yes. He said he was a friend of Cindy's.'

'Oh. Well, look, do you think I could talk to her? Until Mr Vollner gets here?'

'Sure, I don't see why not,' the girl said, and pressed a button in the base of her phone. Into the receiver, she said, 'Cindy, there's a detective here to talk about yesterday. Can you see him? Okay, sure.' She replaced the receiver. 'In a few minutes, Mr ...' She let the sentence hang.

'Kling.'

'Mr Kling. She's got someone in the office with her.' The girl paused. 'She interviews applicants for jobs out at the plant, you see.'

'Oh. Is she in charge of hiring?'

'No, our personnel director does all the hiring.'

'Then why does she interview —'

'Cindy is assistant to the company psychologist.'

'Oh.'

'Yes, she interviews all the applicants, you know, and later our psychologist tests them. To see if they'd be happy working out at the plant. I mean, they have to put together these tiny transistor things, you know, there's a lot of pressure doing work like that.'

'I'll bet there is,' Kling said.

'Sure, there is. So they come here, and first she talks to them for a few minutes, to try to find out what their background is, you know, and then if they pass the first interview, our psychologist gives them a battery of psychological tests later on. Cindy's work is very important. She majored in psychology at college, you know. Our personnel director won't even consider a man if Cindy and our psychologist say he's not suited for the work.'

'Sort of like picking a submarine crew,' Kling said.

'What? Oh, yes, I guess it is,' the girl said, and smiled. She turned as a man came down the corridor. He seemed pleased and even inspired by his first interview with the company's assistant psychologist. He smiled at the receptionist, and then he smiled at Kling and went to the entrance door, and then turned and smiled at them both again, and went out.

'I think she's free now,' the receptionist said. 'Just let me check.' She lifted the phone again, pressed the button, and waited. 'Cindy, is it all right to send him in now? Okay.' She replaced the receiver. 'Go right in,' she said. 'It's number fourteen, the fifth door on the left.'

'Thank you,' Kling said.

'Not at all,' the girl answered.

He nodded and walked past her desk and into the corridor. The doors on the left-hand side started with the number eight and then progressed arithmetically down the corridor. The number thirteen was missing from the row. In its place, and immediately following twelve, was fourteen. Kling wondered if the company's assistant psychologist was superstitious, and then knocked on the door.

'Come in,' the girl's voice said.

He opened the door.

The girl was standing near the window, her back to him. One hand held a telephone receiver to her ear, the blonde hair pushed away from it. She was wearing a dark skirt and a white blouse. The jacket that matched the skirt was draped over the back of her chair. She was very tall, and she had a good figure and a good voice. 'No, John,' she said, 'I didn't think a Rorschach was indicated. Well, if you say so. I'll call you back later, I've got someone with me. Right. G'bye.' She turned to put the phone back onto its cradle, and then looked up at Kling.

They recognized each other immediately.

'What the hell are *you* doing here?' Cindy said.

'So you're Cindy,' Kling said. 'Cynthia Forrest. I'll be damned.'

'Why'd they send *you*? Aren't there any other cops in that precinct of yours?'

'I'm the boss's son. I told you that a long time ago.'

'You told me a lot of things a long time ago. Now go tell your captain I'd prefer talking to another –'

'My lieutenant.'

'*Whatever* he is. I mean, *really*, Mr Kling, I think there's such a thing as adding insult to injury. The way you treated me when my father was killed –'

'I think there was a great deal of misunderstanding all around at that time, Miss Forrest.'

'Yes, and mostly on your part.'

'We were under pressure. There was a sniper loose in the city –'

'Mr Kling, *most* people are under pressure *most* of the time. It was my understanding that policemen are civil servants, and that –'

'We are, that's true.'

'Yes, well, you were anything *but* civil. I have a long memory, Mr Kling.'

'So do I. Your father's name was Anthony Forrest, he was the first victim of those sniper killings. Your mother –'

'Look, Mr Kling –'

'Your mother's name is Clarice, and you've got –'

'Clara.'

'Clara, right, and you've got a younger brother named John.'

'Jeff.'

'Jeff, right. You were majoring in education at the time of the shootings –'

'I switched to psychology in my junior year.'

'Downtown at Ramsey University. You were nineteen years old –'

'Almost twenty.'

'– and that was close to three years ago, which makes you twenty-two.'

'I'll be twenty-two next month.'

'I see you graduated.'

'Yes, I have,' Cindy said curtly. 'Now, if you'll excuse me, Mr Kling –'

'I've been assigned to investigate this complaint, Miss Forrest. Something of this nature is relatively small potatoes in our fair city, so I can positively guarantee the lieutenant won't put another man on it simply because you don't happen to like my face.'

'Among *other* things.'

'Yes, well, that's too bad. Would you like to tell me what happened here yesterday?'

'I would like to tell you nothing.'

'Don't you want us to find the man who came up here?'

'I do.'

'Then –'

'Mr Kling, let me put this as flatly as I can. I don't like you. I didn't like you the last time I saw you, and I *still* don't like you. I'm afraid I'm just one of those people who never change their minds.'

'Bad failing for a psychologist.'

'I'm not a psychologist *yet*. I'm going for my master's at night.'

'The girl outside told me you're assistant to the company –'

'Yes, I am. But I haven't yet taken my boards.'

'Are you allowed to practise?'

'According to the law in this state – I thought you just *might* be familiar with it, Mr Kling – no one can be licensed to –'

'No, I'm not.'

'Obviously. No one can be licensed to practise psychology until he has a master's degree *and* a Ph.D., *and* has passed the state boards. I'm not practising. All I do is conduct interviews and sometimes administer tests.'

'Well, I'm relieved to hear that,' Kling said.

'What the hell is that supposed to mean?'

'Nothing,' Kling said, and shrugged.

'Look, Mr Kling, if you stay here a minute longer, we're going to pick up right where we left off. And as I recall it, the last time I saw you, I told you to drop dead.'

'That's right.'

'So why don't you?'

'Can't,' Kling said. 'This is my case.' he smiled pleasantly, sat in the chair beside her desk, made himself comfortable and very sweetly said, 'Do you want to tell me what happened here yesterday, Miss Forrest?'

When Carella got to the squadroom at ten-thirty that morning, Meyer was already there, and a note on his desk told him that a man named Charles Mercer at the police laboratory had called at 7:45 a.m.

'Did you call him back?' Carella asked.

'I just got in a minute ago.'

'Let's hope he came up with something,' Carella said, and dialled the lab. He asked for Charles Mercer and was told that Mercer had worked the graveyard shift and had gone home at eight o'clock.

'Who's this?' Carella asked.

'Danny Di Tore.'

'Would you know anything about the tests Mercer ran for us? On some gelatin capsules?'

'Yeah, sure,' Di Tore said. 'Just a minute. That was some job you gave Charlie, you know?'

'What'd he find out?'

'Well, to begin with, he had to use a lot of different capsules. They come in different thicknesses, you know. Like all the manufacturers don't make them the same.'

'Pick up the extension, will you, Meyer?' Carella said, and then into the phone, 'Go ahead, Di Tore.'

'And also, there's a lot of things that can affect the dissolving speed. Like if a man just ate, his stomach is full and the capsule won't dissolve as fast. If the stomach's empty, you get a speedier dissolving rate.'

'Yeah, go ahead.'

'It's even possible for one of these capsules to pass right through the system without dissolving at all. That happens with older people sometimes.'

'But Mercer ran the tests,' Carella said.

'Yeah, sure. He mixed a batch of five-percent-solution hydrochloric acid, with a little pepsin. To stimulate the gastric juices, you know? He poured that into a lot of separate containers and then dropped the capsules in.'

'What'd he come up with?'

'Well, let me tell you what he did. He used different brands, you see, and also different sizes. They come in different sizes, you know, the higher the number, the smaller the size. Like a four is smaller than a three, don't ask me.'

'And what's he find out?'

'They dissolve at different rates of speed, ten minutes, four minutes, eight minutes, twelve minutes. The highest was fifteen minutes, the lowest three minutes. That's a lot of help, huh?'

'Well, it's not exactly what I –'

'But most of them took an average of about six minutes to dissolve. That gives you something to fool around with.'

'Six minutes, huh?'

'Yeah.'

'Okay. Thanks a lot, Di Tore. And thank Mercer, will you?'

'Don't mention it. It kept him awake.'

Carella replaced the phone on its cradle and turned to Meyer.

'So what do you think?'

'What am I, a straight man? What *else* can I think? Whether Gifford drank it, or swallowed it, it had to be just before he went on.'

'Had to be. The poison works within minutes, and the capsule takes approximately six minutes to dissolve. He was on for seven.'

'Seven minutes and seventeen seconds,' Meyer corrected.

'You think he took it knowingly?'

'Suicide?'

'Could be.'

'In front of forty million people?'

'Why not? There's nothing an actor likes better than a spectacular exit.'

'Well, maybe,' Meyer said, but he didn't sound convinced.

'We'd better find out who was with him just before he went on.'

'That should be very simple,' Meyer said. 'Only two hundred and twelve people were there last night.'

'Let's call your Mr Krantz. Maybe he'll be able to help us.'

Carella dialled Krantz's office and asked to talk to him. The switchboard connected him with a receptionist, who in turn connected him with Krantz's secretary, who told him that Krantz was out, would he care to leave a message? Carella asked her to wait a moment, and then covered the mouthpiece.

'Are we going out to see Gifford's wife?' he asked Meyer.

'I think we'd better,' Meyer said.

'Please tell Mr Krantz that he can reach me at Mr Gifford's home, will you?' Carella said, and then he thanked her and hung up.

* * *

Larksview was perhaps a half hour outside the city, an exclusive suburb that miraculously managed to provide its homeowners with something more than the conventional sixty-by-a-hundred plots. In a time of encroaching land development, it was pleasant and reassuring to enter a community of wide rolling lawns, of majestic houses set far back from quiet winding roads. Detective Meyer had made the trip to Larksview the night before, when he felt it necessary to explain to Melanie Gifford why the police wanted to do an autopsy, even though her permission was not needed. But now, patiently and uncomplainingly, he made the drive again, seeing the community in daylight for the first time, somehow soothed by its well-ordered, gentle terrain. Carella had been speculating wildly from the moment they left the city, but he was silent now as they pulled up in front of a pair of stone pillars set on either side of a white gravel driveway. A half-dozen men with cameras and another half-dozen with pads and pencils were shouting at the two Larksview patrolmen who stood blocking the drive. Meyer rolled down the window on his side of the car and shouted, 'Break it up here! We want to get through.'

One of the patrolmen moved away from the knot of newspapermen and walked over to the car. 'Who are *you*, Mac?' he said to Meyer, and Meyer showed him his shield.

'87th Precinct, huh?' the patrolman said. 'You handling this case?'

'That's right,' Meyer said.

'Then why don't you send some of your boys out on this driveway detail?'

'What's the matter?' Carella said, leaning over. 'Can't you handle a couple of reporters?'

'A couple? You shoulda seen this ten minutes ago. The crowd's beginning to thin out a little now.'

'Can we get through?' Meyer asked.

'Yeah, sure, go ahead. Just run right over them. We'll sweep up later.'

Meyer honked the horn, and then stepped on the gas pedal. The newspapermen pulled aside hastily, cursing at the sedan as its tyres crunched over the gravel.

'Nice fellas,' Meyer said. 'You'd think they'd leave the poor woman alone.'

'The way *we're* doing, huh?' Carella said.

'This is different.'

The house was a huge Georgian Colonial, with white clapboard siding and pale-green shutters. Either side of the door was heavily planted with big old shrubs that stretched beyond the boundaries of the house to form a screen of privacy for the back acres. The gravel driveway swung past the front door and then turned upon itself to head for the road again, detouring into a small parking area to the left of the house before completing its full cycle. Meyer drove the car into the parking space, pulled up the emergency brake, and got out. Carella came around from the other side of the car, and together they walked over the noisy gravel to the front door. A shining brass bell pull was set in the jamb. Carella took the knob and yanked it. The detectives waited. Carella pulled the knob again. Again, they waited.

'The Giffords have help, don't they?' Carella said, puzzled.

'If you were making half a million dollars a year, wouldn't you have help?'

'I don't know,' Carella said. '*You're* making fifty-five hundred a year, and Sarah doesn't have help.'

'We don't want to seem ostentatious,' Meyer said. 'If we hired a housekeeper, the commissioner might begin asking me about all that graft I've been taking.'

'You too, huh?'

'Sure. Cleared a cool hundred thousand in slot machines alone last year.'

'My game's white slavery,' Carella said. 'I figure to make –'

The door opened.

The woman who stood there was small and Irish and frightened. She peered out into the sunshine and then said, in a very small voice, with a faint brogue, 'Yes, what is it, please?'

'Police department,' Carella said. 'We'd like to talk to Mrs Gifford.'

'Oh.' The woman looked more distressed than ever. 'Oh, yes,' she said. 'Yes, come in. She's out back with the dogs. I'll see if I can find her. Police, did you say?'

'That's right, ma'am,' Carella said. 'If she's out back, couldn't we just go around and look for her?'

'Oh,' the woman said. 'I don't know.'

'You *are* the housekeeper?'

'Yes, sir, I am.'

'Well, *may* we walk around back?'

'All right, but –'

'Do the dogs bite?' Meyer asked cautiously.

'No, they're very gentle. Besides, Mrs Gifford is with them.'

'Thank you,' Carella said. They turned away from the door and began walking on the flagstone path leading to the rear of the house. A woman appeared almost the moment they turned the corner of the building. She was coming out of a small copse of birch trees set at the far end of the lawn, a tall blonde woman wearing a tweed skirt, loafers, and a blue cardigan sweater, looking down at the ground as two golden retrievers ran ahead of her. The dogs saw the detectives almost immediately and began barking. The woman raised her head and her eyes curiously, and then hesitated a moment, her stride breaking.

'That's Melanie Gifford,' Meyer whispered.

The dogs were bounding across the lawn in enormous leaps. Meyer watched their approach uneasily. Carella, who was a city boy himself, and unused to seeing jungle beasts racing across open stretches of ground, was certain they would leap at his jugular. He was, in fact, almost tempted to draw his pistol when the dogs stopped some three feet away and began barking in furious unison.

'Shhh!' Meyer said, and he stamped his foot on the ground. The dogs, to Carella's immense surprise, turned tail and ran yelping back to their mistress, who walked directly towards the detectives now, her head high, her manner openly demanding.

'Yes?' she said. 'What is it?'

'Mrs Gifford?' Carella asked.

'Yes?' The voice was imperious. Now that she was closer, Carella studied her face. The features were delicately formed, the eyes grey and penetrating, the brows slightly arched, the mouth full. She wore no lipstick. Grief seemed to lurk in the corners of those eyes, and on that mouth; grief sat uninvited and omnipresent on her face, robbing it of beauty. 'Yes?' she said again, impatiently.

'We're detectives, Mrs Gifford,' Meyer said. 'I was here last night. Don't you remember?'

She studied him for several seconds, as if in disbelief. The goldens were still barking, courageous now that they were behind her skirts. 'Yes, of course,' she said at last, and then added, 'Hush, boys,' to the dogs, who immediately fell silent.

'We'd like to ask you some questions, Mrs Gifford,' Carella said. 'I know this is a trying time for you, but –'

'That's quite all right,' she answered. 'Would you like to go inside?'

'Wherever you say.'

'If you don't mind, may we stay out here? The house . . . I can't seem to . . . it's open out here, and fresh. After what happened . . .'

Carella, watching her, had the sudden notion she was acting. A slight frown creased his forehead. But immediately, she said, 'That sounds terribly phony and dramatic, doesn't it? I'm sorry. You must forgive me.'

'We understand, Mrs Gifford.'

'Do you really?' she asked. A faint sad smile touched her unpainted mouth. 'Shall we sit on the terrace? It won't be too cool, will it?'

'The terrace will be fine,' Carella said.

They walked across the lawn to where a wide flagstone terrace adjoined the rear doors of the house, open to the woods alive with autumn colour. There were white wrought-iron chairs and a glass-topped table on the terrace. Melanie pulled a low white stool from beneath the table and sat. The detectives pulled up chairs opposite her, sitting higher than Melanie, looking down at her. She turned her face up pathetically, and again Carella had the feeling that this, too, was carefully staged, that she had deliberately placed herself in a lower chair so that she would appear small and defenceless. On impulse, he said, 'Are you an actress, Mrs Gifford?'

Melanie looked surprised. The grey eyes opened wide for a moment, and then she smiled the same wan smile and said, 'I used to be. Before Stan and I were married.'

'How long ago were you married, Mrs Gifford?'

'Six years.'

'Do you have any children?'

'No.'

Carella nodded. 'Mrs Gifford,' he said, 'we're primarily interested in learning about your husband's behaviour in the past few weeks. Did he seem despondent, or overworked, or troubled by anything?'

'No, I don't think so.'

'Was he the type of man who confided things to you?'

'Yes, we were very close.'

'And he never mentioned anything that was troubling him?'

'No. He seemed very pleased with the way things were going.'

'What things, Mrs Gifford?'

'The show, the new stature he'd achieved in television. He'd been a night-club comic before the show went on the air, you know.'

'I didn't know that.'

'Yes. Stan started in vaudeville many years ago, and then drifted into night-club work. He was working in Vegas, as a matter of fact, when they approached him to do the television show.'

'And it's been on the air how many years now?'

'Three years.'

'How old was your husband, Mrs Gifford?'

'Forty-eight.'

'And how old are you?'

'Thirty-seven.'

'Was this your first marriage?'

'Yes.'

'Your husband's?'

'Yes.'

'I see. Would you say you were happily married, Mrs Gifford?'

'Yes. Extremely happy.'

'Mrs Gifford,' Carella said flatly, 'do you think your husband committed suicide?'

Without hesitation, Melanie said, 'No.'

'You know he was poisoned, of course?'

'Yes.'

'If you don't think he killed himself, you must think –'

'I think he was murdered. Yes.'

'Who do you think murdered him, Mrs Gifford?'

'I think –'

'Excuse me, ma'am,' the voice said from the opened French doors leading to the terrace. Melanie turned. Her housekeeper stood there apologetically. 'It's Dr Nelson, ma'am.'

'On the telephone?' Melanie said, rising.

'No ma'am. He's here.'

'Oh.' Melanie frowned. 'Well, ask him to join us, won't you?' She sat immediately. 'Again,' she said.

'What?'

'He was here last night. Came over directly from the show. He's terribly worried about my health. He gave me a sedative and then called twice this morning.' She folded her arms across her knees, a slender graceful woman who somehow made the motion seem awkward. Carella watched her in silence for several moments. The terrace was still. On the lawn, one of the golden retrievers began barking at a laggard autumn bird.

'You were about to say, Mrs Gifford?'

Melanie looked up. Her thoughts seemed to be elsewhere.

'We were discussing your husband's alleged murder.'

'Yes. I was about to say I think Carl Nelson killed him.'

Chapter Four

Dr Carl Nelson came onto the terrace not two minutes after Melanie had spoken his name, going first to her and kissing her on the cheek, and then shaking hands with Meyer, whom he had met the night before. He was promptly introduced to Carella, and he acknowledged the introduction with a firm handclasp and a repetition of the name, 'Detective Carella,' with a slight nod and a smile, as if he wished to imprint it on his memory. He turned immediately to Melanie then, and said, 'How are you, Mel?'

'I'm fine, Carl,' she said. 'I told you that last night.'

'Did you sleep well?'

'Yes.'

'This has been very upsetting,' Nelson said. 'I'm sure you gentlemen can understand.'

Carella nodded. He was busy watching the effect Nelson seemed to be having on Melanie. She had visibly withdrawn from him the moment he stepped onto the terrace, folding her arms across her chest, hugging herself as though threatened by a strong wind. The pose was assuredly a theatrical one, but it seemed genuine nonetheless. If she was not actually frightened of this tall man with the deep voice and the penetrating brown eyes, she certainly appeared suspicious of him; and the suspicion seemingly forced her to turn inward, to flee into icy passivity.

'Was the autopsy conducted?' Nelson asked Meyer.

'Yes, sir.'

'May I ask what the results were? Or are they classified?'

'Mr Gifford was killed by a large dose of strophanthin,' Carella said.

'Strophanthin?' Nelson looked honestly surprised. 'That's rather unusual, isn't it?'

'Are you familiar with the drug, Dr Nelson?'

'Yes, of course. That is, I know of it. I don't think I've ever prescribed it, however. It's rarely used, you know.'

'Dr Nelson, Mr Gifford wasn't a cardiac patient, was he?'

'No. I believe I told that to Detective Meyer last night. Certainly not.'

'He wasn't taking digitalis or any of the related glucosides?'

'No, sir.'

'What *was* he taking?'

'What do you mean?'

'Was he taking any drugs?'

Nelson shrugged. 'No. Not that I know of.'

'Well, you're his personal physician. If anyone *would* know, it'd be you, isn't that so?'

'That's right. No, Stan wasn't taking any drugs. Unless you want to count headache tablets and vitamin pills.'

'What kind of headache tablets?'

'An empirin-codeine compound.'

'And the vitamins?'

'B-complex with vitamin C.'

'How long had he been taking the vitamins?'

'Oh, several months. He was feeling a little tired, run-down, you know. I suggested he try them.'

'You prescribed them?'

'*Prescribed* them? No.' Nelson shook his head. 'He was taking a brand called PlexCin, Mr Carella. It can be purchased at any drugstore without a prescription. But I *suggested* it to him, yes.'

'You suggested this specific brand?'

'Yes. It's manufactured by a reputable firm, and I've found it to be completely relia –'

'Dr Nelson, how are these vitamins packaged?'

'In a capsule. Most vitamins are.'

'How large a capsule?'

'An O capsule, I would say. Perhaps a double O.'

'Dr Nelson, would you happen to know whether or not Mr Gifford was in the habit of taking his vitamins during the show?'

'Why no, I ...' Nelson paused. He looked at Carella and then turned to Melanie, and then looked at Carella again. 'You certainly don't think....' Nelson shrugged. 'But then, I suppose anything's possible.'

'What were *you* thinking, Dr Nelson?'

'That perhaps someone substituted strophanthin for the vitamins?'

'Would that be possible?'

'I don't see why not,' Nelson said. 'The PlexCin capsule is an opaque gelatin that comes apart in two halves. I suppose someone could conceivably have opened the capsule, removed the vitamins, and replaced them with strophanthin.' He shrugged again. 'But that would seem an awfully long way to go to....' He stopped.

'To what, Dr Nelson?'

'Well ... to murder someone, I suppose.'

The terrace was silent again.

'Did he take these vitamin capsules every day?' Carella asked.

'Yes,' Nelson answered.

'Would you know *when* he took them yesterday?'

'No, I –'

'*I* know when,' Melanie said.

Carella turned to her. She was still sitting on the low stool, still hugging herself, still looking chilled and lost and forlorn.

'When?' Carella asked.

'He took one after breakfast yesterday morning.' Melanie paused. 'I met him for lunch in town yesterday afternoon. He took another capsule then.'

'What time was that?'

'Immediately after lunch. About two o'clock.'

Carella sighed.

'What is it, Mr Carella?' Melanie asked.

'I think my partner is beginning to hate clocks,' Meyer said.

'What do you mean?'

'You see, Mrs Gifford, it takes six minutes for a gelatin capsule to dissolve, releasing whatever's inside it. And strophanthin acts immediately.'

'Then the capsule he took at lunch couldn't have contained any poison.'

'That's right, Mrs Gifford. He took it at two o'clock, and he didn't collapse until about eight-forty-four. That's a time span of almost seven hours. No, the poison *had* to be taken while he was at the studio.'

Nelson looked thoughtful for a moment. 'Then wouldn't it be wise to question –' he began, and stopped speaking abruptly because the telephone inside was ringing furiously, shattering the afternoon stillness.

David Krantz was matter-of-fact, businesslike, and brief. His voice fairly crackled over the telephone wire.

'You called me?' he asked.

'Yes.'

'How's Melanie?'

'She seems fine.'

'You didn't waste any time getting over there, did you?'

'We try to do our little jobs,' Carella said drily, remembering Meyer's description of his encounter with Krantz, and wondering whether everybody in television had such a naturally nasty tone of voice.

'What is it you want?' Krantz said. 'This phone hasn't stopped ringing all morning. Every newspaper in town, every magazine, every *cretin* in this city wants to know exactly what happened last night! How do *I* know what happened?'

'You were there, weren't you?'

'I was up in the sponsor's booth. I only saw it on the monitor. What do you want from me? I'm very busy.'

'I want to know exactly where Stan Gifford was last night before he went on camera for the last time.'

'How do I know where he was? I just told you I was up in the sponsor's booth.'

'Where does he usually go when he's off camera, Mr Krantz?'

'That depends on how much time he has.'

'Suppose he had the time it took for some folk singers to sing two songs?'

'Then I imagine he went to his dressing room.'

'Can you check that for me?'

'Whom would you like me to check it with? Stan's dead.'

'Look, Mr Krantz, are you trying to tell me that in your well-functioning, smoothly oiled organization, *nobody* has any idea where Stan Gifford was while those singers were on camera?'

'I didn't say that.'

'What did you say? I'm sure I misunderstood you.'

'I said *I* didn't know. I was up in the sponsor's booth. I went up there about fifteen minutes before air time.'

'All right, Mr Krantz, thank you. You've successfully presented your alibi. I assume that Gifford did not come up to the sponsor's booth at any time during the show?'

'Exactly.'

'Then you couldn't have poisoned him, isn't that your point?'
'I wasn't trying to establish an alibi for myself. I simply –'
'Mr Krantz, who *would* know where Gifford was? Would somebody know? Would *anybody* in your organization know?'
'I'll check on it. Can you call me later?'
'I'd rather stop by. Will you be in your office all day?'
'Yes, but –'
'There are some further questions I'd like to ask you.'
'About what?'
'About Gifford.'
'Am I a suspect in this damn thing?'
'Did I say that, Mr Krantz?'
'No, I said it. Am I?'
'Yes, Mr Krantz, you are,' Carella said, and hung up.

On the way back to the city, Meyer was peculiarly silent. Carella, who had spelled him at the wheel, glanced at him and said, 'Do you want to hit Krantz now or after lunch?'
'After lunch,' Meyer said.
'You seem tired. What's the matter?'
'I think I'm coming down with something. My head feels stuffy.'
'All that clean, fresh suburban air,' Carella said.
'No, I must be getting a cold.'
'I can see Krantz alone,' Carella said. 'Why don't you go on home?'
'No, it's nothing serious.'
'I mean it. I can handle –'
'Stop it already,' Meyer said. 'You'll make me *meshugah*. You sound just like my mother used to. You'll be asking me if I got a clean handkerchief next.'
'You got a clean handkerchief?' Carella asked, and Meyer burst out laughing. In the middle of the laugh, he suddenly sneezed. He reached into his back pocket, hesitated, and turned to Carella.
'You see that?' he said. 'I *haven't* got a clean handkerchief.'
'My mother taught me to use my sleeve,' Carella said.
'All right, may I use your sleeve?' Meyer said.
'What'd you think of our esteemed medical man?'
'Is there any Kleenex in this rattletrap?'
'Try the glove compartment. What'd you think of Dr Nelson?'
Meyer reached into the glove compartment, found a box of tissues, and blew his nose resoundingly. He sniffed again, said, 'Ahhhhhh,' and then immediately said, 'I have a thing about doctors, anyway, but this one I *particularly* dislike.'
'How come?'
'He looks like a smart movie villain,' Meyer said.
'Which means we can safely eliminate him as a suspect, right?'
'There's a better reason than that for eliminating him. He was home during the show last night.' Meyer paused. 'On the other hand, he's a doctor, and would have access to a rare drug like strophanthin.'
'But he was the one who suggested an autopsy, remember?'
'Right. Another good reason to forget all about him. If you just poisoned

somebody, you're not going to tell the cops to look for poison, are you?'

'A smart movie villain might do just that.'

'Sure, but then a smart movie cop would instantly know the smart movie villain was trying to pull a swiftie.'

'Melanie Wistful seems to think he did it,' Carella said.

'Melanie Mournful, you mean. Yeah. I wonder why?'

'We'll have to ask her.'

'I wanted to, but Carl Heavy wouldn't quit the scene.'

'We'll call her later. Make a note.'

'Yes, sir,' Meyer said. He was silent for a moment, and then he said, 'This case stinks.'

'Give me a good old-fashioned hatchet murder any day.'

'Poison is a woman's weapon as a rule, isn't it?' Meyer asked.

'Sure,' Carella said. 'Look at history. Look at all the famous poisoners. Look at Neill Cream and Carlyle Harris. Look at Roland B. Molineux. Look at Henri Landru, look at ...'

'All right, already, I get it,' Meyer said.

Lieutenant Peter Byrnes read Kling's report that Thursday afternoon, and then buzzed the squadroom and asked him to come in. When he arrived, Byrnes offered him a chair (which Kling accepted) and a cigar (which Kling declined) and then lighted his own cigar and blew out a wreath of smoke and said, 'What's this "severe distaste for my personality" business?'

Kling shrugged. 'She doesn't like me, Pete. I can't say I blame her. I was going through a bad time. Well, what am I telling you for?'

'Mmm,' Byrnes said. 'You think there's anything to this prison possibility?'

'I doubt it. It was a chance, though, so I figured we had nothing to lose.' He looked at his watch. 'She ought to be down at the BCI right this minute, looking through their pictures.'

'Maybe she'll come up with something.'

'Maybe. As a follow-up, I called some of the families of Redfield's other victims. I haven't finished them all yet, still a few more to go. But the ones I reached said there'd been no incidents, no threats, nothing like that. I was careful about it, Pete, don't worry. I told them we were making a routine follow-up. I didn't want to alarm them.'

'Yeah, good,' Byrnes said. 'But you don't feel there's a revenge thing working here, is that it?'

'Well, if there is, it'd have to be somebody Redfield knew before we caught him, or somebody he met in stir. Either way, why should anybody risk his own neck for a dead man?'

'Yeah,' Byrnes said. He puffed meditatively on his cigar, and then glanced at the report again. 'Four teeth knocked out, and three broken ribs,' he said. 'Tough customer.'

'Well, Fairchild's a new cop.'

'I know that. Still, this man doesn't seem to have much respect for the law, does he?'

'To put it mildly,' Kling said, smiling.

'Your report says he grabbed the Forrest girl by the arm.'

'That's right.'

POLICE DEPARTMENT		DETECTIVE SQUAD 87th
CRIME CLASSIFICTION	**COMPLAINT REPORT**	PRECINCT 87th
Assault	**COPY**	COMPLAINT NUMBER 306B-41-11
		DATE OF THIS REPORT 10/14

NAME OF COMPLAINANT SURNAME FIRST NAME AND INITIALS	ADDRESS OF COMPLAINANT
Vollner Miles S.	1116 Shepherd Street
DATE AND TIME OF OCCURRENCE October 13 2 P.M.	PLACE OF OCCURRENCE Same as above
DATE AND TIME REPORTED BY THE COMPLAINANT 10/13 2:30 P.M.	DETECTIVE ASSIGNED Bertram Kling

DETAILS:

INTERROGATION OF MILES VOLLNER AND CYNTHIA FORREST:

Miles Vollner is president of Vollner Audio-Visual Components
at 1116 Shepherd Street. He states that ~~anxbes~~ he returned
from lunch at about one forty-five p.m. on Wednesday, October
~~ttth~~ 13th to find a man sitting in his reception room. The
man refused to give his name or state his business, and there-
after threatned Mr. Vollner's receptionist (Janice Di Santo)
when Vollner asked her to call the police. Vollner promptly
went down to the street and enlisted the air of Patrolman
Ronald Fairchild, shield number 36-104, 87th Precinct, who
accompanied him back to the office. When ~~Risn~~ confronted by
Fairchild, ~~igexmx~~ the man stated that he had come there to
see a girl, and when asked which girl, he said, "Cindy."
(Cindy is the nickname for Miss Cynthia Forrest, who is
assistant to the company psychologist.)

Vollner sent for Miss Forrest who looked at the man and
claimed she did not know him. When she attempted to leave, the
man grabbed ger by the arm, at which point Fairchild warned
him to leave her alone, moving toward him and rasing his club.
The man attacked Fairchild, kicking him repeatedl in the head
and chest after he fell to the floor. Fairchild ~~ix~~ was later
sent to Buena Vista Hospital. Four teeth ~~were~~ had been kicked
out of his mouth, and he had suffered three broken ribs.
Vollner states he hd never before seen the man, and Miss
Forrest states so, too.

Miss Forrest is the daughter of the deceased Anthony Forrest
(DD Reports 201A - 46 - 01 through 201A - 46 - 31) first
victim of the sniper killings two years ~~agexx~~ six months ago.
Check of records show that Lewis Redfield was tried and convicted first degree murder, sentenced to death in the electric
chair, executed at Castleview Penitentiary last March. There
seems to be no connection between this case and the sniper
murders, but have arranged for Miss Forrest to look at mug
shots of any prisoners serving time at Castleview (during
Redfield's imprisonment there) and subsequently released.
Doubt if this will come up with a make since Redfield was in
the death house for entire length of term before execution,
although he may have had some contact with general prison
population and arranged for harrassment of Miss Forrest and
other survivors of his victims.

Miss Forrest's previous contact with me on sniper case has
left severe distaste for my personality. If subsequent
investigation is indicated, I respectfully submit that case be
truned over to someone else on the squad.

Bertram Kling

Detective 3rd/Grade Bertram Kling

'I don't like it, Bert. If this guy can be so casual about beating up a cop, what'll he do if he gets that girl alone sometime?'

'Well, that's the thing.'

'I think we ought to get him.'

'Sure, but who is he?'

'Maybe we'll get a make downtown. From those mug shots.'

'She promised to call in later, as soon as she's had a look.'

'Maybe we'll be lucky.'

'Maybe.'

'If we're not, I think we ought to smoke out this guy. I don't like cops getting beat up, that's to begin with. And I don't like the idea of this guy maybe waiting to jump on that girl. He knocked out four of Fairchild's teeth and broke three of his ribs. Who knows what he'd do to a helpless little girl?'

'She's about five-seven, Pete. Actually, that's pretty big. For a girl, I mean.'

'Still. If we're not careful here, we may wind up with a homicide on our hands.'

'Well, that's projecting a little further than I think we have to, Pete.'

'Maybe, maybe not. I think we ought to smoke him out.'

'How?'

'Well, I'm not sure yet. What are you working on right now?'

'Those liquor-store holdups. And also an assault.'

'When was the last holdup?'

'Three nights ago.'

'What's your plan?'

'He seems to be hitting them in a line, Pete, straight up Culver Avenue. I thought I'd plant myself in the next store up the line.'

'You think he's going to hit again so soon?'

'They've been spaced about two weeks apart so far.'

'Then there's no hurry, right?'

'Well, he may change the timetable.'

'He may change the pattern, too. In which case you'll be sitting in the wrong store.'

'That's true. I just thought –'

'Let it wait. What's the assault?'

'Victim is a guy named Vinny Marino, he's a small-time pusher, lives on Ainsley Avenue. About a week ago, two guys pulled up in a car and got out with baseball bats. They broke both his legs. The neighbourhood rumble is that he was fooling around with one of their wives. That's why they went for his legs, you see, so he wouldn't be able to chase around any more. It's only coincidental that he's a pusher.'

'For my part, they could have killed him,' Byrnes said. He took his handkerchief from his back pocket, blew his nose, and then said, 'Mr Marino's case can wait, too. I want you to stay with this one, Bert.'

'I think we'd do better with another man. I doubt if I'll be able to get any co-operation at all from her.'

'Who can I spare?' Byrnes asked. 'Willis and Brown are on that knife murder, Hawes is on a plant of his own, Meyer and Carella are on this damn television thing, Andy Parker –'

'Well, maybe I can switch with one of them.'

'I don't like cases to change hands once they've been started.'

'I'll do whatever you say, Pete, but –'

'I'd appreciate it,' Byrnes said.

'Yes, sir.'

'You can follow up the vendetta possibility if you like, but I agree with you. It'll probably turn out to be a dead end.'

'I know. I just felt –'

'Sure, it was worth a try. See where it goes. Contact the rest of those survivors, and listen to what the Forrest girl has to say when she calls later on. But I wouldn't bank on anything along those lines, if I were you.' Byrnes paused, puffed on his cigar, and then said, 'She claims she doesn't know him, huh?'

'That's right.'

'I thought maybe he was an old boy friend.'

'No.'

'Rejected, you know, that kind of crap.'

'No, not according to her.'

'Maybe he just wants to get in her pants.'

'Maybe.'

'Is she good-looking?'

'She's attractive, yes. She's not a raving beauty, but I guess she's attractive.'

'Then maybe that's it.'

'Maybe, but why would he go after her in this way?'

'Maybe he doesn't *know* any other way. He sounds like a hood, and hoods take what they want. He doesn't know from candy or flowers. He sees a pretty girl he wants, so he goes after her – even if it means beating her up to get her. That's my guess.'

'Maybe.'

'And that's in our favour. Look what happened to Fairchild when he got in this guy's way. He knocked out his teeth and broke his ribs. *Whatever* he wants from this girl – and it's my guess all he wants is her tail – he's not going to let anybody stop him from getting it, law or otherwise. That's where you come in.'

'What do you mean?'

'That's how we smoke him out. I don't want to do anything that'll put this girl in danger. I want this punk to make his move against *you*, Bert.'

'Me?'

'You. He knows where she works, and chances are he knows where she lives, and I'll bet my life he's watching her every minute of the day. Okay, let's give him something to watch.'

'Me?' Kling said again.

'You, that's right. Stay with that girl day and night. Let's –'

'Day and *night*?'

'Well, within reason. Let's get this guy so goddamn sore at you that he comes after you and tries to do exactly what he did to Fairchild.'

Kling smiled. 'Gee,' he said, 'suppose he succeeds?'

'Fairchild is a new cop,' Byrnes said. 'You told me so yourself.'

'Okay, Pete, but you're forgetting something, aren't you?'

'What's that?'

'The girl doesn't like me. She's not going to take kindly to the idea of spending time with me.'

'Ask her if she'd rather get raped some night in the elevator after this guy has knocked out her teeth and broken some of her ribs. Ask her that.'

Kling smiled again. 'She might prefer it.'

'I doubt it.'

'Pete, she hates me. She *really* ...'

Byrnes smiled. 'Win her over, boy,' he said. 'Just win her over, that's all.'

David Krantz worked for a company named Major Broadcasting Associates, which had its offices downtown on Jefferson Street, Major Broadcasting, or MBA as it was familiarly called in the industry, devoted itself primarily to the making of filmed television programmes, but every now and then it ventured into the production of a live show. The Stan Gifford Show was – or at least had been – one of the three shows they presented live from the city each week. A fourth live show was produced bi-monthly on the Coast. MBA was undoubtedly the giant of the television business, and since success always breeds contempt, it had been given various nicknames by disgruntled and ungrateful industry wags. These ranged from mild jibes like Money Banks Anonymous, through gentle epithets like Mighty Bloody Assholes, to genuinely artistic creations like Master Bullshit Artists. Whatever you called the company, and however you sliced it, it was important and vast and accounted for more than sixty per cent of the nation's television fare each week.

The building on Jefferson Street was owned by MBA, and featured floor after floor of wood-panelled offices, ravishing secretaries and receptionists exported from the Coast, and solemn-looking young men in dark suits and ties, white shirts, and black shoes and socks. David Krantz was a solemn-looking man wearing the company uniform, but he wasn't as young as he used to be. His secretary showed Meyer and Carella into the office, and then closed the door gently behind them. 'I've met Mr Meyer,' Krantz said, a trace of sarcasm in his voice, 'but I believe you and I have only had the pleasure on the telephone, Mr Caretta.'

'Carella.'

'Carella, forgive me. Sit down, won't you. I'm expecting a call on the tieline, so if I have to interrupt our chat, I know you'll understand.'

'Certainly,' Carella said.

Krantz smoothed his moustache. 'Well, what is it you want to know?'

'First, did you find out where Gifford went while he was off camera?'

'I haven't been able to locate George Cooper. He's our A.D., he's the man who'd know.'

'What's an A.D.?' Carella asked.

'Assistant director,' Meyer said. 'I talked to him last night, Steve. He's the one who timed that tape for me.'

'Oh.'

'I tried to reach him at home,' Krantz said, 'but no one answered the phone. I'll try it again, if you like.'

'Where does he live?' Carella asked.

'Downtown, in The Quarter. It's his responsibility to see that everyone's in on cue. I'm sure he would know just where Stan went while the folk singers were on. Shall I have my secretary try him again?'

'Please,' Carella said.

Krantz buzzed for his secretary. In keeping with company policy, she was a tall and beautiful redhead wearing a tight green sweater and skirt. She listened attentively as Krantz told her to try Cooper's number again, and then said, 'We're ready on that call to the Coast now, Mr Krantz.'

'Thank you,' Krantz said. 'Excuse me,' he said to Carella and Meyer, and then he lifted the receiver. 'Hello, Krantz here. Hello, Frank, what is it? *Who?* The *writer?* What do you *mean,* the writer? The *writer* doesn't like the changes that were made? Who the hell asked him for his opinion? Well, I *know* he wrote the script, what difference does that make? Just a second now, start from the beginning, will you? Who made the changes? Well, he's a perfectly capable producer, why should the writer have any complaints? He says *what?* He says it's his script, and he resents a half-assed producer tampering with it? Listen, who *is* this fellow, anyway? Who? I never heard of him. What's he done before? The *Saturday Review* says what? Well, what the hell's some literary intelligentsia magazine got to do with the people who watch television? What do I care if he's a novelist, can he write television scripts? Who hired him, anyway? Was this cleared here, or was it a Coast decision? Don't give me any of that crap, Frank, novelists are a dime a dozen. Yeah, even *good* novelists. It's the guy who can write a decent television script that's hard to find. You say he *can* write a decent television script? Then what's the problem? Oh, I see. He doesn't like the changes that were made. Well, what changes *were* made, Frank, can you tell me that? I see, um-huh, the prostitute was rewritten as a nun, um-huh, I see, and she doesn't die at the end, she performs a miracle instead, um-huh, well, how about the hero? Not a truck driver any more, huh? Oh, I see, he's a football coach now, I get it. Um-huh, works at the college nearby the church, um-huh. Is it still set in London? Oh, I see. I see, yes, you want to shoot it at UCLA, sure, that makes sense, a lot closer to the studio. Well, gee, Frank, off the top of my head, I'd say the revisions have made it a much better script, I don't know what the hell the writer's getting excited about. Explain to him that the changes are really minor and that large stretches of his original dialogue and scenes are intact, just the way he wrote them. Tell him we've had pressure from the network, and that this necessitated a few minor – no, use the word "transitional" – a few transitional changes that were made by a competent producer because there simply wasn't time for lengthy consultations about revisions. Tell him we have the highest regard for his work, and that we're well aware of what the *Saturday Review* said about him, but explain that we're all in the same goddamn ratrace, and what else can we do when we're pressured by networks and sponsors and deadlines? Ask him to be reasonable, Frank. I think he'll understand. Fine. Listen, what did the pregnant raisin tell the police? Well, go ahead, guess. Nope. Nope. She said, "I was graped!"' Krantz burst out laughing. 'Okay, Frank, I'll talk to you. Right. So long.'

He hung up. The door to his office opened a second afterwards, and the pretty redhead paused in the doorframe and said, 'I still can't reach Mr Cooper.'

'Keep trying him,' Krantz said, and the girl went out. 'I'm sorry about the interruption, gentlemen. Shall we continue?'

'Yes,' Carella said. 'Can you tell me who was in that booth with you last night?'

'You want the names?'

'I'd appreciate them.'

'I anticipated you,' Krantz said. 'I had my secretary type up a list right after you called this morning.'

'That was very thoughtful of you,' Carella said.

'In this business, I try to anticipate *everything.*'

'It's a pity you couldn't have anticipated Gifford's death,' Carella said.

'Yeah, well, that was unforeseen,' Krantz said absolutely straight-faced, shaking his head solemnly. 'I'll have my secretary bring in that list.' He pushed a button on his phone. 'She used to work for our head of production out at the studio. Did you ever see tits like that before?'

'Never,' Carella said.

'They're remarkable,' Krantz said.

The girl came into the office. 'Yes, sir?'

'Bring in that list you typed for me, would you? How're you doing with Mr Cooper?'

'I'll try him again, sir.'

'Thank you.'

'Yes, sir,' she said and went out.

'Remarkable,' Krantz said.

'While she's getting that list,' Carella said, 'why don't you fill us in, Mr Krantz?'

'Sure. Gladine was in the booth with me, she's usually there to take any notes I might –'

'Gladine?'

'My secretary. The tits,' Krantz said. He gestured with his hands.

'Oh. Sure.'

'My associate producer was up there, too. Dan Hollis is his name, he's been with MBA for close to fifteen years.'

'Who was minding the store?' Meyer asked.

'What do you mean?'

'If you and your associate were in the sponsor's booth –'

'Oh. Well, our unit manager was down on the floor, and our director was in the control booth, of course, and our assistant director was making sure everyone –'

'I see, okay,' Meyer said. 'Who else was in the sponsor's booth with you?'

'The others were guests. Two of them were sponsors' representatives; one was a Hollywood director who's shooting a feature for the studio and who thought Gifford might be right for a part; and the other two were –'

The door opened.

'Here's that list, sir,' Gladine said. 'We're trying Mr Cooper now.'

'Thank you, Gladine.'

'Yes, sir,' she said and walked out. Krantz handed the typewritten list to Carella. Carella looked at the list, and then passed it to Meyer.

'Mr and Mrs Feldensehr, who are they?' Meyer asked.

'Friends of Carter Bentley, our unit manager. He invited them in to watch the show.'

'That's all then, huh? You and your secretary, your associate Dan Hollis ... Who's this Nathan Crabb?'

'The Hollywood director. I told you, he –'

'Yes, fine, and Mr and Mrs Feldensehr, and are these last two the sponsor's men?'

'That's right.'

'Eight people in all,' Carella said. 'And five of them were guests.'

'That's right.'

'You told us there were *six* guests, Mr Krantz.'

'No, I said five.'

'Mr Krantz,' Meyer said, 'last night you told me there were *six*.'

'I must have meant Gladine.'

'Your secretary?' Carella said.

'Yes. I must have included her as one of the guests.'

'That's a little unusual, isn't it, Mr Krantz? Including an employee of the company as a guest?'

'Well ...'

There was a long silence.

'Yes?' Carella said.

'Well ...'

There was another silence.

'We may be investigating a homicide here, Mr Krantz,' Meyer said softly. 'I don't think it's advisable to hide anything from us at this point, do you?'

'Well, I ... I suppose I can trust you gentlemen to be discreet.'

'Certainly,' Carella said.

'Nathan Crabb? The director? The one who was here to look at Stan, see if he was right for –'

'Yes?'

'He had a girl with him, the girl he's grooming for his next picture. I deliberately left her name off the list.'

'Why?'

'Well, Crabb is a married man with two children. I didn't think it wise to include the girl's name.'

'I see.'

'I can have it added to the list, if you like.'

'Yes, we'd like that,' Carella said.

'What time did you go up to the sponsor's booth?' Meyer asked suddenly.

'Fifteen minutes before the show started,' Krantz said.

'At seven-forty-five?'

'That's right. And I stayed there right until the moment Stan got sick.'

'Who was there when you arrived?'

'Everyone but Crabb and the girl.'

'What time did they get there?'

'About five minutes later. Ten to eight – around then.'

The door to Krantz's office opened suddenly. Gladine smiled and said, 'We've reached Mr Cooper, sir. He's on oh-three.'

'Thank you, Gladine.'

'Yes, sir,' she said, and went out.

Krantz picked up the phone. 'Hello,' he said, 'Krantz here. Hello, George, I have some policemen in my office, they're investigating Stan's death. They wanted to ask you some questions about his exact whereabouts during the show last night. Well, hold on, I'll let you talk to one of them. His name's Capella.'

'Carella.'

'Carella, I'm sorry. Here he is, George.'

Krantz handed the phone to Carella. 'Hello, Mr Cooper,' Carella said. 'Are you at home now? Do you expect to be there for a while? Well, I was wondering if my partner and I might stop by. As soon as we leave here. Fine. Would you let me have the address, please?' He took a ballpoint pen from his inside jacket pocket, and began writing the address on an MBA memo slip. 'Fine,' he said again. 'Thank you, Mr Cooper, we'll see you in a half hour or so. Goodbye.' He handed the phone back to Krantz, who replaced it on the cradle.

'Is there anything else I can do for you?' Krantz asked.

'Yes,' Meyer said. 'You can ask your secretary to get us the addresses and phone numbers of everyone who was in the sponsor's booth when you went up there last night.'

'Why? Are you going to check to see that I *really* went up there fifteen minutes before the show?'

'And *remained* there until Gifford collapsed, right?'

'Right,' Krantz said. He shrugged. 'Go ahead, check it. I'm telling the exact truth. I have nothing to hide.'

'We're sure you haven't,' Carella said pleasantly. 'Have her call us with the information, will you?' He extended his hand, thanked Krantz for his time, and then walked out past Gladine's desk, Meyer following him. When they got to the elevator, Meyer said, 'Re*mark*able!'

The Quarter was all the way downtown, jammed into a minuscule portion of the city, its streets as crowded as a bazaar. Jewellery shops, galleries, bookstores, sidewalk cafés, expresso joints, pizzerias, paintings on the kerb, bars, basement theatres, art movie houses, all combined to give The Quarter the flavour, if not the productivity, of a real avant-garde community. George Cooper lived on the second floor of a small apartment building on a tiny, twisting street. The fire escapes were hung with flowerpots and brightly coloured serapes, the doorways were painted pastel oranges and greens, the brass was polished, the whole street had been conceived and executed by the people who dwelt in it, as quaintly phony as a blind con man.

They knocked on Cooper's door and waited. He answered it with the same scowling expression Meyer had come to love the night before.

'Mr Cooper?' Meyer said. 'You remember me, don't you?'

'Yes, come in,' Cooper said. He scowled at Meyer, whom he knew, and then impartially scowled at Carella, who was a stranger.

'This is Detective Carella.'

Cooper nodded and led them into the apartment. The living room was sparsely furnished, a narrow black couch against one wall, two black Bertoia chairs against another, the decorating scheme obviously planned to minimize the furnishings and emphasize the modern paintings that hung facing each other on the remaining two walls. The detectives sat on the couch. Cooper sat in one of the chairs opposite them.

'What we'd like to know, Mr Cooper, is where Stan Gifford went last night while those folk singers were on,' Carella said.

'He went to his dressing room,' Cooper answered without hesitation.

'How do you know that?'

'Because that's where I went to cue him later on.'

'I see. Was he alone in the dressing room?'

'No,' Cooper said.

'Who was with him?'

'Art Wetherley. And Maria Vallejo.'

'Wetherley's a writer,' Meyer explained to Carella. 'Who's Maria – what's her name?'

'Vallejo. She's our wardrobe mistress.'

'And they were both with Mr Gifford when you went to call him?'

'Yes.'

'Would you know how long they were with him?'

'No.'

'How long did *you* stay in the dressing room, Mr Cooper?'

'I knocked on the door, and Stan said, "Come in," and I opened the door, poked my head inside and said, "Two minutes, Stan," and he said, "Okay," and I waited until he came out.'

'Did he come out immediately?'

'Well, almost immediately. A few seconds. You can't kid around on television. Everything's timed to the second, you know. Stan knew that. Whenever he was cued, he came.'

'Then you really didn't spend any time at all in the dressing room, did you, Mr Cooper?'

'No. I didn't even go inside. As I told you, I just poked my head in.'

'Were they talking when you looked in?'

'I think so, yes.'

'They weren't arguing or anything, were they?'

'No, but. . . .' Cooper shook his head.

'What is it, Mr Cooper?'

'Nothing. Would you fellows like a drink?'

'Thanks, no,' Meyer said. 'You're sure you didn't hear anyone arguing?'

'No.'

'No raised voices?'

'No.' Cooper rose. 'If you don't mind, I'll have one. It's not too early to have one, is it?'

'No, go ahead,' Carella said.

Cooper walked into the other room. They heard him pouring his drink, and then he came back into the living room with a short glass containing ice cubes and a healthy triple shot of whisky. 'I hate to drink so damn early in the afternoon,' he said. 'I was on the wagon for a year, you know. How old do you think I am?'

'I don't know,' Carella said.

'Twenty-eight. I look older than that, don't I?'

'No, I wouldn't say so,' Carella said.

'I used to drink a lot,' Cooper explained, and then took a swallow from the glass. The scowl seemed to vanish from his face at once. 'I've cut down.'

'When Mr Gifford left the dressing room,' Meyer said, 'you were with him, right?'

'Yes.'

'Did you meet anyone between the dressing room and the stage?'

'Not that I remember. Why?'

'Would you remember if you'd met anyone?'

'I think so, yes.'

'Then the last people who were with Gifford were Art Wetherley, Maria Vallejo, and you. In fact, Mr Cooper, if we want to be absolutely accurate, the very *last* person was *you*.'

'I suppose so. No, wait a minute. I think he said a word to one of the cameramen, just before he went on. Something about coming in for the close shot. Yes, I'm sure he did.'

'Did Mr Gifford eat anything in your presence?'

'No.'

'Drink anything?'

'No.'

'Put anything into his mouth at all?'

'No.'

'Was he eating or drinking anything when you went into the dressing room?'

'I didn't *go* in, I only *looked* in. I think maybe there were some coffee containers around. I'm not sure.'

'They were drinking coffee?'

'I told you, I'm not sure.'

Carella nodded and then looked at Meyer and then looked at Cooper, and then very slowly and calmly said, 'What is it you want to tell us, Mr Cooper?'

Cooper shrugged. 'Anything you want to know.'

'Yes, but specifically.'

'I don't want to get anybody in trouble.'

'What is it, Mr Cooper?'

'Well ... well, Stan had a fight with Art Wetherley yesterday. Just before the show. Not a fight, an argument. Words. And ... I said something about I wished Stan would calm down before we went on the air, and Art ... Look, I don't want to get him in trouble. He's a nice guy, and I wouldn't even mention this, but the papers said Stan was poisoned and ... well, I don't know.'

'What did he say, Mr Cooper?'

'He said he wished Stan would drop dead.'

Carella was silent for a moment. He rose then and said, 'Can you tell us where Mr Wetherley lives, please?'

Cooper told them where Wetherley lived, but it didn't matter very much because Wetherley was out when they got there. They checked downstairs with his landlady, who said she had seen him leaving the building early that morning, no he didn't have any luggage with him, why in the world would he be carrying luggage at ten o'clock in the morning? Carella and Meyer told the landlady that perhaps he would be carrying luggage if he planned to leave the city, and the landlady told them he never left the city on Thursday because that was when MBA ran the tape of the show from the night before so the writers could see which jokes had got the laughs and which hadn't, and that was very important in Mr Wetherley's line of work. Carella and Meyer explained that perhaps, after what had happened last night, the tape might not be run today. But the landlady said it didn't matter what had happened last night, they'd probably get a replacement for the show, and then Mr Wetherley would have to write for it, anyway, so it was very important that he see the tape today and know where the audience laughed and where it didn't. They thanked her, and then called MBA, who told them the tape was not being shown today and no, Wetherley was not there.

They had coffee and crullers in a diner near Wetherley's apartment, debated putting out a Pickup-and-Hold on him, and decided that would be a little drastic on the basis of hearsay, assuming Cooper was telling the truth to begin with – which he might not have been. They were knowledgeable and hip cops and they knew all about this television ratrace where people slit each others' throats and stabbed each other in the back. It was, after all, quite possible that Cooper was lying. It was, in fact, quite possible that *everybody* was lying. So they called the squadroom and asked Bob O'Brien to put what amounted to a telephone surveillance on Wetherley's apartment, calling him every half hour, and warning him to stay right in that apartment where he was, in case he happened to answer the phone. O'Brien had nothing else to do but call Wetherley's apartment every half hour, being involved in trying to solve three seemingly related Grover Park muggings, so he was naturally very happy to comply with Carella's wishes. The two detectives discussed how large a tip they should leave the waitress, settled on a trifle more than fifteen per cent because she was fast and had good legs, and then went out into the street again.

The late afternoon air was crisp and sharp, the city vibrated with a shimmering clarity that caused buildings to leap out from the sky. The streets seemed longer, stretching endlessly to a distant horizon that was almost visible. The land marks both men had grown up with, the familiar sights that gave the city perspective and reality, seemed to surround them intimately now, seemed closer and more intricately detailed. You could reach out to touch them, you could see the sculptured stone eye of a gargoyle twelve storeys above the street. The people, too, the citizens who gave a city its tempo and its pace, walked with their topcoats open, no longer faceless, contagiously enjoying the rare autumn day, filling their lungs with air that seemed so suddenly sweet. Carella and Meyer crossed the avenue idly, both men smiling. They walked together with the city between them like a beautiful young girl, sharing her silently, somewhat awed in her radiant presence.

For a little while at least, they forgot they were investigating what looked like a murder.

Chapter Five

As Kling had anticipated, Cindy Forrest was not overwhelmed by the prospect of having to spend even an infinitesimal amount of time with him. She reluctantly admitted, however, that such a course might be less repulsive than the possibility of spending an equal amount of time in a hospital. It was decided that Kling would pick her up at the office at noon Friday, take her to lunch, and then walk her back again. He reminded her that he was a city employee and that there was no such thing as an expense account for taking citizens to lunch while trying to protect them, a subtlety Cindy looked upon as simply another index to Kling's personality. Not only was he obnoxious, but he was apparently cheap as well.

Thursday's beautiful weather had turned foreboding and blustery by Friday noon. The sky above was a solemn grey, the streets seemed dimmer, the people less animated. He picked her up at the office, and they walked in silence to a restaurant some six blocks distant. She was wearing high heels, but the top of her head still came only level with his chin. They were both blonde, both hatless. Kling walked with his hands in his coat pockets. Cindy kept her arms crossed over her middle, her hands tucked under them. When they reached the restaurant, Kling forgot to hold open the door for her, but only the faintest flick of Cindy's blue eyes showed that this was exactly what she expected from a man like him. Too late, he allowed her to precede him into the restaurant.

'I hope you like Italian food,' he said.

'Yes, I do,' she answered, 'but you might have asked *first*.'

'I'm sorry, but I have a few other things on my mind besides worrying about which restaurant you might like.'

'I'm sure you're a very busy man,' Cindy said.

'I am.'

'Yes, I'm sure.'

The owner of the restaurant, a short Neapolitan woman with masses of thick black hair framing her round and pretty face, mistook them for lovers and showed them to a secluded table at the rear of the place. Kling remembered to help Cindy off with her coat (she mumbled a polite thank you) and then further remembered to hold out her chair for her (she acknowledged this with a brief nod). The waiter took their order and they sat facing each other without a word to say.

The silence lengthened.

'Well, I can see this is going to be perfectly charming,' Cindy said. 'Lunch with you for the next God knows how long.'

'There are things I'd prefer doing myself, Miss Forrest,' Kling said. 'But, as you pointed out yesterday, I am only a civil servant. I do what I'm told to do.'

'Does Carella still work up there?' Cindy asked.

'Yes.'

'I'd much rather be having lunch with him.'

'Well, those are the breaks,' Kling said. 'Besides, he's married.'

'I know he is.'

'In fact, he's got two kids.'

'I know.'

'Mmm. Well, I'm sure he'd have loved this choice assignment, but unfortunately he's involved with a poisoning at the moment.'

'Who got poisoned?'

'Stan Gifford.'

'Oh? Is he working on that? I was reading about it in the paper just yesterday.'

'Yes, it's his case.'

'He must be a good detective. I mean, to get such an important case.'

'Yes, he's very good,' Kling said.

The table went silent again. Kling glanced over his shoulder towards the door, where a thickset man in a black overcoat was just entering.

'Is that your friend?' he asked.

'No. And he's *not* my friend.'

'The lieutenant thought he might have been one of your ex-boy friends.'

'No.'

'Or someone you'd met someplace.'

'No.'

'You're sure you didn't recognize any of those mug shots yesterday?'

'I'm positive. I don't know who the man is, and I can't imagine what he wants from me.'

'Well, the lieutenant has some ideas about that, too.'

'What were his ideas?'

'Well, I'd rather not discuss them.'

'Why not?'

'Because ... well, I'd just rather not.'

'Is it the lieutenant's notion that this man wants to lay me?' Cindy asked.

'What?'

'I said is it the –'

'Yes, something like that,' Kling answered, and then cleared his throat.

'I wouldn't be surprised,' Cindy said.

The waiter arrived at that moment, sparing Kling the necessity of further comment. Cindy had ordered the antipasto to start, a supposed speciality of the house. Kling had ordered a cup of minestrone. He carefully waited for her to begin eating before he picked up his spoon.

'How is it?' he asked her.

'Very good.' She paused. 'How's the soup?'

'Fine.'

They ate in silence for several moments.

'What *is* the plan exactly?' Cindy asked.

'The lieutenant thinks your admirer is something of a hothead, a

Eighty Million Eyes

reasonable assumption, I would say. He's hoping we'll be seen together, and
he's hoping our man will take a crack at me.'

'In which case?'

'In which case I will crack him back and carry him off to jail.'

'My hero,' Cindy said drily, and attacked an anchovy on her plate.

'I'm supposed to spend as much time with you as I can,' Kling said, and
paused. 'I guess we'll be having dinner together tonight.'

'What?'

'Yes,' Kling said.

'Look, Mr Kling –'

'It's not *my* idea, Miss Forrest.'

'Suppose I've made other plans?'

'Have you?'

'No, but –'

'Then there's no problem.'

'I don't usually go out for dinner, Mr Kling, unless someone is escorting
me.'

'I'll be escorting you.'

'That's not what I meant. I'm a working girl. I can't afford –'

'Well, I'm sorry about the financial arrangements, but as I explained –'

'Yes, well, you just tell your lieutenant I can't afford a long, leisurely
dinner every night, that's all. I earn a hundred and two dollars a week after
taxes, Mr Kling. I pay my own college tuition and the rent on my own
apartment –'

'Well, this shouldn't take too long. If our man spots us, he may make his
play fairly soon. In the meantime, we'll just have to go along with it. Have
you seen the new Hitchcock movie?'

'What?'

'The new –'

'No, I haven't.'

'I thought we'd go see it after dinner.'

'Why?'

'Got to stay together.' Kling paused. 'I could suggest a long walk as an
alternative, but it might be pretty chilly by tonight.'

'I could suggest your going home after dinner,' Cindy said. 'As an
alternative, you understand. Because to tell the truth, Mr Kling, I'm pretty
damned tired by the end of a working day. In fact, on Tuesdays,
Wednesdays, and Thursdays, I barely have time to grab a hamburger before
I run over to the school. I'm not a rah-rah party girl. I think you ought to
understand that.'

'Lieutenant's orders,' Kling said.

'Yeah, well, tell *him* to go see the new Hitchcock movie. I'll have dinner
with you, if you insist, but right after that I'm going to bed.' Cindy paused.
'And I'm *not* suggesting that as an alternative.'

'I didn't think you were.'

'Just so we know where we stand.'

'I know exactly where we stand,' Kling said. 'There are a lot of people in
this city, Miss Forrest, and one of them is the guy who's after you. I don't
know how long it'll take to smoke him out, I don't know when or where he'll
spot us. But I *do* know he's not going to see us together if you're safe and cosy

in your little bed and I'm safe and cosy in mine.' Kling took a deep breath.
'So what we're going to do, Miss Forrest, is have dinner together tonight,
and then see the Hitchcock movie. And then we'll go for coffee and
something afterwards, and then I'll take you home. Tomorrow's Saturday, so
we can plan on a nice long day together. Sunday, too. On Monday –'
'Oh, God,' Cindy said.
'You said it,' Kling answered. 'Cheer up, here comes your lasagna.'

Because a white man punched a Negro in a bar on Culver Avenue just
about the time Cindy Forrest was putting her first forkful of lasagna into her
mouth, five detectives of the 87th Precinct were pressed into emergency
duty to quell what looked like the beginnings of a full-scale riot. Two of
those detectives were Meyer and Carella, the theory being that Stan Gifford
was already dead and gone whereas the Culver Avenue fist fight could
possibly lead to a good many more corpses before nightfall if something were
not done about it immediately.

There was, of course, nothing that could be done about it immediately. A
riot will either start or not start, and all too often the presence of policemen
will only help to enflame a gathering crowd, defeating the reason for their
being there in the first place. The patrolmen and detectives of the 87th could
only play a waiting game, calming citizens wherever they could, spotting
people they knew in the crowd and talking good sense to them, assuring
them that *both* men involved in the fight had been arrested, and not only the
Negro. There were some who could be placated, and others who could not.
The cops roamed the streets like instant father images, trying to bind the
wounds of a century of speaking belated words of peace, by patting a
shoulder tolerantly, by asking to be accepted as friends. Too many of the
cops were not friends and the people knew goddamn well they weren't. Too
many of the cops were angry men with angry notions of their own about
Negroes and Puerto Ricans, inborn prejudices that neither example nor
reprimand could change. It was touch and go for a long while on that windy
October afternoon.

By four o'clock, the crowds began to disperse. The patrolmen were left
behind in double strength, but the detectives were relieved to resume their
investigations. Meyer and Carella went downtown to see Maria Vallejo.

Her street was in one of the city's better neighbourhoods, a block of old
brownstones with clean-swept stoops and curtained front doors. They
entered the tiny lobby with its polished brass mailboxes and bell buttons,
found a listing for Maria in apartment twenty-two, and rang the bell. The
answering buzz was long and insistent; it continued noisily behind them as
they climbed the carpeted steps to the second floor. They rang the bell
outside the door with its polished brass 2s. It opened almost immediately.

Maria was small and dark and bursting with energy. She was perhaps
thirty-two, with thick dark hair pulled tightly to the back of her head,
flashing brown eyes, a generous mouth, and a nose that had been turned up
by a plastic surgeon. She wore a white blouse and black tapered slacks. A
pair of large gold hoop earrings adorned her ears, but she wore no other
jewellery. She opened the door as though she were expecting party guests
and then looked out at the detectives in undisguised puzzlement.

'Yes?' she said. 'What is it?' She spoke without a trace of accent. If Carella had been forced to make a regional guess based on her speech, he'd have chosen Boston or one of its suburbs.

'We're from the police,' he said, flashing his buzzer. 'We're investigating the death of Stan Gifford.'

'Oh, sure,' she said. 'Come on in.'

They followed her into the apartment. The apartment was furnished in brimming good taste, cluttered with objects picked up in the city's better antique and junk shops. The shelves and walls were covered with ancient nutcrackers and old theatre posters and a French puppet, and watercolour sketches for costumes and stage sets, and several enamelled army medals, and black silk fan, and pieces of driftwood. The living room was small, with wide curtained windows overlooking the street, luminous with the glow of the afternoon sun. It was furnished with a sofa and chair covered in deep-green velvet, a bentwood rocker, a low needle-point footstool, and a marble-topped table on which lay several copies of *Paris Match*.

'Do sit down,' Maria said. 'Can I get you a drink? Oh, you're not allowed, are you? Some coffee?'

'I can use a cup,' Carella said.

'It's on the stove. I'll just pour it. I always keep a pot on the stove. I guess I drink a million cups of coffee a day.' She went into the small kitchen. They could see her standing at a round, glass-topped table over which hung a Tiffany lampshade, pouring the coffee from an enamelled hand-painted pot. She carried the cups, spoons, sugar, and cream into the living room on a small teakwood tray, shoved aside the copies of the French magazine to make room for it, and then served the detectives. She went to sit in the bentwood rocker then, sipping at her coffee, rocking idly back and forth.

'I bought this when Kennedy was killed,' she said. 'Do you like it? It keeps falling apart. What did you want to know about Stan?'

'We understand you were in his dressing room with him Wednesday night just before he went on, Miss Vallejo. Is that right?'

'That's right,' she said.

'Were you alone with him?'

'No, there were several people in the room.'

'Who?'

'Gee, I don't remember offhand. I think Art was there, yes . . . and maybe one other person.'

'George Cooper?'

'Yes, that's right. Say, how did *you* know?'

Carella smiled. 'But Mr Cooper didn't come into the room, did he?'

'Oh, sure he did.'

'What I mean is, he simply knocked on the door and called Mr Gifford, isn't that right?'

'No, he came in,' Maria said. 'He was there quite a while.'

'How much time would you say Mr Cooper spent in the dressing room?'

'Oh, maybe five minutes.'

'You remember that clearly, do you?'

'Oh, yes. He was there, all right.'

'What else do you remember, Miss Vallejo? What happened in that dressing room Wednesday night?'

'Oh, nothing. We were just talking. Stan was relaxing while those singers were on, and I just sort of drifted in to have a smoke and chat, that's all.'

'What did you chat about?'

'I don't remember.' She shrugged. 'It was just small talk. The monitor was going and those nuts were singing in the background, so we were just making small talk, that's all.'

'Did Mr Gifford eat anything? Or drink anything?'

'Gee, no. No, he didn't. We were just talking.'

'No coffee? Nothing like that?'

'No. No, I'm sorry.'

'Did he take a vitamin pill? Would you happen to have noticed that?'

'Gee, no, I didn't notice.'

'Or *any* kind of a pill?'

'No, we were just talking, that's all.'

'Did you like Mr Gifford?'

'Well . . .'

Maria hesitated. She got out of the rocker and walked to a coffee table near the couch. She put down her cup, and then walked back to the rocker again, and then shrugged.

'Did you like him, Miss Vallejo?'

'I don't like to talk about the dead,' she said.

'We were talking about him just fine until a minute ago.'

'I don't like to speak *ill* of the dead,' she corrected.

'Then you didn't like him?'

'Well, he was a little demanding, that's all.'

'Demanding how?'

'I'm the show's wardrobe mistress, you know.'

'Yes, we know.'

'I've got eight people working under me. That's a big staff. I'm responsible for all of them, and it's not easy to costume that show each week, believe me. Well, I . . . I don't think Stan made the job any easier, that's all. He . . . well . . . well, really, he didn't *know* very much about costumes, and he pretended he did, and . . . well, he got on my nerves sometimes, that's all.'

'I see,' Carella said.

'But you went into his dressing room to chat, anyway,' Meyer said through his nose, and then sniffed.

'Well, there wasn't a feud between us or anything like that. It's just that every once in a while, we yelled at each other a little, that's all. Because he didn't know a damn thing about costumes, and I happen to know a great deal about costumes, that's all. But that didn't stop me from going into his dressing room to chat a little. I don't see anything so terribly wrong about going into his dressing room to chat a little.'

'No one said anything was wrong, Miss Vallejo.'

'I mean, I know a man's been murdered and all, but that's no reason to start examining every tiny little word that was said, or every little thing that was done. People *do* argue, you know.'

'Yes, we know.'

Maria paused. She stopped rocking, and she turned her head towards the curtained windows streaming sunlight and very softly said, 'Oh, what's the use? I guess they've already told you Stan and I hated each other's guts.' She shrugged her shoulders hopelessly. 'I think he was going to fire me. I heard he wouldn't put up with me any longer.'

'Who told you that?'

'David. He said – David Krantz, our producer – he said Stan was about to give me the axe. That's why I went to his dressing room Wednesday night. To ask him about it, to try to ... well, the job pays well. Personalities shouldn't enter into a person's work. I didn't want to lose the job, that's all.'

'*Did* you discuss the job with him?'

'I started to, but then Art came in, and right after that George, so I didn't get a chance.' She paused again. 'I guess it's academic now, isn't it?'

'I guess so.'

Meyer blew his nose noisily, put his tissue away, and then casually said, 'Are you very well known in the field, Miss Vallejo?'

'Oh, yes, sure.'

'So even if Mr Gifford *had* fired you, you could always get another job. Isn't that so?'

'Well ... word gets around pretty fast in this business. It's not good to get fired from *any* job, I'm sure you know that. And in television ... I would have preferred to resign, that's all. So I wanted to clear it up, you see, which is why I went to his dressing room. To clear it up. If it was true he was going to let me go, I wanted the opportunity of leaving the job of my own volition, that's all.'

'But you never got a chance to discuss it.'

'No. I told you. Art walked in.'

'Well, thank you, Miss Vallejo,' Carella said, rising. 'That was very good coffee.'

'Listen ...'

She had come out of the bentwood rocker now, the rocker still moving back and forth, and she stood in the centre of the room with the sun blazing on the curtains behind her. She worried her lip for a moment, and then said, 'Listen, I didn't have anything to do with this.'

Meyer and Carella said nothing.

'I didn't like Stan, and maybe he was going to fire me, but I'm not nuts, you know. I'm a little temperamental maybe, but I'm not nuts. We didn't get along, that's all. That's no reason to kill a man. I mean, a lot of people on the show didn't get along with Stan. He was a difficult man, that's all, and the star. We blew our stacks every now and then, that's all. But I didn't kill him. I ... I wouldn't know how to begin hurting someone.'

The detectives kept staring at her. Maria gave a small shrug.

'That's all,' she said.

The afternoon was dying by the time they reached the street again. Carella glanced at his watch and said, 'Let's call Bob, see if he had any luck with our friend Wetherley.'

'You call,' Meyer said. 'I feel miserable.'

'You'd better get to bed,' Carella said.

'You know what Fanny Brice said is the best cure for a cold, don't you?' Meyer asked.

'No, what?'

'Put a hot Jew on your chest.'

'Better take some aspirin, too,' Carella advised.

They went into the nearest drugstore, and Carella called the squadroom. O'Brien told him he had tried Wetherley's number three times that afternoon, but no one had answered the phone. Carella thanked him, hung up, and went out to the car, where Meyer was blowing his nose and looking very sick indeed. By the time they got back to the squadroom, O'Brien had called the number a fourth time, again without luck. Carella told Meyer to get the hell home, but Meyer insisted on typing up at least one of the reports on the people they'd talked to in the past two days. He left the squadroom some twenty minutes before Carella. Carella finished the reports in time to greet his relief, Andy Parker, who was a half hour late as usual. He tried Wetherley's number once more, and then told Parker to keep trying it all night long, and to call him at home if he reached Wetherley. Parker assured him that he would, but Carella wasn't at all sure he'd keep the promise.

He got home to his house in Riverhead at seven-fifteen. The twins met him at the door, almost knocking him over in their headlong rush to greet him. He picked up one under each arm, and was swinging them towards the kitchen when the telephone rang.

He put down the children and went to the phone.

'Hello?' he said.

'Bet you thought I wouldn't, huh?' the voice said.

'Who's this?'

'Andy Parker. I just called Wetherley. He told me he got home about ten minutes ago. I advised him to stick around until you got there.'

'Oh,' Carella said. 'Thanks.'

He hung up and turned towards the kitchen, where Teddy was standing in the doorway. He looked at her silently for several moments, and she stared back at him, and then he shrugged and said simply, 'I guess I can eat before I leave.'

Teddy sighed almost imperceptibly, but Mark, the eldest of the twins by five minutes, was watching the byplay with curious intensity. He made a vaguely resigned gesture with one hand and said, 'There he goes.' And April, thinking it was a game, threw herself into Carella's arms, squeezed the breath out of him, and squealed, 'There he goes, there he goes, there he goes!'

Art Wetherley was waiting for him when he got there. He led Carella through the apartment and into a studio overlooking the park. The studio contained a desk upon which sat a typewriter, an ash tray, a ream of blank paper and what looked like another ream of typewritten sheets covered with pencilled hen scratches. There were several industry award plaques on the wall, and a low bookcase beneath them. Wetherley gestured to one of the two chairs in the room, and Carella sat in it. He seemed extremely calm, eminently at ease, but the ash tray on his desk was full of cigarettes, and he lighted another one now.

'I'm not used to getting phone calls from the police,' he said at once.

'Well, we were here –'

'Especially when they tell me to stay where I am, not to leave the apartment.'

'Andy Parker isn't the most tactful –'

'I mean, I didn't know this was a dictatorship,' Wetherley said.

'It isn't, Mr Wetherley,' Carella said gently. 'We're investigating a murder, however, and we were here yesterday, but –'

'I was staying with a friend.'

'What friend?'

'A girl I know. I felt pretty shook up Wednesday night after this ... thing happened, so I went over to her apartment. I've been there the past two days.' Wetherley paused. 'There's no law against that, is there?'

'Certainly not,' Carella smiled. 'I'm sorry if we inconvenienced you, but we did want to ask you some questions.'

Wetherley seemed slightly mollified. 'Well, all right,' he said. 'But there was no need, really, to warn me not to leave the apartment.'

'I apologize for that, Mr Wetherley.'

'Well, all right,' Wetherley said.

'I wonder if you could tell me what happened in Stan Gifford's dressing room Wednesday night. Just before he left it.'

'I don't remember in detail.'

'Well, tell me what you *do* remember.'

Wetherley thought for a moment, crushed out his cigarette, lighted a new one, and then said, 'Maria was there when I came in. She was arguing with Stan about something. At least ...'

'Arguing?'

'Yes. I could hear them shouting at each other before I knocked on the door.'

'Go ahead.'

'The atmosphere was a little strained after I went in, and Maria didn't say very much all the while I was there. But Stan and I were joking, mostly about the folk singers. He hated folk singers, but this particular group is hot right now, and he was talked into hiring them.'

'So you were making jokes about them?'

'Yes. While we watched the act on the monitor.'

'I see. In a friendly manner, would you say?'

'Oh, yes.'

'Then what happened?'

'Well ... then George came in. George Cooper, the show's A.D.'

'He came into the room?'

'Yes.'

'How long did he stay?'

'Oh, three or four minutes, I guess.'

'I see. But *he* didn't argue with Gifford, did he?'

'No.'

'Just Maria?'

'Yes. Before I got there, you understand.'

'Yes, I understand. And what about you?' Carella asked.

'Me?'

'Yes. What about your argument with Gifford before the show went on the air?'

'Argument? Who said there was an argument?'

'Wasn't there one?'

'Certainly not.'

Carella took a deep breath. 'Mr Wetherley, didn't you say you wished Stan Gifford would drop dead?'

'No, sir.'

'You did *not* say that?'

'No, sir, I did not. Stan and I got along very well.' Wetherley paused. 'A lot of people on the show *didn't* get along with him, you understand. But I never had any trouble.'

'*Who* didn't get along with him, Mr Wetherley?'

'Well, Maria, for one, I just told you that. And David Krantz didn't particularly like him. He was always saying within earshot of Stan, that all actors are cattle, and that comedians are only funny actors. And George Cooper didn't exactly enjoy his role of . . . well, handyman, almost. Keeping everyone quiet on the set, and running for coffee, and bringing Stan his pills, and making sure everybody –'

'Bringing Stan his *what*?'

'His pills,' Wetherley said. 'Stan was a nervous guy, you know. I guess he was on tranquillizers. Anyway, George was the chief errand boy and bottle washer, hopping whenever Stan snapped his fingers.'

'Did George bring him a pill Wednesday night?'

'When?' Wetherley asked.

'Wednesday night. When he came to the dressing room.'

Wetherley concentrated for a moment, and then said, 'Now that you mention it, I think he did.'

'You're sure about that?'

'Yes, sir. I'm positive.'

'And did Stan *take* the pill from him?'

'Yes, sir.'

'And did he swallow it?'

'Yes, sir.'

Carella rose suddenly. 'Would you mind coming along with me, Mr Wetherley?' he asked.

'Come along? Where?'

'Uptown. There are a few things we'd like to get straight.'

The few things Carella wanted to get straight were the conflicting stories of the last three people to have been with Gifford before he went on camera. He figured that the best way to do this was in the squadroom, where the police would have the psychological advantage in the question-and-answer game. There was nothing terribly sinister about the green globes hanging outside the station house, or about the high desk in the muster room or the sign advising all visitors to stop at the desk, or even the white sign announcing DETECTIVE DIVISION in bold black letters, and pointing towards the iron-runged steps leading upstairs. There was certainly nothing menacing about the steps themselves or the narrow corridor they opened onto, or the various rooms in that corridor with their neatly lettered signs, INTERROGATION, LAVATORY, CLERICAL. The slatted-wood railing that divided the corridor from the squadroom was innocuous-looking, and the squadroom itself – in spite of the fire-mesh grids over the windows – looked like any business office in the city, with desks, and filing cabinets and ringing telephones, and a water cooler, and bulletin boards, and men working in shirt sleeves. But Art Wetherley, Maria Vallejo, and George Cooper were visibly rattled by their surroundings, and they became more rattled when they were taken into separate rooms for their interrogations. Bob O'Brien, a big cop with a sweet and innocently boyish look, questioned Cooper in the lieutenant's office. Steve Carella questioned Maria in the Clerical Office, kicking out Alf Miscolo, who was busy typing up his records and complained bitterly. Meyer Meyer, suffering from a cold, and not ready to take any nonsense, questioned Art Wetherley at the table in the barely furnished Interrogation Room. The three detectives had decided beforehand what questions they would ask, and what their approach would be. In separate rooms, with different suspects, they went through a familiar routine.

'You said you weren't drinking coffee, Miss Vallejo,' Carella said. 'Mr Cooper tells us there were coffee containers in that room. Were there or weren't there?'
'No. I don't remember. I know *I* didn't have any coffee.'
'Did Art Wetherley?'
'No. I didn't see him drink anything.'
'Did George Cooper hand Gifford a pill?'
'No.'
'Were you arguing with Gifford before Art Wetherley came in?'
'No.'

'Let's go over this one more time, Mr Cooper.' O'Brien said. 'You say you only knocked on the door and poked your head into the room, is that right?'
'That's right.'
'You were there only a few seconds.'
'Yes. Look, I –'
'Did you give Stan Gifford a pill?'
'A pill? No! No, I didn't!'
'But there were coffee containers in the room, huh?'
'Yes. Look, I didn't give him anything! What are you trying . . . ?'
'Did you hear Art Wetherley say he wished Gifford would drop dead?'
'Yes!'

'All right, Wetherley,' Meyer said, 'when did Cooper give him that pill?'
'As soon as he came into the room.'
'And Gifford washed it down with what?'
'With the coffee we were drinking.'
'You were all drinking coffee, huh?'
'Yes.'
'*Who* was?'
'Maria, and Stan, and I was, too.'

'Then why'd you go to that room, Maria, if not to argue?'
'I went to . . . to talk to him. I thought we could –'
'But you *were* arguing, weren't you?'
'No. I swear to God, I wasn't –'

'Then why are you lying about the coffee? Were you drinking coffee, or weren't you?'

'No. No coffee. Please, I ...'

'Now hold it, hold it, Mr Cooper. You were either in that room or not in it. You either gave him a pill or you –'

'I didn't, I'm telling you.'

'Did you *ever* give him pills?'

'No.'

'He was taking tranquillizers, wasn't he?'

'I don't know what he was taking. I never brought him anything.'

'Never?'

'Once maybe, or twice. An aspirin. If he had a headache.'

'But never a tranquillizer?'

'No.'

'How about a vitamin capsule?'

'He handed him the pill,' Wetherley said.

'What kind of a pill?'

'I don't know.'

'Think!'

'I'm thinking. A small pill.'

'What colour?'

'White.'

'A tablet, you mean? Like an aspirin? Like that?'

'Yes. Yes, I think so. I don't remember.'

'Well, you saw it, didn't you?'

'Yes, but ...'

They put it all together afterwards in the squadroom. They left the three suspects in the lieutenant's office with a patrolman watching over them and sat around Carella's desk and compared their answers. They were not particularly pleased with the results, but neither were they surprised by them. They had all been cops for a good many years, and nothing human beings perpetrated against each other ever surprised them. They were perhaps a little saddened by what they discovered each and every time, but never surprised. They were used to dealing with facts, and they accepted the facts in the Stan Gifford case with grim resolution.

The facts were simple and disappointing.

They decided after comparing results that all three of their suspects were lying.

Maria Vallejo *had* been arguing with Gifford, and she *had* been drinking coffee, but she denied both allegations because she realized how incriminating these seemingly isolated circumstances might seem. She recognized quite correctly that someone could have poisoned Gifford by dropping something into his coffee. If she admitted there had been coffee in the dressing room, that indeed she and Gifford had been drinking coffee together, and if she then further admitted they'd been arguing, could she not have been the one who slipped the lethal dose into the sponsor's brew? So Maria had lied in her teeth, but had graciously refused to incriminate anyone else while she was lying. It was enough for her to fabricate her own way out of what seemed like a horrible trap.

Art Wetherley had indeed wished his employer would drop dead, and he had wished it out loud, and he had wished it in the presence of someone else. And that night, lo and behold, Stan Gifford *did* collapse, on camera, for millions to see. Art Wetherley, like a child who'd made a fervent wish, was startled to realize it had come true. Not only was he startled; he was frightened. He immediately remembered what he'd said to George Cooper before the show, and he was certain Cooper would remember it, too. His fear reached new dimensions when he recalled that he had been one of the last few people to spend time with Gifford while he was alive, and that his proximity to Gifford in an obvious poisoning case, coupled with his chance remark during rehearsal, could easily serve to pin a thoroughly specious murder rap on him. When a detective called and warned him not to leave the apartment, Wetherley was certain he'd been picked as the patsy of the year, an award that did not come gold-plated like an Emmy. In desperation, he had tried to discredit Cooper's statement by turning the tables and presenting Cooper as a suspect himself. He had seen Cooper bringing aspirins to Gifford at least a few times in the past three years. He decided to elaborate on what he'd seen, inventing a pill that had never changed hands on the night Gifford died, senselessly incriminating Cooper. But a frightened man doesn't care who takes the blame, so long as it's not himself.

In much the same way, Cooper came to the sudden realization that not only was he one of the last people to be with Gifford, he was *the* last person. Even though he had spent several minutes with Gifford in the dressing room, he thought it was safer to say he had only poked his head into it. And whereas Gifford hadn't stopped to talk to a soul before he went on camera, Cooper thought it was wiser to add a mystery cameraman. Then, to clinch his own escape from what seemed like a definitely compromising position, he remembered Wetherley's earlier outburst and promptly paraded it before the investigating cops, even though he knew the expression was one that was uttered a hundred times a day during any television rehearsal.

Liars all.

But murderers none.

The detectives were convinced, after a gruelling three-hour session, that these assorted liars were now babbling all in the cleansing catharsis of truth. Yes, we lied, they all separately admitted, but now we speak the truth, the shining truth. We did not kill Stan Gifford. We wouldn't know strohoosis from a hole in the wall. Besides, we are kind gentle people; look at us. Liars, yes, but murderers, no. We did not kill. That is the truth.

We did not kill.

The detectives believed them.

They had heard enough lies in their professional lives to know that truth has a shattering ring that can topple skyscrapers. They sent the three home without apologizing for any inconvenience. Bob O'Brien yawned, stretched, asked Carella if he needed him any more, put on his hat, and left. Meyer and Carella sat in the lonely squadroom and faced each other across the desk. It was five minutes to midnight. When the telephone rang, it momentarily startled them. Meyer lifted it from the cradle.

'Meyer, 87th Squad,' he said. 'Oh, hi, George.' To Carella, he whispered,

'It's Temple. I had him out checking Krantz's alibi.' Into the phone again, he said, 'What'd you get? Right. Uh-huh. Right. Okay, thanks.' He hung up. 'He finally got to the last person on Krantz's list, that Hollywood director. He'd been to the theatre, just got back to the hotel. His little bimbo was with him.' Meyer wiggled his eyebrows.

Carella looked at him wearily. 'What'd Temple get?'

'He says they all confirmed Krantz's story. He got to the sponsor's booth a good fifteen minutes before the show went on, and he was there right up to the time Gifford got sick.'

'Mmm,' Carella said.

They stared at each other glumly. Midnight had come and gone; it was another day. Meyer sniffed noisily. Carella yawned and then washed his hand over his face.

'What do you think?' he said.

'I don't know. What do *you* think?'

'I don't know.'

The men were silent.

'Maybe he *did* kill himself,' Carella said.

'Maybe.'

'Oh, man, I'm exhausted,' Carella said.

Meyer sniffed.

Chapter Six

He had followed them to the restaurant and the movie theatre, and now he stood in the doorway across from her house, waiting for her to come home. It was a cold night, and he stood huddled deep in the shadows, his coat collar pulled high on the back of his neck, and his hands thrust into his coat pockets, his hat low on his forehead.

It was ten minutes past twelve, and they had left the movie theatre at eleven-forty-five, but he knew they would be coming straight home. He had been watching the girl long enough now to know a few things about her, and one of those things was that she didn't sleep around much. Last month sometime, she had shacked up with a guy on Banning Street, just for the night, and the next morning after she left the apartment he had gone up to the guy and had worked him over with a pair of brass knuckles, leaving him crying like a baby on the kitchen floor. He had warned the guy against calling the police, and he had also told him he should never go near Cindy Forrest again, never try to see her again, never even try to call her again. The guy had held his broken mouth together with one bloody hand, and nodded his head, and begged not to be hit again – that was one guy who wouldn't be bothering *her* any more. So he knew she didn't sleep around too much, and besides he knew she wouldn't be going anyplace but straight home with this blond guy because this blond guy was a cop.

He had got the fuzz smell from him almost the minute he first saw him, early this afternoon when he came to the office to take her to lunch. He knew the look of fuzz and the smell of fuzz, and he realized right off that the very smart bulls of this wonderful city were setting a trap for him and that he was supposed to fall right into it – here I am, fuzz, take me.

Like fun.

He had stayed far away from the restaurant where they had lunch, getting the fuzz stink sharp and clear in his nostrils and knowing something was up, but not knowing what kind of a trap was being set for him, and wanting to make damn sure before he made another move. The blond guy walked like a cop, that was an unmistakable cop walk. And also he had a sneaky way of making the scene, his head turned in one direction while he was really casing the opposite direction, a very nice fuzz trick that known criminals sometimes utilized, but that mostly cops from here to Detroit and back again were very familiar with. Well, he had known cops all across this fine little country of America, he had busted more cops' heads than he could count on all his fingers and toes. He wouldn't mind busting another, just for the fun of it, but not until he knew what the trap was. The one thing he wasn't going to do was walk into a trap.

In the wintertime, or like now when it was getting kind of chilly and a guy had to wear a coat, you could always tell when he was heeled because if he was wearing a shoulder harness, the button between the top one and the third one was always left unbuttoned. If he was wearing the holster clipped to his belt, then a button was left undone just above the waist, so the right hand could reach in and draw – that was the first concrete tipoff that Blondie was a cop. He was a cop, and he wore his gun clipped to his belt. Watching him from outside the plate-glass window of the second restaurant later that day, there had been the flash of Blondie's tin when he went to pay his check, opening his wallet, with the shield catching light for just a second. That was the second concrete fact, and a smart man don't need more than one or two facts to piece together a story, not when the fuzz smell is all over the place to begin with.

The only thing he didn't know now was what the trap was, and whether or not he should accommodate Blondie by walking into it and maybe beating him up. He thought it would be better to work on the girl, though. It was time the girl learned what she could do and couldn't do, there was no sense putting it off. The girl had to know that she couldn't go sleeping around with no guys on Banning Street, or for that matter anyplace in the city. And she also had to know she couldn't play along with the cops on whatever trap they were cooking up. She had to know it now, and once and for all, because he wasn't planning on staying in the shadows for long. The girl had to know she was *his* meat and his *alone*.

He guessed he'd beat her up tonight.

He looked at his watch again. It was fifteen minutes past twelve, and he began to wonder what was keeping them. Maybe he should have stuck with them when they came out of the movie house, instead of rushing right over here. Still, if Blondie –

A car was turning into the street.

He pulled back into the shadows and waited. The car came up the street slowly. Come on, Blondie, he thought, you ain't being followed, there's no reason to drive slow. He grinned in the darkness. The car pulled to the kerb.

Blondie got out and walked around to the other side, holding open the door for the girl, and then walking her up the front steps. The building was a grey, four-storey job, and the girl lived on the top floor rear. The name on the bell read C. FORREST, that was the first thing he'd found out about her, almost two months ago. A little while after that, he'd broken open the lock on her mailbox and found two letters addressed to Miss Cynthia Forrest – it was a good thing she wasn't married, because if she was, her husband would have been in for one hell of a time – and another letter addressed to Miss Cindy Forrest, this one from a guy over in Thailand, serving with the Peace Corps. The guy was lucky he was over in Thailand, or he'd have had a visitor requesting him to stop writing letters to little Sweetpants.

Blondie was unlocking the inner vestibule door for her now. The girl said good night – he could hear her voice clear across the street – and Blondie gave her the keys and said something with his back turned, and which couldn't be heard. Then the door closed behind her, and Blondie came down the steps, walking with a funny fuzz walk, like a boxer moving towards the ring where a pushover sparring partner was waiting, and keeping his head ducked, though this was a cop trick and those eyes were most likely flashing up and down the street in either direction even though the head was ducked and didn't seem to be turning. Blondie got into the car – the engine was still running – put it into gear, and drove off.

He waited.

In five minutes' time, the car pulled around the corner again and drifted slowly past the grey building.

He almost burst out laughing. What did Blondie think he was playing around with, an amateur? He waited until the car rounded the corner again, and then he waited for at least another fifteen minutes, until he was sure Blondie wasn't coming back.

He crossed the street rapidly then, and walked around the corner and into the building directly behind the girl's. He went straight through the building, opening the door at the rear of the ground floor and stepping out into the back yard. He climbed the clothesline pole near the fence separating the yard from the one behind it, leaped over the fence, and dropped to his knees. Looking up, he could see a light burning in the girl's window on the fourth floor. He walked towards the rear of the building, cautiously but easily, jumping up for the fire-escape ladder, pulling it down, and then swinging up onto it and beginning to climb. He went by each window with great care, especially the other lighted one on the second floor, flitting past it like a shadow and continuing on up to the third floor, and then stepping onto the fourth-floor fire escape, *her* fire escape.

There was a wooden cheese box resting on the iron slats of the fire escape floor, the dried twigs of dead flowers stuck into the stiff earth it contained. The fire escape was outside her bedroom. He peered around the edge of the window, but the room was empty. He glanced to his right and saw that the tiny bathroom window was lighted; the girl was in the bathroom. He debated going right into the bedroom while she was occupied down the hall, but decided against it. He wanted to wait until she was in bed. He wanted to scare her real good.

The only light in the room came from a lamp on the night table near the girl's bed. The bed was clearly visible from where he crouched outside on the fire escape. There was a single chair on this side of the bed, he would have to avoid that in the dark. He wanted his surprise to be complete; he didn't want to go stumbling over no furniture and waking her up before it was time. The window was open just a trifle at the top, probably to let in some air, she'd probably opened it when she came into the apartment. He didn't know whether or not she'd close and lock it before going to bed, maybe she would. This was a pretty decent neighbourhood, though, without any incidents lately – he'd checked on that because he was afraid some cheap punk might burst into the girl's apartment and complicate things for him – so maybe she slept with the window open just a little, at the top, the way it was now. While she was in the bathroom, he studied the simple lock on the sash and decided it wouldn't be a problem, anyway, even if she locked it.

The bathroom light went out suddenly.

He flattened himself against the brick wall of the building. The girl was humming when she came into the room. The humming trailed off abruptly, she was turning on the radio. It came on very loud, for Christ's sake, she was going to wake up the whole damn building! She kept twisting the dial until she found the station she wanted, sweet music, lots of violins and muted trumpets, and then she lowered the volume. He waited. In a moment, she came to the window and pulled down the shade. Good, he thought, she didn't lock the window. He waited a moment longer, and then flattened himself onto the fire escape so that he could peer into the room beneath the lower edge of the shade, where the girl had left a good two-inch gap between it and the window sill.

The girl was still dressed. She was wearing the tan dress she had worn to dinner with Blondie, but when she turned away and began walking towards the closet, he saw that she had already lowered the zipper at the back. The dress was spread in a wide V, the white elastic line of her brassiere crossing her back, the zipper lowered to a point just above the beginning curve of her buttocks. The radio was playing a song she knew, and she began humming along with it again as she opened the closet door and took her nightgown from a hook. She closed the door and then walked to the bed, sitting on the side facing the window and lifting her dress up over her thighs to unhook first one garter and then the other. She took off her shoes and rolled down her stockings, and then walked to the closet to put the shoes away and to put the stockings into some kind of a bag hanging on the inside doorknob. She closed the door again, and then took off her dress, standing just outside the closet and not moving towards the bed again. In her bra and half slip, she walked over to the other side of the room, where he couldn't see her any more, almost as if the lousy little bitch knew he was watching her! She was still humming. His hands were wet. He dried them on the sleeves of his coat and waited.

She came back so suddenly that she startled him. She had taken off her underwear, and she walked swiftly to the bed, naked, to pick up her nightgown. Jesus, she was beautiful! Jesus, he hadn't realized how goddamn beautiful she really was. He watched her as she bent slightly to pull the gown over her head, straightened, and then let it fall down over her breasts and her tilted hips. She yawned. She looked at her watch and then went across the room again, out of sight, and came back to the bed carrying a paperback book. She got into the bed, her legs parting, opening, as she swung up onto it, and then pulled the blanket up over her knees, and fluffed the pillow, and scratched her jaw, and opened the book. She yawned. She looked at her watch again, seemed to change her mind about reading the book, put it down on the night table, and yawned again.

A moment later, she turned out the light.

The first thing she heard was the voice.

It said 'Cindy,' and for the briefest tick of time she thought she was dreaming because the voice was just a whisper. And then she heard it again, 'Cindy,' hovering somewhere just above her face, and her eyes popped wide, and she tried to sit up but something pressed her fiercely back against the pillow. She opened her mouth to scream, but a hand clamped over her lips. She stared over the edge of the thick fingers into the darkness, trying to see. 'Be quiet, Cindy,' the voice said. 'Just be quiet now.'

His grip on her mouth was hard and tight. He was straddling her now, his knees on the bed, his legs tight against her pinioned arms, sitting on her abdomen, one arm flung across her chest, holding her to the pillow.

'Can you hear me?' he asked.

She nodded. His hand stayed tight on her mouth, hurting her. She wanted to bite his hand, but she could not free her mouth. His weight upon her was unbearable. She tried to move, but she was helplessly caught in the vice of his knees, the tight band of his arm thrown across her chest.

'Listen to me,' he said, 'I'm going to beat the shit out of you.'

She believed him instantly; terror rocketed into her skull. Her eyes were growing accustomed to the darkness. She could dimly see his grinning face hovering above her. His fingers smelled of tobacco. He kept his right hand clamped over her mouth, his left arm thrown across her chest, lower now, so that the hand was gripping her breast. He kept working his hand as he talked to her, grasping her through the thin nylon gown, squeezing her nipple as his voice continued in a slow lazy monotone, 'Do you know why I'm going to beat you, Cindy?'

She tried to shake her head, but his hand was so tight against her mouth that she could not move. She knew she would begin to cry within the next few moments. She was trembling beneath his weight. His hand was cruel on her breast. Each time he tightened it on her nipple, she winced with pain.

'I don't like you to go out with cops,' he said. 'I don't like you to go out with *anybody*, but cops especially.'

She could see his face clearly now. He was the same man who had come to the office, the same man who had beaten up the policeman. She remembered the way he had kicked the policeman when he was on the floor, and she began trembling more violently. She heard him laugh.

'I'm going to take my hand off your mouth now,' he said, 'because we have to talk. But if you scream, I'll kill you. Do you understand me?'

She tried to nod. His hand was relaxing. He was slowly lifting it from her mouth, cupped, as though cautiously peering under it to see if he had captured a fly. She debated screaming, and knew at once that if she did he would keep his promise and kill her. He shifted his body to the left, relaxing his grip across her chest, lifting his arms, freeing her breast. He rested his hands palms downwards on his thighs, his legs bent under him, his knees still holding her arms tightly against her side, most of his weight still on her abdomen. Her breast was throbbing with pain. A trickle of sweat rolled down towards her belly and she thought for a moment it was blood, had he made her bleed somehow? A new wave of fear caused her to begin trembling again. She was ashamed of herself for being so frightened, but the fear was something uncontrollable, a raw animal panic that shrieked silently of pain and possible death.

'You'll get rid of him tomorrow,' he whispered. He sat straddling her with his huge hands relaxed on his own thighs.

'Who?' she said. 'Who do you –'

'The cop. You'll get rid of him tomorrow.'

'All right.' She nodded in the darkness. 'All right,' she said again.

'You'll call his precinct – what precinct is it?'

'The eight ... the 87th, I think.'

'You'll call him.'

'Yes. Yes, I will.'

'You'll tell him you don't need a police escort no more. You'll tell him everything is all right now.'

'Yes, all right,' she said. 'Yes, I will.'

'You'll tell him you patched things up with your boy friend.'

'My ...' She paused. Her heart was beating wildly, she was sure he could feel her heart beating in panic. 'My *boy* friend?'

'Me,' he said, and grinned.

'I ... I don't even know you,' she said.

'I'm your boy friend.'

She shook her head.

'I'm your lover.'

She kept shaking her head.

'Yes.'

'I don't *know* you,' she said, and suddenly she began weeping. 'What do you want from me? Please, won't you go? Won't you please leave me alone? I don't even know you. Please, please.'

'Beg,' he said, and grinned.

'Please, please, please ...'

'You're going to tell him to stop coming around.'

'Yes, I *am*. I *said* I would.'

'Promise.'

'I promise.'

'You'll keep the promise,' he said flatly.

'Yes, I will. I told you –'

He slapped her suddenly and fiercely, his right hand abruptly leaving his thigh and coming up viciously towards her face. She blinked her eyes an instant before his open palm collided with her cheek. She pulled back rigidly, her neck muscles taut, her eyes wide, her teeth clamped together.

'You'll keep the promise,' he said, 'because this is a sample of what you'll get if you don't.'

And then he began beating her.

She did not know where she was at first. She tried to open her eyes, but something was wrong with them, she could not seem to open her eyes. Something rough was against her cheek, her head was twisted at a curious angle. She felt a hundred separate throbbing areas of hurt, but none of them seemed connected with her head or her body, each seemed to pulse with a solitary intensity of its own. Her left eye trembled open. Light knifed into the narrow crack of opening eyelid, she could open it no further. Light flickered into the tentative opening, flashes of light pulsated as the flesh over her eye quivered.

She was lying with her cheek pressed to the rug.

She kept trying to open her left eye, catching fitful glimpses of grey carpet as the eye opened and closed spasmodically, still not knowing where she was, possessing a sure knowledge that something terrible had happened to her, but not remembering what it was as yet. She lay quite still on the floor, feeling each throbbing knot of pain, arms, legs, thighs, breasts, nose, the separate pains combining to form a recognizable mass of flesh that was her body, a whole and unified body that had been severely beaten.

And then, of course, she remembered instantly what had happened.

Her first reaction was one of whimpering terror. She drew up her shoulders, trying to pull her head deeper into them. Her left hand came limply towards her face, the fingers fluttering, as though weakly trying to fend off any further blows.

'Please,' she said.

The word whispered into the room. She waited for him to strike her again, every part of her body tensed for another savage blow, and when none came, she lay trembling lest she was mistaken, fearful that he was only pretending to be gone while silently waiting to attack again.

Her eye kept flickering open and shut.

She rolled over onto her back and tried to open the other eye, but again only a crack of winking light came through the trembling lid. The ceiling seemed so very far away. Sobbing, she brought her hand to her nose, thinking it was running, wiping it with the back of her hand, and then realizing that blood was pouring from her nostrils.

'Oh,' she said. 'Oh, my God.'

She lay on her back, sobbing in anguish. At last, she tried to rise. She made it to her knees, and then fell to the floor again, sprawled on her face. The police, she thought, I must call the police. And then she remembered why he had beaten her. He did not want the police. Get rid of the police, he had said. She got to her knees again. Her gown was torn down the front. Her breasts were splotched with purple bruises. The nipple of her right breast looked as raw as an open wound. Her throat, the torn gown, the sloping tops of her breasts were covered with blood from her nose. She cupped her hand under it, and then tried to stop the flow by holding a torn shred of nylon under the nostrils, struggling to her feet and moving unsteadily towards her dressing table, where she knew she'd left her house keys, Kling had returned her house keys, she had left them on the dresser, she would put them at the back of her neck, they would stop the blood, groping for the dresser top, a severe pain on the side of her chest, had he kicked her the way he'd kicked that policeman, get rid of the police, oh my God, oh God, oh God dear God.

She could not believe what she saw in the mirror.

The image that stared back at her was grotesque and frightening, hideous beyond belief. Her eyes were puffed and swollen, the pupils invisible, only a narrow slit showing on the bursting surface of each discoloured bulge. Her face was covered with blood and bruises, a swollen mass of purple lumps, her blonde hair was matted with blood, there were welts on her arms, and thighs, and legs.

She felt suddenly dizzy. She clutched the top of the dressing table to steady herself, taking her hand away from her nose momentarily, watching the falling drops of blood spatter onto the white surface. A wave of nausea came and passed. She stood with her hand pressed to the top of the table, leaning on her extended arm, her head bent, refusing to look into the mirror again. She must not call the police. If she called the police, he would come back and do this to her again. He had told her to get rid of the police, she would call Kling in the morning and tell him everything was all right now, she and her boy friend had patched it up. In utter helplessness, she began crying again, her shoulders heaving, her nose dripping blood, her knees shaking as she clung to the dressing table for support.

Gasping for breath, she stood suddenly erect and opened her mouth wide, sucking in great gulps of air, her hand widespread over her belly like an open fan. Her fingers touched something wet and sticky, and she looked down sharply, expecting more blood, expecting to find herself soaked in blood that seeped from a hundred secret wounds.

She raised her hand slowly towards her swollen eyes.

She fainted when she realized the wet and sticky substance on her belly was semen.

Bert Kling kicked down the door of her apartment at ten-thirty the next morning. He had begun trying to reach her at nine, wanting to work out the details of their day together. He had let the phone ring seven times, and then decided he'd dialled the wrong number. He hung up, and tried it again. This time, he let it ring for a total of ten times, just in case she was a heavy sleeper. There was no answer. At nine-thirty, hoping she had gone down for breakfast and returned to the apartment by now, he called once again. There was still no answer. He called at five-minute intervals until ten o'clock, and then clipped on his gun and went down to his car. It took him a half hour to drive from Riverhead to Cindy's apartment on Glazebrook Street. He climbed the steps to the fourth floor, knocked on her door, called her name, and then kicked it open.

He phoned for an ambulance immediately.

She regained consciousness briefly before the ambulance arrived. When she recognized him, she mumbled, 'No, please, get out of here, he'll know,' and then passed out again.

Outside Cindy's open bedroom window, Kling discovered a visible heel print on one of the iron slats of the fire escape, just below the sill. And very close to that, wedged between two of the slats, he found a small fragment of something that looked like wadded earth. There was the possibility, however small, that the fragment had been dislodged from the shoe of Cindy's attacker. He scooped it into a manilla envelope and marked it for transportation to Detective-Lieutenant Sam Grossman at the police laboratory.

Chapter Seven

Every time Kling went downtown to the lab on High Street, he felt the way he had when he was eleven years old and his parents gave him a Gilbert Chemistry Set for Christmas. The lab covered almost half the first-floor area of the Headquarters building, and although Kling realized it was undoubtedly a most mundane place to Grossman and his cohorts, to him it was a wonderland of scientific marvel. To him, there was truth and justice in the orderly arrangement of cameras and filters, spotlights and enlargers, condensers and projectors. There was an aura of worlds unknown in the silent array of microscopes, common and stereoscopic, comparison and polarizing. There was magic in the quartz lamp with its ultraviolet light, there was poetry in the beakers and crucibles, the flasks and tripods, the burettes and pipettes, the test tubes and Bunsen burners. The police lab was *Mechanics Illustrated* come to life, with balance scales and drafting tools, tape measures and micrometers, scalpels and microtomes, emery wheels and vices. And hovering over it all was the aroma of a thousand chemicals, hitting the nostrils like a waft of exotic perfume caught in the single sail of an Arabian bark.

He loved it, and he wandered into it like a small boy each time, often forgetting that he had come there to discuss the facts of violence or death.

Sam Grossman never forgot the facts of violence or death. He was a tall man, big-boned, with the hands and face of a New England farmer. His eyes were blue and guileless behind thick-rimmed eyeglasses. He spoke softly and with a gentility and warmth reminiscent of an era long past, even though his voice carried the clipped stamp of a man who dealt continually with cold scientific fact. Taking off his glasses in the police lab that Monday morning, he wiped the lenses with a corner of his white lab coat, put them back on the bridge of his nose, and said, 'You gave us an interesting one this time, Bert.'

'How so?'

'Your man was a walking catalogue. We found traces of everything but the kitchen sink in that fragment.'

'Anything I can use?'

'Well, that depends. Come on back here.'

The men walked the length of the lab, moving between two long white counters bearing test tubes of different chemicals, some bubbling, all reminding Kling of a Frankenstein movie.

'Here's what we were able to isolate from that fragment. Seven different identifiable materials, all embedded in, or clinging to, or covering the basic material, which in itself is a combination of three materials. I think you were right about him having carried it on his shoe. Any other way, he couldn't have picked up such a collection of junk.'

'You think it was caught on his heel?'

'Probably wedged near the rear of the shoe, where the sole joins the heel. Impossible to tell, of course. We're just guessing. It seems likely, though, considering the garbage he managed to accumulate.'

'What kind of garbage?'

'Here,' Grossman said.

Each minute particle or particles of 'garbage' had been isolated and mounted on separate microscope slides, all of them labelled for identification. The slides were arranged vertically in a rack on the counter top, and Grossman ticked off each one with his forefinger as he explained.

'The basic compostion is made up of the materials on these first three slides, blended to form a sort of mastic to which the other elements undoubtedly clung.'

'And what are those three materials?' Kling asked.

'Suet, sawdust, and blood,' Grossman replied.

'Human blood?'

'No. We ran the Uhlenhuth precipitin reaction test on it. It's definitely not human.'

'That's good.'

'Well, yes,' Grossman said, 'because it gives us something to play with. Where would we be most likely to find a combination of sawdust, suet, and animal blood?'

'A butcher shop?' Kling asked.

'That's our guess. And our fourth slide lends support to the possibility.' Grossman tapped the slide with his finger. 'It's an animal hair. We weren't certain at first because the granulation resembled that of a human hair. But the medullary index – the relation between the diameter of the medulla and the diameter of the whole hair – was zero point five. Narrower than that would have indicated it was human. It's definitely animal.'

'What kind of an animal?' Kling asked.

'We can't tell for certain. Either bovine or equine. Considering the other indications, the hair probably came from an animal one would expect to find in a butcher shop, most likely a steer.'

'I see,' Kling said. He paused. 'But . . .' He paused again. 'They're *stripped* by the time they get to a butcher shop, aren't they?'

'What do you mean?'

'Well, the hide's been taken off by that time.'

'So?'

'Well, you just wouldn't find a hair from a steer's hide in a butcher shop, that's all.'

'I see what you mean. A slaughterhouse would be a better guess, wouldn't it?'

'Sure,' Kling said. He thought for a moment. 'There're some slaughterhouses here in the city, aren't there?'

'I'm not sure. I think all the slaughtering's done across the river, in the next state.'

'Well, at least this gives us something to look into.'

'We found a few other things as well,' Grossman said.

'Like what?'

'Fish scales.'

'What?'

'Fish scales, or at least a single particle of a fish scale.'

'In a slaughterhouse?'

'It doesn't sound likely, does it?'

'No. I'm beginning to like your butcher shop idea again.'

'You are, huh?'

'Sure. A combined butcher shop and fish market, why not?'

'What about the animal hair?'

'A dog maybe?' Kling suggested.

'We don't think so.'

'Well, how would a guy pick up a fish scale in a slaughterhouse?'

'He didn't have to,' Grossman said. 'He could have picked it up wherever he went walking. He could have picked it up anyplace in the city.'

'That narrows it down a lot,' Kling said.

'You've got to visualize this as a lump composed of suet, blood –'

'Yeah, and sawdust –'

'Right, that got stuck to his shoe. And you've go to visualize him walking around and having additional little pieces of garbage picked up by this sticky wad of glopis –'

'Sticky wad of *what*?'

'Glopis. That's an old Yiddish expression.'

'Glopis?'

'Glopis.'

'And the animal hair was stuck to the glopis, right?'

'Right.'

'And also the fish scale?'

'Right.'

'And what else?'

'These aren't in any particular order, you understand. I mean, it's impossible to get a progressive sequence of where he might have been. We simply –'

'I understand,' Kling said.

'Okay, we found a small dot of putty, a splinter of creosoted wood, and some metal filings which we identified as copper.'

'Go on.'

'We also found a tiny piece of peanut.'

'Peanut,' Kling said blankly.

'That's right. And to wrap it all up, the entire sticky suet mess of glopis was soaked with gasoline. Your friend stepped into a lot.'

Kling took a pen from his jacket pocket. Repeating the items out loud, and getting confirmation from Grossman as he went along, he jotted them into his notebook:

1- Suet
2- Sawdust
3- Blood (animal)
4- Hair (animal)
5- Fish Scale
6- Putty
7- Wood Splinter (creosoted)
8- Metal Filings (copper)
9- Peanut
10- Gasoline

'That's it, huh?'

'That's it,' Grossman said.

'Thanks. You just ruined my day.'

The drawing from the police artist was waiting for Kling when he got back to the squadroom. There were five artists working for the department, and this particular pencil sketch had been made by Detective Victor Haldeman, who had studied at the Art Students League in New York and later at the Art Institute in Chicago before joining the force. Each of the five artists, before being assigned to this special duty, had held other jobs in the department: two of them had been patrolmen in Isola, and the remaining three had been detectives in Calm's Point, Riverhead, and Majesta respectively. The Bureau of Criminal Identification was located at Headquarters on High Street, several floors above the police lab. But the men assigned to the artists' section of the bureau worked in a studio annex at 600 Jessup Street.

Their record was an impressive one. Working solely from verbal descriptions supplied by witnesses who were sometimes agitated and distraught, they had in the past year been responsible for twenty-eight positive identifications and arrests. So far this year, they had made sixty-eight drawings of described suspects, from which fourteen arrests had resulted. In each case, the apprehended suspect bore a remarkable resemblance to the sketch made from his description. Detective Haldeman had talked to all of the people who had been present when Vollner's office was invaded Wednesday afternoon, listening to descriptions of face, hair, eyes, nose, mouth from Miles Vollner, Cindy Forrest, Grace Di Santo, and Ronnie Fairchild, the patrolman who was still hospitalized. The composite drawing he made took three and a half hours to complete. It was delivered to Kling in a manilla envelope that Monday morning. The drawing itself was protected by a celluloid sleeve into which it had been inserted. There was no note with the drawing, and the drawing was unsigned. Kling took it out of the envelope and studied it.

Andy Parker, who was strolling past Kling's desk on his way to the toilet, stopped and looked at the drawing.

'Who's that?'

'Suspect,' Kling said.

'No kidding? I thought maybe it was Cary Grant.'

'You know what you ought to do, Andy?' Kling asked, not looking up at him as he put the drawing back into the manilla envelope.

'What?' Parker asked.

'You should join the police force. I understand they're looking for comical cops.'

'Ha!' Parker said, and went out to the toilet where he hoped to occupy himself for the next half hour with a copy of *Life* Magazine.

Forty miles away from the precinct that Monday morning, twenty-five miles outside the city limits, Detectives Meyer and Carella drove through the autumn countryside on their way to Larksview and the home of Mrs Stan Gifford.

They had spent all day Saturday and part of Sunday questioning a goodly percentage of the 212 people who were present in the studio loft that night. They did not consider any of them possible suspects in a murder case. As a matter of fact, they were trying hard to find something substantial upon which to hang a verdict of suicide. Their line of questioning followed a single simple direction: They wanted to know whether anyone connected with the show had, at any time before or during the show, seen Stan Gifford put anything into his mouth. The answers did nothing to substantiate a theory of suicide. Most of the people connected with the show were too busy to notice who was putting what into his mouth; some of the staff hadn't come across Gifford at all during the day; and those who *had* spent any time with him had definitely not seen anything go into his mouth. A chat with David Krantz revealed that Gifford was in the habit of forestalling dinner until after the show each Wednesday, eating a heavy lunch to carry him through the day. This completely destroyed the theory that perhaps Gifford had eaten again after meeting his wife. But it provided a new possibility for speculation, and it was this possibility that took Meyer and Carella to Larksview once more.

Meyer was miserable. His nose was stuffed, his throat was sore, his eyes were puffed and swollen. He had been taking a commercial cold preparation over the weekend, but it hadn't helped him at all. He kept blowing his nose, and then talking through it, and then blowing it again. He made a thoroughly delightful partner and companion.

Happily, the reporters and photographers had forsaken the Gifford house now that the story had been pushed off the front page and onto the pages reserved for armchair detection. Meyer and Carella drove to the small parking area, walked to the front door, and once again pulled the brass knob set into the jamb. The housekeeper opened the door, peeked out cautiously, and then said, 'Oh, it's you again.'

'Is Mrs Gifford home?' Carella asked.

'I'll see,' she said, and closed the door in their faces. They waited on the front stoop. The woods surrounding the house rattled their autumn colours with each fresh gust of wind. In a few moments, the housekeeper returned.

'Mrs Gifford is having coffee in the dining room,' she said. 'You may join her, if you wish.'

'Thank you,' Carella said, and they followed her into the house. A huge winding staircase started just inside the entrance hall, thickly carpeted, swinging to the upper story of the house. French doors opened onto the living room, and through that and beyond it was a small dining room with a bay window overlooking the back yard. Melanie Gifford sat alone at the table, wearing a quilted robe over a long pink nylon nightgown, the laced edges of the gown showing where the robe ended. Her blonde hair was uncombed, and hung loosely about her face. As before, she wore no makeup, but she seemed more rested now, and infinitely more at ease.

'I was just having breakfast,' she said. 'I'm afraid I'm a late sleeper. Won't you have something?'

Meyer took the chair opposite her, and Carella sat beside her at the table. She poured coffee for both men and then offered them the English muffins and marmalade, which they declined.

'Mrs Gifford,' Carella said, 'when we were here last time, you said something about your husband's physician, Carl Nelson.'

'Yes,' Melanie said. 'Do you take sugar?'

'Thank you.' Carella spooned a teaspoonful into his coffee, and then passed the sugar bowl to Meyer. 'You said you thought he'd murdered –'

'Cream?'

'Thank you – your husband. Now what made you say that, Mrs Gifford?'

'I believed it.'

'Do you still believe it?'

'No.'

'Why not?'

'Because I see now that it would have been impossible. I didn't know the nature of the poison at the time.'

'Its speed, do you mean?'

'Yes. Its speed.'

'And you mean it would have been impossible because Dr Nelson was at home during the show, and not at the studio, is that right?'

'Yes.'

'But what made you suspect him in the first place?'

'I tried to think of who could have had access to poison, and I thought of Carl.'

'So did we,' Carella said.

'I imagine you would have,' Melanie answered. 'These muffins are very good. Won't you have some?'

'No, thank you. But even if he did have access, Mrs Gifford, why would he have wanted to kill your husband?'

'I have no idea.'

'Didn't the two men get along?'

'You know doctors,' Melanie said. 'They all have God complexes.' She paused, and then added, 'In any universe, there can only be one God.'

'And in Stan Gifford's universe, *he* was God.'

Melanie sipped at her coffee and said, 'If an actor hasn't got his ego, then he hasn't got anything.'

'Are you saying the two egos came into conflict occasionally, Mrs Gifford?'

'Yes.'

'But not in any serious way, surely.'

'I don't know what men consider serious. I know that Stan and Carl occasionally argued. So when Stan was killed, as I told you, I tried to figure out who could have got his hands on any poison, and I thought of Carl.'

'This was before you knew the poison was strophanthin.'

'Yes. Once I found out what the poison was, and knowing Carl was home that night, I realized –'

'But if you didn't know the poison was strophanthin, then it could have been anything, any poison, isn't that right?'

'Yes. But –'

'And you also must have known that a great many poisons can be purchased in drugstores, usually in compounds of one sort or another. Like arsenic or cyanide . . .'

'Yes, I suppose I knew that.'

'But you still automatically assumed Dr Nelson had killed your husband.'

'I was in shock at the time. I didn't know what to think.'

'I see,' Carella said. He picked up his cup and took a long deliberate swallow. 'Mrs Gifford, you said your husband took a vitamin capsule after lunch last Wednesday.'

'That's right.'

'Did he have that capsule with him, or did you bring it to him when you went into the city?'

'He had it with him.'

'Was he in the habit of taking vitamin capsules with him?'

'Yes,' Melanie said. 'He was supposed to take one after every meal. Stan was a very conscientious man. When he knew he was going into the city, he carried the vitamins with him, in a small pillbox.'

'Did he take only one capsule to the city last Wednesday? Or *two*?'

'One,' Melanie said.

'How do you know?'

'Because there were two on the breakfast table that morning. He swallowed one with his orange juice, and he put the other in the pillbox, and then put it in his pocket.'

'And you saw him take that second capsule after lunch?'

'Yes. He took it out of the pillbox and put it on the table the moment we were seated. That's what he usually did – so he wouldn't forget to take it.'

'And to your knowledge, he did not have any other capsules with him. That was the only capsule he took after leaving this house last Wednesday.'

'That's right.'

'Who put those capsules on the breakfast table, Mrs Gifford?'

'My housekeeper.' Melanie looked suddenly annoyed. 'I'm not sure I understand all this,' she said. 'If he took the capsule at lunch, I don't see how it could possibly –'

'We're only trying to find out for sure whether or not there were only two capsules, Mrs Gifford.'

'I just told you.'

'We'd like to be sure. We know the capsule he took at lunch couldn't possibly have killed him. But if there was a third capsule –'

'There were only two,' Melanie said. 'He knew he was coming home for dinner after the show, the way he did every Wednesday night. There was no need for him to carry more than –'

'More than the one he took at lunch.'

'Yes.'

'Mrs Gifford, do you know whether or not your husband had any insurance on his life?'

'Yes, of course he did.'

'Would you know in what amount?'

'A hundred thousand dollars.'

'And the company?'

'Municipal Life.'

'Who's the beneficiary, Mrs Gifford?'

'I am,' Melanie replied.

'I see,' Carella said.

There was brief silence. Melanie put down her coffee cup. Her eyes met Carella's levelly. Quietly, she said, 'I'm sure you didn't mean to suggest, Detective Carella –'

'Mrs Gifford, this is all routine –'

'– that I might have had anything to do with the death of –'

'– questioning. I don't know *who* had anything to do with your husband's death.'

'*I* didn't.'

'I hope not.'

'Because, you see, Detective Carella, a hundred thousand dollars in insurance money would hardly come anywhere near the kind of income my husband earned as a performer. I'm sure you know that he recently signed a two-million dollar contract with the network. And I can *assure* you he's always been more than generous to me. Or perhaps you'd like to come upstairs and take a look at the furs in my closet or the jewels on my dresser.'

'I don't think that'll be necessary, Mrs Gifford.'

'I'm sure it won't. But you might also like to consider the fact that Stan's insurance policy carried the usual suicide clause.'

'I'm not sure I follow you, Mrs Gifford.'

'I'm saying, Detective Carella, that unless you can find a murderer – unless you can *prove* there was foul play involved in my husband's death – his insurance company will conclude he was a suicide. In which case, I'll receive only the premiums already paid in, and not a penny more.'

'I see.'

'Yes, I hope you do.'

'Would you know whether or not your husband left a will, Mrs Gifford?' Meyer asked.

'Yes, he did.'

'Are you also a beneficiary in his will?'

'I don't know.'

'You never discussed it with him?'

'Never. I know there's a will, but I don't know what its terms are.'

'Who *would* know, Mrs Gifford?'

'His lawyer, I imagine.'

'And the lawyer's name?'

'Salvatore Di Palma.'

'In the city?'

'Yes.'

'You won't mind if we call him?'

'Why should I?' Melanie paused again, and again stared at Carella. 'I don't mind telling you,' she said, 'that you're beginning to give me a severe pain in the ass.'

'I'm sorry.'

'Does part of your "routine questioning" involve badgering a man's widow?'

'I'm sorry, Mrs Gifford,' Carella said. 'We're only trying to investigate every possibility.'

'Then how about investigating the possibility that I led a full and happy life with Stan? When we met, I was working in summer stock in Pennsylvania, earning sixty dollars a week. I've had everything I ever wanted from the moment we were married, but I'd gladly give all of it – the furs, the jewels, the house, even the clothes on my back – if that'd bring Stan to life again.'

'We're only –'

'Yes, you're only investigating every possibility, I know. Be human,' she said. 'You're dealing with people, not ciphers.'

The detectives were silent. Melanie sighed.

'Did you still want to see my housekeeper?'

'Please,' Meyer said.

Melanie lifted the small bell near her right hand, and gave it a rapid shake. The housekeeper, as though alert and waiting for the tiny sound, came into the dining room immediately.

'These gentlemen would like to ask you some questions, Maureen,' Melanie said. 'If you don't mind, gentlemen, I'll leave you alone. I'm late for an appointment now, and I'd like to get dressed.'

'Thank you for your time, Mrs Gifford,' Carella said.

'Not at all,' Melanie said, and walked out of the room.

Maureen stood by the table, uncertainly picking at her apron. Meyer glanced at Carella, who nodded. Meyer cleared his throat, and said, 'Maureen, on the day Mr Gifford died, did you set the breakfast table for him?'

'For him and for Mrs Gifford, yes, sir.'

'Do you always set the table?'

'Except on Thursdays and every other Sunday, which are my days off. Yes, sir, I always set the table.'

'Did you put Mr Gifford's vitamin capsules on the table that morning?' Meyer asked.

'Yes, sir. Right alongside his plate, same as usual.'

'How many vitamin capsules?'

'Two.'

'Not three?'

'I said two,' Maureen said.

'Was anyone in the room when you put the capsules on the table?'

'No, sir.'

'Who came down to breakfast first? Mr Gifford or Mrs Gifford?'

'Mrs Gifford came in just as I was leaving.'

'And then Mr Gifford?'

'Yes. I heard him come down about five minutes later.'

'Do these vitamin capsules come in a jar?'

'A small bottle, sir.'

'Could we see that bottle, please?'

'I keep it in the kitchen,' Maureen paused. 'You'll have to wait while I get it.'

She went out of the room. Carella waited until he could no longer hear her footfalls, and then asked, 'What are you thinking?'

'I don't know. But if Melanie Gifford was alone in the room with those two capsules, she could have switched one of them, no?'

'The one he was taking to lunch, huh?'

'Yeah.'

'Only one thing wrong with that theory,' Carella said.

'Yeah, I know. He had lunch seven hours before he collapsed.' Meyer sighed and shook his head. 'We're *still* stuck with that lousy six minutes. It's driving me nuts.'

'Besides, it doesn't look as though Melanie had any reason to do in her own dear Godlike husband.'

'Yeah,' Meyer said. 'It's just I get the feeling she's too cooperative, you know? Her and the good doctor both. So very damn helpful. He right away diagnoses poison and insists we do an autopsy. She immediately points to him as a suspect, then changes her mind when she finds out about the poison. And both of them conveniently away from the studio on the night Gifford died.' Meyer nodded his head, a thoughtful expression on his face. 'Maybe that six minutes is *supposed* to drive us nuts.'

'How do you mean?'

'Maybe we were *supposed* to find out which poison killed him. I mean, we'd naturally do an autopsy anyway, right? And we'd find out it was strophanthin, and we'd also find out how fast strophanthin works.'

'Yeah, go ahead.'

'So we'd automatically rule out anybody who wasn't near Gifford before he died.'

'That's almost the entire city, Meyer.'

'No, you know what I mean. We'd rule out Krantz, who says he was in the sponsor's booth, and we'd rule out Melanie, who was here, and Nelson, who was at his own house.'

'That still needs checking,' Carella said.

'Why? Krantz said that was where he reached him after Gifford collapsed.'

'That doesn't mean Nelson was there all night. I want to ask him about that. In fact, I'd like to stop at his office as soon as we get back to the city.'

'Okay, but do you get my point?'

'I think so. Given a dead end to work with, knowing how much poison Gifford had swallowed, and knowing how fast it worked, we'd come to the only logical conclusion: suicide. Is that what you mean?'

'Right,' Meyer said.

'Only one thing wrong with your theory, friend.'

'Yeah, what?'

'The facts. It *was* strophanthin. It *does* work instantly. You can speculate all you want, but the facts remain the same.'

'Facts, facts,' Meyer said. 'All I know –'

'Facts,' Carella insisted.

'Suppose Melanie did switch that lunch capsule? We still haven't checked Gifford's will. She may be in it for a healthy chunk.'

'All right, suppose she did. He'd have dropped dead on his way to the studio.'

'Or suppose Krantz got to him *before* he went up to the sponsor's booth?'

'Then Gifford would have shown symptoms of poisoning before the show even went on the air.'

'Arrrggh, facts,' Meyer said, and Maureen came back into the room.

'I asked Mrs Gifford if it was all right,' she said. She handed the bottle of vitamin capsules to Carella. 'You can do whatever you like with them.'

'We'd like to take them with us, if that's all right.'

'Mrs Gifford said whatever you like.'

'We'll give you a receipt,' Meyer said. He looked at the bottle of vitamins in Carella's hand. The capsules were jammed into the bottle, each one opaque, and coloured purple and black. Meyer stared at them sourly. 'You're looking for a third capsule,' he said to Carella. 'There're a *hundred* of them in that bottle.'

He blew his nose then, and began making out a receipt for the vitamins.

Chapter Eight

Dr Carl Nelson's office was on Hall Avenue in a white apartment building with a green awning that stretched to the kerb. Carella and Meyer got there at one o'clock, took the elevator up to the fifth floor, and then announced themselves to a brunette nurse, who said the doctor had a patient with him at the moment, but she'd tell him they were here, wouldn't they please have a seat?

They had a seat.

In ten minutes' time, an elderly lady with a bandage over one eye came out of the doctor's private office. She smiled at the two detectives, either soliciting sympathy for her wound, or offering sympathy for whatever had brought them to see a doctor. Carl Nelson came out of his office with his hand extended.

'How are you?' he said. 'Come in, come in. Any news?'

'Well, not really, doctor,' Carella said. 'We simply wanted to ask you a few questions.'

'Happy to help in any way I can,' Nelson said. He turned to his nurse and asked, 'When's my next appointment, Rhoda?'

'Two o'clock, doctor.'

'No calls except emergencies until then, please,' Nelson said, and he led the detectives inside. He sat immediately at his desk, offered Carella and Meyer chairs, and then folded his hands before him in a professionally relaxed, patiently expectant way.

'Are you a general practitioner, Dr Nelson?' Meyer asked.

'Yes, I am.' Nelson smiled. 'That's a nasty cold you've got there, Detective Meyer. I hope you're taking something for it.'

'I'm taking *everything* for it,' Meyer said.

'There're a lot of viruses going around,' Nelson said.

'Yes,' Meyer agreed.

'Dr Nelson,' Carella said, 'I wonder if you'd mind telling us a little about yourself.'

'Not at all,' Nelson said. 'What would you like to know?'

'Well, whatever you feel is pertinent.'

'About what? My life? My work? My aspirations?'

'Any of it, or all of it,' Carella said pleasantly.

Nelson smiled. 'Well. . . .' He paused, thinking. 'I'm forty-three years old, a native of this city, attended Haworth University here. I was graduated with a B.S. in January of 1944, and got drafted just in time for the assault on Cassino.'

'How old were you at the time, Dr Nelson?'

'Twenty-two.'

'Was this Army?'

'Yes. The Medical Corps.'

'Were you an officer or an enlisted man?'

'I was a corporal. I was attached to a field hospital in Castelforte. Are you familiar with the country?'

'Vaguely,' Carella said.

'There was some fierce fighting,' Nelson said briefly. He sighed, dismissing the entire subject. 'I was discharged in May of 1946. I began medical school that fall.'

'What school was that, Dr Nelson?'

'Georgetown University. In Washington, D.C.'

'And then you came back here to begin practice, is that it?'

'Yes. I opened my own office in 1952.'

'This same office?'

'No, my first office was uptown. In Riverhead.'

'How long have you been at this location, doctor?'

'Since 1961.'

'Are you married?'

'No.'

'Have you ever been married?'

'Yes. I was divorced seven years ago.'

'Is your former wife alive?'

'Yes.'

'Living in this city?'

'No. She lives in San Diego with her new husband. He's an architect there.'

'Do you have any children?'

'No.'

'You said something about your aspirations, doctor. I wonder ...'

'Oh.' Nelson smiled. 'I hope to start a small rest home one day. For elderly people.'

'Where?'

'Most likely in Riverhead, where I began practice.'

'Now, Dr Nelson,' Carella said, 'it's our understanding that you were at home last Wednesday night when Mr Krantz called to tell you what had happened. Is that correct?'

'Yes, that's correct.'

'Were you home all night, Dr Nelson?'

'Yes, I went home directly from here.'

'And what time did you leave here?'

'My usual evening hours are from five o'clock to eight o'clock. I left here last Wednesday night at about ten minutes past eight.'

'Can anyone verify that?'

'Yes, Rhoda left with me. Miss Barnaby, my nurse; you just met her. We both left at the same time. You can ask her if you like.'

'Where did you go when you left the office?'

'Home. I already said I went directly home.'

'Where do you live, Dr Nelson?'

'On South Fourteenth.'

'South Fourteenth, mmm, so it should have taken you, oh, fifteen minutes at the most to get from here to your house, is that right?'

'That's right. I got home at about eight-thirty.'

'Was anyone there?'

'Just my housekeeper. Mrs Irene Janlewski. She was preparing my dinner when the call came from the studio. Actually, I didn't need the call.'

'Why not?'

'I'd seen Stan collapse.'

'What do you mean, Dr Nelson?'

'I was watching the show. I turned it on the moment I got home.'

'At about eight-thirty, is that right?'

'Yes, that's about when I got home.'

'What was happening when you turned on the show?' Meyer asked.

'Happening?'

'Yes, on the screen,' Meyer said. He had taken out his black notebook and a pencil and seemed to be taking notes as Nelson spoke. Actually, he was studying the page opposite the one on which he was writing. On that page, in his own hand, was the information George Cooper had given him last Wednesday night at the studio. The folk singers had gone off at eight-thirty-seven, and Gifford had come on immediately afterwards, staying on camera with his Hollywood guest for two minutes and twelve seconds. When the guest went off to change . . .

'Stan was doing a commercial when I turned the set on,' Nelson said. 'A coffee commercial.'

'That would have been at about eight-forty,' Meyer said.

'Yes, I suppose so.'

'Actually, it would have been exactly eight-thirty-nine and twelve seconds,' Meyer said, just to be ornery.

'What?' Nelson asked.

'Which means you didn't turn the set on the moment you got into the house. Not if you got home at eight-thirty.'

'Well, I suppose I talked with Mrs Janlewski for a few minutes, asked if there were any calls, settled a few household problems, you know.'

'Yes,' Meyer said. 'The important thing, in any case, is that you were watching Gifford when he got sick.'

'Yes, I was.'

'Which was at exactly eight-forty-four and seventeen seconds,' Meyer said, feeling a wild sense of giddy power.

'Yes,' Nelson agreed. 'I suppose so.'

'What did you think when you saw him collapse?'
'I didn't know what to think. I rushed to the closet for my hat and coat, and was starting out when the telephone rang.'
'Who was it?'
'David Krantz.'
'And he told you that Gifford was sick, is that right?'
'Right.'
'Which you already knew.'
'Yes, I already knew it.'
'But when you saw Gifford collapse, you didn't know *what* was wrong with him.'
'No, I didn't.'
'Later on, Dr Nelson, when I spoke to you at the studio, you seemed certain he'd been poisoned.'
'That's true. But that –'
'It was you, in fact, who suggested that we have an autopsy performed.'
'That's correct. When I got to the studio, the symptoms were unmistakable. A first-year med student could have diagnosed acute poisoning.'
'You didn't know what *kind* of poison, of course.'
'How could I?'
'Dr Nelson,' Carella said, 'did you ever argue with Stan Gifford?'
'Yes. All friends argue every now and then. It's only acquaintances who never have any differences of opinion.'
'What did you argue about?'
'I'm sure I don't remember. Everything. Stan was an alert and well-informed person, with a great many opinions on most things that would concern a thinking man.'
'I see. And so you argued about them.'
'We *discussed* them, might be a better way of putting it.'
'You discussed a wide variety of things, is that right?'
'Yes.'
'But you did not *argue* about these things?'
'Yes, we argued, too.'
'About matters of general concern.'
'Yes.'
'Never about anything specific. Never about anything you might consider personal.'
'We argued about personal matters, yes.'
'Like what?'
'Well, I can't remember any off-hand. But I know we argued about personal matters from time to time.'
'Try to remember, Dr Nelson,' Carella said.
'Has Melanie told you?' Nelson asked suddenly. 'Is that what this is about?'
'Told us what, Dr Nelson?'
'Are you looking for confirmation, is that it? I can assure you the entire incident was idiotic. Stan was drunk, otherwise he wouldn't have lost his temper that way.'
'Tell us about it,' Meyer said calmly.
'There'd been a party at his house, and I was dancing with Melanie. Stan

had been drinking heavily, and he ... well, he behaved somewhat ridiculously.'

'How did he behave?'

'He accused me of trying to steal his wife, and he ... he tried to strike me.'

'What did *you* do, Dr Nelson?'

'I defended myself, naturally.'

'How? Did you hit him back?'

'No. I simply held up my hands – to ward off his blows, you understand. He was very drunk, really incapable of inflicting any harm.'

'When *was* this party, Dr Nelson?'

'Just after Labor Day. In fact, a week before the show went on the air again. After the summer break, you know. It was a sort of celebration.'

'And Stan Gifford thought you were trying to steal his wife, is that right?'

'Yes.'

'Merely because you were dancing with her.'

'Yes.'

'Had you been dancing with her a lot?'

'No. I think that was the second time all evening.'

'Then his attack was really unfounded, wasn't it?'

'He was drunk.'

'And that's why you feel he attacked you; because he was drunk?'

'And because David Krantz provoked him.'

'David Krantz? Was he at the party, too?'

'Yes, most of the people involved with the show were there.'

'I see. How did Mr Krantz provoke him?'

'Oh, you know the stupid jokes some people make.'

'No, what sort of jokes, Dr Nelson?'

'About our dancing together, you know. David Krantz is a barbarian. It's my considered opinion that he's oversexed and attributes evil thoughts to everyone else in the world, as compensation.'

'I see. Then you feel it was Krantz who gave Gifford the idea that you were trying to steal his wife?'

'Yes.'

'Why would he do that?'

'He hated Stan. He hates all actors, for that matter. He calls them *cattle*, that's supposed to *endear* them to him, you know.'

'How did Gifford feel about *him*?'

'I think the feelings were mutual.'

'Gifford hated Krantz, too, is that what you mean?'

'Yes.'

'Then why did he take Krantz seriously that night?'

'What do you mean?'

'At the party. When Krantz said you were trying to steal Mrs Gifford.'

'Oh. I don't know. He was drunk. I guess a man will listen to anyone when he's drunk.'

'Um-huh,' Carella said. He was silent for a moment. Then he asked, 'But in spite of this incident, you remained his personal physician, is that right?'

'Oh, of *course*. Stan apologized to me the very next day.'

'And you continued to be friends?'

'Yes, certainly. I don't even know why Melanie brought this up. I don't see what bearing –'

'She didn't,' Meyer said.

'Oh. Well, who told you about it then? Was it Krantz? I wouldn't put it past him. He's a goddamn troublemaker.'

'No one told us, actually,' Meyer said. 'This is the first we've heard of the incident.'

'Oh,' Nelson paused. 'Well, it doesn't matter. I'd rather you heard it from me than from someone else who was at the party.'

'That's very sensible of you, Dr Nelson. You're being most cooperative.' Carella paused. 'If it's all right with you, we'll simply verify with your nurse that you left here with her at about ten minutes past eight last Wednesday night. And we'll –'

'Yes, you certainly may verify it with her.'

'And we'd also like to call your housekeeper – with your permission, of course – to verify that you arrive home at about eight-thirty, as you say, and remained there until after Krantz's phone call.'

'Certainly. My nurse will give you my home number.'

'Thank you, Dr Nelson. You've been very cooperative,' Carella said, and they went out to talk to Miss Barnaby, who told them the doctor had arrived at the office at four-forty-five last Wednesday afternoon and had not left until office hours were over, at ten minutes past eight. She was absolutely certain about this because she and the doctor had left at the same time. She gave them the doctor's home number so that they could speak to Mrs Janlewski, the housekeeper, and they thanked her politely and went downstairs and then out of the building.

'He's very cooperative,' Carella said.

'Yes, he's very very cooperative,' Meyer agreed.

'Let's put a tail on him,' Carella said.

'I've got a better idea,' Meyer said. 'Let's put a tail on him and Krantz *both*.'

'Good idea.'

'You agree?'

'Sure.'

'You think one them did it?'

'I think you did it,' Carella said, and suddenly slipped his handcuffs from his belt and snapped one of them onto Meyer's wrist. 'Come along now, no tricks,' he said.

'You know what a guy needs like a hole in the head when he's got a bad cold?' Meyer said.

'What?'

'A partner who plays jokes.'

'I'm not playing jokes, mister,' Carella said, his eyes narrowing. 'I happen to know that Stan Gifford took out a seven-million-dollar insurance policy on his life, payable to your wife Sarah as beneficiary in the event that he died on any Wednesday between eight-thirty and nine thirty p.m. during the month of October. I further happen to know –'

'Oh, boy,' Meyer said, 'start up with *goyim*.'

Back at the squadroom, they made two telephone calls.

The first was to the Municipal Life, where they learned that Stanley Gifford's insurance policy had been written only a year and a half ago, and contained a clause that read, 'Death within two years from the date of issue of this policy, from suicide while sane or insane, shall limit the company's liability hereunder to the amount of the premiums actually paid hereon.'

The second was to Mr Salvatore Di Palma, Gifford's lawyer, who promptly confirmed that Melanie Gifford had not been familiar with the terms of her husband's will.

'Why do you want to know?' he asked.

'We're investigating his murder,' Carella said.

'There's nothing in Stan's will that would have caused Melanie to even *consider* murder,' Di Palma said.

'Why do you say that?'

'Because I know what's in the will.'

'Can you tell us?'

'I would not regard it as appropriate for me to reveal the contents of the will to any person until it has first been read to Mr Gifford's widow.'

'We're investigating a murder,' Carella said.

'Look, take my word for it,' Di Palma said. 'There's nothing here to indicate –'

'You mean he doesn't leave her anything?'

'Did I say that?'

'No, *I* said it,' Carella said. 'Does he, or doesn't he?'

'You're twisting my arm,' Di Palma said, and then chuckled. He liked talking to Italians. They were the only civilized people in the world.

'Come on,' Carella said, 'help a working man.'

'Okay, but you didn't hear it from me,' Di Palma said, still chuckling. 'Stan came in early last month, asked me to revise his will.'

'Why?'

'He didn't say. The will now leaves his house and his personal property to Mrs Adelaide Garfein, that's his mother, she's a widow in Poughkeepsie, New York.'

'Go ahead.'

'It leaves one-third of the remainder of his estate to the American Guild of Variety Artists, one-third to the Academy of Television Arts and Sciences, and one-third to the Damon Runyon Cancer Fund.'

'And Melanie?'

'Zero,' Di Palma said. 'That's what the change was all about. He cut her out of it completely.'

'Thank you very much.'

'For what?' Di Palma said, and chuckled again. 'I didn't tell you anything, did I?'

'You didn't say a word,' Carella said. 'Thanks again.'

'Don't mention it,' Di Palma said, and hung up.

'So?' Meyer asked.

'He left her nothing,' Carella said. 'Changed the will early last month.'

'Nothing?'

'Nothing.' Carella paused. 'That's pretty funny, don't you think? I mean, here's this sweet woman who had led a full and happy life with her husband, and who wants to take us upstairs to show us all her furs and jewellery and such – and just last month he cuts her out of his will. That's pretty funny, I think.'

'Yeah, especially since just last month he also took a sock at our doctor friend and accused him of trying to steal his wife.'

'Yeah, that's a very funny coincidence,' Carella said.

'Maybe he really *believed* Nelson was trying to steal his wife.'

'Maybe so.'

'Mmm,' Meyer said. He thought for a moment and then said, 'But she still looks clean, Steve. She doesn't get a cent either way.'

'Unless we find a murderer, in which case it's no longer suicide, in which case she collects a hundred G's from the insurance company.'

'Yeah, but that *still* leaves her out. Because if she's the one who did it, she wouldn't plan it to look like a *suicide*, would she?'

'What do you mean?'

'This thing looks exactly like a suicide. Listen, for all I know, it *is* one.'

'So?'

'So if you're hoping to get a hundred thousand dollars on an insurance policy that has a suicide clause, you're sure as hell not going to plan a murder that looks like a suicide, right?'

'Right.'

'So?' Meyer said.

'So Melanie Gifford looks clean.'

'Yeah.'

'Guess what I found out?' Carella said.

'What?'

'Gifford's real name is Garfein.'

'Yeah?'

'Yeah.'

'So what? *My* real name is Rock Hudson.'

Chapter Nine

Considering the number of *human* killings that took place daily in the five separate sections of the city, Kling was surprised to discover that the city could boast of only one slaughterhouse. Apparently the guiding fathers and the Butchers Union (who gave him the information) were averse to killing animals within the city limits. The single slaughtering-house was on Boswell Avenue in Calm's Point, and it specialized in the slaughtering of lambs. Most of the city's killing, as Grossman had surmised, was done in four separate slaughterhouses across the river, in the next state. Since Calm's Point was closest, Kling hit the one on Boswell Avenue first. He was armed with the list he had compiled at the lab earlier that day, together with the drawing he had received from the BCI. He didn't know exactly what he was looking for, or exactly what he hoped to discover. He had never been inside a slaughterhouse before.

After visiting the one in Calm's Point, he never wanted to step inside another one as long as he lived. Unfortunately, there were four more to check across the river.

He was used to blood; a cop gets used to blood. He was used to the sight of human beings bleeding in a hundred different ways from a thousand different wounds, he was used to all that. He had been witness to sudden attacks with razor blades or knives, pistols or shotguns, had seen the body case torn or punctured, the blood beginning to flow or spurt. He had seen them dead and bleeding, and he had seen them alive and in the midst of attack – bleeding. But he had never seen an animal killed before, and the sight made him want to retch. He could barely concentrate on what the head butcher was telling him. The bleating of the lambs rang in his ears, the stench of blood filled the air. The head butcher looked at the drawing Kling extended, leaving a bloody thumbprint on the celluloid sleeve, and shook his head. Behind him the animals shrieked.

The air outside was cold, it drilled the nostrils. He sucked breath after breath into his lungs, deeply savouring each cleansing rush. He did not want to go across that river, but he went. Forsaking lunch, because he knew he would not be able to keep it down, he hit two more slaughterhouses in succession and – finding nothing – grimly prepared to visit the next two on his list.

There is an intuitive feel to detection, and the closest thing to sudden truth – outside of fiction – is the dawning of awareness of a cop when he is about to make a fresh discovery. The moment Kling drove onto the dock he knew he would hit pay dirt. The knowledge was sudden and fierce. He stepped out of the police sedan with a faint vague smile on his face, looking up at the huge white sign across the top of the building, facing the river, PURLEY BROTHERS, INC. He stood in the centre of the open dock, an area the size of a baseball diamond, and took his time surveying the location, while all the while the rising knowledge clamoured within him, this is it, this is it, this is it.

One side of the dock was open to the waterfront. Beyond the two marine gasoline pumps at the water's edge, Kling could see across the river to where the towers of the city were silhoutted against the grey October sky. His eye lingered on the near distance for a moment, and then he swung his head to the right, where a half-dozen fishing boats were tied up, fishermen dumping their nets and their baskets, leaping onto the dock and then sitting with their booted legs hanging over its edge while they scraped and cleaned their fish and transferred them to fresh baskets lined with newspapers. The grin on his face widened because he knew for certain now that this was pay dirt, that everything would fall into place here on this dock.

He turned his attention back to the slaughterhouse that formed almost one complete side of the rectangular dock area. Gulls shrieked in the air over the river where waste material poured from an open pipe. Railroad tracks fed the rear of the brick building, a siding that ran from the yards some five hundred feet back from the dock. He walked to the tracks and began following them to the building.

They led directly to the animal pens, empty now, alongside of which were the metal entrance doors to the slaughterhouse. He knew what he would find on the floor inside; he had seen the floors of three such places already.

The manager was a man named Joe Brady, and he was more than delighted to help Kling. He took him into a small, glass-partitioned office overlooking the killing floor (Kling sat with his back to the glass) and then accepted the drawing Kling handed to him, and pondered it for several moments, and then asked, 'What is he, a nigger?'

'No,' Kling said. 'He's a white man.'

'You said he attacked a girl, didn't you?'

'Yes, that's right.'

'And he ain't a nigger?' Brady shook his head.

'You can see from the drawing that he's white,' Kling said. An annoyed tone had crept into his voice. Brady did not seem to notice.

'Well, it's hard to tell from a drawing,' he said. 'I mean, the way the shading is done here, look, right here, you see what I mean? That could be a nigger.'

'Mr Brady,' Kling said flatly, 'I do not like that word.'

'What word?' Brady asked.

'Nigger.'

'Oh, come on,' Brady said, 'don't get on your high horse. We got a half a dozen niggers working here, they're all nice guys, what the hell's the matter with you?'

'The word offends me,' Kling said. 'Cut it out.'

Brady abruptly handed back the drawing. 'I've never seen this guy in my life,' he said. 'If you're finished here, I got to get back to work.'

'He doesn't work here?'

'No.'

'Are all of your employees full-time men?'

'All of them.'

'No part-time workers, maybe somebody who worked here for just a few days –'

'I know everybody who works here,' Brady said. 'That guy don't work here.'

'Is he someone who might possibly make deliveries here?'

'What kind of deliveries?'

'I don't know. Maybe –'

'The only thing we get delivered here is animals.'

'I'm sure you get other things delivered here, Mr Brady.'

'Nothing,' Brady said, and he rose from behind his desk. 'I got to get back to work.'

'Sit down, Mr Brady,' Kling said. His voice was harsh.

Surprised, Brady looked at him with rising eyebrows, ready to *really* take offence.

'I said sit down. Now go ahead.'

'Listen, mister –' Brady started.

'No, you listen, mister,' Kling said. 'I'm investigating an assault, and I have good reason to believe this man' – he tapped the drawing – 'was somewhere around here last Friday. Now, I don't like your goddamn attitude, Mr Brady, and if you'd like the inconvenience of answering some questions uptown at the station house instead of here in your nice cosy office overlooking all that killing out there, that's just fine with me. So why don't you get your hat and we'll just take a little ride, okay?'

'What for?' Brady said.

Kling did not answer. He sat grimly on the side of the desk opposite Brady and studied him coldly. Brady looked deep into his eyes.

'The only thing we get delivered here is animals,' he said again.

'Then how'd the paper cups get here?'

'Huh?'

'On the water cooler,' Kling said. 'Don't brush me off, Mr Brady, I'm goddamn good and sore.'

'Okay, okay,' Brady said.

'Okay! Who delivers stuff here?'

'A lot of people. But I know most of them, and I don't recognize that picture.'

'Are there any deliveries made that you would not ordinarily see?'

'What do you mean?'

'Does anything come into this building that you personally would not check?'

'I check anything that goes in or out. What do you mean? You mean *personal* things, too?'

'Personal things?'

'Things that have nothing to do with the business?'

'What'd you have in mind, Mr Brady?'

'Well, some of the guys order lunch from the diner across the dock. They got guys working there who bring the lunch over. Of coffee sometimes. I got my own little hot plate here in the office, so I don't have to send out for coffee, and also I bring my lunch from home. So I don't usually get to see the guys who make the deliveries.'

'Thank you,' Kling said, and rose.

Brady could not resist a parting shot. 'Anyway,' he said, 'most of them delivery guys are niggers.'

The air outside was clean, blowing fresh and wet off the river. Kling sighted the diner on the opposite end of the dock rectangle and quickly began walking towards it. It was set in a row of shops that slowly came into sharper focus as he moved closer to them. The two shops flanking the diner were occupied by a plumber and a glazier.

He took out his notebook and consulted it: suet, sawdust, blood, animal hair, fish scale, putty, wood splinter, metal filings, peanut, and gasoline. The only item he could not account for was the peanut, but maybe he'd find one in the diner. He was hopeful, in fact, of finding something more than just a peanut inside. He was hopeful of finding the man who had stopped at the slaughterhouse and stepped into the suet, blood and sawdust to which the animal hair had later clung when he crossed the pens outside. He was hopeful of finding the man who had walked along the creosoted railroad tracks, picking up a wood splinter in the sticky mess on his heel. He was hopeful of finding the man who had stopped on the edge of the dock where the fishermen were cleaning fish, and later walked through a small puddle of gasoline near the marine pumps, and then into the glazier's where he had acquired the dot of putty, and the plumber's where the copper filings had been added to the rest of the glopis. He was hopeful of finding the man who had beaten Cindy senseless, and the possibility seemed strong that this man made deliveries for the diner. Who else could wander so easily in and out of so many places? Kling unbuttoned his coat and reassuringly touched the butt of his revolver. Briskly, he walked to the door of the diner and entered. The smell of greasy food assailed his nostrils. He had not eaten since breakfast, and the aroma combined with his slaughterhouse memories to bring on a feeling of nausea. He took a seat at the counter and ordered a cup of coffee, wanting to look over the personnel before he showed his drawing to anyone. There were two men behind the counter, one white and one coloured. Neither looked anything at all like the drawing. Behind a passthrough into the kitchen, he caught a glimpse of another white man as he put down a hamburger for pickup. He was not the suspect, either. Two Negro delivery boys in white jackets were sitting in a booth near the cash register, where a baldheaded white man sat poking his teeth with a matchstick. Kling assumed he had seen every employee in the place, with the possible exception of the short-order cook. He finished his coffee, went to the cash register, showed his shield to the baldheaded man and said, 'I'd like to talk to the manager, please.'

'I'm the manager and the owner both,' the baldheaded man said. 'Myron Krepps, how do you do?'

'I'm Detective Kling. I wonder if you would take a look at this picture and tell me if you know the man.'

'I'd be more than happy to,' Krepps said. 'Did he do something?'

'Yes,' Kling said.

'May I ask what it is he done?'

'Well, that's not important,' Kling said. He took the drawing from its envelope and handed it to Krepps. Krepps cocked his head to one side and studied it.

'Does he work here?' Kling asked.

'Nope,' Krepps said.

'Has he ever worked here?'

'Nope,' Krepps said.

'Have you ever seen him in the diner?'

Krepps paused. 'Is this something serious?'

'Yes,' Kling said, and then immediately asked, 'Why?' He could not have said what instinct provoked him into pressing the issue, unless it was the slight hesitation in Krepps's voice as he asked his question.

'How serious?' Krepps said.

'He beat up a young girl,' Kling said.

'Oh.'

'Is that serious enough?'

'That's pretty serious,' Krepps admitted.

'Serious enough for you to tell me who he is?'

'I thought it was a minor thing,' Krepps said. 'For minor things, who needs to be a good citizen?'

'Do you know this man, Mr Krepps?'

'Yes, I seen him around.'

'Have you seen him here in the diner?'

'Yes.'

'How often?'

'When he makes his rounds.'

'What do you mean?'

'He goes to all the places on the dock here.'

'Doing what?'

'I wouldn't get him in trouble for what he does,' Krepps said. 'As far as I'm concerned, it's no crime what he does. The city is unrealistic, that's all.'

'What is it that he does, Mr Krepps?'

'It's only that you say he beat up a young girl. That's serious. For that, I don't have to protect him.'

'Why does he come here, Mr Krepps? Why does he go to all the places on the dock?'

'He collects for the numbers,' Krepps said. 'Whoever wants to play the numbers, they give him their bets when he comes around.'

'What's his name?'

'They call him Cookie.'

'Cookie what?'

'I don't know his last name. Just Cookie. He comes to collect for the numbers.'

'Do you sell peanuts, Mr Krepps?'

'What? Peanuts?'

'Yes.'

'No, I don't sell peanuts. I carry some chocolates and some Life Savers and some chewing-gum, but no peanuts. Why? You like peanuts?'

'Is there any place on the dock where I can get some?'

'Not on the dock,' Krepps said.

'Where then?'

'Up the street. There's a bar. You can get peanuts there.'

'Thank you,' Kling said. 'You've been very helpful.'

'Good, I'm glad,' Krepps said. 'Now, please, would you mind paying for the coffee you drank?'

The front plate-glass window of the bar was painted a dull green. Bold white letters spelled out the name, BUDDY'S, arranged in a somewhat sloppy semicircle in the centre of the glass. Kling walked into the bar and directly to the phone booth some five feet beyond the single entrance door. He took a dime from his pocket, put it in the slot, and dialled his own home phone. While the phone rang unanswered on the other end, he simulated a lively conversation and simultaneously cased the bar. He did not recognize Cindy's attacker among any of the men sitting at the bar itself or in the booths. He hung up, fished his dime from the return chute, and walked up to the bar. The bartender looked at him curiously. He was either a college kid who had wandered into the waterfront area by accident – or else he was a cop. Kling settled the speculation at once by producing his shield.

'Detective Bert Kling,' he said. '87th Squad.'

The bartender studied the shield with an unwavering eye – he was used to bulls wandering in and out of his fine establishment – and then asked in a very polite, prep-school voice, 'What is it that you wish, Detective Kling?'

Kling did not answer at once. Instead, he scooped a handful of peanuts from the bowl on the bar top, put several into his mouth, and began chewing noisily. The proper thing to do, he supposed, was to inquire about some violation or other, garbage cans left outside, serving alcohol to minors, any damn thing to throw the bartender off base. The next thing to do was have the lieutenant assign another man or men to a stakeout of the bar, and simply pick up Cookie the next time he wandered in. That was the proper procedure, and Kling debated using it as he munched on his peanuts and stared silently at the bartender. The only trouble with picking up Cookie, of course, was that Cindy Forrest had been frightened half to death by him. How could you persuade a girl who'd been beaten senseless that it was in her own interest to identify the man who had attacked her? Kling kept munching his peanuts. The bartender kept watching him.

'Would you like a beer or something, Detective Kling?' he asked.

'You the owner?'

'I'm Buddy. You want a beer?'

'Uh-uh,' Kling said, chewing. 'On duty.'

'Well, was there something on your mind?' Buddy asked.

Kling nodded. He had made his decision. He began baiting his trap. 'Cookie been in today?'

'Cookie who?'

'You get a lot of people named Cookie in here?'

'I don't get *anybody* named Cookie in here,' Buddy said.

'Yeah, you do,' Kling said, and nodded. He scooped up another handful of peanuts. 'Don't you know him?'

'No.'

'That's a shame.' Kling began munching peanuts again. Buddy continued watching him. 'You're sure you don't know him?'

'Never heard of him.'

'That's too bad,' Kling said. 'We want him. We want him real bad.'

'What for?'

'He beat up a girl.'

'Yeah?'

'Yeah. Sent her to the hospital.'

'No kidding?'

'That's right,' Kling said. 'We've been searching the whole damn city for him.' He paused, and then took a wild gamble. 'Couldn't find him at the address we had in the Lousy File, but we happen to know he comes in here a lot.'

'How do you happen to know that?'

Kling smiled. 'We've got ways.'

'Mmm,' Buddy said noncommittally.

'We'll get him,' Kling said, and again he took a wild gamble. 'The girl identified his picture. Soon as we pick him up, goodbye, Charlie.'

'He's got a record, huh?'

'No,' Kling answered. 'No record.'

Buddy leaned forward slightly, ready to pounce. 'No record, huh?'

'Nope.'

'Then how'd you get his picture for the girl to identify?' Buddy said, and suddenly smiled.

'He's in the numbers racket,' Kling said. Idly, he popped another peanut into his mouth.

'So?'

'We've got a file on them.'

'On who?'

'On half the guys involved with numbers in this city.'

'Yeah?' Buddy said. His eyes had narrowed to a squint. It was plain to see that he did not trust Kling and was searching for a flaw in what he was being told.

'Sure,' Kling said. 'Addresses, pictures, even prints of some of them.'

'Yeah?' Buddy said again.

'Yeah.'

'What for?'

'Waiting for them to step out of line.'

'What do you mean?'

'I mean something bigger than numbers. Something we can lock them up for and throw away the key.'

'Oh.' Buddy nodded. He was convinced. This, he understood. The devious ways of cops, he understood. Kling tried to keep his face blank. He picked up another handful of peanuts.

'Cookie's finally stepped over the line. Once we get him, the girl takes another look, and bingo! First-degree assault.'

'He used a weapon?'

'Nope, his hands. But he tried to kill her nonetheless.'

Buddy shrugged.

'We'll get him, all right,' Kling said. 'We know who he is, so it's just a matter of time.'

'Yeah, well.' Buddy shrugged.

'All we have to do is find him, that's all. The rest is easy.'

'Yeah, well, sometimes finding a person can be extremely difficult,' Buddy said, reactivating his prep-school voice.

'I'm going to give you a word of warning, friend,' Kling said.

'What's that?'

'Keep your mouth shut about my being in here.'

'Who would I tell?'

'I don't know *who* you'd tell, but it better be *nobody*.'

'Why would I want to obstruct justice?' Buddy said, an offended look coming onto his face. 'If this Cookie person beat up a girl, why then good luck to you in finding him.'

'I appreciate your sentiments.'

'Sure.' Buddy paused, and glanced down at the peanut bowl. 'You going to eat *all* of those, or what?'

'Remember what I told you,' Kling said, hoping he wasn't overdoing it. 'Keep your mouth shut. If this leaks, and we trace it back to you ...'

'Nothing leaks around here but the beer tap,' Buddy answered, and moved away when someone at the other end of the bar signalled him. Kling sat a moment longer, and then rose, put another handful of peanuts into his mouth, and walked out.

On the pavement outside, he permitted himself a smile.

The item appered in both afternoon newspapers later that day.

It was small and hardly noticeable, buried as it was in a morass of print on the fourth page of both papers. Its headline was brief but eye-catching:

Witnesses to Beating Balk

Two witnesses to the brutal beating of Patrolman Ronald Fairchild last Wednesday, October 11, refused today to identify a photograph of the alleged attacker.

The picture was taken from a police file of "numbers racketeers" and had been shown previously to another victim of the same suspect. Miss Cynthia Forrest, recuperating from a bad beating at Elizabeth Rushmore Hospital here, positively identified the photograph and agreed to testify against the known suspect when he is apprehended.

Patrolman Critical

Detective-Lieutenant Peter

Byrnes, whose 87th Squad is investigating both assaults, commented today, "The apathy of these other witnesses is appalling. Patrolman Fairchild has been in coma and on the critical list at Buena Vista Hospital ever since he was admitted last week. If this man dies, we are dealing with a homicide here. Were it not for decent people like Miss Forrest, this city would never get to prosecute a criminal case."

Byrnes read the article in the privacy of his corner office, and then looked up at Kling, who was standing on the other side of his desk, beaming with the pride of authorship.

'Is Fairchild really on the critical list?' he asked.

'Nope,' Kling answered.

'Suppose our man checks?'

'Let him check. I've alerted Buena Vista.'

Byrnes nodded and looked at the article again. He put it aside then, and said, 'You made me sound like a jerk.'

Chapter Ten

Meyer and Carella were in the squadroom when Kling came out of the lieutenant's office.

'How you doing?' Carella asked him.

'So-so. We were just looking over the cheese.'

'What cheese?'

'Ah-ha,' Kling said mysteriously, and left.

'When did the lab say they'd call back on those vitamin capsules?' Carella asked.

'Sometime today,' Meyer answered.

'*When* today? It's past five already.'

'Don't jump on me,' Meyer said, and rose from his desk to walk to the water cooler. The telephone rang. Carella lifted it from the cradle.

'87th Squad, Carella,' he said.

'Steve, this is Bob O'Brien.'

'Yeah, what's up, Bob?'

'How long do you want me to stick with this Nelson guy?'

'Where are you?'

'Outside his house. I tailed him from his office to the hospital and then here.'

'What hospital?'

'General Presbyterian.'

'What was he doing there?'

'Search me. Most doctors are connected with hospitals, aren't they?'

'I guess so. When did he leave his office?'

'This afternoon, after visiting hours.'

'What time was that?'

'A little after two.'

'And he went directly to the hospital?'

'Yeah. He drives a little red MG.'

'What time did he leave the hospital?'

'About a half hour ago.'

'And went straight home?'

'Right. You think he's bedded down for the night?'

'I don't know. Call me in an hour or so, will you?'

'Right. Where'll you be? Home?'

'No, we'll be here a while yet.'

'Okay,' O'Brien said, and hung up. Meyer came back to his desk with a paper cup full of water. He propped it against his telephone, and then opened his desk drawer and took out a long cardboard strip of brightly coloured capsules.

'What's that?' Carella asked.

'For my cold,' Meyer said, and popped one of the capsules out of its cellophane wrapping. He put it into his mouth and washed it down with water. The phone rang again. Meyer picked it up.

'87th Squad, Meyer.'

'Meyer, this is Andy Parker. I'm still with Krantz, just checking in. He's in a cocktail lounge with a girl has boobs like watermelons.'

'What size, would you say?' Meyer asked.

'Huh? How the hell do I know?'

'Okay, just stick with him. Call in again later, will you?'

'I'm tired,' Parker said.

'So am I.'

'Yeah, but I'm *really* tired,' Parker said, and hung up.

Meyer replaced the phone on its cradle. 'Parker,' he said. 'Krantz is out drinking.'

'That's nice,' Carella said. 'You want to send out for some food?'

'With this cold, I'm not very hungry,' Meyer said.

'With this case, I'm not very hungry,' Carella said.

'There should be mathematics.'

'What do you mean?'

'To a case. There should be the laws of mathematics. I don't like cases that defy addition and subtraction.'

'What the hell was Bert grinning about when he left?'

'I don't know. He grins a lot,' Meyer said, and shrugged. 'I like two and two to make four. I like suicide to be suicide.'

'You think this is suicide?'

'No. That's what I mean. I don't like suicide to be murder. I like mathematics.'

'I failed geometry in high school,' Carella said.

'Yeah?'

'Yeah.'

'Our facts are right,' Meyer said, 'and the facts add up to suicide. But I don't like the feel.'

'The feel is wrong,' Carella agreed.

'That's right, the feel is wrong. The feel is murder.'

The telephone rang. Meyer picked it up. '87th Squad, Meyer,' he said. 'You again? What now?' He listened. 'Yeah? Yeah? Well, I don't know, we'll check it. Okay, stick with it. Right.' He hung up.

'Who?' Carella said.

'Bob O'Brien. He says a blue Thunderbird just pulled up to Nelson's house, and a blonde woman got out. He wanted to know if Melanie Gifford drives a blue Thunderbird.'

'I don't know what the hell she drives, do you?'

'No.'

'Motor Vehicle Bureau's closed, isn't it?'

'We can get them on the night line.'

'I think we'd better.'

Meyer shrugged. 'Nelson is a friend of the family. It's perfectly reasonable for her to be visiting him.'

'Yeah, I know,' Carella said. 'What's the number there?'

'Here you go,' Meyer said, and flipped open his telephone pad. 'Of course, there was that business at Gifford's party.'

'The argument, you mean?' Carella said, dialling.

'Yeah, when Gifford took a sock at the doctor.'

'Yeah.' Carella nodded. 'It's ringing.'

'But Gifford was drunk.'

'Yeah. Hello,' Carella said into the phone. 'Steve Carella, Detective/Second, 87th Squad. Checking automobile registration for Mrs Melanie Gifford, Larksview. Right, I'll wait. What? No, that's Gifford, with a G. Right.' He covered the mouthpiece. 'Doesn't Bob know what she looks like?' he asked.

'How would he?'

'That's right. This goddamn case is making me dizzy.' He glanced down at the cardboard strip of capsules on Meyer's desk. 'What's that stuff you're taking, anyway?'

'It's supposed to be good,' Meyer said. 'Better than all that other crap I've been using.'

Carella looked up at the wall clock.

'Anyway, I only have to take them twice a day,' Meyer said.

'Hello,' Carella said into the phone. 'Yes, go ahead. Blue thunderbird convertible, 1964. Right, thank you.' He hung up. 'You heard?'

'I heard.'

'That's pretty interesting, huh?'

'That's *very* interesting.'

'What do you suppose old Melanie Wistful wants with our doctor friend?'

'Maybe she's got a cold, too,' Meyer said.

'Maybe so.' Carella sighed. 'Why only twice?'

'Huh?'

'Why do you only have to take them twice a day?'

Five minutes later, Carella was placing a call to Detective-Lieutenant Sam Grossman at his home in Majesta.

Bob O'Brien was standing across the street from Nelson's brownstone on South Fourteenth when Meyer and Carella arrived. The red MG was parked in front of the doorway, and behind that was Melanie Gifford's blue Thunderbird. Meyer and Carella walked up to where he stood with his shoulders hunched and his hands in his pockets. He recognized them immediately, but only nodded in greeting.

'Getting pretty chilly,' he said.

'Mmm. She still in there?'

'Yep. The way I figure it, he's got the whole building. Ground floor is the entry, first floor must be the kitchen, dining and living room area, and the top floor's the bedrooms.'

'How the hell'd you figure that?' Meyer asked.

'Ground-floor light went on when the woman arrived – is she Mrs Gifford?'

'She is.'

'Mmm-huh,' O'Brien said, 'and out again immediately afterwards. The lights on the first floor were on until just a little while ago. An older woman came out at about seven. I figured she's either the cook or the housekeeper or both.'

'So they're alone in there, huh?'

'Yeah. Light went on upstairs just about ten minutes after the old lady left. See that small window? I figured that's the john, don't you?'

'Yeah, must be.'

'That went on first, and then off, and then the light in the big window went on. That's a bedroom, sure as hell.'

'What do you suppose they're doing in there?' Meyer asked.

'I know what *I'd* be doing in there,' O'Brien said.

'Why don't you go home?' Carella said.

'You don't need me?'

'No. Go on, we'll see you tomorrow.'

'You going in?'

'Yeah.'

'You sure you won't need me to take pictures?'

'Ha ha,' Meyer said, and then followed Carella, who had already begun crossing the street. They paused on the front step. Carella found the doorbell and rang it. There was no answer. He rang it again. Meyer stepped back off the stoop. The lights on the first floor went on.

'He's coming down,' Meyer whispered.

'Let him come down,' Carella said. 'Second murderer.'

'Huh?'

'Macbeth, Act III, scene 3.'

'Boy,' Meyer said, and the entry lights went on. The front door opened a moment later.

'Dr Nelson?' Carella said.

'Yes?' The doctor seemed surprised, but not particularly annoyed. He was wearing a black silk robe, and his feet were encased in slippers.

'I wonder if we might come in,' Carella said.

'Well, I was just getting ready for bed.'

'This won't take a moment.'

'Well ...'

'You're alone, aren't you, doctor?'

'Yes, of course,' Nelson said.

'May we come in?'

'Well ... well, yes. I suppose so. But I *am* tired, and I hope –'

'We'll be as brief as we possibly can,' Carella said, and he walked into the house. There was a couch in the entry, a small table before it. A mirror was on the wall opposite the door; a shelf for mail was fastened to the wall below it. Nelson did not invite them upstairs. He put his hands in the pockets of his robe, and made it clear from his stance that he did not intend moving farther into the house than the entry hall.

'I've got a cold,' Meyer said.

Nelson's eyebrows went up just a trifle.

'I've been trying everything,' Meyer continued. 'I just started on some new stuff. I hope it works.'

Nelson frowned. 'Excuse me, Detective Meyer,' he said, 'but did you come here to discuss your –'

Carella reached into his jacket pocket. When he extended his hand to Nelson, there was a purple-and-black gelatin capsule on the palm.

'Do you know what this is, Dr Nelson?' he asked.

'It looks like a vitamin capsule,' Nelson answered.

'It is, to be specific, a PlexCin capsule, the combination of Vitamin C and B-complex that Stan Gifford was using.'

'Oh, yes,' Nelson said, nodding.

'In fact, to be more specific, it is a capsule taken from the bottle of vitamins Gifford kept in his home.'

'Yes?' Nelson said. He seemed extremely puzzled. He seemed to be wondering exactly where Carella was leading.

'We sent the bottle of capsules to Lieutenant Grossman at the lab this afternoon,' Carella said. 'No poison in any of them. Only vitamins.'

'But I've got a cold,' Meyer said.

Nelson frowned.

'And Detective Meyer's cold led us to call Lieutenant Grossman again, just for the fun of it. He agreed to meet us at the lab, Dr Nelson. We've been down there for the past few hours. Sam – that's Lieutenant Grossman – had some interesting things to tell us, and we wanted your ideas. We want to be as specific about this as possible, you see, since there are a great many specifics in the Gifford case. Isn't that right?'

'Yes, I suppose so.'

'The specific poison, for example, and the specific dose, and the specific speed of the poison, and the specific dissolving rate of a gelatin capsule, isn't that right?'

'Yes, that's right,' Nelson said.

'You're an attending physician at General Presbyterian, aren't you, Dr Nelson?'

'Yes, I am.'

'We spoke to the pharmacist there just a little while ago. He tells us they stock strophantin in its crystalline powder form, oh, maybe three or four grains of it. The rest is in ampules, and even that isn't kept in any great amount.'

'That's very interesting. But what –'

'Open the capsule, Dr Nelson.'

'What?'

'The vitamin capsule. Open it. It comes apart. Go ahead. The size is a double-O, Dr Nelson. You know that, don't you?'

'I would assume it was either an O or a double-O.'

'But let's be specific. This specific capsule that contains the vitamins Gifford habitually took is a double-O.'

'All right then, it's a double-O.'

'Open it.'

Nelson sat on the couch, put the capsule on the low table, and carefully pulled one part from the other. A sifting of powder fell onto the table top.

'That's the vitamin compound, Dr Nelson. The same stuff that's in every one of those capsules in Gifford's bottle. Harmless. In fact, to be specific, beneficial. Isn't that right?'

'That's right.'

'Take another look at the capsule,' Nelson looked. 'No, Dr Nelson, *inside* the capsule. Do you see anything?'

'Why ... there ... there appears to be another capsule inside it.'

'Why, yes!' Carella said. 'Upon my soul, there *does* appear to be another capsule inside it. As a matter of fact, Dr Nelson, it is a number *three* gelatin capsule, which, as you see, fits very easily into the large double-O capsule. We made this sample at the lab.' He lifted the larger capsule from the table and then shook out the rest of its vitamin contents. The smaller capsule fell onto the table top. Using his forefinger, Carella pushed the smaller capsule away from the small mound of vitamins and said, 'The third capsule, Dr Nelson.'

'I don't know what you mean.'

'We were looking for a third capsule, you see. Since the one Gifford took at lunch couldn't possibly have killed him. Now, Dr Nelson, if this smaller capsule were loaded with two grains of stophanthin and placed inside the larger capsule, *that* could have killed him, don't you think?'

'Certainly, but it would have –'

'Yes, Dr Nelson?'

'Well, it seems to me that . . . that the smaller capsule would have dissolved very rapidly, too. I mean –'

'You mean, don't you, Dr Nelson, that if the outside capsule took six minutes to dissolve, the inside capsule might take, oh, let's say another three or four or five or however many minutes to dissolve. Is that what you mean?'

'Yes.'

'So that it doesn't really change anything, does it? The poison still would have had to be taken just before Gifford went on.'

'Yes, I would imagine so.'

'But I have a cold,' Meyer said.

'Yes, and he's taking some capsules of his own,' Carella said, smiling. 'Only has to take two a day because the drug is released slowly over a period of twelve hours. They're called time-release capsules, Dr Nelson. I'm sure you're familiar with them.' Nelson seemed as if he were about to rise, and Carella instantly said, 'Stay where you are, Dr Nelson, we're not finished.'

Meyer smiled and said, 'Of course, my capsules were produced commercially. I imagine it would be impossible to duplicate a time-release capsule without manufacturing facilities, wouldn't it, Dr Nelson?'

'I would imagine so.'

'Well, to be specific,' Carella said, 'Lieutenant Sam Grossman said it *was* impossible to duplicate such a capsule. But he remembered experiments from way back in his Army days, Dr Nelson, when some of the doctors in his outfit were playing around with what is called enteric coating. Did the doctors in your outfit try it, too? Are you familiar with the expression "enteric coating", Dr Nelson?'

'Of course I am,' Nelson said, and he rose, and Carella leaned across the table and put his hands on the doctor's shoulders and slammed him down onto the couch again.

'Enteric coating,' Carella said, 'as it specifically applies to this small *inside* capsule, Dr Nelson, means that if the capsule had been immersed for exactly thirty seconds in a one per cent solution of formaldehyde, and then allowed to dry –'

'What is all this? Why are you –'

'– and then held for two weeks to allow the formaldehyde to act upon the gelatin, hardening it, then the –'

'I don't know what you mean!'

'I mean that a capsule treated in just that way would *not* dissolve in normal gastric juices for at least *three* hours, Dr Nelson, by which time it would have left the stomach. And after that, it would dissolve in the small intestine within a period of *five* hours. So you see, Dr Nelson, we're not working with six minutes any more. Only the outside capsule would have dissolved that quickly. We're working with anywhere from three to eight *hours*. We're working with a soft outer shell and a hard inner nucleus containing two full grains of poison. To be specific, Dr Nelson, we are working with the capsule Gifford undoubtedly took at lunch on the day he was murdered.'

Nelson shook his head. 'I don't know what you're talking about,' he said. 'I had nothing to do with any of this.'

'Ahhh, Dr Nelson,' Carella said. 'Did we forget to mention that the pharmacy at General Presbyterian has a record of all drugs ordered by its physicians? The record shows you have been personally withdrawing small quantities of strophanthin from the pharmacy over the past month. There is no evidence that you were administering the drug to any of your patients at the hospital during that period of time.' Carella paused. 'We know exactly *how* you did it, Dr Nelson. Now would you like to tell us *why*?'

Nelson was silent.

'Then perhaps Mrs Gifford would,' Carella said. He walked to the stairwell at the far end of the entry. 'Mrs Gifford,' he called, 'would you please put on your clothes and come downstairs?'

Elizabeth Rushmore Hospital was on the southern rim of the city, a complex of tall white buildings that faced the River Dix. From the hospital windows, one could watch the river traffic, could see in the distance the smokestacks puffing up black clouds, could follow the spidery strands of the three bridges that connected the island to Sands Spit, Calm's Point, and Majesta.

A cold wind was blowing off the water. He had called the hospital earlier that afternoon and learned that evening visiting hours ended at eight o'clock. It was now seven-forty-five, and he stood on the river's edge with his coat collar raised, and looked up at the lighted hospital windows and once again went over his plan.

He had thought at first that the whole thing was a cheap cop trick. He had listened attentively while Buddy told him about the visit of the blond cop, the same son of a bitch; Buddy said his name was Kling, Detective Bert Kling. Holding the phone receiver to his ear, he had listened, and his hand had begun sweating on the black plastic. But he had told himself all along that it was only a crumby trick, did they think he was going to fall for such a cheap stunt?

Still, they had known his name; Kling had asked for Cookie. How could they have known his name unless there really *was* a file someplace listing guys who were involved with numbers? And hadn't Kling mentioned something about not being able to locate him at the address they had for him in the file? If anything sounded legit, that sure as hell did. He had moved two years ago, so maybe the file went back before then. And besides, he hadn't been home for the past few days, so even if the file was a *recent* one, well then they wouldn't have been able to locate him at his address because he simply hadn't been there. So maybe there was some truth in it, who the hell knew?

But a picture? Where would they have gotten a picture of him? Well, that was maybe possible. If the cops really did have such a file, then maybe they also had a picture. He knew goddamn well that they took pictures all the time, mostly trying to get a line on guys in narcotics, but maybe they did it for numbers, too. He had seen laundry trucks or furniture vans parked in the same spot on a street all day long, and had known – together with everybody else in the neighbourhood – that it was cops taking pictures. So maybe it was possible they had a picture of him, too. And maybe that little bitch had really pointed him out, maybe so, it was a possibility. But it still smelled a little, there were still too many unanswered questions.

Most of the questions were answered for him when he read the story in the afternoon paper. He'd almost missed it because he had started from the back of the paper, where the racing results were, and then had only turned to the front afterwards, sort of killing time. The story confirmed that there *was* a file on numbers racketeers, for one thing, though he was pretty sure about that even before he'd seen the paper. It also explained why Fairchild couldn't make the identification, too. You can't be expected to look at a picture of somebody when you're laying in the hospital with a coma. He didn't think he'd hit the bastard that hard, but maybe he didn't know his own strength. Just to check he'd called Buena Vista as soon as he'd read the story and asked how Patrolman Fairchild was doing. They told him he was still in coma and on the critical list, so that part of it was true. And, of course, if those jerks in the office where Cindy worked were too scared to identify the picture, well then Fairchild's condition explained why Cindy was the only person the cops could bank on.

The word 'homicide' had scared him. If that son of a bitch *did* die, and if the cops picked him up and Cindy said, yes, that's the man, well, that was it, pal. He thought he'd really made it clear to her, but maybe she was tougher than he thought. For some strange reason, the idea excited him, the idea of her not having been frightened by the beating, of her still having the guts to identify his picture and promise to testify. He could remember being excited when he read the story, and the same excitement overtook him now as he looked up at the hospital windows and went over his plan.

Visiting hours ended at eight o'clock, which meant he had exactly ten minutes to get into the building. He wondered suddenly if they would let him in so close to the deadline, and he immediately began walking towards the front entrance. A wide slanting concrete canopy covered the revolving entrance doors. The hospital was new, an imposing edifice of aluminium and glass and concrete. He pushed through the revolving doors and walked immediately to the desk on the right of the entrance lobby. A woman in white – he supposed she was a nurse – looked up as he approached.

'Miss Cynthia Forrest?' he said.

'Room seven-twenty,' the woman said, and immediately looked at her watch. 'Visiting hours are over in a few minutes, you know,' she said.

'Yes, I know, thanks,' he answered, and smiled, and walked swiftly to the elevator bank. There was only one other civilian waiting for an elevator; the rest were all hospital people in white uniforms. He wondered abruptly if there would be a cop on duty outside her door. Well, if there is, he thought, I just call it off, that's all. The elevator doors opened. He stepped in with the other people, pushed the button for the seventh floor, noticed that one of the nurses reached for the same button after he had pushed it, and then withdrew quietly to the rear of the elevator. The doors closed.

'If you ask me,' a nurse was saying, 'it's psoriasis. Dr Kirsch said it's blood poisoning, but did you see that man's leg? You can't tell me that's from blood poisoning.'

'Well, they're going to test him tomorrow,' another nurse said.

'In the meantime, he's got a fever of a hundred and two.'

'That's from the swollen leg. The leg's all infected, you know.'

'Psoriasis,' the first nurse said, '*that's* what it is,' and the doors opened. Both nurses stepped out. The doors closed again. The elevator was silent. He looked at his watch. It was five minutes to eight. The elevator stopped again at the fourth floor, and again at the fifth. On the seventh floor, he got off the elevator with the nurse who had earlier reached for the same button. He hesitated in the corridor for a moment. There was a wide-open area directly in front of the elevators. Beyond that was a large room with a bank of windows, the sunroom, he supposed. To the right and left of the elevators were glass doors leading to the patients' rooms beyond. A nurse sat at a desk some three feet before the doors on the left. He walked swiftly to the desk and said, 'Which way is seven-twenty?'

The nurse barely looked up. 'Straight through,' she said. 'You've only got a few minutes.'

'Yes, I know, thanks,' he said, and pushed open the glass door. The room just inside the partition was 700, and the one beyond that was 702, so he assumed 720 was somewhere at the end of the hall. He looked at his watch. It was almost eight o'clock. He hastily scanned the doors in the corridor, walking rapidly, finding the one marked MEN halfway down the hall. Pushing open the door, he walked immediately to one of the stalls, entered it, and locked it behind him.

In less than a minute, he heard a loudspeaker announcing that visiting hours were now over. He smiled, lowered the toilet seat, sat, lighted a cigarette, and began his long wait.

He did not come out of the men's room until midnight. By that time, he had listened to a variety of patients and doctors as they discussed an endless variety of ills and ailments, both subjectively and objectively. He listened to each of them quietly and with some amusement because they helped to pass the time. He had reasoned that he could not make his move until the hospital turned out the lights in all the rooms. He didn't know what time taps was in this crumby place, but he supposed it would be around ten or ten-thirty. He had decided to wait until midnight, just to be sure. He figured that all of the visiting doctors would be gone by that time, and so he knew he had to be careful when he came out into the corridor. He didn't want anyone to stop him or even to see him on the way to Cindy's room.

It was a shame he would have to kill the little bitch.

She could have really been something.

There was a guy who came back to pee a total of seventeen times between eight o'clock and midnight. He knew because the guy was evidently having some kind of kidney trouble, and every time he came into the john he would walk over to the urinals – the sound of his shuffling slippers carrying into the locked stall – and then he would begin cursing out loud while he peed, 'Oh, you son of a bitch! Oh, what did I do to deserve such pain and misery?' and like that. One time, while he was peeing, some other guy yelled out from the stall alongside, 'For God's sake, Mandel, keep your sickness to yourself.'

And then the guy standing at the urinals had yelled back, 'It should happen to *you*, Liebowitz! It should *rot*, and fall off of you, and be washed down the drain into the river, may God hear my plea!'

He had almost burst out laughing, but instead he lighted another cigarette and looked at his watch again, and wondered what time they'd be putting all these sick jerks to bed, and wondered what Cindy would be wearing. He could still remember her undressing that night he'd beat her up, the quick flash of her nudity – he stopped his thoughts. He could not think that way. He had to kill her tonight, there was no sense thinking about – and yet maybe *while* he was doing it, maybe it would be like last time, maybe with her belly smooth and hard beneath him, maybe like last time maybe he could.

The men's room was silent at midnight.

He unlocked the stall and came out into the room and then walked past the sinks to the door and opened it just a bit and looked out into the corridor. The floors were some kind of hard polished asphalt tile, and you could hear the clicking of high heels on it for a mile, which was good. He listened as a nurse went swiftly down the corridor, her heels clicking away, and then he listened until everything was quiet again. Quickly, he stepped out into the hall. He began walking towards the end of the corridor, the steadily mounting door numbers flashing by on left and right, 709, 710, 711 ... 714, 715, 716 ...

He was passing the door to room 717 on his left, when it opened and a nurse stepped into the corridor. He was too startled to speak at first. He stopped dead, breathless, debating whether he should hit her. And then, from somewhere, he heard a voice saying, 'Good evening, nurse,' and he hardly recognized the voice as his own because it sounded so cultured and pleasant and matter-of-fact. The nurse looked at him for just a moment longer, and then smiled and said, 'Good evening, doctor,' and continued walking down the corridor. He did not turn to look back at her. He continued walking until he came to room 720. Hoping it was a private room, he opened the door, stepped inside quickly, closed the door immediately, and leaned against it, listening. He could hear nothing in the corridor outside. Satisfied, he turned into the room.

The only light in the room came from the windows at the far end, just beyond the bed. He could see the silhouette of her body beneath the blankets, the curved hip limned by the dim light coming from the window. The blanket was pulled high over her shoulders and the back of her neck, but he could see the short blonde hair illuminated by the dim glow of moonlight from the windows. He was getting excited again, the way he had that night he beat her up. He reminded himself why he was here – this girl could send him to the electric chair. If Fairchild died, this girl was all they needed to convict him. He took a deep breath and moved towards the bed.

In the near-darkness, he reached for her throat, seized it between his huge hands and then whispered, 'Cindy,' because he wanted her to be awake and looking straight up into his face when he crushed the life out of her. His hands tightened.

She sat erect suddenly. Two fists flew up between his own hands, up and outward, breaking the grip. His eyes opened wide.

'Surprise!' Bert Kling said, and punched him in the mouth.

Chapter Eleven

Detectives are not poets; there is no iambic pentameter in a broken head.

If Meyer were William Shakespeare, he might have indeed belived that 'Love is a smoke raised with the fume of sighs,' but he wasn't William Shakespeare. If Steve Carella were Henry Wadsworth Longfellow, he would have known that 'Love is every busy with his shuttle,' but alas, you know, he wasn't Henry Wadsworth Longfellow – though he did have an Uncle Henry who lived in Red Bank, New Jersey. As a matter of fact, if either of the two men were Buckingham or Ovid or Byron, they might have respectively realized that 'love is the salt of life', and 'the perpetual source of fears and anxieties,' and 'a capricious power' – but they weren't poets, they were only working cops.

Even as working cops, they might have appreciated Homer's comment (from the motion picture of the same name) which, translated into English subtitles by Nikos Konstantin, went something like this: '*Who love too much, hate in the like extreme.*'

But they had neither seen the picture nor read the book, what the hell can you expect from flatfoots?

Oh, they could tell you tales of love, all right. Boy, the tales of love they could tell. They had heard tales of love from a hundred and one people, or maybe even more. And don't think they didn't know what love was all about, oh, they knew what it was all about, all right. Love was sweet and pure and marvellous, love was magnificent. Hadn't they loved their mothers and their fathers and their aunts and uncles and such? Hadn't they kissed a girl for the first time when they were thirteen or fourteen or something, wasn't that love? Oh boy, it sure was. And weren't they both happily married men who loved their wives and their children? Listen, it wouldn't pay to tell them about love because they knew all about it, yes, sir.

'We love each other,' Nelson said.

'We love each other,' Melanie said.

The pair sat in the 2.00 a.m. silence of the squadroom and dictated their confessions to police stenographers, sitting at separate desks, their hands still stained with the ink that had been used to fingerprint them. Meyer and Carella listened unemotionally, silently, patiently – they had heard it all before. Neither Nelson nor Melanie seemed to realize that they would be taken from the precinct by police van at 9.00 a.m., brought downtown for arraignment, and put into separate cells. They had been seeing each other secretly for more than a year, they said, but they did not yet seem to realize they would not see each other again until they were brought to trial – and then perhaps never after.

Carella and Meyer listened silently as their tale of love unfolded.

'You can't legislate against love,' Nelson said, transforming another man's comment, but making his meaning clear enough. 'This thing between Melanie and me just happened. Neither of us wanted it, and neither of us asked for it. It just happened.'

'It just happened,' Melanie said at the desk nearby. 'I remember exactly when. We were sitting outside the studio in Carl's car one night, waiting for Stan to take off his makeup so the three of us could go to dinner together. Carl's hand touched mine, and the next thing we knew we were kissing. We fell in love shortly afterwards. I guess we fell in love.'

'We fell in love,' Nelson said. 'We tried to stop ourselves. We knew it wasn't right. But when we saw we couldn't stop, we went to Stan and told him about it, and asked him for a divorce. This was immediately after the incident at his party, when he tried to hit me. Last month, September. We told him we were in love and that Melanie wanted a divorce. He flatly refused.'

'I think he'd known about us all along,' Melanie said. 'If you say he revised his will, then that's why he must have done it. He must have known that Carl and I were having an affair. He was a very sensitive man, my husband. He must have known that something was wrong long before we told him about it.'

'The idea to kill him was mine,' Nelson said.

'I agreed to it readily,' Melanie said.

'I began drawing strophanthin from the hospital pharmacy last month. I know the pharmacist there, I often stop in when I'm short of something or other, something I need in my bag or at my office. I'll stop in and say, "Hi, Charlie, I need some penicillin," and of course he'll give it to me because he knows me. I did the same thing with the strophanthin. I never discussed why I needed it. I assumed he thought it was for my private practice, outside the hospital. At any rate, he never questioned me about it, why should he?'

'Carl prepared the capsule,' Melanie said. 'At the breakfast table that Wednesday, after Stan had taken his morning vitamins, I switched the remaining capsule for the one containing the poison. At lunch, I watched while he washed it down with water. We knew it would take somewhere between three and eight hours for the capsule to dissolve, but we didn't know exactly how long. We didn't necessarily expect him to die on camera, but it didn't matter, you see. We'd be nowhere near when it happened, and that was all that mattered. We'd be completely out of it.'

'And yet,' Nelson said, 'we realized that I would be a prime suspect. After all, I am a physician, and I do have access to drugs. We planned for this possibility by making certain that *I* was the one who suggested foul play, *I* was the one who demanded an autopsy.'

'We also figured,' Melanie said, 'that it would be a good idea if I said I suspected Carl. Then, once you found out what kind of poison had been used – how fast it worked, I mean – and once you knew Carl had been home all during the show, well then you'd automatically drop him as a suspect. That was what we figured.'

'We love each other,' Nelson said.

'We love each other,' Melanie said.

They sat still and silent after they had finished talking. The police stenographers showed them transcripts of what they had separately said, and they signed multiple copies, and then Alf Miscolo came out of the Clerical Office, handcuffed the pair, and led them downstairs to the detention cells.

'One for us, one for the lieutenant, and one for Homicide,' Carella told his stenographer. The stenographer merely nodded. He, too, had heard it all already. There was nothing you could tell him about love or homicide. He put on his hat, dropped the requested number of signed confessions on the desk nearest the railing, and went out of the squadroom. As he walked down the corridor, he could hear muted voices behind the closed door of the Interrogation Room.

'Why'd you beat her up?' Kling asked.

'I didn't beat up nobody,' Cookie said. 'I love that girl.'

'You *what*?'

'I love her, you deaf? I loved her from the first minute I ever seen her.'

'When was that?'

'The end of the summer. August. It was on the Stem. I just made a collection in a candy store on the corner there, and I was passing this Pokerino place in the middle of the block, and I thought maybe I'd stop in, kill some time, you know? The guy outside was giving his spiel, and I was standing there listening to him, so many games for a quarter, or whatever the hell it was. I looked in and there was this girl in a dark-green dress, leaning

over one of the tables and rolling the balls, I think she had something like
three queens, I'm not sure.'

'All right, what happened then?'

'I went in.'

'Go ahead.'

'What do you want from me?'

'I want to know why you beat her up.'

'I didn't beat her up, I told you that!'

'Who'd you think was in that bed tonight, you son of a bitch?'

'I didn't *know* who was in it. Leave me alone. You got nothing on me, you
think I'm some snot-nosed kid?'

'Yeah, I think you're some snot-nosed kid,' Kling said. 'What happened
that first night you saw her?'

'Nothing. There was a guy with her, a young guy, one of these advertising
types. I kept watching her, that's all. She didn't know I was watching her,
she didn't even know I existed. Then I followed them when they left, and
found out where she lived, and after that I kept following her wherever she
went. That's all.'

'That's *not* all.'

'I'm telling you that's all.'

'Okay, play it your way,' Kling said. 'Be a wise guy. We'll throw
everything but the goddamn kitchen sink at you.'

'I'm telling you I never laid a finger on her. I went up to her office to let her
know, that's all.'

'Let her know what?'

'That she was my girl. That, you know, she wasn't supposed to go out
with nobody else or see nobody, that she was *mine*, you dig? That's the only
reason I went up there, to let her know. I didn't expect all that kind of
goddamn trouble. All I wanted to do was tell her what I expected from her,
that's all.'

John 'Cookie' Cacciatore lowered his head. The brim of the hat hid his
eyes from Kling's gaze.

'If you'd all have minded your own business, everything would have been
all right.'

The squadroom was silent.

'I love that girl,' he said.

And then, in a mumble, 'You lousy bastard, you almost killed me tonight.'

Morning always comes.

In the morning, Detective Bert Kling went to Elizabeth Rushmore
Hospital and asked to see Cynthia Forrest. He knew this was not the normal
visiting time, but he explained that he was a working detective, and asked
that an allowance be made. Since everyone in the hospital knew that he was
the cop who'd captured a hoodlum on the seventh floor the night before,
there was really no need to explain. Permission was granted at once.

Cindy was sitting up in bed.

She turned her head towards the door as Kling came in, and then her hand
went unconsciously to her short blonde hair, fluffing it.

'Hi,' he said.

'Hello.'

'How do you feel?'

'All right.' She touched her eyes gingerly. 'Has the swelling gone down?'

'Yes.'

'But they're still discoloured, aren't they?'

'Yes, they are. You look all right, though.'

'Thank you.' Cindy paused. 'Did ... did he hurt you last night?'

'No.'

'You're sure.'

'Yes, I'm sure.'

'He's a vicious person.'

'I know he is.'

'Will he go to jail?'

'To prison, yes. Even without your testimony. He assaulted a police officer.' Kling smiled. 'Tried to strangle me, in fact. That's attempted murder.'

'I'm ... I'm very frightened of that man,' Cindy said.

'Yes, I can imagine.'

'But....' She swallowed. 'But if it'll help the case, I'll ... I'd be willing to testify. If it'll help, I mean.'

'I don't know,' Kling said. 'The D.A.'s office'll have to let us know about that.'

'All right,' Cindy said, and was silent. Sunlight streamed through the windows, catching her blonde hair. She lowered her eyes. Her hand picked nervously at the blankets. 'The only thing I'm afraid of is ... is when he gets out. Eventually, I mean. When he gets out.'

'Well, we'll see that you have police protection,' Kling said.

'Mmm,' Cindy said. She did not seem convinced.

'I mean ... I'll *personally* volunteer for the job,' Kling said, and hesitated.

Cindy raised her eyes to meet his. 'That's ... very kind of you,' she said slowly.

'Well ...' he answered and shrugged.

The room was silent.

'You could have got hurt last night,' Cindy said.

'No. No, there wasn't a chance.'

'You could have,' she insisted.

'No, really.'

'Yes,' she said.

'We're not going to start arguing again, are we?'

'No,' she said, and laughed, and then winced and touched her face. 'Oh, God,' she said, 'it still hurts.'

'But only when you laugh, right?'

'Yes,' she said, and laughed again.

'When do you think you'll be out of here?' Kling asked.

'I don't know. Tomorrow, I suppose. Or the day after.'

'Because I thought ...'

'Yes?'

'Well ...'

'What is it, Detective Kling?'

'I know you're a working girl ...'

'Yes?'

'And that you don't normally eat out.'

'That's right, I don't,' Cindy said.

'Unless you're escorted.'

Cindy waited.

'I thought ...'

She waited.

'I thought you'd like to have dinner with me sometime. When you're out of hospital, I mean.' He shrugged. 'I mean, *I'd* pay for it,' Kling said, and lapsed into silence.

Cindy did not answer for several moments. Then she smiled and said simply, 'I'd love to,' and paused, and immediately said, 'When?'

HAIL, HAIL, THE GANG'S ALL HERE!

"The morning hours of the night come imperceptibly here. It is a minute before midnight on the peeling face of the hanging wall clock, and then it is midnight, and then the minute hand moves visibly and with a lurch into the new day...."

(COERCION: A person who with a view to compel another person to do or to abstain from doing an act which such other person has a legal right to do or to abstain from doing wrongfully and unlawfully, is guilty of a misdemeanour. Section 530, New York State Penal Law.)

Chapter One
NIGHTSHADE

The morning hours of the night come imperceptibly here.

It is a minute before midnight on the peeling face of the hanging wall clock, and then it is midnight, and then the minute hand moves visibly and with a lurch into the new day. The morning hours have begun, but scarcely anyone has noticed. The stale coffee in soggy cardboard containers tastes the same as it did thirty seconds ago, the spastic rhythm of the clacking typewriters continues unabated, a drunk across the room shouts that the world is full of brutality, and cigarette smoke drifts up towards the face of the clock, where, unnoticed and unmourned, the old day has already been dead for two minutes. The telephone rings.

The men in this room are part of a tired routine, somewhat shabby about the edges, as faded and as gloomy as the room itself, with its cigarette-scarred desks and its smudged green walls. This could be the office of a failing insurance company were it not for the evidence of the holstered pistols hanging from the belts on the backs of wooden chairs painted a darker green than the walls. The furniture is ancient, the typewriters are ancient, the building itself is ancient – which is perhaps only fitting since these men are involved in what is an ancient pursuit, a pursuit once considered honourable. They are law enforcers. They are, in the words of the drunk still hurling epithets from the grilled detention cage across the room, rotten prick cop bastards. The telephone continues to ring.

The little girl lying in the alley behind the theatre was wearing a belted white trench coat wet with blood. There was blood on the floor of the alley, and blood on the metal fire door behind her, and blood on her face and matted in her blonde hair, blood on her miniskirt and on the lavender tights she wore. A neon sign across the street stained the girl's ebbing life juices green and then orange, while from the open knife wound in her chest, the blood spouted like some ghastly night flower, dark and rich, red, orange, green, pulsing in time to the neon flicker, a grotesque psychedelic light show, and then losing the rhythm, welling up with less force and power. She opened her mouth, she tried to speak, and the scream of an ambulance approaching the theatre seemed to come instead from her mouth on a fresh bubble of blood. The blood stopped, her life ended, the girl's eyes rolled back into her head. Detective Steve Carella turned away as the ambulance attendants rushed a stretcher into the alley. He told them the girl was already dead.

'We got here in seven minutes,' one of the attendants said.

'Nobody's blaming you,' Carella answered.

'This is Saturday night,' the attendant complained. 'Streets are full of traffic. Even *with* the damn siren.'

Carella walked to the unmarked sedan at the kerb. Detective Cotton Hawes, sitting behind the wheel, rolled down his frost-rimed window and said, 'How is she?'

'We've got a homicide,' Carella answered.

The boy was eighteen years old, and he had been picked up not ten minutes ago for breaking off car aerials. He had broken off twelve on the same street, strewing them behind him like a Johnny Appleseed planting radios; a cruising squad car had spotted him as he tried to twist the aerial of a 1966 Cadillac. He was drunk or stoned or both, and when Sergeant Murchison at the muster desk asked him to read the Miranda-Escobedo warning signs on the wall, printed in both English and Spanish, he could read neither. The arresting patrolman took the boy to the squadroom upstairs, where Detective Bert Kling was talking to Hawes on the telephone. He signalled for the patrolman to wait with his prisoner on the bench outside the slatted wooden rail divider, and then buzzed Murchison at the desk downstairs.

'Dave,' he said, 'we've got a homicide in the alley of the Eleventh Street Theatre. You want to get it rolling?'

'Right,' Murchison said, and hung up.

Homicides are a common occurrence in this city, and each one is treated identically, the grisly horror of violent death reduced to routine by a police force that would otherwise be overwhelmed by statistics. At the muster desk switchboard downstairs, while upstairs Kling waved the patrolman and his prisoner into the squadroom, Sergeant Murchison first reported the murder to Captain Frick, who commanded the 87th Precinct, and then to Lieutenant Byrnes, who commanded the 87th Detective Squad. He then phoned Homicide, who in turn set into motion an escalating process of notification that spread cancerously to include the Police Laboratory, the Telegraph, Telephone and Teletype Bureau at Headquarters, the Medical Examiner, the District Attorney, the District Commander of the Detective Division, the Chief of Detectives, and finally the Police Commissioner himself. Someone had thoughtlessly robbed a young woman of her life, and now a lot of sleepy-eyed men were being shaken out of their beds on a cold October night.

Upstairs, the clock on the squadroom wall read 12:30 a.m. The boy who had broken off twelve car aerials sat in a chair alongside Bert Kling's desk. Kling took one look at him and yelled to Miscolo in the Clerical Office to bring in a pot of strong coffee. Across the room, the drunk in the detention cage wanted to know where he was. In a little while, they would release him with a warning to try to stay sober till morning.

But the night was young.

They arrived alone or in pairs, blowing on their hands, shoulders hunched against the bitter cold, breaths pluming whitely from their lips. They marked the dead girl's position in the alleyway, they took her picture, they made drawings of the scene, they searched for the murder weapon and found none, and then they stood around speculating on sudden death. In this alleyway alongside a theatre, the policemen were the stars and the celebrities, and a curious crowd thronged the sidewalk where a barricade had already been set up, anxious for a glimpse of these men with their shields pinned to their overcoats – the identifying *Playbills* of law enforcement, without which you could not tell the civilians from the plainclothes cops.

Monoghan and Monroe had arrived from Homicide, and they watched dispassionately now as the Assistant Medical Examiner fluttered around the dead girl. They were both wearing black overcoats, black mufflers, and black fedoras, both heavier men than Carella, who stood between them with the lean look of an overtrained athlete, a pained expression on his face.

'He done some job on her,' Monroe said.

'Son of a bitch,' Monoghan added.

'You identified her yet?'

'I'm waiting for the M.E. to get through,' Carella answered.

'Might help to know what she was doing here in the alley. What's that door there?' Monroe asked.

'Stage entrance.'

'Think she was in the show?'

'I don't know,' Carella said.

'Well, what the hell,' Monoghan said, 'they're finished with her pocket-book there, ain't they? Why don't you look through it? You finished with that pocketbook there?' he yelled to one of the lab technicians.

'Yeah, any time you want it,' the technician shouted back.

'Go on, Carella, take a look.'

The technician wiped the blood off the dead girl's bag, and handed it to Carella. Monoghan and Monroe crowded in on him as he twisted open the clasp.

'Bring it over to the light,' Monroe said.

The light, with a metal shade, hung over the stage door. So violently had the girl been stabbed that flecks of blood had even dotted the enamelled white underside of the shade. In her bag they found a driver's licence identifying her as Mercy Howell of 1113 Rutherford Avenue, Age 24, Height 5 ft 3 in, Eyes Blue. They found an Actors Equity card in her name, as well as credit cards for two of the city's largest department stores. They found an unopened package of Virginia Slims, and a book of matches advertising an art course. They found a rat-tailed comb. They found seventeen dollars and forty-three cents in cash. They found a package of Kleenex, and an appointment book. They bound a ball-point pen with shreds of tobacco clinging to its tip, an eyelash curler, two subway tokens, and an advertisement for a see-through blouse, clipped from one of the local newspapers.

In the pocket of her trench coat, when the M.E. had finished with her and pronounced her dead from multiple stab wounds in the chest and throat, they found an unfired Browning .25 calibre automatic. They tagged the gun and the handbag, and they moved the girl out of the alleyway and into the waiting ambulance for removal to the morgue. There was now nothing left of Mercy Howell but a chalked outline of her body and a pool of her blood on the alley floor.

*   *   *

'You sober enough to understand me?' Kling asked the boy.

'I was never drunk to begin with,' the boy answered.

'Okay then, here we go,' Kling said. 'In keeping with the Supreme Court decision in *Miranda* v. *Arizona*, we are not permitted to ask you any questions until you are warned of your right to counsel and your privilege against self-incrimination.'

'What does that mean?' the boy asked. 'Self-incrimination?'

'I'm about to explain that to you now,' Kling said.

'This coffee stinks.'

'First, you have the right to remain silent if you so choose,' Kling said. 'Do you understand that?'

'I understand it.'

'Second, you do not have to answer any police questions if you don't want to. Do you understand that?'

'What the hell are you asking me if I understand for? Do I look like a moron or something?'

'The law requires that I ask whether or not you understand these specific warnings. *Did* you understand what I just said about not having to answer ...?'

'Yeah, yeah, I understood.'

'All right. Third, if you *do* decide to answer any questions, the answers may be used as evidence against you, do you ...?'

'What the hell did I do, break off a couple of car aerials? Jesus!'

'Did you understand that?'

'I understood it.'

'You also have the right to consult with an attorney before or during police questioning. If you do not have the money to hire a lawyer, a lawyer will be appointed to consult with you.'

Kling gave this warning straight-faced even though he knew that under the Criminal Procedure Code of the city for which he worked, a public defender could not be appointed by the courts until the preliminary hearing. There was no legal provision for the courts *or* the police to appoint counsel during questioning, and there were certainly no police funds set aside for the appointment of attorneys. In theory, a call to the Legal Aid Society should have brought a lawyer up there to the old squadroom within minutes, ready and eager to offer counsel to any indigent person desiring it. But in practice, if this boy sitting beside Kling told him in the next three seconds that he was unable to pay for his own attorney and would like one provided, Kling would not have known just what the hell to do – other than call off the questioning.

'I understand,' the boy said.

'You've signified that you understand all the warnings,' Kling said, 'and now I ask you whether you are willing to answer my questions without an attorney here to counsel you.'

'Go shit in your hat,' the boy said. 'I don't want to answer nothing.'

So that was that.

They booked him for Criminal Mischief, a Class-A Misdemeanour defined as intentional or reckless damage to the property of another person, and they took him downstairs to a holding cell, to await transportation to the Criminal Courts Building for arraignment.

The phone was ringing again, and a woman was waiting on the bench just outside the squadroom.

The watchman's booth was just inside the metal stage door. An electric clock on the wall behind the watchman's stool read 1:10 a.m. The watchman was a man in his late seventies who did not at all mind being questioned by the police. He came on duty, he told them, at seven-thirty each night. The company call was for eight, and he was there at the stage door waiting to greet everybody as they arrived to get made up and in costume. Curtain went down at eleven-twenty, and usually most of the kids was out of the theatre by quarter to twelve or, latest, midnight. He stayed on till nine the next morning, when the theatre box office opened.

'Ain't much to do during the night except hang around and make sure nobody runs off with the scenery,' he said, and chuckled.

'Did you happen to notice what time Mercy Howell left the theatre?' Carella asked.

'She the one got killed?' the old man asked.

'Yes,' Hawes said. 'Mercy Howell. About this high, blonde hair, blue eyes.'

'They're *all* about that high, with blonde hair and blue eyes,' the old man said, and chuckled again. 'I don't know hardly none of them by name. Shows come and go, you know. Be a hell of a chore to have to remember all the kids who go in and out that door.'

'Do you sit here by the door all night?' Carella asked.

'Well, no, not all night. What I do, is I lock the door after everybody's out and then I check the lights, make sure just the work light's on. I won't touch the switchboard, not allowed to, but I can turn out lights in the lobby, for example, if somebody left them on, or down in the toilets, sometimes they leave lights on down in the toilets. Then I come back here to the booth, and read or listen to the radio. Along about two o'clock, I check the theatre again, make sure we ain't got no fires or nothing, and then I come back here and make the rounds again at four o'clock, and six o'clock, and again about eight. That's what I do.'

'You say you lock this door . . .'

'That's right.'

'Would you remember what time you locked it tonight?'

'Oh, must've been about ten minutes to twelve. Soon as I knew everybody was out.'

'How do you know when they're out?'

'I give a yell up the stairs there. You see those stairs there? They go up to the dressing rooms. Dressing rooms are all upstairs in this house. So I go to the steps, and I yell, "Locking up! Anybody here?" And if somebody yells back, I know somebody's here, and I say, "Let's shake it, honey," if it's a girl, and if it's a boy, I say, "Let's hurry it up, sonny."' The old man chuckled again. 'With *this* show, it's sometimes hard to tell which's the girls and which's the boys. I manage, though,' he said, and again chuckled.

'So you locked that door at ten minutes to twelve?'

'Right.'

'And everybody had left the theatre by that time.'

''Cept me, of course.'

'Did you look out into the alley before you locked the door?'

'Nope. Why should I do that?'

'Did you hear anything outside while you were locking the door?'

'Nope.'

'Or at any time *before* you locked it?'

'Well, there's always noise outside when they're leaving, you know. They got friends waiting for them, or else they go home together, you know, there's always a lot of chatter when they go out.'

'But it was quiet when you locked the door.'

'Dead quiet,' the old man said.

The woman who took the chair beside Detective Meyer Meyer's desk was perhaps thirty-two years old, with long straight black hair trailing down her back, and wide brown eyes that were terrified. It was still October, and the colour of her tailored coat seemed suited to the season, a subtle tangerine with a small brown fur collar that echoed an outdoors trembling with the colours of autumn.

'I feel sort of silly about this,' she said, 'but my husband insisted that I come.'

'I see,' Meyer said.

'There are ghosts,' the woman said.

Across the room, Kling unlocked the door to the detention cage and said, 'Okay, pal, on your way. Try to stay sober till morning, huh?'

'It ain't one-thirty yet,' the man said, 'the night is young.' He stepped out of the cage, tipped his hat to Kling, and hurriedly left the squadroom.

Meyer looked at the woman sitting beside him, studying her with new interest because, to tell the truth, she had not seemed like a nut when she first walked into the squadroom. He had been a detective for more years than he chose to count, and in his time had met far too many nuts of every stripe and persuasion. But he had never met one as pretty as Adele Gorman with her well-tailored, fur-collared coat, and her Vassar voice and her skilfully applied eye makeup, lips bare of colour in her pale white face, pert and reasonably young and seemingly intelligent – but apparently a nut besides.

'In the house,' she said. 'Ghosts.'

'Where do you live, Mrs Gorman?' he asked. He had written her name on the pad in front of him, and now he watched her with his pencil poised and recalled the lady who had come into the squadroom only last month to report a gorilla peering into her bedroom from the fire escape outside. They had sent a patrolman over to make a routine check, and had even called the zoo and the circus (which was coincidentally in town, and which lent at least *some* measure of possibility to her claim) but there had been no ape on the fire escape, nor had any simians recently escaped from their cages. The lady came back the next day to report that her visiting gorilla had put in another appearance the night before, this time wearing a top hat and carrying a black cane with an ivory head. Meyer had assured her that he would have a platoon of cops watching her building that night, which seemed to calm her at least somewhat. He had then led her personally out of the squadroom and down the iron-runged steps, and through the high-ceilinged muster room, and past the hanging green globes on the front stoop, and onto the sidewalk outside the station house. Sergeant Murchison, at the muster desk, shook his head after the lady was gone, and muttered, 'More of them outside than in.'

Meyer watched Adele Gorman now, remembered what Murchison had said, and thought *Gorillas in September, ghosts in October*.

'We live in Smoke Rise,' she said. 'Actually, it's my father's house, but my husband and I are living there with him.'

'And the address?'

'374 MacArthur Lane. You take the first access road into Smoke Rise, about a mile and a half east of Silvermine Oval. The name on the mailbox is Van Houten. That's my father's name. Willem Van Houten.' She paused and studied him, as though expecting some reaction.

'Okay,' Meyer said, and ran a hand over his bald pate, and looked up, and said, 'Now, you were saying, Mrs Gorman ...'

'That we have ghosts.'

'Um-huh. What kind of ghosts?'

'Ghosts. Poltergeists. Shades. I don't know,' she said, and shrugged. 'What kinds of ghosts *are* there?'

'Well, they're *your* ghosts, so suppose you tell me,' Meyer said.

The telephone on Kling's desk rang. He lifted the receiver and said, 'Eighty-seventh Squad, Detective Kling.'

'There are two of them,' Adele said.

'Male or female?'

'One of each.'

'Yeah,' Kling said into the telephone, 'go ahead.'

'How old would you say they were?'

'Centuries, I would guess.'

'No, I mean ...'

'Oh, how old do they *look*? Well, the man ...'

'You've *seen* them?'

'Oh, yes, many times.'

'Um-huh,' Meyer said.

'I'll be right over,' Kling said into the telephone. 'You stay there.' He slammed down the receiver, opened his desk drawer, pulled out a holstered revolver, and hurriedly clipped it to his belt. 'Somebody threw a bomb into a storefront church. 1733 Culver Avenue. I'm heading over.'

'Right,' Meyer said. 'Get back to me.'

'We'll need a couple of meat wagons. The minister and two other people were killed, and it sounds as if there're a lot of injured.'

'Will you tell Dave?'

'On the way out,' Kling said, and was gone.

'Mrs Gorman,' Meyer said, 'as you can see, we're pretty busy here just now. I wonder if your ghosts can wait till morning.'

'No, they can't,' Adele said.

'Why not?'

'Because they appear precisely at two forty-five a.m., and I want someone to see them.'

'Why don't you and your husband look at them?' Meyer said.

'You think I'm a nut, don't you?' Adele said.

'No, no, Mrs Gorman, not at all.'

'Oh, yes you do,' Adele said. 'I didn't believe in ghosts, either, until I saw these two.'

'Well, this is all very interesting, I assure you, Mrs Gorman, but really we do have our hands full right now, and I don't know what we can do about these ghosts of yours, even if we did come over to take a look at them.'

'They've been stealing things from us,' Adele said, and Meyer thought *Oh, we have got ourselves a prime lunatic this time.*

'What sort of things?'

'A diamond brooch that used to belong to my mother when she was alive. They stole that from my father's safe.'

'What else?'

'A pair of emerald earrings. They were in the safe, too.'

'When did these thefts occur?'

'Last month.'

'Isn't it possible the jewellery was mislaid someplace?'

'You don't mislay a diamond brooch and a pair of emerald earrings that are locked inside a wall safe.'

'Did you report any of these thefts?'

'No.'

'Why not?'

'Because I knew you'd think I was crazy. Which is just what you're thinking right this minute.'

'No, Mrs Gorman, but I'm sure you can appreciate the fact that we, uh, can't go around arresting ghosts,' Meyer said, and tried to smile.

Adele Gorman did not smile back. 'Forget the ghosts,' she said. 'I was foolish to mention them, I should have known better.' She took a deep breath, looked him squarely in the eye, and said, 'I'm here to report the theft of a diamond brooch valued at six thousand dollars, and a pair of earrings worth thirty-five hundred dollars. Will you send a man to investigate tonight, or should I ask my father to contact your superior officer?'

'Your father? What's he got to . . .?'

'My father is a retired Surrogate's Court judge,' Adele said.

'I see.'

'Yes, I hope you do.'

'What time did you say these ghosts arrive?' Meyer asked, and sighed heavily.

Between midnight and two o'clock, the city does not change very much. The theatres have all let out, and the average Saturday night revellers, good citizens from Bethtown or Calm's Point, Riverhead or Majesta, have come into the Isola streets again in search of a snack or a giggle before heading home to their separate beds. The city is an ants' nest of after-theatre eateries ranging from chic French cafés to pizzerias to luncheonettes to coffee shops to hot dog stands to delicatessens, all of them packed to the ceilings because Saturday night is not only the loneliest night of the week, it is also the night to howl. And howl they do, these good burghers who have put in five long hard days of labour and who are anxious now to relax and enjoy themselves before Sunday arrives, bringing with it the attendant boredom of too damn much leisure time, anathema for the American male. The crowds shove and jostle their way along The Stem, moving in and out of bowling alleys, shooting galleries, penny arcades, strip joints, night clubs, jazz emporiums, souvenir shops, lining the sidewalks outside plate glass windows in which go-go girls gyrate, or watching with fascination as a roast beef slowly turns on a spit. Saturday night is a time for pleasure, and even the singles can find satisfaction, briefly courted by the sidewalk whores standing outside the shabby hotels in the side streets of The Stem, searching out homosexuals in gay bars on the city's notorious North Side or down in The Quarter, thumbing through dirty books in the myriad 'back magazine' shops, or slipping into darkened screening rooms to watch 16mm films of girls taking off their clothes, good people all or most, with nothing more on their minds than a little fun, a little enjoyment of the short respite between Friday night at five and Monday morning at nine.

But along around 2:00 a.m., the city begins to change.

The citizens have waited to get their cars out of parking garages (more damn garages than there are barbershops) or have staggered their way sleepily into subways to make the long trip back to the outlying sections, the furry toy dog won in the Pokerino palace clutched limply in arms that may or may not later succumb to less than ardent embrace, the laughter a bit thin, the voice a bit croaked, a college song being sung on a rattling subway car, but without much force or spirit, Saturday night has ended, it is really Sunday morning already, the morning hours are truly upon the city now, and the denizens appear.

The hookers brazenly approach any straying male, never mind the 'Want to have a good time, sweetheart?', never mind the euphemisms now. Now it's 'Want to fuck, honey?', yes or no, a quick sidewalk transaction and the attendant danger of later getting mugged and rolled or maybe killed by a pimp in a hotel room stinking of Lysol while your pants are draped over a wooden chair. The junkies are out in force, too, looking for cars foolishly left unlocked and parked on the streets, or – lacking such fortuitous circumstance – experienced enough to force the side vent with a screwdriver, hook the lock button with a wire hanger, and open the door that way. There are pushers peddling their dream stuff, from pot to hoss to speed, a nickel bag or a twenty-dollar deck; fences hawking their stolen goodies, anything from a transistor radio to a refrigerator, the biggest bargain basement in town; burglars jimmying windows or forcing doors with a Celluloid strip, this being an excellent hour to break into apartments, when the occupants are asleep and the street sounds are hushed. But worse than any of these people (for they are, after all, only citizens engaged in commerce of a sort) are the predators who roam the night in search of trouble. In cruising wedges of three or four, sometimes high but more often not, they look for victims – a taxicab driver coming out of a cafeteria, an old woman poking around garbage cans for hidden treasures, a teenage couple necking in a parked automobile, it doesn't matter. You can get killed in this city at any time of the day or night, but your chances for extinction are best after 2:00 a.m. because, paradoxically, the night people take over in the morning. There are the neighbourhoods that terrify even cops in this lunar landscape, and certain places they will not enter unless they have first checked to see that there are two doors, one to get in by, and the other to get out through, fast, should someone decide to block the exit from behind.

The Painted Parasol was just such an establishment.

They had found in Mercy Howell's appointment book a notation that read Harry, 2:00 a.m., The Painted Parasol, and since they knew this particular joint for exactly the kind of hole it was, and since they wondered what connection the slain girl might have had with the various unappetizing types who frequented the place from dusk till dawn, they decided to hit it and found out. The front entrance opened on a long flight of stairs that led down to the main room of what was not a restaurant, and not a club, though it combined features of both. It did not possess a liquor licence, and so it served only coffee and sandwiches, but occasionally a rock singer would plug in his amplifier and guitar and whack out a few numbers for the patrons. The back door of the – hangout? – opened onto a side-street alley. Hawes checked it out, reported back to Carella, and they both made a mental floor plan in case they needed it later.

Carella went down the long flight of steps first, Hawes immediately behind him. At the bottom of the stairway, they moved through a bearded curtain and found themselves in a large room overhung with an old Air Force parachute painted in a wild psychedelic pattern. A counter upon which rested a coffee urn and trays of sandwiches in Saran Wrap was just opposite the hanging beaded curtain. To the left and right of the counter were perhaps two dozen tables, all of them occupied. A waitress in a black leotard and black high-heeled patent leather pumps was swivelling among and around the tables, taking orders. There was a buzz of conversation in the room, hovering, captured in folds of the brightly painted parachute. Behind the counter, a man in a white apron was drawing a cup of coffee from the huge silver urn. Carella and Hawes walked over to him. Carella was almost six feet tall, and he weighed a hundred and eighty pounds, with wide shoulders and a narrow waist and the hands of a street brawler. Hawes was six feet two inches tall, and he weighed a hundred and ninety-five pounds bone-dry, and his hair was a fiery red with a white streak over the left temple, where he had once been knifed while investigating a burglary. Both men looked like exactly what they were: fuzz.

'What's the trouble?' the man behind the counter asked immediately.

'No trouble,' Carella said. 'This your place?'

'Yeah. My name is Georgie Bright, and I already been visited, thanks. Twice.'

'Oh? Who visited you?'

'First time a cop named O'Brien, second time a cop named Parker. I already cleared up that whole thing that was going on downstairs.'

'What whole thing going on downstairs?'

'In the men's room. Some kids were selling pot down there, it got to be a regular neighbourhood supermarket. So I done what O'Brien suggested, I put a man down there outside the toilet door, and the rule now is only one person goes in there at a time. Parker came around to make sure I was keeping my part of the bargain. I don't want no narcotics trouble here. Go down and take a look if you like. You'll see I got a man watching the toilet.'

'Who's watching the man watching the toilet?' Carella asked.

'That ain't funny,' Georgie Bright said, looking offended.

'Know anybody named Harry?' Hawes asked.

'Harry who? I know a lot of Harrys.'

'Any of them here tonight?'

'Maybe.'

'Where?'

'There's one over there near the bandstand. The big guy with the blond hair.'

'Harry what?'

'Donatello.'

'Make the name?' Carella asked Hawes.

'No,' Hawes said.

'Neither do I.'

'Let's talk to him.'

'You want a cup of coffee or something?' Georgie Bright asked.

'Yeah, why don't you send some over to the table?' Hawes said, and followed Carella across the room to where Harry Donatello was sitting with another man. Donatello was wearing grey slacks, black shoes and socks, a white shirt open at the throat, and a double-breasted blue blazer. His long blond hair was combed straight back from his forehead, revealing a sharply defined widow's peak. He was easily as big as Hawes, and he sat with his hands folded on the table in front of him, talking to the man who sat opposite him. He did not look up as the detectives approached.

'Is your name Harry Donatello?' Carella asked.

'Who wants to know?'

'Police officers,' Carella said, and flashed his shield.

'I'm Harry Donatello, what's the matter?'

'Mind if we sit down?' Hawes asked, and before Donatello could answer, both men sat, their backs to the empty bandstand and the exit door.

'Do you know a girl named Mercy Howell?' Carella asked.

'What about her?'

'Do you know her?'

'I know her. What's the beef? She under age or something?'

'When did you see her last?'

The man with Donatello, who up to now had been silent, suddenly piped, 'You don't have to answer no questions without a lawyer, Harry. Tell them you want a lawyer.'

The detectives looked him over. He was small and thin, with black hair combed sideways to conceal a receding hairline. He was badly in need of a shave. He was wearing blue trousers and a striped shirt.

'This is a field investigation,' Hawes said drily, 'and we can ask anything we damn please.'

'Town's getting full of lawyers,' Carella said. 'What's *your* name, counsellor?'

'Jerry Riggs. You going to drag *me* in this, whatever it is?'

'It's a few friendly questions in the middle of the night,' Hawes said. 'Anybody got any objections to that?'

'Getting so two guys can't even sit and talk together without getting shook down,' Riggs said.

'You've got a rough life, all right,' Hawes said, and the girl in the black leotard brought their coffee to the table, and then hurried off to take another order. Donatello watched her jiggling behind as she swivelled across the room.

'So when's the last time you saw the Howell girl?' Carella asked again.

'Wednesday night,' Donatello said.

'Did you see her tonight?'

'No.'

'Were you *supposed* to see her tonight?'

'Where'd you get that idea?'

'We're full of ideas,' Hawes said.

'Yeah, I was supposed to meet her here ten minutes ago. Dumb broad is late, as usual.'

'What do you do for a living, Donatello?'

'I'm an importer. You want to see my business card?'

'What do you import?'

'Souvenir ashtrays.'

'How'd you get to know Mercy Howell?'

'I met her at a party in The Quarter. She got a little high, and she done her thing.'

'What thing?'

'The thing she does in that show she's in.'

'Which is what?'

'She done this dance where she takes off all her clothes.'

'How long have you been seeing her?'

'I met her a couple of months ago. I see her on and off, maybe once a week, something like that. This town is full of broads, you know, a guy don't have to get himself involved in no relationship with no specific broad.'

'What was your relationship with *this* specific broad?'

'We have a few laughs together, that's all. She's a swinger, little Mercy,' Donatello said, and grinned at Riggs.

'Want to tell us where you were tonight between eleven and twelve?'

'Is this still a *field* investigation?' Riggs asked sarcastically.

'Nobody's in custody yet,' Hawes said, 'so let's cut the legal crap, okay? Tell us where you were, Donatello.'

'Right here,' Donatello said. 'From ten o'clock till now.'

'I suppose somebody saw you here during that time.'

'A *hundred* people saw me.'

A crowd of angry black men and women were standing outside the shattered window of the storefront church. Two fire engines and an ambulance were parked at the kerb. Kling pulled in behind the second engine, some ten feet away from the hydrant. It was almost 2:30 a.m. on a bitterly cold October night, but the crowd looked like a mob at an afternoon street-corner rally in the middle of August. Restless, noisy, abrasive, anticipative, they ignored the penetrating cold and concentrated instead on the burning issue of the hour, the fact that a person or persons unknown had thrown a bomb through the plate glass window of the church. The beat patrolman, a newly appointed cop who felt vaguely uneasy in this neighbourhood even during his daytime shift, greeted Kling effusively, his pale white face bracketed by ear-muffs, his gloved hands clinging desperately to his nightstick. The crowd parted to let Kling through. It did not help that he was the youngest man on the squad, with the callow look of a country bumpkin on his unlined face, it did not help that he was blond and hatless, it did not help that he walked into the church with the confident youthful stride of a champion come to set things right. The crowd knew he was fuzz, and they knew he was Whitey, and they knew, too, that if this bombing had taken place on Hall Avenue crosstown and downtown, the Police Commissioner himself would have arrived behind a herald of official trumpets. This, however, was Culver Avenue, where a boiling mixture of Puerto Ricans and Negroes shared a disintegrating ghetto, and so the car that pulled to the kerb was not marked with the Commissioner's distinctive blue-and-gold seal, but was instead a green Chevy convertible that belonged to Kling himself, and the man who stepped out of it looked young and inexperienced and inept despite the confident stride he affected as he walked into the church, his shield pinned to his overcoat.

The bomb had caused little fire damage, and the firemen already had the flames under control, their hoses snaking through and around the over-turned folding chairs scattered about the small room. Ambulance attendants picked their way over the hoses and around the debris, carrying out the injured – the dead could wait.

'Have you called the Bomb Squad?' Kling asked the patrolman.

'No,' the patrolman answered, shaken by the sudden possibility that he had been derelict in his duty.

'Why don't you do that now?' Kling suggested.

'Yes, *sir*,' the patrolman answered, and rushed out. The ambulance attendants went by with a moaning woman on a stretcher. She was still wearing eyeglasses, but one lens had been shattered and blood was running in a steady rivulet down the side of her nose. The place stank of gunpowder and smoke and charred wood. The most serious damage had been done at the rear of the small store, furthest away from the entrance door. Whoever had thrown the bomb must have possessed a damn good pitching arm to have hurled it so accurately through the window and across the fifteen feet to the makeshift altar. The minister lay across his own altar, dead, one arm blown off in the explosion. Two women who had been sitting on folding chairs closest to the altar lay upon each other on the floor now, tangled in death, their clothes still smouldering. The sounds of the injured filled the room, and then were suffocated by the overriding siren-shriek of the arriving second ambulance. Kling went outside to the crowd.

'Anybody here witness this?' he asked.

A young man, black, wearing a beard and a natural hair style, turned away from a group of other youths, and walked directly to Kling.

'Is the minister dead?' he asked.

'Yes, he is,' Kling answered.

'Who else?'

'Two women.'

'Who?'

'I don't know yet. We'll identify them as soon as the men are through in there.' He turned again to the crowd. 'Did anybody see what happened?' he asked.

'I saw it,' the young man said.

'What's your name, son?'

'Andrew Jordan.'

Kling took out his pad. 'All right, let's have it.'

'What good's this going to do?' Jordan asked. 'Writing all this shit in your book?'

'You said you saw what . . .'

'I saw it, all right. I was walking by, heading for the pool room up the street, and the ladies were inside singing, and this car pulled up, and a guy got out, threw the bomb, and ran back to the car.'

'What kind of car was it?'

'A red VW.'

'What year?'

'Who can tell with those VWs?'

'How many people in it?'

'Two. The driver and the guy who threw the bomb.'

'Notice the licence plate?'

'No. They drove off too fast.'

'Can you describe the man who threw the bomb?'

'Yeah. He was white.'

'What else?' Kling asked.

'That's all,' Jordan replied. 'He was *white*.'

There were perhaps three dozen estates in all of Smoke Rise, a hundred or so people living in luxurious near seclusion on acres of valuable land through which ran four winding, interconnected, private roadways. Meyer Meyer drove between the wide stone pillars marking Smoke Rise's western access road, entering a city within a city, bounded on the north by the River Harb, shielded from the River Highway by stands of poplars and evergreens on the south – exclusive Smoke Rise, known familiarly and derisively to the rest of the city's inhabitants as 'The Club'.

374 MacArthur Lane was at the end of the road that curved past the Hamilton Bridge. The house was a huge grey stone structure with a slate roof and scores of gables and chimneys jostling the sky, perched high in gloomy shadow above the Harb. As he stepped from the car, Meyer could hear the sounds of river traffic, the hooting of tugs, the blowing of whistles, the eruption of a squawk box on a destroyer midstream. He looked out over the water. Reflected lights glistened in shimmering liquid beauty, the hanging globes on the bridge's suspension cables, the dazzling reds and greens of signal lights on the opposite shore, single illuminated window slashes in apartment buildings throwing their mirror images onto the black surface of the river, the blinking wing lights of an airplane overhead moving in watery reflection like a submarine. The air was cold, a fine piercing drizzle had begun several minutes ago. Meyer shuddered, pulled the collar of his coat higher on his neck, and walked towards the old grey house, his shoes crunching on the driveway gravel, the sound echoing away into the high surrounding bushes.

The stones of the old house oozed wetness. Thick vines covered the walls, climbing to the gabled, turreted roof. He found a doorbell set over a brass escutcheon in the thick oaken doorjamb, and pressed it. Chimes sounded somewhere deep inside the house. He waited.

The door opened suddenly.

The man looking out at him was perhaps seventy years old, with piercing blue eyes, bald except for white thatches of hair that sprang wildly from behind each ear. He wore a red smoking jacket and black trousers, a black ascot around his neck, red velvet slippers.

'What do you want?' he asked immediately.

'I'm Detective Meyer of the Eighty-seventh ...'

'Who sent for you?'

'A woman named Adele Gorman came to the ...'

'My daughter's a fool,' the man said. 'We don't need the police here,' and slammed the door in his face.

Meyer stood on the doorstep feeling somewhat like a horse's ass. A tugboat hooted on the river. A light snapped on upstairs, casting an amber rectangle into the dark driveway. He looked at the luminous dial of his watch. It was 2:35 a.m. The drizzle was cold and penetrating. He took out his handkerchief, blew his nose, and wondered what he should do next. He did not like ghosts, and he did not like lunatics, and he did not like nasty old men who did not comb their hair and who slammed doors in a person's face. He was about to head back for his car when the door opened again.

'Detective Meyer?' Adele Gorman said. 'Do come in.'

'Thank you,' he said, and stepped into the entrance foyer.

'You're right on time.'

'Well, a little early actually,' Meyer said. He still felt foolish. What the hell was he doing in Smoke rise investigating ghosts in the middle of the night?

'This way,' Adele said, and he followed her through a sombrely panelled foyer into a vast, dimly lighted living room. Heavy oaken beams ran overhead, velvet draperies hung at the window, the room was cluttered with ponderous old furniture. He could believe there were ghosts in this house, he could suddenly believe it. A young man wearing dark glasses rose like a spectre from the sofa near the fireplace. His face, illuminated by the single standing floor lamp, looked wan and drawn. Wearing a black cardigan sweater over a white shirt and dark slacks, he approached Meyer unsmilingly with his hand extented – but he did not accept Meyer's hand when it was offered in return.

Meyer suddenly realized that the man was blind.

'I'm Ralph Gorman,' he said, his hand still extended. 'Adele's husband.'

'How do you do, Mr Gorman,' Meyer said, and took his hand. The palm was moist and cold.

'It was good of you to come,' Gorman said. 'These apparitions have been driving us crazy.'

'What time is it?' Adele asked suddenly, and looked at her watch. 'We've got five minutes,' she said. There was a tremor in her voice. She seemed suddenly very frightened.

'Won't your father be here?' Meyer asked.

'No, he's gone up to bed,' Adele said. 'I'm afraid he's bored with the whole affair, and terribly angry that we notified the police.'

Meyer made no comment. Had he known that Willem Van Houten, former Surrogate's Court judge, had *not* wanted the police to be notified, Meyer would not have been here in the first place. He debated leaving now, but Adele Gorman had begun talking again, and it was impolite to depart in the middle of another person's sentence.

'... is in her early thirties, I would guess. The other ghost, the male, is about your age – forty or forty-five, something like that.'

'I'm thirty-seven,' Meyer said.

'Oh.'

'The bald head fools a lot of people.'

'Yes.'

'I was bald at a very early age.'

'Anyway,' Adele said, 'their names are Elisabeth and Johann, and they've probably been ...'

'Oh, they have names, do they?'

'Yes. They're ancestors, you know. My father is Dutch, and there actually *were* an Elisabeth and Johann Van Houten in the family centuries ago, when Smoke Rise was still a Dutch settlement.'

'They're Dutch, um-huh, I see,' Meyer said.

'Yes. They always appear wearing Dutch costumes. And they also speak Dutch.'

'Have *you* heard them, Mr Gorman?'

'Yes,' Gorman said. 'I'm blind, you know ...' he added, and hesitated, as though expecting some comment from Meyer. When none came, he said, 'But I *have* heard them.'

'Do you speak Dutch?'

'No. My father-in-law speaks it fluently, though, and he identified the language for us, and told us what they were saying.'

'What *did* they say?'

'Well, for one thing, they said they were going to steal Adele's jewellery, and they damn well did.'

'Your *wife's* jewellery? But I thought ...'

'It was willed to her by her mother. My father-in-law keeps it in his safe.'

'*Kept*, you mean.'

'No, keeps. There are several pieces in addition to the ones that were stolen. Two rings and also a necklace.'

'And the value?'

'Altogether? I would say about forty thousand dollars.'

'Your ghosts have expensive taste.'

The floor lamp in the room suddenly began to flicker. Meyer glanced at it and felt the hackles rising at the back of his neck.

'The lights are going out, Ralph,' Adele whispered.

'Is it two forty-five?'

'Yes.'

'They're here,' Gorman whispered.

Mercy Howell's roommate had been asleep for close to four hours when they knocked on her door. But she was a wily young lady, hip to the ways of the big city, and very much awake as she conducted her own little investigation without so much as opening the door a crack. First she asked them to spell their names slowly. Then she asked them their shield numbers. Then she asked them to hold their shields and their I.D. cards close to the door's peephole, where she could see them. Still unconvinced, she said through the locked door, 'You just wait there a minute.' They waited for closer to five minutes before they heard her approaching the door again. The heavy steel bar of a Fox lock was pushed noisily to the side, a safety chain rattled on its track, the tumblers of one lock clicked open, and then another, and finally the girl opened the door.

'Come in,' she said, 'I'm sorry I kept you waiting. I called the station house and they said you were okay.'

'You're a very careful girl,' Hawes said.

'At this hour of the morning? Are you kidding?' she said.

She was perhaps twenty-five, with her red hair up in curlers, her face cold-creamed clean of makeup. She was wearing a pink quilted robe over flannel pyjamas, and although she was probably a very pretty girl at 9:00 a.m., she now looked about as attractive as a Buffalo nickel.

'What's your name, miss?' Carella asked.

'Lois Kaplan. What's this all about? Has there been another burglar in the building?'

'No, Miss Kaplan. We want to ask you some questions about Mercy Howell? Did she live here with you?'

'Yes,' Lois said, and suddenly looked at them shrewdly. 'What do you mean *did*? She still *does*.'

They were standing in the small foyer of the apartment, and the foyer went so still that all the night sounds of the building were clearly audible all at once, as though they had not been there before but had only been summoned up now to fill the void of silence. A toilet flushed somewhere, a hot water pipe rattled, a baby whimpered, a dog barked, someone dropped a shoe. In the foyer now filled with noise, they stared at each other wordlessly, and finally Carella drew a deep breath and said, 'Your roommate is dead. She was stabbed tonight as she was leaving the theatre.'

'No,' Lois said, simply and flatly and unequivocally. 'No, she isn't.'

'Miss Kaplan ...'

'I don't give a damn what you say, Mercy isn't dead.'

'Miss Kaplan, she's dead.'

'Oh Jesus,' Lois said, and burst into tears, 'oh Jesus, oh damn damn, oh Jesus.'

The two men stood by feeling stupid and big and awkward and helpless. Lois Kaplan covered her face with her hands and sobbed into them, her shoulders heaving, saying over and over again, 'I'm sorry, oh Jesus, please, I'm sorry, please, oh poor Mercy, oh my God,' while the detectives tried not to watch. At last the crying stopped and she looked up at them with eyes that had been knifed, and said softly, 'Come in. Please,' and led them into the living room. She kept staring at the floor as she talked. It was as if she could not look them in the face, not these men who had brought her the news.

'Do you know who did it?' she asked.

'No. Not yet.'

'We wouldn't have awoken you in the middle of the night ...'

'That's all right.'

'But very often, if we get moving on a case fast enough, before the trail gets cold ...'

'Yes, I understand.'

'We can often ...'

'Yes, before the trail gets cold,' Lois said.

'Yes.'

The apartment went silent again.

'Would you know if Miss Howell had any enemies?' Carella asked.

'She was the sweetest girl in the world,' Lois said.

'Did she argue with anyone recently, were there ...?'

'No.'

'... any threatening telephone calls or letters?'

Louis Kaplan looked up at them.

'Yes,' she said. 'A letter.'

'A *threatening* letter?'

'We couldn't tell. It frightened Mercy, though. That's why she bought the gun.'

'What kind of gun?'

'I don't know. A small one.'

'Would it have been a .25 calibre Browning?'

'I don't know guns.'

'Was this letter mailed to her, or delivered personally?'

'It was mailed to her. At the theatre.'

'When?'

'A week ago.'

'Did she report it to the police?'

'No.'

'Why not?'

'Haven't you seen *Rattlesnake*?' Lois said.

'What do you mean?' Carella said.

'*Rattlesnake*. The musical. Mercy's show. The show she was in.'

'No, I haven't.'

'But you've *heard* of it.'

'No.'

'Where do you live, for God's sake? On the moon?'

'I'm sorry, I just haven't ...'

'Forgive me,' Lois said immediately. 'I'm not usually ... I'm trying very hard to ... I'm sorry. Forgive me.'

'That's all right,' Carella said.

'Anyway, it's ... it's a big hit now but ... there was trouble in the beginning, you see ... are you *sure* you don't know about this? It was in all the newspapers.'

'Well, I guess I missed it,' Carella said. 'What was the trouble about?'

'Don't *you* know about this either?' she asked Hawes.

'No, I'm sorry.'

'About Mercy's dance?'

'No.'

'Well, in one scene, Mercy danced the title song without any clothes on. Because the idea was to express ... the *hell* with what the idea was. The point is that the dance wasn't at all prurient, it wasn't even sexy! But the police *missed* the point, and closed the show down two days after it opened. The producers had to go to court for a writ to get the show opened again.'

'Yes, I remember it now,' Carella said.

'What I'm trying to say is that nobody involved with *Rattlesnake* would report *anything* to the police. Not even a threatening letter.'

'If she bought a pistol,' Hawes said, 'she would have *had* to go to the police. For a permit.'

'She didn't have a permit.'

'Then how'd she get the pistol? You can't buy a handgun without first ...'

'A friend of hers sold it to her.'

'What's the friend's name?'

'Harry Donatello.'

'An importer,' Carella said drily.

'Of souvenir ashtrays,' Hawes said.

'I don't know what he does for a living,' Lois said. 'But he got the gun for her.'

'When was this?'

'A few days after she received the letter.'

'What did the letter say?' Carella asked.

'I'll get it for you,' Lois said, and went into the bedroom. They heard a dresser drawer opening, the rustle of clothes, what might have been a tin candy box being opened. Lois came back into the room. 'Here it is,' she said.

There didn't seem much point in trying to preserve latent prints on a letter that had already been handled by Mercy Howell, Lois Kaplan, and God knew how many others. But Carella nonetheless accepted the letter on a handkerchief spread over the palm of his hand, and then looked at the face of the envelope. 'She should have brought this to us immediately,' he said. 'It's written on hotel stationery, we've got an address without lifting a finger.'

The letter had indeed been written on stationery from The Addison Hotel, one of the city's lesser-known fleabags, some two blocks north of the Eleventh Street Theatre, where Mercy Howell had worked. There was a single sheet of paper in the envelope. Carella unfolded it. Lettered in pencil were the words:

PUT ON YOUR
CLOSE, MISS!

The Avenging Angel

The lamp went out, the room was black.

At first there was no sound but the sharp intake of Adele Gorman's breath. And then, indistinctly, as faintly as though carried on a swirling mist that blew in wetly from some desolated shore, there came the sound of garbled voices, and the room grew suddenly cold. The voices where those of a crowd in endless debate, rising and falling in cacophonous cadence, a mixture of tongues that rattled and rasped. There was the sound, too, of a rising wind, as though a door to some forbidden landscape had been sharply and suddenly blown open (How cold the room was!) to reveal a host of corpses incessantly pacing, involved in formless dialogue. The voices rose in volume now, carried on that same chill penetrating wind, louder, closer, until they seemed to overwhelm the room, clamouring to be released from whatever unearthly vault contained them. And then, as if two and only two of those disembodied voices had succeeded in breaking away from the mass of unseen dead, bringing with them a rush of bone-chilling air from some world unknown, there came a whisper at first, the whisper of a man's voice, saying the single word 'Ralph!' sharp-edged and with a distinctive foreign inflection, 'Ralph!' and then a woman's voice joining it, 'Adele!' pronounced strangely and in the same cutting whisper, 'Adele!' and then 'Ralph!' again, the voices overlapping, unmistakably foreign, urgent, rising in volume until the whispers commingled to become an agonizing groan and the names were lost in the shrilling echo of the wind.

Meyer's eyes played tricks in the darkness. Apparitions that surely were not there seemed to float on the crescendo of sound that saturated the room. Barely perceived pieces of furniture assumed amorphous shapes as the male voice snarled and the female voice moaned above it in contralto counterpoint. And then the babel of other voices intruded again, as though calling these two back to whatever grim mossy crypt they had momentarily escaped. The sound of the wind became more fierce, and the voices of those numberless pacing dead receded, and echoed, and were gone.

The lamp sputtered back into dim illumination. The room seemed perceptibly warmer, but Meyer Meyer was covered with a cold clammy sweat.

'*Now* do you believe?' Adele Gorman asked.

Detective Bob O'Brien was coming out of the men's room down the hall when he saw the woman sitting on the bench just outside the squadroom. He almost went back into the toilet, but he was an instant too late; she had seen him, there was no escape.

'Hello, Mr O'Brien,' she said, and performed an awkward little half-rising motion, as though uncertain whether she should stand to greet him or accept the deference due a lady. The clock on the squadroom wall read 3:01 a.m., but the lady was dressed as though for a brisk afternoon's hike in the park, brown slacks and low-heeled walking shoes, brief beige car coat, a scarf around her head. She was perhaps fifty-five or thereabouts, with a face that once must have been pretty, save for the overlong nose. Green-eyed, with prominent cheekbones and a generous mouth, she executed her abortive rise, and then fell into step beside O'Brien as he walked into the squadroom.

'Little late in the night to be out, isn't it, Mrs Blair?' O'Brien asked. He was not an insensitive cop, but his manner now was brusque and dismissive. Faced with Mrs Blair for perhaps the seventeenth time in a month, he tried not to empathize with her loss because, truthfully, he was unable to assist her, and his inability to do so was frustrating.

'Have you seen her?' Mrs Blair asked.

'No,' O'Brien said. 'I'm sorry, Mrs Blair, but I haven't.'

'I have a new picture, perhaps that will help.'

'Yes, perhaps it will,' he said.

The telephone was ringing. He lifted the receiver and said, 'Eighty-seventh Squad, O'Brien here.'

'Bob, this's Bert Kling over on Culver, the church bombing.'

'Yeah, Bert.'

'Seems I remember seeing a red Volkswagen on that hot car bulletin we got yesterday. You want to dig it out and let me know where it was snatched?'

'Yeah, just a second,' O'Brien said, and began scanning the sheet on his desk.

'Here's the new picture,' Mrs Blair said. 'I know you're very good with runaways, Mr O'Brien, the kids all like you and give you information. If you see Penelope, all I want you to do is tell her I love her and am sorry for the misunderstanding.'

'Yeah, I will,' O'Brien said. Into the phone, he said, 'I've got *two* red VWs, Bert, a '64 and a '66. You want them both?'

'Shoot,' Kling said.

'The '64 was stolen from a guy named Art Hauser. It was parked outside 861 West Meridian.'

'And the '66?'

'Owner is a woman named Alice Cleary. Car was stolen from a parking lot on Fourteenth.'

'North or South?'

'South. 303 South.'

'Right. Thanks, Bob,' Kling said, and hung up.

'And ask her to come home to me,' Mrs Blair said.

'Yes, I will,' O'Brien said. 'If I see her, I certainly will.'

'That's a nice picture of Penny, don't you think?' Mrs Blair asked. 'It was taken last Easter. It's the most recent picture I have. I thought it would be most helpful to you.'

O'Brien looked at the girl in the picture, and then looked up into Mrs Blair's green eyes, misted now with tears, and suddenly wanted to reach across the desk and pat her hand reassuringly, the one thing he could *not* do with any honesty. Because whereas it was true that he was the squad's runaway expert, with perhaps fifty snapshots of teenage boys and girls crammed into his bulging notebook, and whereas his record of finds was more impressive than any other cop's in the city, uniformed or plainclothes, there wasn't a damn thing he could do for the mother of Penelope Blair, who had run away from home last June.

'You understand . . .'

'Let's not go into *that* again, Mr O'Brien,' she said, and rose.

'Mrs Blair . . .'

'I don't want to hear it,' Mrs Blair said, walking quickly out of the squadroom. 'Tell her to come home. Tell her I love her,' she said, and was gone down the iron-runged steps.

O'Brien sighed and stuffed the new picture of Penelope into his notebook. What Mrs Blair did not choose to hear again was the fact that her runaway daughter Penny was twenty-four years old, and there was not a single agency on God's green earth, police or otherwise, that could force her to go home again if she did not choose to.

Fats Donner was a stool pigeon with a penchant for Turkish baths. A mountainous white Buddha of a man, he could usually be found at one or another of the city's steam emporiums at any given hour of the day, draped in a towel and revelling in the heat that saturated his flabby body. Bert Kling found him in an all-night place called Steam-Fit. He sent the masseur into the steam room to tell Donner he was there, and Donner sent word out that he would be through in five minutes, unless Kling wished to join him. Kling did not wish to join him. He waited in the locker room, and in seven minutes' time, Donner came out, draped in his customary towel, a ludicrous sight at *any* time, but particularly at close to 3:30 a.m.

'Hey!' Donner said. 'How you doing?'

'Fine,' Kling said. 'How about yourself?'

'*Comme ci, comme ça,*' Donner said, and made a see-sawing motion with one fleshy hand.

'I'm looking for some stolen heaps,' Kling said, getting directly to the point.

'What kind?' Donner said.

'Volkswagens. A '64 and a '66.'

'What colour are they?'

'Red.'

'Both of them?'

'Yes.'

'Where were they heisted?'

'One from in front of 861 West Meridian. The other from a parking lot on South Fourteenth.'

'When was this?'

'Both last week sometime. I don't have the exact dates.'

'What do you want to know?'

'Who stole them.'

'You think it's the same guy on both?'

'I doubt it.'

'What's so important about these heaps?'

'One of them may have been used in a bombing tonight.'

'You mean the church over on Culver?'

'That's right.'

'Count me out,' Donner said.

'What do you mean?'

'There's a lot of guys in this town who're in *sympathy* with what happened over there tonight. I don't want to get involved in none of this black-white shit.'

'Who's going to know whether you're involved or not?' Kling asked.

'The same way *you* get information, *they* get information.'

'I need your help, Donner.'

'Yeah, well, I'm sorry on this one,' Donner said, and shook his head.

'In that case, I'd better hurry downtown to High Street.'

'Why? You got another source down there?'

'No, that's where the D.A.'s office is.'

Both men stared at each other, Donner in a white towel draped around his belly, sweat still pouring from his face and his chest even though he was no longer in the steam room, Kling looking like a slightly tired advertising executive rather than a cop threatening a man with revelation of past deeds not entirely legal. They stared at each other with total understanding, caught in the curious symbiosis of law breaker and law enforcer, an empathy created by neither man, but essential to the existence of both. It was Donner who broke the silence.

'I don't like being coerced,' he said.

'I don't like being refused,' Kling answered.

'When do you need this?'

'I want to get going on it before morning.'

'You expect miracles, don't you?'

'Doesn't everybody?'

'Miracles cost.'

'How much?'

'Twenty-five if I turn up one heap, fifty if I turn up both.'

'Turn them up first. We'll talk later.'

'And if somebody breaks my head later?'

'You should have thought of that before you entered the profession,' Kling said. 'Come on, Donner, cut it out. This is a routine bombing by a couple of punks. You've got nothing to be afraid of.'

'No?' Donner asked. And then, in a very professorial voice, he uttered perhaps the biggest understatement of the decade. 'Racial tensions are running very high in this city right now.'

'Have you got my number at the squadroom?'

'Yeah, I've got it,' Donner said glumly.

'I'm going back there now. Let me hear from you soon.'

'You mind if I get dressed first?' Donner asked.

The night clerk at The Addison Hotel was alone in the lobby when Carella and Hawes walked in. Immersed in an open book on the desk in front of him, he did not look up as they approached. The lobby was furnished in faded Gothic: a threadbare oriental rug, heavy curlicued mahogany tables, ponderous stuffed chairs with sagging bottoms and soiled antimacassars, two spittoons resting alongside each of two mahogany-panelled supporting columns. A real Tiffany lampshade hung over the registration desk, one leaded glass panel gone, another badly cracked. In the old days, The Addison had been a luxury hotel. It now wore its past splendour with all the style of a two-dollar hooker in a moth-eaten mink she'd picked up in a thrift shop.

The clerk, in contrast to his ancient surroundings, was a young man in his mid-twenties, wearing a neatly pressed brown tweed suit, a tan shirt, a gold-and-brown silk rep tie, and eyeglasses with tortoiseshell rims. He glanced up at the detectives belatedly, squinting after the intense concentration of peering at print, and then he got to his feet.

'Yes, gentlemen,' he said. 'May I help you?'

'Police officers,' Carella said. He took his wallet from his pocket and opened it to where his detective's shield was pinned to a leather flap.

'Yes, sir.'

'I'm Detective Carella, this is my partner Detective Hawes.'

'How do you do? I'm the night clerk, my name is Ronnie Sanford.'

'We're looking for someone who may have been registered here two weeks ago,' Hawes said.

'Well, if he was registered here two weeks ago,' Sanford said, 'chances are he's still registered. Most of our guests are residents.'

'Do you keep stationery in the lobby here?' Carella asked.

'Sir?'

'Stationery. Is there any place here in the lobby where someone could walk in off the street and pick up a piece of stationery?'

'No, sir. There's a writing desk there in the corner, near the staircase, but we don't stock it with stationery, no, sir.'

'Is there stationery in the rooms?'

'Yes, sir.'

'How about here at the desk?'

'Yes, of course, sir.'

'Is there someone at this desk twenty-four hours a day?'

'Twenty-four hours a day, yes, sir. We have three shifts. Eight to four in the afternoon. Four to midnight. And midnight to eight a.m.'

'You came on at midnight, did you?'

'Yes, sir.'

'Any guests come in after you started your shift?'

'A few, yes, sir.'

'Notice anybody with blood on his clothes?'

'Blood? Oh, no, sir.'

'*Would* you have noticed?'

'What do you mean?'

'Are you generally pretty aware of what's going on around here?'

'I try to be, sir. At least, for most of the night. I catch a little nap when I'm not studying, but usually . . .'

'What do you study?'

'Accounting.'

'Where?'

'At Ramsey U.'

'Mind if we take a look at your register?'

'Not at all, sir.'

He walked to the mail rack and took the hotel register from the counter there. Returning to the desk, he opened it, and said, 'All of our present guests are residents, with the exception of Mr Lambert in 204, and Mrs Grant in 701.'

'When did they check in?'

'Mr Lambert checked in . . . last night, I think it was. And Mrs Grant has been here for four days. She's leaving on Tuesday.'

'Are these the actual signatures of your guests?'

'Yes, sir. All guests are asked to sign the register, as required by state law.'

'Have you got that note, Cotton?' Carella asked, and then turned again to Sanford. 'Would you mind if we took this over to the couch there?'

'Well, we're not supposed . . .'

'We can give you a receipt for it, if you like.'

'No, I guess it'll be all right.'

They carried the register to a couch upholstered in faded red velvet. With the book supported on Carella's lap, they unfolded the note Mercy Howell had received, and began comparing the signatures of the guests with the only part of the note that was not written in block letters, the words 'The Avenging Angel'.

There were fifty-two guests in the hotel. Carella and Hawes went through the register once, and then started through it a second time.

'Hey,' Hawes said suddenly.

'What?'
'Look at this one.'
He took the note and placed it on the page so that it was directly above one
of the signatures:

PUT ON YOUR
CLOSE, MISS!
The Avenging Angel

Timothy Allen Ames

'What do you think?' he asked.
'Different handwriting,' Carella said.
'Same initials,' Hawes said.

Detective Meyer Meyer was still shaken. He did not like ghosts. He did
not like this house. He wanted to go home. He wanted to be in bed with his
wife Sarah. He wanted her to stroke his hand and tell him that such things
did not exist, there was nothing to be afraid of, a grown man? How could he
believe in poltergeists, shades, Dutch spirits? Ridiculous.

But he had heard them, and he had felt their chilling presence, and had
almost thought he'd seen them, if only for an instant. He turned with fresh
shock now towards the hall staircase and the sound of descending footsteps.
Eyes wide, he waited for whatever new manifestation might present itself.
He was tempted to draw his revolver, but he was afraid such an act would
appear foolish to the Gormans. He had come here a sceptic, and he was now
at least *willing* to believe, and he waited in dread for whatever was coming
down those steps with such ponderous footfalls – some ghoul trailing
winding sheets and rattling chains? Some spectre with a bleached skull for a
head and long bony clutching fingers dripping the blood of babies?

Willem Van Houten, wearing his red velvet slippers and his red smoking
jacket, his hair still jutting wildly from behind each ear, his blue eyes fierce
and snapping, came into the living room and walked directly to where his
daughter and son-in-law were sitting.

'Well?' he asked. 'Did they come again?'

'Yes, Daddy,' Adele said.

'What did they want this time?'·

'I don't know. They spoke Dutch again.'

'Bastards,' Van Houten said, and then turned to Meyer. 'Did you see them?' he asked.

'No, sir, I did not,' Meyer said.

'But they were *here*,' Gorman protested, and turned his blank face to his wife. 'I heard them.'

'Yes, darling,' Adele assured him. 'We *all* heard them. But it was like that other time, don't you remember? When we could hear them even though they couldn't quite break through.'

'Yes, that's right,' Gorman said, and nodded. 'This happened once before, Detective Meyer.' He was facing Meyer now, his head tilted quizzically, the sightless eyes covered with their black reflecting glasses. When he spoke, his voice was like that of a child seeking reassurance. 'But you *did* hear them, didn't you, Detective Meyer?'

'Yes,' Meyer said. 'I heard them, Mr Gorman.'

'And the wind?'

'Yes, the wind, too.'

'And felt them? It ... it gets so cold when they appear. You *did* feel their presence, didn't you?'

'I felt something,' Meyer said.

Van Houten suddenly asked, 'Are you satisfied?'

'About what?' Meyer said.

'That there are ghosts in this house? That's why you're here, isn't it? To ascertain ...'

'He's here because I asked Adele to contact the police,' Gorman said.

'Why did you do that?'

'Because of the stolen jewellery,' Gorman said. 'And because ...' He paused. 'Because I ... I've lost my sight, yes, but I wanted to ... to make sure I wasn't losing my mind as well.'

'You're quite sane, Ralph,' Van Houten said.

'About the jewellery ...' Meyer said.

'*They* took it,' Van Houten said.

'Who?'

'Johann and Elisabeth. Our friendly neighbourhood ghosts, the bastards.'

'That's impossible, Mr Van Houten.'

'Why is it impossible?'

'Because ghosts ...' Meyer started, and hesitated.

'Yes?'

'Ghosts, well, ghosts don't go around stealing jewellery. I mean, what use would they have for it?' he said lamely, and looked at the Gormans for corroboration. Neither of them seemed to be in a supportive mood. They sat on the sofa near the fireplace, looking glum and defeated.

'They want us out of this house,' Van Houten said. 'It's as simple as that.'

'How do you know?'

'Because they said so.'

'When?'

'Before they stole the neckace and the earrings.'

'They told this to you?'

'To me and to my children. All three of us were here.'

'But I understand the ghosts speak only Dutch.'

'Yes, I translated for Ralph and Adele.'

'And then what happened?'

'What do you mean?'

'When did you discover the jewellery was missing?'

'The very instant they were gone.'

'You mean you went to the safe ...'

'Yes, and opened it, and the jewellery was gone.'

'We had put it in the safe not ten minutes before that,' Adele said. 'We'd been to a party, Ralph and I, and we got home very late, and Daddy was still awake, reading, sitting in that chair you're in this very minute. I asked him to open the safe, and he did, and he put the jewellery in, and closed the safe and ... and then *they* came and ... and made their threats.'

'What time was this?'

'The usual time. The time they always come. Two forty-five in the morning.'

'And you say the jewellery was put into the safe at what time?'

'About two-thirty,' Gorman said.

'And when was the safe opened again?'

'Immediately after they left. They only stay a few moments. This time they told my father-in-law they were taking the necklace and the earrings with them. He rushed to the safe as soon as the lights came on again ...'

'Do the lights always go off?'

'Always,' Adele said. 'It's always the same. The lights go off, and the room gets very cold, and we hear these ... strange voices arguing.' She paused. 'And then Johann and Elisabeth come.'

'Except that *this* time they didn't come,' Meyer said.

'And one other time,' Adele said quickly.

'They want us out of this house,' Van Houten said, 'that's all there is to it. Maybe we ought to leave. Before they take *everything* from us.'

'Everything? What do you mean?'

'The rest of my daughter's jewellery. Some stock certificates. Everything that's in the safe.'

'Where *is* the safe?' Meyer asked.

'Here. Behind this painting.' Van Houten walked to the wall opposite the fireplace. An oil painting of a pastoral landscape hung there in an ornate gilt frame. The frame was hinged to the wall. Van Houten swung the painting out as though opening a door, and revealed the small, round, black safe behind it. 'Here,' he said.

'How many people know the combination?' Meyer asked.

'Just me,' Van Houten said.

'Do you keep the number written down anywhere?'

'Yes.'

'Where?'

'Hidden.'

'Where?'

'I hardly think that's any of your business, Detective Meyer.'

'I'm only trying to find out whether some other person could have got hold of the combination somehow.'

'Yes, I suppose that's possible,' Van Houten said. 'But highly unlikely.'

'Well,' Meyer said, and shrugged. 'I don't really know what to say. I'd like to measure the room, if you don't mind, get the dimensions, placement of doors and windows, things like that. For my report.' He shrugged again.

'It's rather late, isn't it?' Van Houten said.

'Well, I *got* here rather late,' Meyer said, and smiled.

'Come, Daddy, I'll make us all some tea in the kitchen,' Adele said. 'Will you be long, Detective Meyer?'

'I don't know. It may take a while.'

'Shall I bring you some tea?'

'Thank you, that would be nice.'

She rose from the couch and then guided her husband's hand to her arm. Walking slowly beside him, she led him past her father and out of the room. Van Houten looked at Meyer once again, nodded briefly, and followed them out. Meyer closed the door behind them and immediately walked to the standing floor lamp.

The woman was sixty years old, and she looked like anybody's grandmother, except that she had just murdered her husband and three children. They had explained her rights to her, and she had told them she had nothing to hide and would answer any questions they chose to ask. She sat in a straight-backed squadroom chair, wearing a black cloth coat over blood-stained pyjamas and robe, her handcuffed hands in her lap, her hands unmoving on her black leather pocketbook. O'Brien and Kling looked at the police stenographer, who glanced up at the wall clock, noted the time of the interrogation's start as 3:55 a.m., and then signalled that he was ready whenever they were.

'What is your name?' O'Brien asked.

'Isabel Martin.'

'How old are you, Mrs Martin?'

'Sixty.'

'Where do you live?'

'On Ainsley Avenue.'

'Where on Ainsley?'

'657 Ainsley.'

'With whom do you live there?'

'With my husband Roger, and my son Peter, and my daughters Annie and Abigail.'

'Would you like to tell us what happened tonight, Mrs Martin?' Kling asked.

'I killed them all,' she said. She had white hair, a fine aquiline nose, brown eyes behind rimless spectacles. She stared straight ahead of her as she spoke, looking neither to her right nor to her left, ignoring her questioners completely, seemingly alone with the memory of what she had done not a half-hour before.

'Can you give us some of the details, Mrs Martin?'

'I killed *him* first, the son of a bitch.'

'Who do you mean, Mrs Martin?'

'My husband.'

'When was this?'

'When he came home.'

'What time was that, do you remember?'

'A little while ago.'

'It's almost four o'clock now,' Kling said. 'Would you say this was at, what, three-thirty or thereabouts?'

'I didn't look at the clock,' she said. 'I heard his key in the latch, and I went in the kitchen, and there he was.'

'Yes?'

'There's a meat cleaver I keep on the sink. I hit him with it.'

'Why did you do that, Mrs Martin?'

'Because I wanted to.'

'Were you arguing with him, is that it?'

'No. He was locking the door, and I just went over to the sink and picked up the cleaver, and then I hit him with it.'

'Where did you hit him, Mrs Martin?'

'On his head and on his neck and I think on his shoulder.'

'You hit him three times with the cleaver?'

'I hit him a lot of times, I don't know how many times.'

'Were you aware that you were hitting him?'

'Yes, I was aware.'

'You knew you were striking him with a cleaver.'

'Yes, I knew.'

'Did you intend to kill him with the cleaver?'

'I intended to kill him with the cleaver.'

'And afterwards, did you know you had killed him?'

'I knew he was dead, yes, the son of a bitch.'

'What did you do then?'

'My oldest child came into the kitchen. Peter. My son. He yelled at me, he wanted to know what I'd done, he kept yelling at me. I hit him, too, to get him to shut up. I hit him only once, across the throat.'

'Did you know what you were doing at the time?'

'I knew what I was doing. He was *another* one, that Peter. Little bastard.'

'What happened next, Mrs Martin?'

'I went in the back bedroom where the two girls sleep, and I hit Annie with the cleaver first, and then I hit Abigail.'

'Where did you hit them, Mrs Martin?'

'On the face. Their faces.'

'How many times?'

'I think I hit Annie twice, and Abigail only once.'

'Why did you do that, Mrs Martin?'

'Who would take care of them after I was gone?' Mrs Martin asked of no one.

'Is there anything else you want to tell us?' Kling asked.

'There's nothing more to tell. I done the right thing.'

The detectives walked away from the desk. They were both pale. 'Man,' O'Brien whispered.

'Yeah,' Kling said. 'We'd better call the night D.A. right away, get him to take a full confession from her.'

'Killed four of them without batting an eyelash,' O'Brien said, and shook his head, and went back to where the stenographer was typing up Mrs Martin's statement.

The telephone was ringing. Kling walked to the nearest desk and lifted the receiver. 'Eighty-seventh Squad, Detective Kling,' he said.

'This is Donner.'

'Yeah, Fats.'

'I think I got a lead on one of those heaps.'

'Shoot.'

'This would be the one heisted on Fourteenth Street. According to the dope I've got, it happened yesterday morning. Does that check out?'

'I'll have to look at the bulletin again. Go ahead, Fats.'

'It's already been ditched,' Donner said. 'If you're looking for it, try outside the electric company on the River Road.'

'Thanks, I'll make a note of that. Who stole it, Fats?'

'This is strictly *entre nous*,' Donner said. 'I don't want *no* tie-in with it *never*. The guy who done it is a mean little bastard, rip out his mother's heart for a dime. He hates niggers, killed two of them in a street rumble four years ago, and managed to beat the rap. I think maybe some officer was on the take, huh, Kling?'

'You can't square homicide in this city, and you know it, Fats.'

'Yeah? I'm surprised. You can square damn near anything else for a couple of bills.'

'What's his name?'

'Danny Ryder, 3541 Grover Avenue, near the park. You won't find him there now, though.'

'Where *will* I find him now?'

'Ten minutes ago, he was in an all-night bar on Mason, place called Felicia's. You going in after him?'

'I am.'

'Take your gun,' Donner said.

There were seven people in Felicia's when Kling got there at a quarter to five. He cased the bar through the plate glass window fronting the place, unbuttoned the third button of his overcoat, reached in to clutch the butt of his revolver, worked it out of the holster once and then back again, and went in through the front door.

There was the immediate smell of stale cigarette smoke and beer and sweat and cheap perfume. A Puerto Rican girl was in whispered consultation with a sailor in one of the leatherette booths. Another sailor was hunched over the jukebox, thoughtfully considering his next selection, his face tinted orange and red and green from the coloured tubing. A tired, fat, fifty-year-old blonde sat at the far end of the bar, watching the sailor as though the next button he pushed might destroy the entire world. The bartender was polishing glasses. He looked up when Kling walked in and immediately smelled the law.

Two men were seated at the opposite end of the bar.

One of them was wearing a blue turtleneck sweater, grey slacks, and desert boots. His brown hair was cut close to his scalp in a military cut. The other man was wearing a bright orange team jacket, almost luminous, with the words *Orioles, S.A.C.* lettered across its back in Old English script. The one with the crew cut said something softly, and the other one chuckled. Behind the bar, a glass clinked as the bartender replaced it on the shelf. The jukebox erupted in sound, Jimi Hendrix rendering 'All Along the Watchtower'. Kling walked over to the two men.

'Which one of you is Danny Ryder?' he asked.

The one with the short hair said, 'Who wants to know?'

'Police officer,' Kling said, and the one in the orange jacket whirled with a pistol in his hand, and Kling's eyes opened wide in surprise, and the gun went off.

There was no time to think, there was hardly any time to breathe. The explosion of the gun was shockingly close, the acrid stink of cordite rushed into his nostrils. The knowledge that he was still alive, the sweet rushing clean awareness that the bullet had somehow missed him was only a fleeting click of intelligence accompanying what was essentially a reflexive act. The .38 came free of its holster, his finger was inside the trigger guard and around the trigger, he squeezed off his shot almost before the gun had cleared the flap of his overcoat, fired into the orange jacket and threw his shoulder simultaneously against the chest of the man with the short hair, knocking him backwards off his stool. The man in the orange jacket, his face twisted in pain, was levelling the gun for another shot. Kling fired again, squeezing the trigger without thought or rancour, and then whirling on the man with the short hair, who was crouched on the floor against the bar.

'Get up!' he yelled.

'Don't shoot.'

'Get up, you son of a bitch!'

He yanked the man to his feet, hurled him against the bar, thrust the muzzle of his pistol at the blue turtleneck sweater, ran his hands under the armpits and between the legs while the man kept saying over and over again, 'Don't shoot, please don't shoot.'

He backed away from him and leaned over the one in the orange jacket.

'Is this Ryder?' he asked.

'Yes.'

'Who're you?'

'Frank ... Frank Pasquale. Look, I ...'

'Shut up, Frank,' Kling said. 'Put your hands behind your back! Move!'

He had already taken his handcuffs from his belt. He snapped them onto Pasquale's wrists now, and only then became aware that Jimi Hendrix was still singing, the sailors were watching with pale white faces, the Puerto Rican girl was screaming, the fat faded blonde had her mouth open, the bartender was frozen in mid-motion, the tip of his bar towel inside a glass.

'All right,' Kling said. He was breathing harshly. 'All right,' he said again, and wiped his forehead.

Timothy Allen Ames was a pot-bellied man of forty, with a thick black moustache, a mane of long black hair, and brown eyes sharply alert at five minutes past five in the morning. He answered the door as though he'd been already awake, asked for identification, and then asked the detectives to wait a moment, and closed the door, and came back shortly afterwards wearing a robe over his striped pyjamas.

'Is your name Timothy Ames?' Carella asked.

'That's me,' Ames said. 'Little late to be paying a visit, ain't it?'

'Or early, depending how you look at it,' Hawes said.

'One thing I can do without at five a.m. is humorous cops,' Ames said. 'How'd you get up here, anyway? Is that little jerk asleep at the desk again?'

'Who do you mean?' Carella asked.

'Lonnie Sanford, whatever the hell his name is.'

'*Ronnie* Sanford.'

'Yeah, him. Little bastard's always giving me trouble.'

'What kind of trouble?'

'About broads,' Ames said. 'Acts like he's running a nunnery here, can't stand to see a guy come in with a girl. I notice he ain't got no compunctions about letting *cops* upstairs, though, no matter *what* time it is.'

'Never mind Sanford, let's talk about you,' Carella said.

'Sure, what would you like to know?'

'Where were you between eleven-twenty and twelve o'clock tonight?'

'Right here.'

'Can you prove it?'

'Sure. I got back here about eleven o'clock, and I been here since. Ask Sanford downstairs . . . no, never mind, he wasn't on yet. He don't come on till midnight.'

'Who *else* can we ask, Ames?'

'Listen, you going to make trouble for me?'

'Only if you're *in* trouble.'

'I got a broad here. She's over eighteen, don't worry. But, like, she's a junkie, you know? She ain't holding or nothing, but I know you guys, and if you want to make trouble . . .'

'Where is she?'

'In the john.'

'Get her out here.'

'Look, do me a favour, will you? Don't bust the kid. She's trying to kick the habit, she really is. I been helping her along.'

'How?'

'By keeping her busy,' Ames said, and winked.

'Call her.'

'Bea, come out here!' Ames shouted.

There was a moment's hesitation, and then the bathroom door opened. The girl was a tall, plain brunette wearing a short terry cloth robe. She sidled into the room cautiously, as though expecting to be struck in the face at any moment. Her brown eyes were wide with expectancy. She knew fuzz, and she knew what it was like to be busted on a narcotics charge, and she had listened to the conversation from behind the closed bathroom door, and now she waited for whatever was coming, expecting the worst.

'What's your name, miss?' Hawes asked.

'Beatrice Norden.'

'What time did you get here tonight, Beatrice?'

'About eleven.'

'Was this man with you?'

'Yes.'

'Did he leave here at any time tonight?'

'No.'

'Are you sure?'

'I'm positive. He picked me up about nine o'clock . . .'

'Where do you live, Beatrice?'

'Well, that's the thing, you see,' the girl said. 'I been put out of my room.'

'So where'd he pick you up?'

'At my girl friend's house. You can ask her, she was there when he came. Her name is Rosalie Dewes. Anyway, Timmy picked me up at nine, and we went to eat at Chink's, and we came up here around eleven.'

'I hope you're telling us the truth, Miss Norden,' Carella said.

'I swear to God, we been here all night,' Beatrice answered.

'All right, Ames,' Hawes said, 'we'd like a sample of your handwriting.'

'My *what*?'

'Your handwriting.'

'What for?'

'We collect autographs,' Carella said.

'Gee, these guys really break me up,' Ames said to the girl. 'Regular night-club comics we get in the middle of the night.'

Carella handed him a pen and then tore a sheet from his pad. 'You want to write this for me?' he said. 'The first part's in block lettering.'

'What the hell is block lettering?' Ames asked.

'He means *print* it,' Hawes said.

'Then why didn't he say so?'

'Put on your clothes, miss,' Carella said.

'What for?' Beatrice said. 'I mean, the thing is, I was in bed when you guys ...'

'That's what I want him to write,' Carella explained.

'Oh.'

'Put on your clothes, miss,' Ames repeated, and lettered it onto the sheet of paper. 'What else?' he asked, looking up.

'Now sign it in your own handwriting with the following words: The Avenging Angel.'

'What the hell is this supposed to be?' Ames asked.

'You want to write it, please?'

Ames wrote the words, and then handed the slip of paper to Carella. He and Hawes compared it with the note that had been mailed to Mercy Howell:

PUT ON YOUR
CLOSE, MISS!

The Avenging Angel

PUT ON YOUR CLOTHES,
MISS.

The ~~Avenging~~ ~~Angel~~

'So?' Ames asked.

'So you're clean,' Hawes said.

'Imagine if I was dirty,' Ames answered.

At the desk downstairs, Ronnie Sanford was still immersed in his accounting textbook. He got to his feet again as the detectives came out of the elevator, adjusted his glasses on his nose, and then said, 'Any luck?'

'Afraid not,' Carella answered. 'We're going to need this register for a while, if that's okay.'

'Well ...'

'Give him a receipt for it, Cotton,' Carella said. It was late, and he didn't want a debate in the lobby of a run-down hotel. Hawes quickly made out a receipt in duplicate, signed both copies and handed one to Sanford.

'What about this torn cover?' Hawes asked belatedly.

'Yeah,' Carella said. There was a small rip on the leather binding of the book, and he fingered it briefly now, and then said, 'Better note that on the receipt, Cotton.' Hawes took back the receipt and, on both copies, jotted the words 'Small rip on front cover'. He handed the receipts back to Sanford.

'Want to just sign these, Mr Sanford?' he said.

'What for?' Sanford asked.

'To indicate we received the register in this condition.'

'Oh, sure,' Sanford said. He picked up a ball-point pen from its desk holder, and asked, 'What do you want me to write?'

'Your name and your title, that's all.'

'My title?'

'Night Clerk, The Addison Hotel.'

'Oh, sure,' Sanford said, and signed both receipts. 'This okay?' he asked. The detectives looked at what he had written.

'You like girls?' Carella asked suddenly.

'What?' Sanford asked.

'Girls,' Hawes said.

'Sure. Sure, I like girls.'

'Dressed or naked?'

'What?'

'With clothes or without?'

'I ... I don't know what you mean, sir.'

'Where were you tonight between eleven-twenty and midnight?' Hawes asked.

'Getting ... getting ready to come to ... to work,' Sanford said.

'You sure you weren't in the alley of the Eleventh Street Theatre stabbing a girl named Mercy Howell?'

'What? No ... no, of course ... of course not. I was ... I was ... I was home ... getting ... getting dressed ... to ... to ...' Sanford took a deep breath and decided to get indignant. 'Listen, what's this all about?' he said. 'Would you mind telling me?'

'It's all about *this*,' Carella said, and turned one of the receipts so that Sanford could read the signature:

Ronald Sanford
Night Clerk
The Addison Hotel

'Get your hat,' Hawes said. 'Study hall's over.'

It was twenty-five minutes past five when Adele Gorman came into the room with Meyer's cup of tea. He was crouched near the air-conditioning unit recessed into the wall to the left of the drapes, and he glanced over his shoulder when he heard her, and then rose.

'I didn't know what you took,' she said, 'so I brought everything.'

'Thank you,' he said. 'Just a little milk and sugar is fine.'

'Have you measured the room?' she asked, and put the tray down on the table in front of the sofa.

'Yes, I think I have everything I need now,' Meyer said. He put a spoonful of sugar into the tea, stirred it, added a drop of milk, stirred it again, and then lifted the cup to his mouth. 'Hot,' he said.

Adele Gorman was watching him silently. She said nothing. He kept sipping his tea. The ornate clock on the mantelpiece ticked in a swift whispering tempo.

'Do you always keep this room so dim?' Meyer asked.

'Well, my husband is blind, you know,' Adele said. 'There's really no need for brighter light.'

'Mmm. But your father reads in this room, doesn't he?'

'I beg your pardon?'

'The night you came home from that party. He was sitting in the chair over there near the floor lamp. Reading. Remember?'

'Oh. Yes, he was.'

'Bad light to read by.'

'Yes, I suppose it is.'

'I think maybe those bulbs are defective,' Meyer said.

'Do you think so?'

'Mmm. I happened to look at the lamp, and there are three hundred-watt bulbs in it, all of them burning. You should be getting a lot more illumination with that kind of wattage.'

'Well, I really don't know too much about ...'

'Unless the lamp is on a rheostat, of course.'

'I'm afraid I don't know what a rheostat is.'

'It's an adjustable resistor. You can dim your lights or make them brighter with it. I thought maybe the lamp was on a rheostat, but I couldn't find a control knob anywhere in the room.' Meyer paused. 'You wouldn't know if there's a rheostat control someplace in the house, would you?'

'I'm sure there isn't,' Adele said.

'Must be defective bulbs then,' Meyer said, and smiled. 'Also, I think your air conditioner is broken.'

'No, I'm sure it isn't.'

'Well, I was just looking at it, and all the switches are turned to the "On" position, but it isn't working. So I guess it's broken. That's a shame, too, because it's such a nice unit. Sixteen thousand BTUs. That's a lot of cooling power for a room this size. We've got one of those big old price-fixed apartments on Concord, my wife and I, with a large bedroom, and we get adequate cooling from a half-ton unit. It's a shame this one is broken.'

'Yes. Detective Meyer, I don't wish to appear rude, but it *is* late ...'

'Sure,' Meyer said. 'Unless, of course, the air conditioner's on a remote switch, too. So that all you have to do is turn a knob in another part of the house and it comes on.' He paused. '*Is* there such a switch someplace, Mrs Gorman?'

'I have no idea.'

'I'll just finish my tea and run along,' Meyer said. He lifted the cup to his lips, sipped at the tea, glanced at her over the rim, took the cup away from his mouth, and said, 'But I'll be back.'

'I hardly think there's any need for that,' Adele said.

'Well, some jewellery's been stolen ...'

'The ghosts ...'

'Come off it, Mrs Gorman.'

The room went silent.

'Where are the loudspeakers, Mrs Gorman?' Meyer asked. 'In the false beams up there? They're hollow, I checked them out.'

'I think perhaps you'd better leave,' Adele said slowly.

'Sure,' Meyer said. He put the teacup down, sighed, and got to his feet.

'I'll show you out,' Adele said.

They walked to the front door and out into the driveway. The night was still. The drizzle had stopped, and a thin layer of frost covered the grass rolling away towards the river below. Their footsteps crunched on the gravel as they walked slowly towards the automobile.

'My husband was blinded four years ago,' Adele said abruptly. 'He's a chemical engineer, there was an explosion at the plant, he could have been killed. Instead, he was only blinded.' She hesitated an instant, and then said again, 'Only blinded,' and there was such a sudden cry of despair in those two words that Meyer wanted to put his arm around her, console her the way he might his daughter, tell her that everything would be all right come morning, the night was almost done, and the morning was on the horizon. He leaned on the fender of his car, and she stood beside him looking down at the driveway gravel, her eyes not meeting his. They could have been conspirators exchanging secrets in the night, but they were only two people who had been thrown together on a premise as flimsy as the ghosts that inhabited this house.

'He gets a disability pension from the company,' Adele said, 'they've really been quite kind to us. And, of course, I work. I teach school, Detective Meyer. Kindergarten. I love children.' She paused. She would not raise her eyes to meet his. 'But ... it's sometimes very difficult. My father, you see ...'

Meyer waited. He longed suddenly for dawn, but he waited patiently, and heard her catch her breath as though committed to go ahead now, however painful the revelation might be, compelled to throw herself upon the mercy of the night before the morning sun broke through.

'My father's been retired for fifteen years.' She took a deep breath, and then said, 'He gambles, Detective Meyer. He's a horse player. He loses large sums of money.'

'Is that why he stole your jewels?' Meyer asked.

'You know, don't you?' Adele said simply, and raised her eyes to his. 'Of course you know. It's quite transparent, his ruse, a shoddy little show really, a performance that would fool no one but ... no one but a blind man.' She brushed at her cheek; he could not tell whether the cold air had caused her sudden tears. 'I ... I really don't care about the theft, the jewels were left to me by my mother, and after all it was my father who bought them for her, so it's ... it's really like returning a legacy, I really don't care about that part of it. I ... I'd have *given* the jewellery to him if only he'd asked, but he's so proud, such a proud man. A proud man who ... who steals from me and pretends that ghosts are committing the crime. And my husband, in his dark universe, listens to the sounds my father puts on tape and visualizes things he cannot quite believe and so he asks me to contact the police because he needs an impartial observer to contradict the suspicion that someone is stealing pennies from his blind man's cup. That's why I came to you, Detective Meyer. So that you would arrive here tonight and perhaps be fooled as I was fooled at first, and perhaps say to my husband, "Yes, Mr Gorman, there *are* ghosts in your house." ' She suddenly placed her hand on his sleeve. The tears were streaming down her face, she had difficulty catching her breath. 'Because you see, Detective Meyer, there *are* ghosts in this house, there really and truly are. The ghost of a proud man who was once a brilliant judge and lawyer and who is now a gambler and a thief; and the ghost of a man who once could see, and who now trips and falls in . . . in the darkness.'

On the river, a tugboat hooted. Adele Gorman fell silent. Meyer opened the door of his car and got in behind the wheel.

'I'll call your husband tomorrow,' he said abruptly and gruffly. 'Tell him I'm convinced something supernatural is happening here.'

'And will you be back, Detective Meyer?'

'No,' he said. 'I won't be back, Mrs Gorman.'

In the squadroom, they were wrapping up the night. Their day had begun at 7:45 p.m. yesterday, and they had been officially relieved at 5:45 a.m., but they had not left the office yet because there were still questions to be asked, reports to be typed, odds and ends to put in place before they could go home. And since the relieving detectives were busy getting *their* approaching workday organized, the squadroom at 6:00 a.m. was busier than it might have been on any given afternoon, with two teams of cops getting in each other's way.

In the Interrogation Room, Carella and Hawes were questioning young Ronald Sanford in the presence of the assistant district attorney who had come over earlier to take Mrs Matin's confession, and who now found himself listening to another one when all he wanted to do was go home to sleep. Sanford seemed terribly shocked that they had been able to notice the identical handwriting in 'The Addison Hotel' and 'The Avenging Angel', he couldn't get over it. He thought he had been very clever in mis-spelling the word 'clothes', because then if they ever *had* traced the note, they would think some illiterate had written it, and not someone who was studying to be an accountant. He could not explain why he had killed Mercy Howell. He got all mixed up when he tried to explain that. It had something to do with the moral climate of America, and people exposing themselves in public, people like that shouldn't be allowed to pollute others, to foist their filth upon others, to intrude upon the privacy of others, who only wanted to make a place for themselves in the world, who were trying so very hard to make something of themselves, studying accounting by day and working in a hotel by night, what right had these other people to ruin it for everybody else?

Frank Pasquale's tune, sung in the Clerical Office to Kling and O'Brien, was not quite so hysterical, but similar to Sanford's nonetheless. He had got the idea together with Danny Ryder. They had decided between them that the niggers in America were getting too damn pushy, shoving their way in where they didn't belong, taking jobs away from decent hard-working people who only wanted to be left alone, what right did they have to force themselves on everybody else? So they had decided to bomb the church, just to show the goddamn boogies that you couldn't get away with shit like that, not in America. He didn't seem too terribly concerned over the fact that his partner was lying stone cold dead on a slab at the morgue, or that their little Culver Avenue expedition had cost three people their lives, and had severely injured a half-dozen others. All he wanted to know, repeatedly, was whether his picture would be in the newspaper.

At his desk, Meyer Meyer started to type up a report on the Gorman ghosts, and then decided the hell with it. If the lieutenant asked him where he'd been half the night, he would say he had been out cruising, looking for trouble in the streets. Christ knew there was enough of *that* around. He pulled the report forms and their separating sheets of carbon paper from the ancient typewriter, and noticed that Detective Hal Willis was pacing the room anxiously, waiting to get at the desk the moment he vacated it.

'Okay, Hal,' he said, 'it's all yours.'

'*Finalmente!*' Willis, who was not Italian, said.

The telephone rang.

The sun was up when they came out of the building and walked past the hanging green '87' globes and down the low flat steps to the sidewalk. The part across the street shimmered with early morning autumn brilliance, the sky above it clear and blue. It was going to be a beautiful day. They walked towards the diner on the next block, Meyer and O'Brien ahead of the others, Carella, Hawes, and Kling bringing up the rear. They were tired, and exhaustion showed in their eyes and in the set of their mouths, and in the pace they kept. They talked without animation, mostly about their work, their breaths feathery and white on the cold morning air. When they reached the diner, they took off their overcoats and ordered hot coffee and cheese Danish and toasted English muffins. Meyer said he thought he was coming down with a cold. Carella told him about some cough medicine his wife had given one of the children. O'Brien, munching on a muffin, glanced across the diner and saw a young girl in one of the booths. She was wearing blue jeans and a brightly coloured Mexican serape, and she was talking to a boy wearing a Navy pea jacket.

'I think I see somebody,' he said, and he moved out of the booth past Kling and Hawes, who were talking about the new goddamn regulations on search and seizure.

The girl looked up when he approached the booth.

'Miss Blair?' he said. 'Penelope Blair?'

'Yes,' the girl answered. 'Who are you?'

'Detective O'Brien,' he said, 'the Eighty-seventh Squad. Your mother was in last night, Penny. She asked me to tell you ...'

'Flake off, cop,' Penelope Blair said. 'Go stop a riot someplace.'

O'Brien looked at her silently for a moment. He nodded then, and turned away, and went back to the table.

'Anything?' Kling asked.

'You can't win 'em all,' O'Brien said.

Chapter Two
DAY WATCH

The boy who lay naked on the concrete in the backyard of the tenement was perhaps eighteen years old. He wore his hair quite long, and he had recently begun growing a beard. His hair and his beard were black. His body was very white, and the blood that oozed onto the concrete pavement beneath him was very red.

The Superintendent of the building discovered him at two minutes before 6:00 a.m., when he went to put his garbage in one of the cans out back. The boy was lying face down in his own blood, and the super did not recognize him. He was shocked, of course. He did not ordinarily discover naked dead men in the backyard when he went to put out his garbage. But considering his shock, and considering his advanced age (he was approaching eighty), he managed to notify the police with considerable despatch, something not every good citizen of the city managed to do quite so well or so speedily.

Hal Willis arrived on the scene at fifteen minutes past six, accompanied by Richard Genero, who was the newest man on the squad, having been recently promoted from patrolman to Detective 3rd/Grade. Forbes and Phelps, the two men from Homicide, were already there. It was Willis' contention that any pair of Homicide cops was the same as any other pair of Homicide cops. He had never, for example, seen Forbes and Phelps in the same room with Monoghan and Monroe. Was this not undeniable proof that they were one and the same couple? Moreover, it seemed to Willis that all Homicide cops exchanged clothing regularly, and that Forbes and Phelps could on any given day of the week be found wearing suits and overcoats belonging to Monoghan and Monroe.

'Good morning,' Willis said.

'Morning,' Phelps said.

Forbes grunted.

'Nice way to start a goddamn Sunday, right?' Phelps asked.

'You fellows got here pretty fast,' Genero said.

Forbes looked at him. 'Who're you?'

'Dick Genero.'

'Never heard of you,' Forbes said.

'I never heard of you, neither,' Genero answered, and glanced to Willis for approval.

'Who's the dead man?' Willis asked drily. 'Anybody ever hear of *him*?'

'He sure as hell ain't carrying any identification,' Phelps said, and cackled hoarsely.

'Not unless he's got it shoved up his ass someplace,' Forbes said, and began laughing along with his partner.

'Who found the body?' Willis asked.

'Building superintendent.'

'Want to get him, Dick?'

'Right,' Genero said, and walked off.

'I hate to start my day like this,' Phelps said.

'Grisly,' Forbes said.

'All I had this morning was a cup of coffee,' Phelps said. 'And now *this*. Disgusting.'

'Nauseating,' Forbes said.

'Least have the decency to put on some goddamn clothes before he jumps off the roof,' Phelps said.

'How do you know he jumped off the roof?' Willis asked.

'I don't. I'm only saying.'

'What do you *think* he was doing?' Forbes asked. 'Walking around the backyard naked?'

'I don't know,' Willis said, and shrugged.

'Looks like a jumper to me,' Phelps said. He glanced up at the rear wall of the building. 'Isn't that a broken window up there?'

'Where?'

'Fourth floor there. Isn't that window broken there?'

'Looks like it,' Forbes said.

'Sure looks like it to me,' Phelps said.

'Hal, here's the super,' Genero said, approaching with the old man. 'Name's Mr Dennison, been working here for close to thirty years.'

'How do you do, Mr Dennison? I'm Detective Willis.'

Dennison nodded and said nothing.

'I understand you found the body.'

'That's right.'

'When was that?'

'Just before I called the cops.'

'What time was that, Mr Dennison?'

'Little after six, I guess.'

'Know who it is?'

'Can't see his face,' Dennison said.

'We'll roll him over for you as soon as the M.E. gets here,' Genero said.

'Don't do me no favours,' Dennison answered.

Unlike patrolmen, detectives – with the final approval of the Chief downtown – decide upon their own work schedules. As a result, the shifts will vary according to the whims of the men on the squad. For the past three months, and based on the dubious assumption that the night shift was more arduous than the day, the detectives of the 87th Squad had broken their working hours into two shifts, the first beginning at six in the morning and ending at eight in the evening, the second beginning then and ending at six the next day. The daywatch was fourteen hours long, the nightwatch only ten. But there were more men on duty during the day, and presumably this equalized the load. That some of those men were testifying in court or out on special assignments some of the time seemed not to bother any of the detectives, who considered the schedule equitable. At least for the time being. In another month or so, someone would come up with suggestions for a revised schedule, and they'd hold a meeting in the Interrogation Office and agree that they ought to try something new. A change was as good as a rest, provided the Chief approved.

As with any schedule, though, there were ways of beating it if you tried hard enough. Relieving the departing team at fifteen minutes before the hour was a mandatory courtesy, and one way of avoiding a 5:45 a.m. arrival at the squadroom was to plant yourself in a grocery store that did not open its doors until six-thirty. Detective Andy Parker found himself just such a grocery store on this bright October morning. The fact that the store had been robbed three times in broad daylight during the past month was only incidental. The point was that *some* detective had to cover the joint, and Andy Parker fortuitously happened to *be* that detective. The first thing he did to ingratiate himself with the owner was to swipe an apple from the fruit stand outside the store. The owner, one Silvio Corradini, who was sharp of eye for all his seventy-two years, noticed the petty larceny the moment it was committed. He was about to run out on the sidewalk to apprehend the brigand, when the man began walking directly into the store, eating the apple as he came. It was then Silvio realized the man could be nothing but a cop.

'Good morning,' Parker said.

'Good morning,' Silvio replied. 'You enjoy the fruit?'

'Yeah, very good apple,' Parker said. 'Thanks a lot.' He grinned amiably. 'I'm Detective Parker,' he said. 'I've been assigned to these holdups.'

'What happened to the other detective?'

'Di Maeo? He's on vacation.'

'In October?'

'We can't all get the summertime, huh?' Parker said, and grinned again. He was a huge man wearing rumpled brown corduroy trousers and a soiled tan windbreaker. He had shaved this morning before eating breakfast, but he managed to look unshaven nonetheless. He bit into the apple ferociously, juice spilling onto his chin. Silvio, watching him, thought he resembled a hired gun for the Mafia.

'*Lei è italiano?*' he asked.

'What?'

'Are you Italian?'

'No, are you?' Parker said, and grinned.

'Yes,' Silvio answered. He drew back his shoulders. 'Yes, I'm Italian.'

'Well, good, good,' Parker said. 'You always open the store on Sunday?'

'What?'

'I said . . .'

'I only stay open till twelve o'clock, that's all,' Silvio said, and shrugged. 'I get the people coming home from church.'

'That's against the law in this state, you know that?'

'Nobody ever said anything.'

'Well, just because somebody's willing to look the other way every now and then, that doesn't make it legal,' Parker said. He stared deep into Silvio's eyes. 'We'll talk about it later, huh? Meantime, fill me in on these holdups, okay?'

Silvio hesitated. He knew that talking about it later would cost him money. He was beginning to be sorry he'd ever told the police about the holdups. He sighed now and said, 'It is three times in the past month.'

'Same guy each time?'

'*Two* of them. I don't know if it's the same. They are wearing – *come si dice? Maschere.*'

'Masks?'

'*Si,* masks.'

'Same masks each time?'

'No. Once it was stockings, another time black ones, the third time handkerchiefs.'

Parker bit into the apple again. 'Are they armed?' he asked.

'If they did not have guns, I would break their heads and throw them out on the sidewalk.'

'Handguns?' Parker asked.

'What?'

'Pistols?'

'Yes, yes, pistols.'

'Both of them armed, or just one?'

'Both.'

'What time do they usually come in?'

'Different times. The first time was early in the morning, when I just opened the store. The next time was at night, maybe six, six-thirty. The last time was around lunch, the store was very quiet.'

'Did they take anything but cash?'

'Only cash.'

'Well,' Parker said, and shrugged. 'Maybe they'll come back, who knows? If you don't mind, I'll just hang around, okay? You got a back room or something?'

'Behind the curtain,' Silvio said. 'But if they come back again, I am ready for them myself.'

'What do you mean?'

'I got a gun now.'

He walked behind the counter to the cash register, opened it, and removed from the drawer a .32 Smith & Wesson.

'You need a permit for that, you know,' Parker said.

'I got one. A man gets held up three times, nobody argues about giving him a permit.'

'Carry or premises?'

'Premises.'

'You know how to use that thing?' Parker asked.

'I know how, yes.'

'I've got some advice for you,' Parker said. 'If those hoods come back, leave your gun in the drawer. Let *me* take care of any shooting needs to be done.'

A woman was coming into the store. Without answering, Silvio turned away from Parker, smiled, and said to her, '*Buon giorno, signora.*'

Parker sighed, threw the curtain back, and went into the other room.

'What do you think?' Willis asked the assistant medical examiner.

'Fell or was pushed from someplace up there,' the M.E. said. 'Split his skull wide open when he hit the ground. Probably dead on impact.'

'Anything else?'

'What more do you want? You're lucky we haven't got an omelette here.' He snapped his bag shut, rose from where he was crouched beside the body, and said, 'I'm finished, you can do what you like with him.'

'Thanks, Al,' Willis said.

'Yeah,' the M.E. answered, and walked off.

The body was now lying on its back. Genero looked down at the open skull and turned away. Dennison, the building superintendent, walked over with his hands in the pockets of his bib overalls. He looked down at the boy's bloody face and nodded.

'That's the kid in 4C,' he said.

'What's his name?'

'Scott.'

'That the first name or the last?'

'The last. I got his first name written down someplace inside. I got all the tenants' names written down. You want me to look it up for you?'

'Would you please?'

'Sure,' Dennison said.

'Would that be 4C up there?' Willis asked. 'The apartment with the broken window?'

'That's it, all right,' Dennison said.

The telephone on Arthur Brown's desk was ringing. He lifted the receiver, tucked it between his shoulder and his ear, said, 'Eighty-seventh Squad, Detective Brown,' and then glanced towards the slatted rail divider, where a patrolman was leading a handcuffed prisoner into the squadroom.

'Is this a detective?' the woman on the telephone asked.

'Yes, ma'am, Detective Brown.'

'I want to report a missing person,' the woman said.

'Yes, ma'am, just one second, please.'

Brown opened his desk drawer, took out a block of wood to which was attached the key to the detention cage across the room, and flipped it to the patrolman, who missed the catch. The prisoner laughed. The patrolman picked up the key, led the prisoner to the cage, opened the grillwork door, and shoved him inside.

'Take it easy, man,' the prisoner warned.

The patrolman locked the cage door without answering him. Then he walked to Brown's desk and sat on the edge of it, tilting his peaked cap back on his forehead and lighting a cigarette. On the telephone, Brown was saying, 'Now, what's your name, please, ma'am?'

'Mary Ellingham. Mrs Donald Ellingham.'

'Would you spell that for me, please?'

'E-L-L ...'

'Yep ...'

'... I-N-G-H-A-M.'

'And your address, Mrs Ellingham?'

'742 North Trinity.'

'All right, who's missing, Mrs Ellingham?'

'My husband.'

'That his full name? Donald Ellingham?'

'Yes. Well, no. Donald *E*. Ellingham. For Edward.'

'Yes, ma'am. How long has he been gone?'

'He was gone a week this past Friday.'

'Has this ever happened before, Mrs Ellingham?'

'No. Never.'

'He's never been gone before? Never any unexplained absences?'

'Never.'

'And you say he's been missing since, let's see, that'd be Friday the ninth?'

'Yes.'

'Did he go to work on Monday morning? The twelfth?'

'No.'

'You called his office?'

'Yes, I did.'

'And he wasn't there.'

'He hasn't been there all week.'

'Why'd you wait till today to report this, Mrs Ellingham?'

'I wanted to give him a chance to come back. I kept extending the deadline, you see. I though I'd give him a few days, and then it turned into a week, and then I thought I'd give him just another day, and then Saturday went by, and ... well, I decided to call today.'

'Does your husband drink, Mrs Ellingham?'

'No. That is, he drinks, but not excessively. He's not an alcoholic, if that's what you mean.'

'Has there ever been any problem with ... well ... other women?'

'No.'

'What I'm trying to say, Mrs Ellingham ...'

'Yes, I understand. I don't think he's run off with another woman, no.'

'What *do* you think has happened, Mrs Ellingham?'

'I'm afraid he's been in an accident.'

'Have you contacted the various hospitals in the city?'

'Yes. He's not at any of them.'

'But you still think he may have been in an accident.'

'I think he may be dead someplace,' Mrs Ellingham said, and began weeping.

Brown was silent. He looked up at the patrolman.

'Mrs Ellingham?'

'Yes.'

'I'll try to get over there later today if I can, to get the information I'll need for the Missing Persons Bureau. Will you be home?'

'Yes.'

'Shall I call first?'

'No, I'll be here all day.'

'Fine, I'll see you later then. If you should hear anything meanwhile ...'

'Yes, I'll call you.'

'Good-bye, Mrs Ellingham,' Brown said, and hung up. 'Lady's husband disappeared,' he said to the patrolman.

'Went down for a loaf of bread a year ago, right?' the patrolman said.

'Right. Hasn't been heard from since.' Brown gestured towards the detention cage. 'Who's the prize across the room?'

'Caught him cold in the middle of a burglary on Fifth and Friedlander. On a third-floor fire escape. Jimmied open the window, and was just entering.'

'Any tools on him?'

'Yep. I left them on the bench outside.'

'Want to get them for me?'

The patrolman went out into the corridor. Brown walked over to the detention cage. The prisoner looked at him.

'What's your name?' Brown asked.

'What's yours?'

'Detective Arthur Brown.'

'That's appropriate,' the prisoner said.

'I find it so,' Brown said coolly. 'Now what's yours?'

'Frederick Spaeth.'

The patrolman came back into the room carrying a leather bag containing a hand drill and bits of various sizes, a jimmy, a complete set of picklocks, several punches and skeleton keys, a pair of nippers, a hacksaw, a pair of brown cotton gloves, and a crowbar designed so that it could be taken apart and carried in three sections. Brown looked over the tools and said nothing.

'I'm a carpenter,' Spaeth said in explanation.

Brown turned to the patrolman. 'Anybody in the apartment, Simms?'

'Empty,' Simms replied.

'Spaeth,' Brown said, 'we're charging you with burglary in the third degree, which is a felony. And we're also charging you with Possession of Burglar's Instruments, which is a Class-A Misdemeanour. Take him down, Simms.'

'I want a lawyer,' Spaeth said.

'You're entitled to one,' Brown said.

'I want him *now. Before* you book me.'

Because policemen are sometimes as confused by Miranda-Escobedo as are laymen, Brown might have followed the course pursued by his colleague Kling, who, the night before, had advised a prisoner of his rights even though cruising radio patrolmen had arrested him in the act. Instead, Brown said, 'What for, Spaeth? You were apprehended entering an apartment illegally. Nobody's asking you any questions, we caught you cold. You'll be allowed three telephone calls after you're booked, to your lawyer, your mother, your bail bondsman, your best friend, whoever the hell you like. Take him down, Simms.'

Simms unlocked the cage and prodded Spaeth out of it with his nightstick. 'This is illegal!' Spaeth shouted.

'So's breaking and entry,' Brown answered.

The woman in the apartment across the hall from 4C was taller than both Willis and Genero, which was understandable. Hal Willis was the shortest man on the squad, having cleared the minimum five-feet-eight-inch height requirement by a scant quarter of an inch. Built like a soft shoe dancer, brown-haired and brown-eyed, he stood alongside Genero, who towered above him at five feet nine inches. Hal Willis knew he was short. Richard Genero thought he was very tall. From his father, he had inherited beautiful curly black hair and a strong Neapolitan nose, a sensuous mouth and soulful brown eyes. From his mother, he had inherited the tall Milanese carriage of all his male cousins and uncles – except Uncle Dominick, who was only five feet six. But this lady who opened the door to apartment 4B was a very big lady indeed. Both Willis and Genero looked up at her simultaneously, and then glanced at each other in something like stupefied awe. The lady was wearing a pink slip and nothing else. Barefooted, big-breasted, redheaded, green-eyed, she put her hands on her nylon-sheathed hips and said, 'Yeah?'

'Police officers,' Willis said, and showed her his shield.

The woman scrutinized it, and then said, 'Yeah?'

'We'd like to ask you a few questions,' Genero said.

'What about?'

'About the young man across the hall. Lewis Scott.'

'What about him?'

'Do you know him?'

'Slightly.'

'Only slightly?' Genero said. 'You live directly across the hall from him ...'

'So what? This is the city.'

'Even so ...'

'I'm forty-six years old, he's a kid of what? Eighteen? Nineteen? How do you *expect* me to know him? Intimately?'

'Well, no, ma'am, but ...'

'So that's how I know him. Slightly. Anyway, what about him?'

'Did you see him at any time last night?' Willis asked.

'No. Why? Something happen to him?'

'Did you hear anything unusual in his apartment any time last night?'

'Unusual like what?'

'Like glass breaking?'

'I wasn't home last night. I went out to supper with a friend.'

'What time was that?'

'Eight o'clock.'

'And what time did you get back?'

'I didn't. I slept over.'

'With your friend?'

'Yes.'

'What's her name?' Genero asked.

'Her name is Morris Strauss, *that's* her name.'

'Oh,' Genero said. He glanced at Willis sheepishly.

'When *did* you get home, ma'am?' Willis asked.

'About five o'clock this morning. Morris is a milkman. He gets up very early. We had breakfast together, and then I came back here. Why? What's the matter? Did Lew do something?'

'Did you happen to see him at *any* time yesterday?'

'Yeah. When I was going to the store. He was just coming in the building.'

'What time was that, would you remember?'

'About four-thirty. I was going out for some coffee. I ran out of coffee. I drink maybe six hundred cups of coffee a day. I'm always running out. So I was going up the street to the A&P to get some more. That's when I saw him.'

'Was he alone?'

'No.'

'Who was with him?'

'Another kid.'

'Boy or girl?'

'A boy.'

'Would you know who?' Genero asked.

'I don't hang around with teenagers, how would I ...?'

'Well, you might have seen him around the neighbourhood ...'

'No.'

'How old would you say he was?' Willis asked.

'About Lew's age. Eighteen, nineteen, I don't know. A big kid.'

'Can you describe him?'

'Long blond hair, a sort of handlebar moustache. He was wearing a crazy jacket.'

'What do you mean, crazy?'

'It was like an animal skin, with the fur inside and the, you know, what do you call it, the pelt? Is that what you call it?'

'Go ahead.'

'The raw side, you know what I mean? The skin part. That was the outside of the jacket, and the fur was the inside. White fur. And there was a big orange sun painted on the back of the jacket.'

'Anything else?'

'Ain't that enough?'

'Maybe it is,' Willis said. 'Thank you very much, ma'am.'

'You're welcome,' she answered. 'You want some coffee? I got some on the stove.'

'No thanks, we want to take a look at the apartment here,' Genero said. 'Thanks a lot, though. You've been very kind.'

The woman smiled so suddenly and so radiantly that it almost knocked Genero clear across the hallway to the opposite wall.

'Not at all,' she said in a tiny little voice, and gently eased the door shut. Genero raised his eyebrows. He was trying to remember exactly what he had said, and in what tone of voice. He was still new at this business of questioning people, and any trick he could learn might prove helpful. The trouble was, he couldn't remember his exact words.

'What did I say?' he asked Willis.

'I don't remember,' Willis answered.

'No, come on, Hal, what did I say? What made her smile that way, and all of a sudden get so nice?'

'I think you asked her if she'd like to go to bed with you,' Willis said.

'No,' Genero said seriously, and shook his head. 'No, I don't think so.'

With the passkey the superintendent had provided, Willis opened the door to 4C, and stepped into the apartment. Behind him, Genero was still pondering the subtleties of police interrogation.

There were two windows facing the entrance door. The lower pane of the window on the left was almost completely shattered, with here and there an isolated shard jutting from the window frame. Sunlight streamed through both windows, dust motes rising silently. The apartment was sparsely furnished, a mattress on the floor against one wall, a bookcase on the opposite wall, a stereo record player and a stack of LP albums beside it, a bridge table and two chairs in the kitchen alcove, where another window opened onto the fire escape. A black camp trunk studded with brass rivets served as a coffee table in the centre of the room, near the record player. Brightly coloured cushions lined the wall on either side of the bookcase. Two black-and-white anti-war posters decorated the walls. The windows were curtainless. In the kitchen alcove, the shelves over the stove carried only two boxes of breakfast cereal and a bowl of sugar. A bottle of milk and three containers of yoghurt were in the refrigerator. In the vegetable tray, Willis found a plastic bag of what looked like oregano. He showed it to Genero.

'Grass?' Genero said.

Willis shrugged. He opened the bag and sniffed the greenish-brown, crushed leaves. 'Maybe,' he said. He pulled an evidence tag from his pad, filled it out, and tied it to the plastic bag.

They went through the apartment methodically. There were three coffee mugs on the camp trunk. Each of them smelled of wine, and there was a red lipstick stain on the rim of one cup. They opened the camp trunk and found it stuffed with dungarees, flannel shirts, undershorts, several sweaters, a harmonica, an army blanket, and a small metal cash box. The cash box was unlocked. It contained three dollars in change, and a high school G.O. card encased in plastic. In the kitchen, they found two empty wine bottles in the garbage pail. A sprung mousetrap, the bait gone, was under the kitchen sink. On top of the closed toilet seat in the bathroom, they found a pair of dungarees with a black belt through the trouser loops, an orange Charlie Brown sweatshirt with the sleeves cut off raggedly at the elbows, a pair of white sweat socks, a pair of loafers and a woman's black silk blouse.

The blouse had a label in it.

They came into the grocery store at twenty minutes past seven, each of them wearing a Halloween mask, even though this was only the middle of the month and Halloween was yet two weeks away. They were both holding drawn guns, both dressed in black trench coats and black trousers. They walked rapidly from the front door to the counter, with the familiarity of visitors who had been there before. One of them was wearing a Wolf Man mask and the other was wearing a Snow White mask. The masks completely covered their faces and lent a terrifying nightmare aspect to their headlong rush for the counter.

Silvio's back was turned when they entered the store. He heard the bell over the door, and whirled quickly, but they were almost to the counter by then, and he had time to shout only the single work '*Ancora!*' before he punched the NO SALE key on the register and reached into the drawer for his gun. The man wearing the Snow White mask was the first to realize that Silvio was going for a gun. He did not say a word to his partner. Instead, he fired directly into Silvio's face at close range. The slug almost tore off Silvio's head and sent him spinning backwards against the shelves. Canned goods clattered to the floor. The curtain leading to the back room was suddenly thrown open and Parker stood in the doorway with a .38 Police Special in his fist. The man with the Wolf Man mask had his hand in the cash drawer and was scooping up a pile of bills.

'Hold it!' Parker shouted, and the man with the Snow White mask fired again. His slug caught Parker in the right shoulder. Parker bent low and pulled off a wild shot just as the man at the cash register opened fire, aiming for Parker's belly, catching him in the leg instead. Parker grabbled for the curtain behind him, clutching for support, tearing it loose as he fell to the floor screaming in pain.

The two men in their Halloween masks ran out of the store and into the Sunday morning sunshine.

There were 186 patrolmen assigned to the 87th Precinct and on any given day of the week, their work schedule was outlined by a duty chart that required a PhD in Arabic literature to be properly understood. In essence, six of these patrolmen worked from 8:00 a.m. to 4:00 p.m., Monday through Friday, two of them serving as the Captain's clerical force, one as a highway safety patrolman, and the last two as community relations patrolman and roll call man respectively. The remaining 180 patrolmen were divided into twenty squads with nine men on each squad. Their duty chart looked like this:

SCHEDULE OF DUTY FOR PATROLMEN — 1969

TOURS OF DUTY

DAY ON CHART	12 MID. TO 8 A.M. SQUAD	8 A.M. TO 4 P.M. SQUAD	4 P.M. TO 12 MID. SQUAD
1	(1)2-3-4-5	8-9-10-11-12	15-16-17-18-19
2	(2)3-4-5-6	9-10-11-12-13	16-17-18-19-20
3	3-4-5-6-7	10-11-12-13-14	17-18-19-20-1
4	(4)5-6-7-8	11-12-13-14-15	18-19-20-1-2
5	5-6-7-8-9	12-13-14-15-16	19-20-1-2-3
6	(6)7-8-9-10	13-14-15-16-17	20-1-2-3-4
7	(7)8-9-10-11	14-15-16-17-18	1-2-3-4-5
8	8-9-10-11-12	15-16-17-18-19	2-3-4-5-6
9	9-10-11-12-13	16-17-18-19-20	3-4-5-6-7
10	10-11-12-13-14	17-18-19-20-1	4-5-6-7-8
11	11-12-13-14-15	18-19-20-1-2	5-6-7-8-9
12	12-13-14-15-16	19-20-1-2-3	6-7-8-9-10
13	13-14-15-16-17	20-1-2-3-4	7-8-9-10-11
14	14-15-16-17-18	1-2-3-4-5	8-9-10-11-12
15	15-16-17-18-19	2-3-4-5-6	9-10-11-12-13
16	16-17-18-19-20	3-4-5-6-7	10-11-12-13-14
17	17-18-19-20-1	4-5-6-7-8	11-12-13-14-15
18	18-19-20-1-2	5-6-7-8-9	12-13-14-15-16
19	19-20-1-2-3	6-7-8-9-10	13-14-15-16-17
20	20-1-2-3-4	7-8-9-10-11	14-15-16-17-18

Calendar (1969)

Row	JAN.	FEB.	MAR.	APR.	MAY	JUNE	JULY	AUG.	SEPT.	OCT.	NOV.	DEC.
1	3-23	12	4-24	(13)	(3)23	12	2-22	11-(31)	(20)	10-30	19	9-29
2	(4)24	13	5-25	14	(4)24	13	3-23	12	1-(21)	(11)31	20	10-30
3	(5)25	14	6-26	15	5-(25)	(14)	4-24	13	2-22	(12)	(21)	11-31
4	6-(26)	(15)	7-27	16	6-26	(15)	(5)(25)	14	3-23	13	(22)	12
5	7-27	(16)	(8)28	17	7-27	17	7-(27)	15	4-24	14	3-(23)	(13)
6	8-28	17	(9)(29)	18	8-28	17	7-(27)	(16)	5-25	15	4-24	(14)
7	9-29	18	10-(30)	(19)	8-28	18	8-28	(17)	6-26	16	5-25	(15)
8	10-30	19	11-31	(20)	9-29	19	9-29	18	(27)	(17)	6-26	16
9	(11)31	20	12	1-21	(10)30	20	10-30	19	8-(28)	(18)	7-27	17
10	(12)	(1)21	13	2-22	(11)(31)	(1)(21)	11-31	20	8-(28)	(19)	8-28	18
11	(13)	(2)(22)	14	3-23	12	(2)(22)	(12)	1-21	9-29	20	(8)28	19
12	13	(3)23	(14)	4-24	13	2-22	(13)	(2)22	10-30	1-21	(9)(29)	(20)
13	14	4-24	(15)(16)	(5)25	14	3-23	14	(3)23	11	2-22	11-10	1
14	15	4-24	(16)	(6)(26)	15	4-24	15	4-(24)	12	3-23	11	2
15	16	5-25	17	(7)(27)	16	5-25	16	5-(25)	13	4-(24)	13	3
16	17	6-26	18	8-28	(17)	6-26	17	6-26	16	5-(26)	14	4
17	(8)28	7-27	19	9-29	(18)	7-27	18	7-27	17	6-(26)	(15)	5
18	(9)(29)	(8)28	20	10-30	19	(8)(29)	(19)	8-28	17	7-27	(16)	(5)(6)
19	20	(9)	(1)21	1-30	20	(9)(29)	(20)	9-29	18	8-28	17	(6)
20	1-21	10	(2)(22)	11	1-21	10-30	10-(30)	8-29	18	8-28	18	7
21	2-22	11	3-(23)	(12)	2-22		11-31	10-(30)	19	9-29		8

Legend

O AROUND SQUAD NUMBER INDICATES EXCUSAL EXCEPT WHEN IT CORRESPONDS WITH O AROUND DATE

O INDICATES SATURDAYS & SUNDAYS

TO BE USED BY: PATROL PRECINCTS, EMERGENCY SERVICE, ACCIDENT INVESTIGATION SQUAD, SGTS & PTL OF HARBOR PCT.

eff. 1-1-66

All of which meant that patrolmen worked five tours for a forty-hour week, and then were off for fifty-six hours except when they were working the midnight to 8:00 a.m. shift, in which case they then worked only *four* tours and were off for eighty hours. Unless, of course, the *fifth* midnight tour happened to fall on a Friday or Saturday night, in which case they were required to work. All clear?

Patrolmen were supposed to be relieved on post as soon as possible after the hour by the squad that had just answered roll call in the precinct muster room. But most patrolmen began to drift back towards the station house shortly before the hour, so that seconds after the new shift trotted down the precinct steps, the old one entered the building and headed for the locker room to change into street clothes. There were a lot of cops in and around a police station when the shift was changing, and Sunday morning was no exception. If anything, the precinct was busier on Sunday because Saturday night brought thieves out like cockroaches and their resultant handiwork spilled over onto the day of rest.

This particular Sunday morning was more chaotic than usual because a cop had been shot, and nothing can galvanize a police department like the knowledge that one of their own has been gunned down. Lieutenant Peter Byrnes, who was in command of the sixteen detectives on the 87th Squad, saw fit to call in three men who were on vacation, perhaps on the theory that one wounded cop is worth at least three who were ambulatory. Not content to leave it at that, he then put in a call to Steve Carella at his home in Riverhead, ostensibly to inform him of the shooting.

Sitting behind his desk in the corner room upstairs, looking down at the front steps of the building, where the patrolmen filed out in pairs, the green globes flanking the steps and burning with sunshine as though fired from within, Byrnes must have known that Carella had worked the night shift and that the man did not now need a call from his superior officer. But he dialled the number nonetheless, and waited while the phone rang repeatedly on the other end. When at last Carella answered, Byrnes said, 'Steve? Were you asleep?'

'No, I was just getting into my pyjamas.'

'Sorry to bother you this way.'

'No, no, what is it, Pete?'

'Parker just got shot in a grocery store on Ainsley.'

'No kidding?'

'Yeah.'

'Jesus,' Carella said.

'Two hoods killed the proprietor, wounded Parker in the shoulder and leg. He's been taken to Buenavista Hospital. It looks pretty serious.'

'Jesus,' Carella said again.

'I've already called in Di Maeo, Levine and Meriwether. They're on vacation, Steve, but I had to do it, I don't like it when cops get shot.'

'No, neither do I.'

'I just thought I'd tell you.'

'Yeah, I'm glad you did, Pete.'

The line went silent.

'Pete?'

'Yeah, Steve?'

'What is it? Do you want *me* to come in, too?'

'Well, you had a long night, Steve.'

The line went silent again.

'Well ... what do you want me to do, Pete?'

'Why don't you see how you feel?' Byrnes said. 'Go to bed, get some rest, maybe you'll feel like coming in a little later, okay?' Byrnes paused. 'I can use you, Steve. It's up to you.'

'What time is it, anyway?' Carella asked.

Byrnes looked up at the wall clock. 'Little after eight. Get some rest, okay?'

'Yeah, okay,' Carella said.

'I'll talk to you later,' Byrnes said, and hung up. He rose from behind his desk, hooked his thumbs into his belt just above both hip pockets and walked to the window overlooking the park. He was a compact man with grey hair and flinty blue eyes, and he stood looking silently at the sun-washed foliage across the street, his face expressionless, and then turned suddenly and walked to the frosted glass door of his office, yanked it open, and went out into the squadroom.

A marine corporal was sitting with Detective Carl Kapek at the desk closest to the lieutenant's office. A swollen discoloured lump the size of a baseball sat just over the marine's left eye. His uniform was rumpled and soiled, and he looked extremely embarrassed, his hands clasped in his lap rather like a schoolboy's. He spoke in a very low voice, almost a whisper, to Kapek as the lieutenant walked past them to where Brown was on the telephone at his own desk.

'Right, I'll tell him,' Brown said, and replaced the phone on its cradle.

'That about Parker?' Byrnes asked.

'No, that was Delgado over on South Sixth. Guy was on his way to church, four other guys grabbed him as he came out of his building, damn near killed him. Delgado's on it now.'

'Right. The hospital call back on Parker?'

'Not yet.'

'Who's that in the holding cell downstairs?'

'A burglar Simms picked up on Fifth and Friedlander.'

'You'd better get over to that grocery store, Artie.'

'That'll leave Kapek all alone here.'

'I've got some men coming in. They should be here any time now.'

'Okay then.'

'I want some meat on this, Artie. I don't like my squad getting shot up.'

Brown nodded, opened the top drawer of his desk, and took from it a holstered .38 Detective's Special. He fastened the holster to his belt just slightly forward of his right hip pocket, put on his jacket, and then went to the locker room to get his coat and hat. On his way out of the squadroom, he stopped at Kapek's desk and said, 'I'll be at that grocery store, you need me.'

'Okay,' Kapek said, and turned back to the marine. 'I still don't understand exactly how you got beat up,' he said. 'You mind going over it one more time?'

The marine looked even more embarrassed now. He was short and slender, dwarfed by Kapek, who sat beside him in his shirt sleeves with his tie pulled down, collar open, straight blond hair falling onto his forehead, wearing a shoulder holster from which protruded the walnut butt of a .38.

'Well, you know, I got jumped, is all,' the marine said.

'How?'

'I was walking along, and I got jumped, is all.'

'Where was this, Corporal Miles?'

'On The Stem.'

'What time?'

'Must've been about three in the morning.'

'What were you doing?'

'Just walking.'

'Going any place in particular?'

'I'd just left this bar, you see? I'd been drinking in this bar on Seventeenth Street, I think it was.'

'Anything happen in the bar?'

'Well, like what?'

'Any trouble? Any words?'

'No, no, it was a real nice bar.'

'And you left there about three o'clock and started walking up The Stem.'

'That's right.'

'Where were you going?'

'Oh, just for a little walk, that's all. Before heading back to the ship. I'm on this battleship over to the Navy Yard. It's in dry dock there.'

'Um-huh,' Kapek said. 'So you were walking along and this man jumped you.'

'Mmm.'

'Just one man?'

'Yeah. One.'

'What'd he hit you with?'

'I don't know.'

'And you came to just a little while ago, is that it?'

'Yeah. And found out the bastards had taken my wallet and watch.'

Kapek was silent for several seconds. Then he said, 'I thought there was only one of them.'

'That's right. Just one.'

'You said "bastards".'

'Huh?'

'Plural.'

'Huh?'

'How many were there actually, Corporal?'

'Who hit me, you mean? Like I said. Just one.'

'Never mind who hit you or who didn't. How many were there altogether?'

'Well ... two.'

'All right, let's get this straight now. It was *two* men who jumped you, not ...'

'Well, no. Not exactly.'

'Look, Corporal,' Kapek said, 'you want to tell me about this, or you want to forget it? We're pretty busy around here right now, and I don't have time for this kind of thing, I mean it. You want us to try to recover your stuff, then give us a little help, okay? Otherwise, so long, it was nice meeting you, I hope you get back to your ship all right.'

Miles was silent for several moments. Then he sighed deeply and said, 'I feel like a goddamn jackass, is all.'

'Why? What happened?'

'There was this girl in the bar ...'

'I figured,' Kapek said, and nodded.

'In a red dress. She kept wiggling her ass at me all night long, you know? So I finally started a conversation with her, and she was real friendly and all, I mean she didn't seem to be *after* nothing, I think I maybe bought her only two drinks the whole night long.'

'Yeah, go ahead.'

'So a little before three, she tells me she's awful tired and wants to go home to bed, and she says good night to everybody, and then goes to the door and winks at me and gives me a kind of a little come-on move with her head, you know? Like this, you know? Like just this little movement of her head, you know? To tell me I should follow her. So I paid the check, and hurried on outside, and there she was on the corner, and she starts walking the minute she sees me, looking back over her shoulder, and giving me that same come-on again, trotting her little ass right up the avenue, and then turning off into one of the side streets. So I turned the corner after her and there's this guy standing there, and wham, he clobbers me. Next thing I know, I wake up with *this* —— thing over my eye, and my money gone, and my watch, too. Little bitch.'

'Was she black or white?'

'Black.'

'And the man?'

'White.'

'Would you recognize her if you saw her again?'

'I'll never forget her long as I live.'

'What about the man?'

'I only got a quick look at him. He hit me the minute I come around the corner. Man, I saw stars. They musta moved me after I went out because I woke up in this hallway, you see. I mean, I was laying on the sidewalk when ...' Miles stopped and looked down at his hands.

'Yes, Corporal?'

'What gets me is, I mean, she *kicked* me, the little bitch. When I was down on the sidewalk, she kicked me with his goddamn pointed shoe of hers. I mean, man, *that's* what put me out, not the guy hitting me. It was her kicking me with that pointed shoe of hers.' Corporal Miles looked up plaintively. 'Why'd she do *that*, huh? I was nice to her. I mean it. I was only nice.'

The ambulance had come and gone, carrying away the man who had been attacked as he was leaving his home to go to church. It was now nine o'clock and there was still blood on the front stoop of the building. Detective 3rd/Grade Alexiandre Delgado stood on the steps with the victim's wife and two children, and tried to believe they were unaware of the blood drying in the early morning sunshine. Mrs Huerta was a black-haired woman with brown eyes filled now with tears. Her two daughters, dressed to go to church, wearing identical green wool coats and black patent leather shoes and white ankle socks, resembled their mother except for the tears. Their brown eyes were opened wide in curiosity and fright and incomprehension. But neither of the two was crying. A crowd of bystanders kept nudging towards the stoop, despite the efforts of the beat patrolman to disperse them.

'Can you tell me exactly what happened, Mrs Huerta?' Delgado asked. Like the woman he was questioning, he was Puerto Rican. And like her, he had been raised in a ghetto. Not this one, but a similar one (when you've seen *one* slum, you've seen them all, according to certain observers) in the shadow of the Calm's Point Bridge downtown. He could have spoken to her in fluent Spanish, but he was still slightly embarrassed by his accent when he was speaking English, and as a result he tried to speak it *all* the time. Mrs Huerta, on the other hand, was not so sure she wanted to conduct the conversation in English. Her young daughters understood and spoke English, whereas their Spanish was spotty at best. At the same time, many of Mrs Huerta's neighbours (who were eagerly crowding the front stoop now) spoke *only* Spanish, and she recognized that talking to this detective in English might enable her to keep at least *some* of her business to herself. She silently debated the matter only a moment longer, and then decided to answer in English.

'We were going down to church,' she said, 'the eight o'clock mass. The church is right up the street, it takes five minutes. We came out of the building, José and me and the two girls, and these men came at him.'

'How many men?'

'Four.'

'Did you recognize any of them?'

'No,' Mrs Huerta said.

'What happened?'

'They hit him.'

'With what?'

'Broom handles. Short. You know, they take the broom and saw it off.'

'Did they say anything to your husband?'

'*Nada*. Nothing.'

'Did he say anything to them?'

'No.'

'And you didn't recognize any of them? They weren't men from the *barrio*, the neighbourhood?'

'I never saw them before.'

One of the little girls looked up at her mother and then turned quickly away.

'*Sí, qué hay?*' Delgado asked immediately.

'Nothing,' the little girl answered.

'What's your name?' Delgado said.

'Paquita Huerta.'

'Did you see the men who attacked your father, Paquita?'

'Yes,' Paquita said, and nodded.

'Did you know any of those men?'

The little girl hesitated.

'*Puede usted decirme?*'

'No,' Paquita said. 'I did not know any of them.'

'And you?' Delgado said, turning to the other girl.

'No. None of them.'

Delgado searched their eyes. The little girls watched him unblinkingly. He turned to Mrs Huerta again. 'Your husband's full name is José Huerta?' he asked.

'José Vincente Huerta.'

'How old is he, *señora?*'

'Forty-seven.'

'What does he do for a living?'

'He is a real estate agent.'

'Where is his place of business, Mrs Huerta?'

'In Riverhead, 1345 Harrison Avenue. It is called J-R Realty.'

'Does he own the business?'

'Yes.'

'No partners?'

'Yes, he has a partner.'

'What's his partner's name?'

'Ramon Castañeda. That's how they got the J-R. From José and Ramon.'

'And where does Mr Castañeda live?'

'Two blocks from here. On Fourth Street.'

'The address?'

'112 South Fourth.'

'All right, thank you,' Delgado said. 'I'll let you know if we come up with anything.'

'*Por favor,*' Mrs Huerta said, and took both her daughters by their hands and led them into the building.

The black blouse found in Lewis Scott's bathroom had come from a clothing store called The Monkey Wrench, on Culver Avenue. Since this was a Sunday, the store was closed. The patrolman on the beat spotted Willis and Genero peering through the plate glass window and casually ambled over to them.

'Help you fellows?' he asked.

Both Genero and Willis looked at him. Neither of them recognized him.

'You new on the beat, kid?' Genero said. The patrolman was perhaps three or four years *older* than Genero, but since his rank was lower, Genero felt perfectly free to address him in this manner. The patrolman could not decide whether he was dealing with hoods or fellow law enforcers; the distinction was sometimes difficult to make. He debated whether he should answer smart-ass or subservient. While he was deciding, Willis said, 'I'm Detective Willis. This is my partner, Detective Genero.'

'Oh,' the patrolman said, managing to make the single word sound eloquent.

'How long you been on the beat, kid?' Genero asked.

'Just this past week. They flew me in from Majesta.'

'Special assignment?'

'Yeah. This is a glass post, you know, there's been lots of breakage and looting lately. They almost doubled the force here, from what I understand.'

'Where's the regular beat man?'

'He's catching a cup of coffee at the diner up the street. Anything I can help you with?'

'What's his name?'

'Haskins. You know him?'

'Yeah,' Willis said. 'Diner on the corner there?'

'Right.'

'See you later, kid,' Genero said, and both detectives walked off towards the diner. Behind them, the patrolman shrugged in a manner clearly indicating that he thought all detectives were no-good rotten bastards who were always pulling rank.

The diner at fifteen minutes before ten was empty save for Patrolman Haskins and a man behind the counter. Haskins was hunched over a cup of coffee. He looked as though he had not had much sleep the night before. Genero and Willis walked to the counter and took stools on either side of him.

'Hello, Bill,' Willis said.

Haskins looked up from his coffee. 'Hey, hi,' he said.

'Two coffees,' Genero said to the counterman.

'You looking for me,' Haskins asked, 'or you just happen in?'

'We're looking for you.'

'What's up?'

'How you want those coffees?' the counterman asked.

'Regular,' Willis said.

'One regular, one black,' Genero said.

'Two regulars, one black,' the counterman said.

'*One* regular, *one* black,' Genero said.

'*He* wants a regular,' the counterman insisted, 'and *you* want a regular and a black.'

'What are you, a comedian?' Genero said.

'It's all on the arm anyway, ain't it?' the counterman answered.

'Who says?'

'The day a cop pays for a cup of coffee in here, that's the day they give me a parade up Hall Avenue.'

None of the policemen answered him. They were not, as a matter of fact, in the habit of paying for coffee in local eateries. Neither did they enjoy being reminded of it.

'Bill, we're looking for a kid about eighteen, nineteen,' Willis said. 'Long blond hair, handlebar moustache. See anybody around like that?'

'I seen a hundred of them,' Haskins said. 'Are you kidding?'

'This one was wearing a jacket with the fur inside, the skin side out.' ·

Haskins shrugged.

'Big sun painted on the back of it,' Willis said.

'Yeah, that rings a bell. I think I seen that jacket around.'

'Remember the kid wearing it?'

'Where the hell did I see that jacket?' Haskins asked aloud.

'He might have been with another kid his age, black beard, black hair.'

'No,' Haskins said, and shook his head. 'An orange sun, right? Like an orange sun with rays coming out of it, right?'

'That's right, orange.'

'Yeah, I seen that jacket,' Haskins said. 'Just the other day. Where the hell did I see it?'

'Two coffees, one regular, one black,' the counterman said, and put them down.

'Jerry, you ever seen a kid in here wearing a fur jacket with a sun painted on the back of it?' Haskins asked.

'No,' the counterman said flatly, and walked back into the kitchen.

'White fur, right?' Haskins said to Willis. 'On the inside, right? Like white fur?'

'That's right.'

'Sure, I seen that goddamn jacket. Just give me a minute, okay?'

'Sure, take your time,' Willis said.

Haskins turned to Genero and conversationally said, 'I see you got the gold tin. Who's your rabbi?'

'I was promoted a long time ago,' Genero said, somewhat offended. 'Where the hell have you been?'

'I guess I don't keep up with what's happening around the stationhouse,' Haskins said, and grinned.

'You *know* I was promoted.'

'Yeah, I guess it just slipped my mind,' Haskins said. 'How you like the good life, Genero?'

'Beats laying bricks all to hell,' Genero answered.

'What *doesn't*?' Haskins said.

'About that jacket ...' Willis interrupted.

'Yeah, yeah, just give me a minute, it'll come to me,' Haskins said, and lifted his coffee cup in both hands, and sipped at it and said, 'That new kid covering out there?'

'He's doing fine, don't worry about him.'

'The Monkey Wrench!' Haskins said, snapping his fingers. '*That's* where I seen that damn thing. In the window of The Monkey Wrench. Right up the street.'

'Good,' Willis said, and nodded. 'Got any idea who runs that shop?'

'Yeah, these two dykes who live over on Eighth. Just around the corner from the store.'

'What're their names?'

'Flora Schneider and Frieda something, I don't know what. Flora and Frieda, everybody calls them.'

'What's the address on Eighth?'

'327 North. The brownstone right around the corner.'

'Thanks,' Willis said.

'Thanks for the coffee,' Genero yelled to the kitchen.

The counterman did not answer.

Detective Arthur Brown was a black man with a very dark complexion, kinky hair, large nostrils, and thick lips. He was impressively good-looking, though unfortunately not cast in the Negro mould acceptable to most white people, including liberals. In short, he did not resemble Harry Belafonte, Sidney Poitier, or Adam Clayton Powell. He resembled only himself which was quite a lot since he was six feet four inches tall and weighed two hundred and twenty pounds. Arthur Brown was the sort of black man who caused white men to cross the street when he approached, on the theory that this mean-looking son of a bitch (mean-looking only because he was big and black) would undoubtedly mug them or knife them or do something possibly worse, God knew what. Even after Brown identified himself as a police detective, there were many white people who still harboured the suspicion that he was really some kind of desperate criminal impersonating an officer.

It was therefore a pleasant surprise for Brown to come across a witness to the grocery store shootings who did not seem at all intimidated by either his size or his colour. The person was a little old lady who carried a bright blue umbrella on her arm, despite the fact that the day was clear, with that sharp penetrating bite in the air that comes only with October. The umbrella matched the lady's eyes, which were as clear and as sharp as the day itself. She wore a little flowered hat on her head. If she had been a younger woman, the black coat she was wearing might have been called a maxi. She leaped to her feet as Brown came through the front door of the grocery, and said to him in a brisk resonant voice, 'Ah, at last!'

'Ma'am?' Brown said.

'You're the detective, aren't you?'

'I am,' Brown admitted.

'My name is Mrs Farraday, how do you do?'

'Detective Brown,' he said, and nodded, and would have let it go at that, but Mrs Farraday was holding out her hand. Brown clasped it, shook it, and smiled pleasantly. Mrs Farraday returned the smile and released his hand.

'They told me to wait in here, said a detective would be along any minute. I've been waiting half the morning. It's past ten-thirty now.'

'Well, Mrs Farraday, I've been talking to people in the neighbourhood since a little after eight o'clock. Takes a little while to get around to all of them.'

'Oh, I can well imagine,' she said.

'Patrolman outside says you've got some information for me, though. Is that right?'

'That's right. I saw the two men who held up the store.'

'Where'd you see them?'

'Running around the corner. I was on my way home from church, I always go to six o'clock mass, and I'm generally out by seven, and then I stop at the bakery for buns, my husband likes buns with his breakfast on Sundays, or coffee cake.'

'Um-huh.'

'Never goes to church himself,' she said, 'damn heathen.'

'Um-huh.'

'I was coming out of the bakery – this must have been, oh, close to seven-thirty – when I saw the two of them come running around the corner. I thought at first ...'

'What were they wearing, Mrs Farraday?'

'Black coats. And masks. One of them was a girl's face – the mask, I mean. And the other was a monster mask, I don't know which monster. They had guns. Both of them. But none of that's important, Detective Brown.'

'What *is* important?'

'They took the masks *off*. As soon as they turned the corner, they took the masks off, and I got a very good look at both of them.'

'Can you describe them to me now?'

'I certainly can.'

'Good.' Brown took out his pad and flipped it open. He reached into his pocket for his pen – he was one of the few cops on the squad who still used a fountain pen rather than a ball-point – took off the cap, and said, 'Were they white or black, Mrs Farraday?'

'White,' Mrs Farraday said.

'How old would you say they were?'

'Young.'

'How young? Twenty? Thirty?'

'On, no. In their forties, I would say. They were young, but they were definitely not *kids*, Detective Brown.'

'How tall were they?'

'One was about your height, a very big man. How tall are you?'

'Six four,' Brown said.

'My, that *is* big,' Mrs Farraday said.

'And the other one?'

'Much shorter. Five eight or nine, I would guess.'

'Notice the hair colour?'

'The short one was blond. The tall one had dark hair.'

'I don't suppose you saw the colour of their eyes.'

'They passed close enough, but I just didn't see. They went by very quickly.'

'Any scars? Tattoos? Birthmarks?'

'Not that I could see.'

'Both clean-shaven?'

'Do you mean did they have beards or moustaches?'

'Yes, ma'am.'

'No, both clean-shaven.'

'You say they took the masks off as they came around the corner, is that right?'

'Yes. They just ripped them off. It must be difficult to see through those things, wouldn't you imagine?'

'Was there a car waiting for them?'

'No, I don't think they had a car, Detective Brown. They were running too fast for that. It's my guess they were trying to make their escape on foot. Wouldn't that be your guess as well?'

'I really couldn't say yet, Mrs Farraday. I wonder if you could show me where that bakery store is.'

'Certainly. It's right around the corner.'

They walked out of the grocery, and the patrolman outside said to Brown, 'You know anything about when I'm supposed to be relieved here?'

'What do you mean?' Brown asked.

'I think there's some kind of foul-up. I mean, this ain't even my post.'

'Where *is* your post?'

'On Grover Avenue. Near the park.'

'So what're you doing here?'

'That's just it. I collared this guy around quarter to seven, must've been, and took him back to the station house to book him – he was trying to bust into a Mercedes parked on South Second. By the time I got finished there, it was like seven-fifteen, and Nealy and O'Hara are going by in a patrol car, so I hail them and ask for a lift back to my post. We're on the way when all of a sudden they catch the radio squeal about the shooting here at the grocery store. So we all rush over here, and there's a big hullabaloo, you know, Parker caught some stuff, you know, and Nealy and O'Hara take off on a Ten-Thirteen, and the sergeant tells me to stay outside the door. So I been here all morning. I was supposed to be relieved on post at eight o'clock, but how's my relief supposed to know where I am so he can relieve me? You going back to the station house?'

'Not right away.'

'Listen, I hate to leave here, because the sarge might get sore, you know? He told me to stay right here.'

'I'll call in from the nearest box,' Brown said.

'Would you do that? I certainly would appreciate it.'

'Right away,' Brown said.

He and Mrs Farraday walked around around the corner to the bakery shop. 'This is where I was standing when they ran by,' Mrs Farraday said. 'They were taking off the masks as they came around the corner, and they had them off by the time they passed me. Then they went racing up the street there and ... oh, my goodness!' she said, and stopped.

'What is it, Mrs Farraday?'

'I just remembered what they did with those masks, Detective Brown. They threw them down the sewer there. They stopped at the sewer grating and just threw them away, and then they started running again.'

'Thank you, Mrs Farraday,' Brown said, 'you've been most helpful.'

'Oh, well,' she said, and smiled.

Flora and Frieda did not get back to their apartment on North Eighth until seven minutes past eleven. They were both pretty women in their late twenties, both wearing pants suits and short car coats. Flora was a blonde, Frieda a redhead. Flora wore big gold hoop earrings. Frieda had a tiny black beauty spot near the corner of her mouth. They explained to the detectives that they always walked in the park on Sunday mornings, rain or shine. Flora offered them tea, and when they accepted Frieda went upstairs to the kitchen, to put the kettle on.

Their apartment was in a brownstone that had run the gamut from luxury dwelling fifty years back, to crumbling tenement for as many years to reconverted town house in a block of similar buildings trying desperately to raise their heads above the slime of the neighbourhood. The women owned the entire building, and Flora explained now that the bedrooms were on the top floor, the kitchen, dining room and spare room on the middle floor, and the living room on the ground floor. The detectives were sitting with her in that room now, sunlight streaming through the damask-hung windows. A cat lay before the tiled fireplace, dozing. The living room ran the entire length of the ground floor, and was warmly and beautifully furnished. There was a false sense here of being someplace other than the city – some English country home in Dorset perhaps, or some Welsh manor, quiet and secluded, with gently rolling grassy hills just outside the door. But it was one thing to convert a slum into a beautiful town house, and quite another to ignore the whirlpool surrounding it. Neither Flora nor Frieda were fools; there were iron gates over the windows facing the backyard, and a Fox lock on the front door.

'The store hasn't been burglarized, has it?' Flora asked. Her voice was somewhat throaty. She sounded very much like a torch singer holding the milk too close to her lips.

'No, no,' Willis assured her. 'We merely want to ask about some articles of clothing that may have been purchased there.'

'Thank heavens,' Flora said. Frieda had come down from the kitchen and stood now behind Flora's wingback chair, her hand delicately resting on the lace antimacassar just behind her partner's head.

'We've been burglarized four times since we opened the store,' Frieda said.

'Each time they've taken, oh, less than a hundred dollars worth of merchandise. It's ridiculous. It costs us more to replace the broken glass each time. If they'd just come in the store and *ask* for the damn stuff, we'd give it to them outright.'

'We've had the locks changed four times, too. That all costs money,' Frieda said.

'We operate on a very low profit margin,' Flora said.

'It's junkies who do it,' Frieda said. 'Don't you think so, Flora?'

'Oh, no question,' Flora said. 'Hasn't that been your experience?' she asked the detectives.

'Well, sometimes,' Willis said. 'But not all burglars are junkies.'

'Are all junkies burglars?' Frieda asked.

'Some of them.'

'Most of them?'

'A lot of them. Takes quite a bit of money to support a habit, you know.'

'The city ought to do something about it,' Flora said.

The cat near the fireplace stirred, stretched, blinked at the detectives and then stalked out of the room.

'Pussy's getting hungry,' Flora said.

'We'll feed her soon,' Frieda answered.

'What clothes did you want to ask about?' Flora said.

'Well, primarily a jacket you had in the window last week. A fur jacket with ...'

'The llama, yes, what about it?'

'With an orange sun painted on the back?' Genero said.

'Yes, that's it.'

'Would you remember who you sold it to?' Willis asked.

'I didn't sell it,' Flora said. She glanced up at her partner. 'Frieda?'

'Yes, I sold it,' Frieda said.

'Would you remember who bought it?'

'A boy. Long blond hair and a moustache. A young boy. I explained to him that it was really a woman's coat, but he said that didn't matter, he thought it was groovy and wanted it. It has no buttons, you realize, so that wasn't any problem. A woman's garment buttons differently ...'

'Yes, I know that.'

'This particular coat is held closed with a belt. I remember him trying it *with* the belt and then *without* the belt.'

'Excuse me,' Genero said, 'but is this a coat or a jacket?'

'Well, it's a short coat, actually. Mid-thigh. It's really designed for a woman, to go with a miniskirt. It's about that length.'

'I see.'

'I guess a man could wear it, though,' Frieda said dubiously.

'Do you know who the boy was?'

'I'm sorry, I don't. I'd never seen him before.'

'How much did the coat cost?'

'A hundred and ten dollars.'

'Did he pay for it in cash?'

'No, by ... oh, of course.'

'Yes?' Willis said.

'He gave me a cheque. His name would be on the cheque, wouldn't it?' She turned to Flora. 'Where are the cheques we're holding for deposit tomorrow?' she asked.

'Upstairs,' Flora said. 'In the locked drawer.' She smiled at the detectives and said, 'One drawer in the dresser locks. Not that it would do any good if someone decided to break in here.'

'Shall I get it for you?' Frieda asked.

'If you would,' Willis said.

'Certainly. The tea must be ready, too.'

She went out of the room. Her tread sounded softly on the carpeted steps leading upstairs.

'There was one other item,' Willis said. 'Dick, have you got that blouse?'

Genero handed him a manilla envelope. Willis unclasped it, and removed from it the black silk blouse they had found on Scott's bathroom floor, the police evidence tag dangling from one of its buttons. Flora took the blouse and turned it over in her hands.

'Yes, that's ours,' she said.

'Would you know who bought it from you?'

Flora shook her head. 'I really couldn't say. We sell dozens of blouses every week.' She looked at the label. 'This is a thirty-four, a very popular size.' She shook her head again. 'No, I'm sorry.'

'Okay,' Willis said. He put the blouse back into the envelope. Frieda was coming into the room with a tray upon which was a teapot covered with a cosy, four cups and saucers, a milk pitcher, a sugar bowl, and several sliced lemons in a low dish. A cheque was under the sugar bowl. Frieda put down the tray, lifted the sugar bowl and handed the cheque to Willis.

A name and an address were printed across the top of the cheque:

ROBERT HAMLING
3541 Carrier Avenue
Isola

The cheque was made out to the order of The Monkey Wrench for one hundred thirty-five dollars and sixty-eight cents; it was signed by Hamling in a broad, sprawling hand. Willis looked up. 'I thought the coat cost a hundred and ten dollars. This cheque ...'

'Yes, he bought a blouse as well. The blouse cost eighteen dollars. The rest is tax.'

'A black silk blouse?' Genero asked.

'Yes,' Frieda said.

'*This* one?' Genero asked and pulled the blouse from its envelope like a magician pulling a rabbit from a hat.

'Yes, that's the blouse,' Frieda said.

Genero nodded in satisfaction. Willis turned the cheque over. On the back of it were the penned words: 'Drivers Lic' and the numbers '21546 68916 506607–52'.

'Did you write this?' Willis asked.

'Yes,' Frieda answered.

'He showed you identification, I take it.'

'Oh yes, his driver's licence. We never accept cheques without proper identification.'

'Can I see that?' Genero asked. Willis handed him the cheque. 'Carrier Avenue,' Genero said. 'Where's that?'

'Downtown,' Willis answered. 'In The Quarter.'

'What do you take in your tea, gentlemen?' Flora asked.

They sat sipping tea in the living room streaming with sunlight. Once, during a lull in the small talk over the steaming cups, Genero asked, 'Why'd you name your store the Monkey Wrench?'

'Why not?' Frieda answered.

It was clearly time to go.

The curious thing about fishing in the sewer for those Halloween masks was that it filled Brown with a sense of exhilaration he had not known since he was a boy. He could remember a hundred past occasions when he and his childhood friends had removed an iron sewer grating and climbed down into the muck to retrieve a rubber ball hit by a stickball bat, or an immie carelessly aimed, or even now and then a dime or a quarter that had slipped from a clenched fist and rolled down into the kerbside drain. He was too large now to squeeze through the narrow opening of the sewer, but he could see at least one of the masks some five feet below him, resting on the pipe elbow in a brownish paper-littered slime. He stretched out flat on the pavement, head twisted away from the kerb and tried to reach the mask. His arm, as long as it was, was not long enough. His fingertips wiggled below, touching nothing but stagnant air. He got to his feet, brushed off the knees of his trousers and the elbows of his coat, and then looked up the block. Not a kid in sight. Never a kid around when you needed one. He began searching in his pockets. He found a paper clip holding a business card to one of the pages in his pad. He removed the clip, put the card into his wallet, and then took a sheaf of evidence tags from his inside jacket pocket. Each of the tags had a short length of string tied through a hole at one end. He unfastened the strings from ten tags, knotted them all together and came up with a five-foot-long piece of string. He opened the paper clip so that it resembled a fish hook, and then tied it to one end of the string. Weighting the line with the duplicate key to his station house locker, he grinned and began fishing in the sewer. On the twentieth try, he hooked the narrow piece of elastic clipped to the mask. Slowly, carefully, patiently, he reeled in his line.

He was looking at a somewhat soiled Snow White, but this was the 'seventies, and nobody expected to find virgins in sewers any more.

Still grinning, Brown replaced the grating, brushed himself off again, and headed back for the squadroom.

In the city for which Brown worked, the Identification Section and the Police Laboratory operated on weekends with only a skeleton force, which was often only slightly better than operating with no force at all. Most cases got put over till Monday, unless they were terribly urgent. The shooting of a police detective was considered terribly urgent, and so the Snow White mask Brown despatched to the lab downtown on High Street was given top priority. Detective-Lieutenant Sam Grossman, who ran the lab, was of course not working on a Sunday. The task of examining the mask for latent fingerprints (or indeed *any* clue as to its wearer's identity) fell to Detective 3rd/Grade Marshall Davies, who, like Genero, was a comparatively new detective and therefore prone to catching weekend duty at the lab. He promised Brown he would get back to him as soon as possible, mindful of the fact that a detective had been shot and that there might be all kinds of pressure from upstairs, and then set to work.

In the squadroom, Brown replaced the telephone on its cradle and looked up as a patrolman approached the slatted rail divider with a prisoner in tow. At his desk, Carl Kapek was eating an early lunch, preparatory to heading for the bar in which the marine had encountered the girl with the bewitching behind, bars in this city being closed on Sundays until twelve, at which time it was presumably acceptable for churchgoers to begin getting drunk. The clock on the squadroom wall read fifteen minutes to noon. The squadroom was somewhat more crowded than it might have been at this hour on a Sunday because Levine, Di Maeo and Meriwether, the three detectives who had been called in when they were supposed to be on vacation, were sitting at one of the desks waiting to see the lieutenant, who at the moment was talking to Captain Frick, commander of the precinct, about the grocery store shooting and the necessity to get some more men on it. The three detectives were naturally grumbling. Di Maeo said that next time he was going to Puerto Rico on his vacation because then the lieutenant could shove it up his ass if he wanted him to come back. Cooperman was on vacation, too, wasn't he? But he was in the Virgin Islands, and the loot sure as hell didn't call *him* back there and drag *him* in, did he? Besides, Levine pointed out, Andy Parker was a lousy cop and who the hell cared if he got shot or even killed? Meriwether, who was a mild-mannered hairbag in his early sixties, and a detective/first to boot, said 'Now, now, fellows, it's all part of the game, all part of the game,' and Di Maeo belched.

The patrolman walked over to Brown's desk, told his prisoner to sit down, took Brown aside, and whispered something to him. Brown nodded and came back to the desk. The prisoner was handcuffed, sitting with his hands in his lap. He was a pudgy little man with green eyes and a pencil-line moustache. Brown estimated his age at forty or thereabouts. He was wearing a brown overcoat, a brown suit and shoes, white shirt with a button-down collar, gold-and-brown striped silk tie. Brown asked the patrolman to advise the man of his rights, a job the patrolman accepted with some trepidation, while he called the hospital to ask about Parker's condition. They told him that Parker was doing fine. Brown accepted the report without noticeable enthusiasm. He hung up the phone, heard the prisoner tell the patrolman he had nothing to hide and would answer any questions they wanted to ask, swivelled his chair around to face the man, and said, 'What's your name?'

The man would not look Brown in the eye. Instead, he kept staring past his left ear to the grilled windows and the sky outside.

'Perry Lyons,' he said. His voice was very low. Brown could barely hear him.

'What were you doing in the park just now, Lyons?' Brown said.

'Nothing,' Lyons answered.

'Speak up!' Brown snapped. There was a noticeable edge to his voice. The patrolman, too, was staring down at Lyons in what could only be described as an extremely hostile way, his brow twisted into a frown, his eyes hard and mean, his lips tightly compressed, his arms folded across his chest.

'I wasn't doing nothing,' Lyons answered.

'Patrolman Brogan here seems to think otherwise.'

Lyons shrugged.

'What about it, Lyons?'

'There's no law against talking to somebody.'

'Who were you talking to, Lyons?'

'A kid.'

'What'd you say to him?'

'Just it was a nice day, that's all.'

'That's not what the kid told Patrolman Brogan.'

'Well, kids, you know kids,' Lyons said.

'How old was the kid, Joe?' Brown asked.

'About nine,' Brogan answered.

'You always talk to nine-year-old kids in the park?' Brown asked.

'Sometimes.'

'How often?'

'There's no law against talking to kids. I like kids.'

'I'll bet you do,' Brown said. 'Tell him what the boy told you, Brogan.'

Brogan hesitated a moment, and then said, 'The boy said you asked him to blow you, Lyons.'

'No,' Lyons said. 'No, I never said anything like that. You're mistaken.'

'I'm not mistaken,' Brogan said.

'Well, then, the kid's mistaken. He never heard anything like that from me, nossir.'

'You ever been arrested before?' Brown asked.

Lyons did not answer.

'Come on,' Brown said impatiently, 'we can check it in a minute.'

'Well, yes,' Lyons said. 'I have been arrested before.'

'How many times?'

'Twice.'

'What for?'

'Well ...' Lyons said, and shrugged.

'What *for*, Lyons?'

'Well, it was, uh, I got in trouble with somebody a while back.'

'What kind of trouble?'

'With some kid.'

'What was the charge, Lyons?'

Lyons hesitated again.

'What was the charge?' Brown repeated.

'Carnal Abuse.'

'Your a child molester, huh, Lyons?'

'No, no, it was a bum rap.'

'Were you convicted?'

'Yes, but that don't mean a thing, you guys know that. The kid was lying. He wanted to get even with me, he wanted to get me in trouble, so he told all kinds of lies about me. Hell, what would I want to fool around with a kid like that for? I had a girl friend and everything, this waitress, you know? A real pretty girl, what would I want to fool around with a little kid for?'

'You tell me.'

'It was a bum rap, that's all. These things happen, that's all. You guys know that.'

'And the second arrest?'

'Well, that . . .'

'Yeah?'

'Well, you see what happened, after I got paroled, you know, I went back to live in this motel I used to live in before I got put away, you know?'

'Where'd you serve your time?'

'Castleview.'

'Go ahead.'

'So I had this same room, you know? That I had before they locked me up. And it turned out the kid who got me in trouble before, he was living there with his mother.'

'Just by coincidence, huh?'

'Well, no, not by coincidence. I mean, I can't claim it was coincidence. His mother ran the place, you see. I mean, she and her father owned it together. So it wasn't coincidence, you know. But I didn't think the kid was going to cause me no more trouble, you see what I mean? I done my time, he already got even with me, so I didn't expect no more trouble from him. Only thing is he come around to my cabin one day, and he made me do things to him. He said he'd tell his mother I was bothering him again if I didn't do these things to him. I mean, I was on parole, you know what I mean? If the kid had went to his mother, they'd have packed me off again in a minute.'

'So what *did* you do, Lyons?'

'Argh, the —— little bastard started yelling. They . . . they busted me again.'

'Same charge?'

'Well, not the same 'cause the kid was older now. You know, like there's Carnal Abuse with a kid ten years old or younger, and then there's Carnal Abuse with a kid over ten and less than sixteen. He was eight years old the first time and eleven the next time. It was a bum rap both times. Who the hell needs that kind of stuff, you think I need it? Anyway, this was a long time ago. I already served *both* sentences. You think I'd be crazy enough to risk a third fall?'

'You could've been put away for life the *second* time,' Brown said.

'Don't you think I know it? So why would I take another chance?' He looked up at Brogan. 'That kid must've heard me wrong, Officer. I didn't say nothing like that to him. Honest. I really didn't.'

'We're booking you for Endangering the Morals of a Child, as defined in

Section 483-a of the Penal Law,' Brown said. 'You're allowed three telephone ...'

'Hey, hey, look,' Lyons said, 'give me a break, will you? I didn't mean no harm to the kid, I swear it. We were just sitting there talking, I swear to God. I *never* said nothing like that to him, would I say something like that to a little kid? Jesus what do you take me for? Hey, come on, give me a break, will you? Come on, Officer, give me a break.'

'I'd advise you to get a lawyer,' Brown said. 'You want to take him down, Brogan?'

'Hey, come on,' Lyons said.

Brown watched as the patrolman led Lyons out of the squadroom. He stared at the retreating figure, and thought *The guy's sick, why the hell are we sending him away again, instead of helping him,* and then he thought *I have a seven-year-old daughter* – and then he stopped thinking because everything seemed suddenly too complex, and the telephone on his desk was ringing.

He lifted the receiver.

It was Steve Carella reporting that he was on his way to the squadroom.

José Vicente Huerta was in a bad way. Both of his legs had been broken by the four assailants who'd attacked him, and his face was swathed in bandages, that covered the multiple wounds that had spilled his blood all over the front stoop of the building. He resembled a not so invisible Invisible Man, his brown eyes burning fiercely through the holes left in the bandages.

His mouth, pink against the white, showed through another hole below the eye holes, and looked like a gaping wound itself. He was conscious now, but the doctors advised Delgado that their patient was heavily sedated and might drift in and out of sleep as he talked. Delgado figured he would take his chances.

He sat in a chair by the side of Huerta's bed. Huerta, both legs in traction, his hands lying on the covers, palms up, his head turned into the pillow in Delgado's direction, the brown eyes burning fiercely, the wound of the mouth open and pathetically vulnerable, listened as Delgado identified himself, and then nodded when asked if he felt able to answer some questions.

'First,' Delgado said, 'do you know who the men were?'

'No,' Huerta answered.

'You didn't recognize any of them?'

'No.'

'Were they young men?'

'I don't know.'

'You saw them as they attacked you, didn't you?'

'Yes.'

'Well, how old would you say they were?'

'I don't know.'

'Were they neighbourhood men?'

'I don't know.'

'Mr Huerta, any information you can give us ...'

'I don't know who they were,' Huerta said.

'They hurt you very badly. Surely ...'

The bandaged head turned away from Delgado, into the pillow.

'Mr Huerta?'

Huerta did not answer.

'Mr Huerta?'

Again, he did not answer. As had been promised by the doctors, he seemed to have drifted off into sleep. Delgado sighed and stood up. Since he was at Buenavista Hospital, anyway, and just so his visit shouldn't be a total loss, he decided to stop in on Andy Parker to see how he was doing. Parker was doing about as well as Huerta. He, too, was asleep. The interne on the floor informed Delgado that Parker was out of danger.

Delgado seemed as thrilled by the information as Brown had earlier been.

The trouble with being a detective in any given neighbourhood is that almost everybody in the neighbourhood knows you're a detective. Since detection is supposed to be undercover secret stuff at least some of the time, snooping around becomes a little difficult when 90 per cent of the people you encounter know you're a snoop. The bartender at Bar Seventeen (which was the name of the bar in which the marine had first encountered the girl who later kicked him in the head, such bar being thus imaginatively named since it was located on Seventeenth Street) knew that Carl Kapek was a bull, and Kapek knew that the bartender knew, and since they *both* knew, neither of them made any pretence of playing at cops and robbers. The bartender set up beers for Kapek, who was not supposed to drink on duty, and Kapek accepted them without offering payment, and everybody had a nice little understanding going. Kapek did not even attempt to ask the bartender about the kicking girl and her boyfriend. Nor did the bartender try to find out why Kapek was there. If he was there, he was there for a reason, and the bartender knew it, and Kapek knew he knew it, and so the two men kept a respectful distance, coming into contact only when the bartender refilled Kapek's glass from time to time. It was a cool symbiosis. The bartender merely hoped that Kapek was not there investigating some minor violation that would inevitably cost him money. He was already paying off two guys from the Fire Department, not to mention the police sergeant on the beat; one more guy with his hand out, and it would be cheaper to take care of the goddamn violations instead. Kapek, for his part, merely hoped that the bartender would not indicate to too many of his early afternoon patrons that the big blond guy sitting at the bar was a police detective. It was difficult enough these days to earn a living.

The way he decided to earn his living on this particular bright October Sunday – bright *outside*, dim and cheerless inside – was to engage a drunk in conversation. Kapek had been in the bar for close to an hour now, studying the patrons, trying to decide which of them were regulars, which of them came here infrequently, which of them recognized him from around the streets, which of them had not the faintest inkling that he was fuzz. He did all of this in what he hoped was a surreptitious manner, going to the phone booth once to pretend he was making a call, going to the men's room once, going to the jukebox three or four times, casing everyone in the place on his various excursions, and then settling down on a stool within listening distance of the bartender and a man in a dark blue suit. Kapek opened the Sunday tabloid he had carried with him into the bar, and turned to the sports section. He pretended to be pondering yesterday's racing results, working figures with a pencil in the margin of the newspaper, while simultaneously listening intently to everything the man in the blue suit said. When the bartender walked off to serve someone at the other end of the bar Kapek made his move.

'Damn horse never delivers when he's supposed to,' he said.

'I beg your pardon?' the man in the blue suit said, turning on his stool. He was already very intoxicated, having presumably begun his serious drinking at home before the bar could legally open its doors. He looked at Kapek now with the benign expression of someone anxious to be friendly with anyone at all, even if he happened to be a cop. He did not seem to know that Kapek was a cop, nor was Kapek anxious to let him in on the secret.

'You follow the ponies?' Kapek asked.

'I permit myself a tiny wager every so often,' the man in the blue suit said. He had bleary blue eyes and a veined nose. His white shirt looked unironed, his solid blue tie was haphazardly knotted, his suit rumpled. He kept his right hand firmly clutched around a water tumbler full of whisky on the bar top in front of him.

'This nag's the goddam favourite nine times out of ten,' Kapek said, 'but he never wins when he's supposed to. I think the jocks got it all fixed between them.'

The bartender was ambling back, Kapek shot him a warning glance: *Stay out of this, pal. You work your side of the street, I'll work mine.* The bartender hesitated in mid-strike, then turned on his heel and walked over to his other customers.

'My name's Carl Kapek,' Kapek said, and closed his newspaper, encouraging further conversation. 'I've been playing the horses for twelve years now, I made only one decent killing in all that time.'

'How much?' the man in the blue suit asked.

'Four hundred dollars on a long shot. Had two dollars on his nose. It was beautiful, beautiful,' Kapek said, and grinned and shook his head remembering the beauty of this event that had never taken place. The most he had ever won in his life was a chemistry set at a church bazaar.

'How long ago was that?' the man in the blue suit asked.

'Six years ago,' Kapek said, and laughed.

'That's a long time between drinks,' the man said, and laughed with him.

'I don't think I got your name,' Kapek said, and extended his hand.

'Leonard Sutherland,' the man said. 'My friends all call me Lennie.'

'How do you do, Lennie?' Kapek said, and they shook hands.

'What do *your* friends call *you*?' Lennie asked.

'Carl.'

'Nice meeting you, Carl,' Lennie said.

'A pleasure,' Kapek answered.

'My game's poker,' Lennie said. 'Playing the horses, you'll pardon me, is for suckers. Poker's a game of skill.'

'No question,' Kapek agreed.

'Do you actually *prefer* beer?' Lennie asked suddenly.

'What?'

'I notice you have been drinking beer exclusively. If you would permit me, Carl, I'd consider it an honour to buy you something stronger.'

'Little early in the day for me,' Kapek said, and smiled apologetically.

'Never too early for a little rammer,' Lennie said, and smiled.

'Well I was out drinking late last night,' Kapek said, and shrugged.

'I am out drinking late *every* night,' Lennie said, 'but it's still never too early for a little rammer.' To emphasize his theory, he lifted the water glass and swallowed half the whisky in it. 'Mmm, boy,' he said and coughed.

'You usually do your drinking here?' Kapek asked.

'Hm?' Lennie asked. His eyes were watering. He took a handkerchief from his back pocket and dabbed at them. He coughed again.

'In this place?'

'Oh, I drift around, drift around,' Lennie said, and made a fluttering little motion with the fingers of one hand.

'Reason I ask,' Kapek said, 'is I was in here last night, and I didn't happen to see you.'

'Oh, I was here all right,' Lennie said, which Kapek already knew because this was what he had overheard in the conversation between Lennie and the bartender, a passing reference to a minor event that had taken place in Bar Seventeen the night before, the bartender having had to throw out a twenty-year-old who was noisily expressing his views on lowering the age to vote.

'Were you here when they threw out that young kid?' Kapek asked.

'Oh, indeed,' Lennie said.

'Didn't see you,' Kapek said.

'Oh yes, here indeed,' Lennie said.

'There was a marine ...' Kapek said tentatively.

'Hm?' Lennie asked with a polite smile, and then lifted his glass and threw down the rest of the whisky. He said, 'Mmm, boy,' coughed again, dabbed at his watering eyes, and then said, 'Yes, yes, but he came in later.'

'After they threw that kid out, you mean?'

'Oh, yes, much later. Were you here when the marine came in?'

'Oh, sure,' Kapek said.

'Funny we didn't notice each other,' Lennie said, and shrugged and signalled to the bartender. The bartender slouched towards them, shooting Kapek his own warning glance: *This guy's a good steady customer. If I lose him 'cause you're pumping him for information here, I'm gonna get sore as hell.*

'Yeah, Lennie?' the bartender said.

'I'll have another double, please,' Lennie answered. 'And please see what my friend here is having, won't you?'

The bartender shot the warning glance at Kapek again. Kapek stared back at him implacably and said, 'I'll just have another beer.' The bartender nodded and walked off.

'There was this girl in here about then,' Kapek said to Lennie. 'You remember her?'

'Which girl?'

'Coloured girl in a red dress,' Kapek said.

Lennie was watching the bartender as he poured whisky into the tumbler. 'Hm?' he said.

'Coloured girl in a red dress,' Kapek repeated.

'Oh yes, Belinda,' Lennie answered.

'Belinda what?'

'Don't know,' Lennie said.

His eyes brightened as the bartender came back with his whisky and

Kapek's beer. Lennie lifted the tumbler immediately and drank. 'Mmm, boy,' he said, and coughed. The bartender hovered near them. Kapek met his eyes, decided if he wanted so badly to get in on the act, he'd let him.

'Would *you* happen to know?' Kapek said.

'Know what?'

'There was a girl named Belinda in here last night. Wearing a red dress. Would you know her last name?'

'Me,' the bartender said, 'I'm deaf, dumb, and blind.' He paused. 'This guy's a cop, Lennie, did you know that?'

'Oh yes, certainly,' Lennie said, and fell off his stool and passed out cold.

Kapek got up, bent, seized Lennie under the arms and dragged him over to one of the booths. He loosened his tie and then looked up at the bartender, who had come over and was standing with his hands on his hips.

'You always serve booze to guys who've had too much?' he asked.

'You always ask them questions?' the bartender said.

'Let's ask *you* a couple instead, okay?' Kapek said. 'Who's Belinda?'

'Never heard of her.'

'Okay. Just make sure *she* never hears of *me*.'

'Huh?'

'You were pretty anxious just now to let our friend here know I was a cop. I'm telling you something straight, pal. I'm looking for Belinda, who*ever* the hell she is. If she finds out about it, from whatever source, I'm going to assume you're the one who tipped her. And that might just make you an accessory, pal.'

'Who you trying to snow?' the bartender said. 'I run a clean joint here. I don't know nobody named Belinda, and whatever she done or didn't do, I'm out of it completely. So what's this "accessory" crap?'

'Try to forget I was in here looking for her,' Kapek said. 'Otherwise you're liable to find out *just* what this "accessory" crap is. Okay?'

'You scare me to death,' the bartender said.

'You know where Lennie lives?' Kapek asked.

'Yeah.'

'He married?'

'Yeah.'

'Call his wife. Tell her to come down here and get him.'

'She'll kill him,' the bartender said. He looked down at Lennie and shook his head. 'I'll sober him up and get him home, don't worry about it.'

He was already talking gently and kindly to the unconscious Lennie as Kapek went out of the bar.

Ramon Castañeda was in his undershirt when he opened the door for Delgado.

'*Sí, qué quiere usted?*' he asked.

'I'm Detective Delgado, Eighty-seventh Squad,' Delgado said, and flipped his wallet open to show his shield. Castañeda looked at it closely.

'What's the trouble?' he asked.

'May I come in, please?' Delgado said.

'Who is it, Ray?' a woman called from somewhere in the apartment.

'Policeman,' Castañeda said over his shoulder. 'Come in,' he said to Delgado.

Delgado went into the apartment. There was a kitchen on his right, a living room dead ahead, two bedrooms beyond that. The woman who came out of the closet bedroom was wearing a brightly flowered nylon robe and carrying a hairbrush in her right hand. She was quite beautiful, with long black hair and a pale complexion, grey-green eyes, a full bosom, ripely curving hips. She was barefoot, and she moved soundlessly into the living room, and stood with her legs slightly apart, the hairbrush held just above her hip, somewhat like a hatchet she had just unsheathed.

'Sorry to bother you this way,' Delgado said.

'What is it?' the woman said.

'This is my wife,' Castañeda said. 'Rita this is Detective ... what's your name again?'

'Delgado.'

'You Spanish?'

'Yes.'

'Good,' Castañeda said.

'What is it?' Rita said again.

'Your partner José Huerta ...'

'What's the matter with him?' Castañeda asked immediately. 'Is something the matter with him?'

'Yes. He was attacked by four men this morning ...'

'Oh, my God!' Rita said, and brought the hand holding the hairbrush to her mouth, pressing the back of it to her lips as though stifling a scream.

'Who?' Castañeda said. 'Who did it?'

'We don't know. He's at Buenavista Hospital now.' Delgado paused. 'Both his legs were broken.'

'Oh, my God!' Rita said again.

'We'll go to him at once,' Castañeda said, and turned away, ready to leave the room, seemingly anxious to dress and leave for the hospital immediately.

'If I may ...' Delgado said, and Castañeda remembered he was there, and paused, still on the verge of departure, and impatiently said to his wife, 'Get dressed, Rita,' and then said to Delgado, 'Yes, what is it? We want to see Joe as soon as possible.'

'I'd like to ask some questions before you go,' Delgado said.

'Yes, certainly.'

'How long have you and Mr Huerta been partners?'

The woman had not left the room. She stood standing slightly apart from the two men, the hairbrush bristles cradled on the palm of one hand, the other hand clutched tightly around the handle, her eyes wide as she listened.

'I told you to get dressed,' Castañeda said to her.

She seemed about to answer him. Then she gave a brief complying nod, wheeled and went into the bedroom, closing the door only partially behind her.

'We have been partners for two years,' Castañeda said.

'Get along with each other?'

'Of course. Why?' Castañeda put his hands on his hips. He was a small man, perhaps five feet seven inches tall, and not particularly good-looking, with a pockmarked face and a longish nose and a moustache that sat just beneath it and somehow emphasized its length. He leaned towards Delgado belligerently now, defying him to explain that last question, his brown eyes burning as fiercely as had his partner's through the hospital bandages.

'A man has been assaulted, Mr Castañeda. It's routine to question his relatives and associates. I meant no ...'

'It sounded like you meant plenty,' Castañeda said. His hands were still on his hips. He looked like a fighting rooster Delgado had once seen in a cock fight in the town of Vega Baja, when he had gone back to the island to visit his dying grandmother.

'Let's not get excited,' Delgado said. There was a note of warning in his voice. The note informed Castañeda that whereas both men were Puerto Ricans, one of them was a cop entitled to ask questions about a third Puerto Rican who had been badly beaten up. The note further informed Castañeda that however mild Delgado's manner might appear, he wasn't about to take any crap, and Castañeda had better understand that right from go. Castañeda took his hands from his hips. Delgado stared at him a moment longer.

'Would you happen to know whether or not your partner had any enemies?' he asked. His voice was flat. Through the partially open door of the bedroom, he saw Rita Castañeda move towards the dresser, and then away from it, out of sight.

'No enemies that I know of,' Castañeda replied.

'Would you know if he'd ever received any threatening letters or phone calls?'

'Never.'

The flowered robe flashed into view again. Delgado's eyes flicked momentarily towards the open door. Castañeda frowned.

'Would you have had any business deals recently that caused any hard feelings with anyone?'

'None,' Castañeda said. He moved towards the open bedroom door, took the knob in his hand, and pulled the door firmly shut. 'We're real estate agents for apartment buildings. We rent apartments. It's as simple as that.'

'No trouble with any of the tenants?'

'We hardly ever come into contact with them. Once in a while we have trouble collecting rents. But that's normal in this business, and nobody bears a grudge.'

'Would you say your partner is well liked?'

Castañeda shrugged.

'What does that mean, Mr Castañeda?'

'Well-liked, who knows? He's a man like any other man. He is liked by some and disliked by others.'

'Who *dislikes* him?' Delgado asked immediately.

'No one dislikes him enough to have him beaten up,' Castañeda said.

'I see,' Delgado answered. He smiled pleasantly. 'Well,' he said, 'thank you for your information. I won't keep you any longer.'

'Fine, fine,' Castañeda said. He went to the front door and opened it. 'Let me know if you find the men who did it,' he said.

'I will,' Delgado answered, and found himself in the hallway. The door closed behind him. In the apartment, he heard Castañeda shout, 'Rita, *esta lista?*'

He put his ear to the door.

He could hear Castañeda and his wife talking very quietly inside the apartment, their voices rumbling distantly, but he could not tell what they were saying. Only once, when Rita raised her voice, did Delgado catch a word.

The word was *hermano*, which in Spanish meant 'brother'.

It was close to 2:00 p.m., and things were pretty quiet in the squadroom. Kapek was looking through the Known Muggers file, trying to get a lead on the black girl known only as Belinda. Carella had arrived in time to have lunch with Brown, and both men sat at a long table near one of the windows, one end of it burdened with fingerprinting equipment, eating tuna fish sandwiches and drinking coffee in cardboard containers. As they ate, Brown filled him in on what he had so far. Marshall Davies at the lab, true to his word, had gone to work on the Snow White mask the moment he received it, and had reported back not a half-hour later. He had been able to recover only one good print, that being a thumbprint on the inside surface, presumably left when the wearer was adjusting the mask to his face. He had sent this immediately to the Identification Section, where the men on Sunday duty had searched their Single-Fingerprint file, tracking through a maze of arches, loops, whorls, scars, and accidentals to come up with a positive identification for a man named Bernard Goldenthal.

His yellow sheet was now on Brown's desk, and both detectives studied it carefully:

PRISONER'S CRIMINAL RECORD	POLICE DEPARTMENT	IDENTIFICATION SECTION

NAME ___BERNARD GOLDENTHAL___   B. # 47-61042

ALIAS ___"Bernie Gold," "Goldie," "Goldfinger".___   I.S. # G-21-3479

DATE OF BIRTH ___February 12, 1931___   F.B.I. # 74-01-22

FINGERPRINT CLASSIFICATION ___27 L1T r 20___   89234
                                    L1U

This certifies that the finger impressions of the above named person have
been compared and the following is a true copy of the records of this section.

Date of Arrest	Location	Charge	Arresting Officer	Date, Disposition, Judge and Court
5-7-47	Isola	Burg. Juv. Del.	D of C	Jewish Home for Boys
2-9-48	Calm's Point	Burg. Fin. Chg. Unlaw Entry	Wexner 75 Pot.	Judge McCarthy County Court
6-5-49	Isola	Robbery	Janus 19 Sqd.	6-30-49 Dismissed Judge Evans Sup. Court
8-17-49	Isola	Robbery Gun	Cowper 19 Sqd.	11-28-49 Discharged Judge Mastro Gen. Sess.
1-21-51	Riverhead	Gr. Laro 1st Burg. 3rd	Franklin	3-11-51 5 to 10 Yrs. on Gr. Laro. 5 to 10 Yrs. on Burg. 3rd. Judge Lefkin, County Court.
2-19-59	Isola	Theft from Interstate Shipment	F.B.I.	3 yrs to serve followed by 10 yrs probation Judge O'Hare U.S. So. Dist. Court.
2-23-69	Isola	974 PL	Magruder 2 Div	1-28-70 $50 or 10 days Judge Fields Spec. Sess.
1-9-70	Isola	974 PL	Donovan 2 Div	1-28-70 $100/30 days Judge Fields Spec. Sess.
9-19-70	Isola	974a PL	Donato CIU	11-25-70 Gen. Sess. Unl. Poss. Policy Slips $150 or 60 days. Ashworth.

X represents notations unsupported by fingerprints in Identification Section
files.
"This record is furnished solely for the official use of law enforcement agencies. Unauthorized use of this information is in violation of Sections 554
and 2050, Penal Law."

A man's yellow sheet (so called because the record actually *was* duplicated
on a yellow sheet of paper; bar owners were not the *only* imaginative people
in this city) was perhaps not as entertaining, say, as a good novel, but it did
have a shorthand narrative power all of its own. Goldenthal's record had the
added interest of a rising dramatic line, a climax of sorts, and then a
slackening of tension just before the denouement – which was presumably
yet to come.

His first arrest had been at the age of sixteen, for Burglary and Juvenile
Delinquency, and he had been remanded to the Jewish Home for Boys, a
correctional institution. Less than a year later, apparently back on the streets
again, he had been arrested again for Burglary, with the charge reduced to

Unlawful Entry and (the record was incomplete here) the courts had apparently shown lenience in consideration of his age – he was barely seventeen at the time – and let him off scot-free. Progressing to bigger and better things during the next year, he was arrested first on a Robbery charge and then on a Robbery with a Gun charge, and again the courts showed mercy and let him go. Thus emboldened and encouraged, he moved on to Grand Larceny First and Burglary Third, was again busted and this time was sent to prison. He had probably served both terms concurrently, and was released on parole sometime before 1959, when apparently he decided to knock over a truck crossing state lines, thereby inviting the Federal Bureau of Investigation to step in. Carella and Brown figured the '3 yrs to serve' were the three years remaining from his prior conviction; the courts were again being lenient.

And perhaps this leniency was finally paying off. The violations he'd been convicted of since his second release from prison were not too terribly serious, especially when compared to Grand Larceny or Interstate Theft. Section 974 of the Penal Law was defined as 'keeping a place for or transferring money in the game of policy', and was a misdemeanour. Section 974a was a bit heavier – 'Operating a policy business' – and was a felony punishable by imprisonment for a term not exceeding five years. In either case Goldenthal seemed to have moved into a more respectable line of work, employing himself in the 'policy' or 'numbers game', which many hard-working citizens felt was a perfectly harmless recreation and hardly anything for the Law to get all excited about. The Law had not, in fact, got too terribly excited about Goldenthal's most recent offences. He could have got five years on his last little adventure, when in fact all he had drawn was a fine of a hundred and fifty dollars or sixty days, on a reduced charge of Unlawful Possession of Policy Slips, Section 975 of the Penal Law.

Goldenthal had begun his criminal career at the age of sixteen. He was now almost forty years old, and had spent something better than ten years of his adult life in prison. If they found him, and busted him again, and convicted him of the grocery store holdup and murder, he would be sent away forever.

There were several other pieces of information in the packet the I.S. had sent uptown – a copy of Goldenthal's fingerprint card, with a complete description of him on the reverse side; a final report from his probation officer back in '69; a copy of the Detective Division report on his most recent arrest – but the item of chief interest to Carella and Brown was Goldenthal's last known address. He had apparently been living in uptown Isola with his mother, a Mrs Minnie Goldenthal, until the time of her death three months ago. He had then moved to an apartment downtown, and was presumably still living there.

They decided to hit it together.

They were no fools.

Goldenthal had once been arrested on a gun charge, and either he or his partner had put three bullets into two men not seven hours before.

The show began ten minutes after Carella and Brown left the squadroom. It had a cast of four and was titled *Hookers' Parade*. It starred two young streetwalkers who billed themselves as Rebecca and Sally Good.

'Those are not your real names,' Kapek insisted.

'Those are our real names,' Sally answered, 'and you can all go to hell.' The other two performers in the show were the patrolman who had answered the complaint and made the arrest, and a portly gentleman in a pinstriped suit who looked mortally offended though not at all embarrassed, rather like a person who had wet his pyjamas in a hospital bed, where illness is expected and annoying but certainly nothing to be ashamed of.

'All right, what's the story, Phil?' Kapek asked the patrolman.

'Well, what happened ...'

'If you don't mind,' the portly gentleman said, '*I* am the injured party here.'

'Who the hell injured you, would you mind telling me?' Rebecca said.

'All right, let's calm down here,' Kapek said. He had finished with the Known Muggers file and was anxious to get to the Modus Operandi file, and he found all this tumult distracting. The girls, one black and one white, were both wearing tan sweaters, suede miniskirts, and brown boots. Sally, the white one, had long blonde hair. Rebecca, the black one, had her hair done in an Afro cut and bleached blonde. They were both in their early twenties, both quite attractive, long and leggy and busty and brazen and cheap as a bottle of ninety-cent wine. The portly gentleman sat some distance away from them, on the opposite side of Kapek's desk, as though afraid of contracting some dread disease. His face was screwed into an offended frown, his eyes sparked with indignation.

'I wish these young ladies arrested,' he said. 'I am the man who made the complaint, the injured party, and I am willing to press charges, and I wish them arrested at once.'

'Fine, Mr ...' Kapek consulted his pad. 'Mr Searle,' he said. 'Do you want to tell me what happened?'

'I am from Independence, Missouri,' Searle said. 'The home of Harry S. Truman.'

'Yes, sir,' Kapek said.

'Big deal,' Sally said.

'I am here in the city on business,' Searle said. 'I usually stay midtown, but I have several appointments in this area tomorrow morning, and I thought it would be more convenient to find lodgings in the neighbourhood.' He paused and cleared his throat. 'There is a rather nice hotel overlooking the park. The Grover.'

'Yes, sir,' Kapek said.

'Or at least *I thought* it was a rather nice hotel.'

'It's a fleabag,' Rebecca said.

'How about knocking it off?' Kapek said.

'What the hell for? This hick blows the whistle for no reason at all, and we're supposed ...'

'Let's hear what the man has to say, okay?' Kapek said sharply.

'Okay,' Rebecca said.

'*Whatever* he has to say,' Sally said, 'he's full of crap.'

'Listen, sister,' Kapek warned.

'Okay, okay,' Sally said, and tossed her long blonde hair. Rebecca crossed her legs, and lit a cigarette. She blew the stream of smoke in Searle's direction, and he waved it away with his hands.

'Mr Searle?' Kapek prompted.

'I was sitting in my room reading the *Times*,' Searle said, 'when a knock sounded on the door.'

'When was this, Mr Searle?'

'An hour ago? I'm not sure.'

'What time did you catch the squeal, Phil?'

'One-twenty.'

'Just *about* an hour ago,' Kapek said.

'Then it must have been a little earlier than that,' Searle said. 'They must have arrived at about one-ten or thereabouts.'

'Who's that, Mr Searle?'

'These young ladies,' he answered, without looking at them.

'They knocked on your door?'

'They did.'

'And then what?'

'I opened the door. They were standing there in the corridor. Both of them. They said . . .' Searle shook his head. 'This is entirely incon*ceiv*able to me.'

'What did they say?'

'They said the elevator operator told them I wanted some action, and they were there to supply it. I didn't know what they meant at first. I asked them what they meant. They told me exactly what they meant.'

'What did they tell you, Mr Searle?'

'Do we have to go into this?'

'If you're going to press charges, why, yes, I guess we do. I'm not sure yet what these girls did or said to . . .'

'They offered to sleep with me,' Searle said, and looked away.

'Who the hell would want to sleep with *you*?' Sally muttered.

'Got to be out of your mind,' Rebecca said, and blew another stream of smoke at him.

'They told me they would *both* like to sleep with me,' Searle said. 'Together.'

'Uh-huh,' Kapek said, and glanced at Rebecca. 'Is that right?' he asked.

'Nope,' Rebecca answered.

'So, okay, what happened next?' Kapek asked.

'I told them to come back in five minutes.'

'Why'd you tell them that?'

'Because I wanted to inform the police.'

'And did you?'

'I did.'

'And did the girls come back?'

'In seven minutes. I clocked them.'

'And then what?'

'They came into the room and said it would be fifty dollars for each of them. I told them that was very expensive. They both took off their sweaters to show me what I would be getting for the money. Neither of them was wearing a brassiere.'

'Is that right?' Kapek asked.

'Nobody wears bras today,' Sally said.

'Nobody,' Rebecca said.

'That don't make us hookers,' Sally said.

'Ask the officer here in what condition he found them when he entered the room.'

'Phil?'

'Naked from the waist up,' the patrolman said.

'I wish them arrested,' Searle said. 'For prostitution.'

'You got some case, Fatty,' Rebecca said.

'You know what privates are, Fatty,' Sally asked.

'Must I be submitted to this kind of talk?' Searle said. 'Surely ...'

'Knock it off,' Kapek said to the girls. 'What they're trying to tell you, Mr Searle, is that it's extremely difficult in this city to make a charge of prostitution stick unless the woman has exposed her privates, do you see what I mean? Her genitals,' Kapek said. 'That's been our experience. That's what it is,' he concluded, and shrugged. Rebecca and Sally were smiling.

'They did expose themselves to me,' Searle said.

'Yes, but not the privates, you see. They have to expose the privates. That's the yardstick, you see. For arrest. To make a conviction stick. That's been the, you see, experience of the police department in such matters. Now, of course, we can always book them for disorderly conduct ...'

'Yes, do that,' Searle said.

'That's Section 722,' Kapek said, 'Subdivision 9, but then you'd have to testify in court that the girls were soliciting, you know, were hanging around a public place for the purpose of committing a crime against nature or any other lewdness. That's the way it's worded, that subdivision. So you'd have to explain in court what happened. I mean, what they said to you and all. You know what I mean, Mr Searle?'

'I think so, yes.'

'We could also get them on Section 887, Subdivision 4 of the Code of Criminal Procedure. That's, you know, inducing, enticing or procuring another to commit lewdness, fornication ...'

'Yes, yes, I quite understand,' Searle said, and waved his hand as though clearing away smoke, though Rebecca had not blown any in his direction.

'... unlawful sexual intercourse or any other indecent act,' Kapek concluded. 'But there, too, you'd have to testify in court.'

'Wouldn't the patrolman's word be enough? He saw them all exposed that way.'

'Well, we got half a dozen plays running in this town where the girls are naked from the waist up, and also down, and that doesn't mean they're offering to commit prostitution.' Kapek turned to the patrolman. 'Phil, you hear them *say* anything about prostitution?'

'Nope,' the patrolman answered, and grinned. He was obviously enjoying himself.

'*I* heard them,' Searle said.

'Sure. And like I said, if you're willing to testify in court ...'

'They're *obvious* prostitutes,' Searle said.

'Probably got records, too, no question,' Kapek said. 'But ...'

'I've never been busted,' Sally said.

'How about you, Rebecca?' Kapek asked.

'If you're going to start asking me questions, I want a lawyer. *That's* how about me.'

'Well, what do you say, Mr Searle? You want to go ahead with this, or not?' Kapek asked.

'When would I have to go to court?'

'Prostitution cases usually get immediate hearings. Dozens of them each day. I guess it would be tomorrow sometime.'

'I have business to take care of tomorrow. That's why I'm here to begin with.'

'Well,' Kapek said, and shrugged.

'I hate to let them get away with this,' Searle said.

'Why?' Sally asked. 'Who did you any harm?'

'You offended me gravely, young lady.'

'How?' Rebecca asked.

'Would you ask them to go, please?' Searle said.

'You've decided not to press charges?'

'That is my decision.'

'Beat it,' Kapek said to the girls. 'Keep your asses out of that hotel. Next time, you may not be so lucky.'

Neither of the girls said a word. Sally waited while Rebecca ground out her cigarette in the ashtray. Then they both swivelled out of the squadroom. Searle looked somewhat dazed. He sat staring ahead of him. Then he shook his head and said, 'When they think *that*, when they think a man needs *two* women, they're really thinking he can't even handle *one*.' He shook his head again, rose, put his homburg onto his head, and walked out of the squadroom. The patrolman tilted his nightstick at Kapek, and ambled out after him.

Kapek sighed and went to the Modus Operandi file.

The last known address for Bernard Goldenthal was on the North Side, all the way downtown in a warehouse district adjacent to the River Harb. The tenement in which he reportedly lived was shouldered between two huge edifices that threatened to squash it flat. The street was deserted. This was Sunday, and there was no traffic. Even the tugboats on the river, not two blocks away, seemed motionless. Carella and Brown went into the building, checked the mailboxes – there was a name in only one of them, and it was not Goldenthal's – and then went up to the third floor, where Goldenthal was supposed to be living in Apartment 3A. They listened outside the door and heard nothing. Carella nodded to Brown, and Brown knocked.

'Who is it?' a man's voice asked from behind the door.

'Mr Goldenthal?' Brown asked.

'No,' the man answered. 'Who is it?'

Brown looked at Carella. Carella nodded.

'Police officers,' Brown said. 'Want to open up, please?'

There was a slight hesitation from behind the door. Carella unbuttoned his coat and put his hand on the butt of his revolver. The door opened. The man standing there was in his forties, perhaps as tall as Carella, heavier, with black hair that sprang from his scalp like weeds in a small garden, brown eyes opened wide in enquiry, thick black brows arched over them. Whoever he was, he did not by any stretch of the imagination fit the description on Goldenthal's fingerprint card.

'Yes?' he said. 'What is it?'

'We're looking for Bernard Goldenthal,' Brown said. 'Does he live here?'

'No, I'm sorry,' the man said. 'He doesn't.' He spoke quite softly, the way a very big man will sometimes speak to a child or an old person, as though compensating for his hugeness by lowering the volume of his voice.

'Our information says he lives here,' Carella said.

'Well, I'm sorry,' the man said, 'but he doesn't. He may have at one time, but he doesn't now.'

'What's *your* name?' Carella asked. His coat was still open, and his hand was resting lightly on his hip, close to his holster.

'Herbert Gross.'

'Mind if we come in, Mr Gross?'

'Why would you want to?' Gross asked.

'To see if Mr Goldenthal is here.'

'I just told you he wasn't,' Gross said.

'Mind if we check it for ourselves?' Brown said.

'I really don't see why I should let you,' Gross said.

'Goldenthal's a known criminal,' Carella said, 'and we're looking for him in connection with a recent crime. The last address we have for him is 911 Forrester, Apartment 3A. This is 911 Forrester, Apartment 3A, and we'd like to come in and check on whether or not our information is correct.'

'Your information is wrong,' Gross insisted. 'It must be very old information.'

'No, it's recent information.'

'How recent?'

'Less than three months old.'

'Well, I've been living here for two months now, so he must have moved before that.'

'Are you going to let us in, Mr Gross?'

'No, I don't think so,' Gross said.

'Why not?'

'I don't think I like the idea of policemen crashing in here on a Sunday afternoon, that's all.'

'Anybody in there with you?'

'I don't think that's any of your business,' Gross said.

'Look, Mr Gross,' Brown said, 'we can come back here with a warrant, if that's what you'd like. Why not make it easy for us?'

'Why should I?'

'Why shouldn't you?' Carella said. 'Have you got anything to hide?'

'Nothing at all.'

'Then how about it?'

'Sorry,' Gross said, and closed the door and locked it.

The two detectives stood in the hallway and silently weighed their next move. There were two possibilities open to them, and both of them presented considerable risks. The first possibility was that Goldenthal was indeed in the apartment and armed, in which event he was now warned and if they kicked in the door he would open fire immediately. The second possibility was that the I.S. information *was* dated, and that Goldenthal had indeed moved from the apartment more than two months ago, in which event Gross would have a dandy case against the city if they kicked in the door and conducted an illegal search. Brown gestured with his head, and both men moved towards the stairwell, away from the door.

'What do you think?' Brown whispered.

'There were two of them on the grocery store job,' Carella said. 'Gross might just be the other man.'

'He fits the description I got from the old lady,' Brown said. 'Shall we kick it in?'

'I'd rather wait downstairs. He expects us to come back. If he's in this with Goldenthal, he's going to run, sure as hell.'

'Right,' Brown said. 'Let's split.'

They had parked Brown's sedan just outside the building. Knowing that Gross's apartment overlooked the street, and hoping that he was now watching them from his window, they got into the car and drove north towards the river. Brown turned right under the River Highway, and headed uptown. He turned right again at the next corner, and then drove back to Scovil Avenue and Forrester Street, where he pulled the car to the kerb. Both men got out.

'Think he's still watching?' Brown asked.

'I doubt it, but why take chances?' Carella said. 'The street's deserted. If we plant ourselves in one of the doorways on the end of the block, we can see anybody going in or out of his building.'

The first doorway they found had obviously been used as a nest by any number of vagrants. Empty pint bottles of whisky in brown paper bags littered the floor, together with empty crumpled cigarette packages, and empty half-gallon wine bottles, and empty candy bar wrappers. The stench of urine was overpowering.

'No job's worth *this*,' Brown said.

'Don't care if he killed the goddamn *governor*,' Carella said.

They walked swiftly into the clean brisk October air. Brown looked up the street towards Gross's building. Together, he and Carella ducked into the next doorway. It was better, but only a trifle so.

'Let's hope he makes his move fast,' Brown said.

'Let's hope so,' Carella agreed.

They did not have long to wait.

In five minutes flat, Gross came down the front steps of his building and began walking south, towards the building where they waited. They moved back against the wall. He walked past swiftly, without even glancing into the hallway. They gave him a good lead, and then took off after him, one on each side of the street, so that they formed an isosceles triangle with Gross at the point and Brown and Carella at either end of the base.

They lost him on Payne Avenue, when he boarded an uptown bus that left them running up behind it to choke in a cloud of carbon monoxide. They decided then to go back to the apartment and kick the door in, which is maybe what they should have done in the goddamn first place.

There is an old Spanish proverb which, when translated into city slang, goes something like this: *When nobody knows nothing, everybody knows everything.*

Nobody seemed to know nothing about the José Vicente Huerta assault. He had been attacked in broad daylight on a clear day by four men carrying sawed-off broom handles, and they had beaten him severely enough to have broken both his legs and opened a dozen or more wounds on his face, but nobody seemed to have had a good look at them, even though the beating had lasted a good five minutes or more.

Delgado was not a natural cynic, but he certainly had his doubts about this one. He went through Huerta's building talking to the tenants on each floor, and then he went to the candy store across the street, from which the front stoop of the building was clearly visible, and talked to the proprietor there, but nobody knew nothing. He decided to try another tack.

There was a junkie hooker in the *barrio*, a nineteen-year-old girl who had only one arm. Her handicap, rather than repelling any prospective customers, seemed instead to excite them wildly. From far and wide, the panting Johns came uptown seeking the One-Armed Bandit, as she was notoriously known. She was more familiarly known as Blanca Diaz to those neighbourhood men who were among her regular customers, she having a habit as long as the River Harb, and they knowing a good lay when they stumbled across it, one-armed or not, especially since the habit caused her to charge bargain rates most of the time. Conversely, many of the neighbourhood men were familiarly known to Blanca, and it was for this reason alone that Delgado sought her out.

Blanca was not too terribly interested in passing the time of day with a cop, Puerto Rican or otherwise. But she knew that most of the precinct detectives, unlike Vice Squad cops, were inclined to look the other way where she was concerned, perhaps because of her infirmity. Moreover, she had just had her 3:00 p.m. fix and was feeling no pain when Delgado approached her. She was in fact enjoying the October sunshine, sitting on a bench on one of the grassy ovals running up the centre of The Stem. She spotted Delgado from the corner of her eye, debating moving, thought *Oh, the hell with it*, and sat where she was, basking.

'Hello, Blanca,' Delgado said.

'Hullo,' she answered.

'You okay?'

'I'm fine. I'm not holding, if that's what you mean.'

'That's not what I mean.'

'I mean, if you're looking for a cheap dope bust ...'

'I'm not.'

'Okay,' Blanca said, and nodded. She was not an unattractive girl. Her complexion was dark, her hair was black, her eyes a light shade of brown; her lips were perhaps a trifle too full, and there was a small unsightly scar on her jawline, where she had been stabbed by a pimp when she was just sixteen and already shooting heroin three times a day.

'You want to help me?' Delgado asked.

'Doing what?'

'I need some information.'

'I'm no stoolie,' Blanca said.

'If I ask you anything you don't want to answer, you don't have to.'

'Thanks for nothing.'

'*Querida*,' Delgado said, 'we're very nice to you. Be nice back, huh?'

She looked him full in the face, sighed, and said, 'What do you want to know?'

'Everything you know about Joe Huerta.'

'Nothing.'

'He ever come to visit you?'

'Never.'

'What about his partner?'

'Who's his partner?'

'Ray Castañeda.'

'I don't know him,' Blanca said. 'Is he related to Pepe Castañeda?'

'Maybe. Tell me about Pepe.'

Blanca shrugged. 'A punk,' she said.

'How old is he?'

'Thirty? Something like that.'

'What's he do?'

'Who knows? Maybe numbers, I'm not sure. He used to be a junkie years ago, he's one of the few guys I know who kicked it. He was with this street gang, they called themselves The Spanish Nobles or some shit like that, this was when he was still a kid, you know. I was only five or six myself, you know, but he was a very big man in the neighbourhood, rumbling all the time with this wop gang from the other side of the park, I forget the name of the gang, it was a very big one. Then, you know, everybody started doing dope, the guys all lost interest in gang-busting. Pepe was a very big junkie, but he kicked it. I think he went down to Lexington, I'm not sure. Or maybe he just got busted and sent away and kicked it cold turkey, I'm not sure. But he's off it now, I know that.' She shrugged. 'He's still a punk, though.'

'Have you seen him lately?'

'Yeah, he's around all the time. You always see him on the stoop someplace. Always with a bunch of kids around him, you know, listening to his crap. Big man. The reformed whore,' Blanca said, and snorted.

'Have you seen him today?'

'No. I just come down a little while ago. I had a trick with me all night.'

'Where can I find him, would you know?'

'Pepe or the trick?' Blanca asked, and smiled.

'Pepe,' Delgado said, and did not smile back.

'There's a pool hall on Ainsley,' Blanca said. 'He hangs around there a lot.'

'Let's get back to Huerta for a minute, okay?'

'Why?' Blanca asked, and turned to look at a bus that was rumbling up the avenue.

'Because we got away from him too fast,' Delgado said.

'I hardly know him,' Blanca said. She was still watching the bus. Its blue-grey exhaust fumes seemed to fascinate her.

'You mind looking at me?' Delgado said.

She turned back towards him sharply. 'I told you I'm not a stoolie,' Blanca said. 'I don't want to answer no questions about Joe Huerta.'

'Why not? What's he into?'

'No comment.'

'Dope?'

'No comment.'

'Yes or no, Blanca? We know where you live, we can have the Vice Squad banging on your door every ten minutes. Tell me about Huerta.'

'Okay, he's dealing, okay?'

'I thought he had a real estate business.'

'Sure. He's got an acre of land in Mexico, and he grows pot on it.'

'Is he pushing the hard stuff, too?'

'No. Only grass.'

'Does his partner know this?'

'I don't know what his partner knows or don't know. I'm not his partner. Go ask his partner.'

'Maybe I will,' Delgado said. 'After I talk to his partner's brother.'

'You going to look for Pepe now?'

'Yes.'

'Tell him he still owes me five bucks.'

'What for?'

'What do you think for?' Blanca asked.

Genero was waiting on the sidewalk when Willis came out of the phone booth.

'What'd they say?' he asked.

'Nothing yet. They've got a lot of stuff ahead of what we sent them.'

'So how we supposed to know if it's grass or oregano?' Genero said.

'I guess we wait. They told me to call back in a half-hour or so.'

'Those guys at the lab give me a pain in the ass,' Genero said.

'Yeah, well, what're you gonna do?' Willis said. 'We all have our crosses to bear.' The truth was that Genero gave *him* a pain in the ass. They had arranged for pickup and delivery to the lab of the plastic bag full of oregano/marijuana and had asked for a speedy report on it. But the lab was swamped with such requests every day of the week, the average investigating officer never being terribly certain about a suspect drug until it was checked out downtown. Willis had been willing to wait for the report; Genero had insisted that he call the lab and find out what was happening. Now, at twenty minutes to four, they knew what was happening: nothing. So now Genero was beginning to sulk, and Willis was beginning to wish he would go home and explain to his mother how tough it was to be a working detective in this city.

They were in an area of The Quarter that was not as chic as the section further south, lacking its distinctive Left Bank flair, but boasting of the same high rentals nonetheless, this presumably because of its proximity to all the shops and theatres and coffeehouses. 3541 Carrier Avenue was a brownstone in a row of identical brownstones worn shoddy by the passage of time. They found a nameplate for Robert Hamling in one of the mailboxes in the entrance hallway downstairs. Willis rang the bell for Apartment 22. An answering buzz on the inner door sounded almost immediately. Genero opened the door and both men moved into a dim ground-floor landing. A flight of steps was directly ahead of them. The building smelled of Lysol. They went up to the second floor, searched for Apartment 22, listened outside the door, heard nothing, and knocked.

'Bobby?' a girl's voice said.

'Police officers,' Willis said.

'What do you want?' the girl asked.

'Open the door,' Genero said.

There was silence inside the apartment. They kept listening. They knew that Robert Hamling wasn't in there with the girl, because the first word out of her mouth had been 'Bobby?' But nobody knows better than cops that the female is the deadlier of the species, and so they waited apprehensively for her to unlock the door, their coats open, their guns within ready drawing distance. When the door finally opened, they were looking at a teenage girl wearing dungarees and a tie-dyed T-shirt. Her face was round, her eyes were blue, her brown hair was long and matted.

'Yes, what do you want?' she said. She seemed very frightened and very nervous. She kept one hand on the doorknob. The other fluttered at the throat of the T-shirt.

'We're looking for Robert Hamling,' Willis said. 'Does he live here?'

'Yes,' she said tentatively.

'Is he home?'

'No.'

'When do you expect him?'

'I don't know.'

'What's your name, miss?' Genero asked.

'Sonia.'

'Sonia what?'

'Sonia Sobolev.'

'How old are you, Sonia?'

'Seventeen.'

'Do you live here?'

'No.'

'Where *do* you live?'

'In Riverhead.'

'What are you doing here?'

'Waiting for Bobby. He's a friend of mine.'

'When did he go out?'

'I don't know.'

'How'd you get in here?'

'I have a key.'

'Mind if we come in and wait with you?'

'I don't care,' she said, and shrugged. 'If you want to come in, come in.' She stood aside. She was still very frightened. As they entered, she looked past them into the hallway, as if anxious for Hamling to appear and wishing it would be damn soon. Willis caught this, though Genero did not. She closed the door behind them, and together they went into a room furnished with several battered easy chairs, a foam rubber sofa, and a low, slatted coffee table. 'Well, sit down,' she said.

The detectives sat on the sofa. Sonia took one of the chairs opposite them.

'How well do you know Robert Hamling?' Willis asked.

'Pretty well.'

'When did you see him last?'

'Oh ...' she said, and shrugged, and seemed to be thinking it over.

'Yes?'

'Well, what difference does it make?'

'It might make a difference.'

'Last week sometime, I guess.'

'*When* last week?'

'Well, why don't you ask Bobby when he gets here?'

'We will,' Genero said. 'Meantime, we're asking you. When did you see him last?'

'I don't remember,' Sonia said.

'Do you know anybody named Lewis Scott?' Willis asked.

'No.'

'Ever hear of a clothing store called The Monkey Wrench?'

'Yes, I think so.'

'Ever buy any clothes there?'

'I don't remember.'

'Ever buy a black silk blouse there?' Genero asked.

'I don't remember.'

'Show her the blouse, Dick,' Willis said.

Genero produced the manilla envelope. He took the blouse from it and handed it to the girl. 'This yours?' he asked.

'I don't know.'

'Yes or no?' Genero said.

'It could be, I can't tell for sure. I have a lot of clothes.'

'Do you have a lot of black silk blouses bought at a store called The Monkey Wrench?'

'Well, no, but a person could get confused about her clothes. I mean, it's a black silk blouse, it could be *any* black silk blouse. How do I know it's mine?'

'What size blouse do you take?'

'Thirty-four.'

'This is a thirty-four,' Willis said.

'That still doesn't make it mine, does it?' Sonia asked.

'Were you here in Isola last night?' Willis asked.

'Well, yes.'

'Where?'

'Oh, banking around.'

'Where?'

'Here and there.'

'Here and there *where*?'

'You don't have to answer him, Sonia,' a voice from the doorway said, and both detectives turned simultaneously. The boy standing there was about eighteen, with long blond hair and a handlebar moustache. He had on blue jeans and a blue corduroy shirt, over which he wore an open coat with white fur showing on the inside.

'Mr Hamling, I presume,' Willis said.

'That's me,' Hamling said. He turned to close the entrance door. A bright orange, radiating sun was painted on the back of the coat.

'We've been looking for you,' Willis said.

'So now you found me,' Hamling said. 'This is about Lew, isn't it?'

'You tell *us*,' Genero said.

'Sure, it's about Lew,' Hamling said. 'I figured you'd get to me sooner or later.'

'What about him?'

'He jumped out the window last night.'

'Were you both there when he jumped?'

'We were *both* there,' Hamling said, and glanced at the girl. The girl nodded.

'Want to tell us what happened?'

'He was on a bum trip,' Hamling said. 'He thought he could fly. I tried to hold him down, but he ran for the window and jumped out. End of story.'

'Why didn't you report this to the police?'

'What for? I've got long hair.'

Willis sighed. 'Well,' he said, 'we're here now, so why don't you just tell us everything that happened, and we'll file the damn report and close out the case.'

Genero looked at him. Willis was taking out his pad. 'Want to tell me what time you went over there?'

'It must've been about four-thirty or so. Look,' Hamling said, 'am I gonna get in any trouble on this?'

'Why should you? If Scott jumped out the window, that's suicide, plain and simple.'

'Yeah, well he did.'

'Okay, so help us close it out, will you? This is a headache for us, too,' Willis said, and again Genero looked at him. 'What happened when you got there?'

'Why do I have to be in it, that's all I want to know?' Hamling said.

'Well, you *were* in it, weren't you?'

'Yeah, but . . .'

'So what are we supposed to do? Make believe you *weren't* there? Come on, give us a break. Nobody's trying to get you in trouble. You know how many acid freaks jump out the window every day of the week?'

'I just don't want it to get in the papers or anything,' Hamling said. 'That's why I didn't call you in the first place.'

'We realize that,' Willis said. 'We'll do everything we can to protect you. Just give us the information we need to get a report typed up, that's all.'

'Well, okay,' Hamling said reluctantly.

'So what happened? Did all three of you go up there together, or what?' Willis said.

'No, I ran into him on the street,' Hamling said. 'I was alone at the time. I called Sonia up later, and she came over.'

Willis was writing on the pad. Genero was still watching him. Genero had the strangest feeling that something was going on, but he didn't quite know what. He also had the feeling that he was about to learn something. He was both confused and somewhat exhilarated. He kept his mouth shut and simply watched and listened. 'All right,' Willis said, 'you ran into this friend of yours and . . .'

'No, no, he wasn't a friend of mine,' Hamling said.

'You didn't know him?'

'No, I just ran into him in this coffee joint, and we began talking, you know? So he asked me if I wanted to come up to his place and hear some records, you know, and . . . listen, can I get in trouble if I *really* level with you guys?'

'I'd appreciate it if you would,' Willis said.

'Well, he said he had some good stuff and maybe we could have a smoke.

That's all I thought it was at the time. Just a smoke, you see. I mean, if I'd known the guy had acid in his apartment ...'

'You didn't know that at the time?'

'No, hell, no. I usually try to stay away from these plastic hippies, anyway, they're usually a lot of trouble.'

'How do you mean, trouble?'

'Oh, you know, they're trying to show off all the time, trying to be something they really aren't. Weekend hippies, plastic hippies, same damn thing. None of them are *really* making the scene, they're only *pretending* to make it.'

'How about you?'

'I consider myself genuine,' Hamling said with dignity.

'How about Sonia?'

'Well, she's a sort of a weekend hippie,' Hamling said, 'but she's also a very groovy chick, so I put up with her.' He smiled broadly. Sonia did not smile back. She was still frightened. Her hands were clasped in her lap, and she kept shifting her eyes from Willis to Hamling as though knowing that a dangerous game was being played, and wanting desperately to be elsewhere. Genero sensed this, and also sensed in his inexperienced, newly promoted way that the girl was Willis' real prey and that it would only be a matter of time before he sprang for her jugular. The girl knew this, too. Hamling seemed to be the only person in the room who did *not* know it. Supremely confident of himself, he plunged on.

'Anyway, we went up there and smoked a few joints and drank some wine, and it was then I suggested I give Sonia a ring and have her come over, join in the celebration.'

'What were you celebrating?' Willis asked.

Hamling hesitated. He thought the question over for several moments, and then grinned and said, 'Life. Living. Being alive.'

'Okay,' Willis said.

Genero was still watching very closely, learning as he went along. He knew, for example, that Hamling had just told a lie. Whatever they'd been celebrating, it had not been life or living or being alive. He could not have told *how* he knew Hamling had lied, but he knew it. And Willis knew it. And the girl knew it. And Genero knew that before long Willis would come back to the reason for the celebration, in an attempt to expose Hamling's lie. Genero felt great. He felt as though he were watching a cops-and-robbers movie on television. He didn't want it to end, ever. It never once occurred to him, as he watched and listened to Willis, that he himself was a detective. All he knew was that he was having a great time. He almost asked the girl how she was enjoying herself. He wished he had a bag of popcorn.

'So I went down to the street,' Hamling said. 'He didn't have a phone in the apartment. I went to a pay phone to call Sonia. She ...'

'Where was Sonia?'

'Here. I was supposed to meet her here at seven o'clock, and this was now maybe close to eight. She has a key, so I knew she'd let herself in.'

'*Was* she here?'

'Oh, yeah. So I asked her to meet me uptown. She said she wasn't too familiar with that part of the city, so I told her what train to take, and I met her at the subway stop.'

'What time was that?'

'She must've got there about eight-thirty. Wouldn't you say it was eight-thirty, Sonia?'

The girl nodded.

'Did you go back to the apartment then?'

'Yes,' Hamling said. 'That was the *first* mistake.'

'Why?'

'He was naked when he opened the door. I thought at first . . . hell, I didn't know *what* to think. Then I realized he was high. And then I realized he was on an acid trip. A bummer. I tried to find out what he'd dropped, there's all kinds of stuff, you know, good and bad. Like there's a whole lot of difference between white owsley and green flats; you got shit with strychnine and arsenic mixed into it, man, that's bad news. But he wasn't making any sense at all, didn't know what he'd dropped, didn't know where he was, kept running around the room bare-assed and screaming and yelling he could fly. Scared Sonia half out of her mind, right honey?'

The girl nodded.

'When did he jump out the window?' Willis asked.

'I don't know, we must've been there maybe twenty minutes. I was trying to talk him down, you know, telling him to cool it, calm it, like that, when all of a sudden he jumps up and makes a break for the window. I tried to grab him, but I was too late. The window was closed, you dig? He went through it head first, man oh man. I looked down in the yard, and there he was laying there like . . .' Hamling shook his head.

'So what'd you do?'

'I grabbed Sonia, and we split. I didn't want to get mixed up in it. You got long hair, you're dead.'

'Well, looks open and shut to me,' Willis said, and closed his pad. 'What do you think, Dick?'

Genero nodded. 'Yeah, looks open and shut to me, too,' he said. He was beginning to think he'd been mistaken about Willis. Was it possible his more experienced partner had *really* only been after the details of a suicide? He felt vaguely disappointed.

'Just one more question, I guess,' Willis said, 'and then we can leave you alone. Can't thank you enough for your co-operation. People just don't realize how much trouble they cause when they decide to kill themselves.'

'Oh, I can imagine,' Hamling said.

'We have to treat suicides just like homicides, you know. Same people to notify, same reports to fill out, it's a big job.'

'Oh, sure,' Hamling said.

'Well, thanks again,' Willis said, and started for the door. 'Coming, Dick?'

'Yep,' Genero said, and nodded. 'Thanks a lot,' he said to Hamling.

'Glad to be of help,' Hamling said. 'If I'd known you guys were going to be so decent, I wouldn't have split, I mean it.'

'Oh, that last question,' Willis said, as though remembering something that had momentarily slipped him mind. 'Miss Sobolev . . .'

Hamling's eyes darted to the girl.

'Miss Sobolev, did you take off your blouse before or after Scott jumped out the window?'

'I guess it was before,' Willis said. 'Because you both left immediately after he jumped.'

'Yes, I suppose it was before,' Sonia said.

'Miss Sobolev ... *why* did you take off your blouse?'

'Well ... I don't know why, really. I mean, I guess I just felt like taking it off.'

'I guess she took it off because ...'

'Well, let's let *her* answer it, okay? So we can clear this up, and leave you alone, okay? Why'd you take it off, Miss Sobolev?'

'I guess it was ... I guess it was warm in the apartment.'

'So you took off your blouse?'

'Yes.'

'You'd never met Scott before, but you took off your blouse ...'

'Well, it was warm.'

'He was on a bum trip, running around the place and screaming, and you decided to take off your blouse.'

'Yes.'

'Mmmm,' Willis said. 'Do you want to know how *I* read this, Mr Hamling?'

'How?' Hamling said, and looked at the girl. Genero looked at both of them, and then looked at Willis. He didn't know *what* was going on. He was so excited, he almost wet his pants.

'I think you're protecting the girl,' Willis said.

'Yeah?' Hamling said, puzzled.

'Yeah. It's my guess they were balling in that apartment, and something happened, and the girl here shoved Scott out the window, that's my guess.' The girl's mouth had fallen open. Willis turned to her and nodded. 'We're going to have to take you with us, Miss Sobolev.'

'What do you ... *mean*?' she said.

'Uptown,' Willis answered. 'Mr Hamling, we won't be needing you for now, but the District Attorney may want to ask some more questions after we've booked Miss Sobolev. Please don't leave the city without informing us of your ...'

'Hey, *wait* a minute,' the girl said.

'You want to get your coat, please?' Willis said.

'Listen, *I* didn't push anybody out that damn window!' she said, standing suddenly and putting her hands on her hips.

'Scott was naked, you have your blouse off, what do you expect ...?'

'That was *his* idea!' Sonia shouted, hurling the words at Hamling.

'Cool it, Sonia,' Hamling warned.

'It was *his* idea to get undressed, he wanted to find the damn ...'

'The damn *what*?' Willis snapped.

'The damn money belt!'

Hamling was breaking for the front door. Genero watched in fascinated immobility. Willis was directly in Hamling's path, between him and the door. Hamling was a head taller than Willis and a foot wider, and Genero was certain the boy would now knock his partner flat on his ass. He almost wished he would, because then it would be terribly exciting to see what happened next. Hamling was charging for that front door like an express train, and Genero fully expected him to bowl Willis over and continue running into the corridor, down the steps, into the street, and all the way to China. If he was in Willis' place, he would have got out of the way very quickly, because a man can get hurt by a speeding locomotive. But instead of getting out of the way, Willis started running *towards* Hamling, and suddenly dropped to his right knee. Hamling's right foot was ahead of his left at that moment, with all the weight on it, and as he rushed forward, Willis grabbed his left ankle, and began pulling Hamling forward and pushing him upward at the same time, his right hand against Hamling's chest as he rose. The result was somewhat similar to a football quarterback being hit high and low at the same instant from two opposite directions. Hamling flew over backward, his ankle still clutched in Willis' hand, his head banging back hard against the floor.

Genero blinked.

Willis was stooping over the fallen Hamling now, a gun in his right hand, his handcuffs open in the other hand. He slapped one onto Hamling's wrist, squeezed it closed. The sawtooth edges clicked shut into the retaining metal of the receiver. Willis pulled hard on the cuffs and yanked Hamling to his feet. He whirled him around, pulled his other arm behind his back, and snapped the second cuff shut.

Genero was out of breath.

Danny Gimp was a stool pigeon who told everybody he was a burglar. This was understandable. In a profession where access to underworld gossip was absolutely essential, it was a decided advantage to be considered one of the boys.

Actually, Danny was not a burglar, even though he had been arrested and convicted for burglary in the city of Los Angeles, California, back in the year nineteen hundred and thirty-eight. He had always been a sickly person, and had gone out West to cure himself of a persistent cold. He had met a drinking companion in a bar on La Brea, and the guy had asked Danny to stop by his house while he picked up some more money so that they could continue their all-night revel. They had driven up the Strip past La Cienega and had both entered the guy's house through the back door. The guy had gone into the bedroom and come back a little while later to where Danny was waiting for him in the kitchen. He had picked up several hundred dollars in cash, not to mention a diamond and ruby necklace valued at forty-seven thousand five hundred dollars. But it seemed that Danny was not the only person waiting for his drinking companion to come out of the bedroom. The Los Angeles police were also waiting. In fact, the way Danny found out about the value of the necklace was that the police happened to tell him. Danny tried to explain all this to the judge. He also mentioned to the judge that he had suffered polio as a child, and was a virtual cripple, and that jail would not be very good for his health or his disposition. The judge had kindly considered everything Danny had to say and then sentenced Danny and his drinking companion to a minimum of five and a maximum of ten. Danny never spoke to his drinking companion again after that night, even though the men were in the same cell block. The guy was killed by a black homosexual prisoner a year later, stabbed in the throat with a table knife honed to razor sharpness in the sheet metal shop. The black homosexual stood trial for murder, was convicted, and was executed. Danny served his time thinking about the vagaries of justice, and left prison with the single qualification he would need to pursue a profitable career as a snitch. He was an ex-con. If you can't trust an ex-con, who *can* you trust? Such was the underworld belief, and it accounted for the regularity with which Danny Gimp received choice bits of information, which he then passed on to the police at a price. It was a living, and not a bad one.

Carl Kapek had put in a call to Danny that afternoon. The two men met in Grover Park at seven minutes before five. The afternoon was beginning to wane. They sat together on a park bench and watched governesses wheeling their charges home in baby buggies, watched touch football games beginning to break up, watched a little girl walking slowly by on the winding path, trailing a skip rope behind her and studying the ground the way only little girls can, with an intense concentration that indicated she was pondering all the female secrets of the universe.

'Belinda, huh?' Danny said.

'Yeah. Belinda.'

Danny sniffed. He always seemed to have a cold lately, Kapek noticed. Maybe he was getting old.

'And you don't know Belinda *what*, huh?' Danny said.

'That's why I called you,' Kapek said.

'She's a spade, huh?'

'Yeah.'

'I don't read her right off,' Danny said. He sniffed again. 'It's getting to be winter already, you realize that?'

'It's not so bad,' Kapek said.

'It stinks,' Danny answered. 'Why do you want this broad?'

'She mugged a marine.'

'You're putting me on,' Danny said, and laughed.

'She didn't do it alone.'

'A guy was in it with her?'

'Yeah. She played up to the marine in a bar on Seventeenth, indicated she wanted him to follow her. When he did, she led him to her partner, and they put him out of action.'

'Is the guy a spade, too?'

'No, he's white.'

'Belinda,' Danny said. 'That's a pretty name. I knew a girl named Belinda once. Only girl I ever knew who didn't mind the leg. This was in Chicago one time. I was in Chicago one time. I got people in Chicago. Belinda Kolaczkowska. A Pole. Pretty as a picture, blonde hair, blue eyes, big tits.' Danny demonstrated with his hands, and then immediately put them back in his pockets. 'I asked her one time how come she was going out with a guy like me. I was talking about the limp, you know? She said, "What do you mean, a guy like you?" So I looked her in the eye, and I said, "You know what I mean, Belinda." And she said, "No, I don't know what you mean, Danny." So I said, "Belinda, the fact is that I limp." So she smiled and said, "You *do*?" I'll never forget that smile. I swear to God, if I live to be a hundred and ten, I'll never forget the way Belinda smiled at me that day in Chicago. I felt I could run a mile that day. I felt I could win the goddamn Olympics.' He shook his head, and then sniffed again. A flock of pigeons suddenly took wing not six feet from where the men were sitting, filling the air with the sound of their flight. They soared up against the sky, wheeled, and alighted again near a bench further on, where an old man in a threadbare brown coat was throwing bread crumbs into the air.

'Anyway, that ain't the Belinda you're looking for,' Danny said. He thought a moment longer, and then seemed to suppress the memory completely, pulling his head into his overcoat, thrusting his hands deeper into his pockets. 'Can you give me a description of her?' he asked.

'All I know is she's black, and well built, and she was wearing a red dress.'

'That could mean two thousand girls in this city,' Danny said. 'What about the guy?'

'Nothing.'

'Great.'

'What do you think?'

'I think you're very good for a chuckle on a Sunday when winter's coming, that's what I think.'

'Can you help or not?'

'Let me listen a little, who knows? Will you be around?'

'I'll be around.'

'I'll get back.'

There are times in the city when night refuses to come.

The afternoon lingers, the light changes only slowly and imperceptibly, there is a sense of sweet suspension.

This was just such a day.

There was a briskness to the air, you could never confuse this with a spring day. And yet the afternoon possessed that same luminous quality, the sky so intensely blue that it seemed to vibrate indignantly against encroachment. flatly resisting passage through the colour spectrum to darkness. When the street lights came on at five-thirty, they did so in vain. There was nothing to illuminate, the day was still bright. The sun hung stubbornly over the buildings to the west in downtown Majesta and Calm's Point, defying the earth's rotation, balking at extinction behind roof copings and chimney pots. The citizens of the city lingered in the streets bemused, reluctant to go indoors, as though witnessing some vast astronomical disorder, some realized Nostradamus prediction – it would be daytime forever, the night would never come; there would be dancing in the streets.

The sky to the west yielded at last.

In Herbert Gross's apartment, the light was beginning to fade.

Carella and Brown had been in there for close to three hours now, and whereas they had searched the place from floor to ceiling, wall to wall, timber and toilet tank, they had not found a single clue that told them where Gross had been heading when he hopped that uptown bus.

The clue was everywhere around them. They just hadn't found it yet.

The apartment was a contradiction in itself. It was small and cramped, a cubicle in a crumbling tenement surrounded by warehouses. But it was crowded with furniture that surely had been purchased in the early 'thirties, when solidity was a virtue and inlaid mahogany was the decorative rule. In the living room, a huge overstuffed sofa was upholstered in maroon mohair, its claw feet clutching the faded Persian rug that covered the floor. The sofa alone would have been quite enough to overwhelm the dimensions of the small room, but there were two equally overstuffed easy chairs, and a credenza that seemed to have wandered in from an ornate dining room someplace, and a standing floor lamp with a pink, fringed shade, and an ornately framed painting of snow-clad mountain peaks towering over a placid lake, and a Stronberg-Carlson floor model radio complete with push buttons and a jukebox look, and mahogany end tables on either side of the sofa, each with a tiny drawer, each carrying a huge porcelain lamp with a shade covered in plastic.

The first bedroom had a huge double bed with mahogany headboard and footboard and an unmade mattress. A heavy mahogany dresser of the type that used to be called a 'bureau' when Busby Berkeley was all the rage, complete with its own mahogany-framed mirror, was on the wall oposite the bed. A taller version of it – the male counterpart, so to speak – with longer hanging space for trousers and suits and a row of drawers one atop the other for the storing of handkerchiefs, cuff links, and sundries (Jimmy Walker would have called it a 'chiffonier'), was on the window wall.

The second bedroom was furnished in more modern terms, with two narrow beds covered with simple throws, a Mexican rug hanging on the wall over them. A bookcase was on the wall opposite, alongside a closet without a door. With the exception of the kitchen and the bathroom, there was one other room in the apartment, and this room seemed to have escaped from Arthur Miller's play *The Price*. It was literally packed from floor to ceiling with furniture and china and glassware and marked and unmarked cartons (among those marked was on lettered with the words 'WORLD'S FAIR 1939') and piles of books tied with twine, and cooking utensils, and even old articles of clothing draped over chair or cartons, a veritable child's dream of an attic hideout, equipped with anything needed to serve whatever imaginary excursion suited the fancy.

'I don't get this place,' Carella said.

'Neither do I,' Brown said. He turned on the floor lamp in the living room, and they sat opposite each other, tired and dusty, Carella on the monstrous sofa, Brown in one of the big easy chairs. The room was washed with the glow of the pink, fringed lampshade. Carella almost felt as if he were sitting down to do his homework to the accompaniment of 'Omar the Mystic' flooding from the old Stromberg-Carlson.

'Everything's wrong but that one bedroom,' he said. 'The rest of it doesn't fit.'

'Or maybe vice versa,' Brown said.

'I mean, who the hell has furniture like that nowadays?'

'My mother has furniture like that,' Brown said.

Both men were silent. It was Carella who broke the silence at last.

'When did Goldenthal's mother die?' he asked.

'Three months ago, I think the report said. He was living with her until then.'

'You think all this crap might have been hers?'

'Maybe. Maybe he moved it all here when he left the other apartment.'

'You remember her first name?'

'Minnie.'

'How many Goldenthals do you suppose there are in the telephone book?'

They did not even consider looking in the directories for Bethtown, Majesta, or Calm's Point, because Gross had been heading *uptown*, and access to all those other sections of the city would have required going *downtown*. They did not consider looking in the Riverhead directory, either, because Gross had taken a bus, and transportation all the way to Riverhead was a hell of a slow way to go, when there were express trains running all day long. So they limited their search to the Isola directory alone. (There was one other reason they consulted just this one phone book; it happened to be the *only* one Gross had in the apartment.)

There were eight Goldenthals listed in the Isola directory.

But only one of them was Minnie Goldenthal – now deceased, poor lady, her name surviving in print only until next year's directory would be published by the telephone company.

Sic transit gloria mundi.

The building in which Minnie Goldenthal had lived was a twelve-storey yellow brick structure bristling with television antennae. It was fronted by a small cement courtyard flanked by two yellow brick pillars, atop which sat two stone urns that were probably planted with flowers in the spring, but that now contained only withered stalks. Enclosing this courtyard were the two wings of the building, and a row of apartments connecting both wings, so that the result was an architectural upside-down U facing the low flat entrance steps to the courtyard. The mailboxes for each wing were in the entryway to the right and left. Carella checked one entry, Brown the other. there was no listing for Goldenthal, Minnie or otherwise.

'What do you think?' Carella asked.

'Let's check the super,' Brown suggested.

The superintendent lived on the ground floor, in an apartment behind the staricase. He came to the door in his undershirt. A television set was going somewhere in his apartment, but apparently the show had not completely captured his attention, because he was carrying the Sunday comics in his right hand. The detectives identified themselves. The super looked at Carella's shield. He looked at Carella's I.D. card. Then he said, 'Yes?'

'Was there a Minnie Goldenthal living here recently?' Carella asked.

The super listened attentively to his every word, as though he were being asked a question which, if answered correctly, would cause him to win a hundred-thousand-dollar jackpot.

Then he said, 'Yes.'

'Which apartment?'

'Nine-D.'

'Anyone living in that apartment now?'

'Son's still living in it.'

'Bernie Goldenthal?'

'That's right. Don't know *why* he's living in it, mind you. Moved all the furniture out a little while after Minnie died. Still pays the rent, though.' The super shrugged. 'Tell you the truth, the owners wish he'd get out. That apartment's price-fixed. Nice big old apartment. If he gets out, they can put a new tenant in and legally raise the rent.'

'Anybody up there now?' Carella asked.

'Don't know,' the super said. 'Don't keep tabs on the comings and goings of the people who live here. Their business is their business, and mine is mine.'

'Law requires you have to have a key to all the apartments in the dwelling,' Carella said. 'Have you got one for Nine-D?'

'Yep.'

'All right if we use it?'

'What for?'

'To enter the apartment.'

'That's illegal, ain't it?'

'We won't tell anybody if you won't,' Brown said.

'Well,' the super said, and shrugged. 'Okay,' he said, and shrugged again. 'I guess.'

Carella and Brown took the elevator up to the ninth floor and stepped into the corridor. Neither man said a word to the other, but both simultaneously drew their revolvers. 9D was at the far end of the hall. They listened outside the door and heard nothing. Cautiously, Carella inserted the passkey into the lock. He nodded to Brown, and twisted the key. There was only a small click as the lock turned, but it must have sounded like a warning shot inside that apartment. Carella and Brown burst into a long narrow entrance foyer. At the far end of the foyer, they saw Herbert Gross and a blond man they assumed to be Bernard Goldenthal, both of them armed.

'Hold it right there!' Carella shouted, but neither of the two men were holding anything right there or right anywhere. They opened fire just as Carella and Brown threw themselves flat on the linoleum-covered floor. Goldenthal made a break for a doorway to the right of the long foyer. Brown shouted a warning and fired almost before the words left his lips. The slug caught Goldenthal in the leg, knocked him off his feet and sent him flailing against the corridor wall, where he slid to the floor. Gross held his ground, firing down the long length of the foyer, pulling off shot after shot until his pistol clicked empty. He was reaching into his jacket pocket, presumably for fresh cartridges, when Carella shouted, 'Move and you're dead!'

Gross's hand stopped in mid-motion. He squinted down the corridor, silhouetted in the light that spilled from the room Goldenthal had tried to reach.

'Drop the gun,' Carella said.

Gross did not move.

'*Drop* it!' Carella shouted. 'Now!'

'You, too, Goldie!' Brown shouted.

Goldenthal and Gross – one crouched against the wall clutching his bleeding leg, the other with his hand still hanging motionless over his jacket pocket – exchanged quick glances. Without saying a word to each other, they dropped their guns on the floor. Gross kicked them away as if they were contaminated. The guns came spinning down the corridor one after the other, sliding along the waxed linoleum.

Carella got to his feet, and started towards the two men. Behind him, Brown was crouched on one knee, his gun resting on his forearm and pointing directly at the far end of the foyer. Carella threw Gross against the wall, quickly frisked him, and then bent over Goldenthal.

'Okay,' he called to Brown, and then glanced into the room on the right of the foyer. It, too, was loaded with household goods. But unlike the stuff in the dead woman's home, this was not the accumulation of a lifetime. This was, instead, the result of god knew how many recent burglaries and robberies, a veritable storehouse of television sets, radios, typewriters, tape recorders, broilers, mixers, luggage, you name it, right down to a complete set of the Encyclopaedia Britannica – a criminal bargain basement, awaiting only the services of a good fence.

'Nice little place you've got here,' Carella said, and then handcuffed Gross to Goldenthal and Goldenthal to the radiator. From a telephone on the kitchen wall, the late Minnie's last shopping list still tacked up beside it, he called the station house and asked for a meat wagon. It arrived at exactly 6:00 p.m., not seven minutes after Carella requested it. By that time, Goldenthal had spilled a goodly amount of blood all over his mother's linoleum.

'I'm bleeding to death here,' he complained to one of the hospital orderlies who was lifting him on to the stretcher.

'That's the least of your worries,' the orderly answered.

Delgado had not found Pepe Castañeda in the pool hall, nor had he found him in any one of a dozen bars he tried in the neighbourhood. It was now a quarter past six, and he was about ready to give up the search. On the dubious assumption, however, that a pool shooter might also be a bowler, he decided to hit the Ponce Bowling Lanes on Culver Avenue before heading back to the squadroom.

The place was on the second floor of an old brick building. Delgado went up the narrow flight of steps and came into a fluorescent-lighted room with a counter just opposite the entrance doorway. A bald-headed man was sitting on a stool behind the counter, reading a newspaper. He looked up as Delgado came in, went back to the newspaper, finished the story he was reading, and then put both hands flat on the countertop. 'All the alleys are full,' he said. 'You got maybe a half-hour wait.'

'I don't want an alley,' Delgado said.

The man behind the counter looked at him more carefully, decided he was a cop, gave a brief knowledgeable nod, but said nothing.

'I'm looking for a man named Pepe Castañeda. Is he here?'

'What do you want him for?' the man said.

'I'm a police officer,' Delgado said, and flashed the tin. 'I want to ask him some questions.'

'I don't want no trouble here,' the man said.

'Why should there be trouble? Is Castañeda trouble?'

'*He's* not the trouble,' the man said, and looked at Delgado meaningfully.

'Neither am I,' Delgado said. 'Where is he?'

'Lane number five,' the man said.

'Thanks.'

Delgado went through the doorway adjacent to the counter and found himself in a larger room than the small reception area had promised. There were twelve alleys in all, each of them occupied with bowlers. A bar was at the far end of the place, with tables and chairs set up around it. A jukebox was playing a rock-and-roll song. The record ended as Delgado moved past the racks of the bowling balls against the low wall that separated the lanes from the area behind them. A Spanish-language song erupted from the loudspeakers. Everywhere, there was the reverberating clamour of falling pins, multiplied and echoing in the high-ceilinged room, joined by voices raised in jubilant exclamation or disgruntled invective.

There were four men bowling in lane number five. Three of them were seated on the leatherette banquette that formed a semicircle around the score pad. The fourth man stood waiting for his ball to return. It came rolling down the tracks from the far end of the alley, hit the stop mechanism, eased its way towards his waiting hand. He picked up the ball, stepped back some five feet from the foul line, crouched, started his forward run, right arm coming back, left arm out for balance, stopped dead, and released the ball. It curved down the alley and arced in true between the one and three pins. The bowler hung frozen in motion, his right arm still extended, left arm back, crouched and waiting for the explosion of pins. They flew into the air like gleeful cheerleaders, there was the sound of their leap as the ball sent them helter-skelter, the additional sound of their pell-mell return to the polished alley floor. The bowler shouted, 'Made it!' and turned to the three men on the banquette.

'Which one of you is Pepe Casteñeda?' Delgado asked.

The bowler, who was walking back towards the score pad to supervise the correct marking of the strike, stopped in his tracks and looked up at Delgado. He was a short man with straight black hair and a pockmarked face, thin, with the light step of a dancer, a step that seemed even airier in the red, rubber-soled bowling shoes.

'I'm Castañeda,' he said. 'Who're you?'

'Detective Delgado, Eighty-seventh Squad,' Delgado said. 'Mind if I ask you a few questions?'

'What about?'

'Is Ramon Castañeda your brother?'

'That's right.'

'Why don't we walk over there and talk a little?'

'Over where?'

'The tables there.'

'I'm in the middle of a game.'

'The game can wait.'

Castañeda shrugged. One of the men on the banquette said, 'Go ahead, Pepe. We'll order a round of beer meanwhile.'

'How many frames we got to go?'

'Just three,' the other man said.

'This gonna take long?' Castañeda asked.

'I don't think so,' Delgado said.

'Well, okay. We're ahead here, I don't want to cool off.'

They walked together to the bar at the far end of the room. Two young girls in tight slacks were standing near the jukebox, pondering their next selection. Castañeda looked them over, and then pulled out a chair at one of the tables. The men sat opposite each other. The jukebox erupted again with sound. The intermittent rumble of exploding pins was a steady counterpoint.

'What do you want to know?' Castañeda asked.

'Your brother's got a partner named José Huerta,' Delgado said.

'That's right.'

'Do you know him?'

'Yeah, I know Joe.'

'Do you know he was beaten up this morning?'

'He was? No, I didn't know that. You got a cigarette? I left mine on the table back there.'

'I don't smoke,' Delgado said.

'I didn't used to smoke, either,' Castañeda said. 'But, you know ...' He shrugged. 'You break one habit, you pick up another, huh?' He grinned. The grin was wide and infectious. He was perhaps three or four years younger than Delgado, but he suddenly looked like a teenager. 'I used to be a junkie, you know. Did you know that?'

'Yes, I've heard it.'

'I kicked it.'

'I've heard that, too.'

'Ain't you impressed?'

'I'm impressed,' Delgado said.

'So am I,' Castañeda said and grinned again. Delgado grinned with him. 'So, I still don't know what you want from me,' Castañeda said.

'He got beat up pretty badly,' Delgado said. 'Broke both his legs, chopped his face up like hamburger.'

'Gee, that's too bad,' Castañeda said. 'Who done it?'

'Four men.'

'Boy,' Castañeda said, and shook his head.

'They got him on the front stoop of his building. He was on his way to church.'

'Yeah? Where does he live?'

'On South Sixth.'

'Oh yeah, that's right,' Castañeda said. 'Across the street from the candy store, right?'

'Yes. The reason I wanted to talk to you,' Delgado said, 'is that your brother seemed to think the four men who beat up Huerta were *asked* to beat him up.'

'I don't follow you,' Castañeda said.

'When I asked your brother who disliked Huerta, he said, "No one dislikes him enough to have him beaten up."'

'So? What does that mean?'

'It means ...'

'It don't mean nothing,' Castañeda said, and shrugged.

'It means your brother thinks the men who beat up Huerta were doing it for somebody else, not themselves.'

'I don't see where you get that,' Castañeda said. 'That was just a way of speaking, that's all. My brother didn't mean nothing by it.'

'Let's say he did. Let's say for the moment that somebody *wanted* Huerta beaten up. And let's say he asked four men to do the favour for him.'

'Okay, let's say that.'

'Would you happen to know who those four men might be?'

'Nope,' Castañeda said. 'I really could use a cigarette, you know? You mind if I go back to the table for them?'

'The cigarette can wait, Pepe. There's a man in the hospital with two broken legs and a busted face.'

'Gee, that's too bad,' Castañeda said, 'but maybe the man should've been more careful, you know? Then maybe nobody would've *wanted* him beaten up, and nobody would've talked to anybody *about* beating him up.'

'Who wanted him hurt, Pepe?'

'You interested in some guesses?'

'I'm interested.'

'Joe's a pusher, did you know that?'

'I know that.'

'Grass. For now. But I never yet met a guy selling grass who didn't later figure there was more profit in the hard stuff. It's just a matter of time, that's all.'

'So?'

'So maybe somebody didn't like the idea of him poisoning the neighbourhood, you dig? I'm only saying. But it's something to consider, right?'

'Yes, it's something to consider.'

'And maybe Joe was chasing after somebody's wife, too. Maybe somebody's got a real pretty wife, and maybe Joe's been making it with her, you dig? That's another thing to consider. So maybe somebody decided to break both his legs so he couldn't run around no more balling somebody else's wife and selling poison to the kids in the *barrio*. And maybe they decided to mess up his face for good measure, you dig? So he wouldn't look so pretty to other guys' wives, and so maybe when he come up to a kid in the neighbourhood and tried to get him hooked, the kid might not want to deal with somebody who had a face looked like it hit a meat grinder.' Castañeda paused. 'Those are all things to consider, right?'

'Yes, they're all things to consider,' Delgado said.

'I don't think you're ever gonna find those guys who beat him up,' Castañeda said. 'But what difference does it make?'

'What do you mean?'

'He got what he deserved. That's justice, ain't it? That's what you guys are interested in, ain't it? Justice?'

'Yes, we're interested in justice.'

'So this was justice,' Castañeda said.

Delgado looked at him.

'Wasn't it?' Castañeda asked.

'Yes, I think it was,' Delgado said. He nodded, rose from the table suddenly, pushed his chair back under it, and said, 'Nice talking to you. See you around.'

'Buy you a drink or something?' Castañeda asked.

'Thanks, I've still got an hour before I'm off duty,' Delgado answered, and walked away from the table.

Behind him, Castañeda raised his hand in farewell.

It was 7:00 p.m. by the time Brown finally got around to Mary Ellingham, the lady who had called in twelve hours before to report that her husband was missing. Full darkness was upon the city now, but it was not yet nighttime; it was still that time of day called 'evening', a poetic word that always stirred something deep inside Brown, perhaps because he had never heard the word as a child and only admitted it to his vocabulary after he met Connie, his wife-to-be, when things stopped being merely night and day, or black and white; Connie had brought shadings to his life, and for that he would love her forever.

North Trinity was a two-block-long street off Silvermine Oval, adjacent to fancy Silvermine Road, which bordered on the River Harb and formed the northern frontier of the precinct. From where Brown had parked the car, he could see the waters of the river, and uptown the scattered lights of the estates in Smoke Rise, the brighter illumination on the Hamilton Bridge. The lights were on along Trinity, too, beckoning warmly from windows in the rows of brownstones that faced the secluded street. Brown knew that behind most of those windows, the occupants were enjoying their cocktail hour. One could always determine the socio-economic standing of anybody in this city by asking him what time he ate his dinner. In a slum like Diamondback, the dinner hour had already come and gone. On Trinity Street, the residents were having their before-dinner drinks. Further uptown in Smoke Rise, the dinner hour would not start until nine or nine-thirty – although the cocktail hour may have started at noon.

Brown was hungry.

There were no lights burning at 742 North Trinity. Brown looked at his watch, shrugged, and rang the front doorbell. He waited, rang the doorbell a second time, and then stepped down off the front stoop to look up at the second storey of the building, where a light had suddenly come on. He went back up the steps and waited. He heard someone approaching the door. A peephole flap was thrown back.

'Yes?' a woman's voice asked.

'Mrs Ellingham?'

'Yes?'

'Detective Brown, Eighty-seventh Squad.'

'Oh,' Mrs Ellingham said. 'Oh, just a minute, please.' The peephole flap fell back into place. He heard the door being unlocked.

Mary Ellingham was about forty years old. She was wearing a man's flannel robe. Her hair was disarrayed. Her face was flushed.

'I'm sorry I got here so late,' Brown said. 'We had a sort of busy day.'

'Oh,' Mrs Ellingham said. 'Yes.'

'I won't keep you long,' Brown said, reaching into his pocket for his pad and pen. 'If you'll just give me a description of your husband ...'

'Oh,' Mrs Ellingham said.

'His name is Donald Ellingham, is that correct?'

'Yes, but ...'

'How old is he?'

'Well, you see ...'

Brown looked up from his pad. Mrs Ellingham seemed terribly embarrassed all at once. Before she uttered another word, Brown realized what he had walked in on, and he too was suddenly embarrassed.

'You see,' Mrs Ellingham said, 'he's back. My husband. He got back just a little while ago.'

'Oh,' Brown said.

'Yes,' she said.

'Oh.'

'Yes. I'm sorry. I suppose I should have called ...'

'No, no, that's all right,' Brown said. He put his pad and his pen back into his pocket, and reached behind him for the doorknob. 'Glad he's back, glad everything worked out all right.'

'Yes,' Mrs Ellingham said.

'Good night,' Brown said.

'Good night,' she said.

She closed the door gently behind him as he went down the steps. Just before he got into his automobile, he glanced back at the building. The upstairs light had already gone out again.

Back at the squadroom, the three detectives who had been called in off vacation were bitching about the speed with which Carella and Brown had cracked the grocery store case. It was one thing to interrupt a man's vacation if there was a goddamn *need* for it; it was another to call him in and trot him around all day asking questions and gathering data while two other guys were out following a hot lead that resulted in an arrest.

'You know what I coulda been doing today?' Di Maeo asked.

'What?' Levine said.

'I coulda been watching the ball game on television, and I coulda had a big dinner with the family. My sister is in from Scranton, she come all the way in from Scranton 'cause she knows I'm on vacation. So instead I'm talking to a bunch of people who couldn't care less whether a grocer got shot, and who couldn't care at *all* whether a cop caught one.'

Meriwether the hairbag said, 'Now, now, fellows, it's all part of the game, all part of the game.'

In two separate locked rooms down the corridor, Willis was interrogating Sonia Sobolev, and Genero was interrogating Robert Hamling. Neither of the suspects had exercised their right to an attorney. Hamling, who claimed he had nothing to hide, seemed pleased in fact that he could get his story on the record. He repeated essentially what he had told them in the apartment: Lewis Scott had been on a bum acid trip and had thrown himself out of the window while Hamling had done all he could to prevent the suicide. The stenographer listened to every word, his fingers moving silently over his machine.

Sonia Sobolev apparently felt no need for an attorney because she did not consider herself mixed up in the death of Lewis Scott. Her version of the story differed greatly from Hamling's. According to Sonia, Hamling had met the bearded Scott that afternoon and the two had banked around the city for a while, enjoying each other's company. Scott was indeed celebrating something – the arrival from home of a two-hundred-dollar money order, which he had cashed and which, in the form of ten-dollar bills, was now nestling in a money belt under his shirt. Hamling had gone back to Scott's apartment with him, and tried to get him drunk. When that failed, he asked Scott if he didn't think they needed a little female company, and when Scott agreed that might not be a bad idea, Hamling had gone downstairs to call Sonia.

'What did he tell you when he met you later?' Willis asked.

'Well, I got off the train,' Sonia said, 'and Bobby was waiting there for me. He said he had this dumb plastic hippie in an apartment nearby, and the guy had a money belt with two hundred dollars in it, and Bobby *wanted* that money. He said the only way to get it was to convince the guy to take off his clothes. And the only way to do that was for me to do it first,' Sonia shrugged. 'So we went up there.'

'Yes, what happened then?'

'Well, I went in the john and combed my hair and then I took off my blouse. And I went out to the other room without any blouse on. To see if I could, well, get him excited, you know. So he would take off his clothes. We were all drinking a lot of wine.'

'Were you smoking?'

'Pot, you mean? No.'

'So what happened?'

'Well, he finally went in the john, too, and got undressed. He was wearing blue jeans and a Charlie Brown sweat shirt. And he *did* have a money belt. He was wearing a money belt.'

'Did he take that off, too?'

'Yes.'

'And then what?'

'Well, he came back to the mattress, and we started fooling around a little, you know, just touching each other. Actually, I was sort of keeping him busy while Bobby went through the money belt. Trouble is, he *saw* Bobby. And he jumped up and ran to where Bobby was standing with the money belt in his hands, and they started fighting, and that . . . that was when Bobby pushed him out of the window. We split right away. I just threw on my jacket, and Bobby put on his coat, and we split. I didn't even remember the blouse until much later.'

'Where's the money belt now?' Willis asked.

'In Bobby's apartment. Under his mattress.'

In the other room, Hamling kept insisting that Lewis Scott was an acid freak who had thrown himself out the window to the pavement below. Di Maeo knocked on the door, poked his head inside, and said, 'Dick, you send some suspect dope to the lab?'

'Yeah,' Genero said.

'They just phoned. Said it was oregano.'

'Thanks,' Genero said. He turned again to Hamling. 'The stuff in Lewis Scott's refrigerator was oregano,' he said.

'So what?' Hamling said.

'So tell me one more time about this big acid freak you got involved with.'

In the squadroom outside, Carella sat at his desk typing a report on Goldenthal and Gross. Goldenthal had been take to Buenavista, the same hospital that was caring for Andy Parker whom he had shot. Gross had refused to say a word to anyone. He had been booked for Armed Robbery and Murder One, and was being held in one of the detention cells downstairs. Carella looked extremely tired. When the telephone on his desk rang, he stared at it for several moments before answering it.

'Eighty-seventh Squad,' he said, 'Carella.'

'Steve, this is Artie Brown.'

'Hello, Artie,' Carella said.

'I just wrapped up this squeal on North Trinity. Guy came home, and they're happily in the sack.'

'Good for them,' Carella said. 'I wish *I* was happily in the sack.'

'You want me to come back there, or what?'

'What time is it?'

'Seven-thirty.'

'Go home, Artie.'

'You sure? What about the report?'

'I'm typing it now.'

'Okay then, I'll see you,' Brown said.

'Right,' Carella said, and put the receiver back onto its cradle, and looked up at the wall clock, and sighed. The telephone on Carl Kapek's desk was ringing.

'Eighty-seventh,' he said, 'Kapek speaking.'

'This is Danny Gimp,' the voice on the other end said.

'Hello, Danny, what've you got for me?'

'Nothing,' Danny said.

Di Maeo, Meriwether, and Levine were packing it in, hoping to resume their vacations without further interruption. Levine seemed certain that Brown and Carella would get promotions out of this one; there were always promotions when you cracked a case involving somebody doing something to a cop. Di Maeo agreed with him, and commented that some guys had all the luck. They went down the iron-runged steps and past the muster desk, and through the old building's entrance doors. Meriwether stopped on the front steps to tie his shoelace. Alex Delgado was just getting back to the station house. He chatted for only a moment, said good night to all of them, and went inside. It was almost seven forty-five, and some of the relieving shift was already in the squadroom.

In a little while, the daywatch could go home.

Kapek had been cruising from bar to bar along The Stem since 8:00 p.m. It was now twenty minutes past eleven, and his heart skipped a beat when the black girl in the red dress came through the doors of Romeo's on Twelfth Street. The girl sashayed past the men sitting on stools along the length of the bar, took a seat at the far end near the telephones, and crossed her legs. Kapek gave her ten minutes to eye every guy in the joint, and then walked past her to the telephones. He dialled the squadroom, and got Finch, the catcher on the relieving team.

'What are you doing?' Finch wanted to know.

'Oh, cruising around,' Kapek said.

'I thought you went home hours ago.'

'No rest for the weary,' Kapek said. 'I'm about to make a bust. If I'm lucky.'

'Need some help?'

'Nope,' Kapek said.

'Then why the hell did you call?'

'Just to make some small talk,' Kapek said.

'I've got a knifing on Ainsley,' Finch answered. 'Go make small talk someplace else.'

Kapek took his advice. He hung up, felt in the coin return chute for his dime, shrugged, and went out to sit next to the girl at the bar.

'I'll bet your name is Suzie,' he said.

'Wrong,' the girl said, and grinned. 'It's Belinda.'

'Belinda, you are one beautiful piece,' Kapek said.

'You think so, huh?'

'I do most sincerely think so,' Kapek said. 'May I offer to buy you a drink?'

'I'd be flattered,' Belinda said.

They chatted for close to twenty minutes. Belinda indicated that she found Kapek highly attractive; it was rare that a girl could just wander into a neighbourhood bar and find someone of Kapek's intelligence and sensitivity, she told him. She indicated, too, that she would like to spend some time with Kapek a little later on, but that her husband was a very jealous man and that she couldn't risk leaving the bar with Kapek because word might get back to her husband and then there would be all kinds of hell to pay. Kapek told her he certainly understood her position. Still, Belinda said, I sure would love to spend some time with you, honey. Kapek nodded.

'What do you suppose we can do?' he asked.

'You can meet me outside, can't you?'

'Sure,' he said. 'Where?'

'Let's drink up. Then I'll leave, and you can follow me out in a few minutes. How does that sound?'

Kapek looked up at the clock behind the bar. It was ten minutes to twelve. 'That sounds fine to me,' he said.

Belinda lifted her whisky sour and drained it. She winked at him and swivelled away from the bar. At the door, she turned, winked again, and then went out. Kapek gave her five minutes. He finished his scotch and soda, paid for the drinks, and went out after her. Belinda was waiting on the next corner. She signalled to him, and began walking rapidly up The Stem. Kapek nodded and followed her. She walked two blocks east, looked back at him once again, and turned abruptly left on Fifteenth Street. Kapek reached the corner and drew his pistol. He hesitated, cleared his throat to let them know he was coming, and then rounded the corner.

A white man was standing there with his fist cocked. Kapek thrust the gun into his face and said, 'Everybody stand still.' Belinda started to break. He grabbed her wrist, flung her against the brick wall from the building, said, 'You, too, honey,' and took his handcuffs from his belt.

He looked at his watch.

It was a minute to midnight.

Another day was about to start.

SADIE WHEN SHE DIED

"Detective Steve Carella wasn't sure he had heard the man correctly. This was not what a bereaved husband was supposed to say...."

This is for Charlotte and Dick Condon

Chapter One

Detective Steve Carella wasn't sure he had heard the man correctly. This was not what a bereaved husband was supposed to say when his wife lay disemboweled on the bedroom floor in a pool of her own blood. The man was still wearing overcoat and homburg, muffler and gloves. He stood near the telephone on the night table, a tall man with a narrow face, the vertical plane of which was dramatically broken by a well-groomed grey moustache that matched the greying hair at his temples. His eyes were clear and blue and distinctly free of pain or grief. As if to make certain Carella had understood him, he repeated a fragment of his earlier statement, giving it even more emphasis this time around.

'*Very* glad she's dead,' he said.

'Sir,' Carella said, 'I'm sure I don't have to tell you ...'

'That's right,' the man said, 'you don't have to tell me. It happens I'm a criminal lawyer. I am well aware of my rights, and fully cognizant of the fact that anything I tell you of my own free will may later be used against me. I repeat that my wife was a no-good bitch, and I'm delighted someone killed her.'

Carella nodded, opened his pad, glanced at it, and said, 'Are you the man who notified the police?'

'I am.'

'Then your name is Gerald Fletcher.'

'That's correct.'

'Your wife's name, Mr Fletcher?'

'Sarah. Sarah Fletcher.'

'Want to tell me what happened?'

'I got home about fifteen minutes ago. I called to my wife from the front door, and got no answer. I came here into the bedroom and found her dead on the floor. I immediately called the police.'

'Was the room in this condition when you came in?'

'It was.'

'Touch anything?'

'Nothing. I haven't moved from this spot since I placed the call.'

'Anybody in here when you came in?'

'Not a soul. Except my wife, of course.'

'And you say you got home about fifteen minutes ago?'

'More or less. You can check it with the elevator operator who took me up.'

Carella looked at his watch. 'That would have been ten-thirty or thereabouts.'

'Yes.'

'And you called the police at ...' Carella consulted the open notebook. 'Ten thirty-four. Is that right?'

'I didn't look at my watch, but I expect that's close enough.'

'Well, the call was logged at ...'

'Ten thirty-four is close enough.'

'Is that your suitcase in the entrance hallway?'

'It is.'

'Just returning home from a trip?'

'I was on the Coast for three days.'

'Where?'

'Los Angeles.'

'Doing what?'

'An associate of mine needed advice on a brief he's preparing.'

'What time did your plane get in?'

'Nine forty-five. I claimed my bag, caught a taxi, and came directly home.'

'And got here about ten-thirty, right?'

'That's right. For the third time.'

'Sir?'

'You've already ascertained the fact three times. If there remains any doubt in your mind, let me reiterate that I got here at ten-thirty, found my wife dead, and called the police at ten thirty-four.'

'Yes, sir. I've got that.'

'What's your name?' Fletcher asked suddenly.

'Carella. Detective Steve Carella.'

'I'll remember that.'

'Please do.'

While Fletcher was remembering Carella's name; and while the police photographer was doing his macabre little jig around the body, flashbulbs popping, death being recorded on Polaroid film for instant verification, pull, wait fifteen seconds, beep, rip, examine the picture to make sure the lady looks good in the rushes, or as good as any lady *can* look with her belly wide open and her intestines spilling onto a rug; and while two Homicide cops named Monoghan and Monroe beefed about being called away from their homes on a cold night in December, two weeks before Christmas; and while Detective Bert Kling was downstairs talking to the elevator operator and the doorman in an attempt to ascertain the *exact* hour Mr Gerald Fletcher had pulled up in a taxicab and entered the apartment building on Silvermine Oval and gone up in the elevator to find his once-beautiful wife, Sarah, spread amoeba-like in ugly death on the bedroom rug; while all this was happening, a laboratory technician named Marshall Davies was in the kitchen of the apartment, occupying himself with busy work while he waited for the Medical Examiner to pronounce the lady dead and state the probable cause (as if it took a genius to determine that someone had ripped her open with a switchblade knife), at which time Davies would go into the bedroom and with delicate care remove the knife protruding from the blood and slime of the lady's guts in an attempt to salvage some good latent prints from the handle of the murder weapon.

Davies was a new technician, but an observant one, and the first thing he noticed in the kitchen was that the window was wide open, not exactly usual for a December night when the temperature outside hovered at twelve degrees Fahrenheit, not to mention Centigrade. Davies leaned over the sink and further noticed that the window opened onto a fire escape on the rear of the building. Whereas he was paid only to examine the superficial aspects of any criminal act – such as glass shards in a victim's eyeball, or shotgun pellets in the chest, or, as in the case of the lady in the other room, a knife in the belly – he could not resist speculating that perhaps someone, some intruder, had climbed up the fire escape and into the kitchen, after which he had proceeded to the bedroom, where he'd done the lady in.

Since there was a big muddy footprint in the kitchen sink and another one on the floor near the sink, and several others fading in intensity as they travelled inexorably across the waxed kitchen floor to the door that led to the living room, Davies surmised he was onto something hot. Wasn't it entirely possible that an intruder *had* climbed over the windowsill and into the sink and walked across the room, bearing the switchblade knife that had later been pulled viciously across the lady's belly from left to right, like a rip-top cellophane tab, opening her as effortlessly as it would have a package of cigarettes?

Davies stopped speculating, and photographed the footprint in the sink and the ones on the floor. Then, because the Assistant M.E. was still fussing around with the corpse (Death by stab wound, Davies thought impatiently; evisceration, for Christ's sake!) and seemed reluctant to commit himself without perhaps first calling his superior officer or his mother. (Say, we've got a tough one here, lady's belly ripped open with a knife, got any idea what might have caused death?), Davies climbed out onto the fire escape and dusted the lower edge of the window, which the intruder would have had to grab in order to open the window, and then for good measure dusted the iron railings of the ladder leading up to the fire escape.

Now, if the M.E. ever got through with the goddamn body, and if there were any latent prints on the handle of the knife, the boys of the 87th would be halfway home, thanks to Marshall Davies.

He felt pretty good.

Detective Bert Kling felt pretty lousy.

His condition, he kept telling himself, had nothing to do with the fact that Cindy Forrest had broken their engagement three weeks before. To begin with, it had never been a proper engagement, and a person certainly couldn't go around mourning something that had never truly existed. Besides, Cindy had made it abundantly clear that, whereas they had enjoyed some very good times together, and whereas she would always think upon him fondly and recall with great pleasure the days and months (yea, even years) they had spent together pretending they were in love, she had nonetheless met a very attractive young man who was a practising psychiatrist at Buenavista Hospital, where she was doing her internship, and seeing as how they shared identical interests, and seeing as how he was quite ready to get married whereas Kling seemed to be married to a .38 Detective's Special, a scarred wooden desk, and a detention cage, Cindy felt it might be best to terminate their relationship immediately rather than court the possibility of trauma induced by slow and painful withdrawal.

That had been three weeks ago, and he had not seen nor called Cindy since, and the pain of the breakup was equalled only by the pain of the bursitis in his right shoulder, despite the fact that he was wearing a copper bracelet on his wrist. The bracelet had been given to him by none other than Meyer Meyer, whom no one would have dreamed of as a superstitious man given to beliefs in ridiculous claims. The bracelet was supposed to begin working in ten days (Well, maybe two weeks, Meyer had said, hedging) and Kling had been wearing it for eleven days now, with no relief for the bursitis, but with a noticeable green stain round his wrist just below the bracelet. Hope springs eternal. Somewhere in his race memory, there lurked a hulking ape-like creature rubbing animal teeth by a fire, praying in grunts for a splendid hunt on the morrow. Somewhere also in his race memory, though not as far back, was the image of Cindy Forrest naked in his arms, and the concomitant fantasy that she would call to say she'd made a terrible mistake and was ready to drop her psychiatrist pal. No Woman's Lib man he, Kling nonetheless felt it perfectly all right for Cindy to take the initiative in re-establishing their relationship; it was she, after all, who had taken the first and final step towards ending it. Meanwhile, his bursitis hurt like hell and the elevator operator was not one of those bright snappy young men on the way up (Kling winced; he hated puns even when he made them himself) but rather a stupid clod who had difficulty remembering his own name. Kling went over the same tired ground yet another time.

'Do you know Mr Fletcher by sight?' he asked.

'Oh, yeah,' the elevator operator said.

'What does he look like?'

'Oh, you know, he calls me Max.'

'Yes, Max, but ...'

'"Hello, Max," he says, "How are you, Max?" I say, "Hello there, Mr Fletcher, nice day today, huh?"'

'Could you describe him for me, please?'

'He's nice and handsome.'

'What colour are his eyes?'

'Brown? Blue? Something like that.'

'How tall is he?'

'Tall.'

'Taller than you?'

'Oh, sure.'

'Taller than me?'

'Oh, no. About the same. Mr Fletcher is about the same.'

'What colour hair does he have?'

'White.'

'White? Do you mean grey?'

'White, grey, something like that.'

'Which was it, Max, would you remember?'

'Oh, something like that. Ask Phil. He knows. He's good on times and things like that.'

Phil was the doorman. He was very good on times and things like that. He was also a garrulous lonely old man who welcomed the opportunity to be in a cops-and-robbers documentary film. Kling could not disabuse Phil of the notion that this was a *real* investigation; there was a dead lady upstairs and someone had brought about her present condition, and it was the desire of the police to bring that person to justice, ta-ra.

'Oh, yeah, yeah,' Phil said, 'terrible the way things are getting in this city, ain't it? Even when I was a kid, things wasn't this terrible. I was born over on the South Side, you know, in a neighbourhood where if you wore shoes you were considered a sissy. We were all the time fighting with the wop gangs, you know? We used to drop things down on them from the rooftops. Bricks, eggs, scrap iron, a toaster one time – yeah, I swear to God, we once threw my mother's old toaster off the roof, *bang*, it hit one of them wop's right on the head, bad place to hit a wop, of course, never does him no damage there. What I'm saying, though, is it never was so bad like it is now. Even when we were beating up the wops all the time, and them vice versa, it was fun, you know what I mean? I mean, it was *fun* in those days. Nowadays, what happens? Nowadays, you step in the elevator, there's some crazy fiend, he shoves a gun under your nose and says he'll blow your head off if you don't give him all your money. That happened to Dr Haskins, you think I'm kidding? He's coming home three o'clock in the morning, he goes in the elevator and Max is out taking a leak, so it's on self-service. Only there's a guy in the elevator, God knows how he even got in the building, probably came down from the roof, they jump rooftops like mountain goats, them dope fiends, and he sticks the gun right up under Dr Haskins' nose, right here, right pointing up his nostrils, for Christ's sake, and he says, Give me all your money and also whatever dope you got in that bag. So Dr Haskins figures What the hell, I'm going to get killed here for a lousy forty dollars and two vials of cocaine, here take it, good riddance. So he gives the guy what he wants, and you know what the guy does, anyway? He beats up Dr Haskins. They had to take him to the hospital with seven stitches, the son of a bitch split his forehead open with the butt of the pistol, he pistol-whipped him, you know? What kind of thing is that, huh? This city stinks, and especially this neighbourhood. I can remember this neighbourhood when you could come home three, four, five, even *six* o'clock in the morning, who cared what time you came home; you could be wearing a tuxedo and a mink coat, who cared what you were wearing, your jewels, your diamond cuff links, nobody bothered you. Try that today. Try walking down the street after dark without a Doberman pinscher on a leash, see how far you get. They smell you coming, these dope fiends, they leap out at you from doorways. We had a lot of burglaries in this building, all dope fiends. They come down from the roof, you know? We must've fixed that lock on the roof door a hundred times, what difference does it make? They're all experts, as soon as we fix it, *boom*, it's busted open again. Or they come up the fire escapes, who can stop them? Next thing you know, they're in some apartment stealing the whole place, you're lucky if they leave your false teeth in the glass. I don't know what this city's coming to, I swear to God. It's disgraceful.'

'What about Mr Fletcher?' Kling asked.

'What about him? He's a decent man, a lawyer. He comes home, and what does he find? He finds his wife dead on the floor, probably killed by some crazy dope fiend. Is that a way to live? Who needs it? You can't even go in your own bedroom without somebody jumping on you? What kind of thing is that?'

'When did Mr Fletcher come home tonight?'

'About ten-thirty,' Phil said.

'Are you sure of the time?'

'Positive. You know how I remember? There's Mrs Horowitz, she lives in 12C, she either doesn't have an alarm clock, or else she doesn't know how to set the alarm since her husband passed away two years ago. So every night she calls down to ask me the correct time, and to say would the day-man call her at such and such a time in the morning, to wake her up. This ain't a hotel, but what the hell, an old woman asks a simple favour, you're supposed to refuse it? Besides, she's very generous at Christmas, which ain't too far away, huh? So tonight, she calls down and says, "What's the correct time, Phil?" and I look at my watch and tell her it's ten-thirty, and just then Mr Fletcher pulls up in a taxicab. Mrs Horowitz says will I please ask the day-man to wake her up at seven-thirty, and I tell her I will and then go out to the kerb to carry Mr Fletcher's bag in. That's how I remember exactly what time it was.'

'Did Mr Fletcher go directly upstairs?'

'Directly,' Phil said. 'Why? Where would he go? For a walk in this neighbourhood at ten-thirty in the night? That's like taking a walk off a gangplank.'

'Well, thanks a lot,' Kling said.

'Don't mention it,' Phil said. 'They shot another movie around here one time.'

Back at the ranch, they weren't shooting a movie. They were standing in an informal triangle around Gerald Fletcher, and raising their eyebrows at the answers he gave them. The three points of the triangle were Detective-Lieutenant Peter Byrnes and Detectives Meyer and Carella. Fletcher sat in a chair with his arms crossed over his chest. He was still wearing homburg, muffler, overcoat, and gloves, as if he expected to be called outdoors at any moment and wanted to be fully prepared for the inclement weather. The interrogation was being conducted in a windowless cubicle euphemistically labelled on its frosted glass door INTERROGATION ROOM. Opulently furnished in Institutional Wood, circa 1919, the room sported a long table, two straight-backed chairs, and a framed mirror. The mirror hung on a wall opposite the table. It was (heh-heh) a one-way mirror, which meant that on *this* side you saw your own reflection when you looked into the glass, but if you were standing on the *other* side, you could look into the room and observe all sorts of criminal behaviour while remaining unseen yourself; devious are the ways of law enforcers the world over. Devious, too, are the ways of criminals; there was not a single criminal in the entire city who did not recognize a one-way mirror the minute he laid eyes upon it. Quite often, in fact, criminals with a comic flair had been known to approach the mirror, place a thumb to the nose, and waggle the fingers of the hand as a gesture of esteem and affection to the eavesdropping cops on the other side of the glass. In such ways were mutual respect and admiration built between the men who broke the law and the men who tried to uphold it. Crime does not pay – but it doesn't hurt to have a few laughs along the way, as Euripides once remarked.

The cops standing in their loose triangle around Gerald Fletcher were amazed but not too terribly amused by his honesty; or, to be more exact, his downright brutal frankness. It was one thing to discuss the death of one's spouse without frills or furbelows; it was quite another to court lifelong imprisonment in a state penitentiary. Gerald Fletcher seemed to be doing precisely that.

'I hated her guts,' he said, and Meyer raised his eyebrows and glanced at Byrnes, who in turn raised his eyebrows and glanced at Carella, who was facing the one-way mirror and had the opportunity of witnessing his own reflection raising *its* eyebrows.

'Mr Fletcher,' Byrnes said, 'I know you understand your rights, as we explained them to you . . .'

'I understood them long before you explained them,' Fletcher said.

'And I know you've chosen to answer our questions without an attorney present . . .'

'I *am* an attorney.'

'What I meant . . .'

'I know what you meant. Yes, I'm willing to answer any and all questions without counsel.'

'I *still* feel I must warn you that a woman has been murdered . . .'

'Yes, my dear, wonderful wife,' Fletcher said sarcastically.

'Which is a serious crime . . .'

'Which, among felonies, may very well be the choicest of the lot,' Fletcher said.

'Yes,' Byrnes said. He was not an articulate man, but he felt somewhat tongue-tied in Fletcher's presence. Bullet-headed, hair turning from iron-grey to ice-white (slight bald spot beginning to show at the back), blue-eyed, built like a compact linebacker for the Minnesota Vikings, Byrnes straightened the knot in his tie, cleared his throat, and looked to his colleagues for support. Both Meyer and Carella were watching their shoelaces.

'Well, look,' Byrnes said, 'if *you* understand what you're doing, go right ahead. We warned you.'

'Indeed you *have* warned me. Repeatedly. I can't imagine why,' Fletcher said, 'since I don't feel myself to be in any particular danger. My wife is dead, someone killed the bitch. But it was not me.'

'Well, it's nice to have your assurance of that, Mr Fletcher, but your assurance alone doesn't necessarily still our doubts,' Carella said, hearing the words and wondering where the hell they were coming from. He was, he realized, trying to impress Fletcher, trying to ward off the man's obvious condescension by courting his acceptance. Look at me, he was pleading, listen to me. I'm not just a dumb bull, I'm a man of sensitivity and intelligence, able to understand your vocabulary, your sarcasm, and even your vituperative wit. Half-sitting upon, half-leaning against the scarred wooden table, a tall athletic-looking man with straight brown hair, brown eyes curiously slanted downwards, Carella folded his arms across his chest in unconscious imitation of Fletcher. The moment he realized what he was doing, he uncrossed his arms at once, and stared intently at Fletcher, waiting for an answer. Fletcher stared intently back.

'Well?' Carella said.

'Well what, Detective Carella?'

'Well, what do you have to say?'

'About what?'

'How do we know it *wasn't* you who stabbed her?'

'To begin with,' Fletcher said, 'there were signs of forcible entry in the kitchen and hasty departure in the bedroom – witness the wide-open window in the aforementioned room, and the shattered window in the latter. The drawers in the dining-room sideboard were open ...'

'You're a very observant person,' Meyer said suddenly. 'Did you notice all this in the four minutes it took you to enter the apartment and call the police?'

'It's my *job* to be an observant person,' Fletcher said, 'but to answer your question, no. I noticed all this *after* I had spoken to Detective Carella here, and *while* he was on the phone reporting to your lieutenant. I might add that I've lived in that apartment on Silvermine Oval for the past twelve years, and that it doesn't take a particularly sharp-eyed man to notice that a bedroom window is smashed or a kitchen window open. Nor does it take a sleuth to realize that the family silver has been pilfered – especially when there are several serving spoons, soup ladles, and butter knives scattered on the bedroom floor beneath the shattered window. Have you checked the alleyway below the window? You're liable to find your murderer still lying there.'

'Your apartment is on the second floor, Mr Fletcher,' Meyer said.

'Which is why I suggested he might still be there,' Fletcher answered. 'Nursing a broken leg or a fractured skull.'

'In all my years of experience,' Meyer said, and Carella suddenly realized that *he*, too, was trying to impress Fletcher. 'I have never known a criminal to jump out a window on the second floor of a building.' (Carella was surprised he hadn't used the word 'defenestrate'.)

'*This* criminal may have had good reason for imprudent action,' Fletcher said. 'He had just killed a woman, probably after coming upon her unexpectedly in an apartment he thought was empty. He had heard someone opening the front door, and had realized he could not leave the apartment the way he'd come in, the kitchen being too close to the entrance. He undoubtedly figured he would rather risk a broken leg than the penitentiary for life. How does *that* portrait compare to those of other Criminals You Have Known?'

'I've known *lots* of criminals,' Meyer said inanely, 'and some of them are too smart for their own damn good.' He felt idiotic even as he delivered his little preachment, but Fletcher had a way of making a man feel like a cretin. Meyer ran his hand self-consciously over his bald pate, his eyes avoiding the glances of Carella and Byrnes. Somehow, he felt he had let them all down. Somehow, a rapier thrust had been called for, and he had delivered only a puny mumbletypeg penknife flip. 'What about that knife, Mr Fletcher?' he said. 'Ever see it before?'

'Never.'

'It doesn't happen to be *your* knife, does it?' Carella asked.

'It does not.'

'Did your wife say anything to you when you entered the bedroom?'

'My wife was dead when I entered the bedroom.'

'You're sure of that?'

'I'm positive of it.'

'All right, Mr Fletcher,' Byrnes said abruptly. 'You want to wait outside, please?'

'Certainly,' Fletcher said, and rose, and left the room. The three detectives stood in silence for a respectable number of minutes. Then Byrnes said, 'What do you think?'

'I think he did it,' Carella said.

'What makes you think so?'

'Let me revise that.'

'Go ahead, revise it.'

'I think he *could* have done it.'

'Even with all those signs of a burglary?'

'*Especially* with all those signs.'

'Spell it out, Steve.'

'He could have come home, found his wife stabbed – but not fatally – and finished her off by yanking the knife across her belly. The M.E.'s report says that death was probably instantaneous, either caused by severance of the abdominal aorta, or reflex shock, or both. Fletcher had four minutes when all he needed was maybe four *seconds*.'

'It's possible,' Meyer said.

'Or maybe I just don't like the son of a bitch,' Carella added.

'Let's see what the lab comes up with,' Byrnes said.

There were good fingerprints on the kitchen window sash, and on the silver drawer of the dining-room sideboard. There were good prints on some of the pieces of silver scattered on the floor near the smashed bedroom window. More important, although most of the prints on the handle of the switchblade knife were smeared, some of them were very good indeed. All of the prints matched; they had all been left by the same person.

Gerald Fletcher graciously allowed the police to take *his* fingers, which were then compared with those Marshall Davies had sent over from the police laboratory. The fingerprints on the window, the drawer, the silverware, and the knife did not match Gerald Fletcher's.

Which didn't mean a damn thing if he had been wearing his gloves when he finished her off.

Chapter Two

On Monday morning, the sky above the River Harb was a cloudless blue. In Silvermine Park, young mothers were already pushing baby buggies, eager to take advantage of the unexpected December sunshine. The air was cold and sharp, but the sun was brilliant and it transformed the streets bordering the river into what they must have looked like at the turn of the century. A tugboat hooted, a gull shrieked and swooped low over the water, a woman tucked a blanket up under her baby's chin and cooed to him gently. Near the park railing, a patrolman stood with his hands behind his back, and idly stared out over the sun-dappled river.

Upstairs, in the second-floor rear apartment of 721 Silvermine Oval, a chalked outline on the bedroom floor was the only evidence that a woman had lain there in death the night before. Carella and Kling sidestepped the outline and moved to the shattered window. The lab boys had carefully lifted, packaged, and labelled the shards and slivers of glass, on the assumption that whoever had jumped through the window might have left bloodstains or clothing threads behind. Carella looked through the gaping irregular hole at the narrow alleyway below. There was a distance of perhaps twelve feet between this building and the one across from it. Conceivably, the intruder could have leaped across the shaftway, caught the windowsill on the opposite wall, and then boosted himself up into the apartment there. But this would have required premeditation and calculation, and if a person is going to make a trapeze leap for a windowsill, he doesn't dive through a closed window in haste and panic. The apartment across the way would have to be checked, of course; but the more probable likelihood was that the intruder had fallen to the pavement below.

'That's a long drop,' Kling said, peering over Carella's shoulder.

'How far do you figure?'

'Thirty feet. At least.'

'Got to break a leg taking a fall like that.'

'Maybe the guy's an acrobat.'

'You think he went through the window head first?'

'How else?'

'He might have broken the glass out first, and then gone through.'

'If he was about to go to all that trouble, why didn't he just *open* the damn thing?'

'Well, let's take a look,' Carella said.

They examined the latch, and they examined the sash.

'Okay to touch this?' Kling asked.

'Yeah, they're through with it.'

Kling grabbed both handles on the window frame and pulled up on them. 'Tough one,' he said.

'Try it again.'

Kling tugged again. 'I think it's stuck.'

'Probably painted shut,' Carella said.

'Maybe he *did* try to open it. Maybe he smashed it only when he realized it was stuck.'

'Yeah,' Carella said. 'And in a big hurry, too. Fletcher was opening the front door, maybe already in the apartment by then.'

'The guy probably swung his bag ...'

'What bag?'

'Must've had a bag or something with him, don't you think? To put the loot in?'

'Probably. Though he couldn't have been too experienced.'

'What do you mean?'

'No gloves. Left prints all over the place. Got to be a beginner.'

'Even so, he'd have carried a bag. That's probably what he smashed the window with. Which might explain why there was silverware on the floor. He could've taken a wild swing when he realized the window was stuck, and maybe some of the stuff fell out of the bag.'

'Yeah, maybe,' Carella said.

'Then he probably climbed through the hole and dropped down feet first. That makes more sense than just *diving* through the thing, doesn't it? In fact, what he could've done, Steve, was drop the bag down first . . .'

'If he had a bag.'

'Every burglar in the world has a bag. Even beginners.'

'Well, maybe.'

'Well, *if* he had a bag, he could've dropped it down into the alley there, and *then* climbed out and hung from the sill before he jumped, you know what I mean? To make it a shorter distance.'

'I don't know if he had all that much time, Bert. Fletcher must've been in the apartment and heading for the bedroom by then.'

'Did Fletcher say anything about glass breaking? About hearing glass?'

'I don't remember asking him.'

'We'll have to ask him,' Kling said.

'Why? What difference does it make?'

'I don't know,' Kling said, and shrugged. 'But if the guy was still in the apartment when Fletcher came in . . .'

'Yeah?'

'Well, that cuts it very close, doesn't it?'

'He *must've* been here, Bert. He *had* to hear that front door opening. Otherwise, he'd have taken his good sweet time and gone out the kitchen window and down the fire escape, the way he'd come.'

'Yeah, that's right.' Kling nodded reflectively. 'Fletcher's lucky,' he said. 'The guy could just as easily have waited and stabbed *him*, too.'

'Let's take a look at that alley,' Carella said.

The woman looking through the ground-floor window saw only two big men in overcoats, poking around on the alley floor. Both men were hatless. One of them had brown hair and slanty Chinese eyes. The other one looked younger but no less menacing, a big blond tough with hardly nothing but peach fuzz on his face, the better to eat you, Grandma. She immediately went to the telephone and called the police.

In the alleyway, unaware of the woman who peered out at them from between the slats of her venetian blinds, Carella and Kling studied the concrete pavement, and then looked up at the shattered second-floor window of the Fletcher apartment.

'It's still a hell of a long drop,' Kling said.

'Looks even longer from down here.'

'Where do you suppose he'd have landed?'

'Right about where we're standing. Maybe a foot or so over,' Carella said, and looked at the ground.

'See anything?' Kling asked.

'No. I was just trying to figure something.'

'What?'

'Let's say he *did* land without breaking anything . . .'

'Well, he must've, Steve. Otherwise he'd still be laying here.'

'That's just my point. Even if he *didn't* break anything, I can't believe he just got up and walked away, can you?' He looked up at the window again. 'That's got to be at least forty feet, Bert.'

'Gets longer every minute,' Kling said. 'I still think it's no more than thirty, give or take.'

'Even so. A guy drops thirty feet ...'

'If he hung from the windowsill first, you've got to subtract maybe ten feet from that figure.'

'Okay, so what do we say? A twenty-foot drop?'

'Give or take.'

'Guy drops twenty feet to a concrete pavement, doesn't break anything, gets up, dusts himself off, and runs the fifty-yard dash, right?' Carella shook his head. 'My guess is he stayed right where he was for a while. To at least catch his breath.'

'So?'

'So did Fletcher look out the window?'

'Why would he?'

'If your wife is dead on the floor with a knife in her, and the window is broken, wouldn't you naturally go to the window and look out? On the off chance you might spot the guy who killed her?'

'He was anxious to call the police,' Kling said.

'Why?'

'That's natural, Steve. If the guy's innocent, he's anxious to keep in the clear. He calls the police, he stays in the apartment ...'

'I still think he did it,' Carella said.

'Don't make a federal case out of this,' Kling said. 'I personally would like nothing better than to kick Mr Fletcher in the balls, but let's concentrate on finding the guy whose fingerprints we've got, okay?'

'Yeah,' Carella said.

'I mean, Steve, be reasonable. If a guy's fingerprints are on the handle of a knife, and the knife is still in the goddamn victim ...'

'*And* if the victim's husband realizes what a sweet setup he's stumbled into,' Carella said, 'wife laying on the floor with a knife in her, place broken into and burglarized, why *not* finish the job and hope the burglar will be blamed?'

'Sure,' Kling said. 'Prove it.'

'I can't,' Carella said. 'Not until we catch the burglar.'

'All right, so let's catch him. Where do you think he went after he dropped down here?'

'One of two ways,' Carella said. 'Either through the door there into the basement of the building. Or over the fence there at the other end of the alley.'

'Which way would you go?'

'If I'd just dropped twenty feet or more, I'd go home to my mother and cry.'

'I'd head for the door of the building. If I'd just dropped twenty feet, I wouldn't feel like climbing any fences.'

'Not with the terrible headache you'd probably have.'

The basement door suddenly opened. A red-faced patrolman was standing in the doorway with a .38 in his fist.

'All right, you guys, what's going on here?' he said.

'Oh, great,' Carella said.

*   *   *

Anyway, Marshall Davies had already done the work.

So while Carella and Kling went through the tedious routine of proving to a cop that they were cops themselves, Davies called the 87th Precinct and asked to talk to the detective who was handling the Fletcher homicide. Since *both* detectives who were handling the homicide were at that moment out handling it, or *trying* to, Davies agreed to talk to Detective Meyer instead.

'What've you got?' Meyer asked.

'I think I've got some fairly interesting information about the suspect.'

'Will I need a pencil?' Meyer asked.

'I don't think so. How much do you know about the case?'

'I've been filled in.'

'Then you know there were latent prints all over the apartment.'

'Yes. We've got the I.S. running a check on them now.'

'Maybe you'll get lucky.'

'Maybe,' Meyer said.

'Do you also know there were footprints in the kitchen?'

'No, I didn't know that.'

'Yes, a very good one in the sink, probably left there when he climbed through the window, and some middling-fair ones tracking across the kitchen floor to the dining room. I got some excellent pictures, and some very good blowups of the heel – for comparison purposes if the need arises later on.'

'Good,' Meyer said.

'But more important,' Davies said, 'I got a good walking picture from the footprints on the floor, and I think we can assume it was the man's usual gait, neither dawdling nor hurried.'

'How can you tell that?' Meyer asked.

'Well, if a man is walking slowly, the distance between his footprints is usually about twenty-seven inches. If he's running, his footprints will be about forty inches apart. Thirty-five inches apart is the average for fast walking.'

'How far apart were the prints you got?'

'Thirty-two inches. He was moving quickly, but he wasn't in a desperate hurry. The walking line, incidentally, was normal and not broken.'

'What does that mean?'

'Well, draw an imaginary line in the direction the suspect was walking, and that line should normally run along the inner edge of the heelprints. Fat people and pregnant ladies will often leave a broken walking line because they walk with their feet spread wider apart ... to keep their balance.'

'But *this* walking line was normal,' Meyer said.

'Right,' Davies said.

'So our man is neither fat nor pregnant.'

'Right. Incidentally, it *is* a man. The size and type of the shoe, and also the angle of the foot indicate that clearly.'

'Okay, fine,' Meyer said. He did not thus far consider Davies' information valuable nor even terribly important. They had automatically assumed that anyone burglarizing an apartment would be a man and not a woman. Moreover, according to Carella's report on the size of the footprint in the sink, it had definitely been left by a man – unless a female Russian wrestler was loose in the precinct. Meyer yawned.

'Anyway, none of this is valuable nor even terribly important,' Davies said, 'until we consider the rest of the data.'

'And what's that?' Meyer asked.

'Well, as you know, the bedroom window was smashed, and the Homicide men at the scene ...'

'Monoghan and Monroe?'

'Yes, were speculating that the suspect had jumped through the window into the alley below. I didn't think it would hurt to go downstairs and see if I could get some meaningful pictures.'

'Did you get some meaningful pictures?'

'Yes, I got some pictures of where he must have landed – on both feet, incidentally – and I also got another walking picture and direction line. He moved towards the basement door and into the basement. That's not the important thing, however.'

'What *is* the important thing?' Meyer asked patiently.

'Our man is injured. And I think badly.'

'How do you know?'

'The walking picture downstairs is entirely different from the one in the kitchen. The footprints are the same, of course, no question but that the same person left them. But the walking line indicates that the person was leaning quite heavily on the left leg and dragging the right. There are, in fact, no *flat* footprints for the right foot, only scrape marks where the edges of the sole and heel were pulled along the concrete. I would suggest that whoever's handling the case put out a physician's bulletin. If this guy hasn't got a broken leg, I'll eat the pictures I took.'

A girl in a green coat was waiting in the lobby. Leaning against the wall, hands thrust deep into the slash pockets of the coat, she turned towards the basement door the instant it opened. Carella and Kling, followed by the red-faced patrolman (who was slightly *more* red-faced at the moment), came through the doorway and were starting for the street when the girl said, 'Excuse me, are you the detectives?'

'Yes?' Carella said.

'Hey, listen, I'm sorry,' the patrolman said. 'I just got transferred up here, you know, I ain't too familiar with all you guys.'

'That's okay,' Kling said.

'The super told me you were in the building,' the girl said.

'So, like excuse it, huh?' the patrolman said.

'Right, right,' Kling said, and waved him towards the front door.

'You're investigating the Fletcher murder, aren't you?' the girl said. She was quite soft-spoken, a tall girl with dark hair and large brown eyes that shifted alternately from one detective to the other, as though searching for the most receptive audience.

'How can we help you, miss?' Carella asked.

'I saw somebody in the basement last night,' she said. 'With blood on his clothes.'

Carella glanced at Kling, and immediately said, 'What time was this?'

'About a quarter to eleven,' the girl said.

'What were you doing in the basement?'

'My *clothes*,' the girl said, sounding surprised. 'That's where the washing machines are. I'm sorry, my name is Nora Simonov. I live here in the building.'

'So long, you guys,' the patrolman called from the front door. 'Excuse it, huh?'

'Right, right,' Kling said.

'I live on the fifth floor,' Nora said. 'Apartment 5A.'

'Tell us what happened, will you?' Carella said.

'I was sitting by the machine, watching the clothes tumble – which is simply *fascinating*, you know,' she said, and rolled her eyes and flashed a quick, surprising smile, 'when the door leading to the backyard opened. The door to the alley. You know the door I mean?'

'Yes,' Carella said.

'And this man came down the stairs. I don't even think he saw me. The machines are sort of off to the side, you know. He went straight for the steps at the other end, the ones that go up to the street. There are two flights of steps. One goes to the lobby, the other goes to the street. He went up to the street.'

'Was he anyone you recognized?'

'What do you mean?'

'From the building? Or the neighbourhood?'

'No. I'd never seen him before last night.'

'Can you describe him?'

'Sure. He was about twenty-one, twenty-two years old, your height and weight, well, maybe a little bit shorter, five-ten or eleven. Brown hair.'

Kling was already writing. 'Notice the colour of his eyes?' he said.

'No, I'm sorry.'

'Was he white or black?'

'White.'

'What was he wearing?'

'Dark trousers, high-topped sneakers, a poplin windbreaker. With blood on the sleeve and on the front.'

'Which sleeve?'

'The right one.'

'Any hat?'

'No.'

'Was he carrying anything?'

'Yes. A small red bag. It looked like one of those bags the airlines give you.'

'Any scars, tattoos, marks?'

'Well, I couldn't say. He wasn't that close. And he went by in pretty much of a hurry, considering.'

'Considering *what*?' Carella asked.

'His leg. He was dragging his right leg. I think he was hurt pretty badly.'

'Would you recognize him if you saw him again?' Carella asked.

'In a minute,' Nora said.

What they had in mind, of course, was identification from a mug shot. What they had in mind was the possibility that the I.S. would come up with something positive on the fingerprints that had been sent downtown. What they all hoped was that maybe, just once, it would turn out to be a nice, easy one – the Identification Section would send them the record of a known criminal, and they would pick him up without a fuss, and parade him in a squadroom lineup, from which Nora Simonov would pick him out as the man she had seen in the basement at 10:45 the night before, with blood on his clothes.

The I.S. reported that none of the fingerprints in their file matched the ones found in the apartment.

So the detectives sighed, and figured it was going to be a tough one after all (They are *all* tough ones, after all, they groaned, awash in a sea of self-pity), and did exactly what Marshall Davies had suggested: they sent out a bulletin to all of the city's doctors, asking them to report any leg fractures or sprains suffered by a white man in his early twenties, five feet ten or eleven inches tall, weighing approximately 180 pounds, brown hair, last seen wearing dark trousers, high-topped sneakers, and a poplin windbreaker with bloodstains on the front and on the right sleeve.

And, just to prove that cops can be as wrong as anyone else, it turned out to be a nice, easy one, after all.

The call came from a physician in Riverhead at 4:37 that afternoon, just as Carella was ready to go home.

'This is Dr Mendelsohn,' he said. 'I have your bulletin here, and I want to report treating a man who fits your description.'

'Where are you located, Dr Mendelsohn?' Carella asked.

'On Dover Plains Avenue. In Riverhead. 3461 Dover Plains.'

'When did you treat this man?'

'Early this morning. I have early office hours on Monday. It's my day at the hospital.'

'What did you treat him for?'

'A bad ankle sprain.'

'No fracture?'

'None. We X-rayed the leg here. It was quite swollen, and I suspected a fracture, of course, but it was merely a bad sprain. I taped it for him, and advised him to stay off it for a while.'

'Did he give you his name?'

'Yes. I have it right here.'

'May I have it, sir?'

'Ralph Corwin.'

'Any address?'

'894 Woodside.'

'In Riverhead?'

'Yes.'

'Thank you, Dr Mendelsohn,' Carella said.

'Not at all,' Mendelsohn said, and hung up.

Carella pulled the Riverhead telephone directory from the top drawer of his desk, and quickly flipped to the C's. He did not expect to find a listing for Ralph Corwin. A man would have to be a rank amateur to first burglarize an apartment without wearing gloves, then stab a woman to death, and then give his name when seeking treatment for an injury sustained in escaping from the murder apartment.

Ralph Corwin was apparently a rank amateur.

His name was in the phone book, and the address he'd given the doctor was as true as the day was long.

They kicked in the door without warning, fanning into the room, guns drawn.

The man on the bed was wearing only undershorts. His right ankle was taped. The bedsheets were soiled, and the stench of vomit in the close, hot room was overpowering.

'Are you Ralph Corwin?' Carella asked.

'Yes,' the man said. His face was drawn, the eyes squinched in pain.

'Police officers,' Carella said.

'What do you want?'

'We want to ask you some questions. Get dressed, Corwin.'

'There's nothing to ask,' he said, and turned his head into the pillow. 'I killed her.'

Chapter Three

Ralph Corwin made his confession in the presence of two detectives of the 87th Squad, a police stenographer, an assistant district attorney, and a lawyer appointed by the Legal Aid Society. The man from the D.A.'s office conducted the Q and A.

Q: What is your name, please?

A: Ralph Corwin.

Q: Where do you live, Mr Corwin?'

A: 894 Woodside Avenue. In Riverhead.

Q: Will you relate to us, please, the events that took place on the night of December twelfth. That would be last night, Mr Corwin, Sunday, December twelfth.

A: Where do you want me to start?

Q: Did you enter a building at 721 Silvermine Oval?

A: I did.

Q: How did you enter the building?

A: First I went down the steps from the street, where the garbage cans were. I went in the basement, and through the basement and up the steps at the other end, into the backyard. Then I climbed up the fire escape.

Q: What time was this?

A: I went in the building at about ten o'clock.

Q: Ten p.m.?

A: Yes, ten p.m.

Q: What did you do then?

A: I went in an apartment.

Q: Which apartment?

A: Second-floor rear.

Q: Why did you go into the apartment?

A: To rip it off.

Q: To burglarize it?

A: Yes.

Q: Had you ever been in this building before?

A: No. I never done nothing like this in my life before. Never. I'm a junkie, that's true, but I never stole nothing in my life before this. Nor hurt nobody, either. I wouldn't have stole now, except this girl I was living with left me, and I was desperate. She used to give me whatever bread I needed. But she left me. Friday. She just walked out.

Q: Which girl is that?

A: Do we have to drag her in? She's got nothing to do with it. She never done me no harm, I got no hard feelings towards her, even though she walked out. She was always good to me. I don't want to drag her name in this.

Q: You say you had never been in this building before?

A: Never.

Q: Why did you pick this particular apartment to enter?

A: It was the first one I saw without no lights inside. I figured there was nobody home.

Q: How did you get into the apartment?

A: The kitchen window was open a tiny crack. I squeezed my fingers under the bottom of it, and opened it all the way.

Q: Were you wearing gloves?

A: No.

Q: Why not?

A: I don't have no gloves. Gloves cost money. I'm a junkie.

Q: Weren't you afraid of leaving fingerprints?

A: I figured that was crap. For the movies, you know? For television. Anyway, I don't *have* no gloves, so what difference does it make?

Q: What did you do after you opened the window?

A: I stepped in the sink, and then down to the floor.

Q: Then what?

A: I had this little flashlight. So I used it to find my way across the kitchen to the dining room.

Q: Would you look at this photograph, please?

A: Yeah?

Q: Is this the kitchen you were in?

A: I don't know. It was dark. I guess it could be. I don't know.

Q: What did you do in the dining room?

A: I found where they kept the silverware, and I emptied the drawer and put the stuff in this airlines bag I had with me. I had to go to Chicago last month because my father died, so I went by plane, and I bought this little airlines bag. My girl friend paid for me to fly out there. She was a great girl, I wish I could figure why she left. I wouldn't be in this trouble now, if she'd stayed, you know that? I never stole nothing in my life, nothing, I swear to God. And I never hurt nobody. I don't know what got into me. I must've been scared out of my wits. That's the only thing I can figure.

Q: Where did you go when you left the dining room?

A: I was looking for the bedroom.

Q: Was the flashlight on?

A: Yeah. It's just this little flashlight. A penlight is what they call them. A tiny little thing, you know? So you can have some light.

Q: Why were you looking for the bedroom?

A: I figured that's where people leave watches and rings, stuff like that. I was going to take whatever jewellery I could find and then get out. I'm not a pro, I was just hung up real bad and needed some bread to tide me over.

Q: Did you find the bedroom?

A: I found it.

Q: What happened?

A: There was a lady in bed. This was only like close to ten-thirty, you don't expect nobody to be asleep so early, you know what I mean? I thought the apartment was empty.

Q: But there was a woman in bed.

A: Yeah. She turned on the light the minute I stepped in the room.

Q: What did you do?

A: I had a knife in my pocket. I pulled it out.

Q: Why?

A: To scare her.

Q: Would you look at this knife, please?

A: Yeah, it's mine.

Q: This is the knife you took from your pocket?

A: Yeah. Yes.

Q: Did the woman say anything to you?

A: Yeah, it was almost comical. I mean, when I think back on it, it was comical, though at the time I was very scared. But it was like a movie, you know? Just like a movie. She looks at me and she says 'What are you doing here?' Which is funny, don't you think? I mean, what did she *think* I was doing there?

Q: Did you say anything to her?

A: I told her to keep quiet, that I wasn't going to hurt her.

Q: Then what?

A: She got out of bed. Not all the way, she just threw the covers back, and swung her legs over the side, you know? Sitting, you know? I didn't realize what was happening for a minute, and then I saw she was reaching for the phone. That's got to be crazy, right? A guy is standing there in your bedroom with a knife in his hand, so she reaches for the phone.

Q: What did you do?

A: I grabbed her hand before she could get it. I pulled her off the bed, away from the phone, you know? And I told her again that nobody was going to hurt her, that I was getting out of there right away, to just please calm down.

Q: You said that?

A: What?

Q: You asked her to calm down?

A: I don't know if those were the exact words, but I told her like to take it easy because I could see she was getting hysterical.

Q: Would you look at this photograph, please? Is this the bedroom you were in?

A: Yeah. There's the night table with the phone on it, and there's the window I went out. That's the room.

Q: What happened next?

A: She started to scream.

Q: What did you do when she screamed?

A: I told her to stop. I was beginning to panic by now. I mean, she was really yelling.

Q: Did she stop?

A: No.

Q: What did you do?

A: I stabbed her.

Q: Where did you stab her?

A: I don't know. It was a reflex. She was yelling, I was afraid the whole building would come down. I just ... I just stuck the knife in her. I was very scared.

Q: Did you stab her in the chest?

A: No.

Q: Where?

A: The belly. Some place in the belly.

Q: How many times did you stab her?

A: Once. She ... she backed away from me, I'll never forget the look on her face. And she ... she fell on the floor.

Q: Would you look at this photograph, please?

A: Oh, Jesus.

Q: Is that the woman you stabbed?

A: Oh, Jesus. Oh, Jesus, I didn't think ... oh, Jesus.

Q: Is that the woman?

A: Yes. Yes, that's her. Yes.

Q: What happened next?

A: Can I have a drink of water?

Q: Get him a drink of water. You stabbed her, and she fell to the floor. What happened next?

A: There was ...

Q: Yes?

A: There was somebody at the door. I heard the door opening. Then somebody came in.

Q: Came into the apartment?

A: Yes. And yelled her name.

Q: From the front door?

A: I guess. From some place at the other end of the apartment.

Q: Called her name?

A: Yeah. He yelled, 'Sarah!' and when he got no answer, he yelled, 'Sarah, it's me, I'm home.'

Q: Then what?

A: I knew I was trapped. I couldn't go out the way I come in because this guy was home. So I ran past the ... the woman where she was laying on the floor ... Jesus ... and I tried to open the window, but it was stuck. So I smashed it with the airlines bag and ... I didn't know what to do ... I was on the second floor, how was I going to get out? I threw the bag down first because I figured no matter what happened I was going to need bread for another fix, and then I climbed through the broken window – I cut my hand on a piece of glass – and I hung down from the sill, scared to let go, and finally I let go, I had to let go.

Q: Yes?

A: I must've dropped a mile, it felt like a mile. The minute I hit, I knew I busted something. I tried to get up, and I fell right down. My ankle was killing me, my hand was bleeding. I must've been in that alley ten, fifteen minutes, trying to stand up, falling down, trying again. I finally made it. I finally got out of that alley.

Q: Where did you go?

A: Through the basement and up to the street. The way I come in.

Q: And where did you go from there?

A: I took the subway home. To Riverhead. I turned on the radio right away to see if there was anything about ... about what I done. But there wasn't. So I tried to go to sleep, but the ankle was very bad, and I needed a fix. I went to see Dr Mendelsohn in the morning because I figured it was like life or death, you know what I mean? If I couldn't get around, how was I going to make a connection?

Q: When did you visit Dr Mendelsohn?

A: Early. Nine o'clock. Nine a.m.

Q: Is he your family physician?

A: I never saw him before in my life. He's around the corner from where I live. That's the only reason I picked him, because he was close. He strapped up the ankle, but it didn't do no good. I *still* can't walk on it, I'm like a lousy cripple. I told him to bill me for it. I was going to pay him as soon as I got some bread. That's why I gave him my right name and address. I wasn't going to cheat him. I'm not that kind of person. I know that what I done is bad, but I'm not a bad person.

Q: When did you learn that Mrs Fletcher was dead?

A: I bought a newspaper on the way home from the doctor's. The story was in it. That's when I knew I killed her.

Q: You did not know until then?

A: I did not know how bad it was.

Chapter Four

On Tuesday, December 14, which was the first of Carella's two days off that week, he received a call at home from Gerald Fletcher. He knew that no one in the squadroom would have given his home number to a civilian, and he further knew that the number was unlisted in the Riverhead directory. Puzzled, he said, 'How'd you get my number, Mr Fletcher?'

'Friend of mine in the D.A.'s office,' Fletcher said.

'Well, what can I do for you?' Carella asked. His voice, he realized, was something less than cordial.

'I'm sorry to bother you at home this way.'

'It *is* my day off,' Carella said, fully aware that he was being rude.

'I wanted to apologize for the other night,' Fletcher said.

'Oh?' Carella answered, surprised.

'I know I behaved badly. You men had a job to do, and I wasn't making it any easier for you. I've been trying to understand what provoked my attitude, and I can only think I must have been in shock. I disliked my wife, true, but finding her dead that way was probably more unnerving than I realized. I'm sorry if I caused any trouble.'

'No trouble at all,' Carella said. 'You've been informed, of course, that ...'

'Yes, you caught the murderer.'

'Yes.'

'That was fast and admirable work, Detective Carella. And it only adds to the embarrassment I feel for having behaved so idiotically.'

'Well,' Carella said, and the line went silent.

'Please accept my apologies,' Fletcher said.

'Sure,' Carella said, beginning to feel embarrassed himself.

'I was wondering if you're free for lunch today.'

'Well,' Carella said, 'I was going to get some Christmas shopping done. My wife and I made out a list last night, and I thought ...'

'Will you be coming downtown?'

'Yes, but ...'

'Perhaps, you could manage both.'

'Well, look, Mr Fletcher,' Carella said, 'I know you feel bad about the other night, but you said you're sorry and that's enough, believe me. It was nice of you to call, I realize it wasn't an easy thing to ...'

'Why not meet me at The Golden Lion at one o'clock?' Fletcher said. 'Christmas shopping can be exhausting. You might welcome a break along about then.'

'Well ... where's The Golden Lion?' Carella asked.

'On Juniper and High.'

'Downtown? Near the Criminal Courts Building?'
'Exactly. Do you know it?'
'I'll find it.'
'One o'clock then?' Fletcher said.
'Well, yeah, okay,' Carella said.
'Good, I'll look for you.'

Carella did not know why he went to see Sam Grossman at the Police Lab that afternoon. He told himself that he was going to be in the neighbourhood, anyway, The Golden Lion being all the way downtown in the area bordered by the city's various courthouses. But this did not explain why he rushed through the not-unpleasant task of choosing a doll for his daughter, April, in order to get to Police Headquarters on High Street a full half-hour before he was to meet Fletcher.

Grossman was hunched over a microscope when Carella walked in, but without opening his one closed eye, and without raising his head from the eyepiece, he said, 'Sit down, Steve, be with you in a minute.'

Grossman kept adjusting the focus and jotting notes on a pad near his right hand, never lifting his head. Carella was trying to puzzle out how Grossman had known it was he. The sound of his footfalls? The smell of his aftershave lotion? The faint aroma of his wife's perfume clinging to the shoulder of his overcoat? He had not, until this moment, been aware that Detective-Lieutenant Sam Grossman, he of the spectacles and sharp blue eyes, he of the craggy face and clipped no-nonsense voice, was in reality Sherlock Holmes of 221B Baker Street, who was capable of recognizing a man without looking at him. Grossman's remarkable trick occupied all of Carella's thoughts for the next five minutes. At the end of that time, Grossman looked up from the microscope, extended his hand, and said, 'What brings you to the eighth circle?'

'How'd you know it was me?'

'Huh?' Grossman said.

'I came into the room, and you never looked up, but you said, "Sit down, Steve, be right with you." How'd you know it was me without first *looking* at me?'

'Ah-ha,' Grossman said.

'No, come on, Sam, it's bugging the hell out of me.'

'Well, it's really quite simple,' Grossman said, grinning. 'You will notice that the time is now twenty-five minutes to one, and that the sun, having passed its zenith, is glancing obliquely through the bank of windows lining the laboratory wall, touching the clock ever so faintly and casting shadows the angle of which can easily be measured.'

'Mmm?' Carella said.

'Moreover, the specimen on this microscope slide is particularly light-sensitive, meaning that the slightest deviation of any ray you might care to name – X, ultra-violet, or infrared – could easily have caused recognizable changes on the slide while I was examining it. Couple this, Steve, with the temperature, which I believe is close to ten above zero, and the air pollution level, which is, as *usual* in this city, unsatisfactory, and you can understand how all this might account for immediate identification without visibility being a necessary factor.'

'Yeah?' Carella said.

'Exactly. There's one other important point, of course, and I think we should consider it, too, if we're to understand the complete picture. You wanted to know how I knew you had entered the laboratory and were approaching the worktable. To begin with, when I heard the door opening ...'

'How'd you know it was *me*?'

'Well, here's the single *most* important element in the deductive process that led me to my inescapable conclusion ...'

'Yes, *what*?'

'Marshall Davies saw you in the hall. He popped in just before you opened the door, to tell me you were coming.'

'You son of a bitch,' Carella said, and burst out laughing.

'How do you like the job he did for you guys?' Grossman asked.

'Beautiful,' Carella said.

'Practically handed it to you on a platter.'

'No question.'

'The Police Laboratory strikes again,' Grossman said. 'Pretty soon we'll be able to do without you guys entirely.'

'I know. That's why I came down to see you. I want to turn in my badge.'

'About time,' Grossman said. 'Why *did* you come down? Big case you want us to crack in record time?'

'Nothing more important than a couple of purse snatches on Culver Avenue.'

'Bring the victims in. We'll try to lift some latents from their backsides,' Grossman said.

'I don't think they'd like that,' Carella said.

'And why not? We would treat the ladies with great delicacy.'

'Oh, I don't think the *lady* would mind. But the *guy* whose purse was snatched ...'

'You son of a bitch!' Grossman shouted, and both men began laughing hysterically.

'Seriously,' Carella said, laughing.

'Yes, yes, seriously,' Grossman said.

'Listen, I'm really trying to be serious here.'

'Yes, yes, of course.'

'I came down to thank you.'

'For what?' Grossman said, sobering immediately.

'I was about to go out on a limb. The stuff you got for us clinched the case and made an arrest possible. I wanted to thank you, that's all.'

'What kind of a limb, Steve?'

'I thought the husband did it.'

'Mmm?'

'Mmm.'

'Why?'

'No reason.' Carella paused. 'Sam,' he said, 'I *still* think he did it.'

'Is that why you're having lunch with him today?' Grossman asked.

'Now how the hell do you know *that*?' Carella said.

'Ah-ha,' Grossman answered. 'He was in Rollie Chabrier's office when he called you. I spoke to Rollie a little while after that, and ...'

'Good day, sir,' Carella said. 'You're too much of a smart-ass for me.'

Most policemen in the city for which Carella worked did not very often eat in restaurants like The Golden Lion. They ate lunch at one or another of the greasy spoons in and around the precinct, where the meal was on the arm, tribute to Caesar. Or they grabbed a quick sandwich and a cup of coffee at their desks. On their own time, when they entertained wives or girl friends, they often dropped in on restaurants where they were known as cops, protesting demonstratively when the proprietor said, 'This is on the house,' but accepting the gratuity nonetheless. Not a single cop in the city considered the practice dishonest. They were underpaid and overworked and they were here to protect the average citizen against criminal attack. If some of those citizens were in a position to make the policeman's lot a bit more tolerable, why should they embarrass those persons by refusing a free meal graciously offered? Carella had never been inside The Golden Lion. A look at the menu posted on the window outside would have frightened him out of six months' pay.

The place was a faithful replica of the dining room of an English coach house, circa 1637. Huge oaken beams crossed the room several feet below the vaulted ceiling, binding together the rough white plastered walls. The tables were sturdy, covered with immaculate white cloths, sparkling with heavy silver. Here and there throughout the room there hung the portraits of Elizabethan gentlemen and ladies, white-laced collars and cuffs discreetly echoing the colour of the walls, rich velvet robes or gowns adding muted touches of colour to the pristine candlelit atmosphere. Gerald Fletcher's table was in a secluded corner of the restaurant. He rose as Carella approached, extended his hand, and immediately said, 'Glad you could make it. Sit down, won't you?'

Carella shook Fletcher's hand, and then sat. He felt extremely uncomfortable, nor could he tell whether his discomfort was caused by the room or the man with whom he was dining. The room was intimidating, true, brimming with lawyers discussing their most recent cases in voices best saved for juries. In their presence Carella felt somewhat like a numbers collector in the policy racket, picking up the work to deliver it to the higher-ups for processing and final disposition. The law was his life, but in the midst of lawyers he felt like a menial. The man sitting opposite him was a criminal lawyer, which was intimidating in itself. But he was something more than that, and it was this perhaps that made Carella feel awkward and clumsy in his presence. It did not matter whether or not Fletcher truly *was* cleverer than Carella, or more sophisticated, or better at his work, or handsomer, or more articulate – the truth was unimportant. Carella *felt* Fletcher was all of these things; the man's manner and bearing and attack (yes, it could be called nothing else) utterly convinced Carella that he was in the presence of a superior being, and this was as good as, if not more potent than, the actual truth.

'Would you care for a drink?' Fletcher asked.

'Well, are you having one?' Carella asked.

'Yes, I am.'

'I'll have a scotch and soda,' Carella said. He was not used to drinking at lunch. He *never* drank at lunch when he was on duty, and the next time he would drink at lunch in his own home would be on Christmas day, when the family came to celebrate the holiday.

Fletcher signalled for the waiter. 'Have you ever been here before?' he asked Carella.

'No, never.'

'I thought you might have. It being so close to all the courts. You *do* spend a lot of time in court, don't you?'

'Yes, quite a bit,' Carella said.

'Ah,' Fletcher said to the waiter. 'A scotch and soda, please, and another whisky sour for me.'

'Thank you, Mr Fletcher,' the waiter said, and padded off.

'I cannot tell you how impressed I was by the speed with which you people made your arrest,' Fletcher said.

'Well, we had a lot of help from the lab,' Carella said.

'Incredible, wasn't it? I'm talking about the man's carelessness. But then I understand from Rollie ...' Fletcher paused. 'Rollie Chabrier, in the D.A.'s office. I believe you know him.'

'Yes, I do.'

'He's the one who gave me your home number. I hope you won't think too badly of him for it.'

'No, no, quite all right,' Carella said.

'I called you directly from his office this morning. Quite coincidentally, he'll be prosecuting the case against Corwin.'

'Scotch and soda, sir?' the waiter asked rhetorically, and set the drink down before Carella. He put the second whisky sour on the table before Fletcher and then said, 'Would you care to see menus now, Mr Fletcher?'

'In a bit,' Fletcher said.

'Thank you, sir,' the waiter answered, and went off again.

Fletcher raised his glass. 'Here's to a conviction,' he said.

Carella lifted his own glass. 'I don't expect Rollie'll have any trouble,' he said. 'It looks airtight to me.'

Both men drank. Fletcher dabbed his lips with a napkin and said, 'You never can tell these days. I practise criminal law, as you know, and I'm usually on the other side of the fence. You'd be surprised at the number of times we've won acquittal on cases that seemed cinches for the people.' He lifted his glass again. His eyes met Carella's. 'I hope you're right, though,' he said. 'I hope this one *is* airtight.' He sipped at the drink. 'Rollie was telling me ...'

'Yes, you were starting to say ...'

'Yes, that the man is a drug addict ...'

'Yes ...'

'Who'd never before burglarized an apartment.'

'That's right.'

'I must admit I feel a certain amount of sympathy for him.'

'Do you?'

'Yes. If he's an addict he's automatically entitled to pity. And when one considers that the woman he murdered was a bitch like my wife ...'

'Mr Fletcher ...'

'Gerry, okay?'

'Well ...'

'I know, I know. It isn't very kind of me to malign the dead. I'm afraid you didn't know my wife, though, Mr Carella. May I call you Steve?'

'Sure.'

'My enmity might be a bit more understandable if you did. Still, I *shall* take your advice. She's dead, and no longer capable of hurting me. So why be bitter? Shall we order, Steve?'

The waiter came to the table. Fletcher suggested that Carella try either the trout *au meunière* or the beef and kidney pie, both of which were excellent. Carella ordered prime ribs, medium rare, and a mug of beer. As the men ate and talked, something began happening. Or at least Carella *thought* something was happening; he would never be quite sure. Nor would he ever try to explain the experience to anyone because the conversation with Fletcher seemed on the surface to be routine chatter about such unrelated matters as conditions in the city, the approaching holidays, several recent motion pictures, the effectiveness of the copper bracelet Meyer had given Kling, the University of Wisconsin (where Fletcher had gone to law school), the letters Carella's children had written and were still writing daily to Santa Claus, the quality of the beef, and the virtues of ale as compared to beer. But rushing through this inane, polite, and really quite pointless discussion was an undercurrent that caused excitement, fear, and apprehension. As they spoke, Carella knew with renewed dizzying certainty that Gerald Fletcher had killed his wife. Without ever being told so, he knew it. Without the murder ever mentioned again, he knew it. *This* was why Fletcher had called this morning, *this* was why Fletcher had invited him to lunch, *this* was why he prattled on endlessly while every contradictory move of his body, every hand gesture, every facial expression signalled, indicated, transmitted on an almost extrasensory level that he *knew* Carella suspected him of the murder, and was here to *tell* Carella (without telling him) that, Yes, you stupid cop bastard, yes, I killed my wife. However much the evidence may point to another man, however many confessions you get, I killed the bitch, and I'm glad I killed her.

And there isn't a goddamn thing you can do about it.

Chapter Five

Ralph Corwin was being held before trial in the city's oldest prison, known to law enforcers and law breakers alike as 'Calcutta'. How Calcutta had evolved from Municipal House of Detention, Male Offenders was anybody's guess. The automatic reference, one might have thought, would be to 'The Black Hole', but Calcutta was not bad as prisons went; there were certainly less hanging-suicides among *its* inmates than there were at several of the city's other fine establishments. The building itself was old, but built at a time when masons knew how to handle bricks (and, more important, *cared* how they were handled) and so it had withstood the onslaught of time and weather, yielding only to the city's soot, which covered the rust-red bricks like a malevolent black jungle fungus. Inside the building, the walls and corridors were clean, the cells small but sanitary, the recreational facilities (Ping-Pong, television, and, in the open yard outside, handball) adequate and the guards about as dedicated as those to be found anywhere – which is to say they were brutal, sadistic, moronic clods.

Ralph Corwin was being kept in a wing of the building reserved for heavy felony offenders; his cell block at the moment was occupied by himself, a gentleman who had starved his six-year-old son to death in the basement of his Calm's Point house, another gentleman who had set fire to a synagogue in Majesta, and a third member of the criminal elite who had shot and blinded a gas-station attendant during a holdup in Bethtown. The wounded attendant had rushed out into the highway gushing blood from his shattered face and, because he could not see, was knocked down and killed by a two-ton trailer truck. As the old gag goes, however, he wouldn't have died if he hadn't been shot first. Corwin's cell was at the end of the row, and Carella found him there that Wednesday morning sitting on the lower bunk, hands clasped between his knees, head bent as though in prayer. It had been necessary to get permission for the visit from both the district attorney's office and Corwin's lawyer, neither of whom, apparently, felt that allowing Carella to talk to the prisoner would be harmful to the case. Corwin was expecting him. He lifted his head as soon as he heard approaching footsteps, and then rose from the bunk as the turnkey opened the cell door.

'How are you?' Carella said, and extended his hand.

Corwin took it, shook it briefly and then said, 'I was wondering which one you'd be. I got your names mixed up, you and the blond cop, I couldn't remember which was which. Anyway, now I know. You're Carella.'

'Yes.'

'What'd you want to see me about?'

'I wanted to ask you some questions.'

'My lawyer says ...'

'I spoke to your lawyer, he knows ...'

'Yeah, but he says I'm not supposed to add anything to what I already said. He wanted to *be* here, in fact, but I told him I could take care of myself. I don't even *like* that guy. Did you ever meet that guy? He's this little fink with glasses, he's like a goddamn cockroach.'

'Why don't you ask for another lawyer?'

'Can I do that?'

'Sure.'

'Who do I ask?'

'The Legal Aid Society.'

'Can *you* do that for me? Can you give them a call and tell them ...'

'I'd rather not.'

'Why?' Corwin said, and studied Carella suspiciously.

'I don't want to do anything that might be considered prejudicial to the case.'

'Whose case? Mine or the D.A.'s?'

'Either one. I'm not familiar enough with what the Court might consider ...'

'Okay, so how do *I* call the Legal Aid?'

'Ask one of the officers here. Or simply tell your lawyer. I'm sure if you explain your feelings to him, he would have no objection to dropping out. Would *you* want to defend someone who didn't like you?'

'Yeah, well,' Corwin said, and shrugged. 'I don't want to hurt his feelings. He's a little cockroach, but what the hell.'

'You've got a lot at stake here, Corwin.'

'That's just the point. What the hell difference does it make?'

'What do you mean?'

'I killed her. So what does it matter *who* the lawyer is? Nobody's going to save me. You got it all in black and white.'

Corwin's eyelid was twitching. He wrung his hands together, sat on the bunk again, and said, 'I got to hold my hands together. I got to squeeze them together, otherwise I'm afraid I'll shake myself to pieces, you know what I mean?'

'How bad has it been?'

'Cold turkey's never good, and it's worse when you can't yell. Every time I yell, that son of a bitch in the next cell tells me to shut up, the one who put his own kid in the basement. He scares me. Did you get a look at him? He must weigh two hundred and fifty pounds. Can you imagine a guy like that chaining his own kid in the basement. And not giving him anything to eat? What makes people do things like that?'

'I don't know,' Carella said. 'Have they given you any medication?'

'No. They said this ain't a hospital. Which I *know* it ain't, right? So I asked my cockroach lawyer to get me transferred to the Narcotics Service at Buenavista, and he said the prison authorities would have to make tests before they could transfer me there as a bona-fide addict, and he said that might take a couple of days. So in a couple of days I won't *be* a fuckin' bona-fide addict anymore, because by then I'll vomit up my guts and kick it cold turkey, so what kind of sense does that make? I don't understand rules. I swear to God, I really don't understand rules. That's one thing about junk. It makes you forget all the bullshit rules. You stick a needle in your arm, all the rules vanish. Man, I *hate* rules.'

'You feel like answering some questions?' Carella said.

'I feel like dropping dead is what I feel like.'

'If you'd rather I came back another ...'

'No, no, go ahead. What do you want to know?'

'I want to know exactly how you stabbed Sarah Fletcher.'

Corwin squeezed his hands tightly together. He wet his lips, abruptly leaned forwards as though fighting a sudden cramp, and said, 'How do you *think* you stab somebody? You stick a knife in her, that's how.'

'Where?'

'In the belly.'

'Left-hand side of the body?'

'Yes. I guess so. I'm right-handed, and she was facing me, so I guess that's where I stabbed her. Yes.'

'Then what?'

'What do you mean?'

'What did you do then?'

'I ... you know, I think I must've let go of the knife. I think I was so surprised I stabbed her that I let go of it, you know? I must've let go, don't you think? Because I remember her backing away from me, and then falling, and the knife was still in her.'

'Did she say anything to you?'

'No. She just had this ... this terrible look on her face. Shocked and ... and hurt ... and ... and like wondering why I did it.'

'Where was the knife when she fell?'

'I don't know what you mean.'

'Was the knife on the *right*-hand side of her body or the *left*?'

'I don't know.'

'Try to remember.'

'I don't know. That was when I heard the front door opening and all I could think of was getting out of there.'

'When you stabbed her, did she *twist* away from you?'

'No. She backed away.'

'She didn't twist away while you were still holding the knife?'

'No. She moved straight back. As if she couldn't believe what I done, and ... and just wanted to get *away* from me, you know?'

'And then she fell?'

'Yes. She ... her knees sort of gave way and she grabbed for her belly, and her hands sort of ... it was terrible ... they just ... they were grabbing *air*, you know? And she fell.'

'In what position?'

'On her side.'

'*Which* side?'

'I could still see the knife, so it must've been the opposite side. The side opposite from where I stabbed her.'

'Facing her, how was she lying on the floor? Show me.'

'Well ...' Corwin rose from the bunk and stood before Carella. 'Let's say the toilet bowl there is the window, her feet were towards me, and her head was towards the window. So if you're me ...' Corwin got on the floor and stretched his legs towards Carella. 'This is the position she was in.'

'All right, now show me which side she was lying on.'

Corwin rolled onto his right side. 'This side,' he said.

'Her right side.'

'Yes.'

'And you saw the knife sticking out of the *opposite* side, the left side.'

'Yes.'

'Exactly where you'd stabbed her.'

'I suppose so, yes.'

'Was the knife still in that position when you broke the window and left the apartment?'

'I don't know. I didn't look at the knife again. Nor at her neither. I just wanted to get out of there fast. There was somebody coming, you understand?'

'One last question, Ralph. Was she dead when you went through that window?'

'I don't know. She was bleeding and ... she was very quiet. I ... guess she was dead. I don't know. I guess so.'

'Hello, Miss Simonov?'

'Yes?'

'Detective Kling, 87th Squad. I've ...'

'Who?'

'Kling. Detective Kling. You remember we talked in the hallway ...'

'Oh, yes, how are you?'

'Fine, thanks. I've been trying to get you all afternoon. It finally occurred to me, big detective that I am, that you probably work, and wouldn't be home until after five.'

'I *do* work,' Nora said, 'but I work right here in the apartment. I'm a freelance artist. I really *should* get an answering service, I suppose. I was uptown visiting my mother. I'm sorry you had trouble getting me.'

'Well,' Kling said, 'I've got you now.'

'Just barely. I still haven't taken off my coat.'

'I'll wait.'

'Would you? This apartment's stifling hot. If you close all the windows, they send up steam you could grow orchids with. And if you leave them open the tiniest crack, you come home and it's like an arctic tundra. I'll just be a minute. God, it's suffocating in here.'

Kling waited. While he waited, he looked at his copper bracelet. If the bracelet actually began working, he would send one to his aunt in San Diego, who had been suffering from rheumatism for close to fifteen years. If it didn't work, he would sue Meyer.

'Hello, I'm back.'

'Hello,' Kling said.

'Boy, that's much better,' Nora said. 'I can't stand extremes, can you? It's bitter cold in the street, and the temperature in here *has* to be at least a hundred and four. Wow. What were you calling about, Mr Kling?'

'Well, as your probably know, we apprehended the man who committed the Fletcher murder ...'

'Yes, I read about it.'

'And the district attorney's office is now preparing the case against him. They called us this morning to ask whether you'd be available to make a positive identification of Corwin as the man you saw in the basement of the building.'

'Why is that necessary?'

'I don't follow you, Miss Simonov.'

'The newspapers said you had a full confession. Why do you need ...'

'Yes, of course, but the prosecuting attorney still has to present evidence.'

'Why?'

'Well ... suppose, for example, that *I* confessed to the same murder, and it turned out *my* fingerprints were not on the knife, *I* was not the man you saw in the basement, *I* was in fact in Schenectady on the night of the murder, do you see what I mean? Confession or not, the D.A. has to make a case.'

'I see.'

'So what I'm calling about is to find out if you'd be willing to identify the man.'

'Yes, of course I would.'

'How about tomorrow morning?'

'What time tomorrow morning? I usually sleep late.'

'Name it.'

'First tell me where it'll be.'

'Downtown. On Arbor Street. Around the corner from the Criminal Courts Building.'

'Where's that?'

'The Criminal Courts Building? On High Street.'

'Oh. That's *all* the way downtown.'

'Yes.'

'Would eleven o'clock be too late?'

'No, I'm sure that'll be fine.'

'All right then.'

'I'll meet you downstairs in the lobby. That's 33 Arbor Street. At five to eleven, okay?'

'Yes, okay.'

'Unless I call you back. I want to check with the ...'

'When would you be calling back? If you called.'

'In the next two or three minutes. I just want to contact the D.A.'s office to make sure ...'

'Oh, okay then. Because I want to take a bath.'

'If you don't hear from me within the next – let's say, five minutes, okay? – I'll see you in the morning.'

'Good.'

'Thank you, Miss Simonov.'

''Bye,' she said, and hung up.

Chapter Six

Corwin's attorney, cockroach or otherwise, realized that, if he did not grant the D.A.'s office permission to run a lineup on his client, they would simply get a Supreme Court judge to order such a lineup, so he agreed to it at once. He stipulated only that it be a *fair* lineup and that he be permitted to attend it. Rollie Chabrier, who was handling the case for the people, readily granted both of his demands.

A fair lineup meant that Corwin and the other men in the lineup should be dressed in approximately the same style of clothing, and should be of the same general build, height, and colour. It would not have been considered fair, for example, if the other men in the lineup were all Puerto Rican midgets wearing clown costumes since the witness would then automatically eliminate them and identify the remaining man whether or not he was truly the one she had seen rushing in and out of the basement on the night of the murder. Rollie Chabrier chose six men from the D.A.'s detective squad, all of whom were about the same size and general build as Corwin, asked them all to dress casually, and then trotted them into his office together with Corwin himself, who was wearing civilian clothing for the occasion of his visit from Calcutta.

In the presence of Bert Kling, Nora Simonov, and Corwin's attorney – a cockroach, indeed, whose name was Harvey Johns – Rollie Chabrier said, 'Miss Simonov; would you please look at these seven men and tell me if one of them is the man you saw in the basement of 721 Silvermine Oval on the night of December the twelfth, at or about 10:45 p.m.?'

Nora looked, and then said, 'Yes.'

'You recognize one of these men?'

'I do.'

'Which one is the man you saw in the basement?'

'That one,' Nora said, and pointed unerringly to Ralph Corwin.

The detectives from the D.A.'s squad handcuffed Corwin once again, and walked him up the corridor to the elevator, which whisked him down ten floors to the basement of the building, where he was led up a ramp to a waiting police van that transported him back to Calcutta. In Chabrier's office, Harvey Johns thanked him for the fairness of the lineup he had run, and then advised him that his client had told him he no longer desired his services as defence attorney and that probably a new attorney would be appointed to the case, but this did not mean it had not been a pleasure working with Chabrier anyhow. Chabrier thanked Johns, and Johns went back to his office in midtown Isola. Chabrier also thanked Nora for her cooperation, and Kling for his assistance in getting Miss Simonov downtown, and then he shook hands with Kling, and walked them to the elevator, and said good-bye, and scurried off just before the elevator doors closed, a round, pink-cheeked man with a pencil-line moustache, wearing brown shoes with a dark blue suit. Kling figured he had Presidential aspirations.

In the marble entrance lobby of the building, Kling said, 'Now that was simple, wasn't it?'

'Yes,' Nora answered. 'And yet, I feel ... I don't know. Somewhat like an informer, I guess. I realize the man *killed* Sarah Fletcher, but at the same time I hate to think *my* identification will help convict him.' She shrugged, and then smiled suddenly and apologetically. 'Anyway, I'm glad it's over.'

'I'm sorry it was painful,' Kling said. 'Can the Department make amends by taking you to lunch?'

'Would it be the Department or would it be you?'

'Me, actually,' Kling said. 'What do you say?'

She had, Kling noticed, a direct approach to most matters, asking questions as guilelessly as a child, expecting honest answers in return. Without breaking her stride now, she turned her head towards him, long brown hair falling free over one eye, and said, 'If it's just lunch, fine.'

'That's all,' Kling said, and he smiled, but he could not hide his disappointment. He realized, of course, that he was still smarting from Cindy Forrest's abrupt termination of their relationship, and a nice way for a man to prove he was still attractive to women was to sweep someone like Nora Simonov off her feet and into his arms before Cindy could even raise her eyebrows in astonishment. But Nora Simonov wasn't having any, thanks. 'If it's just lunch, fine,' she had said, making it clear that she wasn't looking for any more meaningful relationship. She had caught the tone of Kling's reply, however, he knew that; her face was a direct barometer of her emotions, pressure-sensitive to every nuance of feeling within. She nibbled at her lip now, and said, 'I'm sorry, I didn't mean to make it sound so ...

terminal. It's just that I *am* in love with someone, you see, and I didn't want
to give the impression that I might be, well, available, or interested or . . . my
God, I'm only screwing it up worse!'
'No, you're doing fine,' Kling said.
'I normally detest people who wear their hearts on their sleeves. *God*, are
they boring! Anyway, do we have to have lunch, I'm not even hungry yet.
What time is it?'
'A little after twelve.'
'Couldn't we walk a little and just talk? If we did, *I* wouldn't feel I was
compromising my *grand amour*,' she said, rolling her eyes, 'and *you* wouldn't
feel you were wasting lunch on a completely unresponsive dud.'
'I would love to walk and talk a little,' Kling said.
They walked.
The city that Thursday nine days before Christmas was overcast with
menacing clouds; the weather bureau had promised a heavy snowfall before
midafternoon. Moreover, a sharp wind was blowing in off the river, swirling
in cruel eddies through the narrow streets of the financial district that
bordered the municipal and federal courts. Nora walked with her head
ducked against the wind, her fine brown hair whipping about her head with
each fierce gust. As a defence against the wind, which truly seemed
determined to blow her off the sidewalk, she took Kling's arm as they
walked, and on more than one occasion turned her face into his shoulder
whenever the blasts became too violent. Kling began wishing she hadn't
already warned him off. As she chattered on about the weather and about
how much she liked the look of the city just before Christmas, he entertained
wild fantasies of male superiority: bold, handsome, witty, intelligent,
sensitive cop pierces armour of young, desirable girl, stealing her away from
ineffectual idiot she adores . . .
'The people, too,' Nora said. 'Something happens to them just before
Christmas, they get, I don't know, grander in spirit.'
Young girl in turn, realizing she has been waiting all these years for
handsome witty, etc., cop lavishes adoration she had previously wasted on
mealy-mouthed moron . . .
'Even though I recognize it's been brutalized and commercialized, it
reaches me, it really does. And that's surprising because I'm Jewish, you
know. We never celebrated Christmas when I was a little girl.'
'How old are you?' Kling asked.
'Twenty-four. Are you Jewish?'
'No.'
'Kling,' Nora said, and shrugged. 'It could be Jewish.'
'Is your boyfriend Jewish?'
'No, he's not.'
'Are you engaged?'
'Not exactly. But we do plan to get married.'
'What does he do?'
'I'd rather not talk about him, if you don't mind,' Nora said.
They did not talk about him again that afternoon. They walked through
streets aglow with lighted Christmas trees, passing shop windows hung
with tinsel and wreaths. Street-corner Santa Clauses jingled their bells and
solicited donations; Salvation Army musicians blew their tubas and

trombones, shook their tambourines, and likewise asked for funds; shoppers hurried from store to store clutching gift-wrapped packages while overhead the clouds grew thicker and more menacing.

Nora told him that she usually kept regular working hours in the studio she had set up in one room of her large, rent-controlled apartment. ('Except once a week, when I go up to Riverhead to visit my mother, which is where I was all day yesterday while you were trying to reach me'), and that she did many different kinds of freelance design, from book jackets to theatrical posters, from industrial brochures to line drawings for cookbooks, colour illustrations for children's books, and what-have-you. ('I'm usually kept very busy. It isn't just the art work, it's running around to see editors and producers and authors and all *sorts* of people. I'll be *damned* if I'll give twenty-five percent of my income to an art agent. That's what some of them are getting these days, don't you think there should be a law?') She had studied art at Cooper Union in New York City, and then had gone on for more training at the Rhode Island School of Design, and then had come here a year ago to work for an advertising firm named Thadlow, Brunner, Growling and Crowe ('His name really *was* Growling, Anthony Growling') where she had lasted for little more than six months, doing illustrations of cans and cigarette packages and other such rewarding subjects before she'd decided to quit and begin free-lancing. ('So that's the story of my life.')

It was almost three o'clock.

Kling suspected he was already halfway in love with her, but it was time to get back to the squadroom. He took her uptown in a taxi, and just before she got out in front of her building on Silvermine Oval, on the offchance that her earlier protestations of undying love were in the nature of a ploy, he said, 'I enjoyed this, Nora. Can I see you again sometime?'

She looked at him with an oddly puzzled expression, as though she had tried her best to make it abundantly clear that she was otherwise involved and had, through some dire fault of her own, failed to communicate the idea to him. She smiled briefly and sadly, shook her head, and said, 'No, I don't think so.'

Then she got out of the taxi and was gone.

Among Sarah Fletcher's personal effects that were considered of interest to the police before they arrested Ralph Corwin was an address book found in the dead woman's handbag on the bedroom dresser. In the Thursday afternoon stillness of the squadroom, Carella examined the book while Meyer and Kling discussed the potency of the copper bracelet Kling wore on his wrist. The squadroom *was* unusually quiet; a person could actually hear himself think. The typewriters were silent, the telephones were not ringing, there were no prisoners in the detention cage yelling their heads off about police brutality or human rights, and all the windows were tightly closed, shutting out even the noises of the street below. In deference to the calm (and also because Carella seemed so hard at work with Sarah Fletcher's address book), Meyer and Kling spoke in what amounted to whispers.

'I can only tell you,' Meyer said, 'that the bracelet is supposed to work miracles. Now what else can I tell you?'

'You can tell me how come it hasn't worked any miracles on *me* so far?'

'When did you put it on?' Meyer said.

'I marked it on my calendar,' Kling said. They were sitting in the corner of the squadroom closest to the detention cage, Kling in a wooden chair behind his desk, Meyer perched on one end of the desk. The desk was against the wall, and the wall was covered with departmental flyers, memos on new rules and regulations, next year's Detectives' Duty Chart (listing Night Duty, Day Duty, and Open Days for each of the squad's six detective teams), a cartoon clipped from the police magazine every red-blooded cop subscribed to, several telephone numbers of complainants Kling hoped to get back to before his tour ended, a photograph of Cindy Forrest (which he'd meant to take down), and several less-flattering mug shots of wanted criminals. Kling's calendar was buried under the morass on the wall; he had to take down an announcement for the P.B.A.'s annual New Year's Eve party to get at it. 'Here,' he said. 'You gave me the bracelet on December first.'

'And today's what?' Meyer asked.

'Today's the sixteenth.'

'How do you know I gave it to you on the first?'

'That's what the MB stands for. Meyer's bracelet.'

'All right, so that's exactly two weeks. So what do you expect? I told you it'd begin working in two weeks.'

'You said ten days.'

'I said two weeks.'

'Anyway, it's *more* than two weeks.'

'Listen, Bert, the bracelet works miracles, it can cure anything from arthritis to ...'

'Then why isn't it working on me?'

'What do you expect?' Meyer asked. 'Miracles?'

There was nothing terribly fascinating about the alphabetical listings in Sarah Fletcher's address book. She had possessed a good handwriting, and the names, addresses, and telephone numbers were all clearly written and easily read. Even when she'd crossed out a telephone number to write in a new listing, the deletion was made with a single sure stroke of her pen, the new number written directly beneath it. Carella leafed through the pages, finding that most of the listings were for obviously married couples (Chuck and Nancy Benton, Harold and Marie Spander, George and Ina Grossman, and on and on), some were for girl friends, some for local merchants and service people, one for Sarah's hairdresser, another for her dentist, several for doctors, and a few for restaurants in town and across the river. A thoroughly uninspiring address book – until Carella came to a page at the end of the book, with the printed word MEMORANDA at its top.

'All I know,' Kling said, 'is that my shoulder still hurts. I'm lucky I haven't been in any fierce pistol duels lately, because I'm sure I wouldn't be able to draw my gun.'

'When's the last time you were in a fierce pistol duel?' Meyer asked.

'I'm in fierce pistol duels all the time,' Kling said, and grinned.

Under the single word MEMORANDA there were five names, addresses, and telephone numbers written in Sarah's meticulous hand. All of the names were men's names. They had obviously been entered in the book at different times because some were written in pencil and others in ink. The parenthetical initials following each entry were all noted in felt marking pens of various colours:

Andrew Hart
1120 Hall Avenue
622 - 8400
   (PB+G) (TG)

Michael Thornton
371 South Lindner
881- 9371
   (TS)

Lou Kantor
434 North 16 Street
FR 7 - 2346
   (TPC) (TG)

Sal Decotto
831 Grover Avenue
FR5 - 3287
   (F) (TG)

Richard Fenner
110 Henderson
593 - 6648
   (QR) (TG)

If there was one thing Carella loved, it was a code. He loved a code almost as much as he loved German measles.

Sighing, he opened the top drawer of his desk and pulled out the Isola directory. He was verifying the address for the first name on Sarah Fletcher's MEMORANDA list when Kling said, 'There are some guys who won't let a case go, even after it's been solved.'

'Who did you have in mind?' Meyer asked.

'Certain very conscientious guys,' Kling said.

Carella pretended neither of them was there. The telephone book address for Andrew Hart matched the one in Sarah's handwriting. He flipped to the back of the directory.

'I knew a very conscientious cop one time,' Meyer said, and winked.

'Tell me about him,' Kling said, and winked back.

'He was walking a beat out in Bethtown, oh, this must have been three or four winters ago,' Meyer said. 'It was a bitter cold day, not unlike today, but he was a very conscientious man, this cop, and he walked his beat faithfully and well, without once taking a coffee break, or even stopping in any of the local bars for a nip.'

'He sounds like a stalwart,' Kling said, grinning.

Carella had found an address for Michael Thornton, the second name on Sarah's list. It, too, was identical to the one in her book.

'Oh, he *was* a stalwart, no question,' Meyer said. 'And conscientious as the day was long. Did I mention it was a bitter cold day?'

'Yes, I believe you did,' Kling said.

'Nonetheless,' Meyer said, 'it was the habit of a very pretty and well-built Bethtown lady to take a swim every day of the year, rain or shine, snow, hail, or sleet. Did I mention she had very big boobs?'

'I believe you did.'

Carella kept turning pages in the directory, checking names and addresses.

'The lady's house was right on the beach, and it was her habit to bathe stark naked because this was a very isolated part of Bethtown, way over near the end of the island. This was before they put a new bridge in, you still had to take a ferry to get out there. It so happened, however, that the lady's house was *also* on the conscientious cop's beat. And on this particularly bitter day some three or four winters ago, the lady rushed out of her back door with her arms crossed just below her big bulging boobs, hugging herself because it was so cold, and the conscientious cop . . .'

'Yes, yes, what about him?' Kling said.

'The conscientious cop took one look at the lady hugging herself as she ran down towards the water, and he yelled, "Stop, police!" and when the lady stopped, and faced him, still clutching herself under those big boobs, she indignantly asked, "What have I done, officer? What crime have I committed?" And the conscientious cop said, "It ain't what you *done*, lady, it's what you were *about* to do. You think I'm going to stand by while you drown those two chubby pink-nosed puppies?" '

Kling burst out laughing. Meyer slapped the top of his desk and roared at his own joke. Carella said, 'Will you guys please shut up?'

He had verified all five addresses.

In the morning, he would go to work.

The letter was the sixth one April Carella had written to Santa Claus. In the kitchen of the Riverhead house, she read it silently over her mother's shoulder:

Dear Santa,
I hope your not getting Too
anoyed with my letters.
I no you must be bizy
this time of year. But
I thought of something,
and wud like to make a
change from my last letter.
Please dont bring the
Craftmaster Sewing like
Kit, but insted I wud like
the Castle Toys doll
Bohnie that wets.
My broter Mark will
be writen to you
personally about his
new idea. So long
for now, and regards.

April Carella

'What do you think, Mom?' she said.

She was standing behind her mother's chair, and Teddy could not see her lips, and had no idea that she had spoken. Teddy was a deaf mute, a beautiful woman with midnight hair and dark luminous brown eyes that cherished words because to her they were visible and tangible; she saw them forming as they tumbled from fingers; she touched them in the dark on her husband's lips, and heard them more profoundly than she would have with normal 'hearing'. She was thoroughly absorbed by the inconsistencies in her daughter's letter, and did not look up as April came round the chair. Why someone should be able to spell a word like 'personally' while making a shambles of simple words like 'busy' or 'would' was beyond Teddy's comprehension. Perhaps she should visit April's teacher, mildly suggest to her that whereas the child possessed undeniable writing ability, wouldn't her style be more effective if her imaginative spelling were controlled somewhat? Some of the avant-garde quality might be lost, true ...

April touched her arm.

Teddy looked up into her daughter's face. The two, in the light of the Tiffany lamp that overhung the old oak table in the large kitchen, were something less than mirror images, but the resemblance, even for mother and daughter, was uncanny nonetheless. More remarkable, however, was the identical intensity of their expressions. As April repeated her question, Teddy studied her lips, and then raised her hands and slowly spelled out her answer, while April's gaze never faltered. It occurred to Teddy, with some amusement, that a child who could not spell 'would' might have difficulty deciphering the letters and words that Teddy deftly and fluidly formed with her fingers, especially when the message she was communicating was 'Your spelling is bad'. But April watched, nodding as she caught letters, smiling as the letters combined to form a word, and then another word, and finally grasping the short sentence, and saying, 'Which ones are spelled wrong, Mom? Show me?'

They were going over the letter again when April heard a key in the front door. Her eyes met briefly with her mother's. A smile cracked instantly across her face. Together, they rose instantly from the table. Mark, April's twin brother, was already bounding down the steps from his bedroom upstairs.

Carella was home.

Chapter Seven

At a little past eight the next morning, on the assumption that most men worked for a living and would be in transit to their jobs after that hour, Carella called Andrew Hart at the number listed in Sarah's address book. The phone was picked up on the fifth ring.

'Hello?' a man's voice said.

'Mr Hart?'

'Speaking.'

'This Detective Carella of the 87th Squad. I wonder ...'

'What's the matter?' Hart said immediately.

'I'd like to ask you some questions, Mr Hart.'

'I'm in the middle of shaving,' Hart said. 'I've got to leave for the office in a little while. What's this about?'

'We're investigating a homicide, Mr Hart ...'

'A *what*? A homicide?'

'Yes, sir.'

'Who? Who's been killed?'

'A woman named Sarah Fletcher.'

'I don't know anyone named Sarah Fletcher,' Hart said.

'She seems to have known you, Mr Hart.'

'Sarah *who*? Fletcher, did you say?'

'That's right.'

'I don't know anybody by that name. Who says she knew me? I never heard of her in my life.'

'Your name's in her address book.'
'My what? My name? That's impossible.'
'Mr Hart, I have her book right here in my hand, and your name is in it, together with your address and your phone number.'
'Well, I don't know how it got there.'
'Neither do I. That's why I'd like to talk to you.'
'Okay, okay,' Hart said. 'What time is it? Jesus, is it ten after eight already?'
'Yes, it is.'
'Look, I've got to shave and get out of here. Can you come to the office later? About . . . ten o'clock? I should be free around then. I'd see you earlier, but someone's coming in at nine.'
'We'll be there at ten. Where *is* the office, Mr Hart?'
'On Hamilton and Reed. 480 Reed. The sixth floor. Hart and Widderman. We've got the whole floor.'
'See you at ten, Mr Hart.'
'Right,' Hart said, and hung up.

Like a woman in her tenth month, the clouds over the city twisted and roiled in angry discomfort but refused to deliver the promised snow. The citizens grew anxious. Hurrying to their jobs, dashing into subway kiosks, boarding buses, climbing into taxicabs, they glanced apprehensively at the bloated skies and wondered if the weather bureau, as usual, was wrong. To the average city dweller, being alerted to a snowstorm was like being alerted to the bubonic plague. Nobody in his right mind liked snow. Nobody liked putting on rubbers and galoshes and skid-chains and boots; nobody liked shovelling sidewalks and cancelling dinner dates and missing theatre parties; nobody liked slipping and sliding and falling on his ass. But worse than that, nobody liked being *promised* all that, and being forced to *anticipate* all that, and then not *having* all that delivered. The city dweller, for all his sophistication, was a creature of habit who dreaded any break in his normal routine. He would accept blackouts or garbage strikes or muggings in the park because these were not breaks in the routine, they *were* the routine. And besides, they reinforced the image he carried of himself as an urban twentieth-century swashbuckler capable of coping with the worst disasters. But threaten a taxicab strike and then postpone or cancel it? Promise a protest and have it dispersed by the police? Forecast snow and then have the storm hover indefinitely over the city like a writhing grey snake ready to strike? Oh no, you couldn't fool with a city person that way. It made him edgy and uncomfortable and insecure and constipated.
'So where the hell is it?' Meyer asked impatiently. One hand on the door of the police sedan, he looked up at the threatening sky and all but shook his fist at the grey clouds overhead.
'It'll come,' Carella said.
'When?' Meyer asked flatly, and opened the door, and climbed into the car. Carella started the engine. 'Damn forecasters *never* know what they're doing,' Meyer said. 'Last big storm we had, they were predicting sunny and mild. We can put men on the moon, but we can't tell if it's going to drizzle on Tuesday.'
'That's an interesting thing,' Carella said.

'What is?'

'About the moon.'

'What about the moon?'

'Why should everything down here be expected to work perfectly just because we've put men on the moon?'

'What the hell are you talking about?' Meyer said.

'We can put men on the moon,' Carella said, 'but we can't get a phone call through to Riverhead. We can put men on the moon, but we can't settle a transit strike. We can put men on the moon . . .'

'I get your point,' Meyer said, 'but I fail to see the parallel. There *is* a connection, between the weather and the billions of dollars we've spent shooting meteorological hardware into space.'

'I merely thought it was an interesting observation,' Carella said.

'It was very interesting,' Meyer said.

'What's the matter with *you* this morning?'

'Nothing's the matter with me this morning.'

'Okay,' Carella said, and shrugged.

They drove in silence. The city was a monochromatic grey, the backdrop for a Warner Brothers gangster film of the thirties. The colour seemed to have been drained from everything – the most vivid billboards, the most vibrant building façades, the most lurid women's clothing, even the Christmas ornaments that decorated the shop windows. Overhung with eternal greyness, the trappings of the yuletide season stood revealed as shabby crap, tinsel and plastic to be exhibited once a year before being returned to the basement. In this bleak light, even the costumes of the street-corner Santa Clauses appeared to be a faded maroon rather than a cheerful red, the fake beards dirty, the brass bells tarnished. The city had been robbed of sunshine and denied the cleansing release of snow. It waited, and it fretted, and it grew crankier by the minute.

'I was wondering about Christmas,' Carella said.

'What about it?'

'I've got the duty. You feel like switching with me?'

'What for?' Meyer said.

'I thought I'd give you Chanukah or something.'

'How long do you know me?' Meyer asked.

'Too long,' Carella said, and smiled.

'How many years has it been?' Meyer said. 'And you don't know I celebrate both Chanukah *and* Christmas? I've had a Christmas tree in the house ever since the kids were born. Every year. You've *been* there every year. You were there *last* year with Teddy. You *saw* the tree. Right in the living room. Right in the *middle* of the goddamn living room.'

'I forgot,' Carella said.

'I celebrate both,' Meyer said.

'Okay,' Carella said.

'Okay. So the answer is no, I don't want to switch the duty.'

'Okay.'

'Okay.'

In this mood of joyous camaraderie, Meyer and Carella parked the car and went into the building at 480 Reed Street, and up the elevator to the sixth floor – in silence. Hart and Widderman manufactured watchbands. A huge advertising display near the receptionist's desk in the lobby proudly proclaimed H&W BEATS THE BAND! and then backed the slogan with more discreet copy that explained how Hart and Widderman had solved the difficult engineering problems of the expansion watch bracelet to present to the world their amazing new line, all illustrated with photographs as big as Carella's head, in gleaming golden tones he felt certain he could hock at the nearest pawnshop. The receptionist's hair was almost as golden, but it did not look as genuine as that in the display. She glanced up from her magazine without much interest as the detectives approached her desk. Meyer was still reading the advertising copy, fascinated.

'Mr Hart, please,' Carella said.

'Who's calling?' the receptionist asked. She had a definite Calm's Point accent, and she sounded as if she were chewing gum, even though she was not.

'Detectives Carella and Meyer.'

'Just a minute, please,' she said, and lifted her phone, and pushed a button in the base. 'Mr Hart,' she said, 'there are some cops here to see you.' She listened for a moment, and then said, 'Yes, sir.' She replaced the receiver on its cradle, gestured towards the inside corridor with a nod of her golden tresses, said, 'Go right in, please. Door at the end of the hall,' and then went back to discovering what people were talking about in *Vogue*.

The grey skies had apparently got to Andrew Hart, too.

'You didn't have to broadcast to the world that the police department is here,' he said immediately.

'We merely announced ourselves,' Carella said.

'Well, okay, now you're here,' Hart said, 'let's get it over with.' He was a big man in his middle fifties, with iron-grey hair and black-rimmed eyeglasses. His eyes behind their lenses were brown and swift and cruel. His jacket was draped over the back of the chair behind his desk, and his shirt sleeves were rolled up over powerful forearms dense with black hair. A gold expansion bracelet, undoubtedly one of his own, held his watch fastened to his thick wrist. 'If you want to know the truth,' he said, 'I don't know what the hell you're doing here, anyway. I told you I don't know any Sarah Fletcher, and I don't.'

'Here's her book, Mr Hart,' Carella said, figuring there was no sense wasting time with a lot of bullshit. He handed the address book to Hart, opened to the MEMORANDA page. 'That's your name, isn't it?'

'Yeah,' Hart said, and shook his head. 'But how it got there is beyond me.'

'You don't know anybody named Sarah Fletcher, huh?'

'No.'

'Is it possible she's someone you met at a party, someone you exchanged numbers with ...'

'No.'

'Are you married, Mr Hart?'

'What's that got to do with it?'

'*Are* you?'

'No.'

'We've got a picture of Mrs Fletcher, I wonder ...'

'Don't go showing me any pictures of a corpse,' Hart said.

'This was taken when she was alive. It's a recent picture, it was on the dresser in her bedroom. Would you mind looking at it?'

'I don't see any sense in this at *all*,' Hart said. 'I told you I don't know her. How's looking at her picture ...?'

'Meyer?' Carella said, and Meyer handed him a manila envelope. Carella opened the flap and removed from the envelope a framed picture of Sarah Fletcher, which he handed to Hart. Hart looked at the photograph, and then immediately looked up at Carella.

'What is this?' he said.

'Do you recognize that picture, Mr Hart?'

'Let me see your badge,' Hart said.

'What?'

'Your badge, your badge. Let me see your identification.'

Carella took out his wallet, and opened it to where his detective's shield was pinned opposite his I.D. card. Hart studied both, and then said, 'I thought this might be a shakedown.'

'Why'd you think that?'

Hart did not answer. He looked at the photograph again, shook his head, and said, 'Somebody killed her, huh?'

'Yes, somebody did,' Carella answered. 'Did you know her?'

'I knew her.'

'I thought you said you didn't.'

'I didn't know Sarah Fletcher, if *that's* who you think she was. But I knew *this* broad, all right.'

'Who'd *you* think she was?' Meyer asked.

'Just who she told me she was.'

'Which was?'

'Sadie Collins. She introduced herself as Sadie Collins, and that's who I knew her as. Sadie Collins.'

'Where was this, Mr Hart? Where'd you meet her?'

'In a bar.'

'Where?'

'Who the hell remembers? A singles' bar. The city's full of them.'

'Would you remember when?'

'At least a year ago.'

'Ever go out with her?'

'Yes.'

'How often?'

'Often enough.'

'*How* often?'

'I used to see her once or twice a week.'

'*Used* to? When did you stop seeing her?'

'Last summer.'

'But until then you used to see her quite regularly.'

'Yeah, on and off.'

'Twice a week, you said.'

'Well, yeah.'

'Did you know she was married?'

'Who? Sadie? You're kidding.'

'She never told you she was married?'

'Never.'

'You saw her twice a week ...'

'Yeah.'

'But you didn't know she was married?'

'How was I supposed to know that? She never said a word about it. Listen, there are enough single girls in this city, I don't have to go looking for trouble with somebody who's married.'

'Where'd you pick her up?' Meyer asked suddenly.

'I told you. A bar. I don't remember which ...'

'When you went out, I mean.'

'What?'

'When you were going out, where'd you pick her up? At her apartment?'

'No. She used to come to my place.'

'Where'd you call her? When you wanted to reach her?'

'I didn't. She used to call me.'

'Where'd you go, Mr Hart? When you went out?'

'We didn't go out too much.'

'What *did* you do?'

'She used to come to my place. We'd spend a lot of time there.'

'But when you *did* go out ...'

'Well, the truth is we never went out.'

'Never?'

'Never. She didn't want to go out much.'

'Didn't you think that was strange?'

'No.' Hart shrugged. 'I figured she liked to stay home.'

'If you never went out, what *did* you do, exactly, Mr Hart?'

'Well now, what the hell do you *think* we did, exactly?' Hart said.

'You tell us.'

'You're big boys. Figure it out for yourself.'

'Why'd you stop seeing her, Mr Hart?'

'I met somebody else. A nice girl. I'm very serious about her. That's why I thought ...'

'Yes?'

'Nothing.'

'That's why you thought *what*, Mr Hart?'

'Okay, that's why I thought this was a shakedown. I thought somebody had found out about Sadie and me and ... well ... I'm very serious about this girl. I wouldn't want her to know anything about the past. About Sadie and me. About seeing Sadie.'

'What was so terrible about seeing Sadie?' Meyer asked.

'Nothing.'

'Then why would anyone want to shake you down?'

'I don't know.'

'If there was nothing terrible ...'

'There wasn't.'

'Then what's there to hide?'

'There's nothing to hide. I'm just very serious about this girl, and I wouldn't want her to know ...'

'To know what?'

'About Sadie.'

'Why not?'

'Because I just wouldn't.'

'Was there something wrong with Sadie?'

'No, no, she was a beautiful woman, beautiful.'

'Then why would you be ashamed ...?'

'Ashamed? Who said anything about being ashamed?'

'You said you wouldn't want your girl friend ...'

'Listen, what *is* this? I stopped seeing Sadie six months ago, I wouldn't even talk to her on the *phone* after that. If the crazy bitch got herself killed ...'

'Crazy?'

Hart suddenly wiped his hand over his face, wet his lips, and walked behind his desk. 'I don't think I have anything more to say to you, gentlemen. If you have any other questions, maybe you'd better charge me with something, and I'll ask my lawyer's advice on what to do next.'

'What did you mean when you said she was crazy?' Carella asked.

'Good day, gentlemen,' Hart said.

In the lieutenant's corner office, Byrnes and Carella sat drinking coffee. Byrnes was frowning. Carella was waiting. Neither of the men said a word. A telephone rang in the squadroom outside, and Byrnes looked at his watch.

'Well, yes or no, Pete?' Carella asked at last.

'I'm inclined to say no.'

'Why?'

'Because I don't know why you still want to pursue this thing.'

'Oh come on, Pete! If the goddamn guy *did* it ...'

'That's only *your* allegation. Suppose he *didn't* do it, and suppose *you* do something to screw up the D.A.'s case?'

'Like what?'

'I don't know like what. They've got a grand jury indictment, they're preparing a case against Corwin, how the hell do I know what you might do? The way things are going these days, if you spit on the sidewalk that's enough to get a case thrown out of court.'

'Fletcher hated his wife,' Carella said calmly.

'Lots of men hate their wives. Half the men in this *city* hate their wives.'

'According to Hart ...'

'All right, so she was playing around a little, so what? She had herself a little fling, who doesn't? Half the women in this *city* are having little flings right this minute.'

'*Her* little fling gives Fletcher a good reason for ... look, Pete, what the hell *else* do we need? He had a motive, he had the opportunity, a golden one, in fact, and he had the means – another man's knife sticking out of Sarah's gut. What more do you want?'

'Proof. There's a funny little system we've got here in this city, Steve. It requires proof before we can arrest a man and charge him with murder.'

'Right. And all I'm asking is the opportunity to *try* for it.'

'Sure. By putting a tail on Fletcher. Suppose he sues the goddamn city?'

'For what?'

'He'll *think* of something.'

'Yes or no, Pete? I want permission to conduct a round-the-clock surveillance of Gerald Fletcher, starting Sunday morning. Yes or no?'

'I must be out of my mind,' Byrnes said, and sighed.

Chapter Eight

At 7:30 p.m. on the loneliest night of the week, Bert Kling did a foolish thing. He telephoned Nora Simonov. He did not expect her to be home, so he really did not know why he was calling her. He could only suppose that he was experiencing that great American illness known as the Saturday Night Funk, not to be confused with the Sunday Evening Hiatus or the Monday Morning Blues, none of which are daily newspapers.

The Saturday Night Funk (or the Snf, as it is familiarly known to those who have ever suffered from it) generally begins the night before, along about eight o'clock, when one realizes he does not have a date for that fabulous flight of **FUN** and **FRIVOLITY** known as S*A*T*U*R*D*A*Y N*I*G*H*T U*S*A.

There is no need for panic at this early juncture, of course. The mythical magical merriment is not scheduled to begin for at least another twenty-four hours, time yet to call a dozen birds or even a hundred, no need for any reaction more potent than a mild sort of self-chastisement for having been so tardy in making arrangements for the gay gaudy gala to follow. And should one fail to make a connection that Friday, there is still all day tomorrow to twirl those little holes in the telephone and ring up this or that hot number – Hello, sweetie, I was wondering whether you'd be available for an entertaining evening of enjoyment and eventual enervation – plenty of time, no need to worry.

By Saturday afternoon at about three, the first signs of anxiety begin to set in as this or that luscious lovely announces that, Oh my, I would have been thrilled and delighted to accompany you even into the mouth of a cannon, but oh goodness here it is Saturday afternoon already and you can't expect to call a girl at the last minute and have her free on D*A*T*E N*I*G*H*T U*S*A, can you? Last minute? What last minute? It is still only three in the afternoon, four in the afternoon, five in the evening. Evening? When did it become evening? And desperation pounces.

A quick brush of the hair, a sprinkle of cologne in the armpits, a bold adventurous approach to the phone (cigarette dangling from the lip), a nonchalant scanning of the little black book, a forthright dialling, and, Oh my, I would have adored going with you to the moon or even Jupiter and back, but here it is almost six o'clock on the most R*O*M*A*N*T*I*C N*I*G*H*T of the week, you don't expect a girl to be free at this late hour, do you? The Snf has arrived. It has arrived full-blown because it is now six o'clock, fast approaching seven, and at the stroke of seven-thirty you will turn into Spiro Agnew.

At the stroke of seven-thirty, Bert Kling called Nora Simonov, certain that she'd be out having a good time, like everybody else in the United States of America on this Saturday night.

'Hullo?' she said.

'Nora?' he said, surprised.

'Yes?'

'Hi. This is Bert Kling.'

'Hullo,' she said, 'what time is it?'

'Seven-thirty.'

'I must've fallen asleep. I was watching the six o'clock news.' She yawned and then quickly said, 'Excuse me.'

'Shall I call you back?'

'What for?'

'Give you a chance to wake.'

'I'm awake, that's okay.'

The line went silent.

'Well ... uh ... how are you?' Kling asked.

'Fine,' Nora said, and the line went silent again.

In the next thirty seconds, as static crackled along the line and Kling debated asking the risky question that might prolong his misery eternally, he could not help realizing how spoiled he had been by Cindy Forrest who, until four weeks ago at least, had been available at any hour of the day or night, and *especially* on Saturday, when no red-blooded American male should be left alone to weep into his wine.

'Well, I'm glad you're okay,' Kling said at last.

'Is that why you called? I thought maybe you had another suspect for me to identify,' Nora said, and laughed.

'No, no,' Kling said. 'No.' He laughed with her, immediately sobered, and quickly said. 'As a matter of fact, Nora, I was wondering ...'

'Yes?'

'Would you like to go out?'

'What do you mean?'

'Out.'

'With you?'

'Yes.'

'Oh.'

In the next ten seconds of silence, which seemed much longer to Kling than the earlier thirty seconds of silence had been, he realized he had made a terrible mistake; he was staring directly into the double-barrelled shotgun of rejection and about to have his damn fool head blown off.

'I told you, you know,' Nora said, 'that I'm involved with someone ...'

'Yes, I know. Well, listen ...'

'But I'm *not* doing anything tonight, and ... if you want to go for a walk or something ...'

'I thought maybe dinner.'

'Well ...'

'And maybe dancing later.'

'Well ...'

'I hate to eat alone, don't you?'

'Yes, as a matter of fact, I do. But Bert ...'

'Yes?'

'I feel sort of funny about this.'

'Funny how?'

'Leading you on,' Nora said.

'I've been warned,' he said. 'You've given me fair warning.'

'I *would* like to have dinner with you,' Nora said, 'but ...'

'Can you be ready at eight?'

'You do understand, don't you, that ...?'

'I understand completely.'

'Mmm,' she said dubiously.

'Eight o'clock?'

'Eight-thirty,' she said.

'See you then,' he said, and hung up quickly before she could change her mind. He was grinning when he looked into the mirror. He felt handsome and assured and sophisticated and in complete control of America.

He did not know who Nora's phantom lover was, but he was certain now that she was only playing the age-old maidenly game of shy resistance and that she would succumb soon enough to his masculine charm.

He was dead wrong.

Dinner was all right, he couldn't knock dinner. They exchanged thoughts on a wide variety of subjects:

'I once did a cover for an historical novel,' Nora said, 'with a woman wearing one of these very low-cut velvet gowns, you know, and I was bored to tears while I was doing the roughs, so I gave her three breasts. The art director didn't even notice. I painted out the third one when I did the final painting.'

'I look at myself,' Kling said, 'and I know I'm *not* a pig. I'm a fairly decent human being trying to do his job. And sometimes my job involves getting into situations that are distasteful to me. You think I *like* going onto a college campus and breaking up a protest by kids who don't want to die in a stupid war? But I'm also supposed to see that they don't burn down the administration building. So how do I convince them that keeping law and order, which is my job, is *not* the same as suppression? It gets difficult sometimes.'

'Contact sports,' Nora said, 'are all homosexual in nature, I'm convinced of it. You can't tell me the quarterback isn't copping a feel off the centre every time he grabs that ball.'

And like that.

But after dinner, when Kling suggested that they go dancing at a little place he knew in the Quarter, three-piece band and nice atmosphere, Nora at first demurred, saying she was awfully tired and had promised her mother she would take her out to the cemetery early tomorrow morning, and then finally acquiescing when Kling said it was still only ten-thirty, and promised to have her home by midnight.

Pedro's, as Kling has promised, was long on atmosphere and good music. Dimly illuminated, ideal for lovers both married and un, adulterated or pure, it seemed to work as a deterrent on Nora from the moment she stepped into the place. She was not good at hiding whatever she was feeling (as Kling had earlier noticed), and the ambience of Pedro's was either threatening or nostalgic (and possibly more), with the result that her eyes took on a glazed look, her mouth wilted, her shoulders slumped, she became the kind of

Saturday-night date red-blooded American males feared and avoided; she became a thorough and complete pain in the ass.

Kling asked her to dance in the hope that bodily contact, blood pulsing beneath flesh, hands touching, cheeks brushing, all that jazz might speed along the seduction he had so successfully launched during dinner. But she held him at bay, with a rigid arm on his left shoulder, so that eventually he tired physically of trying to draw her close, being afflicted with bursitis, and tired mentally of all the adolescent fumbling and manoeuvring. He decided to ply her with booze, having been raised in a generation that placed strong store in the seductive powers of alcohol. (He was, incidentally, a cop who had tried pot twice and enjoyed it. He had realized, however, that he could not very well go around offering grass to young ladies, or even lighting up himself, and had abandoned that pleasant pastime.) Nora drank one drink, count it, or to be more exact, *half* a drink, toying with the remainder of it while Kling consumed two more and asked politely, 'Sure you don't want to drink up and have another?' To which she politely shook her head with a wan little smile.

And then, despite her protestations, two days ago, that she did not want to talk about her *grand amour*, the band began playing the Beatles' 'Something' and her eyes misted over, and the next thing Kling knew he was being treated to a monologue about her lover. The man, she confessed, had until just recently been married, and there were still some complications, but she expected they would be cleared up within the next several months, at which time she hoped to become his wife. She did not say what the complications were, but Kling surmised she was talking about a divorce settlement or some such; at this point, he could not have cared less. He had been warned, true, but spending a Saturday night with someone who talked about another man was akin to taking one's mother to a strip joint, maybe worse. He tried to change the subject, but the power of 'Something' prevailed, and, as the band launched into a second chorus, Nora similarly launched into *her* second chorus, so that the music seemed to be accompanying her little tone poem.

'We met entirely by accident,' she said, 'though we learned later that actually we could have met at any time during the past year.'

'Well, *most* people meet entirely by chance,' Kling said.

'Yes, of course, but this was just the most remarkable coincidence.'

'Mmm,' Kling said, and then launched into what he considered a provocative and perhaps completely original observation on The Beatles Phenomenon, remarking that their rise and fall had encompassed a mere five years or so, which seemed significant when one remembered that they were a product of the space age, where speed was of the essence and ...

'He's so far superior to me,' Nora said, 'that sometimes I wonder what he sees in me at all.'

'What does he do for a living?' Kling asked, thinking Ho-hum.

Nora hesitated for only an instant. But because her face was such a meticulous recorder of anything she felt, he knew that what she said next would be a lie. He was suddenly terribly interested.

'He's a doctor,' Nora said, and turned her eyes from his, and lifted her drink, and sipped at it, and then glanced towards the bandstand.

'Is he on staff any place?'

'Yes,' she said immediately, and again, he knew she was lying. 'Isola General.'

'Over on Wilson Avenue?' he asked.

'Yes,' she said.

Kling nodded. Isola General was on Parsons and Lowell, bordering the River Dix.

'When do you expect to be married?' he asked.

'We haven't set the date yet.'

'What's his name?' Kling asked conversationally, and turned away from her, and lifted his own glass, and pretended to be completely absorbed in the band, which was now playing a medley of tunes from the forties, presumably for the Serutan members of their audience.

'Why do you want to know?' Nora asked.

'Just curious. I have a thing about names. I think certain names go together. If, for example, a woman named Freida did not eventually hook up with a man named Albert, I would be enormously surprised.'

'Who do you think a "Nora" should hook up with?'

'A "Bert",' he said immediately and automatically, and was immediately sorry.

'She's *already* hooked up with someone whose name isn't "Bert".'

'What *is* his name?' Kling asked.

Nora shook her head. 'No,' she said. 'I don't think I'll tell you.'

It was twenty minutes to twelve.

True to his promise, Kling paid the check, hailed a taxicab, and took Nora home. She insisted that it wasn't necessary for him to come up in the elevator with her, but he told her there'd been a woman killed here in this very building less than a week ago, and since he was a cop and all, armed to the teeth and all, he might just as well accompany her. Outside the door to her apartment, she shook hands with him and said, 'Thank you, I had a very nice time.'

'Yes, me, too,' he answered, and nodded bleakly.

He got to his apartment at 12:25, and the telephone rang some twenty minutes later. It was Steve Carella.

'Bert,' he said, 'I've arranged with Pete to put a twenty-four-hour tail on Fletcher, and I want to handle the first round myself. You think you can go with Meyer tomorrow when he hits Thornton?'

'Hits *who*?'

'The second guy in Sarah Fletcher's book.'

'Oh, sure, sure. What time's he going?'

'He'll be in touch with you.'

'Where are you, Steve? Home?'

'No, I've got the graveyard shift. Incidentally, there was a call for you.'

'Oh? Who called?'

'Cindy Forrest.'

Kling caught his breath. 'What'd she say?'

'Just to tell you she'd called.'

'Thanks,' Kling said.

'Good night,' Carella said, and hung up.

Kling put the receiver back on its cradle, took off his jacket, loosened his tie, and began unlacing his shoes. Twice he lifted the receiver from its cradle, began dialling Cindy's number, and changed his mind. Instead, he turned on the television in time to catch the one o'clock news. The weather forecaster announced that the promised snowstorm had blown out to sea. Kling got undressed, and went to bed.

Chapter Nine

Michael Thornton lived in an apartment building several blocks from the Quarter, close enough to absorb some of its artistic flavour, distant enough to escape in high rents. Kling and Meyer did not knock on Thornton's door until 11 a.m., on the theory that a man is entitled to sleep late of a Sunday morning, even if his name is listed in a dead lady's address book.

The man who opened the door was perhaps twenty-eight years old, with blond hair and a blond beard stubble. He was wearing pyjama bottoms and socks, and his brown eyes were still edged with sleep. They had announced themselves as policemen through the wooden barrier of the closed door, and now the blond man looked at them bleary-eyed and asked to see their badges. He studied Meyer's shield, nodded, and, without moving from his position in the doorway, yawned and said, 'So what can I do for you?'

'We're looking for a man named Michael Thornton. Would you happen to be ...?'

'Mike isn't here right now.'

'Does he live here?'

'He lives here, but he isn't here right now.'

'Where is he?'

'What's this about?' the man said.

'Routine investigation,' Kling said.

The words 'routine investigation', Kling noticed, never failed to strike terror into the hearts of man or beast. Had he said they were investigating a hatchet murder or a nursery school arson, the blond man's face would not have gone as pale, his eyes would not have begun to blink the way they did. In the land of supersell, the understatement – 'routine investigation' – was more powerful than trumpets and kettledrums. The blond man was visibly frightened and thinking furiously. Somewhere in the building, a toilet flushed. Meyer and Kling waited patiently.

'Do you know where he is?' Kling said at last.

'Whatever this is, I know he had nothing to do with it.'

'It's just a routine investigation,' Kling repeated, and smiled.

'What's *your* name?' Meyer asked.

'Paul Wendling.'

'Do you live here?'

'Yes.'

'Do you know where we can find Michael Thornton?'

'He went over to the shop.'

'What shop?'

'We have a jewellery shop in the Quarter. We make silver jewellery.'

'The shop's open today?'

'Not to the public. We're not violating the law, if that's what you're thinking.'

'If you're not open to the public ...'

'Mike's working on some new stuff. We make our jewellery in the back of the shop.'

'What's the address there?' Meyer asked.

'1156 Hadley Place.'

'Thank you,' Meyer said.

Behind them, Paul Wendling watched as they went down the steps, and then quickly closed the door.

'You know what he's doing right this minute?' Meyer asked.

'Sure,' Kling said. 'He's calling his pal at the shop to tell him we're on the way over.'

Michael Thornton, as they had guessed, was not surprised to see them. They held up their shields to the plate-glass entrance door, but he was clearly expecting them, and he unlocked the door at once.

'Mr Thornton?' Meyer asked.

'Yes?'

He was wearing a blue work smock, but the contours of the garment did nothing to hide his powerful build. Wide-shouldered, barrel-chested, thick forearms and wrists showing below the short sleeves of the smock, he backed away from the door like a boulder moving on ball bearings and allowed them to enter the shop. His eyes were blue, his hair black. A small scar showed white in the thick eyebrow over his left eye.

'We understand you're working,' Meyer said. 'Sorry to break in on you this way.'

'That's okay,' Thornton said. 'What's up?'

'You know a woman named Sarah Fletcher?'

'No,' Thornton said.

'You know a woman named Sadie Collins?'

Thornton hesitated. 'Yes,' he said.

'This the woman?' Meyer asked, and showed him a newly made stat of the photograph they had confiscated from the Fletcher bedroom.

'That's Sadie. What about her?'

They were standing near Thornton's showcase, a four-foot-long box on tubular steel legs. Rings, bracelets, necklaces, pendants dizzily reflected the sunshine that slanted through the front window of the shop. Meyer took his time putting the stat back into his notebook, meanwhile giving Kling a chance to observe Thornton. The picture seemed to have had no visible effect on him. Like the solid mass of mountain that he was, he waited silently, as though challenging the detectives to scale him.

'What was your relationship with her?' Kling said.

Thornton shrugged, 'Why?' he asked. 'Is she in trouble?'

'When's the last time you saw her?'

'You didn't answer my question,' Thornton said.

'Well, you didn't answer ours, either,' Meyer said, and smiled. 'What was your relationship with her, and when did you see her last?'

'I met her in July and the last time I saw her was in August. We had a brief hot thing, and then good-bye.'

'Where'd you meet her?'

'In a joint called The Saloon.'

'Where's that?'

'Right around the corner. Near what used to be the legit theatre there. The one that's showing skin flicks now. The Saloon's a bar, but they also serve sandwiches and soup. It's not a bad joint. It gets a big crowd, especially on week-ends.'

'Singles?'

'Mostly. A couple of fags thrown in for spice. But it's not a gay bar, not by the usual definition.'

'And you say you met Sadie in July?'

'Yeah. The beginning of July. I remember because I was supposed to go out to Greensward that week-end, but the broad who was renting the bungalow already invited ten other people to the beach, so I got stuck here in the city. You ever get stuck here in the city on a week-end in July?'

'Occasionally,' Meyer said drily.

'How'd you happen to meet her?' Kling asked.

'She admired the ring I was wearing. It was a good opening gambit because the ring happened to be one of my own.' Thornton paused. 'I designed it and made it. Here at the shop.'

'Was she alone when you met her?' Kling asked.

'Alone and lonely,' Thornton said, and grinned. It was a knowing grin, a grin hoping for a similar grin in response from Kling and Meyer, who, being cops, had undoubtedly seen and heard all kinds of things and were therefore men of the world, as was Thornton himself, comrades three who knew all about lonely women in singles' bars.

'Did you realize she was married?' Kling asked, sort of spoiling the Three Musketeers image.

'No. Is she?'

'Yes,' Meyer said. Neither of the detectives had yet informed Thornton that the lady in question, Sarah or Sadie or both, was now unfortunately deceased. They were saving that for last, like dessert.

'So what happened?' Kling said.

'Gee, I didn't know she was married,' Thornton said, seeming truly surprised. 'Otherwise *nothing* would've happened.'

'What *did* happen?'

'I bought her a few drinks, and then I took her home with me. I was living alone at the time, the same pad on South Lindner, but alone. We balled, and then I put her in a cab.'

'When did you see her next?'

'The following day. It was goofy. She called me in the morning, said she was on her way downtown. I was still in bed. I said, "So come on down, baby." And she did. *Believe* me, she did.' Thornton grinned his man-of-the-world grin again, inviting Kling and Meyer into his exclusive all-male club that knew all about women calling early in the morning to say they were on their way down, baby. Somehow, Kling and Meyer did not grin back.

Instead, Kling said, 'Did you see her again after that?'

'Two or three times a week.'

'Where'd you go?'

'To the pad on South Lindner.'

'Never went any place but there?'

'Never. She'd give me a buzz on the phone, say she was on her way, and was I ready? Man, I was *always* ready for her.'

'Why'd you quit seeing her?'

'I went out of town for a while. When I got back, I just didn't hear from her again.'

'Why didn't you call her?'

'I didn't know where to reach her.'

'She never gave you her phone number?'

'Nope. Wasn't listed in the directory, either. No place in the city. I tried all five books.'

'Speaking of books,' Kling said, 'what do you make of this?'

He opened Sarah Fletcher's address book to the MEMORANDA page and extended it to Thornton. Thornton studied it and said, 'Yeah, what about it? She wrote this down the night we met.'

'You saw her writing it?'

'Sure.'

'Did she write those initials at the same time?'

'What initials?'

'The ones in parentheses. Under your phone number.'

Thornton studied the page more closely. 'How would I know?' he said, frowning.

'You said you saw her writing ...'

'Yeah, but I didn't see the actual page. I mean, we were in *bed*, man, this was like after the second time around, and she asked me what the address was, and how she could get in touch with me, and I told her. But I didn't actually see the page itself. I only saw her writing in the book, you dig?'

'Got any idea what the initials mean?'

'TS can only mean "Tough Shit",' Thornton said, and grinned.

'Any reason why she might want to write that in her book?' Meyer asked.

'Hey, I'm only kidding,' Thornton said, the grin expanding. 'We had a ball together. Otherwise, why'd she keep coming back for more?'

'Who knows? She *stopped* coming back, didn't she?'

'Only because I went out of town for a while.'

'How long a while?'

'Four days,' Thornton said. 'I went out to Arizona to pick up some Indian silver. We sell some crap here, too, in addition to what Paul and I make.'

'Gone only four days, and the lady never called again,' Kling said.

'Yeah, well, maybe she got sore. I left kind of sudden like.'

'What day was it?'

'Huh?'

'The day you left?'

'I don't know. Why? The middle of the week, I guess. I don't remember. Anyway, who cares?' Thornton said. 'There are plenty of broads in this city. What's one more or less?' He shrugged, and then looked suddenly thoughtful.

'Yes?' Meyer said.

'Nothing. Just ...'

'Yes?'

'She *was* kind of special, I have to admit it. I mean, she wasn't the kind of broad you'd take home to mother, but she was something else. She was *really* something else.'

'How do you mean?'

'She was ...' Thornton grinned. 'Let's put it this way,' he said. 'She took me places I'd never been before, you know what I mean?'

'No, what do you mean?' Kling said.

'Use your imagination,' Thornton said, still grinning.

'I can't,' Kling answered. 'There's no place I've never been before.'

'Sadie would've *found* some for you,' Thornton said, and the grin suddenly dropped from his face. 'She'll call again, I'm sure of it. She's got my number right there in her book, she'll call.'

'I wouldn't count on it,' Meyer said.

'Why not? She kept coming back, didn't she? We had ...'

'She's dead,' Meyer said.

They kept watching his face. It did not crumble, it did not express grief, it did not even express shock. The only thing it expressed was sudden anger.

'The stupid twat,' Thornton said. 'That's all she ever was, a stupid twat.'

Police work (like life) is often not too tidy. Take surveillance, for example. On Friday afternoon, Carella had asked Byrnes for permission to begin surveillance of Gerald Fletcher on Sunday morning. Being a police officer himself, and knowing that police work (like life) is often not too tidy, Byrnes never once thought of asking Carella why he would not prefer to start his surveillance the very next day, Saturday, instead of waiting two days. The reason Carella did not choose to start the very next day was that police work (like life) is often not too tidy – as in the case of the noun 'surveillance' and the noun/adjective 'surveillant', neither of which has a verb to go with it in the English language.

Carella had 640 odds-and-ends to clean up in the office on Saturday before he could begin the surveillance of Gerald Fletcher with anything resembling an easy conscience. So he had spent the day making phone calls and typing up reports and generally trying to put things in order. In all his years of police experience, he had never known a criminal who was so considerate of a policeman's lot that he would wait patiently for one crime to be solved before committing another. There were four burglaries, two assaults, a robbery, and a forgery still unsolved in Carella's case load; the least he could to was try to create some semblance of order from the information he had on each before embarking on a lengthy and tedious surveillance. Besides, surveillance (like police work) is often not too tidy.

On Sunday morning, Carella was ready to become a surveillant. That is to say, he was ready to adopt a surveillant stance and thereby begin surveillance of his suspect. The trouble was, just as the English language had been exceptionally untidy in not having stolen the verb from the French when it swiped the noun and the adjective, a surveillance (like life and like police work) is bound to get untidy if there is nobody to *surveille*.

Gerald Fletcher was nowhere in sight.

Carella had started his surveillance with the usual police gambit of calling Fletcher's apartment from a nearby phone booth early in the morning. The object of this sometimes transparent ploy was to ascertain that the suspect was still in his own digs, after which the police tail would wait downstairs for him to emerge and then follow him to and fro wherever he went. Gerald Fletcher, however, was *not* in his digs. This being Sunday morning, Carella automatically assumed that Fletcher was spending the week-end elsewhere. But, intrepid law enforcer he, and steadfast surveillant besides, he parked the squad's new (used) 1970 Buick sedan across the street from Fletcher's apartment building, and alternately watched the front door of 721 Silvermine Oval and the kids playing in the park, thinking that perhaps Fletcher had merely spent S*A*T*U*R*D*A*Y N*I*G*H*T some place and might return home momentarily.

At twelve noon, Carella got out of the car, walked into the park, and sat on a bench facing the building. He ate the ham and cheese sandwich his wife had prepared for him, and drank a soft drink that beat the others cold but wasn't so hot hot. Then he stretched his legs by walking over to the railing that overlooked the river, never taking his eyes off the building, and finally went back to the car. His vigil ended at 5 a.m., when he was relieved by Detective Arthur Brown, driving the squad's old 1968 Chevrolet sedan. Brown was equipped with a description of Fletcher as well as a photograph swiped from the bedroom dresser in Fletcher's apartment. In addition, he knew what sort of automobile Fletcher drove, courtesy of the Motor Vehicle Bureau. He told Carella to take it easy, and then he settled down to the serious business of watching a doorway for the next seven hours, at which time he was scheduled to be relieved by O'Brien, who would hold the fort until eight in the morning, when Kapek would report to work for the long daytime stretch.

Carella went home to read his son's latest note to Santa Claus, and then he had dinner with the family and was settling down in the living room with a novel he had bought a week ago and had not yet cracked, when the telephone rang.

'I've got it!' he yelled, knowing that Teddy could not hear him, and knowing this was Fanny's day off, but also knowing that Mark, his son, had a habit these days of answering the telephone with the words 'Automobile Squad, Carella here,' all well and good unless the *caller* happened to be a detective from the Automobile Squad trying to report on a stolen vehicle.

'Hello?' Carella said into the mouthpiece.

'Hello, Steve?'

'Yes?' Carella said. He did not recognize the voice.

'This is Gerry.'

'Who?'

'Gerry Fletcher.'

Carella almost dropped the phone. 'Hello,' he said, 'how are you?'

'Fine, thanks. I was away for the week-end, just got back a little while ago, in fact. I frankly find this apartment depressing as hell. I was wondering if you'd like to join me for a drink.'

'Well,' Carella said, 'it's late, and I was just about to ...'

'Nonsense, it's not even eight o'clock.'

'Yes, but it's Sunday night ...'

'Hop in your car and meet me down here,' Fletcher said. 'We'll do a little old-fashioned pub crawling, what the hell.'

'No, I really couldn't. Thanks a lot, Gerry, but ...'

'Take you half an hour to get here,' Fletcher said, 'and you may end up saving my life. If I sit here alone another five minutes, I'm liable to throw myself out the window.' He suddenly began laughing. 'You know what the Penal Law has to say about suicide, don't you?'

'No, what?' Carella asked.

'Silliest damn section in the book,' Fletcher said, still laughing. 'It says, and I quote *"Although suicide is deemed a grave public wrong, yet from the impossibility of reaching the successful perpetrator, no forfeiture is imposed."* How do you like *that* for legal nonsense? Come on, Steve. I'll show you some of the city's brighter spots, we'll have a few drinks, what do you say?'

It suddenly occurred to Carella that Gerald Fletcher had *already* had a few drinks before placing his call. It further occurred to him that if he played this *too* cosily, Fletcher might rescind his generous offer. And since there was nothing Carella wanted more than a night on the town with a murder suspect who might possibly drink more than was prudent for his own best interests, he immediately said, 'Okay, I'll see you at eight-thirty. Provided I can square it with my wife.'

'Good,' Fletcher said. 'See you.'

Chapter Ten

Paddy's Bar & Grille was on the Stem, adjacent to the city's theatre district. Carella and Fletcher got there at about nine o'clock, while the place was still relatively quiet. The action began a little later, Fletcher explained, the operative theory behind a singles operation being that neither bachelor nor career girl should seem too obvious about wanting to make each other's acquaintance. If you began to prowl too early, you appeared eager. If you got there too late, however, you missed out. The idea was to time your arrival just as the crowd was beginning to reach its peak, wandering in as though casually looking for a phone booth instead of a partner.

'You seem to know a lot about it,' Carella said.

'I'm an observant man,' Fletcher said, and smiled. 'What are you drinking?'

'Scotch and soda,' Carella said.

'A scotch and soda,' Fletcher said to the bartender, 'and a Beefeater's martini, straight up.'

He had drunk whisky sours the day they'd had lunch together, Carella remembered, but he was drinking martinis tonight. Good. The more potent the drinks, the looser his tongue might become. Carella looked around the room. The men ranged in age from the low thirties to the late fifties, a scant dozen in the place at this early hour, all of them neatly dressed in city week-end clothes, sports jackets and slacks, some wearing shirts and ties, others wearing skirts with ascots, still others wearing turtlenecks. The women, half in number, were dressed casually as well – pants suits, skirts, blouses or sweaters, with only one brave and rather ugly soul dressed to the teeth in a silk Pucci. The mating game, at this hour, consisted of sly glances and discreet smiles; no one was willing to take a real gamble until he'd had an opportunity to look over the entire field.

'What do you think of it?' Fletcher asked.

'I've seen worse,' Carella said.

'I'll bet you have. Would it be fair to say you've also seen better?' Their drinks arrived at that moment, and Fletcher lifted his glass in a silent toast. 'What kind of person would you say comes to a place like this?' he asked.

'Judging from appearances alone, and it's still early ...'

'It's a fairly representative crowd,' Fletcher said.

'I would say we've got a nice lower-middle-class clientele bent on making contact with members of the opposite sex.'

'A pretty decent element, would you say?'

'Oh, yes,' Carella answered. 'You go into some places, you know immediately that half the people surrounding you are thieves. I don't smell that here. Small businessmen, junior executives, divorced ladies, bachelor girls – for example, there isn't a hooker in the lot, which is unusual for a bar on the Stem.'

'Can you recognize a hooker by just looking at her?'

'Usually.'

'What would you say if I told you the blonde in the Pucci is a working prostitute?'

Carella looked at the woman again. 'I don't think I'd believe you.'

'Why not?'

'Well, to begin with, she's a bit old for the young competition parading the streets these days. Secondly, she's in deep conversation with a plump little girl who undoubtedly came down from Riverhead looking for a nice boy she can bed and eventually marry. And thirdly, she's not *selling* anything. She's waiting for one of those two or three older guys to make their move. Hookers don't wait, Gerry. *They* make the approach, *they* do the selling. Business is business, and time is money. They can't afford to sit around being coy.' Carella paused. '*Is* she a working prostitute?'

'I haven't the faintest idea,' Fletcher said. 'Never even saw her before tonight. I was merely trying to indicate that appearances can sometimes be misleading. Drink up, there are a few more places I'd like to show you.'

He knew Fletcher well enough, he thought, to realize that the man was trying to tell him something. At lunch last Tuesday, Fletcher had transmitted a message and a challenge: *I killed my wife, what can you do about it?* Tonight, in a similar manner, he was attempting to indicate something else, but Carella could not fathom exactly what.

Fanny's was only twenty blocks away from Paddy's Bar & Grille, but as far removed from it as the moon. Whereas the first bar seemed to cater to a quiet crowd peacefully pursuing its romantic inclinations, Fanny's was noisy and raucous, jammed to the rafters with men and women of all ages, wearing plastic hippie crap purchased in head shops up and down Jackson Avenue. If Paddy's had registered a seven on the scale of desirability and respectability, Fanny's rated a four. The language sounded like what Carella was used to hearing in the squadroom or in any of the cellblocks at Calcutta.

There were half a dozen hookers lining the bar, suffering severely from the onslaught of half a hundred girls in skin-tight costumes wiggling their behinds and thrusting their breasts at anything warm and moving. The approaches were blatant and unashamed. There were more hands on asses than Carella could count, more meaningful glances and ardent sighs than seemed possible outside of a bedroom, more invitations than Truman Capote had sent out for his last masked ball. As Carella and Fletcher elbowed their way towards the bar, a brunette wearing a short skirt and a see-through blouse without a bra, planted herself directly in Carella's path and said, 'What's the password, stranger?'

'Scotch and soda,' Carella said.

'Wrong,' the girl answered and moved closer to him.

'What is it then,' he asked.

'Kiss me,' she said.

'Some other time,' he answered.

'That isn't a command,' she said, giggling, 'it's only the password.'

'Good,' he said.

'So if you want to get to the bar,' the girl said, 'say the password.'

'Kiss me,' he said, and was moving past her when she threw her arms around his neck and delivered a wet open-mouthed, tongue-writhing kiss that shook him to his socks. She held the kiss for what seemed like an hour and a half, and then, with her arms still around his neck, she moved her head back a fraction of an inch, touched her nose to his, and said, 'I'll see you later, stranger. I have to go to the Ladies.'

At the bar, Carella wondered when he had last kissed anyone but his wife, Teddy. As he ordered a drink, he felt a soft pressure against his arm, turned to his left, and found one of the hookers, a black girl in her twenties, leaning in against him and smiling.

'What took you so long to get here?' she said. 'I've been waiting all night.'

'For what?' he said.

'For the good time I'm going to show you.'

'Wow, have *you* got the wrong number,' Carella said, and turned to Fletcher, who was already lifting his martini glass.

'Welcome to Fanny's,' Fletcher said, and raised his glass in a toast, and then drank the contents in one swallow and signalled to the bartender for another. 'You will find many of them on exhibit,' he said.

'Many what?'

'Many fannies. And other things as well.' The bartender brought a fresh martini with lightning speed and grace. Fletcher lifted the glass. 'I hope you don't mind if I drink myself into a stupor,' he said.

'Go right ahead,' Carella answered.

'Merely pour me into the car at the end of the night, and I'll be eternally grateful.' Fletcher lifted the glass and drank. 'I don't usually consume this much alcohol,' he said, 'but I'm very troubled about that boy ...'

'What boy?' Carella said immediately.

'Listen, honey,' the black hooker said, 'aren't you going to buy a girl a drink?'

'Ralph Corwin,' Fletcher said. 'I understand he's having some difficulty with his lawyer, and ...'

'Don't be such a tight-ass,' the girl said. 'I'm thirsty as hell here.'

Carella turned to look at her. Their eyes met and locked. The girl's look said, What do you say? Do you want it or not? Carella's look said, Honey, you're asking for big trouble. Neither of them exchanged a word. The girl got up and moved four stools down the bar, to sit next to a middle-aged man wearing bell-bottomed suede pants and a tangerine-coloured shirt with billowing sleeves.

'You were saying?' Carella said, turning again to Fletcher.

'I was saying I'd like to help Corwin somehow.'

'*Help* him?'

'Yes. Do you think Rollie Chabrier would consider it strange if I suggested a good defence lawyer for the boy?'

'I think he might consider it passing strange, yes.'

'Do I detect a note of sarcasm in your voice?'

'Not at all. Why, I'd guess that ninety percent of all men whose wives have been murdered will then go out and recommend a good defence lawyer for the accused murderer. You've *got* to be kidding.'

'I'm not. Look, I know that what I'm about to say doesn't go over very big with you ...'

'Then don't say it.'

'No, no, I *want* to say it.' Fletcher took another swallow of his drink. 'I feel sorry for that boy. I feel ...'

'Hello, stranger.' The brunette was back. She had taken the stool vacated by the hooker, and now she looped her arm familiarly through Carella's and asked, 'Did you miss me?'

'Desperately,' he said. 'But I'm having a very important conversation with my friend here, and ...'

'Never mind your friend,' the girl said. 'I'm Alice Ann, who are you?'

'I'm Dick Nixon,' Carella said.

'Nice to meet you, Dick,' the girl answered. 'Would you like to kiss me again?'

'No.'

'Why not?'

'Because I have these terrible sores inside my mouth,' Carella said, 'and I wouldn't want you to catch them.'

Alice Ann looked at him and blinked. She reached for his drink then, apparently wishing to wash out her possibly already contaminated mouth, realized it was *his* filthy drink, turned immediately to the man on her left, pushed his arm aside, grabbed his glass, and hastily swallowed a mouthful of disinfectant alcohol. The man said, 'Hey!' and Alice Ann said, 'Cool it, Buster,' and got off the stool, throwing Carella a look even more scorching than her kiss had been, and swivelling off towards a galaxy of young men glittering in a corner of the crowded room.

'You won't understand this,' Fletcher said, 'but I feel grateful to that boy. I'm glad he killed her, and I'd hate to see him punished for what I consider an act of mercy.'

'Take my advice,' Carella said. '*Don't* suggest this to Rollie. I don't think he'd understand.'

'Do *you* understand?' Fletcher asked.

'Not entirely,' Carella said.

Fletcher finished his drink. 'Let's get the hell out of here,' he said. 'Unless you see something you want.'

'I already *have* everything I want,' Carella answered, and wondered if he should tell Teddy about the brunette in the peekaboo blouse.

The Purple Chairs was a bar farther downtown, apparently misnamed, since everything in the place was purple *except* the chairs. Ceiling, walls, bar, tables, curtains, napkins, mirrors, lights, all were purple. The chairs were white.

The misnomer was intentional.

The Purple Chairs was a Lesbian bar, and the subtle question being asked was: Is everybody out of step but Johnny? The chairs were white. Pure. Pristine. Innocent. Virginal. Then why insist on calling them purple? Where did perversity lie, in the actuality or in the labelling?

'Why here?' Carella asked immediately.

'Why not?' Fletcher answered. 'I'm showing you some of the city's more frequented spots.'

Carella strenuously doubted that this was one of the city's more frequented spots. It was now a little past eleven, and the place was only sparsely populated, entirely by women – women talking, women smiling, women dancing to the jukebox, women touching, women kissing. As Carella and Fletcher moved towards the bar, tended by a bull dagger with shirt sleeves rolled up over her powerful forearms, a rush of concerted hostility focused upon them like the beam of a death ray. The bartender verbalized it.

'Sightseeing?' she asked.

'Just browsing,' Fletcher answered.

'Try the public library.'

'It's closed.'

'Maybe you're not getting my message.'

'What's your message?'

'Is anybody bothering *you*?' the bartender asked.

'No.'

'Then stop bothering *us*. We don't need you here, and we don't want you here. You like to see freaks, go to the circus.' The bartender turned away, moving swiftly to a woman at the end of the bar.

'I think we've been invited to leave,' Carella said.

'We certainly haven't been invited to stay,' Fletcher said. 'Did you get a good look?'

'I've been inside dyke bars before.'

'Really? My first time was in September. Just goes to show,' he said, and moved unsteadily towards the purple entrance door.

The cold December air worked furiously on the martinis Fletcher had consumed, so that by the time they got to a bar named Quigley's Rest, just off Skid Row, he was stumbling along drunkenly and clutching Carella's arm for support. Carella suggested that perhaps it was time to be heading home, but Fletcher said he wanted Carella to see them all, see them all, and then led him into the kind of joint Carella had mentioned earlier, where he knew instantly that he was stepping into a hangout frequented by denizens, and was instantly grateful for the .38 holstered at his hip. The floor of Quigley's Rest was covered with sawdust, the lights were dim, the place at twenty minutes to midnight was crowded with people who had undoubtedly awoken at 10 p.m. and who would go till ten the next morning. There was very little about their external appearances to distinguish them from the customers in the first bar Fletcher and Carella had visited. They were similarly dressed, they spoke in the same carefully modulated voices, they were neither as blatant as the crowd in Fanny's nor as subdued as the crowd in The Purple Chairs. But if a speeding shark in cloudy water can still be distinguished from a similarly speeding dolphin, so were the customers in Quigley's immediately identified as dangerous and deadly. Carella was not sure that Fletcher sensed this as strongly as he, himself, did. He knew only that he did not wish to stay here long, especially with Fletcher as drunk as he was.

The trouble started almost at once.

Fletcher shoved his way into position, and a thin-faced young man wearing a dark blue suit and a flowered tie more appropriate to April than December turned towards him sharply and said, 'Watch it.' He barely whispered the words, but they hung on the air with deadly menace, and before Fletcher could react or reply, the young man shoved the flat of his palm against Fletcher's upper arm, with such force that he knocked him to the floor. Fletcher blinked up at him, and started to get drunkenly to his feet. The young man suddenly kicked him in the chest, a flatfooted kick that was less powerful than the shove had been but had the same effect. Fletcher fell back to the floor again, and this time his head crashed heavily against the sawdust. The young man swung his body in preparation for another kick, this time aiming it at Fletcher's head.

'That's it,' Carella said.

. The young man hesitated. Still poised on the ball of one foot, the other slightly back and cocked for release, he looked at Carella and said, '*What's* it?' He was smiling. He seemed to welcome the opportunity of taking on another victim. He turned fully towards Carella now, balancing his weight evenly on both feet, fists bunched. 'Did you say something?' he asked, still smiling.

'Pack your bag, sonny,' Carella said, and bent down to help Fletcher to his feet. He was prepared for what happened next, and was not surprised by it. The only one surprised was the young man, who threw his right fist at the crouching Carella and suddenly found himself flying over Carella's head to land flat on his back in the sawdust. He did next what he had done instinctively since the time he was twelve years old. He reached for a knife in the side pocket of his trousers. Carella did not wait for the knife to clear his pocket. Carella kicked him cleanly and swiftly in the balls. Then he turned to the bar, where another young man seemed ready to spring into action, and very quietly said, 'I'm a police officer. Let's cool it, huh?'

The second young man cooled it very quickly. The place was very silent now. With his back to the bar, and hoping the bartender would not hit him on the head with a sap or a bottle or both, Carella reached under Fletcher's arms and helped him up.

'You okay?' he said.

'Yes, fine,' Fletcher said.

'Come on.'

He walked Fletcher to the door, moving as swiftly as possible. He fully recognized that his shield afforded little enough protection in a place like this, and all he wanted to do was get the hell out fast. On the street, as they stumbled towards the automobile, he prayed only that they would not be cold-cocked before they got to it.

A half-dozen men came out of the bar just as they climbed into the automobile. 'Lock that door!' Carella snapped, and then turned the ignition key, and stepped on the gas, and the car lurched away from the kerb in a squeal of burning rubber. He did not ease up on the accelerator until they were a mile from Quigley's, by which time he was certain they were not being followed.

'That was very nice,' Fletcher said.

'Yes, very nice indeed,' Carella said.

'I admire that. I admire a man who can do that,' Fletcher said.

'Why in hell did you pick *that* sweet dive?' Carella asked.

'I wanted you to see them all,' Fletcher said, and then eased his head back against the seat cushion, and fell promptly asleep.

Chapter Eleven

Early Monday morning, on Kling's day off, he called Cindy Forrest. It was only seven-thirty, but he knew her sleeping and waking habits as well as he knew his own, and since the phone was on the kitchen wall near the refrigerator, and since she would at that moment be preparing breakfast, he was not surprised when she answered it on the second ring.

'Hello?' she said. She sounded rushed, a trifle breathless. She always allowed herself a scant half hour to get out of the apartment each morning, rushing from bedroom to kitchen to bathroom to bedroom again, finally running for the elevator, looking miraculously well-groomed and sleek and rested and ready to do battle with the world. He visualized her standing now at the kitchen phone, only partially clothed, and felt a faint stirring of desire.

'Hi, Cindy,' he said, 'it's me.'

'Oh, hello, Bert,' she said. 'Can you hold just a second? The coffee's about to boil over.' He waited. In the promised second, she was back on the line. 'Okay,' she said. 'I tried to reach you the other night.'

'Yes, I know. I'm returning your call.'

'Right, right,' she said. There was a long silence. 'I'm trying to remember why I called you. Oh, yes. I found a shirt of yours in the dresser, and I wanted to know what I should do with it. So I called you at home, and there was no answer, and then I figured you probably had night duty, and I tried the squadroom, but Steve said you weren't on. So I decided to wrap it up and mail it. I've already got it all addressed and everything.'

There was another silence.

'So I guess I'll drop it off at the post office on my way to work this morning,' Cindy said.

'Okay,' Kling said.

'If that's what you want me to do,' Cindy said.

'Well what would you *like* to do?'

'It's all wrapped and everything, so I guess that's what I'll do.'

'Be a lot of trouble to *un*wrap it, I guess,' Kling said.

'Why would I want to unwrap it?'

'I don't know. Why did you call me Saturday night?'

'To ask what you wanted me to do with the shirt.'

'What choices did you have in mind?'

'When? Saturday night?'

'Yes,' Kling said. 'When you called.'

'Well, there were several possibilities, I guess. You could have stopped here to pick up the shirt, or I could have dropped it off at your place or the squadroom, or we could have had a drink together or something, at which time ...'

'I didn't know that was permissible.'

'Which?'

'Having a drink together. Or *any* of those things, in fact.'

'Well, it's all academic now, isn't it? You weren't home when I called, and you weren't working, either, so I wrapped up the goddamn shirt, and I'll mail it to you this morning.'

'What are you sore about?'

'Who's sore?' Cindy said.

'You sound sore.'

'I have to get out of here in twenty minutes and I still haven't had my coffee.'

'Wouldn't want to be late for the hospital,' Kling said. 'Might upset your friend Dr Freud.'

'Ha-ha,' Cindy said mirthlessly.

'How is he, by the way?'

'He's fine, by the way.'

'Good.'

'Bert?'

'Yes, Cindy?'

'Never mind, nothing.'

'What is it?'

'Nothing. I'll put the shirt in the mail. I washed it and ironed it, I hope it doesn't get messed up.'

'I hope not.'

'Good-bye, Bert,' she said, and hung up.

Kling put the receiver back onto its cradle, sighed, and went into the kitchen. He ate a breakfast of grapefruit juice, coffee, and two slices of toast, and then went back into the bedroom and dialled Nora Simonov's number. When he asked her if she would like to have lunch with him, she politely refused, saying she had an appointment with an art director. Fearful of being turned down for dinner as well, he hedged his bet by asking if she'd like to meet him for a drink at about five, five-thirty. She surprised him by saying she would love it, and they agreed to meet at The Oasis, a quiet cocktail lounge in one of the city's oldest hotels, near the western end of Grover Park. Kling went into the bathroom to brush his teeth.

*　　*　　*

434 North Sixteenth Street was a brownstone within the precinct territory, between Ainsley and Culver avenues. Meyer and Carella found a listing for an L. Kantor in one of the mailboxes downstairs, tried the inner lobby door, found it unlocked, and started up to the fourth floor without ringing the downstairs bell. They had tried calling the number listed in Sarah's address book, but the telephone company had reported it temporarily out of service. Whether this was true or not was a serious question for debate.

'The Telephone Blues' was a dirge still being sung by most residents of the city, and it was becoming increasingly more difficult these days to know if a phone was busy, out of order, disconnected, temporarily out of service, or stolen in the night by an international band of telephone thieves. The direct-dialling system had been a brilliant innovation, except that after directly dialling the digits necessary to place a call, the caller was more often than not greeted with: (a) silence; (b) a recording; (c) a busy signal, or (d) a series of strange beeps and boops. After trying to direct-dial the same number three or four times, the caller was inevitably reduced to dealing with one or more operators (all of whom sounded as if they were in a trainee programme for people with ratings of less than 48 on the Stanford-Binet scale of intelligence) and sometimes actually got to talk to the party he was calling. On too many occasions, Carella visualized someone in desperate trouble trying to reach a doctor, a policeman, or a fireman. The police had a number to call for emergency assistance – but what the hell good was the number if you could never get the *phone* to work? Such were Carella's thoughts as he plodded up the four flights to the apartment of Lou Kantor, the third man listed in Sarah's address book.

Meyer knocked on the door. Both men waited. He knocked again.

'Yes?' a woman's voice said. 'Who is it?'

'Police officers,' Meyer answered.

There was a short silence. Then the woman said, 'Just a moment, please.'

'Think he's home?' Meyer whispered.

Carella shrugged. They heard footsteps approaching the door. Through the closed door, the woman said, 'What do you want?'

'We're looking for Lou Kantor,' Meyer said.

'Why?'

'Routine investigation,' Meyer said.

The door opened a crack, held by a night-chain. 'Let me see your badge,' the woman said. Whatever else they had learned, the citizens of this good city knew that you always asked a cop to show his badge because otherwise he might turn out to be a robber or a rapist or a murderer, and then where were you? Meyer held up his shield. The woman studied it through the narrow opening, and then closed the door again, slipped off the night-chain, and opened the door wide.

'Come in,' she said.

They went into the apartment. The woman closed and locked the door behind them. They were standing in a small, tidy kitchen. Through a doorless doorframe, they could see into the next room, obviously the living room with two easy chairs, a sofa, a floor lamp, and a television set. The woman was perhaps thirty-five years old, five feet eight inches tall, with a solid frame, and a square face fringed with short dark hair. She was wearing a robe over pyjamas, and she was barefoot. Her eyes were blue and suspicious. She looked from one cop to the other, waiting.

'Is he here?' Meyer asked.

'Is who here?'

'Mr Kantor.'

The woman looked at him, puzzled. Understanding suddenly flashed in her blue eyes. A thin smile formed on her mouth. '*I'm* Lou Kantor,' she said. 'Louise Kantor. What can I do for you?'

'Oh,' Meyer said, and studied her.

'What can I do for you?' Lou repeated. The smile had vanished from her mouth; she was frowning again.

Carella took the photostat from his notebook, and handed it to her. 'Do you know this woman?' he asked.

'Yes,' Lou said.

'Do you know her name?'

'Yes,' Lou said wearily. 'That's Sadie Collins. What about her?'

Carella decided to play it straight. 'She's been murdered,' he said.

'Mmm,' Lou said, and handed the stat back to him. 'I thought so.'

'What made you think so?'

'I saw her picture in the newspaper last week. Or at least a picture of somebody who looked a hell of a lot like her. The name was different, and I told myself, No, it isn't her, but Jesus, there was her picture staring up at me, it *had* to be her,' Lou shrugged and then walked to the stove. 'You want some coffee?' she asked. 'I'll get some going, if you like.'

'Thank you, no,' Carella said. 'How well did you know her, Miss Kantor?'

Lou shrugged again. 'I only knew her a short while. I met her in, I guess it was September. Saw her three or four times after that.'

'Where'd you meet her?' Carella asked.

'In a bar called The Purple Chairs,' Lou answered. 'That's right,' she added quickly, 'that's what I am.'

'Nobody asked,' Carella said.

'Your *eyes* asked.'

'What about Sadie Collins?'

'What about her? Spell it out, officer, I'm not going to help you.'

'Why not?'

'Mainly because I don't like being hassled.'

'Nobody's hassling you, Miss Kantor. You practise your religion and I'll practise mine. We're here to talk about a dead woman.'

'Then talk about her, spit it out. What do you want to know? Was she straight? Everybody's straight until they're *not* straight anymore, isn't that right? She was willing to learn. I taught her.'

'Did you know she was married?'

'I knew. So what?'

'She told you?'

'She told me. Broke down in tears one night, lay in my arms all night crying. I knew she was married.'

'What'd she say about her husband?'

'Nothing that surprised me.'

'What, exactly?'

'She said he had another woman. Said he ran off to see her every weekend, told little Sadie he had out-of-town business. *Every* goddamn week-end, can you imagine that?'

'How long had it been going on?'

'Who knows? She found out just before Christmas last year.'

'How often did you say you saw her?'

'Three or four times. She used to come here on week-ends, when he was away. Sauce for the goose.'

'What do you make of this?' Carella said, and handed her Sarah's address book, opened to the MEMORANDA page.

Andrew Hart
1120 Hall Avenue
622 - 8400
    (PB·G) (TG)

Michael Thornton
371 South Lindner
881-9371
    (TS)

Lou Kantor
434 North 16 Street
FR 7 - 2346
    (TPC) (TG)

Sal Decotto
831 Grover Avenue
FR5 - 3287
    (F) (TG)

Richard Fenner
110 Henderson
593 - 6648
    (QR) (TG)

'I don't know any of these people,' Lou said.

'The initials under your name,' Carella said.

'Mmm. What about them?'

'TPC and then TG. Got any ideas?'

'Well, the TPC is obvious, isn't it?'

'Obvious?' Carella said.

'Sure. I met her at The Purple Chairs,' Lou said. 'What else could it mean?'

Carella suddenly felt very stupid. 'Of course,' he said, 'what else could it mean?'

'How about those other initials?' Meyer said.

'Haven't the faintest,' Lou answered, and handed back the book. 'Are you finished with me?'

'Yes, thank you very much,' Carella said.

'I miss her,' Lou said suddenly. 'She was a wild one.'

Cracking a code is like learning to roller-skate; once you know how to do it, it's easy. With a little help from Gerald Fletcher, who had provided a guided tour the night before, and with a lot of help from Lou Kantor, who had generously provided the key, Carella was able to study the list in Sarah's book and crack the code wide open. Well, *almost* wide open.

Last night, Fletcher had taken him, in geographical rather than numerical order, to Paddy's Bar & Grille (PB&G), Fanny's (F), The Purple Chairs (TPC), and Quigley's Rest (QR). For some reason, perhaps to avoid duplication, Sarah Fletcher had felt it necessary to list in code the places in which she had met her various bedmates. It seemed obvious to Carella, now that he knew how to roller-skate, that the TS beneath Michael Thornton's telephone number was meant to indicate nothing more than The Saloon, where Thornton had admitted first meeting her. Gerald Fletcher had not taken Carella there last night, but perhaps the place had been on his itinerary, with the scheduled stop preempted by his own drunkenness and the fight in Quigley's Rest.

But what the hell did TG mean?

By Carella's own modest estimate, he had been in more damn bars in the past twenty-four hours than he had in the past twenty-four years. But he decided nonetheless to hit The Saloon that night. You never learned nothing if you didn't ask, and there were imponderables even in roller-skating.

Three wandering violinists moved from table to table playing a medley of 'Ebb Tide', 'Strangers in the Night', and 'Where or When', none of which seemed to move Nora as much as 'Something' had. Fake potted palms dangled limpid plastic fronds while a small pool, honouring the name of the place, gushed before a painted backdrop of desert sand and sky.

'I'm glad you called,' Nora said. 'I hate to go straight home after the end of a busy day. The apartment always feels so empty. And the meeting today was a disaster. The art director is a man who started in the stockroom forty years ago, after a correspondence course from one of those schools that advertise on matchbook covers. So he had the gall to tell *me* what was wrong with the girl's hand.' She looked up from her drink and said, in explanation, 'It was this drawing of a girl, with her hand sort of brushing a strand of hair away from her cheek.'

'I see,' Kling said.

'Do *you* have to put up with that kind of crap?' she asked.

'Sometimes.'

'Anyway, I'm glad you called. There's nothing like a drink after a session with a moron.'

'How about the company?'

'What?'

'I'm glad you appreciate the drink ...'

'Oh, stop it,' Nora said, 'you *know* I like the company.'

'Since when?'

'Since always. Now just cut it out.'

'May I ask you something?'

'Sure.'

'Why are you here with me, instead of your boyfriend?'

'Well,' Nora said, and turned away preparatory to lying, 'as I told you . . . oh, *look*, the violinsts are coming over. Think of a request, quick.'

'Ask them to play "Something",' Kling said, and Nora turned back towards him immediately, her eyes flashing.

'That isn't funny, Bert,' she said.

'Tell me about your boyfriend.'

'There's nothing to tell you. He's a doctor and he spends a lot of time in his office and at the hospital. As a result, he's not always free when I'd like him to be, and, therefore, I felt it perfectly all right to have a drink with you. In fact, if you wouldn't be so smart all the time, saying I should request "Something" when you know the song has particular meaning for me, you *might* ask me to have dinner with you, and I might possibly say "yes".'

'*Would* you like to have dinner with me?' Kling asked, astonished.

'Yes,' Nora said.

'There isn't a boyfriend at all, is there?' he said.

'Don't make that mistake, Bert. There *is* one, and I love him. And I'm going to marry him as soon as . . .' She cut herself short, and turned away again.

'As soon as *what*?' Kling asked.

'Here are the violinists,' Nora said.

One storm had blown out to sea, but another was approaching, and this time it looked as though the forecasters would be right. The first flakes had not yet begun to fall as Carella walked up the street towards The Saloon, but snow was in the air, you could smell it, you could sense it, the goddamn city would be a frozen tundra by morning. Carella did not particularly like snow. His one brief romance with it had been, oh, several years ago, when some punk arsonists had set fire to him (talk about Dick Tracy!) and he had put out the flames by rolling in a bank of the stuff. But how long can any hot love affair last? Not very. Carella's disaffection had begun again the very next week, when it again snowed, and he again slipped and slogged and sloshed along with ten million other winter-weary citizens of the city. He looked up at the sky now, pulled a sour face, and went inside.

The Saloon was just that: a saloon.

A cigarette-scarred bar behind which ran a mottled, flaking mirror. Wooden booths with patched leatherette seat cushions. Bowls of pretzels and potato chips. Jukebox bubbling and gurgling, rock music babbling and bursting, the smell of steamy bodies and steamy garments, the incessant rise and fall of too many voices talking too loud. He hung his coat on the sagging rack near the cigarette machine, found himself a relatively uncrowded spot at the far end of the bar, and ordered a beer. Because of the frantic activity behind and in front of the bar, he knew it would be quite some while before he could catch the bartender's ear. As it turned out, he did not actually get to talk to him until eleven-thirty, at which time the business of drinking yielded to the more serious business of trying to make out.

'They come in here,' the bartender said, 'at all hours of the night, each and every one of them looking for the same thing. Relentless. You know what that word means? Relentless? That's what the action is here.'

'Yeah, it is kind of frantic,' Carella said.

'Frantic? That's the word, all right. Frantic. Men and women both. Mostly men. The women come for the same thing, you understand? But it takes a lot more fortitude for a woman to go in a bar alone, even if it's *this* kind of place where the only reason anybody comes at all is to meet people, you understand? Fortitude. You know what that word means? Fortitude?'

'Yeah,' Carella said, and nodded.

'Take yourself,' the bartender said. 'You're here to meet a girl, am I right?'

'I'm here mostly to have a few beers and relax,' Carella said.

'Relax? With *that* music? You could just as easy relax in World War II, on the battlefield. Were you in World War II?'

'Yes, I was,' Carella said.

'That was *some* war,' the bartender said. 'The wars they got nowadays are bullshit wars. But World War II?' He grinned fondly and appreciatively. '*That* was a *glorious* war! You know what that word means? Glorious?'

'Yeah,' Carella said.

'Excuse me, I got a customer down the other end,' the bartender said, and walked off. Carella sipped at his beer. Through the plate-glass window facing the side street, he could see the first snowflakes beginning to fall. Great, he thought, and looked at his watch.

The bartender mixed and served the drink, and then came back. 'What'd you do in the war?' he asked.

'Goof off, mostly,' Carella said, and smiled.

'No, seriously. Be serious.'

'I was in the Infantry,' Carella said.

'Who wasn't? Did you get overseas?'

'Yes.'

'Where?'

'Italy.'

'See any action?'

'A little,' Carella said. 'Listen ... getting back to the idea of meeting somebody ...'

'In here, it *always* gets back to that.'

'There *was* someone I was hoping to see.'

'Who?' the bartender said.

'A girl named Sadie Collins.'

'Yeah,' the bartender said, and nodded.

'Do you know her?'

'Yeah.'

'Have you seen her around lately?'

'No. She used to come in a lot, but I ain't seen her in months. What do you want to fool around with her for?'

'Why? What's the matter with her?'

'You want to know something?' the bartender said. 'I thought she was a hooker at first. I almost had her thrown out. The boss don't like hookers hanging around here.'

'What made you think she was a hooker?'

'Aggressive. You know what that word means? Aggressive? She used to come dressed down to here and up to here, which is pretty far out, even compared to some of the things they're wearing today. She was ready for action, you understand? She was selling everything she had.'

'Well, most women try to . . .'

'No, no, this wasn't like *most* women, don't give me that *most* women crap. She'd come in here, pick out a guy she wanted, and go after him like the world was gonna end at midnight. All business, just like a hooker, except she wasn't charging. Knew just what she wanted, and went straight for it, *bam*. And I could always tell *exactly* who she was gonna end up with, even before she knew it herself.'

'How could you tell?'

'Always the same type.'

'What type?'

'Big guys, first of all. You wouldn't stand a chance with her, you're lucky she ain't here. Not that you ain't big, don't misunderstand me. But Sadie liked them gigantic. You know what that word means? Gigantic? That was Sadie's type. Gigantic and mean. All I had to do was look around the room and pick out the biggest, meanest son of a bitch in the place, and that's who Sadie would end up with. You want to know something?'

'What?'

'I'm glad she don't come in here anymore. She used to make me nervous. There was something about her . . . I don't know.' The bartender shook his head. 'Like she was compulsive. You know what that word means? Compulsive?'

He had left Nora at the door to her apartment, where she had given him her customary handshake and her now-expected 'Thank you, I had a very nice time', and rode down in the elevator now, wondering what his next move should be. He did not believe her doctor-boyfriend existed (he seemed to be having a lot of trouble lately with girls and their goddamn doctor-boyfriends) but at the same time he accepted the fact that there *was* a man in her life, a flesh-and-blood person whose identity, for some bewildering reason, Nora chose not to reveal. Kling did not appreciate anonymous competition. He wondered if a *blitz* might not be in order, telephone call when he got back to his apartment, another call in the morning, a dozen roses, a telegram, another dozen calls, another dozen roses, the whole stupid adolescent barrage, all of it designed to convince a girl that somebody out there was madly in love with her.

He wondered if he was madly in love with her.

He decided he was not.

Then why was he expending all this energy? He recalled reading some place that when a man and a woman got divorced, it was usually the man who remarried first. He supposed that what he had shared with Cindy was a marriage, of sorts, and the sudden termination of it . . . well, it was silly to think of it in terms of a marriage. But he supposed the end of it (and it certainly seemed to have ended) *could* be considered a divorce, of sorts. In which case, his frantic pursuit of Nora was merely a part of the reaction syndrome, and . . .

Damn it, he thought. Hang around with a psychologist long enough and you begin to sound like one.

He stepped out of the elevator, swiftly through the lobby, and came out of the building into a blinding snowstorm. It had not been this bad ten minutes ago, when the taxi had dropped them off. The snow was thick and fast now, the wind blowing it in angry swirls that lashed his face and flicked away, successively, incessantly. He ducked his head, and began walking up towards the lighted avenue at the end of the block, his hands in his pockets. He was on the verge of deciding that he would not try to see Nora Simonov again, would not even *call* her again, when three men stepped out of a doorway, directly into his path.

He looked up too late.

A fist came out of the flying snow, smashing him full in the face. He staggered back, his hands still in his pockets. Two of the men seized him from behind, grabbing both his arms, his hands still trapped in his pockets. The one standing in front of him smashed a fist into his face again. His head snapped back. He felt blood gushing from his nose. 'Keep away from Nora,' the man whispered, and then began pounding his fists into Kling's abdomen and chest, blow after blow while Kling fought to free his arms and his hands, his strength ebbing, his struggle weakening, slumping as the men behind him held his arms, and the man in front battered relentlessly with short hard jabs until Kling wanted to scream aloud, and then wanted only to die, and then felt the welcome oblivion of unconsciousness and did not know when they released him at last and allowed him to fall face forward into the white snow, bleeding.

Chapter Twelve

'All right,' Byrnes said, 'I've got a cop in the hospital, now what the hell happened?'

Tuesday morning sunshine assaulted the lieutenant's corner window. The storm had ended, and the snowploughs had come through, and mile-high snowbanks lined the streets, piled against the kerb. It was four days before Christmas, and the temperature was below freezing, and unless the city's soot triumphed, the twenty-fifth would still be white.

Arthur Brown was black. Six feet four inches tall, weighing 220 pounds, with the huge frame and powerful muscles of a heavyweight fighter, he stood before the lieutenant's desk, his eyes squinted against the sunshine.

'I thought you were tailing Fletcher,' Byrnes said.

'I was,' Brown answered.

'All right, Fletcher and this girl live in the same goddamn building. Kling was jumped *leaving* the building. If you were on Fletcher ...'

'I was on him from five o'clock yesterday afternoon, when he left his office downtown.' Brown reached into his inside jacket pocket. 'Here's the timetable,' he said. 'I didn't get back to Silvermine Oval till after midnight. By that time, they'd already taken Bert to the hospital.'

'Let me see it,' Byrnes said, and took the typewritten sheet from Brown's hand, and silently studied it:

SURVEILLANCE GERALD FLETCHER
Monday, December 20

4:55 P.M.—Relieved Detective Kapek outside office bldg 4400 Butler. Suspect emerged 5:10 P.M.,
went to his car parked in local garage, and drove
to home at 721 Silvermine Oval, entered bldg at
5:27 P.M.

7:26 P.M.—Suspect emerged from building, started
to walk south, came back, talked to doorman, and
waited for his car. Drove to 812 North Crane,
parked. Suspect entered apartment building there
at 8:04 P.M.

8:46 P.M.—Suspect emerged from 812 North Crane
in company of redheaded woman wearing fur coat
(black) and green dress, green shoes, approx
height and weight five-six, 120, approx age
thirty. Drove to Rudolph's Restaurant, 127 Har-
row. Surveillant (black) tried to get table, was
told he needed reservation, went outside to wait
in sedan, 9:05 P.M.

Byrnes looked up. 'What's this crap about needing a reservation? Was the
place crowded?'
'No, but ...'
'Anything we can nail them on, Artie?'
'Just try to prove anything,' Brown said.
'Stupid pricks,' Byrnes said, and went back to the timetable.

10:20 P.M.—Suspect and redheaded woman came out
of Rudolph's, drove back to 812 Crane, arrived
10:35 P.M., went into building. No doorman, surveillant entered unobserved, elevator indicator
stopped at eleventh floor. Check of lobby mailboxes showed eight apartments on eleventh floor
(names of occupants not marked as to color of
hair).

Byrnes looked up again, sharply this time. Brown grinned. Byrnes went
back to the report, sighing.

<u>11:40</u> <u>P.M.</u>—Suspect came out of building, walked
north to Glade, where he had parked car, and drove
directly home, arriving there ten minutes past
midnight. 721 Silvermine scene of great activity,
two RMP cars in street, patrolmen questioning
doorman. Suspect said few words to doorman, then
went inside. Detective Bob O'Brien, already on
scene and waiting to relieve, reported Kling had
been assaulted half hour ago and taken to Culver
Avenue Hospital. Relieved by O'Brien at 12:15 A.M.

'When did O'Brien get there?' Byrnes asked.
'I radioed in when I was leaving the woman's building, told O'Brien the suspect was probably heading home, and asked him to relieve me there. He said he arrived a little after midnight. The ambulance had already come and gone.'
'How's Bert?' Byrnes asked.
'I checked a few minutes ago. He's conscious, but they're holding him for observation.'
'He say anything?'
'Three guys jumped him,' Brown said.
'Sons of bitches,' Byrnes said.

Carella had not yet spoken to either Sal Decotto or Richard Fenner, the two remaining people listed in Sarah's book, but he saw no reason to pursue that trail any further. He had been taken to the bars where Sarah (or rather Sadie) had picked them up, and whereas he was not the type of person who ordinarily judged a book by its cover, he had a fair idea of what the men themselves would be like. Big and mean, according to the bartender at The Saloon.
The hardest thing Carella had ever had to learn in his entire life was that there actually *were* mean people in the world. As a young man, he had always believed that people behaved badly only because they'd experienced unhappy childhoods or unfortunate love affairs or deaths in the family or any one of a hundred assorted traumas. He changed his mind about that when he began working for the Police Department. He learned then that there were good people doing bad things, and there were also mean rotten bastards doing bad things. The good ones ended in jail just as easily as the mean ones, but the mean ones were the ones to beware. Why Sarah Fletcher had sought out big, mean men (and apparently one mean woman as well) was anybody's guess. If the place-listings in her book could be considered chronological, she'd gone from bad to worse in her search for partners, throwing in a solitary dyke for good measure (or was Sal Decotto a woman, too?), and ending up at Quigley's Rest, which was no afternoon tea party.
But why? To give it back to her husband in spades? If *he* was playing around with someone each and every week-end, maybe Sarah decided to beat him at his own game, become not only Sadie, but a Sadie who was, in

the words of her various admirers, 'a crazy bitch', 'a stupid twat', and 'a wild one'. It seemed entirely possible that the only thing Carella would learn from Richard Fenner or Sal Decotto was that they shared identical opinions of the woman they had similarly used and abused. And affirmation of a conclusion leading nowhere was a waste of time. Carella tossed Sarah's little black book into the manila folder bearing the various reports on the case, and turned his attention to the information Artie Brown had brought in last night.

Cherchez la femme was a handy little dictum perhaps used more often by the *Sûreté* than by the 87th. But without trying to *cherche* any *femme*, Brown had inadvertently come across one anyway, a thirty-year-old redhead who lived on the eleventh floor of 812 North Crane and with whom Gerald Fletcher had spent almost four hours the night before. It would have been a simple matter to hit the redhead's building and find out exactly who she was, but Carella decided against such a course of action. A chat with the superintendent, however quiet, a question of neighbours, however discreet, might get back to the woman herself, and serve to alert Fletcher. Fletcher was the suspect. Carella sometimes had to remind himself of that fact. Sarah had been playing around with an odd assortment of men and women, five according to her own record (and God knew how many more she had *not* listed, and God knew what the 'TG' after four of the names meant); her blatant infidelity provided Fletcher with a strong motive, despite his own week-end sorties into realms as yet uncharted. So why take Carella to his wife's unhappy haunts, why *show* Carella that he had good and sufficient reason to rip that knife across her belly? And why the hell offer to get a good defence attorney for the boy who had already been indicted for the slaying and who, unless somebody came up with something concrete damn soon, might very well be convicted of the crime?

Sometimes Carella wondered who was doing what to whom.

At five o'clock that evening, he relieved Detective Hal Willis outside Fletcher's office building downtown, and then followed Fletcher to a department store in midtown Isola. Carella did not normally go in for cops-and-robbers disguises, but Fletcher knew exactly what he looked like and so he was wearing a false moustache stuck to his upper lip with spirit gum, a wig with longer hair than his own and of a different colour (a dirty blond whereas his own was brown), and a pair of sunglasses. The disguise, he was certain, would not have fooled Fletcher at close range. But he did not intend to get *that* close, and he felt pretty secure he would not be made. He was, in fact, more nervous about *losing* Fletcher than about being spotted by him.

The store was thronged with late shoppers. This was Tuesday, December 21, fours day to the big one, only three more days of shopping once the stores closed tonight at nine. Hot desperation flowed beneath the cool white plastic icicles that hung from the ceiling, panic in wonderland, the American anxiety syndrome never more evident than at Christmas, when the entire nation became a ruthless jackpot – Two Hundred Million Neediest gifting and getting, with a gigantic hangover waiting just around the new year's corner. Gerald Fletcher shoved through the crowd of holiday shoppers like a quarterback moving the ball downfield without benefit of blockers. Carella, like a reticent tackler, followed some twenty feet behind.

The elevator would be a danger spot. Carella saw the elevator bank at the far end of the store, and knew that Fletcher was heading directly for it, and weighed the chances of being spotted in a crowded car against the chances of losing Fletcher if he did not follow immediately on his heels. He did not know how many thousands of people were in the store at that moment; he *did* know that if he allowed Fletcher to get into an elevator without him, the surveillance was blown. The elevator would stop at every floor, the way most department-store elevators did, and Fletcher could get out at any one of them, and *then* try to find him again.

An elevator arrived. Its door opened, and Fletcher waited while the passengers disembarked and then stepped into the car together with half a dozen shoppers. Carella ungentlemanly shoved his way past a woman in a leopard coat and got into the car with his back to Fletcher, who was standing against the rear wall. The car, as Carella had surmised, stopped at every floor. He studiously kept his back to the rear of the car, moving aside whenever anyone wanted to get out. On the fifth floor, he heard Fletcher call, 'Getting out, please,' and then felt him coming towards the front of the car, and saw him stepping out, and waited for the count of three before he, himself, moved forwards, much to the annoyance of the elevator operator, who was starting to close the door.

Fletcher had walked off to the left. Carella spotted him swiftly up one of the aisles, looking about at the signs identifying each of the various departments, and stopping at one marked INTIMATE APPAREL. Carella walked into the next aisle over, pausing to look at women's robes and kimonos, keeping an eye on Fletcher, who was in conversation with the lingerie salesgirl. The girl nodded, smiled, and showed him what appeared to be either a slip or a short nightgown, holding the garment up against her ample bosom to model it for Fletcher, who nodded, and said something else to her. The girl disappeared under the counter, to reappear several moments later, her hands overflowing with gossamer undergarments, which she spread on the counter before Fletcher, awaiting his further choice.

'May I help you, sir?' a voice said, and Carella turned to find a stocky woman at his elbow, grey hair, black-rimmed spectacles, wearing army shoes and a black dress with a small white collar. She looked exactly like a prison matron, right down to the suspicious smile that silently accused him of being a junkie shoplifter or worse.

'Thank you, no,' Carella said. 'I'm just looking.'

Fletcher was making his selections, pointing now to this garment, now to another. The salesgirl wrote up the order, and Fletcher reached into his wallet to give her either cash or a credit card, it was difficult to tell from this distance. He chatted with the girl a moment longer, and then walked off towards the elevator bank.

'Are you *sure* I can't assist you?' the prison matron said, and Carella immediately answered, 'I'm positive,' and moved swiftly towards the lingerie counter. Fletcher had left the counter without a package in his arms, which meant he was *sending* his purchases. You did not send dainty underthings to a prize fighter, and Carella wanted very much to know exactly which woman was to be the recipient of the 'intimate apparel'. The salesgirl was already gathering up Fletcher's selections – a black half-slip, a wildly patterned Pucci chemise, a peach-coloured baby-doll nightgown with matching bikini panties, and four other pairs of panties, blue, black, white, and beige, each trimmed with lace around the legholes. The girl looked up.

'Yes, sir,' she said, 'may I help you?'

Carella opened his wallet and produced his shield. 'Police officer,' he said. 'I'm interested in the order you just wrote up.'

The girl was perhaps nineteen years old, a college girl working in the store for the Christmas rush. The most exciting thing that had happened on the job, until this very moment, was an elderly Frenchman asking her if she would like to spend the month of February on his yacht in the Mediterranean. Speechlessly, the girl studied the shield, her eyes bugging. It suddenly occurred to Carella that Fletcher might have had the purchases sent to his home address, in which case all this undercover work was merely a waste of time. Well, he thought, you win some, you lose some.

'Are these items being sent?' he asked.

'Yes, *sir*,' the girl said. Her eyes were still wide behind her glasses. She wet her lips and stood up a little straighter, prepared to be a perfect witness.

'Can you tell me where?' Carella asked.

'Yes, *sir*,' she said, and turned the sales slip towards him. 'He wanted them wrapped separately, but they're all going to the same address. Miss Arlene Orton, 812 Crane Street, right here in the city.'

'Thank you very much,' Carella said.

It felt like Christmas Day already.

Bert Kling was sitting up in bed and polishing off his dinner when Carella got to the hospital at close to 7 p.m. The men shook hands, and Carella took a seat by the bed.

'This stuff tastes awful,' Kling said, 'but I've been hungry as hell ever since I got in here. I could almost eat the tray.'

'When are you getting out?'

'Tomorrow morning. I've got a broken rib, nice, huh?'

'Very nice,' Carella said.

'I'm lucky they didn't mess up my insides,' Kling said. 'That's what the doctors were afraid of, internal haemorrhaging. But I'm okay, it seems. They taped up the rib, and whereas I won't be able to do my famous trapeze act for a while, I should be able to get around.'

'Who did it, Bert?'

'Three locomotives, it felt like.'

'Why?'

'A warning to stay away from Nora Simonov.'

'Were you seeing a lot of her?'

'I saw her twice. Apparently someone saw me seeing her. And decided to put me in the hospital. Little did they know I'm a minion of the law, huh?'

'Little did they know,' Carella said.

'I'll have to ask Nora a few questions when I get out of here. How's the case going?'

'I've located Fletcher's girl friend.'

'I didn't know he had one.'

'Brown tailed them last night, got an address for her, but no name. Fletcher just sent her some underwear.'

'Nice,' Kling said.

'Very nice. I'm getting a court order to put a wire in the apartment.'

'What do you expect them to talk about?'

'Bloody murder maybe,' Carella said, and shrugged. Both men were silent for several moments.

'You know what I want for Christmas?' Kling asked suddenly.

'What?'

'I want to find those guys who beat me up.'

Chapter Thirteen

The man who picked the lock on Arlene Orton's front door, ten minutes after she left her apartment on Wednesday morning, was better at it than any burglar in the city, and he happened to work for the Police Department. He had the door open in three minutes flat, at which time a technician went in and wired the joint. It took the technician longer to set up his equipment than it had taken his partner to open the door, but both were artists in their own right, and the sound man had a lot more work to do.

The telephone was the easiest of his jobs. He unscrewed the carbon mike in the mouthpiece of the phone, replaced it with his own mike, attached his wires, screwed the mouthpiece back on, and was instantly in business – or almost in business. The tap would not become operative until the telephone company supplied the police with a list of so-called bridging points that located the pairs and cables for Arlene Orton's phone. The monitoring equipment would be hooked into these, and whenever a call went out of or came into the apartment, a recorder would automatically tape both ends of the conversation. In addition, whenever a call was made from the apartment, a dial indicator would ink out a series of dots that signified the number being called. The police listener would be monitoring the equipment from wherever the bridging point happened to be; in Arlene Orton's case, the location index was seven blocks away.

The technician, while he had Arlene's phone apart, could just as easily have installed a bug that would have picked up any voices in the living room and would also have recorded Arlene's half of any telephone conversations. He chose instead to place his bug in the bookcase on the opposite side of the room. The bug was a small FM transmitter with a battery-powered mike that needed to be changed every twenty-four hours. It operated on the same frequency as the recording machine locked into it, a machine that was voice-actuated and that would begin taping whenever anyone began speaking in the apartment. The technician would have preferred running his own wires, rather than having to worry about changing a battery every twenty-four hours. But running wires meant that you had to pick a place to run them *to*, usually following electrical or telephone circuits to an empty apartment or closet or what-have-you where a policeman would monitor the recording equipment. If a tap was being set up in a hotel room, it was usually possible to rent the room next door, put your listener into it, and go about your messy business without anyone being the wiser. But in this city, empty apartments were about as scarce as working telephones, and whereas the wire was being installed by court order, the technician dared not ask the building superintendent for an empty closet or a workroom in which to hide his listener. Building supers are perhaps not as garrulous as barbers, but the effectiveness of a wiretap is directly proportionate to the secrecy surrounding it, and a blabbermouth superintendent can kill an investigation more quickly than a squad of gangland goons.

So the technician settled upon the battery-powered mike and resigned himself to the fact that every twenty-four hours he and his partner would have to get into the apartment somehow to change the goddamn batteries. In all, there would be four sets of batteries to change because the technician was planting four bugs in the apartment: one in the kitchen, one in the bedroom, one in the bathroom, and one in the living room. While he worked, his partner was down in the lobby with a walkie-talkie in his coat pocket, ready to let him know the moment Arlene Orton came back to the building, and ready to detain her by ruse if necessary. Watching the clock, the technician worked swiftly and silently, hoping the walkie-talkie clipped to his belt would not erupt with his partner's warning voice. He was not worried about legal action against the city; the court order, in effect, gave him permission to break and enter. He worried only about blowing the surveillance.

In the rear of a panel truck parked at the kerb some twelve feet south of the entrance to 812 Crane, Steve Carella sat behind the recording equipment that was locked into the frequency of the four bugs. He knew that in some neighbourhoods a phoney truck was as readily recognizable as the cop on the beat. Put a man in the back of a fake delivery truck, park the truck on the street and start taking pictures of people going in and out of a candy store suspected of being a numbers drop, and all of a sudden the neighbourhood was full of budding stars and starlets, all of whom knew there was a cop-photographer in the back of the truck, all of whom mugged and pranced and emoted shamelessly for the movie camera, while managing to conduct not an iota of business that had anything at all to do with the policy racket. It got discouraging. But Crane Street was in one of the city's better neighbourhoods, where perhaps the citizens were not as wary of cops hiding in the backs of panel trucks doing their dirty watching and listening. Carella sat hopefully with a tuna-fish sandwich and a bottle of beer, prepared to hear and record any sounds that emanated from Arlene's apartment.

At the bridging point seven blocks away and thirty minutes later, Arthur Brown sat behind equipment that was hooked into the telephone mike, and waited for Arlene Orton's phone to ring. He was in radio contact with Carella in the back of his phoney panel truck and could apprise him of any new development at once.

The first call came at 12:17 p.m. The equipment tripped in automatically, and the spools of tape began recording the conversation while Brown simultaneously monitored it through his headphones.

'Hello?'

'Hello, Arlene?'

'Yes, who's this?'

'Nan.'

'Nan? You sound so different. Do you have a cold or something?'

'Every year at this time. Just before the holidays. Arlene, I'm terribly rushed, I'll make this short. Do you know Beth's dress size?'

'A ten. I would guess. Or an eight.'

'Well, which?'

'I don't know. Why don't you give Danny a ring?'

'Do you have his office number?'

'No, but he's listed. It's Reynolds and Abelman. In Calm's Point.'

'Thank you, darling. Let's have lunch after the holidays sometime, okay?'

'Love to.'

'I'll call you. Bye-bye.'

Arlene Orton spoke to three more girl friends in succession. The first one was intent on discussing, among other things, a new birth-control pill she was trying. Arlene told her that she, herself, had stopped taking the pill after her divorce. In the beginning, the very thought of sex was abhorrent to her, and since she had no intention of even *looking* at another man for as long as she lived, she saw no reason to be taking the pill. Later on, when she revised her estimate of the opposite sex, her doctor asked her to stay off the pill for a while. Her friend wanted to know what Arlene was using now, and they went into a long and detailed conversation about the effectiveness of diaphragms, condoms, and intrauterine coils. Brown never did find out what Arlene was using now. Arlene's second girl friend had just returned from Granada, and she gave a long and breathless report on the hotel at which she'd stayed, mentioning in passing that the tennis pro had great legs. Arlene said that she had not played tennis in three years because tennis had been her former husband's sport, and anything that reminded her of him caused her to throw up violently. Arlene's third girl friend talked exclusively about a nude stage show she had seen downtown the night before, stating flatly that it was the filthiest thing she had ever seen in her life, and you know me, Arlene, I'm certainly no prude.

Arlene then called the local supermarket to order the week's groceries (including a turkey, which Brown assumed was for Christmas Day), and then called the credit department of one of the city's bigger department stores to complain that she had left a valise with the superintendent for return to the store, but that the new man they had doing pickups and delivery was an absolute idiot, and the valise had been sitting there in the super's apartment for the past three weeks, and thank God she hadn't planned on taking a trip or anything because the suitcase she ordered to *replace* the one she was returning *still* hadn't been delivered, and she felt this was disgraceful in view of the fact that she had spent something like $2,000 at the store this year and was now reduced to arguing with a goddamn computer.

She had a fine voice, Arlene Orton, deep and forceful, punctuated every so often (when she was talking to her girl friends) with a delightful giggle that seemed to bubble from some adolescent spring. Brown enjoyed listening to her.

At 4 p.m. the telephone in Arlene's apartment rang again.

'Hello?'

'Arlene, this is Gerry.'

'Hello, darling.'

'I'm leaving a little early, I thought I'd come right over.'
'Good.'
'Miss me?'
'Mmm-huh.'
'Love me?'
'Mmm-huh.'
'Someone there with you?'
'No.'
'Then why don't you say it?'
'I love you.'
'Good. I'll be there, in, oh, half an hour, forty minutes.'
'Hurry.'
Brown radioed Carella at once. Carella thanked him and sat back to wait.

Standing in the hallway outside Nora Simonov's apartment, Kling wondered what his approach should be. It seemed to him that, where Nora was concerned, he was always working out elaborate strategies. It further seemed to him that any girl for whom you had to draw up detailed battle plans was a girl well worth dropping. He reminded himself that he was not here today on matters of the heart, but rather on the matters of the rib – the third rib on the right-hand side of his chest, to be exact. He rang the doorbell and waited. He heard no sound from within the apartment, no footsteps approaching the door, but suddenly the peephole flap was thrown back, and he knew Nora was looking out at him; he raised his right hand, waggled the fingers on it, and grinned. The peephole flap closed again. He heard her unlocking the door. The door opened wide.

'Hi,' she said.
'Hi. I happened to be in the building, checking out some things, and thought I'd stop by to say hello.'
'Come in,' Nora said.
'You're not busy, are you?'
'I'm always busy, but come in, anyway.'

It was the first time he had been allowed entrance to her apartment; maybe she figured he was safe with a broken rib, if indeed she *knew* one of his ribs was broken. There was a spacious entrance foyer opening onto a wide living room. What appeared to be an operative fireplace was on the wall opposite the windows. The room was done in bright, rich colours, the fabric on the easy chairs and sofa subtly echoing the colour of the rug and drapes. It was a warm and pleasant room; he would have enjoyed being in it as a person rather than a cop. He thought it supremely ironic that she had let him in too late, and was now wasting hospitality on nothing but a policeman investigating an assault.

'Can I fix you a drink?' she asked. 'Or is it too early for you?'
'I'd love a drink.'
'Name it.'
'What are *you* having?'
'I thought I'd whip up a pitcherful of martinis, and light the cannel coal, and we could sit toasting Christmas.'
'Good idea.' He watched her as she moved towards the bar in the corner of the room. She was wearing work clothes, a paint-smeared white smock over

blue jeans. Her dark hair was pulled back, away from her exquisite profile. She moved gracefully and fluidly, walking erect, the way most tall girls did, as though in rebuttal for the years when they'd been forced to slump in order to appear shorter than the tallest boys in the class. She turned and saw him watching her. She smiled, obviously pleased, and said, 'Gin or vodka?'

'Gin.'

He waited until she had taken the gin bottle from behind the bar, and then he said, 'Where's the bathroom, Nora?'

'Down the hall. The very end of it. You mean to tell me *cops* go to the bathroom, too, the same as mortals?'

He smiled and went out of the room, leaving her busy at the bar. He walked down the long hallway, glancing into the small studio room – drawing board overhung with a fluorescent light, painting of a man jumping up for something, arms stretched over his head, chest muscles rippling, tubes of acrylic paint twisted on a worktable near an empty easel – and continued walking. The bedroom door was open. He looked back towards the living room, closed the bathroom door rather more noisily than was necessary, and stepped quickly into the bedroom.

He went to the dresser first. A silver-framed photograph of a man was on the right-hand end of it. It was inscribed 'To Sweet Nora, with all my love, Frankie'. He studied the man's face, trying to relate it to any of the three men who had jumped him on Monday night. The street had been dark; he had really seen only the one who'd stood in front of him, pounding his fists into his chest and his gut. The man in the photograph was not his attacker. He quickly opened the top drawer of the dresser – panties, nylons, handkerchiefs, brassieres. He closed it, opened the middle drawer, found it full of sweaters and blouses, and then searched the bottom drawer, where Nora kept an odd assortment of gloves, nightgowns, panty-hose, and slips. He closed the drawer and moved rapidly to the night table on the left of the bed, the one upon which the telephone rested. He opened the top drawer, found Nora's address book, and quickly scanned it. There was only one listing for a man named Frank – Frank Richmond in Calm's Point. Kling closed the book, went to the door, looked down the hallway, and wondered how much more time he had. He stepped across the hall, eased open the bathroom door, closed it behind him, flushed the toilet, and then turned on the cold water tap. He went into the hallway again, closed the door gently behind him, and crossed swiftly into the bedroom again.

He found what he wanted in the night table on the other side of the bed – a stack of some two dozen letters, all on the same stationery, bound together with a thick rubber band. The top envelope in the pile was addressed to Nora at 721 Silvermine Oval. The return address in the left-hand corner of the envelope read:

Frank Richmond, 80–17–42
Castleview State Penitentiary
Castleview-on-Rawley, 23751

Whatever else Frank Richmond was, he was also a convict. Kling debated putting the letters back into the night-table drawer, decided he wanted to read them, and stuck them instead into the right-hand pocket of his jacket.

He closed the drawer, went across the hall to the bathroom, turned off the water tap, and went back into the living room, where Nora had started a decent fire and was pouring the drinks.

'Find it?' she asked.

'Yes,' he answered.

Chapter Fourteen

On Thursday morning, two days before Christmas, Carella sat at his desk in the squadroom and looked over the transcripts Miscolo's clerical staff had typed up for him. He had taped five reels the night before, beginning at 4:55, when Fletcher had entered Arlene Orton's apartment, and ending at 7:30, when they left to go out to dinner. The reel that interested him most was the second one. The conversation on that reel had at one point changed abruptly in tone and content; Carella thought he knew why, but he wanted to confirm his suspicion by carefully reading the typewritten record:

```
    The following is a transcript of a conversation
between Gerald Fletcher and Arlene Orton which
took place in Miss Orton's apartment (11D) at 812
Crane Street on Wednesday, December 22. Conversa-
tion on this reel took place commencing at ap-
proximately 5:21 P.M. and ended at approximately
5:45 P.M. on that date.
Fletcher:   I meant after the holidays.
Miss Orton: I thought you meant after the trial.
Fletcher:   No, the holidays.
Miss Orton: I may be able to get away, I'm not
            sure. I'll have to check with my
            shrink.
Fletcher:   What's he got to do with it?
Miss Orton: Well, I have to pay whether I'm there
            or not, you know.
Fletcher:   You mean, oh, I see.
Miss Orton: Sure.
Fletcher:   It would be best if we could . . .
Miss Orton: Sure, coordinate it if we can.
Fletcher:   Is he taking a vacation?
Miss Orton: He went in February last time.
Fletcher:   February, right.
Miss Orton: Two weeks.
```

Fletcher: In February, right, I remember.
Miss Orton: I'll ask him.
Fletcher: Yes, ask him. Because I'd really like to get away.
Miss Orton: Ummm. When do you think the case [Inaudible]
Fletcher: In March sometime. No sooner than that. He's got a new lawyer, you know.
Miss Orton: Do you want some more of this?
Fletcher: Just a little.
Miss Orton: On the cracker or the toast?
Fletcher: What did I have it on?
Miss Orton: The cracker.
Fletcher: Let me try the toast. Mmmm. Did you make this yourself?
Miss Orton: No, I got it at the deli. What does that mean, a new lawyer?
Fletcher: Nothing. He'll be convicted anyway.
Miss Orton: [Inaudible]
Fletcher: Well.
Miss Orton: You making another drink?
Fletcher: I thought . . .
Miss Orton: What time is the reservation?
Fletcher: A quarter to eight.
Miss Orton: Sure, there's time.
Fletcher: Do you want another one?
Miss Orton: Just some ice. One ice cube.
Fletcher: Okay. Is there any more [Inaudible]
Miss Orton: Underneath. Did you look underneath?
Fletcher: [Inaudible]
Miss Orton: There should be some.
Fletcher: Yeah, here it is.
Miss Orton: Thank you.
Fletcher: Because the trial's going to take a lot out of me.
Miss Orton: Ummmm.
Fletcher: I'd like to rest up beforehand.
Miss Orton: I'll ask him.
Fletcher: When do you see him again?

Miss Orton: What's today?
Fletcher: Wednesday.
Miss Orton: Tomorrow. I'll ask him then.
Fletcher: Will he know so far in advance?
Miss Orton: Well, he'll have some idea.
Fletcher: Yes, if he can give you at least an
               approximation . . .
Miss Orton: Sure, we can plan from there.
Fletcher: Yes.
Miss Orton: The trial will be . . . when did you
               say?
Fletcher: March. I'm guessing. I think March.
Miss Orton: How soon after the trial . . .
Fletcher: I don't know.
Miss Orton: She's dead, Gerry, I don't see . . .
Fletcher: Yes, but . . .
Miss Orton: I don't see any reason to wait, do
               you?
Fletcher: No.
Miss Orton: Then why don't we decide?
Fletcher: After the trial.
Miss Orton: Decide after the . . . ?
Fletcher: No, get married after the trial.
Miss Orton: Yes. But shouldn't we in the mean-
               time . . .
Fletcher: Have you read this?
Miss Orton: What is it?
Fletcher: This.
Miss Orton: No. I don't like his stuff.
Fletcher: Then why'd you buy it?
Miss Orton: I didn't. Maria gave it to me for my
               birthday. What I was saying, Gerry,
               is that we ought to set a date now. A
               provisional date. Depending on when
               the trial is.
Fletcher: Mmmm.
Miss Orton: Allowing ourselves enough time, you
               know. It'll probably be a long trial,
               don't you think? Gerry?
Fletcher: Mmmm?
Miss Orton: Do you think it'll be a long trial?
Fletcher: What?
Miss Orton: Gerry?

Fletcher: Yes?

Miss Orton: Where are you?

Fletcher: I was just looking over some of these
              books.

Miss Orton: Do you think you can tear yourself
              away? So we can discuss . . .

Fletcher: Forgive me, darling.

Miss Orton: . . . a matter of some small impor-
              tance. Like our wedding.

Fletcher: I'm sorry.

Miss Orton: If the trial starts in March . . .

Fletcher: It may or it may not. I told you I was
              only guessing.

Miss Orton: Well, say it does start in March.

Fletcher: If it starts in March . . .

Miss Orton: How long could it run? At the out-
              side?

Fletcher: Not very long. A week?

Miss Orton: I thought murder cases . . .

Fletcher: Well, they have a confession, the
              boy's admitted killing her. And
              there won't be a parade of wit-
              nesses, they'll probably call just
              me and the boy. If it runs longer than
              a week, I'll be very much surprised.

Miss Orton: Then if we planned on April . . .

Fletcher: Unless they come up with something
              unexpected, of course.

Miss Orton: Like what?

Fletcher: Oh, I don't know. They've got some
              pretty sharp people on this case.

Miss Orton: In the district attorney's office?

Fletcher: Investigating it, I mean.

Miss Orton: What's there to investigate?

Fletcher: There's always the possibility he
              didn't do it.

Miss Orton: Who?

Fletcher: Corwin. The boy.

Miss Orton: [Inaudible] a signed confession?

Fletcher: I thought you didn't want another
              one?

Miss Orton: I've changed my mind. [Inaudible]
              the end of April?

Fletcher:	I guess that would be safe.
Miss Orton:	[Inaudible]
Fletcher:	No, this is fine, thanks.
Miss Orton:	[Inaudible] forget about getting away in February. That's when they have hurricanes down there, anyway, isn't it?
Fletcher:	September, I thought. Or October. Isn't that the hurricane season?
Miss Orton:	Go after the trial instead. For our honeymoon.
Fletcher:	They may give me a rough time during the trial.
Miss Orton:	Why should they?
Fletcher:	One of the cops thinks I killed her.
Miss Orton:	You're not serious.
Fletcher:	I am.
Miss Orton:	Who?
Fletcher:	A detective named Carella.
Miss Orton:	Why would he think that?
Fletcher:	Well, he probably knows about us by now . . .
Miss Orton:	How could he?
Fletcher:	He's a very thorough cop. I have a great deal of admiration for him. I wonder if he realizes that.
Miss Orton:	Admiration!
Fletcher:	Yes.
Miss Orton:	Admiration for a man who suspects . . .
Fletcher:	He'd have a hell of a time proving anything, though.
Miss Orton:	Where'd he even get such an idea?
Fletcher:	Well, he knows I hated her.
Miss Orton:	How does he know?
Fletcher:	I told him.
Miss Orton:	What? Gerry, why the hell did you do that?
Fletcher:	Why not?
Miss Orton:	Oh, Gerry . . .
Fletcher:	He'd have found out anyway. I told you, he's a very thorough cop. He probably knows by now that Sarah was

	sleeping around with half the men in this city. And he probably knows I knew it, too.
Miss Orton:	That doesn't mean . . .
Fletcher:	If he's also found out about us . . .
Miss Orton:	Who cares what he's found out? Corwin's already confessed. I don't understand you, Gerry.
Fletcher:	I'm only trying to follow his reasoning. Carella's.
Miss Orton:	Is he Italian?
Fletcher:	I would guess so. Why?
Miss Orton:	Italians are the most suspicious people in the world.
Fletcher:	I can understand his reasoning. I'm just not sure he can understand mine.
Miss Orton:	Some reasoning, all right. Why the hell would you kill her? If you were going to kill her, you'd have done it ages ago.
Fletcher:	Of course.
Miss Orton:	When she refused to sign the separation papers.
Fletcher:	Sure.
Miss Orton:	So let him investigate, who cares? You want to know something, Gerry?
Fletcher:	Mmm?
Miss Orton:	Wishing your wife is dead isn't the same thing as killing her. Tell that to Detective Coppola.
Fletcher:	Carella.
Miss Orton:	Carella. Tell him that.
Fletcher:	[Laughs]
Miss Orton:	What's so funny?
Fletcher:	I'll tell him, darling.
Miss Orton:	Good. Meanwhile, the hell with him.
Fletcher:	[Laughs] Do you have to change?
Miss Orton:	I thought I'd go this way. Is it a very dressy place?
Fletcher:	I've never been there.
Miss Orton:	Call them and ask if pants are okay, will you, darling?

According to the technician who had wired the Orton apartment, the living-room bug was in the bookcase on the wall opposite the bar. Carella leafed back through the typewritten pages and came upon the section he wanted:

```
Fletcher:     Have you read this?
Miss Orton:   What is it?
Fletcher:     This.
Miss Orton:   No. I don't like his stuff.
Fletcher:     Then why'd you buy it?
Miss Orton:   I didn't. Maria gave it to me for my
              birthday. What I was saying, Gerry,
              is that we ought to set a date now.
              A provisional date. Depending on
              when the trial is.
Fletcher:     Mmmm.
Miss Orton:   Allowing ourselves enough time, you
              know. It'll probably be a long
              trial, don't you think? Gerry?
Fletcher:     Mmmm?
Miss Orton:   Do you think it'll be a long trial?
Fletcher:     What?
Miss Orton:   Gerry?
Fletcher:     Yes?
Miss Orton:   Where are you?
Fletcher:     I was just looking over some of these
              books.
```

It was Carella's guess that Fletcher had discovered the bookcase bug some nine speeches back, the first time he uttered a thoughtful 'Mmmm'. That was when his attention began to wander, so that he was unable to give any concentration at all to two matters of enormous importance to him and Arlene: the impending trial and their marriage plans. What interested Carella more, however, was that Fletcher had said *after* he knew the place was wired. Certain of an audience now, knowing that whichever cop was actually monitoring the equipment, the tape or transcript would eventually get back to the investigating officer, Fletcher had:

(1) Suggested the possibility that Corwin was not guilty of the murder.
(2) Flatly stated that a cop named Carella suspected him of having killed his own wife.
(3) Expressed the admiration he felt for Carella while wondering if Carella was aware of it.
(4) Speculated that Carella, as a thorough cop, had already doped out the purpose of the bar-crawling last Sunday night, was cognizant of Sarah's promiscuity and knew that Fletcher was aware of it as well.

(5) Made a little joke about 'telling' Carella, when in fact he had *already* told him through the surveillance equipment in the apartment.

Carella felt as eerie as he had when lunching with Fletcher and later when drinking with him. Fletcher seemed to be playing a dangerous game, in which he taunted Carella with bits and pieces of knowledge, and dared him to fit them together into a meaningful whole that would prove he had slain Sarah. On the tape, Fletcher had said in an oddly gentle voice, 'I can understand his reasoning. I'm just not sure he can understand mine.' He had spoken these words after he knew the place was wired, and it could be assumed he was speaking them directly to Carella. But what was he trying to say? And why?

Carella wanted very much to hear what Fletcher would say when he *didn't* know he was being overheard. He asked Lieutenant Byrnes for permission to request a court order putting a bug in Fletcher's automobile. Byrnes granted permission, and the court issued the order. Carella called the Police Laboratory again, and was told that a technician would be assigned to him as soon as he found out where Fletcher parked his automobile.

Reading another man's love letters is like eating Chinese food alone.

In the comparative stillness of the squadroom, Kling joylessly picked over each of Richmond's separate tasty dishes, unable to share them, unable to comment on their flavour or texture. That they were interesting at *all* was a tribute to Richmond's cleverness; his letters were being censored before they left the prison, to make sure they did not contain requests for a file inside a birthday cake, and censorship can somewhat inhibit a man's ardour. As a result, Richmond could write only indirectly about his intense need for Nora, and his longing to rejoin her once he had served his sentence, which he fully expected to be reduced once he went before the parole board.

One letter, however, contained a short paragraph that read somewhat like an open threat:

I hope you are being true to me. Pete tells me he is sure this is so. He is there if you need him for anything, so don't hesitate to call. In any case, he will be watching over you.

Kling read the sentence yet another time, and was reaching for the telephone when it rang. He lifted the receiver.

'Eighty-seventh Squad, Kling.'

'Bert, this is Cindy.'

'Hi,' he said.

'Are you busy?' she asked.

'I was just about to call the I.S.'

'Oh.'

'But go ahead. It can wait.'

Cindy hesitated. Then, her voice very low, she said, 'Bert, can I see you tomorrow?'

'Tomorrow?' he said.

'Yes.' She hesitated again. 'Tomorrow's Christmas Eve.'

'I know.'

'I bought something for you.'

'Why'd you do that, Cindy?'

'Habit,' she said, and he suspected she was smiling.

'I'd love to see you, Cindy,' he said.

'I'll be working till five.'

'No Christmas party?'

'At a *hospital*? Bert, my dear, we deal here daily with life and death.'

'Don't we all,' Kling said, and smiled. 'Shall I meet you at the hospital?'

'All right. The side entrance. That's near the emergency ...'

'Yes, I know where it is. At five o'clock?'

'Well, five-fifteen.'

'Okay, five-fifteen.'

'You'll like what I got you,' she said, and then hung up. He was still smiling when he put his call thru through to the Identification Section. A man named Reilly listened to his request, and promised to call back with the information in ten minutes. He called back in eight.

'Kling?' he said.

'Yes?'

'Reilly at the I.S. I've got that packet on Frank Richmond. You want me to duplicate it or what?'

'Can you just read me his yellow sheet?'

'Well,' Reilly said, 'it's a pretty long one. The guy's been in trouble with the law since he was sixteen.'

'What kind of trouble?'

'Minor crap mostly. Except for the latest one.'

'When?'

'Two months ago.'

'What was the charge?'

'Armed robbery.'

Kling whistled, and then said, 'Have you got the details there, Reilly?'

'Not on his B-sheet. Let me see if there's a copy of the arrest report.'

Kling waited. On the other end, he could hear papers being shuffled. At last, Reilly said, 'Yeah, here it is. Him and another guy went into a supermarket along about closing time, ripped off the day's receipts. Got caught on the way out by an off-duty detective who lived in the neighbourhood.'

'Who was the other guy?'

'Man named Jack Yancy. He's doing time too. You want me to pull his folder?'

'No, that's not necessary.'

'Third guy got off scot-free.'

'I thought you said there were only two of them.'

'No, there was an alleged wheel-man on the job, waiting in the parking lot near the delivery entrance. Caught him in the car with the engine running, but he claimed he didn't know anything about what was going on inside. Richmond and Yancy backed him, said they'd never seen him before in their lives.'

'Honour among thieves?' Kling said. 'I don't believe it.'

'Stranger things happen,' Reilly said.

'What's his name?'

'The wheel-man? Peter Brice.'

'Got an address for him?'

'Not on the report. You want me to hit the file again?'

'Would you?'

'I'll get back,' Reilly said, and hung up.

When the phone rang ten minutes later, Kling thought it would be Reilly again. Instead, it was Arthur Brown.

'Bert,' he said, 'the Orton woman just called Fletcher. Can you get in touch with Steve?'

'I'll try. What's up?'

'They made a date for tomorrow night. They're going across the river to a place named The Chandeliers. Fletcher's picking her up at seven-thirty.'

'Right,' Kling said.

'Bert?'

'Yeah?'

'Does Steve want me on this phone tap while they're out eating? Tomorrow's Christmas Eve, you know.'

'I'll ask him.'

'Also, Hal wants to know if he's supposed to sit in the truck all the while they're out.'

'Because after all, Bert, if they're over in the next state eating, what's there to listen to in the apartment?'

'Right, I'm sure Steve'll agree.'

'Okay. How's everything up there?'

'Quiet.'

'Really?' Brown asked, and hung up.

Chapter Fifteen

The detective who engaged the garage attendant in a bullshit conversation about a hit-and-run accident was Steve Carella. The lab technician who posed as a mechanic sent by the Automobile Club to charge a faulty battery was the same man who had wired Arlene Orton's apartment.

Fletcher's car was parked in a garage four blocks from his office, a fact determined simply by following him to work that morning of December 24. (Carella had already figured that Fletcher would park the car where he finally *did* park it because the pattern had been established in the earlier surveillance; a man who drove to work each day generally parked his car in the same garage or lot.)

On the sidewalk outside the garage, Carella asked invented questions about a damaged left fender and headlight on a fictitious 1968 Dodge, while upstairs the lab technician was installing his bug in Fletcher's 1972 Oldsmobile. It would have been simpler and faster to put in a battery-powered FM transmitter similar to those he had installed in Arlene Orton's apartment, but since batteries needed constant changing, and since access to any given automobile was infinitely more difficult than access to an apartment, he decided on wiring his bug into the car's electrical system instead. With the hood open, with charge cables going to Fletcher's battery from his own two-truck battery, he busily spliced and taped, tucked and tacked. He did not want to put the bug under the dashboard (the easiest spot) because this was wintertime, and the car heater would undoubtedly be in use, and the sensitive microphone would pick up every rattle and rumble of the heater instead of the conversation in the car. So he wedged the microphone into the front cushion, between seat and back, and then ran his wires under the car rug, and up under the dashboard, and finally into the electrical system. Within the city limits, the microphone would effectively broadcast any sounds in the car for a distance of little more than a block, which meant that Fletcher's Oldsmobile would have to be closely followed by the monitoring unmarked police sedan. If Fletcher left the city, as he planned to do tonight when he took Arlene to The Chandeliers, the effective range of the transmitter on the open road would be about a quarter of a mile. In either case, the listener-pursuer had his work cut out for him.

On the sidewalk, Carella saw the technician drive out in his battered tow truck, abruptly thanked the garage attendant for his time, and headed back to the squadroom.

The holiday was starting in earnest and so, in keeping with the conventions of that festive season, the boys of the 87th Squad held their annual Christmas party at 4 p.m. that afternoon. The starting time for the party was entirely arbitrary, since it depended on when the squad's guests began dropping in. The guests, unlike those to be found at most other Christmas parties in the city, were in the crime business, mainly because the hosts were in that same business. Most of the guests were shoplifters. Some of them were pickpockets. A few of them were drunks. One of them was a murderer.

The shoplifters had been arrested in department stores scattered throughout the precinct, the Christmas shopping season being a good time to lift merchandise, Christmas Eve being the last possible day to practise the art in stores still jammed to the rafters. The shoplifters plied their trade in various ways. A skinny lady shoplifter named Hester Brady, for example, came into the squadroom looking like a pregnant lady. Her pregnancy had been caused by stuffing some two hundred dollars' worth of merchandise into the overlarge bloomers she wore under her dress, a risky procedure unless one is skilled at lift, grab, stuff, drop the skirt, move to the next aisle, advance in the space of twenty minutes from a sweet Irish virgin to a lady eight months along; such are the vagaries of birth control.

A man named Felix Hopkins dressed for his annual shopping spree in a trenchcoat lined with dozens of pockets to accommodate the small and quite expensive pieces of jewellery he lifted from counters here and there. A tall, thin, distinguished-looking black man with a tidy moustache and gold-rimmed spectacles, he would generally approach the counter and ask to see a cigarette lighter, indicating the one he wanted, and then rip off five or six fountain pens while the clerk was busy getting the lighter out of the display case. His hands worked as swiftly as a magician's; he had been at the job such a long time now that he didn't even have to unbutton the coat anymore. And though the pockets inside the coat now contained a gold fountain pen, a platinum watch, a gold money clip, a rhinestone necklace, an assortment of matched gold earrings, a leather-bound travelling clock, and a monogrammed ring with a black onyx stone, he still protested to the arresting officer that he had bought all these items elsewhere, had thrown away the sales slips, and was taking them home to wrap them himself because he didn't like the shitty job the stores did.

Most of the other shoplifters were junkies, desperate in their need, unmindful of store detectives and city detectives, sorely tempted by the glittering display of goods in what was surely the world's largest marketplace, knowing only that whatever chances they took might net them a bag or two of heroin before nightfall, guarantee them a Christmas Day free from the pangs of drug-hunger and the pains of withdrawal. They were the pitiful ones, pacing the detention cage at the rear of the squadroom, ready to scream or vomit, knowing that being busted meant cold turkey for Christmas Day, with the only hope being methadone instead – maybe. They were looked upon with disdain by the haughty professionals like Hester Brady of the pregnant bloomers, Felix Hopkins of the pocketed raincoat, and Junius Cooper of the paper-stuffed packages.

Junius Cooper had figured out his dodge all by himself. He was a man of about forty-three, well-dressed, looking somewhat like a harried advertising executive who was rushing around picking up last-minute gifts his secretary had neglected to buy. He came into each department store carrying several shopping bags brimming with gift-wrapped parcels. His *modus operandi* worked in two ways, both equally effective. In either instance, he would stand next to a man or woman who was legitimately shopping and who had momentarily put his own shopping bag on the floor or on the counter top. Junius would immediately: (a) transfer one of the legitimate shopper's gift-wrapped packages into his own shopping bag or (b) pick up the legitimate shopper's bag and leave his own bag behind in its place. The beautifully wrapped boxes in Junius' bag contained nothing but last Sunday's newspapers. His system was a bit pot-luckish, but it provided the advantage of being able to walk innocently past department-store cops, carrying packages actually paid for by bona-fide customers and wrapped by department-store clerks. It was almost impossible to catch Junius unless you saw him making the actual exchange. That was how he had been caught today.

This mixed bag of shoplifters mingled in the squadroom with their first cousins, the pickpockets, who similarly looked upon the frantic shopping days before Christmas as their busiest time of the year. A pickpocket enjoys nothing better than a crowd, and the approaching holiday brought the crowds out like cockroaches from under the bathroom sink: crowds in stores, crowds in the streets, crowds in the buses and subways. They worked in pairs or alone, these light-fingered artists. a nudge or a bump, an 'Oh, excuse me', and a purse delicately lifted from a handbag, a hip pocket slit with a razor blade to release the bulging wallet within. There was not a detective in the city who did not carry his wallet in the left-hand pocket of his trousers, close to his balls, rather than in the sucker hip pocket; cops are not immune to pickpockets. They were surrounded by them that afternoon, all of them innocent, naturally, all of them protesting that they knew their rights.

The drunks did not know their rights, and did not particularly care about them. They had all begun celebrating a bit early and had in their exuberance done one thing or another considered illegal in this fair city – things like

throwing a bus driver out onto the sidewalk when he refused to make change
for a ten-dollar bill, or smashing the window of a taxicab when the driver
said he couldn't possibly make a call to Calm's Point on the busiest day of the
year, or kicking a Salvation Army lady who refused to allow her trombone to
be played by a stranger, or pouring a quart of scotch into a mailbox, or
urinating on the front steps of the city's biggest cathedral. Things like that.
Minor things like that.

One of the drunks had killed someone.

He was unquestionably the star of the 87th's little Christmas celebration,
a small man with vivid blue eyes and the hands of a violinist, beetling black
brows, a mane of black hair, stinking of alcohol and vomit, demanding over
and again to know just what the hell he was doing in a police station, even
though there was blood all over his white shirt front and speckled on his pale
face and staining his long, thin, delicate fingers.

The person he had killed was his sixteen-year-old daughter.

He seemed to have no knowledge that she was dead. He seemed not to
remember at all that he had come into his apartment at three o'clock that
afternoon, little more than an hour ago, having begun his Christmas
celebrating at the office shortly after lunch, and had found his daughter
making love with a boy on the living-room sofa, the television casting unseen
pictures into the darkened room, television voices whispering, whispering,
and his daughter locked in embrace with a strange boy, skirts up over belly and
thighs, buttocks pumping, ecstatic moans mingling with the whisper of
television shadows, not hearing her father when he came into the room, not
hearing him when he went into the kitchen and searched in the table drawer
for a weapon formidable enough, punishing enough, found only a paring
knife and discarded that as unequal to the task, discovered a hammer in the
shoebox under the sink, hefted it on the palm of his hand, and, thin-lipped,
went into the living room where his daughter still moaned beneath the
weight of her young lover, and seized the boy by the shoulder and pulled him
off her, and then struck her repeatedly with the hammer until the girl's face
and head were gristle and pulp and the boy screamed until he fainted from
exhaustion and shock and the woman next door ran in and found her
neighbour still wielding the hammer in terrible dark vengeance for the
unpardonable sin his daughter had committed on the day before Christmas.
'George,' she had whispered, and he had turned to her with blank eyes, and
she had said, 'Oh, George, what have you done?' and he had dropped the
hammer, and could not remember from that moment on what he had done.

It was a nice little Christmas party the boys of the 87th had.

He had forgotten, almost, what she looked like.

She came through the hospital's chrome and glass revolving doors, and he
saw at first only a tall blonde girl, full-breasted and wide-hipped, honey
blonde hair clipped close to her head, cornflower-blue eyes, shoving
through the doors and out onto the low, flat stoop, and he reacted to her the
way he might react to any beautiful stranger stepping into the crisp
December twilight, and then he realized it was Cindy, and his heart lurched.

'Hi,' he said.

'Hi.'

She took his arm. They walked in silence for several moments.

'You look beautiful,' he said.

'Thank you. So do you.'

He was, in fact, quite aware of the way they looked together, and fell immediately into the Young Lovers syndrome, positive that everyone they passed on the windswept street knew instantly that they were mad about each other. Each stranger (or so he thought) cased them quickly, remarking silently on their oneness, envying their youth and strength and glowing health, longing to be these two on Christmas Eve, Cindy and Bert, American Lovers, who had met cute, and loved long, and fought hard, and parted sadly, and were now together again in the great tradition of the season, radiating love like flashing Christmas bulbs on a sixty-foot-high tree.

They found a cocktail lounge near the hospital, one they had never been to before, either together or separately, Kling sensing that a 'first' was necessary to their rediscovery of each other. They sat at a small round table in a corner of the room. The crowd noises were comforting. He suspected an English pub might be like this on Christmas Eve, the voice cadences lulling and soft, the room itself warm and protective, a good place for nurturing a love that had almost died and was now about to redeclare itself.

'Where's my present?' he said, and grinned in mock, evil greediness.

She reached behind her to where she had hung her coat on a wall peg, and dug into the pocket, and placed a small package in the exact centre of the table. The package was wrapped in bright blue paper and tied with a green ribbon and bow. He felt a little embarrassed; he always did when receiving a gift. He went into the pocket of his own coat, and placed his gift on the table beside hers, a slightly larger package wrapped in jingle-bells paper, red and gold, no bow.

'So,' she said.

'So,' he said.

'Merry Christmas.'

'Merry Christmas.'

They hesitated. They looked at each other. They both smiled.

'You first,' he said.

'All right.'

She slipped her fingernail under the Scotch Tape and broke open the wrapping without tearing the paper, and then eased the box out, and moved the wrapping aside, intact, and centred the box before her, and opened its lid. He had brought her a plump gold heart, seemingly bursting with an inner life of its own, the antiqued gold chain a tether that kept it from ballooning ecstatically into space. She looked at the heart, and then glanced quickly into his expectant face and nodded briefly and said, 'Thank you, it's beautiful.'

'It's not Valentine's Day ...'

'Yes.' She was still nodding. She was looking down at the heart again, and nodding.

'But I thought ...' He shrugged.

'Yes, it's beautiful,' she said again. 'Thank you, Bert.'

'Well,' he said, and shrugged again, feeling vaguely uncomfortable and suspecting it was because he hated the ritual of opening presents. He ripped off the bow on her gift, tore open the paper, and lifted the lid off the tiny box. She had bought him a gold tie-tack in the form of miniature handcuffs, and he read meaning into the gift immediately, significance beyond the fact that he was a cop whose tools of the trade included real handcuffs hanging from his belt. His gift had told her something about the way he felt, and he was certain that her gift was telling him the very same thing – they were together again, she was binding herself to him again.

'Thank you,' he said.

'Do you like it, Bert?'

'I love it.'

'I thought ...'

'Yes, I love it.'

'Good.'

They had not yet ordered drinks. Kling signalled for the waiter, and they sat in curious silence until he came to the table. The waiter left, and the silence lengthened, and it was then that Kling began to suspect something was wrong, something was terribly wrong. She had closed the lid on his gift, and was staring at the closed box.

'What is it?' Kling asked.

'Bert ...'

'Tell me, Cindy.'

'I didn't come here to ...'

He knew already, there was no need for her to elaborate. He knew, and the noises of the room were suddenly too loud, the room itself too hot.

'Bert, I'm going to marry him,' she said.

'I see.'

'I'm sorry.'

'No, no,' he said. 'No, Cindy, please.'

'Bert, what you and I had together was very good ...'

'I know that, honey.'

'And I just couldn't end it the way ... the way we were ending it. I had to see you again, and tell you how much you'd meant to me. I had to be sure you knew that.'

'Okay,' he said.

'Bert?'

'Yes, Cindy. Okay,' he said. He smiled and touched her hand reassuringly. 'Okay,' he said again.

They spent a half-hour together, drinking only the single round, and then they went out into the cold, and they shook hands briefly, and Cindy said, 'Good-bye, Bert,' and he said, 'Good-bye, Cindy,' and they walked off in opposite directions.

Peter Brice lived on the third floor of a brownstone on the city's South Side. Kling reached the building at a little past six-thirty, went upstairs, listened outside the door for several moments, drew his service revolver, and knocked. There was no answer. He knocked again, waited, holstered his revolver, and was staring down the hall when a door at the opposite end opened. A blond-headed kid of about eight looked into the hallway and said, 'Oh.'

'Hello,' Kling said, and started down the steps.

'I thought it might be Santa Claus,' the kid said.

'Little early,' Kling said over his shoulder.

'What time does he come?' the kid asked.

'After midnight.'

'When's that?' the kid shouted after him.

'Later,' Kling shouted back, and went down to the ground floor. He found the super's door alongside the stairwell, near where the garbage cans were stacked for the night. He knocked on the door and waited. A black man wearing a red flannel robe opened the door and peered into the dim hallway.

'Who is it?' he said, squinting up into Kling's face.

'Police officer,' Kling said. 'I'm looking for a man named Peter Brice. Know where I can find him?'

'Third-floor front,' the super said. 'Don't do no shootin' in the building.'

'He's not home,' Kling said. 'Got any idea where he might be?'

'He hangs out on the corner sometimes.'

'What corner?'

'Barbecue joint on the corner. Brice's brother works there.'

'Up the street here?'

'Yeah,' the super said. 'What'd he do?'

'Routine investigation,' Kling answered. 'Thanks a lot.'

The streets were dark. Last-minute shoppers, afternoon party-goers, clerks and shopgirls, workingmen and housewives, all of whom had been rushing towards tomorrow since the day after Thanksgiving, now moved homewards to embrace it, put the final fillip on the tree, drink a bit of nog, spend the last quiet hours in peaceful contemplation before the onslaught of relatives and friends in the morning, the attendant frenzied business of gifting and getting. A sense of serenity was in the air. This is what Christmas is all about, Kling thought, this peaceful time of quiet footfalls, and suddenly wondered why the day before Christmas had somehow become more meaningful to him than Christmas Day itself.

Skewered, browning chickens turned slowly on spits, their savoury aroma filling the shop as Kling opened the door and stepped inside. A burly man in a white chef's apron and hat was behind the counter preparing to skewer four more plump white birds. He glanced up as Kling came in. Another man was at the cigarette machine, his back to the door. He was even bigger than the one behind the counter, with wide shoulders and a thick bull's neck. He turned from the machine as Kling closed the door, and the recognition between them was simultaneous. Kling knew at once that this was the man who'd beaten him senseless last Monday night, and the man knew that Kling had been his victim. A grin cracked across his face. 'Well, well,' he said, 'look who's here, Al.'

'Are you Peter Brice?' Kling asked.

'Why, yes, so I am,' Brice said, and took a step towards Kling, his fists already clenched.

Kling had no intention of getting into a brawl with a man as big as Brice. His shoulder still ached (Meyer's copper bracelet wasn't worth a damn) and he had a broken rib and a broken heart besides (which can also hurt). The third button of his overcoat was still unbuttoned. He reached into the coat with his right hand, seized the butt of his revolver, drew it swiftly and effortlessly, and pointed it directly at Brice's gut.

'Police officer,' he said. 'I want to ask you some questions about . . .'

The greasy skewer struck his gun hand like a sword, whipping down fiercely across the knuckles. He whirled towards the counter as the skewer came down again, striking him hard across the wrist, knocking the gun to the floor. In that instant Brice threw the full weight of his shoulder and arm into a punch that caught Kling close to his Adam's apple. Three things flashed through his mind in the next three seconds. First, he realized that if Brice's punch had landed an inch to the right, he would now be dead. Which meant that Brice had no compunctions about sending him home in a basket. Next he realized, too late, that Brice has asked the man behind the counter to 'look who's here, Al.' And then he realized, also too late, that the super had said, 'Brice's brother works there.' His right wrist aching, the three brilliant flashes sputtering out by the time the fourth desperate second ticked by, he backed towards the door and prepared to defend himself with his one good hand, that one being the left and not too terribly good at all. Five seconds gone since Al had hit him on the hand (probably breaking something, the son of a bitch) and Pete had hit him in the throat. Al was now lifting the counter top and coming out front to assist his brother, the idea probably having occurred to both of them that, whereas it was not bad sport to kick around a jerk who was chasing after Frank Richmond's girl, it was bad news to discover that the jerk was a cop, and worse news to let him out of here alive.

The chances of getting out of here alive seemed exceedingly slim to Detective Bert Kling. Seven seconds gone now, ticking by with amazing swiftness as they closed in on him. This was a neighbourhood where people got stomped into the sidewalk every day of the week and nary a soul ever paused to tip his hat or mutter a 'how-de-do' to the bleeding victim. Pete and Al could with immunity take Kling apart in the *next* seven seconds, put him on one of their chicken skewers, hang him on the spit, turn him and baste him in his own juices, and sell him later for sixty-nine cents a pound. Unless he could think of something clever.

He could not seem to think of a single clever thing.

Except maybe you shouldn't leave your undefended gun within striking distance of a brother with a greased skewer.

His gun was on the floor in the corner now, too far to reach.

(Eight seconds.)

The skewers were behind the counter, impossible to grab.

(Nine seconds.)

Pete was directly ahead of him, manoeuvering for a punch that would knock Kling's head into the gutter outside. Al was closing in on the right, fists bunched.

(With a mighty leap, Detective Bert Kling sprang out of the pit.)

He wished he *could* spring out of the goddamn pit. He braced himself, feinted towards Pete, and then whirled suddenly to the right, where Al was moving in fast, and hit him with his left, hard and low, inches below the belt. Pete swung, and Kling dodged the blow, and then swiftly stepped behind the doubled-over Al, bringing his bunched fist down across the back of his neck in a rabbit punch that sent him sprawling across his own sawdust-covered floor.

One down, he thought, and turned just as Pete unleashed a haymaker that caught him on the side opposite the broken rib, thank God for small favours. He lurched back against the counter in pain, brought up his knee in an attempt to groin Pete, who was hip to the ways of the street and sidestepped gingerly while managing at the same time to clobber Kling on the cheek, bringing his fist straight down from above his head, as though he were holding a mallet in it.

I am going to get killed, Kling thought.

'Your brother's dead,' he said.

He said the words suddenly and spontaneously, the first good idea he'd had all week. They stopped Pete cold in his tracks, with his fist pulled back for the blow that could have ended it all in the next thirty seconds, smashing either the bridge of Kling's nose or his windpipe. Pete turned swiftly to look at his brother where he lay motionless in the sawdust. Kling knew a good thing when he saw one. He didn't try to hit Pete again, he didn't even try to kick him; he knew that any further attempts at trying to overpower him physically were doomed to end only one way, and he did not desire a little tag on his big toe. He dived headlong for his gun in the corner of the room, scooped it up in his left hand, the butt awkward and uncomfortable, rolled over, sat up, and curled his finger around the trigger as Pete turned towards him once again.

'Hold it, you son of a bitch!' Kling said.

Pete lunged across the room.

Kling squeezed the trigger once, and then again, aiming for Pete's trunk, just as he had done on the police range so many times, the big target up there at the end of the range, the parts of the body marked with numerals for maximum lethal reward, five points for the head and throat, chest and abdomen, four for the shoulder, three for the arms, two for the legs. He scored a ten with Pete Brice, because both slugs caught him in the chest, one of them going directly through his heart and the other piercing his left lung.

Kling lowered his gun.

He sat on the floor in the corner of the room, and watched Pete's blood oozing into the sawdust, and wiped sweat from his lip, and blinked, and then began crying because this was one hell of a fucking Christmas Eve, all right.

Carella had been parked across the street from The Chandeliers for close to two hours, waiting for Fletcher and Arlene to finish their dinner. It was now ten minutes to ten, and he was drowsy and discouraged and beginning to think the bug in the car wasn't such a hot idea after all. On the way out to the restaurant, Fletcher and Arlene had not once mentioned Sarah or the plans for their impending marriage. The only remotely intimate thing they had discussed was receipt of the lingerie Fletcher had sent, which Arlene just *adored*, and which she planned to model for him later night.

It was now later that night, and Carella was anxious to put them both to bed and get home to his family. When they finally came out of the restaurant and began walking towards Fletcher's Oldsmobile, Carella actually uttered an audible 'At *last*' and started his car. Fletcher started the Olds in silence, and then apparently waited in silence for the engine to warm before pulling out of the parking lot. Carella followed close behind, listening intently. Neither Fletcher nor Arlene had spoken a word since they entered the automobile. They proceeded east on Route 701 now, heading for the bridge, and still they said nothing. Carella thought at first that something was wrong with the equipment, and then he thought that Fletcher had tipped to *this* bug, too, and was deliberately maintaining silence, and then finally Arlene spoke and Carella knew just what had happened. The pair had argued in the restaurant, and Arlene had been smouldering until this moment when she could no longer contain her anger. The words burst into the stillness of Carella's car as he followed close behind, Arlene shouting. Maybe you don't want to marry me at *all*!

That's ridiculous, Fletcher said.

Then why won't you set a date? Arlene said.

I have set a date, Fletcher said.

You haven't set a date. All you've done is say after the trial, after the trial. *When* after the trial?

I don't know yet.

When the hell *will* you know, Gerry?

Don't yell.

Maybe this whole damn thing has been a stall. Maybe you *never* planned to marry me.

You know that isn't true, Arlene.

How do I know there really *were* separation papers?

There were. I told you there were.

Then why wouldn't she sign them?

Because she loved me.

Bullshit.

She said she loved me.

If she loved you ...

She did.

Then why did she do those horrible things?

I don't know.

Because she was a whore, that's why.

To make me pay, I think.

Is that why she showed you her little black book?

Yes, to make me pay.

No. Because she was a whore.

I guess. I guess that's what she became.

Putting a little TG in her book every time she told you about a new one.

Yes.

A new one she'd fucked.

Yes.

Told Gerry, and marked a little TG in her book.

Yes, to make me pay.

A whore. You should have gone after her with detectives. Gotten pictures, threatened her, forced her to sign those damn ...

No, I couldn't have done that. It would have ruined me, Arl.

Your precious career.

Yes, my precious career.

They both fell silent again. They were approaching the bridge now. The silence persisted. Fletcher paid the toll, and then drove onto the River Highway, Carella following. They did not speak again until they were well into the city. Carella tried to stay close behind them, but on occasion the distance between the two cars lengthened and he lost some words in the conversation.

You know she had me in a bind, Fletcher said. You know that, Arlene.
I thought so. But now I'm not so sure anymore.
  She wouldn't sign the papers, and I (   ) adultery because
(   ) have come out.
  All right.
  I thought (   ) perfectly clear, Arl.
  And I thought (   )
  I did everything I possibly could.
  Yes, Gerry, but now she's dead. So what's your excuse now?
  I have reasons for wanting to wait.
  What reasons?
  I told you.
  I don't recall your telling me ...
  I'm suspected of having *killed* her, goddamn it!
  (Silence. Carella waited. Up ahead, Fletcher was making a left turn, off
the highway. Carella stepped on the accelerator, not wanting to lose voice
contact now.)
  What difference does that make? Arlene asked.
  None at all, I'm sure, Fletcher said. I'm sure you wouldn't at all mind
being married to a convicted murderer.
  What are you talking about?
  I'm talking about the possibility ... never mind.
  Let me hear it.
  I said never mind.
  I want to hear it.
  All right, Arlene, I'm talking about the possibility of someone accusing
me of the murder. And of having to stand trial for it.
  That's the most paranoid ...
  It's not paranoid.
  Then what is it? They've caught the murderer, they ...
  I'm only saying suppose. How could we get married if I killed her, if
someone says I killed her?
  No one has said it, Gerry.
  Well, *if* someone should.
  (Silence. Carella was dangerously close to Fletcher's car now, and risking
discovery. But he could not afford to miss a word at this point, even if he had
to follow bumper-to-bumper. On the floor of his own car, the unwinding
reel of tape recorded each word of the dialogue between Fletcher and
Arlene, admissible evidence if ever Fletcher were charged and brought to
trial. Carella held his breath and stayed glued to the car ahead. When Arlene
spoke again, her voice was very low.)
  You sound as if you really *did* do it.
  You know Corwin did it.
  Yes, I know that. That's what ... Gerry, I don't understand this.
  There's nothing to understand.
  Then why ... if you *didn't* kill her, why are you so worried about being
accused and standing trial and ...
  Someone could make a good case for it.
  For what?
  Someone could say I killed her.

Why would anyone do that? They know that Corwin . . .

They could say I came into the apartment and . . . they could say she was still alive when I came into the apartment.

Was she?

They could say it.

But who cares what they . . . ?

They could say that the knife was still in her and I . . . I came in and found her that way and . . . finished her off.

Why would you do that?

To end it.

You wouldn't kill anyone, Gerry.

No.

Then why are you even suggesting such a terrible thing?

If she wanted it . . . if someone accused me . . . if someone said I'd done it . . . that I'd finished the job, pulled the knife across her belly . . . they could claim she *asked* me to do it.

What are you saying, Gerry?

Don't you see?

No, I don't.

I'm trying to explain that Sarah might have . . .

Gerry, I don't think I want to know.

I'm trying to tell you . . .

No, I don't want to know. Please, Gerry, you're frightening me, I really don't want to . . .

Listen to me, goddamn it! I'm trying to explain what *might* have happened, is that so fucking hard to accept? That she might have *asked* me to kill her?

Gerry, please I . . .

I *wanted* to call the hospital, I was *ready* to call the hospital, don't you think I could *see* she wasn't fatally stabbed?

Gerry, Gerry, please . . .

She begged me to kill her, Arlene, she begged me to end it for her, she . . . damn it, can't *either* of you understand that? I tried to show him, I took him to all the places. I thought he was a man who'd understand. For Christ's sake, is it that difficult?

Oh my God, my God, *did* you kill her?

What?

Did you kill Sarah?

No. Not Sarah. Only the woman she'd become, the slut I'd forced her to become. She was Sadie, you see. When I killed her. When she died.

Oh my God, Arlene said, and Carella nodded in weary acceptance. He felt neither elated nor triumphant. As he followed Fletcher's car into the kerb before Arlene's building, he experienced only a familiar nagging sense of repetition and despair. Fletcher was coming out of his car now, walking around to the kerb side, opening the door for Arlene, who took his hand and stepped onto the sidewalk, weeping. Carella intercepted them before they reached the front door of the building. Quietly, he charged Fletcher with the murder of his wife, and made the arrest without resistance.

Fletcher did not seem at all surprised.

And so it was finished, or at least Carella thought it was.

In the silence of his living room, the children already asleep, Teddy wearing a long white hostess gown that reflected the coloured lights of the Christmas tree, he put his arm around her and relaxed for the first time that day. The telephone rang at a quarter past one. He went into the kitchen, catching the phone on the third ring, hoping the children had not been awakened.

'Hello?' he said.

'Steve?'

He recognized the lieutenant's voice at once. 'Yes, Pete,' he said.

'I just got a call from Calcutta,' Byrnes said.

'Mmm?'

'Ralph Corwin hanged himself in his cell, just after midnight. Must have done it while we were still taking Fletcher's confession in the squadroom.'

Carella was silent.

'Steve?'

'Yeah, Pete.'

'Nothing,' Byrnes said, and hung up.

Carella stood with the dead phone in his hand for several seconds, and then replaced it on the hook. He looked into the living room, where the lights of the tree glowed warmly, and he thought of a despairing junkie in a prison cell, who had taken his own life without ever having known he had not taken the life of another.

It was Christmas Day.

Sometimes, none of it made any goddamn sense at all.

LET'S HEAR IT FOR THE DEAF MAN

"Fat balmy breezes wafted in off the park across the street, puffing lazily through the wide-open windows of the Squad room...."

This is for Murray Weller

Chapter One

Fat balmy breezes wafted in off the park across the street, puffing lazily through the wide-open windows of the squadroom. It was the fifteenth of April, and the temperature outside hovered in the mid-sixties. Sunshine splashes drenched the room. Meyer Meyer sat at his desk idly reading a D.D. report, his bald pate touched with golden light, a beatific smile on his mouth, even though he was reading about a mugging. Cheek cradled on the heel and palm of his hand, elbow bent, blue eyes scanning the typewritten form, he sat in sunshine like a Jewish angel on the roof of the *Duomo*. When the telephone rang, it sounded like the trilling of a thousand larks, such was his mood this bright spring day.

'Detective Meyer,' he said, '87th Squad.'

'I'm back,' the voice said.

'Glad to hear it,' Meyer answered. 'Who is this?'

'Come, come, Detective Meyer,' the voice said. 'You haven't forgotten me so soon, have you?'

The voice sounded vaguely familiar. Meyer frowned. 'I'm too busy to play games, mister,' he said. 'Who is this?'

'You'll have to speak louder,' the voice said. 'I'm a little hard of hearing.'

Nothing changed. Telephones and typewriters, filing cabinets, detention cage, water cooler, wanted posters, fingerprint equipment, desks, chairs, all were still awash in brilliant sunshine. But despite the floating golden motes, the room seemed suddenly bleak, as though that remembered telephone voice had stripped the place of its protective gilt to expose it as shabby and cheap. Meyer's frown deepened into a scowl. The telephone was silent except for a small electrical crackling. He was alone in the squadroom and could not initiate a trace. Besides, past experience had taught him that this man (if indeed he was who Meyer thought he was) would not stay on the line long enough for fancy telephone company acrobatics. He was beginning to wish he had not answered the telephone, an odd desire for a cop on duty. The silence lengthened. He did not know quite what to say. He felt foolish and clumsy. He could think only, My *God*, it's happening again.

'Listen,' he said, 'who is this?'

'You *know* who this is.'

'No, I do not.'

'In that case, you're even more stupid than I surmised.'

There was another long silence.

'Okay,' Meyer said.

'Ahh,' the voice said.

'What do you want?'

'Patience, patience,' the voice said.

'Damn it, what do you *want?*'

'If you're going to use profanity,' the voice said, 'I won't talk to you at all.'
There was a small click on the line.

Meyer looked at the dead phone in his hand, sighed, and hung up.

If you happen to be a cop, there are some people you don't need.

The Deaf Man was one of those people. They had not needed him the first
time he'd put in an appearance, wreaking havoc across half the city in an
aborted attempt to rob a bank. They had not needed him the next time,
either when he had killed the Parks Commissioner, the Deputy Mayor, and a
handful of others in an elaborate extortion scheme that had miraculously
backfired. They did not need him now; *whatever* the hell he was up to, they
definitely did not need him.

'Who needs him?' Detective-Lieutenant Peter Byrnes asked. 'Right now,
I don't need him. Are you sure it was him?'

'It sounded like him.'

'I don't need him when I got a cat burglar,' Byrnes said. He rose from his
desk and walked to the open windows. In the park across the street lovers
were idly strolling, young mothers were pushing baby buggies, little girls
were skipping rope, and a patrolman chatted with a man walking his dog. 'I
don't need him,' Byrnes said again, and sighed. He turned from the window
abruptly. He was a compact man, with hair more white than grey, broad-
shouldered, squat, with rough-hewn features and flinty blue eyes. He gave
an impression of controlled power, as though a violence within had been
tempered, honed, and later protectively sheathed. He grinned suddenly,
surprising Meyer. 'If he calls again,' Byrnes said, 'tell him we're out.'

'Very funny,' Meyer said.

'Anyway, we don't even know it's him yet.'

'I think it was him,' Meyer said.

'Well, let's see if he calls again.'

'If it's him,' Meyer said with certainty, 'he'll call again.'

'Meanwhile, what about this goddamn burglar?' Byrnes said. 'He's going
to walk off with every building on Richardson if we don't get him soon.'

'Kling's over there now,' Meyer said.

'As soon as he gets back, I want a report,' Byrnes said.

'What do I do about the Deaf Man?'

Byrnes shrugged. 'Listen to him, find out what he wants.' He grinned
again, surprising Meyer yet another time. 'Maybe he wants to turn himself
in.'

'Yeah,' Meyer said.

Richardson Drive was a side street behind Silvermine Oval. There were
sixteen large apartment buildings on that street, and a dozen of them had
been visited by the cat burglar during the past two months.

According to police mythology, burglars are the cream of the criminal
crop. Skilled professionals, they are capable of breaking and entering in a
wink and without a whisper, making on-the-spot appraisals of appliances or
jewellery, ripping off an entire apartment with speed and dexterity, and then

vanishing soundlessly into the night. According to further lore, they are gentlemen one and all, rarely moved to violence unless cornered or otherwise provoked. To hear the police talk about burglars (except junkie burglars, who are usually desperate amateurs), one would guess that the job required rigorous training, intense dedication, enormous self-discipline, and extraordinary courage. (Not for nothing had the phrase 'the guts of a burglar' entered everyday language directly from the police lexicon.) This grudging respect, this tip of the investigatory hat, was completely in evidence that afternoon of April 15, when Detective Bert Kling talked to Mr and Mrs Joseph Angieri in their apartment at 638 Richardson Drive.

'Clean as a whistle,' he said, and raised his eyebrows in admiration. He was referring to the fact that there were no chisel marks on any of the windows, no lock cylinders punched out, no evidence of any fancy glass cutter or crowbar work. 'Did you lock all the doors and windows when you went away?' he asked.

'Yes,' Angieri said. He was a man in his late fifties, wearing a wildly patterned short-sleeved shirt, and sporting a deep suntan, both of which he had acquired in Jamaica. 'We always lock up,' he said. 'This is the city.'

Kling looked at the door lock again. It was impossible to force this type of lock with a celluloid strip, nor were there any pick marks on it. 'Anybody else have a key to this apartment?' he asked, closing the door.

'Yes. The super. He's got a key to every apartment in the building.'

'I meant besides him,' Kling said.

'My mother has a key,' Mrs Angieri said. She was a short woman, slightly younger than her husband, her eyes darting anxiously in her tanned face. She was, Kling knew, reacting to the knowledge that she had been burglarized – that someone had violated this private space, someone had entered her home and roamed it with immunity, had handled her possessions, had taken things rightfully belonging to her. The *loss* was not the important factor; the jewellery was probably covered by insurance. It was the *idea* that staggered her. If someone could enter to steal, what would prevent someone from entering to kill?

'Might she have been here while you were away? Your mother?'

'What for?'

'I don't know. Just to look in . . .'

'No.'

'Water the plants . . .'

'We don't keep plants,' Angieri said.

'Besides, my mother's eighty-four years old,' Mrs Angieri said. 'She hardly ever leaves Riverhead. That's where she lives.'

'Might she have given the key to anyone else?'

'I don't think she even remembers she *has* a key. We gave it to her years ago, when we first moved in. I don't think she's ever used it.'

'Because, you see,' Kling said, 'there are no marks anywhere. So it's reasonable to assume the man came in with a key.'

'Well, I don't think it was Mr Coe,' Angieri said.

'Who?'

'Mr Coe. The super. He wouldn't do something like this, would he, Marie?'

'No,' Mrs Angieri said.

'I'll talk to him, anyway,' Kling said. 'The thing is, there've been twelve burglaries on this same block, and the M.O.'s been the same – the *modus operandi* – it's been the same in each one, no marks, no signs of entry. So unless there's a ring of burglars who're all building superintendents ...' Kling smiled. Mrs Angieri smiled with him. He reminded her of her son, except for the hair. Her son's hair was brown, and Kling's hair was blond. But her son was a big boy, over six feet tall, and so was Kling, and they both had nice boyish smiles. It made her feel a little better about having been robbed.

'I'll need a list of what was taken,' Kling said, 'and then we'll ...'

'Is there any chance of getting it back?' Angieri asked.

'Well, that's the thing, you see. We'll get the list out to all the hockshops in the city. Sometimes we get very good results that way. Sometimes, though, the stuff's gotten rid of through a fence, and then it's difficult.'

'Well, it isn't likely that he'd take valuable jewellery to a hockshop, is it?'

'Oh, yes, sometimes,' Kling said. 'But to be honest with you, I think we're dealing with a very high-calibre thief here, and it's my guess he's working with a fence. I could be wrong. And it won't hurt to let the hockshops know what we're looking for.'

'Mmm,' Angieri said doubtfully.

'I meant to ask you,' Kling said. 'Was there a kitten?'

'A what?'

'A kitten. He usually leaves a kitten.'

'Who does?'

'The burglar.'

'Leaves a kitten?'

'Yes. As a sort of calling card. A lot of these thieves are wise guys, you know, they like to think they're making fools of honest citizens. And the police, too.'

'Well,' Angieri said bluntly, 'if he's committed twelve burglaries so far, and you *still* haven't caught him, I guess he *is* making fools of you.'

Kling cleared his throat. 'But there was no kitten, I gather.'

'No kitten.'

'He usually leaves it on the bedroom dresser. Tiny little kitten, different one each time. Maybe a month old, something like that.'

'Why a kitten?'

'Well, you know, cat burglar, kitten, that's his idea of a joke, I guess. As I said, it's a sort of calling card.'

'Mmm,' Angieri said again.

'Well,' Kling said, 'would you like to tell me what's missing, please?'

The superintendent was a black man named Reginald Coe. He told Kling that he had been working here in the building ever since his discharge from the United States Army in 1945. He had fought with the infantry in Italy, which was where he'd got the leg wound that caused his noticeable limp. He now received a pension that, together with his salary as building superintendent, enabled him to provide adequately for his wife and three children. Coe and his family lived in a six-room apartment on the ground floor of the building. It was there that he talked to Kling in the waning hours of the afternoon, both men sipping beer at a spotlessly clean enamel-topped table in the kitchen. In another room of the house the Coe children watched an animated television programme, their shrill laughter punctuating the conversation of the two men.

In the Cops-Bending-Over-Backwards Department, Reginald Coe had a great deal going for him. He was black, he was a wounded war veteran, he was a hard-working man, a devoted husband and father, and a genial host. Any cop who did not respond to a man like Coe had to be a racist, a traitor, an ingrate, a loafer, a home wrecker, and a bad guest. Kling tried to be fair in his questioning, but it was really quite impossible to remain unprejudiced. He liked Coe immediately, and knew at once that the man could not have had anything at all to do with the burglary upstairs. But since Coe possessed a duplicate key to the apartment, and since even angelic cherubs have been known to clobber their mothers with hatchets, Kling went through the routine anyway, just so he'd have something to do while drinking the good cold beer.

'Mr and Mrs Angieri tell me they left for Jamaica on the twenty-sixth of March. Does that check out with your information, Mr Coe?'

'That's right,' Coe said, nodding. 'They caught a late plane Friday night. Told me they were going. So I'd keep an eye on the apartment. I like to know who's in the building and who isn't.'

'*Did* you keep an eye on the apartment, Mr Coe?'

'I did,' Coe said, and lifted his beer glass and drank deeply and with obvious satisfaction.

'How?'

'I stopped up there twice.'

'When was that?'

'First time on the Wednesday after they left, and again last Wednesday.'

'Did you lock the door after you?'

'I did.'

'Did it look as if anyone had been in there?'

'Nope. Everything was in its place, all the drawers closed, no mess, no nothing. Not like they found it when they got home last night.'

'This was Wednesday, you say? When you were in there?'

'Yes. Last Wednesday.'

'That would be the . . .' Kling consulted his pocket calendar. 'The seventh of April.'

'If that's what it says there. I wouldn't know the exact date.'

'Yes, the seventh.'

'Then that's when it was,' Coe said, and nodded.

'Which means the place was hit sometime between then and last night. Did you see strangers in the building during that time?'

'No, I didn't. I try to keep a careful eye on what's going on. You get a lot of crooks coming around saying they're repairmen or delivery men, you know, and all they want to do is get in here and carry off anything that ain't nailed down. I watch that very careful. Cop on the beat's a good man, too, knows who lives in the neighbourhood and who don't, stops a lot of strangers on the street just to find out what they're up to.'

'What's his name, would you know?'

'Mike Ingersoll. He's been on the beat a long time.'

'Yes, I know him,' Kling said.

'Started here around 1960, sometime around then. He's younger than I am, must be in his late thirties. He's a good cop, been cited for bravery twice. I like him a lot.'

'When did you discover the burglary, Mr Coe?' Kling asked.

'I *didn't* discover it. Everything was all right last time I went in there. Mr and Mrs Angieri discovered it when they got home last night. They called the police right off.' Coe drank more beer, and then said, 'You think this is connected with the other ones on the block?'

'It looks that way,' Kling said.

'How do you think he gets in?' Coe asked.

'Through the front door.'

'But how?'

'With a key,' Kling said.

'You don't think ...'

'No.'

'If you do, Mr Kling, I wish you'd say so.'

'I don't think you had anything to do with this burglary or with any of the others. No, Mr Coe.'

'Good,' Coe said. He rose, opened the refrigerator, and said, 'Would you care for another beer?'

'Thank you, I've got to be going.'

'It's been nice having you visit,' Coe said.

The call from Joseph Angieri came to the squadroom at close to six o'clock that evening, just as Kling was preparing to go home.

'Mr Kling,' he said, 'we found the cat.'

'I beg your pardon?' Kling said.

'The kitten. You said your man always left a ...'

'Yes, yes,' Kling said. 'Where'd you find it?'

'Behind the dresser. Dead. Tiny little thing, grey and white. Must have fallen off and banged its head.' Angieri paused. 'Do you want me to keep it for you?'

'No, I don't think so.'

'What should I do with it?' Angieri asked.

'Well ... dispose of it,' Kling said.

'Just throw it in the garbage?'

'I suppose so.'

'Maybe I'll take it down and bury it in the park.'

'Whatever you prefer, Mr Angieri.'

'Tiny little thing,' Angieri said. 'You know, I happened to remember something after you left.'

'What's that?'

'The lock on the front door. We had it changed just before we left for Jamaica. Because of all the burglaries on the block, figured we'd better change the lock. If somebody got in here with a *key* ...'

'Yes, Mr Angieri, I follow you,' Kling said. 'What's the locksmith's name?'

Chapter Two

Detective Steve Carella was a tall man with the body and walk of a trained athlete. His eyes were brown, slanting peculiarly downward in an angular face, giving him an oriental appearance that was completely at odds with his Italian background. The downward tilt of the eyes also make him look a trifle mournful at times, again in contradiction to his basically optimistic outlook. He glided towards the ringing telephone now like an outfielder moving up to an easy pop fly, lifted the receiver, sat on the edge of the desk in one fluid motion, and said, '87th Squad, Carella here.'

'Have you paid your income tax, Detective Carella?'

This was Friday morning, the sixteenth of April, and Carella had mailed his income tax return on the ninth, a full six days before the deadline. But even though he suspected the caller was Sam Grossman at the lab, or Rollie Chabrier in the D.A.'s office (both of whom were fond of little telephone gags), he nonetheless felt the normal dread of any American citizen when confronted with a voice supposedly originating in the offices of the Internal Revenue Service.

'Yes, I have,' he said, carrying it off rather well, he thought. 'Who's this, please?'

'No one remembers me anymore,' the voice said dolefully. 'I'm beginning to feel neglected.'

'Oh,' Carella said. 'It's you.'

'Ahh, yes, it's me.'

'Detective Meyer mentioned that you'd called. How are you?' Carella said chattily, and signalled to Hal Willis across the room. Willis looked at him in puzzlement. Carella twirled his forefinger as though dialling a phone. Willis nodded, and immediately called the Security Office at the telephone company to ask for a trace on Carella's line, the Frederick 7-8025 extension.

'I'm all right now,' the voice said. 'I got shot a while back, though. Did you know that, Detective Carella?'

'Yes, I know that.'

'In a tailor shop. On Culver Avenue.'

'Yes.'

'In fact, if I recall correctly, *you're* the man who shot me, Detective Carella.'

'Yes, that's my recollection, too.' Carella looked at Willis and raised his eyebrows inquisitively. Willis nodded and made an encouraging hand gesture – *keep him talking.*

'Quite painful,' the Deaf Man said.

'Yes, getting shot can be painful.'

'But then, *you've* been shot, too.'

'I have indeed.'

'In fact, if I recall correctly, *I'm* the man who shot *you*.'

'With a shotgun, wasn't it?'

'Which makes us even, I suppose.'

'Not quite. Getting shot with a shotgun is more painful than getting shot with a pistol.'

'Are you trying to trace this call, Detective Carella?'

'How could I? I'm all alone up here.'

'I think you're lying,' the Deaf Man said, and hung up.

'Get anything?' Carella asked Willis.

'Miss Sullivan?' Willis said into the phone. He listened, shook his head, said, 'Thanks for trying,' and then hung up. 'When's the last time we successfully traced a telephone call?' he asked Carella. He was a short man (the shortest on the squad, in fact, having barely cleared the Department's 5′8″ minimum height requirement), with slender hands and the alert brown eyes of a frisky terrier. He walked towards Carella's desk with a bouncing stride, as though he were wearing sneakers.

'He'll call back,' Carella said.

'You sounded like two old buddies chatting,' Willis said.

'In a sense, we *are* old buddies.'

'What do you want to do if he calls again? Go through the nonsense?'

'No, he's hip to it. He'll never stay on the line more than a few minutes.'

'What the hell does he want?' Willis asked.

'Who knows?' Carella answered, and thought about what he'd said just a few moments before. *In a sense, we* are *old buddies.*

He had, he realized, stopped considering the Deaf Man a deadly adversary, and he wondered now how much this had to do with the fact that his wife, Teddy, was a deaf mute. Oddly, he never thought of her as such – except when the Deaf Man put in an appearance. There had never been anything resembling a lack of communication in his relationship with Teddy; her eyes were her ears, and her hands spoke volumes. Teddy was capable of screaming down the roof in pantomime and dismissing his own angry response by simply closing her eyes. Her eyes were brown, almost as dark as her black hair. She watched him intently with those eyes, watched his lips, watched his hands as they moved in the alphabet she had taught him, and which he spoke fluently and with a personality distinctly his own. She was beautiful and passionate and responsive and smart as hell. She was also a deaf mute. But he equated this with the lacy black butterfly she'd had tattooed on her right shoulder more years ago than he could recall; they were both superficial aspects of the woman he loved.

He had once hated the Deaf Man. He no longer did. He had once dreaded his intelligence and nerve. He no longer did. In a curious way he was glad the Deaf Man had returned, but at the same time he sincerely wished the Deaf Man would go away. To return again? It was all very puzzling. Carella sighed and wheeled a typing cart into position near his desk.

From his own desk Willis said, 'We don't need him. Not at this time of year. Not with the warm weather starting.'

*   *   *

The clock on the squadroom wall read 10:51 a.m.

A half hour had passed since the Deaf Man's last call. He had not called again, and Carella was not disappointed. As if to support Willis's theory that the Deaf Man was not needed, not with the warm weather starting, the squadroom was now thronged with cops, lawbreakers, and victims – all on a nice quiet Friday morning with the sun shining in a clear blue sky, and the temperature sitting at seventy-two degrees.

There was something about the warm weather that brought them out like cockroaches. The cops of the 87th Precinct rarely enjoyed what could be called a 'slow season', but it did appear to them that less crimes were committed during the winter months. During the winter months, it was the firemen who had all the headaches. Slum landlords were not particularly renowned for their generosity in supplying adequate heat to tenement dwellers, despite the edicts of the Board of Health. The apartments in some of the buildings lining the side streets off Culver and Ainsley avenues were only slightly warmer than the nearest igloo. The tenants, coping with rats and faulty electrical wiring and falling plaster and leaking pipes, often sought to bring a little extra warmth into their lives by using cheap kerosene burners that were fire hazards. There were more fires in the 87th Precinct on any given winter's night than in any other part of the city. Conversely, there were less broken heads. It takes a lot of energy to work up passion when you're freezing your ass off. But winter had all but fled the city, and spring was here, and with it came the attendant rites, the celebrations of the earth, the paeans to life and living. The juices were beginning to flow, and nowhere did they flow as exuberantly as in the 87th, where life and death sometimes got a little bit confused and where the flowing juices were all too often a bright red.

The man clinging to the patrolman's arm had an arrow in his chest. They had called for a meat wagon, but in the meantime they didn't know what the hell to do with him. They had never before had a man up here with an arrow sticking in his chest and protruding from his back.

'Why'd you bring him up here?' Willis whispered to the patrolman.

'What'd you want me to do? Leave him wandering around in the park?'

'Yeah, that's what you should have done,' Willis whispered. 'Let the Department of Hospitals worry about him. This guy can sue us, did you know that? For bringing him up here?'

'He can?' the patrolman whispered, and went immediately pale.

'All right, sit down,' Willis said to the man. 'Can you hear me? Sit down.'

'I got shot,' the man said.

'Yeah, yeah, we know that. Now sit down. Will you please sit down? What the hell's the matter with you?'

'I got shot,' the man said.

'Who did it?'

'I don't know. Are there Indians in this city?'

'The ambulance is coming,' Willis said. 'Sit down.'

'I want to stand up.'

'Why?'

'It hurts more when I sit.'

'You're not bleeding much,' Willis said softly.

'I know. But it hurts. Did you call the ambulance?'

'I just told you we called the ambulance.'

'What time is it?'

'Almost eleven.'

'I was taking a walk in the park,' the man said. 'I felt this sharp pain in my chest, I thought I was having a heart attack. I look down, there's an *arrow* in me.'

'All right, sit down, will you, you're making me nervous.'

'Is the ambulance coming?'

'It's coming, it's coming.'

In the detention cage across the room, a tall blonde girl wearing a white blouse and a short tan skirt paced nervously and angrily, and then stepped up to the grilled metal and shouted, 'I didn't do nothing, let me out of here.'

'The patrolman says you did plenty,' Carella said. 'You slashed your boy friend across the face and throat with a razor blade.'

'He deserved it,' the girl shouted. 'Let me out of here.'

'We're booking you for first-degree assault,' Carella said. 'As soon as you calm down, I'm going to take your fingerprints.'

'I ain't *never* calming down,' the girl shouted.

'We've got all the time in the world.'

'You know what I'm going to do?'

'You're going to calm down, and then we're going to take your fingerprints. And then, if you've got any sense, you're going to start praying your boy friend doesn't die.'

'I *hope* he dies. Let me out of here!'

'Nobody's letting you out. Stop yelling, you're busting my ears.'

'I'm going to rip off all my clothes and say you tried to rape me.'

'Go ahead, we'll enjoy the show.'

'You think I'm kidding?'

'Hey, Hal, the girl here's going to take off her clothes.'

'Good, let her,' Willis said.

'You mother-fuckers,' the girl said.

'Nice talk,' Carella said.

'You think I won't do it?'

'Do it, who cares?' Carella said, and turned away from the cage to walk towards a patrolman who stood behind two teen-age boys handcuffed to each other and to the heavy wooden leg of the fingerprinting table. 'What've we got here, Fred?' Carella asked the patrolman.

'Smashed a Cadillac into the window of a grocery store on the Stem. They're both stoned,' the patrolman said. 'The Caddy was stolen two days ago on the South Side. I've got it on my hot-car list.'

'Take off you blouse, honey,' one of the boys yelled across the room. 'Show us your tits.'

'We'll say they jumped you,' the other boy yelled, giggling. 'Go ahead, baby, do it.'

'Anybody injured?' Carella asked the patrolman.

'Nobody in the store but the owner, and he was behind the counter.'

'How about it?' Carella asked the boys.

'How about what?' the first boy said. He had long black curly hair and a thick black beard. He was wearing blue jeans and a striped polo shirt over which was a tan windbreaker. He kept looking towards the detention cage, where the girl had begun pacing again.

'You crash that car into the window?'

'What car?' he said.

'The blue Caddy that was stolen from in front of 1604 Stewart Place Wednesday night,' the patrolman said.

'You're dreaming,' the boy answered.

'Rip off your blouse, honey!' the second boy shouted. He was shorter than his companion, with long stringy brown hair and pale blue eyes. He was wearing tan chinos and a Mexican poncho. He did not have a shirt on under the poncho. He, too, kept watching the detention cage, where the girl had approached the locked door again and was peering owlishly into the room, as though contemplating her next move. '*Do* it!' he shouted to her. 'Are you chicken?'

'Shut up, punk,' she answered.

'Did you steal that car?' Carella asked.

'I don't know what car you're talking about,' the boy said.

'The car you drove through the grocery-store window.'

'We weren't driving no car, man,' the first boy said.

'We were *flying*, man,' the second boy said, and both of them began giggling.

'Better not book them till they know what's going on,' Carella said. 'Take them down, Fred. Tell Sergeant Murchison they're stoned and won't understand their rights.' He turned to the nearest boy and said, 'How old are you?'

'Fifty-eight,' the boy answered.

'Sixty-five,' the second boy said, and again they giggled.

'Take them down,' Carella said. 'Keep them away from anybody, they may be juveniles.'

The patrolman unlocked the cuff holding them to the leg of the table. As he led them towards the slatted railing that divided the squadroom from the corridor, the bearded boy turned towards the detention cage again and shouted, 'You got nothing to show, anyway!' and then burst into laughter as the patrolman prodded him from behind with his nightstick.

'You think I won't do it?' the girl again said to Carella.

'Sweetheart, we don't care *what* you do,' Carella answered, and walked to Kling's desk, where an old woman sat in a long black overcoat, her hands folded demurely in her lap.

'*Che vergogna*,' the woman said, nodding her head in disapproval of the girl in the cage.

'Yes,' Carella answered. 'Do you speak English, *signora*?'

'I have been in America forty years.'

'Would you like to tell me what happened?'

'Someone steal my pocketbook.'

Carella moved a pad into place before him. 'What's your name, *signora*?'

'Caterina Di Paolo.'

'And your address?'

'Hey, is this a gag?' somebody called from the railing. Carella looked up. A white-suited ambulance attendant was standing there, looking disbelievingly into the squadroom. 'Did somebody *really* get shot with an arrow?'

'There he is,' Willis said.

'That's an arrow, all right,' the attendant said, his eyes bugging.

'Rape, rape!' the girl in the detention cage suddenly shouted, and Carella turned and saw that she had removed her blouse and brassiere.

'Oh, Jesus,' he muttered, and then said, 'Excuse me, *signora*,' and was walking towards the cage when the telephone on his own desk rang.

He lifted the reciever.

'Come on, mister,' the ambulance attendant said.

'They ripped off my clothes!' the girl shouted. 'Look at me!'

'*Che vergogna*,' the old lady said, and began clucking her tongue.

'With your assistance,' the Deaf Man said, 'I'm going to steal five hundred thousand dollars on the last day of April.'

Chapter Three

The manila envelope was addressed in typescript to Detective Steven Louis Carella, 87th Squad, 41 Grover Avenue. There was no return address on the envelope. It had been postmarked in Isola the day before. The picture was inside the envelope, neatly sandwiched between two pieces of grey shirt cardboard.

'That's J. Edgar Hoover, isn't it?' Meyer asked.

'That's who it is,' Carella said.

'Why a photograph of him?'

'It isn't even a photograph,' Carella said. 'It's a photo-*stat*.'

'Federal government is undoubtedly cutting back on expenses,' Meyer said. 'Recession, you know.'

'Undoubtedly,' Carella said.

'What do you think?' Meyer asked seriously.

'I think it's our friend.'

'So do I.'

'His opening gun.'

'Why Hoover?'

'Why not?'

Meyer scratched his bald pate. 'What's he trying to tell us, Steve?'

'I haven't the foggiest notion,' Carella said.

'Well, figure it out, figure it out.'

'Well,' Carella said, 'he told me yesterday that he plans to steal half a million dollars on the last day of April. So now,' he said, and glanced at the wall clock, 'at exactly nine twenty-two the next morning, we receive a photostat of J. Edgar Hoover. He's either trying to tell us something, or trying to tell us nothing, or trying to tell us something that means nothing.'

'That's brilliant reasoning,' Meyer said. 'Have you ever thought of going into police work?'

'I'm basing my deduction upon his past M.O. Remember that first job, whenever the hell it was?'

'More than ten years ago.'

'Right. He led us to believe he was going to hit one bank when he was really after another. Incidentally, wasn't *that* hit also scheduled for the last day of April?'

'It was.'

'And he damn near got away with it.'

'Damn near.'

'He lets us know what he's planning to do, but he doesn't *really* let us know. It's no fun for him otherwise. Look at what he did on his next job. Announced each of his planned murders beforehand, knocked off two city officials in a row, and threatened to knock off the mayor himself. But only because he was trying to extort money from *other* people, and was using those high-calibre murders as warnings. It's all misdirected direction, Meyer. Which is why I say this picture can mean everything or it can mean nothing.'

Meyer looked at the photostat again. 'Hoover,' he said blankly.

The locksmith's name was Stanislaw Janik.

His shop was an eight-by-ten cubicle wedged between a hockshop and a dry-cleaning store on Culver Avenue. The wall behind his counter was made of pegboard upon which hung blank keys. Each blank was identified by a code number that corresponded to a similar number in the manufacturer's catalogue. In the case of automobile keys, the blanks were coded according to year and make. There were six full-grown cats in the shop. The place stank of cat shit.

Janik himself resembled a cross-eyed Siamese, blue eyes magnified behind bifocals, bald save for a tuft of black hair behind each ear. A man in his early fifties, he sat on a stool behind the counter, wearing a tan sweater over a white shirt open at the throat, cutting a key as Kling came into the shop. The bell over the door tinkled, and a cat who had been lying just behind the door growled angrily and leaped halfway across the room.

'Mr Janik?' Kling said.

Janik looked up from the key and turned off the duplicating machine. His teeth were nicotine-stained; a Sherlock Holmes pipe rested in an ashtray near the machine. The counter top was covered with brass filings. He brushed them aside with the back of his hand and said, 'Yes, can I help you?' His speech was faintly accented; Kling could not place the country of origin. He reached into his pocket, opened his wallet to where his shield was pinned to a leather flap opposite his lucite-encased I.D. card, and said, 'Police officer. I'd like to ask you some questions, please.'

'What's the matter?' Janik asked.

'I'm investigating some burglaries on Richardson Drive.'

'Yes?'

'I understand you installed a lock for one of the burglary victims.'

'Who would that be?' Janik asked. A black and white cat leaped suddenly from the floor to the counter and offered its back to Janik. He began stroking the cat idly, not looking at the animal, watching Kling instead from behind his thick spectacles.

'A Mr Joseph Angieri,' Kling said. 'At 638 Richardson.'

'Yes, I installed a lock for him,' Janik said, stroking the cat's arched back.

'What kind of a lock was it?'

'A simple cylinder lock. Not good enough,' Janik said, shaking his head.

'What do you mean?'

'I told Mr Angieri. He was having the lock changed because of the burglaries, do you understand? So I told him this type of cylinder lock was not sufficient protection, that he should allow me to put in a deadlock. Are you familiar with this lock?'

'I am,' Kling said.

'It would have been adequate protection. Even if you remove the cylinder on a deadlock, there is a shutter guard that prevents entry. I suggested a Fox lock, too, as an added precaution. If he was afraid of burglary ...'

'You seem to know a lot about burglary, Mr Janik.'

'Locks are my business,' Janik said, and shrugged. He pushed the cat off the counter. Startled, the cat landed on the floor, scowled up at him, stretched, and stalked off into the corner, where it began licking the ear of a tan Angora. 'I told Mr Angieri that the little extra money would be worth it. For the deadlock, I mean. He said no, he wasn't interested in that kind of investment. So now his place is broken into. So he saved a little money on a cheaper lock, and he lost all his valuable possessions. What kind of thrift is that? Senseless,' Janik said, and shook his head again.

'Would you have any idea what his loss was, Mr Janik?'

'None.'

'Then ... why do you say he lost valuable possessions?'

'I assume if someone breaks into an apartment, it is not to open a piggy bank and steal a few pennies. What are you trying to say, young man?'

'Have you installed locks for anyone else in this neighbourhood, Mr Janik?'

'As I told you before, locks are my business. Of *course* I have installed other locks in the neighbourhood. My *shop* is in the neighbourhood, where would you expect me to install locks? In California?'

'Have you installed other locks on Richardson Drive?'

'I have.'

'Where on Richardson Drive? Which apartments?'

'I would have to consult my records.'

'Would you please?'

'No, I would not.'

'Mr Janik ...'

'I don't believe I care for your manner, young man. I'm very busy, and I don't have time to go through my bills to see just which apartments had locks installed by me. I ask you again, what are you trying to say?'

'Mr Janik ...' Kling said, and hesitated.

'Yes?'

'Would you happen to have duplicate keys for the locks you've installed?'

'I would not. Are you suggesting I'm a thief?'

'No, sir. I merely ...'

'I came to this country from Poland in 1948. My wife and children were killed by the Germans, and I am alone in the world, I earn a meagre living, but I earn it honestly. Even in Poland, when I was starving, I never stole so much as a crust of bread. I am not a thief, young man, and I do not choose to show you my bills. I will thank you to leave my shop.'

'I may be back, Mr Janik.'

'You are free to return. Provided you come with a warrant. I have had enough of storm troopers in my lifetime.'

'I'm sure you understand, Mr Janik ...'

'I understand nothing. Please go.'

'Thank you,' Kling said, and walked to the door. He turned, started to say something else, and then opened the door instead. The bell tinkled, and one of the cats almost ran out onto the sidewalk. Kling hastily closed the door behind him and began walking the six blocks to the station house. He felt he had handled the whole thing badly. He felt like a goddamn Nazi. It was a bright spring day, and the air was clean and fresh, but the stink of cat shit lingered in his nostrils.

At 3:30 p.m., fifteen minutes before Kling was supposed to be relieved, the phone on his desk rang. He picked it up and said:

'87th Squad, Kling.'

'Bert, this is Murchison on the desk. Just got a call from Patrolman Ingersoll at 657 Richardson Drive. He's in 11D with a lady who just got back from a trip abroad. The apartment's been ripped off.'

'I'll get right over there,' Kling said.

He walked to where Hal Willis was sitting at his own desk, two dozen forged cheques spread out before him, and said, 'Hal, I've got another burglary on Richardson. I'll probably head straight home from there.'

'Right,' Willis said, and went back to comparing the signatures on the cheques against a suspect signature on a motel registration card. 'This guy's been hanging paper all over town,' he said conversationally, without looking up.

'Did you hear me?' Kling asked.

'Yeah, burglary on Richardson, heading straight home,' Willis said.

'See you,' Kling said, and went out of the squadroom.

His car was illegally parked on Grover, two blocks from the station house. The visor on the driver's side was down and a hand-lettered sign clipped to it read: POLICE DEPARTMENT VEHICLE. Each time he came back to it at the end of his tour he expected to find it decorated with a parking citation from some overzealous uniformed cop. He checked the windshield now, unlocked the door, shoved the visor up, and drove over to Richardson, where he double-parked alongside a tobacco-brown Mercedes-Benz. He told the doorman he was a police officer, and explained where he had left the car. The doorman promised to call him in apartment 11D if the owner of the Mercedes wanted to get out.

Mike Ingersoll opened the door on Kling's second ring. He was a handsome cop in his late thirties, slightly older than Kling, with curly black hair, brown eyes, and a nose as straight and as swift as a machete slash. He looked in his uniform the way a lot of patrolmen *thought* they looked, but didn't. He wore it with casual pride, as though it had been tailored exclusively for him in a fancy shop on Hall Avenue, rather than picked off a ready-to-wear rack in a store across the street from the Police Academy downtown. 'You got here fast,' he said to Kling, and stepped out of the doorway to let him in. His voice, in contrast to his size, was quite soft and came as a distinct surprise; one expected something fuller and rounder to rumble up out of his barrel chest. 'Lady's in the living room,' he said. 'Place is a complete mess. The guy really cleaned her out.'

'Same one?'

'I think so. No marks on the windows or door, a white kitten on the bedroom dresser.'

'Well,' Kling said, and sighed. 'Let's talk to the lady.'

The lady was sitting on the living-room sofa.

The lady had long red hair and green eyes and a deep suntan. She was wearing a dark green sweater, a short brown skirt, and brown boots. Her legs crossed, she kept staring at the wall as Kling came into the room, and then turned to face him. His first impression was one of total harmony, a casual perfection of colour and design, russet and green, hair and eyes, sweater and skirt, boots blending with the smoothness of her tan, the long sleek grace of crossed legs, the inquisitively angled head, the red hair cascading in clean vertical descent. Her face and figure came as residuals to his brief course in art appreciation. High cheekbones, eyes slanting up from them, fiercely green against the tan, tilted nose gently drawing the upper lip away from partially exposed, even white teeth. Her sweater swelled over breasts firm without a bra, the wool cinched tightly at her waist with a brown, brass-studded belt, hip softly carving an arc against the nubby sofa back, skirt revealing a secret thigh as she turned more fully towards him.

He had never seen a more beautiful woman in his life.

'I'm Detective Kling,' he said. "How do you do?'

'Hullo,' she said dully. She seemed on the edge of tears. Her green eyes glistened, she extended her hand to him, and he took it clumsily, and they exchanged handshakes, and he could not take his eyes from her face. He realized all at once that he was still holding her hand. He dropped it abruptly, cleared his throat, and reached into his pocket for his pad.

'I don't believe I have your name, miss,' he said.

'Augusta Blair,' she said. 'Did you see the mess inside? In the bedroom?'

'I'll take a look in a minute,' Kling said. 'When did you discover the theft, Miss Blair?'

'I got home about half an hour ago.'

'From where?'

'Austria.'

'Nice thing to come home to,' Ingersoll said, and shook his head.

'Was the door locked when you got here?' Kling asked.

'Yes.'

'You used your key to get in?'

'Yes.'

'Anybody in the apartment?'

'No.'

'Did you hear anything? Any sound at all?'

'Nothing.'

'Tell me what happened.'

'I came in, and I left the door open behind me because I knew the doorman was coming up with my bags. Then I took off my coat and hung it in the hall closet, and then I went to the john, and then I went into the bedroom. Everything looked all right until then. The minute I stepped in there, I felt . . . invaded.'

'You'd better take a look at it, Bert,' Ingersoll said. 'The guy went sort of berserk.'

'That it?' Kling asked, indicating a doorway across the room.

'Yes,' Augusta said, and rose from the couch. She was a tall girl, at least five-seven, perhaps five-eight, and she moved with a swift grace, preceding him to the bedroom door, looking inside once again, and then turning away in dismay. Kling went into the room, but she did not follow him. She stood in the doorframe instead, worrying her lip, her shoulder against the jamb.

The burglar had slashed through the room like a hurricane. The dresser drawers had all been pulled out and dumped onto the rug – slips, bras, panties, sweaters, stockings, scarves, blouses, spilling across the room in a dazzle of colour. Similarly, the clothes on hangers had been yanked out of the closet and flung helter-skelter – coats, suits, skirts, gowns, robes strewn over the floor, bed, and chairs. A jewellery box had been overturned in the centre of the bed, and bracelets, rings, beads, pendants, chokers glittered amid a swirl of chiffon, silk, nylon, and wool. A white kitten sat on the dresser top, mewing.

'Did he find what he was looking for?' Kling asked.

'Yes,' she answered. 'My good jewellery was wrapped in a red silk scarf at the back of the top drawer. It's gone.'

'Anything else?'

'Two furs. A leopard and an otter.'

'He's selective,' Ingersoll said.

'Mmm,' Kling said. 'Any radios, phonographs, stuff like that?'

'No. The hi-fi equipment's in the living room. He didn't touch it.'

'I'll need a list of the jewellery and coats, Miss Blair.'

'What for?'

'Well, so we can get working on it. Also, I'm sure you want to report this to your insurance company.'

'None of it was insured.'

'Oh, boy,' Kling said.

'I just never thought anything like this would happen,' Augusta said.

'How long have you been *living* here?' Kling asked incredulously.

'The city or the apartment?'

'Both.'

'I've lived in the city for a year and a half. The apartment for eight months.'

'Where are you from originally?'

'Seattle.'

'Are you presently employed?' Kling said, and took out his pad.

'Yes.'

'Can you give me the name of the firm?'

'I'm a model,' Augusta said. 'I'm represented by the Cutler Agency.'

'Were you in Austria on a modelling assignment?'

'No, vacation. Skiing.'

'I though you looked familiar,' Ingersoll said. 'I'll bet I've seen your picture in the magazines.'

'Mmm,' Augusta said without interest.

'How long were you gone?' Kling asked.

'Two weeks. Well, sixteen days, actually.'

'Nice thing to come home to,' Ingersoll said again, and again shook his head.

'I moved here because it had a doorman,' Augusta said. 'I thought buildings with doormen were safe.'

'*None* of the buildings on this side of the city are safe,' Ingersoll said.

'Not many of them, anyway,' Kling said.

'I couldn't afford anything across the park,' Augusta said. 'I haven't been modelling a very long time, I don't really get many bookings.' She saw the question on Kling's face and said, 'The furs were gifts from my mother, and the jewellery was left to me by my aunt. I saved six goddamn months for the trip to Austria,' she said, and suddenly burst into tears. 'Oh, shit,' she said, 'why'd he have to do this?'

Ingersoll and Kling stood by awkwardly. Augusta turned swiftly, walked past Ingersoll to the sofa, and took a handkerchief from her handbag. She noisily blew her nose, dried her eyes, and said, 'I'm sorry.'

'If you'll let me have the complete list ...' Kling said.

'Yes, of course.'

'We'll do what we can to get it back.'

'Sure,' Augusta said, and blew her nose again.

Chapter Four

Everybody figured it was a mistake.

They were naturally grateful (who wouldn't be?) to receive a second photostated picture of the late beloved leader of our nation's finest security force, but they could not see any reason for it, and so they automatically figured somebody had goofed. It was unlike the Deaf Man to say anything twice when once would suffice. Nor was there any question but that the photostats were identical. The only difference between the one that had arrived in the mail on Saturday, April 17, and the one that arrived today, April 19, were the postmarks on the envelopes. But aside from that, everything was the same, an obvious error. The boys of the 87th were beginning to feel more cheerful about the entire matter; perhaps the Deaf Man was getting senile.

There were five pages of listings for photostat shops in the yellow pages of the Isola directory alone, and perhaps the police should have begun contacting each, on the off chance that one of them had copied Hoover's picture. But nobody was forgetting that thus far no crime had been committed; you could not go around wasting the time of civil servants unless there was something that might conceivably justify such expense. One could, of course, argue that the Deaf Man's past murderous exploits were reason enough for mobilizing the entire police department, getting those men out checking shops, clerks making telephone calls, mailing flyers, and so on. Conversely, one could just as reasonably argue that nobody really knew whether the two pictures of Hoover had indeed come from the Deaf

Man, or whether they were in any way linked with the crime he had said he would commit. Given an overworked, understaffed police force with other pressing matters to worry about – like muggings, knifings, shootings, holdups, rapes, burglaries, forgeries, car thefts, oh you know, nuisance stuff – it was perhaps understandable why the cops of the 87th merely asked the laboratory whether the printing paper was unique and whether or not there were any good latent prints on it. The answers to both questions were depressing. The paper was garden-variety crap, and there were no latent prints on it, good or otherwise.

And then, because police work is not all fun and games and looking at pretty pictures, they got to work on a squeal that came in at 10:27 that morning.

The young man had been nailed to the tenement wall.

Long-haired, with a handlebar moustache, wearing only undershorts, he hung like a latter-day Christ bereft of wooden crucifix, a knife wound on the left side of his chest just below the heart, his arms widespread, a spike driven into the wall through each open palm, legs crossed and impaled with a third large spike, head lolling to the side. A vagrant wino had stumbled upon the body, but there was no telling how long he had been hanging there. The blood no longer ran from his wounds. He had soiled himself either in fright or in death, and his own rank stench mingled with the putrid stink of garbage in the empty room so that the detectives turned away from the open doorframe and went out into the corridor, where the air was only slightly less fetid.

The building was one in a long row of abandoned tenements on North Harrison, infested with rats, inhabited for a time by hippies, discarded by them later when they discovered it was too easy to be victimized there by men and beasts alike. The word LOVE still decorated a wall in the hallway, painted flowers running rampant around it in a faded circle, but the dead man in the empty room stank of his own excrement, and the assistant medical examiner did not want to go in to examine the corpse.

'Why should I get all the bad ones?' he asked Carella. 'All the jobs nobody else wants, I get. The hell with it. He can rot in there, for all I care. Let the hospital people take him down and cart him to the morgue. We'll examine him there, where at least I can wash my hands afterwards.'

The ceiling above their heads was bloated with water, and plaster dangerously loose and close to falling. The room in which the boy hung dead and crucified had one shattered window, and no door in its frame. It had been used as a makeshift garbage dump by the building's squatters, and the garbage was piled three feet high, a thick carpet of mouldering food, rusting cans, broken bottles, newspapers, used condoms, and animal faeces, topped, as though with a maraschino cherry, with a swollen dead rat. For anyone to have entered the room, it would have been necessary to climb *up* onto the ledge formed by the garbage. The ceiling was perhaps twelve feet high, and the man's impaled feet were crossed some six inches above the line of garbage. He was a tall young man. Whoever had driven the spikes through his extended hands had been even taller, but the body had sagged of its own weight since, dislocating both shoulders and wreaking God knew what internal damage.

'You hear me?' the M.E. said.

'Do what you like,' Carella answered.

'I will.'

'Just make sure we get a full necropsy report.'

'You think he was alive when they nailed him there?' Meyer asked.

'Maybe. The stabbing may have been an afterthought,' Carella said.

'I'm not taking him down, and that's that,' the M.E. said.

'Look,' Carella said angrily, 'take him down, leave him there, it's up to you. Send us your goddamn report, and don't forget prints.'

'I won't.'

'Footprints, too.'

'More crazy bastards in this city,' the M.E. said, and walked off sullenly, picking his way through the rubble in the corridor, and starting down the staircase to the street, where he hoped to sell his case to the ambulance people when they arrived.

'Let's check the rest of the floor,' Meyer said.

There were two other apartments on the floor. The locks on the doors to both had been broken. In one apartment there were the remains of a recent fire in the centre of the room. A worn tennis sneaker was in the corner near the window. Meyer lifted it with his handkerchief, and then bagged and tagged it for transportation to the lab. The second room was empty except for a soiled and torn mattress covered with rat leavings.

'What a shit hole,' someone said behind them, and Meyer and Carella turned to find Detective Monoghan in the doorway. Detective Monroe was immediately behind him. Both Homicide cops had grey fedoras on their heads, black topcoats on their backs, and pained expressions on their faces.

'People actually *live* in these shit holes, can you imagine that?' Monroe said.

'Incredible,' Monoghan said, wagging his head.

'Unbelievable,' Monroe said.

'Where's the stiff?' Monoghan asked.

'Down the hall,' Carella said.

'Want to show me?'

'You'll find it,' Carella answered.

'Come on,' Monoghan said to his partner, and both of them went down the hallway, big-shouldered men pushing their way through the empty corridor as though dispersing a crowd. 'Holy mother of God!' Monoghan said.

Carella nodded.

There were footfalls on the steps. Two men in white picked their way over fallen plaster and lathe, looked up when they reached the landing, saw Carella, and walked to him immediately.

'Listen, are you in charge here?' one of them asked.

'It's my case, yes,' Carella said.

'I'm Dr Cortez, what's this about wanting *me* to get somebody off the wall?'

'He's got to be taken to the mortuary,' Carella said.

'Fine, we'll get him to the mortuary. But your medical examiner says he's *nailed* to the goddamn wall. I don't ...'

'That's right.'

'*I* don't plan to take him down, pal.'

'Who do you suggest for the job, pal?' Carella asked.

'I don't *care* who. You look strong enough, why don't you handle it yourself?'

'That's a murder victim in there,' Carella said flatly.

'That's a corpse in there,' Cortez answered, equally flatly.

Monoghan was coming back down the corridor, holding his nose. Monroe was a step behind him, his hand cupped over the lower part of his face.

'These men are from Homicide,' Carella said. 'Talk to them about it.'

'Who's supposed to take down the corpse?' Cortez asked.

'The M.E. through with it?' Monoghan said.

'He won't examine it here,' Carella said.

'He's *got* to examine it here. Those are regulations. We can't move the body till the M.E. examines it, pronounces it dead, and ...'

'Yeah, go tell that to *him*,' Cortez said.

'Where is he?' Monoghan asked.

'Downstairs. Puking out his guts.'

'Come on,' Monoghan said to his partner, and they headed for the staircase. 'You wait here, Carella.'

They listened to the two Homicide cops making their way downstairs. Their footfalls died. There was a strained silence in the corridor.

'Listen, I'm sorry I got so snotty,' Cortez said.

'That's okay,' Carella answered.

'But he knows the regulations as well as I do. He's just trying to get out of a messy job, that's all.'

'Um-huh,' Carella said.

'He knows the regulations,' Cortez repeated.

The assistant medical examiner, if he had not previously known the regulations, knew them letter-perfect by the time Monoghan and Monroe got through with him downstairs. With a handkerchief tied over his nose, and wearing rubber gloves, he took down the impaled body of the unidentified white male, and performed a cursory examination before declaring him officially dead.

Everybody could now begin tackling the *next* unpleasant task of finding out who had made him that way.

Chapter Five

Detective Cotton Hawes looked at the photostat that came in Tuesday morning's mail and decided it was General George Washington.

'Who does that look like to you?' he asked Miscolo, who had come out of the Clerical Office to pick up the weekend's D.D. reports for filing.

'Napoleon Bonaparte,' Miscolo said drily. Shaking his head, he went out of the squadroom muttering. Hawes *still* thought it looked like Washington.

He had been filled in on the latest activities of the Deaf Man, and he

assumed now that the photostat was intended as a companion piece to the pictures of J. Edgar Hoover. He immediately connected Hoover and Washington in the obviously logical way – the main office of the Federal Bureau of Investigation was in the city of Washington, D.C. Hoover, Washington, simple. When dealing with the Deaf Man, however, nothing was simple; Hawes recoiled from his first thought as though bitten by it. If the Deaf Man's planned crime was to take place in Washington, he would not be pestering the hard-working cops (Oh, how hard they worked!) of the 87th. Instead, he would be cavorting on the Mall, taunting the cops of the District of Columbia, those stalwarts. No. This picture of the father of the country was meant to indicate something more than the name of a city. Hawes was certain of that. He was equally certain that J. Edgar's fine face was meant to represent something more than the name of a vacuum cleaner, splendid product though it was. He suddenly wondered what the 'J'. stood for. James? Jack? Jerome? Jules?

'Alf!' he shouted, and Miscolo, down the corridor in the Clerical Office, yelled, 'Yo?'

'Come in here a minute, will you?'

Hawes rose from behind his desk and held the picture of Washington out at arm's length. Hawes was a big man, six feet two inches tall, weighing 190 pounds, give or take a few for sweets or pizza. He had a straight unbroken nose, a good mouth with a wide lower lip, and red hair streaked with white over the left temple, where he had once been knifed by a building superintendent who had mistaken him for a burglar. His eyes were blue, and his vision had been as sharp as a hatpin when he'd joined the force. But that was many years ago, and we all begin to show the signs of age, sonny. He held the picture at arm's length now because he was a trifle far-sighted and not at all certain that Miscolo *hadn't* identified it correctly.

No, it was Washington, all right, no question about it.

'It's Washington,' he said to Miscolo as he came into the squadroom carrying a sheaf of papers.

'You don't say?' Miscolo said drily. He looked harried, and hardly in the mood for small talk. Hawes debated asking his question, figured What the hell, and plunged ahead regardless.

'What does the "J". in J. Edgar Hoover stand for?'

'John,' Miscolo said.

'Are you sure?'

'I'm positive.'

'John,' Hawes said.

'John,' Miscolo repeated.

The two men looked at each other.

'Is that all?' Miscolo asked.

'Yes, thanks a lot, Alf.'

'Don't mention it,' Miscolo said. Shaking his head, he went out of the squadroom muttering.

John Edgar Hoover, Hawes thought. John. And George, of course. Names fascinated him. He himself had been named after the fiery Puritan preacher Cotton Mather. Hawes had never felt comfortable with the name and had debated changing it legally some ten years ago, when he was going with a Jewish girl named Rebecca Gold. The girl had said, 'If you change your name, Cotton, I'll never go out with you again.' Puzzled, he had asked, 'But why, Rebecca?' and she had answered, 'Your name's the only thing I like about you.' He had stopped seeing her the next week.

He still thought wistfully of what he might have become – a Cary Hawes, or a Paul, or a Carter, or a Richard. But more than any of those, the name he most cherished (and he had never revealed this to a soul) was Lefty. Lefty Hawes. Was there a criminal anywhere in the world who would not tremble at the very mention of that dread name, Lefty Hawes? Even though he was right-handed? Hawes thought not. Sighing, he moved the picture of the first President so that it was directly below him on the desk top. Fiercely, he stared into those inscrutable eyes, challenging them to reveal the Deaf Man's secret. Washington never so much as blinked back. Hawes stretched, yawned, picked up the photostat, and carried it to Carella's desk, where it would be waiting when he got back to the office.

The tall blond man, hearing aid in his right ear, came through the revolving doors of the bank at fifteen minutes before noon. He was wearing a custom-tailored beige gabardine suit, an oatmeal-coloured shirt, a dark brown tie, brown socks, and brown patent leather shoes. He knew from his previous visits to the bank that there were cameras focused on the area just inside the revolving doors, and cameras covering the five tellers' cages on the left as well. The cameras, if they operated like most bank cameras he had investigated, took a random picture once every thirty seconds, and did not begin taking consecutive and continuous frames for a motion picture unless activated by a teller or some other member of the bank's staff. He had no fear of his picture being taken, however, since he was a bona-fide depositor here on legitimate business.

He had been here for the first time a month ago, on legitimate business, to deposit $5,000 into a new savings account that paid 5 per cent interest if the money was not withdrawn before the expiration of ninety days. He had assured the assistant manager that he had no intention of withdrawing the money before that time. He had been lying. He had *every* intention of withdrawing his $5,000, plus $495,000 more, on the last day of April. But his visit to the bank had been legitimate.

On two occasions last week, he had again visited the bank on legitimate business – to make small deposits in the newly opened account. Today, he was here on further legitimate business – to deposit $64 into the account. In addition, he was here to determine exactly how he would deploy his task force of five on the day of the robbery.

The bank guard stood just inside the revolving doors, at almost the exact focal point of the camera on the left. He was a man in his sixties, somewhat paunchy, a retired mailroom clerk or messenger who wore his uniform with shabby authority and who would probably drop dead of fright if he was ever forced to pull the .38 calibre revolver holstered at his side. He smiled at the Deaf Man as he came into the bank, his patent leather shoes clicking on the marbled floors. The Deaf Man returned the smile, his back to the camera that angled down from the ledge on the right of the entrance doors. Immediately ahead of him were two marble-topped tables secured to the floor and compartmentalized below their counters to accomodate checking-account deposit slips and savings-account withdrawal and deposit slips. He walked to the nearest table, stood on the side of it opposite the tellers' cages, and began a quick drawing.

Looking into the bank from the entrance, there were three cages on the right side. He stood facing those cages now, his back turned to the clerical office and the loan department. Angling off from these, and running across the entire rear wall of the bank, was the vault, its shining steel door open now, its body encased in concrete and steel mesh interlaced with wires for the alarm system. There was no feasible way of approaching that vault from above it, below it, or behind it. The assault would have to be head-on, but not without its little diversions.

Smiling, the Deaf Man considered the diversions. Or, to be more accurate, the *single* diversion that would ensure the success of the robbery. To say that he considered the police antiquated and foolish would have been unfair to the enormity of his disdain; in fact, he considered them obsolete and essentially hebephrenic. Paradoxically, the success of his scheme depended upon at least some measure of intelligence on the part of his adversaries, so he was making it as simple as he could for them spelling it out in pictures because he sensed words might be too confusing. He had begun explaining exactly where and when he would strike, and he had played fair and would continue to play fair; cheating the police would have been the equivalent of tripping a cripple in a soccer match. Although he suspected himself of sadistic tendencies, he could best exorcise those in bed with a willing wench rather than take advantage of the bumbleheads who worked in the 87th Precinct. He looked upon them almost fondly, like cretinous children who needed to be taken to the circus every now and then. In fact, he rather liked the concept of himself as a circus, complete with clowns and lion-taming acts and high-wire excitement, a one-man circus come to set the city on its ear again.

But in order for the diversion to work, in order for the spectator's eye to become captured by the prancing ponies in the centre ring while man-eating tigers consumed their trainer in the third ring, the diversion had to be plain and evident. The key to his brilliant scheme (he admitted this modestly), the code he had concocted, was simple to comprehend. Too simple? No, he did not think so. They would learn from the photostats only what he wanted them to learn; they would see only the ponies and miss the Bengal tigers. And then, thrilled with their own perception, inordinately proud of having been able to focus on the flashing hoofs, they would howl in pain when bitten on the ass from behind. All fair and above board. All there for the toy police to see, if only they were capable of seeing, if only they possessed the brains of gnats or the imagination of rivets.

The Deaf Man finished his floor plan of the bank. He folded the deposit slip as though he had been making money calculations in the secret manner of bank depositors everywhere, put it into his pocket, and then took another slip from the rack. He quickly filled it out, and walked to the nearest teller's cage.

'Good morning, sir,' the teller said, and smiled pleasantly.

'Good morning,' the Deaf Man said, and returned the smile. Bored, he watched as the teller went about the business of recording the deposit. There were alarm buttons on the floor behind each of the tellers' cages and scattered elsewhere throughout the bank. They did not overly concern him.

The Deaf Man thought it fitting that a police detective would help him rob the bank.

He also thought it fitting that the police detective who would lend his assistance was Steve Carella.

Things had a way of interlocking neatly if one bided his time and played his cards according to the laws of permutation and combination.

'Here you are, sir,' the teller said, and handed back the passbook. The Deaf Man perfunctorily checked the entry, nodded, slipped the book back into its plastic carrying case, and walked towards the revolving doors. He nodded at the security guard, who politely nodded back, and then he went into the street outside.

The bank was a mile outside the 87th Precinct territory, not far from three large factories on the River Harb. McCormick Container Corp. employed 6,347 people. Meredith Mints, Inc. employed 1,512. Holt Brothers, Inc. employed 4,048 for a combined work force of close to twelve thousand and a combined payroll of almost $2 million a week. These weekly salaries were paid by cheque, with roughly 40 per cent of the personnel electing to have the cheques mailed directly to banks of their own choice. Of the remaining 60 per cent, half took their cheques home to cash in supermarkets, whisky stores, department stores, and/or banks in their own neighbourhoods. But some 30 per cent of the combined work force of the three plants cashed their cheques each week at the bank the Deaf Man had just visited. Which meant that every Friday the bank *expected* to cash cheques totalling approximately $600,000. In order to meet this anticipated weekly drain, the bank supplemented its own cash reserve with money shipped from its main branch. This money, somewhere in the vicinity of $500,000, depending on what cash the bank already had on hand, was delivered by armoured truck at nine-fifteen each Friday morning. There were three armed guards on the truck. One guard stayed behind the wheel while the other two, revolvers drawn, went into the bank carrying two sacks of cash. The manager accompanied them into the vault, where they deposited the money, and then left the bank, revolvers now holstered. At eleven-thirty the cash was distributed to the tellers in anticipation of the lunch-hour rush of factory workers seeking to cash their salary cheques.

The Deaf Man had no intention of intercepting the truck on its way from the main branch bank. Nor did he wish to hit any one of the individual tellers' cages. No, he wanted to get that money while it was still neatly stacked in the vault. And whereas his own plan was far less dangerous than sticking up an armoured truck, he nonetheless felt it to be more audacious. In fact, he considered it innovative to the point of genius, and was certain it would go off without a hitch. Ah yes, he thought, the bank will be robbed, the bank will be robbed, and his step quickened, and he breathed deeply of the heady spring air.

The tennis sneaker found in the abandoned building was in shabby condition, a size-twelve gunboat that had seen better days when it was worn on someone's left foot. The sole was worn almost through in one spot, and the canvas top had an enormous hole near the area of the big toe. Even the laces were weary, having been knotted together after breaking in two spots. The brand name was well-known, which excluded the possibility of the sneaker having been purchased (as part of a pair, naturally) in any exotic boutique. The only thing of possible interest about this left-footed sneaker, in fact, was a brown stain on the tip of it, near the small toe. This was identified by the Police Laboratory as microcrystalline wax, a synthetic the colour and consistency of beeswax, but much less expensive. A thin metallic dust adhered to the wax; it was identified as bronze. Carella was not particularly overjoyed by what the lab delivered. Nor was he thrilled by the report from the Identification Section, which had been unable to find any fingerprints, palm prints, or footprints that matched the dead man's. Armed with a somewhat unflattering photograph (it had been taken while the man lay stone-cold dead on a slab at the morgue), Carella went back to the Harrison Street neighbourhood that afternoon and tried to find someone who had known him.

The Medical Examiner had estimated the man's age as somewhere between twenty and twenty-five. In terms of police investigation, this was awkward. He could have been running with a younger crowd of teen-agers, or an older crowd of young adults, depending on his emotional maturity. Carella decided to try a sampling of each, and his first stop was a teen-age coffee house called Space, which had over the years run the gamut from kosher delicatessen to Puerto Rican *bodega* to store-front church to its present status. In contradiction to its name, Space was a ten-by-twelve room with a huge silver espresso machine on a counter at its far end. Like a futuristic idol, the machine intimidated the room and seemed to dwarf its patrons. All of the patrons were young. The girls were wearing blue jeans and long hair. The boys were bearded. In terms of police investigation, this was awkward. It meant they could be (a) hippies, (b) college students, (c) anarchists, (d) prophets, (e) all of the foregoing. To many police officers, of course, long hair or a beard (or both) automatically meant that any person daring to look like that was guilty of (a) possession of marijuana, (b) intent to sell heroin, (c) violation of the Sullivan Act, (d) fornication with livestock, (e) corrupting the morals of a minor, (f) conspiracy, (g) treason, (h) all of the foregoing. Carella wished he had a nickel for every clean-shaven, crew-cutted kid he had arrested for murdering his own brother. On the other hand, he was a police officer and he knew that the moment he showed his badge in this place, these long-haired youngsters would automatically assume he was guilty of (a) fascism, (b) brutality, (c) drinking beer and belching, (d) fornication with livestock, (e) harassment, (f) all of the foregoing. Some days, it was very difficult to earn a living.

The cop smell seeped into the room almost before the door closed behind him. The kids looked at him, and he looked back at them, and he knew that if he asked them what time it was, they would answer in chorus, 'The thirty-fifth of December.' He chose the table closest to the door, pulling out a chair and sitting between a boy with long blond hair and a dark boy with a straggly beard. The girl opposite him had long brown hair, frightened brown eyes, and the face of an angel.

'Yes?' The blond boy asked.

'I'm a police officer,' Carella said, and showed his shield. The boys glanced at it without interest. The girl brushed a strand of hair from her cheek and turned her head away. 'I'm trying to identify a man who was murdered in this area.'

'When?' the boy with the beard asked.

'Sunday night. April eighteenth.'

'Where?' the blond boy asked.

'In an abandoned tenement on Harrison.'

'What'd you say your name was?' the blond boy asked.

'Detective Steve Carella.'

The girl moved her chair back, and rose suddenly, as though anxious to get away from the table. Carella put his hand on her arm and said, 'What's *your* name, miss?'

'Mary Margaret,' she said. She did not sit again. She moved her arm, freeing it from Carella's hand, and then turned to go.

'No last name?' he said.

'Ryan,' she said. 'See you guys,' she said to the boys, and this time moved several paces from the table before she was stopped again by Carella's voice.

'Miss Ryan, would you look at this picture, please?' he said, and removed the photo from his notebook. The girl came back to the table, looked at the picture, and said nothing.

'Does he look familiar?' Carella asked.

'No,' she said. 'See you,' she said again, and this time she walked swiftly from the table and out into the street.

Carella watched her going, and then handed the photograph to the blond boy. 'How about you?'

'Nope.'

'What's your name?'

'Bob.'

'Bob what?'

'Carmody.'

'And yours?' he asked the boy with the beard.

'Hank Scaffale.'

'You both live in the neighbourhood?'

'On Porter Street.'

'Have you been living here long?'

'Awhile.'

'Are you familiar with most of the people in the neighbourhood?'

'The freaks, yeah,' Hank said. 'I don't have much to do with others.'

'Have *you* ever seen this man around?'

'Not if he really looked like that,' Hank said, studying the photo.

'What do you mean?'

'He's dead in that picture, isn't he?'

'Yes.'

'Yeah, well, that makes a difference,' Hank said. 'The juices are gone,' he said, and shook his head. 'All the juices are gone.' He studied the photograph again, and again shook his head. 'I don't know who he is,' he said, 'poor bastard.'

The responses from the other young people in the room were similar. Carella took the photograph around to the five other tables, explained what he was looking for, and waited while the dead man's frozen image was passed from hand to hand. None of the kids were overly friendly (you can get hit on the head by cops only so often before you decide there may not be a basis there for mutual confidence and trust), but neither were they impolite. They all looked solemnly at the picture, and they all reported that they had not known the dead man. Carella thanked them for their time and went out into the street again.

By five o'clock that afternoon he had hit in succession two head shops, a macrobiotic food store, a record store, a store selling sandals, and four other places catering to the neighbourhood's young people – or at least those young people who wore their hair long. He could not bring himself to call them 'freaks' despite their apparent preference for the word; to his way of thinking, that was the same as putting an identifying tag on a dead man's toe before you know who he was. Labels annoyed him unless they were affixed to case report folders or bottles in a medicine cabinet. 'Freaks' was a particularly distressing label, demeaning and misleading, originally applied from without, later adopted from within in self-defence, and finally accepted with pride as a form of self-identification. But how in hell did this in any way lessen its derogatory intent? It was the same as cops proudly calling themselves 'pigs' in the hope that the epithet would lose its vilifying power once it was exorcised by voluntary application. Bullshit. Carella was not a pig, and the kids he'd spoken to this afternoon were not freaks.

They were young people in a neighbourhood as severely divided as any war-torn Asian countryside. In the days when the city was young, or at least younger, the neighbourhood population had been mostly immigrant Jewish, with a dash of Italian or Irish thrown in to keep the pot boiling. It boiled a lot in those days (ask Meyer Meyer, who lived in a similar ghetto as a boy, and who was chased through the streets by bigots shouting, 'Meyer Meyer, Jew on fire!') and eventually simmered down to a sort of armed truce between the old-timers, whose children went to college and learned New World trades and moved out to Riverhead or Calm's Point. The next wave of immigrants to hit the area were United States citizens who did not speak the language and who enjoyed all the rights and privileges of any minority group in the city; that is to say, they were underpaid, overcharged, beaten, scorned, and generally made to feel that Puerto Rico was not a beautiful sun-washed island in the Caribbean but rather a stink hole on the outskirts of a smelly swamp. They learned very rapidly that it was all right to throw garbage from the windows into the backyard, because if you didn't the rats would come into the apartment to eat it. Besides, if people are treated like garbage themselves, they cannot be castigated for *any* way they choose to handle their own garbage. The Puerto Ricans came, and some of them stayed only long enough to earn plane fare back to the island. Some followed the immigration pattern established by the Europeans: they learned the language, they went to school, they got better jobs, they moved into the outlying districts of the city (where they replaced those now-affluent Americans of European stock who had moved out of the city entirely, to private homes in the suburbs). Some remained behind in the old neighbourhood, succumbing to the deadly grinding jaws of poverty, and wondering occasionally what it had been like to swim in clear warm waters where the only possible threat was a barracuda.

The long-haired youths must have seemed like invading immigrants to the Puerto Ricans who still inhabited the area. It is easy to turn prejudice inside out; within every fat oppressor, there lurks a skinny victim waiting to be released. The hippies, the flower children, the 'freaks' if you prefer, came seeking peace and talking love, and were greeted with the same fear, suspicion, hostility, and prejudice that had greeted the Puerto Ricans upon their arrival. In this case, however, it was the Puerto Ricans themselves who were doing the hating – you cannot teach people a way of life, and then expect them to put it conveniently aside. You cannot force them into a sewer and then expect them to understand why the son and daughters of *successful* Americans are voluntarily seeking residence in that very same sewer. If violence of any kind is absurd, then victims attacking other victims is surely ludicrous. Such was the situation in the South Quarter, where the young people who had come there to do their thing had taken instead to buying pistols for protection against other people who had been trying to do *their* thing for more years than they could count. In recent months, bikies had begun drifting into the area, sporting their leather jackets and their swastikas and lavishing on their motorcycles the kind of love usually reserved for women. The bikies were bad news. Their presence added a tense note of uneasiness and unpredictability to an already volatile situation.

The Puerto Ricans Carella spoke to that afternoon did not enjoy talking to a cop. Cops meant false arrests, cops meant bribes, cops meant harassment. It occurred to him that Alex Delgado, the one Puerto Rican detective on the squad (in itself a comment) might have handled the investigation better, but he was stuck with it, and so he plunged ahead, showing the picture, asking the questions, getting the same response each time: *No, I do not know him. They all look alike to me.*

The bikie's name was Yank, meticulously lettered in white paint on the front of his leather jacket, over the heart. He had long frizzy black hair and a dense black beard. His eyes were blue, the right one partially closed by a scar that ran from his forehead to his cheek, crossing a portion of the lid in passing. He wore the usual gear in addition to the black leather jacket: the crushed peaked cap (his crash helmet was on the seat of his bike, parked at the kerb), a black tee shirt (streaked white here and there from bleach-washing), black denim trousers, brass-studded big-buckled belt, black boots. An assortment of chains hung around his neck and the German iron cross dangled from one of them. He was sitting on a tilted wooden chair outside a shop selling posters (LBJ on a motorcycle in the window behind him), smoking a cigar and admiring the sleek chrome sculpture of his own bike at the kerb. He did not even look at Carella as he approached. He knew instantly that Carella was a cop, but bikies don't know from cops. Bikies, in fact, sometimes think they themselves are the cops, and the bad guys are everybody else in the world.

Carella didn't waste time. He showed his shield and his I.D. card, and said, 'Detective Carella, 87th Squad.'

Yank regarded him with cool disdain, and then puffed on his cigar. 'Yeah?' he said.

'We're trying to get a positive identification on a young man who may have been living in the neighbourhood ...'

'Yeah?'

'I thought you might be able to help.'

'Why?'

'Do you live around here?'

'Yeah.'

'How long have you been living here?'

'Three of us blew in from the Coast a few weeks back.'

'Transients, huh?'

'Mobile, you might say.'

'Where are you living?'

'Here and there.'

'Where's that?'

'We drop in various places. Our club members are usually welcome everywhere.'

'Where are you dropping in right now?'

'Around the corner.'

'Around the corner where?'

'On Rutland. Listen, I thought you were trying to identify somebody. What's all these questions about? You charging me with some terrible crime?'

'Have you got a terrible crime in mind?'

'The bike's legally parked, I was sitting here smoking a cigar and meditating. Is that against the law?'

'Nobody said it was.'

'So why all the questions?'

Carella reached into his jacket pocket, took out his notebook, and removed from it the photograph of the dead man. 'Recognize him?' he asked, and handed the picture to Yank, who blew out a cloud of smoke, righted his chair, and then held the picture between his knees, hunched over it, as he studied it.

'Never saw him in my life,' he said. He handed the picture back to Carella, tilted the chair against the wall again, and drew in another lungful of cigar smoke.

'I wonder if I could have your full name,' Carella said.

'What for?'

'In case I need to get in touch with you again.'

'Why would you need to get in touch with me? I just told you I never saw this guy in my life.'

'Yes, but people sometimes come up with information later on. Since you and your friends are so *mobile*, you might just hear something that ...'

'Tell you what,' Yank said, and grinned. 'You give me *your* name. If I hear anything, *I'll* call *you*.' He blew two precise smoke rings into the air, and said, 'How's that?'

'I've already given you my name,' Carella said.

'Shows what kind of memory I've got,' Yank said, and again grinned.

'I'll see you around,' Carella said.

'Don't count on it,' Yank answered.

Chapter Six

At ten minutes to one on Wednesday afternoon, Augusta Blair called the
squadroom and asked to talk to Detective Kling, who was on his lunch hour
and down the hall in the locker room, taking a nap. Meyer asked if Kling
could call her back and she breathlessly told him she had only a minute and
would appreciate it if he could be called to the phone. It had to do with the
burglary, she said. Meyer went down the hall and reluctantly awakened
Kling, who did not seem to mind at all. In fact, he hurried to his desk, picked
up the receiver, and said, quite cheerfully, 'Hello, Miss Blair, how are you?'
   'Fine, thank you,' she said. 'I've been trying to call you all day long, Mr
Kling, but this is the first break we've had. We started at nine this morning,
and I didn't know if you got to work that early.'
   'Yes, I was here,' Kling said.
   'I guess I should have called then. Anyway, here I am now. And I've got to
be back in a minute. Do you think you can come down here?'
   'Where are you, Miss Blair?'
   'Schaeffer Photography at 580 Hall Avenue. The fifth floor.'
   'What's this about?'
   'When I was cleaning up the mess in the apartment, I found something
that wasn't mine. I figure the burglar may have dropped it.'
   'I'll be right there,' Kling said. 'What was it you found?'
   'Well, I'll show you when you get here,' she said. 'I've got to run, Mr
Kling.'
   'Okay,' he said, 'I'll ...'
   But she was gone.

Schaeffer Photography occupied the entire fifth floor of 580 Hall. The
receptionist, a pert blonde with a marked German accent, informed Kling
that Augusta had said he would be coming, and then directed him to the
studio, which was at the end of a long hallway hung with samples of
Schaeffer's work. Judging from the selection, Schaeffer did mostly fashion
photography; no avid reader of *Vogue*, Kling nonetheless recognized the
faces of half the models, and searched in vain for a picture of Augusta.
Apparently she had been telling the truth when she said she'd been in the
business only a short while.
   The door to the studio was closed. Kling eased it open, and found himself
in an enormous room overhung by a skylight. A platform was at the far end
of the room, the wall behind it hung with red backing paper. Four power

packs rested on the floor, with cables running to strobe lights on stands, their grey, umbrella-shaped reflectors angled towards the platform. Redheaded Augusta Blair, wearing a red blouse, a short red jumper, red knee socks, and red patent leather pumps, stood before the red backing paper. A young girl in jeans and a Snoopy sweatshirt stood to the right of the platform, her arms folded across her chest. The photographer and his assistant were hunched over a tripod-mounted Polaroid. They took several pictures, strobe lights flashing for a fraction of a second each time they pressed the shutter release, and then, apparently satisfied with the exposure setting, removed the Polaroid from its mount and replaced it with a Nikon. Augusta spotted Kling standing near the door, grinned, and waggled the fingers of her right hand at him. The photographer turned.

'Yes?' he said.

'He's a friend of mine,' Augusta said.

'Oh, okay,' the photographer said in dismissal. 'Make yourself comfortable, keep it quiet. You ready, honey? Where's David?'

'David!' the assistant called, and a man rushed over from where he'd been standing at a wall phone, partially hidden by a screen over which was draped a pair of purple pantyhose. He went directly to Augusta, combed her hair swiftly, and then stepped off the platform.

'Okay?' the photographer asked.

'Ready,' Augusta said.

'The headline is "Red On Red", God help us, and the idea –'

'What's the matter with the headline?' the girl in the Snoopy sweatshirt asked.

'Nothing, Helen, far be it from me to cast aspersions on your magazine. Gussie, the idea is to get this big *red* feeling, you know what I mean? Everything bursting and screaming and, you know, *red* as hell, okay? You know what I want?'

'I think so,' Augusta said.

'We want *red*,' Helen said.

'What the hell's this proxar doing on here?' the photographer asked.

'I thought we'd be doing close stuff,' his assistant said.

'No, Eddie, get it off here, will you?'

'Sure,' Eddie said, and began unscrewing the lens.

'David, get that hair off her forehead, will you?'

'Where?'

'Right there, hanging over her eye, don't you see it there?'

'Oh yeah.'

'Yeah, that's it, thank you. Eddie, how we doing?'

'You've got it.'

'Gussie?'

'Yep.'

'Okay then, here we go, now give me that big *red*, Gussie, that's what I want, I want this thing to yell *red* all over town, that's the girl, more of that, now tilt the head, that's good, Gussie, smile now, more teeth, honey, red, *red*, throw your arms wide, good, good, that's it, now you're beginning to feel it, let it bubble up, honey, let it burst out of your fingertips, nice, I like that, give me that with a, that's it, good, now the other side, the head the other way, no, no, keep the arms out, fine, that's good, all right now come towards me, no, honey, don't slink, this isn't blue, it's *red*, you've got to *explode* towards, *yes*, that's it, yes, *yes*, good, now with more hip, gussie, fine, I like that, I like it, eyes wider, toss the hair, good, honey . . .'

For the next half hour Kling watched as Augusta exhibited to the camera a wide variety of facial expressions, body positions, and acrobatic contortions, looking nothing less than beautiful in every pose she struck. The only sounds in the huge room were the photographer's voice and the clicking of his camera. Coaxing, scolding, persuading, approving, suggesting, chiding, cajoling, the voice went on and on, barely audible except to Augusta, while the tiny clicking of the camera accompanied the running patter like a soft-shoe routine. Kling was fascinated. In Augusta's apartment the other night, he had been overwhelmed by her beauty, but had not suspected her vitality. Reacting to the burglary, she had presented a solemn, dispirited façade, so that her beauty seemed unmarred but essentially lifeless. Now, as Kling watched her bursting with energy and ideas to convey the concept of red, the camera clicking, the photographer circling her and talking to her, she seemed another person entirely, and he wondered suddenly how many faces Augusta Blair owned, and how many of them he would get to know.

'Okay, great, Gussie,' the photographer said, 'let's break for ten minutes. Then we'll do those sailing outfits, Helen. Eddie, can we get some coffee?'

'Right away.'

Augusta came down off the platform and walked to where Kling was standing at the back of the room. 'Hi,' she said. 'I'm sorry I kept you waiting.'

'I enjoyed it,' Kling said.

'It *was* kind of fun,' Augusta said. 'Most of them aren't.'

'Which of these do you want her in first, Helen?' the photographer asked.

'The one with the striped top.'

'You *do* want me to shoot both of them, right?'

'Yes. The two *tops*. There's only one pair of pants,' Helen said.

'Okay, both tops, the striped one first. You going to introduce me to your friend, Gussie?' he said, and walked to where Kling and Augusta were standing.

'Rick Schaeffer,' she said, 'this is Detective Kling. I'm sorry, I don't know your first name.'

'Bert,' he said.

'Nice to meet you,' Schaeffer said, and extended his hand. The men shook hands briefly, and Schaeffer said, 'Is this about the burglary?'

'Yes,' Kling said.

'Well, look, I won't take up your time,' Schaeffer said. 'Gussie, honey, we'll be shooting the striped top first.'

'Okay.'

'I want to go as soon as we change the no-seam.'

'I'll be ready.'

'Right. Nice meeting you, Bert.'

He walked off briskly towards where two men were carrying a roll of blue backing paper to the platform.

'What did you find in the apartment?' Kling asked.

'I've got it in my bag,' Augusta said. She began walking towards a bench on the side of the room, Kling following. 'Listen, I must apologize for the rush act, but they're paying me twenty-five dollars an hour, and they don't like me sitting around.'

'I understand,' Kling said.

Augusta dug into her bag and pulled out a ballpoint pen, which she handed to Kling and which, despite the fact that her fingerprints were already all over it, he accepted on a tented handkerchief. The top half of the pen was made of metal, brass-plated to resemble gold. The bottom half of the pen was made of black plastic. The pen was obviously a give-away item. Stamped onto the plastic in white letters were the words:

Sulzbacher Realty
1142 Ashmead Avenue
Calm's Point

'You're sure it isn't yours?' Kling asked.

'Positive. Will it help you?'

'It's a start.'

'Good.' She glanced over her shoulder towards where the men were rolling down the blue seamless. 'What time is it, Bert?'

Kling looked at his watch. 'Almost two. What do I call you? Augusta or Gussie?'

'Depends on what we're doing,' she said, and smiled.

'What are we doing tonight?' Kling asked immediately.

'I'm busy,' Augusta said.

'How about tomorrow?'

She looked at him for a moment, seemed to make a swift decision, and then said, 'Let me check my book.' She reached into her bag for an appointment calendar, opened it, said, 'What's tomorrow, Thursday?' and without waiting for his answer, flipped open the page marked Thursday, April 22. 'No, not tomorrow, either,' she said, and Kling figured he had got the message loud and clear. 'I'm free Saturday night, though,' she said, surprising him. 'How's Saturday?'

'Saturday's fine,' he said quickly. 'Dinner?'

'I'd love to.'

'And maybe a movie later.'

'Why don't we do it the other way around? If you won't mind how I look, you can pick me up at the studio ...'

'Fine ...'

'Around six, six-fifteen, and we can catch an early movie, and then maybe grab a hamburger or something later on. What time do you quit work?'

'I'll certainly be free by six.'

'Okay, the photographer's name is Jerry Bloom, and he's at 1204 Concord. The second floor, I think. Aren't you going to write it down?'

'Jerry Bloom,' Kling said, '1204 Concord, the second floor, at six o'clock.'

'Gussie, let's go!' Schaeffer shouted.

'Saturday,' she said and, to Kling's vast amazement, touched her fingers to her lips, blew him an unmistakable kiss, grinned, and walked swiftly to where Rick Schaeffer was waiting.

Kling blinked.

*   *   *

Ashmead Avenue was in the shadow of the elevated structure in downtown Calm's Point, not far from the bustling business section and the Academy of Music. When Kling was seventeen years old he had dated a girl from Calm's Point, and had sworn never again. The date had been for eight-thirty, and he had left Riverhead at seven sharp, taking the train on Allen and riding for an hour and a half before getting off at Kingston Parkway as she had instructed him. He had then proceeded to lose himself in the, labyrinthine streets with their alien names, arriving at her house at 10 p.m., to be told by her mother that she had gone to a movie with a girl friend. He had asked if he should wait, and the girl's mother had looked at him as though he were retarded and had said simply, 'I would not suggest it.' Rarely did he come to Calm's Point anymore, unless he was called there on an investigation.

Sulzbacher Realty was in a two-storey brick building sandwiched between a supermarket and a liquor store. The entrance door was between two plate-glass windows adorned with photographs of houses in and around the area. Through the glass Kling could see a pair of desks. A man sat at one of them studying an open book before him. He looked up as Kling came into the office.

'Good afternoon,' he said, 'may I help you?'

He was wearing a brown business suit, a white shirt, and a striped tie. A local Chamber of Commerce pin was in his lapel, and the tops of several cigars protruded from the breast pocket of his jacket.

'I hope so,' Kling said. He took out his wallet, and opened it. 'I'm Detective Kling,' he said, '87th Squad. I'd like to ask you some questions.'

'Have a seat,' the man answered, and indicated the wooden chair alongside his desk. 'I'm Fred Lipton, be happy to help you any way I can.'

'Mr Lipton, one of your company pens was found at the scene of a burglary, and we ...'

'Company pens?'

'Yes, sir. The name of the company lettered on the barrel.'

'Oh, yes. *Those.* The ones Nat bought to advertise the business.'

'Nat?'

'Nat Sulzbacher. He owns the company. I'm just a salesman.' Lipton opened the top drawer of his desk, reached into it, opened his hand, and dropped a half-dozen ballpoint pens onto the desk top. 'Are these the ones you mean?'

Kling picked one up and looked at it. 'Yes,' he said, 'a pen similar to these.'

The front door opened, and a tall, dark-haired man entered the room. 'Afternoon, Fred,' he said. 'Selling lots of houses?'

'Mr Sulzbacher, this is Detective ...'

'Kling.'

'Kling. He's investigating a burglary.'

'Yeah?' Sulzbacher said, and raised his eyebrows in appreciation.

'They found one of our pens at the scene of the crime.'

'One of ours?' Sulzbacher said. 'May I see it, please?'

'I don't have it with me right now.'

'Then how do I know it's ours?'

'Our name's on it,' Lipton said.

'Oh. So what would you like to know, young man?'

'Since the pen was found at the scene of a crime ...'

'You don't think we're criminals here, do you?'

'No. I was merely wondering ...'

'Because if that's what you think, you're mistaken. We're real estate agents here. *That's* what we are.'

'No one's suggesting you or Mr Lipton burglarized an apartment. All I wanted to know is whether you give these pens to anybody special, or whether ...'

'You know how many of these pens I ordered?' Sulzbacher asked.

'How many?'

'Five thousand.'

'Oh,' Kling said.

'You know how many of them we've given out in the past six months? At least half that amount. Certainly two thousand, anyway. So you expect us to remember who we gave them to?'

'Were these customers or ...?'

'Customers, sure, but also strangers. Somebody come in, asks about a house, we give him a little pen so he won't forget the name. There are a lot of real estate agents in Calm's Point, you know.'

'Mmm,' Kling said.

'I'm sorry,' Sulzbacher said.

'Yeah,' Kling said. 'Me too.'

This time, they did not think it was a mistake.

The duplicate photostat arrived in the afternoon mail, and was promptly added to the gallery on the bulletin board, so that the squad now proudly possessed two pictures of J. Edgar Hoover and two pictures of George Washington.

'What do you think he's driving at?' Hawes asked.

'I don't know,' Carella said.

'It's deliberate, that's for sure,' Meyer said.

'No question.'

The three men stood before the bulletin board, hands on hips, studying the photostats as though they were hanging on the wall of a museum.

'Where do you suppose he got the pictures?' Hawes asked.

'Newspapers, I would guess. Books. Magazines.'

'Any help for us there?'

'I doubt it. Even if we located the source, what good ...'

'Yeah.'

'The important thing is what he's trying to tell us.'

'What do we know so far?' Meyer asked.

'So far we know he's going to steal half a million dollars on April thirtieth,' Hawes said.

'No, that's not it exactly,' Carella said.

'What is it exactly?'

'He said, "With your assistance..." remember? "With your *assistance*, I'm going to steal five hundred thousand dollars on the last day of April."'

'*Whose* assistance?' Meyer asked.

'Ours, I guess,' Carella said.

'Or maybe yours *personally*,' Hawes said. 'You're the one he was talking to.'

'That's right, yeah,' Carella said.

'And the pictures have all been addressed to you.'

'Yeah.'

'Maybe he figures you've got something in common. Maybe all this crap is pegged directly at you.'

'We *have* got something in common,' Carella said.

'What's that?'

'We shot each other. And survived.'

'So what do you think?' Hawes said.

'What do you mean?'

'If he's pegging it at you, what do you think? Have you got any ideas?'

'Not a single one,' Carella said.

'Hoover and Washington,' Meyer said thoughtfully. 'What have *they* got in common?'

Chapter Seven

'The Jesus Case,' as it was playfully dubbed by the heathens of the 87th Squad, was going nowhere very quickly. The dead man had still not been identified, and Carella knew that, unless a positive identification was made within the next few days, the case was in danger of being buried as deep as the corpse had been. Until they knew who he was, until they could say with certainty that *this* man with *this* name was slain by person or persons unknown, why then he would remain only what Dr Cortez had labelled him last Monday: a corpse. Labels. A corpse. Anonymous. A lifeless heap of human rubble, unmissed, unreported, unidentified when it was buried in the municipal cemetery. There were too many murder victims in the city, all of them with names and addresses and relatives and histories. It was too much to ask of any over-worked police department that it should spend valuable time trying to find the murderer of someone who had namelessly roamed the streets. A cipher never evokes much sympathy.

On Thursday morning, as Carella made his way from shop to shop in the Harrison Street area, it began raining heavily. The Jesus Case was now four days old. Carella knew that, unless he came up with something soon, the case would be thrown into the squad's Open File. For all intents and purposes, such disposition would mean that the case was closed. Not solved, merely closed until something accidentally turned up on it weeks or months or years later, if ever. The idea of burying the case a scant two days after the body itself had been buried was extremely distasteful to Carella. Aside from his revulsion for the brutality of the crucifixion (if such it could be called; there had, after all, been no cross involved), Carella suspected that something deeper within him was being touched. He had not been inside a church since the day his sister got married, more than thirteen years ago, but he felt vague stirrings now, memories of priests with thuribles, the heavy musk of incense, altar boys in white, the crucified form of Jesus Christ high above the altar. He had not been a religious child, nor was he a religious man. But the murdered man was curiously linked in his mind to the spiritual concept of someone dying for humanity, and he could not accept the idea that the man in the abandoned tenement had died for nothing at all.

The rain swept the pavements like machine-gun fire in some grey disputed no-man's land. A jagged lance of lightning crackled across the sky, followed by a boom of thunder that rattled Carella to his shoelaces. He ran for the nearest shop, threw open the door, shook water from his trench coat, and mopped his head with a handkerchief. Only then did he look around him. He first thought he was in an art gallery having a one-man show. He then realized he was in a sculptor's shop, the artist's work displayed on long tables and shelves, female nudes of various sizes sculpted in wood and stone, cast in plaster and bronze. The work was quite good, or at least it seemed so to Carella. Naturalistic, almost photographic, the nudes sat or stood or lay on their sides in frozen three-dimensional realism, some of them no larger than a fist, others standing some three or four feet tall. The artist had used the same model for all of the pieces, an obviously young girl, tall and slender, with small well-formed breasts and narrow hips, long hair trailing halfway down her back. The effect was of being in a mirrored room that reflected the same girl in a dozen different poses, shrinking her to less than human size and capturing her life force in materials firmer than flesh. Carella was studying one of the statues more closely when a man came out of the back room.

The man was in his late twenties, a tall blond man with dark brown eyes and a leonine head. He was on crutches. His left leg was heavily bandaged. A tattered white tennis sneaker was on his right foot.

There were, Carella surmised, possibly ten thousand men in this city at this moment who were wearing white tennis sneakers on their right feet, their left feet, and perhaps even *both* feet. He did not know how many of them had a shop on King's Circle, though, four blocks from Harrison Street, where a boy had been nailed to the wall five days ago, and where a left-footed tennis sneaker had been found in an empty apartment down the hall.

'Yes, sir?' the man said. 'May I help you?'

'I'm a police officer,' Carella said.

'Uh-huh,' the man said.

'Detective Carella, 87th Squad.'

'Uh-huh,' he said again. He did not ask for identification, and Carella did not show any.

'I'm investigating a homicide,' he said.

'I see.' The man nodded, and then hobbled on his crutches to one of the long tables. He sat on the edge of it, beside a sculpture of his slender young model at repose in bronze, legs crossed, head bent, eyes downcast like a naked nun. 'My name's Sanford Elliot,' he said. 'Sandy, everybody calls me. Who was killed?'

'We don't know. That's why I've been going around the neighbourhood.'

'When did it happen?' Elliot asked.

'Last Sunday night.'

'I was out of town last Sunday,' Elliot said, and Carella suddenly

wondered why he felt compelled to establish an alibi for a murder that had
thus far been discussed only in the most ambiguous terms.

'Really?' Carella said. 'Where were you?'

'Boston. I went up to Boston for the weekend.'

'Nice up there,' Carella said.

'Yes.'

'Anyway, I've been showing a picture of the victim ...'

'I don't know too many people in the neighbourhood,' Elliot said. 'I've
only been here in the city since January. I keep mostly to myself. Do my
work in the studio back there, and try to sell it out front here. I don't know
too many people.'

'Well, lots of people come in and out of the shop, don't they?' Carella said.

'Oh, sure. But unless they buy one of my pieces, I never get to know their
names. You see what I mean?'

'Sure,' Carella said. 'Why don't you take a look at the picture, anyway?'

'Well, if you like. It won't do any good, though. I really don't know too
many people around here.'

'Are you from Boston originally?'

'What?'

'You said you went up to Boston, I figured ...'

'Oh. No, I'm from Oregon. But I went to art school up there. School of
Fine Arts at B.U. Boston University.'

'And you say you were up there Sunday?'

'That's right. I went up to see some friends. I've got a lot of friends in the
Boston area.'

'But not too many around here.'

'No, not around here.'

'Did you hurt your leg before you went to Boston, or after you came
back?'

'Before.'

'Went up there on crutches, huh?'

'Yes.'

'Did you drive up?'

'A friend drove me.'

'Who?'

'The girl who poses for me.' He made a vague gesture at the pieces of
sculpture surrounding them.

'What's wrong with the leg, anyway?' Carella asked.

'I had an accident.'

'Is it broken.'

'No. I sprained the ankle.'

'Those can be worse than a break, sometimes.'

'Yeah, that's what the doctor said.'

'Who's the doctor?'

'Why do you want to know?'

'Just curious.'

'Well,' Elliot said, 'I don't think that's any of your business.'

'You're right,' Carella said, 'it isn't. Would you mind looking at this
picture?'

'I mean,' Elliot said, gathering steam, 'I've given you a lot of time as it is. I

was working when you came in. I don't like being disturbed when I'm ...'
'I'm sorry,' Carella said. 'If you'll just look at this picture ...'
'I won't know who he is, anyway,' Elliot said. 'I hardly know any of the
guys in this neighbourhood. Most of my friends are up in Boston.'
'Well, take a look,' Carella said, and handed him the photograph.
'No, I don't know him,' Elliot said, and handed it back almost at once.
Carella put the photograph into his notebook, turned up the collar of his
coat, said, 'Thanks,' and went out into the rain. It was coming down in
buckets; he was willing to forsake the goddamn May flowers. He began
running the instant he hit the street, and did not stop until he reached the
open diner on the corner. Inside, he expelled his breath in the exaggerated
manner of all people who have run through rain and finally reached shelter,
took off his trench coat, hung it up, and sat at the counter. A waitress
slouched over and asked him what he wanted. He ordered a cup of coffee and
a cheese Danish.
       There was a lot that bothered him about Sanford Elliot.
       He was bothered by the tattered white tennis sneaker, and he was
bothered by the fact that Elliot's *left* foot was in bandages – or was it only
coincidence that the sneaker they'd found was left-footed? He was bothered
by the speedy alibi Elliot had offered for his whereabouts on the night of the
murder, and bothered by the thought of a man on crutches taking a long car
trip up to Boston, even if he was being driven by someone.
       Why hadn't Elliot been willing to tell him the name of his doctor? And
how had Elliot known that the murder victim was a man? Even before
Carella showed him the photograph, he had said, 'I won't know who he is,
anyway.' *He*. When up to that time Carella had spoken of the dead man only
as 'the victim'.
       Something else was bothering him.
       The waitress put his cup of coffee on the counter, sloshing it into the
saucer. He picked up his Danish, bit into it, put it down, lifted the coffee
cup, slipped a paper napkin between cup and saucer, drank some coffee, and
suddenly knew what was nudging his memory.
       He debated going back to the shop.
       Elliot had mentioned that he'd been working when Carella came in; the
possibility existed that the girl was still with him. He decided instead to wait
a while and talk to her alone, without Elliot there to prompt her.
       He finished his coffee and Danish, called the squadroom to find out if
there had been any messages, and was informed by Meyer that another
manila envelope had arrived in the mail. Carella asked him to open it. When
Meyer got back on the line, he said, 'Well, what is it this time?'
       'An airplane,' Meyer said.
       'A what?'
       'A picture of an airplane.'
       'What kind of an airplane?'
       'Beats the hell out of me,' Meyer said.
       It was Cotton Hawes who positively identified the airplane.
       'That's a Zero,' he said, looking at the photostat now pinned to the
bulletin board at the end of the row that contained two pictures of J. Edgar
Hoover and two pictures of George Washington. Hawes had been Chief
Torpedoman aboard a PT boat throughout the war in the Pacific and

presumably knew whereof he spoke; Meyer accepted his word without
hesitation.

'But why?' he said.

'Who the hell knows? How does a picture of a Japanese fighter plane tie in
with Hoover and Washington?'

'Maybe the Japanese are planning an attack on the FBI in Washington,'
Meyer said.

'Right,' Hawes said. 'Six squadrons of Zekes zooming in low over
Pennsylvania Avenue.'

'Pearl Harbor all over again.'

'Beginning of World War III.'

'Must be that,' Meyer said. 'What else could it be?'

'And the Deaf Man, realizing we're the nation's only hope, is warning us
and hoping we'll sound the clarion.'

'Go sound the clarion, Cotton.'

'You know what I think?' Hawes said.

'Tell me, pray.'

'I think this time he's putting us on. I don't think there's any connection at
all between those stats.'

'Then why send them to us?'

'Because he's a pain in the ass, plain and simple. He snips unrelated
pictures out of newspapers, magazines, and books, has them photostated,
and then mails them to us, hoping they'll drive us crazy.'

'What about the threat he made?'

'What about it? Carella's going to help him steal half a million bucks, huh? Fat chance of that happening.'

'Cotton?' Meyer said.

'Mmm?'

'If this was anybody else we were dealing with here, I would say, "Yes, you're right, he's a bedbug." But this is the Deaf Man. When the Deaf Man says he is going to do something, he does it. I don't know what connection there is between those stats, but I know there *is* a connection, and I know he's hoping we're smart enough to figure it out.'

'Why?' Hawes said.

'Because once we figure it out, he'll do something related but unrelated. Cotton . . .'

'Yes, Meyer?'

'Cotton,' Meyer said, and looked up seriously, and said with great intensity, 'Cotton, this man is a diabolical *fiend!*'

'Steady now,' Hawes said.

'Cotton, I detest this man. Cotton, I wish I had never heard of this villain in my entire life.'

'Try to get hold of yourself,' Hawes said.

'How can we *possibly* figure out the associations his maniacal mind has concocted?'

'Look, Meyer, you're letting this . . .'

'How can we *possibly* know what these images mean to him? Hoover, Washington, and a goddamn Jap Zero!' Meyer stabbed his finger at the photostat of the airplane. 'Maybe that's *all* he's trying to tell us, Cotton.'

'What do you mean?'

'That so far we've got nothing. Zero. A big fat empty circle. Zero, zero, zero.'

'Would you like a cup of coffee?' Hawes asked kindly.

Carella hit four apartment buildings on Porter Street before he found a mailbox listing for Henry Scaffale. He climbed the steps to the third floor, listened outside Apartment 32, heard voices inside but could not distinguish what they were saying. He knocked on the door.

'Who is it?' a man's voice asked.

'Me,' Carella said. 'Detective Carella.'

There was a short silence. Carella waited. He heard someone approaching the door. It opened a crack, and Bob Carmody looked out.

'Yes?' he said. 'What do you want?'

'Mary Margaret here?'

'Maybe.'

'I'd like to talk to her.'

'What about?'

'Is she here?'

'Maybe you'd better come back with a warrant,' Bob said, and began closing the door.

Carella immediately wedged his foot into it, and said, 'I can do that, Bob, but going all the way downtown isn't going to sweeten my disposition by the time I get back. What do you say?'

'Let him in, Bob,' a girl's voice said.

Bob scowled, opened the door, and stepped aside to let Carella in. Mary Margaret was sitting on a mattress on the floor. A chubby girl wearing a pink sweater and jeans was sitting beside her. Both girls had their backs to the wall. Hank was straddling a kitchen chair, his chin on his folded arms, watching Carella as he came into the room.

'Hello, Mary Margaret,' Carella said.

'Hello,' she answered without enthusiasm.

'I'd like to talk to you.'

'Talk,' she said.

'Privately.'

'Where would you suggest? There's only this one room and a john.'

'How about the hallway?'

Mary Margaret shrugged, shoved her long hair back over her shoulders with both hands, rose with a dancer's motion from her cross-legged position, and walked barefooted past Carella and into the hallway. Carella followed her out and closed the door behind them.

'What do you want to talk about?' she asked.

'Do you pose for an artist named Sandy Elliot?'

'Why?' Mary Margaret asked. 'Is that against the law? I'm nineteen years old.'

'No, it's not against the law.'

'So, okay, I pose for him. How'd *you* know that?'

'I saw some of his work. The likeness is remarkable.' Carella paused. 'Do you also *drive* for him?'

'What are you talking about?'

'Did you drive him up to Boston last weekend?'

'Yes,' Mary Margaret said.

'Were you posing for him today when I went to the shop?'

'I don't know when you went to the shop.'

'Let's take just the first part. Were you posing for him today?'

'Yes.'

'What time?'

'From ten o'clock on.'

'I was there about eleven.'

'I didn't know that.'

'Sandy didn't mention my visit?'

'No.'

'When did he hurt his leg, Mary Margaret?'

'I don't know.'

'When was the last time you posed for him?'

'Before today, do you mean?'

'Yes.'

'Last Thursday.'

Carella took a small celluloid calendar from his wallet and looked at it. 'That would be Thursday, the fifteenth.'

'Yes, I guess so.'

'Was he on crutches at that time?'

'Yes.'

'When did you pose for him before that?'

'I pose for him every Thursday morning.'

'Does that mean you posed for him on Thursday, April eighth?'

'Yes.'

'Was he on crutches then?'

'No.'

'So he hurt himself sometime between the eighth and the fifteenth, is that right?'

'I guess so. What difference does it make *when* he ...'

'Where'd you go in Boston?'

'Oh, around.'

'Around where?'

'I don't know Boston too well. Sandy was giving me directions.'

'When did you leave here?'

'Friday.'

'Mmm.'

'Was it?'

'Yes, it was. Last Friday. Right.'

'What kind of car did you use?'

'Sandy's.'

'Which is what?'

'Little Volkswagon.'

'Must have been uncomfortable. Crutches and all.'

'Mmm.'

'How long did it take you to get up there?'

'Oh, I don't know. Four, five hours. Something like that.'

'What time did you leave?'

'Here? The city?'

'Yes.'

'In the morning.'

'What time in the morning?'

'Nine? Ten? I don't remember.'

'Did you come back down that night?'

'No. We stayed a few days. In Boston.'

'Where?'

'One of Sandy's friends.'

'And came back when?'

'Late Monday night.'

'And today you posed for Sandy again.'

'That's right.'

'How much does he pay you?'

Mary Margaret hesitated.

'How much does he pay you?' Carella asked again.

'Sandy's my boy friend,' she said. 'He doesn't pay me anything.'

'Where do you pose?'

'In the back of his shop. He's got his studio there. In the back.'

'Are you living with him, Mary Margaret?'

'I live here. But I spend most of my time with Sandy.'

'Would you know the name of the doctor who treated his foot?'

'No.'

'What happened to it, anyway?'

'He had an accident.'
'Fell, did he?'
'Yes.'
'And tore the Achilles' tendon, huh?'
'Yes.'
'Mary Margaret, do you think Sandy might have known that man in the picture I showed you?'
'Go ask Sandy.'
'I did.'
'So what did he say?'
'He said no.'
'Then I guess he didn't know him.'
'Did you know him?'
'No.'
'You want to know what I think, Mary Margaret?'
'What?'
'I think Sandy was lying.'
Mary Margaret shrugged.
'I think you're lying, too.'
'Why would I lie?'
'I don't know yet,' Carella said.

He had been inside the apartment for perhaps twenty minutes when he heard a key turning in the lock. He knew that the Ungermans would be gone until the end of the week, and at first he thought the building superintendent was making an inopportune, routine check, but then he heard a man say, 'Good to be home, eh, Karin?' and realized the Ungermans were back, and he was in the bedroom, and there were no exterior fire escapes; the only way out was through the front door, the way he had come in. He decided immediately that there was no percentage in waiting, the thing to do was make his move at once. The Ungermans were a couple in their late sixties, he would have no trouble getting past them, the difficult thing would be getting out of the building. They were moving towards the bedroom, Harry Ungerman carrying a pair of suitcases, his wife a step behind him, reaching up to take off her hat, when he charged them. He knocked Ungerman flat on his back, and then shoved out at Mrs Ungerman, who reached out towards him for support, clutching at his clothes to keep from falling backwards the way her husband had done not ten seconds before. They danced an awkward, silent little jig for perhaps four seconds, her hands grasping, he trying to shove her away, and finally he wrenched loose, slamming her against the wall, and racing for the front door. He got the door unlocked, opened it, and was running for the stairway at the far end of the hall when Mrs Ungerman began screaming.
Instead of heading down for the street, he went up towards the roof of the twelve-storey building. The metal door was locked when he reached it. He backed off several paces, sprang the lock with a flat-footed kick, and sprinted out onto the roof. He hesitated a moment in the star-drenched night, to get his bearings. Then he ran for the parapet, looked down at the roof of the adjacent building, and leaped.
By the time Harry Ungerman put in his call to the police, the man who had

tried to burglarize his apartment was already four blocks away, entering his own automobile.

But it had been a close call.

Chapter Eight

If you are going to go tiptoeing into empty apartments, you had best make certain they are going to *stay* empty all the while you are illegally on the premises. If they suddenly become anything less than empty, it is best not to try pushing around an elderly lady with a bad back, since she just might possibly grab you to keep from falling on her coccyx, and in the ensuing gavotte might get a very good look at you, particularly if she is a sharp-eyed old bat.

Karin Ungerman was a very sharp-eyed old bat, and mad as a hornet besides. What annoyed her particularly was the kitten. The kitten was a fluffy little tan thing who had wet on the gold brocade chaise in the Ungerman bedroom. Mrs Ungerman was certain the stain would not come out, despite liberal and repeated sprinklings of a highly touted spot remover. The first thing she asked Kling when he arrived that morning was whether or not her insurance company would pay damages for the kitten's indiscretion. The kitten had, after all, been brought there by a burglar and she was covered for fire and theft, so why shouldn't they pay? Kling did not know the answer. Kling – who had arrived at the squadroom at 8 a.m., and been promptly informed of last night's events – had rushed over to 641 Richardson Drive immediately, and was interested only in getting a description of the man both Ungermans had seen.

The Ungermans informed him that the only thing missing was a gold and pearl pin but that perhaps Karin Ungerman had given that to her sister who lived in Florida, she wasn't quite sure. The burglar had undoubtedly been in the apartment for only a very short while; only the top drawer of the dresser had been disturbed. Luckily, Mrs Ungerman hid all her good jewellery in a galosh in the closet whenever she went on a trip. If you lived to be sixty-eight years old, and have been burglarized four times in the past seventeen years, you learn how to deal with the bastards. But bringing in a cat to pee all over your gold brocade chaise! Really!

'What did the man look like, can you tell me that?' Kling asked.

'He was a tall man,' Mrs Ungerman said.

'How tall?'

'Taller than you,' she said.

'Six feet two inches, around there,' Mr Ungerman said.

'How was he dressed?'

'In dark clothes. Black, I think.'

'Blue,' Mr Ungerman said.

'Dark, anyway,' Mrs Ungerman said. 'Trousers, jacket, shirt, all dark.'

'What kind of shirt?'

'A turtleneck,' Mrs Ungerman said.

'Was he a white man or a black man?'

'White. The part of his face we could see.'

'What do you mean?'

'We only saw his eyes and forehead. He was wearing a mask.'

'What kind of a mask?'

'A handkerchief. Over the bridge of his nose, hanging down over his face.'

'You say you saw his eyes ...'

'Yes, and his forehead.'

'And his hair, too,' Mr Ungerman said. 'He wasn't wearing a hat.'

'What colour were his eyes?' Kling asked.

'Brown.'

'And his hair?'

'Black.'

'Was it straight, wavy, curly?'

'Curly.'

'Long or close-cropped?'

'Just average length,' Mrs Ungerman said.

'Anything else you may have noticed about him?'

'Nothing. Except that he moved very fast.'

'I'd move fast, too,' Mrs Ungerman said, 'if I'd just let a cat make a mess all over somebody's gold brocade chaise.'

That morning Detective Steve Carella went down to the Criminal Courts Building and, being duly sworn, deposed and said in writing:

1. I am a detective in the Police Department assigned to the 87th Detective Squad.

2. I have information based upon my personal knowledge and belief and facts disclosed to me by the Medical Examiner that a murder has been committed. Investigation discloses the following:

On April 19th, at 10:15 A.M., George Mossler, a vagrant, discovered the body of an unidentified man in Apartment 51 of an abandoned tenement building at 433 North Harrison Street. The victim had been stabbed in the chest and nailed to the wall, a spike through each extended palm and a third spike through his crossed feet. Medical Examiner states cause of death to be cardiac hemorrhage due to penetrating knife wound; and sets time of death as sometime during the night of April 18th.

A search of the building at 433 North Harrison Street resulted in the finding of a size twelve, left-footed, white tennis sneaker in Apartment 52 which is down the hall from Apartment 51 where the body was discovered.

On April 22nd, while showing pictures of the body of the dead man to people in the neighborhood where the body was found, investigator entered the shop of Sanford Elliot, located at 1211 King's Circle, approximately four blocks from the North Harrison Street address. Sanford Elliot was on crutches and his left foot was bandaged. On his right foot was a white tennis sneaker believed to be the mate to the left-footed sneaker found at the murder scene. When questioned, Sanford Elliot stated that he had been in Boston on the night of April 18th and did not know or recognize the picture of the man found murdered at the North Harrison Street address.

Based upon the foregoing reliable information and upon my personal
knowledge, there is probable cause to believe that aforementioned
tennis sneaker constitutes evidence in the crime of murder and may
be found in the possession of Sanford Elliot or at premises 1211
King's Circle, ground floor rear.

Wherefore, I respectfully request that the court issue a warrant
and order of seizure, in the form annexed authorizing the search
of Sanford Elliot and of premises 1211 King's Circle, ground floor
rear, and directing that if such property or evidence or any part
thereof be found that it be seized and brought before the court,
together with such other and further relief that the court may deem
proper.

No previous application in this matter has been made in this or
any other court or to any other judge, justice, or magistrate.

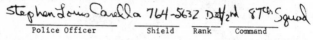

| Police Officer | Shield | Rank | Command |

Carella realized that the application was weak in that there was no way of connecting Elliot with the murder except through the sneaker, and sneakers were, after all, fairly common wearing apparel. He knew, too, that a warrant issued on his application might possibly be later controverted on a motion to suppress the evidence seized under it. He was somewhat surprised, but nonetheless grateful, when a supreme court judge signed and dated the application, and issued the requested warrant.

Which meant that Carella now had the legal right to arrest an inanimate object, so to speak.

If Carella was getting a little help from the courts, Kling was simultaneously getting a little help from the Identification Section. As a matter of routine, he had asked them to run checks on both Fred Lipton and Nat Sulzbacher, the Calm's Point real estate agents whose give-away pen had been found in Augusta Blair's apartment. Much to his surprise, the I.S. had come back with a positive identification that immediately catapulted old Fred Lipton into the role of prime suspect in the burglary case. Kling had not yet eliminated Stanislaw Janik as a contender for best supporting player and possible supplier of kittens and keys, but the physical description given by Mrs Ungerman ruled him out as the man actually entering the apartments. The burglar was tall, with black curly hair and brown eyes. Janik was short, almost totally bald, and his blue eyes were magnified by thick eyeglasses.

So Kling was pleased to learn that whereas Nat Sulzbacher had no criminal record (he could have obtained a licence to sell real estate after having been convicted of a misdemeanor), his salesman, Frederick Horace Lipton, had been in trouble with the law on two previous occasions, having been arrested for Disorderly Conduct back in 1954 and for First-Degree Forgery in 1957. The disturbance in 1954 was only a misdemeanor, defined as any crime other than a felony, but it still might have netted Lipton as much as six months' imprisonment in a county jail or workhouse. Instead, all he'd got was a $50 fine. The 1957 paper-hanging rap was a felony, of course, defined as a crime punishable by death or imprisonment in a state prison. Considering the offence, the court was equally charitable in sentencing Lipton this second time; he could have got twenty years, but he drew only ten.

He had served three and a half of those at Castleview State Prison, and had been released on parole in 1961. As far as society was concerned, he had paid his debt and was now a hard-working real estate salesman in Calm's Point. But one of his employer's give-away pens had been found at the scene of a burglary. Nat Sulzbacher did not have a criminal record; he was therefore an ordinary respectable everyday citizen. But Fred Lipton was an ex-con. So Kling naturally asked Lieutenant Byrnes for permission to begin surveillance of him as a suspect, and Byrnes naturally granted permission, and the tailing began that afternoon.

Never let it be said that policemen look with prejudice upon citizens who have previously been convicted of a crime.

Of the four guests in the Deaf Man's room at the Devon Hotel, three had previously been convicted of crimes. The fourth was a plain-looking woman in her late thirties, and she had never so much as received a parking ticket. The hotel was one of the city's lesser-known dumps, furnished economically and without imagination. There was only one easy chair in the room, and the men had graciously allowed the lady to claim it. They themselves sat on straight-backed wooden chairs facing a small end table that had been pulled up and placed within the semicircle they formed. A child's slate was propped up on the end table. The Deaf Man had served drinks (the lady had politely declined), and they sat sipping them thoughtfully as they examined the chalked diagram on the slate.

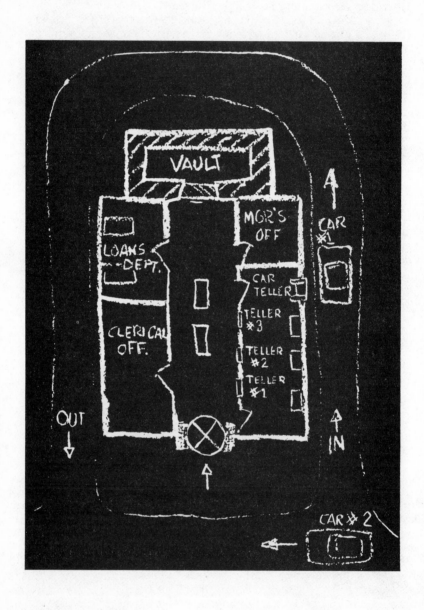

'Any questions?' the Deaf Man said.

'I've got one.'

'Let's hear it, John.'

John Preiss was a tall slender man with a pock-marked face. He was the only man in the room who had not dressed for the occasion. The others, as though attending a church social, were all wearing jackets and ties. John was wearing a cardigan sweater over an open-throated sports shirt. 'Where's the alarm box?' he asked.

'I don't know,' the Deaf Man answered. 'It's not important. As I've told you before, I *expect* the alarm to be sounded.'

'I don't like it,' John said.

'Then this is the time to get out. None of you yet know where the bank is, or when we're going to hit. If anything about the job doesn't appeal to you, you're free to pass.'

'I mean,' John said, 'if the damn alarm goes off ...'

'It *will* go off, it *has* to go off. That's the least of our worries.'

'Maybe you'd better explain it again, Mr Taubman,' the woman said.

'I'd be happy to, Angela,' the Deaf Man replied. 'Where shall I begin?'

'The beginning might be a good place,' one of the other men said. He was portly, partially balding, chewing on a dead cigar. His name was Kerry Donovan.

'Very well,' the Deaf Man said, and picked up a pointer from the end table. 'This is the vault. Forget about getting into it any other way than through the door. The door is opened at eight-thirty every morning, and is not closed until the employees leave at close to five in the evening.'

'What time do we hit?' Rudy Manello asked. He was younger than any of the others, a narrow-faced man, with brown hair combed straight back without a part. He was smoking a cigarette, the ash dangerously close to spilling all over the floor.

'I'll let you know the time and place as soon as we're all committed, Rudy.'

'Why all the secrecy?' Rudy asked.

'I do not intend spending any amount of time in prison,' the Deaf Man said, and smiled. 'Whereas I trust you all implicitly, I must take certain precautions at this stage of the planning.'

'So let's hear the plan again,' Angela said, and crossed her legs, a move that had no visible effect on any of the men in the room. Angela Gould was perhaps the least attractive woman the Deaf Man had ever met. Long-nosed, thin-lipped, bespectacled, blessed with curly hair in an age that demanded sleekness, dumpy, with an irritating, whiny voice – impossible, utterly impossible. And yet perfect for the part she would play on the last day of April.

'Here is the plan again,' the Deaf Man said, and smiled graciously. He did not much like any of the people he was forced to deal with, but even the best football coach needs a team to execute the plays. 'On the day of the robbery, Kerry will enter the bank, carrying a rather large case in which there will be architectural plans and a scale model of a housing development for which he needs financing. He will previously have made an appointment with the manager, and he will be there ostensibly to show him the plans and the model.'

'Where do we get this stuff?' Kerry asked.

'It is being prepared for us now. By a legitimate architectural firm that believes it to a bona-fide land-development project.'

'Okay, go ahead.'

'Once inside the manager's office, you will explain your project and then put your plans and your model on his desk, asking him to come around to *your* side of the desk so that he can read the plans better. You will do this in order to get him away from the alarm button, which is on the floor under his desk, and which he will be unable to reach from your side.'

'I thought you *expected* the alarm to go off,' John said.

'Yes, but not until we have the money.'

'The money that's in the vault.'

'Yes. As I've already told you, there will be five hundred thousand dollars in payroll money in the bank's vault. It will be necessary for Kerry to get *into* the vault ...'

'That's the part I don't like,' Kerry said.

'There will be no problem about getting into the vault, Kerry. The moment the manager comes around to your side of the desk, you will put a gun in his back and inform him that a holdup is in progress. You will also tell him that, unless he escorts you to the vault immediately, you will blow his brains out.'

'That's exactly what bothers me,' Kerry said. 'Suppose he says, "Go ahead, blow my brains out." What do I do then?'

'The bank is insured. You will rarely find heroic bank employees nowadays. They all have instructions to press the alarm button and sit tight until the police arrive. In this case, we are depriving Mr Alton – that's the manager's name – of the opportunity to sound the alarm. I can assure you he will not avail himself of the alternate opportunity – that of having his brains blown out. He will escort you to the vault, quietly and without fuss.'

'I hope so,' Kerry said. 'But what if he doesn't? Since I'm the only guy inside the bank, I'm automatically the fall guy.'

'I will also be inside the bank,' the Deaf Man said.

'Yeah, but you won't be holding a gun on any manager.'

'I chose you for the job because you'd had previous experience,' the Deaf Man said. 'I assumed you would have the nerve to ...'

'Yeah, I got *caught* on my previous experience,' Kerry said.

'Do you want the job or don't you?' the Deaf Man asked. 'You can still get out. No hard feelings either way.'

'Let me hear the rest of it again.'

'You go into the vault with Mr Alton, carrying your leather case, the architectural contents of which are now in Mr Alton's office.'

'In other words,' Angela said, 'the case is empty now.'

'Precisely,' the Deaf Man said, and thought, *Impossible*. 'As soon as you are inside the vault, Kerry, you will transfer the payroll to your case, and then allow Mr Alton to escort you back to his office ...'

'Suppose there's somebody else in the vault when we get in there?'

'You will already have informed Mr Alton that should anyone question your presence, he is to say you're there to test the alarm system. Presumably, that is why you are carrying a big black leather case.'

'But suppose somebody's actually *in* the vault?' Kerry said. 'You didn't answer the question.'

'Mr Alton will ask that person to leave. The testing of an alarm system is not something normally open to casual scrutiny by insignificant bank personnel.'

'Okay. So I'm in the vault transferring all that money into my case ...'

'Correct. The moment I see you *leaving* the vault to head back for Mr Alton's office, I will step outside the bank and set the second phase of the plan in motion.'

'This is where *we* come in,' Angela said, and smiled. *Utterly impossible*, the Deaf Man thought, and returned her smile.

'Yes,' he said pleasantly enough, 'this is where you come in. If you'll all look at the diagram again, you'll see that a driveway comes in off the street on the right of the bank, runs around the rear of the bank, and then emerges into the street again on the left. The driveway was put in to accommodate the car teller's window. It is only wide enough to permit the passage of a single automobile. Two things will happen the moment I step out of the bank. First, John and Rudy, in Car Number One, will drive up to the teller's window. Second, Angela, in Car Number Two, will park across the mouth of the driveway, get out of the car, and open the hood as though searching for starter trouble.'

'That's so no other cars can get in the driveway after Rudy and John pull up to the teller's window,' Angela said.

'Yes,' the Deaf Man answered blankly.

'Meanwhile,' Kerry said, and the Deaf Man was pleased to see that he had managed to generate some sort of enthusiasm for the project, '*I'll* be in the manager's office, tying him up and sticking a gag in his mouth.'

'Correct,' the Deaf Man said. 'John?'

'I'll get out of the car at the teller's window and smash the glass there with a sledge hammer.'

'Which is precisely when the alarm will go off. You won't hear it. It's a silent alarm that sounds at the 86th Precinct and also at the Security Office.'

'But *I'll* hear the glass smashing,' Kerry said, and grinned. 'Which is when I open the door leading from the manager's office to the tellers' cages, go through the gate in the counter, and jump through the busted window into the driveway.'

'Yes,' the Deaf Man said. 'You get into the car, and Rudy, at the wheel, will drive around the rear of the bank and out into the street again. I will meanwhile have entered the car Angela is driving, and we will all go off together into a lucrative sunset.'

'How long does it take the police to answer that alarm?' Rudy asked.

'Four minutes.'

'How long does it take to drive around the bank?'

'A minute and a half.'

The group was silent.

'What do you think?' The Deaf Man asked. He had deliberately chosen nonthinkers, and he fully realized that his task today was one of selling an idea. He looked at them hopefully. If he had not completely sold them, he would replace them. It was as simple as that.

'I think it'll work,' John said.

'So do I,' Rudy said.

'Oh, how can it miss?' Angela said in her whiny voice, and the Deaf Man winced.

'Kerry?' he asked.

Kerry, of course, was the key man. As he had rightfully pointed out, he was the only one of the group who would actually be *inside* the bank, holding a gun, committing a robbery. The question Kerry asked now was the only question he should have asked; the Deaf Man was beginning to think he had chosen someone altogether too smart.

'How come *you* don't go into the manager's office and stick the gun in his back?' Kerry asked.

'I'm known at the bank,' the Deaf Man said.

'How?'

'As a depositor.'

'Why can't a depositor also be somebody who's asking for financing on a housing development?'

'There's no reason why he couldn't be. But my face has been recorded by the bank's cameras too many times already, and I don't wish to spend the rest of my life dodging the police.'

'What about *my* face?' Kerry asked. 'They'll know what *I* look like, won't they? What's to stop them from hounding *me* after the job?'

'*You'll* be in disguise.'

'You didn't mention that.'

'I know I didn't,' the Deaf Man said. He hadn't mentioned it because he hadn't thought of it until just this moment. 'You will grow a moustache and shave your head before the job. As far as they'll ever know, the bank was robbed by a Yul Brynner with a hairy lip.' Everyone laughed, including Kerry. The Deaf Man waited. They were almost in his pocket. It all depended on Kerry.

Kerry, still laughing, shook his head in admiration. 'I got to hand it to you,' he said. 'You think of everything.' He took a long swallow of the drink, and said, 'I don't know about the rest of you, but it sounds good to me. He raised his glass to the Deaf Man and said, 'Count me in.'

The Deaf Man did not mention to Kerry that his next logical question should have been, 'Mr Taubman, why don't *you* shave your head and grow a moustache?' or that he was extremely grateful to him for not having asked it. But then again, had the question come up, the Deaf Man would have thought of an answer. As Kerry had noted, the Deaf Man thought of everything, even when he *didn't* think of everything. Grinning now, he said to the others, 'May I count *all* of you in?' and turned away not three seconds later to mix a fresh round of drinks in celebration.

The second photostat of the Japanese Zero came in the afternoon mail, just as Carella was leaving the squadroom. Carella studied it solemnly as Meyer tacked it to the bulletin board alongside the five other stats. Then he picked up the manila envelope in which it had been delivered and looked again at the typewritten address.

'He's still addressing them to me,' he said.

'I see that.'

'And still spelling my name wrong. It's Stephen with a *p-h*, not Steven with a *v*.'

'*I* didn't even know that,' Meyer said.

'Yeah,' Carella said, and then turned to look at the row of stats again. 'Do you suppose he knows I have twins?'

'Why?'

'Because that's all I can figure. He's addressing the stuff to me, he's putting it on an entirely personal level. So maybe he's also duplicating it because I have twins.'

'You think so?'

'Yeah.' Carella paused. 'What do *you* think?'

'*I* think you're getting slightly paranoid,' Meyer said.

Sanford Elliot was working when Carella went over with his search warrant. The long wooden table at which he sat was spattered with daubs of wax. A round biscuit tin was near his right elbow, half full of molten wax, a naked electric light bulb shining into its open top to keep it soft. Elliot dipped into the can with fingers or wire-end tool, adding, spreading, moulding wax onto the small figure of the nude on the table before him. He was thoroughly engrossed in what he was doing, and did not look up when Carella walked into the studio from the front of the shop. Carella did not wish to startle him. The man may have figured in a murder, and a startled murderer is a dangerous one. He hesitated just inside the curtain that divided the studio from the front, and then coughed. Elliot looked up immediately.

'You,' he said.

'Me,' Carella answered.

'What is it this time?'

'Do you always work in wax, Mr Elliot?'

'Only when I'm going to cast something in bronze.'

'How do you mean?'

'I don't give art lessons,' Elliot said abruptly. 'What do you want?'

'This is what I want,' Carella said, and walked to him and handed him the search warrant:

IN THE NAME OF THE PEOPLE OF THIS STATE TO ANY POLICE OFFICER IN THIS CITY:

Proof by affidavit having been made this day by Detective Stephen L. Carella that there is probable cause for believing that certain property constitutes evidence of the crime of murder or tends to show that a particular person has committed the crime of murder:

YOU ARE THEREFORE COMMANDED, between the hours of 6:00 A.M. and 9:00 P.M. to make an immediate search of the ground floor rear of premises 1211 King's Circle, occupied by Sanford Elliot and of the person of Sanford Elliot and of any other person who may be found to have such property in his possession or under his control or to whom such property may have been delivered, for a size twelve, right-footed, white tennis sneaker, and if you find such property or any part thereof to bring it before me at the Criminal Courts Building in this county.

This warrant must be executed within ten days of the date of issuance.

Elliot read the warrant, checked the date and the signature of the supreme court justice, and then said, '*What* sneaker? I don't know what you're talking about.'

Carella looked down at his right foot. Elliot was no longer wearing the sneaker; instead, there was a leather sandal on his foot.

'You were wearing a sneaker the last time I saw you. That search warrant gives me the right to look for it.'

'You're out of your mind,' Elliot said.

'Am I?'

'I've never worn sneakers in my life.'

'I'll just look around, if you don't mind.'

'How can I stop you?' Elliot said sarcastically, and went back to work.

'Want to tell me about the wax?' Carella said. He was roaming the studio now, looking for a closet or a cupboard, the logical places one might put a sneaker. There was a second curtain hanging opposite the door leading to the shop, and Carella figured it might be covering the opening to a closet. He was mistaken. There was a small sink-refrigerator-stove unit behind the curtain. He stepped on the foot lever to open the refrigerator door and discovered that it was full of arms, legs, breasts, and heads. They had all been rendered in wax, to be sure, but the discovery was startling nonetheless, somewhat like stumbling upon the remains of a mass Lilliputian dismemberment. 'What are these?' Carella said.

'Parts,' Elliot answered. He had obviously decided not to be cooperative, responsive, or even polite. His attitude was not exactly surprising; his visitor had come into the studio with a piece of paper empowering him to go through the place from top to bottom.

'Did you mould them?'

'Yes,' Elliot said.

'I suppose you keep them in here so they won't melt.'

'Brilliant.'

'Why do you keep them at all?'

'I made up a batch from rubber moulds,' Elliot said. 'I use them as prototypes, changing them to fit a specific pose.'

Carella nodded, closed the refrigerator, and began wandering the studio again. He found what he thought was a packing crate, but when he lifted the lid he discovered that Elliot stored his clothes in it. He kneeled and began going through the crate, being careful not to disturb the order in which blue jeans and sweaters, shirts and socks, underwear and jackets were arranged. A single sandal was in the crate, the mate to the one Elliot was now wearing. There were also two pairs of loafers. But no sneaker. Carella put the lid onto the crate again.

'Why do you model in wax if it's so perishable?' he asked.

'I told you, I only do it when I'm going to be casting in bronze.' Elliot put down the wire-end tool in his hand, turned to Carella, and patiently said, 'It's called *cire perdue*, the lost-wax method. A mould is made of the piece when it gets to the foundry, and then the wax is melted out, and molten bronze is poured into the mould.'

'Then the original wax piece is lost, is that right?'

'Brilliant,' Elliot said again, and picked up a fettling knife.

'What do you do when you get the bronze piece back?'

'Chisel or file off the fins, plug any holes, colour it, polish it, and mount it on a marble base.'

'What's in here?' Carella asked, indicating a closed door.

'Storage.'
'Of what?'
'Larger pieces. Most of them in plaster.'
'Mind if I take a look?'
'You're hot stuff, you know that?' Elliot said. 'You come around with a search warrant, and then you go through the charade of asking me whether or not you can ...'
'No sense being uncivilized about it, is there?'
'Why not? I thought you were investigating a murder.'
'I didn't think you realized that, Mr Elliot.'
'I realize it fine. And I've already told you I don't know who the dead man ...'
'Yes, you've already told me. The trouble is, I don't happen to believe you.'
'Then don't be so fucking polite,' Elliot said. 'If I'm a murder suspect, I don't need your good manners.'
Carella went into the storage room without answering. As Elliot had promised, the room contained several larger pieces, all done in plaster, all unmistakably of Mary Margaret Ryan. A locked door was at the far end of the room. 'Where's that door go?' Carella asked.
'What?' Elliot said.
'The other door here.'
'Outside. The alley.'
'You want to unlock it for me, please?'
'I don't have a key. I never open that door. It's locked all the time.'
'I'll have to kick it open then,' Carella said.
'Why?'
'Because I want to see what's out in that alley.'
'There's nothing out in that alley.'
There were prints in the plaster dust on the floor. Easily identifiable prints left by someone's right foot; on either side of them, there were circular marks that might have been left by the rubber tips of crutches. The prints led directly to the alley door.
'What do you say, Elliot? Are you going to open it for me?'
'I told you I don't have a key.'
'Fine,' Carella said, and kicked the door in without another word.
'Are you allowed to do that?' Elliot said.
'Sue me,' Carella said, and went out into the alley. A garbage can and two cardboard boxes full of trash were stacked against the brick wall. In one of the cardboard cartons Carella found the sneaker Elliot had been wearing yesterday. He came back into the studio, showed the sneaker to Elliot and said, 'Ever see this before?'
'Never.'
'I figured you wouldn't have,' Carella said. 'Mr Elliot, at the risk of sounding like a television cop, I'd like to warn you not to leave the city.'
'Where would I go?' Elliot asked.
'Who knows? You seem to have a penchant for Boston. Take my advice and stay put till I get back to you.'
'What do you hope to get from a fucking mouldy sneaker?' Elliot said.
'Maybe some wax that *didn't* get lost,' Carella answered.

*   *   *

The cop who picked up the surveillance of Frederick Lipton at five o'clock that evening was Cotton Hawes. From his parked sedan across the street from the real estate office, he watched Lipton as he locked up the place and walked down the block to where his Ford convertible was parked. He followed him at a safe distance to a garden apartment a mile and a half from the real estate office, and waited outside for the next four hours, at which time Lipton emerged, got into his Ford again, and drove to a bar imaginatively named the Gee-Gee-Go-Go. Since Lipton had never met Hawes and did not know what he looked like, and also since the place advertised topless dancers, Hawes figured he might as well step inside and continue the surveillance there. The place was no more disappointing than he expected it to be. Topless dancing, in this city, was something more than topless – the something more being pasties or filmy brassieres. Hookers freely roamed the streets and plied their trade, but God forbid a mammary gland should be exposed to some unsuspecting visitor from Sioux City. The dancers, nonetheless, were usually young and attractive, gyrating wildly to canned rock music while the equivalent of front-row centre in a burlesque house ogled them from stools lining the bar. Not so at the Gee-Gee-Go-Go. The dancers here were thirtyish or better, considerably over the hill for the kind of acrobatics they performed or the kind or erotic response they attempted to provoke. Hawes sat in bored silence while the elaborate electronics system buffeted him with waves of amplified sound and the dancers, four in all, came out in succession to grind away in tempo along the length of the bar. Keeping one eye on Lipton, who sat at the other end of the bar, Hawes speculated that the sound system had cost more than the dancing girls, but this was Calm's Point and not Isola; one settled for whatever he could get in the city's hinterlands.

Lipton seemed to know one of the dancers, a woman of about thirty-five, with bleached blonde hair and siliconed breasts tipped with star-shaped pasties, ample buttocks, rather resembling in build one of the sturdy Clydesdale horses in the Rheingold commercials. When she finished her number, she kneeled down beside him on the bar top, chatted with him briefly, and then went to join him at a table in the rear of the place. Lipton ordered a drink for the girl, and they talked together for perhaps a half hour, at the end of which time she clambered onto the bar top again to hurl some more beef at her audience, all of whom watched her every move in pop-eyed fascination, as though privileged to be witnessing Markova at a command performance of *Swan Lake*. Lipton settled his bill and left the bar. Without much regret, Hawes followed him back to the garden apartment, where he put his car into one of a row of single garages on the ground level of the building, and then went upstairs. Figuring he was home for the night, Hawes drove back to the Gee-Gee-Go-Go, ordered a scotch and soda, and waited for an opportunity to engage the beefy blonde in conversation.

He caught her after she finished her number, a tiresome repetition of the last three, or five, or fifty numbers she had performed on the bar top. She was heading either for the ladies' room or a dressing room behind the bar when he stepped into her path, smiled politely, and said, 'I like the way you dance. May I buy you a drink?'

The girl said, 'Sure,' without hesitation, confirming his surmise that part of the job was getting the customers to buy watered-down booze or ginger ale masquerading as champagne. She led him to the same table Lipton had shared with her, where a waiter appeared with something like lightning speed, pencil poised. The girl ordered a double bourbon and soda; apparently the champagne dodge was a mite too sophisticated for the Calm's Point sticks. Hawes ordered a scotch and soda and then smiled at the girl and said, 'I really do like the way you dance. Have you been working here long?'

'Are you a cop?' the girl asked.

'No,' Hawes said, startled.

'Then what are you? A crook?'

'No.'

'Then why are you carrying a gun?' the girl said.

Hawes cleared his throat. 'Who says I am?'

'*I* say you are. On your right hip. I saw the bulge when we were talking in the hallway there, and I brushed against it when we were coming over to the table. It's a gun, all right.'

'It's a gun, yes.'

'So, *are* you a cop?'

'No. Close to it, though,' Hawes said.

'Yeah? What does that mean? Private eye?'

'I'm a night watchman. Factory over on Klein and Sixth.'

'If you're a night watchman, what are you doing here? This is the nightime.'

'I don't start till midnight.'

'You always drink like this before you go to work?'

'Not always.'

'Where'd you go when you left here before?' the girl asked.

'You noticed me, huh?' Hawes answered, and grinned, figuring he'd get the conversation onto a socio-sexual level and move it away from more dangerous ground.

'I noticed,' the girl said, and shrugged. 'You're a big guy. Also you've got red hair, which is unusual. Do they call you "Red"?'

'They call me Hamp.'

'Hamp? What kind of name is that?'

'Short for Hampton.'

'Is that your first name or your last?'

'My last. It's Oliver Hampton.'

'I can see why you settled for Hamp.'

'What's *your* name?'

'It's on the card outside. Didn't you see it?'

'I guess I missed it.'

'Rhonda Spear.'

'Is that your real name?'

'It's my show business name.'

'What's your real name?'

'Why do you want to know? So you can call me up in the middle of the night and breathe on the phone?'

'I might call you, but I wouldn't breathe.'

'If a person doesn't breathe, he drops dead,' Rhonda said. She smiled, consumed her drink in a single swallow, and said, 'I'd like another double bourbon, please.'

'Sure,' Hawes said, and signalled for the waiter to bring another round. 'How many of those do you drink in a night?'

'Ten or twelve,' she said. 'It's only Coca-Cola,' she said. 'You're a cop, you know damn well it's Coca-Cola.'

'I'm not a cop, and I didn't know it was Coca-Cola,' Hawes said.

'*I* know cops,' Rhonda said. 'And *you* know Coca-Cola.' She hesitated, looked him straight in the eye, and said, 'What do you want from me, officer?'

'Little conversation, that's all,' Hawes said.

'About what?'

'About why you would tell a cop, if that's what you think I am, that he's paying for bourbon and getting Coca-Cola.'

Rhonda shrugged. 'Why not? If this joint was gonna be busted, they'd have done it ages ago. Everybody in this precinct, from the lieutenant on down, is on the take. We even dance without the pasties every now and then. Nobody ever bothers us. Is that why you're here, officer,' she asked sweetly, 'to get your share of the pie?'

'I'm not a cop,' Hawes said, 'and I wouldn't care if you danced bare-assed while drinking a whole crate of Coca-Cola.'

Rhonda laughed, suddenly and girlishly. Her mirth transformed her face, revealing a fleeting glimpse of what she must have looked like when she was a lot younger, and a lot softer. The laughter trailed, the image died. 'Thanks, honey,' she said to the waiter, and lifted her glass and said to Hawes, 'Maybe you're *not* a cop, after all. Who gives a damn?'

'Cheers,' Hawes said.

'Cheers,' she answered, and they both drank. 'So if you're not a cop, what do you want from me?'

'You're a pretty woman,' Hawes said.

'Um-huh.'

'I'm sure you know that,' he said, and lowered his eyes in a swift covetous sweep of the swelling star-tipped breasts.

'Um-huh.'

'Saw you talking to a guy earlier. I'm sure he ...'

'You did, huh?'

'Sure.'

'You've been watching me, huh?'

'Sure. And I'll bet *he* didn't want to talk about the price of Coca-Cola, either.'

'How do *you* know what he wanted to talk about?'

'I don't. I'm just saying that a pretty woman like you ...'

'Um-huh.'

'Must get a lot of attention from men. So you shouldn't be so surprised by *my* attention. That's all,' he said, and shrugged.

'You're kind of cute,' Rhonda said. 'It's a shame.'

'What is?'

'That you're a cop.'

'Look, how many times ...'

'You're a cop,' she said flatly. 'I don't know what you're after, but something tells me to say good night. Whatever you are, you're trouble.'

'I'm a night watchman,' Hawes said.

'Yeah,' Rhonda replied. 'And I'm Lillian Gish.' She swallowed the remainder of her drink, said, 'You'll settle with the waiter, huh?' and swiveled away from the table, ample buttocks threatening the purple satin shorts she wore.

Hawes paid for the drinks, and left.

Chapter Nine

On Saturday morning, while Carella was waiting for a lab report on the sneaker he had found in Elliot's trash, he made a routine check of the three hospitals in the area, trying to discover if and when a man named Sanford Elliot had been treated for a sprained ankle. The idea of calling all the private physicians in the area was out of the question, of course; if Carella had not hit pay dirt with one of the hospitals, he would have given up this line of investigation at once. But sometimes you get lucky. On Saturday, April 24, Carella got lucky on the second call he made.

The intern on duty in the Emergency Room of Buenavista Hospital was a Japanese named Dr Yukio Watanabe. He told Carella that business was slow at the moment and that he was free to check through the log; had Carella called an hour ago, he'd have been told to buzz off fast because the place had been thronged with victims of three-car highway accident.

'You never saw so much blood in your life,' Watanabe said, almost gleefully, Carella thought. 'Anyway, what period are you interested in? I've got the book right here in front of me.'

'This would have been sometime between the eighth and fifteenth,' Carella said.

'Of this month?'

'Yes.'

'Okay, let's take a look. What'd you say his name was?'

'Sanford Elliot.'

There was a long silence on the line. Carella waited.

'I'm checking,' Watanabe said. 'Sprained ankle, huh?'

'That's right.'

'Nothing so far.'

'Where are you?'

'Through the eleventh,' Watanabe said, and fell silent again. Carella waited.

'Nothing,' Watanabe said at last. 'You sure it was between those dates?'

'Could you check a bit further for me?'

'How far?'

'Through the next week, if you've got time.'

'We've always got time here until somebody comes in with a broken head,' Watanabe said. 'Okay, here we go. Sanford Elliot, right?'

'Right.'

Watanabe was silent. Carella could hear him turning pages.

'Sanford Elliot,' Watanabe said. 'Here it is.'

'When did he come in?'

'Monday morning, April nineteenth.'

'What time?'

'Ten past seven. Treated by Dr Goldstein.' Watanabe paused. 'I thought you said it was a sprained ankle.'

'Wasn't it?'

'Not according to this. He was treated for third-degree burns. Foot, ankle, and calf of the left leg.'

'I see,' Carella said.

'Does that help you?'

'It confuses me. But thanks, anyway.'

'No problem,' Watanabe said, and hung up.

Carella stared at the telephone. It was always good to stare at the telephone when you didn't have any ideas. There was something terribly reassuring about the knowledge that the telephone itself was worthless until a bell started ringing. Carella waited for a bell to start ringing. Instead, Miscolo came in with the morning mail.

The lady was lovely, to be sure, but nobody knew who she was. There was no question about *what* she was. She was a silent film star. There is a look about silent film stars that immediately identifies their profession and their era, even to people who have never watched any of their films. None of the detectives looking at the lady's picture were old enough to have seen her films, but they knew immediately what she was, and so they began riffling through their memories, calling up ancient names and trying to associate them with printed photographs they'd seen accompanying articles probably titled 'Whatever Happened To?'

'Gloria Swanson?' Hawes asked.

'No, I know what Gloria Swanson looks like,' Meyer said. 'This is definitely not Gloria Swanson.'

'Dolores Del Rio?' Hawes said.

'No, Dolores Del Rio was very sexy,' Carella said. 'Still *is*, as a matter of fact. I saw a recent picture of her only last month.'

'What's the matter with *this* girl?' Meyer said. 'I happen to think *this* girl is very sexy.'

'Norma Talmadge, do you think?' Hawes said.

'Who's Norma Talmadge?' Kling asked.

'Get this bottle baby out of here, will you?' Meyer said.

'I mean it, who's Norma Talmadge?'

'How about Marion Davies?'

'I don't think so,' Carella said.

'Who's Marion Davies?' Kling asked, and Meyer shook his head.

'Janet Gaynor?' Hawes said.

'No.'

'Pola Negri?'

'I know who Pola Negri is,' Kling said. 'The Vamp.'

'Theda Bara was The Vamp,' Meyer said.

'Oh,' Kling said.

'Dolores Costello?'

'No, I don't think so.'

'Mae Murray?'

'No.'

The telephone rang. Hawes picked up the receiver. '87th Squad,' he said, 'Detective Hawes.' He listened silently for a moment, and then said, 'Hold on, will you? I think you want Carella.' He handed the receiver to him, and said, 'It's the lab. They've got a report on your tennis sneaker.'

Through the plate-glass window of Sandy Elliot's shop, Carella could see him inside with two bikies. He recognized one of them as Yank, the cigar-smoking heavyweight he had spoken to on Tuesday. Yank was wandering around the shop, examining the pieces of sculpture, paying scant attention to Elliot and the second bikie, who was wagging his finger in Elliot's face like a district attorney in a grade-C flick. Elliot leaned on his crutches and listened solemnly to what was being said, occasionally nodding. At last the second bikie turned away from the counter, tapped Yank on the arm, and started out of the shop. Carella moved swiftly into the adjacent doorway. As the pair passed by, he caught a quick glimpse of Yank's companion – short, brawny, with a pock-marked face and a sailor's rolling gait, the name 'Ox' lettered on the front of his jacket. As they went off, Carella heard Yank burst into laughter.

He waited several moments, came out of the doorway, and went into Elliot's shop.

'See you had a couple of art lovers in here,' he said. 'Did they buy anything?'

'No.'

'What did they want?'

'What do *you* want?' Elliot said.

'Some answers,' Carella said.

'I've given you all the answers I've got.'

'I haven't given you all the questions yet.'

'Maybe you'd better advise me of my rights first.'

'This is a field investigation, and you haven't been taken into custody or otherwise detained, so please don't give me any bullshit about rights. Nobody's violating your rights. I've got a few simple questions, and I want a few simple answers. How about it, Elliot? I'm investigating a homicide here.'

'I don't know anything about any homicide.'

'Your sneaker was found at the scene of the crime.'

'Who says so?'

'*I* say so. And the police lab says so. How did it get there, Elliot?'

'I have no idea. I threw that pair of sneakers out two weeks ago. Somebody must've picked one of them out of the trash.'

'When *I* picked it out of the trash yesterday, you said you'd never seen it before. You can't have it both ways, Elliot. Anyway, you couldn't have thrown them out two weeks ago, because I saw you wearing one of them only two *days* ago. What do you say? You going to play ball, or do you want to take a trip to the station house?'

'For what? You going to charge me with murder?'

'Maybe.'

'I don't think you will,' Elliot said. 'I'm not a lawyer, but I know you can't build a case on a sneaker you found in a goddamn abandoned tenement.'

'How do *you* know where we found that sneaker?'

'I read about the murder in the papers.'

'How do you know which murder I'm investigating?'

'You showed me a picture, didn't you? It doesn't take a mastermind to tie the newspaper story to ...'

'Get your hat, Elliot. I'm taking you to the station house.'

'You can't arrest me,' Elliot said. 'Who the hell do you think you're kidding? You've got nothing to base a charge on.'

'Haven't I?' Carella said. 'Try this for size. It's from the Code of Criminal Procedure. *A peace officer may, without a warrant, arrest a person when he has reasonable cause for believing that a felony has been committed, and that the person arrested has committed it ...*'

'On the basis of a *sneaker*?' Elliot said.

'*Though it should afterwards appear,*' Carella continued, '*That no felony has been committed, or, if committed, that the person arrested did not commit it.* All right, Elliot, I *know* a felony was committed on the night of April eighteenth, and I *know* an article of clothing belonging to you was found at the scene of the crime, and that's reasonable cause for believing you were there either before or after it happened. Either way, I think I've got justifiable cause for arrest. Would you like to tell me how you sprained your ankle? Or is it a torn Achilles' tendon?'

'It's a sprained ankle.'

'Want to tell me about it? Or shall we save it for the squadroom?'

'I would not like to tell you anything. And if you take me to the squadroom, you'll be forced to advise me of my rights. Once you do that, I'll refuse to answer any questions, and ...'

'We'll worry about that when we get there.'

'You're wasting your time, Carella, and you know it.'

The men stared at each other. There was a faintly superior smirk on Elliot's mouth, a confident challenge in his eyes. Against his better judgment, Carella decided to pick up the gauntlet.

'Your ankle *isn't* sprained,' he said. 'Buenavista Hospital reports having treated you for third-degree burns on April nineteenth, the morning after the murder.'

'I've never been to Buenavista Hospital in my life.'

'Then someone's been using your name around town, Elliot.'

'Maybe so.'

'You want to unwrap that bandage and show me your foot?'

'No.'

'Am I going to need another warrant?'

'Yes. Why don't you just go get yourself one?'

'There were remains of a small fire in one of the rooms ...'

'Go get your warrant. I think we're finished talking.'

'Is that where you had your accident, Elliot? Is that where you burned your foot?'

'I've got nothing more to say to you.'

'Okay, have it your way,' Carella said angrily, and opened the front door. 'I'll be back.'

He slammed the door shut behind him and went out onto the street, no closer to a solution than he had been when he walked into the shop. There were three incontrovertible facts that added up to evidence of a sort, but unfortunately not *enough* evidence for an arrest. The sneaker found in that tenement was unquestionably Elliot's. It had been found in the corner of a room that contained the dead ashes of a recent fire. And Elliot had been treated for burns on April 19, the morning after the murder. Carella had hoped Elliot might be intimidated by these three seemingly related facts, and then either volunteer a confession or blurt out something that would move the investigation onto firmer ground. But Elliot had called the bluff. A charge on the basis of the existing evidence alone would be kicked out of court in three minutes flat. Moreover, Elliot's rights were securely protected: if arrested, he would have to be warned against saying anything self-incriminating, and would undoubtedly refuse to answer any questions without an attorney present. Once a lawyer entered the squadroom, he would most certainly advise Elliot to remain silent, which would take them right back to where they'd started: a charge of murder based on evidence that indicated only possible presence at the scene of a crime.

Carella walked rapidly towards his parked car.

He was certain of only one thing: if Sanford Elliot *really* knew nothing at all about what had happened on the fifth floor of 433 North Harrison on the night of April 18, he would be answering any and all questions willingly and honestly. But he was *not* answering willingly, and he was lying whenever he *did* answer. Which brought Carella to the little lady with the long brown hair, the frightened brown eyes, and the face of an angel – Mary Margaret Ryan, as sweet a young lass as had ever crossed herself in the anonymous darkness of a confessional. Mary Margaret Ryan, bless her soul, had told Carella that she and Elliot had come down from Boston late Monday night. But Elliot's foot had been treated at Buenavista on Monday *morning*. Which meant that Mary Margaret perhaps had something to tell her priest the next time she saw him. In the meantime, seeing as how Mary Margaret was a frightened, slender little wisp of a thing, Carella decided it was worth trying to frighten her a hell of a lot more.

He slammed the door of his car, stuck the key into the ignition switch, and started the engine.

The trouble was, Kling could not stop staring at her.

He had picked up Augusta at six o'clock sharp, and whereas she had warned him about the way she might look after a full day's shooting, she looked nothing less than radiant. Red hair still a bit damp (she confessed to having caught a quick shower in Jerry Bloom's own executive washroom), she came into the reception room to meet Kling, extended her hand to him, and then offered her cheek for a kiss he only belatedly realized was expected. Her cheek was cool and smooth, there was not a trace of makeup on her face except for the pale green shadow on her eyelids, the brownish liner just above her lashes. Her hair was brushed straight back from her forehead, falling to her shoulders without a part. She was wearing blue jeans, sandals, and a ribbed jersey top without a bra. A blue leather bag was slung over her right shoulder, but she shifted it immediately to the shoulder opposite, looped her right hand through his arm, and said, 'Were you waiting long?'

'No, I just got here.'

'Is something wrong?'

'No. What do you mean?'

'The way you're looking at me.'

'No. No, no, everything's fine.'

But he could not stop staring at her. The film they went to see was *Bullitt*, which Kling had seen the first time it played the circuit, but which Augusta was intent on seeing in the presence of a *real* cop. Kling hesitated to tell her that, real cop or not, the first time he'd seen *Bullitt* he hadn't for a moment known what the hell was going on. He had come out of the theatre grateful that he hadn't been the cop assigned to the case, partially because he wouldn't have known where to begin unravelling it, and partially because fast car rides made him dizzy. He didn't know what the movie was about *this* time either, but not because of any devious motivation or complicated plot twists. The simple fact was that he didn't *watch* the picture; he watched Augusta instead. It was dark when they came out into the street. They walked in silence for several moments, and then Augusta said, 'Listen, I think we'd better get something straight right away.

'What's that?' he said, afraid she would tell him she was married, or engaged, or living with a high-priced photographer.

'I *know* I'm beautiful,' she said.

'What?' he said.

'Bert,' she said, 'I'm a model, and I get *paid* for being beautiful. It makes me very nervous to have you staring at me all the time.'

'Okay, I won't ...'

'No, please let me finish ...'

'I thought you *were* finished.'

'No. I want to get this settled.'

'It's settled,' he said. 'Now we *both* know you're beautiful.' He hesitated just an instant, and then added, 'And modest besides.'

'Oh, boy,' she said. 'I'm trying to relate as a goddamn *person*, and you're ...'

'I'm sorry I made you uncomfortable,' he said. 'But the truth is ...'

'Yes, what's the truth?' Augusta said. 'Let's at least *start* with the truth, okay?'

'The truth is I've never in my life been out with a girl as beautiful as you are, that's the truth. And I can't get over it. So I keep staring at you. That's the truth.'

'Well, you'll have to get over it.'

'Why?'

'Because I think you're beautiful, too,' Augusta said, 'and we'd have one hell of a relationship if all we did was sit around and *stare* at each other all the time.'

She stopped dead in the middle of the sidewalk. Kling searched her face, hoping she would recognize that this was not the same as staring.

'I mean,' she said, 'I expect we'll be seeing a lot of each other, and I'd like to think I'm permitted to *sweat* every now and then. I *do* sweat, you know.'

'Yes, I suppose you do,' he said, and smiled.

'Okay?' she said.

'Okay.'

'Let's eat,' she said. 'I'm famished.'

★   ★   ★

It was Detective-Lieutenant Peter Byrnes himself who identified the photostat of the silent silver-screen star. This was only reasonable, since he was the oldest man on the squad.

'This is Vilma Banky,' he said.

'Are you sure?' Meyer asked.

'Positive. I saw her in *The Awakening*, and I also saw her in *Two Lovers* with Ronald Colman.' Byrnes cleared his throat. 'I was, naturally, a very small child at the time.'

'Naturally,' Meyer said.

'Banky,' Hawes said. 'He can't be *that* goddamn corny, can he?'

'What do you mean?' Byrnes said.

'He isn't telling us it's a *bank*, is he?'

'I'll bet he is,' Meyer said. 'Of *course* he is.'

'I'll be damned,' Byrnes said. 'Put it up there on the bulletin board with the rest of them, Meyer. Let's see what else we've got here.' He watched as Meyer tacked the picture to the end of the row. Two of Hoover, two of Washington, two of a Japanese Zero, and now Miss Banky. 'All right, let's dope it out,' Byrnes said.

'It's her last name,' Hawes said. 'Maybe we're supposed to put together all the last names.'

'Yeah,' Meyer said. 'And come up with the name of the bank.'

'Right, right.'

'Hoover Washington Zero Bank,' Byrnes said. 'That's *some* bank.'

'Or maybe the first names,' Hawes suggested.

'John George Japanese Bank,' Byrnes said. 'Even better.'

The men looked at the photostats and then looked at each other.

'Listen, let's not ...'

'Right, right.'

'He's not that smart. If *he* doped it out, *we* can dope it out.'

'Right.'

'So it isn't the last names, and it isn't the first names.'

'So what is it?' Byrnes said.

'I don't know,' Hawes said.

'Anyway, Cotton, he *is* that smart,' Meyer said.

'That's right, he is,' Byrnes said.

The men looked at the photostats again.

'J. Edgar Hoover,' Hawes said.

'Right.'

'Director of the FBI.'

'Right.'

'George Washington.'

'Right, right.'

'Father of the country.'

'Which gives us nothing,' Byrnes said.

'Zero,' Meyer said.

'Exactly,' Byrnes said.

'Let's start from the beginning,' Hawes said. 'The first picture we got was Hoover's, right?'

'Mmm.'

'And then Washington and the Zero,' Meyer said.

'All right, let's associate,' Hawes said.

'What?'

'Let's free-associate. What do you think of when I say Washington?'

'General.'

'President.'

'Martha.'

'Mount Vernon.'

'D.C..'

'State of.'

'Let's take it back. General.'

'Revolution.'

'Valley Forge.'

'Delaware.'

'Cherry tree,' Meyer said.

'Cherry tree?'

'He chopped down a cherry tree, didn't he?'

'How about President? What can we get from that?'

'Chief Executive.'

'Commander in Chief.'

'We're getting no place,' Byrnes said.

'How about Hoover?'

'FBI.'

'Federal Bureau of ...'

'Federal!' Hawes said, and snapped his fingers. 'A *federal* bank!'

'Yes,' Byrnes said, and nodded, and the men fell silent.

'A federal bank in Washington?'

'Then why bother us with it?'

'What about the Zero?'

'Never mind the Zero, let's get back to Washington.'

'No, wait a minute, maybe the Zero's important.'

'How?'

'I don't know.'

'Let's try it. Zero.'

'Nothing.'

'Goose egg.'

'Zip.'

'Zed.'

'Zed?'

'Isn't that what they say in England?'

'For zero? I don't think so.'

'Zero, zero ...'

'Zero, one, two, three, four ...'

'Love,' Meyer said.

'Love?'

'That's zero in a tennis match.'

'Let's get back to Washington.'

'It *has* to be a federal bank in Washington,' Byrnes said.

'Then why send us a picture of Washington himself? If he's trying to identify a *place* ...'

'A bank *is* a place, isn't it?'

'Yes, but wouldn't it have been easier to send a picture of the White House or the Capitol dome or ...'

'Who says he's trying to make it easy?'

'All right, let's see what we've got so far, all right? Federal Washington Zero Bank.'

'Come on, Cotton, that doesn't make any sense at all.'

'I know it doesn't but that's the order they arrived in, so maybe ...'

'Who says there has to be any special order?'

'Bank came last, didn't it?'

'Yes, but ...'

'So that's where I've put it. Last.'

'And Hoover came first,' Meyer said. 'So what?'

'So that's where I've put him.'

'Federal Washington Zero Bank. It still doesn't make sense.'

'Suppose the Zero means nothing at all? Literally zero. Suppose it's just there to be cancelled out?'

'Try it.'

'Federal Washington Bank.'

'That's just what I said,' Byrnes said. 'A federal bank in Washington.'

'If the bank's in Washington, why's he telling us about it?'

'Washington,' Hawes said.

'Here we go again,' Meyer said.

'Washington.'

'President?'

'Federal President Bank?'

'No, no.'

'General?'

'Federal General Bank?'

'Federal *Martha* Bank?'

'What the hell *was* he besides a general and the first President of the United ...'

'*First* Federal Bank,' Meyer said.

'What?'

'First *President*, First goddamn Federal *Bank!*'

'That's it,' Byrnes said.

'That's *got* to be it.'

'First Federal Bank,' Meyer said, grinning.

'Get the phone book,' Byrnes said.

They were all quite naturally proud of the deductive reasoning that had led them to their solution. They now felt they knew the name of the bank as well as the exact date of the planned holdup. Gleefully, they began going through the Yellow Pages, confident that the rest would be simple.

There were twenty-one First Federal Banks in Isola alone, and none of them were located in the 87th Precinct.

There were seventeen First Federal in Calm's Point.

There were nine in Riverhead, twelve in Majesta, and two in Bethtown, for a grand total of sixty-one banks.

It is sometimes not so good to work in a very big city.

Chapter Ten

Sunday.

Take a look at this city.

How can you possibly hate her?

She is composed of five sections as alien to each other as foreign countries with a common border; indeed, many residents of Isola are more familiar with the streets of England or France than they are with those of Bethtown, a stone's throw across the river. Her natives, too, speak dissimilar tongues. It is not uncommon for a Calm's Point accent to sound as unintelligible as the sounds a Welshman makes.

How can you hate this untidy bitch?

She is all walls, true. She flings up buildings like army stockades designed for protection against an Indian population long since cheated and departed. She hides the sky. She blocks her rivers from view. (Never perhaps in the history of mankind has a city so neglected the beauty of her waterways or treated them so casually. Were her rivers lovers, they would surely be unfaithful.) She forces you to catch glimpses of herself in quick takes, through chinks in long canyons, here a wedge of water, there a slice of sky, never a panoramic view, always walls enclosing, constricting, yet how can you hate her, this flirtatious bitch with smoky hair?

'She's noisy and vulgar; there are runs in her nylons, and her heels are round (you can put this lady on her back with a kind word or a knowing leer because she's a sucker for attention, always willing to please, anxious to prove she's at least as good as most). She sings too fucking loud. Her lipstick is smeared across her face like an obscene challenge. She raises her skirt or drops it with equal abandon, she snarls, she belches, she hustles, she farts, she staggers, she falls, she's common, vile, treacherous, dangerous, brittle, vulnerable, stupid, obstinate, clever, and cheap, but it is impossible to hate her because when she steps out of the shower smelling of gasoline and sweat and smoke and grass and wine and flowers and food and dust and death (never mind the high-pollution level), she wears that blatant stink like the most expensive perfume. If you were born in a city, and raised in a city, you know the scent and it makes you dizzy. *Not* the scent of all the half-ass towns, hamlets, and villages that pose as cities and fool no one but their own hick inhabitants. There are half a dozen *real* cities in the world, and this is one of them, and it's impossible to hate her when she comes to you with a suppressed female giggle about to burst on her silly face, bubbling up from some secret adolescent well to erupt in merriment on her unpredictable mouth. (If you can't personalize a city, you have never lived in one. If you can't get romantic and sentimental about her, you're a foreigner still learning the language. Try Philadelphia, you'll love it there.) To know a real city, you've got to hold her close or not at all. You've got to breathe her. Take a look at this city.

How can you possibly hate her?

The Sunday comics have been read and the apartment is still.

The man sitting in the easy chair is black, forty-seven years old, wearing an undershirt, denim trousers, and house slippers. He is a slender man, with brown eyes too large for his face, so that he always looks either frightened or astonished. There is a mild breeze blowing in off the fire escape, where the man's eight-year-old daughter has planted four o'clocks in a cheese box as part of a school project. The balmy feel of the day reminds the man that summer is coming. He frowns. He is suddenly upset, but he does not know quite why. His wife is next door visiting with a neighbour woman, and he feels neglected all at once, and begins wondering why she isn't preparing lunch for him, why she's next door gabbing when he's beginning to get hungry and summer is coming.

He gets out of the easy chair, sees perhaps for the hundredth time that the upholstery is worn in spots, the batting revealed. He sighs heavily. Again; he does not know why he is agitated. He looks down at the linoleum. The pattern has been worn off by the scuffings of years, and he stares at the brownish-red underlay and wonders where the bright colours went. He thinks he will turn on the television set and watch a baseball game, but it is too early yet, the game will not start until later in the day. He does not know what he wants to do with himself. And summer is coming.

He works in a toilet, this man.

He has a little table in a toilet in one of the hotels downtown. There is a white cloth on the table. There is a neat pile of hand towels on the table. There is a comb and a brush on the table. There is a dish in which the man puts four quarters when he begins work, in the hope that the tips he receives from male urinators will be at least as generous. He does not mind the work so much in the winter-time. He waits while his customers urinate, and then he hands them fresh towels, and he brushes off their coats and tries not to appear as if he is waiting for a tip. Most of the men tip him. Some of them do not. He goes home each night with toilet smells in his nostrils, and sometimes he is awakened by the rustling of rats in the empty hours, and the stench is still there, and he goes into the bathroom and puts salt into the palm of his hand and dilutes it with water and sniffs it up into his nose, but the smell will not go away.

In the winter, he does not mind the job too much.

In the summer, in his airless cubicle stinking of the waste of other men, he wonders whether he will spend the rest of his life unfolding towels, extending them to strangers, brushing coats, and waiting hopefully for quarter tips, trying not to look anxious, trying not to show on his face that those quarters are all that stand between him and welfare, all that stand between him and the loss of whatever shred of human dignity he still possesses.

Summer is coming.

He stands bleakly in the middle of the living room and listens to the drip of the water tap in the kitchen.

When his wife comes into the apartment some ten minutes later, he beats her senseless, and then holds her body close to his, and rocks her, keening, keening, rocking her, and still not knowing why he is agitated, or why he has tried to kill the one person on earth he loves.

In the April sunshine four fat men sit at a chess table in the park across the street from the university. All four of the men are wearing dark cardigan sweaters. Two of the men are playing chess, and two of them are kibitzing, but the game has been going on for so many Sundays now that it seems almost as though they are playing four-handed, the players and the kibitzers indistinguishable one from the other.

The white boy who enters the park is seventeen years old. He is grinning happily. He walks with a jaunty stride, and he sucks deep draughts of good spring air into his lungs, and he looks at the girls in their abbreviated skirts, and admires their legs, and feels horny and alive and masculine and strong.

When he comes abreast of the chess table where the old men are in deep concentration, he suddenly whirls and sweeps his hand across the table top, knocking the chessmen to the ground. Grinning, he walks off, and the old men sigh and pick up the pieces and prepare to start the game all over again, though they know the one important move, the crucial move, has been lost to them forever.

The afternoon dawdles.

It is Sunday, the tempo of the city is lackadaisical. Grover Park has been closed to traffic, and cyclists pedal along the winding paths through banks of forsythia and cornelian cherry. A young girl's laughter carries for blocks. How can you possibly hate this city with her open empty streets stretching from horizon to horizon?

They are sitting on opposite sides of the cafeteria table. The younger one is wearing a turtleneck sweater and blue jeans. The older one is wearing a dark blue suit over a white shirt open at the throat, no tie. They are talking in hushed voices.

'I'm sorry,' the one in the suit says. 'But what can I do, huh?'

'Well, yeah, I know,' the younger one answers. 'I thought ... since it's so close, you know?'

'Close, Ralphie, but no cigar.'

'Well, only two bucks short is all, Jay.'

'Two bucks is two bucks.'

'I thought maybe just this once.'

'I'd help you if I could, Ralphie, but I can't.'

'Because I plan to go see my mother tomorrow, you know, and she's always good for a hit.'

'Go see her tonight.'

'Yeah, I would, only she went out to Sands Spit. We got people out there. My father drove her out there this morning.'

'Then go see her tomorrow. And after you see her, you can come see me.'

'Yeah, Jay, but ...' I'm starting to feel sick, you know?'

'That's too bad, Ralphie.'

'Oh, sure, listen, I know it ain't your fault.'

'You *know* it ain't.'

'I know, I know.'

'I'm in business, same as anybody else.'

'Of course you are, Jay. Am I saying you ain't? Am I asking you for freebies? If it wasn't so close, I wouldn't ask you at all.'

'Two dollars ain't close.'

'Maybe for strangers it ain't, Jay. But we know each other a long time, ain't that true?'

'That's true.'

'I'm a good customer, Jay. You know that.'

'I know that.'

'You carry me till tomorrow, Jay ...'

'I can't, Ralphie. I just can't do it. If I did it for you, I'd have to do it for everybody on the street.'

'Who'd know? I wouldn't tell a soul. I swear to God.'

'Word gets around. Ralphie, you're a nice guy, I mean that from the bottom of my heart. But I can't help you. If I knew you didn't have the bread, I wouldn't even have come to meet you. I mean it.'

'Yeah, but it's only two bucks.'

'Two bucks here, two bucks there, it adds up. Who takes the risks, Ralphie, you or me?'

'Well, you, sure. But ...'

'So now you're asking me to lay the stuff on you free.'

'I'm *not*. I'm asking you to carry me till tomorrow when I get the bread from my old lady. That's all.'

'I'm sorry.'

'Jay? Jay, listen, have I ever asked you before? Have I ever once come to you and *not* had the bread? Tell the truth.'

'No, that's true.'

'Have I ever complained when I got stuck with shit that wasn't ...'

'Now wait a minute, you never got no bad stuff from me. Are you trying to say I laid bad stuff on you?'

'No, no. Who said that?'

'I thought that's what you said.'

'No, no.'

'Then what did you say?'

'I meant when the stuff was bad all *over* the city. When the heat was on. Last June. You remember last June? When it was so hard to get anything halfway decent? That's what I meant.'

'Yeah, I remember last June.'

'I'm saying I never complained. When things were bad, I mean. I never complained.'

'So?'

'So help me out this once, Jay, and ...'

'I can't, Ralphie.'

'Jay? Please.'

'I can't.'

'Jay?'

'No, Ralphie. Don't ask me.'

'I'll get the money tomorrow, I swear to God.'

'No.'
'I'll see my mother tomorrow ...'
'No.'
'And get the money for you. Okay? What do you say, huh?'
'I got to split, Ralphie. You go see your mother ...'
'Jay, please. Jay, I'm sick, I mean it. Please.'
'See your mother, get the money ...'
'Jay, please!'
'And *then* talk to me, okay?'
'Jay!'
'So long, Ralphie.'

Dusk moves rapidly over the city, spreading through the sky above Calm's Point to fill with guttering purple the crevices between chimney pot and spire. Flickers of yellow appear in window slits, neon tubes burst into oranges and blues, race around the shadowed sides of buildings to swallow their sputtering tails. Traffic signals blink in fiercer reds and brighter greens, emboldened by the swift descent of darkness. Colour claims the night. It is impossible to hate this glittering nest of gems.

The patrolman does not know what to do.

The woman is hysterical, and she is bleeding from a cut over her left eye, and he does not know whether he should first call an ambulance or first go upstairs to arrest the man who hit her. The sergeant solves his dilemma, fortuitously arriving in a prowl car, and getting out, and coming over to where the woman is babbling and the patrolman is listening with a puzzled expression on his face.

The person who hit her is her husband, the woman says. But she does not want to press charges. That's not what she wants from the police.

The sergeant knows an assault when he sees one and is not particularly interested in whether or not the woman wants to press charges. But it is a nice Sunday night in April, and he would much rather stand here on the sidewalk and listen to the woman (who is not bad-looking, and who is wearing a nylon wrapper over nothing but bikini panties) than go upstairs to arrest whoever clobbered her over the eye.

The woman is upset because her husband has said he is going to kill himself. He hit her over the eye with a milk bottle and then he locked himself in the bathroom and started running the water in the tub and yelling that he was going to kill himself. The woman does not want him to kill himself because she loves him. That's why she ran down into the street, practically naked, to find the nearest cop. So he could stop her husband from killing himself.

The sergeant is somewhat bored. He keeps assuring the woman that anybody who's going to kill himself doesn't go around advertising it, he just goes right ahead and *does* it. But the woman is hysterical and still bleeding, and the sergeant feels he ought to set a proper example for the young patrolman. 'Come on, kid,' he says, and the two of them start into the tenement building while the patrolman at the wheel of the r.m.p. car radios in for a meat wagon. The lady sits weakly on the fender of the car. She has just begun to notice that she is pouring blood from the open cut over her eyes, and has gone very pale. The patrolman at the wheel thinks she is going to faint, but he does not get out of the car.

On the third floor of the building (Apartment 31, the lady told them), the sergeant knocks briskly on the closed door, waits, listens, knocks again, and then turns to the patrolman and again says, 'Come on, kid.' The door is unlocked. The apartment is still save for the sound of running water in the bathroom.

'Anybody home?' the sergeant calls. There is no answer. He shrugs, makes a 'Come on, kid' gesture with his head, and starts for the closed bathroom door. He is reaching for the knob when the door opens.

The man is naked.

He has climbed out of the tub where the water still runs, and his pale white body is glistening wet. The water in the tub behind him is red. He has slashed the arteries of his left wrist, and he is gushing blood onto the white tile floor while behind him water splashes into the tub. He holds a broken milk bottle in his right hand, presumably the same bottle with which he struck his wife, and the moment he throws open the bathroom door he swings the bottle at the sergeant's head. The sergeant is concerned about several things, and only one of them has to do with the possibility that he may be killed in the next few moments. He is concerned about grappling with a naked man, he is concerned about getting blood on his new uniform, he is concerned about putting on a good show for the patrolman.

The man is screaming, 'Leave me alone, let me die,' and lunging repeatedly at the sergeant with the jagged ends of the broken bottle. The sergeant, fat and puffing, is trying desperately to avoid each new lunge, trying to grab the man's arm, trying to stay out of the way of those pointed glass shards, trying to draw his revolver, trying to do all these things while the man keeps screaming and thrashing and thrusting the bottle at his face and neck.

There is a sudden shocking explosion. The bleeding man lets out a final scream and drops the bottle. It shatters on the tile, and the sergeant watches in bug-eyed fascination as the man keels over backwards and falls into the red-stained water in the tub. The sergeant wipes sweat from his lip and turns to look at the patrolman, whose smoking service revolver is in his hand. The patrolman's eyes are squinched in pain. He keeps staring at the tub where the man has sunk beneath the surface of the red water.

'Nice going, kid,' the sergeant says.

The city is asleep.

The streets lamps are all that glow now, casting pale illumination over miles and miles of deserted sidewalks. In the apartment buildings the windows are dark save for an occasional bathroom, where a light flickers briefly and then dies. Everything is still. So still.

Take a look at this city.

How can you possibly hate her?

Chapter Eleven

He had been searching for Mary Margaret Ryan without success since Saturday afternoon. He had tried the apartment on Porter Street, where she said she was living, but Henry and Bob told him she hadn't been around, and they had no idea where she was. He had then tried all the neighbourhood places she might have frequented, and had even staked out Elliot's shop, on the off chance she might go there to see him. But she had not put in an appearance.

Now, at ten o'clock on Monday morning, April 26, four days before the Deaf Man had promised to steal $500,000 from the First Federal Bank (though God knew which one), Carella roamed Rutland Street looking for a silver motorcycle. During their brief conversation last Tuesday, Yank had told Carella that he'd blown in a few weeks back and was living in an apartment on Rutland. He had not given the address but Carella didn't think he'd have too much trouble finding the place – it is almost impossible to hide something as large as a motorcycle. He did not honestly expect Yank or his friends to know anything about the whereabouts of Mary Margaret Ryan; she hardly seemed the kind of girl who'd run with a motorcycle gang. But Yank and a bikie named Ox had been in Elliot's shop the day before, and the argument Carella had witnessed through the plate-glass window seemed something more than casual. When you run out of places to look, you'll look anywhere. Mary Margaret Ryan had to be someplace; *everybody's* got to be someplace, man.

After fifteen minutes on the block, he located *three* bikes chained to the metal post of a banister in the downstairs hallway of 601 Rutland. He knocked on the door of the sole apartment on the ground floor, and asked the man who answered it where the bikies were living.

'You going to bust them?' the man asked.

'What apartment are they in?'

'Second-floor front,' the man said. 'I wish you'd clean them out of here.'

'Why?'

'Because they're no damn good,' the man said, and closed the door.

Carella went up to the second floor. Several brown bags of garbage were leaning against the wall. He listened outside the door, heard voices inside, and knocked. A blond man, naked to the waist, opened the door. He was powerful and huge, with hard, tight muscles developed by years of weight-lifting. Barefooted, with blue jeans stretched tight over bulging thighs, he looked out at Carella and said nothing.

'Police officer,' Carella said. 'I'm looking for some people named Ox and Yank.'

'Why?' the blond said.

'Couple of questions I want to ask them.'

The blond studied him, shrugged, said, 'Okay,' and led him into the apartment. Ox and Yank were sitting at a table in the kitchen, drinking beer.

'Well, well,' Yank said.

'Who's this?' Ox asked.

'A gentleman from the police,' Yank said, and added with mock formality, 'I fear I've forgotten your name, officer.'

'Detective Carella.'

'Carella, Carella, right. What can we do for you, Detective Carella?'

'Have you seen Mary Margaret around?' Carella asked.

'Who?'

'Mary Margaret Ryan.'

'Don't know her,' Yank said.

'How about you?' Carella said.

'Nope,' Ox answered.

'Me, neither,' the blond said.

'Girl about this high,' Carella said, 'long brown hair, brown eyes.'

'Nope,' Yank said.

'Reason I ask ...'

'We don't know her,' Yank said.

'Reason I ask,' Carella repeated, 'is that she poses for Sanford Elliot, and ...'

'Don't know him either,' Yank said.

'You don't, huh?'

'Nope.'

'None of you know him, huh?'

'None of us,' Yank said.

'Have you had any second thoughts about that picture I showed you?'

'Nope, no second thoughts,' Yank said. 'Sorry.'

'You want to take a look at this picture, Ox?'

'What picture?' Ox asked.

'This one,' Carella said, and took the photograph from his notebook. He handed it to Ox, looking into his face, looking into his eyes, and becoming suddenly unsettled by what he saw there. Through the plate-glass window of Elliot's shop, Ox had somehow appeared both intelligent and articulate, perhaps because he had been delivering a finger-waving harangue. But now, after having heard his voice, after having seen his eyes, Carella knew at once that he was dealing with someone only slightly more alert than a beast of the field. The discovery was frightening. Give me the smart ones anytime, Carella thought. I'll take a thousand like the Deaf Man if you'll only keep the stupid ones away from me.

'Recognize him?' he asked.

'No,' Ox said, and tossed the photograph onto the table.

'I was talking to Sanford Elliot Saturday,' Carella said. 'I thought *he* might be able to help me with this picture.' He picked it up, put it back into his notebook, and waited. Neither Ox nor Yank said a word. 'You say you don't know him, huh?'

'*What* was the name?' Ox said.

'Sanford Elliot. His friends call him Sandy.'

'Never heard of him,' Ox said.

'Uh-huh,' Carella said. He looked around the room. 'Nice place, is it yours?' he asked the bare-chested, bare-footed blond man.

'Yeah.'

'What's your name?'

'Who says I have to tell you?'

'That garbage stacked in the hallway is a violation,' Carella said flatly. 'You want me to get snotty, or you want to tell me your name?'

'Willie Harcourt.'

'How long have you been living here, Willie?'

'About a year.'

'When did your friends arrive?'

'I told you ...' Yank started.

'I'm asking your pal. When did they get here, Willie?'

'Few weeks ago.'

Carella turned to Ox and said, 'What's your beef with Sandy Elliot?'

'What?' Ox said.

'Sandy Elliot.'

'We told you we don't know him,' Yank said.

'You've got a habit of answering questions nobody asked you,' Carella said. 'I'm talking to your friend here. What's the beef, Ox? You want to tell me?'

'No beef,' Ox said.

'Then why were you yelling at him?'

'Me? You're crazy.'

'You were in his shop Saturday, and you were yelling at him. Why?'

'You must have me mixed up with somebody else,' Ox said, and lifted his beer bottle and drank.

'Who else lives in this apartment?' Carella asked.

'Just the three of us,' Willie said.

'Those your bikes downstairs?'

'Yes,' Yank said quickly.

'Pal,' Carella said, 'I'm going to tell you one last time ...'

'Yeah, *what* are you going to tell me?' Yank asked, and rose from the table and put his hands on his hips.

'You're a big boy, I'm impressed,' Carella said, and, without another word, drew his gun. 'This is a .38 Detective's Special,' he said. 'It carries six cartridges, and I'm a great shot. I don't intend tangling with three gorillas. Sit down and be nice, or I'll shoot you in the foot and say you were attempting to assault a police officer.'

Yank blinked.

'Hurry up,' Carella said.

Yank hesitated only a moment longer, and then sat at the table again.

'Very nice,' Carella said. He did not holster the pistol. He kept it in his hand, with his finger inside the trigger guard. 'The silver bike is yours, isn't it?' he asked.

'Yeah.'

'Which one is yours, Ox?'

'The black.'

'How about you?' he said, turning to Willie.

'The red one.'

'They all properly registered?'

'Come on,' Yank said, 'you're not going to hang any bullshit violation on us.'

'Unless I decide to lean on you about the garbage outside.'

'Why you doing this?' Ox asked suddenly.

'Doing what, Ox?'

'Hassling us this way? What the hell did we do?'

'You lied about being in Elliot's shop Saturday, that's what you did.'

'Big deal. Okay, we were there. So what?'

'What were you arguing about?'

'The price of a statue,' Ox said.

'It didn't look that way.'

'That's all it was,' Ox said. 'We were arguing about a price.'

'What'd you decide?'

'Huh?'

'What price did you agree on?'

'We didn't.'

'How well do you know Elliot?'

'Don't know him at all. We saw his stuff in the window, and we went in to ask about it.'

'What about Mary Margaret Ryan?'

'Never heard of her.'

'Okay,' Carella said. He went to the door, opened it, and said, 'If you were planning to leave suddenly for the Coast, I'd advise against it. I'd also advise you to get that garbage out of the hallway.' He opened the door, stepped outside, closed the door behind him, and went down the steps. He did not return the gun to its holster until he was on the ground floor again. He knocked on the door at the end of the hall there, and the same man answered it.

'Did you bust them?' the man asked.

'No. Mind if I come in a minute?'

'You should have busted them,' the man said, but he stepped aside and allowed Carella to enter the apartment. He was a man in his fifties, wearing dark trousers, house slippers, and an undershirt with shoulder straps. 'I'm the superintendent here,' he said.

'What's your name, sir?' Carella asked.

'Andrew Halloran,' the super said. 'And yours?'

'Detective Carella.'

'Why didn't you bust them, Detective Carella? They give me a hell of a lot of trouble, I wish you would have busted them for something.'

'Who's paying for the apartment, Mr Halloran?'

'The one with all the muscles. His name's William Harcourt. They call him Willie. But he's never there alone. They come and go all the time. Sometimes a dozen of them are living in there at the same time, men and women, makes no difference. They get drunk, they take dope, they yell, they fight with each other and with anybody tries to say a decent word to them. They're no damn good, is all.'

'Would you know the full names of the other two?'

'Which two is that?' Halloran asked.

'Ox and Yank.'

'I get mixed up,' Halloran said. 'Three of them came in from California a few weeks back, and I sometimes have trouble telling them apart. I think the two up there with Willie ...'

'*Three* of them, did you say?' Carella asked, and suddenly remembered that Yank had given him this same information last Tuesday, when he'd been sitting outside the candy store with his chair tilted back against the brick wall. '*Three of us blew in from the Coast a few weeks back.*'

'Yeah, three of them, all right. Raising all kinds of hell, too.'

'Can you describe them to me?'

'Sure. One of them's short and squat, built like an ape with the mind of one besides.'

'That'd be Ox.'

'Second one's got frizzy hair and a thick black beard, scar over his right eye.'

'Yank. And the third one?'

'Tall fellow with dark hair and a handlebar moustache. Nicest of the lot, matter of fact. I haven't seen him around for a while. Not since last week sometime. I don't think he's left for good, though, because his bike's still here in the hall.'

'Which bike?'

'The red one.'

'I thought that belonged to Willie.'

'Willie? Hell, he's lucky if he can afford roller skates.'

Carella took the notebook from his jacket pocket, removed the photograph from it, and asked, 'Is this the third bikie?'

'That's Adam, all right,' Halloran said.

'Adam *what*?' Carella said.

'Adam Villers.'

He called the squadroom from a pay phone in the corner drugstore, told Meyer he'd had a positive identification of the dead boy in the Jesus Case, and asked him to run a routine I.S. check on Adam Villers, V-I-L-L-E-R-S. He then asked if there had been any calls for him.

'Yeah,' Meyer said. 'Your sister called and said not to forget Wednesday is your father's birthday and to mail him a card.'

'Right. Anything else?'

'Kling wants to know if you feel like taking your wife to a strip joint in Calm's Point.'

'What?'

'He's tailing a guy on those burglaries, and the guy knows what he looks like, and Cotton was spotted for a cop first crack out of the box.'

'Tell Kling I've got nothing better to do right now than take Teddy to a strip joint in Calm's Point. Jesus!'

'Don't get sore at *me*, Steve.'

'Any other calls?'

'Did you have a mugging on Ainsley back in March? Woman named Charity Miles?'

'Yes.'

'The Eight-eight just cracked it. Guy's admitted to every crime of the past century, including the Brink's Robbery.'
'Good, that's one less to worry about. Anything else?'
'Nothing.'
'Any mail?'
'Another picture from our Secret Pen Pal.'
'Who'd he send this time?'
'Who do you think?' Meyer said.

He did not find Mary Margaret Ryan until close to midnight. It had begun drizzling at 11:45 p.m., by which time he had tried the apartment on Porter again, as well as all the neighbourhood hangouts, and was ready to give up and go home. He recognized her coming out of a doorway on Hager. She was wearing an army poncho, World War II salvage stuff, camouflaged for jungle warfare. She walked swiftly and purposefully, and he figured she was heading back for the apartment, not two blocks away. He caught up with her on the corner of Hager and McKay.
'Mary Margaret,' he said, and she turned abruptly, her eyes as wide and frightened as they had been that first day he'd talked to her.
'What do you want?' she said.
'Where are you going?' he asked.
'Home,' she said. 'Excuse me, I ...'
'Few things I'd like to ask you.'
'No,' she said, and began walking up McKay.
He caught her elbow and turned her to face him, and looked down into her eyes and said, 'What are you afraid of, Mary Margaret?'
'Nothing, leave me alone. I have to get home.'
'Why?'
'Because ... I'm packing. I'm getting out of here. Look,' she said, plaintively, 'I finally got the money I need, and I'm splitting, so leave me alone, okay? Let me just get the fuck *out* of here.'
'Why?'
'I've had this city.'
'Where are you going?'
'To Denver. I hear the scene's good there. *Anything's* better than here.'
'Who gave you the money?'
'A girl friend. She's a waitress at the Yellow Bagel. She makes good money. It's only a loan, I'll pay her back. Look, I got to catch a plane, okay? I got to go now. I don't like it here. I don't like anything *about* this city. I don't like the look of it, I don't like the people, I don't like ...'
'Where've you been hiding?'
'I *haven't* been hiding. I was busy trying to raise some bread, that's all. I had to talk to a lot of people.'
'You were *hiding*, Mary Margaret. Who from?'
'Nobody.'
'Who the hell are you *running* from?'
'Nobody, nobody.'
'What was Sandy doing in that abandoned building on the eighteenth?'
'I don't know what you mean.'
'Were *you* there, too?'

'No.'

'*Where* were you?'

'I told you. In Boston. We were both in Boston.'

'*Where* in Boston?'

'I don't know.'

'How'd Sandy burn his foot?'

'Burn? It's not burned, it's ...'

'It's *burned*. How'd it happen?'

'I don't know. Please, I have to ...'

'Who killed Adam Villers?'

'Adam? How ... how do you ...?'

'I know his name, and I know when he got here, and I know his friends have been to see Sandy. Now how about it, Mary Margaret?'

'Please, please ...'

'Are you going to tell me what happened, or ...?'

'Oh my God, oh my God,' she said, and suddenly covered her face with her hands and began sobbing. They stood in the rain, Mary Margaret weeping into her hands, Carella watching her for only a moment before he said, 'You'd better come with me.'

The three of them had only arrived a few days before, and still hadn't caught up with their friend, the blond one with the muscles, I don't know his name. So they were flopping in the building on Harrison when they first made contact with Sandy. It was Adam Villers who came into the shop. He was a decent person, Adam. There's nothing that says bikies can't be decent. He was honestly trying to set something up. And it cost him his life.

What he did was he came into the shop to tell Sandy how much he liked his work. He's a good artist, you know, a really good one, well, you saw his stuff, you know how good he is. But he just wasn't <u>selling</u> much, and it costs a lot to cast those things in bronze, and he was running low on bread, which is why Adam's idea sounded like such a good one. Adam said the guys he ran with could pack the stuff in their bike bags, and try to sell it, you know, like wherever they traveled. He said they couldn't pay what Sandy was asking in the shop, but they'd take a <u>lot</u> of it, you see, and he could make it up in volume. So Sandy agreed to go up there—to where they were living on Harrison—and talk price with them, to see if it would be worth it to him. Adam really thought . . . I mean, Adam had no idea what the other two were after. You

read a lot about bikies, and you get all these
ideas about them, but Adam was okay. He really
dug the work Sandy was doing, and figured we could
all make a little money out of it. That's why he
took us there that night.

They were living in two rooms on the fifth floor.
One of the rooms had a mattress in it. In the other
room, they had built a small fire in the center of
the floor. The one called Yank was trying to fix
something from his bike when we came in. I don't
know what it was, something that had fallen off
his bike. He was trying to hammer a dent out of it.
Anyway, we all sat around the fire, and Sandy offered them some grass, and we smoked a little
while Adam explained his idea about buying Sandy's
work at discount and selling it on the road, which
he figured would pay for all their traveling expenses. The one called Ox said that he had looked
over the stuff in the shop window the other day
and thought the girl was very sexy.

I think that was when I first began to get scared.

But . . . anyway, we . . . we went on talking
about how much the sculpture was worth. Adam was
still very excited about the whole thing, and trying to figure out how much Sandy should get for
pieces that were this big or that big, you know,
trying to work out a legitimate business deal. I
mean, that's why we'd gone up there. Because it
looked like a good way to make a little bread. So
all of a sudden Ox said How much do you want for
the girl?

We were all, I guess, I mean, surprised, you
know? Because it came out of the blue, like, when
we were talking about Sandy's work and all, and
we just sat there sort of stunned and Ox said You
hear me? How much you want for the girl?

What girl? Sandy said.

This one, Ox said, and reached over and . . . and
poked my breast, poked his finger at my breast.

Hey, come on, Adam said, knock it off, Ox, we're
here to talk about the guy's work, okay?

And Ox said I'd rather talk about the guy's girl.

Sandy got up and said Come on, Mary Margaret,

let's get out of here, and that was when Ox hit
him and it all started. I screamed, I guess, and
Ox hit me, too, hard, he punched me in the ribs,
it still hurts where he hit me. They . . . Adam
started to yell at them, and Yank grabbed him
from behind and held his arms while Ox . . . Ox
dragged Sandy over to the fire and pulled off his
sneaker and stuck his foot in the flames, and
told him next time they asked a question about the
price of something he should answer nice instead
of being such a wise guy. Sandy passed out, and I
began screaming again because . . . Sandy was
. . . his foot was all black and . . . and Ox hit
me again and threw me on the floor and that was
when Adam broke away from Yank, to try to help
me. They both turned on him. Like animals. Like
sharks. Like attacking their own, do you know?
In frenzy, do you know? They went after him, they
chased him down the hallway, they . . . I heard
sounds like . . . hammering, I knew later it was
hammering, and I heard Adam screaming, and I ran
down the hall and saw what they had done and
fainted. I don't know what they did to me while I
was unconscious. I was . . . I was bleeding bad
when I woke up . . . but they were gone, thank God,
they were gone at last.

I didn't know what to do. Sandy could hardly
walk and there . . . there was a dead man down the
hall, Adam was dead down the hall. I . . . put
Sandy's arm over my shoulder, and we started down
the steps, all I could think of was getting away
from there. Have you seen that place? The steps
are covered with all kinds of crap, it's like
walking through a junkyard. But I got him down to
the street, he was in such pain, oh God, he kept
moaning, and we couldn't find a taxi, there are
never any taxis in this neighborhood. But finally
we got one, and I took him over to the clinic at
Buenavista Hospital, and they treated his foot,
and we hoped it was all over, we hoped we'd seen
the last of them.

They came back to the shop the next day. They
said we'd better keep our mouths shut about what

```
happened or the same thing would happen to us. We
made up the story about Boston, we knew the police
might get to us, we figured we needed an alibi.
And . . . we've been waiting for them to leave,
praying they'd go back to California, leave us
alone, get out of our lives.
Now they'll kill us, won't they?
```

He was not foolish enough to go after them alone.

The three bikes were still chained to the metal hall banister, silver, red, and black. He and Meyer went past them swiftly and silently, guns drawn, and climbed to the second floor. They fanned out on both sides of the door to Apartment 2A and then, facing each other, put their ears to the door and listened.

'How many?' Carella whispered.

'I can make out at least four,' Meyer whispered back.

'You ready?'

'Ready as I'll ever be.'

The worst part about kicking in a door is that you never know what might be on the other side of it. You can listen for an hour, you can distinguish two different voices, or five, or eight, and then break in to find an army with sawed-off shotguns, determined to blow you down the stairs and out into the gutter. Meyer had heard four distinctly different voices, which was exactly what Carella thought he had heard. They were all men's voices, and he thought he recognized two of them as belonging to Ox and Yank. He did not think the bikies would be armed, but he had no way of knowing whether his supposition was true or not. There was nothing to do but go in after them. There was nothing to do but take them.

Carella nodded at Meyer, and Meyer returned the nod.

Backing across the hall, gun clutched in his right hand, Carella braced himself against the opposite wall, and then shoved himself off it, right knee coming up, and hit the door with a hard flat-footed kick just below the lock. The door sprang inwards, followed by Carella at a run, Meyer behind him and to the left. Ox and Willie were sitting at the kitchen table, drinking wine. Yank was standing near the refrigerator, talking to a muscular black man.

Ox threw back his chair, and a switchblade knife snapped open in his hand. He was coming at Carella with the knife clutched tight in his fist when Carella fired. The first slug had no effect on him. Like a rampaging elephant, he continued his charge, and Carella fired again, and then once more, and still Ox came, finally hurling himself onto Carella, the knife blade grazing his face and neck as he pulled off another shot, the muzzle of the gun pushed hard into Ox's belly. There was a muffled explosion. The slug knocked Ox backwards onto the kitchen table. He twisted over onto his side, bubbling blood, and then rolled to the floor.

Nobody was moving.

Yank, at the refrigerator with the muscular black man, seemed ready to make a break. The look was in his eyes, the trapped look of a man who knows it's all over, there's nothing to lose, stay or run, there's nothing to lose.

Meyer recognized the look because he had seen it a hundred times before. He did not know who any of these men were, but he knew that Yank was the one about to break, and was therefore extremely dangerous.

He swung the gun on him.

'Don't,' he said.

That's all he said.

The gun was steady in his hand, levelled at Yank's heart. A new look came into Yank's eyes, replacing the trapped and desperate glitter that had been in them not a moment before. Meyer had seen this look, too; there was nothing new under the sun. It was a look composed of guilt, surrender, and relief. He knew now that Yank would stay right where he was until the cuffs were closed on his wrists. There would be no further trouble.

Willie Harcourt sat at the kitchen table with his eyes wide in terror. Ox was at his feet, dead and bleeding, and Willie had urinated in his pants when the shooting began. He was afraid to move now because he thought they might shoot him, too; he was also ashamed to move because if he did they would see he had wet himself.

'Is there a phone in here?' Carella asked.

'N-n-no,' Willie stammered.

'What's *your* name, mister?' Carella asked the black man.

'Frankie Childs. I don't know these guys from a hole in the wall. I came up for a little wine, that's all.'

'You're bleeding, Steve,' Meyer said.

Carella touched his handkerchief to his face.

'Yeah,' he said, and tried to catch his breath.

Chapter Twelve

The boys were beginning to enjoy themselves.

After all, if there had to be bank robberies (and in their line of work, there most certainly had to be bank robberies), they preferred dealing with a criminal who at least *tried* to make it all a little more interesting. For where indeed was there any joy in coping with some jerk whose idea of a brilliant holdup was to walk in and stick a gun in a person's face? The boys had to admit it – the Deaf Man brought a spot of needed cheer to that dingy old squadroom.

'Who do you suppose it is?' Byrnes asked.

Hawes looked at the photostat, which had arrived in Tuesday morning's mail, and then said, 'He looks a lot like Meyer.'

'Except Meyer hasn't got as much hair.'

'I fail to see the humour,' Meyer said, and then studied the picture more carefully. 'Now that you mention it, he does resemble my Uncle Morris in New Jersey.'

'You think he's an actor?' Hawes asked.

'My Uncle Morris? He's a haberdasher.'

'I mean this guy.'

'I doubt it,' Byrnes said. 'He looks too intelligent.'

'He might be an actor, though,' Meyer said. 'Somebody out of *Great Expectations*.'

'He does look English.'

'Or *Bleak House*,' Meyer said.

'He looks like an English lawyer,' Hawes said.

'Maybe he's Charles Dickens himself,' Meyer said.

'Maybe. English lawyers and English writers all look alike.'

'Maybe he's a famous English murderer.'

'Or a famous English sex fiend.'

'*All* the English are famous sex fiends.'

'He *does* look very sexy,' Byrnes said.

'It's the hair. It's the way he's got the hair teased.'

'I like his tie, too.'

'His cravat.'

'Yes, but also his tie.'

'Who the hell is he?' Byrnes asked.

'Who the hell knows?' Meyer said.

The Deaf Man held out the slate and asked, 'Do you understand all of it so far?'

'Yes,' Harold said. 'I go into the vault with the bank manager ...'

'His name is Alton.'

'Right. I clean out the place, and then take him back to the office.'

'Meanwhile,' Roger said, 'Danny and me are in the car, right outside the teller's window.'

'And you, Florence?'

'I'm in my stalled car at the head of the driveway.'

'In the manager's office,' Harold said, 'I clobber him and tie him up.'

'I'm out of the car by then,' Danny said, 'busting the window.'

'I run out of the manager's office, go through the gate, and jump out the broken window.'

'I help him climb through.'

'We both get in the car ...'

'I step on the gas,' Roger said.

'I pick you up, Mr Taubman, at the front of the bank,' Florence said.

'And we're off and running.'

'Perfect,' the Deaf Man said. 'Any questions?'

'Do we come straight back here, or what?'

'No. I've already reserved rooms for all of us at the Allister.'

'Why there?'

'Why not?'

'Why not right here at the Remington?'

'This is a flea bag. I chose it for our meetings only because it's inconspicuous.'

'That's just my point. The Allister's right in the middle of everything.'

'Exactly. You, Roger, and Danny are three respectable businessmen checking into one of the biggest hotels in the city. Florence and I are man and wife arriving from Los Angeles. We'll meet in Roger's room at three o'clock, and share the money at that time. On Saturday morning, we'll all check out and go our separate ways.'

'Five hundred thousand bucks,' Harold said, and whistled softly.

'Give or take a few thousand,' the Deaf Man said. 'Any other questions?'

'The only part that bother me is the double cross,' Roger said.

'Let *me* worry about that,' the Deaf Man said. 'All *you* have to worry about is doing your part. I rather imagine a hundred thousand dollars will ease your conscience considerably.'

'Still . . .'

'I don't want second thoughts about this, Roger. If you're not with us, say so now. We won't be going through the dry run until Thursday, and I won't reveal the location of the bank until then. You're free to go. Just have the decency to do it now, while I can still find a replacement.'

'I guess I'm in,' Roger said.

'No guesswork, Roger. Yes or no?'

'Yes.'

'Good. Does the duplicity bother anyone else?'

'I only worry about number one,' Danny said.

'I never met a man I could trust,' Florence said, 'and I don't expect nobody to trust me, either.'

'How about you, Harold?'

'I want that hundred thousand dollars,' Harold said simply.

'Then I take it we're all committed,' the Deaf Man said.

Patrolman Mike Ingersoll came into the squadroom at four o'clock that afternoon. He had been relieved on post fifteen minutes ago, and had already changed into street attire – brown trousers and tan sports shirt, a poplin, zippered jacket. Kling was sitting at his desk with Mrs Ungerman, showing her mug shots in the hope she might be able to identify the man with whom she had briefly waltzed last Thursday night. He motioned to Ingersoll to come in, and Ingersoll motioned back that if Kling was busy, and Kling motioned back, No, that's okay – and all the pantomime caused Mrs Ungerman to turn curiously towards the railing.

'Hello, Mrs Ungerman,' Ingersoll said, and smiled pleasantly.

Mrs Ungerman looked at him in puzzlement.

'Patrolman Ingersoll,' he said.

'Oh,' she said. 'Oh, of course. I didn't recognize you without the uniform.'

'I'll just be a minute, Mike,' Kling said.

'Sure, sure, take your time,' Ingersoll said, and wandered over to the bulletin board and studied the Deaf Man's art gallery. He knew nothing about the case, and thought the photostats were some kind of little joke the detectives were playing up here in the rarefied atmosphere on the second floor of the building. At Kling's desk Mrs Ungerman kept looking at photographs of known burglars and shaking her head. At last she rose, and Kling thanked her for her time. She waved at Ingersoll, said, 'Nice seeing you,' and went out of the squadroom.

'Any help? Ingersoll said, coming over to the desk.

'None at all.'

Ingersoll pulled up a chair and sat. 'Have you got a minute?' he asked.

'Don't tell me we've had another burglary.'

'No, no,' Ingersoll said, and knocked the desk with his knuckles. 'Been very quiet this week, thank God. This is what I want to talk to you about.' Ingersoll paused, and then shifted his weight and leaned closer to Kling, lowering his voice, as if he did not want his words to be overheard even within the sanctified walls of a detective squadroom. 'How would you like to set a trap for our heist artist?' he said.

'Stick a man in one of the empty apartments, you mean?'

'Yeah.'

'I thought of that, Mike, but I'm not sure it'd work.'

'Why not?'

'If these are inside jobs, the guy's probably watching all the time, don't you think? He'll know we've got a stakeout going.'

'Maybe not. Besides, we're up a dead-end street right now. Anything's worth a chance.'

'Well, I've got a lead, you know. Let's see what happens there before we go spending the night ...'

'What kind of lead, Bert?' Ingersoll said, and took out his notebook. 'Anything I should know?'

'The guy dropped a ballpoint pen in the Blair apartment.'

'Pretty girl,' Ingersoll said.

'Yeah,' Kling said, and hoped he sounded noncommittal. 'Anyway, I tracked it to an ex-con named Fred Lipton, two previous convictions.'

'For Burglary?'

'No, Dis Cond and Forgery One.'

'He live around here?'

'Calm's Point.'

'Whereabouts? *I* live in Calm's Point, you know.'

'He works for a real estate agency on Ashmead Avenue, and lives in a garden apartment on Ninety-eighth and Aurora.'

'That's not too far from me,' Ingersoll said. 'Anything I can do for you out there?'

'You look too much like a cop,' Kling said, and smiled.

'What do you mean?'

'Lipton's friendly with a dancer at a joint called the Gee-Gee-Go-Go.'

'Yeah, I know the place, it's a real dive.'

'Hawes tried to pump the girl the other night, but she made him for a cop right off.'

'Well, he *does* look kind of like a cop,' Ingersoll said, and nodded. 'You sure you don't want me to take a whack at it?'

'I thought I'd ask Willis.'

'Yeah, he'd be perfect,' Ingersoll said. 'But meanwhile, can't we set something up right here? In case you *don't* get anything on Lipton?'

'I really think it'd be a waste of time, Mike.'

'The Ungerman hit was the last one, am I right? That was five days ago, Bert. It's not like this guy to stay inactive for such a long time.'

'Maybe he's cooling it because the old lady got a look at him.'

'What's that got to do with it? He wouldn't go back to the same apartment twice, would he?'

'No, that's right.'

'The way I figure it, Bert, he's trying to knock off as many places as he can while people are still taking winter vacations.'

'I don't get you, Mike.'

'Look at the M.O., Bert. A dozen places in February and March, and three more in the last ... how long has it been? Two weeks?'

'About that, yeah.'

'Okay, this is still April, people are still going away a little. We get into May and June, most of them'll be staying home. Until the summer months, you know? So he hasn't got much time before he has to lay off. And he *missed* on the Ungerman job, don't forget that. I figure he's got to be coming out again real soon.'

'So what's your idea?'

'I've been talking to some of the supers in the neighbourhood, there are maybe three or four apartments with people away. I figure we can stake out at least two of them every night, more if the Loot'll let you have additional men. We rotate the apartments, we stay in touch with walkie-talkies, and we take our chances. What do you think?'

'I don't think the Loot'll give me any men.'

'How about Captain Frick? You think I should ask him?'

'I wouldn't, Mike. If you want to try this just the two of us, I'm game. But I can guarantee we won't get any help. Things are just too goddamn busy around here.'

'Okay, so you want to do it?'

'When?'

'Tonight?'

'Okay, sure.'

'Maybe we'll get lucky. If not, we'll try again tomorrow night. I don't go on the four-to-midnight till next week sometime, but even then I'm willing to stick with this till we get the son of a bitch.'

'Well, we do have to sleep every now and then,' Kling said, and smiled.

'We catch this guy, we can all take a rest,' Ingersoll said, and returned the smile. 'Look, Bert, I'll level with you. I'm anxious to grab him because it might help me get the gold tin. Even an assist might do it for me. I've been on the force twelve years now, been commended for bravery twice, and I'm still making a lousy eleven thousand a year. It's time I started helping myself, don't you think? I'm divorced, you know, did you know that?'

'No, I didn't.'

'Sure. So I got alimony to pay, and also I'd like to get married again, I'm thinking about getting married again. There's a nice girl I want to marry. If we can crack this one together, it'd be a big help to me, Bert. I'm talking to you like a brother.'

'I understand what you mean, Mike.'

'You can understand how I feel, can't you?'

'Sure.'

'So look, let me check out those apartments again, make sure the people didn't come back all of a sudden. I'll call in later and let you know where to meet me, okay?'

'Fine.'

'You want to requisition the walkie-talkies, or shall I take care of it?'

'Why do we need walkie-talkies?'

'Well, the guy got careless on his last job. He may be armed this time, who knows? If we run into any kind of trouble, be nice to know we're in contact with each other.'

'I'll get the walkie-talkies,' Kling said.

'Good. I'll call you later.'

'See you,' Kling said, and watched Ingersoll go through the gate in the railing and down the corridor to the iron-runged stairway. He suddenly wondered why Ingersoll had set his promotion sights so low; the guy was *already* behaving like the goddamn commissioner.

Hal Willis was an experienced cop and a smart one. At the Gee-Gee-Go-Go that night he talked to Rhonda Spear for close to forty minutes, buying her six drinks during the course of their odd discussion. At the end of that time, he had elicited from her exactly nothing.

Willis did not look like a cop, and he was not carrying a gun, having been previously warned that Rhonda was quite adept at detecting the presence of hardware. Yet he was certain she had not given a single straight answer to any of his seemingly innocent questions. He could only assume that Hawes' abortive attempt to reach her had served as a warning against further conversation with any men who weren't regulars in the place. If you're not sure who's a cop and who isn't, it's best to behave as though *everyone* is. Especially if you've got something to hide. That was the one thing Willis came away with: the intuitive feeling that Rhonda Spear had a hell of a lot to hide.

Aside from that, the night was a total loss.

The night, for Kling and Ingersoll, was no more rewarding; it was merely longer. They sat in separate empty apartments three buildings away from each other, and waited for the burglar to strike. The walkie-talkie communication was sketchy at best, but they did manage to maintain contact with each other, and their infrequent conversations at least kept them awake. They did not leave the apartments until seven in the morning – no closer to solving the case than they had been at the start of the stakeout.

Chapter Thirteen

At ten minutes past two, shortly after the second mail had been delivered, the squadroom telephone rang, and Carella picked it up.

'87th Squad, Carella,' he said.

'Good afternoon, Detective Carella.'

He recognized the voice at once, and signalled for Meyer to pick up the extension.

'Good afternoon,' he said. 'Long time no hear.'

'Has the mail arrived yet?' the Deaf Man asked.

'Few minutes ago.'

'Have you opened it yet?'

'Not yet.'

'Don't you think you should?'

'I have a feeling I already know what's in it.'

'I may surprise you.'

'No, I don't think so,' Carella said. 'The pattern's been pretty well established by now.'

'Do you have the envelope there?'

'Yes, I have,' Carella said, and separated the manila envelope from the rest of his mail. 'By the way, it's Stephen with a *p-h*.'

'Oh, forgive me,' the Deaf Man said. 'Open it, why don't you?'

'Will you hold on?'

'Surely,' the Deaf Man said. 'Not too long, though. We can't risk a trace, now can we?'

Carella tore open the flap, reached into the envelope, and pulled out the photostat:

'Big surprise,' Carella said. 'Who is this guy, anyway?'

'You mean you don't know?'

'We haven't been able to dope out *any* of it,' Carella said.

'I think you're lying,' the Deaf Man said, and hung up.

Carella waited. He knew the phone would ring again within the next few minutes, and he was not disappointed.

'87th Squad,' he said, 'Carella.'

'Please forgive my precautionary measures,' the Deaf Man said. 'I'm not yet convinced of the effectiveness of telephone traces, but one can't be too careful these days.'

'What's this picture gallery supposed to mean?' Carella said.

'Come, come, Carella, you're disappointing me.'

'I'm serious. We think you've lost your marbles this time. Do you want to give us a hint or two?'

'Oh, I couldn't do that,' the Deaf Man said. 'I'm afraid you'll simply have to double your efforts.'

'Not much time left, you know. Today's Wednesday, and you're pulling your big job on Friday, isn't that right?'

'Yes, that's absolutely true. Perhaps you ought to circle the date, Carella. So you won't forget it.'

'I already have.'

'Good. In that case, you're halfway home.'

'What do you mean?'

'Think about it,' the Deaf Man said, and again hung up.

Carella thought about it. He had a long time to think about it because the Deaf Man did not call again until three-thirty.

'What happened?' Carella asked. 'Get involved in a big executive meeting?'

'I merely like to keep you off balance,' the Deaf Man said.

'You do, you certainly do.'

'What do you make of the most recent picture?'

'Have no idea who he is. Nor the woman, either. We recognized Hoover and Washington, of course ... you're not planning a raid on the FBI, are you?'

'No, nothing as clever as that.'

'We thought maybe you were going to fly to Washington in a Jap Zero and strafe ...'

'Ah, then you *did* recognize the zero?'

'Yes, we did. We're very well oriented up here.'

'Please, no puns,' the Deaf Man said, and Carella could swear he was wincing.

'But none of it makes any sense,' Carella said. 'Hoover, Washington, this guy with the mutton chops. What are you trying to tell us?'

'Does it really seem that difficult to you?'

'It certainly does.'

'In that case, I'd merely accept the facts as they are, Carella.'

'What facts?'

'The fact that you're incompetent ...'

'Well, I wouldn't ...'

'The fact that you're incapable of stopping me.'

'Do you *want* us to stop you?'

'I'd like you to try.'

'Why?'

'It's the nature of the beast, Carella. The delicate symbiosis that keeps us both alive. You might call it a vicious circle,' he said, and this time the word registered, this time Carella realized its use was deliberate. *Circle.*

'Might I call it that?' Carella said.

'I would strongly suggest it. Otherwise, you may merely come up with a zero,' the Deaf Man said, and hung up.

Carella quickly put his own phone back onto the cradle, opened his top drawer, and removed from it the Isola telephone directory. The zero was a circle; the Deaf Man had just told him as much. And if he correctly recalled his cursory inspection of directory addresses ...

He ran his finger swiftly down the page:

FIRST FEDERAL BANK
Main office 1265 Highland 380–1764
304 S 110 780–3751
60 Yates Av...................................... 271–0800
4404 Hrsy Blvd 983–6100
371 N 84 642–8751
14 VnBur Cir 231–7244

Carella went through the entire list in the Isola directory, and then checked all the First Federal addresses in the other four books as well. Only one of them seemed to fit. He buttoned the top button of his shirt, pulled up his tie, and was leaving the squadroom just as Meyer came back from the men's room down the hall.

'Where you off too?' Meyer asked.

'The library,' Carella said.

That's who it was, all right.

The man with the fancy hair styling was none other than:

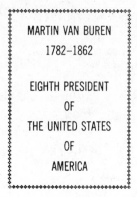

MARTIN VAN BUREN

1782–1862

EIGHTH PRESIDENT

OF

THE UNITED STATES

OF

AMERICA

In a city where streets, avenues, boulevards, bridges, airports, high schools, and even race tracks were named after past Presidents, it was perhaps no great honour to have a mere circle so-named – but then again, who remembered Van Buren except perhaps in Kinderhook, New York, where he'd been born? Anyway, there it was, Van Buren Circle. And at 14 Van Buren Circle, there was branch of the First Federal Bank. At last it all made sense – or at least Carella *thought* it made sense. Which is exactly why he was suddenly so troubled. If everything made sense, then nothing made sense. Why would the Deaf Man pinpoint the exact location of a bank he planned to rob on a date he had already announced? Symbiosis aside, something else was surely coming, and Carella could not guess what.

An apartment is alive only when the people who live in it are there. When they are away, it becomes nothing more than a random collection of possessions, essentially lifeless. To a policeman sitting in the dark in the empty hours of the night, the place resembles a graveyard for furniture.

In the living room of 648 Richardson Drive that night, Bert Kling sat in an easy chair facing the front door, the walkie-talkie in his lap, his revolver in his right hand. It was difficult to stay awake. Occasionally, to relieve the monotony, he would contact Mike Ingersoll, who was in a similarly vacant apartment at 653 Richardson, across the street. Their conversations were almost as dreary as their separate vigils.

'Hello, Mike?'

'Yes, Bert.'

'How's it going there?'

'Quiet.'

'Same here.'

'Talk to you later.'

At ten minutes to midnight, the telephone rang. Sitting in the darkness, Kling nearly leaped out of the chair on the first ring, and then realized it was only the phone. He listened as it rang six times and then went silent. In as long as it took for the caller to re-dial, the phone began ringing again. This time there were fourteen rings before it went still. The caller might have been someone who did not know the tenants of the apartment were away; he had called once, assumed he'd misdialled, and tried again. On the other hand, the caller might have been the burglar, checking and then double-checking to make certain the tenants were *still* away. In which case, he now had his information and would come tiptoeing up to unlock the front door, let himself in, and burglarize to his heart's content.

Kling waited.

At twelve-thirty, Ingersoll contacted him on the walkie-talkie.

'Hello, Bert? Anything?'

'Telephone rang a while back, that's all.'

'Nothing here, either.'

'It's going to be long night, Mike.'

'No longer than last night,' Ingersoll said.

'Talk to you.'

'Right.'

They talked to each other every forty minutes or so. Not one single burglar tried to enter either of the apartments all night long. At the first sign of light in the east, Kling contacted Ingersoll and suggested that they knock off. Ingersoll sighed and said, 'Yeah, I guess so. You want some coffee before we head home?'

'Good idea,' Kling said. 'Meet you downstairs.'

A patrol car was parked on the street in front of 657 Richardson, the building in which Augusta lived. Kling and Ingersoll walked to it rapidly. The patrolman behind the wheel recognized them and asked if they'd been sent over on the squeal.

'What squeal?' Kling asked.

'Guy ripped off an apartment in there.'

'You're kidding,' Kling said.

'Would I kid about a felony?' the patrolman asked, offended.

Kling and Ingersoll went into the building and knocked on the superintendent's door. It was answered by a woman in a bathrobe, who said her husband had gone upstairs to 6D, with the cop. Kling and Ingersoll took the elevator up, got out on the sixth floor, glanced down the hallway, and walked immediately to the left, where the partner of the patrolman in the car was examining a door and jamb for jimmy marks, the super standing just beside him.

'Anything?' Kling asked.

'No, it's clean, Bert,' the patrolman said. 'Guy must've got in with a key.'

'Let's take a look, Mike,' Kling said. To the patrolman, he said, 'Have you called this in, Lew?'

'Henry took care of it downstairs. We knew what it was already 'cause the super'd been in here. In fact, I thought you was the detective they sent over.'

'No,' Kling said, and shook his head, and walked through the foyer into the apartment, Ingersoll directly behind him. The layout was identical to Augusta's apartment on the eleventh floor, and so he knew exactly where the bedroom was. The place was in total disorder, clothing strewn all over the room, drawers pulled from dressers and overturned.

'Something's missing,' Ingersoll said.

'Huh?'

'No kitten.'

They walked to the dresser. Kling, remembering Mr Angieri's experience, looked behind the dresser, thinking the kitten might have fallen there.

'Wait, here it is,' Ingersoll said.

The kitten was a small glass figurine, white, with a blue bow around its neck. It sat next to a sterling-silver comb-and-brush set, which the burglar had apparently decided not to steal.

'Guess he's running out of live ones,' Ingersoll said.

'Might get some prints from this, though,' Kling said.

'I doubt it.'

'Yeah, he's too smart for that.'

'How do you like this son of a bitch?' Ingersoll said. 'We're sitting in two apartments so close we could spit at him, and he's got the guts to rip off this joint. Jesus!'

'Let's talk to the super,' Kling said.

The super's name was Phillip Trammel. He was a thin man in his sixties wearing bib overalls and a blue denim work shirt.

'How'd you discover the burglary?' Kling asked him.

'I was coming up to get the garbage. We ain't got no incinerator in this building. What the tenants do is they usually leave their garbage outside the service entrance in plastic bags, and I take it down to the basement for them. It's a little service we perform, you know? Ain't nothing says the super's supposed to go around picking up garbage, but I don't mind, it's a little extra service.'

'So what happened?'

'I saw the door to 6D was open, and I knew we'd had that burglary in Miss Blair's apartment little more'n a week ago, so I went inside and looked around. Somebody'd been there, all right. So I called the police, and here you are.'

'Here we are,' Ingersoll said, and sighed.

Chapter Fourteen

When you are dealing with a man who sends you a picture of a football team, you have to believe he is crazy – unless you think you understand the way his mind works. The boys of the 87th would never in a million years have presumed to understand the workings of the Deaf Man's mind. But since they now possessed a considerable body of knowledge upon which to base some speculations, they turned to the latest photostat with something resembling scientific perspective.

If Washington meant First ...

And Hoover meant Federal ...

And Vilma Banky meant Bank ...

What did a football team mean?

Van Buren, of course, meant only Van Buren, which was not much help.

But Zero meant Circle.

So what did a football team mean?

'Why not a baseball team?' Meyer asked.

'Or a hockey team,' Carella said.

'Or a basketball, swimming, soccer, or lacrosse team,' Hawes suggested.

'Why football?'

'What's he trying to tell us?'

'He's already told us all we need to know.'

'Maybe he's just saying it's all a game to him.'

'But why a *football* game?'

'Why not? A game's a game.'

'Not to the Deaf Man.'

'This isn't even the football season.'

'Baseball's the game right now.'

'So why football?'

'Anyway, he's already *told* us everything.'

'That's what *I* said two minutes ago.'

'Did somebody call the Eight-six?'

'I did. Yesterday afternoon.'

'Will they be covering the bank tomorrow?'

'Like a dirty shirt.'

'Maybe he's going to use eleven men on the job,' Hawes said.

'What do you mean?'

'A football team. Eleven men.'

'No, wait a second,' Carella said. 'What's the only thing he *hasn't* told us?'

'He's told it all. The date, the name of the bank, the address ...'

'But not the *time*.'

'Eleven,' Hawes said.

'Eleven o'clock,' Meyer said.

'Yeah,' Carella said, and reached for the phone. 'Who's handling this at the Eight-six?'

The cops of the 86th Precinct were similar to the cops of the 87th Precinct, except that they had different names. Cops, like all other minority groups, are difficult to tell apart. Before Carella's call, Detective First-grade Albert Schmitt had already been in touch with Mr Alton, the manager of the First Federal Bank. But now, supplied with new information about the anticipated holdup, he paid him another visit.

Mr Alton, a portly little man with thinning white hair, was still visibly distressed over the first visit from the police. This new visit, pinpointing the *time* the bank would be robbed, contributed little towards soothing his dyspepsia.

'But I don't understand,' he said. 'Why would they be telling us exactly when they're coming?'

'Well, I don't quite know,' Schmitt said thoughtfully. 'Maybe they won't be coming at all, sir. Maybe this is just an elaborate hoax, who knows?'

'But you say this man has a record of ...'

'Oh yes, he's given us trouble before. Not me personally, but the department. Which is why we're taking these precautions.'

'I don't know,' Mr Alton said, shaking his head. 'Friday is our busiest day. We cash cheques for three payrolls on Friday. If you substitute ...'

'Well, that's just what we think he's after, Mr Alton. Those payrolls.'

'Yes, but if you substitute your men for my tellers, how can we possibly serve our customers?'

'Would we be serving them better if we allowed this man to walk off with a million dollars?'

'No, of course not, but ...' Alton shook his head again. 'What time will your men be here?'

'What time do you open?'

'Nine o'clock.'

'That's what time we'll be here,' Schmitt said.

In the squadroom of the 87th, perhaps because the boys felt they would soon be rid of the Deaf Man forever, they were telling deaf jokes.

'This man buys a hearing aid, you see,' Meyer said, 'and he's explaining to his friend how much he likes it. "Best investment I ever made in my life," he says. "Before I put this thing in my ear, I was deaf as a post. Now, if I'm upstairs in the bedroom and the tea kettle goes off, I can hear it immediately. If a car pulls into the driveway, I can hear it when it's still a mile away. I'm telling you, this is the best investment I ever made." His friend nods and asks, "How much did it cost?" The guy looks at his watch and answers, "A quarter to two."'

The telephone rang.

Kling, laughing, picked it up and said, '87th Squad, Detective Kling.'

'Bert, it's me.'

'Oh, hi, Augusta.'

'There's this guy,' Hawes said, 'Who plays the violin beautifully. Whenever he plays the violin, people stop fighting, dogs and cats stop clawing at each other, he figures it's a real instrument for world peace.'

'Bert, I'll be finished here in about a half hour,' Augusta said. 'How soon can you get away?'

'Not till four,' Kling said. 'Why?'

'I though we might make love this afternoon.'

'So he goes to the United Nations,' Hawes said, 'and they finance a test trip to the African jungle, figuring if he can play his violin for the wild animals there and make them stop fighting with each other, why then they'll finance a world-wide tour to promote peace.'

'Well, uh,' Kling said, and glanced at the other men, 'I guess I can get away a little earlier. Where are you now?'

'I'm ...'

'Just a second, let me find a pencil.'

'In the middle of the jungle, he stops under a huge cork tree, takes out his violin, and begins playing,' Hawes said.

'Go ahead,' Kling said into the phone.

'The animals begin gathering around him – lions, rhinos, hippos, jackals, giraffes, all the animals of the jungle. The beautiful music is pouring from the violin, and the wild animals are all sitting around him in a circle, with their arms around each other, nobody fighting, everybody listening peacefully.'

'Yes, I've got it,' Kling said into the phone.

'But as the guy keeps playing,' Hawes said, 'a leopard creeps along a branch of the tree over his head, and suddenly leaps down on him, and eats him alive.'

'See you in half hour,' Kling said, and hung up.

'The animals are appalled,' Hawes said. 'A lion steps out of the circle and says to the leopard, "Why did you do that? This man came all the way from America to the wilds of the jungle here, and he brought his violin with him, and he played this beautiful music that made us all stop fighting. Why did you do such a terrible thing?" And the leopard cups his paw behind his ear and says, "Huh?"'

Everyone burst out laughing except Kling.

'If Mike Ingersoll stops by,' he said gruffly, like a detective investigating an important case, 'I'll be at the Blair apartment.'

In the dim silence of Augusta Blair's bedroom, they made love.

It was not so good.

'What's the matter?' Augusta whispered.

'I don't know,' Kling whispered back.

'Am I doing something wrong?'

'No, no.'

'Because if I am ...'

'No, Augusta, really.'

'Then what is it?'

'I think I'm a little afraid of you.'

'Afraid?'

'Yes. I keep thinking. What's a dumb kid from Riverhead doing in bed with a beautiful model?'

'You're not a dumb kid,' Augusta said, and smiled, and touched his mouth with her fingertips.

'I feel like a dumb kid.'

'Why?'

'Because you're so beautiful.'

'Bert, if you start that again, I'll hit you right on the head with a hammer.'

'How'd you know about a hammer?'

'What?'

'A hammer. About it being the best weapon for a woman.'

'I didn't know.'

They were both silent for several moments.

'Relax,' she said.

'I think that's exactly the problem,' Kling said.

'If you want me to be ugly, I can be ugly as hell. Look,' she said, and made a face. 'How's that?'

'Beautiful.'

'Where's my hammer?' she said, and got out of bed naked and padded out of the room. He heard her rummaging around in the kitchen. When she returned, she was indeed carrying a hammer. 'Have you ever been hit with a hammer?' she asked, and sat beside him, pulling her long legs up onto the bed, crossing them Indian fashion, her head and back erect, the hammer clutched in her right hand.

'No,' he said. 'Lots of things, but never a hammer.'

'Have you ever been shot?'

'Yes.'

'Is that what this is?' she asked, and pointed with the hammer at the scar on his shoulder.

'Yes.'

'Did it hurt?'

'Yes.'

'Think I'll kiss it,' she said, and bent over from the waist and kissed his shoulder lightly, and then sat up again. 'You're dealing with the Mad Hammer Hitter here,' she said. 'One more word about how good-looking I am and, pow, your friends'll be investigating a homicide. You got that?'

'Got it,' Kling said.

'This is the obligatory sex scene,' she said. 'I'm going to drive you to distraction in the next ten minutes. If you fail to respond, I'll cleave your skull with a swift single blow. In fact,' she said, 'a swift single blow might not be a bad way to start,' and she bent over swiftly, her tongue darting. 'I think you're beginning to get the message,' she murmured. 'Must be the goddamn hammer.'

'Must be,' Kling whispered.

Abruptly, she brought her head up to the pillow, stretched her legs, and rolled in tight against him, the hammer still in her right hand. 'Listen, you,' she whispered.

'I'm listening.'

'We're going to be very important to each other.'

'I know that.'

'I'm scared to death,' she said, and caught her breath. 'I've never felt this way about any man. Do you believe me, Bert?'

'Yes.'

'We're going to make love now.'

'Yes, Augusta.'

'We're going to make beautiful love.'

'Yes.'

'Yes, touch me,' she said, and the hammer slipped from her grasp.

The telephone rang four times while they were in bed together. Each time, Augusta's answering service picked it up on the first ring.

'Might be someone important,' Kling whispered after the last call.

'No one's more important than you,' she whispered back, and immediately got out of bed and went into the kitchen. When she returned, she was carrying a split of champagne.

'Ah, good,' he said. 'How'd you know I was thirsty?'

'You open it while I think up a toast.'

'You forgot glasses.'

'Lovers don't need glasses.'

'My grandmother does. Blind as a bat without them.'

'Is she a lover?'

'Just ask Grandpa.'

Kling popped the cork with his thumbs.

'Got that toast?' he asked.

'You're getting the bed wet.'

'Come on, think of some people we can drink to.'

'How about John and Martha Mitchell?'

'Why not? Here's to . . .'

'How about us?' Augusta said. She gently took the bottle from him, lifted it high, and said, 'To Bert and Augusta. And to . . .' She hesitated.

'Yes?'

Solemnly, she studied his face, the bottle still extended. 'And to at least the possibility of always,' she said, and quickly, almost shyly, brought the bottle to her lips, drank from the open top, and handed it back to Kling. He did not take his eyes from her face. Watching her steadily, he said, 'To us. And to always,' and drank.

'Excuse me,' Augusta said, and started out of the room.

'Leaving already, huh?' Kling said. 'After all that sweet talk about . . .'

'I'm only going to the bathroom,' Augusta said, and giggled.

'In that case, check the phone on the way back.'

'Why?'

'I'm a cop.'

'Hell with the phone,' Augusta said.

But she nonetheless dialled her service, and then reported to Kling that the third call had been for him.

'Who was it?' he asked.

'A man named Meyer. He said Mrs Ungerman is ready to make a positive identification.'

Kling knocked on the door of Mike Ingersoll's Calm's Point apartment at ten minutes past eleven. He had heard voices inside, and now he heard footsteps approaching the door.

'Who's there?' Ingersoll asked.

'Me. Bert Kling.'

'Who?'

'Kling.'

'Oh. Oh, just a second, Bert.'

Kling heard the night chain being slipped off, the lock turning. Ingersoll, wearing pyjamas and slippers, opened the door wide, and said, 'Hey, how are you? Come on in.'

'I know it's late,' Kling said. 'You weren't asleep, were you?'

'No, no, I was just watching the news on television.'

'Are you alone?'

'Yeah,' Ingersoll said. 'Come in, come in. Can I get you a beer?'

'No, Mike, thanks.'

'Mind if I have one?'

'Go right ahead.'

'Make yourself comfortable,' Ingersoll said. 'I'll be with you in a minute.'

Kling went into the living room and sat in an easy chair facing the television set. Ingersoll's gun and holster were resting on top of the cabinet, and a newscaster was talking about the latest sanitation strike. A cigarette was in an ashtray on an end table alongside the easy chair. There were lipstick stains on its white filter tip. In the kitchen, Kling heard Ingersoll closing the refrigerator. He came into the room a moment later, glanced at a closed door at the far end, tilted the beer bottle to his lips, and drank. Briefly, he wiped the back of his hand across his mouth, and then said, 'Something new on the case?'

'I think so, Mike.'

'Not another burglary?'

'No, no.'

'What then?'

'A positive identification,' Kling said.

'Yeah? Great, great.'

'That depends on where you're sitting, Mike.'

'How do you mean?'

'Mrs Ungerman called the squadroom earlier tonight. I was out, but I spoke to her just a little while ago.' Kling paused. 'She told me she knew who the burglar was. She hadn't made the connection before because she'd only seen him in ...'

'Don't say it, Bert.'

'She'd only seen him in uniform. But the other day, in the squadroom ...'

'Don't, Bert.'

'It's true, isn't it?'

Ingersoll did not answer.

'Mike? Is it true?'

'True or not, we can talk it over,' Ingersoll said, and moved towards the television set.

'Don't go for the gun, Mike,' Kling warned, and pulled his own service revolver.

'You don't need that, Bert,' Ingersoll said with an injured tone.

'Don't I? Over there, Mike. Against the wall.'

'Hey, come on ...'

'*Move* it!'

'All right, take it easy, will you?' Ingersoll said, and backed away towards the wall.

'What'd you do, Mike? Steal a set of skeleton keys from the squad-room?'

'No.'

'Then how'd you get them?'

'I was on a numbers investigation last October. Remember when they brought a lot of us in on ...'

'Yes, I remember.'

'We put in wires all around town. I was working with the tech guys who planted the bugs. That's when I got hold of the keys.'

'What else are you into, Mike? Are you just burglarizing apartments?'

'Nothing, I swear!'

'Or are you selling dope to school kids, too?'

'Come on, Bert, what do you think I am?'

'I think you're a cheap thief!'

'I needed money!'

'We all need money!'

'Yeah, so name me a cop in the precinct who *isn't* on the take. When the hell did *you* get so fucking pure?'

'I've never taken a nickel, Mike.'

'How many meals have you had on the arm?'

'Are you trying to equate a free cup of coffee with a string of felonies? Jesus Christ!'

'I'm trying to tell you ...'

'Yeah, *what*, Mike?'

The room went silent. Ingersoll shrugged and said, 'Look, I wanted to keep you out of this. Why do you think I suggested the stakeout? I didn't want anybody to think you were connected. I was ...'

'The stakeout was a smoke screen,' Kling said flatly. 'That's why you wanted to the walkie-talkies, isn't it? So I'd think you were sitting in the dark where you were *supposed* to be, when instead you were ripping off an apartment down the block. And the glass kitten! "*Guess he's running out of live ones*," isn't that what you said, Mike? Running out, my ass. You couldn't carry a live one last night because even a dummy like me would've tipped to a goddamn cat in your coat pocket.'

'Bert, believe me ...'

'Oh, *I* believe you, Mike. It's the lieutenant who might not. Especially when he hears Fred Lipton's story.'

'I have no connection with Fred Lipton.'

'No? Well, we'll find out about that in just a little while, won't we? Hawes is picking him up right this minute. It's my guess he's your fence. Yes or no, Mike?'

'I told you I don't know him.'

'Then why were you so anxious to get us off his trail? What'd you do, give Rhonda Spear a description of every cop in the squadroom? We were beginning to think she was a goddamn mind reader!' Kling paused, and then said, 'Get her out here, Mike. We might as well take her along with us.'

'What? Who?'

'The broad in the other room. It *is* Rhonda Spear, isn't it?'

'No, there's nobody ...'

'Is she the one you were telling me about? The nice girl you want to marry, Mike? The reason you were so anxious to catch the burglar?'

'Bert ...'

'Well, we've caught him. So how about introducing me to the bride? Miss!' he shouted. 'Come out here with your hands over your head!'

'Don't shoot,' a woman's voice said from behind the closed door. The door opened. A beefy blonde wearing a blue robe over a long pink nightgown came into the living room, her hands up over her head, her lip trembling.

'What's your name, miss?' Kling asked.

'Which one?' she asked.

'What?'

'Stage or real?'

'Are you Rhonda Spear?'

'Yes.'

'Get dressed, Miss Spear. You, too, Mike.'

'Bert, for Christ's sake ... give me a break, will you?'

'Why?' Kling asked.

The motion picture had been a bad choice for Teddy Carella. It was full of arty shots in which the actors spoke from behind vases, trees, lampshades, or elephants, seemingly determined to hide their lips from her so that she would not know what was happening. When they weren't speaking with their faces hidden or their backs turned, the actors made important plot points offscreen, their voices floating in over the picture of a rushing locomotive or a changing traffic light.

Teddy normally enjoyed films, except when she was submitted to the excesses of a sadistic *nouvelle vague* camera. Tonight was such a night. She sat beside Carella and watched the film in utter helplessness, unable to 'hear' long stretches of it, grateful when it ended and they could leave the theatre.

It had been almost balmy when they'd left the house, and they had elected to walk the six blocks to the theatre on Dover Plains Avenue. The walk home was a bit chillier, the temperature having dropped slightly, but it was still comfortable, and they moved without hurry beside old trees that spread their branches over the deserted Riverhead sidewalks. Carella, in fact, seemed to be dawdling. Teddy was anxious to ask him all sorts of questions about the movie as soon as they got home; he was breathing deeply of the night air and walking the way an old man does in the park on Sunday morning, when there are pigeons to imitate.

The attack came without warning.

The fist was thrown full into his face, as unexpected as an earthquake. He was reaching for his gun when he was struck from behind by a second assailant. A third man grabbed for Teddy's handbag, just as the first attacker threw his clenched fist into Carella's face again. The man behind him was wielding a sap. Carella's gun came clear of his topcoat just as the sap grazed him above and behind the ear. There was the sound of the gun's explosion, shockingly loud on the still suburban street, and then the sap caught him again, solidly this time, at the base of the skull, and he toppled to the sidewalk.

The embarrassment was almost worse than the pain. A half hour later, in the muster room of the 103rd Precinct, he explained to an incredulous desk sergeant that he was a police officer and that he and his wife had been mugged on the way home from the movies. The attackers had stolen his wife's handbag and wristwatch, as well as his own watch, his wallet, and, most shameful to admit, his service revolver.

The sergeant took down all the information, and promised to get in touch.

Carella felt like a horse's ass.

Chapter Fifteen

Something was wrong with the day.

Heady breezes blew in off the River Harb, brilliant sunshine touched avenue and street; May was just around the corner, and April seemed bent on jubilant collision.

But there was no further communication from the Deaf Man. The first mail had already been delivered, and there was no manila envelope addressed to Carella, no duplication of the football team. Had this been an oversight, or was it a deliberate act of omission with deep significance? The detectives of the 87th Squad pondered this with the concern of a proctological convention considering oral hygiene. The case had been turned over to the stalwarts of the 86th; let *their* mothers worry.

The clock on the sidewalk outside the bank read twelve minutes past nine. Sitting on a bench in the small park around which ran Van Buren Circle, the Deaf Man checked his own watch, and then glanced up the street. In three minutes, if the armoured truck followed its usual Friday morning routine, enough cash to cover the combined McCormick, Meredith, and Holt payrolls would be delivered to the bank. At eleven o'clock, the money would be withdrawn, despite the efforts of the toy police, who were already inside the bank. The Deaf Man had seen them arriving at a little past nine, three burly detectives and one lady cop, undoubtedly there to replace the tellers. He credited them with having enough intelligence to realize he might strike at some time other than the announced eleven o'clock, but then even a cretin might have surmised that. And besides, they were wrong. The bank *would* be robbed at eleven. Whatever else the Deaf Man was, he was scrupulously fair. When dealing with inferiors, there was no other way.

The armoured truck was coming up the street.

It pulled to the kerb outside the bank. The driver got out and walked swiftly to the rear of the truck, taking up position near the door, a rifle in his hands. The door on the kerbside opened, and the second guard got out and followed his partner, pistol still holstered. From a key attached to his belt with a chain, he unlocked the rear door of the truck. Then he took the pistol from its holster, turned up the butt, and rapped sharply on the door, twice, the signal for the guard inside to unlock the door from within. The rear door of the truck opened. The guard with the rifle covered his companions as they transferred the two sacks of cash from the truck to the pavement. The guard inside the truck climbed down, pistol in hand, and picked up one of the sacks. The second guard picked up the other sack. As they walked towards the revolving doors, the guard with the rifle covered the sidewalk. It was all very routine, and all very efficient.

As they disappeared inside the bank, the Deaf Man nodded, smiled, and walked swiftly to a pay phone on the corner. He dialled his own number, and the phone on the other end was lifted on the second ring.

'Hello?' a voice said.

'Kerry?'

'Yes?'

'This is Mr Taubman.'

'Yes, Mr Taubman.'

'The money is here. You and the others may come for it at once.'

'Thank you, Mr Taubman.'

There was a click on the line. Still smiling, the Deaf Man replaced the receiver on the hook and went back to his command post on the park bench.

Inside the bank, Detective Schmitt of the 86th was briefing Mr Alton yet another time. The clock on the wall opposite the tellers' cages read 9:21.

'There's nothing to worry about,' Schmitt said. 'I've got experienced men at windows number one and two, and an experienced policewoman at the car teller's window. I'll be covering window number three myself.'

'Yes, thank you,' Alton said. He hesitated, and glanced nervously around the bank. 'What do I do meanwhile?'

'Just go about your business as usual,' Schmitt said. 'Try to relax. There's no sense upsetting your customers. Everything's under control. Believe me, Mr Alton, with the four of us here, nobody's going to rob this bank.'

Schmitt didn't realize it, but he was right.

At 9:37 a.m. Kerry Donovan, his head shaved bald and gleaming in the sun, a new but nonetheless rather respectable moustache under his nose, entered the bank carrying a large black rectangular case. He asked the guard where the manager's office was, and the guard asked whether he had an appointment. Donovan said yes, he had called last week to make an appointment with Mr Alton. The guard asked Donovan his name, and he replied, 'Mr Dunmore. Karl Dunmore.'

'One second, Mr Dunmore,' the guard said, and signalled to one of the bank clerks, an attractive young girl in her twenties, who immediately came over to him.

'Mr Karl Dunmore to see Mr Alton,' the guard said.

'Just a moment, please,' the girl said, and walked to the rear of the bank and into Alton's office. She came out not a moment later, walked back to where the guard and Donovan where engaged in polite conversation about the beautiful weather, and asked Donovan if he would come with her, please. Donovan followed her up the length of the bank, passing the Deaf Man, who stood at one of the islands making out a deposit slip. She opened the door to Alton's office, ushered him in, and closed the door behind him.

The Deaf Man thought it a pity that Kerry Donovan did not know the bank was full of policemen.

'Mr Dunmore,' Alton said, and extended his hand. 'Nice to see you.'

'Good of you to make time for me,' Donovan said.

'What have you brought me?'

'Well, as we discussed on the phone, I thought we might make more progress once you'd actually seen the plans and scale model of our project. I know we're asking for an unusually large amount of development money, but I'm hoping you'll agree our expectations for profit are realistic. May I use your desk top?' Donovan asked, and quickly realized that the model was too big for Alton's cluttered desk. 'Or perhaps the floor would be better,' he said, improvising. 'We can spread the plans out that way, get a better look at them.'

'Yes, certainly,' Alton said. 'As you wish.'

Donovan opened the black case and carefully removed from it a scale model of a forty-unit housing development, complete with winding roads, miniature trees, lamp-posts, and fire hydrants. He put this on the floor in front of the desk, and then reached into the case for a rolled sheaf of architectural drawings. He removed the rubber band from the roll, and spread the plans on the floor.

'I wonder if I could have something to hold these down?' he said.

'Will this do?' Alton asked.

'Yes, thank you,' Donovan said, and accepted the offered cut-glass paperweight. 'Just to hold down this one end of it.'

'Yes,' Alton said.

'If you'll come around here, Mr Alton, I think you'll be able to ...'

'Where's the proposed location?' Alton said, coming around the desk.

'I explained that in my initial ...'

'Yes, but we deal with so many ...'

'It's on Sands Spit, sir.'

'Have you sought development money out there?'

'No, sir. Our offices are here in Isola. We thought it preferable to deal with a local bank.'

'I see.'

'This top drawing is a schematic of the entire development. If you compare it with the model ...'

Alton was standing just to Donovan's left now, looking down at the model. Donovan rose, drew a pistol from his coat pocket, and pointed it at Alton's head.

'Don't make a sound,' he said. 'This is a holdup. Do exactly what I tell you to do, or I'll kill you.'

Alton, his lip trembling, stared at the muzzle of the gun. The Deaf Man had deliberately armed Donovan with a Colt .45, the meanest-looking handgun he could think of.

'Do you understand?' Donovan asked.

'Yes. Yes, I do.'

'Good. We're going into the vault now,' Donovan said, and stopped, and quickly snapped the case shut. 'If we meet anyone on the way, you're to tell them I'm here to inspect the alarm. If there's anyone in the vault, you will ask that person to leave us alone. Clear?'

'Yes.'

'No signals to anyone, no attempts to indicate that anything out of the ordinary is happening. I promise you, Mr Alton, a felony conviction will send me to jail for life, and I have no qualms about shooting you dead. I'm going to put this gun back in my pocket now, but it'll be pointed right at *you*, Mr Alton, and I'll fire through the pocket if you so much as raise an eyebrow to anyone. Are you ready?'

'Yes, I'm ready.'

'Let's go then.'

From where he stood at the island in the centre of the bank, the Deaf Man saw Donovan and Alton coming out of the office and heading for the vault. Donovan was smiling and chatting amiably, the black case in his left hand, his right hand in the pocket of his coat. Both men went into the vault, and the Deaf Man headed swiftly towards the revolving doors at the front of the bank. According to the outlined plan, he was supposed to initiate the second phase of the plan only *after* Donovan was safely out of the vault and back in the manager's office. Instead, he walked out of the bank now, his appearance on the sidewalk being the signal to the two automobiles parked on the other side of the small park. He saw Rudy Manello pulling the first car away from the kerb. Angela Gould's car followed immediately behind it. In less than a minute Rudy had driven around the curving street and turned into the driveway on the right-hand side of the bank, Angela following in the second automobile. When Angela's car was directly abreast of the driveway, she cut the engine, and pretended helpless female indignation at things mechanical. An instant later John Preiss stepped out of the first car and swung a sledge hammer at the car teller's window.

An instant after that, both he and Rudy were shot dead by the police-woman behind the shattered window. Kerry Donovan, still in the bank vault stuffing banded stacks of bills into the black case, heard the shots and realized at once that something had gone wrong. He dropped the bills in his hand, rushed out of the vault, saw that the woman in the car teller's window was armed, and recognized in panic that he could not make his escape as planned. He was running for the revolving doors at the front of the bank when he was felled by bullets from the guns of the three separate detectives manning the interior tellers' cages.

Outside the bank Angela Gould heard all the shooting and immediately started the car. In her panic she would not have stopped to pick up the Deaf Man even if he'd been waiting on the sidewalk where he was supposed to be. But by that time he was in a taxicab half a mile away, heading for a rendezvous with the second team.

Something was still wrong with the day, only more so.

When Albert Schmitt of the 86th called Carella to report that the attempted robbery had been foiled, Carella was somewhat taken aback.

'What do you mean?' he asked, and looked up at the wall clock. 'It's only ten-thirty.'

'That's right,' Schmitt said. 'They hit early.'

'When?'

'Almost an hour ago. They came in about twenty to ten. It was all over by ten.'

'Who? How many?'

'One guy inside, two outside. I don't know what the plan was, but how they ever expected to get away with it is beyond me. Especially after all the warning beforehand. I don't get it, Carella, I really don't.'

'Who were the men involved in the attempt?' Carella asked.

'Identification we found on the bodies . . .'

'They're all dead?'

'All three of them. Rudy Manello, John Preiss, and Kerry Donovan. Names mean anything to you?'

'Nothing at all. Any of them wearing a hearing aid?'

'A what?'

'A hearing aid.'

'No.'

'Any of them tall and blond?'

'No.'

'Then he got away.'

'Who did?'

'The guy who masterminded it.'

'Some mastermind,' Schmitt said. 'My six-year-old kid could've planned a better caper. It's like nothing ever happened, Carella. The glazier already had the window fixed before I left. I pulled my people out because even the guys from the security office were leaving. Anyway, we can forget about it now. It's all over and done with.'

'Well, good,' Carella said, 'good,' and hung up feeling mildly disappointed. The squadroom was unusually silent, the windows open to the sounds of light morning traffic. Carella sat at his desk and sipped coffee from a cardboard container. This was not like the Deaf Man. If Carella had figured him correctly (and he probably hadn't), the 'delicate symbiosis' of which he had spoken was composed of several interlocking elements.

Not the least of these was the Deaf Man himself. It now seemed apparent that he worked with different pickup gangs on each job, rather like a jazz soloist recruiting sidemen in the various cities on his tour. In the past any apprehended gang members did not know the true identity of their leader; he had presented himself once as L. Sordo and again as Mort Orecchio, the former name meaning 'the deaf one' in Spanish, the latter meaning 'dead ear' in Italian. The hearing aid itself may have been a phony, even though he always took pains to announce that he was hard of hearing. But whatever he was or whoever he was, the crimes he conceived were always grand in scale and involved large sums of money.

Nor was conceiving crimes and executing them quite enough for the Deaf Man. The second symbiotic element consisted of telling the police what he was going to do long before he did it. At first Carella had supposed this to be evidence of a monumental ego, but he had come to learn that the Deaf Man used the police as a sort of *second* pickup gang, larger than the nucleus group, but equally essential to the successful commission of the crime. That he had been thwarted on two previous occasions was entirely due to chance. He was smarter than the police, and he used the police, and he let the police know they were being used, and that was where the third element locked into place.

Knowing they were being used, but now *how*; knowing he was telling them a great deal about the crime, but not *enough*; knowing he would do what he predicted, but not *exactly*, the police generally reacted like country bumpkins on a hick police force. Their behaviour in turn strengthened the Deaf Man's premise that they were singularly inept. Given their now-demonstrated ineffectiveness, he became more and more outrageous, more and more daring. And the bolder *he* became, the more *they* tripped over their own flat feet. It was, indeed, a delicate symbiosis.

But the deception this time seemed unworthy of someone of his calibre. The cheapest thief in the precinct could just as easily have announced that he would rob a bank at eleven and then rob it at nine-thirty. Big deal. A lie of such petty dimensions hardly required duplication. Yet the Deaf Man had thought it necessary to tell them all about it twice. So apparently he himself was convinced that he was about to pull off the biggest caper in the history of criminal endeavour, gigantic enough to be announced not only once, but then once again – like 50 DANCING GIRLS 50.

Carella picked up the container and sipped at his coffee. It was getting cold. He swallowed the remainder of it in a single gulp and then almost choked on the startling suddenness of an exceptionally brilliant thought: the Deaf Man had *not* said everything twice. True enough, he had said almost everything twice, but there had been only *one* photostat pinpointing the time of the holdup. Carella shoved back his chair and reached for his jacket. He had brought another gun to work with him this morning, the first revolver he'd owned, back when he was a patrolman. He eased it out of the holster now, the grip unfamiliar to him, and hoped he would not have to use it, hoped somehow he was wrong. But it was a quarter to eleven on the face of the squadroom clock, and Carella now thought he knew why there'd been any duplication at all, and it did not have a damn thing to do with his twins or the Deaf Man's ego.

Oddly, it had only to do with playing the crime game fair.

He came through the revolving doors at ten minutes to eleven, walked directly to the bank guard, and opened his wallet.

'Detective Carella,' he said, '87th Squad. I'd like to see Mr Alton, please.'

The bank guard studied the detective's shield pinned to a leather tab opposite an identification card. He nodded, and then said, 'Right this way, sir,' and led him through the bank to a door at the far end, adjacent to the vault. Discreetly, he knocked.

'Yes?' a voice said.

'It's me, Mr Alton. Corrigan.'

'Come in,' Alton said.

The bank guard entered the office, and came out again not a moment later. 'Go right in, Mr Carella,' he said.

Alton was sitting behind his desk, but he rose and extended his hand at once. 'How do you do?' he said.

'How do you do, sir? I'm Detective Carella of the 87th Squad.' He showed his shield and I.D. card again, and then smiled. 'How do you feel after all that excitement?' he asked, and pulled a chair up to the desk, and sat.

'Much better now,' Alton said. 'What can I do for you, Detective Carella?'

'Well, sir, I won't be more than a few minutes. We're the squad that caught the original squeal and later turned it over to the 86th. My lieutenant asked me to stop by and complete this check list, if that's okay with you.'

'What sort of check list?' Alton asked.

'Well, sir, I hate to bother you with interdepartmental problems, but that's exactly what this is, and I hope you'll bear with me. You see, because the case was turned over to another squad, that doesn't mean it isn't still officially ours. The final disposition of it, I mean.'

'I'm not sure I understand,' Alton said.

'We're responsible for it, sir. It's as simple as that.'

'I see,' Alton said, but he still looked puzzled.

'These questions are just to make sure that the 86th handled things properly. I'll be honest with you, Mr Alton, it's our insurance in case there's any static later on. From the brass upstairs, I mean.'

'I see,' Alton said, finally comprehending. 'What are the questions?'

'Just a few, sir,' he said, and took a sheet of paper from his pocket, unfolded it, and put it on the desk. There were several typewritten questions on the sheet. He took out a ballpoint pen, glanced at the first question, and said, 'how many police officers were inside the bank at the time of the attempted robbery?'

'Four,' Alton said.

'Would you know their names?'

'The man in charge was Detective Schmitt. I don't know the names of the others.'

'I can get that from the 86th,' he said, and wrote 'Schmitt' on the typewritten sheet, and then went on to the next question. 'Were you treated courteously by the police at all times?'

'Oh yes, most definitely,' Alton said.

He wrote the word 'Yes' alongside the question, and then said, 'Did any of the police officers have access to cash while they were inside the bank?'

'Yes. The ones at the tellers' windows.'

'Has this cash been tallied since the police officers left the bank?'

'No, Mr Carella, it has not.'

'When will a tally be made?'

'This afternoon.'

'Would you please give me a call after the tally is made, sir? The number is Frederick 7-8025.'

'Yes, I'll do that.'

'Just so I'll know it's all there,' he said, and smiled.

'Yes,' Alton said.

'Just a few more questions. Did any of the police officers enter the vault at any time while they were inside the bank?'

'No.'

'Sir, can you tell me how much cash was actually delivered to the bank this morning?'

'Five hundred thousand, three hundred dollars.'

'Was it counted after the holdup, sir?'

'It was.'

'By whom?'

'My assistant manager. Mr Warshaw.'

'Was it all there?'

'Every penny.'

'Then the perpetrators were entirely unsuccessful.'

'Entirely.'

'Good. I'd like to get Mr Warshaw's signature later, stating that he counted the money after the attempted holdup and after the police officers had left the bank ...'

'Well, they were still *in* the bank while he was counting.'

'But not in the vault?'

'No.'

'That's just as good, Mr Alton. I only need verification, that's all. Could we go into the vault now?'

'The vault? What for?'

'To satisfy my lieutenant's request.'

'What *is* your lieutenant's request, Detective Carella?'

'He wants me to make sure the cash is all there.'

'I've just told you it's all there.'

'He wants me to ascertain the fact, sir.'

'How?'

'By counting it.'

'That's absurd,' Alton said, and looked at his watch. 'We'll be sending the cash out to the tellers in just a little while. An accurate count would take you ...'

'I'll be very quick about it, Mr Alton. Would it be all right if we went into the vault now? So I can get started?'

'No, I don't think so,' Alton said.

'Why not, sir?'

'I've just told you. I don't mind cooperating with a departmental request, but not if it's going to further upset the bank's routine. I've had enough confusion here today, and I don't need ...'

'Sir, this is more than just a departmental request. In order to close out the investigation and satisfy my lieutenant's ...'

'Perhaps I'd best discuss this with your lieutenant then,' Alton said, and reached for the telephone. 'What did you say your number was?'

'Don't touch that phone, Mr Alton.'

The man was holding a revolver in his fist, and pointing it directly at Alton's head. For a moment Alton had a terrible feeling of *déja vu*. He thought, No, this cannot possibly be happening twice in the same day, and then he heard the man saying, 'Now listen to me very carefully, Mr Alton. We are going into the vault and you are going to tell anyone we meet on the way or in the vault itself that I am Detective Carella of the 87th Squad and that we are taking the cash to your office for a count according to police regulations. If you say anything to the contrary, I'll put a hole in your fucking head. Have you got that, Mr Alton?'

Alton sighed and said, 'Yes, I've got it.'

From where he stood at the island counter, the Deaf Man saw Harold and Alton leaving the manager's office. Harold's right hand was in the pocket of his coat, undoubtedly around the butt of his pistol. He watched as they entered the vault. On the withdrawal slip before him, he wrote the date, and the number of his account, and then he filled in the amount as *Five hundred thousand and no/100*, and in the space provided wrote the amount in numerals, $500,000, and then signed the slip *D. R. Taubman*.

Alton was coming out of the vault already, carrying a sack of cash. Harold was directly behind him, carrying the second sack, his right hand still in his coat pocket. Together, they went into Alton's office. The door closed behind them, and the Deaf Man started for the front of the bank.

He was feeling quite proud of himself. Folklore maintained that lightning never struck twice, especially within the space of less than an hour and a half. Yet Harold already had all that sweet cash in his possession, and in just several minutes more (as soon as the Deaf Man stepped outside the bank) Danny and Roger would drive up to the car teller's window, Florence would park her car across the driveway, and the robbery would happen all over again. The only difference was that this time it would work. It would work because it had already failed, and nobody expects failure to be an essential *part* of any plan. Having foiled a daring robbery attempt, everyone was now content to sit back and bask in the glory of the achievement. When that teller's window was smashed in just a very few minutes, and the alarm sounded at the 86th Precinct and the Security Office, the Deaf Man would not be surprised if everyone considered it an error. He was willing to bet that the phone in Mr Alton's office would ring immediately, asking if this was legit or if there was something malfunctioning. In any case, Harold would be out of the office the moment he heard the glass smashing, and they would all be on their way before the police responded. It was almost too simple. And yet it was delicious.

He reached the revolving doors and started through them.

A man was pushing his way through from the street side.

It had been a long time since the Deaf Man had seen Carella. But when you've once fired a shotgun at a man and he later returns the compliment with a .38 Detective's Special, you're not too terribly likely to forget his face. The Deaf Man knew at once that the man shoving his way into the bank was Detective Steve Carella, whom his cohorts had clobbered and robbed of identification the night before. In that split second of recognition, the Deaf Man found himself *outside* the bank, while Carella moved *inside* and walked directly to the guard.

Carella had not seen him.

But the Deaf Man's appearance on the sidewalk was the signal for Roger and Danny to start their car and head for the teller's window, which they did now with frightening alacrity. Similarly, it was the signal for Florence to move *her* car across the mouth of the bank's driveway, and the Deaf Man was dismayed to see that she had learned her job only too well, and was proceeding to perform it with all possible haste. Carella was talking to the bank guard, who looked extremely puzzled, as well he might when presented with two detectives in the space of fifteen minutes, each of whom claimed to be the same person. The Deaf Man figured the jig was up. He did what any sensible master criminal would have done in the same situation. He got the hell out of there, fast.

A lot of things happened in the next few minutes.

Following the guard to the manager's office, Carella heard glass shattering on his right. He turned and saw a man smashing the car teller's window with a sledge hammer. He did what any sensible crack detective would have done in the same situation. He drew his revolver and fired at the man, and then ran to the counter and fired across it at a second man, sitting in the driver's seat of a car outside the window. In that instant a third man came running out of the manager's office carrying two sacks of cash. The bank guard, thinking he had somehow lived through all of this before, in the not-too-distant past, nonetheless drew his own pistol and began firing at the man with the cash, whom he had previously met as Detective Carella; it was all very confusing. He hit the vault door, he hit the door of Mr Alton's office, and he also hit Mr Warshaw, the assistant manager, in the right arm. But he did not hit the man carrying the sacks of cash. The man dropped one sack, pulled a pistol from his coat pocket, and began spraying the centre aisle with bullets. He leaped the counter, and was heading for the broken teller's window when Carella shot him in the leg. He whirled and, dragging himself towards the window, fired at Carella, shoved the frightened car teller out of his way, and attempted to climb through the broken glass to where one of his colleagues lay dead at the wheel of the car. Carella felled him with his second shot, and then leaped the counter himself and rushed to the broken window. The man who had smashed it with the sledge hammer was badly wounded and trying to crawl up the driveway to where a car engine suddenly started. Carella leaned out and fired at the car as it pulled away, tyres screeching. One of the lady tellers screamed. A uniformed policeman rushed into the bank and started firing at Carella, who yelled, 'I'm a cop!' And then the bank was swarming with policemen from the 86th and private security officers, all of them answering the alarm for the second time that day. Two blocks away from the bank, the lady driving the getaway car ran a traffic light and was stopped by a patrolman. She tried to shoot him with a .22 calibre revolver she pulled from her purse, so the patrolman hit her with his nightstick and clapped her into handcuffs.

Her name was Florence Barrows.

Florence had once told the Deaf Man that she'd never met a man she could trust and didn't expect anyone to trust her, either.

She told the detectives everything she knew.

'His name is Taubman,' she said, 'and we had our meetings in a room at the Hotel Remington. Room 604. I'd never met him before he contacted me for the caper, and I don't know anything else about him.'

This time, they had him.

They didn't expect to find anybody at the Hotel Remington, and they didn't. But now, at least, they had a name for him. They began going through all the city directories, encouraged by the scarcity of Taubmans, determined to track down each and every one of them until they got their man – even if it took forever.

It did not take nearly that long.

Detective Schmitt of the 86th Squad called while they were still going through the directories and compiling a list of Taubmans.

'Hey, how *about* that?' he said to Carella. 'Son of bitch really *did* try to bring it off at eleven, huh?'

'He sure did,' Carella said.

'I understand he got away, though,' Schmitt said.

'Yeah, but we've got a lead.'

'Oh? What've you got?'

'His name.'

'Great. Has he got a record?'

'We're checking that with the I.S. right this minute.'

'Good, good. Is it a common name?'

'Only eleven of them in the Isola directory. Five in Calm's Point. We're checking the others now.'

'What's the name?' Schmitt asked.

'Taubman.'

'Yeah?'

'Yeah,' Carella said. There had been a curious lilt to Schmitt's voice just then, a mixture of incredulity and mirth. 'Why?' Carella asked at once.

'Didn't you say the guy was deaf?'

'Yes, I did. What ... ?'

'Because, you know ... I *guess* you know ... or maybe you don't.'

'What?'

'It's German. Taubman.'

'So?'

'It means the deaf man. "*De taube mann*." That means "the deaf man" in German.'

'I see,' Carella said.

'Yeah,' Schmitt said.

'Thank you,' Carella said.

'Don't mention it,' Schmitt said, and hung up.

Carella put the phone back onto its cradle and decided to become a fireman.